Crescent
Island

XANA

Dasu

Daye

Gaing Gulf

Mt. Kiji

Rui

Kigo Yezu

Kriphi

Big Island

Lake Tututika

Mira River

HAAN

Lutho Beach

amu Mountains

Ginpen

Mt Fithoweo

Temple of
Peace

RIMA

Zathin Gulf

Silkworm Eggs

Na Thion

FAÇA

HIGHLANDS

Boama

Shinané Mountains

Rufizo Falls

W

*Tazu
Whirlpool*

Ogé

S

N

Big Toe

Wolf's Paw

E

SPEAKING BONES

SPEAKING BONES

BOOK FOUR of the DANDELION DYNASTY

KEN LIU

SAGA  PRESS

LONDON SYDNEY **NEW YORK** TORONTO NEW DELHI

SAGA PRESS

AN IMPRINT OF SIMON & SCHUSTER, INC.

1230 AVENUE OF THE AMERICAS, NEW YORK, NEW YORK 10020

• Copyright © 2022 by Ken Liu • Map illustrations copyright © 2021 by Robert Lazzaretti •
For information, address Saga Press Subsidiary Rights Department, 1230 Avenue of the Americas, New York, NY 10020. • First Saga Press hardcover edition June 2022 • SAGA PRESS and colophon are trademarks of Simon & Schuster, Inc. • For information about special discounts for bulk purchases, please contact Simon & Schuster Special Sales at 1-866-506-1949 or business@simonandschuster.com. • The Simon & Schuster Speakers Bureau can bring authors to your live event. For more information or to book an event, contact the Simon & Schuster Speakers Bureau at 1-866-248-3049 or visit our website at www.simonspeakers.com. • Interior design by Kathryn A. Kenney-Peterson • Manufactured in the United States of America • 10 9 8 7 6 5 4 3 2 1 • Library of Congress Cataloging-in-Publication Data is available. • ISBN 978-1-9821-4897-3 • ISBN 978-1-9821-4899-7 (ebook)

For all those who left their teeth
on the board in service of mutagé

TABLE OF CONTENTS

FALLING LEAVES

A NOTE ON PRONUNCIATION, TRANSLITERATION, AND TRANSLATION

Many names in Dara are derived from Classical Ano. The transliteration for Classical Ano in this book does not use vowel digraphs; each vowel is pronounced separately. For example, "Réfiroa" has four distinct syllables: "Ré-fi-ro-a." Similarly, "Na-aroénna" has five syllables: "Na-a-ro-én-na."

The *i* is always pronounced like the *i* in English "mill."

The *o* is always pronounced like the *o* in English "code."

The *ü* is always pronounced like the umlauted form in German or Chinese pinyin.

Other names have different origins and contain sounds that do not appear in Classical Ano, such as the *xa* in "Xana" or the *ha* in "Haan." In such cases, however, each vowel is still pronounced separately. Thus, "Haan" also contains two syllables.

The notion that Classical Ano is one fixed language, unaltered for millennia, is attractive and commonly held among the less erudite in Dara. It is, however, false. As the (primarily) literary language of learning and officialdom, "Classical" Ano has continued to evolve, influencing and influenced by the vernacular as well as contact with new peoples, new ideas, new practices.

Scribes and poets create neologisms based on Classical Ano roots, along with new logograms to write them with, and even novel grammatical forms, at first deemed solecisms, become accepted over time as stylists adopt them with little regard to the carping of Moralist grammarians.

The changes in Classical Ano are most readily seen in the logograms themselves. However, it's possible to see some of the changes even through transliterations (we leave aside, for now, the problem of how even the way Classical Ano is spoken has changed over time). The Classical Ano in which Kon Fiji wrote most of his observations is not the same language in which Vocu Firna wrote his poems.

To emphasize the different register that the language evokes for the people of Dara, Classical Ano words and phrases are always italicized in the text.

The representation of Lyucu and Agon names and words presents a different problem. As we come to know them through the people(s) and language(s) of Dara, the scrubland words given in this work are doubly mediated. Just as English speakers who write down Chinese names and words they hear with Latin letters will achieve only a rough approximation of the original sounds, so with the Dara transliteration of Lyucu and Agon.

Lyucu and Agon do not pluralize nouns in the manner of English. For the benefit of the anglophone reader, certain words, such as "pékyu" and "garinafin," are pluralized in this book as though they have become "naturalized" English words. On the other hand, other words and phrases, less common, retain the character of their non-English origins.

"Dara," "Lyucu," and "Agon" can refer to a language, the people who speak that language, the culture of that people, or even a single individual of that culture—a practice closer to the way these languages represent such concepts natively.

Also, in contrast to Classical Ano, Lyucu and Agon words and phrases are not (with very few exceptions) italicized in the text. For the people who speak the language(s), they are not foreign.

Like most matters involving translation, transliteration, assimilation, adaptation, and migration, these practices represent an imperfect compromise, which, given the nature of the tale re-remembered here, is perhaps appropriate.

LIST OF MAJOR CHARACTERS

THE CHRYSANTHEMUM AND THE DANDELION

KUNI GARU: Emperor Ragin of Dara, who died during the Battle of Zathin Gulf, though his body was never recovered.

MATA ZYNDU: deceased Hegemon of Dara, worshipped by some cults in Tunoa and among the common soldiers as the pinnacle of martial prowess and honor.

THE DANDELION COURT

JIA MATIZA: Empress and Regent of Dara; a skilled herbalist.

RISANA: an illusionist and accomplished musician; posthumously given the title Empress of Dara.

KADO GARU: Kuni's elder brother; holds the title of King of Dasu without the substance; father of Prince Gimoto.

COGO YELU: Prime Minister of Dara, one of the longest-serving officials at the Dandelion Court.

ZOMI KIDOSU: Farsight Secretary; prized student of Luan Zyaji and a noted inventor in her own right; Princess Théra's lover; daughter of a Dasu farming-fishing family (Oga and Aki Kidosu).

GIN MAZOTI: Marshal of Dara and Queen of Géjira; the greatest battlefield tactician of her time; posthumous victor at the Battle of Zathin Gulf; Aya Mazoti is her daughter.

THAN CARUCONO: First General of the Cavalry and First Admiral of the Navy.

PUMA YEMU: Marquess of Porin; noted practitioner of raiding tactics.

SOTO ZYNDU: Jia's confidante and adviser; aunt of Mata Zyndu.

WI: leader of the Dyran Fins, who serve Empress Jia.

SHIDO: a Dyran Fin.

LADY RAGI: an orphaned girl raised by Jia; serves the empress on special missions.

GORI RUTHI: nephew of the late Imperial Tutor Zato Ruthi and husband of Lady Ragi; a noted Moralist scholar.

CHILDREN OF THE HOUSE OF DANDELION

PRINCE TIMU (NURSING NAME: TOTO-*TIKA*): Emperor Thaké of Ukyu-taasa; Kuni's firstborn; consort of Tanvanaki; son of Empress Jia.

PRINCESS THÉRA (NURSING NAME: RATA-*TIKA*): named by Kuni as his successor and once known as Empress Üna of Dara; yielded the throne to her younger brother Phyro in order to journey to Ukyu-Gondé to war with the Lyucu; daughter of Empress Jia.

PRINCE PHYRO (NURSING NAME: HUDO-*TIKA*): Emperor Monadétu of Dara; son of Empress Risana.

PRINCESS FARA (NURSING NAME: ADA-*TIKA*): an artist and collector of folktales; youngest of Kuni's children; daughter of Consort Fina, who died in childbirth.

PRINCESS AYA: daughter of Gin Mazoti and Luan Zyaji; given the title of Imperial Princess by Empress Jia to honor the sacrifices of her mother.

PRINCE GIMOTO: son of Kado Garu, Kuni's elder brother.

SCHOLARS OF DARA

LUAN ZYAJI: Kuni's chief strategist; Gin Mazoti's lover; he journeyed to Ukyu-Gondé and discovered the secret of the periodic openings in the Wall of Storms; known during life as Luan Zya.

ZATO RUTHI: Imperial Tutor; leading Moralist of modern times.

KON FIJI: ancient Ano philosopher; founder of the Moralist school.

POTI MAJI: ancient Ano philosopher; the most accomplished student of Kon Fiji.

RA OJI: ancient Ano epigrammatist; founder of the Fluxist school.

ÜSHIN PIDAJI: ancient Ano philosopher; the most renowned student of Ra Oji.

NA MOJI: ancient Xana engineer who studied the flights of birds; founder of the Patternist school.

GI ANJI: modern philosopher of the Tiro states era; founder of the Incentivist school.

MIZA CRUN: renowned scholar of the silkmotic force; once a street magician.

UKYU-TAASA

TENRYO ROATAN: seized position of Pékyu of the Lyucu by murdering his father Toluroru; conqueror of the scrublands; leader of the Lyucu invasion of Dara; died at the Battle of Zathin Gulf.

VADYU ROATAN (NICKNAMED "TANVANAKI"): the best garinafin pilot and current pékyu of Ukyu-taasa; daughter of Tenryo.

TODYU ROATAN (NURSING NAME: DYU-TIKA): son of Timu and Tanvanaki.

DYANA ROATAN (NURSING NAME: ZAZA-TIKA): daughter of Timu and Tanvanaki.

VOCU FIRNA: a thane close to Timu; a poet.

CUTANROVO AGA: a prominent thane, commander of the Capital Security Forces.

GOZTAN RYOTO: a prominent thane; rival of Cutanrovo.

SAVO RYOTO: Goztan's son; also known by the Dara name Kinri Rito.

NAZU TEI: a scholar; teacher of Savo.

NODA MI: a minister at the court of Tanvanaki and Timu; betrayed Gin Mazoti at the Battle of Zathin Gulf.

WIRA PIN: a minister at the court of Tanvanaki and Timu; once tried to persuade Prince Timu to surrender to the Lyucu under Pékyu Tenryo.

OFLURO: a skilled garinafin rider.

LADY SUCA: one of the few non-Lyucu to learn to ride a garinafin; wife of Ofluro.

THE SPLENDID URN AND THE BLOSSOM GANG

RATI YERA: leader of the Blossom Gang; an illiterate inventor of ingenious machines.

MOTA KIPHI: member of the Blossom Gang; a man rivaling Mata Zyndu in pure strength; survivor of the Battle of Zathin Gulf.

ARONA TARÉ: member of the Blossom Gang; an actress.

WIDI TUCRU: member of the Blossom Gang; a paid litigator.

WIDOW WASU: head of the Wasu clan; she knew Kuni Garu as a youth.

MATI PHY: sous-chef at the Splendid Urn.

LODAN THO: head waitress at the Splendid Urn; Mati's wife.

TIPHAN HUTO: the youngest son of the Huto clan, rival of the Wasu clan.

MOZO MU: a young chef employed by Tiphan Huto; granddaughter of Suda Mu, legendary cook in the time of the Tiro kings.

LOLOTIKA TUNÉ: Headgirl of the Aviary, Ginpen's leading indigo house.

KITA THU: head of the Imperial laboratories in Ginpen; once led the effort to discover the secret of garinafin fire breath during the war against the Lyucu.

SÉCA THU: a scholar; nephew of Kita Thu.

DARA AT LARGE

ABBOTT SHATTERED AXE: head of the Temple of Still and Flowing Waters in the mountains of Rima.

ZEN-KARA: a scholar; daughter of Chief Kyzen of Tan Adü.

RÉZA MÜI: a troublemaker.

ÉGI and ASULU: a pair of soldiers in the city garrison of Pan.

KISLI PÉRO: a researcher at one of the Imperial laboratories.

THE CREW OF *DISSOLVER OF SORROWS*

RAZUTANA PON: a scholar of the Cultivationism school.

ÇAMI PHITHADAPU: a Golden Carp scholar; an expert on whales.

MITU ROSO: an admiral, commander-in-chief of the expedition to Ukyu-Gondé.

NMÉJI GON: captain of *Dissolver of Sorrows*.

TIPO THO: former air ship officer; commander of the marines aboard *Dissolver of Sorrows*.

THORYO: a mysterious stowaway.

THE LYUCU

TOLURORU ROATAN: unifier of the Lyucu.

CUDYU ROATAN: leader of the Lyucu; son of Tenryo; grandson of Toluroru.

TOVO TASARICU: Cudyu's most trusted thane.

TOOF: a garinafin pilot.

RADIA: a garinafin rider.

THE AGON

NOBO ARAGOZ: unifier of the Agon.

SOULIYAN ARAGOZ: youngest daughter of Nobo Aragoz; mother of Takval.

VOLYU ARAGOZ: youngest son of Nobo Aragoz; Chief of the Agon.

TAKVAL ARAGOZ: pékyu-taasa of the Agon; husband of Théra.

TANTO GARU ARAGOZ (NURSING NAME: KUNILU-*TIKA*): eldest son of Théra and Takval.

ROKIRI GARU ARAGOZ (NURSING NAME: JIAN-*TIKA*): second son of Théra and Takval.

VARA RONALEK: an old thane who refuses to give up riding garinafins into battle.

GOZOFIN: a warrior, skilled in the crafting of arucuro tocua.

NALU: Gozofin's son.

ADYULEK: an aged shaman, skilled in the taking of spirit portraits.

SATAARI: a young shaman.

ARATEN: a thane trusted by Takval.

THE GODS OF DARA

KIJI: patron of Xana; Lord of the Air; god of wind, flight, and birds; his *pawi* is the Mingén falcon; favors a white traveling cloak; in Ukyu-taasa he is identified with Péa, the god who gave the gift of garinafins to the people.

TUTUTIKA: patron of Amu; youngest of the gods; goddess of agriculture, beauty, and fresh water; her *pawi* is the golden carp; in Ukyu-taasa she is identified with Aluro, the Lady of a Thousand Streams.

KANA AND RAPA: twin patrons of Cocru; Kana is the goddess of fire, ash, cremation, and death; Rapa is the goddess of ice, snow, glaciers, and sleep; their *pawi* are twin ravens: one black, one white; in Ukyu-taasa they are identified with Cudyufin, the Well of Daylight, and Nalyufin, the Pillar of Ice and the hate-hearted.

RUFIZO: patron of Faça; Divine Healer; his *pawi* is the dove; in Ukyu-taasa he is identified with Toryoana, the long-haired bull who watches over cattle and sheep.

TAZU: patron of Gan; unpredictable, chaotic, delighting in chance; god of sea currents, tsunamis, and sunken treasures; his *pawi* is the shark; in Ukyu-taasa both he and Lutho are identified with Péten, the god of trappers and hunters.

LUTHO: patron of Haan; god of fishermen, divination, mathematics, and knowledge; his *pawi* is the sea turtle; missing from Dara when he became mortal to hitch a ride on *Dissolver of Sorrows*.

FITHOWÉO: patron of Rima; god of war, the hunt, and the forge; his *pawi* is the wolf; in Ukyu-taasa he is identified with the goddess Diasa, the she-wolf club-maiden.

PART ONE
HAIL-PUMMELED FLOWERS

CHAPTER ONE

BACK IN THE FLOW

WORLD'S EDGE MOUNTAINS: THE FIFTH MONTH
IN THE NINTH YEAR AFTER THE DEPARTURE
OF PRINCESS THÉRA FROM DARA FOR UKYU-
GONDÉ (TWELVE MONTHS UNTIL THE LYUCU MUST
LAUNCH THEIR NEW INVASION FLEET TO DARA).

For much of the winter and spring, the last remnants of the rebels of Kiri Valley lived in constant fear.

They would find some hidden valley on the western side of the World's Edge Mountains and make camp, careful to mask smoke, middens, noise, and other signs of their presence. But a few days later the pursuing garinafins of the Lyucu would be sighted in the sky to the south, and they would have to pack up and be on the run again.

Tipo Tho, with her newborn son strapped to her chest, suggested several times that perhaps the group should attempt to scale the massive peaks to the east and cross over the mountain range, but most of the surviving Agon warriors strenuously objected to the plan. To cross the mountains was to move into the realm of the gods, and that was simply something mortals did not do.

"But that is also why we would be safe," Tipo said. "Cudyu wouldn't think of chasing us beyond the mountains either."

The other surviving Dara fighters nodded. This seemed the most obvious choice.

But Takval and his warriors looked at her as though she were babbling nonsense.

"Look at how tall the mountains are," said Takval, pointing to the snow-capped peaks. They were about halfway up one of the mountains, and already everyone was shivering and having trouble breathing. "The cold gets worse the higher we go, and Alkir can't fly that high."

"We can make the crossing on foot," said Çami Phithadapu. "There are ways to keep everyone warm. We can come up with *some* plan—"

The old shaman Adyulek swore and walked away, disgusted.

"With all due respect, I don't think this is the best time for Dara to be suggesting any more changes to the ways of the Agon," said Gozofin.

Tipo, Çami, and the others held their tongues. After the disaster at Kiri Valley, the reputation of the Dara allies among the Agon was in tatters. Takval's people blamed Théra for pushing them to farm instead of pasturing and hunting, for putting their trust in weapons enhanced with Dara magic instead of the known ways of the Agon, for insisting on delaying the attack until the Lyucu had returned to Taten instead of following Volyu's original suggestion of a quick strike at Aluro's Basin. . . . Among the people of the scrublands, the only argument that ultimately swayed was victory in war. And since Théra had been responsible for the greatest defeat of the Agon since the death of Pékyu Nobo Aragoz, everything she had pushed for was worthless.

And so, as spring came to the mountains, they continued to meander north, following no clear plan beyond survival.

While the rest of the Dara survivors seethed at what they saw as the unjust treatment of their princess, Théra was unperturbed.

More accurately, she remained in the near-catatonic state she had fallen into after the loss of Kunilu-*tika* and Jian-*tika*. Most of her waking hours were spent fingering the bag of baked clay logogram playing blocks and an old silk mask with an edging of embroidered tolyusa berries, so worn that it was nearly in tatters. She made no suggestions and gave no orders; she obeyed whatever instructions were given to her docilely; the very act of survival seemed to her a burden more than she could bear.

Takval, though weighed down with the responsibility of keeping the small band alive by himself, never stopped trying to help Théra. He held her in their tent and spoke to her of his love and need, even if she never responded. He asked Adyulek to intercede with the gods on Théra's behalf, but the old shaman shook her head, explaining that there wasn't much she could do when the princess had neither trust in nor fear of the gods of Gondé.

"She isn't Agon, and she's too proud to accept our wisdom," said Adyulek. "Perhaps because it's rare among her people to lose children, she lacks the inborn strength to recover from such a blow. Leave her to her deserved suffering—she is, after all, responsible for our plight with her obduracy."

Takval didn't agree with this assessment, but he could hardly compel the old shaman to put aside her suspicion and prejudice. In the end, he asked Thoryo to become Théra's caretaker, hoping that the originless young woman with a gift for speech could offer some comfort to Théra in the accents of Dara.

So Thoryo spent all her time with the princess. She fed her, bathed her, sang to her quietly, and strapped her into the netting on the garinafin, next to herself, when the band needed to take flight again.

She also talked to Théra. She didn't speak to her of strategies and plots, of plans and grand ideals. She simply took her to quiet clearings in the mountainside forests, where spring alpine flowers bloomed in all their finery, or to cliffside overlooks at sunset, when birds swooped through crimson and gold clouds like colorful fish in a painted sea. She spoke to the princess softly of the beauty around them.

One day, after a spring shower, Thoryo took Théra to a high point in the valley the band was bivouacking in. They sat down on a rock. Everything—the trees, the grass, the glistening red berries in the bushes, the eggshell-yellow mushrooms peeking out from under the rock they sat on—shone with a vivid, wet light. A rainbow arched across the sky opposite from the sun.

"This is my favorite moment, climbing onto a high spot right after rain," exclaimed Thoryo. "The world has been reborn!"

As always, Théra said nothing. But Thoryo heard a scratching noise that made her glance to the side. To her surprise, she saw that Théra's hands were fluttering in her lap like frightened birds, searching for something that didn't exist. Gingerly, she placed a hand over Théra's, stilling those restless fingers. For the first time in a long while, she saw that the princess's lips were moving, as though trying to speak.

She leaned in. Théra's voice was so soft that she could barely make out the words.

". . . climbing onto a high place . . . after a spring rain . . ."

"Princess! Are you all right?" she called out, frightened.

Théra blinked, as though awakening from a long dream. Tension and color returned to the slack muscles in her cheeks as she focused her gaze on Thoryo. She cleared her throat, and spoke in a voice raspy from disuse. "A great lady I met years ago told me that gazing upon the rejuvenated world after rain was one of the greatest of pleasures in the world."

Thoryo nodded. "I agree."

Tears spilled from Théra's eyes as her body convulsed. Thoryo pulled her into an embrace and cradled the princess's head against her shoulder, the same way Théra used to hold her in Lurodia Tanta, when Thoryo was certain that they would never make it out of the desert alive.

"Zomi . . . Takval . . . Dara . . . my family . . . my sons . . . all the dead . . . everyone I touch is hurt, lost, gone, ruined . . . my heart is bitter."

Thoryo gently caressed her back, saying nothing. It was a long time before Théra's lamentation abated.

"When you first found me," said Thoryo, "when I saw the bodies of all those people from the Lyucu city-ship and the Dara marines adrift at sea, I was inconsolable. I couldn't understand how the gods could be so cruel as to give the gift of life only to snatch it away."

Théra sat up and wiped her eyes, listening intently.

"I wondered why we should even believe in the existence of the gods. The Ano sages speak of the River-on-Which-Nothing-Floats, and the Agon speak of riding beyond the World's Edge Mountains on cloud-garinafins. But who has ever returned from the country of death to verify these claims? There seems to be nothing but the terror of death in this world; death is the one single truth against which all courage and struggle is vanity. Why doesn't everyone just give up?"

Théra shuddered, hearing her own fears echoed in the words of Thoryo.

"I've found no answers in the words of the Ano sages or the stories of the Agon shamans. But I *have* experienced the world through my senses. Death *does* come to everything: flowers wilt, trees wither and shed leaves, the sun sets, the strongest ewe or cow weakens with old age, voices fade, sweet fragrances dissipate, the light in the brightest eyes winks out. Yet, beauty never dies. Beauty always refreshes itself."

She pointed, and Théra followed her finger, taking in the promise of the rainbow.

"After every winter comes the spring, and every death is accompanied by the promise for more life. With his dying breath, Admiral Mitu Roso tried to save the children of Kiri Valley from wolves. On the night of the Lyucu assault, Souliyan Aragoz and Nméji Gon chose to buy more time for us with their own lives. It isn't that they weren't afraid of death. But they also saw themselves as part of something grander, a greater Life that never dies so long as each individual life refuses to yield to despair."

"You speak of the Flow," muttered Théra, "as did that great lady who once shared some lotus seeds with me. She spoke of the infinite potential in a heart of emptiness, of the ever-renewing pleasure of simply *being*. But my errors—"

"I am not wise enough to know the will of the gods or the right course in life," said Thoryo. "I only know that the world is too large, too beautiful, too interesting to let one act define us. Death only triumphs when we stop learning and growing. So long as our lungs sing with the gift of life, we cannot cease to give back to Life."

Théra said nothing. She stilled her heart and opened her senses, to the intense carmine glow of the berries, to the woodsy fragrance of the mushrooms, to the distant song of an answer-me-now, to the warm caress of the spring breeze. She let herself sink into the Flow as though diving into the eternal sea.

CHAPTER TWO

CITY OF GHOSTS

TATEN-RYO-ALVOVO: THE FIFTH MONTH IN THE
NINTH YEAR AFTER THE DEPARTURE OF PRINCESS
THÉRA FROM DARA FOR UKYU-GONDÉ (TWELVE
MONTHS UNTIL THE LYUCU MUST LAUNCH THEIR
NEW INVASION FLEET TO DARA).

With the coming of the spring, the hilly region on the eastern shore of the Sea of Tears, known as Taten-ryo-alvovo, the City of Ghosts, came back to life.

As it neared the Sea of Tears, the Ghost River gave up the urgency of its youthful source back in the snowmelt mountains, slowed down, and spread itself to embrace the land with the mellow kindness that came with age. Long before it reached the vast lake at the end of its journey, most of its waters had seeped into the ground, turning the land around the eastern shore into a giant swamp.

The mounds that made up the City of Ghosts, called barrows, rose out of this wetland-dotted terrain. Covered with a thick layer of lush grass, the mounds resembled furry, massive beasts at rest. Between the mounds, where marsh alternated with dry land, one could see bushes and even copses of trees, bedecked with flowers in every hue of the rainbow, promising berries and fruits in fall. Flitting shadows of birds and animals could be glimpsed between the dappled shadows.

It had been a hard winter for the small band of refugees. Water had to be obtained by melting ice chipped from the frozen salt lake— luckily, the edge of the barrows provided plenty of dried grass and firewood for fuel. At first, Razutana was afraid of drawing pursuers with smoke, but Sataari told him there was no need to worry. No one ever approached the City of Ghosts, not Lyucu, not Agon, not tanto-lyu-naro, not even the gods.

Although neither Sataari nor Razutana were great hunters, the Agon children, led by the redoubtable Nalu, Tanto and Rokiri's close friend, took up the burden of the band's sustenance. In this endeavor they were aided by the fact that the barrows were never visited by hunting parties, and prey had not yet learned to fear humans. Even through the worst part of the winter, Nalu and his band caught hares, voles, hibernating lizards, brumating snakes, and Razutana and Sataari dug for tubers and roots and caches of nuts hidden by moonfur rats near the mounds. They succeeded in keeping starva-tion at bay. Mostly.

Five small bodies lay at the edge of the barrows, almost hidden by the rejuvenated vegetation. Now that insects and larger animals were active again, the dead children would soon begin pédiato savaga, a journey that would end with reunion with their parents on the backs of cloud-garinafins.

Grief, like snow, had to yield before the quickening demands of life, the compulsion to go on.

A few times during the winter, Razutana had urged that the band move their encampment deeper into the barrows, where he believed more and better food would be available than at their site on the border of the salt flats. But Sataari would not hear of it, and none of the Agon children—not even levelheaded Nalu—treated this sug-gestion as sensible either. Eventually, Razutana dropped the idea.

But with the arrival of spring, Razutana renewed his pleas. His hunch during the winter had proven right. The vibrancy and fecun-dity of the barrows was plain to anyone. To avoid a repeat of the tragedy of the past winter, it seemed obvious that they should move deep into the barrows proper, build shelters and storage pits, and spend much of the summer and autumn gathering a food store against the next winter.

Sataari shook her head, explaining that the blood price she had paid to the All-Mother gave them the right only to skim from the very edge of the mounds, but not to penetrate into the interior. To set foot within the City of Ghosts was to bring ruin on the whole band.

Most of the Agon children nodded at this explanation, but Tanto and Rokiri were bewildered. They still didn't understand the nature of this place.

"Why do you act as though the place is filled with boiling lava or poisonous miasma?" asked an exasperated Razutana. "Why have the Lyucu and the Agon never settled here, even though it's a perfect oasis?"

"Because we are not allowed to."

"That explains nothing! Is the City of Ghosts . . . sacred?"

Sataari shook her head, and then nodded, and then shook her head again.

Baffled, Razutana tried again. "Is it . . . cursed?"

Sataari nodded her head, and then shook it, and then nodded again.

"I'm afraid that I'm completely at a loss."

"This place is why we live in the Sixth Age," said Sataari. In her voice was awe and revulsion, reverence as well as terror.

"I know about the Ages of Mankind," said Razutana, "but never have I heard of the barrows of Taten-ryo-alvovo."

"That's because it's a sad story, not often told," said Sataari.

A small bonfire was built, and a set of tiny drums, made from the vertebrae of snakes and the pelts of voles, had to serve in place of true cactus drums. As the children gathered around the grass-fed fire, thick with smoke, Sataari began to chant and dance.

The people of the scrublands believed that the world had been born out of primordial chaos with the coupling of the All-Father and the Every-Mother, but just as parents on the scrublands could not count on every child surviving into adulthood, the pair of Prime Deities could not count on their creations' permanence.

The world was as mortal as its inhabitants.

(Razutana, Tanto, and Rokiri leaned in, rapt.)

The Lyucu and Agon were not the first people. The gods had remade the world again and again. Before Afir and Kikisavo, there had been other peoples.

During the First Age of Mankind, the world was as flat as a freshly scraped piece of voice-painting vellum and as dry as Lurodia Tanta. People—they were not shaped like the humans of the present age— stood rooted in the ground like cactus lobes. The only water they could drink was dew and the only breath they drew in and let out was the result of the action of the wind. Sunlight was all they needed to sustain themselves, and they offered lethargic praise to the gods with their slow-swaying, vegetal poses.

The gods found this world too lacking in motion, too complacent in demeanor. Thus, they sent forth an eagle with a burning stick in its beak, who started fires all over the world until it was consumed in a fiery tide.

(As Sataari danced and chanted, she sketched figures in the ground with the tips of her pointed feet. Startled, Razutana and the pékyus-taasa recognized the figures: smaller versions of those fantastical, immense designs they had seen in the salt flats from the air on the way here.)

During the Second Age of Mankind, the gods took another approach. They flooded Ukyu-Gondé, and a great ocean covered the entire world. This time, humans were remade to be as sleek as fish, and they swam the world-ocean in pursuit of smaller fish and shrimp, crunching their jaws on crabs and oysters. The humans could not speak—for with water in their lungs, how could they produce thinking-breath?—nor could their finned appendages grasp instruments capable of making voice paintings.

The gods found this world too silent, too close to a living death. Thus, they sent forth a whale with icicle teeth, who left crystalline trails and hail-foam wakes that refused to dissolve wherever it swam until the whole world became a solid block of ice.

During the Third Age of Mankind, the gods remade the world by bringing the clouds down, and humans were remade as birds. Each tribe sang in a different style, and the chittering, twittering, chirping music pleased the immortal ears very much. But then some of the bird-humans grew bold and decided that they would prefer to fly ever higher instead of remaining in the sublunary realm, and their cacophony shook the stars loose in the firmament.

The gods, unable to put up with the disturbance, decided to destroy this world by sending forth a thousand-thousand bolts of lightning, incinerating the clouds and the winged humans in one brilliant flash.

During the Fourth Age of Mankind, the gods decided to punish their mortal kin for daring to reach for the stars. They remade the world with bone and dung, and humans were reborn as insect-like creatures forever mired in death and corruption. Driven by hunger, they consumed everything they touched, regardless of the stench and filth, and yet their hunger remained unsatiated.

The gods did not have to do much to end this age, for the humans soon ended the world by themselves. After devouring everything, they were trapped in empty darkness, the absence that outlasted all substance.

Having learned from their previous attempts, the gods created the Fifth Age of Mankind as a paradise. There was a balance of rich soil and fresh water, of sweet wind and mild sunlight. Milk bubbled from springs in the ground, and honey pooled into fragrant, indulgent lakes. Lambs and calves willingly lay down next to the people to be slaughtered, and fruits and nuts that were so nourishing that you were full after just three bites sprouted everywhere. Horrid wolves and tusked tigers stayed far away from the people, subsisting only on the dead. Humans lived lives of leisure and abundance, and they gave birth to more children with every passing year. No grandparent ever had to walk into the winter storm, nor did fathers and mothers have to strangle newborn babes so that other children could have enough to eat.

The gods hoped that humans would be able to live in this world where everything was good and offer pious praise to their makers.

And at first, the humans did exactly that. But as the population swelled, their hearts became restless. Bored with praising the divine, in their idleness they invented fantastical contraptions that imitated the power of the gods, built grand storytelling mind-scars out of piles of bones and logs and stones that sought to surpass the grandeur of the All-Father—

(*Are the gigantic stone paintings we saw mind-scars?* asked Razutana. *Are they remnants of a past age?*

Sataari ignored him and went on.)

—and entertained themselves with songs and poems and never-ending tales that sought to exceed the wisdom of the Every-Mother. They believed that by their own efforts, they were close to achieving godhood for themselves, forgetting that they were but another iteration in the gods' endless attempts at perfecting their own creation.

Humans grew ambitious and greedy. Rather than living off the bounty of the land, as the gods had intended, they began to enslave it. With no predators, no droughts, no storms to plague them, they decided that they should stop roaming around so that they could accumulate possessions. They gathered into large tribes and divided the land into separate parcels with stone fences at the borders so that the fruits and nuts and tubers that came out of each parcel would belong only to the tribe staking a claim to that parcel. They settled into tent-cities rooted to one place and penned up sheep and cattle so that they could no longer graze freely and wander about. They clogged and shackled the rivers with weirs so that the fish had nowhere to go except into their cooking pots. They built ever more elaborate edifices and apparatuses that celebrated the power of humankind but turned their faces away from the gods.

As the tribes continued to multiply and stopped roaming to new pastures, they gave the land no time to recover. The teeming clans tried to extract every bit of nourishment from the world with their clever inventions, devices that enslaved the land, the water, and the air. As the people clamored for *More! More! More!* they began to war among themselves, and they turned their cleverness to devising fearful weapons and dark magic that could slaughter thousands at a single blow.

They became so wicked that, instead of offering up their own bodies after death to the vultures and wolves who were also gods' creatures, they decided to bury their dead in the ground, as though hoarding themselves in storage pits, and heaped their corpses with treasures and magical weapons, as if they could take such things with them into the afterlife.

Then they covered these selfish vaults with mounds of earth, to deny the carrion eaters their rightful claim and to erect monuments to their own greed. The land was littered with with many such barrows, as though mindless moles had tunneled under the earth, pushing up earthen bumps in their ignorance and blindness.

The gods, sorrowful that their perfect creation had been desecrated by the people in this manner, sent forth monsters to punish the ungrateful. Garinafins made of only bones flew across the land, burning down their huts and charring their storage pits; tigers with star-metal tusks broke into their pens and slaughtered the animals they had imprisoned; horrid wolves with stone teeth and claws tore apart men, women, and children alike, showing no mercy. And there were many other monsters besides, all indescribably terrible.

The rivers dried up and the lakes shrank. Water that had once been sweet and refreshing turned salty and bitter. Land that had once been lush with vegetation turned into dry desert. Wind whipped dust into the air, blinding the people and grating against their skin until they were covered in blood. The world that used to be a paradise became so inhospitable that humans had no choice but to leave their bordered parcels, abandon their rooted settlements, and stop the enslavement of the land.

And that was how the Sixth Age of Mankind came to be, when humans were driven into the scrublands, full of harsh storms and brutal droughts, lashed by lightning bolts and cleansed by prairie fires. The people forgot all their vain knowledge, discarded their false wisdom, and huddled in the darkness—until the coming of Kikisavo and Afir, who warred against the gods and won the tribes the wisdom they needed to survive in this debased world.

Tribes were no longer free to have as many children as they liked, but must cull the aged and the infirm much as they culled their own flocks and herds. Sheep and cattle must roam widely so as not to overburden the land, sparsely covered in hardy shrubs, spiny cacti, and brittle, skin-lacerating grass. Smaller versions of the monsters that had destroyed their ancestors' lives provided a constant reminder of the arrogance of humankind and how we had displeased the gods. Of the grand settlements of the people during the Fifth Age, nothing was left save these burial barrows, the mounds at the eastern shore of the Sea of Tears called the City of Ghosts.

The barrows were a reminder of what happened when humans gave in to their hubris, monuments to the depravities of lives sustained through extraction and exploitation of the land, rather than submission to its wisdom.

Despite the appearance of bounty, the barrows were forbidden ground. Anyone who entered the barrows would incur the wrath of the gods and be cursed never to escape. The refugees had obtained the Every-Mother's blessing to stay on the very edge of the barrows because of their desperate predicament, but to ask for more was to commit the same error as those who had lived at the end of the Fifth Age, whose pride and greed had brought about their fall.

Though Sataari was a skilled storyteller, the tale of Taten-ryo-alvovo faded from the minds of most of the children after a few days. They knew the story already, at least in outline, and there was too much to do at the settlement to linger on old myths.

Led by Razutana, they built a purification system modeled on the experiences of Takval and Théra in Lurodia Tanta, which turned the salt lake into an adequate source of potable water. At the edge of the barrows, Nalu led the other children in hunting for partridges, hares, moonfur rats, and the occasional moss-antlered deer. They also picked tidal tern eggs on the rocky lake shore and fished for hairy crabs and giant brine shrimp in the shallows. What they couldn't eat right away, they tried to turn into jerky and pemmican.

Razutana and Sataari took the children on expeditions to pick berries and nuts and to dig for tubers. The pair complemented each other well. Sataari drew on the shamanistic lore of medicinal and edible plants; Razutana had studied the native flora for years using the techniques of Dara cultivators. There were many plants near the barrows that neither knew, and in such cases, the pair learned to combine their skills and instincts to experiment cautiously, dividing those that were safe and useful from those that were toxic and devoid of value.

Back in Kiri Valley, due to the mutual suspicion between Agon shamans and Dara scholars, they had not known each other well. But thrust into a situation where the two had to work together to keep a large group of children alive in an unfamiliar environment, they discovered a previously unknown appreciation for each other's domain of expertise.

Even more unexpectedly, Razutana found that he enjoyed Sataari's company. His mind quickened at the way she danced and moved in the firelight, her lithe, youthful figure animating the stories of the ancients; his heart sped up whenever she praised him for a clever bit of herbal deduction; he tried to make her laugh, despite the stress and pressure of the unknown all around them, because hearing her laugh made him feel like he was walking on clouds.

To preserve this happy mood, he resisted the urge to suggest that they try to cultivate some of the new plants in gardens near the settlement to provide a more reliable source of food. Now that he had a better understanding of the origin of the Agon's vehement distaste for farming, he could predict her reaction without voicing the idea.

However, unlike the Agon children, Razutana could not get the story of Taten-ryo-alvovo out of his head.

Imbued with the Dara scholars' general skepticism of the existence of the supernatural, Razutana couldn't help trying to make sense of the stories of the Agon by comparing them to the sagas of Dara. Did the cyclical pattern of these tales signal a fundamental philosophical difference in the Lyucu and Agon way of thinking, as compared to the people of Dara, whose philosophies tended to emphasize humankind's perfectibility and progress through change? Or did the yearning for a mythical golden age represent a mental escape to offset the harsh conditions of the present, much as the Dara myth of the Ano's perfect homeland, now sunken in the western sea, offered hope to the people in times of war and turmoil?

Though Razutana, much like Théra, didn't put much stock in a realm beyond the mortal world, he believed that old stories that had survived many generations likely held a truth—but a truth cast in the language of metaphors that could no longer be read. His mind never stopped trying to decipher the real history that lay beneath the fantastical lore of the scrublands.

There was one other person whose imagination was seized by the legend of Taten-ryo-alvovo: Tanto.

All the children of the settlement suffered nightmares and were prone to bouts of melancholy. Though young minds were resilient, losing their parents and grandparents, or at least prolonged separation without knowing their fates, left deep scars. Add in the fact that the community of Kiri Valley, the only tribe and home they had ever known, was gone, it was a wonder that they were holding up as well as they did.

Sataari and Razutana kept the children busy with constant work and chores. This was only partly because there really were many tasks that had to be done for their survival; it was also a way to distract their traumatized minds with a sense of purpose. Sataari tried to entertain the children with nightly renditions of traditional scrubland tales: "Tiger Witch and Naro-with-Eleven-Toes," "How the Horrid Wolf Got His Hair," "The Tanto-Lyu-Naro Lost in the Boneyard," and so on. Since these were not sacred stories, she could simply narrate them without a storytelling dance. Razutana, for his part, re-remembered episodes from Dara's history, with the exploits of the hero Iluthan during the Diaspora Wars and the deeds of the Hegemon being particular favorites among the children.

One night, as Razutana recounted for a circle of children the story of how the Hegemon obtained Na-aroénna, the Doubt-Ender, Tanto made his way quietly around the circle to Sataari.

"Tell me more about the magical weapons that people used during the Fifth Age," he begged.

"Why do you want to hear about *them*?" asked Sataari with a frown. "Those were wicked weapons, invented in a sinful age and wielded with false pride."

"I want to know more about them so that . . . I can tell if the weapons my mother wanted to teach us to build are also dangerous."

Sataari relaxed and nodded with approval. "All right. It is said in the old tales that the vainglorious chiefs of the Fifth Age learned to harness the power of lightning so that a single warrior could stun a hundred-hundred naros with but one sweep of her magical staff. It is also said that they learned to bind the power of thunder so that merely by playing a set of drums, they could make a noise that made a thousand-thousand culeks fall at once, with blood oozing from their eyes and ears. It is finally said that they learned to tame the power of the wind so that simply by aiming a set of bone trumpets at the air, they could imitate the voices of the gods and make insects, birds, and even garinafins fall out of the sky."

Tanto's eyes widened as he listened intently. "They were *that* powerful? Would the warriors and riders commanded by my father's father have been able to withstand these weapons?"

Sataari shook her head. "Of course not. Weren't you paying attention? Those weapons were from another age, and they unleashed powers that humans were simply not meant to have."

"What about the Lyucu? Would they have been able to withstand them?"

"Pékyu Cudyu may frighten children," Sataari said with contempt in her voice, "and he is certainly following in the footsteps of those arrogant chiefs from the Fifth Age by pitching his Taten in the same place, year after year. But he and all his garinafins and thanes wouldn't stand a chance against those powerful weapons either."

"If only those ancient chiefs could return on the cloud-garinafins and fight with us—"

"Don't blaspheme!" said a stern Sataari. "No matter how powerful their weapons were, because the haughty hearts of the barrow-dwellers had turned away from the ways of their ancestors and their lungsongs no longer honored the gods, they were ultimately driven out of paradise. That's the most important lesson of all taught by the City of Ghosts."

Tanto nodded, as though he understood.

CHAPTER THREE

BANDIT QUEENS

TOAZA: THE SEVENTH MONTH IN THE NINTH YEAR
OF THE REIGN OF SEASON OF STORMS AND THE
REIGN OF AUDACIOUS FREEDOM (TWENTY-TWO
MONTHS UNTIL THE REOPENING OF THE WALL OF
STORMS).

Tiphan Huto popped a grape into his mouth, savoring the sweet burst. Then he lay back on his bed and stretched out his limbs, enjoying the feel of smooth silk sheets and a soft mattress.

Servants had brought blocks of ice out of the cellar and placed them in cubbies all around the room. A windmill on top of the house drove fans behind the cubbies, filling his room with cool breezes that kept the scorching summer heat at bay.

It's nice to be home, he thought.

He was lucky; he knew that.

Back in Pan, when he had first been brought before the stern judges in the underground courtroom, he had been so terrified that his knees refused to support his weight, and he had to be held up by soldiers on either side. He began to whimper when he saw that a deputy minister of justice had been sent to act as the prosecutor for the Throne. And when the chief judge had slammed the block of ironwood, his symbol of office, against the bench to bring the court to order, he had lost control of his bladder and sphincter simultaneously.

After he had been taken away to be hosed down and changed into a fresh set of prison scrubs, he was brought back to kneel before the judges again. Witnesses—mostly pirates and hired swords who had turned against him in order to save their own hides—described in detail his various schemes: frauds upon the public, lies and forgeries to gain advantages over his competitors, betraying business partners to pirates, smuggling contraband from Unredeemed Dara, conspiracy to kidnap and enslave. . . .

His family had mortgaged what assets they could still access to hire the most expensive paid litigators possible to defend him. Much as his siblings and cousins despised him for selling out the Huto clan to benefit himself, their only chance of preventing the Huto business empire from escheating to the Throne was to save Tiphan from conviction on the most heinous charges, however futile that effort appeared.

The litigators had advised Tiphan that his best course was to plead guilty to the lesser charges and throw himself at the mercy of the judges. But Tiphan rejected their counsel because he knew that no mercy would be granted. Treason prosecutions were extremely rare; the Throne never brought such charges unless they intended to seek the death penalty. And after what he had done . . .

He forced his remarkable brain to focus on the task of survival despite the terror, to devise some scheme to conjure a miracle.

The Throne's case was built on circumstantial evidence, he realized. He had been paid with gold ingots with stamps that could be traced back to tribute fleets to Rui; many of the pirates caught working with him wielded Lyucu-sourced bone weapons; the rescued victims had overheard conversations that strongly hinted that they were destined to be slaves for the Lyucu.

But Tiphan clung to the hope that the Throne had no direct proof. The anti-piracy raids had not caught any of the pirate kings who negotiated the deals with him, only low-level flunkies. He had been careful to transact with his "partners" only through intermediaries and to leave no written trail. Moreover, none of his own people had ever heard him make an unambiguous, clear reference to abducting skilled workers for the Lyucu—he had insisted that everyone speak in code.

The Throne had to prove that he knew or should have known that the abducted mechanics and engineers were being sold to the Lyucu. That was the heart of the treason charge; everything else he had done paled in significance next to that. So long as the requisite mental element of the crime was lacking, he could not be convicted.

Deny, deny, deny! he instructed his litigators.

But the litigators told him that the Throne intended to call on other witnesses, farseers whose testimony would have to be in camera and sealed. Apparently the farseers had secret intelligence about the Lyucu plans and would be able to show that Tiphan Huto had been acting as their agent. A full confession that gave the farseers additional information was his only chance for leniency.

No! Never!

Cold sweat drenched his back; he couldn't sleep the whole night. If the farseers were involved, then he was sure to be convicted. Telling the truth would only make things worse. No one bargained with the farseers and came out ahead, not even a business genius like Tiphan Huto.

And so, in the morning, when he was brought to court to confront the new witnesses, he was ready to soil himself a second time in order to delay the inevitable by another hour. Unfortunately, due to nervousness, he had neither eaten nor drunk anything for most of a day, and he lacked the ammunition to carry out this last, desperate tactic.

Terror and regret so clouded his mind as he knelt there that it took him a while to understand the chief judge sitting behind the bench as he read from a scroll.

. . . Empress Jia has directly intervened . . . farseers will not testify . . . We deem the defendant's actions extraordinarily base and heinous . . . insufficient evidence to support a charge of treason, which is hereby withdrawn in a confession of error . . . is convicted on all other charges . . . Empress Jia pleads for mercy . . . therefore a fine will be imposed instead . . .

He knelt there, stunned, as the realization gradually sank in. His gambit had worked. He had called the farseers' bluff.

His best guess was that the farseers either did not know as much as they claimed or didn't want to reveal the extent of their knowledge of Lyucu plans (even in sealed testimony). To minimize the embarrassment of a failed treason prosecution, Secretary Kidosu had appealed to the empress to intervene and grant him what essentially amounted to a pardon. To be sure, the Huto clan would pay a heavy price, as the fine levied to compensate the victims and to send a message would certainly eject the family from the top rank of trading clans in Wolf's Paw. But compared to what could have happened . . .

"Just be glad you weren't prosecuted during the Principate or the Reign of Four Placid Seas," his litigators told him, looking smug, as though his salvation was the result of their useless, wagging tongues, instead of the victory of his own clever stratagem of denial and delay, executed by himself with flawless verve and battle-hardened resolve. Tiphan told them to get out of his sight immediately.

Still, Tiphan agreed with the litigators in one respect: He had been lucky. Kuni Garu had abolished paid litigators, simplified the criminal code, and given the farseers free rein over the investigation and punishment of traitors. Tiphan wouldn't have lasted a day under that system. Thank Tazu that Empress Jia and Prime Minister Cogo Yelu had built up the bureaucracy, with intricate rules of evidence and burdens of proof. Sure, the system avoided harming the innocent, but Tiphan was most glad that it also gave him the room to wiggle free.

"Bring me some iced sour-plum soup!" Tiphan called out, and shifted to a cooler spot on the bed.

After he returned to Toaza, the angry elders of the clan had berated and lectured him for three days and three nights, while he knelt before the mourning tablets of the Huto ancestors. What was left of the mercantile empire he had built was taken away from him and divided among his timid siblings and cousins, who couldn't recognize a good trading opportunity if it bit them in the ass. Then the elders had confined him to his room and told him he was to reflect on his errors and would have nothing more to do with the family's business.

Tiphan had seethed and stewed the whole time he knelt in the ancestral hall. How could the elders be so cruel? Didn't they see that everything Tiphan had done had been aimed at bringing more wealth and prestige to the family? How could his siblings and cousins be so shortsighted? Even with the losses from the fine, the clan retained enough capital to rise again—and meteorically so if he were in charge. This should be an occasion for celebration, and he, Tiphan Huto, should be hailed as a conquering hero in the field of business!

Never mind. He would bide his time.

Let my siblings and cousins worry about making money and bringing honor to the Huto name for a while. I need a break anyway.

Staying in his room wasn't so bad. He could order whatever food and drink he wanted, and maybe later, after the elders and his older siblings got busy and didn't watch him so closely, he could sneak in an indigo house girl or two and bet on the boat races by sending messenger pigeons to a bookie.

Eventually, after his siblings and cousins had bumped into a few walls and found out just how hard it was to engineer the rise of the Huto clan without their master tactician, they would surely come back to him begging. He would make them pay *then*.

For this was the most important lesson Tiphan Huto had learned from his experiences in Ginpen, the one fact about himself that he had not known before but now understood as bedrock truth, the one secret weapon that was more valuable than any skill or knowledge:

He was lucky.

He had dodged conviction for treason; evaded the near certainty of the death penalty; eluded the mysterious farseers, the self-righteous deputy minister of justice, the stone-faced judges, the meddling fools of the Blossom Gang . . . not because of the work of the overpaid litigators or his insincere displays of remorse (insisted on by the elders), but because *he was lucky*.

Incredibly, impossibly, Tazu-pleasing-and-Lutho-defyingly lucky.

And everyone knew that good fortune was the greatest, most desirable, and least replicable asset in business; everyone except his foolish relations.

So no, he regretted nothing and would have changed nothing. He would simply bide his time until he could take command of the clan again.

He took a sip of the iced sour-plum soup. A baby plum, tiny but incredibly sweet, landed on the tip of his tongue: an omen of good fortune. He sighed contentedly.

It's better to be lucky than right.

∾

- Do you know what Jia is up to, my sister, my other self?
- No, but when have we ever truly understood the heart of our favorite girl?
- Risana could never see into her mind—
—and neither can we. That is probably why, after all this time, we still
find her interesting.

Tiphan Huto was counting his winnings in the boat races when he felt something cold and hard pressing against his neck.

Impatiently, he tried to shove it away. The object bit into his hand, and he yelped in pain as he jolted awake in the darkness.

Actually, he wasn't sure he *was* awake. Gingerly, he ran his finger over the object: long, flat, two sharp edges . . . *there was a sword against his throat!*

He opened his mouth to scream, but a rough, knotted piece of rope forced its way between his teeth and was jammed right down his throat. He gagged, but the forceful hand behind the rope didn't relent.

"Are you always this slow?" demanded a harsh voice in the darkness. "Or did all that greasy food at dinner clog up that slimy, slippery organ you call a brain?"

"*Mfff!*"

A light flickered to life: a lit candle.

A woman stood on either side of the bed; both wore kerchiefs covering the lower halves of their faces. Their eyes glinted as coldly as the sword held at his throat.

"We just want to talk," said the woman with the candle, who seemed to be the older of the two. Her voice wasn't unkind.

"Our sisters are stationed near the rest of your family," said the woman with the sword, whose tone was far harsher and more threatening. "If you don't behave—" She drew the sword slowly across Tiphan's throat, drawing blood.

Tiphan couldn't care less about the rest of his family. But he nodded, not too vigorously, lest the sword cut deeper into his skin.

The woman lifted the blade away and pulled the knotted rope out of his mouth. "Sit up."

Tiphan did and tried to compose himself as the two women found cushions and sat down opposite him in *thakrido*. He saw that they were dressed in black leggings and black fitted tops that allowed them to move silently and efficiently, with no loose fabric to snag or catch on obstacles and corners. Their hair was coiled tightly atop their heads and pinned in place with plain black coral pins, the only decorative element a delicate silk flap at the end that shimmered in the firelight like a butterfly's wings or a dyran's fins.

The women were obviously hardened criminals, likely bandits who kidnapped for ransom.

He cleared his throat. "Err . . . Mistresses, no—Master Mistresses—no—" *How does one address robbers in a way that doesn't offend?* "Most Noble Bandit Queens—"

The two women looked at each other and grinned.

"I like that," said the older woman, the one with the candle. "You can call me Queen . . . Lightbringer."

"And you can call me Queen Blooddrinker," said the woman with the sword. She lifted the scarf over her face to reveal a snarl, her teeth glinting against the dim candle light.

"Yes, yes! Queen Lightbringer and Queen Blood . . . Blooddrinker—" He shuddered at this terrifying image. "Your humble servant is most honored to be visited by two such noble queens. I despise the government as much as you do! No, I despise it even more, especially that foolish Cogo Yelu and wicked Jia—"

Lightbringer and Blooddrinker both frowned at this attempt to curry their favor.

"No-no-no! I misspoke, misspoke!"—*of course women bandits would sympathize with Jia, a thief who had usurped the throne from her child*—"I despise the government exactly the right amount, not one whit more or less than is appropriate. Uh . . . um . . . if the noble queens could instruct this foolish servant how much . . . er, contribution you would like for your benevolent cause, I will endeavor to obtain it the soonest—"

"We're not here for ransom," said Blooddrinker impatiently. "Are you trying to insult us?"

"No, no! I misspoke again. The contribution would be *entirely* voluntary. It's to build a more magnificent mountain fortress befitting the dignity of the two noble queens—"

"Calm yourself, Master Huto," said Lightbringer gently. "We want to do business with you."

Tiphan paused. "What . . . what kind of business?"

"A business you're familiar with. We know you have certain connections with buyers who are . . . shall we say, in a *similar* trade as us."

Tiphan's mind churned. "Certain events lately have largely severed those connections."

"We know all about the trial. But the pirates captured by Aya Mazoti are just lowly henchmen. We know you can get back in touch with the pirate kings."

Tiphan tried to keep his voice noncommittal. "Even if I could— and I'm speaking purely in hypotheticals here—what exactly is it that you have to sell?"

"You don't need to worry about that. Suffice it to say that it'll be more profitable than anything else you can get your hands on, though you may sell it *only* to these buyers. We'll bring you a regular supply. You can mix it with your ordinary trading goods on shipments around the Islands and then make certain detours to meet with your buyers on the open seas. We'll split the profits half-and-half."

"Just *how* profitable?"

"Let's put it this way: If you manage the business well, the Huto clan may become the wealthiest trading clan of Wolf's Paw in three years."

A surge of excitement shot through Tiphan like a silkmotic bolt. "But I'm currently not allowed to do any trading. The elders have placed me under house arrest."

"That is a simple matter to take care of. In a couple of days there will be a messenger from the magistrate of Toaza to your clan heads, explaining that it is the Throne's policy to encourage the rehabilitation of criminals like you by putting them back to work in their trade as soon as possible."

"You can do that?"

"We have our ways," said Lightbringer.

Tiphan Huto pondered the proposal. His luck really was his

greatest asset. He had just been plotting his return earlier today, and look how many things were turning out exactly the way he wanted already!

"Are the goods you want me to trade dangerous?"

"Possibly," said Blooddrinker. "Especially if you try to steal any of it." She waved her sword threateningly again.

"I mean to ship! Whether it's dangerous to ship!"

"No," said Lightbringer. "In fact, it's likely that the customs inspectors won't even know what it is . . . but to be safe and to make sure you're focused, we'll want you to stop trading in all the other contraband you used to ship: antiques, saltpeter, pig iron, weapons, abducted individuals—especially abducted individuals. The risk is simply too great."

Tiphan started to object. "I'm not admitting *anything*—"

Lightbringer ignored him. "Don't worry, the profits from our goods will more than make up for your losses. Now, we all know that the pirates are just middlemen, and they won't appreciate the true value of what you'll be selling; so you may have to convince the pirates to carry a few trial boxes to the ultimate buyers first, just to prove that there is a market."

Tiphan nodded thoughtfully. If what these bandits were claiming was true, he would find ways to raise the prices once the market was proven, especially if he had a monopoly. As for dividing the profits half-and-half . . . *ha*, he was confident he could outwit a few simpleton bandits and make the deal even more favorable for himself.

To be sure, if the ultimate buyers were really willing to pay such an exorbitant price, then the goods were likely restricted to military use. That wasn't his problem, though. He was a clever merchant, not a dumb hero—just look at how poor the veterans were, even after losing an arm or a leg for Dara.

"I think we have a deal," he said. "Soon as you get the elders to let me trade again, we can start."

"Very good," said Lightbringer.

Before he could react, Blooddrinker had gotten up from her sitting cushion and closed the distance between them without appearing to move. Astonished, his jaw dropped reflexively. The woman pushed something into his mouth, pinched his nose shut, and slapped him squarely on the lips. The blow caused him to swallow whatever had been forced into his mouth.

"What . . . what was that?" he sputtered, trying to keep his shocked and terrified voice low since Blooddrinker had picked up that sword again.

"Consider it . . . insurance," said Lightbringer.

"You've just ingested a rare mushroom called Blooddrinker," said the woman with the same name. "In an hour it will take root in your stomach, and there will be no way to remove it from your body short of a surgeon slicing you open and ripping out your viscera along with it. Once rooted, the mushroom's mycelia will spread through-out your vessels and muscles, subsisting on your blood. In a month or so, you'll start to feel the most excruciating pain all over your body before a slow, agonizing death."

"But why!?" Tiphan trembled with rage and horror. "Why would you do this—"

"Not to worry. Though the mushroom can never be removed, we can give you a medicine to keep its growth under check. As long as you take it once every month, you'll live on indefinitely with no ill effects. Every time we meet to deliver you the goods and to get our profit, we'll give you a dose of the medicine."

Tiphan breathed hard as the implications sank in. Apparently these bandits were more sophisticated than he thought. This would guarantee his cooperation and honesty.

"Why don't we work out the details over the next hour?" said Lightbringer. "It will give the mushroom a chance to settle in your gut. Also, it's rather rude that you haven't offered us any tea."

Tiphan nodded in resignation as he went about preparing tea in the glow of the single candle. He was a little trepidatious at the idea of a deadly mushroom being implanted in his belly, but all in all, considering he would soon get everything he desired and more, he still thought he was blessed with extraordinary luck.

Tiphan Huto will rise again!

CHAPTER FOUR

A LONG JOURNEY REVEALS THE TRUE STRENGTH OF A HORSE

WORLD'S EDGE MOUNTAINS: THE SEVENTH MONTH IN THE NINTH YEAR AFTER THE DEPARTURE OF PRINCESS THÉRA FROM DARA FOR UKYU-GONDÉ (TEN MONTHS UNTIL THE LYUCU MUST LAUNCH THEIR NEW INVASION FLEET TO DARA).

The band managed to stay just out of the reach of the pursuing Lyucu, but they never could shake the hunters completely. No matter how obscure the valleys they hiked through or how unexpected the direction of their flight, always, at most a few days later, the Lyucu would appear on the edge of the horizon.

Though he tried to maintain a confident demeanor, with each failed attempt to be free of the pursuit, Takval grew more worried.

One morning, as the camp awakened in late afternoon—they always traveled at night and slept much of the day to reduce the possibility of discovery—Takval found that the two Agon warriors posted as lookouts were missing. There were no signs of predators or struggle.

Takval sighed. Apparently, the pair had finally lost faith and stolen away while the rest of them were sleeping. Considering that all the rebels, Dara and Agon, remaining with Takval now numbered less than twenty, this was a tremendous blow.

"Do they really think they can just fade away into the scrublands, to be adopted into some Lyucu or Agon tribe where they can live out the rest of their days in peace?" fumed Takval, as though talking to himself. "Every tribe will be on the lookout. Capturing one of the escapees from Kiri Valley will bring them great rewards from Cudyu."

There was no response. Everyone understood that Takval had delivered that monologue as a warning.

Théra beckoned Takval to come with her on a walk away from the campsite.

"You can't do that," she said quietly.

Ever since that rainy-day talk with Thoryo, Théra had begun to rouse herself. Though she was no longer the confident, determined leader of Kiri Valley, she took part in discussions with Takval and the others, and offered ideas and suggestions from time to time. With each passing day, more strength seemed to return to her, and she took an active role in hunting, pitching the tent, tending to Alkir's needs, even asking Takval to teach her how to ride, something she had never shown much interest for in the past.

"What do you mean?"

"You're the pékyu," said Théra. "Our cause may look hopeless, but we haven't lost. It's only when you stop trying to inspire them and resort to threats that they'll lose all faith in you."

Takval gazed at Théra. The mask of resolution and strength, which he had kept up for months, fell away in an instant, revealing a tired and frightened man. In a barely audible whisper, he said, "What can we do with one garinafin and less than twenty people, many of whom aren't even fighters?"

"I don't know," said Théra. "But I do know that Tenryo Roaten was once just an escaped hostage with a single garinafin, and that my father began his rebellion with a band of prisoners and deserters about equal in number to ours. And I seem to recall an Agon prince who wasn't afraid to dive into the endless sea from a city-ship, alone, armed only with the hope that he would find a way to free his people."

Takval pulled Théra into an embrace and kissed her deeply. "My breath, the mirror of my soul," he said when he finally let her go. "I have missed you."

"I'm sorry that I haven't been there for you," said Théra, tears in her eyes. "Kunilu-*tika* and Jian-*tika* may be gone, but the beauty of the world remains. We must not let the storm make us forget the rainbow."

"Now that you're with me again, I already feel as strong as Afir."

As they turned back toward the encampment, Théra whispered to herself, "There's always a second act. Always."

True to his word, Takval made no more threats. Instead, he rallied the Agon warriors to practice and drill, making plans to capture more garinafins if they should chance upon a lone Lyucu hunting party in the foothills. Meanwhile, Théra kept up the spirits of Tipo, Çami, and the other Dara members of the party, reminding them that they still had the opportunity to avenge their friends and loved ones, and to carry out the mission that their homeland had entrusted to them.

One day, Takval returned to the camp from a scouting flight unexpectedly early. Behind Alkir, his mount, was another garinafin, so badly injured that it could barely keep aloft. The pilot was Araten, one of the Agon thanes of Kiri Valley, who everyone thought had been lost along with the others. Riding with him were six other Agon warriors, all of them beyond their prime fighting years or injured at the time of the Lyucu assault.

The newcomers were a sorry sight: emaciated, covered in scars—the older ones clearly from fighting and the newer ones signs of struggle against the elements. Their eyes looked haunted, as though they had witnessed horrors beyond the ken of mere mortals.

Théra was amazed. "How did—"

"Later," said Takval gently but firmly. "There will be time enough."

Quickly, ventilated fire pits were stoked to life. Based on a traditional Agon design with improvements made by Çami, these pits minimized smoke and firelight, keeping the risk of discovery to a minimum. Hot water revived the spirits of the newcomers, and they wolfed down the roast meat and berry sauce Takval and Théra offered.

"You cannot imagine how glad we are to see you," said Théra, once Araten and the others had eaten their fill.

"I think I can, Princess," said Araten, his gaunt and scarred face relaxing into a wan smile. "So many have died, and I can't tell you how many times the doubt that I'd never find you and the pékyu again assaulted me."

It did not escape Théra's notice that Araten had emphasized that he had been looking for both her and Takval, and had in fact mentioned her first. This small gesture almost moved her to tears.

"But an Agon warrior never gives up," said Araten, "and the gods have seen fit to reward my faith. Votan." He struggled to his feet, swaying unsteadily, and saluted Takval by lifting both his arms and crossing them at the wrists. Then he turned to Théra. "Votan," he repeated, giving a Dara-style bow.

After the desertion of the lookouts earlier, the steadfastness of the irascible Araten, who had never seemed to respect her back in Kiri Valley and who she had never really liked, overwhelmed her. The scars on the thane's body and face bore witness to the tortures and terrors he must have suffered to escape from the Lyucu and make his way here.

"In my land," said Théra, keeping her voice even with great effort, "it is said that only a long journey can reveal the true strength of a horse—that's a kind of land-bound garinafin, and much smaller. Only with the passage of time can we see the true characters of our companions. I'm sorry we weren't better friends in the past."

Araten also cried, and there wasn't a pair of dry eyes in attendance.

Takval lengthened his patrols with Alkir. With a wounded garinafin and fighters still on the mend, it was even more important they get advance warning when the Lyucu approached.

No Lyucu pursuers were sighted over the next week—the longest stretch the refugees had been able to stay in one place. Some attributed the respite to the seclusion of the valley they were in— perhaps Cudyu's hunting parties had overshot their location and were now to the north, moving farther away with each passing day. Others thought the Lyucu pékyu had finally given up after such a long, fruitless search.

Takval told Théra that though he couldn't be sure, he believed that Araten's escape had something to do with it. Fearful that more enslaved Agon would follow the example of Araten, Cudyu had probably decided to call off the pursuit and gather his warriors and prisoners back in Taten to consolidate his position. Théra, though skeptical of such wishful thinking, hoped that he was right.

In any event, the break was welcome as it gave Araten and the other wounded a chance to recuperate. The new members of the band recounted their adventures.

Most of the captives from Kiri Valley had been sent to Taten, explained Araten, but he and some of the other Agon prisoners, since they had resisted so fiercely before finally succumbing to their wounds, needed time to recover at the valley. Cudyu left the wounded Lyucu behind as well, as he set off in pursuit of Takval and Théra. Volyu, the hated traitor, left long before Araten and the others had recovered enough to seek him out for vengeance—

"Wait!" Théra cried, speaking for everyone in Takval's band. "Did you say our uncle was the traitor?"

Thus did Volyu's plot come to light. There was much pounding of the ground and cursing of his name. Tears of grief flowed afresh. To think that so many had died because of a single craven man was nigh intolerable.

Adyulek went to one knee before Théra. "Princess, forgive me for having wronged you. You were not the cause of our fall. I have not always agreed with your decisions, but I should never have allowed our discord to cloud my judgment. There is no excuse for my obdurate error."

The other Agon followed her lead.

But Théra sat there, stunned. The revelation did not lessen her feelings of guilt. If anything, it made them worse.

For it had been at her insistence, years ago, that Takval spared his uncle. She had thought Volyu could be won over or controlled, that having his help was better than more bloodshed. But she had not seen through Volyu's nature, and the blood of all those who had died at Kiri Valley was even more indelibly on her hands.

My father betrayed the Hegemon on the shore of the Liru, knowing that keeping him alive would lead to many more deaths down the road. I chose mercy when I was faced with a similar decision, and fate proved me wrong. Am I too weak to make the hard decisions?

Araten went on. He explained that he'd gone around in secret, testing out which of the Agon captives still believed in the pékyu's cause. It wasn't easy, for after the escape of the pékyus-taasa, security around the remaining prisoners had been redoubled—

"WHAT?" asked a shocked Théra, halting the narrative once more.

Thus did it come to light that the guards escorting the children had gotten drunk one night, leaving Toof and Radia in charge of the prisoners. Razutana, Sataari, and the children had somehow managed to free themselves, overcame Toof and Radia, and escaped into the wilderness with the garinafins. When the dazed guards finally followed the Blood River on foot back to a Lyucu encampment and reported the missing prisoners to Cudyu, the Lyucu pékyu had immediately realized that Toof and Radia were responsible for a plot. They were stripped of all rank and sent to Taten as slaves—death, as Cudyu put it, would be "too kind" for these two traitors.

The band was overjoyed as Araten explained that despite Cudyu's best efforts, the children had not been found. The garinafins they stole had been recovered later, hundreds of miles from where they had gone missing. Though many thought the children must have died of exposure and starvation over the winter, just as many believed that they had in fact managed to find some obscure hideout and survived.

"I'm certain they're alive," said Gozofin to Takval and Théra. "My Nalu is a good hunter, and Sataari and Razutana, though no warriors, are resourceful. The gods are watching over them!"

Takval and Théra embraced and shed tears of joy. If Théra had already found Araten likable earlier, this second revelation filled her with glowing gratitude toward the stouthearted warrior. Everyone's spirits lifted.

Once the tide of joy had ebbed a bit, Théra became thoughtful again. Now that Toof and Radia's loyalty had been reaffirmed, their actions had to be reinterpreted. By carrying out the ruthless scrubland tactic of leaving the children behind to distract Cudyu, the pair had not only saved the children, but Takval and Théra as well. Having experienced months of strenuous hikes and desperate flights through the mountains, the princess had to agree that had they kept the children with them, it would have been far more difficult, if not impossible, for the band to have evaded capture. It was hard enough to stay ahead of the Lyucu pursuit with able-bodied adults and one fighting garinafin. An additional garinafin laden with helpless children would have doomed everyone.

A difficult decision had to be made, and Toof and Radia had made it in an instant, risking their lives and honor both. The contrast between their hard resolve and her own useless vacillation couldn't be greater. She was filled with guilt, admiration, self-doubt, and gratitude. She vowed to rescue the two adopted Agon and find the children at the first chance—but . . . did she really have what it would take?

Volyu, who she had believed was loyal and true, had turned out to be the architect of their downfall. Toof and Radia, who she had condemned as traitors, had turned out to be the saviors of both the children of Kiri Valley and the lone surviving band of rebels. Was there anything more mysterious and complicated than the human heart? How could one tell true hearts apart from false ones?

"You're indeed messengers of good news," said Takval. "But you haven't explained how *you* escaped from Cudyu's clutches."

All winter, Araten and the other wounded Agon prisoners recuperated in what remained of the razed settlement in Kiri Valley. As time went on, the Lyucu guards slackened in their vigilance. And when spring arrived, one night, Araten and a band of warriors loyal to Takval overcame their guards and seized a garinafin, making their way north in search of their lost lord.

Araten and his band had evaded the notice of the Lyucu search parties by disguising themselves as tanto-lyu-naro, tribeless wanderers of the scrublands who had given up all warfare. The "warriors who do not make war" worshipped an aspect of the god of healing called Toryoana of Still Hands and renounced all violence—an alternate name for their god was Toryoana Pacific. Though they were scorned by all the tribes of the scrublands, Lyucu and Agon alike, fear of retribution from the god also kept them from harm. Since they made their living by scavenging and begging, this gave Araten and his band a chance at gathering information about Cudyu's political maneuverings and plans.

"Cudyu has been summoning the most skilled shamans and the cleverest Dara slaves to Taten," said Araten.

"What for?" asked Théra.

"Volyu told Cudyu that the Wall of Storms around Dara is going to reopen again. Cudyu wants his gathering of the knowledgeable to repeat the steps of Luan Zya and calculate the exact time so that he can send another invasion fleet to Dara."

Théra realized that this was again most likely her own fault. Though she had been careful to keep the reopening of the Wall a secret, Volyu must have deduced, based on her interest in attacking Taten, that such a reopening was likely.

Time and again, she had been outfoxed.

Théra pondered this new development. To discern the patterns in the Wall of Storms and to calculate its future openings were feats as difficult as the prediction of eclipses. It was the crowning achievement of the great Luan Zyaji in a long career of brilliant computations and inventions. Even the gifted Zomi Kidosu had to rely on Luan's clues to re-create his calculations. The idea that the Lyucu, without the benefit of centuries of Dara learning and a literate culture, could solve such a problem on their own appeared facially absurd.

But hadn't she been consistently wrong precisely because she had underestimated those she dealt with? Volyu, Toof and Radia, Cudyu . . . the list was long.

"Rumors say that they're making good progress in Taten," said Araten. "The group has already narrowed the timing of the next opening down to the year."

"Do you know if it's the year after the next?" she asked. Her chest felt tight. She had already paid for her arrogance; she was not going to repeat that mistake. *Death only triumphs when we stop learning.*

Araten shook his head. "I've heard only rumors without details."

"As soon as you've recovered enough, you must go back to the scrublands and find out more," said Théra. *Oh, please, please let it not be true!* she prayed. There was literally nothing she could do at this point to stop another invasion fleet. If Cudyu succeeded in computing the moment the wall would reopen, her journey to Ukyu-Gondé and the sacrifices of so many would all be for naught.

Araten was reluctant to return to the scrublands, as the chances of being discovered by Cudyu's people increased with each encounter with the other tribes. But Takval supported Théra, knowing how much the matter gnawed at his wife's heart. Preventing another Lyucu invasion fleet was the foundation of the alliance between the Agon and Dara and her most important strategic goal.

A few days later, Araten announced that he was ready and left alone, without his garinafin or companions.

Meanwhile, Théra continued her riding lessons. Now that the band had two war mounts, it seemed especially important for every able-bodied member of the group to learn to ride garinafins effectively to give them the most tactical flexibility.

Takval taught Théra personally. She proved a decent student, and within a couple of weeks, she was able to guide Ga-al, the old bull garinafin brought by Araten, with some confidence as Takval sat on the saddle behind her. Ga-al had apparently been raised as a war garinafin under the Lyucu method of absolute obedience induced through terror and abuse so that he could be ridden by any pilot. Now past the prime age of a war mount, Ga-al had been relegated to transportation duty, and would have been retired to the slaughter grounds in a year or so. The lackadaisical security around the aged animal was how Araten had been able to steal him. Though the bull was docile, he was also skittish and timid, flinching each time someone approached his head, as though fearing some punishment. Taking pity on the abused creature, Théra tended to the garinafin's wounds while he recuperated, and the beast seemed to be slowly developing a bond of trust with her.

Staying on the garinafin proved to be the easy part. Unless she asked Ga-al to perform aerial acrobatics—which she had no intention of doing—the bull in level flight was surprisingly steady. But the system of giving commands to the garinafin through knee squeezes, foot kicks, strokes against the neck, and verbal commands delivered through the spine-tapping trumpet proved to be as challenging as learning a new language.

Riders on a speeding garinafin were practically deaf. The roaring wind, generated by the beating wings as well as turbulence from the rushing air, made it impossible for riders to converse with one another, much less to speak to their mount. To solve the problem, the people of the scrublands relied on a garinafin-bone trumpet: the narrow end of the device was pressed against the spinous process of the last vertebra at the base of the mount's neck, and the pilot then shouted simple commands into the flared mouthpiece.

Sa-sa, for instance, meant that the garinafin was supposed to execute a quick turn in the air in order to spot any enemies tight on its tail. *Ruga-to*, on the other hand, meant that the garinafin was supposed to give chase to the nearest enemy and bathe it in flames. *Péte-péte* meant the garinafin was supposed to repeat the last maneuver, and *ta-sli* meant that the garinafin needed to twist and buckle as violently as possible—the command was usually issued by the pilot to throw off aerial boarders from hostile garinafin crews. *Tek* was the most common command given during patrols—it meant to stay alert—while *te-vote* was probably the order least often issued— it meant that the garinafin was to wrestle with the enemy with talons and teeth, a tactic of last resort when the garinafin's fire breath was depleted. There was a whole system of these verbal commands that Théra needed to learn, supplemented by physical gestures that covered more basic maneuvers.

The first time Théra was asked to try to command Ga-al, she found the process utterly baffling.

"I can't even hear what I'm saying; how can he hear it?" Théra asked. She had to lean back and turn her head until she was practically screaming into Takval's ear for him to hear her question.

"He can hear it through the bones," shouted Takval. "You just have to trust it. The trumpet works."

Half disbelieving, she turned back around, pressed the narrow end of the bone trumpet against the base of the trunk-thick neck, and spoke into the mouthpiece.

"Sa-sa."

The garinafin obediently turned around in a tight circle, banking steeply, before returning to their former heading and continuing.

She marveled both at the fact that the animal could hear her through his spine and the fact that he could understand her. She had known that garinafins were intelligent, but it was one thing to know this intellectually, and quite another to experience a mountain of muscle and sinew heeding her commands.

A week more of practice sessions later, Théra asked to ride alone.

"Are you sure?" asked Takval. "You are new to this—"

"I have to be able to do this on my own," said Théra adamantly.

"All right," said Takval. "But remember to stay low so you won't be spotted from afar and don't leave the valley. If you see anything suspicious, return immediately."

Théra took off at the crack of dawn. The sensation of freedom, of soaring through the air, was exhilarating. Flying on the back of a garinafin was nothing like riding in an airship. An airship, despite its feathered oars and complement of contracting and expanding lift gas bladders inspired by the Mingén falcon, was ultimately a machine and not a living thing. To be an airship rider was to be a passive passenger.

Piloting a garinafin, on the other hand, required constant movement and participation—a dance between the rider and her mount. She had to shift her center of gravity as the beast turned to maintain balance, squeeze and flex her legs to stay in the saddle, match her breathing to the beast's heaving rhythms. To move in sync with her partner-mount, to feel the garinafin's body heat against her thighs, and to vibrate in sympathy with the tremors in the massive body made the experience organic, as though she had melded into another being.

Gaining confidence, she practiced diving, climbing, tight and slow turns, some common defensive maneuvers, and even a few mock attacks. The chilly winds slicing across her skin, despite the warm summer morning air rising in the valley, made her appreciate the thick furs and leggings favored by the Lyucu.

Satisfied with her progress, Théra decided to take a break midmorning. For her landing site, she picked a wide stone ledge jutting out halfway up a steep mountainside. While dense foliage covered the sheer cliffs above and below, the stone platform was bare, making it seem almost man-made. She thought it a good perch to refresh herself with a snack, as she was not confident enough to try eating on the back of a soaring garinafin.

As soon as Ga-al landed, however, he strained and squealed, seeming to want to take off again immediately.

"Wait!" said Théra, laughing. She gently but firmly brushed the side of the beast's neck to calm him down, the way Takval had shown her. "You may be full of vim and vigor, but I need a break and a bite to eat."

The garinafin, however, refused to be placated. He snorted and lowed, shuffling in place and preventing Théra from climbing off his back. In the end, Théra had no choice but to use the bone trumpet and speak in a severe voice of authority to compel obedience.

"Kiru-kiru!"

Reluctantly, Ga-al twisted his neck around and placed his head right below his shoulder, so that Théra could step on it and dismount.

Despite the garinafin's fussing, Théra found the ledge a pleasant resting stop. Broad-leafed vines dangling from the rock face above provided plenty of shade, and the jutting platform afforded her an unimpeded view of much of the valley floor and the mountains on the other side. Now that she wasn't consumed with the effort of hanging on to the back of a massive beast hurtling through the air, she could appreciate the beauty of the magnificent valley with a calmer heart and a more leisurely gaze.

The mountains that walled the valley were sharp and steep, like clumps of swords, their outlines deepened by the long shadows of early morning. Here and there, a peak seemed to have been sheared off, leaving behind a flat platform covered by grass and wildflowers, resembling the intricate designs Dara bladesmiths etched into their weapons. Crags carved by the wind into strange and fantastic shapes teetered on ledges, and the bottom of the valley was shrouded in fog. Everything seemed pristine, unexplored, untouched by the hand of man, as the people of the scrublands stayed away from these sacred mountains—except for desperate refugees like them.

Théra knew that after months of meandering north, they had by now entered the foothills of one of the branch ranges of the World's Edge Mountains, known as the Foot among the Agon and the Wing among the Lyucu. If she were to ascend to the top of her side of the valley, she would catch a glimpse of the tall mountains to the east, the spine of the titanic imaginary garinafin that was the barrier to the realm of the gods. Those snowbound peaks, disappearing into the clouds like spears thrust into the domain of the stars, were among the tallest peaks in all Ukyu-Gondé—indeed, in the whole known world.

Gingerly, she sat down at the edge of the platform, her legs dangling over the side. She took out a skin pouch filled with smoked meat and fresh berries, and began to eat.

As she savored the chewy treat, she couldn't help but reflect on the differences between the landscapes of Dara and Ukyu-Gondé.

The dominant feature of Dara was the sea. Against that endless, blue, shimmering liquid mirror, everything in the Islands appeared delicate, fragile, refined, as though etched in wax by a Creator wielding an ivory writing knife. Stately cliffs, pounded by waves, formed the semantic roots; frozen lava, smoothed by dancing rain and singing wind, made up the motive modifiers; lakes, gouged out by silent glaciers and filled by the clear ink of winding rivers, served as inflection glyphs; and over it all was a cacophony of phonetic adapters: the *thaké-thaké* of spring rain, the twittering of brightly plumaged summer birds, the rustling of crimson autumn leaves, the skittering of bolting winter hares, the squeaking and moaning of sailors' spars and cables, the clinking and clanking of merchants' coins, the susurration of scholars unfolding scrolls and turning pages, the murmurs and chants of monks and nuns in incense-shrouded temples, the rainbow-hued music of the endless variety of topolects in markets, forums, restaurants, teahouses, lecture halls, hamlets, palaces. . . .

Dara was a colorful book of logograms, and the people of Dara were the scribes who read, wrote, revised, edited, amended, emended, annotated, compiled, arranged, polished. The landscape was like a pruned garden or a cultivated field, over which the gods, human-shaped though hero-scaled, roamed gently as caretakers and horticulturists, frequently intervening as much for the benefit of their charges as for their own amusement.

In contrast, the dominant feature of the scrublands was the bare earth itself, and the Sculptor seemed to have wielded an axe as grand as a shooting star and as rough as the growl of a horrid wolf. The lakes were wide as seas; the rivers inconstant and unpredictable as youthful hearts; the mountains hewn out of prime chaos with a carelessness that left jagged scars. The boundless wilderness resembled a vast sheet of taut skin stretched over the skeleton of the universe, over which tribes of humans, herds of cattle and aurochs, flocks of sheep and mouflon, packs of horrid wolves, ambushes of tigers, flights of garinafins, and the scraggly bushes and spiny cactus lobes and clumps of grass careened and vibrated, handfuls of colorful sand impelled by the storytelling dance of a Shaman. The gods, distant and amorphous presences, surveyed this vast painting dispassionately, disdaining to be involved.

Everything in Ukyu and Gondé was oversized, expansive, tending to extremes. Even the tallest peak in Dara could not match the height of an unnamed spike in the Wing or the Foot, let alone the magnificent spine that was the World's Edge Mountains. Even the deepest canyons in Dara were mere gullies when placed next to this valley, so wide and spacious that it allowed a garinafin to stretch its wings and work up a sweat—and they had already passed through hundreds of such valleys in their journey. Entire islands from Dara could fit inside Aluro's Basin or the Sea of Tears, and it was said that there were a thousand-thousand ice floes up north in Nalyufin's Pasture, each as big as a mountain. A dust storm racing across the scrublands could be the size of Arulugi or Rui, entire kingdoms swallowed up in a single puff of divine breath.

How can I understand this land, which is so different from the land of my birth? How can I understand its gods, which are so different from the gods of my childhood? How can I learn its mysterious ways, which are not the ways of my people?

What did that goddess-like lady say? If you do not like the stories you've been told, fill your heart with new stories. If you do not like the script you've been given, design for yourself new roles.

I am neither an exile nor a sojourner in Ukyu-Gondé. I belong here.
To start a second act, I must first say goodbye to the first.

As she continued to gaze out at the magnificent natural wonder that was the valley, Théra felt herself transported to that day years ago, when she had sat atop another mountain with the world spread out at her feet, next to someone she loved.

> *How far will they go? What will they behold?*
> *What distant shores will they touch and visit*
> *Before they sink and sprout and grow and bloom—*
> *To sway over sun-dappled waves anew!*

"O Zomi, my wakeful weakness," she whispered. She looked up at the sun and prayed that the golden orb, like the moon, would agree to carry a message to her beloved. She was now a mother and the wife of another, with many more attachments and threads of love about her, but the bond between her and Zomi had not weakened with the passage of time. She hoped that the other woman was also looking up at the sun and could feel her thoughts.

What are you thinking? What are you doing? Are you helping Phyro to be the best emperor he can be? Have you, my mother, my brother, and all the people of Dara, found a way to defeat the Lyucu invaders or at least hold them back? Have you—

Abruptly, she was pulled out of her reverie. Ga-al was moaning loudly and looking at her inquiringly. He turned his pupil-less eyes to the cliff at the back of the ledge and snorted with hostility.

"What's the matter?"

The garinafin shook his head and shuffled back away from the cliff until he was near the lip of the ledge. He swung his long neck through the air above her and stopped when his head was pointing into the valley, like a long and very large finger.

Annoyed to be interrupted, Théra snapped at the garinafin, "I know you want to fly again. But I want a little more time to just be by myself, all right?"

The garinafin snorted, looking at her pleadingly.

Théra had to laugh. She was getting mad at an *animal*, even if a very clever animal. "I'm sorry," she said, taking a deep breath to calm herself. "I haven't felt like myself for a long time. So much has . . . happened."

It was relaxing to talk to the garinafin, who didn't judge her, doubt her, ponder ways to take advantage of her, or scheme against her. She could understand how Toof used to claim that he preferred to be with garinafins than people.

Ga-al cocked his massive head to look at her quizzically as she continued to talk to him. He scratched at the ground impatiently with his claws like a chicken searching for grubs.

"I've been trying to do the right thing, the best thing for both the Agon and the Dara, but things keep on not working out. But I've been wondering if maybe the problem is that I haven't really learned to think the way this land wants me to think, to no longer be a Princess of Dara but a true Bride of the Agon. The gods and stories here are shaped by this land, as much as the gods and stories of Dara are shaped by the islands. And until I start to learn, truly learn—"

And in that moment, she saw Ga-al's neck stiffen.

A strange sensation descended over her.

No, that wasn't quite right. It was as though the strange sensation had descended over the *world*. Abruptly, the world had fallen silent and still, and an overwhelming *presence* enveloped her.

There was an indescribable quality to this presence, an ineffable purity and ethereal clarity. She was familiar with it because she had experienced something like it twice before: once with the lady by Lake Tututika, who had taught her the parable of lotus seeds with empty hearts, and once with a man in the palace at Pan, who played the *moaphya* and taught her the unity between sound and light.

She felt like she was cradled in the hand of some giant—no, it was more like she was nestled in the *ear* of some giant. She was surrounded by a powerful, awe-inspiring, sublime being who truly *listened* to her. Perhaps this was what newborns felt as they were held close to the breast of their mothers, an all-consuming sense of peace, of trusted ease, of unconditional love that withstood all storms.

She let herself give in to the sensation. After so much guilt, self-doubt, and heart-wrenching loss, she yearned for someone who truly listened and heard the voice in her heart while she plucked out a hesitant tune. Takval and Thoryo tried their best and came close, but no one could *hear* her heart-voice the way she wanted to be heard, no one except, perhaps, Zomi.

The world faded away from her consciousness, and all she wanted was to sink into this all-enveloping sea of love, this undulating eternity of being listened to and heard, forever.

Annoyingly, there were noises demanding her attention, flittering, stinging nibbles from little fish that assaulted her as she drifted in the peaceful sea. She dove deeper, out of their reach.

Ga-al leapt across the platform, brandishing his claws as he landed.

. . . *as though he has spotted some threat.*

But the movements of the garinafin felt as unreal as a shadow play. Reality was this sea of the numinous. She had dived so deep that her feet touched the bottom, and now she found herself standing on a vast plain covered by a vaster sky, and all around her, bushes with crooked limbs and waxy leaves cowered like humans coming face-to-face with the divine. Lightning bolts crisscrossed the sky, and towering tornadoes danced across the scrublands, each a pillar reaching from the earth to the heavens.

The dancing storms seemed to form and re-form into different figures, titans who struggled on a stage as large as the world. She saw generations rise and fall, some looking like birds, some looking like fish, some looking like the clenched-fist cacti that stood mutely in the desert. She saw tribes rising out of the ashes and remnants of destroyed worlds. She saw human beings construct grand works that rivaled the magnificence of the gods, only to have them ruined by monsters that knew nothing of pity or remorse. She saw a paradise on earth, and then a hell fallen from heaven. She saw the Agon and the Lyucu make their entrances on the stage, migrating across the land as fluidly as their cattle and sheep, taking to the air on the backs of garinafins to fight against gods and men, fearless of the consequences.

Ga-al leapt back to the lip of the platform, squealing in terror.

. . . *as though he had lost some encounter.*

It didn't matter. She was an observer safely in the embrace of the divine, watching the grandest storytelling dance in the universe, lit by the fire of godhead. She wept as villains triumphed in darkness; she cheered as heroes won through guile and strength; she read the narrative strands in these tales that unified them with the stories of Dara, the foundational truth in all myths that survived the eons; she also understood the distinctions that made the stories uniquely the expressions of the scrublands, as innate to this land as its fauna and flora, its harsh climate and axe-hewn mountains, its peoples and gods.

She was sure that this was what the shamans meant when they were possessed by the gods and spirits of ancient warriors. Her body no longer belonged to her or to this world, and whatever happened on this stone ledge had no connection to her essence, to her soul at all.

She felt immortal.

Ga-al leapt again, straight over her head, and she ducked out of instinct. She turned around to see what he was so worked up about.

A gigantic feline form gracefully approached her out of the dancing storms, sharp tusks protruding from its jaws. The creature was at least the size of an elephant from back home on Écofi. Its cave-like maw was yawning open as it roared, but there was no sound.

It felt out of place, like the presence of an actor who suddenly stood up in front of a shadow-puppet screen, breaking the illusion.

Théra felt no fear at all. If the tusked tiger decided to tear her to shreds, she would be liberated, no longer tethered to this sublunary plane.

Descending, Ga-al tried to attack the tiger with his left claw, his wings buffeting the air to maintain balance. The tusked tiger swiped back at the garinafin with one of its massive paws, batting the claw out of the way. Ga-al shrieked and backed away on frantic wings.

Théra wanted to tell the two of them to cut it out. There was no place for violence, for fighting, in this world of pure love. She wished they could feel what she was feeling. How could they not?

Ga-al struggled into the air, the narrow space on the ledge making the takeoff arduous. He swooped around the outside of the ledge and assaulted the tiger once more, this time from behind the predator's head. The tusked tiger had no choice but to duck down and roll away. The tiger turned its head away from Théra and toward the garinafin, roaring silently. Ga-al twisted his long neck to whip his head out of the way, as though the tiger were spitting invisible venom.

The vast scrubland stage and the dancing tornadoes disappeared in an instant, and Théra gasped, as though she had been rudely plucked out of a warm pool and plunged back into the icy cold physicality of this world. The sounds and colors of reality rushed back into her consciousness in a flood.

She screamed as the realization struck her. She was going to be killed by the tusked tiger looming over her like a mountain of death, and there was nothing she could do to save herself. She scrambled back on her hands and knees, heedless of the sheer drop behind her, intent only on getting as far away from the animal as possible.

The tusked tiger whipped its head back and locked eyes with her. It opened its maw and roared silently once more.

The *presence* descended over her, and Théra stopped trying to get away. She was back in the ear of the giant, in the warm, numinous sea, on the divine scrublands where the storms danced eternally.

There is absolutely nothing to worry about.

She smiled at the approaching tiger and beckoned it closer.

A shadow loomed above her. She looked up. The wings of a garinafin blotted out the sun momentarily as the beast and the rider dove down at her.

CHAPTER FIVE

INTO THE BARROWS

TATEN-RYO-ALVOVO: THE SEVENTH MONTH IN
THE NINTH YEAR AFTER THE DEPARTURE OF
PRINCESS THÉRA FROM DARA FOR UKYU-GONDÉ
(TEN MONTHS UNTIL THE LYUCU MUST LAUNCH
THEIR NEW INVASION FLEET TO DARA).

One sunny summer day, as Sataari and Razutana organized the children to go to the shore to catch brine shrimp and dig for marsh clams, Tanto complained of a stomachache. Concerned, Razutana offered to stay with him, but the boy declined.

"Are you sure?"

"I just need to lie down for a bit."

"Drink plenty of water."

The boy nodded, his brows knotted as though suppressing a groan.

"Are you in a lot of pain?" asked Razutana. "Let me get Sataari to see if she can give you some medicine."

"No, no! I'll be fine," said Tanto. "Probably just ate too many puckerberries last night." He showed Razutana a relaxed face, though Razutana saw the boy's fingers tighten around the clay Ano logogram for "*mutagé*" that he wore on a leather cord around his neck.

Tanto had never been lazy, and so Razutana didn't think that he was pretending an illness to get out of work.

"All right," he said in a gentle voice, and stroked the boy's forehead, brushing aside a lock of hair. "Anything you particularly want to eat?"

The boy looked thoughtful. "Maybe . . . when you get back you can make that fried shrimp paste that my mother used to put in scrambled eggs?"

Scrambled eggs wasn't something the Agon ate normally, but Théra had made it for both Tanto and Rokiri as they grew up.

The boy had shifted to Dara instead of the language of the scrublands, something he seldom did in front of the other children except his brother. Without bringing attention to it, Razutana switched to speaking Dara as well. "I can try. I'll ask Nalu to keep an eye out for tern eggs. As for the shrimp paste, the version your mother made was different from how we did it in Dara since there's no lard here in Gondé—"

"I like *her* version."

"Of course." Razutana's heart clenched in sympathy. The boy missed his mother but always tried to put on a brave face. "I'll do my best to re-create her recipe. Maybe I'll use moonfur rat fat instead of tallow . . . it should be close, if not exactly the same."

"Add bits of crispy fried skin. She used to do that."

"Definitely."

"And instead of tern eggs, can you get something bigger? She would use mountain goose eggs. . . ."

Razutana knew that marsh ducks nested among the reeds on the banks of the brackish ponds to the east, in the opposite direction of the Sea of Tears. It would mean a longer trip than the one he and Sataari had been planning, but he nodded all the same. "All right; we'll see what we can do."

Moments after Razutana and Sataari had led the children out of the campsite on their fishing-foraging expedition, Tanto threw off his deerskin blanket and crept out of the lean-to shelter. Cautiously, he looked around to be sure that he was truly alone, and then ran toward the large pit just south of the camp, the settlement's midden heap.

He walked along the edge of the pit until he reached a large white rock. Then he began to dig.

Tanto had been preparing for this moment for months. From every meal, he snuck away pieces of pemmican and dried fruits, adding to his secret cache. He practiced his slingshot and tracking skills with Nalu until he was almost as good a hunter as his friend. He studied with Sataari until he was sure he knew how to find the softest spots in copses and dig until water seeped out and filled the hole. He begged for lessons from Razutana on how to filter dirty water with a skull cup filled with sand and pebbles so that it became potable. He dried the segmented roots of the cogon grass in the sun and secreted the pieces in a leather pouch, knowing that no hunter or warrior would go on a journey without a supply of the herb, good for so many injuries and illnesses.

His fingers found the stash under the soft soil.

Tanto's heart leapt like a prancing hare. He had done it! By dispatching the rest of the camp on an egg hunt that would take them most of the day, he had hopefully bought himself enough time to carry out his plan.

Wrapping all his supplies in the deerskin blanket, he tied the neat bundle to his back. Then, with his slingshot tucked into his belt, he set off northward, the direction of the barrows.

He jogged and ran, knowing that the pace was unsustainable. But he wanted to put as much distance between himself and the camp as possible. Only after he had entered the copse in the valley between two barrows that stood like the posts of a massive gate did he slow down. This was as far as Sataari ever let anyone go into the City of Ghosts.

Innumerable restless spirits were condemned to roam the barrows for eternity because they had destroyed paradise and couldn't ascend to the realm beyond on cloud-garinafins.

He knelt down and prayed to the All-Father and the Every-Mother.

"I am Tanto Aragoz, son of Takval, son of Nobo, Pékyu-taasa of the Agon. I know that this is forbidden ground, but I come not to taunt the trapped ghosts or to challenge the gods. I wish . . . to beg for a favor."

He had been composing this prayer in his mind for months, trying to imitate the rhythm of Sataari's and Adyulek's dance-stories as well as the tone of the ancient sages in his mother's bedtime stories. The words now flowed out of him in an unstoppable torrent.

"The Lyucu are following the path of wickedness first trod by the arrogant people of the Fifth Age. They have not moved the site of Taten in a generation, relying on the labor of slaves for sustenance and pleasure. They have driven the Agon into the remotest corners of Gondé, hoarding good grazing for themselves. They have become infatuated with the city-ships, monstrous machines brought here by evil-hearted strangers contemptuous of the people of the scrublands." Here, the boy paused, wondering if the gods might reject him for his blood ties to those strangers from beyond the seas. But . . . surely the gods could see that Admiral Krita was nothing like his mother, and his mother's people were victims of the Lyucu too, weren't they? He shook off his doubts and pressed on. "The Lyucu are so powerful that most good people dare not rise up to oppose them, and the few who do are mercilessly slaughtered. In short, the Lyucu have begun to enslave the land, to exploit it rather than to roam over it freely, living a life of luxury and corruption, abandoning the ever-renewing spirit of the scrublands embodied in the deeds of Afir and Kikisavo.

"The Lyucu have taken away my parents, my grandmother, my grandfather in Dara, my mother's family there that I never even knew, my friends, my teachers, my elders—and I do not know if any of them are still alive."

He paused again, choking back tears. Taking deep breaths to calm himself, he went on.

"They must be confronted lest the darkness marking the end of the Fifth Age once again descend upon the scrublands, and you be forced to destroy humanity once more for forgetting your lessons. Therefore, I have come to this forbidden place in search of those mighty weapons once wielded by the haughty chiefs of the last age.

"The shamans say that the weapons of the Fifth Age were unnatural and wicked, but I do not agree. My mother always told me that there is nothing inherently good or wicked in the nature of tools, for they only serve to amplify what is already present in the hearts of humankind. The Lyucu are wicked and seek to enslave, and in their hands the city-ships of Dara further evil. My parents are good and seek to free the Agon, and in their hands the weapons of Dara bolster good. We show our character not by the weapons we choose, but through the purpose for which we fight and manner in which we wield them.

"I speak not of a new wisdom, but lessons taught by Afir and Kikisavo. The people were cast out of paradise, but the heroes defied the gods by seeking weapons and skills that would allow the people to return to paradise. Though you disapproved of their quest, in the end you were moved by their courage and pure hearts, and you gifted them valuable tools so that the people would have warmth in their tents, light in their pits, weapons to defeat predators, food to sustain their strength, garinafins to serve as their allies, and babies in mothers' bellies. Surely similar tools had been available to those living during the Fifth Age, but in their hands the tools only spurred pride and boosted immorality. You took paradise away, but you handed back Afir and Kikisavo the tools to construct new bubbles of paradise in the harsh landscape."

Tanto paused once more, hoping that the gods would be convinced by his unorthodox interpretation of the shamans' dance-stories. In truth, he had drawn this line of argument from the stories of Dara told by his mother: In the hands of the Hegemon, Na-aroénna drank the blood of innocents and laid waste to the Islands; in the hands of the Marshal, the Doubt-Ender became an instrument of peace, the dam that held back the Lyucu killing tide.

It's really too bad that the gods of Gondé don't know about the heroes of Dara, he reflected. *It would be so much easier to persuade them if they did.*

"I am a pékyu-taasa of the Agon, and if my father has already ridden the cloud-garinafins, then I am the pékyu in his stead. I am not strong enough to defeat the Lyucu on my own, but if my strength can be multiplied by the weapons hidden here, I will have a chance.

"If you agree with my quest, then allow me passage into the City of Ghosts. Test me as you once tested Afir and Kikisavo, and judge me with the same fairness you judged them. My heart is pure, and once the Lyucu have been defeated, I will return and lay the borrowed weapons to rest."

He listened hard for the gods' response. The thick shade in the copse was like twilight, save for occasional shafts of sun that penetrated the canopy to paint a mottled pattern on the ground. He watched the shifting shadows, listened to the rustling of the wind among the leaves, and hoped to catch a glimpse of the divine will, a sign to guide him.

No answer came, which was also a kind of answer.

He pressed on.

It took him most of the day to hike through the dense wood in the valley. When he emerged, he saw barrows looming all around him, each grander than the last. Between the mounds were valleys filled with trees or grass, with marshy rivers winding through.

The sun was sinking in the west; he decided to climb the mound on the left before it got dark to get a better sense of the geography of the barrows. The mound wasn't tall, really not much more than a knoll by the standards of the World's Edge Mountains. But after the journey through the salt flats and the shoreside plain on which he had spent the winter, he felt as though he were ascending toward heaven.

By the time he reached the top, panting from the exertion, the first stars were emerging in the sky. He stood still and looked around.

To the south, he could see the dark forest he had just traversed. Beyond it was the tiny settlement, where he hoped his little brother was getting ready for bed and not giving away his secret. Already, he felt the first pangs of fear, loneliness, and yearning for the safety of friends and tribe. He pushed those feelings away. He was only at the beginning of a journey that was likely to grow much harder.

He turned to the west and saw the shimmering waves of the Sea of Tears beyond a few more low knolls. The sun was just setting over the great salt lake, a bare sliver of reddish-gold on the horizon.

He looked to the northeast, and the sight took his breath away.

Earthen tumuli stood in neat rows and columns, as far as the eyes could see. Though covered by vegetation, it was impossible to mistake them for the work of nature. For one thing, they were all carefully shaped and positioned: Roughly oval at the base, with the major and minor axes aligned perfectly in the cardinal directions, the artificial hills gradually grew more angular with increasing height, until the round sides turned into steep, flat faces that converged to sharp apexes. For another thing, the barrows were arranged in a grid, though some of them were many times larger than others. The smaller mounds could perhaps be circled by a running herd of cattle in a few hours, while the larger ones would take days.

Is this what a city in Dara looks like? he wondered. His mother had told him and his brother about the marvelous cities of her homeland and drawn sketches for them, but he had never been able to really envision a *city*, a landscape filled with outsized artificial constructions, with *buildings*, until now.

Since he had never seen a Dara city, a more apt comparison came to his mind: how a fly might see a herd of resting cattle. The slumbering, monumental, man-made hill-beasts stretched into the distance, ready to settle down for the night.

And then he saw something else in the fading twilight: In the far distance, at the very center of the City of Ghosts, there rose a mound so gargantuan that it was like seeing a garinafin at rest, guarding the long-haired cattle all around. A true mountain in a tribe of hills, it seemed scarcely possible that it had been constructed by human hands. Surely a shaman standing at the very top would be able to reach out and pluck down a star.

The gods decided to punish their mortal kin for daring to reach for the stars.

He shivered as he recalled the hypnotic words of Sataari.

That's where I must go.

The journey through the barrows was neither easy nor fast.

From east to west, the Ghost River branched out among the artificial hills like a spider's web, gradually ramifying into marshes indistinguishable from grassland. And where the river did not flow, thick forests filled the flat regions between the mounds. Tanto was constantly trudging through mud, wading through water, fighting his way through thick brambles, or climbing up the side of one of the mounds when the vegetation below proved too thick.

Mosquitoes swarmed around his face and arms, and soon his skin was covered by itchy red bumps. Though the landscape was filled with strange fruits that gave off tempting sweet odors, so rich that they verged on rotten, he dared not eat them lest they prove poisonous. Because he wanted to conserve the supplies he had brought for as long as possible, he stuck to foraging for the few tubers and wild greens that he knew were safe to eat, and he dug for grubs and insects to supplement his diet. Once in a while, if he was lucky, he managed to use his slingshot to kill a bird or hare, and he roasted these over fire pits, grateful for the rich nourishment.

Day after day, he drew closer to the gigantic mound at the center of the City of Ghosts.

Many sights along the way puzzled him. There were stone steps built into the sides of some of the barrows, indicating that they had once been climbed, perhaps often. He passed by wide-open plazas of packed earth and gravel, empty except for a few large broken rocks, making him wonder if massive engines, now decayed, had once occupied such spaces. The number of steep, planar faces at the tops of the mounds varied: three, four, five, six, seven . . . and some remained ovalish from bottom to top, looking more like natural hills.

Most barrows had sides honeycombed with caves, with stone-lined walls and floors. He thought they might have served as dwellings, based on faint traces of pictures left on some of the walls. Some of the caves seemed to wind deep into the earthen interior, but he didn't follow them to the end, fearful of getting lost.

The best weapons must be secreted deeper in the city.

Sataari had said that the barrows were burial mounds, graves that kept the bodies of the deceased away from their natural fate as food for scavengers and robbed their souls of the uplifting light of the Eye of Cudyufin. But now Tanto wondered if Sataari was entirely right; he couldn't imagine people would live on top of such horrific structures.

In the shadow of one large tumulus, he passed through a field filled with stone heaps, miniature versions of the barrows. The stone piles were of varying heights, though none much taller than he was. Most had become overgrown with weeds and vines, and the harsh winters had reduced many to mere rubble. He imagined himself as a vole scurrying through a patch of mushrooms.

As he wound his way between them, he experienced the strange sensation of being watched. He whipped about, but there was nothing: no bird, beast, nor man. Goose bumps appeared on his arms, though it was a hot afternoon, and a chill tingled along his spine. He began to run.

It was similar to the sensation he had felt when he visited the small graveyard at the end of Kiri Valley, where Admiral Mitu Roso and the other deceased of Dara had been interred after the custom of their homeland. Théra always took the boys there on the day of the Grave-Mending Festival to clear off weeds and repair the logograms on the tablets marking the tombs. Both Tanto and Rokiri had hated it.

He collapsed to the ground when he finally escaped that field of stone piles. It was a long time before he caught his breath and found enough strength to get up.

He pressed on and did not look back.

In other places, he found signs that the ground had been flattened and shaped. The vegetation in these plots grew in rows, reminding him of the crops that his mother and the people of Dara had worked so hard to cultivate back in Kiri Valley.

Curious, he went into the straight-edged plots to investigate, and he found that the earth had been divided into long, narrow rows with low banks of stone. Soil had covered the stones, and because of the difference in elevation and water accumulation, different kinds of plants grew on the peaks and in the troughs.

What had happened here? He shuddered, wondering if he was seeing signs of the enslavement of the land by the wicked people of the Fifth Age.

Occasionally, he came across human skeletons on the side of a mound or by the shore of a stream. The lack of pelts or other clothing indicated that they had been dead a long time, and the unfamiliar bone and stone implements near the remains showed that they were likely not members of the scrubland tribes, or at least not Agon. Were they people of the Fifth Age who had died when the gods cleansed this city of pride? Were they brave adventurers who later dared to defy the wrath of the gods to explore this forbidden ground? Were they also refugees who tried to escape their pursuers by hiding in the City of Ghosts? There was no way to know.

Being a child of the scrublands, Tanto was not afraid of bones. He took the skeletons apart, picked out pieces that he thought could be useful as tools, and broke the rest into smaller fragments. These he assembled into arucuro tocua creations—playing with them soothed his spirit, and it was a way to honor the spirit of the dead. Into each bone beast he incorporated a Dara logogram made of bone fragments: "father," "mother," "mouth," "heart," "faith," "fish," "bird," and so on. Back in Kiri Valley, he had hated the logogram lessons, but now making them felt like a way to speak to his mother.

As he got up to continue his journey, he left behind his arucuro tocua, unique constructions melding the wisdom of the Ano sages and the craft of the people of the scrublands. The wind and the rain would propel them to explore the barrows on their own.

Once, confused by the fog that hung in the valleys between the mounds and refused to lift even after sunrise, he climbed a tall barrow to get his bearings. At the top, he found a circular stone platform with marks incised into the edge. Lines from these marks converged to a single point at the center of the circle. He guessed that the marks showed the positions of stars or landmarks seen from the platform, but he could not guess what they were for.

At night, he always tried to sleep up the side of a barrow, preferably sheltered in one of the stone-lined caves. It allowed him to stay out of the chill of the wet marshes, and he also hoped that the elevation provided some protection from predators. He hadn't run into anything as dangerous as a horrid wolf or a tusked tiger, but he slept lightly, his hand always on his slingshot or child-sized bone axe.

He developed a rash along the inside of his thighs that refused to go away; he fell sick from a skull cup of water that he hadn't filtered as well as he should have and lay in a delirium until he recovered; he lost count of the number of days he had been in Taten-ryo-alvovo; he cried at night, missing his brother, Nalu, Razutana, Sataari, and the others; he realized he had gone too far now to turn back; he had no choice but to press on.

The fog in the valleys grew thicker. Like Afir and Kikisavo when they approached the gods, much of the time Tanto was just trudging forward without knowing where he was going.

Finally, after another night of aimless hiking, he was ready to give up from exhaustion and despair, ready to lie down and never get up again, yielding his body to the scavengers.

In the morning, I'll climb up the nearest barrow and die in the gaze of the Eye of Cudyufin.

It took all his strength to struggle up the mound the next dawn. He waited for the last sunrise of his short life. "Papa, Mama, I'm sorry," he whispered, and couldn't stop the tears that spilled from his eyes.

The sun jumped above the horizon to the east, and the fog dissipated in the golden heat. He looked in the direction of the sun, and a cry of joy was torn from his throat.

The artificial structure was so close he thought he could reach it just by stretching out his hands.

He had arrived at the largest mound of them all, standing like a mountain in the center of the City of Ghosts.

He was certain that the most powerful weapons of the Fifth Age, if they existed at all, would be hidden inside this central barrow. It dominated the City of Ghosts like the Great Tent of the Lyucu pékyu dominated Taten, and was surely the site of honor for the arrogant chiefs of a sinful age.

Energized, he spent the next few days hiking and climbing the massive mound, hoping to discover a way in. But, unlike most of the other barrows he had passed, he found no caves or hidden entrances, no stairs or paths, no platform at the top or retaining walls on the sides. It was perfectly symmetrical, oval from bottom to top, the curves smooth and graceful, like a tortoise shell. If one ignored the perfect symmetry, the giant barrow could almost be mistaken for a natural hill, covered by lush grass and wildflowers of every hue.

Having come so close to his prize, he found this denial at the threshold intolerable. At the top of the giant barrow, he knelt down and wept bitterly. Had the gods of Agon allowed him to get this far only to mock him for his powerlessness?

When he was done crying, he got up and searched again. The stories his mother and the shamans had told him gave him renewed strength. Kikisavo and Afir didn't give up when they were lost in the fog, and the hero Iluthan didn't yield when he was trapped in the lair of the beautiful demons. He wouldn't, either.

From the apex, he surveyed the base of the mound with care. The long axis of the mound ran north-south, and on each of the shorter sides, after a short gap of packed earth, were fields of those small stone heaps that reminded him of the graveyard in Kiri Valley. In the west, the direction he had come from, stood a copse that divided the mound from smaller barrows beyond.

It was in the direction of the sunrise that he noticed something unusual. A marshy grassland began at the foot of the mound and stretched miles to the east before being interrupted by more barrows—like a lake of grass. During his explorations, he had avoided going too close to this side of the mound as he was unfamiliar with this kind of landscape, and it seemed too monotonous to arouse his curiosity. But now, from this high vantage point, he noticed circles and ovals in the grass that appeared slightly lighter in color compared to the rest of the green backdrop.

He scrambled most of the way down the side of the mound to examine them closer.

The discolored patches in the vast grassland on the eastern side of the great tumulus formed a long arc hugging the base, like a string of pearls worn around the neck of a Dara princess in one of his mother's tales. One, in particular, attracted Tanto's attention. It was larger than the rest, about a hundred paces across, and the kind of grass that grew in the patch was unlike anything he had ever seen. In the sunlight, the broad, circular leaves seemed to bob up and down, as though they were floating. And there was an unfamiliar odor, half-sweet, half-fetid, a stench that simultaneously caused Tanto's stomach to growl and made him want to retch.

Fascinated, he shuffled closer, making sure his hands and feet were secure against the steep incline. He reached a spot on the slope leading directly to the patch. The smell was even stronger here. Gingerly, he inched lower, keeping his eyes on the patch. Yes, there was no doubt about it: The grass in the patch was undulating.

Abruptly, a bird burst out of the patch, screeching angrily as it flew straight at his face, a blur of iridescent, fluttering wings. Reflexively, he raised his arms to protect his face, putting all his weight on his feet. The small stone against which he braced his right foot gave way, and he began to slide down the sloping side, out of control.

The bird swooped by his face, screeching as it winged away. Desperately, Tanto scrambled for purchase. As he fell, he plucked handfuls of grass out of the soil, the sharp grass blades slicing his hands and making him wince, but the effort failed to slow his descent. Dizzily, he rolled over, once, twice, thrice, and then struck the green patch.

The round leaves opened up like the maw of some monster, and he disappeared into it before he could scream.

The grasslands that stretched between some of the larger barrows in the City of Ghosts were unfamiliar to Tanto, born and raised in Kiri Valley. But the tribespeople who lived on the backs of garina-fins and roamed from one end of Ukyu-Gondé to the other would have instantly recognized these regions as miniature versions of the grass seas.

In parts of the scrublands where conditions were particularly favorable, the usual sparse ground cover of low, prickly shrubs and cacti gave way to lush grassland, pastures in high demand. Some of the larger grassland regions stretched for hundreds of miles in each direction. Standing in the middle of one of these patches, one experienced the illusion of being in the middle of an ocean, as passing breezes caressed waves of nodding blades, and different types of grass, in darker and lighter bands, imitated the shading of the sea.

Although the vegetal surface gave the appearance of monotonous uniformity, underneath, the grass seas were every bit as complex and variegated as their aquatic counterparts. The trampling hooves of millions of roaming cattle, aurochs, mouflon, and sheep gouged pits and depressions; dung heaps and scavenger-scoured skeletons hid among the roots like shoals and reefs; sudden flash floods carved channels and trenches across the land that were quickly concealed by regenerating vegetation; and minor, local changes in elevation created choke points and high grounds contested by warring armies of seeds and seedlings, as different species fought to dominate the landscape and establish their own miniature virid empires. If grasses and ferns and cacti and shrubs could sing and chant, they would no doubt compose their own epics to celebrate these grand battles fought among the green tribes season after season.

A view from the ground level didn't fully exhaust the complexity of life in the grass seas. Beneath the earth, other creatures lived out their allotted spans in the darkness. Gophers and voles and moles and ground squirrels burrowed mazes of tunnels in the soil, subsisting on roots and tubers and grubs and worms. Some of them lived solitary lives, like unschooled fish in a solid sea, but others congregated in tribes, all paying homage to a queen, like mammalian versions of ants, constructing vast underground warrens rivaling the complexity of megalopolises in faraway Dara. They excavated immense underground chambers to store up food for the long winters and built cavernous halls where the queens lay in luxurious ease on beds of fermenting vegetation, listening to chirped and squeaked reports of the distant surface frontier brought by fur-clad servants and descendants.

From time to time, these underground palaces collapsed from herds trampling overhead or overambitious excavation. The cave-ins left in the grasslands deep craters, mute monuments to the glory of an alien civilization. As the rodent subjects carried their queen elsewhere to re-establish their domain, grass and ferns sprouted at the bottom of the depressions, colonizing the ruins of a bygone age. When it rained, these cavities filled with water, drowning the grass at the bottom, where the dead, rotting vegetation formed a waterproof layer that prevented drainage. The pool of dead water then became covered by aquatic weeds, whose verdant hue blended into the surrounding grass sea and disguised their existence except for the rotten stench.

These covered dead pools of water became traps for unwary

navigators of the grass seas. Though migrating herds sometimes used them as sources of drinking water, it was not uncommon for calves and lambs, or even the occasional adult animal, to slip into one and drown. The people of the scrublands called these pools in the grass seas water bubbles, and some of the larger, deeper bubbles persisted for years, claiming skeleton after skeleton.

Slimy weeds filled his mouth and nostrils and blinded his eyes as Tanto sank beneath the surface.

The cold, rancid taste immediately made him want to gag, but he forced himself to bite down, to squeeze his eyes shut, and to tamp down the urge, knowing that to panic was to guarantee his own death. He floundered and kicked, hoping to find the bottom of the pool or a wall.

Nothing.

He forced his eyes open, and was shocked to find the water around him clear enough to see. Although the surface of the pool was covered by drifting aquatic weeds, debris in the water had long since sunk to the bottom, leaving the water limpid. Sunlight, filtered by the green leaves on top, flickered in the water, imbuing the realm around him with an eerie, otherworldly aura.

To the surface. He had to head to the surface.

Ignoring the burning sensation in his lungs, he bit down even harder on the slimy mess in his mouth and swam toward the green ceiling. He was glad that his mother had insisted that he learn how to swim, a skill that few Agon, excepting those who lived on the coast, knew.

Out of the corner of one eye, a ray of sunlight glinted off something. His heart convulsed in disbelief. But there was no time to investigate. He had to get to the surface *now*.

He kicked and pulled as the pressure in his lungs built and his vision narrowed to a tunnel, with the shimmering green surface at the other end. Just as he was about to give up, he erupted out of the weed-strewn surface, into bright sunlight.

He spat out the slimy weeds and gulped for air before retching uncontrollably. He swam to the edge of the pool and held on to some dangling roots, resting in the water as his heart gradually calmed down and his body grew more used to the cold water.

As he readied himself to climb out onto the safety of solid shore, doubt gnawed at his heart. He had seen *something* down there. He couldn't just leave without finding out what it was.

Untying the bundle from his back, he tossed it onto the side of the mound. Without its bulk, he would be able to move through the water with speed and agility.

He took several deep breaths to prepare himself, grateful that his nose was no longer as bothered by the overwhelming stench. Then he closed his mouth and dove, swimming toward where he had seen the white glint earlier.

It turned out to be a human skeleton, lying still at the bottom of the pool as though it had gone to sleep. The pale ribs and thigh bones gleamed strangely in the green light. He swam for the bones, hoping to recover a hand or rib so that he would be able to expose it to the gaze of the Eye of Cudyufin and release the unfortunate soul that had been trapped here.

But as he reached the skeleton and dragged a hand through the mud at the bottom of the pool, his fingers brushed against something unexpected. Beneath the thin layer of mud and rotten plant matter, he felt stone.

Startled, he felt around. The entire bottom of the pool was lined in stone. Could it be that this pool wasn't the work of burrowing animals but the work of human hands?

He grabbed onto the skeleton's left arm and pulled. Instead of coming apart, the whole skeleton lifted off the bottom. Adrift in the water, the skeleton waved its limbs as though in a slow, dreamlike dance. Tanto watched, mesmerized. Perhaps the skeleton was telling him that it preferred to stay in this pool.

He noticed that the fingers of the bony hand that he had tried to pull off were curled, except for the index finger, which seemed to be pointing at something. He followed the finger and saw a stone opening where the skeleton had been resting.

A tiny crab skittered and retreated into the opening.

He broke the surface once more and gulped for air as he considered his options. The opening in the stone was large enough for him to swim through, and it led in the direction of the mound.

In the old stories, the heroes always heeded signs. He had just been given one; he was sure of it.

He had to try at least.

Closing his eyes, he prayed to the gods. *I'm not coming up again. If you want me to find the weapons that will free the Agon people, then help me!*

He dove.

Pulling himself along the claustrophobic underwater tunnel with both hands and feet, Tanto was crawling more than swimming. He tried to move as fast as he could, hoping that the tunnel would start to curve up soon.

The light from the water bubble behind him dimmed. He peered ahead into the darkness and saw nothing.

The pressure in his lungs was now painful; he was close to bursting. Every instinct in his body screamed for him to go back.

He stopped and tried to turn around, but the tunnel was too narrow. Trying to crawl backward would be much too slow. He would never make it back to the bubble; he was stuck.

A stubborn pride rose in his heart. An Agon warrior preferred to die facing the enemy. He would crawl as far ahead as possible and die fighting.

He scrabbled even harder with his knees and elbows, chanting the fight song of Afir in his heart.

His mind grew sluggish. The pain in his chest and throat throbbed like an approaching thunderstorm. This was it. He had gone as far as he could. He was going to open his mouth and let the water into his lungs. He had given his all to this quest, but it wasn't enough.

He stopped fighting and let himself drift. He opened his mouth—

And felt his face break through the surface of the water. The sudden flood of life-giving breath rasped painfully against his throat and lungs. He screamed with relief, a sound halfway between laughter and sobbing.

Gradually, his eyes adjusted. He was in a large cavern inside the great mound. Above him, tiny lights glowed in the dark like stars. If those glowing dots indicated the ceiling of the cavern, then the space was grander than any cave he had ever been inside of, including the largest storage pit in Kiri Valley, where a year's supply of pemmican and smoked meat could be held.

The lights above were reflected in the shallow lake that he found himself in, making him feel as though he was floating among the stars.

Even if the leaders of the Fifth Age were wicked, he was awed by the magnificence of their resting place.

"Thank you," he croaked, "O chiefs of the Fifth Age. Whether you're heroes or villains, I am humbled to be in your presence."

The inside of the mound turned out to be a maze of branching tunnels and mysterious caverns. Much of the time, he was mired in darkness. Having shucked off his pack before diving into the water bubble, he had no access to a fire starter. The fire starter, modeled after the operation of garinafin canine teeth, was one of the few pieces of machinery introduced by his mother that had been widely adopted by the Agon. He regretted his rashness now.

But tiny clumps of glowing mushrooms sprouting from ceilings and walls provided some illumination. Trickles of water flowed down the walls, lined with moss-covered stone. He guessed that the water from rain and mist above drained through the body of the mound and eventually gathered at the bottom into the lake through which he had entered.

He had no idea where he should go or what he was looking for, but relying on instinct, he tried to always pick the branch that slanted up whenever there was a fork in the tunnels. Several times, he ended up in dead ends with collapsed tunnels blocking the way, forcing him to backtrack.

Many of the chambers he wandered through were empty— or at least seemed that way in the dim light of the mushrooms. Sometimes he found stone vessels and shelves, but he couldn't discern their purpose or the nature of the rituals that had perhaps been conducted with them. In some chambers, he found skeletons laid out on stone biers, perhaps the bodies of great warriors and chiefs. Excited, he rushed up to the biers, but next to the bodies he found only unfamiliar weapons made of bone or stone. The bone weapons were short, delicate, and thin, and had none of the hard knobs and sharp teeth that he was used to. The stone weapons had dull edges and were very clumsy, and he couldn't imagine how they could be wielded effectively in battle.

Unwilling to abandon them without more testing, he picked up some of the bone weapons and swung them through the air, hoping to see crackling lightning or hear booming thunder. But the bones were so old that they often crumbled in his hands as he picked them up.

Feeling pangs of hunger, he thought he should backtrack until he found the cavern through which he had entered and swim back out. Now that he knew the way into the mound, he would come back better prepared, with his supplies. By picking the downward-tending branch every time there was a fork in the tunnels, he returned to the large cavern with the lake at the bottom. Taking deep breaths and mentally preparing himself for the cold, he dove in, searching for the tunnel that led to the water bubble outside.

After an hour of diving and exploration, he found himself huddled on the shore of the lake, shivering uncontrollably. In his initial excitement, he had failed to mark the location of the entrance tunnel, and he couldn't find it in the frigid, dark water. Indeed, he couldn't even be sure this was the same cavern he had entered from at all. The mound was so large that it easily could have accommodated multiple similar caverns in the base.

Trapped in the Great Barrow, he had to find other sources of sustenance. Since both Sataari and Razutana had warned the children of the dangers of ingesting unknown mushrooms, he knew he should stay away from the glowing fungi. Fortunately, the lake at the bottom of the mound was inhabited by fish whose bodies also luminesced, and they seemed rather unused to the idea of being hunted. He was able to catch them with a ladle fashioned from a skull he picked up in one of the chambers. The fish were pale and almost translucent, and wriggled in his mouth like slimy worms.

The food helped with the shivering and made him realize just how tired he felt. He lay down, telling himself he would rest his eyes a bit. He was asleep before his eyes were even fully closed.

When he woke up, he felt feverish and light-headed. His limbs felt heavy and his joints ached. He was lost and hadn't done a very good job of taking care of himself—an intense longing for Théra and Takval seized his heart, and he wept and smiled by turns as he imagined how his parents would berate him for the foolish risks he had taken before embracing him to make everything better.

In his weakened state, it was even more impossible for him to escape from the artificial mountain. Lost and confused, he began to wander the tunnels aimlessly. Invisible creatures skittered away at his approach, and from time to time, he felt slimy presences slither over his feet, making him jump and cry out in alarm. Pairs of tiny glowing eyes stared at him out of the darkness, and though he tried to stay very still to catch them, they always dodged out of the way as he lunged.

His tongue felt parched. He approached one of the walls and, heedless of the danger, licked the water trickling over the glowing mushrooms; the taste was both bitter and sweet, and tingled against his tongue.

He slept when exhaustion overtook him, and when he woke up again, he would wander around some more. Time ceased to have meaning, and he tried to stave off the ever-present, dull throbs of hunger with mouthfuls of caustic moss scraped off the walls. Sometimes he seemed to fall asleep on his feet, lost in hallucinatory visions of his life in Kiri Valley and the settlement outside Taten-ryo-alvovo for minutes or hours at a time.

Abruptly, the hallucinatory haze lifted. He licked his cracked lips and wiped the sweat from his fevered brow. He was in a large cavern, perhaps even larger than the one he had first encountered upon entering the mound. Entire walls seemed to gleam dimly like pieces of the moon, brighter than any light he had encountered in the tunnels. On an elevated platform up front, he saw two skeletons lying in repose.

He staggered up to the platform. The skeletons were tall, broad shouldered, and arranged with the feet of each next to the head of the other. Around them were arranged more of the strange, useless weaponry that he had seen too much of already. But there was something odd about these weapons . . . were they longer? He should look closer—

A loud, echoing racket made him jump out of his skin. He cowered, squeezed his eyes shut, and whimpered, waiting for the spirits trapped in this sunless mound to wreak their vengeance against him for disturbing their afterlife.

At length, when nothing more happened, he opened his eyes carefully. He felt around the foot of the platform and gradually discovered the source of the earlier noise. Around the platform stood rows and rows of cylindrical vessels, and his careless approach had broken several. They weren't made from skulls, as was the custom of the scrublands, but baked clay. Heart racing, he reached into the broken containers, hoping to find objects imbued with magic. His trembling fingers wrapped tightly around whatever he found.

Unable to see clearly, he pulled his hands out, uncurled his fingers, and smelled and touched the contents with the tip of his tongue.

Seeds or dried husks.

Hunger roared to life in his belly like a stoked fire. He bit down, and pain shot along his gums as his teeth cracked against the hard shells. A horrible, revolting taste filled his mouth, whether from blood or the contents of the husks he couldn't tell.

He dropped his hands and wept bitterly. The fever and weakness were getting worse, and he no longer had the strength to keep on exploring. He had risked his life for nothing. There were no magical weapons here that he could take back to defeat the Lyucu and avenge his parents. He was not Afir or Kikisavo. After all he had been through and overcome, the gods had not found him worthy.

He lay down next to the skeletons and closed his eyes. He wondered if in the far future, when other explorers came into the forbidden lands and found his small skeleton next to the two already here, they'd think he was one of the attendants of the great chiefs of the Fifth Age.

Being mistaken for a hero is not the worst way to go, even if out of the sight of the Eye of Cudyufin.

He closed his eyes and fell into a deep slumber from which he knew he would not awaken.

CHAPTER SIX

THAT WHICH CANNOT BE HEARD

Théra's injuries turned out to be relatively minor. The tusked tiger had only grazed her with its claws, leaving four ugly gashes in her arm. But with Adyulek's medicine and Thoryo's care, she would recover.

"The tusked tiger is known to stun its victims with a silent roar," said Takval. "The males, who hunt alone, can be good climbers. It's my fault that I didn't scout the area better."

"How did you know I was in trouble?" asked Théra.

"Ga-al called us. Garinafins can hear each other over long distances, even though we cannot always hear their rumbles and cries."

Théra thought back to the way the garinafins had become agitated in the camp in Kiri Valley just before Cudyu's assault, even though no one had heard anything. The world was full of wonders.

Takval, concerned that Ga-al's desperate cries for help had also given away their location to Lyucu search parties still in the area, intensified patrols of the surrounding peaks. Fortunately, once again no signs of Lyucu pursuers were found.

No matter how much Takval and Tipo Tho tried to insist on discipline, remaining in one place had a tendency to reduce the vigilance of lookouts and guards. Departing for a new campsite was obviously prudent. But the refugees were reluctant to leave, since they had grown attached to this valley that had sheltered them for so long. After much debate, Takval and Théra decided they would take the risk of staying until Araten returned.

"He has suffered so much to rejoin us," said Théra. "We must wait for him."

While recuperating, Théra summoned Çami Phithadapu to discuss her experience with the tusked tiger.

"Tales of inaudible sounds that can be perceived only by animals aren't unknown in Dara," said the scholar. "For instance, hunters in Écofi spoke of elephants being able to converse over vast distances in secret by talking in voices that even the sharpest human ears couldn't detect."

"But do these inaudible sounds ever . . . affect people?" asked Théra.

Çami looked thoughtful. "Some pearl divers in Wolf's Paw told me that when diving in the vicinity of giant whales, sometimes they would suddenly feel that they were in the presence of Tazu—a dangerous lassitude and languor seized them like a giant hand underwater. They insisted that they heard no whale song."

What was that line that Zomi and Luan Zyaji both said so often? Oh, that's right: The universe is knowable.

"Let's look into it," urged Théra. "I feel that there is a mystery here . . . whose resolution can be helpful."

Çami and Théra spoke to Takval and the other Agon, gathering stories of garinafins communicating with each other across long distances, of prairie voles and moonfur rats running away from sea coasts hours before the arrival of tsunami waves, of bands of hunters falling prey to the silent roars of tusked tigers.

But the stories were just that, stories. Çami couldn't conjure up a tsunami or an earthquake and observe the reaction of the fauna, nor could she demand that a tusked tiger be captured to experiment with. The garinafins did seem to be ideal research subjects, but try as she might, she couldn't discern when they were singing inaudibly. She devised a series of sound amplification instruments: echo chambers at the bottoms of cliffs, oversized trumpets, even a totally dark and silent cave into which she coaxed Alkir . . . But never could she be sure that she was hearing something that would otherwise be *inaudible.*

"If only there were some way to make sound visible," lamented Çami, "a way to hear that which cannot be heard, to see that which cannot be seen."

Long after Çami had left, Théra pondered her comment.

She wondered if she was going about solving this mystery the wrong way. Çami, like Zomi and Luan Zyaji, preferred to explain the world without resort to the supernatural, and that would have been Théra's preference as well. Yet, she *had* experienced something decidedly *extraordinary* on that ledge, and it was impossible for her to forget that sense of belonging, of being one with the scrublands and the myths of the Agon, of participating in a grand storytelling dance in the presence of the divine.

Is the universe knowable? she wondered. *Even if one could describe with mathematical precision every heartbeat and breath, reproduce with camera obscura fidelity every wrinkle and fold, capture with absolutely no loss every coo and babble, would one, in the end, know anything about her own joy as she beheld Kunilu-tika and Jian-tika for the first time? Even if one could hear every whispered conversation and observe every blushing glance, read every heartfelt letter and listen in on every secret prayer, observe every heart-fluttering kiss and fumbled caress, would one, in the end, understand the nature of her loves for Zomi and for Takval?*

There were things that could not be seen, voices that could not be heard, truths that could not be known, but only experienced.

Is it possible to strive to know the universe while also believing in mysteries?

She wondered if she had the courage to keep her heart empty, to open herself to possibilities, to truly immerse herself into the patterns of her adopted homeland.

In the morning, she sought out Adyulek, the old shaman.

"Tongue-of-the-Every-Mother," the princess said, "is it possible for you to teach me the mysteries?"

The shaman looked at her guardedly. The princess had never

seemed spiritual or pious to her, and she had never shown any interest in the Agon mysteries.

Théra described for Adyulek how she had felt on the ledge, in the presence of the tusked tiger. "I believe . . . I was in the presence of the gods."

"Could it be," muttered the old shaman, "that the Dara princess has taken the first steps toward fearing and trusting our gods?" At length, she shook her head. "Our mysteries . . . are reserved for the children of Afir."

"I am an Agon by marriage," said Théra. "Is it not the custom of the scrublands to adopt the willing stranger into the tribes? Surely the gods will not reject me simply because I *became* a child of Afir instead of being born as one."

The shaman looked at her for a long time, and then, with the barest hint of a smile curving up the corners of her mouth, she nodded and held out her hand.

Araten returned with more worrisome news.

"They say that Cudyu's gathering of clever minds has narrowed the date of the opening of the Wall of Storms further," said Araten.

"What is their latest guess?" asked Théra.

"The shamans and divination experts are divided into three camps. One faction believes that the Wall will open in the last moon of the summer after the next, close to the fall."

Théra nodded. That estimate overshot the actual reopening—which only she and Takval knew. She stared intently into Araten's eyes. "Go on."

"The second faction thinks it will be in fall proper."

Théra nodded again. That estimate overshot the real date even more. If all three factions were pushing for a date in the second half of the year after the next, then perhaps she had nothing to worry about. If Cudyu were to launch an invasion based on these erroneous computations, the fleet would arrive long after the opening in the Wall had closed.

"The last faction thinks it will be in the first moon of the summer, near the end of spring."

Théra's heart sped up. If Cudyu chose to believe *this* faction, then the fleet *would* succeed. To reach the Wall by then, he would have to launch the fleet in about ten months, leaving her almost no time to stop him.

"Do you know which faction has the most support?"

Araten seemed to draw back a bit at the intensity of her gaze. "I . . . don't know."

Théra's mind churned. She didn't know how there could be *factions* on a matter of calculation—the only reasonable explanation was that Cudyu's people were not strictly treating this as a problem whose answer could be computed, but a subject open to argument, omens, lucky guesses, superstition. That gave her a chance: Opinions on the interpretation of the unknowable could be swayed.

"Is there any way for us to sow rumors among the Lyucu to influence the debate among these 'experts' one way or the other?"

Araten pondered this. "I can go back and try. But in which direction do you wish the rumors to push?"

"The later the better. The last faction in your summary must not be allowed to win the debate."

A complicated look of resignation mixed with other emotions, both lighter and darker in tone, appeared on Araten's face.

Théra felt terrible. The old warrior must be dreading going back into danger again. "Please! This is vital for both the Dara and Agon."

Araten nodded. "I understand, Princess."

"Oh . . . if possible, please try to find out more news about the pékyus-taasa and the other children."

This time, Araten wanted to take the warriors who he had brought to Takval as well as Ga-al.

"More wagging tongues make spreading rumors easier," the old thane said. "Ga-al will help us travel farther and faster."

Takval didn't like this plan at all. Sending Araten back to spy and spread rumors meant that the band would have to stay in the valley yet longer to wait for him. Though the old thane assured them that Cudyu was now obsessed with the puzzle of the reopening of the Wall of Storms and few Lyucu seemed interested in catching the escapees, he felt that he had to minimize the risks.

"If you and your band intend to continue to pass as tanto-lyu-naro, it would be more convincing if you didn't have a garinafin with you. Don't try to do too much. Go do as Théra asks, and then return as soon as you can."

Araten had to concede that the pékyu had a point.

Théra was rather relieved that Ga-al would stay behind—she enjoyed learning to ride with him.

The old Agon thane and his warriors left the hidden valley, promising to return at the end of the next month.

While waiting for Araten, Théra continued her studies under Adyulek in the Agon mysteries as well as her investigation with Çami and Thoryo into the nature of inaudible sounds.

The princess recalled for Çami an experience from her girlhood, when she had witnessed how the metal plates of a *moaphya* could be seen to be vibrating under the grid lines of a silk screen.

"The same is true of the strings of a zither," said Çami.

"Do all sounds come from vibrations in some medium?" asked Thoryo.

Çami looked thoughtful. "That is an interesting theory. . . . It certainly seems to be true of musical instruments. . . . I wish Razutana were around; he may know of an obscure reference in some ancient tome—"

"Forget about old tomes," said Théra. "We're on our own here. Let's go with my theory, which suggests that even inaudible sounds are also vibrations. Therefore, the way to study sounds that cannot be heard is to *feel* them rather than to *listen* for them."

Çami looked startled. Then she chuckled. "Like the way you can feel the vibrations in the ground at the storytelling dances! Thank you, Princess. It seems so obvious now that you've mentioned it."

"Sometimes a paving stone is essential on the path to mine pure jade," said Théra.

"You need not be so modest, Princess," said Çami. "When one becomes obsessed with a problem, there's a tendency to become stuck in well-trodden paths that lead nowhere. I needed your fresh perspective to be jolted out of those ruts."

"As long as it helps," said Théra, laughing. "I'm not embarrassed to voice my opinions, no matter how foolish they may be."

Guided by this new direction of research, Çami and Théra devised a new experiment.

They found a sharp bend in the valley. Théra and Thoryo took Ga-al to one side of the bend; Çami took Alkir to the other. The women and the garinafins could hear each other but not see each other. Then they taught the two garinafins to play a game where Ga-al would make a sound, and Alkir would repeat it, at which point both garinafins would receive a treat—a rather sour crabapple-like fruit that the garinafins seemed to enjoy.

Ga-al and Alkir, though raised separately by the Lyucu and the Agon and of differing ages, seemed to have developed a deep mutual affection. Théra thought it made sense. After all, they were both alone, away from their families, and probably found in each other a substitute family.

After the garinafins learned the basic idea, the women changed the rules. Now if the garinafins repeated a sound that they had already made earlier, they wouldn't receive a treat. Only by constantly "innovating" in their song would they keep the treats coming.

Somewhat to Théra's surprise, the garinafins had a rather large vocal repertoire of moans, lows, squeals, snarls, snorts, whinnies, screeches, trumpets, roars, and so on. Here, Thoryo's skill with languages once again proved crucial. Though she couldn't imitate the vocalizations of the garinafins with perfect fidelity, she could memorize their performances and tell right away if a sound made by the garinafins was something that they had heard before. With Thoryo acting as an audio "notebook," the garinafins could be kept honest.

It took multiple sessions before the garinafins finally seemed to exhaust their vocal repertoire and began to repeat themselves. Théra and Çami stayed firm and refused to hand out the treats, and so Alkir and Ga-al began to try out more unusual vocal patterns.

Finally, Ga-al stretched out his neck and stared intently into space. After a few seconds of silence, he twisted his neck around, looking down at Théra and Thoryo expectantly.

Théra hollered at Çami, out of sight. "Ga-al just went! Did you hear anything?"

"No," replied Çami. "But Alkir perked up and looked like he was talking just now—also no sound I could hear. Heh, he's looking at me like I owe him something."

Théra turned back to Ga-al. "Can you do it again? The same thing you just did."

Ga-al looked uncomprehendingly at Théra. Flustered, the princess turned to Thoryo. "Can you talk to him?"

Thoryo shook her head. "I can't speak garinafin."

"How are we going to get them to do that again?" Çami was vexed. "I didn't get a chance to feel Alkir's throat."

Théra groaned with frustration. They had been so focused on teaching the garinafins that they couldn't repeat any of the sounds they made that they had neglected to devise a way to instruct the garinafins to repeat the desired "silent" vocalization.

"Wait!" Théra's eyes brightened. "I have an idea."

She snapped her fingers and pointed at her knees, indicating that Ga-al should place his head at the ground near his shoulder so that she could mount up. The beast obeyed; Théra scrambled onto his back.

"Péte-péte!" she said, giving the command for a war garinafin to repeat the last maneuver in battle.

Ga-al, his antlered head still twisted around, regarded her with puzzlement.

"Péte-péte!" she said again.

Ga-al stretched out his neck and stared intently into space.

"Yee-haw!" shouted Théra triumphantly, reverting back to her time as a temporary cattle hand on her grandmother's ranch in Faça.

"Alkir is doing it too!" Çami shouted. "Keep them at it. I'm climbing up."

Ga-al turned around to look at Théra. She gestured for Thoryo to toss him a piece of sour fruit as a reward.

"Yee-haw!" shouted Théra again, her excitement bubbling over.

Ga-al stretched out his neck and stared intently into space. Evidently, he was interpreting *yee-haw* as a new command.

Gingerly, Théra placed her hand against the throat of the garina-fin. Her face lit up.

"Yee-haw!" she shouted. "Thoryo! Çami! Can you feel it?"

"I can! Alkir's neck is throbbing! He's definitely hearing Ga-al's call and repeating it, though I can't hear anything."

"I can feel the vibrations! I can feel the trembling!"

It felt like the purr of a cat, a very large and contented cat.

Théra leaned against Ga-al's neck and wrapped her arms around the leathery skin. She relaxed, putting as much of her own body in contact with the garinafin as possible. Her heartbeat slowed down. The deep pulses of the inaudible song seemed to fill her with an overwhelming sense of peace, a feeling of being cradled in the palm of a loving presence that would protect her from all harm. . . .

"Wake up, Princess! Wake up!"

Thoryo's worried cries jolted her back to reality. She took deep breaths, as though emerging from a sea.

"I'm all right," she reassured the young woman. "I just need a few moments."

Is this how the tusked tiger stuns its victims? she wondered. *Can the inaudible sound touch the heart so deeply that it lulls the mind to sleep?*

If that is the case, then I didn't come into contact with the divine, but merely an illusion of it.

Disappointment flooded her heart.

She thought back to her visions of that vast land under the vaster sky, of the air crackling with the numinous as storms danced out stories of the past and the future. The idea that none of it was real, but only a physiological reaction, a quirk of her body, felt like lead over her heart, ashes in her mouth.

"Oh, how lovely!" exclaimed Thoryo.

Théra looked where she was pointing, and saw Çami walking toward them, Alkir in tow. The two had evidently been walking through some dripping foliage, and were soaked in water. As they approached, both shook their heads, throwing off drops of water. The sun lit up the droplets, refracting into brilliant, golden star-bursts. Alkir's antlers were studded with diamonds, while Çami was crowned with a webbed coronet of pearls.

Théra sat transfixed.

The dazzling sight brought to mind more images: Zomi standing by the carcass of the dissected garinafin, explaining to her the beauty of the garinafin's intricate anatomy; Takval standing by the side of Alkir, teaching her how to mount up; Kunilu-*tika* and Jian-*tika* standing by the self-locomoting arucuro tocua beast, proud of their achievement; her father in the Palace Garden, pointing at a floral map of Dara and recounting his ride on the back of a cruben; her mother and herself, a little girl, wandering through a hedge maze, as Consort Risana conjured monsters out of fog and smoke to frighten and delight her. . . .

Beauty-drunkenness and love-weakness are also mind-pleasures derived from the senses, she thought, *mere physiological reactions. But that doesn't mean they aren't real, that they don't describe some deeper Truth.*

Knowing that a garinafin relies on fermented gas to breathe fire enhances the wonder of the sight with understanding; knowing that monsters are summoned with smokecraft augments the thrill of wanting to be frightened with recognition of skill; knowing that a story is a filtered and constructed view of reality complements the joy of a tale well told with appreciation of craft; knowing that grace and pulchritude and charm and affection are rooted in the flesh only makes it more marvelous to descry in them reflections of the invisible soul, to hear in them echoes of the inaudible spirit, to feel in them traces of the incorruptible.

Who's to say that the divine can't also be experienced through the mundane, that the numinous isn't also based on the knowable? After dissecting the dead garinafin, the living creature still inspires. After weighing the fish, the dyran's dance remains indescribable.

". . . it's a wave of sound in which the pulses are so far apart that they're beyond our ability to hear, yet it has the power to affect our bodies, much like earthquake tremors." Çami finished her lecture.

"I can't believe we heard that which cannot be heard," said Thoryo, looking dazed.

"Another mystery solved," said Çami, sighing contentedly. "There's no need to resort to mysticism; the universe is knowable."

"Some mysteries only become more magnificent after you solve them," said Théra, smiling enigmatically.

Seek wonder, the only interesting thing in the world.

∾

The women returned to Takval and reported their findings.

"We've known since forever that garinafins could call to each other like that," said Takval, confused why the three were so excited.

"But you never explained *how*," said Théra, exasperated.

"What's the point of telling you that?" said Takval. "We can't do anything with calls that we can't hear. Sometimes really bad-tempered garinafins will sing silently to get other garinafins riled up without alerting the trainers, and it's a bad habit we have to break them of when they're young."

"But don't you see that if garinafins can make inaudible sounds, then probably tusked tigers can as well. And maybe the silent roar is really—"

Théra stopped. There were just too many unknowns for her to speculate responsibly. Still, she was extremely pleased that she, Çami, and Thoryo had figured out the mechanism behind a mystery on their own. The scrublands seemed just a little bit more like home now.

Takval wasn't completely sure he understood why the three of them had devoted so much energy to rediscovering a bit of common knowledge, but the fact that they had trained the garinafins to make the inaudible calls on command could be useful. He knew that the inaudible sound traveled long distances through the ground, and in fact garinafins in the wild would communicate with each other this way, especially when terrain or distance made normal calls useless. Now, even if their band were divided up into two groups, it was possible to send messages to each other across long distances.

Once he explained the idea to the other Agon warriors, they were all suitably impressed. The seemingly frivolous experiments of the Dara scholar and the princess had led to a new tactic in garinafin warfare.

CHAPTER SEVEN

PAINTED WALLS

TATEN-RYO-ALVOVO: THE EIGHTH MONTH IN THE
NINTH YEAR AFTER THE DEPARTURE OF PRINCESS
THÉRA FROM DARA FOR UKYU-GONDÉ (NINE
MONTHS UNTIL THE LYUCU MUST LAUNCH THEIR
NEW INVASION FLEET TO DARA).

Water. Cold, fresh water. He swallowed greedily.

The thirst slaked, his stomach knotted painfully with hunger. He groaned.

Something savory and salty and warm was in his mouth.

Maybe it's my tongue.

He didn't care. Even if it was his tongue, he was so hungry that he would eat it. He bit down, fully anticipating the excruciating agony. But there was no pain, only the rush of receiving nourishment after being denied for too long, only the sensation of life flowing back into him.

Tentatively, he chewed again. There was still no pain. He chewed harder and faster.

I had no idea that even after death you would have roasted meat to eat.

He swallowed.

"Good. You need to keep on drinking and eating," a voice said. The language of Dara, the language of his mother.

His eyes snapped open.

There was light, blinding light. After who knew how long in the darkness, even the light of a tallow torch seemed too bright to his eyes. He forced himself to look despite the pain, and was welcomed by the sight of Razutana.

"Are you also . . . dead?"

"Not a chance," he said. "Unlike a certain pékyu-taasa I know, I don't believe in the Agon philosophy of always running headlong into certain death. If there's even a sliver of hope of living, like squirming out from under the feet of a rampaging garinafin, I seize it."

Tanto laughed and struggled to sit up. A wave of dizziness overtook him, and his vision blacked out.

"Easy," said Razutana, supporting him by his shoulders. "You're very dehydrated and that fever is no joke either. You have to listen to your body."

Tanto relaxed and allowed himself to be helped to lie back down. Razutana put something under his head so that he was able to look about a bit while remaining on his back. He saw a bright sphere of light in the distance, slowly roaming along the wall of the large chamber. The pacing figure in the center of the sphere of light: Sataari.

"Did you come for me?"

As Razutana tore off strips of meat and stuffed them into Tanto's mouth, alternating with sips from the waterskin, the scholar explained to the boy what had happened.

After discovering that Tanto had disappeared from the camp, both Sataari and Razutana were frantic. They searched everywhere, worried that he had fallen into the midden pit or been snatched away by some predator that had not attacked the camp before.

They grew suspicious when they realized that Rokiri seemed more excited than anxious about his brother's vanishing act. But no matter how much they cajoled or threatened the young boy, Rokiri professed ignorance.

Sataari then decided to take a different tack. She sighed deeply. "The young pékyu-taasa must have been so frightened by the Lyucu. . . ."

Catching on, Razutana wrung his hands. "You don't think . . . oh, that's too dreadful to contemplate. . . ."

Sataari nodded reluctantly. "I'm afraid that . . ."

"Who knew that the boy would be so lacking in courage! How can we possibly face the pékyu and the princess when we meet them again!"

"I know. I am so ashamed!"

Rokiri could hold himself back no more. "What are you talking about? What do you think happened to Tanto?"

"Why, isn't it obvious?" asked Razutana. "Tanto has lost the heart to fight."

"Your brother—" Sataari swallowed, as if what she had to say pained her. "He has decided to sneak out of the salt flats to surrender to the Lyucu."

Rokiri screamed with rage and rushed at the shaman and the scholar, his fists windmilling, demanding that the two retract this most false contumely against his brother. Tears welling in his eyes, the young boy revealed Tanto's secret plan to explore the barrows to bring back magical weapons to defeat the Lyucu and rescue their parents.

There was much hand-wringing and debate over what to do. Razutana was determined to go into the barrows to find Tanto, a course of action Sataari objected to strenuously. Razutana tried to argue that the gods would not punish him for entering the forbidden grounds to rescue a child who sought to emulate the great Afir herself.

"Since when do you speak for the gods?" demanded Sataari. "Perhaps the gods do not agree with this parallel being drawn by the pékyu-taasa and Afir."

"That is yet more reason for me to go into the barrows," insisted Razutana. "Perhaps the gods wish for me to intervene before Tanto somehow succeeds. If he should revive the dreaded weapons of the Fifth Age, the gods may punish us even more for not stopping him."

Sataari sighed. "You and the other scholars of Dara seem to speak with double tongues. You can always find more than one reason to do something, even if the reasons are contradictory. The gods don't work that way."

"You're right," said Razutana, after a pause. "The reasons are just rationalizations, and they don't matter. All I care about is helping a boy who may have bitten off more than he can chew, and who's willing to risk his life for his parents, for us, for his people. I don't care what the gods think; I'm going."

"All right, then I'm coming with you," said Sataari. As Razutana gaped at her in amazement, she added, "With that attitude, someone is going to have to go in and save *you* later. Might as well give myself a head start. *Someone* has to try to talk to the gods on behalf of bull-headed fools."

He would swear to all the gods of Dara and Gondé that there was a smile on her face and a tenderness in her voice before she turned all serious again.

After giving the rest of the children strict orders to remain in the camp and stay safe, Razutana and Sataari set out to find Tanto two days after his departure. They followed the trail left by the boy easily and, though the journey took many days, they steadily closed in on Tanto. Indeed, only hours after Tanto dove into the water bubble, they found his pack at the base of the Great Barrow.

"But are you trapped here like me? I couldn't find—"

"Don't worry," said Razutana, putting a comforting hand on his shoulder. "At every turn, we shaped the glowing mushrooms on the walls into a sign. I've already gone back out once to bring in some supplies."

Tanto was ashamed that he had not thought of such a simple thing to do. His grand adventure had been a debacle. "I came to look for weapons—"

"I know," said Razutana. "But staying alive is the most important weapon of them all. Don't you dare do something this foolish ever again." Seeing the dejected look on the boy's face, he relented. "You've been incredibly brave. If it hadn't been for you, none of us would have seen the wonders of the City of Ghosts."

"What's Sataari doing?" asked Tanto, trying to shift the topic away from himself.

"Are you strong enough to walk? Let's go join her."

The boy leaned against the scholar as the pair slowly approached the shaman, deeply absorbed by the wall in front of her. Without disturbing her, they examined the wall by the light of Sataari's torch as well.

The walls of the chamber were covered by paintings in shades of red, yellow, and black. Some of the strokes had apparently been made with branches or fingers; other parts of the paintings had been made with droplets of paint spewed from mouths against hands or other stencils; still other parts had been done with soot and smoke, probably from torches similar to the one now lighting the scene.

On the scrublands, a painted story usually began in the west, the direction of night, darkness, and the mysteries of the unknown. Could he orient himself and determine the cardinal directions in this enclosed space?

With his belly filled and thirst quenched, Tanto found himself thinking more clearly than before. He looked back at the skeletons on the platform behind him. Bodies undergoing pédiato savaga on the scrublands were always placed with their heads pointing toward the rising sun. Perhaps the people who had built the Great Barrow followed a similar custom? However, since the bodies in this burial chamber had been arranged with the feet of each next to the head of the other, the orientation of the skeletons didn't help.

Wait! He realized that there was a stone pillar topped by a sphere some distance from one end of the stone platform. That had to represent the sun, right? He couldn't be sure, but it seemed as good a guess as any, so he decided to go with it.

Along the western wall, where they were standing, the painted scene was full of garinafins, tusked tigers, horrid wolves, moss-antlered deer, spiral-horned mouflon, and aurochs with long horns and broad shoulders. These last resembled the long-haired cattle herded by the people of the scrublands, but leaner, with flowing lines that suggested great strength. Around them were groups of small humans wielding spears and axes, chasing after prey many times larger in size.

"Were these the people of the Fifth Age?" asked Razutana. "Or is this a scene from after they had been driven out of paradise?"

Startled by the question, Sataari almost dropped the torch. The figures on the wall seemed to come alive as the flame trembled. "I don't know," she said, her voice distant. She walked along the wall, beckoning them to follow.

As darkness swallowed the vibrant painting, Tanto gasped. Where the eyes of the animals and humans had been, there now appeared eerie, glowing dots. The luminescent mushrooms had apparently grown in the painted eyes, perhaps the result of some nutrient in the pigment.

Tanto's eyes darted around the dark chamber, and cold sweat broke out on his back. All the glowing points of light around the chamber were eyes, staring at him and offering silent judgment. He wondered if all the other chambers were decorated like this. Without torches, he hadn't been able to see the paintings earlier.

Razutana's warm, steady hand wrapped around his. "It's all right," the scholar said to him. "Think of the paintings as stars in the sky, guiding us to the truth."

The boy nodded and stayed close to the Dara scholar as they followed Sataari's torch.

Along the northern wall, the painted scene changed drastically. Here, large barrows dominated the background, many of them studded with strange structures. Tiny human figures appeared on the mounds: some tending to fires in front of cave-like dwellings, others standing at the top, dancing or performing unknown rituals.

In the foreground was a large lake or sea. Ships of strange design, like giant water-striding insects, plied the waves. If the human figures on them were to scale, then these ships were far larger than the coracles used by the tribespeople on the coast of Ukyu and Gondé. Some of the people on the ships strained to lift nets heavy with catch. Fish leapt from the waves, and waterfowl swam or glided above them.

"Is that the Sea of Tears?" asked Tanto excitedly. "Look at all those fish! We've never seen anything like that."

"It must not have been as salty as it is now," muttered Razutana.

Between the barrows and the lake, the middle of the painting bustled with the most activity. Here, on one side of the estuarine flat, herds of long-haired cattle and knob-horned sheep grazed inside stone fences. The penned animals looked far fatter than their wild counterparts on the first wall. At the left and right edges of the painting, beyond the limits of the mound city, some humans rode on broad-shouldered bulls to face off against tusked tigers and horrid wolves.

In the center of the estuarine flat, other humans clustered around strange engines and structures. Some of the artificial structures took up as much space as a small mound, while others were so tall that their tops disappeared in the smoky clouds in the sky. Shaped like skeletal beasts with dozens or even hundreds of limbs and wings, the gargantuan machines appeared to be harnessed by long cables attached to various parts of their bodies, with teams of humans and cattle pulling on them. Some of the bone beasts were moving earth to heap upon new mounds; some of the beasts were coming from afar, laden with cut stone; still others were working near the many small rivers winding their way through the city of mounds toward the lake, constructing dams or dredging channels.

On the opposite side of the estuarine flat from the penned animals, many more humans could be seen laboring in fields filled with neat rows of vegetation.

Razutana bent closer to examine the painted fields, mumbling as he took out a piece of rolled bark and a charcoal stylus to take notes in shorthand.

"They're farming!" exclaimed Tanto. "Just like Mother and the people from Dara!"

Still silent, Sataari led them to the next wall, along the eastern side of the chamber.

The scene changed yet again. Many human skeletons lay next to deserted fields and empty pens. There were no more fish or birds or ships in the sea, and the rivers that had once crisscrossed the land were gone as well. The towering structures that had moved earth and water in the previous scene lay in fragments between the mounds. A bright sun shone in a sky devoid of clouds.

Two large groups of humans were engaged in heated battle at the bottom of the mural. Garinafins spat fire at one another in the sky, while warriors on the ground fought with slingshots, clubs, axes, slings, and spears in dense formation. Behind them, small groups of people climbed the mounds, carrying vessels and stretchers piled high with various goods, as well as skeletons of the dead on their backs.

"The end of the Fifth Age," whispered Razutana.

Sataari showed no reaction.

Finally, they came to the southern wall. This time, the scene was of the heart of the city, where a giant barrow, larger than any of the others, loomed in the center. Atop the mound, a group of warriors stood around their chief, who had been drawn to appear larger than life. Her features were twisted in anguish, and she held her hands out supplicatingly to the viewer.

At the foot of the barrow, a long line of people wound its way from the base of the earthen structure to somewhere outside the frame of the painting. They were passing large vessels from hand to hand, and those standing directly at the foot of the mound poured the contents out on the ground. Water? Blood? Kyoffir for the gods?

In the foreground was a long procession headed toward the Great Barrow: humans, cattle, sheep, dogs. . . . They carried heavy bundles on their backs, but held no weapons in their hands. At the head of the procession was a large bier, with a man dressed as a chief lying on it. This figure had also been drawn to appear larger than life, and his hands, laced together, rested atop his chest.

Numerous garinafins circled over the procession, not in battle, but more like an honor guard.

"The barrows weren't built to house the dead," said Razutana. "This was once a living city. The mounds were palaces, temples, hive-houses. They domesticated animals and farmed here, and fished in the freshwater sea."

Sataari said nothing.

"Was this enslavement of the land?" asked Tanto.

Sataari said nothing.

"Are you all right?" Razutana said, putting a hand gently on her shoulder.

Jolted out of her reverie, the shaman nodded slowly, as though still caught in a dream-haze. "I've . . . I've never been in a place so quiet," she croaked.

"Tanto and I can make more noise if you want," said Razutana, grinning.

She shook her head impatiently. "You don't understand. When I'm out there, the gods are always talking to me, even though I can't always understand their voices—the wind moaning over the scrublands, the birds chittering in the bushes and cactus nest-holes, the voles skittering underground, the stars twinkling their silent music . . .

"But in here, I can't hear their voices at all."

Razutana and Tanto looked at each other. "Do you feel the presence of evil?" asked Razutana cautiously.

"No . . . more like the gods are staying away, out of fear or respect . . . as though they're reluctant to guide us, as though we're truly on our own."

The other two didn't know what to say.

At length, Sataari shook off the invisible weight on her shoulders and knelt down. The base of the wall, now illuminated by torchlight, turned out to be more than bare stone. Tanto and Razutana also knelt down to get a closer look.

Strips of thin membrane sheets were tacked all around the bottom of the chamber, reminding Razutana of the pliable vellum, almost translucent, that he had seen Adyulek and Sataari use for the voice paintings at the Winter Festival. However, instead of the explosion of color and tangled dynamic curlicues that froze the movements of the dancer and fixed the music of the drums, the membranous strips were covered in a uniform layer of something the color of smoky haze, and through that featureless tract, a single thin line wandered, like the course of a lazy river meandering over a desert plain or the route of a confused traveler in the pathless grass seas.

The abstract image seemed both meaningless and full of significance.

"What is that material?" asked Razutana, whispering out of awe. "It looks just like paper."

"That's the lining from a garinafin stomach," said Sataari, her tone strangely distant. "It's very thin but strong, and if properly prepared, endures generations of winters."

Fascinated, Tanto extended a finger.

"Don't!" Razutana cried out, and Tanto jerked back. But it was too late. The boy's finger had already touched the strip of lining. The scholar winced, thinking that the fragile markings would be damaged.

But the markings stayed true. A layer of transparent glaze sealed the marks and protected them from the elements, similar to the glue used to make Adyulek's voice paintings permanent.

"It's a spirit portrait," said Sataari, her voice raspy. "Maybe more than one is in this chamber," she added, glancing at the skeletons. "I've never seen one this old or well-made, but the principle is the same. They are taken of great warriors just before death, in order to capture the breath of life, the flow of their spirit."

"Capture the breath of life . . . How? Like the voice paintings?" asked Razutana.

Sataari shook her head. "Only the children of Afir can be shown the mysteries."

"But *I* am Agon, and I fear and trust the gods," said Tanto.

Sataari looked at the boy affectionately. "Brave as you are, you're not yet a warrior. Only after you've spilled your first blood will you be initiated into the deepest of the mysteries. Leave these sacred portraits alone. You can look, but don't touch."

"Do the stories told in these paintings match up with any of the lore you know?" asked Razutana.

After a long pause, Sataari said, "It's still too quiet." Her face looked haunted, as though she was not quite able to believe some revelation that only she could see.

Razutana didn't understand Sataari's odd reaction. He would bet good money that the two larger-than-life figures in the last painting were the same individuals entombed in this chamber and memorialized in the spirit portraits. Based on what he remembered of Sataari's stories, they were thus likely the sinful chiefs of the arrogant Fifth Age, who had angered the gods with their pride and wicked ways of living. They were reprobates, villains, the very embodiment of the antithesis of the Agon spirit. Yet instead of treating them with contempt and disdain, Sataari acted with great reverence and protectiveness.

Did Sataari know more about the occupants of this chamber than she was willing to share?

"Tanto and I will look around a bit more," said Razutana. He lit a torch from the one held by Sataari, and, leaving the shaman standing alone contemplatively next to the spirit portraits, the scholar and the boy returned to the central platform of the chamber, upon which the two skeletons rested.

Razutana stuck the torch into a hole at one end of the platform to brighten the area. Though not a pious man, he nonetheless whispered a prayer to the gods of Dara and of Gondé to give the spirits of the dead a peaceful repose. The two deceased were tall and powerfully built, their bones showing signs of breakage and healing that hinted at lives consumed in violence.

While Tanto inspected the weapons on the stone platform, unwilling to give up the idea of finding potent magic among them, Razutana got on his hands and knees to look at the baked clay jars at the foot of the platform. Seeds spilled from the few jars that Tanto had broken earlier, and Razutana chuckled in delight.

As a Cultivationist, Razutana found the seeds to be far more interesting than weapons or "spirit portraits," whatever they were. Back in Kiri Valley, he had tried to domesticate some of the native tubers and wild grains with little success. That was why the valley settlement had been so dependent on crops from Dara. But if the people who had lived in this mound-city had once practiced agriculture, then they must have domesticated crops that were well suited to local conditions. He didn't have the time or equipment to study the seeds properly in the burial chamber, so he simply collected as many varieties as he could and stuffed them into the pouches at his waist.

"I think I found something!" said Tanto excitedly.

Razutana got up. "What is it?"

Tanto pointed at the stone and bone tools. "Look at where they're placed. How could these two reach them?"

The scholar saw what the boy meant. The tools—wedges, hammers, spikes, flat and curved blades—were all relatively short. But instead of being placed next to the hands of the deceased, where they would be easily accessible in the afterlife—assuming that was the intent—the weapons were located next to their feet, well out of reach.

"And they didn't look like this earlier," said Tanto.

"What do you mean?"

"I don't know how to explain it." Tanto was frustrated. "Before you came, I checked these weapons in the dark, and they looked different. . . . They've been moved!"

"That's impossible. Sataari and I didn't touch anything."

"I know what I know! They moved!" Tanto clenched his fists. "Maybe . . . it's the light. Ghosts don't like light, right?"

No matter how much Razutana took pride in his identity as a man of reason and not of superstition, standing here inside a burial mound next to two skeletons and hearing that the weapons of the dead had moved on their own sent chills down his spine. He took a deep breath to steady himself.

"I'm not saying that you're wrong," said Razutana. "Let's test your theory, all right?"

"Weigh the fish," said Tanto, letting out a held breath.

Razutana smiled. The young pékyu-taasa probably didn't realize how much he sounded like his mother sometimes. He picked up the torch and walked away, placing it behind a large stone statue of a sleeping bull before returning.

Gradually, their eyes adjusted to the darkness, and glowing dots reappeared on the stone platform like creatures of the deep. But besides the dots, there was something more.

"There! That's what I saw!" cried Tanto.

Faint luminescent lines materialized on the stone platform, connecting the weapons with the hands of the skeletons like ghostly handles.

"It *is* magic," said Tanto. "That was how they wielded the weapons: with invisible handles!"

Razutana retrieved the torch and inspected the platform closely, his nose almost touching the stone.

Now that he had an idea of what to look for, it was easy to notice faint black lines on the surface, corresponding to the luminous handles in the dark. He thought back to the glowing eyes of the animals and people in the paintings.

"I think . . . I know what happened," said Razutana.

He explained to Tanto that the bone and stone weapons likely had been attached to handles constructed of some perishable material, such as wood. Over time, the handles had rotted away, leaving behind only traces on the stone. These traces, however, provided ideal beds for the luminescent fungi that colonized the interior of the mound, thus creating the illusion of "ghost handles."

Tanto looked disappointed at this explanation.

"But I think you've discovered something much more interesting," said Razutana. "If you imagine long handles attached to these, the weapons appear not to be weapons at all, but likely farming implements."

Tanto saw that it was true. Once he mentally added long handles to the "weapons," they did resemble the rakes, hoes, shovels, and similar tools Théra and the others had used to till the fields in Kiri Valley.

He tried to imagine these two great chiefs of the Fifth Age laboring in the fields. His gaze landed on the fingers of the skeleton nearest him, and he pictured them wrapped around a clod-breaking hoe instead of a thunder-dealing war club. It was such an incongruous change that the corners of his mouth lifted up in a smile.

He froze.

"The fingers!" He pulled on Razutana's hand and pointed. The scholar looked confused for a moment before his eyes also widened.

Together, they counted the fingers to be sure: one, two, three, four, five, six. There were six fingers on each hand.

They stared at each other, stunned. Then they ran to the foot of the other skeleton and counted the toes: one, two, three, four, five, six. There were six toes on each foot.

They ran toward Sataari, still motionless before the painting on the southern wall. By the glow of the torch, they counted the fingers in the interlaced hands of the large man lying on the bier at the head of the procession: one, two, three, four, five, six.

The great hero Kikisavo had six fingers on each hand, which gave him the strength of ten bears; the great hero Afir had six toes on each foot, which gave her the endurance of ten mouflon.

"Afir and Kikisavo had muddy feet and arms," Sataari muttered. The revelation was impossible, but the tools they had been buried with, the seeds found around the stone bier, and the paintings on the walls of the chamber made denial of the truth impossible.

The heroic pair were not innocents who had been cast out of paradise unjustly, but responsible for the very works—or at least some of them—that had supposedly brought down the wrath of the gods. The people who had built these barrows and tended these fields were the ancestors of the Agon and the Lyucu. They had made the same kinds of spirit portraits, worshipped the same gods, and told many of the same stories.

"The old stories are all true," Sataari whispered. "But we didn't understand them."

Tanto and Razutana didn't interrupt her, though there were so many questions they wanted to ask. What kind of lives did the people who built these mounds live? What had happened to turn the lush paradise of the earlier painting into this City of Ghosts? Why did Kikisavo part from Afir only to return after his death?

"What do you think happened here?" asked Razutana in the end.

Sataari shook her head. "The gods are still silent."

"Maybe we're meant to make sense of it all ourselves."

One thing was clear: Afir and Kikisavo had tried their hardest to preserve their way of life. If they had enslaved the land by doing so, they never regretted it even unto death.

Though he brought back no magical weapons, Tanto gained the admiration of all the children at camp. No warrior in any legend had ever entered the City of Ghosts and returned alive.

"You are as brave as your father, the pékyu," said Nalu solemnly.

Tanto blushed and muttered his thanks.

In the months that followed, Tanto entertained the band with tales of his adventures. With a natural storyteller's instinct, he doled them out at a slow trickle, and only after much embellishment. Every night ended with raucous demands from the other children for "just one more barrow" as Tanto smiled enigmatically, shaking his head.

"You'll have to return tomorrow night."

The experience also brought Sataari and Razutana closer. When Razutana suggested that they plant some of the seeds retrieved from the Great Barrow, Sataari didn't object. In fact, she joined him in digging the ditches for irrigation and wielded the hoes and spades, which Razutana modeled after the ones he had seen in the burial chamber. After all, if Afir had so valued farming that she chose to be buried with agricultural implements instead of weapons, then maybe there was something to the idea of digging for food out of the earth.

As the crops sprouted and then thrived, Razutana turned his attention to devising techniques of harvest, storage, and ultimately, cooking. He experimented with various recipes to extract the most taste and nourishment from these unfamiliar tubers and grains. Sataari and the children, to his surprise and pleasure, eagerly joined in the experiments. Sometimes, as the camp raucously debated the appropriate roasting and boiling techniques, combinations of spices, strength of cooking fire, and similar topics, Razutana would grin and shake his head, thinking that he had somehow been transported to a test kitchen in one of the great restaurants back in Dara.

No one would starve in the coming winter.

CHAPTER EIGHT

THE SPRUNG TRAP

WORLD'S EDGE MOUNTAINS: THE NINTH MONTH
IN THE NINTH YEAR AFTER THE DEPARTURE
OF PRINCESS THÉRA FROM DARA FOR UKYU-
GONDÉ (EIGHT MONTHS UNTIL THE LYUCU
MUST LAUNCH THEIR NEW INVASION FLEET TO
DARA).

The deadline for Araten's return was in three days.

Théra flew to the valley entrance every day to wait for him, praying that he was all right and that there would be more news about her children.

Suddenly, Ga-al snorted, flared his nostrils, and jerked up from his haunches, looking alarmed. Then he twisted his neck to stare at her, a look of terror in his pupil-less eyes.

"What is it? Another tusked tiger?" asked Théra. She looked about in alarm.

Ga-al shook his head and snorted again. No matter how much Théra stroked the base of the neck, he refused to calm down. Bending his serpentine neck back, he nudged Théra with one of his antlers, urging her to *get going*.

Théra complied, having learned to trust the garinafin's ability to hear that which cannot be heard. By the time the pair returned to camp, she saw everyone was rushing about to get Alkir ready, draping the war webbing on the garinafin and strapping their supplies and gear in securely.

"I had to risk having Alkir warn you," said Takval. "Let's just hope that the Lyucu garinafins, even if they heard Alkir's silent cry, can't tell their riders."

"They've found us?"

"Sighted them just beyond the ridge. I rushed back as quickly as possible. We have to get out of here now."

"But Araten isn't back yet!" she said, her voice cracking from fright and worry. The trusty thane was their only connection with the outside world and her only hope of finding out more news of her children.

"We'll lose everyone if we wait any longer," said Takval.

"What if he and his band were to return after Cudyu has taken over the valley?"

Takval said nothing. But his resolute look, the same expression he wore when he had suggested that Théra and the rest of the fleet flee while he stayed behind to fight the Lyucu city-ship, told her everything.

They have to be sacrificed to buy us more time.

Her chest felt tight and she labored to get enough air into her lungs, but she knew he was right. She had always been unwilling to make sacrifices, but by now that obstinacy had been worn down by the pain of so many lives lost because of her. She had to be more ruthless, think of the grander picture.

They took off before noon, abandoning the camp in the Foot Range that had been their home for the last few months.

They didn't even get out of the valley before realizing that they were trapped.

The Lyucu raiding party Takval had spotted was but one small part of an overwhelming force that had encircled the valley, sealing off every exit route. No matter which way the refugees turned in their flight, they sighted teams of garinafins sneaking up on them from below, conserving lift gas by hiking through the mountainous terrain. Takval kept them flying close to the valley floor and executed tight turns, hoping that they hadn't been sighted.

There was no choice but to land.

"We've been betrayed," said Takval, his voice heavy with rage and regret.

"How?"

Takval and Théra looked at each other. The timing of the attack made the answer obvious.

"Why didn't they attack earlier? Araten must have led them here the first time he left—"

Théra felt her blood run cold. She thought back to the conversations between her and Araten, the questions he had asked, the enigmatic expressions in response to her answers. . . .

"O gods," she whispered. "He was prying from me when the Wall of Storms would reopen."

There had likely never been any attempt by Cudyu to gather shamans and diviners to calculate the time at all. Why bother doing the hard work when it was so much easier to gain her trust with news of her children, to worm into her heart through guilt and gratitude, to probe and poke and unsettle her with lies until she spilled the secret herself?

"Why?" asked Théra, swaying unsteadily from the emotional blow. *"Why would Araten do this?"*

"I should have been much less trusting," said Takval, his jaw clenched. "I should have learned my lesson after Volyu's treachery!"

There was no way to know the complexity of the human heart. Perhaps Araten had agreed to serve the Lyucu under duress, or perhaps he had done so in order to secure his position in Cudyu's new order. Betrayal, like love, had a thousand-thousand forms.

Théra's mind was a tangled mess, and she was surrounded by doubt on all sides, much as they were encircled by the Lyucu. What could she *believe?* Had everything Araten told her been false?

Almost without realizing it, she began to pray to the gods of Ukyu-Gondé. Abruptly, Takval's self-recriminations and the curses of their Agon and Dara retinues faded from her awareness. Once more, she was on that vast plain under a vaster sky, where the air was filled with the limpid light of the numinous. Powerful storms raged across this scrubland of the interior—dancing, singing, guiding, questioning; jagged branches of defiant shrubs and ephemeral lightning flashes divided the world into a thousand-thousand chiaroscuro fragments.

She prayed for clarity, and she felt, rather than heard, the deep rumbling of distant thunder. The truth tumbled into her heart like drops of life-giving rain.

"Tanto and Rokiri are all right!" said Théra, gasping as she emerged from that other plane of consciousness. "As are the rest of the children."

Takval and the others looked at her, confused.

"Don't you see?" she said. "If Cudyu had actually managed to get his hands on our children, there would have been no need for this ruse. They could have captured us and extracted whatever they needed from us by threatening harm to them. The only reason they resorted to the gambit with Araten is because Toof and Radia succeeded in their plot."

Hope flared once more in everyone's heart.

But it was short-lived.

"How can we possibly stop the invasion fleet now that they know when to launch it?" Théra asked in anguish.

Çami, Tipo, and the other Dara fighters looked at one another helplessly. Had all their sacrifices and plans come to naught because of her carelessness?

"The tolyusa blooms in the heart of winter," said Takval. "When things look the worst is also when our fortunes will start to turn. I promise you that if we get out of this alive, we won't stop until we're in Taten and their city-ships are in flames."

The sun was lower in the west. It was almost time for Araten and his raiding party to attack.

Earlier in the day, he had sighted Takval and Théra's band at their camp down in the valley, right where he had left them. Rather than launching an attack right away, he had ordered the party to wait until hunting parties approaching from the other sides had completely sealed off all routes of escape.

All afternoon, he had kept his garinafins out of sight, resting in the shade of a low ridge in the valley. He knew that it was Takval's habit to perform daily patrols. Hopefully, he would catch Takval's garinafins after they had already used up some of their lift gas while his were at their strongest. Sure, the Lyucu garinafins vastly outnumbered the two garinafins under Takval's command; it was still best to minimize the risk.

His caution was a reflection of his master's approach. Cudyu was by nature suspicious, and he became even more paranoid after being deceived by Toof and Radia. Even after all Araten had done for the Lyucu cause in Kiri Valley, the Lyucu pékyu didn't trust the Agon defector completely. Though Araten had come up with the whole plot to trick Théra into yielding up the information Cudyu wanted, Cudyu nonetheless opted to hold Araten's family as hostages to ensure his loyalty. The scars on Araten's body, which had helped to buy Théra's trust, had been inflicted by Cudyu to impress upon Araten the reality of his threats.

Araten sighed. When Théra had unwittingly given up the secret, he had almost blurted out the truth—the shame of abusing her trust was so great. But he had survived that bout of erupting conscience without doing anything foolish. Betrayal, once committed, led only to more betrayals. There was no middle path.

He tried to tell himself that he really had no choice. How could Takval and Théra believe it was possible to defy the might of Cudyu, the greatest pékyu the scrublands had ever seen? After the destruction of the base in Kiri Valley, Cudyu's sway over the Agon tribes was even more absolute than Tenryo's had been.

Araten had no interest in sharing the fate of the other captives from Kiri Valley, now relegated to hard labor in Taten. Indeed, if one thought about it, he was acting in the best interests of the Agon by capturing the pretender pékyu and his barbarian bride—it was the only way to bring about peace, to give his people a chance to survive, albeit as slaves. (It was, of course, also a way for him and his followers to prove their loyalty to Cudyu and perhaps become full-fledged Lyucu, but he preferred to think of himself in a more selfless and heroic mode.)

Only half of the sun peeked above the mountains in the west now. He gestured for his warriors to ready the garinafins and strap themselves into battle positions. It was time to end this.

"After our victory today," he whispered to his band, "maybe all of you will be promoted to naros-votan."

"And we should all congratulate you on your imminent adoption into the Tasaricu clan!" one of his followers simpered.

"May it please the pékyu," he said, smiling back.

Abruptly, two shadows swooped low overhead, heading westward. The gusts from beating wings made him wince and duck down.

"Garinafins! Garinafins away!" shouted his followers.

He looked up and cursed. Takval and Théra must have seen him and waited until this moment to seize the initiative.

Araten had to admire the princess and the pékyu for their boldness. They had most likely crept up on him all afternoon, intending to catch him by surprise. Instead of making a useless last stand in the valley, the rebels were hoping to prey on the would-be predator, breaking through the encirclement and finding refuge in the descending night.

"After them!"

His raiding party scrambled. Soon, four garinafins with full crews took off in hot pursuit of the two rebel garinafins. Many of Araten's riders were Lyucu, placed under his command for the nonce. He was uncertain whether they would obey his orders diligently, considering that he was just a surrendered Agon, his loyalty in question. Fortunately, his own crew was mostly made up of other Agon who had surrendered to Cudyu alongside him. They shared his fate and would do whatever he demanded of them.

Although Alkir and Ga-al were heavily laden with people and goods, they seemed to speed through the air with unusual ease. Slowly, they pulled away from the pursuing garinafins. Considering that Ga-al was too old to even be considered a proper war mount, the feat was astonishing and confused Araten.

The sun had almost dipped below the horizon, and once darkness descended, there was a real possibility that the rebels could get away.

Terror gripped Araten's heart. He had begged to be allowed to lead a band of garinafins in this final assault in the hope of seizing Takval and Théra personally and gaining more glory. But now that Takval had picked him as the soft spot in the encirclement, he would be held responsible if they escaped. The paranoid Cudyu might even believe Araten was like Toof and Radia. . . .

No . . . NO!

He shouted into his bone trumpet, urging his mount to fly harder and faster. But the garinafin's breathing was already labored.

Time for desperate measures.

He turned around and gave the prearranged signal to one of his riders.

The woman scrambled out of her harness, crawled over the netting until she was next to him. "Are you certain, votan?" she shouted into his ear.

He nodded vigorously.

The woman crawled past him and climbed out on the long, sinuous neck of the garinafin. The war beast, trained by the Lyucu to be absolutely obedient, did not react at this unusual maneuver. Once the woman was perched between the antlers, she used twisted sinew to bind herself securely in place. Then she took off a pouch from her back, and carefully poured the contents over the eyelids of the garinafin.

Araten turned around to make sure all his crew were secure in their harnesses. They were about to experience some flight turbulence.

The woman capped the pouch and held on.

The garinafin screamed. The skin over its eyelids bubbled and hissed, and a faint smoke rose from the wounded flesh. It whipped its head around in agony, wings flapping madly.

Concentrated gash cactus juice was occasionally used by the Lyucu as a weapon or torture device. When applied to the sensitive eyelids of the garinafins, it caused unbelievable pain. If given in combination with tolyusa, it could drive war mounts into sustained bouts of frenzy during which they ignored their injuries and exhaustion and performed physical feats far beyond their normal endurance. Of course, they often died after such induced mania, completely drained.

Wounding or killing a Lyucu war garinafin this way would surely draw Cudyu's wrath; his only hope was to capture Takval and Théra to make up for it.

As Araten's crew held on, their mount burst through the air, leaving the other pursuing garinafins far behind. Breath rasping, heart thundering, it flapped its wings with crazed strength, paying no heed to the damage it was doing to its delicate tissues.

Gradually, it gained on the two escaping Agon garinafins.

Straining against the buffeting wind, Araten's crew launched slingshot missiles and spears against the fleeing riders huddled on their mounts, their skull helmets bowed. A fire breath attack was out of the question, as the goal was to capture the rebels alive. Several of the missiles struck true, and Araten's crew cheered. The struck Agon riders flopped and convulsed, but did not otherwise react. Araten hoped the strikes weren't fatal. He had given explicit orders to avoid the heads.

The Lyucu riders ducked as their garinafin swept past the enemy, ready for returning shots. But strangely, Takval and Théra's crew didn't fire back.

A feeling of dread grew in Araten's heart. Something was very wrong. Based on what he knew of Takval's personality, he had expected the pékyu to engage him with Alkir, thereby buying more time for Ga-al to escape with his wife and their followers. But the two garinafins weren't even swerving to avoid the missiles and continued to fly side by side, making no attempt to separate or counterattack. Indeed, they took no evasive maneuvers at all, apparently intent on outrunning the pursuit by speed alone.

Tamping down his unease, he guided his frenzied mount to race ahead of the two fleeing garinafins, heading them off as the rest of the raiding party caught up. His slingshot scouts pelted the Agon riders with missiles as they overtook the fliers, hoping to disable as many as possible without killing any outright.

The barrage seemed to have an effect. The rebel garinafins turned sharply to avoid injury, but didn't put up much of a fight. Corralled by Araten's frenzied mount's superior speed, the rebels were soon surrounded by the four Lyucu garinafins. After a few warning fire breaths from the Lyucu, the refugee mounts were forced to land.

As soon as his own garinafin landed, Araten scrambled down the webbing, dropping the rest of the way when he was below the garinafin's shoulders. Paying no attention to the agonized groans of the wounded garinafin—its eyelids had been completely burned away by the acid, and it was unlikely to live through the night—he ran toward Ga-al, his war club raised and ready. Other riders climbed down and joined him, racing to seize the prisoners.

The three uninjured Lyucu garinafins growled threateningly, and the two captured garinafins moaned in terror. They cowered, adopting the submissive stance of garinafins whose riders had given up all resistance.

Araten whistled loudly.

His old mount turned to him and lowed in recognition.

Araten's heart leapt with joy. Perhaps Takval had been unable to put up much resistance because Ga-al refused to obey him! Ga-al, though also brutally raised in the Lyucu manner, had been assigned to him for a few months, and maybe that was enough time for a bond to form.

He skidded to a stop next to the heaving masses of Ga-al and Alkir, his mouth agape as he saw the riders on the back of the two garinafins clearly for the first time in the darkening twilight.

All the riders drooped lifelessly in the webbing. Not a single skull helmet was moving.

Araten recovered and scrambled up Alkir's webbing until he reached the pilot's saddle. He grabbed the man by the shoulder and turned him around. After a moment of stunned silence, Araten cursed and laughed, though the noise betrayed no mirth, only a profound sadness and resignation.

Instead of a muscled shoulder, his fingers were wrapped around a crooked branch clad in animal skin; instead of Takval's face, he was staring into the hollow sockets of a deer skull.

None of the riders on the garinafin were real. They were human-shaped frames made from lightweight branches and sticks, covered in furs and pelts. Empty animal skulls served as heads.

No wonder the fleeing garinafins had moved as though they carried no weight; no wonder the riders hadn't reacted when shot; no wonder the war beasts hadn't put up any fight.

He looked up and saw that Ga-al had curled his sinuous neck

around to look at him. In those pupil-less eyes, Araten saw hints of emotions that should be beyond the ken of such a dumb beast: pity and mockery.

Araten laughed and laughed. As tears streamed down his face, he ignored his followers' pleas for direction.

There was nothing else to do. His fate was sealed. The other Lyucu hunting parties would soon converge on this spot, and then he would have to face Cudyu's judgment. Even if he were endowed with a hundred mouths and a thousand tongues, he would never be able to convince Cudyu that he hadn't been in on Takval's scheme, that he hadn't helped the Agon pékyu escape through this devious trick. Despite his repeated betrayals and all the lives he had sacrificed for his own ambition and his family's welfare, he was about to die as a loyal member of the Agon rebellion.

He laughed, though the hacks were indistinguishable from sobs. The gods sure liked to play jokes.

After a very long and circuitous journey, he was about to see his true character revealed in the merciless, cold gaze of Cudyu Roatan.

Araten was right that Takval's first instinct had been to engage the Lyucu with Alkir, affording Théra and the others a chance to escape on Ga-al. But Théra had convinced him of an alternate plan.

The plot to use decoy riders to distract the Lyucu pursuit was inspired by the Hegemon, who had once used a similar trick to capture Zudi back in Dara. While Alkir and Ga-al fled west, leading the Lyucu on a fruitless chase, Théra and Takval led their band east on foot, hiking into the spine of the World's Edge Mountains.

"They'd never believe we would voluntarily breach the realm of the gods," said Théra, "just as they'd never expect us to abandon our garinafins. When everything you've tried has failed, the only path left is to do something impossible, something new."

Takval expected Adyulek to object to this plan, which seemed to him a sacrilege. One did not go over the World's Edge unless one did so on the back of a cloud-garinafin. But surprisingly, the old shaman supported the princess.

"The Every-Mother speaks in interesting ways and through

unusual messengers," she said. "Didn't Afir once attempt to cross into the realm of the gods in order to save her people? The princess's thinking-breath recalls our origins."

Takval shook his head. Would wonders never cease?

Wrapping their bodies in thick furs and their hearts in renewed resolve, they set off toward the east, toward the towering mountains that seemed to reach into the sky, toward hope that glinted as faintly as starglow.

CHAPTER NINE

SECRET

After finally ridding herself of Cutanrovo for the night, Tanvanaki seethed alone in the Great Tent.

Every conversation with the single-minded thane ended the same way. Cutanrovo would dream up some outrageous project to further "purify" Ukyu-taasa of native influence—impose strict limits on the number of children natives might have, to be enforced by infanticide; reclaim all agricultural fields for pasturing, with the farmers pressed into labor gangs; abolish the system of native officials and reduce the status of all natives to livestock—and Tanvanaki would have to point out that these projects ran contrary to the goal of turning the natives into obedient fighters for Ukyu-taasa.

"They'll obey only if they still believe submission will allow them to preserve what little they have left," said Tanvanaki. "If they should conclude that they have nothing to lose, then *we* will lose everything."

But Cutanrovo kept on pushing and pushing, and it was getting harder and harder for Tanvanaki to hold her line.

She got up, strode to the middle of the empty Great Tent, and began to punch and kick at the air, imagining her fists and feet landing against Cutanrovo's face. There was nothing more frustrating than debating a sincere zealot.

She didn't want to go back to her bed, where Timu lay still, as welcoming as a block of ice. He had withdrawn into himself, spending his days muttering Classical Ano poetry, reading histories, and teaching Dyana only gods knew what. He rarely spoke to her except to argue.

Time and again, she had explained to him that she had no choice but to allow Cutanrovo and the hard-liners to carry out their rampage against the natives if she wanted to remain the pékyu. The warriors loved Cutanrovo; the hard-liner thane made them feel like masters of Ukyu-taasa, blessed kin of the gods, omnipotent, invincible. If she moved against Cutanrovo now, who would fight for her when Cudyu arrived to challenge her?

"Do you think your people will fare better under my brother?" she demanded. "With me in charge, we can still realize the dream of a kinder fate for the people of Dara once the crisis posed by the arrival of my brother's fleet is resolved."

He simply looked at her, as though no longer believing anything she said.

"I need Cutanrovo's support," she said, a note of pleading in her voice, willing him to understand. "She is the only hope I have of holding on to Ukyu-taasa."

"Be careful that your guard dog doesn't turn into a wolf that rips out your throat," he said. Then he turned away, burying himself in his old books, which Tanvanaki had saved from Cutanrovo's burning campaigns for his benefit—not that he appreciated her efforts. Dyana, sitting by her father, looked at her with accusing eyes, as though blaming her for the state of strife in the household.

Neither could she seek comfort from her son, who was now always found in the company of the hard-liner thanes, gleeful to be paraded about as the symbol of the future of Ukyu-taasa: a young man who, despite the admixture of native blood, acted even more Lyucu than the pure-blooded and was as eager to attack native scholars and tear down native structures as Cutanrovo herself. Tanvanaki sometimes wondered if Todyu now thought of Cutanrovo as a greater hero than his own mother.

I can control Cutanrovo, she thought, panting as she continued to fight shadows in the air. *I'm just using her.* She repeated the thought with each punch and kick, as though trying to convince herself.

"Votan."

She whirled around, her fist stopping barely inches from the face of the spy, who had silently materialized inside the Great Tent.

"What is it?" She relaxed into a resting pose. The exercise had done her good, clearing her head of the feeling of powerlessness.

"A purification pack composed of two culeks and some native soldiers descended on Phada three days ago."

Tanvanaki held her breath. The hamlet of Phada was the site of the entrance to the underwater tunnel that led to Dasu, now sealed up as the Lyucu preferred to travel between the two islands of Ukyu-taasa by ship or garinafin. It was also where Tanvanaki kept her secret.

In an emotionless voice, the spy went on. "After harassing the villagers and confiscating a few books and some idols of native gods, they built a bonfire to eliminate the contraband. To celebrate the victory, they danced around the bonfire late into the night, drinking kyoffir and smoking tolyusa leaves. They fell asleep a few hours before dawn."

Tanvanaki pictured the scene. Phada was an isolated village with little to offer. The land around it was infertile, and though it was close to the coast, it was blocked from the sea by a range of low but steep hills. Its remoteness had preserved it from the roaming purification packs earlier, and that was also why Tanvanaki, Goztan, and Vocu had chosen it for their covert project.

"But just before dawn, one of the culeks awakened to relieve himself. Stumbling in the darkness, he failed to return to his companions but wandered far afield, eventually ending up near the crater east of the village. There, he noticed light coming from behind the stones piled at the entrance at the bottom—"

"I've heard enough," said Tanvanaki. "Have you taken care of it?"

The spy nodded.

"You got everyone in the pack?"

Another nod.

Tanvanaki sighed. She hated the very idea of killing any Lyucu, but there was no choice—these days, so many things she did or condoned felt that way. The operation inside the sealed-off tunnel between Dasu and Rui had to be concealed from Cutanrovo at all costs. She had learned her lesson after Cutanrovo's destruction of the camp among the Roro Hills, where Tanvanaki had attempted to force scholars abducted from the core islands to work for the benefit of the Lyucu.

"What did you do with the bodies?"

"I've come for your instructions."

Tanvanaki contemplated the situation. Cutanrovo wasn't particularly detail-oriented, which was how Tanvanaki had been able to divert some of the tribute goods intended for the native auxiliary troops to her secret project. But news of a missing purification pack would eventually make its way to the thane's ears, and that would mean trouble.

"Dispose of them near another native village, one at some distance from Phada."

The spy nodded and turned go.

"Wait," Tanvanaki said. After the briefest of hesitations, she added, "Kill everyone in Phada as well."

The spy waited.

"They can't be left alive if they've seen the purification pack," Tanvanaki said, though she knew no explanation was needed. He always did as she commanded. "Besides, Goztan will need a clear area to practice."

The spy disappeared as silently as he had appeared.

Once the bodies of the purification pack were discovered, that unfortunate other village would be blamed, and there would be a new round of reprisals and killings from Cutanrovo. That was the cost of keeping the secret in the tunnel.

She hated herself. The tactic was so cowardly, so deceptive, unworthy of a true pékyu of the Lyucu.

She resumed kicking and punching at wavering shadows in the dimly lit Great Tent, swirling with smoke from the tallow torches, her only companion the voice in her head.

I can control Cutanrovo. I'm just using her.

CHAPTER TEN

ICE BLOSSOMS

ON THE PLAINS WEST OF THE TAIL RANGE: THE
ELEVENTH MONTH IN THE NINTH YEAR AFTER THE
DEPARTURE OF PRINCESS THÉRA FROM DARA FOR
UKYU-GONDÉ (SIX MONTHS UNTIL THE LYUCU MUST
LAUNCH THEIR NEW INVASION FLEET TO DARA).

With frigid winter winds slicing across their faces, the band of rebels finally emerged from the mountains known as the Tail to the Agon and the Antler to the Lyucu. Before them lay the great plains in the north of Ukyu-Gondé, a snowscape dotted here and there with a few stunted coniferous copses.

After what they had gone through, this might as well be the blessed realm of the gods.

Théra's initial plan to climb over the World's Edge Mountains had been defeated by the most unlikely of causes: air.

At first, the ascent into the towering mountains was physically demanding but manageable. Takval and Théra instructed the band to take plenty of breaks, minimize heat loss, and eat frequently. But after a few days, everyone began to feel light-headed and exhausted no matter how much they slept. Breathing became difficult. The air felt thin, hollow, unsatisfying. No matter how deeply or quickly they tried to draw air, they couldn't get enough of it.

Things got worse.

The higher they climbed up the snowbound peaks, the more rarefied grew the air.

Tipo Tho's baby cried so much from the effort to breathe that he fainted. Tipo had to breathe into his mouth to revive him. Everyone began to see sights and hear sounds that weren't real.

"We're drowning," panted Takval. "We'll never make it."

Théra was plagued by doubt again. Had she made another error that would doom everyone?

Adyulek, too exhausted to even stand up, beckoned for Théra. The princess leaned in, placing her ear against the old shaman's lips.

"We haven't been caught by Cudyu," the shaman whispered. "So you've already led us into a better place. If the gods won't let us go join them, maybe it's because they think we still have more to do on this side of the world. I fear the gods, but I trust you."

Théra cried. Trust was a heavy burden, one that had to be earned.

She went to Takval, and the two huddled in council. Was there any untapped reservoir of strength, any potential source of aid, any unlikely refuge that they could aim for?

In the morning, they began to descend from the spine of the garinafin guarding the realm of the gods. They had a new goal.

To the north.

Far in the north of Ukyu-Gondé, where the scrublands gradually gave way to swampy taiga and then tundra, where the only vegetation consisted of lichen and moss and stunted trees that found little nourishment in the permafrost, people nonetheless eked out a living.

The tribes that lived this far north were few in number, and they did not consider themselves Lyucu or Agon. They had their own sacred stories, as different from the tales of Afir and Kikisavo as snow differed from sand. They lived in shelters constructed with ice and frozen mud, dressed in thick hooded seadog fur coats, and carried their children around on whalebone cradleboards. They burned peat and dung for heat and light. They herded moss-antlered deer and hunted for fish, whales, and seacows on canoes fashioned from bones and animal hide. They crossed the broad, snowy plains and the icebound waterways with sleds pulled by teams of oversized dogs, the domesticated descendants of horrid wolves.

Though their languages were mutually intelligible, the tribes of the scrublands, proud of their larger populations and wealth of live-stock, had long disdained to acknowledge the far weaker ice tribes as equals. Though Toluroru Roatan of the Lyucu and Nobo Aragoz of the Agon both, in their times of ambition, had launched raids against the far north to decorate their skull helmets with more vic-tory marks, the people of the scrublands generally left the ice tribes alone, as there was little reason for them to covet the harsh land these poor cousins called home. Compared to the frozen northern plains, the heart of the scrublands was a mild paradise.

But things had changed with the rise of Tenryo. His policy of driv-ing the defeated Agon tribes into the periphery of Ukyu-Gondé had cascading repercussions. In the south, some of the displaced Agon tribes settled in oases in Lurodia Tanta, and in the north, the exiles came into conflict with the ice tribes.

Unable to thrive in the unfamiliar landscape by relying on their ancestral wisdom, the Agon refugees became robbers, raiding and pillaging and looting and causing mayhem. The small ice tribes, plagued by repeated incursions, gradually gathered under the com-mand of esteemed war chiefs to fight back. Though they were not numerous, their knowledge of the unforgiving patterns of their desolate homeland gave them an advantage. They won against the Agon invaders more than they lost.

Some of the defeated Agon then fled back into Ukyu proper, pre-ferring enslavement to starvation. Others, however, abandoned their tribal identities in defeat and joined the ice tribes, adopting their ways.

"They'll help us. They are our votan-sa-taasa in suffering."

This was Takval's rallying cry, and the mantra of the lonely band of rebels.

Just as Kuni Garu once built his army from the weedlike common people disdained by the grand Lords of Dara, Takval and Théra hoped that the despised ice tribes, provoked into restlessness by the pressures emanating from Lyucu expansionism, would give the ref-ugees succor and infuse their rebellion with fresh blood.

But could the ice tribes be persuaded to see that the Agon

marauders were only a symptom, not the root cause? Could an Agon pékyu and a princess from a faraway land convince the natives of this icebound land to trust them and go to war against the Lyucu as allies of Dara and the Agon?

To the north. To the north.

Hiking any length along the World's Edge Mountains without the aid of garinafins was incredibly arduous. Two peaks separated by a single day's flight could be connected only by a treacherous, winding path that took weeks to traverse on foot: steep slopes covered in jagged rocks; bottomless canyons requiring long detours; thick, pathless jungles in perpetual twilight; high passes blocked by ice and snow; slimy swamps enveloped in miasma; rushing mountain streams swelling with white water. . . .

Death was a merciless traveling companion. A few members of the band would never leave the mountains except as memories and stories recounted by loved ones.

But the gods were not without mercy. Tipo Tho and her baby, who were always given the best of the band's meager supplies, survived. Once she realized that the baby would not die in infancy despite the hard trials, Tipo Tho named him Crucru, the Dara onomatopoeia for the sound a cruben or whale made when diving, to commemorate her husband's life as a submariner.

Through the long fall, as they fought against mudslides, predators, disease, frost, starvation, poison . . . and slogged on, the goal of getting to Taten, of wreaking havoc on Cudyu's plan to launch a fresh invasion and freeing the Agon captives held there, was the lone beacon of hope that kept the band going.

But Taten was thousands of miles away, literally on the other side of the world. Abandoning the garinafins had saved them from being caught, but garinafin-less, how would they cross the endless expanse of Ukyu-Gondé to get to where they needed to be in time?

They'll help us. To the north.

Three days after emerging from the Tail onto the frozen tundra, the band arrived at the mud-and-ice settlement of a large ice tribe.

More than a few of the carved whalebone ancestor poles in front of the shelters showed distinctive Agon designs. This ice tribe must have adopted many exiled Agon.

By the side of a deer-dung flame, Takval negotiated with the tribe's chief.

"In the time of my grandfather Nobo Aragoz, we Agon were not kind to the people of the north," said Takval. "I apologize now for those ancient insults."

The chief, Kitos, was not only the leader of his tribe, but also a voice held in high esteem by many of the smaller ice tribes in the region. He looked at Takval suspiciously, saying nothing.

"Ancient enmities may yet give birth to fresh friendships," said Takval. "Know that the Agon raiders who fled into your land came not by choice, but were driven by the greed of the Lyucu. So long as the Lyucu dominate the scrublands, both the Agon and the ice tribes will suffer."

Kitos was noncommittal. True, the people of the north had seen and heard enough of Lyucu atrocities to know that what Takval said was sensible, but Cudyu was a mighty warlord, and so far he had not directly encroached upon the tundra. There was no reason to awaken a sleeping tusked tiger by tweaking its whiskers.

The ice tribes would not go to war over a possibility, a hypothetical, a mere dream. Theirs was not a land forgiving of flights of fancy.

"We ask for no warriors, no weapons, no commitment to stand by us," pleaded Takval. "We ask only that you help us get to where we could fight. In return, I promise that should we defeat Cudyu in Taten, the Agon shall honor the people of the north as votan-sataasa, even unto the tenth generation."

Still, Kitos hesitated. Takval's offer promised much gain for little risk . . . but a promise weighed even less than a snowflake and was worth about as much.

Théra laid upon the ground all the jewelry on her person, as well as curios such as silk handkerchiefs, a bronze writing knife, a pair of lacquered eating sticks. . . . These were the last remnants of her life in Dara, kept by her side more out of sentiment than utility. She offered them reluctantly and with a heavy heart, knowing that in some way, she was bidding farewell to yet another part of her past.

The offer finally proved to be enough—ever since the time of Admiral Krita's ill-fated expedition, Dara artifacts had been highly valued by the scrubland tribes as well as the people of the north. Kitos agreed to transport Takval's band along the northern coast to the western shore of Ukyu-Gondé, whence they would have to find their own way down to Taten. The powerful dogs could cover hundreds of miles in a week, and they represented the fastest way across the tundra.

A convoy of dogsleds was quickly outfitted, and the rebels were on their way.

After losing the rebels in the Wing Range as a result of Araten's treachery, Cudyu executed the traitorous former Agon thane in a fit of rage and vowed never to return to Taten until Takval and Théra were caught. The pair—and their children—had eluded him for months, and his reputation would be in tatters unless he found them as quickly as possible and killed them in the most painful and slowest way. He declared that he would devote a thousand garinafins to comb through the World's Edge Mountains and burn off every tree, shrub, flower, and mushroom until he succeeded.

After much pleading and counsel from his thanes, reason eventually prevailed. After all, they pointed out, the pékyu had already discovered the date when the Wall of Storms would reopen, arguably the only practical value to be extracted from Théra. Surely there were more worthy victories to pursue and better ways to glorify the eminent pékyu's name than to obsess over a few insignificant failed rebels.

Thus mollified, Cudyu decided to return to Taten to prepare the invasion fleet to Dara and left Tovo Tasaricu, his most trusted garinafin-thane, in charge of finding and capturing the rebel remnants. Once seized, the captives who had embarrassed the pékyu would be offered as sacrifices to guarantee a swift and safe voyage for the invasion fleet.

Luckily for Takval and Théra, Thane Tovo was a meticulous and thorough man, but rather lacking in imagination.

For much of the fall, he sent garinafins on patrols over an

ever-widening circle centered on the last known location of Takval's band. Reasoning that the rebels had to find shelter in a relatively mild valley over the winter, he concentrated his efforts in the south. The idea that Takval might lead his paltry band to the north and attempt to cross the entire continent to attack Taten was so preposterous that he didn't even consider sending any patrols to the north.

But news of Kitos's caravan eventually reached Tovo's ears. As much as Takval warned him to be discreet, it was impossible to prevent Kitos from showing off the treasures that Théra had given him each time they stopped to replenish supplies from one of the ice tribes. After all, the treasures gave him prestige, and what use was prestige without display?

As soon as Tovo heard a description of the opulent Dara treasures and the strangers traveling with the ice tribe chief, he realized that the rebels had slipped out from right under his nose.

It wasn't too late to remedy his error. Dogsleds might be fast, but garinafins were faster.

Though Cudyu demanded periodic tribute from the ice tribes, he was content to leave them mostly alone—except by driving displaced Agon into their territory. Tovo now thought it was high time to change the policy. The Lyucu pékyu's generosity had clearly not been appreciated if the ice fleas—for that was the term the Lyucu used to refer to the tiny tribes of the north—dared to harbor fugitives and assist in their escape.

It was time to conquer them once and for all.

Tovo took all the garinafins and warriors left under his command and invaded the tundra. He burned and pillaged, killed and mutilated. He massacred some settlements for psychological intimidation and took captives from other settlements to strengthen his army. To dilute the shame of having allowed Théra and Takval to escape (again), he had to erect a monument of terror in the hearts of the ice fleas: They must submit absolutely to Cudyu Roatan, Pékyu of Pékyus, Lone Voice of Ukyu and Gondé.

But as Tovo's invasion force headed farther north, the garinafins began to fall sick. Some were lethargic; some vomited and suffered the runs; still others couldn't take off or stay aloft.

This was in fact one of the reasons that Takval had led his band into the far north. Winters in the desolate region were far harsher than even the worst years in the heart of the scrublands. As creatures of fire, garinafins became sluggish and weak under prolonged exposure to extreme cold.

After Tovo realized that he couldn't catch the fugitives by air, he sent away to the south all remaining garinafins that could still fly. The earthbound garinafins, stricken with cold-sickness, were slaughtered to provide the warriors with a splendid and fortifying blood meal. Their bellies full of kyoffir and their minds buoyed with tolyusa smoke, the Lyucu slammed their bone weapons against the earth, quaking the frozen ground with battle-lust.

"The Agon rebels and Dara barbarians must die!" Tovo led them in fervent chants. "Long live the Lyucu! Long live Pékyu Cudyu!"

Tovo forced the ice fleas to supply the Lyucu with dogsleds, and so began a long pursuit across the bleak, frost-bound north.

Over hundreds of miles of dreary tundra, the Agon and the Lyucu raced.

Tovo's warriors cared little about the welfare of the dogs, pushing them until they died of exhaustion, and then the carcasses were fed to new dogs forcefully drafted from the ice fleas. With this brutal approach, they gained on their prey despite the lack of flight.

Refugees fleeing the callous Lyucu invasion scattered in all directions, passing on the news like cracks spreading in the ice. Takval's band realized that they were running out of time.

"We'll never outrun them," said Kitos, "not when they don't need to plan for more than one journey."

Takval considered their situation. The featureless, flat expanse of the tundra wasn't like the World's Edge Mountains, full of nooks and crannies where one could hide.

"What if we stopped running west?" Takval asked. "What if we turned . . . north again?"

Kitos regarded him curiously. "What do you have in mind?"

The northern shore of Ukyu-Gondé faced the icebound islands of Nalyufin's Pasture across a narrow channel. The ice tribes crossed to the nearest islands in spring and summer to hunt for seacows and toddling auks. No one knew how many islands there were or how far to the north they continued.

"Can we flee over the sea and disappear among the thousand-thousand islands?"

"The ice tribes don't live on the islands," said Kitos. "This late in winter there will be nothing there to eat: only endless mountains of ice and treacherous crevasses that devour without noise."

"Exactly," said Takval. "The more dangerous the terrain, the more easily we could shake off our pursuers."

"Interesting," mused Kitos, stroking his frost-encrusted beard. "But remember, would-be pékyu of the Agon, our deal is for me to transport you, not to make you into our lord. You get to pick where you want to go, but if there's not enough food, I won't feed you at the expense of my warriors or even my dogs."

Takval gave a bitter smile. "You've made that abundantly clear. So, is my plan possible?"

"Anything is *possible*. This late in winter, the sea between the mainland and the nearest islands should be frozen solid. Dogsleds can cross it—so long as we're careful."

Instead of a solid sheet of ice, a roiling ocean in the throes of a winter storm greeted them at the headland. Across the channel, on the horizon, they could barely discern the outlines of Spotted Heifer, the nearest island in the archipelago known as Nalyufin's Pasture.

"The sea freezes late in some winters," said Kitos.

Takval cursed their bad luck. "Is it possible to make the crossing by boat?"

Kitos laughed. "Would-be pékyu of the Agon, you speak out of ignorance. Though it is true that we take our skin canoes over to the islands to hunt in spring and summer, they'll never survive a winter storm like this. You have to wait."

"How long?"

"There's no way to know. The sea is as unpredictable as the whims of a child."

The idea of waiting for the sea to freeze while the Lyucu were getting closer with every passing minute seemed like madness to Takval. Evidently, Kitos agreed.

"We've taken you as far as we can," declared Kitos. "Our agreement ends here."

"You'd abandon us to the Lyucu?" asked Takval.

"I'm the chief of my people, not of the Agon," said Kitos. "What would you do if you were in my place?"

Takval considered the position of the ice tribe chief. How could he demand that Kitos risk the lives of his people for a band of rebels numbering less than twenty? The very idea that they could overthrow the mighty Lyucu was ludicrous.

Dejected, he returned to Théra. "Kitos will not stand with us. We'll have to face the Lyucu alone."

Instead of despair, he saw only tranquility in her eyes.

"Are you afraid?"

He nodded, ashamed.

"I don't think you're afraid of dying," said Théra. "I think you're afraid that by asking Kitos to stand with you, you'll be asking them to make a meaningless sacrifice."

Takval pondered Théra's judgment and realized it was true.

"We've both made mistakes," said Théra. "You were all too willing to sacrifice yourself, and I was too unwilling to accept any sacrifices at all. But sometimes we have to demand that others make sacrifices and accept them."

"What if we're wrong?"

"Then we must be willing to leave our teeth on the board—to put our own lives on the line, or, if we should survive, live with the guilt."

"That sounds like the kind of justification that would have worked equally as well for Tenryo or Volyu."

"You're not wrong," said Théra. "In Dara, it is said that there is often little to divide the madness of tyrants from the grace of kings, and heroes and villains alike demand sacrifices of others. The difference, if there is one, lies in why the sacrifices are being sought: to satisfy the ambition of the few or to secure the freedom of the many."

Takval gazed into her eyes. "Is this the gods speaking through you, my breath?"

Théra smiled. "The gods always speak in our hearts. You just have to listen."

A short distance away, Thoryo listened to the exchange, her eyes troubled.

Takval came to Kitos. The ice tribespeople were getting ready to depart with their sleds and dogs. As a last gesture of mercy, they would leave the band of rebels stacks of peat cut from the swamp a little to the south, as well as some venison and seadog jerky.

"The Lyucu will not stop once we're gone," said Takval. "Conquest, once tasted, is a dish they cannot resist. Your people will become slaves."

Kitos halted. Without turning around, he said, "The troubles of tomorrow should be left for tomorrow."

"If you stand with us, there will be a chance that such a tomorrow will never come true."

"What good is a chance that is as remote as a bone-and-skin canoe surviving this storm?"

"The more of you who stand with us, the greater that chance becomes."

Kitos whipped around. "You're asking me to go to war with the Lyucu, to die for you. What gives you the right to demand that? What can you offer to buy our lives?"

"Nothing," said Takval. "I call myself Pékyu of the Agon, but in truth I command less than twenty, and many of them not skilled warriors. Yet a single snowflake heralds the coming of winter, and a single drop of water is the source of the mighty ocean. I can offer you nothing but the chance to become part of something grand: a future of freedom. Seize it."

"I am an old man," said Kitos, "with not many years left. Such fairy tales do not interest me."

"Then consider your children, and their children. Someday, when they're dying under the clubs and axes of the Lyucu or groaning in bondage, they may remember you, who had a chance, however remote, of preventing that fate but chose to stand by and do nothing. They'll be ashamed to call themselves the descendants of a coward."

Kitos laughed, flecks of ice flying off his beard. "That is an old trick. Do you think me so easily manipulated?"

"No," said Takval. "But I think you can still be inspired. A true coward has no heart-kindling for the spark of hope."

Kitos regarded Takval. At length, he said, "I think you're mad."

"It was also madness that made Tenryo think he could defeat my grandfather, and madness that made your ancestors think it possible to kill a whale in a boat made of bones and skins," said Takval. "It's madness to fall in love, and madness to have children, knowing that the world is a cruel and harsh place and death our constant companion. It's madness to fight to be free when the chances of success are so slim. Anything worth doing is at least a little bit mad."

"Anything worth doing is at least a little bit mad," muttered Kitos. "I don't know if that's wisdom or foolishness."

Then he whistled loudly. His warriors stopped packing the sleds and turned to gaze at their chief.

"We're staying," said Kitos. "From this moment on, the Agon are no longer our passengers, but fellow warriors."

Thoryo, listening in again on the conversation, looked even more troubled.

Kitos dispatched messengers to other ice tribe chiefs, asking for aid.

Warriors came, swelling Takval's band to nearly a hundred. Some were former Agon who still revered the Aragoz name. Others, however, were ice people from tribes raided by the Lyucu. They came to show that the people of the far north were not afraid. Even fleas could bite hard.

"We're still vastly outnumbered," fretted Théra. "If only there were a way to build a fortress."

Like the people of the scrublands, the ice tribes relied on mobility in warfare and were not skilled in the construction of fortifications—the harsh landscape provided little in the way of suitable materials, in any event. But they did know how to build simple defenses for semi-permanent camps in winter: low walls made of packed snow, dung, branches, antlers, and similar material, sufficient to stop wolves and provide some protection against raiding parties from other tribes.

That was what they did now. About a hundred ice tribe warriors, along with the Agon and Dara rebels, hastily constructed a semi-circular wall around the headland. They would wait here for the sea to freeze, hoping that the Lyucu wouldn't arrive first.

Théra and Thoryo strolled by the sea. Even wrapped in multiple layers of fur, they shivered. The frigid wind seemed to always manage to find a way between the seams, no matter how carefully the women overlapped the skins and tightened the sashes.

"Our clothes are as leaky as our defenses," muttered Théra. "We've got to find—"

A sob from Thoryo stopped her.

"What's wrong?" Théra asked. Ever since their escape from the Lyucu in the Foot Range, the young woman had seemed to grow more morose, her spirits sinking along with the temperature. Lately, she had become more gloomy than Théra ever remembered, her vivacity and hunger for life distant memories.

Thoryo shook her head, not speaking.

Théra pulled her into her arms. "Are you scared?"

She said nothing.

"Are you worried about the Lyucu?"

She said nothing.

No matter what questions Théra asked, the young woman continued to cry inconsolably.

Remembering how Thoryo had once rescued her from a similar state of unresponsive melancholy, Théra decided to stop asking questions. She simply hugged Thoryo tightly and spoke to her of the beauty of the world.

"Look at how the sea tries to stay alive even in the heart of winter," she whispered. "Look at the flowers of ice blooming in the face of death."

Wordlessly, Thoryo looked.

The stormy sea roared and raged, refusing to be stilled by the cold. Foamy sprays at the tips of towering waves froze into crystal flowers. Before they could plunge back into the sea, the wind seized them, carrying them aloft like dandelion seeds, and scattered them on the beach. The delicate petals broke as the frozen foam-flowers rolled along the sand, tinkling like fistfuls of pearls. They huddled together, sparkling until the very end, when they broke into a thousand-thousand shards in the howling wind.

"What a useless thing is such beauty," whispered Thoryo, her voice hoarse. "Crushed almost as soon as it's born."

Théra squeezed her tighter and continued to listen.

"I once thought the brevity of life not something to be feared: Life could never die so long as each individual life refuses to yield to despair. But what if each individual life isn't part of Life, but only a shadow of Death?

"All around me, everyone speaks and thinks of killing. Takval and you demand sacrifices; Kitos talks of the wisdom of madness. The Lyucu wish to kill and enslave, and in return you wish to slaughter the Lyucu in vengeance. How can Life triumph if Death rules all?"

"Death isn't at all what we yearn for," said Théra. "To defend yourself and your loved ones, to sustain—"

"I know about the needs of survival," said Thoryo. "But the Lyucu would say that they must kill lest they be overthrown by those they've conquered. What, then, separates you from Cudyu if both justify fighting and killing in the name of necessity, under the banner of survival?"

"You ask a question that is harder to answer than it may appear at first," said Théra. "No one is a villain in their own stories, and justifications can always be found to condone killing as being in the service of life. Like the goddesses Rapa and Kana, to die and to live are two aspects of the same Flow.

"I understand your confusion. The Lyucu drove the Agon to the ends of Gondé and invaded Dara under the rallying cry of freedom, and we fight them now, in both Dara and Gondé, also through an appeal to freedom. Cudyu speaks of a better life for the Lyucu under his empire; and Takval speaks of a better life for everyone who isn't Lyucu with the empire gone.

"I can describe for you the principle of reduction in suffering; I can point you to the words of the Ano sages and the teachings of the gods of two lands; I can offer you a hundred reasons why these causes are different, but a clever mind will also find a hundred arguments for why my explanations are wrong. Good isn't always accomplished through beneficent means, and Evil isn't always committed without some sympathetic cause."

"Then how do you know what is *right*?" asked Thoryo, tears frozen on her face. "Do you make an appeal to blood? But I am neither Dara nor Agon, whether by birth or marriage. Do you pray for guidance of the gods? But I neither fear nor trust the gods."

"I can't tell you the answer," said Théra, "for conscience is the only scale that can tell truth apart from lies, separate gold from dross. But conscience belongs to you and you alone, and can be calibrated by no philosophy or religion, only experience."

There was a momentary lull in the storm, and the surface of the sea seemed to crystallize into a sheet of ice, only to shatter into a million fragments with the next rising wave.

"I don't know what to do," muttered Thoryo. "I love you, I love Takval, I love the people who have become my tribe, though I know not my origins. But I also know that I will never kill."

"Then don't," said Théra. "You have the right to refuse to fight. I will never ask you to do something that your conscience does not approve of."

She continued to hold the young woman. Gradually, Thoryo stopped crying. The two of them stood gazing at the sea and the blooming and breaking of ice-foam flowers.

"They are indeed beautiful," said Thoryo.

"It's as if we're seeing the shape of wind in the ice," said Théra, quoting the Amu poet Nakipo. More ice shards struck against one another, clinking like the distant clang of sword on armor.

Already the princess's mind had moved on to the immediate needs of their fortress in the distance. The walls were so low that it seemed impossible to imagine that the Lyucu horde would even be slowed down by it, let alone kept at bay.

A look of determination came into Théra's eyes. "Let's go back and get warmed up." Wrapping her arm around the young woman protectively, she began the long walk back with Thoryo.

Every few miles, another drafted sled dog collapsed from exhaustion, never to get up again. Tovo ignored the pleas of the enslaved drivers, whipping them mercilessly so that they would make their remaining beasts work harder too. Nothing mattered except catching the Agon pékyu and his Dara princess. They would *not* slip from his grasp again.

No one made Pékyu Cudyu and Thane Tovo look foolish without paying a heavy price.

The Lyucu arrived at the headland on a cold and stormy morning.

Tovo could see the rebels hiding behind their hastily constructed barrier of peat and snow and almost laughed. For a moment, he was sorry that he didn't have any garinafins with him. He would love to see these slaves trapped inside their hideout, scrabbling and screeching like moonfur rats being roasted alive.

No matter. He would lead his warriors to victory by the strength of their arms alone. It was more satisfying to see the despair in the eyes of one's enemies up close as they realized how complete their defeat would be.

He gave the order to attack. There was no need for preparation, no need for formations, no need for tactics when the foe put their trust in such flimsy defenses.

Hundreds of Lyucu naros and culeks thundered across the tundra toward the beach fort. The rebels peeked out above the low wall like prairie voles. Tovo imagined that he could see the fear in their eyes even from such a distance. Behind them was the merciless sea, and before them was an even deadlier tide of war clubs and axes. The Agon and Dara slaves had nowhere to run to escape the righteous fury of their indomitable Lyucu masters.

As Tovo and his horde approached the fortress, he realized that the wall wasn't quite as low as they had first thought. Unlike the typical temporary fortifications built by the ice fleas—barely as tall as a man—the wall of this fort rose to the height of several warriors stacked in a column. Tovo couldn't fathom how they had been able to build such a structure; he had never seen anything like it.

Still, he couldn't imagine how packed snow could stop his rampaging warriors. "Faster! Faster!" he shouted. "Whoever captures the barbarian princess will be made a naro-votan on the spot!"

Stones zoomed through the air from the defenders' slingshots, and a few of the Lyucu warriors in the front screamed and faltered. One fell, his skull smashed by the missile.

Tovo was unconcerned. Even if all the defenders were master marksmen, the Lyucu were closing in so fast that the casualties would be barely felt.

Like the waves crashing against the shore behind the defenders, the Lyucu assault arrived at the base of the wall. As those in the back aimed their slingshots up at the defenders, fighters in front began to scramble up the wall. The defenders ducked back out of the way. The battle was going to be over in minutes.

Except . . . the Lyucu couldn't climb up the wall.

What they had thought from afar to be a barrier of loose logs covered in packed snow turned out to be a solid cliff of ice. No matter how much the warriors strained and scrambled, they could gain no purchase against the slippery surface.

"Break the ice!" Tovo shouted. "Make footholds!"

The naros and culeks slammed their axes against the ice wall, hoping to gouge big enough holes to fashion a makeshift ladder. But the bone weapons bounced harmlessly off the stone-hard ice.

"Boost each other!" Tovo shouted. "Get up there no matter what!"

Some of the Lyucu warriors dropped their weapons and tried to form human pyramids to allow their comrades to reach the top of the wall. Since they had such an advantage in numbers, even if they could get only a small proportion of fighters over the barrier, they would surely overwhelm the defenders.

But that was when the defenders peeked out over the wall again. Some held up garinafin-hide shields to deflect the slingshot missiles while others raised skin pots and poured their contents over the outside of the ice wall.

The liquid that spilled from the pots was foul-smelling, golden-brown in color, and boiling hot. As the strange "soup" spilled over the human pyramids, wherever the liquid touched exposed flesh, skin boiled, sizzled, and burst.

Amidst howls of outrage and screams of agony, the human pyramids collapsed. The scalding liquid had spilled into the eyes of a few unlucky fighters, and they rolled around at the foot of the ice wall, cursing, blinded, and helpless.

Those warriors in the back shrank from this scene of carnage. Even as Tovo urged them on, they hesitated. No one wanted to be denied the gaze of the Eye of Cudyufin, wounded and bleating like lambs about to be slaughtered. The Lyucu abandoned such crippled people as useless drains on the tribe's resources.

Tovo had no choice but to order a retreat. The Lyucu tide, full of bloodlust and confident of victory but minutes earlier, now receded quietly.

The fort held.

Princess Théra, inspired by Nakipo's poem, had come up with the idea that the ice tribes could reinforce their fortifications with the most abundant construction material available in the region: ice itself.

By boiling chunks of ice retrieved from the shoreline in skin pots over fire fueled with peat and dung, the defenders soon produced a great quantify of hot water. This they poured over the sides of the fort. The extreme cold quickly froze the water into a slippery, hard shell, as tough as metal.

Tipo Tho, the most experienced Dara fighter in the band, instantly saw the wisdom in the plan and devised improvements to it. By using the ice as a kind of cement, the defenders could build the wall far higher than the traditional method of packed snow and loose logs, adding even more strength to the fortress.

The boiling water also inspired Théra and Tipo Tho to revive an ancient technique from Dara's long history of warfare centered around city walls, a weapon they unleashed upon the hapless Lyucu trying to build human pyramids.

By boiling water mixed with human and animal excrement, they produced the euphemistically named "golden soup." Not only did the bubbling liquid injure the attackers, but the stench also had the benefit of psychological intimidation. Furthermore, the foul water left festering wounds in the attackers that were slow to heal and induced diseases, akin to a death sentence, given the harsh climate.

True to the promise of Princess Théra, Thoryo took no part in these death-dealing activities. She did, however, help Adyulek with healing and acted as a nurse to the wounded.

After the Lyucu retreat, Thoryo pleaded to be allowed to attend to some of the wounded Lyucu outside the fort. Adyulek shook her head and muttered that she would not allow her medicines to be used on the Lyucu.

Thoryo went out alone. However, the crippled Lyucu survivors responded to her ministrations by cursing at her, and no matter how the young woman tried to reason with them, they called her a witch and snarled as she got close. Finally, a culek attacked Thoryo when she attempted to bandage her wounds, and Gozofin, watching over the young woman, had no choice but to bash in the skull of the unyielding Lyucu. The other wounded were eventually dispatched similarly as an act of mercy.

Their dying howls would haunt Thoryo for days.

Unfamiliar with the basics of siege warfare, Tovo adapted slowly.

For the next assault, he ordered his warriors to leave their weapons strapped to their backs and to assemble into teams, each carrying a long piece of bone or a bundle of sticks, obtained by smashing some of the dogsleds. The plan was to charge up to the foot of the fort and to pile the bones and sticks into a ramp to get over the ice wall.

The plan fell apart when the Lyucu warriors, enduring a barrage of slingshot missiles, approached the wall. By now, the foul water that had been poured by the defenders had frozen into slick sheets of ice on the ground, and the attackers, their movements clumsy due to the burden they carried, slipped and fell down. Some of the warriors managed to maintain their footing by shuffling slowly, but this exposed them to more slingshot fire, and others flailing around them knocked them down in the end.

The defenders peered over the wall and poured down yet more boiling golden soup. They concluded the brief battle with a fusillade of hunting spears and whale harpoons.

By the time Tovo ordered another retreat, close to a hundred Lyucu bodies were pinned to the ground or had their skulls crushed.

Despite their success in holding off the siege, Théra's anxiety grew. Trapped inside the fort, they were running out of food and fuel. Meanwhile, the storm continued to rage over the sea, which showed no signs of freezing over.

Over the next few days, Tovo launched multiple assaults on the ice fort, each more desperate than the last.

Thinking that the defenders would run out of stones for their slingshots and bone-spears to hurl, Tovo urged his warriors to attack in waves. But the ice fort defenders were ready with ice balls for the slingshots and icicle spears, which could be produced overnight in large quantities. Next, teams of Lyucu, protected by sheets of gari-nafin hide over their heads, tried to crack the ice wall with battering rams fashioned from the hardest and heaviest whale and dog bones; the defenders responded by dropping blocks of ice on them, crushing some and maiming many. The Lyucu tried to build a fire to melt the ice barrier; the defenders doused the fire with seawater. The Lyucu sought to intimidate the defenders by heaving bloody dog carcasses over the wall; the defenders responded by lobbing back the heads of the dead Lyucu.

It was as if the two sides were recapitulating the evolution of siege warfare in Dara around this little fort. Tovo showed a dogged determination as well as a resourcefulness exceeding his reputation, but Tipo Tho was able to devise counters to all his ideas by drawing on her reservoir of experience in Dara.

"Even your father would have to be impressed," boasted Tipo to baby Crucru. "I'd like to see him defend a city as well. Maybe he'll finally admit that submariners aren't the equal of aviators." Then she nuzzled the baby and added softly, "But when we see him and your siblings on the other side of the River-on-Which-Nothing-Floats, we'll be too happy to quarrel, won't we?"

Tovo's relentless assaults failed to weaken the fortress. In fact, the ice wall was growing taller and thicker with every passing day, as the defenders poured new pots of water over the side, letting the wintry winds do the work of patching any cracks and dents. The temperature continued to fall.

One morning, as the first rays of the sun lit up the battle-worn landscape, the defenders woke to the sight they had been both hoping for and dreading for weeks: The sea had frozen overnight, and the broad plain of ice extended all the way to Spotted Heifer on the northern horizon.

CHAPTER ELEVEN

NALYUFIN'S PASTURE

ACROSS THE CHANNEL FROM SPOTTED HEIFER:
THE ELEVENTH MONTH IN THE NINTH YEAR AFTER
THE DEPARTURE OF PRINCESS THÉRA FROM DARA
FOR UKYU-GONDÉ (SIX MONTHS UNTIL THE LYUCU
MUST LAUNCH THEIR NEW INVASION FLEET TO
DARA).

"Can we cross?" asked Takval. His lips were blue, and he was shivering uncontrollably. The other defenders weren't faring much better.

"I don't recommend it," answered Kitos. "It may look solid to you, but there will be thin patches that are almost impossible to detect until we're right on top. Best to wait another few days."

"We can't wait another few days," said Tipo Tho. "With the sea frozen, the Lyucu can bypass the wall and attack us from the other side. As soon as they figure that out, we're doomed."

"Even if the Lyucu don't attack, we may not be able to last much longer," said Théra. Many of the defenders were wounded, and they were down to their last reserves of food and fuel.

Takval and Théra looked at each other. Escaping over the sea wasn't a great option—as Kitos pointed out, there would be no food—but it seemed their only choice. If they could shake off the Lyucu, perhaps the gods would show them another way to Taten.

"What do you want to do?" asked Takval.

"Sometimes you have to gamble," said Théra. "After all the calculations and plans, sometimes you still have to take a leap."

∾

Tovo was planning to spend the day recuperating and plotting. Lying in his tent, he imagined building a tower out of bones so that his warriors could shoot down at the defenders over the wall—

The flap of his tent lifted, and a naro rushed in, accompanied by a blast of cold air. "Votan, they've escaped!"

Tovo ran to the ice fort. Indeed, the place had been abandoned overnight, and the Lyucu warriors had already gained entry. Tovo went inside the fort and climbed the steps onto the wall to gain a better view. On the horizon, he could see a stream of dogsleds winding its way across the frozen sea.

"After them!"

The drafted ice flea drivers and drudges begged Tovo not to do this. The ice wasn't strong enough. The foolish rebels were sure to die by falling into some crack.

Tovo bashed in the skull of the loudest complainer and whipped the rest for their insolence. The ice fleas were weaklings and cowards, and like all slaves, they had to understand that the will of the Lyucu was never to be defied.

"We've already lost too much time," he said. "The next one who complains will be harnessed like a dog and added to the teams."

And so the sleds that hadn't been torn down to make weapons for the siege were hastily readied, and the Lyucu broke camp. In preparation for a long chase, all the sleds were heavily laden with goods and warriors.

"Form a single column," ordered Tovo. "That way, the sleds in the back can draft in the wake of the sleds in front. We'll move faster."

The conscripted ice flea drivers wanted to object, but the threat from Tovo earlier kept their mouths shut.

Over the endless expanse of the frozen sea, two groups of dogsleds raced north like a few caterpillars chased by a long column of ants.

The ants were closing in.

While Théra and Kitos led the convoy and scouted for a safe path across, Takval's sled took up the tail so he could keep an eye on the pursuit.

As his sled glided across the ice, a metal blade was pulled along behind. One of the few Dara weapons that had survived the long trek from Kiri Valley, it was now scoring a deep groove in the ice.

In the featureless icescape, the trail left by the metal blade seemed like a promise. The dogs that pulled the sleds of the pursuers naturally followed it.

The lead driver, a woman with years of experience on the ice, found the unnaturally deep groove suspicious and was reluctant to follow it. But Tovo dismissed her concerns with a slap across the face. Anybody could see that the safest path was to follow the exact course taken by the rebels. Freed from having to gauge the safety of the ice, the Lyucu could concentrate on plunging ahead as speedily as possible. This was how they would catch their prey despite a head start.

In the afternoon, as the weak sun warmed the air slightly, the ice began to groan. As the first sled in the Lyucu convoy passed over a particularly thin patch, the ice bent and buckled, but did not break.

A second sled crossed, and the ice still held.

Another. Thin cracks appeared in the surface, radiating from the groove cut by Takval's blade like spiderwebs.

Yet one more. The patch now resembled the back of a turtle shell. As long as no more weight was placed on it, the frosty winds would heal it in time.

But that was not to be. Another sled, this one driven by Tovo himself, screeched over the weakened surface. Tovo had surrounded himself with his strongest, biggest warriors, maximizing his own chances of landing the killing blow against the Agon pékyu.

The ice gave up.

The loud snap reverberated far across the crystalline sea. The rebels glanced back and cheered.

Théra urged the driver of the lead sled to slow down and turn around so they could get a better look.

"That's not a good idea," warned Kitos. "The ice is going to weaken more in the sun. We need to get to Spotted Heifer as quickly as possible."

"We'll be careful," said Théra. "But we need to make sure."

The drivers slowed their dogs and brought the sleds around in a gentle curve until they were facing the way they had come. Riders got out of the sleds and congregated on the ice, shading their eyes against the glare of the slanting sun.

In the distance, they could see that a giant gash had appeared in the eggshell-like surface, stretching half a mile across. Dozens of Lyucu sleds, unable to pull away in time, had tumbled into the gaping maw. Warriors and dogs were floundering in the heart-stopping, bone-numbing waves. Those who had not fallen in were no longer pursuing the rebels but doing their best to rescue the unfortunate victims.

Théra couldn't help but let out a yelp of relief and triumph. The gods were with them!

That was when the ice below their feet groaned and cracked, mutating into a spiderweb within which all of them were trapped.

"No sudden movements," shouted Kitos, his voice trembling. In all his years of living by and on the sea, he had never been placed in such peril.

Théra, terrified, wrapped her arms around Takval and squeezed her eyes shut. "It's not such a bad fate to die in the arms of someone I love."

He hugged her back. "Who says we're going to die?" he whispered. "I promised you we'd all get to Taten in time, didn't I? I've never broken a promise to you, and I'm not about to start now."

Théra smiled, already feeling calmer. She let go of Takval. Everyone stood still. The ice, though cracked, held.

Takval directed everyone to walk away from the strained patch of ice, one person at a time. "Slow and steady," he whispered, his tone calm. "We can make it."

Despite the cold, beads of sweat rolled down the warriors' faces as they gingerly shuffled to safety on thicker ice. As the number of people over the patch dwindled, those who remained let out sighs of relief. When most of the people had reached the safety of more stable ice, Kitos began to whistle and direct the dogs to pull the sleds away as well. They'd need them if they were to reach Spotted Heifer before nightfall.

Takval waited until everyone else had stepped out of the danger zone. The last few warriors to go left with cheerful smiles, confident that they would escape unscathed. Takval saw the cracks widen and lengthen behind their steps, but he kept up a stream of calm and cheerful patter, as though nothing was happening.

At last, it was his turn. As the rest of the band cheered from the thick ice, he took the first step away from the center of the web of cracks. A second step. A third.

He let out a held breath. He was going to make it.

The ice gave way. Takval disappeared into the sudden hole in the ice.

Théra screamed and tried to run back. Thoryo and Kitos grabbed her and pulled her back.

"You can't help him if you fall in too!" Kitos screamed into her ear.

Takval floundered to the surface, gasping for air. He tried to pull himself onto the ice, but the weakened edge of the hole wouldn't support his weight, and more pieces broke off, enlarging the hole. He couldn't get any purchase. The frigid water was already slowing his movements. He wouldn't last more than a few minutes.

Kitos dropped onto the ice and rolled toward the edge of the ice hole, bringing with him a sinew rope. But the ice buckled under his weight, and he had to stop dozens of paces away. "I'm too heavy," cried the old ice tribe chief in despair.

"Let me!" said Thoryo. "I'm the lightest."

Kitos rolled back and handed Thoryo the rope. The young woman rolled all the way to the edge of the hole in the ice. She tried to hand the rope to Takval, but his limbs were too stiff and his fingers too numb to grab on. The churning water subsided. He was drifting away and sinking.

"No!"

Without warning, Thoryo rolled into the water as cries of surprise and terror filled the air.

The cold was shocking.

Her skin had been ripped away; a thousand needles pierced her at once, throbbing, twisting, worming their way into the weakening flame of life that was her heart. The agony almost made her blank out before her raw nerves mercifully dulled. The light dimmed; the voices of the others faded.

What a useless thing is such beauty. Crushed almost as soon as it's born.

She knew that she had only seconds before the cold so numbed her muscles that they stopped responding to her will. She would then be doomed along with Takval. Her limbs already felt so heavy, requiring so much effort to move.

What's the point of trying to save anyone?

The wounded Lyucu warriors at the foot of the ice fort had refused her help, had in fact tried to kill her. Of those who escaped Kiri Valley, so many more had died along the way. Murder-minded Lyucu were chasing after them, but if she managed to save Takval, he would try, in turn, to kill those killers. There was no end, no respite, no escape. She was surrounded by death and the potential of death.

How can Life triumph if Death rules all?

Was the right thing to do to stop struggling, to let go? What if she allowed herself and Takval to drown? Would the world be any the worse for it? Would, perhaps, Takval's death even lead to fewer people dying?

It was all so confusing.

She remembered her time in the hold of *Dissolver of Sorrows*, before light and shadows had resolved into shapes, before sound and fury had resolved into syllable and thinking-breath, before she had understood life and death and beauty and wonder and disappointment and heartache. If only she could return to that time, to a time before awareness and confusion.

She looked at Takval. He was on his last breath, his head about to go under. He wasn't looking at her; he was looking toward the ice shore.

Dimly, she heard Théra's voice. *You promised! Come back to me. You promised!*

She saw no fear in Takval's eyes, only regret and tenderness, only acceptance and love, as deep and eternal as the tides.

She remembered the way Takval and Théra looked at each other, the way they held each other, the way they spoke of their children and parents, the way they told the stories of their peoples. So much beauty; so much wonder; so utterly useless against the ultimate meaninglessness of all existence, the futility of mortality.

Théra spoke of the Flow, of life and death as its two aspects, like the rise and ebb of the tide. What was one life or two, against the endless ocean? What was one woman or one man, against an unfeeling sky of stars?

An image came unbidden to her mind: frozen foam flowers lifting off the tips of waves like dandelion seeds, brilliant crystal sparks in the wind and sun, barely glimpsed before being dashed to pieces on the beach. They huddled together, as though unaware of anything else in the grand universe, as though it was enough to have tinkled together, to have heard the music of one another's soul for a fraction of a moment.

There is no need for philosophy or religion, no need for appeals to blood or affirmations of the gods. It is enough that we have loved and are loved. There is no meaning in eternity; only now, only here.

The light brightened; the world rushed back in a roar. She gasped and swallowed a mouthful of bitter water before clamping her lips shut. With her last ounce of strength, she looped the rope around herself and Takval. As she cinched the knot, her fingers slipped off, numb, helpless.

Dogs and men strained until, finally, the pair were pulled out.

Théra wrapped Takval and Thoryo in thick layers of fur. Kitos and the others lit fires and swept the embers into auk and dog skulls. Wrapping the hot skulls in skins, they tucked them into the armpits and around the torsos of the two chilled bodies, infusing them with the heat of life. As the sleds continued north, Théra stripped off her clothes and nestled herself against Takval's frigid skin, trying to give him as much of her body heat as possible.

Behind them, the Lyucu wailed and cursed.

At nightfall, the surviving Lyucu made their way back to the abandoned ice fortress, where they kept fires going all night as they attempted to revive as many of the frozen that had been hauled out of the sea as they could.

Tovo survived.

Not all of him, to be sure. Prolonged exposure to the sea in Nalyufin's Pasture would ultimately cost him his left arm as well as four blackened toes that shriveled and then fell off. Nonetheless, that made him far luckier than many of the thanes and warriors under his charge, who would never return from this expedition to the far north at all.

It took two weeks for Tovo to recover enough of his wits to contemplate the next step. The dogsled drivers assured him that by now the sea was rock solid. Still, Tovo had learned his lesson. Gingerly, he scattered his sleds widely apart, with scouts running far ahead to find and mark safe paths with waybones. Whenever the ice shifted or buckled and the loud snaps ripped through the silence, the Lyucu froze in place, as though expecting to be thrown into the deadly maw of the ocean again.

By the time they reached Spotted Heifer, the first island to the north, all traces of the rebels had been erased by intervening storms. Tovo looked to the north at the other distant islands, peeking out of the deserted landscape like bleached skeletons in the salt flats, and shivered uncontrollably. The idea of pursuing the rebels into this no-man's-land seemed the very definition of madness.

"They're already dead," said the leader of the conscripted ice flea drivers, her voice trembling. "They can't hunt; they can't fish. There's nothing to eat. Most likely, they're at the bottom of some crevasse."

Rather than slap her for offering an opinion that wasn't solicited, Tovo nodded with approval. After all, the ice fleas lived here year-round and knew the land well. If even they thought the rebels couldn't survive in this cursed wasteland, who was he to argue?

He immediately ordered a retreat. The other thanes were only too glad to obey, and when the ragged warriors, half-frozen, missing fingers and toes and limbs, finally limped back to the mainland, they couldn't wait to return to the warmth and comforts of Taten, secure in the knowledge that their enemies were turning into pillars of ice in the desolate north.

The optimism of the Lyucu wasn't unwarranted.

After crossing the sea, the rebels found shelter in an ice cave on the western edge of Spotted Heifer. They had no clear plans except to stay out of the view of their pursuers.

And while Thoryo recovered from her ordeal in the icy sea,

Takval was much less fortunate. He remained in a coma as a high fever raged throughout his body. Théra remained by his side at all hours, wiping down his scalding skin with ice chips.

As the days passed, the fever did not abate.

"We have only a week's worth of food left for people," reported Kitos.

"Reduce everyone's rations," said Théra, "except Adyulek, Tipo, and her baby. Give the order for all to bundle up and sleep as much as possible. You told me that the star-snout bears of the north sleep and don't eat all winter, didn't you? We can follow their example. And we don't even have to wait all winter, only until the Lyucu retreat, and then we can make our way back to the mainland."

"I'm afraid you haven't understood me completely," said Kitos. "I spoke of food for people, but we must also think of the dogs. If they starve, we'll have no hope of getting out of here alive."

Théra gritted her teeth. She had seen how much the large dogs, descendants of the horrid wolves, ate to maintain their strength. "How long can the food last if we starve people and feed the dogs?"

"Maybe three days."

"Is there really no way to get food in this land?"

Kitos looked at her with pity. "If it were that easy to survive in Nalyufin's Pasture, don't you think we would have settled here? No, there's no food that we can get to."

Going back to the mainland now, when the Lyucu were most likely still waiting for them, would be suicide. "Feed the dogs," said Théra. "We'll worry about people later."

Takval remained in his feverish coma, muttering incomprehensibly from time to time. Théra pried open his jaws to pour in water, and she chewed up small pieces of the tough jerky until they softened, which she then stuffed into his mouth until he swallowed, without waking.

Even with careful rationing, food ran out on the fifth day of the vigil. Several of the warriors who had accompanied them this far had died from a combination of their wounds, the cold, and lack of nourishment. Kitos believed that the band had to start back toward the mainland if they were to have a chance at all. But a storm was rampaging across the island, and it was impossible to find their way in the blinding snow and ice.

Théra reluctantly gave the order to slaughter some of the dogs to be used as food. She knew this was a choice that only deferred the date of death. Without dogs, they would have no hope of making their way off this icebound island, but without eating the dogs, all of them would die.

She fasted and prayed to the gods of Dara and to the gods of Gondé. She stretched her mind into the icy void. There seemed nothing else she could do.

Once again, she found herself on that vast plain under a vaster sky, surrounded by the liquid air that crackled with the energy of lightning and thunder. Storms danced around her.

She felt at peace. They were not going to make it, but that was all right. She was going to die next to someone she loved, and that was a better fate than most.

A voice spoke to her out of the dancing storms.

We have only a week's worth of food left for people.

She laughed to herself. Kitos spoke in such peculiar ways. It had taken her longer than Takval to adjust to Kitos's topolect, and even though now she could understand his speech, there were still patterns in the way he phrased things that sometimes tripped her up. Maybe he just assumed that she would know things that she didn't, like the fact that dogs had to be fed before people.

No, there's no food that we can get to.

Her eyes snapped open. "He didn't say there was no food at all," she muttered to herself.

"Kitos!" she called. "We must speak immediately."

"Is there food that we *can't* get to?" asked Théra, her heart hanging in her throat.

Kitos nodded.

"Where is this food?" Théra spoke slowly and deliberately, not daring to let hope inch too far out along the thin ice above despair.

Kitos closed his eyes and looked deep in thought.

She fully expected him to say something like "back on the mainland." It would be literally true and completely useless.

Kitos opened his eyes. "About half a day's journey by dogsled. We passed it on the way here."

Théra wanted to hug the man and thrash him at the same time.

"What. Do. You. Mean?"

Kitos explained.

The ocean around Nalyufin's Pasture was so cold and dark that most of the time the water was an empty abyss.

But during the brief summers, the sea exploded with activity and life. Majestic whales and seacows drifted through, filtering mouthfuls of tiny shrimp with their baleen bristles. Seadogs playfully dove for blockhead mackerel, surfacing to sneeze and to bark for mates. Toddling auks, with their sharp beaks and flipper-like swimming wings, dashed through the water for beaked needlefish and small fry, simultaneously evading the sharp claws and teeth of opportunistic seadogs. Star-snout bears, the exalted sovereigns of these northern lands, prowled the islands and the brine, eating anything and everything to fatten up for the long, dark winter.

A few animals, however, chose to make these waters home year-round.

One of these rare finny permanent residents of Nalyufin's Pasture was the ice shark. Slow-moving and filled with blood barely warmer than the surrounding water, these giant predators relied on stealth and camouflage more than speed and ferocity. They preyed on unwary toddling auks, careless seadogs who mistook the massive drifting fish for reefs, and even the occasional seacow or juvenile whale too stunned or inexperienced to get out of the way of their languid but nonetheless deadly jaws.

The lethargic sharks were easy prey for bands of nimble human hunters, and the ice tribes would have devoted all their summer hunts to this fish except for one problem: The flesh of the ice shark was toxic. Even a small quantity, if consumed right after the fish was caught, would render an adult unconscious and could kill a child.

Legend had it that the ice sharks were Nalyufin's special creations, helping her maintain the frozen pasture much as sheepdogs aided the people of the scrublands with their flocks.

The harsh conditions this far north meant that no potential source of nourishment could be overlooked. After generations of experimentation, the ice tribes developed a method to render the ice shark's flesh safe for consumption. The process involved digging a shallow trench in the ground, placing the dressed carcass inside, stuffing the internal cavity with a pungent mixture derived from animal fat and a tongue-numbing seaweed, and then covering the ice shark with layers of gravel, sand, and rocks.

In this shallow grave, the weight of the rocks and sand slowly pressed much of the toxic secretions out of the shark carcass while the flesh, stewed in seaweed juice, fermented. Only after many months—sometimes years—would the flesh be considered safe to eat. At that point, the hunters dug up the fermented flesh, dried it, and cut it into strips for storage. The result was a fatty preserve emitting a strong, revolting odor, but it tasted delicious and provided plenty of nutrients.

Since the fermentation process took so long, sharks caught in one season would have to be left in their caches, sealed away by ice and the frozen earth, until the next summer.

"Why don't we just go and dig up this nearby cache?" asked Théra.

"Because we can't get to it," said Kitos, a hint of impatience creeping into his voice.

"Why not? Surely we have enough dogs left to make the journey."

Kitos laughed. "Come with me, Princess."

They exited the temporary shelter of the ice cave, and Kitos slammed his seacow horn staff against the ice beneath their feet. It barely chipped.

"You built a fortress out of ice that held the Lyucu at bay for days," said Kitos. "The ice shark lies under ice and frozen earth as hard as the walls of that fortress, except ten times thicker. Do you understand now?"

"I do," said Théra. "But there is hope."

During their long escape, Théra and Takval had been forced to abandon just about everything they took from Kiri Valley—weapons, spirit portraits, objects of sentimental value. But even after their arduous journey on foot through the World's Edge Mountains, there were a few pieces of equipment they refused to give up.

Among these were a steel drill bit and firework powder—both of which had been instrumental in the battle between *Dissolver of Sorrows* and the Lyucu city-ship. The pékyu and the princess had believed the tools essential in an assault on the city-ships of Taten. As for how a single drill bit and a few pouches of firework powder could make much difference against a fleet of city-ships . . . they avoided thinking that far.

Sometimes the flame of hope, centered on a talisman, couldn't survive the strong winds of close examination.

In any event, the needs of the future had to yield to the crisis of the present. Under Théra's direction, Gozofin and Tipo led a team of workers to drill a deep hole into the thick layer of ice covering the cache. Then they packed it full of firework powder and lit the fuse.

The rebels' ears rang from the explosion; smoke cleared; chunks of fermented shark flesh rained down; there was a giant hole in the frozen ground, like the opening to a cellar promising full bellies for dogs *and* people.

The unfamiliar flesh smelled so foul that the Dara and the Agon both retched, but the food did give them strength, and the crisis was temporarily resolved. They would be able to wait out the Lyucu on the mainland.

However, Takval's condition continued to decline, and Théra could see that he was literally wasting away before her eyes. Sores and lesions appeared on his skin, no matter how often she turned his comatose body. In spite of the pungent and bitter medicines Adyulek poured down his throat and the pleas she made to the Every-Mother, his fever didn't abate.

The princess continued to pray to the gods of Dara and of Gondé, but all she received in return was silence.

The days were so short that it seemed the sun barely peeked above the horizon before it went back to bed. The mood of the rebels grew correspondingly darker. Some of the Agon and the Dara spoke to

Kitos tentatively about becoming members of the ice tribes. By the time of the thaw next spring, it wasn't clear how many would still respond to her commands.

"I have failed," muttered Théra to herself as she wiped Takval's forehead with ice chips on the longest night of the year, more to keep herself busy than out of any real belief that it was doing the patient much good.

The Lyucu would launch their invasion in the spring, bringing a fresh tide of slaughter and death to Dara. The Agon and the ice tribes would suffer more than ever before. She had come to this foreign land to unleash a revolution, to free a people. But in the end, she couldn't even save her own children or husband.

"I love you," she sobbed, and wrapped her arms around his shrunken body, placing her cheek against his burning skin. Tears spilled from her eyes and drenched his face. "Everything we've built is gone; everything we've dreamed of is impossible. I don't know what to do."

She was a dandelion seed who found only unyielding rock, a lotus seed with a bitter heart. She did not dissolve sorrows; she was sorrow incarnate.

"My breath."

At first, she thought she had imagined the faint voice, but then she felt the skin under her cheek move. She sat up and saw that for the first time in days, Takval was awake.

His face was flushed; his breath rasped in his throat; there was a brightness in his eyes, like the spark on a fuse. Her heart leapt with hope, but then she remembered that sometimes, when people were about to die, they showed a last burst of vitality, like the brief glimpse of the sun above the horizon this far north, on the longest night of the year.

"Mother," Takval whispered hoarsely.

Was he delirious? "It's me, Théra."

He shook his head. "Mother spoke to me in a dream," he whispered, his voice hoarse. "And all our friends who died with her in Kiri Valley."

A terrible foreboding seized her heart, as bleak as the icebound landscape around her.

His voice was so faint that she had to lean close to hear him.

"I'll be with them soon."

"No," she said. "No! Spring is coming. You'll get better—"

"I promised to get you to Taten, my breath," he whispered. "I'm sorry I won't be able to keep my word—"

"No! I won't release you from your vow. You cannot—"

"Listen to me, please! Don't let my breath fade away like the whimpers of a slaughtered lamb on the scrublands; don't let my blood freeze in darkness like a coward concealing himself under fallen comrades in battle." He wheezed from the exertion, and his voice lowered even more so that she had to press her ear against his feverish lips, straining to hear him above the roar of blood rushing through her arteries. As he continued to speak, her eyes widened.

"No!" Her body convulsed; her head shook. "I can't. I'm not Agon."

"You can and you must. You belong to this land. You love the people of the scrublands as much as I do."

Hot tears spilled from Théra's eyes.

"Remember what you told me: Sometimes we have to demand that others make sacrifices and accept them. It's the grace of kings and the burden of pékyus." He gazed into her eyes, and they both saw in the eyes of the other the mirror of infinite longing.

She sealed her lips against his, and as they kissed she blew her breath into his weakened lungs, willing as much of her strength into him as possible.

Then she stood up and summoned Adyulek.

PART TWO

THUNDER-AWAKENED FOREST

CHAPTER TWELVE

LYUCU KYO! UKYU KYO!

IN THE WATERS NORTH OF RUI AND DASU, NEAR
THE WALL OF STORMS: THE FIFTH MONTH OF
THE ELEVENTH YEAR OF THE REIGN OF SEASON
OF STORMS AND THE REIGN OF AUDACIOUS
FREEDOM (EXACTLY TEN YEARS AFTER THE LAST
TIME THE WALL OPENED).

The city-ship *Toryoana's Gift* drifted in the calm sea. Though it was still miles from the Wall of Storms, the tumult aboard the ship seemed an echo of the distant mountain range made of water and wind, lit up by bright forks of lightning.

The vessel was but a distillation of the waves of trepidation and anxiety gripping every heart in Ukyu-taasa. After ten years of peace, the treaty with the Dara-raaki had expired earlier this year. Although the tribute fleets continued to come to Kriphi, bearing food and treasure, and the cowardly barbarians, their faces turned to the mud at their feet and their hearts stewing in the filthy lucre of commerce, showed no signs of gearing up for war, everyone, even the pathetic accommodationists, thought it was only a matter of time before hostilities would resume between the two sides.

And the fate of that oncoming war would be decided today, for the Wall of Storms was about to reopen, revealing the long-awaited reinforcements from Ukyu.

Shamans danced on the deck as well as among the spars, where they swung and pivoted among the rigging as easily as upon the netting on a garinafin. Booming cactus drums, blaring Péa pipes, and honking bone trumpets created a thunderous soundscape in which the shamans, dressed in feathered capes and antlered skull helmets, twirled and leapt, re-enacting the great deeds of past Lyucu heroes and pékyus. Naros and culeks, their minds uplifted with tolyusa smoke, watched the storytelling dances, rapt. From time to time, they chanted in unison.

> *Dara-raaki must be destroyed!*
> *Dara-raaki must be destroyed!*

Cutanrovo Aga, the captain of *Toryoana's Gift*, surveyed the scene with pride and mounting excitement. Since that fateful day three years ago in Kigo Yezu, when she had begun the process of dismantling the disastrous accommodationist policies that would have doomed Ukyu-taasa, she had accomplished so much.

Cleansing Ukyu-taasa of native cultural taint had been only the first step. Virtually every shrine or temple dedicated to native idols in Rui and Dasu had been razed; all books, disgusting insect-spun shrouds covered in word-scars, had been found and burned; speaking the native tongue was a crime punished not only with death of the speaker, but also the castration of all the speaker's male family members within three degrees of relatedness.

Next had come the much harder process of reminding the pure-blooded Lyucu of their sacred supremacy, of encouraging the togaten to become worthy of the superior strain in their blood, of binding and lashing the natives into embracing their nature as mindless drones dedicated to the welfare of their true masters.

Agricultural fields were trampled into pastures for long-haired cattle and knob-horned sheep (or, as Cutanrovo put it, the enslaved land had to be liberated); native villagers were assigned to Lyucu households much like livestock; the birth of every pure Lyucu child was celebrated by the sacrifice of three native infants to Nalyufin, the hate-hearted; traditional native burials were forbidden; togaten and native youths who desecrated ancestral graves were celebrated publicly; while grandparents and children were penned in stockaded camps under the watchful gaze of garinafins, natives of prime fighting age were conscripted into the army, where they worshipped the spirit of Tenryo and Tanvanaki, the earthly representative of the gods; native scholars who professed love for mud-legged "wisdom" had their tongues cut out and hands amputated. . . .

Every step along the way, she had had to face down challenges from the accommodationists.

"There will be nothing to eat if you destroy the fields and force all the villagers into the army," fretted Goztan Ryoto.

"We'll demand more tribute from Pan," said Cutanrovo.

"That will make us even more dependent on the very people who, by your account, are our inveterate enemies," objected Vocu Firna.

"All the more reason to build up the army so that we can take what belongs to us when they refuse," answered Cutanrovo.

Tanvanaki presided over these debates, vacillating like a banner in a storm. But in the end, she always sided with Cutanrovo. What else could she do? Cutanrovo had set in motion a process that was like the coming of the tide, and the pékyu had no choice but to go with the flow.

Every concession to Cutanrovo strengthened the hard-liners and weakened the accommodationists, which made the next concession even harder to resist. Fear and hatred were self-sustaining, mutually reinforcing. Every policy of terror required ten more policies of terror to prevent an explosive backlash.

After all that had already been done, there was no more possibility of accommodation with the natives, no room for Tanvanaki to retreat without damaging her own aura of infallibility. She had no hope of securing the loyalty of the hard-liners—required to strengthen her hand against the challenge posed by the coming of Cudyu's reinforcements—except to do as Cutanrovo suggested.

Dara-raaki must be destroyed!

Dara-raaki must be destroyed!

And the accommodationists had not helped their own cause. By chance, Cutanrovo had discovered that Vocu Firna was sheltering native scholars from her cleansing squads by disguising them as his slaves. One of these Dara-raaki word-scar carvers, under torture, had confessed an even more damning fact: Vocu Firna had continued to write poetry in Classical Ano, and called the native scholar his master in composition.

A search of the grounds of Vocu Firna's old mansion—a pile of rubble now—had turned up a buried trove of proscribed native artifacts: antiques, books, figurines of native gods, paintings, ritual vessels, even . . . *histories*. His heart had been poisoned and tainted by the mudlegs beyond redemption. Such an act of treachery could not be borne.

Still, Cutanrovo held on to hope for her old political rival—he was Lyucu, and she wanted to save him, if she could. She heaped the proscribed goods atop a pile of firewood, along with the trussed native scholars that Vocu had been protecting. If he would light the fire to annihilate the goods and slaves, she would still call him ru-votan.

"I will not," said Vocu Firna. "We have no right to erase those who lived here before we did. We have no claim to destroy the re-rememberings and ancestral goods of the people of Dara. Even Admiral Krita never sought to wipe out the memories of our people. You will incur the wrath of all the gods, Lyucu and Dara, if you continue down this path!"

It was with a grieving heart that Cutanrovo prepared to execute this traitor. But Goztan, desperate to save her last major political ally, interceded with the pékyu. In the end, Tanvanaki, always too willing to listen to her old friend's false counsel, granted a reprieve on Vocu Firna's life. But he was stripped of his command and rank and sentenced to hard labor like a native slave.

After that, even Goztan stopped overtly interfering with Cutanrovo's grand task of revitalizing the Lyucu spirit.

There had been whispers among the thanes that when the time came for Tanvanaki to take her spirit portrait, perhaps Cutanrovo would become the next pékyu instead of one of the togaten pékyustaasa. Cutanrovo squashed these rumors mercilessly. She was enraged that they would misunderstand her so. Yes, she had become the most powerful thane, the first among equals; yes, she had had herself elevated to the post of chief shaman, despite the fact that she was a warrior, not a speaker for the gods; however, she had done everything not for personal ambition, but to push Tanvanaki into fulfilling her duty to realize Pékyu Tenryo's dream: turning Ukyutaasa into a new paradise for the Lyucu people.

Couldn't they see that?

More than anything else, she was comforted by the current state of Ukyu-taasa. Only the speech of the scrublands could be heard in Kriphi now, from the Great Tent to the hovels of the slaves; every Lyucu youth was a master of garinafin riding and traditional warfare, having honed their skills against native captives and rebels during stints leading cleansing squads; every togaten child saw their highest goal in life as becoming more Lyucu; and the large native armies loyally maintained order in Ukyu-taasa, ready to do whatever the Lyucu commanders demanded of them. Combined with the systematic castrations and infanticides, she could foresee a time, perhaps in only a few more generations, when native bloodlines would be virtually extinct, and Tenryo's vision would be finally complete.

Hot tears welled in her eyes. For the sake of her children and their children, for the survival of the Lyucu people and the glory of the gods, she had had to endure suspicion and doubt from Tanvanaki, as well as hostility and rancor from softheaded fools like Goztan and Vocu. But she was fighting for their children too, and she would bear any trial to ensure a secure future for all Lyucu in this treacherous land.

And today, she would welcome more Lyucu blood. Having been dispatched to guide Cudyu's reinforcement fleet to Kriphi, she and her crew would be the face of Ukyu-taasa. It was up to them to impress upon the newcomers how much Tanvanaki had already succeeded in her mission, and to demonstrate the blossoming of the Lyucu spirit in this barbaric realm.

Time to add a little magic and bring focus to the proceedings, she thought.

The cactus drums, Péa pipes, and bone trumpets quieted; the shamans stood still; all the eyes of the naros and culeks were on Cutanrovo Aga, erect on a raised dais near the city-ship's bow.

In addition to the garinafin skull helmet of a high-ranking thane, she wore a bulky war cape of pure white, full of round protuberances that covered her from shoulder to the ground. An impatient observer from Dara might have concluded after a hasty glance that the garment was woven from chain links or armor plates, but a closer examination would have revealed that the bumps in the cape were far more sinister: human skulls, one hundred and eight in number.

The lurona ryo lurotan, or literally "tent of head-tents," was traditionally fashioned from the bleached skulls of the vanquished. As the Lyucu didn't have a habit of wearing bulky armor into battle, the lurona ryo lurotan was not a garment intended for fighters, but for shamans praying for divine aid in battle. Diasa, the club-maiden and huntress, supposedly made the first such cape from the skulls of the sinful people of the Fifth Age, whose pride angered the gods before the redemption of the tribes of the scrublands by Kikisavo (and his sidekick and ultimate betrayer, Afir).

Cutanrovo lifted her hands toward the heavens and began to chant.

> *Ten dyudyu cupéruna?*
> *Lyucu kyo!*
> *Ten dyudyu cupéruna?*
> *Ukyu kyo!*
> *Lurona ryo lurotan saten ra pécu,*
> *Saten ra pécu!*
> *Pégoz nara kita kita.*

Gradually, the assembled naros and culeks joined Cutanrovo's lone voice, until the mighty chorus shook the very deck of the city-ship with their thunder-roar, their flood-breath.

More than a few eyes on the ship were wet as the warriors recalled the dangerous journey across the seas and the terrible battles that had followed to secure themselves this foothold in Dara.

> *Who do the gods favor above all?*
> *The Lyucu people!*

They hoped that the many comrades who hadn't lived to see this day would smile from the backs of the cloud-garinafins as they gazed upon this scene of celebration; they hoped that the gods of Ukyu would nod with approval as they observed Cutanrovo in her splendor, draped in the skulls of their enemies.

> *What do the gods favor above all?*
> *The land of Ukyu!*

In truth, the tradition of making and wearing skull capes had long fallen into disuse among the Lyucu, and was mentioned only in old stories. Even Tenryo, who slaughtered thousands upon thousands, first in his drive to unite the Lyucu to overthrow the hated Agon, and then during the long conquest of the mud-legged Dara-raaki, had never revived the lapsed custom, believing that such gruesome symbolism was unnecessary because his victories spoke for themselves. It was enough to leave that ancient vision of horror to song and story.

> *Spread the tent of head-tents,*
> *Spread it!*
> *There is nothing we cannot do.*

But Cutanrovo understood that it was not enough to merely replicate Ukyu's way of life in Ukyu-taasa. In order to fully revitalize the Lyucu spirit, dulled after years of accommodationist misrule and compromise, it was necessary to, in some sense, "out-Lyucu" the homeland. By reviving these customs from a mythical and even bloodier age, she and her followers could instill in the natives even more terror and boost the cohesion of the Lyucu conquerors.

And the skull cape was only the beginning.

Behind Cutanrovo's dais, a dozen Lyucu warriors, all naros-votan, stood on the foredeck, massive clubs fashioned from whale bone and shark's teeth over their shoulders. At their feet lay a group of seven Dara-raaki prisoners, the only survivors of the most recent rebellion in Dasu. Sedated with tolyusa juice and dream herbs, the prisoners were completely docile, unable to tell their fantastical hallucinations apart from the nightmarish reality around them.

Her opening chant at an end, Cutanrovo turned toward the naros-votan guarding the prisoners and clapped her hands together, causing the skulls in her cape to rattle and clatter like the singing dunes of Lurodia Tanta.

"Let the music begin!"

Two of the warriors picked up one of the sedated rebels and dragged her to the prow of the ship. They pushed her upper body out over the foaming sea and held her in place by her arms. The other ten warriors lined up behind her in a column.

The prisoner moaned, uncertain of where she was. Before her the Wall of Storms loomed, as unreal as the swirling haze in her mind.

Cutanrovo stood still, waiting for the skulls in her cape to stop rattling against one another. The naros and culeks held their breath. A solemn silence descended over the ship. Cutanrovo nodded at the naros-votan waiting in line.

The first naro-votan strode forward and slammed her massive club into the prisoner's right ankle. The sickening, wet crack of shattering bone reverberated over the city-ship.

The woman faltered, but the two naros-votan on either side of her held her up. A moment later, as the pain pierced her drugged mind, she let out an inhuman scream, something not of this world.

Cutanrovo turned back to the rest of the ship, and raised her arms under the skull cape. "Gods of Ukyu, we seek your aid in opening the Wall of Storms and granting our votan-ru-taasa and votan-sa-taasa safe passage. There is no music more pleasing than the lamentation of our foes as they're driven before you, and we offer this gift to you now in gratitude."

The keening of the woman with the broken ankle gradually subsided. A second naro-votan strode up to her and slammed his toothed club into her left ankle. A fresh howl of pain tore through the air. The woman convulsed and jerked like a hooked fish.

Cutanrovo nodded, and the two naros-votan holding her up let go of her arms. The prisoner collapsed to the deck, screaming again, her broken ankles unable to support her.

As Cutanrovo watched, the other six prisoners were led up in turn against the prow of the ship. One by one, their legs were also shattered, adding their agonized screams and howls to the grotesque chorus that Cutanrovo was conducting for the pleasure of her gods.

Whenever one of the prisoners slackened in their wailing, one of the naros-votan would stride up to inflict a new injury: breaking arms; smashing fingers; shattering ribs; slamming the teeth-studded club heads into the prisoners' private parts; slashing open their bellies to extract the entrails slowly, one loop at a time. . . . Only when a victim could no longer be roused through torture or could no longer scream due to choking on their own blood would one of the naros-votan end their life with a precise bash in the skull.

By the time the ritual sacrifice was complete, the last victim silent and dead, more than a few of the naros-votan, naros, and culeks were trembling. Even for battle-hardened veterans, the intensity of the ritualistic torture they had had to inflict and witness was over-whelming.

Cutanrovo smiled at the naros-votan who had made the prison-ers sing for a divine audience. "The gods are pleased."

The naros-votan nodded, their faces twitching.

Cutanrovo clapped her hands together several times loudly.

Shamans scrambled up from the interior of the city-ship, skull bowls full of crimson berries in their arms. They went first to the naros-votan and then among the rest of the crew, distributing the sacred fruits. The assembled warriors grabbed handfuls of berries and chewed them as though satisfying a desperate hunger, careless of the blood-like juice spilling down their chins. As the magic spread through their veins, their twitching faces relaxed. Visions of feasting gods and proud warriors on cloud-garinafins crowded their minds, and a manic energy suffused their limbs, seeking an outlet.

Cutanrovo laughed with pleasure. These tolyusa berries were a lucky find. The pirates were actually good for something.

Tanvanaki's secret dealings with the pirates had always bothered her. The pékyu's obsession with acquiring native artisans and their expertise seemed to her to betray a lack of faith in Lyucu traditions. However, she reluctantly accepted Tanvanaki's reasoning that an army of natives had to be equipped with native weaponry, as the mud-legs couldn't be allowed to learn to ride garinafins or to fight with bone weapons.

However, she kept a tight watch on the pirates, as they were prone to smuggling contraband into Ukyu-taasa for profit—mostly small carved idols of false gods consecrated at temples in the core islands and books of the words of Ano sages, which were very much in demand among native officials who continued to covertly practice their barbaric customs. (In truth, she fervently wished she could get rid of all the native officials, but they did serve a purpose in making the large population of slaves easier to control, like sheepdogs. *We must cull the herd and reduce the number of mud-legs even further,* she mused. *It's the solution to all problems.*)

It was from one of these pirate smuggling crews that she had seized the first supply of special tolyusa berries. While she wasn't surprised that the plant had become established on other islands in Dara—Ukyu-taasa's supply had been derived from a patch discovered on Crescent Island, after all—she was amazed at how round and lush the berries were, far more appealing in appearance than the familiar variety in military-controlled patches on Rui and Dasu.

Instantly, Cutanrovo saw yet another opportunity to enhance her own power. Tolyusa was vital to the health and breeding of garinafins, and Goztan Ryoto, the last accommodationist in power, controlled the meager supply of tolyusa in Ukyu-taasa because Tanvanaki entrusted the garinafin force to her. However, tolyusa was also an important component in religious service, and Cutanrovo, even as chief shaman, had to beg Goztan for it, which the latter doled out only reluctantly. If Cutanrovo could secure her own independent supply of tolyusa, then she would be one step closer to toppling Goztan completely.

Her plan to keep the pirate-sourced tolyusa to herself, however, had almost been thwarted by Tanvanaki's nameless spy. He found out about the smugglers and wanted to report the finding to the pékyu. Cutanrovo caught him just in time and tried to persuade him to see things her way—surely there was no reason to bother the pékyu with such a minor matter when she already had so many other things to worry about!

But neither enticements nor threats worked. He refused to contemplate the idea of keeping anything from Tanvanaki. She was a goddess, infallible, all-wise, ever-aware. . . . Cutanrovo heard enough. She killed him.

Cutanrovo regretted having to do such a thing to a fellow Lyucu, but the man *had* always made her uneasy. Clanless, tribeless, nameless, he just didn't fit. That he was such a good swimmer, unheard of among the Lyucu, further marked him as strange, tainted, unnatural. She had been wanting to get rid of him for a long time.

What Cutanrovo feared most of all was that the man represented Tanvanaki's eyes and ears, and could tell the pékyu things without going through Cutanrovo. She had already gradually replaced the guards and servants around Tanvanaki with people she trusted, but she had not been able to persuade Tanvanaki to assign the spy to her command.

Cutanrovo believed it was important to protect the pékyu by controlling the information she received. Facts were never found in nature, but shaped by mindset. There were simply too many "facts"—the harvest figures, the number of natives being killed, the health of the herds and flocks—that required the proper context and interpretation to be (correctly) understood as successes of hard-liner policies. Tanvanaki, on the other hand, often showed an unfortunate resistance to the necessary hard-liner mindset. To allow the pékyu to be exposed to information without proper filtering, therefore, was to leave her vulnerable to deception and manipulation by the wily accommodationists.

Viewed in the proper light, killing the nameless spy was a supreme act of loyalty. Cutanrovo was willing to stain her own hands with Lyucu blood in order to save the pékyu from deception-by-fact.

So she had blamed the death of the spy on native saboteurs, and executed a whole village as vengeance to comfort the grieving pékyu.

Her own sacrifices had been worth it. The pirate berries turned out to be much more potent than the traditional variety, and those who ingested them reported longer, more intense dream-hazes that brought them closer to the gods.

Cutanrovo saw the new tolyusa berries as a kind of sign. If a plant from Ukyu could take root in Dara and grow into a more intense, powerful version of itself, didn't it presage that the people of Ukyu would also take root in Dara and become a more intense, powerful version of themselves? The Lyucu of Ukyu-taasa would evolve to be even more Lyucu than the Lyucu back home, exactly as she envisaged.

The pirates were vague about where they had obtained the berries, and Cutanrovo understood their reticence. Even outlaws among the Dara-raaki were as obsessed with profit and commerce as the rest of that benighted race. No matter; once all of Dara was conquered, the Lyucu would discover the source and have as much of the new tolyusa as they liked. Meanwhile, it was no trouble to advise the pékyu to demand more tributary gold from that coward Jia and divert some into her private coffers to pay the pirates for a steady supply.

And so Cutanrovo kept the source of the new supply secret. She increased the use of tolyusa at all religious ceremonies and dispensed berries liberally as rewards to warriors and togaten (and even a few favored, loyal natives) who devised particularly clever ways of promoting Lyucu interests. The native Wira Pin, for instance, received some tolyusa berries when he came up with the idea of requiring every native village to construct an elaborate statue of Tanvanaki in a competition to demonstrate their loyalty. Once the statues were finished, all natives were compelled to pledge allegiance to the village statue each morning and to confess their sins to the same statue each night.

Fortuitously, the new berries also bolstered her project to make the Lyucu *more* Lyucu. Shamans reported feeling closer to the gods; warriors reported more strength and energy; the togaten thought it made them feel closer to their Lyucu roots. The only people who objected were the surviving accommodationists, who, ironically, argued that such extensive use of tolyusa was "un-Lyucu."

Cutanrovo didn't even deign to dignify their whining with a response.

Now that everyone was in a proper festive mood, Cutanrovo decided to bring the ceremony to a climax.

"Let's welcome our votan-ru-taasa and votan-sa-taasa with a fitting display of our Lyucu spirit!"

Music started again, as did the dancing. The twirling shamans leapt even higher and the frenzied musicians played even louder. Naros and culeks picked up their bone weapons and slammed them against the masts and gunwales while stomping their feet against the deck.

Cutanrovo extended her hands toward the Wall of Storms, as though beseeching the wind and the water directly, and intoned:

> *Cu na goztenva va péfir!*
> *Cu na tatenva va péfir!*

Yes, she thought, *yes. Why can't we build a paradise with our own arms? Why can't we open the Wall by the strength of our own voices? The Lyucu spirit is indomitable!*

The prayer, amplified and repeated by all the fervent throats on *Toryoana's Gift,* expanded outward from the city-ship like the rumbling of thunder.

The Wall shimmered, as though ready to reveal the next stage in the grand conquest of Dara by the Lyucu.

At that moment, somewhere to the east of *Toryoana's Gift,* below the horizon, Admiral Than Carucono paced the deck of the tiny fishing barge *Toru-noki.* A few guards, dressed as fishermen, gazed alertly out upon the empty sea.

Toru-noki was alone. Given the expiration of the peace treaty with Unredeemed Dara, everyone, from Empress Jia and Prime Minister Cogo Yelu to the junior analysts in the College of Advocates, thought it was best to refrain from any action that might be interpreted by Tanvanaki as a provocation. Thus, Than couldn't be escorted by warships, including mechanical crubens or airships.

He was here to observe, not to start a fight.

The aged admiral peered north at the roiling columns of water and clouds. He didn't pray to any of the gods of Dara, though he thought he could see the shapes of the gods in those ever-shifting storms and hear their voices in the dull clamor of distant thunder. Years of watching the great engineers of the empire at work—first Luan Zyaji, his old friend, and then Zomi Kidosu, the student who came to surpass her master—had taught him that it was better to trust the arcane symbols and the abstruse mathematics that they used to divine the future than the ambivalent signs of the gods. If Zomi Kidosu said that the Wall of Storms would reopen today, then it was as certain to occur as that the sun would set in the west.

The only uncertainty was who and what would come through, and that, he knew, had already been decided more than a year ago, since a year was how long it took to travel from Ukyu to Dara on the great belt current.

"Grand Princess Théra," he muttered, "the die has been cast and the arrow loosed from its string. Have you succeeded?"

Than Carucono squinted at the Wall of Storms, waiting for the fate of Dara to be changed once again from outside.

CHAPTER THIRTEEN

THE WOLF-THANE

TATEN: THE FIFTH MONTH IN THE TENTH YEAR
AFTER THE DEPARTURE OF PRINCESS THÉRA
FROM DARA FOR UKYU-GONDÉ (WHEN THE LYUCU
MUST LAUNCH THEIR NEW INVASION FLEET TO
DARA).

Another spring had arrived in Ukyu-Gondé. The scrublands, after a harsh winter, revived with a vengeance. Meltwater refilled dry riverbeds; spiny frog tadpoles wriggled in mud pools; flowers bloomed in the grass seas as well as on the shores of Aluro's Basin and the Sea of Tears. Babies born during the winter sniffed for the first time the moist scent of cactus dew carried on fresh breezes instead of the perpetual smoky haze inside sealed tents, and all the earth seemed to have awakened from a long slumber.

In Taten, thousands busied themselves. Agon and Dara slaves, many of them captured from Kiri Valley and supervised by whip-wielding naros, labored over the city-ships, restoring them to seaworthiness. Butchered cattle and sheep carcasses waited in heaps outside smoke tents, where teams of culeks would turn them into provisions for the expedition. Agon slaves cut, dried, and tied bundles of waxtongue, thornbush, and long-ear grass, loading them onto the city-ships as feed for garinafins. Young naros wrestled and competed in feats of strength for the chance to be chosen as members of the expedition, while thanes jostled for political advantage— either to be designated as leaders in the fleet to Dara or to take up juicy posts left behind in Ukyu.

Having pacified the Agon-Dara rebellion and subjugated the ice tribes—though it was regretful that Tovo couldn't bring back Takval and Théra, either alive or dead (Cudyu had been hoping to demonstrate his power by using Takval's skull as a drinking bowl and making Théra his pleasure slave)—the pékyu now turned his attention to new victories and conquests.

He had, by guile and cunning (or rather, by divine revelation, if one were to listen to his explanation to his followers), discovered the next opening in the Wall of Storms, and now he would lead the greatest expedition in the history of the scrublands through it. He wasn't rash and impulsive like his father; he would learn from the old man's mistakes and be prepared. With the aid of the Dara captives taken from Kiri Valley, he would make these city-ships stronger and better. Through torture and threats, he would extract from them the most up-to-date intelligence concerning the strategic situation in Dara. Unlike the last expedition he'd sent, a perfunctory effort to fulfill his duties as a son and an opportunity to be rid of thanes he didn't like, this one would be a serious effort drawing on the strength of all Lyucu. He would bring many more garinafins and riders; he would pack plenty of provisions and tolyusa; he would lead the bravest naros and the wiliest thanes.

After all, this time he wouldn't be fighting to support someone else, but to carve his own legacy.

The young pékyu vowed not only to complete the quest left unfinished by his father and sister, but also to seize the secret of those Dara ships that had brought Théra to Ukyu, ships that could cross the Wall at will. He would then return to Ukyu triumphant, bringing undreamed-of treasures and docile slaves from that distant, indolent land.

There was no pékyu grander than Cudyu in all the voice paintings and spirit portraits of the Lyucu, declared the shamans, not Toluroru, not Tenryo, not even Kikisavo himself.

"Votan! Votan!" Two naros rushed into the Great Tent and fell to one knee before Pékyu Cudyu.

"What is it?"

"A sign! A sign in the gulf!"

In their eyes the pékyu saw both wonder and terror.

He got up and gestured for the naros to lead the way.

Saof was tired. Piloting garinafin patrols for seven days in a row was a lot, even for an eighteen-year-old who felt as strong as Kikisavo when he had first set out to demand answers from the gods. Even his mount, a seven-year-old male who had just been added to the regular garinafin pool, showed the effects of the nonstop flights. The leathery lids of his eyes drooped, and every flap of the wing seemed a struggle.

But the pékyu's orders had been clear. The launch of the fleet to Dara was the most important occasion in decades; every effort had to be made to prevent acts of sabotage from the subjugated and the enslaved.

Wait, who are they?

In the distance, a group of people and animals were heading for Taten from the north, kicking up a cloud of dust.

Saof guided his mount toward them. As the garinafin made a low, wide circle over the caravan, he took stock of the strangers. A single rider sat on top of a long-haired bull, followed by a line of cows. A string of captives, about twenty in number, their necks connected by sinew ropes, marched alongside the cattle. Some of them were dressed like Agon slaves, while others wore sleek furs from animals he didn't recognize. On each side of the marching group, running up and down to keep the cows and captives in line, were several large white-haired dogs who could almost be mistaken for horrid wolves.

Saof landed in front of the convoy.

The wing gusts ruffled the long hair of the bull rider, who pulled back on the reins connected to a ring in the nose of her mount. A horrid-wolf skull helmet covered her visage, but her eyes, star-bright, shone through the sockets in the skull.

"Show your face, stranger!" demanded Saof. "How dare you remain in battle dress when you approach Taten, the seat of the Lone Voice of Ukyu and Gondé?"

"I was scarred as a child by the claw of a garinafin calf," said the woman in a haughty tone. "I don't reveal my face except to my enemies, so that I can see them shrink back in terror."

She was young, Saof realized, probably no older than himself. In her lilting accent he heard the rustling of the grass seas around Aluro's Basin, the rich ancestral grazing grounds of the Roatan clan, unifier of the scrublands. It was an accent that many of the thanes of Cudyu's Great Tent struggled to imitate, but this woman spoke it with the natural assurance of one born to it.

"Will you give me your name and lineage at least?" said Saof, his tone now much more polite. He felt both envious and a bit intimidated. "Uh . . . pékyu's orders."

"I am Rita, daughter of Kyogo, son of Lu. I serve the pékyu as Wolf-Thane of Nalyufin's Hounds."

Saof had never heard of the Tribe of Nalyufin's Hounds. He dismounted from his garinafin and approached Rita. "Forgive my ignorance—" He bit back the urge to address her as "votan"; after all, though he was only a naro, he served the pékyu directly, a source of considerable pride. "I know not of your tribe."

"It is new," said Rita. "My clan was allowed to establish the tribe for meritorious service."

It wasn't uncommon for feuding clans to split into new tribes when there was new land and spoils from war to be divided among them. "Then where does your tribe roam?"

"By the shores of Nalyufin's Pasture," came the reply. "Garinafin-Thane Tovo sent me to wipe up the remnants of the ice fleas who dared to join the Agon rebels, and I've brought fresh captives and cattle to honor the pékyu."

To Saof, Rita appeared as a bundle of contradictions. Covered from neck to toe in layers of fur, the diminutive woman looked frail, as though unable to endure even the chill of the early spring breeze. But if she held the rank of wolf-thane at such a young age, she must be a warrior of considerable skill.

Wait, how and why would a wolf-thane travel across the scrublands without a retinue of warriors or even a garinafin?

Saof's eyes narrowed in suspicion. Something about this situation didn't seem right. Keeping Rita in view, he slowly backed toward his garinafin.

Rita's pose remained relaxed, unaware of his intention.

Behind Rita, however, the ice flea captives seemed to notice his hesitation. The one in the lead, an old man with a hoary beard, glanced at the others. All of a sudden, it was as if an unspoken command had been issued, and all the captives tensed their bodies, their eyes directed at the young woman sitting on the bull.

Saof could sense the incipient rebellion in their poses. Perhaps the ice fleas saw this confrontation between Saof and Rita as an opportunity to rise up against their captor. For a brief moment, he wondered if he should warn her, but then decided against it. Even if the captives overcame Rita, he would have plenty of time to get on his mount and take care of them. The assault would provide him an opportunity to better evaluate this mysterious "wolf-thane."

The old man grunted, and a wild look came into the eyes of the captives as they rushed at the young woman riding on the bull.

Still holding Saof's gaze, Rita swept her right arm behind her, pointing at the old captive in the lead. Though she held no club or axe, it was as though some invisible force shot out of her fingertips, and the old man collapsed to the ground with a surprised howl, dragging the other captives connected to his neck to the ground in a confused heap.

Rita finally turned around and glanced at the captives contemptuously. "Again?" She spoke in that accent Saof had heard so often from the pékyu himself and Thane Tovo, the accent of power and prestige. "You haven't had enough after all these miles?"

She stabbed her finger through the air at the old man and the other captives, and the ice fleas hollered and shrieked, as though lashed by an invisible whip.

"Nalyufin loves the cries of captives in pain," said Rita calmly. Saof imagined that the hate-hearted goddess probably sounded exactly like this woman. "Maybe I'll make you sing for her all night. What do you think of that?"

Tears and mucus covered the faces of the ice fleas as they writhed on the ground, babbling piteous pleas for mercy in their uncouth topolect in between screams of pain. The gigantic dogs surrounded the captives and snarled, howling like horrid wolves.

Doubt evaporated from Saof's heart. It was obvious why this

young woman had been promoted to wolf-thane at such a tender age, and why she was confident enough to journey across the scrublands, guarding the captives all by herself.

He dropped to one knee before Rita. "Votan! I had heard stories that shamans favored by the Pillar of Ice can defeat their foes from a distance. But I never thought I would witness such a demonstration of power with my own eyes!"

Rita glanced back at the naro and smiled. "Oh, this is nothing. You should have seen how I overcame the wily Dara barbarians on Spotted Heifer."

Saof had indeed heard some of the exploits of Tovo's expedition to the far north. The naros and culeks spoke in hushed tones of facing thousands of dastardly Agon and Dara rebels allied with the contemptible ice fleas. The evil rebels deployed terrifying and unnatural weapons: calling upon ice giants, burning monsters, and even abominations made of excrement. Outnumbered, Tovo's brave warriors had beaten back the rebel assault for days, sustained by nothing except the indomitable Lyucu spirit. In the end, Thane Tovo had to summon the aid of Nalyufin herself to defeat the rebels, and that was why so many of the naros and culeks came back missing toes, fingers, and even limbs, like Tovo himself, who showed off his sole remaining arm as a sign of proven courage and favor of the grim goddess.

Saof had thought these stories exaggerations, but having witnessed Rita's power, he was now convinced of their truth. If Tovo had to call on powerful shamans like Rita to deal pain and death to the rebels from a distance, then he could readily imagine how incredibly stirring and tragic that final battle on Spotted Heifer must have been.

"All the Lyucu will remember your courage in song and story," said Saof to Rita, awed by the great thane. "Do you wish to be shown the slaughter grounds for the tribute cattle?"

"I want to go to the garinafin pens first," said the woman imperiously.

"But, votan . . ." Saof was confused. "You don't have a garinafin."

"Thank you for that astute observation," said Rita sarcastically.

Saof's face reddened. "Nalyufin's Pasture is much too cold for gari-nafins and long-haired cattle. My tribe must rely on ice flea slaves and their herds of moss-antlered deer, as well as what they can haul out of the sea in summer. Since the pékyu is asking for contributions for the expedition to chastise Dara, I brought these slaves and dogs as my offering. On the way here, I also raided an Agon settlement to swell my tribute with some cattle."

"The pékyu will surely appreciate all you've brought," said Saof, looking at her with admiration.

"But I'm not walking all the way home after the launch of the fleet! I shall borrow a garinafin from the pékyu to ride to visit my aunt, who's roaming next to Aluro's Basin. She can then escort me back to my grazing grounds and return the garinafin later. I must go to the pens now to pick out a good mount before the celebrations begin, when it will be too chaotic."

Saof nodded. "You'll want to head that way then, beyond the tents flying the tusked tiger tail banners." He pointed to make sure the thane understood. Then he got off his knee, grabbed one of the signaling spears strapped to his back—a foxtail tied to a whale-rib shaft—and presented it to her with both hands. "This will let the other patrols know that you've already been checked, so you won't lose any more time."

"Thank you," said the wolf-thane. She slapped the neck of her mount, and the long-haired bull shook his head from side to side impatiently as he began to stride forward. The dogs growled and urged the cows and captives, stumbling quickly to their feet, to keep up.

Saof stood next to his garinafin and bowed his head respectfully as the procession passed.

Cudyu stared at the mountain of ice floating a few miles out from the shore. Contrasted against its bulk, even the silhouettes of the city-ships anchored nearby seemed puny.

"Praise be to Nalyufin," intoned Cudyu piously. He held out his right hand, the thumb and index finger extended so that they resembled the crescent moon.

Using his hand as a gauge, he squinted to measure the iceberg.

It wasn't quite as large as the one that had arrived at Taten near the beginning of his reign, but it was certainly large enough to be considered an auspicious gift from the goddess of the north.

The two naros imitated their pékyu and made the same gesture in honor of the goddess. Their expressions, however, revealed more trepidation than gratitude.

Cudyu noticed and frowned. "What's the matter with you?"

"Err . . ." "Um . . ." The naros looked at each other, neither willing to speak.

"The gift isn't merely a good sign for our expedition; it's practical!" said Cudyu, thinking that perhaps the naros needed more convincing. "We can break off pieces from this mountain of ice and load the chunks onto the city-ships to preserve fresh provisions. Our warriors will now have more than just smoked meat and pemmican on their long journey to Dara!"

The two naros bobbed their heads to show agreement and gritted their teeth, rather unconvincing caricatures of joy.

"Out with it!" demanded an impatient Tovo, who had joined the pékyu. "You!" He pointed to one of the naros. "Speak up! What's bothering you?"

The naro ducked his head timidly. "Votan, I think it's best that we show you."

Uncertain just what had so spooked his warriors, Cudyu nodded.

The two naros led Cudyu and Tovo to one of the round coracles. They boarded, and the naros began to row.

Cudyu admired the iceberg as they approached. In the bright spring sun it seemed to glow blue, like a piece of the sky that had fallen into the sea. He imagined himself ensconced within one of the city-ships as the fleet sailed toward Dara. He was determined to enjoy not only fresh meat but also ice-chilled kyoffir infused with tolyusa essence. He saw no need to skimp on luxuries. After all, wasn't he the greatest pékyu who had ever ruled the scrublands? Wasn't he the equal of all the heroes of old? Hadn't the gods delivered him this gift to show that he would rule over two lands, Ukyu and Dara, much as this iceberg bridged the sky and the sea?

The naros oared the coracle to one side of the iceberg, where the ice sloped down into the sea like a long, white tongue. The tip of the tongue served as a natural berth. The naros docked carefully, tying the coracle to a bone stake driven into the ice.

"Votan, we need to climb to the top."

"Why?" asked Cudyu. Even though the ice slope was gentle, he could tell a hike up this slippery mountain was going to be arduous.

"There is a . . . wonder atop that we wish to show you. The crews loading the city-ships discovered it this morning, and none of us know what to do."

Cudyu looked to Tovo, but the garinafin-thane shook his head in incomprehension. "This is the first I've heard of it."

No matter how Cudyu yelled and threatened, the naros refused to describe this "wonder," insisting that the pékyu had to see for himself.

"All right," said Cudyu, resigned. "Let's go."

An hour later, they reached the top of the iceberg, a flat, circular expanse about two hundred paces across. Winded from the long climb, Cudyu walked slowly along the lip of the platform to catch his breath. The height gave him a pleasant view of the city-ship fleet, like a pod of sleeping whales. Behind the city-ships, massive bone-and-skin coracle-rafts bobbed on the gentle waves like small islands. These rafts, towed by the city-ships, added greatly to the carrying capacity of the fleet and were the means by which Cudyu would bring many more warriors and garinafins on this expedition than his father and sister. He could already imagine the garinafins taking off from these floating islands to deal death and terror to the natives of Dara—and perhaps even other garinafin riders. . . .

As though reading his mind, Tovo spoke. "Once in Dara, votan, you'll have a far stronger garinafin force than your sister."

Cudyu smiled. The Dara captives had given him detailed accounts of the exploits of Tenryo and Tanvanaki in Dara. Publicly, he had mourned his father and rallied the thanes with vows of vengeance for the beloved pékyu-votan, but privately, he had celebrated his good fortune. Tanvanaki, by the captives' accounts, had assumed the title of Pékyu of the Lyucu in Dara after Tenryo's death, but considering how few garinafins and warriors were under her command, she wasn't going to put up much of a fight when he demanded her surrender.

"Strength isn't measured only by the number of garinafins under one's command," he chided. "Real strength comes from warriors' hearts."

"Wherever you toss your signaling spear, there goes my axe," said Tovo. "My heart beats in sync with yours. In the hearts of all your warriors, there is only room for you."

Cudyu nodded. Tovo had echoed Tenryo's old rule that wherever he threw his war axe, Langiaboto, his warriors were to attack without question. This was how he had murdered his father, Toluroru, and become the pékyu of the scrublands. He imagined himself tossing his garinafin-antler signaling spear at Tanvanaki, and a grim look of triumph came onto his face.

"Votan, please come and see!"

Annoyed by the interruption, he turned around. The two naros were some distance away, at the center of the flat top of the iceberg. They were looking down at their feet, their poses and expressions anxious. Both were muttering as they moved their hands through the air, fingers trembling as though trying to ward off evil spirits.

Cudyu and Tovo strode over and looked down, and instantly Cudyu felt his blood turn to ice.

Through the crystalline surface of the floe, he could see six long and narrow rectangular black boxes. He knew what they were: Dara burial boxes for the dead.

Passing by other garinafin sentries unchallenged, Wolf-Thane Rita and her captives approached the massive garinafin pens of Taten. The stench of garinafin dung and the noise of too many animals packed into too tight a space was overwhelming.

Rita patted the head of the bull, causing it to stop.

"Is everything all right?" asked the old captive.

"I just need a moment . . . ," said Rita. "What happened back there . . ."

"It was just an act," said the old captive, grinning. "You weren't hurting us."

"I know." Rita's voice was low. "Still, it seemed like you were in pain, and it was all I could do not to cry myself. It's a clever plan."

The old man beamed with pride. "I'm impressed at how well you imitate the speech of Tovo's people. We got by largely on your accent."

Rita gave a wan smile. "I heard enough of the wounded speak before they died. . . . I wish we could stop all the killing."

The old man said nothing; theirs wasn't a mission of peace.

"Enough of this," said Rita determinedly. "Time to get to work."

The garinafin pens were the spine of the Lyucu military. They formed the foundation of Tenryo's empire, and the bulwark of Cudyu's.

The exact construction of the garinafin corral had changed over time, but the basic principle remained the same: It was, above all, a prison.

A long fence made of ribs and thigh bones marked the perimeter, but the flimsy barrier was not the primary means of confining the powerful beasts. Psychological chains proved far more effective.

While Pékyu Nobo Aragoz of the Agon was the first to exploit the familial bonds of garinafins to enslave them, it was Pékyu Tenryo Roatan who elevated the process into an art. Following the basic pattern established by Tenryo, the area within the bone fence was divided into two regions. The first, not much bigger than the Great Tent itself, was reserved for the personal mounts of Cudyu and the most powerful garinafin-thanes. These beasts were bred from sires and dams selected for exceptional speed, strength, endurance, ferocity, and other qualities. From the time they were hatchlings, each had a team of slave grooms who pampered them for every need. Cudyu and the other powerful thanes even took time to build personal bonds with the elite war beasts, a vestige of the traditional scrubland approach.

The other region, far larger, stabled the vast bulk of the garinafins of the Lyucu army. Upon reaching sexual maturity, garinafins who showed promise in war were mated, and the hatchlings were allowed to stay with their families until about two years old. This wasn't a concession to tender sentiment, however, but a period deliberately calculated to cement the bonds between the juveniles and their parents.

At that point, the young garinafins were taken away from the parents, and as the adult garinafins watched, the weakest calf in each brood was slaughtered. The resulting meat was considered a delicacy, and the immature skulls and bones were fashioned into helmets, signaling spears, and other items of utility. Garinafin calf-skin, being more supple and easier to work with than adult skin, was prized as the raw material for blankets and garments for the great thanes.

The slaughter wasn't needed to cull the herd, but to emphasize to the parents the absolute nature of their servitude and the consequences of disobedience.

From that point on, the juveniles were imprisoned in underground warrens apart from their parents, who underwent constant training for war. The adults had to learn to accept any pilot and to obey a series of simple commands that followed standardized formats. A disobedient garinafin was brought back to the corral, where his or her children were brought out to be tortured in front of them. The young garinafins were struck with teeth-studded clubs on the tender skin between their legs, burned with gash cactus juice, starved, or had their heads held under water as they flailed until they ceased moving. Sometimes young garinafins died during the torture sessions.

Most adult garinafins needed no more than one such reminder to stop rebelling and became extremely docile. The submission continued even when the garinafins were away at war, or even when all their children had been slaughtered—habits of mind, instilled in moments of vulnerability, shackled beasts as well as men. Occasionally, a few garinafins, overstressed by the relentless cruelty, went mad and stopped responding to all orders, heedless of the consequences. They and their children were put to death, the lineages deemed untrainable.

In dark, cramped subterranean cells, the young garinafins were staked to the walls and grew up in chains. Upon reaching maturity, and before they had hatchlings of their own, their parents would be tortured in front of them. The role reversal was the start of their own journey into submission.

Old garinafins no longer fit for war were usually slaughtered for meat, leather, and bones, though a few were kept around as beasts of burden. The killing and butchering typically occurred within hearing and sight of their children and grandchildren.

The diabolical cycles continued generation after generation, links in an unbreakable chain of bondage.

Rita demanded to be shown the garinafins not on regular patrol duty so that she could pick one to borrow.

"What would votan like to do with her slaves?" asked the head groom. Once, he had been a good garinafin pilot and was charged with training new pilots for Tenryo. But he had incurred Cudyu's wrath when the new pékyu overheard him enthusiastically praising Tanvanaki's skills to a group of student pilots. Cudyu had accused him of disloyalty ("Excessive admiration of the past is no more than a coward's way of denigrating the current leadership")—a charge against which there could be no defense—and then demoted him to this post. There was little hope that he would ever be elevated beyond the rank of naro-votan.

"I brought them to do whatever needs to be done," said Rita carelessly. Then her eyes lit up. "Ah, I know! They are good with animals, since they trained these dogs that my tribe has found very useful in the far north. They'd be perfect for you here in the stables!"

The head groom said nothing. There was no use in pointing out that dogs were nothing like garinafins. A lowly naro out of the pékyu's favor didn't object to the opinions—even worthless ones—of a young thane clearly esteemed by both Tovo and Cudyu (especially with that accent, a sign of her noble birth and powerful clan affiliation).

"Why don't you take them and teach them what they need to know so they can be useful?" said Rita. It really wasn't a request.

The head groom summoned a few grooms to take the ice flea captives away. Rita untied the rope binding their necks together.

"Kitos, from now on, obey him as if he were me," Rita said to the old man at the head of the line.

The old ice flea nodded submissively.

The head groom could see how the ice fleas visibly relaxed as they were taken away from the wolf-thane, who had probably been terrorizing them nonstop since their capture. Even he felt a sense of revulsion, wondering just how horribly disfigured the woman was under that helmet-mask that she refused to take off. But if the ice fleas thought they would get some reprieve here, they were sorely mistaken. The garinafin pens were among the worst places a slave could be assigned to.

Well, no matter. Their fate wasn't his problem. The head groom had enough troubles of his own.

He accompanied the young wolf-thane on a tour through the regular pens. The garinafins dozed in the afternoon sun, chewing the thornbush branches listlessly. The foul odor of garinafin dung hung in the air, along with clouds of buzzing slisli flies. Some of the beasts looked rather malnourished, and they showed little interest as the wolf-thane and the head groom walked past.

"Why are conditions here so poor?" asked Rita, frowning. "Don't you *care*? Even cattle-guarding garinafins of the gutless Agon look much healthier."

The head groom sighed inwardly. Thanes from outside Taten invariably made such comments when visiting the pens. But what did they know of his difficulties? Cudyu and the senior thanes lavished attention on their personal mounts, but they cared little for the rank-and-file war beasts. The head groom was never given enough resources, and in any event, obedience from the garinafins was valued far more than their vigor. He had no choice but to focus most of his attention on discipline. To be sure, he thought this posed a long-term danger to the Lyucu, but he knew better than to voice his real opinions to Cudyu or his close advisers.

"The pékyu is pleased with the state of the garinafin force," he said, his voice devoid of any emotion. "The victory in Kiri Valley was complete."

Rita was dismissive. "That was due entirely to surprise and advantage in numbers. Do you really think one of these poor specimens can win against an Agon garinafin in one-to-one combat?"

The head groom lowered his head, keeping his face expression-less.

Rita shook her head and walked on. After a moment, the head groom followed.

Teams of Agon slaves labored around the pens, replenishing the feeding troughs and taking away the dung on stretchers. They moved with little urgency or interest, only quickening their pace when Lyucu overseers walked by, whips at the ready. Many of the garinafins would soon be driven onto the city-ships for the grand invasion fleet to Dara.

The head groom hoped the wolf-thane would pick a mount quickly; he was running out of patience for her unsought opinions. But Rita was a picky pilot and kept on shaking her head at every choice the head groom offered. Always, she managed to find some fault: "The snout is too large. . . . I don't like the shape of the antlers. . . . Why are his eyes so red? Do you know *anything* about garinafins?"

Of course the eyes look bloodshot, thought the seething head groom. The pékyu had been pushing the garinafins hard for weeks with-out upping their feed. The beasts were overworked and not getting enough sleep. They probably felt as exhausted as the Agon slaves who took care of them.

Halfway around the corral, they came upon a dozing old garina-fin bull. Two grooms were giving him a bath with a moss brush and a skin-tub of dirty water.

The head groom stopped. "Why is this *thing* still here?" he asked.

The two grooms turned around. "He's doing better today," the woman said, bowing submissively. The man next to her nodded vig-orously.

Surprisingly, the woman spoke in a Lyucu topolect, though both were dressed in the same dirty, ragged furs as the rest of the slave grooms.

"I don't *care* if he's doing better," said the head groom. "His foot is broken." He pointed at a clawed foot, gingerly curled under the beast. "I told you to send him to the slaughter grounds."

"But he'll heal if he's properly taken care of," said the man. "Radia and I have nursed many injured garinafins back to health."

After the escape of the pékyus-taasa and the other children of Kiri Valley, Toof and Radia had lost Cudyu's trust. Although he couldn't prove that they had schemed the escape, the enraged pékyu had stripped them of their ranks and made them slaves in Taten's garina-fin pens.

"That isn't necessary," said the head groom. "There are plenty of healthy garinafins to take his place without wasting feed and time. Send him to the slaughter grounds now!"

"Please," begged Toof. "He's a veteran war mount, and he has plenty of wisdom to teach the others."

"Not this again," said the head groom with a groan. "You two sometimes act as if these beasts are more than mere brutes. I've already indulged you too far by letting you two keep that obstinate Agon garinafin alive—the traitor pretender's useless mount. And now you're saving cripples! Ridiculous! The only brain that matters on a garinafin belongs to the pilot, and the only thing these dumb animals comprehend is the value of obedience!"

"But they *can* understand us, really! Radia and I can tell that the heart of a warrior still beats within him—"

"ENOUGH! I WILL NOT DEBATE—"

Rita broke in. "This one. I want this one."

The garinafin lifted his head to look in her direction. Scarred and battered, he had clearly been much abused. His nostrils flared as he sniffed the air, as though trying to place a familiar scent.

The head groom looked at Rita in disbelief. "But votan, he's injured! The useless thing can't even stand up properly. Besides, you should know that he used to be—"

"My mind is made up," said the wolf-thane. "I'll be staying in Taten until the departure of the fleet, so there's plenty of time for him to heal."

Toof and Radia looked at her gratefully.

The head groom threw up his hands. "As you wish, votan."

"You may return to your duties," said Rita, her tone brooking no disagreement. "I wish to get acquainted with my new mount."

The head groom nodded, turned around, and left, glad to finally be rid of the insufferably arrogant thane.

The wolf-thane extended a hand and gently caressed the nose of the bull garinafin.

"I'm sorry, Ga-al, my friend," she muttered, "you've really suffered. Is Alkir here too?"

Toof and Radia stared at her, amazed.

"How . . . how do you . . ."

The wolf-thane shushed them as she drew closer. Glancing around to be sure that no one else in the corral was paying attention, she lifted her skull helmet just enough to reveal her face.

"Pékyu Théra sends you her greetings."

Toof and Radia gaped. They were looking at someone they never thought they'd see again: Thoryo.

CHAPTER FOURTEEN

BURIAL BOXES

TATEN: THE FIFTH MONTH IN THE TENTH YEAR
AFTER THE DEPARTURE OF PRINCESS THÉRA FROM
DARA FOR UKYU-GONDÉ (WHEN THE LYUCU MUST
LAUNCH THEIR NEW INVASION FLEET TO DARA).

It took garinafin fire and teams of axe-wielding culeks chipping away nonstop for most of three days to excavate the burial boxes from the ice.

They now lay on the shore in a neat row.

Four of the boxes were smaller, about six feet in length and three in width. The other two were bigger, about ten feet in length and five in width. All were surprisingly heavy for their size. The boxes were fashioned from black seacow hide wrapped around some kind of rigid internal frame and then tied in place with loops of sinew. After baking in the sun for most of the morning, clouds of slisli flies swarmed around them, attracted by the faint odor of decay and rot.

Up close, the Lyucu could see that the boxes were decorated in a strange manner. Bits of shell embedded in the top of each box formed the vague outline of a human figure. Polished turtle shells, etched with face portraits, looked up from where the heads would be, like masks.

"This is a barbaric custom from Dara," whispered Cudyu to Tovo. "They seal the dead within and then bury them, a manifestation of their everlasting shame in their evil ways."

Years ago, he and his sister had, in fact, supervised the construction of a simulated Dara graveyard as part of the deception of Luan

Zya. Though there were no bodies in the counterfeit graves, he understood the principle behind coffins.

Tovo stared at the black boxes with a mixture of fascination and horror. The idea of being placed inside such a thing, to be deprived forever of the gaze of Cudyufin and the gaze of Nalyufin, to be held back from pédiato savaga through the strength of horrid wolves, tusked tigers, eagles, and vultures—the idea was too horrible to endure.

Cudyu walked among the body boxes, examining the shell-portraits thoughtfully. The crowd of thanes and warriors pressed forward, drawn by curiosity, but stopped some paces away, fearful of contamination.

The pékyu stopped by the pair of large boxes and waved away the swarming flies. Two faces, a man and a woman, lay under his gaze serenely, as though asleep. A Dara captive from Kiri Valley was summoned. She confirmed what Cudyu already knew: The portraits depicted the faces of Takval Aragoz, the self-proclaimed Pékyu of the Agon, and Princess Théra Garu of Dara.

Cudyu returned to Tovo's side.

"What do you think happened?" he asked. "I thought you said you saw them all fall to their deaths in a crevasse in Nalyufin's Pasture? But some must have survived to construct these."

Tovo cursed Takval and Théra silently. Even in death the pair continued to embarrass him. "My initial report . . . simplified things somewhat."

Cudyu lifted his eyebrows. "Perhaps it's time to re-remember?"

Tovo swallowed. "Before reaching Spotted Heifer, Takval and I both fell . . . into a hole in the thin ice. We fought for hours in the bone-numbing water, and I wounded him grievously before his warriors managed to rescue him. They were able to slip away due to their advantage in numbers. But I knew he was not long for the world. We had to tend to the wounded and regroup before resuming the chase."

He squared his shoulders, deliberately presenting the stump of his left arm to the pékyu, reminding him of his sacrifices. Cudyu's face showed no reaction.

"And then," Tovo continued, "after fasting for a few days to pray for Nalyufin's aid, we set out for Spotted Heifer again. It must have been during that time when Takval and Théra died, and the remaining rebels desecrated their bodies in this manner. By the time my warriors and I caught up to the fugitives and watched them tumble into the crevasse, they must have been . . ." His eyes brightened, as though coming to a sudden realization. "They must have been leaderless! That explains why they panicked as soon as they saw us and scampered, heedless of the death trap they were heading into."

Cudyu looked at him skeptically.

Tovo plunged on. Once a lie had been told, there was no choice but to shore it up with more lies. "Clearly, the Agon pretender had converted to the false religion of his barbarian bride. That's why his followers would resort to such barbaric funeral rites. The other four burial boxes must contain the bodies of their most loyal attendants, willing to give up the chance to ascend on cloud-garinafins in order to accompany the lost pair into eternal perdition."

Cudyu pondered Tovo's account. *A pékyu must be able to tell true stories apart from false ones*, his father had always said. He expected Tovo's story to be embellished—such was the nature of all battle reports—but did it contain a kernel of truth?

He closed his eyes and imagined the scene: the rebels' mad scramble across the ice-covered sea; the desperate seeking of shelter in the snowy realm; the realization that they had not found a refuge but only an extended death; the despair that settled in as their lord expired in front of their eyes.

Yes, it seemed plausible. But could he be *sure*? Though Tovo had followed him all these years, did he know the color of the man's heart?

"We must open the boxes," said Cudyu.

"Why?" asked Tovo. The thought of opening these abominations made the hairs on his back stand up straight. "If they wished to desecrate their own bodies, then let them."

"For proof," said Cudyu, his eyes glowing hungrily.

Tovo understood. The pékyu was a suspicious man, and Tovo's changing stories had stoked his doubt. Cudyu would never be able to leave Ukyu on his expedition without having held Takval's skull in his own hands.

Cudyu strode up to the box with Takval's portrait and was just about to slam his war axe into it when he paused. The boxes were surprisingly heavy, he remembered.

What if they contain more than just corpses?

He had made it this far, in part, because he didn't take unnecessary risks.

He looked over at Tovo, who shuddered in the pékyu's unwavering gaze.

Cudyu smiled. "I wouldn't dream of depriving you of the honor of personally exposing the proof of your hard-won battle in the north."

Tovo gritted his teeth. He dared not reveal that the battle at the ice fort had instilled in him a dread of barbaric magic, and the moans and groans of his warriors, dying from pus-filled wounds caused by boiling water charged with Dara witchcraft, haunted his dreams. What kind of evil spirits lurked within these burial boxes? Could the Agon pékyu and the Dara princess have booby-trapped them to deal more death?

"The rebels are dead, Tovo," said Cudyu, a hard edge coming into his voice. "The dead have no power over the living, especially not barbarians who do not fear or trust the gods. You *did* see them die, yes? Or perhaps you think another re-remembering is needed?"

Tovo knew there was no way out. He nodded in resignation. "Thank you for giving me this honor."

Cudyu led the crowd of onlookers until they were several hundred paces away, well out of the range of any Dara booby traps. As an extra measure of caution, shamans were summoned to slice their palms and drip blood barriers to ward off evil spirits that might emerge—just in case Tovo's tales of Dara witchcraft turned out to be true. Only then did Cudyu shout at Tovo, alone among the grim body boxes, "Open them up!"

Tovo shuffled to the nearest small black box. It seemed safer to start with one of these instead of the two bigger boxes.

"Try not to damage the contents," advised Cudyu from a distance. "An intact trophy is better than a mangled one."

Tovo ignored the bleating pékyu to concentrate on his task. Wielding a tusk knife in his trembling hand, he sliced through the loops of sinew around the box and let them fall away. He got down on his hand and knees to examine the container more closely and noticed a seam in the side, going all the way around. Apparently, the box had been made in two pieces, top and bottom, which were then bonded together with glue.

The portrait of a man in repose in the top of the box looked so serene that Tovo was almost sorry to have to disturb him.

He pressed the tip of the knife against the seam. There was some resistance; whoever made the box had done their work well. Taking a deep breath and gripping the handle tightly with his one hand, he began to cut. The blade glided smoothly—like skinning a cow or sheep. He tried to keep the pressure steady so that the knife wouldn't slice too deeply and damage what was inside.

Tovo followed the seam and cut all the way around the box until the top was separated from the bottom. In the warm spring sun, a faint odor of putrefaction filled the air. He put the knife away, took another deep breath to still his beating heart, and lifted the top.

Two garinafin grooms rolled around on the dirty earthen floor of the corral, locked in a fight. As they hurled insults at each other and pummeled each other's faces, slaves from other parts of the enclosure abandoned their tasks and ran over.

The addition of the ice fleas brought by the wolf-thane Rita had disrupted the existing hierarchy among the slave grooms, and tension had simmered over the last two days. Finally, Kitos, the leader of the ice fleas, and Allek, a burly Agon who all the other grooms deferred to, decided that a physical debate was the only way to rearrange or preserve the social order.

Lyucu overseers gathered as well. Instead of trying to break up the altercation and whipping the slaves back to work, they excitedly made wagers on which fighter would win. Life in the corral was monotonous, and the Lyucu assigned to supervise the slaves, typically long past their prime fighting years, appreciated the thrill of a good brawl. Besides, the Lyucu were keenly aware that strife among slave factions was invaluable in preventing rebellions: The best way to maintain control over the subjugated population was to encourage them to hate each other more than they hated the Lyucu.

Kitos got plenty of bets, but most of the money was on Allek. The Agon woman, a skilled wrestler and cagey boxer, had maimed and killed plenty of challengers to her authority before.

As the other slaves shouted encouragement, as fists landed with dull thuds and the occasional wet thunk of cracking cartilage, as teeth and spurts of blood fell on the dung-streaked floor . . . Toof and Radia, out of sight of the distracted Lyucu overseers, slipped into the underground cells in which young garinafins were imprisoned as hostages.

Toof approached one of the calves and showed her the bone knife in his hand—slaves were not allowed to possess weapons, though many secretly fashioned crude utensils from midden bones to cut the tough, leathery meat in their meals and save their teeth.

The young garinafin shrank back. But chained to the wall with thick bundles of sinew, there wasn't much room for the juvenile to move. She opened her jaws to screech in terror, thinking she was about to be tortured again to reinforce her parents' obedience.

"Shhh, shhh," whispered Toof. He kept the knife in the calf's view and held out his other hand, a few sliced tolyusa berries showing in the palm. "I'm not going to hurt you. Calm down. Just try to be quiet." His voice was low and reassuring.

The calf calmed and tentatively licked at Toof's hand. Toof cooed at her encouragingly, and the calf picked up the tolyusa berries with her nimble tongue and chewed contentedly. While she held still, Toof slowly moved the knife closer and began to slice away at the sinew ropes tethering her to the cell wall.

The young garinafin tensed briefly as she felt the vibrations of the knife against the ropes, but soon she relaxed under the combined effects of the tolyusa and Toof's soothing voice. She didn't know what was going on, but she did sense that Toof could be trusted not to hurt her. Many of the grooms, abused by the Lyucu overseers, took out their humiliation and pain on the defenseless baby garinafins, and sometimes the calves were deprived of feed or stewed in their own filth for days. Worse, some of the crueler grooms enjoyed forcing the calves to fight one another for sport, making bets on who would break an antler or snap a tooth. The injured juvenile garinafins would then be sent to the slaughter grounds, as a garinafin who lost her dagger-like

canine teeth also lost the ability to breathe fire. Toof and Radia, however, never treated the calves with anything but tenderness and care.

The bout between Kitos and Allek lasted far longer than anyone
anticipated. Each time one of them seemed to gain the upper hand, the
other somehow found a fresh reserve of strength. The contest was so
exciting that no one noticed when Toof and Radia returned to the crowd
of onlookers. As the wrestling pair rolled close to the side of the ring
where the two Lyucu stood, Radia let out a low whistle of admiration.

Abruptly, Kitos stopped. "I yield," he said, panting, and spat
out a mouthful of blood with two teeth. Then he wrapped his arms
protectively about his head as the winded Allek landed a few more
blows before falling off him, exhausted.

The ice fleas groaned, despondent, while the Agon jeered. The
Lyucu overseers settled the bets among themselves before scattering
the crowd with loud snaps of their whips.

Toof and Radia approached the head groom and suggested that
since Allek had won, the Agon slaves should be given a day off while
the ice fleas and Kitos were punished with extra work. The head groom
approved, happy to stoke the hatred between the slave factions further.

Thus, while the experienced Agon grooms napped or played
games in the shade of the enclosure fence, the captives that Thane
Rita had brought labored under the supervision of Toof and Radia.
Even Kitos, his face swollen and bruised, wasn't spared. The slaves
from the far north carried away garinafin dung, refilled feeding
troughs, cleaned and mended the saddle cables, greased the hinges
on the doors to the underground cells. . . .

Toof and Radia walked among the adult garinafins, whispering
into their ears. A few, including Ga-al and Alkir, seemed to perk up,
and a few others looked at the two Lyucu strangely. But most of the
garinafins didn't react, staring dully into the dust swirling in the sun.

Tovo squeezed his eyes shut as he stumbled back from the opened
burial box, certain that he was about to be assaulted by vengeful spirits.

Nothing happened.

He forced one eye open. The sun continued to shine brightly as
before, and the buzzing of slisli flies was as loud as ever.

Cautiously, Tovo shuffled back to the body box and peeked over the edge.

The stench of putrefaction wasn't nearly as bad as he had feared. The corpse's decomposition must have been slowed down considerably by the ice in which it had been embedded. The dead Agon warrior inside was wrapped in a seacow hide as though ready for pédiato savaga. The face that poked out of the hide appeared pale and swollen, but otherwise unmarred.

Tovo stood up and waved at Cudyu.

The throng of onlookers followed the pékyu back to the burial boxes. Cudyu and Tovo lifted out the sheathed corpse and unwrapped the seacow hide.

The removal of the body also revealed the source of the box's unexpected weight: layers of heavy stones lining the bottom. Close examination disclosed their purpose. The stones had been heated before being placed inside, and that was how the burial box had been able to sink into the ice. Some of the stones were stained from a brown liquid that pooled on the bottom.

Cudyu turned his attention back to the well-preserved corpse. There was some bloating, especially in the belly area, but there were no writhing maggots, no missing chunks of flesh torn away by vultures and carrion feeders. A few unhealed wounds over the chest and shoulders were likely the cause of death. The face was serene and relaxed, as though the warrior were simply asleep. Considering the man had died months ago, it was a most unnatural sight.

Wordlessly, Cudyu strode up to another small black box, slid his dagger through the sealing glue, and kicked off the top.

The corpse inside was a woman of Dara, perhaps a scholar. Her body was as well preserved as the body of the Agon man, save for the severe frostbite on her hands and feet.

"It is indeed as you reported," said Cudyu to Tovo, who sighed inwardly with relief.

It was obvious now to the pékyu what had happened. Trapped on the frozen island, some rebels had succumbed to their injuries and the cold. Lacking earth in which to excavate Dara-style graves, the survivors had modified their barbaric custom by burying body boxes inside ice. After Tovo chased the remnants of the band into the crevasse, the icebound graves would have remained hidden forever. But with the coming of the spring, the chunk of ice housing the bodies had calved, much as new garinafin and long-haired cattle calves are born in the spring, and drifted with the sea currents into Péa's Sea.

The corpses, Cudyu realized, not the iceberg, was the real gift from Nalyufin.

Tovo strode toward the bigger boxes, bone knife in hand.

"No!" Cudyu cried out. "Don't open them. Better yet, keep them buried in ice to prevent spoilage."

He laughed at Tovo's look of surprise.

"Summon all the thanes and shamans in Taten for a grand assembly tomorrow. We'll pray to the gods and offer up the best sacrificial feast of all in advance of our expedition."

Understanding dawned in Tovo's eyes. He fell to one knee before Cudyu. "Votan, you're wise beyond measure. Even the corpses of our enemies cannot escape being exploited to our advantage."

Cudyu smiled as he imagined the scene. Under the expectant gaze of the gathered multitudes, he would solemnly unseal the boxes to reveal the lifelike bodies of Takval and Théra to their awe and admiration. He would act as though they were still alive and bash in their skulls from the back in the full gaze of the Eye of Cudyufin, completing the humiliation of the Agon and the Dara. And then . . .

It would be the best way to boost the morale of his warriors while crushing the spirit of the Agon and Dara captives.

He would daub Takval's and Théra's blood on the bow-eyes of the city-ships to endow them with sight for the passage through the Wall of Storms. He would polish their femurs to shore up the Great Tent. He would feast on meat presented on trenchers fashioned from their pelvises. Having consumed the cunning of the rebel leaders and incorporated their strength into his own body, he would then begin the final conquest of the islands on the other side of the turbulent ocean.

Throughout the night, as the rest of the grooms slept, the ice fleas, who had been assigned the night watch, labored in the garinafin corral. The pékyu had called for a grand assembly the next day, and the head groom guessed the loading of the city-ships would begin soon after. He wanted his overseers and trusted slaves well rested.

Radia and Toof volunteered to supervise the ice fleas, and the head groom was happy to accept, failing to notice the excited glances passing between the two Lyucu grooms and Kitos.

A glorious, sunny morning in Taten.

In front of the Great Tent, thanes and shamans assembled in neat ranks. The garinafin-thanes stood up front, varicolored antler signaling spears sticking out of backpacks like the quills of the scrubland porcupine; after them came the tiger-thanes, bundles of polished semaphore tusks in quivers strapped to their shoulders; behind them the wolf-thanes were arrayed, with wolf- and foxtails flapping over their heads; and beyond them still were the naros-votan and naros in dense concentric semi-rings.

At the very center of this martial theater, just before the entrance to the Great Tent, an earthen platform had been erected overnight, like a raised stage. Venerated shamans from every Lyucu tribe sat around this stage, muttering prayers to the gods they individually spoke for. The platform itself was empty save for two large burial boxes, like altars ready to receive sacrifices. The boxes were so heavy that it had taken eight culeks to carry each onto the platform during the night, and only the gods knew how many stones were packed at the bottom of each.

Overhead, about a dozen garinafins patrolled in wide circles, led by Thane Tovo himself. They would ensure that no saboteur from afar could disturb this sacred occasion.

The mournful song of the Péa pipes washed over the assembly like a rising tide, and the chatter among the warriors died down. As the powerful music inundated every body, all hearts seemed to beat to the same rhythm. Spontaneously, the Lyucu host burst into song.

> *Ten dyudyu cupéruna?*
> *Lyucu kyo!*
> *Ten dyudyu cupéruna?*
> *Ukyu kyo!*

Lurona ryo lurotan saten ra pécu,
Saten ra pécu!
Pégoz nara kita kita.

The combined voices reached a crescendo as signaling spears were thrust high into the air and hot tears spilled from every eye.

It wasn't obvious that the gods always favored the Lyucu people or the land of Ukyu. The oldest thanes recalled the suffering of the tribes under the cruel Agon Pékyu Nobo Aragoz; slightly younger thanes thought of Admiral Krita and his reign of terror. Yet, hadn't Pékyu Tenryo, who was now riding the cloud-garinafins beyond the World's Edge, led them to overcome their enemies and drive them to lamentation? Hadn't Tenryo's children, Tanvanaki, as brilliant and mercurial as a flash of lightning connecting sky and earth, and Pékyu Cudyu, as steady and strong as the rumbling thunder quaking land and roiling ocean, led them to ever-higher peaks of supreme victory and dominance over their foes by dint of strength and cunning?

Indeed, there is nothing we cannot do!

Abruptly, the Péa pipes fell silent, and the singing voices faded away. But the very air remained charged, like the scrublands right before a thunderstorm.

Cudyu emerged from the Great Tent and climbed onto the earthen platform. Slowly, he stepped up to the two large burial boxes, his hands lifted to the heavens. Every pair of eyes was on him.

"Votan-ru-taasa, votan-sa-taasa, today we give thanks to the gods for their aid as we deal the final blow to the evil alliance between the Agon and Dara. There is no better way to begin a new venture than by ending an old war, no better vellum to take on a new voice painting than the skin ripped from the bodies of our ancient foes, no better way to invigorate our courage by consuming the blood and bones of defeated rivals.

"Takval Aragoz, the last of the Agon pékyus, and Théra, the sly barbarian witch, plotted against us but were foiled by the indomitable Lyucu spirit. To achieve his impossible dream, he was willing to worship her false idols, to fall under the sway of her foreign ways, to betray the grazing grounds of his ancestors for her promised mirages—but what could you expect of a sniveling Agon, a descendent of the treacherous Afir?"

The Lyucu host laughed and jeered.

Cudyu gestured for them to be quiet. "Cowardice was in his nature, just as malevolence was in hers. Yet, even a poisonous snake's flesh may provide nourishment to the wise, and a runt's meat can replenish a hero's strength. We can seize the weapons and treasures of the decadent Dara and enslave the bodies and descendants of the cowardly Agon, making us stronger in the process.

"The gods have delivered a gift to us, the unspoiled bodies of our enemies. Let us make use of them. I have consulted the gods through the shamans, and they tell me that we can, by reviving an ancient ritual, ensure that the false hope of rebellion never enter the hearts of the Agon again and pledge the lives of the Dara to the eternal glory of the gods. From this day on, the Agon will be a people without a name, forever our thralls in bondage. From this day on, the Dara will be doomed, as bereft of hope as prey caught in the silent roar of the tusked tiger!"

The warriors watched him, holding their breath, hanging on his every word.

"Let's break open these abominations and reveal the bodies deprived of pédiato savaga; let's complete the journey the gods intended for their souls; let's chew the still-pliant flesh and smash the bones to suck out the still-juicy marrow. Let's eat our enemies to make their strength ours, as it was done in the days of the oldest pékyus. What say you, votan-ru-taasa and votan-sa-taasa?"

A full-throated roar of approval; a cacophonous racket of signaling spears and weapons slamming together.

Smiling, Cudyu picked up two large bone daggers from the ground, backed away until he was standing between the two large burial boxes, and, almost casually, thrust the blades out to either side. The tips sank into the hide noiselessly.

The noise from the crowd grew louder.

Satisfied, Cudyu spread his legs to plant himself securely, changed his grip on the dagger handles, and began to pull, expecting to slice through the soft seal between the top and bottom halves of the burial boxes as easily as he had a day earlier.

Nothing happened.

The clamor from the crowd grew hesitant, no longer as loud as before.

Cudyu checked—his aim had been true, and both daggers had plunged into the seams in the boxes. He grunted and pulled harder. There was a surprising amount of resistance.

The noise died down. The Lyucu host craned their necks, uncertain if something had gone wrong.

Cudyu would have liked to slow down, to investigate the cause, but with so many eyes watching, he couldn't appear indecisive. He gritted his teeth and pulled harder.

The blades jerked through the sealing material, leaving gashes of a few inches. A putrid odor, far worse than the smell from the smaller burial boxes, spilled forth.

Is this Takval's last breath? Is he bringing upon me contagion and corruption?

Cudyu suppressed a shudder, held his breath, and pulled even harder. It was possible that the bodies of Takval and Théra had spoiled beyond his plans for them, but at this point, there was no choice but to get the boxes open as quickly as possible.

A faint rumbling rolled across the scrublands from afar, perhaps the start of a thunderstorm.

"The gods of Ukyu are watching us open our gift, ready to celebrate with us!" shouted Cudyu. He had to act like everything was going as planned, to control the situation. The assembly was expecting him to present the trophies inside the boxes, and he couldn't afford the loss of prestige should he show any sign of hesitation.

The tip of one of the daggers caught on something hard in the box on the right. Takval's box. A bone? He bit down and pulled with every ounce of strength.

Whatever was resisting his blade gave way. He felt something inside the burial box snap.

Nothing stands in the way of the Lyucu people, he thought triumphantly. *Nothing stands in the way of Pékyu Cudyu!*

The burial box disappeared in a brilliant flash of light and engulfed him, and he was dead before he even heard the explosion.

CHAPTER FIFTEEN

SPIRIT PORTRAIT

SPOTTED HEIFER: FIVE MONTHS EARLIER.

Adyulek explained to Théra what must be done.

Théra shuddered. The old shaman had confirmed Takval's instructions. "Why? Why can't I just take his garinafin gallbladder stone pendant?"

"The pendant is just an empty symbol, like one of your word-scars; it has no breath, no power, no mystery," Adyulek said. "Only a shaman or a warrior may speak true thinking-breath, may know the deepest mysteries."

"I fear and trust the gods. I'm responsible for the deaths of thousands." Théra swallowed, choking back a sob. "Isn't that enough?"

"Though you fear and trust the gods, you do not know the pain and terror of speaking for them. Though you've led armies and ridden garinafins, you've never spilled blood or taken a life by your own hand. It isn't enough." The old shaman placed a hand on her arm compassionately.

Théra closed her eyes. She understood the wisdom behind the restrictions. It was the same in Dara as in Gondé. *Teeth on the board.* One who would wield power must understand the consequences of that power not through abstract philosophy, but with bloodied hands and bruised nerves stripped of the last shred of innocence.

But the act Adyulek demanded of her was revolting. She felt its wrongness with every fiber of her being. There was nothing in the words of the Ano sages to support it.

"This is what the gods want," whispered Takval, lying next to her.

"How can we possibly know what the gods want?" asked Théra, seizing upon doubt like a drowning woman clutching at a drifting straw.

"How do we know that the sun will rise again after a long night or that spring will come after a hard winter?"

"That's different."

"It isn't." Takval struggled to get air into his lungs. At length, he rasped, "No matter how many miles you've flown, you must still will yourself to trust that the next wingbeat will keep you aloft. No matter how much you experience and plan and calculate, you must still leap into the unknown."

Théra squeezed her eyes shut and held her hands against her ears, blocking out the oil flame struggling to illuminate the murky future and the desperate voices urging her to accept the unacceptable.

The translucent, shadow-plagued walls of the ice cave faded away; the bone-piercing air lifted from her numbed skin; the acrid odor of fish oil smoke vanished from her nostrils.

She was surrounded by air as dense as water, as warm as mother's milk. The vast scrubland plain on which she stood was covered by a vaster empyrean dome. But the numinous plane didn't bring her peace or understanding, didn't reify the comforting metaphor of the Flow, didn't suffuse her with the irresistible shiver of acceptance. Though gods and heroes danced in the immense storms all around her, she felt utterly alone.

I've already lost so much! she screamed voicelessly.

She had lost the guidance of her parents; departed from the embrace of her lover; been torn from her children, whose fate she knew not; left behind the world of her birth, islands as sweet as lotus-paste moonbread, as familiar as the voices of her brothers and sister, as comforting as the curves of Ano logograms indelibly carved into the topography of her mind. And now she was being asked to lose the man she loved, her confidant, her bedrock, the father of her children, the mirror of her soul—no, not just to *lose* him, but to commit an unforgivable act.

What do you want? she shouted silently at the gods.

There was no answer. The great storms danced on, following

patterns and steps only they knew. Perhaps the universe was know-able, but the will of the gods was not.

The wisdom of the Ano sages was useless here, as was the experi-ence of her life's journey so far. The boundless scrublands of Gondé were not the Islands of Dara, no more than voice paintings and spirit portraits were the ancient scrolls of Ano sages. The faceless, distant deities of the Agon were not the gods of her home, who liked to take on human form and interfere in mortal affairs. She would never again see the family of her birth, kiss her first love, teach her children the beauty of that land on the other side of the ocean. The people who surrounded her and demanded of her the impossible were not her people; they did not understand the world through her stories.

She had never missed home so much. The pain of longing bent her like a blade of long-ear grass in the storm, and she wept, bereft, alone, silenced. She would remain here forever, as though at the bottom of a water bubble in the grass sea, abandoning and aban-doned by the mortal world.

A hand, the skin cool and rough, grabbed her right hand. It was the hand of a woman, the speaker for the Every-Mother. There was strength and compassion in the grip.

Come back to us, you who have ridden the garinafin, you who have heard that which cannot be heard, you who became a child of Afir.

A hand, hot and trembling, grabbed her left hand. It was the hand of a man, the dying Pékyu of the Agon. There was hope and passion in the grip, though weakened like the last rays of the winter sun.

Come back to us, my beloved, my breath.

Lightning flashed across the murky landscape, freezing the danc-ing storms in their indecipherable poses. And as she gazed at the indistinct shapes, they seemed to suggest, in their abstract outlines, memory after memory:

Ice-foam flowers tumbling along the beach, crystalline dandelion seeds singing of the beauty of life even as they broke apart . . .

Souliyan telling her that she had the heart of an Agon and entrust-ing her son to her . . .

Volyu, sly and despicable Volyu, recounting for them the tale of

Cudyu seeing the iceberg in Péa's Sea, explained as a sign from the gods for him to assume the title of pékyu . . .

Kunilu-*tika* and Jian-*tika* looking proud next to their arucuro tocua creation, a blend of the bones of scrubland warriors and pieces of clay Ano logograms . . .

Sitting next to Thoryo and admiring the beauty of a valley in the World's Edge Mountains, a valley deeper and bigger than any in Dara . . .

The thrill of flying on the back of a garinafin, of gaining the trust of a partner who was a mountain of muscle and sinew, a living storm, a breathing cloud, of feeling the rumbling voice that could not be heard . . .

Çami and Alkir walking toward her in the sunlight, the glistening raindrops on their heads more dazzling than priceless jewels . . .

Hearing and watching stories of Kikisavo and Afir being told by the shamans at the Winter Festival, while the tune of the Péa pipes still rang in her ears, while the contrasting flavors of the ten meats still lingered at the tip of her tongue . . .

Standing in the moonlight, facing Takval.

The heart isn't a fixed pool like a water bubble in the grass sea; it grows and swells like the ocean. Your mother has become my mother, and your people my people.

Sometimes we have to demand that others make sacrifices and accept them. To secure the freedom of the many.

Without realizing it, she had stopped crying. She had lost so much that her heart had emptied out, and only in that emptiness did she discover how much she had gained.

She did love this land, its people, its stories, its gods, its traditions, its living bone creations. She wanted to see the scrublands free, not just the enslaved Agon, but also the ice tribes of Nalyufin's Pasture, the exiles in the oases of Lurodia Tanta, and even the Lyucu themselves, in bondage to their own twisted stories about who they were.

She had come to this land hoping to bring about a revolution, but how could she do that if she didn't first effect a revolution in her own mind? Only when she had lost herself in the stories of the scrublands, when she had abandoned herself to the mores and customs of her adopted people, when she had opened her heart to the austere beauty of another creation myth—only then would she truly find herself.

The lotus seed had found her turbulent pond; the dandelion seed had found her rocky perch.

Goodbye, Dara.

She squeezed the hands holding hers and opened her eyes. The mortal plane rushed back into her awareness in such a flood that for a moment her mind was without thinking-breath.

"I can do it," she gasped. After a pause, she added, "And I have a plan. Beloved, you will keep your promise after all."

As Takval and Adyulek listened, she explained.

Takval's face glowed as bright as the fish-oil flame. He smiled at her, and she smiled back. There was no need to speak.

Adyulek bowed. "You've always been a noble princess of Dara, and I see in you now a worthy pékyu of the Agon people."

Adyulek explained that they would need assistants to take Takval's spirit portrait. Though her connection to the Every-Mother was as strong as ever, Adyulek was no longer a young woman like Sataari, with steady hands and sharp eyes. Though Théra trusted and feared the gods, she spoke Agon with an accent, without the purity demanded by the gods watching over such a holy ceremony.

None of the Agon warriors had the necessary skills: They were not shamans practiced in the art of sacred arucuro tocua.

"There is no one with more mechanical expertise than Çami Phithadapu," said Théra. "And Thoryo speaks the languages of the scrublands with a perfection none can match."

Though it was not the custom to allow outsiders to witness this most sacred of the mysteries, Adyulek assented. "The gods accept human frailty. There is precedent for those with speech impediments or palsy to be assisted by trusted companions who were neither warriors nor shamans."

As Théra, Thoryo, and Çami sat next to Takval in the cramped ice cave, Adyulek took out her implements and instructed Çami on what to do.

First, Çami cut a sheet of garinafin stomach lining, as light and thin as paper, into slender strips. The strips were then sewn together, end to end, into a long tape.

Next, she mixed bone charcoal powder into a pot of boiled tallow, creating a thick, dark paste. This she brushed onto one side of the long garinafin stomach lining tape, where it hardened into a smoky black-gray coating. The long tape was then rolled up into a thick scroll.

Adyulek directed Çami to put together a bone frame that reminded Théra of an upside-down cart with two axles and no wheels. The tape scroll was mounted onto one axle and stretched across to the other, to which was attached an articulated arm that could be turned like a hand crank.

The next item Adyulek produced confused both Théra and Thoryo, but Çami recognized it right away.

"That's a garinafin ear!"

Indeed, the organ was bigger than Takval's torso. In addition to the cartilaginous auricle, the attached ear canal and assorted organs at the other end had been retained as well.

Çami, who had some experience with taxidermy and the anatomy of hearing, marveled at the skill with which this specimen had been prepared and preserved. The organ remained supple and flexible, nearly in lifelike condition. There was a faint sheen, likely from grease, over the fleshy surfaces, and even the eardrum itself remained translucent. The chain of bones behind the eardrum trembled gently in the chilled air of the cave.

"How did you do this?" she couldn't help but ask. "What concoction? What treatment—"

Adyulek shook her head and gestured for her to be quiet. This wasn't the time.

To the last bone in the delicate chain behind the eardrum, Adyulek attached a slender but strong bone needle, made from the tip of a garinafin's wing. With Çami's help, she draped the garinafin ear over Takval until the auricle hung just above Takval's face, as though he were whispering into it. The rest of the auricular apparatus was then strapped to the bone frame until the thin bone stylus at the other end just touched the surface of the suspended tape.

As she chanted and prayed for the Every-Mother's assistance,

Adyulek ground up some dried tolyusa berries and mixed the powder, with other dried herbs, into a pungent broth. Théra watched Adyulek work, her mind in turmoil. The tolyusa berries were known in Dara as zomi berries—this seemed significant to her. Perhaps one of her loves could help the other in this weighty moment. The gods did like to arrange coincidences like that.

She helped Takval sit up and drink the broth.

"What does it do?" whispered Thoryo.

"Those who are about to mount the cloud-garinafins sometimes need a last burst of strength," said Adyulek, her tone calm.

Çami and Thoryo turned away to wipe their eyes. But Théra kept her gaze locked with Takval's. Every second remaining between them was precious.

Théra helped Takval lie down again beneath the garinafin ear.

"I'm ready," he said, his voice more steady and strong than it had been in days.

Adyulek nodded at Çami, who began to crank the arm attached to the empty axle. The old shaman chanted quietly, clapping her hands to keep time. Çami made sure that she was cranking the axle to her beat.

As Théra held Takval's hands, the Pékyu of the Agon spoke into the garinafin ear.

Her vision blurred. She wanted this moment to last forever. All the memories she and Takval had built together tumbled into her mind: their courtship on *Dissolver of Sorrows*; the tears and laughter they shared in Kiri Valley as they brought their sons into the world and watched them grow; Cudyu's assault and the long march to escape; the deadly flight across the ice. . . .

Théra was so distraught that only snippets of his words came to her ears.

". . . *rejuvenate the Agon people* . . . *all those who call themselves children of Afir* . . . *Princess Théra of Dara, now known as the Pékyu of the Agon people* . . . *my last wish* . . ."

Çami continued to crank the arm to the beat of Adyulek's chants. She watched as the garinafin stomach lining scroll unwound from one axle onto the other. As the tape spooled past the thin bone stylus, the needle vibrated and traced out a stark white line against the smoky, black background.

Wonder filled Çami's heart. The Agon had indeed reserved their most amazing arucuro tocua creations for the divine mysteries. As Takval spoke into the garinafin ear, Çami saw, his voice caused the eardrum at the end of the canal to vibrate. The vibrations were then passed on through the chain of linked bones, which amplified the tremors in the membrane, causing the bone needle at the end to move up and down. The rise and fall in Takval's voice was replicated by the stylus against the scroll, leaving behind an undulating trail.

The arucuro tocua is making his voice visible, Çami realized. *The living bones are re-remembering thinking-breath.*

In Dara, it was said that while a wild goose flies over a pond, leaving behind a voice in the wind, a man passes through this world, leaving behind a name.

With bone and skin, Takval is painting a portrait of his speech, the truest essence of his spirit.

She cranked the scroll and watched the portrait take shape against the murky future.

Takval stopped speaking.

Adyulek stopped chanting.

Çami stopped cranking.

The spirit portrait was complete.

The glow was fading from Takval's face. The tolyusa had given him a last burst of strength, but now the tide was ebbing. He was fading away before their eyes.

"Now," he rasped. "Now."

Théra wouldn't let go of his hands. Her body was racked by sobs.

"My breath, you must do it now. Take my breath into your lungs; take my blood into your veins; let my fading life add to your strength."

Adyulek began to speak in a solemn, faraway voice.

"Takval Aragoz, son of Souliyan Aragoz, daughter of Nobo Aragoz, you have served the Agon people as pékyu faithfully. The time has come for you to mount the cloud-garinafin."

Takval nodded. "I accept the judgment of the Every-Mother."

"Who do you designate as the next pékyu, to speak and fight as you have done?"

"My wife, Théra."

Adyulek turned to Théra. "Who comes with fear and trust of the gods in her heart, love of the people in her actions, pride in our land in her spirit? Who comes to claim the duties of the next pékyu?"

With a tear-choked voice that could barely be understood, Théra spoke as she had been taught. "I am Théra Garu, daughter of Kuni Garu, son of Féso Garu. I came to the Agon people as a princess of Dara; now I wish to serve them as the pékyu."

Thoryo, fulfilling her role in the ceremony, repeated Théra's words in pure Agon so that the gods would be without doubt.

"Without breath, there is no spirit. Without blood, there is no strength. Without death, there is no life," said Adyulek. "You have no lineage traceable back to Afir; you are no shaman nor warrior; you must rectify these faults to be the pékyu."

There was only one way for Théra to do so by the custom of the scrublands, only one way for her to gain the trust of the people she would lead.

The old shaman pressed a bone dagger into Théra's hands; Théra shook uncontrollably, like a leaf in autumn.

"Let's demand sacrifices of each other," said Takval, barely a whisper. "Let's accept each other's sacrifices. My breath, lead my people, which is also your people, to victory."

"Théra," intoned Adyulek, "will you become the pékyu?"

Still shaking, Théra dragged the blade of the dagger through her left palm, drawing blood. The pain of the wound seemed to infuse her with a new awareness, and her body stilled.

Everyone watched her, holding their breath.

With a sudden, anguished scream, Théra raised the dagger and plunged it deep into Takval's chest, right at the center of the charcoal circle on his naked chest that had been drawn to show the location of his heart.

Even knowing what was supposed to happen, Thoryo nearly fainted at the sight. Çami caught her and held her up.

Takval's body buckled like a bow being strung, but he did not cry out. Théra's right hand held the dagger in place as blood spurted from the wound. She brought up her left hand, placed it gently on his chest, letting the hot blood cover her hand, letting his blood commingle with her own.

A pékyu must know what it feels like to bleed as well as to kill.

They looked at each other, and there was so much longing and despair and hope and pain that the others could not bear to watch.

Slowly, Théra leaned down and locked her lips with his in a deep kiss, taking his breath into her lungs as his heart stopped beating.

Takval's eyelids drooped and closed; his body relaxed.

With infinite gentleness, Théra let go of Takval and sat up.

"I am Théra Garu Aragoz, wife of Takval Aragoz, son of Souliyan Aragoz. I claim kinship to Afir by blood and breath. I have taken a life and incorporated its strength into mine. I now serve the Agon people as pékyu."

With great difficulty, Thoryo repeated Théra's words in perfect Agon.

Adyulek stood up and exited the ice cave.

Théra fell down and wrapped her arms around the cooling body of Takval, crying inconsolably. Thoryo and Çami waited, knowing this was not the time to offer comfort.

Outside, Adyulek was making some kind of announcement. Her voice was too faint to be heard.

But then the cave walls shook as the assembled rebels, Agon, Dara, and the ice tribes of the north, shouted in unison: "The pékyu is dead! Long live Pékyu Théra Garu Aragoz!"

As spring thawed Ukyu-Gondé, the rebels in Nalyufin's Pasture also emerged from their winter preparations.

Several rebels had died during the difficult and bleak winter. Their bodies, along with Takval's, had been preserved in ice. These were now encased in Dara-style coffins fashioned from local materials. The Agon abhorred the foreign custom, but they accepted Pékyu Théra's explanation that the corpses of their comrades would become the implements of their enemy's destruction, and to fight on beyond death was a fate all warriors craved.

Two coffins, larger than the others, were decorated with the death masks of Théra and Takval.

In actuality, the coffin with Théra's mask contained no corpse at all. Instead, one found inside a waterproof barrel of seacow hide, reinforced with bone hoops, packed tightly with all the remaining firework powder in Théra's possession, along with sharp-edged gravel, stones suitable for slingshots, and even some rusty metal shards. The idea was to launch a hailstorm of deadly missiles when the bomb finally exploded.

To trigger the bomb, Théra settled on a design based on the fire starter of the Adüans, which she and Zomi had studied back in Dara when they were searching for the secret of garinafin fire breathing. The device had become popular among the Agon in Kiri Valley, and she thought it would be easy to make such a thing.

But where would they find a baby garinafin canine tooth on Spotted Heifer?

The problem stumped Théra and her advisers until Gozofin, skilled with arucuro tocua, came to the rescue. He built a piston out of a sled dog's femur and rib—a complementary set of hollow tube and straight rod that, when slammed home, generated sufficient heat in the compressed air to start a fire. A sprinkling of firework powder in the femur provided kindling, and then the rib and femur were installed respectively in the upper and lower halves of the coffin, carefully aligned to allow one to slide smoothly into the other. Keeping the plug and the cylinder separated with a wad of dried ice-shark flesh, Gozofin then wrapped strong bundles of sinew around the two and twisted the sinew to add tension. As soon as the wad of ice shark flesh, tough and resilient, was removed, the tensed sinews would snap the rib into the femur, creating the spark to detonate the bomb.

As Théra watched Gozofin demonstrate the arucuro tocua fire starter, her mind returned to the first time she had seen the living bones in action, that long-ago day in Kiri Valley when Kunilu-*tika* and Jian-*tika*'s bone creature filled her with wonder and love for her new homeland. Tears streamed from her eyes as she tried in vain to assure Gozofin that he had done nothing wrong.

The other large coffin held Takval's body.

All the decoys, including the four smaller coffins, were weighed down with stones so that they would not appear out of place compared to the heft of the bomb-laden coffin. Knowing that Cudyu was cautious and would suspect booby traps, Théra planned on the smaller coffins being opened first, perhaps by someone Cudyu thought of as disposable. That was why they had to be filled with real corpses to assure Cudyu that there was no danger. But since Cudyu was also vain and obsessed with the crafting of his own mythology, Théra gambled that the Lyucu pékyu would personally open the larger coffins, thereby bringing about his own demise.

Since she couldn't be sure Cudyu would leave her own coffin to the last, it was vital for Takval's body to be packed into the other decoy coffin, as a final layer of deception. But in addition to such practical considerations, Théra also found the gesture poetically appropriate. It felt right to have Takval present at the scene of Cudyu's defeat.

You promised you would bring me to Taten in the spring, she thought, her heart aching. *You've always kept your word.*

A group of ice tribe warriors then carried the coffins by dogsled to the edge of Nalyufin's Pasture, where icebergs calved every spring. There, they tested crevasses and cracks until they found a mountain of ice about to fall into the sea. Using heated stones, they melted deep shafts into the ice so that the coffins could be entombed.

Their hard work had only begun. Once the iceberg calved into the sea, herding it in the right direction was not something a few warriors could accomplish. But by now, Kitos's stand against the Lyucu the previous winter had become legendary, and hundreds of bone-and-skin canoes from dozens of ice tribes heeded Kitos's call for help. Without understanding the full plan, they disregarded their own needs during the busy spring hunting season and put their trust in Kitos. Like ice fleas swarming after a star-snout bear fearful of their tiny but irritating bites, the fleet of tiny boats nudged the iceberg slowly but inexorably into the ocean current heading south, toward Péa's Sea.

Meanwhile, Kitos and Thoryo departed with a small band of warriors toward Taten, and Théra led the remaining rebels to a spot northeast of Taten. Each group had their own separate parts to play in Théra's scheme.

CHAPTER SIXTEEN

"FEEL MY BREATH AGAINST YOU . . ."

TATEN: THE FIFTH MONTH IN THE TENTH YEAR
AFTER THE DEPARTURE OF PRINCESS THÉRA FROM
DARA FOR UKYU-GONDÉ (WHEN THE LYUCU MUST
LAUNCH THEIR NEW INVASION FLEET TO DARA).

By the time Tovo got his startled mount under control and surveyed the scene below, all was chaos.

The explosion had instantly killed Cudyu as well as a large number of shamans and garinafin-thanes closest to the platform. Projectiles from the death-dealing burial box shot deep into the rows of the lower-ranking thanes, and many had been blinded, maimed, or injured. The survivors rolled around on the ground, howling in agony.

As Lyucu commanders thronged in confusion, the leaderless naros and culeks scattered in terror, stampeding to get away in case another bomb was waiting for them.

Tovo knew that he had to restore order right away. The fear that had lain dormant in his heart all these months—that Takval's rebellion had not, in fact, been snuffed out in the frozen wastes of Nalyufin's Pasture—flared back to life. What if this was only the first blow in a general assault on Taten?

But with the terror also came the growing thrill at a possibility he had barely dared to imagine before.

He ordered his mount to fly lower.

The pékyu is dead. Who will be the next pékyu?

～

In the general confusion that followed the explosion, nobody noticed Thoryo, disguised as a masked wolf-thane, running away from the assembly.

Naros and culeks, drawn by the loud noise, emerged from tents all over Taten and converged on the scene of carnage. Thoryo found it as difficult to move through the thickening crowd as a fish swimming upriver.

In truth, she wanted to join them. Even knowing the cruelty of the Lyucu thanes, her instinct was to go and help, to tend to the wounded.

But she had a mission. She whistled loudly.

Dogs as large as horrid wolves emerged from the tent assigned to her. Barking, howling, snarling, they barreled through the crowd until they were next to her. She climbed onto the back of one, and the pack of dogs shoved Lyucu warriors aside as they forced a path out of Taten.

A group of Dara captives staggered from one of the tents. Their guards had deserted them in the general pandemonium. Emaciated, scarred, flinching at every noise, it was all they could do to stare, slack-jawed, at the bedlam all around.

"Get on! Get on!" Thoryo shouted. She whistled loudly; the dogs stopped and crouched.

The captives couldn't understand why a Lyucu thane with a pack of giant dogs was urging them to ride with her. Too many unexpected things were happening all at once. But she was speaking to them in the comforting syllables of Dara—that meant she could be trusted, didn't it?

Thoryo would have liked to find and save all the captives from Kiri Valley in Taten, but there was simply no time. As she whistled and trilled, the dogs carried her and the rescued captives toward the garinafin pens.

The grooms congregated at the gates of the garinafin compound dove out of the way as the pack of giant barking dogs charged inside.

The head groom, who had tumbled to the ground from the violent entrance, scrambled back to his feet. He blinked, uncomprehending, at the shivering Dara captives riding the dogs. Then he noticed the wolf-thane among them.

"What happened, votan? We heard a thunderous noise, but . . ."

Thoryo ignored him. She looked around frantically until she found Ga-al, dozing nearby in the corner of the enclosure reserved for cargo garinafins. "Yee-haw!" she shouted.

Instantly, Ga-al's eyes popped open. He stretched out his neck and stared intently into space.

On the far side of the corral, among the war mounts, Alkir also stretched out his neck and stared intently into space, as though in response to some silent call.

"Why have you brought these slaves here?" demanded the head groom. *"What is going on?"*

Paying him no heed, Thoryo coaxed the Dara captives off the dogs and then directed the dogs to form a protective ring around the huddle. After months of maltreatment, the captives would be of no use in the coming confrontation. She had to keep them safe.

Neither Ga-al nor Alkir had made any noise. But by now all the garinafins in the pens were snorting and lowing, looking agitatedly about as though sensing an impending attack.

"Get your beasts under control!" Thoryo spoke to the head groom imperiously. "Stop asking questions!"

The head groom had no idea why everything seemed to be going wrong. The Agon grooms shrank away from the agitated garinafins, unwilling to risk being trampled. The head groom had to dispatch the Lyucu overseers to calm the agitated garinafins, but they were having no success.

Unnoticed in the general confusion, Radia and Toof snuck away from the other grooms and made their way toward Alkir and Ga-al.

"Yee-haw!" Thoryo shouted again.

The two garinafins stretched out their necks in mute concentration.

Doors to the underground cells where the juvenile garinafins were shackled slammed open. Young garinafins stumbled out of their dark prison, blinking in the bright sun, keening and whimpering. Around their necks, some still wore the remnants of their sinew bonds, which Toof and Radia had sawn through the day before.

The adult garinafins, seeing their offspring suddenly free, called out in joy and distress. Soon garinafins were lumbering across the enclosure in every direction, calves rushing to their parents, sibling ambling to join sibling, none heeding the shouts of the grooms and the whips of the Lyucu overseers.

Seated on her dog, Thoryo clapped her hands together happily.

Finally, it dawned on the head groom that this was all somehow the wolf-thane's doing. He pointed at Thoryo and screamed, "A witch! She's a saboteur!"

The giant dogs snarled, enlarging their defensive ring around the huddled captives to include Thoryo. Kitos and the ice tribe warriors dashed over and joined them. Though they had no weapons other than dung shovels and carrying poles, they brandished these threateningly, daring the Lyucu to approach.

For the moment, the Lyucu overseers weren't too concerned with the out-of-control garinafins. Most of the beasts were busily licking and nuzzling their young, paying no attention to the human conflict in the middle of the compound. Even though they now had their offspring back, none of the garinafins seemed to be thinking of escape or turning on the Lyucu. Habits of obedience, instilled through a lifetime of terror and confinement, could not be shaken off so easily.

The head groom was confident that the unthinking brutes, directionless without their pilots, could always be muzzled and brought to heel later. It was far more important to take care of the traitorous wolf-thane witch first.

"Wedge formation. Charge!"

Armed with bone axes and clubs and garinafin-hide shields, the Lyucu overseers gathered into a dense, triangular battle-throng and charged at a steady pace toward Thoryo and the ice tribe warriors.

A sled dog broke from the ring and ran at the Lyucu. The warriors stopped and crouched in defensive poses. With a snarl, the dog leapt. A naro's head disappeared into its jaws.

Thoryo screamed.

But none of the Lyucu reacted to the demise of their comrade. Methodically, they converged on the dog, axes and clubs ready.

Incredibly, the warrior with her head inside the dog's mouth remained on her feet. Arms waving about blindly, she grabbed the front paws of the dog and wrestled the much larger creature, holding it in place.

The dog tried to clamp down, but found that it couldn't. The naro's head somehow refused to yield against the pressure. The dog then tried to spit out the half-swallowed naro, but the naro had become lodged in its throat. As the dog moaned and shuffled helplessly in place, its teeth and claws useless, the other Lyucu slammed their axes and clubs against its massive body in coordinated waves, killing it after a few rounds.

Only after the dog was dead did the other Lyucu pry open its jaws to release their comrade. The skull helmet, its antlers hardened with the woody ribs of the gash cactus, had protected her head from being crushed and also caught in the dog's throat.

The woman adjusted her helmet, ignored the blood oozing from wounds in her arms and shoulders, and rejoined the other Lyucu as though nothing had happened. Even Kitos was impressed by this display of discipline and martial prowess.

The Lyucu were seasoned warriors, and a few overgrown dogs and shovel-wielding ice fleas didn't frighten them. They had put down slave rebellions before and would do so again.

Ripping off her skull helmet to reveal her face, Thoryo sat up as tall as possible on her dog-mount and shouted at the Agon grooms cowering behind the charging Lyucu.

"In the name of Théra Garu Aragoz, wife of Takval Aragoz, son of Souliyan Aragoz, now serving the Agon people as pékyu, I command all the children of Afir to rise up and reclaim their freedom!"

The Agon slave grooms stared at her, dumbfounded. The Lyucu wolf-thane was speaking in the topolect of the Aragoz clan, an accent that, for the older grooms, brought back memories of the glory days of Pékyu Nobo Aragoz, an accent that they had not heard in many years. What was happening?

"Rise! Rise!" shouted Thoryo. "Seize the Lyucu overseers! Free the garinafins! This is your chance!"

The Lyucu had reached the defenses around Thoryo. Kitos and

his warriors fought back ferociously. But the Lyucu were too strong. Another sled dog was dispatched; two ice tribe warriors fell.

The Agon grooms looked at one another, hesitating. Thoryo's words awakened in them urges they had suppressed for years, rekindled a fighting spirit that they had thought long snuffed out in ashes. But what she was demanding of them was impossible. Like the garinafins, they had been subjected to too much terror and witnessed too many failures to believe that rebellion could ever succeed.

"Kill her!" screamed the head groom, swinging his club as he stood at the head of the Lyucu formation. "Kill them all!"

"Help us!" Thoryo's voice was tearful. "Please help us!"

Still, the Agon grooms didn't move. There were so many Lyucu, and the voice calling for them to rise was so alone.

A loud roar split the air. Alkir, with Radia on his back, charged through the clumps of reunited garinafin families, heading straight for the Lyucu overseers.

The head groom's eyes widened. He cursed himself for not dispatching the recalcitrant bull to the slaughter grounds earlier. This was the problem with keeping alive poorly trained garinafins captured from the Agon. "Heel!" he screamed. "Heel!"

Alkir sped up, his wings folded back.

"Scatter!" shouted the head groom. "Mount up! We need riders on garinafins!"

The Lyucu warriors around him broke from the formation and scattered, but the head groom remained where he was. He had once been a great garinafin pilot, in the retinue of the peerless Tanvanaki, and he was *not* going to back down from a feckless Agon mount, a defeated prisoner, ridden by a slave.

He raised his club threateningly, eyes locked with the beast's pupil-less orbs. "I'm going to enjoy skinning you while you're still alive; I'm going to make it last as long as possible—"

Alkir opened his jaws, snapped them shut, and opened them again. A long tongue of flame curled out and engulfed the head groom.

Everyone stopped and gaped at the screaming ball of flames rolling on the ground: the Agon grooms; the Lyucu overseers; the huddled Dara captives; Thoryo, Kitos, and his warriors; the garina-fin families; the sled dogs . . .

No one could recall the last time such an act had been committed. Lyucu war garinafins bred and raised in Taten *never* attacked their grooms.

Just like that, the mental chains around the Agon slaves and the penned garinafins shattered.

With full-throated roars, the Agon grooms picked up dung shov-els, long-handled cleaning brushes, bundles of thornbush, whatever was at hand, and charged after the Lyucu overseers. The Lyucu tried to defend themselves, but they were vastly outnumbered by their former drudges, who had suddenly rediscovered the warrior spirit. Even with their axes and clubs, the overseers were forced slowly back toward the smaller, separate pen in which the elite mounts of the senior thanes were kept.

"Why?" muttered Thoryo. People were killing and dying, and her words had been at least partly responsible. She had not thought it would feel so agonizing, so awful. Why must death herald every revolution? Why did freedom have to cost lives? Why was it necessary to kill to preserve the beauty of the world? She would never understand it.

"Go, go!" shouted Kitos at the rebels. "We have to free the gari-nafins before Lyucu reinforcements arrive!"

With buffeting wings, Ga-al and Alkir took off, Toof and Radia on their backs. The pair circled overhead, trumpeting and lowing. The two garinafins were the most unlikely of friends: old against young, cargo animal against war beast, common flier enslaved to the Lyucu army against personal mount bonded to the Pékyu of the Agon—yet, as a result of their intense experiences and shared adventures, they had developed a common understanding and affection rarely found even in blood families.

In the manner of garinafinkind, the pair sang of the years they had flown from one corner of Ukyu-Gondé to the other; of strange sights in the World's Edge Mountains; of distant valleys where the ancestors of the garinafins had once lived and where their wild descendants might live still; of grass seas too remote for the herds and flocks of the tribes and of salt flats where humans feared to tread; of dreams of freedom, dreams buried deep in the heart of every enslaved garinafin who dared to imagine a life without Man.

And the garinafins below responded.

Parents helped young calves, yet incapable of flight, onto their backs. Grandparents and older siblings lowed in encouragement as the frightened youngsters clung to their mothers and fathers. One by one, families of garinafins took off, heading for remote corners of the scrublands. Life in the wild would not be easy. They would have to defend themselves against ambushes of tusked tigers and watch out for packs of horrid wolves who might strike at night, while they were asleep. They would have to fend for themselves over the long winters, when feed was scarce and the storms brutal. But calves would no longer have to grow up in confinement, darkness, and terror, and parents would no longer have to live with guilt, heartache, and minds numb from scars inflicted by the enslavers.

They would be free.

The remaining Lyucu rallied to beat back the rebelling Agon grooms and retreated into the small pen for the elite garinafins. If they could mount these pedigree war beasts, they would be able to incinerate all the rebels in short order and still have a chance at recapturing most of the escaping garinafins.

But the Lyucu hadn't counted on the lingering influence of their pékyu, who was by now only a few bloody smears in the smoky crater in front of the Great Tent.

Suspicious of the loyalty of thanes who had risen to prominence during the many long and glorious campaigns of his father, Cudyu had tried to counteract their clout by elevating his own friends and followers into the highest ranks of Lyucu society. But as he chose them more for their willingness to do his bidding than their prowess in war, most of the new garinafin- and tiger-thanes were not battle-tested veterans. (This was, in fact, why the Battle of Kiri Valley had lasted as long as it did. Other than Tovo, Cudyu could find few commanders who he trusted *and* who could also fight well.)

Thus, many of Cudyu's senior thanes took to the air only rarely, preferring to spend their time on the ground in luxurious Taten year-round, leaving the affairs of their tribes to elders at home. Even thanes who did ride regularly flew mostly for sport or to terrorize the Agon tribes, but were lackadaisical in their military training.

It was said among the elders that pilot and mount paired for a long time grew to resemble each other. This was certainly true of the elite garinafins in Taten's corral. Pampered, rarely ridden, and almost never called on to fight, these descendants of the most cunning and ferocious sires and dams, thanes of garinafinkind, had become as indolent and unready as their in-name-only riders. Even those who were regularly exercised acquired from their noble pilots an obsession with human status—after all, in Cudyu's Taten, the pékyu's favor, more than success in war, determined one's place. A garinafin bonded to a garinafin-thane would allow a tiger-thane to ride her only reluctantly, even if her mistress lent her to the lower-ranking thane, and would outright spurn a mere wolf-thane, stinking of blood and battle-sweat. The senior thanes found this habit in their mounts endearing and in fact encouraged it as evidence of the beasts' noble lineages.

Alas, the highborn war mounts chose this moment of desperation and crisis, when the Lyucu overseers needed their aid the most, to proclaim their superior nature. Certainly the garinafins were familiar with the would-be riders clamoring at their feet, but the garinafins were also keenly aware that they were lowly naros, little better than the drudges they whipped and drove to cart feed and haul water. Why, they even stank of common garinafin dung, just like the grooms!

The garinafins snorted, and, stretching out their long, elegant necks to keep their noble heads as high in the air as possible, they turned their noses away disdainfully. No lowly, foul-smelling naro was going to step on *these* heads!

The rebelling Agon grooms, rather astounded by this most unexpected source of assistance, laughed and cheered. Having obtained better weapons from the barracks of the Lyucu overseers, they attacked again.

The Lyucu, sensing they were doomed, ran to the tails of the highborn garinafins. Mounting from the back rather than the front was both dangerous and inefficient, to be resorted to only in desperate straits or by the unskilled, but the Lyucu were beyond caring. They had to get onto the garinafins one way or another.

The garinafins whipped their tails about like long-haired cattle shaking off irksome slisli flies. Some of the Lyucu screamed as they were hurled through the air; others groaned as they lay on the ground, crushed by the weight of the oversized appendage. The Agon grooms rushed up and bashed in their skulls, some jokingly offering praise to the garinafins.

The highborn garinafins, disgusted by the bloody mess in their once-pristine pen, lowed for the Agon grooms to clean up. When the grooms, instead of rushing to take care of their charges, simply abandoned the bodies and returned to the larger enclosure, the arrogant creatures were utterly baffled. They continued to moan and low, hoping the grooms would stop this nonsense and return to their familiar patterns.

The rebels ignored the useless highborns. They had a more immediate concern: escape.

Thoryo tumbled off the back of her sled dog, too sickened by the carnage.

Kitos caught her. "You've done well," he said gently. For some reason, the ice tribe chief didn't find Thoryo's distaste for killing and fighting contemptible or cowardly. Rather, he sensed in Thoryo—though she neither feared nor trusted the gods—a connection to a realm beyond the mortal plane, as though she were a shaman of Toryoana of Still Hands, the god of the tanto-lyu-naro.

The corral—at least the part that used to hold the regular army garinafins—was now practically empty, as most of the garinafins had escaped. Only a few loners remained, watching the unfolding human rebellion with somber eyes.

Ga-al and Alkir landed, panting.

"The Lyucu are heading this way!" said Toof.

"Let's get out of here," said Kitos, cradling Thoryo.

"But the city-ships," said Radia. "We haven't gotten to the city-ships."

"Pékyu Théra said . . ." The world seemed to swim in Thoryo's eyes. She tried to push away the terror and revulsion that threatened to overwhelm her—more deaths, more killings, no end in sight. ". . . said that after Cudyu is dead, our top priority is to free the garinafins and get out."

"But we have a lot more people with us now than we planned for," said Kitos. "If we . . ." His voice trailed off.

Everyone knew what he meant. The ice tribe warriors and their dogs had been joined by the Agon grooms who had rebelled and the Dara captives Thoryo had saved. But with only Ga-al and Alkir to carry so many, their flight would be slow and ponderous, vulnerable to pursuit.

It was a repeat of the escape from Kiri Valley.

"We must *all* get out. . . ." Thoryo fainted in Kitos's arms.

"We need a distraction," said Radia slowly. They both knew that the "distraction" would likely never return alive.

Toof looked her in the eye. "You should go with Ga-al and bring everyone to safety. I'm the better pilot. I'll stay behind with Alkir."

"No," said Radia. "Ever since Thane Vara died—"

"We were *both* responsible for her death!" said Toof.

There was a moment of silence. Vara Ronalek, the Agon thane who had adopted Radia and Toof into her clan, had died during the struggle over the garinafin that carried the children of Kiri Valley. There had been no time for Toof and Radia to explain to her their plan.

"But we can't both throw our lives away," said Radia. "*Someone* has to get everyone out of here; *someone* has to help the pékyu find her children—only you and I know where we left them—"

"Maybe nobody has to die," said Kitos.

Toof and Radia looked at him, uncomprehending.

Kitos pointed to the regular army garinafins still in the corral, those who had chosen to stay instead of leaving with their families, about a dozen in number. They had lowered their heads to the ground, inviting the former Agon slaves to mount up.

"I think they want to fight with us."

With great effort, Tovo and the garinafin crews patrolling in the air at the moment of the explosion brought the panicked Lyucu host back to some semblance of order. Swooping and gliding over the leaderless naros and culeks swarming among the tents, he shouted encouragement and instruction, letting everyone know where they should go and how to secure Taten against the anticipated rebel assault.

It wasn't unlike herding long-haired cattle, he mused.

Now that he had seized the moment to establish his own authority, he was in a position to dictate to the shamans and surviving thanes which one of Cudyu's young pékyus-taasa should be the next pékyu—to rule with his guidance and approval, of course . . .

. . . or perhaps he would keep the white garinafin antler signaling spears, the symbol of the authority of the Pékyu of the Lyucu, for himself.

All in good time. All in good time.

"The garinafin corral is on fire, votan!" shouted the naros and culeks around him, pointing at the pillar of smoke rising in the distance.

Earlier, while Tovo was preoccupied with the frightened Lyucu crowd near the Great Tent, he had seen many garinafins taking off from the corral in the distance. The sight had cheered him at the time, as he assumed that alert crews were taking the initiative to fly off to reconnoiter for rebels. Only now did he realize that his earlier thinking made no sense. Most of the pilots had gathered at the Great Tent to watch Cudyu's ceremony, and only a small band of naros were stationed at the corral. Who could have piloted so many garinafins?

Cursing his own carelessness, he summoned his crew and flew to investigate. Other Lyucu followed on foot.

The scene at the corral was pure chaos. The main section, where hundreds of army garinafins had been penned, was deserted; the underground cells, where juvenile garinafins were confined to ensure the obedience of their parents, were empty; dead Lyucu overseers were scattered here and there; the fencing and barracks were on fire; the only garinafins left were the highborn mounts of the senior thanes (most of whom were dead after the explosion of the burial box), and these rampaged around the smaller pen reserved to them, moaning and keening in terror and confusion, demanding that *someone* come and take care of them.

While Tovo tried to put on a brave face as he dispatched troops to put out the fire and muzzle the complaining noble garinafins, his mind reeled. Hundreds of garinafins, the very fount of Lyucu strength over the scrublands, all gone!

And once news of this disaster got out, the Lyucu tribes would surely view it as *his* fault—he had, after all, assumed command in the immediate aftermath of Cudyu's death. And Agon tribes everywhere would surely rise up in rebellion, knowing that Taten no longer had the power to punish them. The scrublands would be consumed with war of all against all—

"Votan! Patrols have returned with witnesses!" Several naros, herders in the region around Taten, were brought in, all vying to speak with him.

Tovo listened to their reports impatiently. The herders outside the Lyucu capital reported similar sights in every direction: garinafin families carrying juveniles flying away from their former masters as fast as possible; no riders.

Tovo actually sighed with relief. Apparently the army garinafins had merely escaped to feral life and had not been stolen by the Agon. It was a small blessing, but he would certainly thank the gods. He would have to come up with a plan to recapture the escapees—

"The garinafins *I* saw weren't like that," offered the last herder.

"What?" demanded Tovo. "Speak more!"

"There were about six of them, led by an old bull with a crippled foot. The netting on their backs was crawling with Agon, Dara, and ice fleas. I saw as well some large dogs strapped in harnesses. They were flying slowly to keep pace with the old bull—"

"Which way were they heading?" Tovo asked.

"To the north, in the direction of the Boneyard."

Tovo's heart pounded and his mind raced. *Escaping Agon and ice fleas . . . they must be the saboteurs responsible for this mess. And they must be running toward the rebel base!*

"Summon all available garinafin crews! We must begin pursuit immediately. With that old bull slowing them down—"

"Votan, votan! Saboteurs are attacking the city-ships!" A naro ran into the corral at that moment and shouted, out of breath.

Tovo barely held back the urge to punch her in the face. Who cared about the city-ships now? This was obviously a distraction intended to secure the escape of the other saboteurs—perhaps with an important rebel leader among them. Cudyu's dream of conquering distant

Dara had gone up in smoke the moment the burial box exploded. At this point, the top priority was to capture the escaping saboteurs and find out where the rebel base was—

But more messengers ran into the corral, each with a report more dire than the last.

"Thane Tekal has left Taten, taking the baby Pékyu-taasa Yote with her!"

"Votan, three shamans are telling the culeks that the gods are angry with us, and we must reflect upon the errors of Pékyu Cudyu!"

"Thane Risli and Thane Cutakyo are fighting over Pékyu-taasa Rudia, each claiming to be her most trusted guardian. The pékyu-taasa is too young to speak, so the thanes are about to come to blows!"

. . .

"Silence!" Tovo roared.

He tried to slow his mind down, to think through the situation.

It's already happening. I'm not the only one dreaming of taking over now that Cudyu is gone. Even if I chase down the escaping saboteurs, what good will it do?

In the ensuing chaos, whoever secures the loyalty of the most thanes and warriors will emerge victorious. To support a large army, I need provisions . . .

. . . the city-ships are full of provisions and water, as well as garinafin eggs and weapons.

The more he thought about it, the more attractive the idea became. Even if the assault on the city-ships was merely a diversion, it was more to his advantage to seize control of the fleet at this moment.

Moreover, if the other restive Lyucu thanes refused to heed his authority, the fleet gave him another way out. Instead of staying behind to deal with the mess left by Cudyu, *he* could lead the invasion fleet to Dara.

He knew when the Wall of Storms would open again, and he knew that Tanvanaki had established a secure foothold among those islands. He would take the warriors he trusted and bring all remaining garinafins with him. While he wasn't so bold as to think that he could challenge Tanvanaki, Pékyu Tenryo's favorite daughter, surely Pékyu Vadyu would be appreciative of the reinforcements he would bring and perhaps elevate him to be the first among her garinafin-thanes. . . .

"Mount all available garinafins!" he barked. "We must keep alive the dream of Pékyu-votan Tenryo and Pékyu Cudyu. Lyucu kyo! Ukyu kyo!"

The plan was simple.

Radia, piloting Alkir, would lead the assault on the city-ships.

Five Agon grooms, skilled garinafin pilots in their former lives, volunteered to join her. Their mounts were also volunteers, garinafins who wanted to fight the Lyucu instead of escaping into the wilderness.

Toof, piloting Ga-al, would lead the other volunteer garinafins, laden with Agon rebels, freed Dara captives, Kitos and the ice tribe warriors, and the unconscious Thoryo, to fly back to Théra's new base in the Boneyard.

"Stay only long enough to create chaos," admonished Toof, before he left. He placed his lips against Radia's ear so that she could feel his breath against her cheek, the most intimate gesture they shared in all the years they had been together. "Your job isn't to fight them head-on. The garinafins under your command have no crew and won't be a match against the Lyucu, but they *can* get away because they are much lighter. Don't play the hero."

Radia nodded, blushing. It seemed like a sensible plan. After all, the city-ships were practically undefended, and the Lyucu had lost almost all their garinafins. What could go wrong?

The coracle-rafts towed by the city-ships were easy to destroy, but the city-ships proved much tougher than she anticipated. The thick hulls refused to burn easily, even with six garinafins breathing fire at the same time. Again and again, she had to direct the team of garinafins to sweep low over the ships, concentrating their flames to maximize the damage.

One ship was burning; another; yet one more. . . .

Next to the floating iceberg, the Lyucu city-ship fleet smoked and blazed brilliantly.

"Incoming!" shouted one of the Agon pilots on another garinafin.

Radia looked. At least a dozen garinafins were winging her way from the shore.

∽

Tovo's garinafins, after patrolling and herding panicked Lyucu all morning, were no longer in the best fighting shape. The garinafins returning from perimeter patrols farther out weren't faring much better. He needed fresh garinafins to take on the rebels attacking the city-ships.

He turned his attention to the highborn garinafins complaining in their special pen. As before, many of them refused to be mounted by Tovo's naros, thinking it beneath their dignity.

Enough of this.

Tovo tossed his signaling spear at the largest, most arrogant bull, Pékyu Cudyu's own personal mount. After only a moment of hesitation, Tovo's loyal riders, still mounted on the patrol garinafins, attacked. The haughty creature didn't even let out more than one terrified scream before he had been torn apart. The other garinafins in the pen watched in stunned silence. They never thought the day would come when they'd be treated no different from any common army beast.

When the naros approached the remaining highborn garinafins again, they lowered their heads to the ground submissively.

We've been too easy on our thralls, reflected Tovo. *Cudyu had become soft. If Pékyu Tenryo were still in charge, none of this would have happened. If I ever get the other thanes under control, I must never forget this lesson. If you are too kind to those with slavish natures, they'll rebel. Terror, more terror, is the only way to ensure obedience.*

But more delays ensued when the riders tried to outfit the garinafins. Most of the webbing and saddles in storage had been sabotaged—probably by the ice fleas over the last few days. The extensive planning behind the rebellion was stunning.

In the end, Tovo had no choice but to take off with the dozen garinafins he had already flown with for most of the day. They were running low on lift gas, but at least they were properly rigged for combat.

If he wanted to save the city-ships, he couldn't afford to wait.

By the time Tovo approached the city-ships with his garinafins from the east, most of the fleet was beyond saving. Several ships had already sunk after the garinafins dropped onto their fire-weakened frames, shattering hull planks and collapsing internal isolation bulkheads.

The skeletal crew on three of the city-ships, however, had raised anchor and cut the towing cables to the coracle-rafts. They were lumbering away from the rest of the doomed fleet, attempting to find refuge in the lee of the hulking floating iceberg.

The other rebel pilots guided their mounts to fly close to Alkir so that they could hold an aerial council with Radia.

"Should we retreat?" asked one of the pilots.

"We've probably done as much damage as we can," said a second pilot.

"No way to fight them," said a third. "I've got no slingshot scout or spearhand."

Radia considered. After so much fire-breathing, the six rebel garinafins were low on lift gas. If they fled immediately, there was a chance that they could get out of visual range before exhaustion forced them to land somewhere to hide and recover. Given that each rebel garinafin carried only a pilot, outflying the fully crewed pursuers shouldn't be a problem.

But those three city-ships . . .

She knew how important destroying the city-ships was to Théra, now the pékyu of the Agon. It was, in fact, the very foundation of the Agon-Dara alliance. Yet, Théra had specifically said that it was more important for them to free the garinafins and get out. Surely destroying the last three city-ships wasn't as essential as getting out with six more garinafins?

She gave the order for everyone to turn south. They would lead the Lyucu on a diversionary chase in the opposite direction from Théra's new base in the Boneyard to give Toof and the others more time to flee.

Alkir snorted to show that he understood, and led the others on a southeasterly course that would take them over Taten.

As they passed over the tent-city, Radia was suddenly seized by an impulse to see the results of Théra's booby trap for herself. She guided Alkir to fly lower. Below her, naros and culeks scattered, thinking that the hostile garinafins were about to launch an attack.

"Little do they know that we can't afford to waste any more fire breath on them," Radia muttered to herself.

A shallow crater lay in front of the Great Tent, and the bloody body pieces scattered about testified to the violence of the bomb. Radia was hoping to catch a glimpse of Cudyu's corpse, to reassure herself that the man responsible for all the deaths in Kiri Valley was truly gone. But the state of the crater made it clear that it was unlikely she would be able to tell which crimson streak belonged to Cudyu, and in any event, the overflight was too fast for her to make out details.

Alkir let out a plaintive cry and turned tightly around to pass over the Great Tent again.

"What are you doing?" Radia shouted into the bone trumpet placed against the base of Alkir's spine. She issued several orders for Alkir to resume course, but the great war beast, who had followed her commands thus far, ignored her as he continued circling over the crater.

Then, without warning, Alkir landed, the turbulence from his beating wings stirring up the bloodstained dust. He staggered forward a few steps, folded his wings back, and leaned down to nuzzle something on the ground.

It was part of a human head, the features too mutilated to be recognizable.

Radia didn't interfere. Alkir's plaintive moans meant that he had found the head of Takval Aragoz, Alkir's true pilot. She lifted both arms and crossed them at the wrists, a silent salute for a great pékyu struck down in his prime.

The other rebel garinafins landed around them.

Alkir twisted his serpentine neck and locked eyes with Radia. He snorted and turned to look in the direction of Péa's Sea, from which they had just escaped and over which their pursuers were fast approaching. The beast stared at Radia, the fire of vengeance burning in his pupil-less orbs.

"Are you sure?" asked Radia.

Alkir moaned with conviction.

A wave of complicated emotions washed over Radia: awe, ecstasy, anguish, acceptance—a combination that some might call the heroic spirit. She was unfamiliar with it, never having wanted to be a hero. But she welcomed it the way a shaman welcomed possession by the gods.

"Votan-ru-taasa, votan-sa-taasa," she shouted at the other pilots, "Pékyu Takval avenged himself against Cudyu even in death. Shall we emulate him?"

The other pilots sat still on their mounts, uncertain what she meant.

"The city-ships are the symbol of the power of Tenryo and Cudyu. If we can sink all of them, it will be more than a distraction; it'll be a blast from the Péa pipes to all the corners of the scrublands that the Lyucu are not invincible, that Taten can fall!"

Alkir raised his head high into the air and began to keen and moan. A few moments later, the other garinafins stamped their clawed feet against the ground and moaned in response.

The Agon riders shouted in unison, "Sink the city-ships! Sink the city-ships!"

Tears came into Radia's eyes. Though she believed that the garinafins were far more sentient than most humans credited, she could not understand their speech. She didn't know their stories. She could only imagine how they had watched, powerless to intervene, as parents and grandparents died to build the mound that was Tenryo's empire, their bones the arucuro tocua bearing up Tenryo's ambition. She could only imagine how they felt as their offspring were taken away and then abused or slaughtered in front of their eyes, their hearts shackled as they learned to be helpless.

The garinafins did not speak as humans did, but the fire of vengeance burned in their hearts as strong as in the hearts of women and men.

They took off, heading back the way they had come.

The fight over the city-ships was brief but fierce. While Tovo had the advantage of numbers and discipline, the rebels, led by Radia, rode garinafins who were fearless. While the two sides twisted, dove, climbed, bit, clawed, and shot tongues of flames at each other, the rebel fighters made sure to attack the city-ships at every opportunity.

Two of the last three city-ships caught on fire, burned, and sank, but Tovo's garinafins managed to isolate and surround the rebel garinafins, eliminating them one by one. Even in their death throes, the rebel garinafins thrashed and whipped their necks and tails about, refusing to yield. One of the rebel garinafins crashed into the iceberg, and her blazing body melted a hole in the ice as she and her pilot sank, both with eyes wide open, staring contemptuously at their enemies even as they were entombed in the ice.

Radia and Alkir were the only rebels left. She guided the garinafin down toward the last city-ship, heedless of the Lyucu garinafins right on their tail. As the garinafin dove, the few sailors on deck scattered, screaming, leaping headlong into the sea. Alkir opened his jaws, snapped them shut, and opened them again to bathe the ship in flames.

Nothing came out.

With great, laboring strokes of his wings, Alkir heaved himself back up into the air. His body trembled with exhaustion beneath Radia, and his breathing sounded like the notes of an ill-tuned set of Péa pipes.

Radia's heart sank. She knew that Alkir was almost out of lift gas, which also fueled the fire breath.

The Lyucu riders and their mounts howled with pleasure. They knew they had won. Without fire breath, Alkir and Radia were as good as dead.

Radia looked about: They were surrounded by Lyucu garinafins. There was no way out—and even if there were, Alkir lacked the lift to stay aloft much longer. Below them was the city-ship, a floating man-made island in the endless sea.

That's a familiar sight, she thought. A decade ago, she and Toof had ridden another garinafin above another lonely city-ship in the boundless sea. That was how they had come to meet Takval and Théra, the couple who would change their lives forever. Did life, like the great belt current, like to revisit the same place after circumnavigating the world?

Alkir's wings faltered and they dropped for a breathless second before he managed to halt their descent. One of the Lyucu garinafins left the circling pack and approached, ready to deal the coup de grâce.

The gods always demand sacrifices, reflected Radia. No favor was ever granted for free. Takval and Théra had given them a new home, a place where she and Toof could help raise garinafins the way the magnificent creatures deserved, a happiness that they could never have found as Lyucu. To repay Takval and Théra for making their vision come true, they had tried to secure their escape as well as saving their children. It would have all worked out, but for Vara Ronalek.

Everything seemed to slow down as Radia watched the approaching Lyucu garinafin.

She was hanging on for dear life from the webbing draped over the garinafin carrying the pékyus-taasa and the other children, the cold wind whipping by her face and the deadly winter ground hundreds of feet beneath her. Above, she could see Toof struggling to bring the young cow garinafin under control, to stabilize her flight, while unbeknownst to him, Vara Ronalek crawled over the harness from behind, ready to lunge at him.

She wanted to yell at the old thane. We have a plan! We're loyal to Takval!

But would the old thane believe her? Was there enough time to explain? Or would Vara come to the conclusion that the two Lyucu were like the proverbial wolf pups taken in by the foolish herder, revealing their nature and betraying their benefactors at the moment when they were most vulnerable?

It was impossible to believe that the old thane wouldn't heed the wisdom of the ancient stories.

So, instead, she stayed silent. She watched and waited, and at the last possible moment, when she was sure that the old thane was about to lunge at Toof from behind, she yelled, as loud as possible, "Duck!"

Toof ducked and flattened himself against the garinafin's neck, and Vara hurtled right past him, falling over the shoulder of the garinafin.

"O gods," muttered Radia. Not a single day had gone by since when she had not questioned her decision. Yes, she and Toof had saved the pékyus-taasa as well as their parents, making the hard decision to unburden Takval and Théra of the children who would have slowed them down. But they had also betrayed the beloved old thane who had taken them in as though they were her own children, given them full status as members of the tribe.

The gods always demand sacrifices, and I must pay for my acts as well as omissions.

The Lyucu garinafin was very close now. It opened its jaws and snapped them shut. When it opened them again, she knew, she and Alkir would be bathed in flames.

"I'm so sorry, old friend," she said into the bone trumpet planted at the base of Alkir's neck, hoping that he understood. The bull seemed to have accepted his fate and given up. He made no effort to get away from impending death; it was possible that he had no strength left even to dodge.

She and Toof had spent all their lives trying to care for garinafins, to give them a good life, but in the end, what had they accomplished? They saved Ga-al from the slaughter grounds, but instead of a comfortable senescence, the old bull would have to spend the remainder of his life fighting against Lyucu enslavers. They took care of Alkir and convinced the head groom that he didn't need to be killed, but now he would die, exhausted and surrounded by enemies. They had raised Tana from a hatchling, but then had to watch as she drowned in the endless ocean, blinded, terrified, utterly alone. . . .

Yes! That's it!

A blazing light filled Radia's mind—as brilliant as Razutana's wall-buster. The entirety of her life seemed to replay before her like a storytelling dance from the shamans or that shadow play she had seen long ago from the Dara fleet being pursued by *Boundless Pastures*. Everything in life was connected, a great circle like the belt current. The end was the beginning, and the beginning was also the end.

Is this the Flow spoken of by Pékyu Théra?

"Ruga-to! Te-vote!" she screamed into the flared mouthpiece of the bone trumpet, as loud and authoritative as possible.

Approach the enemy! Wrestle it to the ground!

Time snapped back into its normal flow. Just like Toof on that horrible night over Kiri Valley, Alkir reacted more out of instinct than conscious thought. Instead of dodging away from the flame tongue shooting out of the attacking Lyucu garinafin, he turned toward it, crashed through the flames, and embraced the attacker, wrapping his wings and clawed feet around the torso of the other.

Alkir's primal, terrified screams of pain filled Radia's ears. The fire breath had blinded the bull and charred one side of his neck, and Radia could feel the unbearable pain in her own left arm, incinerated into a charred stump. The surprised Lyucu garinafin kicked out with its sharp claws, and left deep gashes in Alkir's vulnerable belly.

She was again hanging on to the webbing of a garinafin for dear life.

"Te-vote! Te-vote!" she shouted. The bone trumpet was gone. She could only scream at the top of her lungs, hoping Alkir could somehow hear her through the madness of pain, through the terror of blindness.

Alkir clung to the attacking garinafin, digging his claws into the other beast's back and refusing to let go. The other garinafin flapped its wings mightily, but it was unable to keep both itself and Alkir's deadweight aloft.

Slowly, the mess of flapping wings and biting heads and scratching claws, like a monster from the end of the Fifth Age of Mankind, sank out of the air and tumbled toward the city-ship.

Even in death, Takval managed to strike back at his foes. Even as she sank, Tana managed to save those she loved. So now would Alkir and Radia sink and die.

"I am Radia Ronalek," Radia shouted. "I claim descent by blood and spirit from both Kikisavo and Afir. I am not afraid. *I am not afraid!*"

Ignoring the pain of the ruined arm, Radia sang at the top of her lungs:

> *Tents sprout across the scrublands like mushrooms after rain,*
> *People roam the endless grass like stars through the cloud-sea.*
> *Feel my arms around you, my eyes on you . . .*

No matter how much the other garinafin struggled and bit and clawed, Alkir held on. The frenzied ball of fighting flesh struck the city-ship with a thunderous bang and crashed through the decking.

The impact knocked Radia out of her saddle and the wind out of her lungs.

She lay still in the darkness of the interior of the ship, knowing that her back was broken, and she would not live for long. She heard the struggle continue next to her, heard the other garinafin's terrified screams and the death shrieks of her riders, heard Alkir's defiant trumpeting as he clutched the other garinafin's long neck like the hose of a living flamethrower.

A bright lance of flames lit up the darkness. The other garinafin was breathing fire, careless of the consequences in such a confined space. Before the heat consumed her, Radia spat the blood out of her mouth and croaked, hoping that her weak voice would still carry to Alkir, would still bring him the comfort of the song that she sang to him when he was a little calf just learning to fly in Kiri Valley.

> *Feel my breath against you, my voice through you.*
> *You're never alone when you hear the tribe's lungsong . . .*

Overhead, Tovo and his other garinafins circled helplessly in disbelief as the last city-ship caught fire and slowly sank beneath the waves.

To the north, Ga-al and the other rebel garinafins flew across miles of empty scrubland until they reached the Boneyard, badlands full of steep buttes, cracked mesas, dusty ravines, dry gullies.

Pékyu Théra welcomed them.

"Is it done?" she asked.

Thoryo, Kitos, and Toof nodded and then shook their heads. How could mere words capture what had taken place in Taten?

Théra gave them a wan smile. "Get some rest. There's lots more to do, and not a moment to lose."

CHAPTER SEVENTEEN

SELF-RELIANCE

ONE YEAR LATER, IN THE WATERS NORTH OF RUI
AND DASU, NEAR THE WALL OF STORMS.

Cu na goztenva va péfir!
Cu na tatenva va péfir!

Tolyusa and the bloody sacrificial rites had driven the shamans and warriors into a feverish mania, the combination of dancing and singing and drum-beating and trumpet-blowing and club-slamming and feet-stomping on the verge of spilling over into an intoxicated brawl—always a danger with Cutanrovo's raucous rallies even back on land. Several naros who had partaken of too much of the sacred herb were frothing at the mouth, and one shaman had fallen down, writhing against the deck, her eyes rolled into the back of the head.

Cutanrovo Aga abandoned herself to the intoxicating throb of power as she led the chorus that channeled the hopes and fears of a whole nation. She was the head of a One formed out of Many, the voice of a Self coalesced out of innumerable selves. United, the Lyucu really were invincible.

She was almost sorry when the gods finally answered their prayers.

It was not a sudden thing, the opening of the Wall. In one part of the perpetual roiling barrier, the cyclones and twisters began to slacken, and the flashes of lightning gradually dimmed. Like a skilled opera troupe that quietly drew the curtains at the Imperial Theater so that the first notes of the prelude would steal upon the murmuring audience before they had noticed the yawning cave that was the stage, the watery cliffs gently parted, as if unwilling to steal attention from the drama that was to follow.

The frenzied dancing and shouting on the deck subsided. Necks craned; eyes peered into the widening gulf.

Cutanrovo gazed up at the lookouts perched on the crow's nests.

"Which tribes' banners do you see? How many ships?"

Than Carucono squinted at the tiny square among the clouds, motionless and enigmatic.

He pulled his eyes back to the giant winch at the prow of the ship. The capstan crew had locked their bars and were resting against them. The strike plate at the end of the thick cable curving into the sky remained stubbornly empty. The tension and anxiety felt as thick as the humid sea breeze.

"Ask the question again!" he shouted to the flag officers next to the capstan. "Tell her that there's no need to get an exact count. A rough estimate will do."

The flag officers nodded and manipulated the long bamboo poles, extending far beyond the sides of the ship like a pair of airship oars. The giant white and red flags at the ends of the poles began to dance in an intricate pattern. From her high perch among the clouds, the lookout on the reconnaissance kite should be able to see the message against the blue backdrop of the sea and answer by dropping signaling rings down the kite's cable. A silver ring was a counter representing a single city-ship, a gold ring five, and a jade ring ten.

Than wished he were on the kite himself so that he could assess the enemy fleet with his own eyes. Wryly, he thought of the moment, decades ago, when he had been the stable master for the Mayor of Zudi, standing on the hill outside of the city and craning his neck, terrified but also a little excited to catch sight of the army of the Xana Empire that was expected to come and crush Kuni Garu's nascent rebellion.

"More horses," he muttered. *"I need more horses."*

"Than, you'll have to make do with what you've got," said Kuni Garu, *his friend and then lord.*

The years since then had been mostly spent either on the back of a galloping horse or the deck of a wave-leaping ship. And though he had accumulated little in the way of personal wealth, he was rich with memories.

He and Puma Yemu were the only surviving senior military commanders who had served Kuni Garu since before he was Emperor
Ragin, and he was the only one who knew Kuni in all the phases
of his life: wastrel son, street gangster, minor Xana official, bandit
king, duke by acclamation, resourceful rebel, unorthodox Tiro king,
and finally, Emperor of Dara. He had watched the man grow into a
legend and played a role in that myth-making drama himself; he had
devoted all his adult life, including these waning years, to serving
Kuni and his legacy.

He knew those who fought with him and for him better than he
knew his own family—and he didn't regret that choice. He had seen
old comrades rise in esteem like New Year's fireworks and fall from
grace like shooting stars. He had helped to build and then defend
Kuni's empire against a shifting cast of enemies: the cruel Xana, the
haughty Hegemon, the faithless rebels who sought to tear Kuni's
creation apart, the implacable Lyucu with their fire-breathing monsters, the small-minded bureaucrats who prized the ease of peace
over all virtues. . . .

Yet, despite the constant strife, the seemingly inexhaustible
stream of setbacks, the mind-numbing palace politics, and the ever-
fresh pain of losing old friends, he had never yielded to despair. He
wasn't fighting for the House of Dandelion—no single man, woman,
or family was worth that—but for the dream of a happier Dara.

Squinting up at the minuscule, blurry shadow of the kite high
above, like a circling bird of prey, Than sighed. Though he wished
to be the rider, he knew that his joints were too stiff, his movements
too slow, his eyesight too dim. In his heart, he was still the fearless
young man who would follow his lord into any battle, careless of
the odds, but age was an implacable opponent that even he had to
concede ground to.

A pang of helpless anguish struck his heart. *Age, unforgiving age!*
One by one, companions who had marched and fought next to him
on this longest of campaigns had fallen by the wayside: ambitious
Théca Kimo, sly Rin Coda, fearless Mün Çakri, loyal Dafiro Miro,
peerless Gin Mazoti, even legendary Kuni himself. . . . Sometimes
he felt very alone, the last member of a shrinking tribe, a dying

generation. Would all those memories, that mountain of insubstantial treasure, that knowledge of what it took to craft and hold an empire by the sword, die with him?

Yet that wisdom, that martial knowledge, was exactly what Dara needed the most. Empress Jia, always suspicious of military commanders, was content to let Kuni's legacy fade into a half empire subsisting in cowardly peace, to consign the people of Unredeemed Dara to enslavement and butchering by the Lyucu. In the years since Kuni Garu's death, against Jia's relentless drive to weaken and defund the military, it had taken every bit of bureaucratic wile he possessed and shameless begging to even maintain a shadow of the proud army, navy, and air force that Marshal Mazoti had built.

Without the empress's support, courageous Phyro, the very spitting image of his father, lacked the matériel and soldiers to reclaim Kuni's dream. Than had thought it impossible to overcome these difficulties, but the young emperor had proven him wrong. Relying only on himself and a few clever advisers, Phyro had devised a daring plan to achieve that dream, and Than was more than willing to offer the young man his experience and guidance. After all, hadn't Kuni done the same when he started his rebellion—

A faint, sustained trill broke his reverie. Than's heart pounded as he shaded his eyes against the sun, hoping to catch the glint of the incoming signaling rings so that he could discern their significance in advance. How many rings and in what combination of the green glow of jade, the sunlit gleam of gold, or the bright, cold glare of silver?

One single, tiny ring materialized against the haze, vibrating on the silk cable, whistling louder and louder as it approached, and before he could get a clear look, the ring struck the bronze plate at the end of the cable, resulting in a resonant, heavy clang.

The burly sailors resting against their capstan bars straightened in wordless amazement. Than Carucono rushed up to the strike plate to be sure that his eyes had not deceived him.

No, they had not. The ring was thick and black, made of iron.

"Ask again!" Than shouted to the flag officers. "Tell her to be absolutely certain."

An interval of time as long as it took to boil a pot of tea later, a second ring fell through the sky and struck the previous ring.

Again, black iron.

You did it, Théra. You did it.

Than Carucono let out a breath that he hadn't realized he was holding. As the tension drained from his body, he swayed unsteadily on his legs.

"Admiral! Admiral!" The crew of *Toru-noki* rushed over.

"I'm all right!" the old warrior assured them. There was laughter in his voice even though tears were flowing down his wrinkled face. "Winch down the kite so Po can get some rest; she's been up there in the cold far too long. Be sure to stay out of sight of the Lyucu ship, and we'll make another confirmatory observation in an hour."

But in his heart, he already knew that the faith of the empress and the Farsight Secretary had been rewarded. Grand Princess Théra had succeeded in her mission, and Emperor Monadétu would finally get his war.

The iron ring meant that there were no Lyucu ships coming through the Wall at all.

- *Don't look so dejected, Tazu. I know you were hoping that more Lyucu would come, to add to the chaos and slaughter.*

- *I've got plenty to work with already, my high-flying brother—and who says I've been stirring the pot? The mortals seem perfectly capable of making a mess of things on their own. It's you that I feel sorry for. You still thought you could secretly aid Tanvanaki against her brother and awaken her conscience once she was secure in her hold on Ukyu-taasa and grateful for the help of Dara's gods and people. Well!*

- *I've long learned not to plan too far in advance. That way lies madness.*

"Votan! Votan!"

Cutanrovo stood still and mute, like a reef in the sea of warriors clamoring for her attention.

The lookouts' initial reports had been easy to dismiss. The fleet could still be too far away for them to see. After all, based on the calculations of the Dara mind-slaves, the opening in the Wall of Storms should remain stable for most of a day.

And so she had ordered more celebration aboard *Toryoana's Gift*, more prayers and dancing, more kyoffir and tolyusa.

But as the day went on and reports from the lookouts remained unchanged, she could sense the mood shift among the crew. There was doubt, uncertainty, fear. She had to do something.

With great fanfare, one of the two garinafins carried aboard the city-ship was readied and launched at the opening in the Wall to investigate. Cutanrovo had originally intended to send aloft the garinafins only when the Lyucu fleet had been spotted, as a subtle show of force to demonstrate that Tanvanaki was firmly in control, and that the newcomers should not expect to take over the young pékyu's domain. Such political calculations, however, had to be put aside in the face of a brewing crisis of confidence with no reinforcement fleet at all.

After hours of fruitless searching through the pass, the garinafin returned with no better news. Indeed, the crew reported no sign of a fleet on the other side of the Wall at all.

Cutanrovo ordered all remaining kyoffir to be brought out to keep up the revelry and dispatched the other garinafin to continue the search. Timidly, the crew from the first garinafin reported the presence of a Dara fishing ship in the vicinity, but Cutanrovo angrily dismissed the news. This was no time to worry about a few Dara-raaki fisherfolk.

Where is the Lyucu fleet?

In the back of her mind, Cutanrovo already knew the answer.

Everyone—Cutanrovo realized—from hard-liners like herself to accommodationists like Goztan Ryoto, and even Tanvanaki herself, had been deceived by a lie of their own weaving. They had assumed that the turtle messages, showing the sign of the garinafin, had been sent by Cudyu as the promise of a reinforcement fleet. But what evidence did they have for that interpretation?

Indeed, in the cold light of disappointing reality, Cutanrovo realized how absurd the hope had been. How could Cudyu, without the aid of Dara mathematicians, have deciphered the abstruse calculations employed by the Dara-raaki to predict the patterns in the Wall of Storms? As much as she despised the barbaric natives, she knew there was a kind of magic in their ways of knowing the world that was beyond the ken of Lyucu shamans.

Instead, she and the others of Ukyu-taasa had been telling themselves a dream-story, a collective hallucination fueled by wishful thinking.

The second garinafin returned in the westering sunlight.

It thumped down on the deck and faltered from fatigue. The dancing shamans and sweating drummers and red-faced trumpeters stilled, equally exhausted. Even kyoffir could not keep up this facade of hope much longer. All eyes were on the crew of the garinafin.

Slowly, they climbed down, and though their despondent poses said everything that needed to be said, the warriors waited. Until it was spoken aloud, despair could still be held at bay with wild, senseless hope.

The crew came up to Cutanrovo, draped in her terrible, rattling lurona ryo lurotan, and fell to one knee.

"What news?" croaked Cutanrovo.

The crew looked at one another and then turned to her. Silent tears flowed down their faces.

They talked, but Cutanrovo wasn't listening. What good did it do to hear their description of their long and arduous search? Of how they had skimmed over the empty sea, peering in every direction until their eyes had almost been blinded by the bright sun reflecting off the calm water? Of how closely they had flown to the towering walls of water and wind at the edges of the opening in the hope of seeing some wreckage, some sign that they had not believed in a mere myth, a fantasy?

"Votan! Votan!"

Cutanrovo stood still, the eye of the growing storm that was her restless crew. She heard whispered suggestions that the gods of this land were punishing the Lyucu for their treatment of the natives, mumbled confessions that perhaps those who had continued to offer prayers to the native gods were the wise ones, muttered conjectures that maybe the gods of their homeland had abandoned them in this inhospitable land, filled with swarming hostile hordes.

"Votan! Votan! Where is the fleet? Where are the reinforcements?"

She could well imagine how Tanvanaki would respond to this revelation. Cutanrovo's own rise to power had been premised on a mirage fleet that would never materialize. The pékyu would blame her for this shocking turn, and use the excuse to drive her and her hard-liner allies out of power.

Next, Goztan Ryoto and her cronies would no doubt revive the idea of seeking accommodation with the Dara-raaki, of corrupting the Lyucu with native influence, of giving the puppet Emperor Thaké more power. And then? What next? Even the cowardly Empress Jia would know to seize this moment of weakness to attack, to slaughter, to drive the Lyucu into the sea.

The impending loss of her own hard-won power didn't bother Cutanrovo—a warrior gambled and accepted the consequences—but the looming disaster facing Ukyu-taasa, facing her people, had to be halted at all costs. No matter how much pain she had to endure personally, she had to save her people.

"Votan! Votan! The Wall is closing! What should we do?"

Cutanrovo shook herself as if awakening from a nightmare, and she looked toward the horizon. There, the two disconnected parts of the Wall were drawing together, much like the curtains at the end of a native stage play—another corrupt Dara practice that she had stamped out.

But . . . the mud-legs' ridiculous stories do contain a kernel of wisdom: They say that there is a second act, don't they? It's . . . like the triumph of Kikisavo and Afir after the horrors at the end of the Fifth Age.

She held up her hands, and the cacophony around her ceased.

"Votan-ru-taasa, votan-sa-taasa," she began. *Brothers, sisters.* This was how Pékyu Tenryo had once begun the speech that rallied a despondent people into seeking vengeance, how every great hero of the Lyucu people had started the word dances that would lift them out of the cold, dark night into a sunlit morning.

"We are faced with a greater challenge now than we have ever faced in these islands. There will be no reinforcements from beyond the Wall of Storms, no aid from the homeland."

Everyone was transfixed, their faces stony. Though Cutanrovo had simply voiced aloud what everyone was already thinking, there was a power to the articulation of truth with thinking-breath that shook them to the core.

"I know your hearts are heavy, and your limbs tired. I know you're full of doubt and question. Without reinforcements, how can we overcome the crafty barbarians who breed like moonfur rats? How can we withstand their endless hordes, even if each Lyucu warrior fights with the strength of ten, nay, a hundred Dara-raaki? Even a sturdy reef will be worn down by the relentless tides, and even a brave wolf cannot vanquish a thousand bleating sheep in a mindless, cowardly stampede. Have we been walking down the wrong path? Is this how the gods intend to finish us?"

Shamans, thanes, naros, culeks hung on her every word. Somehow, speaking aloud the fear in their hearts also made it less frightening.

"I do not know the answers, votan-ru-taasa, votan-sa-taasa. Only the gods know the future, and they may have indeed abandoned us."

The crowd murmured in agitation. Cutanrovo was speaking the unspeakable.

"However, it's not the gods we should count on, but ourselves. It is in times of despair that we most need to remember who we are. Do you recall how Kikisavo and Afir had once stood naked in the world, without weapons, helmets, allies, mounts? Do you recall how Pékyu Tenryo had once been confronted with a fleet the likes of which no Lyucu had ever seen, each ship bigger than the biggest whale, each laden with barbarians wielding weapons that dealt death from a distance, that seemed as terrifying and powerful as the weapons of the end of the Fifth Age?

"Did the gods help Kikisavo and Afir willingly? Did the gods tell Pékyu Tenryo what to do?"

The crowd was mesmerized. Cutanrovo seemed to be showing them a new way of seeing the world. Even the shamans did not protest this challenge to their authority from their chief.

"No!" Cutanrovo roared. "The gods did not aid our ancestors until our ancestors proved that they didn't need them! Kikisavo and Afir challenged the gods and defeated them through cunning and audacity, and Pékyu Tenryo enslaved the strangers with mortal guile and living courage. These stories are in our blood; they affirm our nature; we are the people who overcome gods and demons without anyone's help but our own. We earn the fear of our foes and the trust of our divine kin!

"Pékyu Tenryo's axe was called Langiaboto, and though it now lies at the bottom of the sea, its spirit, the spirit of self-reliance, abides with us. Even if the gods have abandoned us, we cannot abandon who we are.

"Ten dyudyu diakyoga?"

She waited.

The responses came in scattered, hesitant.

She asked again, louder, "Ten dyudyu diakyoga?"

This time, the responses were more coherent, in sync.

She screamed, her face red with blood, *Ten dyudyu diakyoga?*

The responding chorus boomed with confidence and strength, as though many tiny streams had commingled into a powerful river.

"Lyucu kyo!"

She turned to issue fresh orders to her guards. As they ran off, she turned back to the crowd.

"The answer for every new challenge can be found in our past, in the stories that have been passed down from generation to generation, through living breath. The barbarians have nothing to rely on but the dead wax word-scars of their ancestors—as mindless as the tracks left by aurochs herds hurtling over cliffs, as disgusting as mouflon dung piled by water bubbles in grass seas, as lifeless as charred prairie partridge carcasses in the wake of scrubland fires, as breathless as moonfur corpses buried in their trampled tunnels. What should we do with them? What should the tusked tiger do to the silence-shocked calves? What should the wolf do to the trembling lambs?"

The crowd roared, stomped their feet, slammed their weapons against the masts and gunwales. "Kill them!" "Castrate them!" "Roast them!"

Cutanrovo's guards returned, pushing through the crowd. The two in the front carried a large wooden barrel. Behind the guards came twenty Dara slaves in chains—many of them had served the crew as cooks, drudges, garinafin grooms, sexual outlets for the warriors.

"What should we do with them?" Cutanrovo asked again.

"Dara-raaki must be destroyed! Kill! *Kill!* KILL!"

Cutanrovo raised her fists and slammed them together. She took several steps back, the skull cape rattling on her body. Her guards left the chained slaves on the foredeck, where they stood, dazed. They carried the wooden barrel in front of Cutanrovo and popped off the lid.

Cutanrovo reached in and grabbed handfuls of the rich, bright red tolyusa of Dara, the only good thing in this gods-forsaken land, and scattered them among the crowd.

"Feast! And manifest your nature!"

The fevered crowd rushed forward and grabbed the tolyusa berries, catching them in the air or picking them off the deck before they were trampled. This was a supply that would have lasted days for thousands at the Winter Festival, but now it would be consumed by the ship's crew in a single afternoon.

As the berry juice boiled their blood and filled their minds with visions of glorious battle, the warriors turned on the terrified slaves. Screams and piteous howls filled the air as the Lyucu beat, kicked, bit, tore. Soon, the Dara slaves were submerged beneath a bloody tide of nails and teeth.

By the time the tide finally receded, the slaves were gone. Some of the Lyucu warriors held up torn limbs or pieces of flesh, many had blood dripping from their lips, and the deck was streaked with gore.

Cutanrovo stepped forward, bending to pick up a severed head. The white skull showed through where the flesh had been bitten off. She poked a short bit of sinew through the eye sockets and attached the bloody trophy to her skull cape.

"Ten dyudyu diakyoga?"

"Lyucu kyo!"

"Who don't need the favor of the gods at all?"

"The Lyucu people!"

Clouds raced across the sky, never settling into any form. As the Wall of Storms closed, a new storm was brewing in Dara itself. The will of the gods, native or otherwise, remained elusive.

CHAPTER EIGHTEEN

CONSPIRACY

GINPEN: THE SIXTH MONTH OF THE ELEVENTH
YEAR OF THE REIGN OF SEASON OF STORMS AND
THE REIGN OF AUDACIOUS FREEDOM.

Historically, Ginpen had never been a great trading hub. The city's Moralist scholars disdained commerce, which they viewed as a distraction from the high-mindedness of Haan's people. The Tiro kings of Haan taxed the harbor heavily and didn't allow much to be done in the way of expansion or maintenance.

The Xana conquest, which sank most of the Haan fleet in the harbor, further reduced the attractiveness of sea routes to the city. It took years of dredging and salvaging under the reign of Emperor Ragin to clear out the wrecks and restore full access to the docks.

But the tributary trading missions to the conquered islands of Rui and Dasu gave the port of Ginpen a new significance. Fear of a Lyucu invasion led to heavy investment by Empress Jia in the naval presence at Ginpen—one of the few military expenditures she approved of—and the harbor had to be deepened and the wharves expanded to accommodate the large, deep-draft warships and cargo vessels. Large warehouses were constructed to store the goods destined for Unredeemed Dara and many stevedores had to be hired to load the ships.

Once all this infrastructure had been built, it made little sense for it to remain idle for much of the year, in between tributary trading missions. Since the civil service code by which roaming Imperial officials were judged and promoted measured, as one of their accomplishments, the economic productivity of the regions under their charge, successive governors of Haan and mayors of Ginpen sought ways to promote more efficient use of Ginpen's modernized harbor. In this endeavor they were also helped by the sensible Imperial tax policies initiated by Prime Minister Cogo Yelu, which promoted trade to make Dara more robust against natural disasters, to encourage the mingling of Dara's peoples, and to reduce lingering regional prejudices.

In this manner, Ginpen became one of the busiest port cities in all Dara. Even if the city wasn't quite as prosperous as sprawling Dimushi or old-money Toaza, it was a far more commerce-driven city than elegant Müning or fog-shrouded Boama.

At first, the city's elders and taste-making noble families saw the influx of barely literate merchants obsessed with profit as an assault on the city's scholarly character—not only did they make everything more expensive, but they also hired away the best servants with higher wages and caused a veritable flood of uncouth peasants into the city in hopes of finding jobs as laborers. But over time, as Imperial officials wisely encouraged merchants to donate to Ginpen's civic and religious institutions, opinion began to shift. The new money gave ancient public academies modern lecture halls and state-of-the-art laboratory equipment (powerful silkmotic generators were not cheap); attracted scholars from afar to found private schools teaching fresh ideas; expanded existing temples; funded new shrines (the biggest new shrines were for Luan Zyaji, the great explorer—many merchants braving the seas for profit claimed to see themselves reflected in the man's maritime exploits—and to Mata Zyndu, the Hegemon, now improbably worshipped by the marines and sailors of the navy and scholars cramming for the Imperial examinations alike, as both groups claimed "courage" as their defining trait); renovated the statues of the gods; and brought artists, craftspeople, folk opera troupes, street performers, and inventors from every corner of Dara into Ginpen's bustling markets.

The Moralists now spoke of Ginpen's new golden age, a time when scholarship flourished as never before. They might still disdain petty commerce, but they enjoyed its fruits.

All of which was to say that Ginpen, as a microcosm of Dara under the regency of Empress Jia, was the perfect stage for political drama.

～

Aya Mazoti, the newly appointed Admiral of the Tributary Fleet, couldn't understand how a routine tributary mission had turned into such a disaster before she had even set foot aboard her flagship.

Riding tall on a horse at the head of a cargo convoy escorted by a full regiment of the empire's elite soldiers, a ceremonial cape embroidered with a thousand sword-petaled dandelions draping over her golden armor, a giant flag showing a blue breaching cruben on a red field flapping over her head—she was the very embodiment of the authority of the Dandelion Throne. This should be a moment of triumph: the full redemption of the Mazoti name. She had finally fulfilled the expectation of her mentors and teachers. The daughter of an accused traitor was now an admiral!

But instead of celebrating, the agitated crowd lining both sides of the street screamed and cursed at her. Behind her, soldiers cowered in silent resentment. In front of her, a young woman, an official, lay in the middle of the road. To make forward progress, Aya would have to trample her with her horse's hooves.

Hundreds of scholars—*toko dawiji, cashima*, even a few *pana méji*—knelt in neat rows beyond the official, holding up silk scrolls with giant logograms: *Traitor, Coward, Death before dishonor, The writing knife stands with the fighting sword!*

And beyond the last row of scholars, she saw ranks of men and women standing in silence, all of them middle-aged or even silver-haired. Some were dressed in the hemp clothing of the peasantry, some were in tattered rags, and a few looked like prosperous artisans or merchants. Many stood with the aid of a crutch or wooden leg, some sported an artificial arm, and a few sat in wheeled chairs.

No matter their wealth or station, the silent protesters were united by the same resolute expression and the small wooden tablets they held up, covered in wax military insignia: red for the air force; blue for the navy; green for the army; five bars for the rank of fifty-chief; a circle for the rank of hundred-chief; cruben scales in increasing numbers for ensigns, sergeants, corporals, captains; a sword for a soldier or a marine; an oar for a sailor; falcon wings for an aviator; stylized flowers for distinguished service, acts of bravery, wounds suffered in battle. . . .

They were veterans from Dara's wars, and even without armor or weapons, their disciplined mute formation offered a solemn rebuke to Aya even more severe than the clamorous commoners.

Back in Pan, Princess Fara had warned Aya.

"You must decline the appointment!"

"Why should I do that?" asked Aya, miffed that her best friend wasn't more excited for her.

Fara had changed a great deal in the two years after those hectic months in Ginpen, the first time she had been away from the palace on her own. Though she still took delight in provoking insufferable Prince Gimoto and mocking his friends, she was more subdued at riddle parties and no longer obsessed after every bit of gossip about handsome actors. In fact, often she turned down Aya's invitations to playhouses and amusing outings, claiming to be too busy. Fara's maids told Aya that the princess painted, wrote poetry, read histories, played music, and often went to the markets alone, watching the performances of folk troupes and talking to the rustic performers. Aya had no idea why Fara found these plebeian, sentimental stories interesting. All she knew was that the two of them, once inseparable as sisters, were no longer as close.

"Haven't you been paying attention?" asked Fara. "The empress's desk is groaning under the weight of petitions from the College of Advocates denouncing this mission."

"I don't care how many of those young hotheads are carping about the empress's choice," said Aya contemptuously. "She is the decider and she has made her will known."

"It's not that simple," said Fara. "Oh, by the Twins, I'm no good at politics and intrigue, but even I can tell you that there is more to this than what the empress wants."

Aya resented the way Fara sounded . . . so adult. "I'm so glad to have your tutelage, my wise sister. I hadn't realized that you are much more experienced with the world than I."

Fara ignored the sarcasm. "Having traveled around Dara, I can tell you there are many who don't want this peace. The veterans' societies are influential, and there are more and more folk operas celebrating resistance."

That was another thing that had changed. Fara would often leave on long trips by herself to Ginpen, Boama, or remote hamlets in Faça and Rima. Ostensibly, these were trips to visit Widow Wasu or distant relatives from her mother's side of the family, but Aya found Fara's answers about what she did on these trips evasive and vague. Mystified, she had abused her authority as an anti-piracy commander and demanded that the farseers keep the princess under surveillance on the pretext of protecting her from pirate abduction attempts. The farseers' reports showed that Fara spent a lot of time visiting refugees from Unredeemed Dara who had settled in small communities all over the northern shore of the Big Island.

"Who cares what some aged veterans think?" said Aya. "The holder of the Seal of Dara decides to go to war or not, and it's the job of the army to carry out the sovereign's will. Anyway, this appointment is a great honor. I'll be the youngest person ever to be given command of a fleet of this size!"

"But it's a fleet to deliver tribute and a treaty akin to terms of surrender—" Fara paused. "It's hardly an . . . honor."

"Says who?" Aya's face reddened. "'To achieve a peace without slaughter is the highest of victories.' My mother said so. Even if my job appears to be only delivering a message, it *is* an important command and a crucial step in my military career."

"Since when have you cared about your military career?" Fara asked in disbelief. "It was always Zomi and Phyro who pushed this life on you, trying to tell you that you must fulfill a destiny. But you don't have to live up to the stories others tell about you."

Fara is right, but she doesn't understand, not really, Aya thought.

Reluctantly, Aya dismounted and approached the official lying on the ground. She covered the short distance on foot with some difficulty—the heavy golden armor and clingy water-silk cape looked good but weren't very practical.

This official, whoever she was, was clearly the leader of the protest.

She tried to kneel down in *mipa rari*, but found that the stiff armor prevented her from doing so. Making a mental note to adjust her costume—no, *uniform*—for more comfort and range of movement in the future, Aya bent forward awkwardly, placing her hands on her knees.

"Perhaps there is some misunderstanding," she began. She tried to imitate the demeanor and tone of Prime Minister Cogo Yelu: authoritative but not arrogant, firm but also understanding. "My mission is of great importance, authorized and commanded by Empress Jia herself. It cannot be delayed. If you have some grievance that you wish to bring to the attention of—"

"There is no misunderstanding here," said the official lying on the ground. "Delaying you—no, *stopping* you from carrying out your treasonous mission is exactly our goal."

Aya's face flushed with heat. Nothing set her off like the word "treason." She had emphasized the empress's name in order to impress upon this official the fact that interfering with an Imperial envoy's tributary mission was tantamount to treason—an implied accusation this woman had thrown back in her face.

"What is your name?" she asked, her voice now cold.

"Réza Müi," the young woman said. "I'm a *pana méji* from the last session of the Grand Examination, currently serving as secretary to Magistrate Zuda of Ginpen."

"Ah, I remember you," Aya blurted out. "You were the one who . . ." Her voice trailed off.

"That's all right, Your Highness," said Réza, a smile on her face. "I was the troublemaker who led the scholars to protest Farsight Secretary Kidosu's ill-advised attempt to abolish the use of Ano logograms during the last Grand Examination. As you can tell, I have no fear of speaking out against errors committed by those in positions of power, even an error committed by the empress herself."

"Ada-*tika*, why can't you just be happy for me? However controversial the peace treaty may be, it's still a fact that *I* have been picked—"

"That's precisely *why* I worry!"

Aya's eyes narrowed. "What exactly do you mean by that?"

Fara wrung her hands helplessly. "Why do you think you've been picked?"

"I am a skilled theoretician as well as an able field commander." Aya paused. Since breaking up the nest of pirates and Lyucu spies in the Silkworm Eggs and rescuing the abducted artisans, she had been given more responsibility and promoted several times—but she could still count only that first anti-piracy patrol as a true victory. Keenly aware that Fara was as responsible as she for that particular achievement, she pressed on, willing herself to believe the story she was telling. "Among the younger generation of military commanders, there's no one who can claim having accomplished as much. Even Gori Ruthi's sarcastic reports as monitor couldn't turn the empress against me—"

"Oh, Aya, do you still think this is actually about what you've done or not done? Your victories—you really think—" Fara paused, an anguished look distorting her features. "The . . . the truth is, you were picked because the Marshal and Luan Zyaji are symbols of Dara's defiance against Lyucu aggression. Your mother killed Pékyu Tenryo; your father tricked him and stranded the Lyucu here with no reinforcements. Sending *you*, their child, as the emissary bearing tribute is the ultimate sign of our submission and obeisance to the Lyucu—"

"You think I'm picked to be a *symbol*? Because of my *parents*?" Disbelief warred with the pain of betrayal in her face. "I thought you were my friend."

"I *am* your friend. That's why I must tell you what you don't want to hear," said Fara. "I don't know why my aunt-mother is so intent on sending a message of appeasement to the Lyucu . . . but I do know that a symbol is no longer a person, but a tool—"

"So now I'm useless *and* an idiot," said Aya. "You really think highly of your friends, don't you?"

Fara stamped her foot in frustration. "Listen to me! You're caught up in a political game that neither of us understands. Should anything go wrong with this mission, you will be an easy scapegoat. Should those favoring war gain the upper hand, there will be no better way to celebrate their victory than to ruin you, the symbol of appeasement. You must do all you can to refuse this false honor. Fake an illness, manufacture an injury, anything—"

Aya laughed bitterly. "Listen to you!? Oh, my perspicacious and sagacious Imperial Princess Fara, since I'm so unaccomplished and undeserving of honor, please enlighten me: What have *you* attained in life that isn't because of *your* parentage?"

"I've never claimed to—" Fara gritted her teeth. She took a deep breath. When she spoke again, her voice was calm but strained. "I know that my talents are limited. I have neither the fortitude nor the desire to follow in the footsteps of my father. That's why I've stayed away from the conflict between Phyro and the empress—"

"You've been moping about because of a stupid boy who didn't like you as much as you liked him! You're as pathetic as the love-lorn girls in those silly plays." As soon as the words left her mouth, Aya regretted them, but Fara had hurt her, and she wanted to hurt her back. "You spend your days visiting refugees who speak the Dasu topolect so you can pretend you're talking to him, penning silly love poems he'll never read, and painting pictures no one even understands—"

Fara flinched as though she had been slapped. "You . . . you have no idea. . . . That isn't fair—"

"You may be content with hopeless crushes and a life spent resting in the shade of your parent's glory, but I'm not! My family is the reason I *must* accept this mission."

"I . . . don't understand."

"My mother died fighting for Dara, but she's still labeled a traitor by the court historians!" shouted Aya. "How can you understand what it's like to be Gin Mazoti's child?"

She choked up, unable to continue. True, Fara had never known her mother, who died giving birth to her. But she had grown up surrounded by siblings and aunt-mothers, at the knees of a father who always took time to tell her stories or inquired after her homework. Fara would never know the pain of growing up alone in a palace, her father a mystery, her mother always away at war or busy with the minutiae of administration. Even when Gin had been alive, she was little more than a severe voice, a source of discipline, an unapproachable presence Aya knew more through larger-than-life tales recounted by admiring generals and terrified courtiers than familial intimacy. The closest she ever felt to her mother was . . . when she worked on *The Mazoti Way of War*, long after Gin was dead.

More than anything else, she was taught that *Your mother is a grand lord, the greatest warrior in all Dara. She is the very embodiment of* mutagé. *You must live up to the Mazoti name and never bring her shame.*

No other path had ever been open to her. None.

And then, it had all come crashing down. Her mother was denounced, imprisoned, vilified. She lost everything she had overnight.

"Her fief—which ought to be *my* fief—was taken away, as well as her good name and honor!" Aya screamed. The words were inadequate, a pale shadow of the inarticulable fury and shame warring in her heart.

"Oh, Aya . . ." Fara's voice trailed off. "You don't know . . . I can't . . . You can't believe everything . . ."

"What are you talking about?"

Fara looked helpless. "I know the Marshal was no traitor."

"You have proof?"

Fara shook her head, forlorn.

The protestation of faith from Fara sounded hollow. What did a pampered princess know of politics and truth?

How could Aya accept that her own venerated mother was a traitor? Yet, how could she not when everyone said it was so? Her mother had also told her that the accusations were lies; but, in the end, she had gone to fight for the Dandelion Throne without demanding that her name be cleared. What conclusion could Aya draw other than that her mother *was* guilty, that Gin had brought shame to the very name and betrayed the very ideals that Aya had been taught to revere?

Even Zomi Kidosu, who had recanted her accusation and visited her mother in tears to beg for forgiveness, never wanted to discuss the truth about Gin's trial with Aya after the Marshal's death. *Some truths are best left unspoken.* That was the most Zomi would ever say on the subject. What cold comfort was Aya supposed to take from *that*?

All she could do was to try to rebuild what her mother had wrecked, to recapture that which her mother had lost. She had to live up to the story others told about her mother, for good or ill. Her mother was brilliant, but she was also disloyal, a legacy that Aya had to accept, learn from, and redeem.

No other path had ever been open to her. None.

"I don't know what happened to my mother to make her rebel, but even death couldn't wash away the stain of treason down the generations." Aya cleared her face of tears with one fierce swipe. "However, now I've been given the chance to be elevated into the ranks of trusted commanders of the empire, to prove that my inherited nature isn't incompatible with honor, to restore the Mazoti name to the Hall of Mutagé. *How can I refuse that?*"

All of that seemed a distant memory now.

Aya had imagined that delivering the tribute and the sealed treaty to Kriphi would be easy—even the most ferocious pirates wouldn't dare to attack a tribute fleet, would they?

She had not counted on being reviled by such a large crowd, had not imagined her mission would be denounced as treasonous. She was a lone barque about to be torn apart by the tidal waves of protest around her.

Where had all these veterans come from? Who had gathered the scholars? Why was Réza Müi being so stubborn?

PAN: A MONTH EARLIER.

After Than Carucono returned with the news that no Lyucu reinforcements had come through the Wall of Storms, there was much celebration of Grand Princess Théra's peerless accomplishment. She had not only survived the passage through the Wall of Storms, but delivered a mortal blow against Lyucu ambition in their homeland.

But soon talk returned, as it always did, to the here and now, to mundane politics. Everyone in Pan expected Tanvanaki to beg for a second peace treaty. Her strategic situation had worsened considerably, and in this grand game of *zamaki*, she simply didn't have the pieces to launch another invasion against the core islands.

There was much speculation over what kind of concessions the Lyucu would offer. Some, led by Prince Gimoto, predicted that Tanvanaki would be so overcome by gratitude for the empress regent's merciful Moralist restraint that she would at least return Dasu to the Throne, and maybe even pay tribute to Pan.

Within a week, a Lyucu envoy came to Pan onboard *Grace of Kings*, the fast airship that had once carried Kuni Garu and was later taken by the Lyucu as a prize. The envoy's message was indeed one of peace—so long as the Dandelion Court agreed to *double* all tribute paid to the Lyucu.

In the confused uproar that followed, the court soon divided into two factions. One party, led by governors of provinces that had flourished under the peace and officials from prominent, wealthy families, advocated capitulating to the Lyucu demands. They reasoned that a decade of peace had brought unprecedented prosperity to Dara: the harvests were plentiful, trade was thriving, the number of scholars who passed the Imperial examinations at all levels had risen, and though Prime Minister Cogo Yelu had lowered the tax rate three times, the Imperial Treasury's surpluses increased every year. Tanvanaki's tribute demand could be satisfied with ease.

"The fruits of our enlightened regent's labors must not be so casually consigned to the flames of unnecessary war," declared Prince Gimoto, bowing reverently to Empress Jia.

But the other party, led by old military commanders like Than Carucono and Puma Yemu, and ancient noble families like the Cosugi clan of Haan, strenuously objected. Emperor Ragin's death remained unavenged, and the people of Unredeemed Dara were suffering under the yoke of Lyucu misrule. How could the Dandelion Court abandon them to more terror and anguish while living in ease, paying tribute to sustain the very regime that enslaved them? Dara was now stronger and richer than ten years ago, and it was past time to declare war against the invaders and liberate the people of Rui and Dasu.

"Those of us living in freedom have a duty to fight for those under tyranny and bondage," declaimed an impassioned Than Carucono, surveying the assembled ministers and generals, daring any to disagree.

Both sides appealed to the authority of venerated Ano philosophers.

Didn't Kon Fiji say that "Peace should be the prime pursuit of a wise ruler?" War with the Lyucu was against Moralism.

But didn't Kon Fiji also say that "A virtuous man should not shore up a wall erected through slave labor?" To pay the Lyucu for peace was against Moralism.

Ah, but Poti Maji, Kon Fiji's best student, had elaborated that the most important Moralist virtue of all was concern for the common people. War would lead to brother parting from brother, husband from wife; deserted fields and empty fishing weirs as peasants and fishermen were conscripted to fight; death, dismemberment, bloodshed. To advocate for war was to treat the common people as kindling for the glory of the Throne. War was contrary to the well-being of the voiceless and powerless, completely immoral.

But wait! Poti Maji had also said that it was error to presume that the sole concern of the common people was survival. Justice, a higher principle, presented also a weightier claim. To abandon the people of Rui and Dasu to Lyucu depredation so that the rest of Dara might live in gilded prosperity was to attribute to the people a pusillanimity and selfishness that they did not possess. To speak against war was to force the voiceless to chorus for injustice and to abduct the powerless to serve oppression, utterly immoral.

The debate in formal court raged on for three days, and though plenty of speeches were made, everyone understood that the real contest was backstage, out of sight of the performances. Every day of continued peace paying tribute to the Lyucu was another day that cemented the power of Empress Jia as permanent regent (and laid another stone in Prince Gimoto's sly, long road to the throne as her favorite); to seize the reins of power, Phyro had to press for war so that he could bypass Jia's vast Imperial bureaucracy and become Emperor Monadétu in fact as well as in name.

Prime Minister Cogo Yelu, as the architect of Empress Jia's elaborate machinery of state, was presumed to be the leader of the party for peace, whereas Farsight Secretary Zomi Kidosu, as the emperor's most powerful ally in court, was presumed to be the leader of the party for war.

Oddly, both Cogo and Zomi remained silent during the debates, expressing no opinion one way or the other. While Empress Jia presided over the deliberations, letting both sides put on a show, Phyro stayed away in the Wisoti Mountains, refusing to come and confront his regent.

Finally, Empress Jia broke her silence. "The decision to go to war or to seek peace should not be taken lightly. Emperor Ragin always said that in any decision, the welfare of the people of Dara must be given the greatest weight, followed by the stability of the Throne, and only if all other factors are in equipoise should the inclinations of the person sitting on the throne be considered."

The arguing officials and generals looked at one another in consternation. The empress had paraphrased a gloss by Poti Maji on Kon Fiji's long essay *The Just King*. But invoking the great sage (as filtered through Kuni Garu, who had a way of reinterpreting the words of the sages in unorthodox ways) at this point was as good as saying nothing—both sides could use that quote to support their own positions.

The empress went on. "But 'the people of Dara' is *not* a monolithic entity—when the interests of the few are weighed against the interests of the many, the few must yield."

After a stunned pause, urgent whispers passed through the Grand Audience Hall like an autumn breeze rustling leaves.

When the debate resumed, the tone had shifted strikingly. The empress's speech had reframed the conflict between the pro-war and pro-peace factions as a contest between the interests of the people of the core islands and the interests of the people living in Unredeemed Dara.

Despair descended over the hearts of Than Carucono, Puma Yemu, and the other generals. How could two islands' yearning for freedom outweigh the desire for security and stability in all the rest? Simply by producing the scale on which each party's proposal would be measured, the empress had determined the outcome.

Cogo Yelu, as the most senior of the civil ministers, and Zomi Kidosu, as the most senior of the security-military officers, stood mutely across from each other in the Grand Audience Hall. As the arguments raged on around them, neither met the gaze of the other.

Messenger pigeons from Zomi brought news of the empress's new treaty with the Lyucu to the secret base of Tiro Cozo, deep in the Wisoti Mountains.

Phyro finished Zomi's letter, dangled it over a candle, and watched as the silk burst into flames and the wax logograms deformed and dripped into an unrecognizable lump.

Phyro had been deliberately avoiding going back to Pan during the crisis. The palace was Empress Jia's *zamaki* castle, and every piece there had been carefully placed by the empress. A direct confrontation would have done more harm than good.

But there was a grander *zamaki* board outside the castle, and Phyro had been hard at work during the last two years, both in Tiro Cozo and outside. Meanwhile, Zomi and Than had been covertly advising him, helping him place *his* pieces.

The words of Ra Oji, the irreverent Fluxist, came to mind.

> *In Damu the scarlet Phaédo sits,*
> *For three years, snowbound, all sounds he omits.*
> *Then, one morn he sings to call forth the sun.*
> *Stunned, the world stands still to listen as one.*

Even with the best advisers by his side, it was up to the lord to play the game. Was he ready to emerge from his cocoon of seeming disinterest? Should he continue to bide his time?

He imagined the consequences of waiting. He had accomplished a great deal in the two years since Zomi had agreed to help him build his private army, but he was still working from a position of weakness. With every passing day, his strength grew.

Yet, with the increased tribute to the Lyucu under the new treaty, Dara would be helping the butchers and enslavers grow stronger as well. Each passing day was another day in which the people of Rui and Dasu suffered, died, became sacrifices to an insatiable appetite for cruelty.

What was it that Auntie Gin had always said? *The best-made plans in the world must ultimately be put to the test of reality.*

Who knew what kind of sacrifices and horrors Théra had gone through to buy them this chance? Could he afford to throw away this opportunity his sister had won for the people of Dara?

Phyro retrieved a small bundle tucked under his pillow and unwrapped it, revealing a pile of tiny golden decorative pins. The pins were of four types, all sculpted to fit a floral motif: bamboo leaves, pine cones, safflowers, orchids.

Rati Yera was here in Tiro Cozo, working with him every day. It was time to call upon the others to help the Phaédo spread its wings.

He stayed up all night, his writing knife slicing and carving furiously. With the first rays of the sun, three pigeons took off from the secluded valley, each carrying a slender bamboo tube sealed with a wax plug, in which was embedded a golden pin.

The first pigeon alighted at the window of a small house in Pan. It cooed a few times and tapped at the sash with its beak.

A moment later, the window opened to reveal a most singular man, a collection of contradictions. He sported the double scroll-bun of a *toko dawiji* as well as the handlebar mustache favored by merchants contemptuous of book learning. His showy bright blue robe suggested a man of some means, but that impression was immediately belied by the many patches covering the robe, in all colors and shapes and sizes, badges of an itinerant beggar. In his left hand was a writing knife of polished ivory, the implement of a refined member of the literati, but instead of hot wax from the composition of a serious essay, mouthwatering grease dripped from the blade—evidently the man had been wielding it to carve up his peasant-style fried chicken.

He was none other than Widi Tucru, the orchid with the wagging knife-tongue.

"Aha!" Widi exclaimed. "Just in time for dinner."

The pigeon tilted its head and glanced accusatorially at the writing knife.

"Oh, sorry! I meant that you should be *joining* me for dinner, not that I view you in the same manner as your delicious avian cousin. Well, squab *is* also delicious, but—never mind."

He brought the pigeon in, set out a dish of quality sorghum seeds and a bowl of clean water, and then carefully removed the bamboo tube from one of the pigeon's legs. He popped off the wax plug with the orchid pin, tipped the bamboo tube, and unrolled the scroll that fell out.

While the pigeon ate and drank, he read.

Two years earlier, Zomi had introduced the Blossom Gang to Phyro in Tiro Cozo, explaining that the four eccentric characters could be valuable allies for the young emperor.

Phyro was immediately impressed by Mota's strength, Rati's ingenuity, Arona's facility with disguises, and Widi's encyclopedic knowledge of rules as well as how to bend them. But even more than their skills, he appreciated the gang's refusal to be constrained by conventional propriety and stuffy Moralist ethics. Talk of treason didn't faze them—they had broken into one of the most secure research facilities of the empire to satisfy their curiosity and to make the dream of a friend come true. As Widi put it, "I consider it a greater crime to betray a friend than to defy the Throne."

The Blossom Gang, in turn, was touched by Phyro's sincerity and lack of airs. He exclaimed like a child over Rati's inventions, agreed vehemently with Widi's critiques of the Imperial bureaucracy, sympathized with Mota's indignation over the unjust treatment of the Marshal and the veterans to the point of weeping, and laughed with merriment and wonder as Arona put on comic one-woman plays in which she portrayed a dozen characters. He didn't care that Rati Yera was born a *raye*, the lowest of the low. He didn't question Widi Tucru's lack of interest in advancing in the Imperial examinations, a decision most found incomprehensible. He embraced Mota like a brother after a demonstration of martial prowess, careless that the man's sweat stained his robe. He praised Arona's masks and listened to her disquisitions on the history of theater, never treating her as a frivolous actress. He simply took them as they were, pouring beer for all and sitting in *géüpa* as though they were all equals.

He didn't fit the image of a recluse emperor or an idle prince; instead, to the gang, he seemed like an overgrown child who still delighted in the performances of street magicians, who still believed in teahouse tales about good and evil, who still held fast to the idea that the knotty problems of the world could all be solved with enough courage and smarts.

The gang, along with Zomi and Phyro, stayed up several nights in a row, drinking and talking, not going to bed until saffron-fingered dawn had pulled aside the curtain of night. Phyro spoke to them of his dreams of liberating the people of Unredeemed Dara, of reunifying the Islands, of ushering forth a golden age in which all, not just some, would live in freedom and justice.

"It isn't power for the sake of power that I seek," said Phyro. "My aunt-mother is an able administrator, and the people of Dara have prospered under her. But she is too willing to appease an implacable enemy, too driven to compromise with the unconscionable. The people of Rui and Dasu *are* also people of Dara, and they must not be sacrificed for a so-called greater good.

"I seek not a rebellion against Empress Jia, but only to compel her to do what is right. Will you join me, as men and women of talent once rallied to the banner of my father? Together, we can build a better Dara, a Dara bathed in the light of true *mutagé*."

Privately, Widi shared his doubts with the other members of the gang.

"It's no wonder that the Dandelion Throne remains empty and veiled," he said. "Though he's intelligent and charming, he seems unseasoned, lacking an understanding of the shades of gray that can reside in human hearts."

"What do you mean?" asked Arona.

"I spoke to him of the many ways I've seen by which the wealthy prey upon the poor. He was sympathetic and vowed to put me in charge of simplifying and reforming the legal code once he has defeated the Lyucu."

"Isn't that what you want?"

"No . . . well, yes . . . but it isn't that simple. Emperor Ragin once outlawed the hated profession of paid litigators, but then they had to be brought back, for in their absence different abuses prevailed. There are consequences for every change, most of which cannot be anticipated. The belief that all wrongs can be righted merely by the desire to do good is . . . worrisome. Even the wisest laws and the most dedicated ministers will produce injustice, so long as humans are frail and selfish."

"So you want him to listen to your complaints and do nothing?" asked Arona.

Widi shook his head. "Of course not. But I wanted to hear less optimism and more humility, more understanding of the corrupt nature of humankind." He tried to think of some way to explain himself better to his friends. "Take, for instance, the fact that he has revealed the secret of the garinafins being trained in this valley. What does he know about us that he would trust us so? What if we're Lyucu spies?"

"Zomi thinks we can help him, and that is enough for the emperor," said Rati.

"But to be so liberal with trust . . ." Widi struggled to find the right words.

"Emperor Ragin made Gin Mazoti his marshal because he trusted the judgment of Cogo Yelu," Mota pointed out.

"That's different," said Widi. "That's just a legend, and my point is that nothing in life is ever as simple as legends."

"The emperor is no fool," said Mota, surprisingly loquacious. "Trust is rewarded with trust. I was once a rebel against the Marshal, but she trusted me to fight for her. The emperor has that same fearless charisma. Do you know that his chief garinafin trainer is a Lyucu? I've spoken with the man, Ofluro; he aids the emperor because rather than compelling Ofluro's service against his will, Phyro was not afraid to let him go. That grandness of spirit inspires love in his soldiers."

"But that can't work in every situation," said Widi. "He may be a good war leader, but he is too trusting, too willing to think the best of everyone."

"Not *everyone*," said Arona. "He's made it clear that no compromise with the regime of Tanvanaki is possible. The enslavers in Unredeemed Dara are evil, and evil must be confronted."

"But don't you see?" Widi grew frustrated. "To speak of good and evil like that betrays a discomfort with compromises, with . . . ambiguities. It's unsophisticated, unwise, almost naive. He will never be a match against his regent politically, and I fear that he will prove to be a terrible ruler."

"What you really mean," said Rati Yera, "is that he isn't cynical. He dares to love those who love him without reservation, dares to hate those who hate him without qualification."

Widi hadn't thought of it that way, but he realized that Rati was right.

"But what's wrong with believing in ideals, in good and evil?" asked Rati.

"Nothing. I just don't want us to get caught up in something that is doomed to fail," Widi said weakly.

"A bamboo stalk is just a straight tube, without sly twists and cunning turns, yet do you think me naive?" asked Rati.

Widi's face reddened. "I didn't mean that—"

Rati glanced at Mota, Arona, and Widi in turn. "A pine refuses to bend with every passing wind, yet you wouldn't speak of Mota as lacking in wisdom. A safflower is pure and plain in its hue, yet you wouldn't accuse Arona of being unsophisticated. Even you, the tongued orchid, strive to converse with and give succor to common working bees rather than offer your nectar to the menacing praying mantis, and I daresay you don't think of yourself as doomed to fail."

Widi didn't object.

Rati went on. "Phyro spoke to me of designing machines both for war and peace, of changing the lives of hundreds of thousands, even millions. Never in my life have I been given such a vision for the application of my skills. Though I know it won't be as simple as he says, his belief elevates me, fills me with hope."

Mota and Arona nodded. Phyro had also spoken to them of wondrous visions for their skills.

"You're not wrong to doubt, Widi. The emperor isn't much of an Incentivist and is unskilled in the art of political intrigue. But in that, he and we are kindred souls. Our abiding love as siblings who have found one another rather than being born of the same blood isn't motivated by thoughts of profit or advancement, but by shared ideals for the pursuit of knowledge. The love between the emperor and his soldiers, similarly, isn't rooted in ambition or vanity, but faith in a vision of *mutagé*, of bettering the world."

"The path to that vision will be full of danger and difficulties," said Widi. "Indeed, it may prove to be impassable."

"There is strength in simplicity, power in trust, beauty in plain-speaking, and grandness of spirit in believing in ideals," said Rati. "I know the world is complicated, but some questions really are as simple as good and evil. I know that the hearts of mankind are intricate and mazy, but I'm tired of being cynical. He has painted for me a future in which I, a *raye*, matter to the world because of what I can do. Even a slim chance, a mere sliver of hope, of achieving it is worth any danger, any risk. I will follow him."

"Me too," said Arona.

"And I," said Mota.

After a moment, Widi nodded as well. "Kon Fiji said that men should be willing to die for great lords who recognize their talent. Never have I understood the weight of those words until now."

Like a master *cüpa* player planning for the endgame from the first stone, Zomi had placed the members of the Blossom Gang in different parts of Dara, best suited to the unique talent of each.

While Rati Yera stayed in Tiro Cozo to work closely with Phyro on outfitting his army, Mota Kiphi and Arona Taré traveled around Dara, carrying out missions aligned with their own visions. Widi Tucru, as the one most familiar with the machinery of bureaucracy, had been assigned to Pan, where he made a name for himself as a litigator and built up the nonmilitary organizations that would be just as important as the army in the emperor's quest.

The latest message from Phyro contained no master plan. The intricate web of alliances and rivalries at the court changed daily, sometimes hourly, and the emperor, no great politician himself, could not possibly dictate the moves of his coconspirators from afar.

Therefore he could only suggest a general strategic goal, and leave the tactical implementation to his followers, trusting they had laid the necessary groundwork ahead of time.

By the time the pigeon was cooing contentedly and Widi had cleaned off the last wing of his fried chicken, the broad outlines of a plan had taken shape in the mind of the sly litigator.

Deviating from his typical routine of befriending members of the College of Advocates with drink and collecting gossip, Widi Tucru went to the Imperial Library and searched through old archives, focusing in particular on diplomatic records between the Tiro states.

A few hours later, he emerged with a triumphant grin. Prior to the Xana Conquest, when the Seven States had warred incessantly with one another, Cocru had at one point invaded Amu each harvest season for seven years, bringing great suffering to the people. Péshi, King of Amu, petitioned Cocru for peace by ceding a vast swath of farmland in Géfica. An ambassador from Cocru was summoned, and a treaty confirming the territorial handover was signed with the Seal of Amu.

The Cocru ambassador began the trip home to deliver the treaty to his king. But before he could cross the Amu-Cocru border, nobles who disagreed with Péshi's decision had staged a coup in Müning. The new ruler of Amu, Queen-Regent Üthephada, then dispatched speedy riders to the border crossing and intercepted the Cocru ambassador, seizing the signed treaty.

The ensuing war lasted many years, claimed many lives, and contributed to the weakening of both Amu and Cocru, but for Widi, what mattered was only one thing: The incident established the legal principle that a signed treaty was not effective until it had been delivered to the capital of the counterparty. The precedent was obscure, and there was little commentary, but every knife-tongue worth his fee knew that what mattered wasn't the inherent heft of the precedent, but how one leveraged that weight.

He went to see Zomi Kidosu. The two holed up in her study and dismissed the servants, conversing in hushed whispers all night.

The next morning, more messenger pigeons took off from Pan for Mota and Arona, who were in Ginpen at the moment.

∽

Since the competition between the Splendid Urn and the Treasure Chest, Arona and Lolotika Tuné, head girl of the Aviary, had become partners in a new venture.

It had begun because Lolo wanted to hire Arona to teach her girls some advanced techniques for stage makeup and quick-change masks. With the abolition of indentured servitude in indigo houses, a subtle change had come over these establishments. The owner-partners, often themselves working girls, improved conditions, protected the employees better, and branched out into other entertainment services. Since many of the girls were already excellent dancers and singers, Lolo thought the Aviary could explore putting on burlesque shows or even family-friendly comedy and serious drama.

Arona and Lolo took to each other like fish and water. Both their fathers, it turned out, had died in the Chrysanthemum-Dandelion War, and the two had entered business at an early age to provide for their families. The shared experience entailed a natural trust. When Arona explained to Lolo a new scheme, Lolo was enthusiastic. Making a profit while doing some good was the best of all possible worlds.

Thus, Arona's performance company, Foundational Myths, was funded and staffed by the Aviary. The troupe put on pageants, operas, and plays that recounted episodes from the Chrysanthemum-Dandelion War as well as the war against the Lyucu.

"There is unmet demand for stories about our heroes," declared Arona.

An early hit of the company, *The Women of Zudi*, told the story of a pair of sisters, Imuri and Rogé. At the start of the opera, the two helped Kuni Garu and Mata Zyndu defend the city against the army of Tanno Namen by carting stones and logs onto the city walls and caring for the wounded. The opera then followed their lives through the years: Imuri rose through the ranks in Gin Mazoti's auxiliary corps while Rogé became a spy for Kuni Garu against the Hegemon.

At their moment of triumph, when both were discharged honorably after the founding of the Dandelion Throne, tragedy struck. Corrupt officials pocketed Imuri's pension and accused Rogé of collaborating with the enemy, and the two families were forced to pawn everything they owned in order to bribe the unscrupulous officials and free the falsely accused Rogé.

The two ruined families then settled in Ginpen, toiling as laborers until they accumulated enough savings to start a dumpling cart together. Although Emperor Ragin tried to do right by his veterans, the two sisters, as a result of the unjust treason charge against Rogé, couldn't benefit. But by dint of hard work and frugal living, they managed to build back to a comfortable life. Their children went to private academies and studied hard, and Imuri and Rogé became respected elders in their neighborhoods.

At that point, the Lyucu invasion began. Without hesitation, Imuri volunteered for the air force.

"Why, sister? Why?" asked the bitter Rogé, who had lost the use of an arm as the result of tortures in prison. "Have we not suffered enough for the Dandelion Throne?"

Imuri replied with a song:

> *The Four Placid Seas are as wide as the years are long.*
> *A wild goose flies over a pond, leaving behind a voice in the*
> *   wind.*
> *A man passes through this world, leaving behind a name.*
>
> *A wild goose cares naught for honor, gold, fame, ambition.*
> *We are but links in the endless chain of love through the*
> *   generations.*
> *I fight not for any throne, but to tell my children:*
> *   Dara is you;*
> *   You are Dara.*
> *   Never surrender.*

Imuri was among the initial wave of aviators who sacrificed themselves to detonate firebombs against the garinafins, achieving the first victory in Dara's war against the Lyucu. At the conclusion of the opera, as her final letter, written before that last mission, was delivered home, Rogé fell to the stage, keening inconsolably.

Then she got up, and, as the curtains fell, volunteered for Marshal Mazoti's army, along with her husband, Imuri's husband, and all their children.

Not a single eye was dry in the playhouse.

The subject of war was not a popular topic for the playhouses. In part, it was because Empress Jia's well-known anti-militarism had chilled many performers from a politically sensitive topic. But the reluctance was also because the long years of peace had fostered a certain unspoken consensus among the literati: There was a collective sense of shame in the general prosperity of the Reign of Season of Storms, achieved only at the cost of paying tribute to the Lyucu and abandoning the people of Dasu and Rui to the mercy of the butchers. But there was no way to address the shame without confronting the cowardice and selfishness that lurked behind each individual mask of virtue. All in Dara were guilty.

To assuage their guilt, Moralists and Incentivists alike invented excuses to justify this state of affairs: war was the last resort of the uncivilized; true patriotism required absolute obedience to the decisions of the Throne; the most "efficient" strategy was to incentivize the Lyucu to continue to "trade" with Dara; by submitting to the Lyucu, Dara had in fact achieved a superior moral victory; the right response to aggression was universal love; learned scholars should not sully their minds by thinking about killing; one should always empathize with the enemy and engage with them to find accommodation; and so on.

In Jia's Dara, in other words, it was best not to talk about war at all.

But Arona's opera, unabashedly sentimental, melodramatic, lurid, old-fashioned, and sincere, ripped away those cynical veils, celebrated the bravery and sacrifices of those who had fought, and castigated the hypocrisy of those who advocated peace out of self-interest. Drama critics and sophisticated aesthetics lecturers at the academies scoffed and denounced *The Women of Zudi* as mere trash, meaningless entertainment to be consumed by simpletons packed into a theater on a summer night, sucking on candied monkeyberries as their minds rotted. It was obvious to them that the opera had been written by a hack, little better than a street performer.

Yet, crowds continued to show up for the shows: peasants, kitchen maids, merchants, giggling lovers, respected elders, minor nobles, scholars. . . . To be sure, Arona and Lolo spared no expense so that the opera had the highest production values: the actors and actresses were famous talents drawn from the best scarlet and indigo houses; the opulent costumes came from leading fashion ateliers; the orchestra employed retired Imperial master musicians as consultants; the special effects—many of them designed by Séca Thu, one of Lolo's most ardent suitors—made the garinafins and airships come alive onstage, and every night a few members of the audience fainted from fright.

Ultimately, however, these were mere details. The crowd came because the shows satisfied a hunger they had not known they had, filled a void in their hearts that they had not felt. People yearned for stories that told them who they were.

Over time, Foundational Myths toured around Dara and branched into other media. On giant screens, shadow puppets portrayed the suffering of the people in Unredeemed Dara based on accounts of the refugees; tumbling carts on rails, similar to those the Splendid Urn had deployed in the third competition, re-created for riders the experience of battling garinafins on Gin Mazoti's silkmotic airships; and Arona even partnered with re-enactors—history aficionados who gathered in their free time to act out famous battles from the past using replica armor and mock swords—to put on semi-educational shows, thereby bringing some measure of respectability to their eccentric hobby.

Gold and silver flowed in from these ventures, evenly divided between the Aviary and Arona Taré. Arona sent most of her share to Tiro Cozo, as Phyro and Rati desperately needed the funds to equip the private army. The rest she delivered to Mota Kiphi, who also needed money for his veterans' societies.

The veterans' mutual beneficial societies that popped up all over Dara were the brainchildren of Mota Kiphi and Widi Tucru. Empress Jia's distrust of the military extended to reduction of pensions for veterans and a general refusal to recognize them for their sacrifices, even symbolically. The Minister of Rituals, for instance, declined to issue official military insignia for discharged veterans, and there were no parades or ceremonies honoring them at important holidays such as New Year's or the Grave-Mending Festival.

But Widi, drawing on his experience organizing tenant farmers and laborers in collective action against landlords and workshop owners, suggested that recognition didn't have to come from above. It was possible to have the veterans organize themselves and tap into the reverence the common people had for those who put their lives on the line and left their teeth on the board for Dara.

Mota went around Dara, organizing local chapters of veterans' mutual benefit societies. Veterans of Dara's wars came together to share stories and reminisce about their experiences, and these oral histories were recorded by scribes (some of these stories became the foundation for Arona's plays and operas). Old friends and comrades who had lost touch over the years reconnected and pooled funds to help one another's families: pensions for widows, widowers, and orphans; funeral expenses; prosthetics and wheeled chairs for those who had lost limbs or mobility; advanced medical treatment such as silkmotic therapy; and so on. The veterans' societies also solicited funds from the public, and as a result of the rising patriotic fervor stoked by Arona's shows, many donated.

Though Emperor Ragin had taken care of his veterans by distributing land, unscrupulous landlords and merchants had cheated many out of their farms through predatory mortgages and springing-interest loans. The veterans of the war against the Lyucu, on the other hand, never received much from Empress Jia. Most of the surviving veterans were thus poor and looked down upon by Dara society.

To combat the low morale among veterans and to change public perception, Mota devised a system of tablets to display the honors each had earned during service. Widow Wasu and Arona began to offer discounts and special seating to patrons who presented such "honor tablets," and other merchants in Ginpen and elsewhere soon followed suit. Slowly but steadily, veterans held their backs straighter and strode through the streets of Dara with more pride, and the gazes that greeted them were no longer ones of pity or contempt, but admiration.

The veterans' societies performed yet one more function, known only to those who had gained Mota's trust: recruiting for Emperor Monadétu's private army.

The core of Phyro's private army in Tiro Cozo was his personal guard. Members of this unit had been responsible for his safety, and many had campaigned with him against various rebellions, starting as far back as the Reign of Four Placid Seas, when Phyro was but a boy. Around this aging core, Phyro had added new recruits slowly, usually idealistic individuals in whom Phyro detected a sympathetic spark: scholars who failed to advance in the Imperial examinations because they criticized Empress Jia's servile stance toward the Lyucu; sword fighters whose laments in small-town pubs regarding the lack of heroes in this degraded age had been overheard by the emperor traveling in disguise; people of talent—like the Blossom Gang—recommended by Zomi, Than, and other trusted allies. . . . But this process was slow and unpredictable, and very few recruits were added every year.

The veterans' societies, however, by spreading the message of heroism and sacrifice, acted as focal points to attract many endowed with a martial spirit receptive to the emperor's message. Working with a trusted staff, Mota was soon able to send a steady stream of new recruits to Tiro Cozo, swelling the ranks of Phyro's army.

Arona and Mota had begun to mobilize their resources as soon as they received Phyro's note. By the time Widi and Zomi informed them of the specific plan, they were ready for action.

Mota dispatched messengers to veterans' societies around the Islands, bearing instructions that he needed as many members as possible to muster in Ginpen. Arona reached out to Réza Müi to recruit her as the liaison to Ginpen's pro-war scholars, who were generally younger and came from impoverished backgrounds.

Zomi had told Arona that Réza would be a good potential coconspirator because she possessed the right combination of ambition, charisma, and tolerance for risk to lead a movement that could easily be misconstrued as treason.

"She reminds me of a younger me," as Zomi put it.

While Arona believed in Zomi's judgment, she had another reason to trust Réza: The young official was a Foundational Myths season ticket holder and a huge fan of *The Women of Zudi*.

Aya Mazoti could not have known that by the time she arrived in Ginpen, she would be stepping into a trap years in the making.

GINPEN: THE SIXTH MONTH OF THE ELEVENTH
YEAR OF THE REIGN OF SEASON OF STORMS AND
THE REIGN OF AUDACIOUS FREEDOM.

After multiple rounds of fruitless negotiations, Aya finally gave the order for her troops to remove Réza Müi and the other protesters by force.

The scholars and veterans linked their arms and began to sing.

> *A wild goose cares naught for honor, gold, fame, ambition.*
> *We are but links in the endless chain of love through the*
>   *generations.*
> *I fight not for any throne, but to tell my children . . .*

The immense crowd watching the confrontation joined in. Many of them had seen *The Women of Zudi*, ridden the tumbling carts against imaginary garinafins, attended battle re-enactments, or listened to proud veterans at teahouses recounting their campaigns as they displayed their tablets and scars. Empress Jia's craven capitulation to Lyucu demands contrasted sharply against the heroic images presented by the protesters, and they made their rage and displeasure known.

As Aya's soldiers dismounted from their horses and reluctantly approached the protesters, intending to shove or lift them out of the way, the crowd screamed at them.

"Shame! Shame! Shame!"

"You should be fighting the Lyucu barbarians, not *Anojiti*!"

"Have you seen the refugees from Rui and Dasu? Some were boys and girls younger than you, and they dared to rise up against the Lyucu for freedom!"

The crowd surged, threatening to overwhelm the two lines of soldiers holding them back.

Soldiers closing in on the protesters hesitated and stopped, looking pleadingly at Aya.

Aya gripped Réza by her collar and pulled her upper body off the ground. "Tell your mob to back down!"

"Never! Not unless you rip up that humiliating treaty," said Réza. "How can you do this? Your mother would turn her face away in shame to see you reduced to a lapdog of the Lyucu."

I am not a traitor. I must obey the empress, the holder of the Seal of Dara.

Aya leaned down and pressed her nose right against Réza's. "Don't you *dare* bring up my mother," she growled. "The job of a soldier is to carry out the orders of the sovereign."

"Not when the order is unjust."

"This. Is. Treason."

"Then arrest everyone here. We have more bodies willing to lie down in your path than you have prison cells."

"Traitor! Shame!" the crowd continued to scream.

"Draw your weapons! Beat the mob back!" Aya Mazoti cried as she shoved Réza away. Her eyes turned bloodred—the cries of the mob made her blood boil, and a doubt that had been growing in her since the conversation with Fara threatened to overwhelm her.

Could Réza be right? Would my mother be ashamed of me?

"I am not a traitor . . . ," she muttered to herself. "I will redeem the Mazoti name. . . ."

Troops moved toward the protesters once more. The scholars and veterans standing in their way linked arms and stared at them defiantly, singing even louder.

> *Dara is you;*
> *You are Dara.*
> *Never surrender!*

The crowd pressed against the soldiers like a storm-slung wave against the seawall.

"Arrest them all!" screamed Aya Mazoti. "*They* are the traitors! They are! Use all necessary force!"

Two soldiers put their hands on an old man who wore a wooden peg in place of his missing left leg. Two young scholars linked arms with him, one on each side. The old veteran refused to budge, and the soldiers tried to pry him away from the human chain. After a brief scuffle, they succeeded; the old man fell, smashing his nose bloody against the ground.

A roar erupted from the crowd like a peal of thunder, followed by a hailstorm of arcing objects—bits of rotten fruit, raw eggs, worm-bitten leafy vegetables, small pebbles, broken shingles, hastily shucked shoes. . . .

The struck soldiers, shocked rather than injured, staggered back into a clump and ducked behind their shields. Soon, the shields were covered by streaks of slimy albumen, broken shells, and smashed fruit. A pile of garbage grew around the cowering troops.

Aya Mazoti screamed for her troops to get up and fight the mob, but they refused to budge.

"What are you scared of?" Aya Mazoti shouted at them.

"I'm not afraid," said a young soldier, turning to face her. "But I joined the army to fight pirates and invaders, not to push maimed veterans around or to draw my sword against defenseless scholars. *My* mother would be ashamed of me."

Aya's face crumpled as she broke into helpless tears of humiliation. Garbage rained down around her, on her, over her; she kept her hands by her side, enduring the buffeting storm silently.

CHAPTER NINETEEN

TREASON BY THE BOOK

PAN: THE SIXTH MONTH OF THE ELEVENTH YEAR
OF THE REIGN OF SEASON OF STORMS AND THE
REIGN OF AUDACIOUS FREEDOM.

"Auntie Soto, you better go back."

"So eager to get rid of me, child? It may be a while before we see each other again."

"It's not that! I . . . I'm grateful for your help in sneaking me out of the palace. I just don't want you to get in trouble. If they find me missing while you're absent from the palace—"

"Your aunt-mother will suspect me anyway, even if I stayed in her sight this whole time. She didn't become the most powerful person in Dara by trusting. . . . Not anyone, not anything."

"Do you think she'll send the Dyran Fins after me?"

A pause. "No, I don't think so. As much as she worries about you, she knows you can take care of yourself. Besides, there are too many other things for her to worry about right now." A sigh. "Dara is about to be engulfed in a fierce and fiery storm."

A nervous glance and brush of the hair. "Do you think I'm wrong to run away?"

"Not at all. I understand how you feel. You sense the crackling in the tense air and the oppressive change in the political winds, but you have no power to steer the ship of state, to avert bloodshed and war. Some people, like Aya and Phyro, are eager to become kites in the storm to test the strength of their ideals and the height of their ambition, but that isn't the only way to live a worthy life. The

Fluxists say that when you cannot save the world, there is virtue also in retreating from the world. In a quiet cove, away from the storm, you may preserve the beauty of a single soul."

A quiet little laugh, and then melancholy again. "You speak too highly of me. I wonder sometimes if I'm too silly, despite all the Ano sages I've studied. I . . . never mind, I should go."

A step. Two steps. Three.

"You're not silly, child. This isn't about that boy, but about your-self."

A stumble. "How did you—"

"I may be old, but I haven't forgotten what it's like to be young. You want to go wander around Dara by yourself, away from atten-dants, away from the secret protection of the farseers, because you're afraid of leading them to him. But I daresay that in seeking him, you are really seeking your own nature. To know if you've found the mirror of your soul, don't you have to first know yourself? Or as the Ano sages would say, *gitré üthu*. That is the most serious journey any of us can undertake."

Tears sparkling in the moonlight. "Thank you, Auntie Soto."

"Be well, Ada-*tika*."

The College of Advocates, where the eponymous body performed its duties, glowed in the night like a bright lantern, the many windows along its octagonal sides lit up from within by silkmotic lamps and whale-oil candles.

At this late hour, most businesses in Pan, even the pubs and indigo houses, had shut down. But ambitious young advocates, most of them *firoa* and *pana méji* from the last session of the Grand Examination, remained at their desks, furiously wielding writing knives or gently rubbing blocks of ice under silk scrolls to fix the soft, finished wax logograms.

Zomi approached the building and paused before its imposing gate. As the author of the questions on the last session of the Grand Examination, she would be viewed by many of the young advocates as a teacher figure—despite the controversy surrounding the use of Ano logograms or zyndari letters. What she had to say to them would be immensely influential. It was a power that she had never used or abused . . . until now.

She thought back to her own time as a young advocate, when everything was new and the possibilities of government service seemed endless. How ambitious and full of ideas she had been then, imagining that if she just stayed at her desk later than her colleagues, read more books in the Imperial Library, consulted with more experts in the Imperial laboratories . . . she would be able to locate the perfect Ano quotation, discover the perfect invention, devise the perfect policy that would change the fate of all Dara.

What had happened to that fire that once burned in her heart, as bright as zomi berries, since then?

Objectively, she knew she should be proud of her accomplishments. She was the Farsight Secretary. She had contributed to the victory at Zathin Gulf, administered and reformed the Imperial examinations, created the system of circuit intendants to keep the bureaucracy honest, oversaw research in the system of Imperial laboratories . . . but she couldn't be objective. As soon as she had remedied one ill, she discovered ten more imperfections. What she had done had fallen so far short of her ever-expanding expectations.

She had not been able to help Phyro take his rightful place as the Emperor of Dara; she had not been able to drive the Lyucu out of her home island; she had not been able to right all the injustices she saw. She made mistakes; she overreached; she lost touch with the very people she thought she was representing.

Instead of speaking plainly and fearlessly, relying only on facts and principles, she was now resorting to plots and schemes and conspiratorial intrigue.

Had she become too willing to compromise? Had the cynical air at the court smothered her heart? Had she become as useless and myopic as the officials she once despised?

Worse, she seemed to lose everyone she loved: She had betrayed and then killed the Marshal, watched as her mother was incinerated before her very eyes, held her teacher's hand as he wrote his last words, buried her father as soon as she met him, forced her long-lost brother—her only kin—into exile, sent the woman she loved onto a journey from which she would never return . . . and now, just tonight, wept as her benefactors' only daughter was publicly disgraced. A sense of helplessness, of absolute and complete failure, overwhelmed her.

She looked up at the stars. *Théra, O my Théra.*

The reopening of the Wall of Storms had broken her tranquility. Without daring to admit the truth to herself, she had been hoping that Théra would seize the opportunity to return to her, like those messages etched into the backs of the turtles. When no ships came through and the storms resealed the opening, they seemed to also have cut off her last ray of hope.

She had always known that the hope was remote, ridiculous, foolish, but love made one do strange things.

She felt abandoned, lost. *Why didn't you come back? Have you forgotten me?* The stars blurred in her vision; she swayed on her feet.

Two shooting stars crossed the sky, like brilliant dyrans passing each other in the deep. An omen.

The most beautiful visage in the world seemed to take shape among the stars, and the most mellifluous voice in the universe spoke to her from the empyrean.

Just because we'll be apart doesn't mean that our love ends. You and I will both have many other loves, many grand romances and devotions and enlargements of the soul. But this is our first, and it will always be special. No matter how much time passes or how far apart we are, our love will remain true. We're dyrans streaking past each other in the vast deep, but our shared lightning-flash will illuminate the darkness ahead until we are embraced by the eternal storm.

I love you, Zomi, but this is what I want. Respect that.

"I love you, too, Théra," she whispered to the stars.

And in that moment, she knew, as certain as she ever knew anything in life, that Théra was alive, that she had succeeded in stopping another Lyucu invasion, that she had stayed in Ukyu-Gondé because her work was not done.

A surge of incandescent strength charged her from head to toe.

We're defined by the web of our loves, not one grand romance.

Théra has done her part; what about me?

We are Dara; Dara is us. There is a war going on, and we have not even begun to fight.

She still believed in ideals, trusted the vision of liberation, loved the people of Dara. Phyro, Than, Rati, Widi, Mota, Arona . . . so many friends fought by her side; she was not alone.

Actions reify ideals. If treason is the only path to mutagé, *then treason it must be.*

Resolutely, she strode through the gate and into the College of Advocates. It was time to make the humiliation of Aya Mazoti in Ginpen do some good.

Jia walked through the streets of Pan in the evening.

It was the middle of the weeklong Lantern Festival, and all around her, bright, beautiful lanterns of every conceivable design and color hung from eaves, tree branches, gate lintels, the hands of running children and the shafts of rolling carriages. Some spun, some swayed, some rose into the air like miniature hot-air balloons, tethered with a string. Many of the lanterns were painted with scenes from history and myth, the pictures often serving as logogram riddles. Passersby who guessed the right logogram would receive a prize.

From their street-side stalls, vendors tempted the strolling lantern viewers with snacks: candied monkeyberries, cold lotus-seed soup, mutton skewers roasted in the manner of the Lyucu but sprinkled with Dasu spices—the sellers were probably refugees. . . . The warm spring breeze, still with a hint of chill, carried the mouthwatering aromas to her.

Grand mansions and humble hovels alike participated in the festive displays. Laborers crowded in tenement buildings pooled funds to purchase communal lanterns and hired letter writers in markets to draft generic folk logogram riddles for a few coppers. Wealthy merchants vied with one another to put on the most opulent light shows, bedecking the curved roofs of their grand manors with hundreds, even thousands of lanterns—some of them powered by silkmotic candles—exhibiting bespoke logogram riddles crafted by erudite firoa or even officials at court.

This was a festival celebrating the arrival of spring, the return of light, and the eternal recurrence of the grand mystery that was life. To solve a logogram riddle was to symbolically break through the weight of wintry death and sprout the soul anew.

This is very odd, *Jia thought. Isn't it summer already?*

She paused before a large lantern slowly spinning in front of a small dress shop. A group of young people about fifteen or sixteen in age, dressed in shimmering silk and wearing jade hairpins, were looking up at the lantern and trying to guess the logogram. An old woman sat under the lantern, evidently the dress shop proprietor.

The painting on the sides of the hexagonal lantern showed a scene of devastation. Dead horses and soldiers lay scattered on a battlefield, interspersed with discarded weapons and broken siege engines. In the middle of the field stood a lone soldier, his body covered in wounds and armor askew, holding a dejected horse by the reins.

"Does anyone have a guess?" a girl asked the rest of the group. Two red pearls, each as big as a quail egg and worth its weight in gold, dangled from her earlobes. She glanced at a tall boy dressed in a bright yellow water-silk robe. "Mosoa isn't allowed to guess. He's too quick."

The other boys and girls shouted their conjectures. "Solitude!" "Patience?" "Grief."

The old woman shook her head at each answer.

Jia pondered the riddle herself. Usually, logogram riddles for the Lantern Festival tilted toward positive sentiments: fortune, health, many children. The desolation of this scene cast a pall over the celebratory mood.

"Rénga, you're looking well."

Jia snapped around at the familiar voice. The middle-aged woman standing next to her was bald, muscular, not very tall. The eyes that gazed at her out of the brown, leathery face, lightly lined, were piercing and clear.

"Gin," she blurted. Now she understood why she was walking through the streets of the capital devoid of attendants, and no one was paying attention to her. This isn't real.

She wasn't sure if these visits by apparitions from the beyond were messages from the gods or stirrings from her troubled conscience. However, so long as her children, Timu and Théra, remained out of her dreams, she was content. Perhaps irrationally, she took it as a sign that Théra was thriving beyond the Wall of Storms and Timu was enduring his fate with patience.

She would accept the slings and arrows of other ghosts.

"This is quite a puzzle," said Gin, gesturing at the riddle on the lantern. Jia's heart sped up. "Did you make it?"

Gin held a finger to her lips, indicating that they should watch and listen.

Mosoa, the quick-witted boy, looked around at his companions, an arrogant smirk on his face. "You've all been fooled by the mood of the painting. A man in shattered armor obviously stands for the semantic root of 'load,' written as the logogram for 'person' overlaid with the broken triple-bar motive modifier for 'weight.' Next to that is 'horse,' or koda *in Classical Ano, which here serves as both phonetic adapter and secondary semantic root. Put all of them together and you get* godawi, *meaning 'to promote, to elevate.' Despite the rather depressing visuals, this is a most auspicious logogram for all of us who seek to be elevated to the rank of* toko dawiji *at the next session of the Town Examinations."*

His friends exclaimed in admiration.

"Marvelous!"

"So well-deciphered!"

"Nothing can stump our Needle-Mind Mosoa."

The old woman sitting under the lantern nodded and handed Mosoa a small silk bundle. "Here is your prize, young master. It's a charm from the Temple of Fithowéo. May it bring you good fortune at the examinations."

Mosoa smiled and accepted the charm, tucking it away in his voluminous sleeve.

The old woman looked at the well-dressed teens and lifted a wooden bowl. "I'm working with the veterans' mutual benefit society, raising money to send the orphans of departed friends to school. Would any of the young masters and mistresses like to make a donation?"

Mosoa's face hardened. "If you're trying to sell the charms, you should just say so."

"No, it's nothing like that," said the old woman. "My husband was a sailor with the Imperial Navy, and he died at the Battle of Zathin Gulf. In fact, the soldier in the painting is based on his appearance. I've been blessed to have a little success with my business, so I thought I'd commission a large lantern this year to draw a bigger crowd and tell them about the scholarship fund—"

"What is the point of sending the children of dead soldiers to school?" Mosoa said disdainfully. He whipped his sleeves through the air and turned around to go.

"Wait!" the girl with the pearl earrings called out. "I saw a shadow puppet show about the lives of veterans. They're really pitiable—"

"You have to think with your head, Tenami," said Mosoa. "Veterans are typically drunkards, inveterate gamblers, criminals, cripples, or soft in the head—that is why they're so poor. How can children who come from such stock amount to anything? If you give them money, they'll just piss and gamble it away—"

"That is a most outrageous slur, young master!" The old woman stood up and pointed a trembling finger at the boy. "How can you speak with such contempt of people who have bled and died for Dara?"

Mosoa flushed, but he refused to back down. "I never told them to go fight and die, so they have only themselves to blame. Everyone knows that only simpleton peasants with overdeveloped muscles would join the army— if they were clever enough, they would have distinguished themselves in the Imperial examinations or figured out how to make fortunes."

"You . . . you . . . how dare you! My husband fought under the Marshal. You'll never find a quicker mind or a nobler soul in Dara."

"You speak of Gin Mazoti, a traitor who fought because she had no choice," said Mosoa with a snicker. "I certainly wouldn't call her clever or noble. She was born in a whorehouse and didn't even know how to read until she was an adult."

Jia glanced at stone-faced Gin.

"Besides, I find war morally objectionable," Mosoa continued. "There's no conflict that cannot be peacefully resolved through the proper study of the words of the Ano sages, the exercise of our natural human empathy, and judicious adjustment of incentives and trading opportunities. Everyone wants profit. As far as I'm concerned, all who fight in wars are equally foolish and wrong."

Sparks seemed to fly out of the old woman's eyes as she spat at the boy, "If it weren't for the Marshal and people like my husband on that day in Zathin Gulf, you would be dead now, or at best a slave speaking Lyucu."

That arrogant smirk reappeared on the boy's face. "Don't be so sure of that, old fool. The terror of the Lyucu has no doubt been exaggerated—we've been living in peace with them all these years, haven't we? Besides, I hear native ministers over there with talent do quite well. Even if the Lyucu should rule all Dara, some of us will always find success because we have this—" He pointed at his head. "Anyway, thanks for the charm." He turned and strode away.

His friends went with him, simpering and praising his sharp mind and sharper tongue—except for Tenami, who remained behind, hesitating.

The old woman turned to look up at the spinning lantern. Tears flowed down her wrinkled face; her shoulders heaved silently.

Tenami fished a few silvers out of the purse tucked into her sleeve and dropped them into the wooden bowl at the old woman's feet.

Mosoa's voice came from afar. "Come on, Tenami! I bet you can't figure this one out."

"I'm sorry," Tenami whispered to the old woman, and ran off.

The old woman said nothing. She continued to stare up at the lantern, her lips moving as she murmured silently to the painted likeness of her dead husband.

Gin turned and strode away. After a moment, Jia ran to catch up to her. They walked through the wide avenues of Pan, turned down side streets and narrow alleys, neither speaking.

Abruptly, Gin stopped. Jia saw that they had arrived at the largest cemetery in Pan. Here, there were no bright lanterns, no laughing crowds, no vendors selling greasy snacks. Endless columns of gravestones marched off into the night, mute tenements and ghostly mansions in this city of the dead.

Gin was staring at one corner of the graveyard, where some veterans from the Battle of Zathin Gulf were buried. It was supposed to be a resting place of honor, reserved for those who could not be interred in their ancestral graves either because they came from Rui and Dasu or because they were orphans with no certain lineage. But the gravestones were unadorned and plain, with tiny altars devoid of offerings. Jia had not allocated any funds to the Ministry of Rituals to maintain the tombs.

Cautiously, Jia walked up behind Gin. "Are you angry?"

Gin kept her face turned away. Jia waited patiently.

When Gin finally spoke, her voice was subdued. "No. My heart is heavy with sorrow, not fury."

"Sorrow for your comrades?"

Gin shook her head. "All those who go to war for home and country know that there will always be people like Mosoa. Soldiers risk their life and limb not because they wish to be thanked, but because it's the right thing to do. I am sad for Mosoa: A boy who doesn't understand the price others paid for his life and freedom will never become a man; he is, in fact, even worse off than a slave, for he has enslaved himself and cast away his soul, something that no conqueror can ever take from a man without his consent."

Jia sighed. "I feared you would feel that way. But Dara is better off with ten thousand cowards like Mosoa than one martial soul like you."

Gin turned around. "You were once a worthy Empress of Dara. Are you so afraid of the Lyucu?"

"I once stared down Tanvanaki on a garinafin, ready to incinerate me, and I can do so again."

Gin's eyes narrowed. "Is this about Timu then? You fear harm would come to him in a war?"

Jia laughed, a dry and bitter bark. "Being an apparition of my mind, you should know that I've already put my son in more danger than a heartless serpent would her wormlike young, and taken better care of your daughter than my own flesh and blood. Think not so little of me, Gin; such pettiness suits you ill."

"Then why? Why have you cut off veterans' pensions? Why have you allowed their tombs to be neglected? Why have you squeezed the army, navy, and air force until barely a skeleton remains? Why do you thwart Phyro at every turn and beg the Lyucu for an unjust peace? Why not fight them?"

"Because they cannot be defeated."

"What? Have you forgotten the Battle of Zathin Gulf?"

"A battle is not the war."

"A war is simply the accumulation of battle upon battle."

"Spoken like a tactician," said Jia. "But it is possible to lose a war even if you win every battle. Théra has stabilized the strategic situation by eliminating any hope of Lyucu reinforcements, curbing the aggression of the hard-liners in Unredeemed Dara. The peace can last. I will not throw away all that my daughter has achieved at who knows what price in a meaningless, doomed effort that will result in nothing but death and suffering."

"I don't understand you at all. Théra has given you the perfect opportunity to strike."

Jia took a deep breath. "Do you remember why Kuni chose to be taken hostage by the Lyucu at Naza Pass instead of escaping by airship?"

Gin was silent. The horrors of that day, as hundreds of villagers were executed by garinafin fire, were unspeakable.

"The Lyucu have turned Rui and Dasu into one giant military camp and enslaved the entire population," said Jia. "An invasion will lead to hundreds of recurrences of the scene at Naza Pass; nay, tens of thousands. All the people on those islands, also a part of the people of Dara, are hostages."

"Surely when the Lyucu see that defeat is inevitable, they will surrender?"

"Then you don't understand the nature of the Lyucu at all," said Jia. "The Tiro kings and even the Hegemon, despite their pride and ambition, ultimately viewed themselves as members of the people of Dara. The Lyucu, on the other hand, do not. They will prefer the extermination of the entire population under their control to surrender. You won't find a Jizu or Timu among them. The people of Dara are not their people, and there is too much history, too much hatred and fear in their hearts, to change that. They will measure success not by battles won, but by how many people of Dara they can kill before they can kill no more."

Gin shuddered. "You speak of a great evil."

"I do. Yet, it is an evil that cannot be confronted, for the price we must pay is too high."

"Is there no hope?"

For a moment, Jia almost wanted to reveal her secret. It was only a dream, after all, and what harm could there be in telling the secret to a figment of her imagination?

The impulse passed, unheeded. She was the empress regent, the holder of the Seal of Dara. She was watched, observed, spied upon. Even a dream-utterance could betray her and risk everything she had worked so long and so hard to achieve.

"So you pay for peace," said Gin, "appease the Lyucu to keep the hostages alive. You wait, hoping something will change."

Jia nodded. "And to succeed, I must remove the very possibility of an invasion from the minds of the people. Patriotism is like fire, a dangerous sentiment that can easily roar out of control when stoked. If the Throne holds military parades in Pan, if Imperial airships fly over temple consecrations, if the banner of Dara were flown above government buildings and public forums, if veterans were esteemed and honored at festivals, if Imuri's song were chorused as a patriotic anthem before the Imperial examinations—then it would be natural for the people to feel roused to war, to account little of its cost. That is why I have starved the military, neglected the veterans, suppressed accounts of the suffering of the people of Unredeemed Dara, hobbled commanders with civilian monitors. . . . The people of Dara must not be allowed to think a military invasion is the answer."

"You've always been suspicious of Kuni's generals," said Gin. "But to treat the military as though they were the enemy . . . to subject the veterans to contempt and chill their hearts . . . You've seen what happens when you carry that suspicion too far."

"I have made mistakes," acknowledged Jia. "But too little investment in defense can be easily remedied in a crisis, for there will always be brave men and women like you willing to take up the banner of Dara against our enemies. The opposite error, of trusting the army too much, is a far more perilous condition for the body politic. Courage can all too easily metastasize into a darker ambition with no cure. You remember what happened during the Principate: War became its own end, and warlords ruled the land.

"A standing army is an insatiable beast: It demands foes and growth. More, always more. More funds, more weapons, more soldiers, more victories. It comes to dominate the economy, as inventors devote their minds to methods of killing and industry becomes entwined with the machinery of war. Expropriation and conquest become more valued than cultivation and production.

"And when the army has run out of enemies, it will manufacture them. War is a drug that creates an unquenchable thirst. After Mapidéré conquered the Six States, he sent Admiral Krita's fleet beyond the Wall of Storms in search of the land of immortals. After Tenryo Roatan was finished with the Agon and Admiral Krita's fleet, he set his eyes on the Islands of Dara, though we had nothing to do with Mapidéré's folly. What will Phyro do, when he has 'liberated' Unredeemed Dara into charred reefs strewn with bones? Will he not want to launch an expedition to Ukyu to punish the Lyucu and avenge the dead? When will the cycles of slaughter end?

"In facing our enemies, we must take care not to become like them. As founders of a new dynasty, Kuni and I must always keep in mind that our actions are constitutive acts for subsequent generations, and weighty as precedent. If we do not prize peace, it becomes harder for successive sovereigns to do so. To protect the people of Dara from the dark future of militarism, the army must be caged and the generals chained."

Gin gazed into Jia's impassioned eyes. At length, she said, "You speak of broad trends as though they are certainties; you speak of historical patterns as though they dictate the future. But how can you claim to know the future when even the gods speak ambivalently? Time may not be a cycle. History is not the only story we can tell. Honor and courage do not have to devolve into ambition and zealotry."

"I wish I could have your faith," said Jia. "But I cannot gamble with the lives of the people of Dara, whether they live in Pan or Kriphi. Peace must prevail."

"You are a worthy Empress of Dara, but as always, I'm saddened by your way of looking at the world, an ugly, brutal world that I do not want to live in."

"It is the only world we have," said Jia. "I expect we'll never be able to convince each other of the truth of our respective visions."

Both smiled, reminded of a very similar debate they had had a long time ago.

The stars began to fade; the dream was about to end.

"It's good to see you, Gin," Jia said. She meant it.

"One last thing, Rénga," said Gin. "You say that the price of confronting evil is too high. But if in your peace, the people of Dara devolve to be all like Mosoa, is that not also too high a price?"

She strode away, leaving Jia alone with her thoughts.

These days, it was getting harder and harder for officials to secure a private audience with Empress Jia. She sometimes even skipped meetings of the Inner Council, complaining of headaches or other sources of discomfort. She preferred to spend her time in seclusion with Lady Soto, playing *cüpa* or reminiscing about the past. Soto never lobbied her for some policy or other, and such tranquil company was hard to find.

But this time, even Soto didn't know where the empress was. Unable to locate her in either the public sector of the palace or the private quarters of the Imperial family, Prime Minister Cogo Yelu eventually came to the Pellucid Cocoon Shrine.

A pair of Dyran Fins barred his way at the shrine door.

"Our mistress is meditating," said Teké, one of the Dyran Fins, her tone polite but firm. Like all Jia's bodyguards, she spoke in the distinctive accent of Boama, their mistress's home topolect, different from the courtly accent derived from Kuni's Central Cocru. Though only about twenty in age, she acted with no deference toward Cogo's station or seniority.

Cogo nodded and knelt down on the brick-lined path. "I'll wait here. It's important." He placed the tray laden with thick bundles of scrolls on the grass next to him.

Teké made no move to report his presence to the empress—not that Cogo expected her to. To the Dyran Fins, nothing mattered except what Jia wanted. The two Dyran Fins remained at the shrine door, looking vigilantly ahead. A distinctive birthmark next to Teké's right eye, shaped like a plum, seemed to glare at Cogo like a third eye, ensuring that he was no trouble.

Cogo sighed and closed his eyes, contemplating the shrine before him in his mind.

Located on the former site of the Moon-Gazing Tower, the Pellucid Cocoon Shrine was both the tallest and most distinctive structure in the entire palace complex. Unlike most buildings in Pan, which sported angular, sweeping roofs and stately columns of thick oak, the shrine was constructed from a bamboo frame wrapped in layers of gray and white silk. Cylindrical at the base, the shrine narrowed as it rose into the air, twisting and gyrating like a climbing vine or a wriggling silkworm until it came to a narrow tip topped by a giant pearl. Viewed from a distance, it resembled the tall spire of a sea snail shell, or a column of coiling smoke.

The shrine was dedicated to the memory of Empress Risana, who had fallen to her death here from atop the Moon-Gazing Tower (the guilty edifice had been torn down after the event to remove the taint of ill fortune). Every year, on the day of the Grave-Mending Festival, Empress Jia honored her sister-wife with another title that was recorded by the court historians and added to the row of stone tablets erected along the bamboo groove path leading to the entrance of the shrine: Sea-Compassionate Empress, Cloud-Fair Consort of the Dandelion Throne, Mountain-Wise Mother of Dara, Breeze-Gentle

Sister, Clear-Seeing Smokecrafter, Earth-Sturdy Adviser, Paragon of Faith and Piety, Counselor of Victory-Without-Shedding-Blood, Most Moral Exemplar of Feminine Virtue, Merciful Advocate for the War-Torn. . . .

Some poets praised Empress Jia for her solicitousness of the memory of Risana. It was but one sign of the grandness of her soul, the poets wrote, because Risana was rumored to have claimed a greater portion of Emperor Ragin's affections, especially in his later years. Yet, instead of seeking to bury her in oblivion out of jealousy, Jia highlighted Risana's achievements—though they were obviously outshone by Jia's own accomplishments as regent and supreme ruler of Dara—and heaped lavish honors upon her, going so far as to grant the junior consort the title of empress posthumously.

Others saw something more sinister in Empress Jia's actions. After all, Consort Fina, youngest consort of Emperor Kuni, who had died giving birth to Princess Fara, never received even a fraction of the honors given to Risana. Could it be, these gossips whispered, that Empress Jia was using the effusive titles stacked on his mother's memory to placate the young Emperor Monadétu? Was it perhaps a way to compensate him, at least symbolically, for the seemingly interminable regency? Fara, by all signs devoid of ambition, needed no such psychic bribery.

Whatever her real motives, Empress Jia often came to the Pellucid Cocoon Shrine to offer incense and to meditate, especially when momentous decisions had to be made, claiming to seek her sister-wife's spiritual counsel.

"Cogo." The empress's voice came from the door of the shrine. "My apologies. Have you been waiting long?"

Eyes snapping open, Cogo bowed deeply. "Not at all."

Eyeing the scrolls lying next to him on the grass, and without changing her expression, Jia backed into the shrine and swept one arm in a gesture of invitation. "Come inside." She turned to the Dyran Fins. "Go to the edge of the grove and keep everyone away." After a brief pause, she added, "Including Koko and Tutu." The empress never bothered to learn the names of her lovers-of-the-month, preferring to rename them like pets.

Cogo grabbed the tray of scrolls and followed the empress into the shrine. Though it was high summer, the inside was cool and comfortable. They climbed the long, spiraling bamboo staircase. From time to time, both paused to catch their breath.

Neither of us can move as effortlessly as we did in our youth, reflected Cogo. *Time catches up with all. . . . How much longer can we wait?*

Eventually, they reached the small sanctum at the top. Calming incense burned in a brazier, and comfortable cushions lined the floor. The empress sat down in *géüpa* and sighed with contentment.

"You must not strain yourself, Your Imperial Majesty," said Cogo. Carefully, he knelt down in *mipa rari*. It was his habit when in her presence never to break protocol, the same way he never called her *Rénga*. If Jia noticed, she never commented on it. "Be solicitous of your own health. So much depends on you."

"You seemed to desire privacy for your audience," she said, catching her breath. "Climbing up here is the quickest way to achieve it."

"There is nothing so urgent that I would presume to risk your well-being."

Coolly, Jia regarded Cogo, who did not meet her gaze. The corners of her mouth turned up in a bitter smile.

"I *am* getting old," she said, "much as I dislike to admit it. But you're an old friend, Cogo, and I think we have earned the right to demand honesty from each other."

"My thoughts have always been as transparent to you as my speech," Cogo said, without looking up from the silk-lined floor.

Jia sighed as she poured tea for Cogo and herself. This was always Cogo's way. Despite her declaration, she couldn't be sure they *were* friends. They were more like partners in a boat, rowing in the same direction and with the same stroke, most of the time.

When she pushed, he often yielded and then flowed around her like water, giving her no purchase. He never confronted her, but there were times when he arranged things in a way that carried out the letter of her orders instead of the spirit. Alone among all the ministers, he seemed to understand what she feared and what she hoped to accomplish. Yet, she couldn't trust him with the totality of her vision.

"I assume this isn't about Fara."

Cogo shook his head. "The farseers haven't been able to locate the princess. Secretary Kidosu can't spare more people on the task until the crisis in Ginpen—"

"Tell Zomi to call off the search," said Jia, her voice weary. "Fara is old enough to take care of herself. If she doesn't want to be found, so be it. Children, even princesses, go where they will."

She took a sip of tea and then pointed to the tray of scrolls. "What are these? More petitions from the College of Advocates complaining about the treaty? The fact that Aya was halted by a few warmongering fools means nothing. Delivery of the treaty is a mere formality. I've already ordered that a new emissary be nominated."

Instead of answering, Cogo handed her one of the scrolls. Reluctantly, she accepted it.

As Jia scanned the columns of logograms, her expression didn't change. Wordlessly, she set the scroll down, and picked up a second one.

Cogo looked around the sanctum. He had not been up here in some time. Behind the incense burners hung an embroidered portrait of Empress Risana. In line with the ethereal, light design of the shrine itself, instead of an elaborate, gilded statue, this simple portrait was the only object of veneration.

But what a portrait it was! Done entirely in shades of black and gray, the figure of Risana was realized with only abstract lines rather than the detailed, lifelike brushstrokes characteristic of the hand of a painter trained in the camera obscura and at formal model sittings. A short black dash evoked her left shoulder; three short curves elicited the shape of her face; a series of wavy silver ripples filled in the rest of her half-glimpsed body; two long, sinuous gray swirls, as airy as smoke trails, suggested the motion of her famed long sleeves in dance.

The entire creation was reminiscent both of Lady Mira's abstractionist portraits of the Hegemon and of Risana's own unique style of smokecraft. It was, of course, the work of Princess Fara, who had made it as a present for her elder brother when they were younger. Phyro had kept the portrait in his room and wept in front of it daily. When his attendants informed Empress Jia, she praised the portrait and ordered it removed from the young emperor's room so that it could be hung here, replacing the gaudy gold-and-ivory memorial statue that had been commissioned by Jia herself. Phyro had refused to speak to her for months after that.

She finished reading the last scroll. "These petitions may come from different hands, but the arguments show a remarkable unity."

Cogo Yelu bowed slightly. "Members of the College of Advocates do work closely."

Empress Jia chuckled without mirth. "Someone is feeding them arguments—someone who enjoys crawling through musty, worm-ridden scrolls for specious legal reasoning."

"The precedent set by Üthephada of Amu is good law," said Cogo, his tone even.

"There is no such thing as 'law' when it comes to relations between states," said Empress Jia, an edge coming into her voice. "All that matters is power. Do you think the Lyucu care about these precious 'precedents' set by the petty Tiro states? The treaty has been signed; the debate is over."

"The Lyucu may not care," said Cogo, his voice as gentle as water, "but the Dandelion Court does. There is a building consensus among the ministers and generals that since the treaty has not been delivered, debate isn't over."

Jia sighed. "What is the point of further debate? We've all heard everything we need to hear. A decision has been made."

"Not one that takes into account the new argument," said Cogo, pointing at the scrolls.

"These don't contain any *new* argument. Most of the petitions circle around the same theme: the desire of the few for a safe and peaceful life must not outweigh the yearning of the many for justice. This is nothing but a clever way to twist my words and clothe the same old argument in fresh garments."

"The argument comes now with previously unweighed support," said Cogo. "The people have spoken. The advocates describe vividly the scale and vehemence of the protests in Ginpen that stopped Princess Aya—"

"It's the fault of that foolish girl!" said Jia. "Why did she have to march through the streets of Ginpen as though she were returning from a triumph, making herself a convenient target for political drama? She should have relied on stealth, secrecy—"

Cogo shook his head. "Aya should not be blamed. Veterans' societies from all around Dara are unified in their opposition to the treaty, and many scholars are standing with them—"

"I've told you that I don't trust these veterans' societies," said Jia. "This protest has all the signs of being stirred up by pro-war agitators."

When the veterans' societies began popping up around Dara a couple of years ago, Jia had been suspicious and ordered Zomi, as Farsight Secretary, to investigate them. Zomi claimed that she found nothing incriminating. Unconvinced, Jia had then asked Cogo to conduct an investigation, but the Prime Minister pleaded lack of resources and expertise. Jia would have liked to conduct her own surveillance with the Dyran Fins, but unfortunately, Wi and Shido had their hands full overseeing the secret trade arrangement with Tiphan Huto.

"Even if some of the veterans have been manipulated," said Cogo, "it doesn't make their sentiments inauthentic. To lure all the fish into one weir may be a trick, but that only works if the river is already full of fish."

"A few veterans can hardly represent the voice of the people. I will not back down from the right path for Dara because some disgruntled old soldiers—"

"It's far more than that," said Cogo. "The people of Dara are speaking out through multiple channels: members of the College of Advocates fill your desk with petitions; hundreds of veterans have pledged not to ingest a single grain of rice until you relent; hundreds of monks and nuns have declared ill omens seen in the sky and the sea, showing the gods' displeasure with this treaty; fifty-eight ministers kneel at this moment in the Grand Audience Hall, demanding that you reopen the debate in formal court; stevedores and students in Ginpen have formed human chains around the docks of Ginpen, vowing to stop anyone from boarding the tribute ships; elders in fishing villages along the northern coast have organized fleets to blockade the port of Ginpen, promising to ram their boats into the tribute fleet if it tries to depart; in Boama, Dimu, Çaruza, Müning, and other cities, crowds have gathered around government buildings, chanting songs from patriotic operas—"

Empress Jia glared at Cogo and spoke slowly, enunciating each word carefully. "Are you telling me there will be mutiny if I refuse their demands? Is this a threat of rebellion? That's an act of treason."

Cogo shook his head. "The protests have remained peaceful. If this is considered rebellion or treason, then it's rebellion within the lines, treason by the book. The people are not threatening, but pleading for you to heed your own pronouncement: When the interests of the few are weighed against the interests of the many, the few must yield."

Jia closed her eyes.

And who belongs to the many, who the few?

Can the suffering of the people be weighed like fish?

Who is speaking for the voiceless people of Unredeemed Dara? Who is advocating for the interests of the hostages who are about to be sacrificed in the name of "justice"? They cannot march through streets or sing patriotic songs; they cannot make rousing speeches or debate legal precedents. All they can do is survive, and hope.

Many are speaking, but many more have been silent. The voice of the people is as hard to discern as the will of the gods.

It's easy to say that those living in freedom have a duty to fight for those under tyranny and bondage—but what good is freedom when those you aim to save are dead?

She tried one last time. "You know as well as I do why peace is the only course. It's why you've backed me against Phyro for so many years. What has changed?"

"The voice of the people," said Cogo. "You and I have tried to maintain this peace, thinking it's for the greater good. But we are old, and perhaps our wisdom has grown outdated.

"Could you have predicted that despite all our attempts at suppressing the sentiments of patriotism, it has flared into such bright flames? Would you have believed that despite our plans at building an all-encompassing machinery of state, the people have framed their own institutions outside the bureaucracy? The world continues to surprise us because it is eternally young, while we march closer to death with each passing day.

"So how can we be certain of the future? How can we know the Lyucu will never surrender? How can we know that the enslaved people of Dasu and Rui will not succeed in an uprising when we attack? How can we be so sure that Phyro, because he is inexperienced, must be wrong, and that we, because we have seen much, must be right?"

"Phyro wants to gamble with the lives of the soldiers," said Jia, "and the lives of the people of Unredeemed Dara. Do we have the right to make that choice for them?"

"But how can we know they do not wish to gamble on their own? To deny them that chance is also making a choice for them."

"This is sophistry!" said Jia. "You have converted entirely to Phyro's idealized militarism, and now you're finding reasons to justify that leap of faith."

"It isn't Phyro's opinion that matters," said Cogo. "No single person, whether emperor or regent, can stand in the way of the voice of the people of Dara, channeled through their own institutions."

"The people do not understand the horror they are about to unleash! Those who are speaking are but a hotheaded minority as rash as the emperor. I'll send the navy to scatter the fishing boats; I'll order the army to break up the protests; I'll arrest any scholar, monk, peasant, laborer—the treaty must be delivered—"

"Your Imperial Majesty!" Cogo's words pounded against her heart like angry waves against the shore. "You have always wanted a Dara in which it doesn't matter who holds the Seal of Dara, because the hand that holds the seal must be guided by the voice of the people. Now that your vision has been realized, will you embrace it or shrink back in fear? The people do not wish to live like cattle and sheep, to be milked and fleeced by the Lyucu. If you defy the will of the people, then you'll be a sovereign in name only, a mere tyrant."

The words of Gin Mazoti came to her mind unbidden.

"You say that the price of confronting evil is too high. But if in your peace, the people of Dara devolve to be all like Mosoa, is that not also too high a price?"

You should be comforted, Gin, Jia thought. *The people have decided that they prefer a bloody war to a soul-bleaching peace.*

Jia began to laugh, a sound more horrifying than sobs.

Cogo remained in *mipa rari*, his head bowed. But it was a posture more of defiance than respect.

If only I had a little more time. The amount being shipped by Tiphan Huto still isn't enough, though I've come so close.

But the people have spoken.

Abruptly, she swept her hands through the pile of scrolls and tossed them far away into the corner, where they slammed against the wall of the shrine and fell in a jumble.

"Summon Phyro from Tiro Cozo."

CHAPTER TWENTY

OPENING SALVOS

A FEW DAYS' SAILING OFF THE SOUTHERN SHORE
OF RUI ISLAND: THE SEVENTH MONTH OF THE
ELEVENTH YEAR OF THE REIGN OF SEASON OF
STORMS AND THE REIGN OF AUDACIOUS FREEDOM.

As she surveyed the silhouettes of the opposing fleet from the crow's nest of the city-ship *Péa's Beak*, Goztan Ryoto felt no fear, only pity.

The Dara invasion armada consisted of more than thirty vessels, but even the largest warships on the horizon had less than one-fiftieth the displacement of a city-ship in the Lyucu fleet. It was like watching a school of tuna trying to challenge a pod of whales—the outcome was so obvious that the contest seemed hardly honorable.

"As you can see, the intelligence I derived from the Dara envoys has proven true," said Noda Mi, standing next to Goztan. "The Dara-raaki haven't been constructing city-ships of their own. The Great Lyucu will surely dismantle these toy ships as easily as wolves feast on mere bleating sheep."

Goztan didn't acknowledge the simpering man with so much as a nod. The Loyal Hound's efforts to ingratiate himself with the Lyucu thanes at every turn—going so far as to pepper his own speech with the most extreme anti-Dara slurs employed by Cutanrovo and her party—nauseated Goztan. She found his attempt to out-Lyucu the Lyucu almost laughable, except she could derive no pleasure from the slaughter she was about to commit—if his advice turned out to be right.

"One wonders what kind of rotten dream herbs that usurper, Jia the Whore, had smoked that made her dare to challenge the perspicacious, the merciful, the fair Tanvanaki!" Noda Mi declaimed, waving his arms about excitedly, oblivious to the growing disgust of his commander. "She's throwing away the lives of all the poor sailors on those ships with this mad venture! I'm ashamed to think that I once called her my empress. Oh, if only the Dara-raaki had been wise enough to accept the compassionate terms of our omnipotent pékyu! I weep with sorrow, thinking of the blood about to flow! But then I tremble with admiration as I imagine the pity that would have been on Pékyu-votan Tenryo's face—"

"That's enough," said Goztan. "Your patter grows wearisome."

Noda Mi jackknifed into a bow so deep that his buttocks stuck out over the side of the crow's nest, making his form resemble that of a chicken ready to defecate. "Oh, I do apologize, votan! I'm beyond embarrassed. Of course I didn't mean to lament the loss of Dara-raaki sheep lives. I only wanted to express my sincerest regret that brave Lyucu warriors would have to dirty their awesome weapons with the unworthy blood—"

"Silence!" Goztan took a deep breath and turned away from the odious little man. "Let me focus on the battle at hand. Dara commanders have always been resourceful, and there may be a trick here. We must tread with caution."

Noda Mi shut up, but he bowed again and again, abjectly knocking his head against the mast.

Goztan ignored him. The tactical situation had to be analyzed carefully.

To counter the Dara armada, Goztan had under her command five city-ships, escorted by ten smaller warships that formed a defensive line ahead of them. The formation was designed to prevent mechanical crubens from sneaking up on the city-ships, which carried the primary weapons of the Lyucu: garinafins.

A second line of Lyucu defenders floated in the air above the calm water between the fleets. These silk-and-bamboo airships, propelled by feathered oars, had been seized from the natives during the Lyucu conquest. Instead of the banner of the House of Dandelion, a blue breaching cruben on a red field, they flew the ensign of Ukyu-taasa: a string of wolf tails flapping in the wind.

Goztan was grateful that Tanvanaki, despite fierce objections from Cutanrovo, had authorized her use of these airships to augment the Lyucu fleet.

"Votan, how can you ask our brave warriors to fight with the feeble weapons of the vanquished?" Cutanrovo had demanded of Tanvanaki.

"Airships are *not* feeble," said Goztan. "They complement garinafin riders and city-ships. Besides, we already use airships to patrol the coasts. It hardly seems radical to add them to the fleet against the invasion."

"You remain as blind as ever, enamored of native ways," said Cutanrovo, her voice dripping with contempt. "You are even tainted with their muddy patterns of thinking!"

Since returning from the Wall of Storms with the terrible news that no reinforcements had come through, Cutanrovo had become even more dedicated to the project of eradicating all native influence from Ukyu-taasa. She held more rallies, launched more campaigns to destroy farmland and convert it to pasturing, revived the ancient custom of human sacrifice for more celebrations, and stepped up efforts at total militarization of the state. She dispensed tolyusa at every ritual and gathering. (Goztan wondered where Cutanrovo was finding so much wild tolyusa, but so long as Cutanrovo didn't endanger the military supply, she couldn't really accuse her of impropriety.) Lately, Cutanrovo's anti-native diatribes had grown so extreme that sometimes Cutanrovo sounded to Goztan like a parody of herself.

At first, Goztan had been hopeful that Ukyu-taasa's increasingly untenable strategic position would finally force Tanvanaki to turn away from the hard-liner party. After all, much of the justification for Cutanrovo's rise, that Cudyu would be sending more Lyucu to join them in Dara, had turned out to be a mirage.

But Tanvanaki continued to accede to Cutanrovo's demands. When Goztan finally found a chance to confront the pékyu in private, her answer was brief.

"When gash cactus juice has been poured over the eyes of the garinafin, there's nothing the pilot can do to stop the frenzy except hang on."

In a flash, Goztan saw Tanvanaki's dilemma. The pékyu was trapped.

Tanvanaki, no less than Cutanrovo, had shaped the policy of Ukyu-taasa around the expected arrival of Cudyu. She had ceded more and more control to the hard-liners in order to secure her own power against the assumed challenge from her brother. To admit now that the forecasting of more reinforcements was an error, that the blind faith in the reopening of the Wall was unwarranted, would be to cast doubt upon Tanvanaki's judgment, to erode the myth of the pékyu's infallibility.

She had no choice but to go along with Cutanrovo's explanation: The reinforcements had been withdrawn because the gods were testing Ukyu-taasa; the pékyu and her warriors had to triumph, right here, right now, by manifesting the self-reliant destiny of the indomitable Lyucu spirit.

During the intervening years, Cutanrovo had unleashed a self-reinforcing mass movement among the Lyucu, and the madness was no longer confined to a few thanes or even one party. The killing of natives who showed the least sign of defiance had become so routine that the court re-rememberers had ceased to keep track. Lyucu and togaten youths as young as ten participated in competitions to hunt native villagers for sport. Step by step, Cutanrovo's vision of Lyucu supremacy, founded upon the complete subjugation (and eventual elimination) of the native population, had become an article of faith among the naros and culeks, as revered as the tales of the adventures of Kikisavo and Afir.

Indeed, the culeks and low-ranking naros, despite their lives being noticeably worse as a result of hard-liner policies, were among Cutanrovo's most ardent supporters. Though Goztan had no access to the census records and reports from the remnants of the native bureaucracy—Cutanrovo classified all such information as state secrets and controlled access strictly—she could tell anecdotally that the economy of the Lyucu-conquered islands was weakening. Only tribute from Dara proper allowed Ukyu-taasa to maintain the appearance of prosperity. Farms were failing; new pastures were unproductive; herds and flocks were collapsing; culeks and low-ranking naros had lost what little wealth they had as everything became more scarce and expensive. As their lives worsened, they clung even harder to the ideal of Lyucu supremacy. Only by slaughtering the natives and by committing atrocities against them could they maintain the feeling that they were stronger, fiercer, *better*.

Cutanrovo knew how to take advantage of their state of desperation. She distributed to the culeks and low-ranking naros more tolyusa and kyoffir than they had ever gotten from Tanvanaki. She was celebrated as the great kyoffir-giver, the reviver of the Lyucu spirit, the best and most loyal thane of them all.

Even the least sign of disapproval of Cutanrovo from Tanvanaki led to howls of protest at court and beyond—and a full-scale civil war would no doubt flare up if the pékyu actually attempted to move against the garinafin-thane. Ukyu-taasa had become so dependent on the tribute fleets that their absence for an extended period would lead to the total collapse of Ukyu-taasa, and the only way to keep the tribute flowing was to maintain the hard-liners' relentless policy of threats and intimidation against Dara proper.

"When you've gone down one path far enough," said Tanvanaki, her voice weary, "it's no longer possible to turn back and pick another. You think I wield Power, but it's Power now that wields me."

Goztan heard in the pékyu's declaration a thousand-thousand unspoken regrets, but also a thousand-thousand defiant affirmations. The pékyu saw her own empathetic nature as a liability, a weakness. She could not allow her own revulsion at the consequences of the occupation to manifest as vacillation, believing it would invite rebellion, attack, the end of Ukyu-taasa. She had to look away as she unleashed Cutanrovo upon the land. Step by step, she had done what she thought was the right thing, even if she *felt* otherwise, and at some point, it no longer mattered what she felt.

Even after the expiration of the last peace treaty, Jia had continued to send tribute, but it was unclear how long the Dandelion Throne would do so once it realized that there would be no more Lyucu reinforcements from beyond the Wall. Tanvanaki tried to secure a future for Ukyu-taasa by demanding even more tribute in exchange for a new peace treaty, but the bluff had failed in spectacular fashion. Somehow, the young emperor had succeeded in a power struggle against the empress, and instead of a tributary fleet, Dara had sent an invasion force.

"Let me explain why these useless native gasbags must not be added to our glorious fleet." Cutanrovo strode around the Great Tent, waving her arms about passionately. "Using airships to patrol for escaping slaves is like fashioning garinafin muzzles out of garinafin leather—there's nothing wrong with employing the tools of the slaves to control slaves. But war is the most sacred act of the Lyucu people, a manifestation of the Lyucu spirit! Using slave weapons in war will pollute the Lyucu spirit with the contagion of defeat!"

Goztan wanted to wrap her hands around the neck of the strutting garinafin-thane and *squeeze* until her tongue hung limp. Instead of focusing on the practical matter of how to defend Ukyu-taasa from this invasion, Cutanrovo was obsessing over symbolism. Goztan could no longer tell if Cutanrovo was a fool who really believed the nonsense she spouted about the "pure Lyucu spirit" or a cynic trying to use this debate to advance the power of her faction at the expense of Goztan's. Either way, Cutanrovo was going to get them all killed.

She had had enough. But before Goztan could unleash her fury on Cutanrovo, the pékyu stepped in.

"Airships can do things garinafins cannot." Tanvanaki's voice was calm, rational. "The flight power of our lightning-fast garinafins must be conserved as much as possible, but these native airships, though slow and cumbersome, may stay in the air indefinitely. They make ideal scouts, especially against underwater mechanical crubens."

Cutanrovo would have none of it. "The pékyu-votan didn't conquer Ukyu-taasa with airships. The spirit of the Lyucu, our most potent weapon, is weakened when we turn away from the ways of our fathers and abandon the practices of our mothers."

A hint of impatience surfaced on Tanvanaki's face. "My father's father didn't sail across the sea on floating wooden islands captured from the barbarians. My mother's mother didn't feed the tribe with meat obtained from people who dug most of their food out of mud.

Circumstances change. If my father didn't dilute the Lyucu spirit by coming to Ukyu-taasa on city-ships, then how can I be accused of straying from his path by deploying airships to defend his legacy?"

"You are not the pékyu-votan," said Cutanrovo.

"What do you mean by that?" Tanvanaki said after a pause. She didn't raise her voice, but there was an edge to it, as cold as a metal blade.

Cutanrovo didn't flinch. "A great Lyucu like the pékyu-votan is born once in a hundred generations. He rode the will of the gods with as much skill as you, votan, ride Korva. Like the heroes Kikisavo and Afir, he could show the Lyucu a new way of life. But you . . . forgive me, votan, you do not wield Langiaboto."

Tanvanaki surveyed the thanes standing in the Great Tent. Those who were of Cutanrovo's party stared back, flickers of defiance in their eyes. She could not remember such an open challenge to her authority.

She leapt into motion, a blur like the flashing shadow of a garinafin diving through the clouds. Before anyone could even exclaim with shock, the fight was over. She knelt with one knee on the back of the prone figure of Cutanrovo, her war club held aloft above the thane's head.

"You forget yourself," she said, her voice reverberating in the suddenly silent tent. "I've been patient with you because I don't wish to see votan-sa-taasa and votan-ru-taasa at one another's throats. Perhaps, like so many of your frenzied followers, you've been ingesting too many tolyusa berries to think straight. But let me clear away the haze in your mind: Where *I* point, *you* go."

Cutanrovo remained submissively immobile. The other hardliner thanes stood rooted to their spots, none daring to move.

Tanvanaki got up and stepped back onto the throne. When she spoke again, it was as if nothing had happened. "Incorporate all combat-worthy airships into the fleet."

"As you command, votan," said Goztan.

"Since Goztan will have to concentrate on readying the ships," said Tanvanaki as she turned to Cutanrovo, who was slowly climbing back to her feet, "you'll be responsible for provisioning her with slave labor and preparing our defenses on land. You've talked often enough of an army of native thralls; it's time to see you put your vision into practice."

"As you command, votan," said Cutanrovo.

Goztan sighed inside, disheartened. True, the pékyu had just crushed a brewing challenge against her authority, but she lacked the will and the resources to eliminate Cutanrovo and her faction altogether. Instead, Tanvanaki had to appease Cutanrovo's pride by granting her yet more power over the defenses of Ukyu-taasa.

As the sun descended toward the western horizon, the Dara ships raised their sails and steered for the Lyucu fleet.

Goztan, standing at the bow of *Pea's Beak*, looked up at the sentry airships. The signal flags showed that the observers aloft had detected no signs of mechanical crubens.

Instead of relief, Goztan only felt even more unease.

Why would they initiate an attack when their ships are clearly inferior?

Intelligence gathered by Noda Mi from past Dara tribute envoys indicated that Jia had been starving the military, with no funds allocated for the construction of powerful naval vessels to challenge the supremacy of Lyucu city-ships or the creation of a new air force capable of taking on garinafins. The ragtag fleet before her, devoid of air support, seemed to confirm Noda's findings.

Goztan turned to Noda Mi. She had conscripted the man as her field adviser in part because of his familiarity with Dara's generals and admirals. "Can you tell who's commanding the enemy fleet?"

Noda Mi squinted at the approaching ships.

Besides the breaching cruben flag of the Dandelion Throne, the attacking ships also flew smaller banners charged with a rampant horse atop stylized undulating lines.

Noda answered confidently, "That's the banner of Puma Yemu, Marquess of Porin."

"The raider," mused Goztan.

"Votan speaks true," said Noda Mi. "He is a coward, unwilling and unable to engage a superior force in open combat. I despise the man with all my heart."

Goztan didn't bother responding. Puma was known for hit-and-run tactics, both on land and water. If he was in charge of the Dara fleet, then this attack was almost certainly a feint. But even feints could turn deadly if she was careless.

Since the wind was southerly, Goztan ordered the smaller, nimbler ships in the protective line to tack into the wind and meet the oncoming Dara armada. Lyucu naros shouted orders, and native slave sailors scrambled to obey. The city-ships would stay back and observe the engagement from a safe distance, ready to respond to any barbarian trick.

Overhead, culeks aboard airships beat a steady cadence on cattle-skin drums, and under the watchful eyes and swinging whips of Lyucu overseers, Dara slave rowers pulled on the large feathered oars. The graceful airships, like exotic birds, headed into the wind, giving aerial cover to the surface vessels below.

Goztan watched the maneuvers of her fleet with some trepidation. Although she was confident of her own and Tanvanaki's preparations for the invasion, the weak link in the Lyucu defense had always been their small numbers. Most of the available Lyucu warriors were aboard the city-ships to augment the garinafin crews. The smaller naval vessels and airships must thus rely on a large number of native slaves, and their loyalty was questionable.

She didn't exactly blame them—why would the natives, after all that they had been put through, fight for the Lyucu except when coerced? Memories of her own days of silent rage in the company of Captain Dathama came unbidden to her mind, but she forced them away. She was a thane of the Lyucu, and she had to fight for the survival of her people. Everything else had to yield before that unshirkable duty.

As if reading her mind, Noda Mi, Loyal Hound of the Lyucu, spoke up again. "Votan, you may have complete confidence in the native crew. Each slave serving the pékyu today in our glorious fleet has family back in Ukyu-taasa. Thane Cutanrovo has gathered the family members and chained them at the bottom of a pit. Unless we achieve victory today, Thane Cutanrovo will execute them."

Goztan closed her eyes and sighed. She had never been comfortable with the way Pékyu Tenryo controlled large armies of garinafins by threatening harm to their young. Cutanrovo had simply expanded the technique to people.

Noda Mi went on, oblivious of her unease. "Now, to provide additional incentive to the slaves, the wise thane made it clear to them that the execution of their families would be slow and painful. For instance, one might be put to death by a thousand slow cuts, each gouging out a thumb-sized piece of her flesh. Another might be held under water until he passed out, only to be retrieved, revived, and returned to the water again. The methods were most ingenious and creative!" A tone of glee crept into his voice, and he licked his lips excitedly.

Goztan shuddered with revulsion.

"Not that I would dare to take any credit away from wise Thane Cutanrovo," said Noda, "but I feel it's only honest to mention that I did suggest a few of the execution ideas to her." He bowed and looked up hopefully at Goztan, just like a dog who had done a good trick.

Goztan could no longer stand his presence. "Go down and make sure the garinafin crews are ready to launch on my command."

The two fleets were still so far apart that they would not come within range of each other's catapults for some time yet.

Abruptly, massive stones shot off the decks of the Dara armada. Screeching through the air at speeds far too fast to be the work of catapults, most of the stones splashed into the sea near the Lyucu ships, throwing up tall columns of water like breaching crubens. But a few struck home, and smashed spars and splintered beams tumbled through the air, accompanied by the bloody limbs of crushed sailors and the wailing of the dying.

The Lyucu ships were thrown into confusion. How did Dara catapults suddenly gain such power?

Puma Yemu, Marquess of Porin, laughed heartily. He had been skeptical when the emperor equipped his ships with these newfangled weapons, but now he could see that they were indeed worth all the training he had put the crew through.

Back in Tiro Cozo, Phyro had studied the Lyucu way of war in depth, poring over eyewitness accounts of the Battle of Zathin Gulf and the engagements on Rui, as well as interviewing refugees from Unredeemed Dara. The hand weapons of the garinafin riders drew his particular interest.

The slingshots, operating on a similar principle as Dara bows, were easy to understand, but the slings and spear-throwers favored by some of the Lyucu fighters were unfamiliar. He asked Rati Yera to study them and to extract their principles of mechanical advantage.

After experimenting with these weapons, Rati devised a new kind of stone-throwing machinery that she named Fithowéo's arm. The machines, a kind of enhanced catapult, were powered by gravity rather than torsion. A heavy counterweight at the short end of a swinging beam powered the far longer throwing arm so that the end of the arm swung through a much longer arc as the weight was released. This mechanical advantage was further amplified by a set of sling cables attached to the end of the throwing arm, modeled on the Lyucu hand sling, to accelerate a missile even more. The result was a stone-throwing machine that was compact and operable with a small crew, but capable of launching missiles to much greater distances than even the most powerful torsion catapults previously used in Dara.

"Fire at will," ordered Puma Yemu, his white hair and bushy beard lifted by the wind. "Ha! This is my favorite sort of fight. We can hit them but they can't hit us!"

"Shame! Shame!" cried an animated Noda Mi. "Even that coward Kuni Garu never deployed such decadent and unnatural weapons! Surely this is a novel contraption devised by some dark-hearted Dara-raaki bookworm, preferring dead machines to superior courage, which the Lyucu possess in abundance—" He flinched and ducked involuntarily as another screaming stone missile splashed into the water, though still half a mile from the hulking *Péa's Beak*.

Goztan paid little attention to Noda's blathering—she knew that the primary goal of his little performance was to clear himself of all responsibility in case she suspected him of collaborating with the Dara invaders by withholding knowledge of these weapons of terror.

Calmly, she observed the swinging Fithowéo's arms and issued a series of new orders, which were transmitted to the defending fleet by flag signals.

Sails were lowered on the smaller Lyucu ships, and native sailors and marines as well as their Lyucu commanders scrambled below-decks as though preparing for a storm. Then, oars poked through the open oar-ports and propelled the ships at a rapid rate toward the oncoming Dara ships.

More stones whizzed through the air, many of them overshooting the speeding Lyucu ships and splashing into the sea harmlessly. A few struck masts and hulls, but since the ships were no longer powered by sails and there was no crew on the exposed decks, little damage resulted.

"Oh, brilliant!" cried Noda Mi. "Look how the enemy flees before true courage!"

Goztan heaved a sigh of relief. Once the shock of seeing them for the first time had faded, she realized that Fithowéo's arms were more terrifying than practical, at least on the sea. Although the machines had great range, they lacked accuracy. Reloading and adjusting their aim took time. By closing in on the enemy at full speed, the Lyucu ships minimized their exposure to the missiles. Although resorting to oars this early threatened to deplete her fleet of maneuverability in a long engagement, she was glad to have found a counter.

The Dara ships, realizing that the Lyucu vessels were trying to duck under their fire, turned and zigzagged away, though they continued to lob stones in the pursuers' direction.

"Stop the pursuit and rest the rowers," ordered Goztan.

"But votan, they're on the run!" Noda Mi said. "We should give chase and sink them all in one decisive strike by our invincible garinafins!"

Goztan shook her head. "Puma's preferred tactic has always been to hit and run. If we give chase at full speed, he'll simply retreat out of range with his smaller ships and then strike back when our rowers are exhausted."

"But if we don't chase, he'll continue to harass our ships from afar."

Goztan pondered this. "While the surface vessels are resting, send the airships to hound the enemy. And when the airship crews are tired, send the surface vessels."

The orders were issued via flag signals. The airships added new banks of feathered oars and sped after the retreating Dara fleet. Without air support, the Dara ships would be particularly vulnerable against firebombs from above.

The bombardment was brutal. Burning oil and tar rained down; sails burned; masts smoked. Even with wet sand covering the decks, several of the larger ships caught fire after sustained aerial sorties.

When fire suppression measures proved ineffective, the captains gave orders to abandon ship. The Dara crews squeezed into lifeboats, but the Lyucu airships descended and caught them with more firebombs. Sailors and marines leapt into the ocean and swam for other ships, but many were overwhelmed by the waves and never made it.

"Marquess, two more ships lost in the left wing!"

"*Golden Armor* reports that her rudder is jammed and she can no longer steer!"

"Captain Iré of *Tenth Month* is dead. First Officer Azokéda has assumed command, but the ship's crew sustained heavy losses and can no longer staff the Fithowéo's arms."

Puma Yemu, standing on the foredeck of *Réfiroa*, a sleek war sloop that served as his flagship, received these reports with a grim expression.

"Rescue as many survivors from the water as we can," he ordered. "But keep on tacking and firing at the surface ships. We have to hold out as long as possible."

Ki Aten, a middle-aged official in the Ministry of Rituals who had been drafted as Puma's monitor, piped up. "Marquess, maybe . . . uh . . . discretion is the better part of valor?" His hands, legs, and lips were all trembling uncontrollably. The man was completely unnerved by the smell of burning tar and the groans of the wounded all around him.

"No!" snarled Puma Yemu. "They're expecting me to run, which is why we must stay and give them a fight they won't forget." He turned to his personal guards. "Stay here and protect Monitor Aten!"

The guards rushed over and surrounded the cowering official.

Holding up their immense ironwood pavises, they formed a nigh-impenetrable protective barrier, which, perhaps not entirely by coincidence, also prevented Ki Aten from following or approaching Puma Yemu.

With the monitor out of the way, Puma Yemu ran toward the single mast of the sloop. Upon reaching it, he unsheathed his heavy steel sword and hacked at the base.

"Come on, you lazy beavers! Help me gnaw this thing down!"

After a moment of consternation, the crew of *Réfiroa* came to the aid of their lord. About half of the crew were sailors drawn from the regular navy, while the rest were soldiers in Phyro's private army; there was lack of coordination among them due to the short time they'd spent training together. Still, the regular sailors, unaccustomed to the unorthodox tactics and weapons of the emperor, were adjusting quickly. Wielding axes, swords, hatchets—whatever they could get their hands on—the crew made short work of the mast.

Ki Aten, peeking from seams in his personal miniature fortress-prison, screamed in terror. "What are you doing, marquess? Stop! I order you to immediately cease this senseless act!"

Technically, the monitor had the authority to countermand any order of the commanding officer. But since Ki Aten was trapped at the bow of the ship, none of the mast-chopping sailors heard him.

Puma Yemu had the same order transmitted to other ships in the fleet. Soon, the crew of every Dara warship was chopping down masts as though felling trees, leaving the decks an open space without obstructions.

Lyucu commanders aboard the airships and the pursuing surface fleet watched this scene in total disbelief. Without masts, how would the Dara fleet escape? The Marquess of Porin, known for striking and running away, had trapped himself.

Goztan, sensing a trick—Puma's apparent self-sacrifice *must* be covering for some new assault—ordered her commanders to refrain from swallowing the bait and increase their vigilance against threats from beyond the horizon or beneath the waves.

This did not sit well with everyone. A few of the hard-liner thanes, chafing under Goztan's command, began to mock Goztan's caution, demanding an immediate, all-out assault. Others, more loyal to the garinafin-thane, angrily demanded obedience.

While the Lyucu commanders contended with one another in confusion, the Dara ships hummed with activity, as busy as anthills and beehives. Sailors swarmed onto the cleared decks, carrying bamboo frameworks and bundles of silk. As Puma and the other captains strode across the decks, barking orders, the crews divided into smaller groups and fell to work. Soon, giant battle kites lay on the deck of every ship.

Traditionally, battle kites in Dara were used for ancillary military tasks such as surveillance and signaling. In ancient times, they were also used to carry individual champions into the air for duels—an outdated ritual last revived by the Hegemon. Since the advent of airships, their use had grown increasingly rare.

The battle kites now being readied by the Dara fleet, however, were far larger than specimens from Dara's past: Each could be ridden by a crew of three.

As signal flags danced, the battle kites took off, anchored to the rotating platforms and winches of the Fithowéo's arms.

By now, Goztan had reasserted her authority over the fleet by stripping command from a particularly recalcitrant hard-liner thane. The chastened Lyucu commanders refocused on the new threat. Cautiously, the airships came about and began another bombing run.

Only now did Puma's earlier order to dismast his own ships make sense. With the decks cleared of all interfering superstructures, crews could guide the kites in virtually any direction without fear of entangling the control lines. Swooping, diving, flipping, rolling, the kites circled the air above each ship like Mingén falcons, their silk wings flapping loudly.

Still, it was hard to imagine a battle kite, even one as large as these, doing much damage to an airship. Even if the battle kites were equipped with ramming blades, a direct collision with an airship would leave them in tatters. Thus, the airship captains urged their crews to maintain their approach, firebombs at the ready.

"Aim for Puma's ship," shouted the captain of the lead airship, a naro-votan. "Ignore the silk birds."

The chief of his bombing crew, a native, instructed his men, "Open bombing-bay doors." There was both weariness and resignation in his voice. He hated what he had already done, what he was about to do. But his family members were all chained at the bottom of a pit on Rui, and disobedience was out of the question.

Wide doors along the sides of the gondola and at the bottom slid open. The crew scrambled into position with ceramic jars filled with tar and oil, torches ready to light the fuses. As soon as the airship was in range, the firebombs would be tossed out of the gondola, dealing death and carnage to the ship below.

Puma's sailors sang and labored at their winch, bringing the giant battle kite around. As it swept past the gondola of the airship, the bombing crew craned their necks to get a better look at the kite, expecting to see a defiant Dara warrior brandishing a sword like a hero out of the ancient sagas.

Time seemed to slow down for the bombing crew as the kite loomed into view.

Below the billowing wings of the kite was a small horizontal platform, barely more than a suspended bar. A large crossbow, as wide as a man was tall, was mounted on it. Three kite fighters were strapped to the wings of the kite, each performing a distinct job: loading the next bolt; drawing the crossbow (with feet so as to utilize the strength of the whole body); and aiming and firing the weapon.

For a moment, the stunned firebombers looked into the grim eyes of Puma Yemu, his flowing silvery beard and hair like the feathers of an aged Mingén falcon. Then, the old raider general, who had personally taken to the skies to inspire his crew, mercilessly squeezed the trigger of the crossbow.

The bolt zinged through the air like the darting tongue of a snake, twisting, flexing, covering the distance between the kite and the gondola in the blink of an eye.

The bolt thwacked into the chest of a soldier standing near the open bombing-bay doors of the gondola. He didn't even let out a scream as the force of the projectile carried him back into the gondola, stumbling. The firebomb fell from his grasp and rolled along the floor, its fuse lit.

"Smother it!" shouted the bombing crew chief. He jumped at the firebomb. The faces of his father, his mother, his wife, his two children, flashed through his mind in an instant. "I'm sorry," he muttered.

The bomb exploded.

Smoke and flames shot out of the windows of the gondola as survivors leapt from the burning wreckage, screaming, flailing, falling, until the cold sea silenced them.

As she watched the fragile-seeming battle kites hold their own against much larger airships, Goztan experienced a deepening sense of unease.

Though she had not been present at the Battle of Zathin Gulf, accounts of the deadly weapons employed by the natives under Marshal Gin Mazoti had made a deep impression on her. She had felt relief (as well as a hint of disappointment) when she realized that this invasion fleet didn't come with Imperial airships dangling enormous spheres that unleashed the mysterious silkmotic force.

She hoped that it was a sign that the natives could no longer afford the magnificent military force they had fielded more than a decade ago. Cutanrovo had been insistent that Empress Jia lacked both the resolve and the resources for war. Perhaps, just perhaps, this invasion had been launched out of desperation rather than confidence.

But once she saw what Fithowéo's arms and the new battle kites could do, Goztan began to rethink her conclusion. These new weapons were simple in operation, demanded little maintenance, and appeared cheap to build. They were cost-effective modifications to known weapons rather than entirely new inventions. The architect of this invasion had apparently been forced to work within tight constraints and had to find ways to win without the kind of resources Gin Mazoti could call on, with a whole empire behind her.

It reminded her of the way Tenryo had always achieved victory: not with overwhelming advantage in matériel, but by surprise, guile, and the skillful deployment of the tried-and-true.

She wondered if she should have been even more cautious in ordering the aerial assault—perhaps she should have launched the newly equipped garinafins. . . .

No. The existence of those weapons had to be kept secret as long as possible. It was the tendency of all armies to fight the last war, and she suspected that neither the Lyucu nor the natives were wholly exempt from this bias. The longer she concealed her true capabilities from the Dara commanders, the more of an advantage she obtained.

Even after Jia had been forced to resume a state of war against the Lyucu, she refused to commit to Phyro the level of resources he needed for an all-out invasion. Puma Yemu's navy, for example, had to be scraped together from the small fleets maintained at various harbors across Dara for anti-piracy patrols.

Phyro didn't blame his aunt-mother; indeed, he had anticipated and planned for this exact scenario. He knew that support for the war, though fervent at the moment, was fragile. The voice of the people was powerful, but it was also fickle. After so many years of peace, few were willing to give up the prosperity gained during the regency or to sacrifice much to free others—selfishness was the natural state of all humankind.

The total mobilization Dara had undertaken a decade ago had only been possible because all the Islands faced an existential threat, and the martial spirit from the Dandelion-Chrysanthemum War still lingered. Things were different now, and a war to liberate Unredeemed Dara would remain popular only so long as most people didn't feel its effects. In this, the empress and the emperor reached an unspoken consensus.

Thus, it was vital that victory be achieved quickly and with the least amount of resources. There was neither the time nor the funds to build up Dara's ill-maintained military, and Phyro had to rely for the most part on his private army, drawing on the regular military only for support roles.

No powerful Imperial airships existed to complement the invasion fleet; Phyro had to find some other way to neutralize the threat posed by Lyucu airships.

Though battle kites had been used to defend against airships in the earliest days of the Xana conquest, the practice had fallen out of favor during the Principate, since most Tiro kings fielded their own airship fleets. Phyro decided to revive the use of these cheap aircraft but upgraded them with more advanced weapons.

He was also gambling on the fact that the Lyucu, being devotees of garinafin warfare, would not bother to learn how to fight effectively with airships. Events proved him correct. Goztan deployed her airships as scouts and equipped them only with bombs, instead of staffing them with full complements of archers. Since archery required long training and crossbows demanded skilled mechanics, the Lyucu never adopted these weapons for themselves. Lyucu commanders also didn't like the idea of arming their native crews—despite Cutanrovo's reassurances, they couldn't trust that native auxiliaries wouldn't mutiny.

As a result, Goztan's airships were ill-equipped to deal with the battle kites. The only ranged weapons available were slingshots and slings, and the kite riders were clad in light armor made of layers of paper that, to the surprise of the Lyucu, stopped the bullets very effectively.

Still, as the battle went on, the Lyucu commanders learned to deal with the kites. Some airships used their bulk to foul the control lines of the kites, causing them to fall into the sea. Still others improvised by tossing firebombs or fuse-lighting torches at the kites, and successful strikes sent the silk-and-bamboo constructions diving into the sea like fiery meteors.

By far the most effective countermeasure, of course, was to close off the bombing-bay doors, preventing the crossbows from targeting the interior of the gondolas. In response, the kite riders directed their bolts at the airship hulls, and the powerful missiles were able to penetrate the light armor to puncture the gasbags inside.

More experienced airship commanders would have realized that given the number of gasbags and the relatively small size of the punctures, their vessels had plenty of excess lift to deal with the kite riders or escape. But the Lyucu captains, already spooked by the sight of several airships going down in flames early on due to well-placed crossbow hits, were panicked by this move that they should have anticipated. As they screamed for their crews to gain altitude, ballast bags were carelessly discarded and the constricting straps around the gasbags loosened to the maximum. A few Lyucu captains even resorted to throwing hapless oar slaves out of the gondolas so that their ships could ascend more quickly out of the range of the battle kites.

Puma Yemu watched the receding airships with satisfaction. He signaled for the battle kites to be retracted, landing nimbly on the deck himself.

"Now that we've humiliated them properly, we should run before their surface vessels come at us again, perhaps with garinafins this time."

"That's the first sensible thing you've said all day." Ki Aten poked his head out from between the protective pavises like a timid snail. "But how are we going to run? We have no masts and no sails. We can't possibly row our way back to the Big Island!"

"The emperor has thought of that . . . and who says we're heading back to the Big Island?" Puma turned away to issue more orders.

"Wait, wait!" cried Ki Aten. "Then where are we going? Our battle plan was to engage with the enemy and find out their strength. Now that we've done so, what else are we supposed to do besides retreat home?"

"There are many details not fully elucidated in the battle plan the emperor gave you," said Puma Yemu, waving his hands vaguely. "Now, if you'll excuse me—"

"How am I supposed to provide oversight if you keep your battle plans secret from me? The empress made it clear—"

"You're welcome to complain to the empress after we've liberated Unredeemed Dara," said Puma brusquely. He strode away to supervise the sailors as they rushed around to build a new contraption, leaving Ki Aten to sputter impotently behind him.

It felt good to be out of Pan, where petty bureaucrats ran everything and he felt like a prisoner.

Finally, the generals are free.

The airship captains observed the commotion far below with puzzlement: Long oars were brought up from holds and laid out in parallel on the decks instead of being dipped into water; bundles of sailcloth spread open; sailors climbed over the large winglike objects gradually taking shape. . . .

"What in the world are they building?"

"Is that a giant battle kite?"

"Are they trying to fly all the way up here?"

Indeed, on the surviving Dara ships, the crews seemed to be assembling long oars into diamond-shaped frames and stretching canvas over them, creating massive kites almost as big as the ships themselves. On top of these immense kite-sails, they attached the smaller battle kites that had been used earlier to fend off the airships.

Once more, the smaller battle kites were launched into the air.

Goztan realized that something was wrong. "Quick," she ordered, "full speed ahead! Give general chase!"

But it was too late. As the smaller battle kites lifted into the air, they pulled the big kite-sails up with them. And as the billowing, free-floating sails filled, the mastless Dara ships began to move. The kite-sails climbed higher and higher, even above the height of the airships, and the fleet sped away to the west.

"I've heard of this invention!" volunteered Noda Mi, always eager to be of service. "By harnessing high-altitude winds, they allow surface ships to move at speeds far in excess of what can be achieved by ordinary sails. Indeed, I believe these kite-sails were an experimental device first used by the traitor Luan Zya—" Noda stopped talking, suddenly realizing that he might be blamed for not bringing up this information earlier.

"Never mind," said Goztan. "If the device is experimental, I doubt they can sustain this high speed for long. Signal for the airships to land on the city-ships. We'll pursue the enemy by sea."

She was relieved by the outcome of the battle. Though she had suffered some casualties, she had also gotten a good look at the capabilities of the Dara invasion force. The new weapons were clever, but hardly the kind of terrifying engines of death like the silkmotic airships at Zathin Gulf.

The kite-sails evidently provided the enemy with little ability to steer. If they continued west, they'd hit the eastern shore of Crescent

Island before long. She was confident that she could trap the Dara fleet there and force them to surrender.

A victory over the invasion fleet would finally give her enough political capital and support among the thanes of Kriphi to challenge Cutanrovo and put an end to the madness she had unleashed among the Lyucu. After that, she should be able to persuade Tanvanaki to seek peace again with Dara, but this time with much more reasonable terms.

The sooner she could end this senseless war, the better.

CHAPTER TWENTY-ONE

AN UNEXPECTED MIRROR

DIMUSHI: MORE THAN A YEAR EARLIER.

There was a saying that Dara had three capitals: the Capital of the Empire, the Capital of the Mind, and the Capital of Magic.

The Capital of the Empire was Pan, where the avenues were wide and the traffic orderly, and even the stately buildings lining the streets seemed to sit in *mipa rari*. This was where you lived if you craved power or proximity to it. Browsing the open-air markets, one might rub shoulders with a general or deputy minister; praying at the many magnificent temples, one might find oneself kneeling next to a duchess or the chatelain of a great house; brunching at a restaurant, one might overhear conversations from the next table that changed the fate of industries and provinces. Founded by Mapidéré to rule over an empire larger than any Tiro state, Pan was a young city already steeped in history, and every glazed brick or fluted column seemed to whisper, *If only you knew what I have seen. . . .*

The Capital of the Mind was Ginpen, which produced the largest portion of successful scholars in the Imperial examinations. The city's libraries, both public and private, contained more books than all the rest of Dara combined, and seven of the ten top-ranked academies in the Islands were located here. *Toko dawiji* could be found in the markets, writing calligraphic letters for the illiterate, and *cashima* were so numerous that jealous visitors from other cities joked that they were like the fleas on a monkey. Ginpen was where the latest fashionable academic trends started, where the cleverest logogram riddles were born and then spread to the rest of Dara, where inventors gathered to consult with like-minded colleagues. Whether the subject was literary analysis of the classics, advanced symbolic mathematics, history of Adüan folklore, mechanical and silkmotic engineering, mating habits of the whales, cultivation of orchid breeds . . . Ginpen was where one went to find the experts.

But for fun and temptation, there was no place like Dimushi, the Capital of Magic.

Once merely a satellite port of Dimu, across the wide mouth of the Liru, Dimushi over time became a refuge for artists who despised traditional notions of beauty; poets who felt stifled by classical forms; young people escaping from arranged marriages they dreaded; cult founders driven away by angry mobs and concerned magistrates; radical philosophers dreaming up new, perfect societies; scholars who failed in the Imperial examinations and felt their genius was unrecognized; . . . and of course, lots and lots of criminals, from petty thieves to gang bosses. Even in the days of the Tiro states, when Dimushi was under the administration of Amu, it had a reputation as a place where *anything* went. Moralist values were flouted; unconventional manners and fashions flaunted; the unwary fleeced; and square jaws floored.

Clever merchants soon realized the opportunity Dimushi presented. It was a wilderness of sorts, a fount of thrills for those weary of the staid rituals of civilization. Indigo houses, casinos, pleasure inns of every description sprang up, offering avenues for visitors to experience the delights of this city in a prepackaged, safe manner. To protect the tax revenue skimmed from these generous but naive wallets, the magistrates of Dimushi and the gang bosses reached a silent understanding that allowed everyone to prosper.

Dimushi flourished under the peace of the regency. Dress designers came to be inspired by its street art and graffiti; court poets came to steal the slangy vernacular of hawkers and beggars, which captured the life of the people more vividly than ancient logograms; singers, dancers, magicians, and performers of every stripe tried to break out in the grand theaters and music halls, filled with the most profitable but also jaded audience in the empire. Bars served drinks at outrageous prices, promising tastes not found anywhere else in Dara; smokecrafters put on shows that blurred the line between reality and illusion, claiming to have learned their technique from Empress Risana; casino-inns offered group tours where guests rode around Dimushi in opulent carriages, listening to narration that was nine parts lies and one part exaggeration, gawking at sites such as the colorful shanties in the Artists' Quarter, the ruin of the indigo house where Gin Mazoti had been born, the teahouse where Empress Risana had once performed with her mother, dark alleys where herbalists were said to brew concoctions that allowed drinkers to converse with the gods, and walled compounds where gang bosses held invitation-only sword-fighting tournaments with eye-popping wagers. . . . In a thousand ways, the city's wildness was tamed, bottled, and sold to swell the purses of the wealthy, while the poor gathered in teahouses to lament rising property prices and the loss of the city's "authentic character."

Still, if you needed services that couldn't be found anywhere else in Dara, chances were that you could obtain them in Dimushi.

Zen-Kara strolled through the street, deep in thought.

Few people walked by the docks this late at night. The district was considered a part of the seamy underbelly of the city, and darkness was the friend of smuggler gangs, pirate liaisons, swaggering swordsmen-for-hire, drunkards looking for trouble, and other unsavory characters.

Clad in a pearl-white silk robe, face covered in blue tattoos, braided blond hair under a smoky-hued scholar's cap, Zen-Kara seemed as out of place here as a blooming orchid next to a fetid pool. But she was unconcerned. It wasn't just because she was a good fighter; she was used to being out of place, no matter where she was.

A warm breeze caressed her face, bringing with it the odor of rotting garbage floating in the wide, slow-flowing Liru, invisible beyond the warehouses. She sighed, thinking about her father's message. *Come home, child. It's time to stop drifting like a coconut in the ocean.*

Home. She repeated the word to herself in both Dara and Adüan. Neither felt completely right on the tongue. The Islands were so varied and the ocean limitless; yet, she didn't know where she belonged.

The sounds of argument; a shout of outrage.

She was passing by a dilapidated warehouse. Having constructed the oversized structure in a bout of optimism, the owner, a Wolf's Paw trading clan, had then failed to find the anticipated tide of trade that was supposed to lift its fortunes. Unwilling to throw good money after bad, the clan decided to abandon ship, leaving the warehouse empty and stranded. As the years passed by, the roof leaked, rats moved in, and scavengers had long since picked the inside clean. It became the abode of vagabonds and a meeting house for street gangs.

Muffled running steps; a loud crack as something—or someone—smashed into a wall, about two stories up from where she stood.

She backed away, looking up in alarm.

Another loud crack as rotted wooden planks splintered overhead, and a man tumbled out of the fresh hole in the side of the warehouse. He managed to land on his feet and rolled along the packed earth to absorb the force of the impact.

With great difficulty, he staggered back up. The crash through the warehouse wall had bruised and bloodied his shoulder, visible through his torn tunic. One leg was clearly having trouble supporting his weight. Zen-Kara and he locked eyes.

Despite this shocking entrance into her life, she found a natural charm in his eyes. Though he winced from the pain in his leg, his posture was confident as he brought up his arms in a defensive stance.

"Impressive," he said. "Uluhara had this trap all planned out." There was neither arrogance nor fear in his voice, only determination. "Come get me then, but I won't make it easy for you."

"I'm not with them," she blurted out, "whoever they are."

His eyebrows lifted skeptically as he examined her tattoo-covered face.

More noises as feet pounded up stairs within the warehouse; wooden treads snapping under strain; loud curses; bodies crashing; groans; more shouting.

She frowned. The shouts were in Adüan.

He turned and tried to run, and groaned as his knee buckled. He turned back to her. She tensed.

"Help me out of here," he said, gritting his teeth.

"Why?" she asked. "I don't know you; I don't know—"

"Because if they catch me, terrible things will happen to Tan Adü, though I don't want them to."

She looked into his eyes and saw that it wasn't a threat, simply a statement of fact.

She stripped off her eye-catching white robe and dropped it carelessly to the ground. She walked up to him, crouched, and waited until he had climbed onto her back.

More pounding steps inside the warehouse; shouts. "Hurry!" "Get the ladder!" "Go out the back door!"

Straining, she straightened up, his weight on her back. She began to run, at first stumbling, and then with more confidence as he trusted her with his weight and relaxed.

By the time the pursuers emerged from the warehouse, their prey had melded into the darkness.

They staggered into her shack, one like many others lining the anonymous alley in the old Artists' Quarter. These were now mostly rented out as dormitories for workers at the grand casinos. The transient population tended to keep to themselves and asked few questions.

She helped him sit down on the lone bed. He looked exhausted, but nonetheless smiled assuredly as he took in his surroundings.

"I never got a chance to ask your name," he said.

"Zen-Kara," she said, "of Tan Adü."

"I'm Phyro," he said, ". . . of Zudi. Thank you, Zen-Kara, for saving my life."

She wasn't surprised that he withheld his clan name. After all, many in Dimushi came to the city because they wanted nothing to do with their families. She was relieved that upon confirming her Adüan origin, he didn't respond with "Nomi, nomi." She hated that. So many people in Dara did that to her, either as a joke or because they thought it made them sound worldly.

She found herself liking the way he said her name. Over the years, she had grown used to the way the people of Dara butchered her name, and even introduced herself sometimes with those twisted phonemes to make it easier for the others. Phyro, however, didn't pronounce the syllables the way most in Dara did, forcing them into the patterns of Dara, but melded Adüan tones into the Dara-inflected syllables, a kind of compromise that she herself had adopted.

"What were you doing with an Adüan gang?" she asked.

"I had certain goods that I couldn't transport with officially stamped manifests and customs receipts," he said.

Though many Adüans came to Dara to study, many more signed up to be crew on the trading ships. Over time, some Adüans settled in coastal cities and took up other work, including criminal enterprises—especially after Chief Kyzen had called for all Adüans in Dara to return home. There were still chiefs and shamans in Tan Adü who resisted the intrusion of Dara medicines, figurines of the gods, and various luxuries such as lacquerware and silk, though their tribes craved these things. Neither could Dara's demand for Adüan crafts such as scrimshaw, feather accoutrements, and shell carvings be satisfied through the officially sanctioned trading fleets. Smuggling was lucrative, and every big port city in the south had Adüan gangs specializing in the trade.

"So you were trying to take advantage of the Adüan gangs for your own profit?" Zen-Kara asked. She couldn't keep the disappointment and incipient anger out of her voice.

Because the Adüans had aided Emperor Ragin in his rise to be the "All-Chief," officials of the Dandelion Court had always enforced the rules more laxly when Adüan shippers were involved—their way of respecting the special bond between Tan Adü and Pan.

"As I told you," Phyro said, "I swear on the grave of my mother that I intended no harm to the people of Tan Adü. There are things proscribed by the Dandelion Court that are nonetheless beneficial to all the Islands, and I needed the help of the gangs."

His expression was so earnest that she wanted to believe him, and the fact that he said "the people of Tan Adü" instead of "your people" endeared him to her. It was almost as if he sensed instinctively the confusion in her heart, the doubt that surrounded her like a fog.

Noticing his drooping eyelids and the way he struggled to support himself on the bed, she said, "Rest. We'll talk more in the morning."

He cooperated as she stripped off his leggings and helped him take off his tunic and undershirt, grinning to reassure her that it was all right even as she blushed at his mostly nude state. She cleaned his shoulder wound, bandaged and wrapped his ankle, and then left to empty out the washbasin with the bloodstained water. By the time she returned, he was already snoring. He seemed to feel at home no matter where he was.

Zen-Kara stared, amazed at his deep and untroubled sleep, alone in a stranger's house and having just escaped from a vicious gang.

How she wished she could act that way.

She knelt down next to the bed and gazed at his placid expression, finding the smooth, young face, though unadorned with tattoos, not unattractive.

One day, while Zen-Kara was a little girl of eight on Tan Adü, a merchant from the Big Island showed her a wooden carving of Tututika, a goddess his people worshipped. It looked exactly like a miniature human, with eyes that seemed about to blink and lips that seemed about to part.

She was fascinated by the way the carver had taken advantage of the grain in the wood to represent the folds and pleats of her flowing dress, as though the goddess had been hidden within the aspen and only waited for the artist's chisel to be revealed. The wood had then been varnished and painted, with decorative bits of gold added.

The Adüans did not make figurines of the gods like that, since divinity couldn't reside in something so small. But Zen-Kara also knew that in old times, many generations ago, her ancestors had made large idols to which they prayed. She wondered if those had looked anything like this statue.

The merchant also showed her a silk handkerchief covered in lumps of painted wax, each carved into a different shape like the burls found on the staffs of shamans and chieftains. She caressed them gingerly, afraid to damage the miniature sculptures.

She was not unfamiliar with goods from the Big Island. As the chief's youngest daughter, she had grown up surrounded by luxuries like porcelain and silk, lacquerware and metal weapons. Merchants bearing such goods came to the village regularly to trade for cruben scales and dyran fins, whale scrimshaw and shark jaws. But never had she seen anything like the objects this merchant showed her.

"These contain the wisdom of Kon Fiji," said the merchant, "the greatest way-finder in history."

She had never heard a man of Dara speak without the aid of an interpreter. His speech sounded strange, as though he had something in his mouth, making the words come out all gnarled and misshapen.

But the import of his words was even more shocking. How could lumps of wax contain wisdom? Were they, perhaps, similar to the cocoons of moths, and when sliced open would reveal their winged magic? What sort of name was "Kon Fiji"? And way-finders were people of great skill who led hunting bands across trackless waves and through dense woods, but she had always been told that the people living on other islands did not know how to do these things at all.

Before she could ask more questions, her father, Chief Kyzen, appeared with his warriors and drove the merchant away.

"These goods are forbidden!" her father shouted at the merchant. "You must obey our laws!"

Later, she begged him to explain. He was reluctant, telling her only that the objects brought by that particular merchant contained a toxin that poisoned the mind.

But the memory of those wax lumps and that lifelike statue stayed with her, and she worried that her mind had already been poisoned somehow.

As she grew up, the village and Tan Adü changed with her.

After a trading mission to another village some days away, venturing villagers returned home with porcelain and wood figurines. They set these up in cubby-shrines at home and made offerings to them. When Kyzen objected, the villagers explained that the gods of Dara could bring about good harvests and heal diseases—statues of Rufizo, in particular, came with little hollow recesses at the bottom filled with powdered herbal medicine in various colors, efficacious against many diseases. The shamans in other villages said these were the same gods as the ones the Adüans already prayed to, just given new names and armed with more powerful magic. What was the harm?

Though Chief Kyzen, as a result of the treaty he had negotiated with Kuni Garu, held the title of All-Chief of Tan Adü, he could not command the hundreds of chiefs and chieftains of the smaller tribes, only advise.

"Better to welcome the gods home than to force the people to pray to them in secret," one of Chief Kyzen's shamans said. "As the tide alters the patterns of the waves, so we must change how we surf."

Kyzen sighed and stopped objecting. A feast was held to celebrate the "homecoming" of gods who had never left. The figurines were set up in a hut of their own, and shamans pledged to make regular offerings.

After that, scrolls with wax logograms began to dangle at hut doors for good luck, and traders came regularly with new figurines and packets of medicines to refill Rufizo as he emptied out. Rather than relying on scribes hired from Dara, some of the village's youngsters left to study with way-finders on the Big Island. When they returned, they brought back idols constructed from driftwood, coral, bone, shell, coconut, or grass, objects of veneration made by their ancestors, which had been seized by invading armies from the Big Island long ago, before All-Chief Kuni Garu put a stop to them.

The idols that had truly returned home sat next to the shiny, colorful statues carved by the hands of the people of Dara, and it was unclear which was more at home.

Zen-Kara knelt on the cold paving stones of the alley as she prepared breakfast. Huts for the poor like hers had no room for a kitchen. Everyone cooked outside, in the street.

"Good morning."

She turned around from fanning the stove and saw him leaning against the doorpost, a bright smile on his wan face. He had struggled back into his clothes, muddy and tattered from last night's struggles.

"What are you doing up?" she chided. "You've lost a lot of blood. I'm making you monkeyberry porridge."

"Perfect. I'm as restless as a monkey. Let me help?" He approached, but winced as the injured leg took his weight.

She dropped the fan and rushed to him, supporting his weight as she eased him onto the little stool before the stove. The inhabitants of the other shacks along the lane, many also cooking breakfast in the open, paid little attention to them. But she blushed nonetheless from their intimate pose.

"Do you know how to cook porridge?" she asked, looking at him skeptically. She didn't know anything about Phyro, but judging by his elegant courtly accent, she doubted he made his own breakfast much.

"I know how to use a soldier's field kit. Does that count?"

"Sort of." She handed him the fan and showed him how to keep the flame in the stove at the right temperature while she busied herself with stirring and flavoring. "So you come from a soldiering family?"

"You sound surprised," he said, still smiling. "What did you think I did?"

"I would have pegged you as a merchant's son . . . or maybe the scion of an official trying to make some money after frustration at the Imperial examinations."

He chuckled at this. "You're likely far more knowledgeable about the classics than I am."

Irked at the thought that he was probably just trying to be polite, the kind of condescending friendliness so many people of Dara put on in her presence because she was a well-spoken Adüan, she pressed. "How do you know that?"

"I saw the scroll on your desk this morning. I didn't recognize all the logograms, but the calligraphic style reminded me of Lurusén. My old master used to berate me for never infusing the logograms with any kind of spirit—though I was! He just didn't like my monkey nature. Anyway, you write with a beauty and strength he would have admired."

He had seen a half-finished scroll in the novel script Zen-Kara was developing: a hybrid of modified Classical Ano logograms and zyndari Adüan transcriptions. She basked in the pleasure of the sincerity of his praise—she had always admired Lurusén, the great Cocru poet-official, and she felt closer to him already for recognizing her model.

Mollified, she returned to the porridge, slowly pouring in the monkeyberries that were said to be good for replenishing blood. Thick steam rose out of the pot, mixing with the fragrant smoke from the stove into a mouthwatering brew. "If you weren't much of a scholar, what did you devote your time to?"

"Tales of adventure and heroism," he said, "and lots of pranks on my master."

"What? Nothing productive then?"

With a mischievous glint in his eyes, Phyro began to wield the fan like a sculpting knife. A swipe here, a tuck there, and soon he had corralled the smoke into a straight column. As he continued to tend to the smoke with gentle flutters from the fan, he puckered his lips and blew at the smoke as he oscillated his head from side to side. The column of smoke curved into a spiral, dancing in the morning air like a charmed snake, like a staircase to the cloud palaces of the immortals, like the turbulent wake of a dyran's tail.

"Oh!" exclaimed Zen-Kara. "That's . . . lovely. I've heard of smokecraft but haven't seen it much."

"My mother was a master of the art," said Phyro with pride. But the glow in his eyes soon faded. "I never was a dedicated student, not even with her. This is as much as I can do."

The melancholy and regret was unmistakable. The young man, who had seemed so confident and self-possessed, appeared for the first time vulnerable. Zen-Kara had to suppress the impulse to wrap her arms around him in comfort. A line of classical poetry came to her mind, perfectly capturing the beauty of the smoke. She recited, *"'A nimbus in the wake of a stride, a moonbow the aftermath of strife—'"*

"'*You and I, both fate misunderstood, need no shared history for this duet,*'" he finished for her.

They locked eyes, the bubbling porridge forgotten for the moment. Both felt their hearts connected by a link as insubstantial as smoke but also as real as the empathy that transfixed the lonely in company.

When Zen-Kara was thirteen, she left Tan Adü for the Big Island.

"Why do you wish to go away, my youngest daughter, the comfort of my old age, as beloved as the taste of the sea against the tip of my tongue?" asked Chief Kyzen. "All who have gone to Dara to study have been much older than you."

She didn't know how to answer him. The adventures recounted by older children who had studied abroad stirred her heart; the way they giggled and spoke to each other in Dara, thinking that no one else could follow their conversation, aroused her envy. If she were completely honest, she knew it was because she couldn't stop dreaming of the painted wax logograms, couldn't forget their soft and cool touch against her fingertips. But that wasn't a reason that she thought her father could understand.

So she told him what she thought he wanted to hear: "Every fledgling tern must learn to make her own way across the sea."

Chief Kyzen sighed and nodded.

Accompanied by several other older Adüan youths, she began her studies in Canfin, the Cocru trading hub closest to Tan Adü. She learned to speak Dara, to read and write, to unravel the Ano logograms like the silk makers who unwound the tight moth cocoons into ethereal strands of meaning. The other students her age, none of them Adüan, laughed at her halting attempts at speaking and clumsy logograms. At night she cried herself to sleep, missing the tastes and smells of home, the comforting sound of evening breezes whispering through the banana leaves and the sensation of a smooth, cool woven-grass sleeping mat against her cheek.

This is what I want, she told herself. *I must not fail.*

Gradually, the confusing sounds around her coalesced into meaningful syllables, and the profusion of angles and surfaces resolved into logograms she could decode. When she felt confident about her language skills, she left Canfin to travel around Dara on her own, learning from teachers both inside and outside classrooms.

She studied history, mathematics, geography, botany, and zoology; she learned to give labels to things and to divide them into new categories. Clouds were no longer mere exhalations of the gods in diverse moods, presaging storm or drought, but *cumulus, stratus, cirrus, cumulonimbus* . . . sonorous names that rolled off her tongue like thunder and gave her a sense of mastery; plants and animals were no longer just useful, dangerous, good to eat, or curative, but specimens divided into species and families, clans, tribes, provinces, nations . . . a tree of life as solemn as the chart of the bureaucratic ministries and organs of the empire; instead of dreaming about the warriors and gods in the stories she had heard from elders as a child, she read about the deeds of the heroes of the Diaspora Wars, the pride of the Tiro kings, the wrath of the Hegemon.

There were some who laughed at her accent or pretended not to understand when she spoke, some who gawked at her dark complexion and fair hair—an unusual combination in Dara—some who asked about the meaning behind the tattoos on her face and made ignorant comments. She let these insults roll off her like water off the back of a wax-billed duck; most of her teachers and classmates accepted her as a member of their fellowship, dedicated to the pursuit of knowledge, and she was too immersed in the joy of learning to let a few fools bother her. If anyone made her feel unwelcome, she repeated to herself the mantra attributed to Kon Fiji, to whom she secretly attached the sobriquet the One True Way-Finder: *Within the Four Seas, all men are brothers.*

She attended the performances of famous opera troupes; she gaped at the stalls of street vendors; she marveled at the temples of the gods of Dara, filled with statues a thousand-thousand times grander than that tiny figurine of Tututika from long ago; she tried foods that she had never imagined: the spicy sauces of Dasu refugees; the elegantly sculpted canapés of Amu; the sweet, textured compotes of Wolf's Paw; the savory caterpillar medley salad from Cocru's countryside; the raw fish and shellfish of Gan garnished with herbs, so similar and yet so different from the foods of her homeland; the roasted mutton and beef of Faça, where every cut was paired with a different wine. . . .

The world was so grand, so rich, so layered. She savored the words of the Ano philosophers, who constructed models in her mind that allowed her to see the world from so many different perspectives. She delighted in the way her teachers and the older students thought and debated, as though there were no secrets in the universe that would not yield before the blade of a honed intellect. She felt at once humbled and uplifted by the chants of the monks and nuns in the grand temples, as though the rising columns of incense brought her prayers straight to the ears of the gods of Dara, a connection at once intimate and open.

Her life in that village in Tan Adü seemed so limited, so confined, so *small*.

I am a woman of Dara, she thought. *This is where I'm meant to be.*

She enrolled in a cram school in Ginpen and began to prepare for the Imperial examinations. This was the path all men and women of learning took to ascend into the upper echelons of society, to become players, not mere audience members, in the magnificent pageant that was Dara.

Because she was a vagabond, with no fixed abode or family in the empire, she had to sit for the Town Examination in Ginpen, with her teacher, Master Tathu, acting as her sponsor. The competition in this city of learning was intense, and she would be taking the test alongside scholars who had been studying the classics for at least a decade longer than she had. But as she walked into the examination hall in her district, she felt no trepidation, only excitement.

Nonetheless, on the day the examination results were posted, she was too fearful to go to the Hall of Learning. The terror of failure, of having her dream shattered, paralyzed her. She waited in her room and prayed to Fithowéo while her friends dressed up in formal scholar's robes and traipsed out of the dormitories.

They returned with the news that out of the twenty students at the cram school, five had made it onto the list of newly minted *toko dawiji*. Zen-Kara had obtained the highest score of the five, fifteenth-highest overall in Ginpen. It was the best rank in the Town Examination any of Master Tathu's students had ever achieved.

"In a less erudite part of Dara, your name would surely be at the very top of the list," declared Master Tathu with pride.

A celebratory banquet was held at the Splendid Urn, Ginpen's best restaurant, and Zen-Kara, wearing her blond hair for the first time in the double scroll-bun reserved for ranked scholars, felt she had truly become a woman of Dara. Her friends toasted her, their eyes filled with equal measures of envy and admiration.

Master Tathu asked for a copy of her essay so that she could use it as an example for students of the next class. Later that night, she summoned Zen-Kara to her study.

"Yours is a beautiful essay," Master Tathu said. "Since the topic is 'On the Nature of Time,' most examinees naturally expounded on quotations drawn from the Fluxists, who wrote much about the brevity of life in the face of eternity, or from the Moralists, who tended to wax eloquent on the lasting value of virtue as exemplified through history. But you chose to root your essay in the arguments of the Incentivists, on observations about the ebb and flow of desire as the metronome of life in a modern metropolis like Ginpen. It's startlingly original."

She blushed and thanked her teacher.

"But—"

Her heart tensed at the shift in tone.

"But there is almost nothing of yourself in your writing. The most powerful instrument of a writer isn't her sharpened writing knife or heated wax spoon; it's her voice, the embodiment of her soul. Zen-Kara, you conceal yourself from your reader; you speak from behind a mask."

The sound of blood rushing through her arteries, a rising tide, filled her ears as her teacher continued.

"Why are you so reluctant to embrace the authority of your own experience, the only teacher more wise than the Ano sages? Only someone who had not grown up in Dara could have offered the insight that the way we slice up time, the way we obsess over efficiency and fear its waste, is not natural. Yet you offer no examples from your life in Tan Adü, shrink from proclaiming the difference of the Adüan worldview, refuse to draw upon that treasure trove of cultural experience to strengthen your case and make your essay truly stand out.

"Where is your description of a days-long boar roast with the whole tribe? Where is your reminiscence of a clam-gathering trip with your sisters? Where is the smell, the taste, the sounds and colors of life in a hut in Tan Adü, surrounded by your loved ones, away from the hubbub of Dara? Had I not known you were the writer, I would not have been able to tell that it *wasn't* written by a woman of Dara."

Zen-Kara looked into the expectant face of her teacher, and, after a long, awkward pause, croaked out "Thank you" before turning away.

Back in her room, disappointment and rage warred in her heart.

It wasn't written by a woman of Dara.

Master Tathu had meant well, but how could she have understood how her words had wounded Zen-Kara?

She was hardly the first *toko dawiji* from Tan Adü. Curious young men and women from her island, mostly the children of chiefs and chieftains, had been coming to the core islands since the founding of the Dandelion Throne, and more than a few had obtained that first rung in the ladder of scholastic honors. Most had then returned to Tan Adü, content to use their learning to obtain better deals for their people in negotiations with Dara merchants and officials, or to make the lives of the people better with new crops and tools obtained from Dara. A few, however, had chosen to remain in Dara and became storytellers, actors, or aides to emissaries from Tan Adü.

Some of her Dara friends had taken her to see a performance by one of these storytellers, thinking it would assuage her homesickness. The storyteller reminisced about his life in Tan Adü, described in great detail the feel and texture and taste of mashed taro, sang the sacred songs used to converse with the crubens, demonstrated the techniques for paddling an Adüan canoe, recalled the first time he looked at a woman with a longing he had never experienced as a boy, chronicled the harsh manner in which his father administered corporal punishment and the fearful rumors his mother repeated about life on the Big Island, told anecdotes about the errors he had made when he had first come to Dara—he didn't know how to clean himself in the bathroom ("What are these neat little grass-woven pads for? To wipe my face?"); he didn't know how to eat a dumpling ("The hot soup spilled out and I thought I had a mouthful of lava!"); he didn't know how to sit properly ("Can you imagine? The whole time I was dining with my benefactor and her husband, I sat in *thakrido!*") . . .

The teahouse audience had, by turns, laughed, dabbed at their eyes, sat mesmerized. Afterward, as they dropped coins into the storyteller's tipping bowl, Zen-Kara's friends had excitedly whispered to her their admiration for the man.

"He's so spiritual! So in harmony with nature!"

"What a hard life he's led! His father probably beat him so much because he didn't know if the boy was really his. . . ."

"I love the way he laughs. So at peace! You can just tell the Adüans are much more in tune with the gods. . . ."

"The primitive tribes have much wisdom that we've forgotten, with our books and money and busy lives."

. . .

She had said nothing, her face red from shame and anger. She wanted to shout at her friends that the storyteller's tales were not *her* tales, that her father had not beaten her, that her father and mother loved each other, that she did not like mashed taro at all, that she was bothered to hear the sacred cruben songs sung in a teahouse full of strangers who didn't understand the words, that she had never made those mistakes the storyteller had, that she did not feel particularly "primitive" or "spiritual" or in communion with the gods, that one Adüan, whoever they were, could not possibly *represent* her experience, her village's experience, the experiences of a whole people.

But how could her friends understand? They thought they were complimenting her people. To berate them for it would be churlish.

She didn't know how to feel about the storyteller and other Adüans like him. They had succeeded in Dara essentially by acting as "professional Adüans," spinning sentimental and silly tales that packaged up what it meant to be a person from Tan Adü into neat, digestible dumplings that oozed exoticism, that were redolent with "primitive charm," that flattered the prejudices of the people of Dara and made them laugh. They served up the "authentic Adüan experience" in exchange for fame and coin. They were responsible for all those people in the markets who greeted her with "Nomi, nomi," which always set her teeth on edge and ruined her mood for the day.

Yet, could she really say that the stories they told were lies? No, she could not. Some fathers did beat their children on Tan Adü, the same as it happened in Dara. Some mothers in Tan Adü did believe in outrageous stories about other peoples, the same as it was in Dara. Some Adüans probably really did take pride in being "primitive" and "closer to the gods" as a way to feel superior to the people of Dara, a lie they told themselves to assuage feelings of inferiority. But could she really claim that it was a false consciousness, a kind of self-exoticization that was inauthentic?

What did "authentic" mean anyway when it came to defining what it meant to be Adüan? Sure, the storyteller no longer lived in Tan Adü, but neither did she. The storyteller couldn't possibly know what life was like in every village on Tan Adü, but neither could she. So what right did she have, any more than the "professional Adüans," to authoritatively declare what it meant to be Adüan? To dictate how the people of Dara perceived her people?

She had responded to her distaste for the storyteller's performance by bleaching all traces of her homeland from her writing and speech. She would out-Dara her Dara classmates and studiously avoid any trace of foreignness in her arguments and essays. She vowed to write as though Tan Adü were a blank space on the map, as though she had been immersed in the words of the Ano sages from birth, as though she had played with the logogram blocks before she had even walked. She couldn't eliminate her accent—she had come to Dara too late for that—but she would ensure that her wax logograms were as perfect as her teacher's, cleansed of all solecisms, stripped of even a whiff of Tan Adü.

She would succeed as a woman of Dara or not at all.

And for the briefest of moments, she thought she had. To place so high in the examinations was a validation she had not dared to even contemplate. The examination administrators did not know who she was, could not see her Adüan face, could not hear her Adüan accent, could judge her only by her logograms. And they had found her worthy.

But all that had come crashing down with a single sentence from her teacher.

If a woman of Dara had written that essay, Master Tathu would have praised the writer for her intellect. But because it was Zen-Kara, her teacher had attributed the insight to the fact that she was Adüan, and found it wanting . . . because it failed to imitate her teacher's idea of Adüan-ness.

No matter how much she strove, Zen-Kara realized, Dara would never be her home. No matter how much she accomplished, her teacher would never treat her the same as her other students. No matter how well she could recite the Ano Classics, her classmates would notice first the tattoos on her face. No matter how beautiful and refined her calligraphy, no one could forget the accident of her birth. No matter how deeply she thought about the topic or how much she revered the Ano sages and feared the gods of Dara, the people of this land would always see her as an outsider, reduce her insights to the mere product of her origin.

It wasn't written by a woman of Dara.

They would never accord her the respect due to any other *toko dawiji*; they only expected her to write autobiography. They wanted her, needed her, pushed her to become a professional Adüan. They demanded her to smile when they said "Nomi, nomi."

After she changed his bandage, they sat down together to breakfast. Something had changed between them. The very air seemed permeated with longing and tension.

He reached into his money purse and retrieved something and placed it in her hand. She was about to object, but he shook his head and directed her gaze to the middle of her palm.

It was a gold medallion. Gingerly, she caressed the stylized floral burst design on the front, the crest of the House of Dandelion. Her heart raced. His courtly accent, his self-possession, his easy manners, his smokecraft, his knowledge of the Ano Classics despite a self-proclaimed lack of erudition—everything fell into place. This Phyro of Zudi hadn't just been named *after* the young Emperor of Dara.

She looked at him, her eyes full of confusion. *What is Phyro Garu, Emperor Monadétu, doing in Dimushi in disguise?*

"My mother had the skill to see through appearances, to know who to trust," he said. "I don't have her power. But you sense it too, don't you? This connection between us. Maybe the gods meant for me to confide in you."

Which gods? she wondered. But she let him go on.

He told her of his plan to transport certain goods and people to Crescent Island, in preparation for a grand act to reshape the map of Dara. The plan was so bold that it sounded impossible, like something one read in ancient tomes whose veracity was suspect.

"Do you crave tales of adventure and heroism of your own?" she asked, thinking of rumors of how much the emperor seethed under the iron fist of his regent. "Do you wish to stride across the Islands, leaving strife-born wails and smoking ruins in your wake?"

"No!" he said, his face flushed with rage. "That is how I've been misunderstood, misconstrued, misinterpreted."

"But you seek to end the peace that has lasted a decade," she said. "You aim to break the pacific reign of Empress Jia."

"Change is coming whether my aunt-mother wants it or not," he said. "A peace bought with the suffering of tens of thousands is not a peace worth keeping."

Change is coming. She repeated in her mind. Strange, to hear the sentiment that had long gripped her mind emerge from the lips of another.

He stood up, swaying unsteadily on his feet. She put his arm around her shoulders and supported his weight as they circled the room, the exercise invigorating his body as well as freeing his speech. Their closeness brought heat into her face.

He spoke to her of the terror of life in Unredeemed Dara, glimpsed through the fog of Lyucu secrecy in harrowing tales told by refugees and meager clues gathered by spies on the tribute missions. He spoke to her of the steady buildup of a private army at his remote base, and the rising sentiment for war, like bubbling porridge above the fanned flames of rekindled patriotism.

He told her of approaching the Adüan gang in the guise of a smuggler. He told her of the heated negotiations, in which he tried to weave a maze of smoke to conceal the true nature of the goods. He told her of greed coalescing in the eyes of the gang leader as he decided that holding the young smuggler for ransom would be far more profitable than any deal. He told her of the desperate fight that ensued, and the fortuitous escape.

"You're reckless," she chided. "You trust too easily."

He laughed, acknowledging the justness of the accusation. "My father always said that there should be a little bit of Tazu in everyone's life. It's more interesting that way."

Despondent over her master's reaction to her success, Zen-Kara turned down the invitation to meet Magistrate Zuda with the other new *toko dawiji*, leaving her classmates and teacher in consternation.

She returned to Tan Adü, the home she had not seen in five years.

Her parents were overjoyed to see her, and there was much feasting and fussing and fierce hugs and flicking of tears. She had not realized how much she missed hearing the language of her homeland, how much pleasure she took in the foods cooked by sisters and aunts and grandmothers—she even found mashed taro to be more tasty than she had recalled. She allowed herself to revert to the role of a child, to be immersed in the love of family and tribe as the instincts of living on Tan Adü slowly returned to her.

She went swimming and canoeing in the ocean, reacquainting herself with the way-finding techniques of her people. She practiced the whalebone trumpet that the Adüans used to converse with the great crubens, the sovereigns of the sea. She took pride in addressing the gods only by their Adüan names and forms, and tried to push the idols of Dara out of her mind.

Because she had left home so young and had not spoken Adüan for so long, she found to her own horror that the words of her own language no longer came easily to her. To reteach herself her mother tongue, she set herself the task of recording the village's stories in writing. After years immersed in tales of Dara's kings and generals, poets and princesses, she realized with a heart-piercing pang how much deeper the stories of her own people moved her. The connection she felt to Taro Girl and the Hero-with-Six-Arms was one forged of blood and ancestral memory, far more powerful than the intellectual appreciation she had cultivated for the sagas of the Diaspora Wars or the chronicles of the Tiro kings.

Older students who had gone to Dara before her had, with the help of their teachers, devised a method of writing Adüan using zyndari letters. It was mainly employed by curious Dara scholars who wished to collect Adüan folktales. She used this system now to record the oral histories of the great warriors and chiefs of her people.

But try as she might, she found the system unsatisfactory. Classical Ano, which was the first language she learned to write, was full of literary devices that delighted the senses: rhetorical tropes that moved the heart as well as the mind, clusters of near synonyms that ramified and filled the semantic space, phonetic dances that twisted the tongue, visual puns that amused the eye. A scribe could draw on a panoply of sophisticated techniques to add to the appeal of the written word: a sentence written with logograms that all contained the same semantic root provided a subtle hint of a unifying theme; a point illustrated by an apropos quotation derived authority from the classics; a line constructed with logograms of increasing height yielded a simulation of the rising tension in the argument, to be punctuated by a squat final logogram as the emphatic conclusion; the judicious use of four-, five-, and seven-logogram phrases led to euphonious balance and visual symmetry; a grammatical chiasmus or rhetorical parallelism could be literally laid out on the page through the placement and shaping of wax lumps; different calligraphic styles could be combined in the same text to evoke changing moods or opposing speakers; and on and on.

In contrast, writing Adüan with zyndari letters was intolerably crude. The stories that had been so full of magic in her childhood, when written down, lost all hints of the fantastic.

The Story of Xina the Taro Girl. She was born from, uh, a taro. One time, the villager, his name was Wuluweno, um, he was the villager with the taro patch. The taro patch, it was not so large. . . .

The feeble zyndari letters, imprisoned in their little word-squares, could not capture Grandmother's wrinkled smile or the twinkle in her eyes, could not re-create her hands waving through the air, sketching out the shape and heft of the taro that would burst apart to give birth to a future great warrior. The vivid characters that her grandmother's narration had brought to life in her mind appeared as mere paper-craft puppets on the page. A living cruben in orality was a lifeless skeleton when reduced to transcription, a ruin that she was too ashamed to even read over.

Only when she was away from Dara did she realize how deep was her love for those islands.

Never had she felt the gap between speech and writing so acutely. Her keen analytical mind told her the reasons for the felt difference between written Classical Ano and transcribed vernacular Adüan. Classical Ano, as a primarily literary language, was rarely spoken without reference to a text. Even during poetry recitations, the audience imagined the logograms appearing on a virtual scroll. It was a language that had grown over millennia to adapt to life in writing, so much so that certain Classical Ano compositions were impossible to decipher by sound alone.

No Dara author ever wrote alone—even in the solitude of a mountain hut, she always wrote with and against all the mute texts that had come before her and would come after her. No Dara reader ever read alone—even in the seclusion of a library carrel, he derived meaning from the text only by juxtaposing it against a thousand-thousand other texts, packing it with expectations and assumptions shaped by prior models of good prose, arguing silently with critical voices subversive as well as dominant, repeatedly going over dense passages with the finger as well as the eye, logogram by logogram, stroke by stroke, identifying allusions, deciphering neologisms, teasing out graphical paronomasias, completing enjambments. The techniques of beautiful prose and poetry that she loved so much had been developed by generations of writers and readers working together, like a grand palace built up over the centuries, one brick at a time.

How could she expect Adüan, a language that had just entered literacy from orality, to evolve the rich repertoire of accumulated literary frameworks, models, and meta-structures to support that kind of beauty? It was doubtful that such a task could even be completed in five generations, much less five years.

She spoke of her doubts to her older siblings and cousins, who had studied in Dara before her.

"Why do we need to write down the old stories at all?" asked her older brother.

"So that they won't be forgotten," she said, confused by the question.

"Ah, you speak like one of *them*," said her older sister.

She knew what her sister meant, and her face burned. "No. There is beauty in our stories, and I'm unwilling to consign them to the vagaries of memory between the generations. Our ancestors left us petroglyphs on the mountains, but now even the oldest shamans cannot be certain of their meaning. If the people of Dara have invented a way to preserve love and beauty across time, what's wrong with us learning to use it for ourselves?"

"But why do we need to write like them?" asked her older sister. "Why do you judge our stories by their standards? If you must write, write the words as they're spoken."

"In Dara they write for the approval of their critics," said her older brother, "but we tell stories for our own pleasure."

She tried to see things their way. Wasn't there a raw beauty, direct and unaffected, in the transcription of Adüan oral tales absent from the literature in Dara? Wasn't there a transparency of expression in the mapping of living sounds to letters, that, when enhanced by the knowledge of readers steeped in the oral tradition, re-created the sympathy between a rapt audience and a storyteller speaking straight from the heart, a consensus of purpose that rivaled the harmony between Dara authors and readers as they played hide-and-seek in the labyrinthine palace of millennia of literary tradition?

To be ashamed of transcriptions of Adüan oral stories in the face of the opulent tapestry of Ano logograms was akin to disdaining the dive of an eagle in the face of the strut of a peacock, to deriding the homely mashed taro with fish flakes in the face of a sumptuous, sophisticated Dara banquet. They were simply two different kinds of beauty, each suited to the tastes of a people.

Yet, she wondered if such a framing of the contrasts between Tan Adü and Dara—simplicity versus ornamentation, directness versus sophistication, authenticity versus always speaking from behind a mask—wasn't just playing into the judgments of Dara concerning Tan Adü. Wasn't she, in her own way, submitting to the notion of irreconcilable differences between so-called "Adüan" and "Dara" mindsets, held to be self-evident among the Dara literati? Was she really different from those pandering "professional Adüans" she held in such contempt?

It was incontrovertible, however, that while her heart beat to the rhythm of Adüan tales, her mind thrilled to the beauty of Classical Ano expression. Rather than trying to transcribe the tales of the elders using zyndari letters, she tried to translate them into Classical Ano and then fixed the translations in logograms. Finally, she could bring to bear all the tricks of literary composition she had learned in Dara: the visual puns, the skip-hop metaphors, the roll-drop hyperbole-litotes, the Eighty-One Rhetorical Tropes, the Forty-Nine Extended Idioms. . . . She was painfully aware of the irony of what she was doing. To write down the stories of her ancestors in a manner she felt worthy of her love for them, she had to resort to making allusions to the heroes of another culture, employing a language the elders didn't speak, recasting the gods of her people into the molds of foreigners.

But she didn't write everything in Classical Ano. Many were the instances where Classical Ano lacked the mot juste, the apt phrase, the precise constellation to guide the reader to the intended port across the infinite sea that was all inchoate meaning. The experiences of her ancestors, and of herself, could not be captured by Classical Ano without modification.

And so she did modify. She invented new logograms, or shoe-horned word-squares of transcribed Adüan into the columns of Classical Ano. She borrowed and stole, hammered and cut, levered and wedged, tore apart and put the pieces back together, until she had devised a script that mixed zyndari letters transcribing Adüan with logograms taught to signify something new. She thought of it as the first step on the long journey to a truly Adüan vernacular *literature*, and not merely a crude, lossy shadow of orality.

Translation was as inevitable in the transition of her people from orality to literacy as in the translocation of herself from Tan Adü to Dara.

"What is this you've been writing?" said her older sister, laughing. "This is neither Dara nor Adüan, neither fish nor fowl."

"We went to Dara to bring back our own gods," said her older brother, looking confused and disappointed. "I thought you were going to write down our own stories so that they may never be taken from us again, not to turn Tan Adü into an imitation of Dara."

Melancholy blanketed her heart much as fallen autumnal leaves covered the ground. No one seemed to understand her. She wasn't trying to turn Tan Adü into Dara. She was trying to paint the beauty of her homeland in colors that she had learned to see through other eyes, to lay the foundation for a future Adüan literature with stones borrowed from other islands, to ensure that the ancient stories and gods of Tan Adü had a future.

For Tan Adü was *changing*, and the village of her girlhood was no more. The people now worshipped Fithowéo and Tututika, paid for medicines imported from Dimu and Çaruza, vied to buy Ginpen silks and Müning porcelains.

"What difference does it make if the shamans call the gods by other names?" said her older brother carelessly. "Who cares if people want more colorful clothes and sturdier pots? The spirit of Tan Adü will endure."

Her older siblings and cousins seemed content to negotiate with traders from the Big Island and Wolf's Paw, to act as interpreters, to treat what they had learned in Dara as merely a tool, no different from metal spades or water screws.

They didn't understand that it was not possible to import the material culture of another people without also importing the spirit of the inventor, that the apparent stasis only disguised a brewing crisis of faith. They didn't see the need for a more fundamental transformation, changes that must be made if the spirit of Tan Adü *was* to endure.

"It's enough for some of us to know how to speak Dara and read Classical Ano—enough to make sure the traders don't cheat us," said her older sister. "The people don't need to learn your strange script or your odd ways of telling old stories in new shapes."

But it isn't enough! she wanted to scream. Over time, more young Adüans, like her, would want to study the ways of Dara. Unless they strengthened the culture of their ancestors, made the stories of the elders feel as beautiful as the stories recorded in Dara books, built an Adüan literature that could stand shoulder to shoulder with the loaded shelves of Dara, many more Adüans would go through what she had gone through and lose faith in their own heritage, as she almost had.

"There is no need to change," said her oldest cousin. "The fear is yours alone."

But things are already changing! She fervently believed that her clumsy experiments at a hybrid literary language, at strengthening Adüan traditions with bits and pieces taken from Dara, was not only the best way forward, but the *only* way forward.

"Why don't any of them see what I see?" she lamented to her father. "Why don't they feel my urgency? Father, do you not sense the tsunami looming in the distance, about to wash away all we know?"

Chief Kyzen, who loved the fearless passion of his youngest daughter, asked, "Why do you care so much about the people of Dara? Why do you direct your way-finding by their landmarks? Don't you see that it is your love of those people, who will never accept you, that has curdled into this fear, that makes you yearn for a Tan Adü that is more like Dara?"

Zen-Kara was shocked. It wasn't at all what she thought her father would say. Hadn't he, when she was younger, worried so much about the soft invasion of Dara influence? Did he not understand how much greater the threat was now than before? Traditions died when they ceased to adapt, to evolve, to *grow*. Without pursuing the changes she advocated, Tan Adü would cease to be Tan Adü, at first slowly, then all at once.

"The difference between your older siblings and cousins and you," said Chief Kyzen, unpersuaded, "is that they went to study in Dara only when they already knew who they were. You left home a fledgling tern, but you've returned an albatross who has forgotten how to walk on her ancestral shores."

The words of her father, though harsh, rang true. She wondered if she had indeed gone to Dara too young, exposed to a powerful foreign beauty before she had grown fully confident in the tastes of home.

But wasn't there value in her experiences as well? She loved both Dara and Tan Adü with the purity of a child, embraced the experiences of both lands with the malleable mind of youth. She knew Dara better than any Adüan, and with that knowledge, she thought she could see Tan Adü, both its past and future, as no one else could.

"I shall forbid any future Adüan students from going to Dara," declared her father. "We have enough knowledge to trade with. We must not lose our youths to the lures of that decadent land."

"No! That you must not do!" The thought of denying all young Adüans her own experience, a mind-cleaving exposure to the wonders of Dara, was unbearable. How could her father be so blind to the consequences of his actions? "The more you forbid it, the stronger the yearning grows—"

"You are Adüan," said her father. "Remember that. Kuni Garu promised me that no armed invasion of Tan Adü will ever take place so long as the Dandelion Throne stands, and we need not trouble ourselves with thoughts of changing to suit the ways of Dara."

She was misunderstood. Misconstrued. Misinterpreted.

Chief Kyzen prohibited her from continuing to develop her hybrid literary language and script. He told her to shadow her older sister and learn to negotiate with traders from Dara, the only good use of her learning.

The next day, she ran away from home and returned to the Big Island.

The more Zen-Kara learned of Phyro's life, the more she saw echoes of her own journey.

When Phyro spoke of his devastation upon discovering Kuni Garu's betrayal of the Hegemon, she thought of her own disappointment when she found out that her father lacked the courage to embrace the change that ideas from Dara represented. Parents were always gods and heroes in the eyes of their children until they were revealed to be ordinary people with mortal failings, and children's paths were defined in that moment when they vowed to correct the errors committed by their forbearers.

When Phyro spoke of the sense of rootlessness he suffered, having been orphaned so young, she thought of her own homeless wandering. He thought he had all the time in the world to get to know his parents, to learn from them, not realizing he would lose them both, while she thought she had all the time in the world to become both Adüan and Dara, not realizing that she'd be exiled from both.

They had both found refuge in their work. He was dedicated to the task of building up an army that would free his people from bondage, while she was devoted to the invention of a transformative literature that would prepare her people to soar into the future, tethered securely by their traditions.

Hesitantly, shyly, she explained her hybrid script to him.

He didn't react with the patronizing glee of encountering the exotic. He simply nodded.

"New ways of living require new ways of naming," he said.

"What do you mean by that?" She couldn't imagine how the Emperor of Dara could empathize with her, understand what she went through. But she dared to hope, just a little.

"I'm reminded of Farsight Secretary Zomi Kidosu's efforts to promote writing in the vernacular, using only zyndari letters."

"I know," she said. "It seems such a terrible idea, to abandon the beauty of Classical Ano."

"Maybe she pushes a bit too hard," he said. "But I can see the point of it. Some voices can't be captured in Classical Ano: thieves' cant in dark alleys, ribald jokes from scarlet houses, soldiers' slang, sailors' patois and pidgin, vernacular words specific to village topolects, neologisms invented in the Artists' Quarter here in Dimushi—but they all deserve to be written, the same as the words of the Ano sages. I've seen some poets and even members of the College of Advocates mix in zyndari word-squares with their logograms, or adopt folk logograms found in no dictionary at all."

She scrunched up her nose. "I've seen scribes do that in Ginpen's markets. It's a shameful sign of the decline of standards. 'Irregardless' is not a word! Neither is 'magnidazzlelicious'!"

He laughed. "If you say it and I understand it, how can it not be a word? Irregardless of the denunciations of Moralist grammarians, isn't it magnidazzlelicious to have poems and stories that reflect the way the people of Dara speak, rather than having to translate them into Classical Ano?"

"But the classics—"

"The classics will be fine," he said. "They have always adapted to changing readers. The *Morality* that Kon Fiji wrote and that Poti Maji glossed was not the same text that Master Zato Ruthi tried to teach me and that my father so gleefully reinterpreted. The logograms may remain the same, but the context is constantly shifting. If they continue to be meaningful to us, it's because we have, without recognizing it, translated them."

"What?" Zen-Kara looked at him as though he were mad.

"I believe the classics have survived because they are self-modernizing, self-translating. The ephemeral and the fashionable are washed away by the relentless pounding of time's tides. Only hard shoals of deep wisdom could withstand the cycles—not because they're unchanging, but because they are without vanity, without affectation, without pretension, humble enough to embrace new interpretations without yielding their essential nature. New readers are like the hermit crabs, sea urchins, anemones, snails, and seaweeds that colonize a tidal pool—only by first filling the bare rock of the classics with the colors of their own experience could the endless forms of meaning in the grandness of Life then blossom in the interaction of reader and text. The classics are always-already in translation."

How similar to hers were his thoughts on reading and writing! How startling and pleasurable to hear her own view reflected in a new pool!

He used the vernacular *always-already*, a calque from the Classical Ano original, a word coined by Ra Oji, the irreverent Fluxist, to describe the awareness of eternal existence by a mortal conscious-ness. Ordinarily, Zen-Kara would have found the vernacular form vulgar, but in Phyro's impassioned defense of the inherent translat-edness and translatability of the classics, it seemed perfect.

"But how can the classics live vigorously if they remain in a lan-guage the people do not speak?" Phyro went on. "Dara is chang-ing, with more students in schools, more documents and records, more people hungering for the written word—what was it that the ancient sages said? 'Man is the word-hungry animal.' Let the classics be translated into the vernacular; let the people write with a mix of logograms and folk logograms and letters and rebuses; let new voices be reflected with honor and grace.

"I like your invention, Zen-Kara. I think Secretary Kidosu would enjoy seeing it; perhaps she'll find in it an inspiration for Dara's future."

She was stunned. The Emperor of Dara thought her invention admirable. He craved to marry orality with literacy as much as she did. He saw, in her very Adüan creation, a path forward for Dara— and yet, she felt no sense of being condescended to, as she had with Master Tathu, when the teacher had referred to her heritage; he treated her as an equal, with a mind and spirit as grand as his, unbounded by her origin.

"How can you be so"—she hesitated, struggling for the right word—"open?"

"To confront evil, one must be open to all that is good in the world," he said. It was a Moralist cliché; yet, she had never heard it spoken with such conviction.

His easy trust in strangers and unfamiliar ideas, she saw, was a mirror image of her constant doubt. His sweet belief in good and evil, almost naive in its purity, was as much a defense against the world as her own cynical outlook. His faith in heroes and villains, in the potential of children rectifying the errors of their fathers and teachers, made him as alone among his people as she was among hers from a yearning to hold that same faith.

She had never expected to find the mirror of her soul in the Emperor of Dara.

In their mutual isolation, she felt a sense of belonging, of home.

Upon Zen-Kara's return to Ginpen, Master Tathu gladly took her in as an assistant tutor for the fresh crop of cram school students. Zen-Kara corrected their grammar, taught calligraphy sessions, gave tips on how to handle the nervousness of being inside the examination hall, and performed other duties around the school.

Once, passing through the dormitories, she overheard two of the girls in their room mocking her accent.

"She sounds like a rooster with a cold," said one of the girls, giggling. "Nooooomi! Nooooomi!"

"She told me to change the inflection glyph for the Twins from the dual to the singular!" said the other girl. "Can you imagine? I'm sure the graders gave her special consideration because she's, you know, one of those."

Zen-Kara felt blood rush to her face.

She imagined herself sliding open the door and marching in calmly to explain that she had never said, "Nomi, nomi" to anyone in Dara. She wanted to demand that they produce proof that Moralist masters who viewed their reputation as dearer than life would resort to breaking the veil of anonymity in the Imperial examinations to give her special treatment. She wanted to drag them by their ears to the library and show them classical verses composed by Dipa of Amu, Séthuwi of Gan, and Lurusén of Cocru, all of whom used the singular instead of the dual to refer to the goddesses as a way of emphasizing their divine unity, a mystery.

But she did none of those things. She simply walked away. If achieving the rank of *toko dawiji* did not give her the respect she craved, then what good would yelling at a few schoolgirls do?

She loved Dara. There was no heartache more piercing than a love unrequited.

Her old classmates, who were now studying for the Provincial examinations, sometimes invited her to the teahouses and beer pubs with them. At these reunions, her old friends were too polite to comment on the way she no longer wore her blond tresses in the double-scroll bun of a *toko dawiji* or to ask why Zen-Kara, the best student in their class, had decided not to advance further in her studies. A few did ask after her necklace of shark's teeth, something they could not recall seeing her wear in the old days. She deflected their questions until they slid away like the water cascading off a cruben's iridescent back; she did not want to tell them about her grandmother or the stories the old woman had told her, one for each tooth; she did not want to translate from Adüan to Dara; she did not owe them an explanation at all.

They spoke of the latest trends in scholastic philosophy and literary analysis, of new discoveries by the Imperial laboratories, of gossip from the court in Pan, of rumors of changes to the Imperial examinations advocated by Prime Minister Cogo Yelu and Farsight Secretary Zomi Kidosu, of the newest beaus of the actresses at Foundational Myths. For the most part, Zen-Kara listened while they chatted, disengaged. Once she would have hung on their every word, but now, it seemed as if her former classmates inhabited a separate world. The problems that troubled them were not her problems; the puzzles that absorbed them she found tedious. They were at home; she was not.

Messengers dispatched by her father came to Ginpen, telling her how much her parents missed her. Holding back tears, she shook her head. There was no way to explain to them why she was exiling herself. She wasn't sure even *she* understood.

The performances of the Adüan storytellers now took on a new significance. Looking past the cringe-inducing words and gestures, she found not cynicism, but a yearning for a homeland that no longer existed, like a flower dropped into the fast-moving river of time, destined to slip through the grasping fingers of hope. Once, she even stopped in Temple Square, tears filling her eyes as she listened to two street performers of Dara imitate the throat-singing of her homeland in the middle of some restaurant competition. Would her children, and her children's children, still sing like that? Or would they find the singing crude and grating, a dying art best consigned to oblivion?

Only when she was away from Tan Adü did she realize how abiding was her love for the island of her birth.

She decided to leave Ginpen; it was too painful to remain in a place imbued with memories of how she had tried but failed to belong. She didn't want to go back to Tan Adü, but she didn't know where in Dara she would be at peace. The Islands were many and the sea boundless, but there was no place that felt like *home*.

So she came to Dimushi, where everyone was from somewhere else, where to be rootless and homeless was not so strange at all.

Wordlessly, she eased him down into her bed. Their eyes still locked, she disrobed and stood proudly before him, naked except for the tattoos covering her skin, an aspect of herself she had never shared with anyone from Dara. Had never wanted to. Until now.

She sighed, pleased, as she saw the heat of desire fanned to life in his eyes.

He swallowed. "I'll make you breakfast later. It's my turn."

"All right," she said, feeling her skin tingle where his fingers touched.

Afterward, they lay together in bed, curled against each other like the crescent moon and her halo.

He kissed her neck. "Maybe it's time you told me your story, Zen-Kara of Tan Adü."

And for the first time, without feeling she was exploiting her own experience to pander to the tastes of other people, without feeling constrained by the expectations and condescensions of another culture, without feeling stifled by the suppressed voices of her family and tribe trying to speak through her, for her, she told her story.

He listened without commentary, understanding without being told that what she needed wasn't response, guidance, help—only to be heard.

Together in bed, their limbs entwined, the lovers fought against the loneliness that was universal to dreamers, whether emperor or exile.

When she was done, when it was clear that she had said as much as she wished to, he held her as lovingly and securely as the sea held the Islands of Dara.

Then he began to speak. Though he had already confided his plans to her, he had never revealed as much of himself as he now did. The anecdotes were not woven into a coherent whole. This was not a performance, a crafted literary creation, a shaped just-so narrative to give coherence to a sequence of days, but raw glimpses into a living soul: hesitant and therefore glorious, full of doubt and thus magnificent.

Their parallel tales were like two great crubens swimming together in the ocean. Neither needed the other; yet there was comfort in their parallel solitudes.

He spoke to her of his alienation at court: the severe aunt-mother who disapproved of everything he did; the nurse-governess who forever treated him as a child; his father's generals and nobles, who judged his every move against the shadow of his father.

He spoke to her of his longing for loved ones he could not reach: the big brother who was trapped in the enemy camp; the big sister who was fighting abroad; the little sister who lived in her own world; parents beyond the River-on-Which-Nothing-Floats, whose approval he craved but knew he would never win.

Only with his friends, companions who shared his dream, did he feel fully himself. "We're born into one family, but then we must build another for ourselves. As my big sister used to say, we're always the heroes of our own stories."

She weighed his words in her mind, the sight of their entangled legs and arms a comfort. Where was her tribe, she who belonged to neither Dara nor Tan Adü?

Scenes of other exiles surfaced in her memory: storytellers in teahouses whose performances had made her cringe; tattooed sailors whose broken Dara vernacular had embarrassed her; Adüans who had refused the call to return home because their hearts had already taken root in Dara though they were not Dara. Did they not share her loneliness? Could she not kindle in them the same dream that moved herself?

She did not need to belong to either Dara or Tan Adü; she was already of both. In that vacillation, in that instability, in that uncertain rootlessness, she found also her strength. Contrary to the short-sighted caution of her father, she could see that the futures of Dara and Tan Adü were as entangled as the bodies of Phyro and herself. It was the defining insight, born of both experience and long reflection, that would form the plot of her own story.

She recalled Phyro's plan.

Had the gods conspired to bring them together? Was this fate?

Heart racing, she turned to Phyro. "There are no merchant ships large enough to do what you want. There is only one course, a route pointed to by wayposts from history and legend."

After a moment, he understood. "But years ago, Chief Kyzen asked for their aid against the Lyucu on our behalf, and that plea was rejected. Since then, he has steadfastly refused to be involved in the conflict between Dara and Lyucu."

"My father's voice is loud and sonorous, but it is hardly the only voice in Tan Adü. They may listen to me where they did not listen to him."

He looked at her, awed. "I did not expect to meet a way-finder here." After a pause, he added, "I may be emperor in name, but I can offer Tan Adü no treasure nor concession in recompense—"

She stopped him with a firm shake of her head. "The fates of Tan Adü and Dara are as inseparable as you and I. I offer you my aid not in expectation of some material advantage, but because the creation of a great literature requires not only words and scripts, but also deeds worthy of being recorded."

They looked into each other's eyes, two hearts ready for a duet with no misunderstanding.

CHAPTER TWENTY-TWO

THE BATTLE OF CRESCENT ISLAND, PART I

CRESCENT ISLAND: THE SEVENTH MONTH OF THE ELEVENTH YEAR OF THE REIGN OF SEASON OF STORMS AND THE REIGN OF AUDACIOUS FREEDOM.

Waves gently lapped the craggy shore, the pattern unaltered for eons.

There was no oracular storm, no prophesying volcanic eruption. The sky yielded no lightning bolts to sketch the shapes of wolves or stags, nor shooting stars to prognosticate the fall of empires or warlords. The earth didn't quake; bats didn't crow in the morning; moonbows didn't appear on a rainless night of the new moon.

On the eve of the upcoming grand battle, there were no signs from the gods at all.

Perhaps even the grandest deeds of mortals were but a passing flash in the eye of eternity.

- What a somber bunch! Aren't you going to cheer on your champions? Some of you have been clamoring for war for forever; I'd have expected a bit more spirit now it's finally happening.

There was no response to Tazu's taunts.

The gods of Dara, confounded by the plots and counterplots of mortals, were assembled not in council, but to bear silent witness.

Crescent Island, though one of the Islands of Dara, always set itself apart. It was never occupied by the original inhabitants of the Islands, whose tribes were now concentrated in Tan Adü; it was not settled by the Ano and then later abandoned during the Diaspora Wars, like

Écofi; it did not sprout great cities and Tiro states like the rest of the islands from Dasu to the Tunoas.

Instead, it remained a wilderness where the veil of nature was peeled back only in the environs of a few scattered settlements in the misty mountains. Poets imagined it to be the retreat of the gods of Dara when they were tired of the squabbling humans.

While there were numerous flat beaches and sheltered coves along the western coast, the island's rocky eastern coast, full of jagged reefs and steep cliffs, presented few natural harbors. The lush jungle crowded all the way to the shore, where the waves roared and swirled under overhanging headlands and inside steep, narrow inlets carved into the coast, as though by the hand of Fithowéo, the divine bladesmith. Their sides were dotted with caves that wound deep into the rock, as though giant worms or prehistoric rivers had once tunneled through the landscape.

In years past, these isolated inlets had offered shelter for refugees, both poor and wealthy, seeking to escape the ravages of war on the core islands, as well as pirates wishing to hide from pursuing navies. But the dense, inhospitable jungle had never been welcoming to large, permanent settlements.

One of these inlets, perhaps a bit wider than the rest, housed a large troop of chattering monkeys. They swung from branch to branch in the jungle atop the cliffs, feasting on juicy monkeyberries dangling from vines. From time to time, bold and curious members of the troop climbed down the sheer cliffs to collect the soft-shelled crabs that skittered across the slimy rocks revealed at low tide. Away from the influence of humankind, they lived lives of leisure and plenty, like immortals in legends.

But one day, the monkeys stopped chattering and stared in amazement as their inlet transformed before their eyes.

Great floating islands surged into the inlet through the thick mist of dawn, their backs covered in iridescent scales more mesmerizing than any pirate treasure, their dome-shaped heads topped by horns more stout than any ship's mast. Booming moans reverberated through the water, and the very cliffs shuddered in the waves thrown up by their powerful flukes.

Crubens, the greatest living beings in the known world, were visiting this sleepy inlet.

And they weren't alone.

Teams of men and women, both Adüan and Dara by dress and appearance, rode on the backs of the giant scaled whales with chests and mysterious bundles in waterproof canvas.

But the monkeys paid the humans little mind. The crubens carried far more impressive passengers. Winged monstrosities with serpentine necks perched atop some of the living islands, gazing about curiously like long-necked cranes sometimes seen riding atop water buffaloes in the rice paddies of the Big Island.

Led by a wise old monkey whose hair had turned all white, the simian troop faded into the jungle with nary a peep. They knew, instinctively, that their home would never be the same again.

Three days after the skirmish in the open sea, the Lyucu fleet caught up to the escaping Dara ships on the shore of Crescent Island.

The dismasted Dara fleet made a sorry sight, more wreckage than functioning vessels. To avoid crashing into the reefs, the Dara crew had cut off the kite-sails as they approached land, and then crawled the rest of the way with makeshift oars fashioned from broken planks. The looming rocky coastline blocked any further thought of progress to the west, and the Lyucu fleet, composed of city-ships, warships, and airships, pressed in from the east.

The Dara ships were literally sitting ducks, bobbing at the mouth of a narrow inlet that disappeared into the interior of the island.

Goztan sent forth an emissary, a native official who she had saved from Cutanrovo's waves of purges, in a small pinnace to parley with Puma Yemu.

"If you surrender, Thane Goztan Ryoto, daughter of Dayu Ryoto, son of Péfir Vagapé, Thane of the Five Tribes of the Antler, promises you and all those under your command your lives."

Puma Yemu looked at the emissary solemnly. "Will we be brought back to Unredeemed Dara as slaves?"

"You'll come to Ukyu-taasa as the thane's captives," said the emissary.

"That's not answering my question," said Puma.

"The thane can promise that you, and all officers above the rank of hundred-chief, will not be enslaved."

"That's tempting . . . ," mused Puma. "But the offer feels slight. Is there room for negotiation?" A mocking light came into his eyes. "Perhaps I could be given a title just a little bit more impressive than yours. Say, Dog Walker of the Lyucu?"

"What are you doing?" demanded an anxious Ki Aten of Puma. Three days of tumbling over rough waves at the mercy of giant kite-sails had made him vow to get back on land—any land, whether held by the Lyucu or Dara—as soon as possible. "He's very clear that we'll be safe. Don't anger him!"

"Do not be too bold, barbarian," said the emissary. He adjusted his official's hat, a tall Dara-style cap whose silk flaps had been recut and decorated to resemble garinafin wings. Since he was wearing his hair loose in the Lyucu manner, instead of the scroll-bun of Dara scholars, the hat kept on sliding out of place. "It's the law of the Lyucu that captives in war are at the disposal of the victor, much as sheep bare their throats for the wolf. The thane is more than gener-ous to offer you and your officers these terms."

Puma Yemu whistled as though impressed. "Ah, my apologies. I hadn't realized I was talking to a mighty Lyucu warrior. Aren't you a barbarian, the same as I?"

The emissary's face flushed bright red. "How dare—dare—dare—"

Puma Yemu laughed. "Now that *is* bleating like a sheep! I'm afraid that as a mere barbarian, I'm rather unimpressed with the 'generosity' on offer here. Tell your master that the fighting hearts of Dara will never yield—"

"Silence!" roared Ki Aten. "Honored Ambassador of the Lyucu, pay no mind to the ravings of my rude associate, an unlettered ruf-fian of little import. As the military monitor and his superior, I think votan's terms are very fair."

"Oh, good," said the relieved emissary. "Our most merciful Thane Goztan does not wish to see lives needlessly lost. Why don't you draft a letter of surrender—"

"I'll get to it right away," said Ki Aten.

The Dara sailors and marines on the dismasted flagship looked at him with utter contempt and silent rage, but none dared to move. Under the regulations promulgated by Empress Jia, Ki Aten had the power to override Puma Yemu's orders in situations like this.

"A letter of surrender isn't yours to give," said Puma Yemu.

Every pair of eyes was on him.

"Wh-what are you talking about?" Ki Aten sputtered.

"According to the Code of Imperial Military Conduct, Article the Fifth, Section One, a military monitor is the highest authority in strategic decisions away from the battlefield," said Puma Yemu, "but the field officer is the highest authority when there is an active engagement."

"Exactly," said Ki Aten. "There is no fighting right now. This is a diplomatic negotiation and I'm in charge."

"Except there is fighting," said Puma. Almost casually, he strode up, gripped the emissary by the scruff of the neck to lift him up like a baby rabbit, spun him around, and planted a firm kick right in his scrawny ass.

The emissary, flailing his limbs and screaming in terror, sailed through the air to collapse in a heap in his pinnace. Puma grabbed a sword from a nearby marine and cut through the ropes tying the pinnace to his ship in one stroke. The pinnace toppled off the side of the ship, landing in the sea with a loud splash.

"Asslicker—oops, I meant Ambassador of the Lyucu," Puma yelled, "do you agree that we're in the middle of an active battle right now?"

The emissary finally scrambled up from the bottom of the pinnace. "Row away! Row away!" he yelled at his stunned oarsmen.

"Inform Thane Goztan that we'll be ready to fight her in the morning," Puma Yemu shouted. Around him, and on the other ships, Dara troops cheered thunderously.

The emissary ducked down in his boat as though the waves of noise were volleys of arrows.

Soon, the pinnace was too far away for any more parley to be possible.

"You've doomed us all, you fool!" screamed Ki Aten, stamping his foot. "How are we going to get out of this alive?"

"See, that's the difference between you and me," said Puma Yemu. "I don't think remaining alive is the only thing that matters."

"Your insubordination will become a permanent stain on your record," fumed Ki Aten. "You may be sure of that. When I'm back in Pan—"

"Why don't you get a head start on drafting that report?" said Puma. He ordered his guards to take the military monitor back to his cabin and keep him there.

Then he turned back to his troops. "Pull into the inlet. We have much to do before tomorrow."

Goztan, Noda, and the Lyucu warriors gazed at the rising sun with equal measures of trepidation and relief.

After the return of the failed emissary, Goztan had placed the entire fleet, anchored outside the inlet, on high alert. Stories of Dara ghost airships using flamethrowers were known to every Lyucu warrior, and Puma Yemu's reputation for raiding tactics made a night attack—in direct violation of his untrustworthy promise to battle in the morning—almost a certainty.

Thus, all night long, garinafin grooms kept their charges ready to launch from the decks of the city-ships at a moment's notice; smaller warships patrolled back and forth to create a screen between the city-ships and the yawning mouth of the inlet, with bright torches blazing on every deck; even airships kept watch in the starry sky at different altitudes, intent on uncovering any Dara mischief.

To stay alert and keep up morale, the thanes and naros-votan demanded that tolyusa be distributed to them and their troops. Goztan disliked the idea, believing the sacred berries would affect the judgment of commanders and warriors. But Cutanrovo had been so liberal with the sacred berries that many of the fighters believed it was their due. In the end, she gave in, drawing on the supply that Cutanrovo had pushed on her. Goztan suspected that Cutanrovo had been maintaining her own private tolyusa patches outside the official military preserves—which would, ironically, be a violation of the traditions established by Pékyu-votan Tenryo—but she had no proof.

In the end, all the preparations were for naught. The Dara fleet spent the night just inside the mouth of the inlet in peaceful slumber. A few of the ships sported bright bonfires, but native divers sent in as spies reported that the crew of those ships were roasting meat and dancing and singing, as though celebrating some holiday.

As the first rays of the waking sun gilded the undulating waves behind them, the Lyucu warriors, their taut nerves stretched to the breaking point after a night of fruitless vigilance, sighed with exhaustion and relief. The ragtag Dara ships, mastless, sailless, barely afloat, had emerged from the morning mist shrouding the inlet and oared their way into the open water in front of the inlet.

Goztan quietly cursed herself for her error. A nighttime assault into the unknown waters of the inlet would have been a mistake, but she shouldn't have kept her troops up all night based on Puma Yemu's reputation, blunting their readiness.

She didn't relish the prospect of the slaughter to come. *Once I fought to free my people,* she thought, *and now . . . what am I fighting for? To preserve Cutanrovo's cloak of skulls? To shore up the bars of the cage that imprisons the population of enslaved Ukyu-taasa? What have we become?*

It was too late for regrets. The survival of the Lyucu in Dara was at stake.

She steeled herself and held aloft Gaslira-sata, the Peace-Bite, her war axe. *To survive in peace, the wolf must bite. That is my nature.*

Cries of consternation arose from the Lyucu ranks.

"Another sun?"

"But it's in the west!"

"Maybe it's the moon?"

"But it's the night of the new moon. . . ."

Goztan turned to look behind her, squinting against the rising sun to be sure it was still there. Then she turned back to the west and rubbed her eyes hard to be sure that she wasn't seeing things.

There was indeed another golden orb rising in front of her, behind the sorry shapes of the almost-wrecked Dara vessels, through the swirling fog in the shaded gap of the inlet, above the dense, impenetrable jungle on either side, above the shoreline hills that hid the many valleys that filled this rugged island.

How can this be?

As the Lyucu watched, mouths agape, more giant orbs rose in the west, some behind the first, some in front. All of them golden, resplendent, radiant.

Martial drumbeats originating from the jungles onshore drifted to their ears over the restless sea, punctuated by a few blaring blasts from horns.

Once the shock of witnessing a scene out of some primordial creation myth had worn off, Goztan realized that the rising orbs were not, in fact, duplicates of the sun. For one thing, they were much too close—the panicked seabirds that swerved away from the rising blobs informed her that they were sublunary entities, not celestial bodies. For another thing, the orbs were not in fact spherical, but flattened and puffy, like the caps of jellyfish. The shiny surfaces undulated in the breeze, billowing like wind-filled sails.

Airships.

A shiver of recognition scampered down Goztan's spine. Though she had not been present at the Battle of Zathin Gulf, the accounts of the survivors of that battle had haunted her mind for the last ten years. This was the sight that had greeted Tanvanaki's garinafin riders as they prepared for the assault on Ginpen on that fateful day, when the dream of a quick conquest of all Dara had died.

Somehow, in this inhospitable, uninhabited corner of the Islands of Dara, Phyro's little band of misfits had managed to assemble a fleet of Imperial airships rivaling, no, surpassing the fleet Gin Mazoti had fielded with the resources of the entire empire behind her.

From the very beginning of his preparations, Phyro understood that in the war against the Lyucu, he had two opponents. One was tightly knit, cruel, resourceful, and dedicated to war as a way of life; the other was disordered, indolent, self-indulgent, and so enamored of peace that the martial spirit had deserted the body politic.

Not only did he have to overcome the militaristic Lyucu, he also had to find a way to win over the cacophonous, many-minded multitudes of Dara.

Even if he successfully shifted the popular opinion toward war, and even if Jia didn't actively sabotage his efforts, Phyro knew that he couldn't count on wielding the resources of the whole empire, certainly not for long. The crowd's opinion was fickle and the inertia of entrenched bureaucracies—unwilling to stray from established patterns—enormous. There would be but a brief window for war, a window that demanded a quick victory. It was difficult to move a free people at peace to fight for strangers enslaved on other islands, a cause that didn't yield an immediate dividend in their daily lives, and harder still when the price of war was long and continuous sacrifice.

Thus, when the opportunity for an invasion presented itself, Phyro knew he would have to rely for the most part on his private army, and not count on more support than the matériel and manpower already present in the Dara military.

He would not, for example, be constructing large-scale floating platforms from which to launch garinafins, like the city-ships of the Lyucu. Neither would he be building a vast fleet of underwater crubens, or financing the exploratory trips necessary to map out the submarine volcanoes necessary for their propulsion. He could not redirect the research priorities of the Imperial Academy and the Imperial laboratories to expensive new weapons. He could not conscript an army of hundreds of thousands or recruit volunteers from the breadth and length of Dara. . . . There was simply not enough time, and besides, his aunt-mother would never have approved such a drastic redirection of Dara's economy to war.

Thus, he had to plan for a fast and (relatively) cheap war, not one that required sustained backing from the common people and the court. His most powerful weapons, the garinafins, had to be launched from land. He could only rely on a small workshop financed by patriotic plays and veterans' donations to build weapons, not the Imperial Treasury or the manufacturing might of the empire. He had no hope of acquiring the costly weapons that Jia had deployed against the Lyucu invasion ten years ago, such as the diamond-tipped silkmotic lances, each worth as much as a city's taxes, or the silkmotic spheres that emptied the palace of silver and delivered the power of lightning against the enemy.

His only allies were surprise, guile, and a boundless appetite for risk. Not very powerful allies at first glance, to be sure.

These same allies built my father an empire and won Auntie Gin her greatest victory, he reminded himself.

So, he had to sketch his battle plans years in advance, using a trickle of resources that escaped the empress's attention. He had to craft a confrontation against the Lyucu in a place and manner of his choosing.

Puma Yemu had been instructed to give as good a fight to the Lyucu as he could muster with his outmatched fleet, but his goal was always losing and drawing the enemy to the coast of Crescent Island, where Phyro had prepared a trap.

Phyro knew that he couldn't possibly win against the Lyucu with only his secret garinafins. Any well-balanced army required many different parts all working together like the pieces of a *zamaki* player.

To counter the Lyucu fleet and airships, he needed airships of his own. Phyro didn't have the luxury of large shipyards where hundreds of skilled engineers spent months building each airship. Not only could he not afford such facilities, but industrial efforts at such a scale risked drawing Empress Jia's attention and, ultimately, the suspicions of the Lyucu.

He needed a new kind of airship: something that could be produced and transported in secret and then deployed quickly in the field.

This was a challenge that Zomi Kidosu and Rati Yera took up with gusto. Their solution was a design that could be prefabricated in small pieces, which could then be assembled on the battlefield by a relatively small team of aviators unskilled in the art of ship construction.

Instead of long keels and girders that provided overall structural strength, these new ships relied on short sections of bamboo that were secured together just before launch. In this, Zomi and Rati were inspired by the mortise-and-tenon construction technique used in temples devoted to Tututika. The goddess of beauty and nature was said to abhor the symbolism of man-made iron stakes piercing wood, so the builders of old Amu devised a system of notches and recesses to bind together the structural elements of temples without any nails.

Rati and Zomi came up with a similar system of studs and holes at the ends of bamboo segments, which could be joined into keels and girders. Moreover, the protrusions and recesses were uniquely coded so that assemblers could find the right segments without reference to an engineering drawing.

Instead of hulls made by wrapping long bolts of silk around the frame, strengthened with lacquer, the hulls of the new ships were made from small squares of lacquered material designed to be patched together with a series of tiny hooks and loops inspired by burrs. Battlefield assembly of these new airships could be accomplished in a few hours.

To be sure, these new airships were not nearly as airworthy or strong as traditional airships, and they were incapable of long cruises. But they were more than adequate for the decisive, explosive encounter that Phyro had in mind.

To avoid detection by Lyucu spies or Empress Jia's officials, during the year before Réza Müi's little rebellion, airship components were secretly shipped to Crescent Island, bamboo girder by bamboo girder, square of varnished silk by square of varnished silk. Some of the work was accomplished by Adüan smugglers, while Widow Wasu's merchantmen fleet handled the rest—the aged widow had been only too glad to join the conspiracy when Arona Taré and Mota Kiphi approached her. ("How can the Wasu clan prosper by ourselves when all Dara is under the threat of the Lyucu? Everyone must do their duty. Besides, I already helped Kuni obtain the throne; might as well help his son defend it.")

But there was yet another hurdle: How would the airships, once assembled, take off? The standard source of lift gas in Dara, after the fall of Rui, was manure gas. But where would Phyro's private army find manure in wild Crescent Island?

A chance discovery by one of the researchers in the Imperial laboratories in Pan provided the breakthrough. While attempting to understand the exact means by which the bovine digestive system produced manure gas, she generated a flammable, lighter-than-air gas from rotting vegetation in a sealed chamber. In essence, she re-created a cow's insides.

Zomi, who as Farsight Secretary had access to all the research results of the various Imperial laboratories, passed on this information to Rati. The technique was then scaled up and adapted to the underground caverns of Crescent Island. Using fresh leaves, vines, and other chopped up bits of vegetation—taking care not to disturb the appearance of the jungle from the sky too much—the troops Phyro stationed on Crescent Island in advance of the invasion practically engineered underground swamps that bubbled with a steady supply of manure gas. The gas was then piped out and stored in other underground chambers so that it could be used to fill the gasbags of airships once they were assembled.

While Puma Yemu's sailors put on a show for the benefit of the Lyucu observers overnight, Phyro's troops had been busy in the jungle above the inlet. As the morning sun rose, the battle-ready airships lifted off, ready for the long-planned confrontation.

Aboard the city-ships, Lyucu warriors admired the floating engines of war, jellyfish that had propelled themselves into a rarefied medium.

Since the Battle of Zathin Gulf, silkmotic airships had played a prominent role in the nightmares of young Lyucu naros and culeks training for the inevitable day when they had to fight for the survival of Ukyu-taasa, and Thane Cutanrovo had portrayed them as symbols of Dara-raaki's unnatural way of life, mechanical monstrosities that exemplified the corrupt nature of Dara.

But the Lyucu had never expected the airships to be so . . . beautiful.

The giant vessels shimmered in the brightening sunlight, their billowing surfaces flexing, undulating, heaving, wobbling, more like living, breathing creatures than machines of war.

"Votan-ru-taasa, votan-sa-taasa," Goztan called out, her cry breaking through the silence like the clarion trumpet of a garinafin.

The warriors turned to her, like sunflowers turning to the brightest star.

Though she had worked so hard to avoid war, now that slaughter was inevitable, Goztan felt a preternatural calm descend over her, like the peace of the gods that the shamans spoke of. For the last three days, she had suspected, in the back of her mind, that her victory over Puma Yemu had been too easy. The sudden appearance of

Imperial airships at this deserted island was not really a surprise; in a way, the world was making sense again. By setting this trap for her, Phyro was only following in the footsteps of the great Gin Mazoti, and that was something she had anticipated.

Goztan sent her most trusted naros-votan belowdecks to begin the secret preparations as soon as she saw the airships. She didn't want to fight, but now that the natives had come to invade Ukyutaasa, she knew her duty.

"Rare are the moments when our actions may divert the flow of time into the future, like a well-considered garinafin sweep may turn a stampeding herd away from the precipice. I believe we've come to such a moment.

"Many of us remember the time, many winters ago, when Pékyu Tenryo first told us of his dream of finding a new homeland for us, where we would be free from the horrors of starvation; where we would escape the life-taking axes of winter storms, summer droughts, merciless packs of horrid wolves, ambushes of tusked tigers, and plagues that decimate the herds; where we would find exotic foods, soft beds, rich grazing land, sweet fresh water, and beautiful and pliant slaves.

"Since then, we have labored hard and long to fulfill that dream. We learned to sail the ships built by our enemies; we defied heaven, sea, and strange gods to pass through the Wall of Storms; we survived a journey longer and more arduous than any our ancestors had taken. Yet even after our landing, our ordeal did not end. We faced hostile natives bent on our destruction; we found a land that was rich but not hospitable to our way of life; we watched our brothers and sisters and mothers and fathers and sons and daughters die in that struggle.

"We performed these deeds not for ourselves, votan-ru-taasa and votan-sa-taasa. We strove and fought and bled and died so that our grandmothers and grandfathers would no longer have to walk out into the storm to leave enough food for our children, so that our families would no longer be at risk of being enslaved by those stronger than us, so that those we love would always live free.

"We dared to take up arms against fate because we wished to change the future."

Tears flowed down the faces of the Lyucu warriors standing at attention as they recalled the price they'd paid to realize Pékyu Tenryo's dream. Spontaneously, they began to cheer, their hearts pounding as loudly in their ears as their clubs and axes struck the wooden decks of the city-ships.

> *Ten dyudyu cupéruna?*
> *Lyucu kyo!*
> *Ten dyudyu cupéruna?*
> *Ukyu kyo!*

Goztan waited until the cheers gradually subsided.

"Let me speak to you now of this moment.

"I'm not ashamed to admit that the machines of the barbarians are terrifying. Each of them seems as imposing as an aerial city-ship, and we can all recall tales of the deadly magic they contain. It is certain that many of us will never return to see our loved ones, to offer rich, fatty sheep sponge to the aged, or chewy, flavorful cartilage to the little ones. Some of us will never again experience the pleasure of the embrace of our husbands or wives, or slaves on whom we have lavished our affection."

More tears flowing down scarred and rugged faces; more sporadic shouts of defiance.

"But more than fear of these machines, I harbor doubt, and I know that I am not alone. Even more terrifying than the threat posed by our enemy is the internal strife among us."

The Lyucu quieted at this unexpected turn in the speech.

"Sometimes I fear we've become monsters in the pursuit of a dream. We sought freedom, not just for ourselves, but also for this land, which had been enslaved by the iron implements of farming, and also for its inhabitants, who had been enslaved by the Lords of Dara, known to us as tyrants.

"But as we look back on the re-rememberings of Ukyu-taasa, we know we've done things we aren't sure will be judged as righteous in the eyes of the gods and the memories of those who'll come after us. Some of you, myself included, sense the growing doubt in our cause. Are we right to enslave the natives? Are we certain that all those who have been executed are traitors and spies? Can we truly claim to be free if we've come to depend upon the plunder and tribute the natives give us?"

The ranks of Lyucu warriors became agitated. Whispers filled the air as confused faces looked at one another and then back at Goztan. But there were also some who gazed at her with expressions of gratitude; she had given voice to what lay concealed deep in their hearts.

"I don't know the answers to these questions, votan-ru-taasa and votan-sa-taasa. Perhaps these are not inquiries meant for mere mortals at all. But I do know that we cannot resolve these questions unless we live beyond today, unless we preserve the existence of Ukyu-taasa, home to our elders, lovers, and children.

"In this moment of doubt, I'm reminded of the great warlord Mata Zyndu, revered by the natives. We never had the pleasure of testing his mettle, but it is said that he wielded a great sword called the Doubt-Ender.

"Let's resolutely wield the Doubt-Ender against the tangled mess in our hearts. No matter what your thoughts are concerning the justness of our cause, we cannot afford to show the enemy mercy or let hesitation stay our arm in this moment. The enemy will plunge us all into the merciless sea today if they're able, and unless we're victorious, we have *no* future.

"Doubt is a luxury enjoyed only by those who survive."

The Lyucu warriors roared with approval, their hearts now as hardened as garinafin skulls.

Cu na goztenva va péfir!
Cu na tatenva va péfir!

Goztan gave the order to open the large hatches, and garinafins took off from the city-ships.

Concealed among the dense jungle topping the cliffs south of the inlet, Phyro prayed silently to the gods of Dara as he watched his new airships gain altitude. This was, without a doubt, the greatest gamble he had ever made in his life, and the wager involved not chips or jewels, but the very future of the Islands.

While Marshal Gin Mazoti had stopped the Lyucu invasion force with only six airships, Phyro was launching twelve. He hoped that the Lyucu were suitably impressed.

A giant antlered head snorted nervously next to him, enveloping him in blasts of warm breath redolent of semi-digested vegetation. Phyro placed a comforting hand against the side of the massive deer-like cranium, which belonged to his mount, a young female garina-fin named Ginki.

"Not yet," he whispered into one of the twitching ears, as big as his torso. "Not yet."

He held on to the thought of Zen-Kara, held on to the vision of the future he had promised her. To realize that future, he first had to win this war.

Once the airships had risen high enough, gigantic feathered oars, like tentacles, emerged through slits in the side of the hull. As teams of oarswomen grunted and pulled, the ships began to glide grace-fully forward, gaining even more altitude on dynamic lift, as they were designed to do. Beneath the billowing hulls, massive spheres dangling on chains came into view as the ships cleared the tree-lined ridge and the mist-shrouded inlet.

The drumbeats grew more rushed, like a summer storm. The sonorous horn blasts were like claps of thunder.

As if intent on demonstrating the vessels' power, small squares of cloth were pulled away from the rippling bows of the airships, revealing weapon ports. Arrows, with clumsy burr-shaped tips about the size of a person's head, poked through the holes.

Twelve aerial jellyfish, their stingers bared, pressed menacingly toward the Lyucu fleet.

Goztan looked up. The garinafins were circling above her ship, wait-ing for orders. Turbulence from their beating wings stirred the hair of Noda Mi and her guards.

Melancholy weighed down her heart. There was a time when she would have been with them, riding at their head. But age was an enemy none could overcome. She had her experience and knowledge, but she lacked the agility and endurance of a younger woman. It was the fate of all great warriors to yield their spots to younger rivals, and that eternal law applied in Dara as well as the scrublands.

She took a deep breath and pushed the sorrow-tinged heart-cloud away. There was no use in lamenting the passage of time. She had her place, as did those who followed her.

She swung her signaling spear high overhead, and pointed it at the approaching airships.

"Garinafin! Garinafin!" Lyucu warriors shouted from the city-ships.

Ten garinafins pulled out of their circling pattern and headed for the golden, shimmering Imperial airships.

The younger naros and culeks cheered with the thrill of finding themselves face-to-face with monsters known only from legends. But for the older thanes and naros-votan, who had been present at the Battle of Zathin Gulf, this moment felt always-already familiar, as though they had been violently cast back in time.

Once again, garinafins streaked toward airships like hungry wolves heading toward slow, overfed cattle. Once again, airships bared their arrow-shaped teeth like steady fortresses ready for any assault. Once again, the fate of two peoples hung in the balance, between the sky and the roiling sea, between lightning-fast garinafin and cloud-elegant airship, as men and women intent on rewriting the future of Dara pledged their lives.

But there were important differences, too.

For one, all the garinafins shone with a bright, metallic glint, as though their naturally varicolored leathery hides had been replaced with steel and iron. Instead of living creatures, they resembled automata constructed by the hand of Fithowéo.

For another, the garinafin riders were not armed with slingshots and bone-spears; instead, they carried bundles of iron-tipped spears on their backs and held aloft steel axes in their hands.

"Diasa, club-maiden and huntress, protect my warriors," whispered Goztan. She had not prayed to the goddess for a long time, not since the day her father had died at the hand of her mother. She had hated the goddess for not intervening to save him, though he had devoted his life to her service and denied himself to secure the goddess's protection for his daughter.

"If you should see fit to reward us with a victory today, I pledge to never let the flesh of animals pass between my teeth again," Goztan whispered. In this moment, she was willing to forgive the goddess, if any remnants of the special bond between them still survived. She was willing to do as her father had done, if only her warriors would survive and carry the day.

The Lyucu's secret was out. This was why history would not repeat itself, and why the rematch between Ukyu-taasa and Dara would have a different outcome.

The garinafins were draped in plate armor and chain mail, and the riders wielded weapons derived from Dara.

In the course of human affairs, it is almost never possible to fix an old mistake. Yet, at this moment, Goztan and her warriors were being given that rarest of jewels: a chance to remedy an error from the past, to refight a battle that they had lost.

A decade ago, the mighty Lyucu invasion force that had threatened to overwhelm the Islands like a tsunami had crashed into an immovable barrier at Ginpen and receded to the islands of Rui and Dasu. Since that day, Tanvanaki and her thanes had obsessed over the reasons for their failure.

At the root of the cascade of Lyucu tactical errors at Zathin Gulf, Tanvanaki found, lay a piece of humble and easily overlooked equipment: the collapsible bamboo caltrop that the Dara defenders had used to jam open the jaws of the garinafins, thereby depriving them of fire breath. Everything had gone wrong for the Lyucu after that.

Tanvanaki had then instructed Goztan, her most trusted ally and the only person whose knowledge of garinafins she respected, to devise a counter.

Thankfully, Cutanrovo's chaos-inducing purification campaigns had largely left the garinafin force alone, and Goztan was able to focus on retraining. As a first step, she drilled the garinafins never to open their jaws unless their riders gave an explicit order to breathe fire.

Moreover, in contravention of standard practice among the people of the scrublands, Goztan ordered the first wave of ten garinafins to approach the Imperial airships with their mouths muzzled. In Ukyu-Gondé, muzzling mounts was typically only done during war games, but in this case, Goztan wanted to probe the defenses of the airships.

As pilots guided their garinafins to swoop past the billowing bows of the airships, archers hidden within, not realizing that the garinafins were muzzled, launched volleys of caltrop-tipped bolts. Though a few of the garinafins panicked under the assault, the muzzles nonetheless kept their jaws shut, and the burred arrows bounced harmlessly off their metal armor.

The armor was part of Tanvanaki's meticulous preparation for the inevitable invasion from Dara. Although Cutanrovo had advocated passionately for a return to the purity of traditional Lyucu fighting techniques, Tanvanaki and Goztan were not so foolish as to leave Dara advances only in the hands of unreliable native auxiliaries. Though Dara's counterespionage efforts had put an end to Tanvanaki's plan of acquiring advanced knowledge of the silkmotic force by kidnapping engineers and mechanics from the core islands, the pékyu was able to protect some of Ukyu-taasa's native smiths from Cutanrovo's zealotry under the guise of the need to arm the native auxiliaries with weapons familiar to them.

Tanvanaki and Goztan had then set up a secret workshop in the vast underwater tunnel between Dasu and Rui. Staffed with the most skilled smiths of Ukyu-taasa and supplied with metal diverted and melted down from the quarterly tribute goods from Dara, the workshop was dedicated to producing weapons and armor based on native designs for the garinafin crews—a project that certainly would have sent Cutanrovo into a frenzy of opposition, had she known about it.

Goztan's key insight was that Gin Mazoti's oversized silkmotic bolts, which had caused so many casualties among the garinafins, had to penetrate the hide to do maximum damage. Thus, the workshop invented Dara-style armor for the flying mounts. Though Goztan had been training covertly with armored garinafins and crews absolutely loyal to her for some time now, this was the first time they had been deployed in battle. Most of the Lyucu warriors in the fleet—especially the hard-liners—hadn't even known of their existence until this moment.

The feinting garinafins retreated and joined the rest of the circling garinafins above the city-ships. None of them had been disarmed by the caltrops or even suffered a scratch from the arrows.

Although the metal garinafin armor was unfamiliar, the watching naros and culeks on the city-ship decks quickly discerned their utility after such a powerful demonstration. Though no hideous silkmotic bolts—no doubt the Dara airships' most potent weapon—had yet been launched, it seemed not unreasonable to expect that they would be as ineffective against armored garinafins as the burred caltrops.

Spontaneous cheers broke out all over the Lyucu fleet.

As if realizing the futility of their efforts, archers aboard the airships retracted their caltrop-tipped arrows, leaving the bows as smooth and vulnerable as the exposed flesh of clams.

"The gods are with us," intoned Noda Mi piously. "Such wisdom from the all-seeing pékyu! Such courage from the never-wavering dragon-thanes! Such . . ."

Goztan smiled grimly. There was no need for the aid of the gods as long as the Lyucu learned from their mistakes. Phyro, true to the report she had received from Noda Mi, was following exactly in the steps of Gin Mazoti, his hero.

She waved her signaling spear again, and trumpeters blew into their booming instruments, announcing a new round of attacks, no longer probing feints.

In the air above the city-ships, the most nimble members of the garinafin crews scampered over the network of ropes draped over the heavy armor toward the mouths of the beasts, intent on untying the muzzles.

The extension of the traditional webbing to which riders attached themselves all the way to the heads of the garinafins was yet another innovation by Goztan. Besides allowing crews to unmuzzle the gari-nafins without having to land, the new webbing also gave riders a safer way to access the heads of the giant beasts to remove any cal-trops that managed to lodge in their jaws during battle.

After one more long blow from the bone trumpets, forty garina-fins headed for the Imperial air force.

Goztan kept her eyes fixed on the airships, fully expecting them to rotate in midair and interlock with one another, transforming into one or two aerial fortresses. The gondolas should drop their walls to reveal the powerful silkmotic bolt launchers.

"Spirit of Gin Mazoti," Goztan whispered, "now you'll see how we're ready for your tricks."

Phyro grinned confidently as he saw the massive cloud of leathery wings approach his airships. The Lyucu, having assured themselves that these airships were imitations of the vessels Gin Mazoti had deployed, had committed the bulk of their garinafin force.

He gave no orders for the airships to assume the Plum Formation or the Box Formation, and the aviators aboard didn't scramble to winch back giant crossbows.

Why? Because such maneuvers were impossible for his airships.

Despite a superficial resemblance, Phyro's airships were in no way the equals of the magnificent vessels that had carried the Marshal to victory a decade ago. Powerful but expensive weapons like silkmotic lances and silkmotic bolts were simply beyond Phyro's small work-shop and meager budget. Moreover, the hull and structural skeleton, designed for ease of production, transport, and assembly, lacked the strength to support the mechanisms that allowed Gin Mazoti's ships to maneuver and attack as they did. How else could Phyro have produced so many airships with less than a hundredth of the funds available to the Marshal?

Even the giant dangling spheres were not fashioned out of coiled garinafin gut filled with captured lightning. In fact, they were simply papier-mâché shells designed to *look* like weapons of mass destruction.

Without realizing it, Phyro had struck upon the same trick that had once served Théra so well. The airships, like those kites with painted tusked tigers, were crafted to evoke the memories of a dif-ferent war in his enemy.

He knew as well as Gin Mazoti that the first rule of war was never to fight the same battle twice.

The garinafins, clad in silver armor, approached the ponderous golden airships like a school of sharks approaching a pod of sleeping whales, or a bundle of sharp knifes held to a plate of billowing puff pastry.

Around Goztan, Lyucu warriors cheered and banged their weapons against the gunwales and masts, hungry for the sight of airships decimated by the fiery tongues of their most potent weapons, augmented by that most Dara of materials: metal.

But growing unease crept over the garinafin-thane. The hovering airships weren't shedding their silk skins or false gondola bottoms to transform. Where were the silkmotic lances and giant crossbows?

The first garinafins were finally within striking distance of the front-most Imperial airships. The winged beasts slowed down and twisted their sinuous necks so that their heads faced away from the target, as they were trained to do. The unnatural pose allowed them to open their jaws away from the enemy in order to prevent a last-minute caltrop shot before breathing fire.

Slender nozzles poked through arrow slits in the hulls of the airships.

The garinafin pilots, some of them veterans, were unmoved. The nozzles appeared similar to the flamethrowers on the ghost airships that had once raided Rui in the first failed invasion of Ukyu-taasa. Such weapons, paltry imitations of true garinafin fire, posed little threat against trained garinafins with tough skin and armor. Besides, garinafin fire breath had much better range.

The front-most garinafins snapped their jaws shut, whipped their heads about, and reopened their jaws as bright columns of fire streaked forth from their maws.

Sparkling columns of water shot out of the nozzles, meeting the fiery garinafin breath head-on.

Sizzling steam filled the air. Multiple, additional streams of water, arcing out of other slits in the floating fortresses, doused each attacking garinafin head. Clouds of white steam soon surrounded each airship, like mountains poking through the clouds.

The shocked garinafins circled away, their heads and riders all drenched in water. The airships survived this first assault largely unscathed. A few of the garinafins did manage to set one of the airships on fire, but the airship crew quickly aimed their hoses at these spots and put the fire out.

"Cowards! Fools!" sputtered Noda Mi. "How dare you defy the Great Lyucu?"

Goztan pondered the sight with furrowed brows, deeply puzzled. On the one hand, she had to admire the ingenuity of the natives. Using water to defend against fire was both elegant and quite natural. But she couldn't see the point of this novel tactic. Water was extremely heavy and took away valuable lift capacity on airships that could have gone to weaponry and crew—presumably that was why earlier Dara airships had not adopted this approach.

Even these gigantic airships could only carry a comparatively small volume of water. A few more strafing garinafin attacks would force the crews to use up the purely defensive substance, leaving them at the mercy of the Lyucu. What was the young Emperor of Dara thinking?

Something wasn't quite right, Goztan realized. The steam-fog clouds around the airships didn't dissipate in the breeze, but had only grown thicker. Was there something unique about the water used to douse the flames, or were the crews of the airships thickening the mist with smoke? In any event, the airships were now entirely veiled behind curtains of clouds, like whales lost in the frothy sea.

Briefly, Goztan wondered if she should call off the assault. But it was too late. Already, the garinafins had shaken off the water on their heads, turned around, and began another attack approach.

Abruptly, the Dara drummers onshore changed to a different beat, and long, blaring horn blasts seemed to call for a new war dance. Loud, unfamiliar noises came from the mist-hidden airships, as though a thousand-thousand sheets of paper were being ripped or a hundred-hundred bolts of cloth were being torn.

The garinafin riders widened their eyes, and a few muttered curses in consternation.

Hundreds, thousands of pairs of iridescent wings emerged from the billowing steam clouds around each airship, swarming toward them like a living nightmare.

CHAPTER TWENTY-THREE

ORNITHOPTERS

TIRO COZO: MORE THAN A YEAR EARLIER.

Despite Phyro's deep admiration for military commanders who showed great personal courage and boldness of style—as exemplified by Mata Zyndu, the Hegemon—he was at heart a very different kind of tactician. Rather than trusting to the myth of personal invincibility to turn the tide of battle, he preferred to weigh advantages and disadvantages, to analyze honestly the strengths of his enemies and the weaknesses of his own army, to draw up orders of battle based on columns and rows of numbers that slowly but inexorably shifted the contest in his favor.

Though he probably would have bristled at the comparison, the historical war leader closest to him in approach was none other than Kindo Marana, the onetime-tax-collector-turned-marshal of Xana, who viewed war as a species of accounting, who prized logistics and calculation over mere martial prowess.

Takval's gift of garinafins offered the opportunity for a fundamental shift in the strategic positions of Ukyu-taasa and Dara, but Phyro wasn't so foolish as to think that victory required only that he ride to Kriphi on the back of a garinafin, laying waste to everything as portrayed in some patriotic propaganda pageant.

Only the most arrogant and deluded would believe that the people of Dara, merely a decade after acquiring these flying mounts, could magically out-Lyucu the Lyucu and win in direct garinafin-to-garinafin combat against an enemy who had existed in symbiosis with these creatures for countless generations.

Dara's garinafins would be smaller, younger, and fewer than the force commanded by the Lyucu. Dara's pilots and riders would be less experienced and skilled than their Lyucu counterparts. Dara would be without the benefit of centuries of experience and lore, acquired through thousands of garinafin battles. To challenge the Lyucu directly with garinafins was suicide.

Phyro was reminded of an old tale from the days of the Tiro states. Many centuries ago, the King of Gan, a chariot-racing enthusiast, spent lavishly to breed the fastest horses, to build the lightest chariots, and to hire the most skilled drivers. After ten years, he had the best racing team in the whole world. No other Tiro king could beat him, and he won race after race, wager after wager. Eventually, no one would even agree to race against his team.

A bandit by the name of Dophino—it was said that he was brought up as a girl but preferred to go about the world as a man—then came to challenge the King of Gan. He had become famous by leading a rebellion of prostitutes, and he and his followers were incredibly fierce warriors, bowing to no duke nor king.

"What kind of horses do you race with?" asked the king.

"I went to the market in the south of Toaza," replied Dophino. "I haggled with the horse vendors there until I got a good deal."

"What kind of chariot do you race with?" asked the king, rather astonished.

"I saw a night-soil carrier at the city gates," replied Dophino. "I thought his cart looked very sturdy, so I bought it from him. After I open up a few side panels and remove a couple of wheels, it will look great."

"What is the name of your driver?" asked the king, even more amazed.

"Why, myself, of course."

"How long have you been studying the art of chariot racing?" asked the king, more than a bit nervous. Dophino must be the world's greatest driver if he had come to challenge the king with cheap market-bought draft horses and a cargo cart.

"I don't know how to drive a chariot at all, not yet anyway," said Dophino. "I never needed to before because my bandits fight on foot. But racing a chariot looks like fun, and I heard you would give anyone who beat you a city. Well, here I am. Let's race."

The King of Gan laughed and laughed. "Do you know that I have been racing chariots since before I could walk? I can tell the quality of a horse just by looking into its eyes. I can judge the weight and ride of a chariot just by listening to its wheels. I have memorized the names of the five hundred best drivers in the whole world. I dream of racetracks and eat all my meals at the stables. Do you really think you can beat me?"

"I'll never know until I try," said Dophino.

"Fine," said the king, his voice now imbued with a hint of menace. "But if I win, I want your head."

No, Phyro would not commit such a basic mistake and challenge the Lyucu to a head-to-head garinafin fight. The garinafins *were* important, but Phyro would have to add to his side of the ledger many other entries to balance out the books.

In Dara, the dream of flight had taken many forms. From the very first prayer lanterns powered by air heated by candles to Emperor Mapidéré's gigantic airships filled with the mysterious lift gas from Lake Dako, generations of engineers had attempted to realize the fantasy of humans being as free as the birds.

Luan Zyaji, driven by the desire to avenge his family against the Xana tyrant, was among the first to investigate the potential of heavier-than-air flight. He studied the flight of kites in detail and elucidated the principles by which they stayed aloft. The tethers that anchored kites to the earth, as it turned out, were in fact critical to the upward force that kept them off the ground: the strings provided a kind of forward propulsive force against the wind, and it was the flow of air over the wings of the kites that lifted them into the sky.

From these principles and the flight of birds he invented the stringless kite. Wings driven by the rider's muscles propelled the machine forward, which also created upward lift as a result of air currents flowing over the surfaces of the wings. Although the stringless kite was not advanced significantly beyond the prototype used against the tyrant Mapidéré in an assassination attempt, Luan later taught its secrets to his favorite student, Zomi Kidosu.

For a time after Dara lost its sole source of lift gas at Lake Dako, Imperial researchers looked into the military potential of heavier-than-air flight. However, the eventual discovery of manure gas as an alternative to Lake Dako's lift gas halted that particular avenue of research. Nonetheless, after the conspiracy was formed, Zomi shared what she knew of stringless kites with the Blossom Gang, hoping that the gang, coming at the problem with fresh eyes, would find new applications for this type of machine in Phyro's quest to counter Lyucu superiority in garinafin warfare.

Rati Yera initially drew up plans for garinafin-sized stringless kites as a direct answer to the garinafins. Thickly armored and mounted with powerful weapons, heavier-than-air mechanical garinafins might challenge flesh-and-blood garinafins much as mechanical crubens had replaced actual crubens in Kuni Garu's original assault on the Big Island during the Chrysanthemum-Dandelion War.

But Phyro almost immediately scrapped the idea as impractical. To engineer such a mechanical wonder would require years of experiments and research, and even if they somehow managed to arrive at a workable design in time, Phyro could see no way to marshal the resources needed to build it.

"What if we go with a less ambitious version of the plan and build numerous man-sized stringless kites?" asked Phyro. "You know, closer to Luan Zyaji's original idea?"

"Master Zyaji's machine was more glider than true flier," said Rati Yera. "The biggest problem with his prototype, which the Imperial laboratories also struggled with, is the need for constant power to maintain forward movement and generate lift. Human muscle can barely keep even just a frame aloft, leaving little room for armor or weaponry."

With so little excess lift, Phyro knew that the machines weren't good for much except delivering boarding parties onto enemy garinafins. A similar tactic had been used by Gin Mazoti's ghost ships to conduct suicide attacks on garinafins. But that was a time of desperation, and sacrificing so casually the lives of his tiny band of fighters in a war of liberation was abhorrent to the young emperor.

He encouraged Rati to keep working at the problem. Instinctively, he felt that heavier-than-air flight would be important to the overall task.

One day, while Rati Yera propelled herself past the garinafin training grounds in her wheeled chair, she saw a curious young garinafin investigating a copse in which a flock of starlings roosted. The starlings, though individually tiny and weak compared to the juvenile garinafin, swarmed around the creature and pecked at its eyes and ears relentlessly until the garinafin fled from the copse, moaning and snorting with terror.

The old inventor returned to her workshop and shut the doors, only to emerge weeks later with prototypes of what she called "ornithopters."

Shaped like the small birds that had inspired them, the ornithopters were built with light frames of bamboo and wings of paper and silk—essentially tiny, articulated kites. Due to their small size and weight, especially relative to their wing area, a wound-up spring or twisted piece of sinew provided enough power for flights lasting half an hour or even longer. As for weaponry, Rati planned for each to be endowed with a sharp bite: a spring-driven steel beak, a tiny silkmotic Ogé jar shocker, a slingshot or pneumatic pellet-launcher, or even an explosive bolt propelled by firework powder.

"But how do you guide these miniature stringless kites?" asked a puzzled Phyro, when Rati Yera presented the invention to him. "Are you also going to create an army of miniature pilots?"

"*Rénga*, this is why the gods brought us together," said a chuckling Rati. "I solved that problem before we even met!"

Now that Rati Yera was working directly with the emperor himself, she no longer felt the shame of the ignominious origins of her proudest invention. Freely, she elaborated on the principles of the instructible carts and their instant application.

Inside each ornithopter, the power source—the wound-up sinew or mainspring—drove two independent axles connected to the wings. The amount of energy released to each axle was regulated via a separate escapement mechanism that rocked back and forth on a spring-loaded balance wheel, advancing and locking a set number of teeth on the drive gear on each swing of the escapement bar. Each oscillation of one of the balance wheels corresponded to a single beat of one wing, resulting in a heartbeat-like sound.

However, unlike escapements used in clocks, the size of the arc swept by the wing-escapement bar was not uniform, but changed on each oscillation. When the arc was narrow, the drive gear advanced only a small distance, resulting in less movement; when the arc was wide, the drive gear advanced a longer distance, resulting in more movement. The size of the arc traced by the variable escapement was determined by a probe attached to the balance wheel, which pressed into one of a succession of holes drilled along a tight spiral winding up the side of a rotating piece of cork. When the hole was shallow, the probe prevented the balance wheel from reaching the full extent of its rotation, resulting in a narrower arc in the variable escapement and a weaker wingbeat; when the hole was deep, on the other hand, the balance wheel swung through a wider angle, advancing a larger number of teeth under the escapement to yield a stronger wingbeat. With each wing flap, the piece of cork also rotated a fraction of a degree, presenting the next hole in the spiraling series to the probe on the following oscillation.

In addition to the two rotating cork cylinders for controlling the motion of the wings, there was also a third cylinder with drilled holes that regulated the position of a gimbaled flywheel at the center of each ornithopter. The use of a gimbaled flywheel, called a gyro for short, to maintain the stability of an airship or mechanical cruben was well-known in Dara. Shifting the internal position of the gyro altered the angles of the wings, which caused the ornithopter to ascend or descend.

Thus, by altering the depth of the holes etched into the sides of the rotating cork cylinders, the entire flight plan of an ornithopter could be "written" by the pilot ahead of time, to be read and enacted by the machine later.

After days of intense labor, Rati Yera had produced three pro-totype ornithopters and three sets of instruction cylinders. The diminutive cylinders had been by far the hardest part: Near the end, her fingers trembled uncontrollably from the tension of the precise movements required and her eyes swam in tears.

But all that suffering seemed worth it as she demonstrated the ornithopters to Emperor Monadétu. She sat in her wheeled chair, her chest puffed out with pride, as the little mechanical birds executed impressive aerial maneuvers: diving, swooping, climbing, circling. . . .

"How do these stringless kites attack?" Phyro asked, his voice calm.

Rati was a bit miffed that the emperor didn't seem more impressed. She had, after all, just shown him mechanical birds that could fly like the real thing, a wonder never before witnessed in Dara. She sighed inside. It was the fate of all great engineers to be underappreciated.

"Well, these are just proofs of concept," she said. "I suppose depending on the type of weapon, the ornithopters could be set to be triggered on contact or by a timed fuse—"

"But they're so small that you'd need a lot of them to do real damage," mused Phyro.

"Yes, that's true." Rati's annoyance grew. Did the emperor not *see* what was so amazing about these machines? "*Rénga*, you have to understand that the ornithopters are *instructible*. Just by swapping in cork plugs with different patterns of holes drilled into them, they could instantly learn a new flight pattern. Imagine these flying in formation—"

Phyro stopped her by holding up one hand. He squinted at the tiny cork cylinders in her palm and seemed to work through some calculations in his head.

"This is a wonderful invention, Rati," he said at last, "but how long did it take you to make these three ornithopters and nine instruction cylinders?"

"The design took about a week, and the construction took two weeks from start to finish," said Rati.

"With practice, how fast can you make them?" asked the emperor.

"I can probably make one ornithopter a day," said Rati cautiously.

"What about the cork plugs? Did you drill the holes with a nail?"

"With an embroidery needle, actually," said Rati. "The instruction cylinders will always take much longer than the ornithopters. They're delicate components that require a steady hand and clear eyes."

"Then the invention won't be of any use to us," said Phyro, his voice not unkind. "By my estimate, we'll need tens of thousands of them to have any hope of making a dent against garinafins, and even if you taught everyone at Tiro Cozo your method, we can't make enough in time. And that's not even accounting for repairs and replacements."

Rati Yera was silent.

"Besides," Phyro added, "I don't see how we can teach anyone else to make these drilled cork cylinders like you. Most of my soldiers are fighters, far more comfortable with a sword than an embroidery needle."

The problems posed by Phyro's levelheaded accounting seemed insurmountable. He had doused her enthusiasm with a bucket of ice water.

Gently, he sat the ornithopters down in her lap, and, after resting a comforting hand momentarily on her shoulder, strode away.

"*Rénga*," she called out, "I'm sorry."

He turned around. "What for?"

"For . . . wasting your time."

Phyro shook his head. "You haven't wasted my time. It's my duty to point out problems, and yours to solve them. You've discovered a promising idea, but now comes the hard part of making it practical. I believe in you."

Rati wasn't sure *she* did. She felt as dispirited as the mechanical birds in her lap, flapping their wings erratically as they dissipated the last of their energy.

Deep into the night, Rati tossed and turned in her bed, berating herself.

She had allowed the excitement of pure invention to lead her astray, not keeping the true goal in sight. Yes, the ornithopters were fantastic and would no doubt make a wonderful part of her street magic repertoire alongside the maze-navigating carts "piloted" by animals. But she was part of a team now, and her job was to find cheap, effective weapons that the emperor could deploy against the Lyucu, weapons that would liberate the people of the two unredeemed islands.

Was Zomi wrong to have trusted her?

Things were so much easier back when the Blossom Gang had no responsibilities, when they were free to pursue their own interests and help whoever they wanted in their own disorganized, ad-hoc manner. True, their work back then was buried in obscurity and she was embarrassed by her *raye* origins, but there were days, like today, when she almost wished she could have her old life back.

Freedom and responsibility, obscurity and respect, aimless creative exploration and the pressure of deadlines and budgets that came with projects that *mattered*—were these always doomed to be incompatible?

She wondered how the young emperor could remain unbowed after a whole life spent under the weight of responsibility, of being aware that everything he said, everything he did, mattered. Had he ever gotten to live as carefree as the Blossom Gang did? Maybe only when he was a small child.

A faint smile appeared on her face as a comforting memory came to her mind unbidden.

She was in the kitchen of the Splendid Urn, watching with satisfaction as her system was being tested for the first time. Mati, the stout sous-chef, stood at one cooking station and gingerly guided the chopping knife held in a mechanical hand. And as she chopped, so did twenty other knives at twenty cooking stations all around the kitchen, mimicking her movements with precision.

"Ah! This feels so weird," complained Mati. "It's like I suddenly grew twenty extra arms."

"In a way, you have," said Savo, laughing. "The Lyucu speak of a god named Kyonaro-naro, the Many-Armed, who baffles his enemies with his many tentacles. And now you're experiencing what it's like to be a god."

"I just want to cook," muttered Mati, moving to guide another mechanical hand to nudge the lotus root into position on the cutting board in front

of her. Around the kitchen, twenty mechanical arms repeated the motion exactly.

"*This is better than having twenty human helpers,*" *observed Rati Yera.* "*If you tried to teach twenty cooks to make your dishes, you'd end up with twenty variations on a theme. But this way, all the food will come out exactly the way you want it to be.*"

"*That's not necessarily a good thing,*" *said Mati.*

"*We'll debate this another time,*" *said Rati.* "*Right now, we just need to beat the Treasure Chest.*"

Rati Yera sat up in her bed, heart pounding. She reached for the bell placed on the nightstand to summon her assistants.

Phyro was far more impressed by the second demonstration from Rati Yera. A hundred ornithopters took off into the air, fluttering, dancing, soaring, spinning . . . their silk wings iridescent in the bright sunlight.

"By tomorrow, I can show you a hundred more," said Rati, beaming.

"All right," said the emperor, gazing at the old engineer with amusement and admiration, "tell me what you've done."

Instead of crafting individual ornithopters by hand, Rati Yera had constructed a novel kind of workshop next to one of the rapid streams that ran down the side of the steep valley in which Tiro Cozo was nestled. Workers had dug a millrace next to the stream, and the flow through the sluice could be regulated by a gate at the head. Inside this channel was a waterwheel whose speed depended on the amount of water flowing through.

The wheel, connected to a series of cams and axles, drove gear trains attached to individual machines that operated saws, chisels, fabric cutters, hammers, and so on. As moving belts, also driven by the waterwheel, carried pieces of bamboo and silk past these machines, the tools cut and shaped the raw material into wings, frame segments, gears, bearings, axles, and other components of the ornithopter. These were collected into bins and put together in final assembly by soldiers sitting at a long table following simple directions—similar to the procedure by which the new airships would be assembled in the field. Since all instances of each component processed by the machines were of the exact same size and shape, the parts were interchangeable, greatly simplifying the process.

"A system is better than mere craft," said Rati Yera. "What can't be done by a hundred master artisans can be accomplished by ten unskilled soldiers with the aid of mechanized precision and standard parts."

Phyro was reminded of Empress Jia's insistence that a bureaucratic system built around standardized rules was better than ad-hoc decisions made on the fly by wise ministers.

"This also solves the problem of repairs and replacements," said Rati. "There will be plenty of spare parts without any need for customization."

Phyro nodded. He wasn't sure if he was more impressed or saddened by the fact that Rati had come to the same conclusion as his aunt-mother, albeit in different domains.

But it was in the crafting of the "brain" of each ornithopter that Rati Yera achieved her greatest triumph.

Initially, Rati had tried to apply the lessons she had learned in Mati's kitchen directly. She built a machine that rotated a hundred cork cylinders at once, placing them under a hundred repurposed embroidery needles. All the needle-drills moved in sync, copying the movements of her hand. It was as if she had sprouted a hundred arms in imitation of the Lyucu god Kyonaro-naro.

But she also needed to compensate for her aging eyes and shaky fingers, as the cork cylinders were no bigger than wine cask plugs. Her solution was inspired by the "copying machine," said to be invented by the ancient Patternist master Na Moji, which used a mechanical linkage between a tracing brush and an inking brush to enlarge an existing picture. Rati reversed the linkage from the copying machine so that large, sweeping movements of her hands, guiding a chisel carving into a large cylinder of wax, would be reduced to minuscule, precise movements of the embroidery needles at the other end, drilling into the plugs of cork.

The idea worked, for the most part, but Rati found the mental exertion of plotting out an entire flight plan one hole at a time beyond

taxing. Compared to the task of instructing a self-driving cart to navigate a maze, one wheel-turn at a time, the work of holding in her
mind a whole flight plan, which involved thousands upon thousands of synchronized wingbeats and angle shifts in three dimensions, pushed her beyond the breaking point. Worst of all, a single
mistake ruined the entire set of half-drilled cork cylinders, forcing
her to start over again.

Flight plans for the ornithopters had to be varied, elaborate, and
complex to be effective against the garinafins. Some would have to
stay in holding patterns to patrol the space near the airships, while
others would have to swerve and zigzag to confuse the beasts. But
it was almost impossible to create these paths when she could only
think in terms of tiny holes punched into cork cylinders.

Her mind was suffocating under the weight of having to consider
each wingbeat, each tilt of the silk vanes, each twist of the bamboo
frame. Just as a general could not command an army by concentrating on every soldier, she could not reason about complex flight
patterns by focusing on every basic movement. Just as the reverse
copying machine linkage translated her broad strokes into precise
gestures at the other end, she needed a way to translate high-level
patterns into constituent, atomic wingbeats.

She began by breaking down the motion of an ornithopter into
the most primitive components: "a weak stroke of the left wing," "a
strong stroke of the right wing," "a normal beat with both wings,"
"shift gyro forward/backward one click," and so on. Though Rati
was illiterate, she, like almost everyone in Dara, had some knowledge of basic and folk logograms. Thus, she devised a system of mnemonic pseudo-logograms for recording these fundamental primi-
tives, including wax symbols for numbers, directions, and degrees.

By combining these basic logograms into bigger compounds, Rati
could use wax to write out a series of instructions, akin to the rope-
maps for the self-driving carts, that anyone could read once they
learned her system of pseudo-logograms:

Fly forward for ten strong strokes;
Turn left by one-tenth of a circle;
Fly forward for one hundred normal strokes;

Turn right by three-tenths of a circle;

Fly forward for fifty strokes while inclining the ornithopter upward at an angle of one-tenth of a circle;

And so on.

Rati Yera devised yet another refinement to this system. Once these high-level instructions were reified on the page as wax logograms, she realized that they themselves could be manipulated by yet higher-level instructions. That is, by inventing more pseudo-logograms that encoded meta-directives that targeted the instructions themselves, she could now write (and think) in more abstract terms:

Repeat the following three lines of instructions five times;

Keep repeating the following block of instructions until the ornithopter is flying straight up;

Repeat the following block of instructions six times, but make the stroke stronger each time by one-tenth of a full swing of the escapement arc;

And so on.

The system of pseudo-logograms allowed her to reason and describe the planned flight path for ornithopters in terms closer to the way she saw the world, rather than forcing her mind to work at the level of primitive wing strokes. The system was like her wheeled chair, a tool that gave her freedom.

Once she had drafted various flight plans on long scrolls of silk, there remained the problem of how to render them as patterns of holes. For this, Rati returned to her cork-encoder.

With the silk scroll next to her, Rati translated each line of high-level pseudo-logogram instruction into the corresponding pattern of holes and chiseled them into a large master wax cylinder about as tall as herself, seated. The process was not entirely mechanical, as she would sometimes have to correct logical errors in the program of instructions or devise optimizations at the level of wingbeats that were not obvious in the high-level code. Rati rather enjoyed this part, as chiseling into a large column of wax was far more pleasant and physically satisfying than fiddling with tiny needles. Moreover, as holes in the wax column could be refilled, she could correct errors, resulting in much less stress.

Once the master cylinder was made, Rati could set the encoder to copy it into a hundred cork cylinders at a time. She added a "reader" to the encoder, which was basically a long probe that pressed into each successive hole in the wax cylinder as she spun it in place. The reader actuated the linkage mechanism to the encoder, and a hundred needle-drills repeated the same motion of the probe at a smaller scale, drilling holes of corresponding depths into the sides of a hundred cork cylinders.

What once would have taken Rati Yera weeks of labor could now be accomplished in less time than it took to boil a pot of water for tea. The vision of building thousands upon thousands of ornithopters to harass garinafins no longer seemed impossible.

Thinking back fondly on her time with Savo, Fara, Mati, Lodan, and the rest of the Blossom Gang at the Splendid Urn, Rati said, "I guess all my aimless wandering around Dara as a street magician has been good for something after all. *Rénga*, I could not have taught the ornithopters without having had my soul enlarged and my mind instructed by idle play in the company of my friends."

Phyro laughed. "I never doubted that for a second. Dara's best inventions have not come from the rarefied air of Imperial laboratories, but busy street corners and grease-stained workshop floors. My mother was a street magician, just like you, and I always knew you would find me real magic. Come, we must now plan."

He pushed Rati's wheeled chair ahead of him to give her arms some much needed respite, and Rati's heart soared as high as the demonstration ornithopters, still dancing far above the swaying trees.

CHAPTER TWENTY-FOUR

THE BATTLE OF CRESCENT ISLAND, PART II

CRESCENT ISLAND: THE SEVENTH MONTH OF THE
ELEVENTH YEAR OF THE REIGN OF SEASON OF
STORMS AND THE REIGN OF AUDACIOUS FREEDOM.

Tens of thousands of ornithopters emerged from the thick, steamy fog surrounding the airships and swarmed toward the garinafins. As though guided by the hand of Kiji, god of birds, they soared, dove, swerved, spun, looped, separated into clouds of buzzing and whir-ring wings, and soon enveloped the stunned garinafins.

In place of beaks, many of the fastest ornithopters had menac-ing blades that scissored or spun. Though the miniature weapons couldn't penetrate thick garinafin hide, they did pose a threat to the riders, who wore no armor in order to preserve their agility. They paid for this decision now as the deadly mechanical birds pecked and sliced at their faces, hands, chests, arms. . . . Some of the flock-ing ornithopters also severed the webbing securing the riders, and numerous naros tumbled into the merciless ocean below.

Other ornithopters, slower and more ponderous, were packed with firework powder as well as a small Ogé jar as spark-fuse. Swerving from side to side like drunken bats, these autonomous bombs crashed into the garinafins and exploded on contact, maim-ing riders and starting fires along the webbing.

Still other ornithopters spewed a viscous and oily liquid that siz-zled against the hides of the garinafins and burned right through the skin of any rider unfortunate enough to be sprayed.

The air was filled with yelps and howls, from beast and human alike.

In truth, the direct damage caused by the swarming ornithopters was minimal. The mechanical birds were flapping about blindly with no coordination, striking targets more by chance than design. But the same principle by which a burly man would jump about and swat the air in terror when approached by a few buzzing wasps and by which a herd of elephants on Écofi would stampede at the sight of a nest of mice was at work: The garinafins and their riders panicked.

The flying behemoths swatted at the swarming ornithopters with their claws and long tails, and the riders batted at the nettlesome artificial creatures with their war clubs and axes. But the nimble ornithopters darted about in unpredictable ways, and most of the strikes missed. And when the Lyucu did succeed in hitting the zig-zagging ornithopters, it only made the situation worse, for often the destruction of the ornithopter resulted in a firework-powder explosion or a spray of burning acid.

Fortunately, the explosions were so small and the acid so weak that they caused no serious injury to the riders, and the garinafins, already protected by their thick hides, were further insulated from the ineffective ammunition by armor.

However, by chance one of the firework ornithopters crashed against the head of a garinafin and exploded, blinding its left eye. As the injured beast flailed about in the air, screaming, it clawed at its pain-racked face. The effort did nothing to assuage the pain, but it did suc-ceed in grabbing a Lyucu rider who was climbing up its neck to tend to the wound. The unfortunate rider died almost instantly as her spine snapped, and the lifeless body dangled from the garinafin's clawed foot as the creature whipped its serpentine neck about, menacing the other riders. Its strict training forgotten, the garinafin snapped its jaws and began to breathe fire, aiming it at the swarming ornithopters, the screaming riders scurrying over its back, and nearby garinafins.

The pain-crazed war mount now posed more of a threat to the Lyucu than the swarming ornithopters. Reluctantly, the pilots of sev-eral nearby garinafins congregated on the wounded animal to put it out of its misery before it could wreak more havoc.

As more ornithopters crashed against the vulnerable eyes, ears, and noses of garinafins, the frenzy grew. Although Goztan, observing from her flagship at a distance, repeatedly gave the order to retreat, few of the pilots noticed the signals—even if they did, it was doubtful they could have gotten their panicked mounts to obey.

Amid the general chaos, one of the Lyucu pilots, a clever young man named Rufira Tan, had the presence of mind to notice something: The swirling cloud of steamy fog and thickening smoke around the airships was finally dissipating, and although dense flocks of ornithopters swarmed around the garinafins, the space immediately next to the airships was relatively clear.

This was a consequence of the ornithopter's limits. Although they could follow complicated paths described by their internal instructions, they were, after all, not alive and not endowed with true intelligence. To prevent the swarming ornithopters from striking the airships by mistake, Rati had designed all the flight plans to take them a safe distance away from the airships before commencing the zigzagging attack patterns. Thus, the area right next to the airships became an ornithopter-free zone.

Rufira Tan communicated his discovery to his crewmates. With the shock of the unfamiliar fading, most of the crew had by now realized that the ornithopters were not nearly as dangerous as their own overreaction to the machines. Rufira scampered up the neck of his garinafin and gently massaged its massive eyelids, trying to persuade it to close its eyes.

Silently, Rufira thanked the gods that he had been assigned to this particular garinafin, which had once been the personal mount of a disgraced accommodationist thane. As such, it had been raised with a gentle hand and bonded with the intended pilot, before it was thrown into the general military pool when the thane was executed. Though ordinary garinafins would never close their eyes when surrounded by such a terrifying swarm, *this* garinafin's experience as a juvenile made it far more trusting of humans. Rufira hoped that it was enough for the beast to do as he asked.

Reluctantly, the garinafin obeyed. Rufira almost whooped with delight. Deprived of the sight of the ornithopter swarm, it calmed down almost instantly. As the rest of the crew pressed their bodies flat against their mount to minimize their profiles, Rufira shouted directions into the garinafin's ear, coaxing it to fly through the thick swarm and aim for the airships. Ignoring the stings from numerous circling mechanical birds, armored garinafin and crew eventually emerged into the clear space next to the airships.

Rufira Tan told the garinafin to open its eyes, and the beast bellowed in triumph. Other garinafins, encouraged by this demonstration, imitated the maneuver. One by one, the armored garinafins squeezed their eyes shut and plowed through the ornithopter cloud, intent on exacting vengeance against the airships on the other side.

"Hold it," Mota Kiphi, captain of *Spirit of Kiji*, muttered to his crew. "Let them get right up against us."

It was hard for him not to recall that nightmarish day a decade ago, when he was aboard another ship with the same name. Back then, Captain Atamu had given her crew the same command, though the nature of the surprise he now had in store was so different.

A garinafin pulled up right in front of the gondola, its sail-like wings blotting out the sun. Patches of viscous acid could be seen over its head, neck, and shoulders, the result of having smashed through so many acid-carrying ornithopters in the swarm. However, since the acid wasn't strong enough to eat through the armor and hide, it served only to enrage the creature, not disable it.

Mota stared into the eyes of the Lyucu pilot, whose wolfish grin showed that he was about to give the order for the garinafin to spew fire.

"Give 'em hell!" shouted Mota.

Rufira surveyed the clumsy airship's boxy gondola with confidence. It was by no means an accident that he had called for the other pilots to gather their mounts here. Earlier, he had observed the defenses of the airship with care and noticed that the gondola was the most heavily defended part of the ship, thus the likely locus of the bridge and the senior officers.

The Imperial airship in front of him was like an imposing floating island. But no arrows poked through the slits next to the hoses, and no clacking flocks of ornithopters emerged for a last, desperate gambit. The barbarians had run out of tricks.

He raised his arm, and all the garinafins aimed their heads in the same direction. As soon as he swept his arm down, five tongues of fire would lance into *Spirit of Kiji*, turning the airship into a true second sun, a ball of fire.

As he had anticipated, the water hoses began to spray. Rufira paid them no mind, convinced that the concentrated garinafin fire would overwhelm them.

Streams splashed onto the garinafins. The globs of thick, oily acid that had stuck to the hide and armor earlier began to hiss and sizzle, bubble and explode. The acrid smell of burning flesh filled the air, and smoke rose in thick plumes. It was as if the garinafins were covered by miniature erupting volcanoes.

The garinafins howled and buckled in midair, the command to attack forgotten. The acid explosions were eating through their skin. Their armor was of no use as the bubbling mixture dripped between the seams.

Twisting, screaming, lashing, flailing, whipping, flapping, the garinafins clawed at one another and lashed out with fire tongues, as though their agony could only be assuaged with more cauterizing pain. Scores of Lyucu warriors, in order not to be roasted alive, leapt away from their mounts and fell to their deaths.

Miraculously, Rufira managed to get his mount under control and pulled away from the pandemonium of tearing limbs and fiery jaws. The pilots of garinafins in the back of the attack group managed to pull away as well, but it seemed certain that the garinafin force would suffer an unprecedented carnage today.

Aboard *Spirit of Kiji*, the crew cheered.

Empress Jia, had she been present, would have probably grinned from recognition. The airship's success in thwarting the garinafins relied on an old herbalist trick in which two components, each relatively harmless in isolation, could be combined for deadly effect.

Oil of vitriol, used for decades in Dara as a solvent for stripping paint and to clean off rust from metal, had a tendency to react explosively with water. In workshops, the careless addition of water to tubs of oil of vitriol often maimed and even killed.

Zomi and Rati had taken advantage of this property to design a two-step counter to the tough skin of garinafins. The initial, ineffective attack with oil of vitriol alone served to convince the garinafins and their riders that the acid was harmless, encouraging them to push through the swarm and approach the airships. Only then would the water bath unleash the acid's full, deadly potential.

Goztan made her decision. Garinafins and warriors were being lost, and the tide of battle was turning against her. She had to do what she could to stave off defeat, no matter the political costs.

She turned to her personal guards and said, "Launch the special reserves."

Noda Mi kept up his obsequious patter as the guards passed on her order to the other ships, and soon, the last of the garinafins took off from the decks of the city-ships. When he squinted and saw the crew on these new garinafins clearly, however, the unceasing stream of nonsensical praise died in his throat.

The reserve garinafins were armored just like the others—but with one crucial difference: Instead of slingshots, spears, and axes, many of the riders shouldered longbows and quivers of arrows. Each of them also held aloft a torch, their grim faces peering out from beneath metal helmets.

These riders were natives of Ukyu-taasa, not Lyucu.

The Lyucu warriors congregated on the decks of the city-ships were completely silent, as astonished as Noda Mi. Never in the history of Ukyu-taasa had any native auxiliaries ridden into battle on the back of a garinafin.

"Now we'll see if your greatest contribution to the Lyucu cause is going to work, Loyal Hound," Goztan said quietly to the stunned native official standing by her side.

Just as Phyro had to prepare for war with the Lyucu against the inertia of Dara's prosperous indolence, Goztan had to arrange for the defense of Ukyu-taasa while holding the fanaticism of Lyucu hard-liners at bay.

The dominance of hard-liners in Ukyu-taasa couldn't be entirely explained by accommodationist missteps or Tanvanaki's ambivalence; indeed, Cutanrovo was able to create and then lead such a powerful movement because she tapped into the deepest grievances and fears of ordinary Lyucu naros and culeks, rooted in an existential terror that the Lyucu could not survive in Dara without ceasing to be Lyucu.

Cutanrovo's exhortations that the Lyucu could and should triumph over the natives by becoming more Lyucu assuaged these fears, much as the tolyusa offered comfort to dispirited warriors who felt abandoned by the gods. It was a powerful vision that none, not even the great Tanvanaki, dared to openly defy.

Goztan knew that in order to lead her army to victory, she could not ignore the feelings of the rank and file. She had acquiesced to the use of slave labor and the forceful conscription of native auxiliaries via threats against their families largely out of necessity—there was simply no other way to marshal the resources needed to defend Ukyu-taasa—but she also understood that such measures were good for morale by reinforcing feelings of racial superiority among her warriors. She was not above exploiting the darkness that lurked in every heart to motivate her fighters. In war, one had to make compromises in order to achieve victory.

Any tactical decision deviating from Cutanrovo's narrative of absolute Lyucu supremacy would therefore incur a heavy cost in morale, a trade-off that Goztan had to weigh carefully against military advantages. Cladding war garinafins in native-style metal armor was already risky, since it implied acceptance of the superiority of native knowledge, but Goztan and Tanvanaki both felt it an essential adaptation against Dara weaponry. They believed that when the time came, they could justify it against Cutanrovo's certain opposition, much as they justified the use of airships in sentry duty to assist the garinafins, because it represented merely an augmentation of traditional Lyucu customs.

But putting native auxiliaries, seen by most Lyucu warriors as little better than beasts of burden, on the backs of the pride of the

Lyucu military went far beyond these concessions. The symbolism of the act would be missed by no one.

That the Lyucu fleet had survived the Battle of Zathin Gulf only because of Noda Mi's surprise backstabbing attack on Gin Mazoti's airships was a source of great shame among the Lyucu. Because it went counter to Cutanrovo's narrative of Lyucu invincibility, hard-liners tended to minimize the role played by Noda Mi's soldiers and preferred to emphasize the courage of the garinafin fighters earlier during the battle.

Nonetheless, Tanvanaki and Goztan both realized that adopting native fire arrows was critical to overcoming the airships. At first, they had wanted to train Lyucu warriors in the art of archery, but Cutanrovo's fervor in cleansing the Lyucu of all native influence closed off that path. Goztan dared not even propose the idea lest she be accused of betraying the vaunted Lyucu spirit. And Tanvanaki believed that forcing her warriors to adopt a method of fighting seen by Cutanrovo as a submission to native culture would shake the foundation of her rule.

Thus, the pékyu and the garinafin-thane had no choice but to turn to recruiting native archers willing to be trained in secret in the art of garinafin riding. Despite the general conscripted status of native auxiliaries, there were a few native commanders that Goztan and Tanvanaki trusted. Some of them were former Imperial officers who had surrendered early during the war and knew their lot was bound up with the fate of the conquerors; others were ambitious individuals who sought to profit from the political division between the accommodationists and hard-liners; still others were former pirates who enjoyed the idea of carrying on their days of pillaging and robbery with the protection of a like-minded sovereign.

Whatever their motivations, these native fighters were willing to gamble their lives in the service of the Lyucu. Goztan then turned to her most trusted pilots, veterans who were sympathetic to the accommodationist cause, and explained the importance of a fire-arrow unit to the Lyucu. Reluctantly, they agreed to the scheme. Once Tanvanaki secured for the unit a deserted training ground near Phada, the pilots and would-be riders went to work in earnest.

By participating, both groups were taking substantial risks. The native archers knew that if they were discovered by Cutanrovo, Tanvanaki and Goztan would have no choice but to disavow them and abandon them to the purification packs. As for the pilots, they would be branded traitors or worse. Nonetheless, the pilots continued to teach and the archers continued to train, the former out of a sense of duty to give Ukyu-taasa the best chance at surviving an invasion, and the latter hoping to be treated as heroes if they did turn out to be the key to the salvation of Ukyu-taasa against their own people.

Goztan had been hoping that she would be able to defeat Phyro's airships without the use of garinafin-riding native archers, but events had left her little choice. It was a political gamble. Even if the native archers succeeded, the Lyucu would likely suffer a spiritual defeat since they had been forced to resort to native weapons and tactics, and Cutanrovo would surely seize the opportunity to topple Goztan once and for all.

But she had to save Ukyu-taasa. She had to.

She prayed to Diasa again.

The new armor-clad garinafins soared higher and higher, beyond the reach of ornithopter swarms, beyond the fiery tongues and flailing limbs of the pain-panicked pack. From their precipitous vantage point, they surveyed the billowing masses of the Imperial airships and the dying garinafins like the gods looking down upon the Islands of Dara.

Streaks of fire, arrows lit with torches, fell from them like a sublunary meteor shower. It was a beautiful sight. Deadly, but also wondrous.

Than Carucono, commander-in-chief of the airship fleet, gazed up at the approaching fiery missiles from the observation bubble atop *Sword Chrysanthemum*, the flagship.

"Admiral!" begged one of his personal guards, "please descend into the gondola for safety."

"Admiral!" asked another guard in a shaky voice, "should we initiate evasive maneuvers?"

Than said nothing. How could an egg be safe when the whole

nest was on fire? How could a lumbering, ponderous jellyfish escape the darting stings of a school of Tazu's needles?

Ignoring the pleas of his subordinates, he remained where he was. Tears welled in the eyes of the old man, not tears of terror or sorrow, but rage and regret.

Through blurry eyes, he seemed to see the figure of a bald woman, a woman he had admired and loved since that day long ago when she had sat down across from him at a table, explaining to him and Mün Çakri her vision for building Dasu's puny army into a force that would challenge the might of the Hegemon.

"Marshal," the old warrior croaked.

"It's good to see you again, Than," said Gin Mazoti.

The arcing fiery bolts were closer now, like falling stars, like the sparks of the bonfires Kuni used to light in Dasu to feast his followers and companions, like the hope that young Phyro had stoked to life in his heart.

His guards tried to drag him below, but he refused to budge, like an aged oak rooted to his spot.

"I'm sorry, Marshal," he said.

"For what?" asked Gin.

"For the loss of so many lives . . . for not anticipating this . . . for not being as good an adviser to Phyro as you and Luan had been to Kuni—" He choked and could not continue. This had always been his secret fear. He was never as brilliant a strategist as Luan Zyaji, never as brave a warrior as Mün Çakri, never as resourceful an administrator as Cogo Yelu, never as adaptable as Puma Yemu, never as skilled a field tactician as Gin Mazoti. In all the years he had fought under the banner of the House of Dandelion, he often wondered if he deserved to be included among his companions. Did Kuni only keep him around out of pity, out of a sense of obligation because he was an old friend?

Fire bolts thwacked into the hull of the airship around him, starting conflagrations that spread quickly over the varnished silk hull. Below, he heard barked commands and the noises of aviators scrambling to rescue the doomed ship. All around, he could see other airships straining to get away from the rain of fire arrows.

"You were the lone voice that supported Phyro on the Inner Council," said Gin. "You kept the memory of Kuni's generation alive in the hearts of the young. You devoted your life to the people of Dara, serving them the best you knew how. If that isn't *mutagé*, then the word has no meaning."

"But it isn't enough!" cried Than. "To die this way . . . not to see Phyro free Unredeemed Dara and take his rightful place on the Veiled Throne . . . how can I face you, face Mün, face Luan and Rin and the emperor himself in the land beyond the River-on-Which-Nothing-Floats?"

"There's no shame in an honorable defeat," said Gin. "Even I, elevated as I've been in legend and song, lost plenty of battles and soldiers during my life. No general is invincible, so long as they are mortal. It isn't the outcome that matters, but the cause. You may hold your head high, knowing that you fought to free others."

Teams of women, some of them mere teenagers, emerged from the hull of *Sword Chrysanthemum*, dragging water hoses and pumping tanks. Though terror was written plain on their faces, there was no panic as they worked efficiently, fighting to get the spreading fire under control. Since the days of their origin in distant Dasu, the aviators of the Dandelion Throne had always been mostly women.

Than Carucono wept inconsolably. Tears flowed freely down his cheeks, filling the deep lines on his face like spring floods following gullies in the Gonlogi Desert. These young aviators would never be mothers and grandmothers, cherished repositories of stories about their time, beacons of wisdom for future generations. And it was his fault. His.

"Don't condescend to them, Than. They knew the risks when they joined Phyro. Yes, it was your job to command and their duty to obey, and you're responsible for their deaths. But they pledged their lives to the vision of a liberated Dara of their own free will, and you will honor them not with pity or self-recrimination, but by joining them, never yielding no matter how long the odds."

A hot tide rose from Than Carucono's belly, gradually suffusing his limbs. He hadn't felt like that in years, as though the decline that came with age was but an illusion. He climbed out of the observation bubble and strode toward one of the fire suppression teams.

More fire bolts struck the hull in front of, behind, all around him. The silk hull buckled and swayed from wind and fire. He fell down to his hands and knees and crawled, finding a way over the disintegrating hull. Despite the unceasing firefighting efforts of the aviators, large parts of the hull had burned away, leaving widening holes that revealed the bamboo skeleton and organ-like bags of lift gas. The ship was doomed, but the knowledge only made him more determined to do his job. He crawled even faster.

He reached the fire suppression team. "Let me help—" he said to the hundred-chief in charge, but before he could finish, the air around him suddenly brightened.

Almost instinctively, he leapt toward her, covering her with his body. A fire bolt thunked into his back, and he felt his body go limp, all strength seeping out.

The world was fading away. He didn't smell the odor of burning flesh, didn't hear the cries of *Admiral! Admiral!* from the aviators, didn't feel the pain that seared his nerves and made his limbs flop helplessly. He wanted to shout, *Don't give up!* but his body no longer obeyed his will.

Dimly, he saw a few fire arrows plunge right through one of the yawning gaps in the hull and strike the lift-gas bags.

With the last of his dissipating consciousness, he heard Gin.

"You've done your part. Trust the others to do theirs."

The fire arrows disappeared inside the gasbags. For the briefest of moments, the interior of *Sword Chrysanthemum* glowed like a lava-filled crater.

Everything was consumed by light.

Like Cutanrovo, Phyro never expected the Lyucu to fight like the people of Dara.

Everything he had learned from the refugees, defectors, farseers, and historical records told him that the Lyucu disdained Dara learning, that they viewed native military traditions with contempt, that they were too proud to adopt wholesale the arts and crafts of a conquered people.

To be sure, the Lyucu weren't above using tools seized from their enemies to further their own goals. Pékyu Tenryo, after all, had come to Dara on city-ships seized from Admiral Krita, and Tanvanaki had been quick to repurpose captured Dara airships for sentry and support duty. But these were superficial changes, like a Lyucu thane putting on native dress for play or equipping garinafins with metal armor instead of bone plates—there was no fundamental interest in learning to think like their enemies.

His own experiences with the Lyucu only confirmed the reports. For instance, Ukyu-taasa's rumored plot to kidnap Dara engineers, which would have been evidence of Lyucu interest in learning from the natives, had turned out to be a mere mirage. The only prosecution of a supposed Lyucu collaborator, a wealthy merchant from Wolf's Paw, had ended in a verdict of not guilty due to lack of evidence. Truth be told, Phyro suspected that the rumors were spread by Empress Jia herself so that she could claim false credit for stopping a manufactured Lyucu plot, when she in fact had no intention to do anything about the true Lyucu threat.

Puma Yemu's engagement with the Lyucu had only reinforced Phyro's opinion. Throughout that naval battle, the Lyucu commander had treated her own airships and conscripted native soldiers only as disposable scouts, and never once did the airships use archers against the battle kites. Moreover, the Lyucu had held back their garinafins so long as Puma continued to retreat, suggesting that they saw the flying beasts, with their limited range, as heavy-strike weapons to be used to deal the decisive blow against a cornered enemy. Everything indicated adherence to traditional Lyucu battlefield thinking, not new tactics.

Ofluro had lectured Phyro at length on the importance of garinafins to the Lyucu way of life, and the young emperor had come to appreciate the almost sacred place garinafins held in the Lyucu imagination. Techniques for fighting with garinafins, honed over many generations, were not to be altered lightly, and Phyro had seen the proof with his own eyes at Crescent Island. The addition of armor and anti-caltrop muzzles were cosmetic changes intended to allow the garinafins to be used *as they always had been*. There was no fundamental shift in thinking, no attempt to complement them with different support units, no addition of equipment that would lead to revolutionary capabilities.

All this was to say, Phyro expected that the Lyucu would fight as they always had, but not that they would literally refight the last war, using the weapons of their enemies.

He screamed with anguish as the air above the inlet lit up with the light of a dozen suns.

"Ready the riders!" he shouted at the stunned signaling corps behind him. "We must launch immediately!"

Onboard *Spirit of Kiji*, senior aviators gave Mota the unwelcome news.

"We've used up the last of the water," one of them said.

"I've pulled all the fire suppression teams back inside to shield the lift-gas bags," said another. "But it's only a matter of time until one of the fire arrows gets through."

This was not how Phyro's plan was supposed to work, but Mota adjusted.

"Launch all remaining ornithopters," he ordered. "Use attack pattern 'Garinafin's Den'!"

The crew scrambled to find the cork cylinders with the designated flight plan and inserted as many of them as possible into the remaining ornithopters.

Several airships had already been engulfed by flames. Maimed and dead aviators tumbled out of the slow-falling wreckage, much as Lyucu riders had fallen from their dying garinafins earlier. The remaining airships, some of them partially shielded by the unlucky sister ships, desperately tried to row out of the way.

Flocks of ornithopters emerged from the surviving airships. Unlike the ornithopters from earlier, these didn't swarm in holding patterns nearby, but scattered and headed for the city-ships in the distance.

An explosion rocked *Spirit of Kiji*, throwing Mota to the deck. Regretfully, he gave the order, "Abandon ship!"

Goztan watched the horror unfolding in the air above the inlet silently.

Like graceful jellyfish glowing with an inner light, the wrecks of the Imperial airships slowly fell toward the sea. From time to time, explosions erupted from what was left of their skins, like a brief flare of some defiant life force.

The sun was already westering; the aerial battle had lasted most of the day.

The celebration among the Lyucu on the city-ships was muted. They had won, but at what cost? Garinafins were being ridden by slaves, and the hated Dara-raaki had been defeated only when the Lyucu deployed native archers. It was one thing to send out some slaves on their toylike, fragile airships—these benighted people had, after all, been denied the gift of the magnificent garinafins by their gods—but quite something else to send aloft slave archers on garinafins to deal death like cowards from afar, like those hated Dara-raaki who had come to Ukyu with Admiral Krita.

The shame of Zathin Gulf had not been erased, only deepened.

Dark mutterings could be heard among the naros and culeks.

"It's unnatural to fight with garinafins from such a distance. Where's the risk? Where's the honor? Where's the glory?"

"The gods will punish us for trying to act like the Dara-raaki."

"Not just 'act like'—those archers *are* Dara-raaki."

"If Thane Cutanrovo were in charge of the defenses, this would *never* have happened."

"Why does the pékyu still listen to the fools who have forgotten how to be Lyucu? Is she so enamored of that weakling concubine of hers?"

. . .

Goztan pretended not to hear. She would willingly suffer the political fallout back in Kriphi, so long as Ukyu-taasa was safe, so long as her people were safe.

To vent their frustration and self-loathing, the Lyucu warriors turned to mocking and ridiculing the dying Dara aviators.

Aviators leapt from their doomed ships, some on fire themselves. A few lucky souls had time to strap on rescue kits, and silk balloons, much like those that had once enabled Mata Zyndu's aerial assault on Zudi, sprouted from their backs to slow their descent toward the sea or the jungle on each side of the inlet. On the water below, Puma Yemu's sailors leaned into their oars, rushing to save as many of the fallen aviators as they could.

"Look at that muddy monkey flailing her arms!"

"I bet her sponge would taste pretty good, after a good roasting like that."

"Listen to those screams! I've slaughtered ewes who showed more courage."

As if trying to salvage the cool reception the native-archers-led victory was earning among their comrades, pilots who had earlier pulled away from the maelstrom of oil-of-vitriol-crazed garinafins urged their mounts to move in for the kill. By now, most of the ornithopters had run out of energy and sunk harmlessly into the sea, and archers on the high-altitude garinafins had run out of bolts, leaving the air around the sinking Imperial airships clear.

Rufira Tan and the other pilots guided their garinafins to roast the ballooning aviators or to shred them in midair. It was more sport than fight, as the women tried to ward off the giant beasts with daggers and short swords to little effect. With the death of each aviator, the Lyucu on the city-ships cheered louder. *This* was how garinafin warfare was supposed to be conducted; *this* was an affirmation of the Lyucu spirit.

Meanwhile, unnoticed by the blood-crazed Lyucu, the last ornithopters released by the Imperial airships prior to their demise reached their target. Traveling in ones or twos, the mechanical birds plunged into the rigging and sails and instantly exploded, spewing fire and burning oil everywhere.

Lyucu warriors and native slaves scrambled to put out the fires, and some of the garinafin crews, seeing the smoke from their home bases, returned to help. But the giant beasts did more harm than good, as they could do little to stop the tiny ornithopters darting about erratically, while their flapping wings fanned the flames and their bulk got in the way of firefighting sailors.

By the time the last of the fires were put out and all the ornithopters destroyed, the garinafins and their crews were near exhaustion. The heavy armor, combined with the multiple mad rushes and constant hovering to deal with the ornithopters, had cost the beasts most of their strength and lift gas. Despite the victory over the Dara airships, morale was low. Of the fifty-plus garinafins the expedition had brought, only thirty-six survived.

They were very much ready for a rest, and Goztan ordered them to land. With his airships destroyed and naval fleet dismasted, Phyro wasn't going anywhere.

"We'll crush the Dara-raaki in the morning," declared Noda Mi. "Our garinafin-thane is most merciful, most wise, most compassionate to allow these cowards another night of life—"

Goztan didn't need to tell Noda Mi to shut up; the tiresome man had stopped speaking of his own accord.

Everyone turned to stare at the dense trees and vines atop the cliffs.

Out of the lush vegetation came a new noise, a noise none of them ever expected to hear from any army of Dara: the long, low moan of a garinafin bone trumpet.

Giant winged beasts were rising from the jungle.

CRESCENT ISLAND: MONTHS EARLIER.

It was twilight, the hour when sight was the sense least to be trusted, when magic was most believable in the ambiguous border between day and night, between sky and sea.

Like a painting in the dream-style of Umbrist brush painters, winged shadows rose from shimmering living reefs. The shadows, each as grand as a merchantman's mainsail, blotted out entire constellations painted on the starry vault. The reefs left behind bobbed a bit higher in the water before spewing forth misty spouts that turned into dozens of moonbows.

It took some coaxing for the last few garinafins, more timid than their mates, to relax their clenched claws, sunk deep into the seams between the scales on the backs of their cruben hosts. They were exhausted, having flown from Tiro Cozo to the Karo Peninsula over several nights, only to then climb onto crubens for the multiday sea journey. The ordeal of their most unusual voyage was not something they'd forget soon. But at length, the pilots persuaded them to spread their wings and head for the cliffs on each side of the inlet.

Adüan-style canoes, filled with Phyro's soldiers and Adüan stevedores, began to paddle out to the resting crubens in the middle of the inlet to unload the other cargo carried by this living fleet.

"What a ride!" exclaimed Phyro, standing at the lip of the cliff and wringing out his sea-drenched hair. The water sparkled in starlight as it cascaded to the surf far below.

He had ridden here on the back of a cruben, his arms around his beloved, his face washed in salty mist, his eyes filled with the lone horn of the sovereign of the seas defiantly pointing out a path through the waves.

Zen-Kara laughed at his expression of pure joy. "It's my first time also. But to be honest, I think riding a cruben isn't nearly as fun as surfing."

"You'll have to teach me."

"Will you ever have the time to learn?"

"After the Lyucu are defeated, I'll come to Tan Adü with a treasure fleet of gifts and ask your parents for your hand. Then we'll have all the time in the world to surf and cruise around the Islands on crubens. Will you say yes?"

The image made her smile. "I doubt we'll ever get a chance to ride a cruben again. The scaled whales don't obey summonses. They interfere in the affairs of humankind only when they wish." Deliberately, she left his proposal unanswered.

"They certainly responded to the future Empress of Dara," said Phyro. "There's a special bond between the crubens and the House of Dandelion, you know? The crubens agree with me: Please, be a part of my family."

Zen-Kara wasn't sure she wanted to be part of the House of Dandelion. The palace intrigues, the factions at court, the constant plots and counterplots—what Phyro had told her of life at court didn't sound attractive at all. And she imagined the looks of contempt that courtiers would surely give an Adüan woman. . . .

As if reading her thoughts, Phyro pulled her into an embrace. "You and I will reform Pan to cast out the old and bring in the new.

My father had the counsel and aid of my mother during his rise, but I never had a companion to sing a duet of the heart with until I met you. With your help, I've now ridden on the back of a cruben, the same as my father. Is there any doubt that we'll accomplish even more than my parents did?"

She kissed him, still uncertain of the future he painted so confidently. But she didn't want to let doubt mar this moment of intimacy.

Gently, he let go and grabbed her by the shoulders to direct her attention to the middle of the inlet. "I've composed a logogram riddle for you. . . . Look over there. Do you dare to venture a guess?"

Zen-Kara noted the mischievous glint in his eyes. She looked where he was pointing. The last garinafin, more timid than the others, had just taken off from its cruben. Its wings still stiff from the long ride, it barely struggled to the top of the cliff before plunging, almost collapsing, into the dense jungle. Cries of surprised monkeys, perhaps awakened from their slumber, filled the air. Down below, the cruben, relieved of its burden, sneezed a languid spray into the air before diving under.

The answer came to her mind almost immediately. The Classical Ano logogram for "beauty" was a compound made from two sub-logograms: "feather" above, and "fish" below. The etymology was somewhat obscure, but most scholars believed that it was derived from the ancient Ano practice of wearing feather head-dresses and fish-scale jewelry to enhance their appearance.

But such pedestrian explanations from philologists could hardly satisfy the people's yearning for romance. And so a folk etymology had sprung up. It was best exemplified by a surviving fragment of Suzaré, praising her lover, Jito of White Sleeves:

> *wild geese fall*
> *stunned*
> *by your grace*
>
> *golden carp dive*
> *dazed*
> *in your glow*

No matter how many times he told her she was beautiful, she loved to hear it. Blushing, she chided, mock-serious, "A garinafin may fly, but it has no feathers and is no bird. A cruben may swim, but it is no fish. You may know a few logograms, Emperor of Dara, but it's clear you need to spend more time studying biology."

Phyro shook his head like a rattle drum. "You have not guessed the correct answer to the riddle. The word I'm thinking of is definitely not 'beautiful.'"

Zen-Kara's face felt as hot as a roasted taro. She glared at him. "What?"

Unfazed, Phyro alternately nodded and shook his head like a Moralist tutor expounding upon some fine point of philosophy. "Jito of White Sleeves was deemed beautiful because wild geese fell from the sky when they saw her, forgetting how to fly, and ornamental fish dove away in her presence, ashamed to compare themselves to her aura. That is obviously not what you do—"

"Still talking? Are you really—"

"You, the mirror of my soul, managed to stun a *garinafin* out of the sky and shamed away a *cruben*. How can a common word like 'beautiful' be sufficient for a deed like that? No. I will not allow it. A more appropriate word would be 'beautilicious' or 'alluretravagant' or maybe 'megapulchritudinous,' none of which can be written in Classical Ano logograms. So, I was inventing a new script— *Ouch!*"

She jabbed at him a few more times playfully before she kissed him.

Long garinafin necks craned in the jungle at their giggles.

"Over there, that's where Zomi thinks the Lyucu discovered a source of tolyusa," shouted Phyro over the rushing wind, pointing at a vein of solidified lava atop a bluff, like a scar etched into the dense jungle. He guided Ginki, his young garinafin, to dive and sweep low over the area.

Behind him, Zen-Kara instinctively tightened her arms around his waist. Fighting against the terrifying sinking sensation that made her heart jump into her throat, she kept her eyes open, drinking in the vertiginous wonder of flight. As a student in Dara, she had ridden once on an airship when Master Tathu hired one to take all the girls on a harbor cruise over Zathin Gulf in spring, but the freedom and thrill of riding a garinafin exceeded that a thousandfold.

"Hold on tight," he shouted. "I'm going to show you something fun."

Placing the point of the bone trumpet against the base of Ginki's neck, he spoke some commands into it. The young garinafin flapped her wings, climbed sharply until she was flying straight up, but continued to arch her back so that she began to tilt backward.

"O gods!" Zen-Kara screamed. She wrapped her arms even tighter around Phyro's waist and buried her face against his back.

A force seemed to press her body against the saddle as the garinafin continued to flap her wings, flying upside down, and then diving, until she leveled out again. She had finished one inside loop.

"Let's do that again," shouted Phyro, laughing. "But try to keep your eyes open this time."

One after another, Phyro guided Ginki through a series of aerobatic moves: inside loops, outside loops, spire snail climbs, spinning-drill dives, barrel rolls, bowl-rim glides, double scroll-buns, triple scroll-buns, "Tututika's kiss," "Fithowéo's lunge". . .

Gradually, Zen-Kara stopped screaming and began to enjoy the experience. Sky and land and jungle and sea ceased to have meaning, all mere patches of color in an infinite, spinning, ever-changing universal sphere of which she and Phyro were the center. She had no words for the exhilaration she felt. For the first time, she began to see the merit in Phyro's made-up vocabulary.

Sensing that the young garinafin cow was tiring, Phyro directed her into a level glide. Zen-Kara sighed. She put her lips against Phyro's ear. "Even the gods may not have this much fun. And you get to do this every day!"

"No," said Phyro. "This is a thousand times better than any flight I've ever had before."

Zen-Kara smiled. *Because you're here.*

"If all your riders are this skilled," said Zen-Kara, growing serious, "then it must be easy to defeat the Lyucu."

Phyro shook his head. "Let's talk after we land."

He guided the garinafin back to their jungle camp and helped Zen-Kara dismount by using Ginki's antlered head as a kind of elevator. Affectionately, he patted Ginki's cheek in farewell. While the grooms rushed up to water and feed the garinafin and to take off the saddle, Phyro took Zen-Kara on a walk.

When he spoke again, his tone was somber. "Ofluro and Lady Suca have told me, in no uncertain terms, that I and my riders stand no chance against the Lyucu."

Methodically, he explained that the oldest Dara garinafins, being all hatched from Takval's eggs, were still considered too young to be prime fighters. They would be outclassed by the older garinafins among the Lyucu by mass, strength, and battle experience. Moreover, the kind of aerial acrobatics he had shown her were considered child's play among the Lyucu, though he was already the most skilled rider in Dara. Despite the constant drills, with no real fighting experience, he and his greenhorns would be slaughtered by Lyucu veterans in direct combat.

"Then why are you taking this risk?" she asked. "Why not wait until you're stronger?"

"Because the Lyucu will grow stronger as well, once the Wall of Storms opens. Empress Jia is convinced there will be no reinforcements, but how can she know the future? Even without reinforcements, more of their juvenile garinafins will grow into prime fighting beasts. You can't achieve victory by waiting and praying. With each passing day, the people of Unredeemed Dara are suffering and dying. They cannot wait."

"But if going to war with them is suicide—"

"No, I didn't say that. There are ways of evening out the disparities in skill and strength. Gin Mazoti was never the strongest on the battlefield, but she won by taking calculated risks with the help of clever advisers. I will do the same."

Zen-Kara remained unconvinced. Back in Dimushi, his risk-taking with the smuggling gang might have cost him his life if she hadn't happened to pass by. His confidence in himself and his companions was admirable, but mere confidence was not enough.

"There are tides in the affairs of humankind, no different from the eternal sea," said Phyro. "I cannot tell you exactly how, but soon there will be a sea change in public opinion in Dara to press for war against the Lyucu. If I don't seize this brief window of opportunity and make the most of it, the tide will recede and the people of Unredeemed Dara will be plunged into a darkness devoid of all light of hope. You told me that the crubens do not heed summonses, and we can ride them only when they wish to be ridden. It is the same with war. Fate does not allow us to fight when we want, and we must take up the sword and leap into the wave at its apex."

Zen-Kara didn't try to dissuade him. How could one romance be weighed against the fate of a people? If she loved him, then she must not change him.

"I will go back to Dimushi on the morrow," she said. "I can't help you by staying here."

"Wait for me there," he said.

She shook her head. "I have my own work to pursue."

She thought about her own battles ahead: persuading the elders and chieftains of Tan Adü to join her in opposing Chief Kyzen's policy of forbidding more youngsters to go to Dara to study; organizing the Adüan exiles in Dara into a community that could become a bridge between Tan Adü and the rest of Dara; developing her hybrid script so that Tan Adü would have the tools for entering literacy without leaving behind all the treasures of orality; encouraging her people to embrace the changes that would come with learning the ways of Dara without the fear of ceasing to be Adüan. . . .

"I don't know where I'll be," she said. "Come find me when you're victorious. The world is grand and the sea boundless, but two hearts in sync will always find each other."

He didn't try to dissuade her, as she knew he wouldn't. That was also part of why she loved him.

"I promise you that when this war is over," said Phyro, "I'll give you my sword. I'll seek no more battles alone."

They embraced, and listened to the duet of their beating hearts against the endless chorus of the tides.

~

The race goes not always to the swift, nor the battle always to the strong.

This lament by the Hegemon, like so many proverbs, had many interpretations. Some found it a cry of despair, others a cynical justification for acts of dishonor. But to Phyro, the young emperor, it was an inspiration.

Here's how the story of Dophino, the bandit who had never driven chariots but nonetheless challenged the King of Gan to a race, ended.

On the morning of the race, Dophino came to see the king, claiming that he needed to be taught the rudiments of driving. After all, he reasoned, the king would surely enjoy a fairer race than one in which Dophino didn't even know how to get a chariot to start and stop.

The king readily assented. He summoned his best team of horses, lightest racing chariot, and most skilled driver. Since a racing chariot had no room for passengers, the king and Dophino climbed onto the back, securing themselves by grabbing straps tied to the driver's seat.

"I'm not quite ready for the racetrack just yet," said Dophino. "Perhaps we can learn on some country roads first."

And so the king had the driver take them out into the countryside, demonstrating for Dophino how to guide the horses to speed up and slow down, how to take sharp turns and accelerate out of them.

After an hour of this, Dophino pointed to a nearby steep hill. "Though the reputation of your horses reverberates throughout Dara like thunder, I'm not convinced that your horses are strong enough to crest that slope. I don't want to race against horses that are weak."

The king laughed at his ignorance and ordered the driver to put Dophino's qualms to rest. The horses raced up the hill, as swift as a pack of hunting hounds.

While the horses panted from their exertion, Dophino pointed to the tangled cow paths at the foot of the hill. "Though the nimbleness of your chariot is praised by poets on all the Islands, I don't believe they can navigate such tight turns. I don't want to race against a chariot that is clumsy."

The king laughed at this bumpkin and ordered the driver to refute Dophino's doubts. The driver guided the chariot around the mazy paths, turning this way and that like an eel darting around a coral reef.

While the wheels of the chariot squeaked from these maneuvers, Dophino pointed to an apple orchard in the distance. "Though the skill of your drivers is spoken of with awe by the people of Gan, I think the tales are exaggerated. I don't want to race against someone with inferior skill. Do you think your driver can ride through that orchard, weave around every tree, and use his whip to pick an apple from each without breaking the skin?"

The king laughed at this arrogant bandit and ordered the driver to meet Dophino's challenge. Motivated by a desire to show off and the terror of disappointing his king, the driver concentrated hard and retrieved dozens of apples with the tip of his whip like the trunk of an elephant, piling them at his feet.

"I'm satisfied that I have an worthy opponent," declared Dophino. "Let's race."

The king's horses were exhausted after a day of hill climbing and maze running; the king's chariot rattled and creaked from the many extreme turns it had been forced to make earlier; the king's driver had to race with a sore wrist and flagging concentration after that apple-picking demonstration. Dophino's market horses and night-soil cart easily crossed the finish line first.

The shamed King of Gan had to grant Dophino and his bandits a city. From that new base, Dophino continued to terrorize the Tiro kings, often sitting before them in *thakrido* when negotiating for ransom. But he was said to also give lavishly to the poor, and many were the legends praising the noble bandit. Even Kon Fiji, who at one time had taught Dophino as a student, recorded some of the bandit-king's exploits in his books.

Like Dophino, Phyro realized that to overcome his faster, stronger, more experienced opponent, he would have to hold his own garinafins back for as long as possible. Before that, he would wear the Lyucu down, baffle them, blunt their concentration, confuse and harass and befuddle and amaze . . . and only then deal the fatal blow.

Though the airships had never been intended as more than decoys, he had not planned to sacrifice them either. Goztan's surprise assault with fire arrows forced him to launch the garinafins far earlier than anticipated.

Nonetheless, while the Lyucu riders and garinafins had been flying and fighting all day against strange weapons, his own aerial cavalry was fresh and rested. He hoped that he had done enough.

A teahouse storyteller from Dara, had one been present at Crescent Island, might have summarized the clash of garinafins thusly:

> Wing-sails flap across a sun-sanguinary sky,
> A sight more storm-charged than the famed fleets of Métashi;
> Fire-tongues accuse and counter in a star-stripped void,
> A debate more ferocious than factions at Pan.
>
> On one side, ironclad demons of tooth and claw;
> On the other, hope-mounted youths craving triumph.
> Wing batter wing; tined tail bash against antlered skull.
> Lady Kana faints at this ceaseless slaughter;
> Fithowéo pales at this carnage carnival.
> Fire breath roasts flesh; flame-lances sear gushing gashes.
> The Hegemon would have wept at the dying wails;
> The Marshal would have cursed the curdling horror-howls.
>
> The fate of the parted Islands hangs in balance;
> The future of divided Dara is in doubt.
> Will Tenryo's nightmarish garinafins prevail?
> Or will Phyro's living fleet a new dream unveil?

As the sun gradually sank behind the mountains of Crescent Island, the stars blinked into existence in the twilight one by one, like so many celestial spectators coming to bear witness to a bloody and desperate battle that had no equal in the annals of Dara.

After losses suffered during the assault on the Imperial airships, the Lyucu had thirty-six garinafins remaining, most of them war beasts of prime fighting age. The Dara garinafin force was about fifty strong, but all were fairly young and inexperienced, not unlike their riders.

Recovering from the initial shock of seeing garinafins in the Dara invasion force, Goztan issued three orders in quick succession: First, all the armored garinafins would shed their armor immediately; second, the fire-bolt garinafins should land so native archers could be exchanged for Lyucu crews armed with traditional weapons; third, a tight defensive perimeter must be established around the city-ships.

Armor, while helpful against Dara archers and silkmotic bolts, slowed down the garinafins too much against nimble foes. Besides, after having fought most of the day in armor, the garinafins needed to lighten their load to stay in the air.

As well, native archers would have hindered more than helped in the chaotic, fast-paced setting of garinafin-to-garinafin combat. Since Goztan had never imagined that Dara would gain garinafins of their own, the archers had only been training for scenarios against slow-moving airships. In fact, they were such poor riders that they had to be secured to the garinafins' netting like cargo for the duration of the assault on the airships, despite the smooth and calm flight paths.

Moreover, by discarding native-style armor and switching back to traditional Lyucu crews, Goztan hoped that the boost in morale would appease the brewing mutiny among her troops and compensate for the error of having committed all her garinafins too early and too fast.

Goztan's last order, in particular, reflected her recognition of Phyro's plot. Like an arrow near the end of its flight, the Lyucu garinafin force had spent the bulk of its lift gas. The priority now was defense of the city-ships. Outnumbered and worn down, the Lyucu had to rely on guile and experience rather than brute strength. Thus, despite the small number of garinafins still at her disposal, Goztan insisted on sending only half of her mounted force aloft to patrol the airspace above the city-ships in tight patterns to conserve their lift gas, sortieing forth only when Dara garinafins were dangerously close. When the patrolling garinafins were exhausted, the reserves would relieve them.

Tolyusa was distributed to the beasts and riders resting on the city-ships. Goztan would have liked to avoid using so much tolyusa in so short a period of time, but she had little choice. The sacred berries would offer her garinafin force temporary relief from injuries and infuse them with a burst of strength and alertness, at the cost of likely long-term harm.

The destruction of the airships and the death of Than Carucono struck Phyro hard. The old general had been like a second father to him, and the young emperor vowed to avenge his death as well as the deaths of the many aviators who had been cruelly killed by the Lyucu and their traitorous native auxiliaries.

"Attack! Attack!" he shouted, directing his signaling corps to blow into the bone trumpets.

He wanted nothing more than to ride into the air himself, leading the charge like the berserking Hegemon at Wolf's Paw. But Puma and Than, perhaps anticipating a moment just like this, had made him swear before the battle in the name of Empress Risana not to risk his life in this way.

"Stick to the plan," Than had told him that morning, before the launch of the decoy airships. "No matter how the battle goes, you must not ride forth today."

"But I'm our best rider."

"It doesn't matter. Your father always listened to counsel and trusted his generals to accomplish what they were meant to do. Do you have so little faith in us that you think the battle cannot be won without you?"

Reluctantly, he had agreed.

How he regretted that decision now. He should have known that the best-made battle plans never survived an encounter with the enemy.

Again and again, he demanded his riders to strike harder, to fly faster, to break through the Lyucu defensive perimeter.

Gin Mazoti had always admonished against battlefield judgments clouded by emotion. Had she been present, she would have sighed with sorrow at how the desire for vengeance led Phyro to commit a fundamental tactical mistake. Rather than continuing to wear down his opponent by taking advantage of his garinafin force's superiority in numbers, agility, and youthful stamina, Phyro's attempt at a quick victory pitted his weakness against the enemy's strength.

Just as Phyro had worn down the Lyucu earlier with his decoy airships, Goztan now needed a way to wear down the Dara garinafins slamming against her defenses like an enraged hurricane.

Grim-faced, she ordered the airships, until now hovering out of the way as lookouts, to join the fray. The native auxiliaries aboard, deprived of the use of arrows and crossbows, posed little threat against fast-moving garinafins—this was by design, as the Lyucu lived in perpetual terror of a native rebellion. Nonetheless, Goztan commanded them to reinforce the defensive line around the city-ships.

Compelled by threats against their families on Ukyu-taasa, the airship crews oared their vessels into the maelstrom. Those few who refused were soon overcome by their fellow enslaved comrades. Love, when twisted and corrupted by ruthless minds, could be more effective than any chain in bondage.

Phyro's garinafin riders fell on the airships with a ferocity that matched, if not exceeded, their assault on the Lyucu garinafins. It was natural to despise the traitor even more than the enemy, and the incensed Dara riders were intent on avenging their comrades who had perished earlier from the fire arrows of native auxiliaries. They couldn't understand why these natives, also the people of Dara, would fight for the enemy.

The airship crews, armed only with tar bombs, were virtually defenseless. With cold determination and hot fury, Dara garinafin riders carved up the slow-moving Lyucu airships in short order. Fire tongues, claws, teeth all played their roles, and within a quarter of an hour, native auxiliaries were tumbling into the sea like dumplings being tossed into a pot, while their aircraft disintegrated above them.

Goztan grimaced with revulsion. Cutanrovo had envisioned using native auxiliaries as disposable meat shields in exactly this manner. To be sure, the sacrifice of the airships had bought her a little more time and allowed her to assess the skills of Phyro's riders, but the fact that she could justify the practice by military necessity didn't make her feel any less sullied.

Perhaps I am no less a monster than Cutanrovo.

But doubt is a luxury enjoyed only by those who survive.

The assault on the airships had revealed the Dara riders to be unskilled in the ways of garinafin warfare. Even against such defenseless targets, the Dara garinafin crews had been uncoordinated in their attack patterns, demonstrating little mastery of formation flying or awareness of mutual support. Their rage and thirst for vengeance only magnified these flaws.

Goztan wasn't the only one who noticed. Aided by an instinctual understanding achieved through decades of unceasing warfare, the Lyucu riders set up aerial traps with only a few laconic exchanges.

Feigning injury, one of the Lyucu garinafins would begin to retreat. Sensing an opening, several Dara garinafins would race ahead in hot pursuit, only to find themselves caught in the crossfire of multiple Lyucu garinafins in waiting, incinerating the Dara crews with well-timed fire breaths.

Another Lyucu garinafin would fly close to the surface of the sea, apparently so exhausted that it could barely stay airborne. Trying to take advantage, a Dara garinafin would dive down from above, intent on slamming the weakened creature into the sea. But at the last minute, the wily Lyucu garinafin would flip over in midair, slice deep gashes into the wings of the pursuer with its sharp talons, and then dodge out of the way as the maimed Dara garinafin tumbled into the water, drowning as its damaged wings flailed uselessly against the weight of the brine.

Over and over, experienced Lyucu pilots guided their veteran mounts into maneuvers that seemed physically impossible: a sharp, midair somersault that allowed a garinafin to bathe its Dara pursuer in flames; a last-minute swerve that caused the Dara opponent to slam into the cliffs of the inlet; an unexpected, sudden pull-up that led an attacking Dara garinafin to overshoot, while a hail of slingshot stones and bone-spears rained down upon the stunned crew. . . .

As the garinafins strafed one another with fire breath, rolled, dove, swerved, clawed, and bit, riders scrambled across the netting over their mounts to find refuge and to strike at one another with spears and slingshots, in the case of the Lyucu, and with crossbows and acid-bombs, in the case of the Dara. Occasionally, when two garinafins were tangled together, claws and wings a buffeting mess, the crews even jumped across the aerial gap, boarding each other's mounts. The hand-to-hand combat that resulted was beyond brutal, as swords and clubs rose and fell, and hacked-off limbs and bashed-in brains rained down upon the city-ships below.

While battle raged above them, the Lyucu warriors on the city-ships weren't idle either.

Contrary to speculation by some Dara military analysts during the early days of the conflict with the Lyucu, ground units were not entirely helpless against garinafin assault. In the long centuries during which garinafin tactics had been developed, the people of the scrublands also invented a variety of anti-garinafin tactics for occasions when friendly garinafins were unavailable. By taking advantage of local terrain or garinafin habits, well-trained warriors on foot could repel garinafin raids or even kill them.

The naros and culeks on the city-ships put some of these tactics into practice now. Some aimed their slingshots at the sensitive eyes of garinafins as they dove within range; others doused themselves with water and then climbed up tall masts in order to leap onto the backs of low-flying garinafins trying to strafe the decks. The naros-votan organized multiple fire-suppression teams to put out the fires sprouting all over the wooden ships as friendly and hostile garinafins contended for supremacy overhead.

Some of the most quick-witted warriors seized upon an old but effective trick. By blowing into the bone trumpets a certain way, it was possible to create a highly realistic imitation of the keening of a hatchling garinafin. Much as a crying infant will nearly always break the concentration of nearby human adults, the distressed keening of garinafin hatchlings produced in adults and older juveniles a nearly irresistible urge to come to their aid.

While garinafins in the professional armies of both the Lyucu and the Agon had been trained to disregard such tricks, they were completely new to Phyro's war mounts. In part this was the result of Phyro's reliance on Ofluro as his trainer. The defector's vow to teach the young emperor how to ride garinafins *without* revealing the military secrets of Ukyu-taasa forced him to walk a fine line. To Ofluro, standard garinafin aerobatics were part of the repertoire of any garinafin rider, but techniques for fighting against garinafins on foot were "underhanded tricks." As a result, Phyro's garinafins were never immunized against this tactic of deception.

Thus, many of the Lyucu warriors began to torment Phyro's garinafins with phantom calls. To the inexperienced war beasts, it sounded as though nests of helpless hatchlings were being tortured. Disregarding the orders of their pilots, they dove down toward the city-ships, frantically searching for the source. But when they finally found where the piteous cries were coming from, instead of a nest of babies waiting to be rescued, they were greeted with a fusillade of spears, slingshot bullets, or pouches filled with caustic scorpion venom that blinded them and left them thrashing and lashing about, a menace to friend and foe alike.

Night. No moon.

All was chaos and confusion. The air above the city-ships was a roiling maelstrom of shredded wings and charred bones, with occasional eruptions of fire that illuminated the terror and bloodlust in the eyes of the combatants.

There was no mood-echoing storm to show the displeasure of the gods, no future-foretelling omen to reveal divine sentiment. After all, this was life and death, not the re-remembering of a teahouse storyteller. Perhaps even the gods were too stunned by the savagery of the scene before them to react.

Phyro's impetuous and ill-advised all-out assault had taken its toll. Despite the fact that his garinafins had been fresh while Goztan's had been fighting for most of the day, the Dara riders were no match for their Lyucu counterparts. Young garinafin after young garinafin fell from the sky, laden with the burnt bodies of slain warriors. There were only eighteen Dara garinafins left now against twenty-five Lyucu garinafins. In the all-consuming darkness, where sound and instinct surpassed sight, the inexperienced Dara garinafins faced an even greater disadvantage.

A smile finally began to appear on Goztan's weary and grim visage. Despite the disadvantage in numbers and strength at the beginning of the battle, she appeared to be on the verge of victory. Perhaps that famed Lyucu spirit, spoken of so often by Cutanrovo, did mean something.

Short blasts from the shore of Crescent Island told her all she needed to know. The Dara garinafins had lost the heart to fight, and they were being recalled to shore.

She hesitated. Should she order her warriors to give chase and destroy the last remaining hope of the native invasion force? Or should she exercise caution and consolidate her gains by recalling her own garinafins? After fighting for most of the day and much of the night, and in spite of her best efforts to conserve their strength, all her garinafins were on the verge of collapse from exhaustion. If her enemy hadn't lost the will to fight, she doubted she could have held on much longer.

The Dara garinafins turned and fled from the battle, winging swiftly away from the city-ships. The Lyucu riders in the air ululated in celebration, and their cheers were echoed by howls of victory from the city-ships below.

"Lyucu kyo! Lyucu kyo! Lyucu kyo!"

"Kill them! Kill them! Kill them!"

The frenzied shouts reverberated over the sea in thunderous waves, but still Goztan hesitated. She looked at the faces of the celebrating Lyucu warriors, clustered around bright torch flames like moths swarming around bonfires. Something about the situation felt wrong, but she couldn't articulate the source of her unease.

Certainly the victory had not come easy, and the Lyucu had paid a heavy price. The smell of charred flesh was all around her, and the decks and rigging were slick with gore. Though many Dara garinafins had been killed, she had lost half of her own complement as well, not to mention the many riders who would never see Ukyutaasa or their families again.

But she couldn't shake the uncomfortable feeling that the enemy's retreat wasn't so much a forced concession as a deliberate choice.

What am I missing?

Then it struck her. Throughout the battle, she couldn't recall having ever seen the opposing commander, Emperor Monadétu.

She turned to Noda Mi. "You say that Phyro has always worshipped the Hegemon?"

Noda Mi nodded vigorously, though his eyes betrayed his terror, uncertain why Goztan was asking him this.

Impatient with the garinafin-thane's hesitation, many of the garinafin pilots had decided to give chase on their own. They were determined to not only kill the enemy garinafins, but also seek out the hideouts for the Dara-raaki sailors and soldiers, and burn the Dara base down to the ground.

Goztan thought furiously. The Hegemon was known for leading his troops into battle personally, risking his life to inspire the soldiers. That Phyro wasn't among the riders, following the example of his role model, *had* to mean something.

The escaping Dara garinafins and pursuing Lyucu garinafins had by now both left the gentle glow of the torches on the city-ships. Their progress could only be tracked as shadowy wings occluding the pinprick stars, flapping steadily toward the shore of Crescent Island.

Goztan held up her hands and waved them vigorously. She thought she heard *something*. The raucous cheering subsided.

Across the water, a shrill whistle sounded, roving about, sometimes to the south, sometimes to the north. Some invisible *thing* was tearing through the darkness, as though hunting for prey.

CHAPTER TWENTY-FIVE

OCULIUM

TIRO COZO: MORE THAN A YEAR EARLIER.

The complex of long, low buildings nestled in the heart of the valley had originally been built as stables for horses. When Phyro first arrived in Tiro Cozo, he and his retinue spent long hours practicing horsemanship in preparation for a different kind of riding.

Once the garinafin hatchlings had grown old enough to be bonded to each pilot, there was no more need for a large contingent of warhorses in the valley. The stable complex was largely abandoned and neglected.

When Rati Yera joined Phyro's secret base, however, she took an immediate liking to the stables. The buildings were spacious and remote from the rest of the army camp, the perfect setting for a workshop for her experiments. This was the place in which she invented the ornithopters as well as the machinery to construct and instruct them.

On any typical day, the workshop hummed with activity. Rati had recruited a group of assistant engineers from sailors, discharged veterans, examination-phobic scholars, artisans, adventurers, street magicians, silk weavers—men and women who were curious about the workings of the universe and who believed in Phyro's vision of a united Dara liberated from Lyucu domination. Drawing, measuring, sawing, hammering, sanding, debating, drinking, playing games, and singing work songs, they labored to weigh the fish and to realize Rati's vision.

But today, a strange quiescence enveloped the longest and largest building in the complex. Rati had given strict orders that no one was to enter the warehouse-like structure without her explicit authorization.

"What exactly is so exciting that you have to show me this instant?" Phyro asked, a trace of annoyance in his voice, as he followed Rati Yera's wheeled chair through the imposing stable doors at the end of the building. The tall figure of Mota Kiphi brought up the rear.

"You'll see," said Rati Yera mysteriously. She winked at Mota Kiphi, who smiled back but said nothing.

Rati and Mota had dragged Phyro away from the training grounds, and the emperor was worried. The garinafin riders were nowhere near ready.

"And don't think I've forgotten you," said Phyro, turning to Mota. "I haven't seen you in months! You'd better be ready to stay up all night to wrestle and drink with me."

Mota, always a man of few words, lifted his eyebrows inquiringly.

"Ha! Don't be so certain of your victory. Ofluro has been teaching me the fundamentals of Lyucu wrestling. I think you'll find me a much worthier opponent than last time. . . . Anyway, what brought you back? I thought you were helping Arona with her new show."

"Widi is taking over—he's much better at composing librettos. Rati asked me to help her out with a mission—"

"Shhh!" Rati held up a finger before her lips. "Don't spoil the surprise!"

Mota went to close the stable doors. Shades had been drawn over the windows lining both sides of the long room, and the only illumination came from the silkmotic lamps dangling from the ceiling. Phyro looked around and saw that the floor was covered by numerous canvas bundles. Some of the largest were about the girth of a man, but many times as long.

"What are these?" asked Phyro. "Some kind of new weapon?"

"Not exactly *new*," said Rati.

"I told you, we can't rely on old ways of doing things," said Phyro. "A good general—"

"Yes, yes, 'A good general never fights the same battle twice.'"

I know the lecture. You've given it at least a hundred times and I can repeat it in my sleep. The bundles on the floor aren't the main attraction—not right now anyway." Rati pointed to a much smaller bundle, about as long as Phyro, lying on a table next to the wall. "That's what I wanted to give you right away."

Stepping gingerly over the bundles on the floor, Phyro approached the table. His hands hovered apprehensively over the gift.

"Go on. Open it!" urged Rati.

Taking a deep breath, Phyro lifted the bundle with both hands—it was much heavier than he expected and he almost faltered from the weight—and Mota came over to help him unwrap it. As layer after layer of canvas was pulled away, Phyro's heart sped up.

Finally, the last layer of canvas was lifted, and Phyro found himself holding a giant sword.

The center of the blade was forged from bronze—that accounted for the weapon's unusual weight—but the two edges were cold and blue, showing the fine wave patterns of thousand-hammered steel. Both sides of the blade were full of intricately etched logograms. By the light of the silkmotic lamp overhead, he read:

> *Let a man fall with each ten steps you take;*
> *Walk a thousand miles a new path to make.*

Turning over the blade, he read the other side:

> *Lament not that the days are short,*
> *But that they are without glory.*
> *Where doubt ends, so does courage.*
> *May each of your days be a day of battle.*

> . . .

Phyro couldn't finish. He looked up so that tears wouldn't spill from his eyes.

He was holding the legendary Na-aroénna, the Doubt-Ender, the most wondrous creation of the master bladesmith Suma Ji. It was the weapon of the peerless Mata Zyndu, Hegemon of Dara, as well as of Gin Mazoti, the greatest tactician of the Islands.

"I know that you said you don't care about the past except to avoid its mistakes," said Rati, her voice kind but solemn. "Yet, I also know how much you admired the two who wielded this sword."

Phyro struggled to compose himself. "But how . . . where . . . it was lost—"

"Have you forgotten my old profession?" asked Rati, pride in her voice and a mischievous glint in her eyes.

During the Battle of Zathin Gulf, Gin Mazoti died on the burning deck of *Pride of Ukyu*, the Lyucu flagship. The charred remains were recovered and then interred near Dimushi—the closest thing to an ancestral home for the Marshal, who was born in an indigo house and never knew a father.

However, Na-aroénna, the sword that she had wielded against Pékyu Tenryo in one of the most iconic and legend-shrouded moments of the battle, was lost.

City-ship wrecks and sunken Dara vessels lay at the bottom of the gulf, an aquatic city of the dead entombing thousands of souls from both sides who had fought on that fateful day. The only attendants of their eternal rest were crabs scuttling over the barnacle-encrusted surfaces and fish weaving in and out of gaping holes.

But with tombs came tomb robbers, whose domain of expertise extended far beyond mere audacity to break into ancient graves.

To retrieve valuable antiquities required detailed knowledge of history (especially the sort of history not recorded in books), geography, hydrology, climate and weather, construction, and of course, advanced engineering. Indeed, notorious grave robbers sometimes claimed that many of the techniques in that science respectable scholars termed *archaeology* had been first invented and developed in *their* disreputable trade.

One of the most lucrative sources of antiquities was found not on land, but in the sea. Ancient shipwrecks were filled with treasure of all kinds, and their recovery posed special challenges. Only by studying historical trade routes and navigation records in detail could one locate the shipwrecks, and then, a great deal of ingenuity and effort had to be expended to find, retrieve, and restore the lost artifacts.

One of Mota's new veterans' societies' projects was a comprehensive oral history of the Battle of Zathin Gulf, collecting eyewitness accounts from as many of the survivors as possible. Rati had combed through these and meticulously triangulated and plotted the movements of the vessels during the battle until she was reasonably certain of where the Lyucu flagship, *Pride of Ukyu*, had sunk. She had then asked Mota to head up a secret expedition—staffed by members of her old gang—to locate the wreck and to retrieve everything he could find there.

Posing as the crew of a fishing boat and as pearl divers, Mota's expedition had spent several weeks over the region of the sea pinpointed by Rati, systematically exploring the seafloor in a grid pattern. With the aid of devices such as lodestones and dragnets, Mota's crew finally found the wreck of *Pride of Ukyu*. They then deployed diving bells and mechanical dolphins—modeled on the mechanical crubens but much smaller and tethered to the surface vessel—to recover many artifacts from the wreck and the surrounding seafloor.

Among the many treasures was Na-aroénna, though that hadn't been Rati Yera's goal at all.

It was some time before Phyro could speak again.

"It doesn't look like a sword that has been immersed in salt water for ten years."

"It was in pretty bad shape when Mota first found it," said Rati. "But some careful scouring with oil of vitriol and polishing with pangolin scales soon restored it to its former glory. Shedding a layer of rust renews the old, much as a snake is reborn when it shucks its former skin."

Phyro pondered his chief engineer's words, wondering if they were a subtle hint that more value should be given to tradition than he had been willing to concede. "Thank you, Master Yera," he said. "The recovery of this mighty blade is surely a favorable omen from the gods."

"I don't know much about the will of the gods," said Rati. "But I do know that many in Dara have waited to see the day when someone raises this sword to free those groaning under the yoke of slavery."

"I can only hope that I'm worthy of it," said Phyro.

"Of that I have no doubt," said Mota.

Taking another deep breath, Phyro composed himself and reverently set down the sword. Then he turned to the other bundles on the floor. "What are these?"

"Other artifacts recovered from and near the wreck of *Pride of Ukyu.*"

Slowly, Phyro and Mota walked around the long room and unwrapped some of the smaller bundles. There was a large assortment of weapons, both Lyucu and Dara, as well as structural fragments from the Imperial airship *Silkmotic Arrow*, which had crash-landed on the city-ship.

"We recovered the remains of some of the fighters as well," said Mota, his voice somber. "The bones are held at the port of Ginpen."

"Can the bodies be identified?" asked Phyro.

"A few, yes, based on personal effects found with the bodies," said Mota. "But most cannot. It's not even clear which are Lyucu and which are Dara."

Phyro's eyes dimmed, and Mota waited in respectful silence. Kuni Garu's body had never been recovered after the Battle of Zathin Gulf, and Mota's expedition had no luck on that front either.

At length, Phyro said, "Where the bodies can be identified, send the remains to their families so that they may be interred in their ancestral plots. Make honor tablets to recognize their service in the battle, and I'll personally deliver each to the family with a stipend—pay for it by auctioning off more of my jewels and books."

"But . . ." Mota looked uncomfortable.

Phyro understood. "Are they all gone? Then . . . sell off the items I've kept to remember my parents. Even from the other shore of the River-on-Which-Nothing-Floats, they'll approve."

Mota nodded and said nothing. Though Phyro was nominally the emperor, he had no authority over the Imperial Treasury, and Empress Jia had given Tiro Cozo a meager budget, barely enough to keep the garinafins fed. Before Arona had come along to generate funds with her patriotic plays, Phyro had kept the base running with donations from his father's old retainers, like Puma Yemu and Than Carucono, and sold off the jewels and rare books from his personal collection, mostly gifts from prominent families who had tried to curry favor with his mother during that period when Jia and Risana had been locked in a palace battle over whose son should be the heir to the Dandelion Throne. He ate the same food as the other soldiers at the base and slept on the same straw mattresses. He patched his own war cape and resoled his own shoes. He shoveled garinafin dung with the other laborers and filled feeding troughs alongside the grooms.

However, there were a few pieces of jewelry, given to him by Kuni and Risana on special occasions, that he had always kept for sentimental reasons—until now.

This is why you're a lord so many are willing to follow, thought Mota.

"As for the remains that cannot be identified, inter them in a mass grave at the Imperial graveyard, and commemorate all with a tablet describing the Battle of Zathin Gulf," said Phyro.

"But some of the bodies may belong to the Lyucu," objected Rati, "including Tenryo himself."

Phyro looked at Mota.

"It's possible," said Mota. "We really can't tell. Na-aroénna wasn't found embedded in a body, but the bones nearby came from multiple individuals, too entangled to be identified."

"It's better to mistakenly honor an enemy than to neglect the reverence due those who died so that we may live," said Phyro. "Besides, even the dead Lyucu believed that they were fighting for a just cause. We cannot triumph by mistreating the dead."

Mota nodded again. It was an extraordinary decision to inter with honor what were likely the remains of Tenryo Roatan while Kuni Garu's body remained lost. The streak of compassion in the emperor reminded him of stories about Emperor Ragin and the Hegemon, who both tried to treat their veterans with respect and their foes with dignity.

The very long bundles turned out to be the oversized silkmotic bolts that had been launched from giant crossbows mounted on Imperial airships. Diamond-tipped and packed with firework powder with an Ogé jar fuse, these had dealt terror and death to the invading garinafins alongside the current-channeling silkmotic lances. Some of the bolts were remarkably intact—though of course the firework powder had long spoiled—as they had missed their marks on launch and fell harmlessly into the sea.

Phyro caressed the shafts, imagining the bloody and terrible battle that he had not witnessed. As the presumptive heir at the time, he had been safely hidden away in Pan.

"These probably don't have much military value in their present form," said Rati, "especially since we cannot afford the capital ships capable of launching them. I actually ordered the expedition because I was interested in their tips. Combined with the silver recovered from those massive garinafin-gut Ogé jars dangled by the Imperial airships, we can raise a great deal more money on the black market—"

"No," said Phyro decisively. "We must not be grave robbers intent only on profit. They should be preserved as they are. Someday, perhaps we can build a hall to commemorate the war, and we can display these objects to remind all the price for their freedom." He wrapped his fingers around the handle of Na-aroénna. "There's a visceral reality to old objects that transcends mere descriptions in books. The weight of history requires the tangible."

In her capacity as Farsight Secretary, Zomi Kidosu was also required to give Empress Jia reports on Phyro's actions at Tiro Cozo. While Zomi avoided any hints of the brewing conspiracy to force the Throne to approve an invasion of Unredeemed Dara in these accounts, she saw little reason to censor herself concerning Phyro's research into new weapons.

Such weapons would also be useful in *resisting* a Lyucu invasion. While the empress refused to contemplate a war of liberation, Zomi thought she could be convinced to tolerate or even support Phyro's work if framed as an effort to enhance Dara's security. Jia did, after all, approve a minimal military budget in order to maintain a credible defense, invaluable in deterring Lyucu aggression and sustaining the status quo.

In practice, Jia never commented on these sections of Zomi's reports. Taking that as tacit approval, Zomi also began a program of sending select scholars from various Imperial laboratories around Dara to visit Tiro Cozo and present their interesting discoveries to Phyro's weapons-research staff. Although the Imperial laboratories tended to focus on projects of peace, both Zomi and Rati believed that such intellectual exchanges were beneficial, even crucial.

"Good ideas are like children," said Rati. "You never know how they'll develop and grow."

"All Creation is connected," said Zomi. "Inventions in one area may spur invention in another seemingly unconnected area, much as the shuttling bee brings fructifying pollen from one flower to another on the other side of a river."

Ever since Ofluro and Lady Suca joined Tiro Cozo, Phyro had relaxed the strict security of the base to be more humane. Ofluro sometimes liked to go into the mountains outside the valley to hunt, and Lady Suca wanted to visit her aged aunts and uncles from time to time. Unwilling to chill the hearts of his garinafin instructors, in the end, Phyro gave in and agreed to institute a system of regular family furlough for all base personnel. He even set up mail delivery by airship to the outside world, though all the letters had to be censored to be sure they betrayed no military secrets.

But visitors were still forbidden at the base. Rati and Zomi had to convince Phyro that the benefits of intellectual exchange outweighed the risks, though Phyro insisted that Zomi vet the approved scholars with extreme care—and even so, he admonished them that the existence of the garinafins must be concealed. It was critical to limit the number of people who knew that Dara possessed garinafins.

Rati enjoyed these visits from Imperial scholars immensely. There was nothing like the stimulation of talking with others equally passionate about concocting new ways to manipulate natural forces to achieve fantastical deeds.

The visiting scholar arriving in Tiro Cozo today was an old friend, Kisli Péro. Ever since they met at Last Bite, the two had maintained an active correspondence. (To cover up what had really happened, Zomi later explained to the laboratory staff that the Blossom Gang's breach of the security at Last Bite had been a planned test.) Though Kisli had been shocked at first to find out that Rati was not a ranked scholar—in fact, Rati had to employ a scribe for her letters because she didn't know how to read or write—she didn't look down on the old woman. After years of dealing with the Imperial laboratory's administrative bureaucracy, she was well aware that those who performed the best on the examinations were not always the best engineers. After all, Miza Crun, one of Dara's greatest silkmotic experts, made most of his discoveries as a street magician. What mattered to Kisli was one's skill as an artificer and engineer.

After the requisite warnings about maintaining secrecy, Rati showed Kisli prototypes of the ornithopters and solicited her advice on several problems she had been struggling with, primarily the miniaturization of Ogé jars as fuses for the firework-powder bombs and the storage of oil of vitriol. Kisli admired the flying machines, and after clarifying the principles of their operation, began to discuss Rati's difficulties in earnest. The design charrette lasted about an hour, and Rati was very pleased with their progress.

"Some tea?" suggested Rati. "Arona just sent me some orchid tea from Müning, supposed to be very relaxing."

"Nothing better than orchid tea after such an invigorating discussion. Well, nothing except a good long bath."

In deference to Rati's age and her wheeled chair, the younger woman happily got up and brought over the service tray to steep and pour for both of them. As the two women sipped the fragrant beverage contentedly, Kisli said in a mysterious voice, "I brought something interesting to show you."

Intrigued, Rati leaned forward eagerly. Kisli took out pieces of a machine from her traveling case and set them on the table.

"Archon Thu recently assigned me a new problem," said Kisli, emphasizing the formal title of Kita Thu, the head of the Imperial laboratories in Ginpen. She paused for effect but was disappointed to see no sign from Rati of being impressed. For a junior researcher like Kisli to be assigned a research topic directly by such a senior administrator was a sign of great esteem and boded well for her own career.

"And the problem is?" prodded Rati.

Kisli sighed inwardly. She couldn't expect her friend, who was working directly with the emperor, to be impressed by her own modest success. Brushing aside her slight vexation, she went on, "How to keep a silkmotic mill spinning at a constant rate."

"Isn't that generally taken care of by the flywheel?" asked Rati.

"Yes, but that wastes energy and isn't practical for smaller devices. Sometimes we need to power a silkmotic mill from Ogé jars that can't be constantly recharged—such as in a portable fan or a cart in a warehouse. As the charge is depleted, the mill slows down, and we have to move the jars closer to the blades to maintain the same spin rate. It would be nice if the mill could take care of that adjustment itself."

While she explained, Kisli set up the model silkmotic mill that Rati had seen before: a vertical bamboo pole tipped with a needle, a ceramic plate with radiating strips of silver foil, and two Ogé jars. She began to charge the jars with a glass rod and a piece of silk.

"Hmm," mused Rati. "This sounds like a problem in automatic control, where you need the machine to adjust itself in response to changing conditions. It's not unlike how windmill builders have to design their vanes to keep spinning despite the shifting directions of the wind."

"Exactly," said Kisli, pleased with Rati's quick understanding. "In the case of windmills, the solution is a fantail, a small windmill mounted behind the main sails and perpendicular to them. When the wind is at an angle to the fantail, it spins, which provides the power to rotate the axle of the main sails until they're directly facing into the wind. At that point, the fantail, being parallel to the wind, stops by itself. I need something similar that would automatically channel more power into the blades of the silkmotic mill as the charge in the Ogé jars is depleted."

Kisli picked up the ceramic plate with silver foil blades—the component that was supposed to go on top of the needle spindle—and handed it to Rati, who examined it carefully.

Right away, Rati noticed some differences from the last time she had seen the model. The foil blades at the plate's rim no longer flared out horizontally; instead, they were tilted downward at a sharp angle. The tip of each foil was connected by a thin bamboo skewer to the upper rim of a short cylinder—more like a finger ring—sized so that it could just slide up and down the bamboo mill axle. From the bottom of the ring dangled two arms tipped with small stone weights. Though the arms were fixed to opposite spots in the lower rim of the ring, they could swing up and down freely as the ring spun.

"How does this work?" asked Rati, puzzled.

"It's easier to show you," said Kisli. She slid the ring onto the axle, centered the plate over the needle, and then moved the Ogé jars close enough to the strips of foil to start the plate spinning.

As the plate accelerated, the two hanging arms at the bottom of the ring began to fan out.

"Centrifugal force pushes the weights away from the ring," said Kisli. "The faster the plate spins, the higher the arms are raised."

Rati nodded. That much seemed obvious.

Soon, the plate was spinning so fast that the arms were almost horizontal. This apparently triggered some mechanism inside the ring because it clicked down a fraction of an inch.

"The axle is notched to catch on small gears inside the ring," explained Kisli. "If the arms spread out beyond a certain angle, they'll snap the ring one notch down."

The lowering of the ring meant that the thin skewers attached to its upper rim pulled on the foil blades, angling them down even more sharply.

"This increases the distance between the foil blades and the Ogé jars, which is the same as moving the Ogé jars farther away," said Kisli. "And that reduces the amount of charge flowing across the mill."

The spinning plate slowed down. As a result, the weights at the tips of the two outstretched arms pulled them down until they were almost vertical. At that point, the gears in the ring tripped again, pushing the ring a notch up the axle, which in turn caused the skewers to raise the foil blades to move closer to the Ogé jars, thereby causing more charge to flow across the mill, speeding up the plate again.

Rati watched, fascinated, as the ring oscillated up and down the axle, opening and closing the foil blades like an umbrella until the mill eventually stabilized at a constant speed, with the two weighted arms stretched out at an angle about midway between vertical and horizontal.

"As the charge in the Ogé jar is slowly depleted, the ring will stabilize at an equilibrium point higher up the axle, raising the blades to draw more charge out of the jars. The mill maintains a constant speed all on its own, without any human intervention," said Kisli, beaming with pride. "I call this invention the 'even-tempered archon.' Like those ideal rulers spoken of by Moralists, the even-tempered archon neither rushes nor tarries. It spurs the indolent to be more industrious, while tempering the impatient so as not to deplete reserves in a burst of wasteful extravagance."

"This is utterly brilliant," exclaimed Rati.

"A mere curiosity," said Kisli, blushing with pleasure.

"This is far beyond a mere curiosity!" said Rati. "Without operator supervision, a regular silkmotic mill will discharge too fast at the beginning and leave not enough to finish the job. Your even-tempered archon, on the other hand, allows the mill to regulate itself, meting out the reservoir of silkmotic force to deliver a constant amount of power for much longer. It couldn't have been easy to design this."

"I did suffer through many failed prototypes," allowed Kisli. "But it was such an interesting problem! I slept several nights in my office and skipped as many as three baths in a row! The key was figuring out a way to feed the output of the mill back into itself in order to control its speed—to allow the mill to observe its own actions and reflect on what to do, so to speak."

"It's almost as if you've built a machine with intelligence," said Rati admiringly. "You've artificed intelligence."

"Oh, that's too grand a claim," said Kisli with a laugh. "Legends from the time of the Diaspora Wars speak of Fithowéo building mechanical wolves that could hunt and fight on their own. Now *that* would be artificed intelligence. This is merely a crude shadow of the work of the gods."

"Listen to you! So modest and pious," said Rati. A teasing look came into her eyes. "I haven't even commented on the most ingenious aspect of this invention: its name."

"Err . . . I don't know what you're talking about," said Kisli. "I told you, it's just a reference to the ideal rulers—"

"Really? Hmm, let's see. 'Even-tempered archon.' Are you certain you weren't thinking of the reaction of Archon Kita Thu when you present the solution to his problem?"

"Heh," said Kisli, reddening. Apparently Rati wasn't as ignorant of the subtleties of bureaucratic office politics as she let on. Kisli chuckled awkwardly. "Even in an Imperial laboratory, it isn't a bad idea to flatter your boss when the occasion arises."

"He ought to be a lot more impressed by the substance of your invention. It is truly one of the most beautiful things I've ever seen."

"Thank you. But not all of us have the good fortune to work for bosses free from vanity."

The two women admired the spinning mill in silence until it finally stopped, a long time later.

For days after Kisli's departure, Rati couldn't get the image of that spinning silkmotic mill out of her head.

A powerful silkmotic mill could perform wonders—the elevator at Last Bite had shown her that. Surely it would be useful in the emperor's war preparations?

Phyro had said to avoid repeating techniques of the past—both because the Lyucu would be prepared against them and because he didn't have the resources to re-create Gin Mazoti's awe-inducing fleet. But perhaps there was a way to be inspired by the past while overcoming both objections.

A vision came to life in her head.

She went into her workshop and told everyone to leave her alone. Working in a frenzy, she sketched and built and calculated and modeled, interacting with the outside world only when meals were delivered to her through a slot in the workshop door.

A cool, crisp autumn day in the month of fog and mist.

After the long sere-month, the days were getting shorter, and garinafin riders could finally run drills in the middle of the day without tiring out their mounts too quickly.

Ofluro and Suca were teaching Phyro and the other riders a tricky maneuver called "Péa's dive." An offensive aerobatic move designed to break through defensive formations of garinafins circling in a tight cluster, Péa's dive involved distracting the defensive perimeter with multiple feints from supporting garinafins, while a single lead garinafin, taking advantage of cloud cover or the general confusion, snuck above the cluster to attempt a hard and fast dive into its heart like a streaking comet.

The maneuver was particularly difficult for the pilot of the lead garinafin, who would be plunging down at the enemy garinafins milling about below at a rate far exceeding free fall. Disregarding the terrifying sensation that their inner organs were about to erupt from their throat, the pilot had to maintain focus throughout the dive, find a momentary opening in the cloud of flailing limbs through which to guide his hurtling mount, and then launch a fire breath attack the moment they were inside the cluster.

Phyro guided Ginki far above the roiling clouds that often hung over the valley like a lace tablecloth during this time of the year. Through the openings in the sea of clouds, he could glimpse the cluster of garinafins below, his intended target. He took a deep breath, whispered a prayer to Fithowéo and Péa both, and prepared to spur Ginki into the long dive.

Suddenly, an elongated object, like a flash of lightning, erupted out of the clouds to his right, and arcing up gently, swept right past him and his garinafin, barely yards away.

Ginki panicked and bolted to the left, her wings flapping so hard that Phyro felt his organs had been left behind. Fighting against the disorienting sensation, Phyro finally brought the young garinafin back under control. Panting, heart thumping from the ordeal, his mind lingered over the astonishing sight he had just witnessed.

It was like watching a graceful dyran leap out of the ocean to skim above the waves, except this particular flying fish had a body of bamboo over twenty yards in length and a sparkling head that reflected sunlight with dazzling brilliance. Along its length were numerous translucent fin-wings that fluttered and flapped in a coordinated manner, and behind it was a whirring tail that spun too fast ·

to be seen clearly. As the missile shot through the clouds, the twirling tail stirred and spun the wisps into a mist that refracted the sunlight into a rainbow, much like the real dyran's rainbow-hued tail. It wriggled through the air as though it were born for this element, swimming-flying as adroitly as a dolphin at sea.

By the time Phyro got to the open field some distance from the long, low-slung workshop complex, a large crowd had already gathered around where the mechanical dyran had plunged into the ground.

"What do you think?" asked an excited Rati Yera from her wheeled chair, parked next to the long, slender missile sticking out of the ground at a sharp angle. Twenty yards above her, the whirring tail of the machine continued to spin weakly. The motion was now slow enough for Phyro to see that the tail consisted of long, revolving angled blades shaped like the vanes of a windmill, or the wings of the bamboo-copters that children in Amu spun between their hands so that the contraptions leapt into the air like tiny dragonflies. The blades of the missile tail, however, were closed in and pointed straight back, not spread out like the petals of a flower.

"I don't know *what* to think," said Phyro. "That thing almost hit me up there!"

Rati was aghast. "That . . . wasn't part of the plan."

Phyro took several deep breaths to calm himself. No matter how terrifying he had found the experience, he knew he had to show no fear in front of so many. "What—what is that? I've never seen anything like it!"

Rati Yera, despite having never sat for the Imperial examinations, clearly relished the chance to lecture to an audience. Interpreting Phyro's amazement as an invitation, she expounded on her invention.

"Historically, missiles have relied on an application of force only at the beginning of their trajectory—think of catapult stones, arrows, and crossbow bolts—"

"What about fire arrows driven by firework-powder rockets?" asked one of the observers, an archer.

"Even in their case, the acceleration is only near the beginning of the flight," said Rati. "A firework powder rocket doesn't burn for very long, not even if you link several together in stages. The dependence on the injection of force at launch limits the range of missiles."

Everyone nodded.

"But what if we built missiles that could fly like living things?" asked Rati. "What if we gave them beating hearts that powered them throughout their flight?"

"We already have ornithopters," said Phyro.

"Yes, yes, but ornithopters are tiny. Wound-up sinew and compressed springs cannot generate enough power for large missiles, missiles that will do real damage."

Rati went on to paint a vision of how silkmotic mills regulated by even-tempered archons could power mechanical dyrans to change the course of battle.

The silkmotic bolts that had almost become synonymous with Marshal Gin Mazoti's triumph against the garinafins were not, strictly speaking, "silkmotic" at all. They were essentially giant versions of traditional crossbow bolts, which drew on silkmotic power only in the form of a fuse to detonate the firework powder once the bolt had penetrated the tough skin of the garinafins with its diamond-studded tip. They relied on heavy launch machinery carried by capital airships, which Phyro couldn't afford, and their range was still very limited.

But everything changed once Rati reimagined the bolts as living things, creatures with their own engines independent of an expensive launch system.

Along with the intact silkmotic bolts, Mota's expedition to Zathin Gulf had also retrieved some of the silkmotic reservoirs created from coiled garinafin gut coated in silver. Essentially Ogé jars in the form of long, sinuous tubes, they could be cut up into shorter coils that would fit inside the slender body of a silkmotic bolt.

As a consequence of their large surface area, the garinafin gut coils made capacious silkmotic reservoirs. Once charged, they could power a spinning silkmotic mill for a long time. Rati simplified the design of the mill by attaching the Kana and Rapa poles for driving the silkmotic charge across the blades to the inner and outer surfaces of a single garinafin-gut Ogé jar. An even-tempered archon regulated the rate of discharge and the speed of the mill, though Rati modified Kisli Péro's original design by using compressed springs in place of weighted arms so that the archon could function regardless of the orientation of the missile.

And by adopting the propeller design of a bamboo-copter, Rati created a spinning tail that could be driven by the silkmotic mill to deliver thrust to the missile. Stabilizing fins along the outside kept the missile heading in a specific direction and allowed it to be steered. A mechanism similar to that used in the ornithopters guided the missile along a predetermined flight program, with the spinning mill itself providing the timing signal for the instructions.

"How long can a mechanical dyran like this fly?" Phyro asked.

"This mill, which I've been charging with a water-powered silk-motic generator for several days, managed to keep the prototype flying for half an hour," Rati said. "I'm sure we can increase the range with more refinement to the reservoir as well as the charging technique. Once we pack the body with firework powder and another small Ogé jar as the fuse, a mechanical dyran can be launched by a single soldier to destroy a garinafin from miles away. Even the Marshal didn't have weapons like this."

Ofluro, who was also among the onlookers, shuddered involuntarily. A survivor of the Battle of Zathin Gulf, he recalled vividly how the silkmotic bolts had terrorized the Lyucu host. Though he now served the Emperor of Dara, he couldn't help but feel conflicted about this new terror about to be unleashed against his own people.

"*Rénga*, I know you wanted to preserve the silkmotic bolts as memorials to history," said Rati. "But just as your parents would be honored to see you giving up mementos of them to aid the families of martyred veterans, I think it would honor the Marshal and those who fought with her to see us adapt the old into the new, turning their dead bolts into living mechanical dyrans to bring freedom to the people of Unredeemed Dara."

Phyro was moved by the speech, but he didn't react visibly. Instead, he continued to silently ponder the prototype missile sticking out of the ground before him. He could see its potential. With that increased range, it was hundreds of times more powerful than the Marshal's old bolts. And Rati had managed to make the weapon practical by recycling costly components that he could not possibly afford.

Yet, it was useless.

"We can't use this," said Phyro, his voice cracking with regret, "at least not in the way you envision."

"Why not?" Rati asked in confusion.

"A range of many miles is of little import if a missile cannot be aimed," said Phyro, putting a comforting hand on her shoulder. "A mechanical dyran is, after all, not a true living being. It's blind and without intelligence, like an ornithopter. The even-tempered archon is like a man trapped inside a camera obscura with the pinhole welded shut. He can contemplate and regulate his own breathing, but he has no awareness of the world outside.

"How can we possibly hope to strike a target from miles away by plotting in an unalterable course at the start? By the time the missile arrived at its destination, the garinafin would have long seen its approach and moved out of the way. Ornithopters can be useful because we'll be deploying them in large swarms at short range, but we can't possibly make enough mechanical dyrans for that tactic to work."

As Phyro spoke, Rati's face went through a complicated series of emotions: surprise, denial, defiance, thoughtfulness, and eventually, defeat.

One consequence of working for a boss who was free from vanity was unvarnished criticism.

"Once again, I've been so blinded by the pleasures of inventing something new," said Rati, dejected, "that I neglected to keep in mind the aim for which we invent."

"Don't be so hard on yourself," said Phyro. "Without blind exploration, perhaps nothing interesting would *ever* be invented."

Before heading back to the garinafin training grounds, Phyro offered a few thoughts—most of them impractical—on how the mechanical dyrans *could* still be used. For instance, he suggested, with sufficient scouting, it might be possible to instruct the missiles with the coordinates of distant Lyucu city-ships when the fleet was still below the horizon, and strike them from afar. However, such precision seemed well beyond the realm of what was feasible.

Nonetheless, Rati was grateful for the emperor's solicitude.

Rati tried to focus on other challenges, but the dream of the mechanical dyrans would not leave her alone. Sometimes, when she tried to work out other problems, her mind would wander and drift off, and then she would be startled to find herself staring at another sketch of a mechanical dyran on the page.

Meanwhile, Phyro sent more expeditions to Zathin Gulf to retrieve the remains of dead warriors and artifacts from the old battle. He was adamant that the souls of the martyrs should find rest under the earth and that their history not be forgotten.

Rati couldn't help but see this as a sign. She recalled an old folk myth concerning the dyran. It was said that the rainbow-tailed flying fish never died of old age. Rather, in their senescence, dyrans with faded scales and ragged tails dove into underwater volcanoes, only to emerge moments later with their tails resplendent and scales glowing, sleek as though they had been reborn.

The past wasn't dead. It cried to be reborn.

But how? How could mechanical dyrans be given intelligence and sight? How could the even-tempered archon open the hole in the camera obscura and let the light in?

She wrote to Kisli Péro, seeking advice.

My Dearest Rati,

Thank you for your latest letter. The puzzle you pose is most intriguing.

But first, let me update you on a few other matters of mutual interest.

I showed sketches of your bamboo-copter-inspired propellers to colleagues in the underwater engineering group. They're very excited, thinking it might provide a more efficient means of driving mechanical crubens than the waving tails currently used. They'll perform some trials and may follow up with more questions for you.

You mentioned in passing the need for large quantities of oil of vitriol, from which I deduce that you might be interested in a novel method for its manufacture. As it happens, a friend, an alchemist at the Imperial Academy in Pan, has been assigned to study more efficient ways to produce various compounds needed for industry. While he was visiting Ginpen this week, I asked him about oil of vitriol. He told me that the most promising method involves the roasting of sulfur-reeking ores from Mount Kana and Mount Rapa in a steam furnace along with acid-decomposed saltpeter. To contain the highly corrosive oil that results from this procedure, large vats lined with sheets of lead must be used. Early prototypes resulted in several explosions, but luckily no one was seriously injured. If you wish to learn more about this method, I can ask him to apply to Farsight Secretary Kidosu for a chance to visit you.

Much to my chagrin, my even-tempered archon turned out to be not entirely unprecedented. When I presented it at a seminar here at Last Bite, mechanical engineering colleagues informed me that a similar idea had been devised to regulate the output of steam engines on mechanical crubens as far back as the time of Emperor Ragin, and mill owners in Géjira also use a similar mechanism to regulate the pressure of millstones in variable winds. To be sure, no one had ever sought to extend their principles to silkmotic mills, and I'm sure you'd comfort me by pointing out that no invention is ever wholly original. Still, my pride was hurt—and I treated myself to a long, hot bath.

In the aftermath, my thoughts turned to the process of discovery. If only there were a better way to quickly spread new discoveries to all the men and women interested in weighing the great fish that is the wonder of nature! It is impossible, even for a researcher at one of the Imperial institutions, to know all the new discoveries and inventions being made in far-flung corners of the empire: by scholars in Imperial laboratories, by street magicians, by monastics in temples, by master artisans in commercial workshops. Whether we seek knowledge for the sake of knowledge, to entertain, to glorify the *gods, or to make profit, we should all benefit by the free exchange of ideas, much as flowers bear sweeter fruit when bees bring pollen from afar.*

Sometimes I feel that we're like the proverbial group of creatures summoned by Lord Tazu to describe to him the nature of a cruben. The crane says the cruben is a featureless floating island; the squid says the cruben is a bottomless pit lined with death-dealing spikes; the remora says the cruben is an ocean-cruising ship that drops food generously; the barnacles say that the cruben is a flat, peltate plate, a good homestead; and the corals say that the cruben is a sharp spear that wreaks havoc. All of us can see merely one corner of this grand universe but are blind to everything else; only by piecing together all the multiplicity of insights can we grasp the whole.

But that is probably more philosophical than practical, which ought to be our focus. And so we come to your question: To endow a mechanical contrivance with intelligence is perhaps a challenge that would stump even the greatest engineer of them all, Na Moji. Rather than trying to soar into the realm of the gods in one leap, perhaps it's best to start with a much more modest approach: Why not harness the intelligence of lesser creatures?

I remain, Artificer, your
obedient servant, Kisli Péro

Kisli's suggestion led to a head-slapping moment for Rati. Once again, her hunger for innovation had forced her to forget the obvious and old. For years, she had made a living through tricks that seemed to borrow animal intelligence for the use of her mechanical contrivances, so why not make what was merely show real? Surely an animal pilot could be trained to guide the mechanical dyrans to home in on enemy garinafins!

First, she added a tiny cockpit to the missile, just behind the tip. Ensconced within, the occupant could see what was directly ahead through the transparent diamond, like a set of windows. Silk strings attached to the stabilizing fins were gathered into the cockpit and connected to a minuscule baton that could be manipulated by paw or snout to steer the missile. It took some time for Rati to design an intricate system of gears and levers to translate the jerky movements of the animal pilot into smooth, precise motion in the fins so that the missile wouldn't tumble out of control.

Once the control mechanism was perfected, it was time to find a suitable pilot. Rati Yera considered the requirements from all angles: The creature had to fit inside the cockpit, be trainable, possess enough intelligence to understand what a garinafin was, and be sharp-eyed so that it could steer a fast-flying missile toward a distant target. These criteria ruled out most insects and reptiles. Mammals such as cats and weasels, natural hunters, were considered but ultimately rejected because most of them panicked when placed inside a flying vehicle. Monkeys, with their natural intelligence, would have been a good choice except they were too rare and just a little too big. This left birds as the only reasonable and practical choice.

Rati asked Widi and Arona to scour the markets of metropolises throughout Dara to recruit street performers with interesting acts involving birds. After they were vetted and inducted into the emperor's cause, the expert trainers were brought to Tiro Cozo.

Rati explained what she had in mind; the trainers reacted with disbelief.

"How are we supposed to train the birds to pilot a living weapon when we won't be in the sky with them?" demanded the trainers. "What you ask is impossible."

"The first time Luan Zyaji soared over Mapidéré's procession on his stringless kite, many also exclaimed the sight impossible," said Rati. "Our job, ladies and gentlemen, is to make the impossible real."

The trainers huddled, and after days of heated debate, emerged with a plan: a simulated training environment that they called "ersatz reality."

They began with a replica of the transparent tip and cockpit of the mechanical dyran. A segment of bamboo was cleft down the middle to create a semi-tubular "seat" in the cockpit. A pilot trainee—a sparrow, siskin, crested mynah, or pigeon—was then strapped into the seat, head first, leaving it free to peck at the control baton. This replica dyran's head was then suspended in the middle of a large room whose floor, ceiling, and walls were covered with scale models of mountains, coasts, forests, fields, rivers, and even clouds—generated by piped steam—to simulate the bird's-eye view. In response to the tiny avian pilot's pecking at the control baton, the model dyran's head would be moved around and the scenery around the room scrolled to reflect the results of the bird pilot's actions.

This ersatz reality mechanism allowed the trainers to teach their charges how to pilot the mechanical dyran without having to launch them into the sky. The scheme caught the young emperor's fancy and he adopted a version of ersatz reality to train his garinafin riders. Using actual garinafins for every training exercise would have overworked the beasts and put inexperienced riders in too much danger. Therefore, a scale-model replica of the terrain of Crescent Island was constructed in an open field, over which trainees could "fly" with hobbyhorses between their legs—except that the horse heads were replaced with shrunken versions of antlered garinafin heads. Although it wasn't quite the same as training with actual garinafins, riders could practice maneuvers, get more "flight time," and familiarize themselves with what they would see from their aerial mounts without much danger or expense. Indeed, after a while, hobby-garinafin racing became a favorite pastime among garinafin riders, especially after the consumption of multiple flasks of rice beer.

However, in spite of the dedication of the trainers, progress on teaching birds to be pilots soon stalled. Birds were meant to fly under their own power, and being strapped into a confined space and forced to alter their position by pecking at a tiny stick proved an experience too alien for their nature. Moreover, when confronted with a fire-breathing model garinafin, the avian pilot's instinct was to swerve away, not to head toward it.

After weeks of fruitless effort, Rati Yera had to abandon the failed experiment. In truth, she had to admit that she felt more relieved than disappointed. The notion of training tiny avian minds so that they could act as suicide weapons in a war without their understanding or consent bothered her. Even if the tactic worked, it would be a stain upon the idealistic emperor's war of liberation. She didn't feel silly or weak for such scruples.

Ideals are why we follow him, after all.

My Dearest Rati,

I am so excited that I hardly know where to start.

As I must have already told you, Master Miza Crun is the leader of the silkmotic group here at Last Bite. Recently, he has tasked me with investigating the silkmotic channeling and damming capacities of various substances in the hope of discovering an even better channeling material than silver, which would aid the construction of more capacious Ogé jars and more efficient circuits.

I decided to focus my efforts on unusual substances and consulted my colleagues and friends for suggestions. Do you recall the novel method of producing oil of vitriol that you're trying to adopt? My alchemist friend wrote back and informed me that after cooking each batch of oil of vitriol, the furnace and lead-lined tanks are coated with a noxious sludge, in which are found various substances, some known, some unknown, all likely refined from the sulfur-odored ore. Along with his letter, my friend sent samples of some of these materials. Curious, I began experimenting with them right away.

It's well known that channeling capacity is an inherent characteristic of the substance that, though it may change with temperature, humidity, and other conditions, is generally unique with respect to each substance. It may be used, in conjunction with other features, to identify different materials.

To measure the channeling capacity of a substance, we normally employ a device invented by Master Miza Crun called a crunometer, which takes advantage of the tendency for the silkmotic current flowing through a wire to deflect a compass needle placed near the wire. The stronger the silkmotic current, the greater the deflection.

I was able to identify many of the sludge-derived substances, but one particular material puzzled me. The specimens I received came in the form of grayish beads, and none of my alchemical colleagues knew what they were. They did not appear to be metallic, and my initial crunometer tests, conducted after a long day of other investigations, revealed little to no silkmotic channeling capacity. I pushed the gray pellets into the growing pile of damming materials and lost interest in them.

The next day, I lost a whole morning to drafting a report justifying my travel expenses for the past month—oh, how I envy you, Rati, for not having to deal with auditors from the dreaded Budget Office. After a long soak in the tub—I find midday baths so invigorating—I was only too glad to be able to return to my experiments in the afternoon. It's my habit, when resuming an investigation after a long bureaucratic interruption, to repeat the last experiment performed before the break. The practice eases my mind back into the flow of work. Thus, I tested the channeling capacity of the gray pellets again.

Imagine my surprise, if you can, when the pellets appeared to channel the flow of the silkmotic force almost as well as a metal! I repeated the test several times just to be sure. I congratulated myself on the fortuitous decision to repeat the test, as the crunometer had apparently been malfunctioning the evening before. I moved the gray beads back over to the pile of channeling materials, determined to examine them closer later.

After dinner, I returned to the laboratory to try out the gray substance as a component in a silkmotic mill. To my annoyance, the mill refused to spin at all. On a hunch, I brought out the crunometer again, and this time, the pellets showed almost no channeling capacity.

I was most puzzled. Clearly something was wrong. I went and borrowed a few other crunometers from other junior investigators, but they all showed the same result. The gray substance did not allow the flow of the silkmotic force.

I examined my notes of the previous experiments. There did not seem to be any changes in conditions that would result in such a drastic difference in outcome. What was I missing?

Just then, a cleaning crew came to my laboratory. Secretary Kidosu was about to arrive in Last Bite for an inspection, and

Archon Thu wanted every room to look spotless and orderly. Maids and footmen entered with mops, buckets, dust rags, and brooms, and I told them to carry on with their work and not mind me, as I just needed to wrap up my investigation notes and then head to bed to puzzle over the mystery.

I like to keep the laboratory fairly dim in the evenings—it makes it easier to see the sparks from the silkmotic force, a sight that I never tire of. But this made the cleaning crew's jobs harder. They asked if they could turn up the silkmotic lamps and bring in more light, and I assented. Soon, the place was as bright as day.

Just then I seemed to hear a voice, gentle as a bubbling spring, whispering in my ear, "Look at the crunometer."

No member of the cleaning crew was anywhere near me. Confused, I looked up from the unfinished notes and my eyes landed on the crunometer, still connected to a gray bead: The needle was jumping, indicating the flow of a silkmotic current.

I couldn't believe it. The unknown substance that had earlier dammed the silkmotic current was channeling again. I leaned over the crunometer to take a closer look, and the needle, like an eel retreating into its reef hideout, swung back to showing no current. Yet, as soon as I sat back, the needle jumped wildly. It was like the needle was playing hide-and-seek with me!

I turned my head to look at the bright lights behind me; I turned back and saw the sharp shadow I cast against the desk and wall. I realized that when I first tested the substance it had also been in the evening and the second time it had been the middle of the day.

Could it be?

I moved my hand over the gray pellet in the crunometer, immersing it in shadow. The needle swung to zero. I moved my hand away, bathing it in light. The needle began to jump.

The cleaning crew must have thought I had lost my mind as I rushed over, wild-eyed, and grabbed one of the lamps out of the hands of a young maid. I placed the lamp right next to the crunometer and watched as the needle swung far to the right. I danced and whooped with joy as the crew stared at me, dumbfounded.

Rati, can you believe it? I've found a substance that channels the silkmotic force only when it is doused in light! I've discovered ocu-lium, a substance that can see.

What fortune, what luck, what unimaginable coincidence has allowed me to discover this wondrous secret of nature!

I remain, Artificer, your
obedient servant, Kisli Péro

Rati Yera woke Phyro before the first crow of the rooster, insisting that he dispatch his personal airship to Ginpen to fetch Kisli Péro.

"There's not a moment to waste!" she shouted.

Kisli arrived late in the evening, long after the stars had spun halfway through their nightly course and everyone was supposed to be in bed. Thinking she would relax a bit before going to sleep, she hauled water from the well, heated it over the stove, and filled her bath barrel—it had been a long, tiring journey; they were flying against a headwind almost the whole way, and at one point she had taken up an oar herself because the pilot explained that the emper-or's orders had been to "make all haste."

She sprinkled some bath salts given to her by an alchemist friend from Müning—supposed to do wonders for the skin—and inhaled the fragrant steam appreciatively. Just as she was sinking into the bath barrel to give her sore muscles a much-needed treat, Rati Yera barged in—literally. She had augmented her wheeled chair with a silkmotic mill, which allowed her to roam the workshop and train-ing grounds freely, checking in on the progress of various projects and shouting at her apprentices, much like a dockmaster inspecting a busy harbor on her barge.

Kisli ducked into the water so that only her head was peeking out the top. "By the Twins! What is the matter—"

"Get out and get dressed. We have work to do."

"It's the middle of the night! I'm tired—"

"Did you bring all the oculium you have on hand like I asked? Teach me everything you know about it. Everything!"

Reluctantly, Kisli climbed out of her bath. When Rati Yera used that tone, it was like she was everyone's grandmother. Disobedience wasn't an option.

Alone among the cabins and tents of Tiro Cozo, Kisli's guest-house remained lit throughout the night. Moths swarmed outside the window, tapping against the screen like whispering spirits, straining toward the brilliant whale oil lamps inside.

By sunrise, the floor of the guesthouse was covered with engi-neering diagrams and sketches. Between the time of her last letter and now, Kisli had devised numerous machines taking advantage of the light-sensitive nature of oculium: an intruder detector for under-ground vaults; a case for secret letters that would incinerate the con-tents if its seal was tampered with; a mechanical rooster that crowed as soon as the sky grew bright enough; a self-filling bath barrel that began heating as soon as it got dark so that the water would be at the temperature for a bath at bedtime. . . .

"You're entirely too obsessed with hot baths," said Rati, shaking her head.

"There are two kinds of people in the world," said Kisli, "those who understand that the progress of civilization is measured by better ways to take baths, and barbarians."

"Enough theorizing," said Rati. "Show me!"

Yawning and squinting against the rising sun, Kisli set up the model silkmotic mill to give Rati a demonstration of the properties of this most marvelous material. Rati watched as the Ogé jars, mod-ified with oculium probes, were pushed closer to the silkmotic mill, causing it to spin under the bright sun. When Kisli leaned over the contraption and shaded the oculium probes from the sunlight, the mill stopped.

"That's it?" asked Rati.

"Uh . . . yes," said Kisli.

"Can it distinguish shapes, colors, sizes?" asked Rati.

Kisli shook her head.

"Can it be taught to respond to silhouettes of a certain design?"

Kisli shook her head.

Rati stared at the gray, unremarkable lumps of oculium. The fan-tastic machines Kisli had sketched had led Rati to expect far more from this substance. "It's not really an eye at all," she said, dejected. "The oculium is no more sensitive than an orchid that knows to open its petals at dusk and to close them at dawn. How can this be used to guide a missile to a garinafin?"

"My mother used to tell me a story about Fithowéo, the god of war," said Kisli. "After he was blinded by Kiji's lightning bolts, an orchid in a dark, dank cave taught him to 'see' even though he could no longer detect a single pinprick of light."

"Are you suggesting that we should think about how to see like Fithowéo?" asked Rati, bemused.

Kisli gestured grandly. "Not at all. But we possess many more advantages than Lord Fithowéo in that cave."

"How so?"

"Here we are, able to tell light from shadow like that orchid, able to wield the silkmotic force like Lord Kiji, and best of all, able to take a hot bath whenever we want to."

Rati had to laugh, shaking her head.

"I think we should continue that bath you interrupted. Trust me, every problem will seem easier after a nice long hot bath."

Rati and Kisli soaked in their bath barrels side by side.

"Hey, don't go to sleep on me," said Rati. Despite the fragrant steam wafting around her head, she didn't sound relaxed at all. "You said you wanted a bath, not a nap."

"Who can sleep with you yammering incessantly like that?" said Kisli, her head resting against the rim of the barrel with a folded washcloth over her eyes. She sighed. Clearly, Rati would not be dissuaded from working even now. "Go ahead. I'm ready to be the dutiful floor on which you bounce your ideas."

"When Grand Princess Théra and Secretary Kidosu led the effort to discover the secret of garinafin fire breathing," said Rati, "they gathered knowledge of fire-making techniques from all the Islands so that they could study them in detail and derive the garinafin mechanism by analogy."

"Right," said Kisli. "Oh, and there was such a romantic story about the two of them—"

"Stay focused," said Rati. "I'm thinking we could use that as a model for understanding the secret of sight. We should study how real eyes work—whether they belong to fish, fowl, or fellow beast—so we can build a mechanical eye that can really *see*."

"But neither of us is an expert in zoology—" Kisli took the washcloth off her eyes and looked over at Rati. "Oh no, you've got that look—"

"Listen!" said Rati, her eyes glowing with excitement. "The two of us may not be able to solve this problem, but there are many more clever minds in Dara. You must have lots of colleagues at the Imperial laboratories and the Imperial Academy who specialize in the secrets of living beings. Can't you ask for their help?"

"I can try," said Kisli, looking troubled. "But it's one thing to ask me and my friends to share with you incidental insights related to our assigned research, and quite another to ask for a comprehensive review of animal vision. No one I know is working on that subject right now, so people will have to be reassigned and the budget reallocated—"

"Surely Secretary Kidosu can make this into a top priority for all the Imperial research institutions, much as understanding garinafin anatomy was the dedicated focus of the top minds of Dara a decade ago—"

Kisli shook her head. "That was a time of war, before the present system of bureaucratic oversight had been instituted. Farsight Secretary Kidosu administers the system of Imperial research laboratories, but she doesn't have free rein. All the laboratories have specific research goals and budgets, approved in advance by the Inner Council. Empress Jia has always said that since the Imperial laboratories are funded by the taxes of the people of Dara, our work must benefit everyone."

"But developing weapons against the Lyucu *does* benefit everyone."

"Empress Jia doesn't want there to be war at all. And while the emperor may focus his team here in Tiro Cozo on weapons research, military application is not at all a priority for the rest of us."

Rati was finally getting an inkling of the inertia of the peaceful prosperity Phyro was running up against. "So how does the Inner Council determine the budgets and research directions for the various laboratories?"

"Like with most things under Empress Jia's regency, the decisions are made through a system designed to balance competing interests. Every year, the budget process begins with the College of Advocates and the roaming circuit intendants soliciting petitions from various grassroots groups—"

Rati's head throbbed. As much as she enjoyed designing and building machines, the specifics of Dara's elaborate political machinery always bored her. "Can you just stick to the big picture?"

"All right. The point is, there's an ongoing process for associations of business owners, guilds, farmers' leagues, and prominent noble families to submit requests for aid from the Imperial Academy and the Imperial laboratories. After the College of Advocates collates these requests into formal petitions, they're submitted to the Inner Council, where ministers debate the needs of the various regions and industries in order to arrive at a list of research priorities and budgets. For instance, in one year, zoology experts may be directed to focus on the blight decimating the silkworm farms in Haan, while the mechanical engineers are supposed to improve the efficiency of water mills in Géjira. And in the year after that, they may be directed to look into the diseases affecting the cattle herds in Faça and the maintenance of dams in Géfica instead."

"I never realized that the Imperial laboratories worked on so many practical problems," marveled Rati. In her mind, she had pictured the researchers at the Imperial institutions like scholars in the old folk operas, walking about with their heads among the clouds.

"You're not alone," Kisli said, more than a hint of bitterness in her voice. "Unlike the other ministries like justice, treasury, rituals, and agriculture, whose work is more readily visible, the work of the Imperial laboratories tends to be undervalued because we don't always succeed in solving our problems. Every year, some freshly minted *pana méji* considers themselves brilliant for proposing a reduction in the Imperial laboratories' budget in order to lower taxes, and every year, the heads of the laboratories have to come before the

Inner Council to justify what they've accomplished in the past year. I always feel like my job is hanging by a thread. But the truth is, lots of people, from wealthy landlords and tycoons with hundreds of workshops to laborers and peasants struggling to eke out a living, benefit from the fruits of our research. We've found countless ways to improve the yield of crops, to grow healthier pigs and chickens, to weave smoother silk, to build stronger bridges, to fulfill Emperor Ragin's dream of a better Dara."

"I guess that makes it difficult to have everyone drop what they're working on to help me figure out how to make mechanical eyes," said Rati, feeling sheepish.

"That's right," said Kisli. "Even Secretary Kidosu can't dictate what everyone should be working on just by snapping her fingers. Under the regency, things are no longer so loose and informal as in the days of yore—"

She was interrupted by a loud and long meow.

"How cute!" exclaimed Kisli. There was a cat with fur the color of a purebred snow dove in the corner of the guest room. "It's like a little dandelion puff ball, all white."

"I've never seen that cat before," said Rati. "Wonder if it belongs to one of the cooks. They've been saying that there's a mouse problem in the kitchen."

Kisli made kissing noises at the cat from her bath barrel and dangled a hand down to pet it, but the cat stayed in its corner and licked its paws, ignoring Kisli.

"Proud little puff ball, that one," said Kisli. "Reminds me of the doves I saw at the hot bathing pools near the Rufizo Falls, all aloof while they preened themselves. Maybe if I go get a treat—"

"Forget about the cat," said Rati. "So if I can't make animal vision into a research priority at the Imperial laboratories, what else can I do? Should I speak to doctors and surgeons? Glass-eye makers? Painters? Surely one of them has a deeper understanding of how sight works."

"It's worth a try," said Kisli noncommittally. She dangled her wet washcloth and waved it around to try to attract the cat, who steadfastly continued to ignore her.

"Or maybe I should speak to the blind to learn how they compensate for the sense of sight," mused Rati. "Maybe your story about Lord Fithowéo should be our inspiration." The white cat stopped licking its paws and shook its head rapidly, as though trying to get rid of a bothersome fly. "There are lots of animals who don't have good eyes—I seem to recall that moles can barely tell when it's light out—and they may be a good model—"

"Honestly, Rati, I think you're coming at this the wrong way," said Kisli. She dropped the wet washcloth, apparently giving up on the quest to get the white cat to come to her. Picking up a small hand mirror by the bath barrel, she wiped away the condensation.

"What do you mean?"

"When you have a problem, you always want to confront it head-on," said Kisli. "That's an admirable trait. But sometimes you have to consider whether you're solving the right problem. For example, I was not having much success in getting Puff Ball to play with me, but really, I should have been thinking like a cat."

Kisli was using the mirror to reflect the sun onto the opposite wall. The white cat leapt after the bright, dancing spot excitedly, totally absorbed by the game.

Rati looked thoughtful as she sank back into her barrel.

Am I trying to solve the right problem? Is it really the secret of sight that I'm after?

She glanced at the window, which had misted over from the steam of the baths. A few planters sat on the windowsill, growing trained bamboo shoots, dwarf pines, clumps of safflower, and a few orchids. She had kept these plants around the compound as a reminder of the Blossom Gang, now that they were scattered all across the Islands. The safflowers and orchid flowers leaned toward the window, like curious cats peering at the sun.

There was also a planter of sunflowers. She had planted these because the sunflower was said to be the favorite flower of Lord Lutho, the patron of those seeking knowledge. The Ano poets used to compare scholars hungry for knowledge to sunflowers hungry for the light of enlightenment. On this south-facing windowsill, the sunflowers had followed the course of the sun from east to west every day, silently turning back to the east during the night to await the next dawn.

Kisli was saying something, but Rati no longer heard her, her thoughts filled with visions of swarming moths tapping against the screen, an excited cat chasing after a bright spot of light, and the orderly, almost imperceptibly slow turning of thousands of golden faces in unison in a sunflower field.

The demonstration was scheduled at night.

"Why can't I bring a torch?" complained Phyro as he almost tripped over a rock in the field. "And on a night with the new moon, too."

"*Rénga*, I picked tonight *because* it's the new moon," said Rati Yera. "You should have listened to me and stayed in darkness for at least half an hour to allow your eyes to adjust."

It was pitch-black. Rati had ordered all torches and lanterns near the testing field extinguished, and none of the dozen or so observers invited along were allowed to bring a light.

"I had way too many reports to read," said Phyro.

"You should have turned off the lights and read the logograms by touch," chided Rati. "Wasn't that how scholars too poor to afford lighting oil studied the Ano Classics at night in old stories?"

"Many of the petitions are from veterans who only know how to write with zyndari letters," said Phyro gently. "They haven't been able to get the magistrates and the circuit intendants to address their grievances and now write to me out of desperation. I may not be able to solve all their problems, but I want to respond to them individually."

Rati fell silent. Even now, her lord sometimes surprised her.

"Why do we have to be in complete darkness?" asked Phyro as Rati brought the procession to a halt.

"With more refinement over time, the system will be more tolerant of some stray light. But for now, it's much too sensitive to risk a test except on the darkest of nights."

"All right," said Phyro, "let's get this demonstration started before the mosquitoes eat all of us alive."

Rati gave a shrill long whistle, soon answered by a short toot from some distance away. A loud *pop*, like an exploding firework, sounded in the same direction, accompanied by a brief flare. Then, everyone heard the distinct sound of large beating wings rising into the night.

"What *is* that?" asked Phyro. "A bat?"

"You'll see," said Rati enigmatically.

Gradually, a glowing shape materialized in the darkness above the observers, its luminosity growing more intense with each passing second. It was a cold, blue light, the ethereal fire of otherworldly life.

Phyro wasn't completely unfamiliar with the phenomenon. Miners in Dara harvested glowing mushrooms from caves and preserved them by drying. When pulverized and rehydrated, the resulting paste luminesced upon exposure to air. It was traditionally used by miners as a safe source of illumination to minimize the risk of subterranean fires.

Phyro squinted at the flapping, glowing wings. "Wait . . . is that a . . . a *baby garinafin?!* Why is it glowing like that? WHAT HAVE YOU DONE?"

"*Rénga*, calm down!" said Rati. "You have to be more observant and patient. Pay attention to its jerky flight path; take note of the stiff motion of the wings—"

"I don't care about any of that! Baby garinafins that size shouldn't be flying at night! What if it gets lost? What if it tires and lands in the wolf-infested mountains? You cannot experiment with irreplaceable—"

"*Rénga! Rénga!*" Rati was growing exasperated. "That isn't a baby garinafin at all! It's an exact one-thirty-sixth scale *model* of a garinafin. At that size, the wound-up sinew won't be able to keep the model aloft for long, so you need to—"

"That—that—that's a giant ornithopter?"

"Yes, I guess you can think of it that way—though technically, since it glides more than it flies—"

"Why didn't you just say that in the first place?"

"Err . . . I wanted to add a little drama to the demonstration—"

Phyro gritted his teeth. "When it comes to garinafins, I don't want any 'drama.' Do you understand?"

"All right. All right. Anyway, the garinafin model isn't the point. It's just a target."

"A target? For what?"

Instead of answering, Rati put two fingers in her mouth and gave another two quick shrill whistles. Two quick toots from a spot nearby but hidden in darkness responded, and with another loud *pop*, some invisible *presence* shot into the air. A high-pitched droning noise whined overhead.

"What *is* that?" asked Phyro.

"Just watch. I'll explain everything later."

The glowing model garinafin continued to flap its wings jerkily, following an erratic, unpredictable course: diving one second, swooping the next, soaring straight up for dozens of wingbeats before turning sharply to the left and gliding down in tight spirals.

Phyro felt dizzy just trying to follow the luminescent creature with his eyes.

"The exact course followed by the garinafin is known only to the apprentice who drilled the instruction cork," said Rati. "To ensure the integrity of the experiment, I asked her to work alone, and to plot out the flight plan by rolling a pair of dice so that no predictable pattern would be unwittingly encoded into the instructions. No one knows where the model garinafin is going to go."

The droning from the invisible hunter whirled overhead as it circled around in the darkness. Far above, the model garinafin shone as brightly as the full moon.

Suddenly, the pitch of the droning changed as the hunter seemed to have caught the scent of its prey. The noise grew fainter but more high-pitched as it sped away.

"What's going on—" a confused Phyro began, but then had to duck and avert his eyes as the model garinafin disappeared in a blinding flash. A moment later, the observers heard the dull, deep rumble of the explosion.

By the time Phyro's eyes had recovered and he could look up again, there was a brilliant ball of fire in the sky that slowly crumbled into a shower of fading sparks.

Rati whooped, as did her apprentices and assistants. Amidst cheers and applause, torches were lit and lamps uncovered.

"Explain," said Phyro, squinting in the sudden abundance of light.

～

Back inside Phyro's command tent, surrounded by the emperor's most trusted aides and garinafin riders, Rati waxed professorial concerning her new secret weapon, the "sunflower."

The group stood around a partially disassembled missile lying on a table. Half of the tubular bamboo shaft had been removed to reveal an interior packed full of components: thin but strong silk strings, spinning gears, levers actuating vanes and flaps, coiled garinafin gut like loops of sausage. . . .

"You're looking at a quarter-scale model of a sunflower, just like the prototype that shot down the decoy garinafin earlier," said Rati. "Don't worry, this one has been completely disarmed."

The sunflower was a modified version of the mechanical dyran. Like the "unintelligent" missiles, the sunflower used the exact same silkmotic bolt shell, diamond-tipped head, varnished silk fins for steering and stability, and spinning propellers driven by silkmotic mill for propulsion. But instead of relying on a predrilled instruction cork for guidance, the sunflower was piloted by a system Rati designated the "phototropic archon."

Carefully, Rati took apart the head of the missile to reveal a ring with multiple gray beads embedded around it, like a miniature diadem. The royal imagery was only emphasized as Rati lifted it up, revealing a cascade of thin wires trailing from the rim like the veil of the Imperial crown.

"This device, called the ring-eye, is the key to the operation of the phototropic archon. These gray beads are made of oculium, a mineral that channels silkmotic force in proportion to the amount of light it's exposed to."

The ring-eye was placed immediately behind the diamond tip of the missile (though in this model, the tip was glass). The diadem-frame contained multiple flaring teeth, each one curled over a single bead of oculium, such that each oculium bead could only be fully illuminated by light coming from a specific direction. Each oculium bead was then connected to a circuit powered by a tiny silkmotic mill that controlled a fin on the same side of the missile as the bead. The ring-eye and the associated set of silkmotic mills together made up the phototropic archon.

"I'm not sure I fully understand the principle of this apparatus," said Phyro, his brows still furrowed after carefully examining the bundle of wires.

Rati proceeded to sketch a picture on the table.

"Take the simplified example of a missile with two oculium sensors, one on the left, one on the right. And suppose there is a source of light ahead of the missile, but off to the left side. The amount of light falling on the left oculium sensor will be greater than the light falling on the right oculium sensor, meaning that the silkmotic mill connected to the left fin will be spinning with more force than the one connected to the right fin. The greater force applied against the left fin deforms it, which increases the drag on the left side of the missile. The net effect will be to curve the flight path of the missile to the left, bending it toward the source of light.

"But as the missile continues to turn to the left, it will eventually overshoot, placing the source of light on the right side of the missile's nose. The amount of light falling on the right oculium bead will be greater than the amount falling on the left oculium bead, and the mill connected to the right fin will now spin with more force than the one connected to the left bead. Therefore, the fin on the left relaxes and return to its previous shape, while the right fin is deformed. The net effect will be to curve the flight path of the missile back to the right, once again bending it toward the source of light.

"By waving back and forth like this, the phototropic archon plots a course toward the source of light, taking into account the missile's own motion, gradually homing in on the source of light like a snake slithering toward its prey through the grass."

Understanding and admiration flooded Phyro's face. "You've opened the pinhole in the camera obscura, bringing light to the oscillation of the even-tempered archon."

"That's the gist of it," said Rati, nodding with approval. "The actual control scheme of the sunflower is more complicated because it operates in three dimensions. But it is simply an elaboration of the principle illustrated by my example."

"What happens when there is no light hitting any of the oculium beads?"

"Ah, you're thinking of a situation when the light source is too faint or far away, or when there's no illuminated target at all. In that case, there is a default cork cylinder that will take over. The instructions on that cork will keep the missile flying around in a circular pattern, with occasional sudden changes of direction. The sunflower will maintain that hunting pattern until light actuates one of the silkmotic mills—meaning a target has been sighted—at which point the phototropic archon takes over."

"You've really thought of everything."

Phyro asked Rati to reconnect the wires in the model and bid his aides extinguish all the lamps in the tent. Then, opening a flap in a shaded lamp to let out a narrow beam of light, he directed the light-finger against the separate beads in the ring-eye in turn to actuate the associated mills, control fins, and stabilizing vanes so that he really grasped how the weapon functioned. Just as he had to know the limits and capabilities of his soldiers to command them, the emperor believed that he had to understand the limitations and functional principles of his weapons to wield them effectively.

Satisfied, he put the lamp away and asked for the tent to be relit.

"During the day, the system cannot function effectively because there's too much light everywhere," said Rati.

As if to illustrate her point, all the mills whirled to life and all the fins became deformed. The sunflower writhed on the table like a worm. She quickly disconnected the wires and sighed with relief as the chaotic movements subsided.

"I'm sure we can improve the system in various ways, *Rénga*. For instance, we can increase the sensitivity of the ring-eye with purer beads of oculium. As well, we can use lenses to gather and focus more light on the oculium sensors to enhance the range of vision. But I suspect the sunflower will always work best when there are only a handful of strong light sources around for it to home in on—"

"You never stop thinking of ways to improve, do you? Oh, but I love that name, Rati. A sunflower looks just like a dandelion, only much grander. It's a most auspicious name for a weapon that will allow the House of Dandelion to smite the Lyucu as decisively as Na-aroénna once smote the army of the tyrant Mapidéré."

Rati chuckled to herself and shook her head. If Kisli were around, the sly woman would probably tease Rati that she had picked the name to flatter her lord. But she really had named it literally, because following the "sun" was exactly what the missile did. How the gods loved to play jokes.

"I don't want you to be overconfident," cautioned Rati. "As you can see, the sunflower has many weaknesses, and you'll have to plan carefully before deploying it—"

"In time, Rati, in time. I can only absorb so much information at once; right now, my head is spinning like one of your silkmotic mills. . . . I haven't been this amazed since the day Miza Crun first showed me the wonders of the silkmotic force. How did you come up with all of this? You're the greatest engineer in Dara! Not even Luan Zyaji or Zomi Kidosu is your equal."

All of us can see merely one corner of this grand universe but are blind to everything else; only by piecing together all the multiplicity of insights can we grasp the whole.

Rati thought over everything that had led to this moment: Miza Crun's experiments with the silkmotic force; Zomi, Grand Princess Théra, and Marshal Gin Mazoti's joint invention of the silkmotic bolts; Kisli's even-tempered archon; the plants on the windowsill, reminding her of the constant support of her knowledge-craving companions; the discovery of oculium by Kisli's alchemist friend; the playful kitten; the light-following sunflower, Lord Lutho's favorite blossom; all Creation was connected. . . .

"If I can soar so high," she said, looking up with moist eyes at the emperor from her wheeled chair, "it's only because I'm carried on the wings of many others."

CHAPTER TWENTY-SIX

THE BATTLE OF CRESCENT ISLAND, PART III

CRESCENT ISLAND: THE SEVENTH MONTH OF THE
ELEVENTH YEAR OF THE REIGN OF SEASON OF
STORMS AND THE REIGN OF AUDACIOUS FREEDOM.

"Retreat! Retreat!" Goztan shouted. Bone trumpets began to moan, carrying her despondent order across the waves.

The Lyucu garinafins, though startled and tired, beat their wings furiously and turned for the safety of the warmly lit city-ships. Despite the howling monstrous presence in the darkness behind them, there was no panicked scattering, no mindless loss of discipline. The garinafins kept pace with one another, flying in close formation so that those behind could draft in the wing-wake of the leaders to conserve energy.

The shrill whistling, still roving about uncertainly, seemed to grow louder.

"Faster! Fly faster!" Goztan screamed into the night.

But even in retreat, the garinafin riders didn't abandon their fighting instincts. Pursuant to standard Lyucu practice, one of the garinafins, designated as a rearguard for situations like this, turned abruptly in midair and let out a long tongue of fire, sweeping it through the air both as a warning and as an illuminated lure. The other garinafins also turned to hover near it, ready to pounce on whatever threat emerged. In the glow of the bright fire breath, their silhouettes stood out like the shadow puppets of traditional Dara folk opera troupes.

The shrill whistling stopped wandering about and quickly increased in volume.

The garinafin's fire breath grew even more fierce, ready to incinerate whatever peril dared to emerge from the darkness.

The whistling, now so strident that it seemed as though the very stars were screeching, was cut off suddenly as an invisible missile slammed into the fire-breathing garinafin.

An ear-piercing howl of surprise and pain. The fire breath was extinguished. In the darkness, a brief flare of light. A muffled explosion.

The Lyucu riders pressed their bodies against their mounts, expecting to feel the searing heat from a firework-powder bomb. In their experience, such bombs, though ineffective against tough garinafin hide, could kill or maim riders closest to the source.

Instead, they felt cool droplets of water against their faces and arms, as though they were flying through morning fog. Gingerly, they opened their eyes.

The garinafin struck by the missile was unharmed. The explosion had only released a fine mist around the cluster of garinafins. A few wingbeats propelled them out of the mist-cloud.

Fearful that the mist was some caustic acid—though it was hard to imagine how much damage it could do in such small quantities—the riders wiped their faces vigorously. There was no burning sensation, no discomfort at all.

As the riders looked at one another, confused, an eerie glow began to suffuse the air.

The light was coming from the faces and arms of the riders, from the shoulders, necks, and wings of the garinafins, from every spot, wrinkle, crease where the fine droplets clung. And the light was growing brighter by the minute.

Everyone, on the city-ships or in the air, gasped. The garinafins gleamed in the darkness, as though they had been dipped in silver or painted with diamond dust. It was a cold blue light, like the glow of jellyfish and fireflies, but so bright that it was hard to gaze at it directly without squinting.

A new shrill whistling arose in the darkness, growing louder with each passing moment. Unlike before, it didn't wander about in the darkness, but seemed to be headed straight for the glowing garina-fins like a hound that had scented its prey.

Horror washed over Goztan like a tide. "Don't cluster! Scatter!" she cried out, her voice cracking.

The shining garinafins tried to obey, but it was too late. The whistling stopped as another invisible missile struck one of them.

Instead of an explosion, however, there was only a dull thud. Time seemed to slow down as a new source of light, this one red and hot instead of blue and cold, came to life inside the struck gari-nafin, growing heartbeat by heartbeat. Its whole body swelled, the skin stretched taut, the wings spread in agony. Against the dark sky, the glowing figure of the garinafin reminded Goztan of a giant paper-and-bamboo construction found at the native Lantern Festival before Cutanrovo had forbidden the custom.

And then, the garinafin exploded.

A great fireball engulfed the creature, and the riders still aboard were incinerated in an instant. Nearby garinafins scattered like fragments of this new midnight sun as the deafening noise reached the stunned Lyucu observing from the city-ships.

Gradually, the fiery glow faded as chunks of charred garinafin flesh plunged into the cold sea.

Only now did Goztan notice that the shore of Crescent Island was completely dark, without even a single lit torch on any of the Dara ships. The only bright spots in the all-consuming darkness were the blue-glowing garinafins, hovering uncertainly like self-illuminating denizens of the inky deep, and the red-glowing decks of the city-ships, limned and colored by flickering torches like pockets of civilization in a lightless wilderness.

More shrill screeches pierced the darkness, and moments later, a second moon-garinafin turned into a fiery exploding sun. Almost simultaneously, a missile slammed into the center of a glowing ring of torches on one of the city-ships, and the resulting explosion killed or maimed dozens of warriors nearby.

It was as though Fithowéo, the blind war god of Dara, who never saw but also never missed, was hurling spears leisurely at the Lyucu from the darkness.

Finally, Goztan understood. She turned to the trumpeters and screamed, "Douse all the torches on all the city-ships! They're attracted by light! Tell the garinafins to dive into the sea and wash off the glow-paint!"

The trumpeters repeated her order with a series of patterned toots. Naros and culeks on the city-ships scrambled to extinguish the torches while the surviving garinafin riders guided their mounts to descend into the dark sea.

The maneuver was highly dangerous. Garinafins were not natural swimmers, and taking off from the water in their exhausted state was no sure thing. At least one garinafin, with too little lift gas left, drowned with all its riders. And one more garinafin was struck by an invisible missile before it could be fully cleansed. But the rest managed to wash off the glowing paint and heaved themselves back into the air, their riders clinging to the netting, coughing, hacking, half-drowned.

The invisible hunters continued to roam the air, emitting that shrill, intolerable screech. Goztan, now in complete darkness, gritted her teeth. She had no choice. "Order the garinafins to search the shoreline for the launch point of these weapons," she barked to the trumpeters. "We have to destroy the source! But don't breathe fire. Claw and maw only!"

The sea-drenched riders guided their mounts, now on their last reserves of lift gas, over the featureless cliffs of the Crescent Island shoreline. Sweeping this way and that, they desperately sought some sign of the enemy. Surely, with thousands of souls gathered here, there must be a spark, a hint of where the deadly light-seeking bolts were coming from.

Multiple loud whistles roamed the air, screaming from every direction. Invisible terrors seemed omnipresent: above, below, west, east, south, north.

The riders felt themselves sliding toward total panic as they strained against the darkness. Meanwhile, their mounts whipped their heads about and flicked their ears back and forth, beating their wings wildly as they tried to dodge the unseen threats. The cacophony of whistling grew to ear-shattering volume as multiple *presences*, large and menacing, darted past the hovering garinafins, like giant sharks herding a school of fish in the lightless abyss.

The garinafins could no longer bear the strain. Disregarding their pilots and training, they snapped their jaws and began to spew fire, giving in to the instinct to do *something, anything*, to ward off the invisible predators. Bright plumes of fire dotted the dark shore, like a fireworks display on New Year's.

"No! No!" Goztan howled, beating her fists helplessly against the gunwale of the city-ship.

Once again, Rufira Tan, the clever Lyucu pilot who had evaded the swarms of ornithopters earlier, decided to try something unorthodox. While his panicked mount thrashed and tossed, breathing fire randomly and buckling off riders who weren't strapped in, he wrapped his arms and legs about the slender neck of the beast and shimmied up until he was next to its head. Stroking the massive cranium gently, he sang into its ears.

> *Feel my arms around you, my eyes on you;*
> *Feel my breath against you, my voice through you.*
> . . .

The old lullaby worked. Gradually, the garinafin calmed down. Once again, Rufira thanked the gods for assigning him to such a trusting creature and vowed to take care of it if he managed to escape this night alive. Shouting into the garinafin's ear, he directed it to turn back toward the city-ships.

Rufira wasn't proud of this cowardly act. Leaving the other garinafin crews to the mercy of the invisible hunters while escaping himself was very much against Thane Cutanrovo's idea of the Lyucu spirit. A Lyucu warrior was always supposed to stand and fight, never turning his back. But he was beyond caring. If Thane Goztan decided to execute him later for desertion, then so be it. At least he wouldn't die here, without even knowing what these dreaded shadow hunters looked like.

Clinging to one of the garinafin's massive antlers, he continued to shout encouragement into its ear: "Good boy! Just keep your mouth shut and fly."

Loud explosions sounded behind them.

The garinafin whipped its head around in fright, and after a dizzying moment as the world shifted around him, Rufira found himself staring at a sight at once horrifying and beautiful.

The remnants of several exploded garinafins hung in the air near the shore, like shattered constellations. As he watched, invisible bolts slammed into the remaining garinafins, still breathing fire, and each blossomed into eye-searing eruptions before fading into the eternal night.

As the noises from the explosions subsided, the persistent whistling returned. The demonic predators continued to circle in the night, looking for prey.

"Fly! Fly!" shouted Rufira. "But don't breathe fire! O gods, please, *please* don't breathe fire!"

The drained garinafin put on a final burst of speed. It was running out of lift gas, and it could feel itself sinking lower in the air. The demonic whining grew louder.

Rufira peered into the darkness ahead. Torches came to life in the distance, outlining the decks of the city-ships. His heart beat wildly. Thane Goztan and the rest of the Lyucu were doing what they could to help. By putting up torches, they were trying to lure away the light-seeking shadows and guide him home!

But the city-ships were still so far.

The garinafin knew it would never make it.

Defiantly, it whipped its wings and turned in midair. It wasn't going to go down without a fight.

"No! *No!*" screamed Rufira, scrambling over the gigantic head to wrap his arms about the jaws of the beast, hoping to act as a human muzzle.

But it was no use. The garinafin was no longer his to command. It had returned to that primal state in which it lived only by instinct. With a quick snap of its neck, it tossed Rufira away, as casually as it might rid itself of a nettlesome parasite. The pilot grunted as his spine was broken by the force of the sudden motion, and he was dead before his body hit the cold sea.

The garinafin snapped its jaws shut and reopened them, roaring forth an audacious tongue of flames. It was a challenge to the shadow hunters, to this life of peril, to this cold, dark, unfeeling universe.

Goztan watched as a slender, dark shape plunged into the open maw of the garinafin, like a graceful sleeve-tailed fish leaping into a red-hot caldera filled with bubbling lava.

For a moment, the hovering beast seemed frozen in air. Its fire breath faded and winked out. Its jaws closed. All was darkness.

But then, in that darkness, a new light began to glow. Muffled, shaded, like the embers of a banked fire. The glow brightened, and the garinafin reappeared in the sky, lit up from within, the veined skin glowing like varnished silk, the quivering muscular sheath like a jellyfish pulsating in the dark sea.

Goztan knew that she was looking at the garinafin's agonized death throes. The mysterious missile, guided by the light of the fire breath, had plunged straight down the gullet and exploded deep inside. Somehow, the people of Dara had devised weapons that could hunt on their own, killing lances that could see in the dark and home in on the light of life.

The garinafin-shaped lantern in the sky shattered. Burning, smoking, tumbling pieces were flung in every direction, leaving glowing fireworks-like trails that gradually faded.

Finally, there was silence. The demonic hunting lances, having caught their last prey, ceased their shrieks.

Bright torches sprang to life all over the shore, and the noise of celebratory cheers drifted over the waves. In the hazy glow of those distant torches, the enemy's garinafins were taking off.

The Lyucu on the city-ships were too stunned to move.

"Votan!" Noda Mi was kneeling next to her, his body shaking like a leaf in autumn. "Wh-what are your orders?"

As though waking from a dream, she spoke in a tired, toneless voice. "Get Safin ready."

Goztan's personal mount, Safin, was so old that his once pure-white hide had become mottled and cracked, like the drought-plagued fields in parts of Rui. The aged garinafin had been brought along on this expedition not to fight, but to provide a calming presence for the younger war beasts. To ride such aged mounts—who by their very survival were seen as talismans of good luck—into war was not something the tribes of the scrublands would ever contemplate except as a last resort.

Though it had been many years since he had been rigged for battle, Safin showed no hesitation as Goztan settled into the saddle and pressed the bone trumpet to the base of his neck. "Time to fight for fire pit and breath, my old friend."

Straining hard, Safin took off and spiraled up slowly. Below him, warriors raised bright torches to light his way.

The approaching Dara garinafins and their riders hesitated, uncertain what to do with this single approaching garinafin. They could see that the pilot was riding with no crew. Even more shocking: The garinafin was muzzled, unable to breathe fire.

Goztan spread her arms to the side and opened her hands to show that she held no weapons. She was invoking the right to parley.

The Dara riders allowed her to approach until they could see her face, a fearless mien of determination.

"I am called Goztan Ryoto, daughter of Dayu Ryoto, son of Péfir Vagapé. I serve the pékyu as the Garinafin-Thane of the Five Tribes of the Antler. I command the forces of Ukyu-taasa. Tell your emperor to come see me, if he dares."

"This a trick," said Puma Yemu. "They are demoralized and out of options. We must press our advantage and defeat them once and for all."

But the young emperor looked thoughtful. All day long, he had been like a lone lifeboat seized by a storm, alternately lifted high above the angry sea on mountainous swells of hope and plunged into deep troughs of despair: the thrill of seeing the decoy airships and ornithopters carry out their plan to perfection; the grief that pierced his heart as he witnessed the deaths of Than and his aviators; the wave of hot rage that led to his rash decision to commit all his forces to a battle of attrition; the helpless horror of watching his beloved garinafins and riders die at the hands of the experienced

Lyucu; the cold determination that then enclosed his heart like armor, allowing him to calculatedly sacrifice his troops to prolong the battle until nightfall, whereupon the sunflowers could be deployed. . . .

"We have no more sunflowers," beseeched Puma Yemu. "*Rénga*, now is not the time to vacillate."

In the wake of the storm, as his heart drifted over a sea full of burning wreckage and charred corpses; as his mind was left exhausted after years of planning had been consumed by reality; as the full weight of the consequences of his decisions pressed down on his shoulders: aviators he had called sisters, soldiers he had personally recruited, sailors he had gone drinking with, riders he had thought of as brothers, garinafins he had raised from hatchlings, and Than, old, faithful Than who was like a second father to him—dead, all dead . . . he felt numb, insubstantial, ashamed.

They died for my vision, he thought. *They fought and died under my orders, while I watched, safely hidden in the jungle. Is this how the Emperor of Dara should behave?*

"Do not talk to her," pleaded Puma Yemu. "Order the final assault, *Rénga*, please."

"The Emperor of Dara must not be a coward," said Phyro. "I will parley with her."

He mounted his garinafin, Ginki, and after impatiently waiting for this chance all day and all night, the garinafin was only too glad to finally stretch her wings. In no time at all, Ginki had arrived in the warmly lit air above the city-ships.

The two garinafins circled around each other in tight loops, wary, tense, like arrows nocked to their bows.

"I've come to parley, garinafin-thane of the Lyucu," said Phyro. "What do you wish to say besides an immediate offer of surrender?"

Goztan laughed. "You may think you've won the battle, but my heart remains unconvinced."

Phyro was startled. "Why?"

"You tried to exhaust our garinafins before coming at them with fresh ones, and even then, you could only achieve a stalemate. In the end, we lost only because you had more magical weapons and more deceitful tricks, not because you were stronger or more courageous. It wasn't fair."

Phyro felt his face color with ire. "A battle isn't just fought on the backs of fire-breathing garinafins or over the decks of swaying ships. It's also fought by smiths swinging hammers in the workshops and inventors honing their minds in the laboratories. We pitted our strengths against your weaknesses. What's unfair about that?"

"I should have known that a descendant of the House of Dandelion would deem deception compatible with honor, and consider glory obtained through the sacrifice of others his own," said Goztan, her voice dripping with contempt. "You are your father's son, after all, and theft and betrayal are in your blood."

Phyro's face darkened even more. The Lyucu thane had evoked two episodes during his father's rise that always brought him shame: Kuni Garu's theft of Pan while Mata Zyndu risked his life to hold off the might of the Xana Empire on Wolf's Paw, and the King of Dasu's later betrayal of the Hegemon on the bank of the Liru. For Phyro, these were stains in the origin of the dynasty that would never fade.

Goztan, seeing him at a loss for words, pressed further. "Go ahead, call upon your garinafins to slaughter me and mine. Hide behind the magic crafted by others and veil yourself in borrowed honor and stolen glory. Yet the spirit of the Lyucu remains indomitable, and my heart will never accept that you won at all."

Phyro's heart grew somber. Honor and glory were not empty words; he had grown up with stories of courage and chivalry, and the defiance in the garinafin-thane's voice stirred him in a way that he could not explain. "Then what will make you yield?"

"It was the custom of the people of Dara in old times to decide the outcome of a battle in single combat, was it not?" said Goztan. "That was the way of the scrublands as well."

"Are you challenging me to a duel?" Phyro asked, incredulous.

"Terrified?" asked Goztan.

"You . . . you can't possibly be serious. We've won the battle." Visions of the dead bodies floating on the invisible sea below filled Phyro's head, and his voice cracked. "Only a fool would throw away a victory secured with so much blood by wagering it on an outdated ritual."

Goztan shook her head. "You misunderstand me. A duel cannot alter the reality on the battlefield, but it can sway the hearts of the vanquished and victorious alike. If you win, we'll surrender immediately with no more resistance, having been convinced of your superiority. But if I should emerge victorious, I ask that you send me and my warriors home on rafts so that we may live to fight again, and we'll leave behind all our ships and weapons as your spoils."

Heat suffused Phyro's body, as though lava instead of blood was flowing through his veins. He felt himself turning into one of the characters in his boyhood legends, heroes who never borrowed honor nor stole glory: the great Xana general Tanno Namen, the incomparable Hegemon Mata Zyndu, the peerless Marshal Gin Mazoti.

Solemnly, Phyro intoned, "I accept."

"Then let's fight in the morning, after we've both had a chance to rest our mounts."

Phyro's generals and monitors vehemently opposed the idea.

"You promised Than and me that you would not ride forth and risk your life!" raged Puma Yemu. "You promised to listen to counsel!"

Phyro tried to explain how the duel was a way to secure a decisive victory without the loss of more lives, how it would lay the groundwork for the ultimate liberation of Unredeemed Dara.

"Even if you win, how can you trust the word of a Lyucu!?"

Phyro tried to list the pros and cons, to measure out for his advisers the risks and benefits, to demonstrate that it was a rational decision justified by military necessity.

"How unseemly to have the emperor swinging a sword and riding a fire-breathing beast like some common brute or bandit!" fretted Ki Aten, who had finally been released from his cabin because Phyro thought there was little danger that he would further disrupt his plans. "The Emperor of Dara should be like the sage-kings spoken of by Kon Fiji, even-tempered, gentle-hearted, preferring the ivory writing knife to the bronze butcher's blade!"

Phyro was about to quote some lines of Kon Fiji back at Ki Aten, to the effect that winning over the heart of the enemy was more moral than merely vanquishing him on the field, but he was tired of such meaningless debates. He simply shook his head as his guards dragged the complaining military monitor away.

But in his heart, he knew that none of the reasons he was offering mattered.

What moved him was a feeling, an impulse, an instinctive yearning.

His father had not bested the Hegemon in a fair fight, but Kuni had descended from *Grace of Kings* to save the lives of his people. His Auntie Gin had won plenty of victories through guile and deceit, as well as weapons crafted by the ingenuity of others, but in the end, she had taken up the sword to face Pékyu Tenryo alone on the deck of a burning ship.

How could he be a leader without risking his own life? How could he send his soldiers to die without being ready to join them? After all, wasn't that why the Moralists spoke of "teeth on the board"? Wasn't that the very foundation of *mutagé*?

His father had always exhorted him to live an interesting life; his mother had always told him that he should trust his instincts. Once he had worked out all the odds, he still had to toss the dice, to take that leap of faith, to believe that his foe was honorable.

He lifted Na-aroénna, feeling the full weight of the peerless sword, and read from the blade:

> *Lament not that the days are short,*
> *But that they are without glory.*
> *Where doubt ends, so does courage.*
> *May each of your days be a day of battle.*

"I cannot be a worthy Emperor of Dara," he announced to the assembled generals and advisers, "unless I go."

And so, as the sun rose upon the carnage of the night before, two garinafins took off from their respective camps. One was mottled and wrinkled with age, the other still fuzzy around the antlers and not fully grown. Each was piloted by a single rider without a crew—a fitting cast for an ancient ritual that transcended all space and time.

Among the people of the scrublands, when two great chiefs decided to duel by garinafin, it was the custom that they fight alone. Victory was achieved by skill and daring, as each tried to dismount the other or to singe the opponent with well-timed blasts of fire breath. Few survived such duels, which was part of the reason why they gradually grew out of fashion. Even someone as proud and arrogant as Tenryo Roatan never participated in such a ritual himself.

But on this day, thousands of miles from the land of Ukyu-Gondé, that ancient custom came to life again. As the armies of Ukyu-taasa and Dara watched in awed silence, Goztan and Phyro circled each other, diving, climbing, charging, twisting, snapping, dodging, clawing, breathing, smashing, slashing. . . .

Two champions tired of slaughter,
As distinct as fire from water,
Or glistening pearl from fiery garnet,
Glory in the flesh, honor incarnate.

One dives like a coruscant comet streaking through the sky;
The other climbs like a crowned cruben breaching from Tazu's
   sphere.
One shoots a tongue of flame like Fithowéo's unerring spear;
The other twists like Diasa dodging Nalyufin's vile eye.

Speed is matched by endurance,
Guile met with strength.
In silence the gods observe,
Obscuring who they'll preserve.

Na-aroénna brooks no doubt of dominion;
Gaslira-sata will suffer no piecemeal peace.
Though two have entered the arena disdainful of death,
Only one shall emerge with beating heart and heaving breath.

Summoning all the training from Ofluro and Suca, all the skills gained over years of drills, Phyro performed feats of aerobatics he never thought possible. He had never felt so well-matched to Ginki—she was an extension of him and he of her. As he swung Na-aroénna to deflect a slashing talon or to strike at Goztan as they swept past each other at impossible speeds, he thought he finally understood the exhilaration of Mata Zyndu as he dueled over Zudi on a battle kite and the purity of purpose of Luan Zyaji as he glided toward Mapidéré's procession.

Goztan, despite her advanced age, put on a fight that rivaled any in her youth. Here, on the back of her trusty mount, she finally felt free for the first time since she had come to Dara. Gone were the simpering blandishments of Noda Mi, the crazed ravings of Cutanrovo, the anguished compromises of Tanvanaki, the self-loathing and doubt of an unworthy cause. She was pure Lyucu, the embodiment of defiant survival, of fire pit and tribe, of motion and breath.

Many were the times that one rider or the other was on the verge of annihilation by fire or fall, only to be saved at the last moment by a skilled maneuver from their mount or a quick scramble to the other side of the netting. Claws and wings clashed, as bone rang against steel. Garinafins and riders alike were covered in bloody wounds and singed scars. Warriors from both sides cheered and gasped in turn, mesmerized by this aerial display of power and grace.

The two fought from morning till noon, took a break by mutual agreement, and then continued again until the sun was low in the west.

Phyro lay Na-aroénna across his saddle; Goztan rested Gaslira-sata on her thigh. The two sweat-drenched pilots, as exhausted as their drooping mounts, parleyed again.

"Shall we continue on the morrow?" called out Goztan. There was a respect in her voice.

Phyro secured his sword to the saddle, let go of the reins, and raised both arms to cross them at the wrist, saluting in the Lyucu manner. "It would be an honor to fight you again."

Goztan, stunned momentarily, fumbled to tie her war axe to her back and let go of the reins to return the salute—

- *What are you doing, Tazu?*
  - *Making things more interesting, of course. Think of it . . . as a tribute to our absent brother.*

∾

Over time, the eagles of Crescent Island had developed a taste for the juicy flesh of the turtles that could be found plodding along the rocky beaches. But the delicacy was encased in a hard shell immune to claws or beak. To obtain the treat, the eagles had to learn a new way to hunt.

One such eagle circled above the island, a turtle clutched in its claws. By dropping turtles from a great height, the raptor could smash the hard shell and extract the delicious flesh.

The last few days had been most vexing for the eagle, as strange creatures—smoke-bellowing, fire-breathing, wind-buffeting, nonstop-screaming—had come to war near its home, sending every creature of the jungle and beach scurrying into concealment. The eagle had hidden itself until now, but hunger had finally forced it into making a move.

It had intended to fly high above the clouds and away from the confusion, dropping the turtle on a distant rocky beach to enjoy a much-needed meal. But as it was straining to gain more height, a wisp of cloud suddenly seemed to solidify before it, taking on the vague form of a shark.

The eagle screamed and veered away, dropping the turtle.

The turtle plunged through the air, tumbling end over end, until it struck Safin, Goztan's mount, right over his left eye.

Startled, Safin screamed and jerked his head away, buckling violently and throwing Goztan out of her saddle. As watching warriors from both sides cried out in alarm, the garinafin-thane plunged toward the sea, arms and legs flailing helplessly. Safin, half-blinded and confused, flapped his wings wildly, unsure what had happened or what to do.

Phyro grabbed the reins of Ginki and dug his heels into her shoulders. "Go, go!" he shouted, sending Ginki into Péa's dive.

It was low tide. Falling woman and diving garinafin raced for the half-submerged reefs below, and just before Goztan's body would have smashed into the jagged reefs, Ginki extended her neck and broke the thane's fall. While Phyro grabbed her by the waist and held her securely against the back of Ginki's neck, the garinafin flapped her wings mightily, pulling out of her dive and lifting all out of harm's way.

Waves crashed against the reefs, and overhead the clouds roiled, as though the gods were rendering judgment.

"Thank you," said Goztan, when she had recovered her breath. "But why? You would have won had you done nothing and let me fall. It was a sign from the gods."

Phyro looked into the eyes of the proud garinafin-thane. For a moment he was again that wide-eyed young boy in that teahouse from long ago, nestled safely between Rata-*tika* and Toto-*tika*, listening to the storyteller recounting tales of great heroes.

"A great warrior deserves not to have her life end by chance," he said. "The world may not be fair, but we must strive to make it so."

Goztan smiled and closed her eyes. "You win, Emperor Monadétu. My heart accepts."

Down in the dark hold of the city-ship, the native slaves of Ukyu-taasa whispered to one another. They were not desperadoes who fought for the Lyucu for profit or pleasure; they were not collaborators who had thrown their lot in with the invaders; they were not mind-scrubbed zealots who had become convinced that the cause of their captors was just.

They were simple peasants who had been drafted to pull the oars, to shovel garinafin dung, to serve the pleasure and whims of the Lyucu. They obeyed because their families were held hostage in death pits back on Rui and Dasu. They had not read the books of the Ano sages; they didn't dream about words like honor and glory; they didn't know the meaning of *mutagé*. All they knew was the need to survive, and to cling to love.

"Why are the Lyucu celebrating?"

"Because by surrendering, they won't have to die."

"So we're heading back home?"

"Yes."

"What will happen to our masters?"

"Nothing. They're Lyucu."

"What will happen to us?"

"We'll be blamed for the loss, and our families as well as ourselves will be executed. Thane Cutanrovo said so."

"Then what can we do?"

"We must save our families."

The Lyucu warriors and native auxiliaries left their weapons on the city-ships as they rowed to shore in lifeboats. The mood was subdued but not lachrymose. They had lost, it was true, but they had not been slaughtered or enslaved. Some comforted themselves with the thought that the Dara-raaki had won only by adopting the method of warfare of the Lyucu, so in a way, the Lyucu spirit had indeed triumphed.

Puma Yemu guided his fleet out to take over the city-ships. Sailors and marines climbed up rope ladders as though ascending towering cliffs on draping vines. The city-ships, relics of Mapidéré's megalomaniacal engineering style, were awe-inducing even so many decades later.

But just before the sailors and marines had reached the top of the rope ladders, enslaved natives of Rui and Dasu rushed out of the holds of the city-ships. Emaciated, dirty, dressed in rags, they picked up the discarded weapons of the Lyucu and rushed to the gunwales, beating back the boarding party as though defending a city. A few of the sailors and marines lost their grip and fell to their deaths. The rest scrambled back down the rope ladders.

Phyro, taking this all in from atop the cliffs to the side of the inlet, whipped around on Goztan.

"An ambush?" He unsheathed Na-aroénna.

Goztan shook her head but kept her eyes locked with Phyro's. "They are natives. All the Lyucu are now onshore. We neither planned this nor do we have any control over them."

"But why?" demanded Phyro. "They're our people! We're liberating them."

Goztan sighed. While Phyro's garinafin riders were scrambling to mount and Puma Yemu's fleet was pulling back, the rebelling slaves had set the city-ships on fire.

Faintly, the voices of many chanting in unison on the burning ships carried across the water:

Ten dyudyu cupéruna?
Lyucu kyo!
Ten dyudyu cupéruna?
Ukyu kyo!

"They believe that if they allow themselves to be liberated, they and their families will all die in horrific ways once we return to Ukyu-taasa," said Goztan. "But if they resist you to the utmost, then perhaps there's a chance that their families may be spared—if I speak of their martyrdom to Tanvanaki and Cutanrovo."

Not all the enslaved natives joined the chant. Some, believing that the Lyucu would not keep their promise to spare the families of the loyal, fought back against the rebels. Others, despairing that they would be blamed no matter what happened, gave up and plunged into the sea to wait for their loved ones on the other side of the River-on-Which-Nothing-Floats. But those who clung to hope were the most numerous, and they refused to yield even as their bodies were immolated, meaningless sacrifices to the doomed Lyucu cause.

Na-aroénna thunked to the ground as Phyro buried his face in his hands and wept.

As the garinafins circled helplessly over the burning city-ships, as the Dara fleet circled the smoldering wooden islands, as the Lyucu stood in ordered ranks somberly observing the smoking pyres in the sea, Goztan spoke to Phyro.

"I do not think you understand what life is like in Ukyu-taasa. . . ."

A WEEK LATER.

As the towering profile of Tenryo's Peak (the new name for Mount Kiji chosen by Cutanrovo) poked above the horizon, the Lyucu huddled on the rafts cheered. They had been at sea for days, and many didn't think they would survive the arduous journey.

Goztan staggered to her feet and gazed hungrily at the horizon. *Home. I'm finally home.*

But she knew that arriving in Rui was only the first step in an even more taxing journey: She had promised to act as Phyro's emissary to Ukyu-taasa, to negotiate for a full surrender of the Lyucu.

Enough evil has been committed in the name of our people. Enough blood has been shed for the sake of the Lyucu spirit.

She knew that behind her, behind the ragtag flotilla of rafts carrying the Lyucu survivors of the Battle of Crescent Island, was Phyro's invasion fleet. A few city-ships had survived the slave rebellion to carry his garinafins, provisions, and army. For the first time in a decade, a Dara fleet had returned to reclaim what was rightfully theirs.

"But how will we convince Thane Cutanrovo and her warriors?" one of the thanes asked. "How can we trust that the Dara emperor won't slaughter all the Lyucu even if the pékyu agrees to surrender?"

"I fought him to know him," said Goztan. "He can be trusted because he has the soul of a Lyucu."

CHAPTER TWENTY-SEVEN

WHAT PRICE VICTORY?

KRIPHI: A LONG TIME AGO.

Millennia earlier, Ano refugees arrived in Dara from beyond the endless sea. While the precise history of how they settled among the Islands and mixed with the natives to give birth to the people who would later call themselves the people of Dara was lost in the mists of time, it was clear that the amount of Ano influence differed significantly from island to island. The Big Island seemed to have been changed the most by the Ano, while Rui and Dasu the least—except for places like Tan Adü, where the Ano never set foot.

The palace at Kriphi had begun as a simple hut of stone and thatch, just a little bigger than the other huts around it. Mo-Xana, the man who lived in it, called himself king and his hut a war-hall, but he was really no better than the chief of a band of bandits who had accumulated more loot than other competing bandit bands in this corner of Rui. They terrorized the shepherds and farmers and fisherfolk in the surrounding countryside, taking what they wanted in exchange for keeping the other bandits away. They drank mead and beer and feasted on roasted mutton from morning till evening, and wrestled one another in between for entertainment.

Mo-Xana was proud that he owned a bronze sword and three gold rings, while the rest of his band had to make do with wooden clubs and bamboo spears.

But Mo-Xana's heart was as restless as the turbulent waves that lapped Rui's shores. He didn't know what he wanted, except that he craved *more*.

Then news came of a great war breaking out among the core islands, and Mo-Xana crossed the sea with his warriors in wave-weaving boats not much bigger than the pots they cooked dolphins in. He cared not for what cause he fought, so long as it allowed him to have *more*.

On the Big Island, he saw men who rode on tall horses and fought in gleaming armor; he saw women in silk dresses who divined the will of the gods using ivory sticks; he heard scholars who had read all twelve books that existed in the world; he tasted fine foods and beverages whose names were unknown to him; he met kings and queens who actually lived in palaces that had more than one room.

He felt embarrassed as they looked at him in consternation and whispered to one another behind raised sleeves. He felt aggrieved as guests on either side of him at banquets shifted away, frowning— and one even had the audacity to ask if he would perhaps like a bath before the meal. He gazed into a mirror and experienced deep shame as he finally saw himself the way they saw him: an ignorant brute from a barbarous land who had no trove of treasure, no gift from the gods, no praise by the poets, who had lost all claims to the heritage of the civilization of the Ano.

He set out to transform the image in the mirror.

He fought with a ferocity that his enemies could not match. He hacked off their limbs and took their bronze swords. He bashed in their skulls and took their shining armor. When he conquered cities, he slaughtered the recalcitrant and distributed the pliant captives to his followers—while hoarding treasure in heavy heaps. But he was a generous lord, and he gave away a larger share of his treasure to warriors who came to fight for him than any other lord, friend or foe.

Even hero-hearted Iluthan once asked him to lead his vanguard; even wily-willed Séraca twice conceded he was not unbrave. He saw the gods stride through the battlefield like living colossi, killing hundreds in a single blow, and did not lose his nerve. He opened the famed ivory vaults of Écofi and bestowed all the living jade to his war band. The natives of the islands and the descendants of the Ano alike came to know his name.

Now, when he attended the banquets of the great kings and

queens, he rode in on a giant horse that was taller than any of theirs, with a louder retinue of warriors and poets, with greener jade pendants around his neck, with heavier gold rings on his fingers, with loftier corals and feathers resting atop his head.

He had *more*.

But still the other Lords of Dara kept their distance from him, paused in their conversation awkwardly when he interjected a remark, discussed books and art and fine food as though he were not there.

At the end of the war, when Aruano, the great lawgiver, declared the names and boundaries of the sixty-four Tiro states, Mo-Xana was named last, his territory but the tip of Rui. Though all the Tiro states were supposed to be equal, everyone knew that to be named earlier meant *more*.

"Why?" he stood up and demanded. "I have a hoard larger than most ranked before me."

The assembled Lords of Dara were silent. After a moment, the aged sage, frost-faced Aruano, spoke. "Rui is among the last of the Islands to be settled by the Ano but among the first to forget the grace of our ancestors. That decline is revealed by your rude question."

"What's so rude about demanding my due? I've given and spilled more blood than all but a few present."

"You may have more rings in your chests, but you have no precious breast-hoard, that refinement of the soul, nor a capacious skull-dwelling, that grandness of spirit. You may sit among the *tiro*, but you're not their equal."

Enraged, Mo-Xana stormed out and returned to Rui, where he waged war until he had conquered the territories of the other Tiro states on the islands of Rui and Dasu. He razed the stone hut of his origin and rebuilt it into a castle with sixty-four rooms, and he vowed to one day make the other Lords of Dara regret not giving him the respect that he deserved. They spoke of breast-hoards and skull-dwellings, but in the end, the only hoards that counted were piles of gold and jade to buy the loyalty of the war band, and the only dwellings that mattered were grand palaces that made visitors look up in awe and rattle their knees in fear.

～

In the sagas of the Diaspora Wars popular among the core islands, Mo-Xana's name was often absent—though there were some versions that alluded to Mo-Xana's deeds in a few couplets. But on Rui and Dasu, the bards sang of Mo-Xana's many feats of valor and guile, of how Iluthan had yielded to his sword, of how Séraca had fled from his plots. Above all, they spoke of how the Tiro kings of the core islands had denied Mo-Xana his due, of the respect owed to a man who had *more*.

As for which version was closer to the truth, the gods were silent.

It would be simplistic to trace the origin of a national preoccupation to a legend, but sometimes the breast-hoards of a people lean toward a myth like sunflowers yearning for the golden orb's bright rays, and the skull-dwellings of a people can be shaped by an oft-repeated story like pebbles polished by the relentless tides.

Successive generations of Xana's kings added to the palace begun by their bitter ancestor in the quest for *more*. Mithon, who crushed a brief-lived rebellion on Dasu, added two wings containing one hundred and eight new rooms; Nozé, who fought the pirates plaguing Dasu's shores and forced them to pay *him* tribute, filled a hall with bronze mirrors polished with the blood of the mirror makers; Domita, the queen who ruled in the name of her son and sacrificed nine cauldrons of ears and noses from war captives to Kiji, was responsible for the first iteration of the Mingén Tower, at the time of its construction the tallest structure in all the Islands; Hushitoda, who cut out the tongues of the envoys of Cocru and Loye (a Tiro state that once existed in Géfica) and sent the mute men back instead of paying tribute, expanded the palace grounds to include three layers of walls; Dézan, who witnessed the invention of the modern airship and acted as the architect of his son's grand unification, added nine mooring masts for airships . . . And eventually, Réon, better known as Mapidéré, enlarged the palace with six more layers of walls before eventually deciding that the palace in Kriphi was simply not enough—he had to build a whole new city from scratch: the Immaculate City of Pan.

Even cowardly Éodüna, known by the sobriquet "the Languid,"

managed to add one room, which he lined with walls of amber. The room, though it did little to raise the esteem of Xana, did impress visiting paleontology scholars and led to some entries in the annals of the other Tiro states.

Even Kuni Garu, who rose from Dasu and resided in the palace of Kriphi for less than six months, kept alive the tradition by adding fireplaces to the Tertiary Audience Hall—he stayed away from the Great Hall, finding it too austere—so that he and his advisers wouldn't shiver on winter nights as they plotted the downfall of the Hegemon.

The point was: The palace of Kriphi always grew *more*.

KRIPHI: THE EIGHTH MONTH OF THE ELEVENTH YEAR OF THE REIGN OF SEASON OF STORMS AND THE REIGN OF AUDACIOUS FREEDOM.

The aged falcon circled over Kriphi, crying plaintively.

He was so old that even staying aloft was a chore, and he doubted that he had the strength or agility to attempt to dive down to the market to steal a fish—not that such a thing would have been possible anymore: Kriphi hadn't had anything resembling a functioning market for many months, years even.

Below him, the city that he had lived in since he was a hatchling was unrecognizable. Gone were the densely packed houses and tenement buildings, the winding stone-paved streets and alleyways perpetually shrouded in shadow, the once-bustling markets and open squares filled with people. In their place were vast, empty fields of rubble, over which small herds of emaciated long-haired cattle roamed, trying to feed on tough clumps of grass that managed to grow in this inhospitable landscape.

Here and there, white tents like patches of mushrooms sat among the ruins, but even they sagged and looked dirty and in ill repair. The few humans who sat on the ground outside them looked as old as the falcon felt, and they did not look up as the raptor glided overhead. Instead, they sat as still and as bored as statues, reaching up once in a while to pick a louse out of their hair and beard or to scratch vigorously at a bite.

The falcon remembered seeing crowds of people demolish the buildings and cart the debris away to be tossed into the wetlands that had once embraced the city; the wetlands were gone, as were the fish, frogs, toads, scholar's geese, and migratory cranes. The falcon recalled observing the vigorous humans who once lived in these tents march away—though he didn't know that they had gone to the great stratovolcano in the southwestern corner of the island, where they whipped other humans to dig up earth and chisel stone from the mountain so that the rubble could be loaded in carts heading to the shore and dumped into the sea. The falcon didn't understand why any of these things were happening; he only knew that even the harbor was so fouled by the earth being discharged into it that there were no more fish.

Even his old home, the man-made mountain that the humans called Mingén Tower, was gone. It had been dismantled, stone by stone, much like the rest of the palace, until it had collapsed like a mighty oak being felled, tossing up a cloud of dirt and ash that remained in the air for days.

In the middle of the field of rubble that had once been the palace of Kriphi stood a giant white tent, around which were piles of bones and pits full of shit, in which thin rats with tough, chewy meat and patchy fur scrabbled and hissed.

The palace was not only *less*; it was in fact no more.

The falcon had returned out of a sense of nostalgia. But this was no longer home.

The falcon did not sigh—that was not the way of raptors—but he turned to the east, away from the ruins of Kriphi. He was heading for the killing fields where he knew that every day, some of the humans who lived in tents bashed in the skulls of some of the humans who used to live in houses. He didn't exactly enjoy the taste of carrion, but it was better than starving.

Inside the Great Tent was the biggest assembly of the thanes of Ukyu-taasa in quite some time. Except for the thanes commanding the remaining city-ships and garinafins facing off against the Dara armada off the southern coast of Rui, every single Lyucu commander of note was present. Even the aged thanes who could barely pick up an axe and who were therefore assigned to watch over the native slave gangs at Tenryo's Peak had returned.

Tanvanaki seethed at the three figures before her.

There was Noda Mi, kneeling with his forehead against the ground like a groveling dog. There was Goztan, standing with her shoulders hunched, the very image of defeat. Then there was Cutanrovo, circling around the two of them like a prowling wolf, declaiming at the top of her lungs, every phrase spat out like an invective.

". . . to plead for the lives of the families of the saboteur slaves? Where is your fighting spirit? Where is your wolf-virtue? Why are you even alive? I should like to tear open your rib cage to see if you have the heart of a sheep—"

"That's enough," said Tanvanaki. "Goztan hasn't even delivered the demands of the Dara invaders."

"Why do we care? Dara-raaki must be destr—"

Tanvanaki growled and bared her teeth at Cutanrovo. The two locked gazes, and after a long moment, Cutanrovo backed up and lowered her eyes.

Everyone in the tent held their breath and listened as Goztan continued her interrupted account in a weary, dry voice. "I recite for you now the terms offered by Emperor Monadétu of Dara—"

Next to Tanvanaki, the huddled figure of Timu jerked involuntarily. In his mind, his brother remained the young teenaged boy with no patience for the books of the Ano sages and loved games of war. It was difficult for him to reconcile that image with the resourceful and audacious commander who had vanquished the might of the Lyucu expedition.

"—demands your immediate surrender and the cessation of all Lyucu resistance. All remaining city-ships and garinafins shall be turned over to the Dara fleet. All Lyucu warriors must disarm and yield themselves to the custody of native auxiliary commanders, who will cooperate with the landing of the invasion force and the subsequent liberation."

"I see," said Tanvanaki, her calm tone betraying no emotion. "Obviously, if we refuse, he will follow with a direct assault on Ukyu-taasa. But what will become of us if we agree to these terms?"

"Emperor Monadétu didn't reveal his full intentions to me," said Goztan. "But he did say that for each native who dies from this moment on, the debt must be repaid threefold, even if we attempt to escape beyond the Wall of Storms."

Tanvanaki said nothing. Neither did anyone else in the tent.

The voice that finally broke the silence belonged to Timu. In halting Lyucu, he said, "My brother speaks harshly but has a compassionate heart. If we surrender and cooperate, I'm certain he will show us mercy just as he showed Thane Goztan mercy."

Cutanrovo barked a harsh laugh of disbelief. "You think the Dara-raaki emperor will show us *mercy*? After that threat?"

"I agree with Emperor Thaké," said Goztan. "Emperor Monadétu can be trusted."

"Why?" sneered Cutanrovo. "Because he spared you in a moment of weakness? It's a plot. The Dara-raaki can never be trusted because they are not Lyucu."

Goztan was at a loss for words. She didn't know how to articulate the feelings she had when she saw him fight her like a garinafin rider of the scrublands, when he put his sword away to salute her in the Lyucu style, when he dropped his weapon to weep for the senseless deaths of the native slaves.

Unbidden, the image of Oga Kidosu came to her mind.

He was sitting on the deck of Captain Dathama's city-ship, gutting and cleaning fish in the predawn starlight.

"The sea laps the shores of Dara as well as of Ukyu," he said. "Before the sea, all are brothers."

"Because I have fought him," she croaked, forcing the memory away. "I have seen the nature of his soul."

Cutanrovo's lips curled in contempt, but before she could say anything, Tanvanaki broke in.

"What will happen to us isn't up to Phyro. He doesn't hold the Seal of Dara because Jia remains the regent. Can you say you know the nature of *her* soul?"

Goztan held her tongue. She had been pinning her hopes on the young Emperor of Dara, but Tanvanaki was right. There was no telling what Jia would do to the surrendered Lyucu.

"You have lost, old friend," said Tanvanaki, her voice weary. "The defeated have no voice, no claim to be heard."

Goztan continued to hold her tongue. What Tanvanaki said was the rule of the scrublands, and how could she claim that it didn't apply equally to Dara, to Ukyu-taasa, to this very tent?

Timu spoke again. "I will plead for mercy from my mother."

Around the Great Tent, many Lyucu thanes, even those in the hard-liner faction, looked hopeful at this. Timu was, after all, Jia's flesh and blood. It was rumored that she had always wanted him to ascend to the Dandelion Throne rather than his brother. The puppet Emperor Thaké, whom they'd always despised, now seemed the best bulwark against the mighty Dara invasion fleet.

"Please, Tanvanaki, there is no point in sending more warriors to die. Dyu-*tika* and Zaza-*tika* are my mother's grandchildren. If all four of us go to her and beg for the lives of the Lyucu people, she *will* soften. We're family—"

Tanvanaki turned and struck him with a quick blow to the side of the face. Timu tumbled to the ground. After a moment, he climbed up and wiped the blood from the corner of his mouth. He did not speak again.

Tanvanaki looked around the tent. "Twice I've looked into the eyes of Jia and sounded her soul. At the Battle of Zathin Gulf, she ordered her marshal to target her husband in order to win. And now, though Phyro has been full grown for years, she refuses to let go of the reins of power. This is a woman consumed by ambition without an ounce of human feeling. Do any of you really think she'll give in to the sniveling tears of a weak boy and two grandchildren she's never met?"

The spark of hope that had lit up in the eyes of some of the thanes dimmed.

"The moment we disarm ourselves and turn ourselves over to the native auxiliaries," continued Tanvanaki in her calm voice, as though discussing a new way to divide up pasturing land, as opposed to the very survival of Ukyu-taasa, "what do you imagine will happen? Think about what we've done to them and put yourselves in their place. Do you trust that your slaves will show *mercy* to you?"

She glared at the assembled thanes in turn, and each averted their eyes.

Cutanrovo, her eyes burning with fervor, spoke. "Votan, the Lyucu spirit remains unbowed. Goztan's failure comes from her refusal to trust in the traditions of our people—"

Goztan couldn't let this stand. "Had I not deployed the fire archers, we would have lost even earlier and perhaps none of us would have returned alive—"

"You have learned nothing!" roared Cutanrovo. "You corrupted the spirits of our warriors by advocating change! You lost because you put slaves on our sacred garinafins! Are you so blind? Even the mud-footed Dara-raaki could only triumph by learning our ways. We are the predators and they the prey. If only we would return to our pure ancient virtues, if only we would follow the example of the pékyu-votan—"

"What exactly do *you* propose we do?" interrupted Tanvanaki, her voice icy. "Should I re-create Langiaboto and board a leaky bone raft to charge at the invading fleet, invoking the name of my father? Would you be satisfied if I ordered everyone in this tent to drink kyoffir and smoke tolyusa until they lived in dream-haze and rode forth on the last of our garinafins? Do you believe the Lyucu spirit will magically make us invulnerable to their light-seeking missiles? Look around, Cutanrovo. What. Do. You. Want?"

Cutanrovo looked around the tent. So many of her old comrades had died to subdue this cursed land, and the survivors were either too old or too young. The invasion force that Pékyu Tenryo had taken to these islands had been decimated, and so many of their children were togaten, weakened by native taint.

For a moment, her heart ached with despair and sorrow.

If only the pékyu had listened to me earlier. If only she had attended my spirit rallies and smoked tolyusa with my warriors. If only she hadn't been deceived by her weakling concubine and the defeatist Goztan!

But she straightened her spine and proudly strode toward the pékyu.

"I am not advocating meaningless suicide, votan. We still have thousands of native troops who would fight for us willingly: some because they had betrayed the Dandelion Throne and they know they'd suffer the same fate as us in the event of a Dara conquest; others because they've suffered under the lash for so long that they've become arucuro tocua, obedient shells without their own will—"

Tanvanaki broke into her impassioned oration with a long, bitter series of guffaws. "You fool! Your idea of compelling obedience through a regime of terror might have once had some merit, but you carried it too far. You've torn down their temples and cities; you've desecrated their ancestral graves and spiritual shrines; you've turned fertile fields into drought-baked ground; you've killed tens of thousands through hard labor and mindless slaughter. You left them with no hope that obedience will improve their lot!"

Cutanrovo refused to back down. "They *should* have no hope. That is the point."

"No, you left them with no hope from *us*," snarled Tanvanaki. "What do you think will happen if you bring them to the battlefield and they see the hope represented by the invading army of Dara? And as for the Imperial troops who had betrayed the Dandelion Throne and surrendered to us—why do you think Phyro has released the native auxiliaries along with our Lyucu warriors from Crescent Island? He's sending a message that he's willing to grant them mercy—"

"Then let's take away their hope," countered Cutanrovo. "Votan, you fear a battlefield mutiny by the natives, but the dead slaves at Crescent Island show that we can eliminate that possibility. Let's augment our strength with an army of able-bodied native slaves between the ages of twelve and sixty and compel their cooperation by gathering their families in killing pits." Her voice grew louder and louder until it cracked. "If that whelp Phyro tries to invade Ukyutaasa, his army will pay a heavy price for every inch of ground. What if ten slaves die for every invader? They'll only be killing their own. We will never yield! We will fight in the beaches, in the fields, among the forests, in the torn towns, across rivers, on the mountains—"

"How exactly do you suggest that we carry out this grand plan of yours with a few thousand surviving Lyucu against tens of thousands of restless natives?" Tanvanaki shouted back just as loudly. "How will you hold half the population of Ukyu-taasa prisoner while forcing the other half to fight? I know that calculation and planning have never been your strength, but surely even you understand that our precarious position has been sustainable only because, despite the horrors you've visited upon them, the natives have so far had enough to eat. But we've been able to feed them and ourselves only because of tribute shipments from Dara, which have stopped. We can't even look toward a harvest this fall because your endless purification campaigns have destroyed the agricultural base. When the natives realize that the only choice is between certain death by starvation or a general uprising against us, how do you think that will end?"

"I've been working on solving that problem," protested Cutanrovo. "I've already increased the amount of grazing land—"

"Oh, yes, you've certainly done that. You've razed cities and towns and declared them pastures. You're driving native slave gangs to dig earth from the mountains to fill in the sea to create more land. But what do you have to show for these efforts? Only the most stubborn of grasses that cut the lips of the cattle grow there, salty and bitter, and our herds are thinner than ever—" Tanvanaki stopped, as though choking on the torrent of words pouring out of her.

The gathered thanes, including Cutanrovo and Goztan, were stunned. Never had the pékyu spoken so forcefully against the hardliner faction.

At length, Tanvanaki continued in a frosty, calm tone. "At first, I listened to you because you seemed to speak for many warriors who doubted my path, and then, I listened to you because I feared civil strife among the Lyucu. But step by step, I lost my way. I should have pushed hard for Ukyu-taasa to be truly independent, to develop our own agriculture and economy and not become addicted to Dara tribute. It's too late now; all too late. O Father, how I've failed you." The anguish in her voice was like the cry of a wounded garinafin calf.

Cutanrovo was unrelenting. "That way would have been mad-ness, votan. We cannot become as the barbaric natives and enslave the land to dig food out of mud. It's not our nature. We came to lib-erate the land—"

"You speak of liberating the land, but look around you: We live in a land of ashes and waste. There isn't enough meat and milk for the children—"

"It's still better than eating rice and sorghum like the slave sheep! Votan, if we must, we can *eat* the slaves—"

"If I may be granted a few moments of your time, votan."

Everyone stared at the speaker. It was the forgotten Noda Mi, still kneeling with his forehead pressed into the earthen floor.

"There is no place for you to speak here, slave," snarled Cutanrovo.

But Tanvanaki held up a hand. "We might as well listen to him—"

"He's already failed at Crescent Island—"

"He's about the only native we can trust now," said Tanvanaki. "He's hated by his people as much as we are. After all he's done, you can be sure Jia will show him no more mercy than she'll show us. Since fighting and surrendering are both terrible choices, perhaps the Loyal Hound can pull something out of his knotty, twisted intestines."

Noda Mi slammed his head against the ground. "Most Merciful Pékyu, this loyal slave does think there is a third way, beyond sur-render and a fight to the last brave Lyucu. . . ."

When he was finished, the inside of the Great Tent was so quiet that even the angry screeching of falcons fighting over carrion in the distance could be heard clearly.

Cutanrovo was the first to recover. Gradually, the stunned expres-sion on her face turned to hope, excitement, pleasure. She was about to step forward to offer her support—

A bloodcurdling howl shattered the silence. "Have you lost all decency?" Timu screamed at the kneeling figure. "Are you even human? Tanvanaki, please, oh please! This will enrage the gods—"

A hard punch drove the air out of his lungs and left him curled up on the ground. Tanvanaki waved her hand, and two naros ran up to drag the spasming body of the emperor away.

"I will not be part of this," said Goztan, her voice quiet but resolute. "Tanvanaki, when will you stop? Is there no line you won't cross?"

"We must win," said Tanvanaki. Both her voice and gaze were pleading. "The defeated have no voice."

Goztan shook her head. "No victory can come from Noda's proposal. It is a betrayal of the very Lyucu spirit that you hold so dear."

Cutanrovo took a threatening step toward her. "Do you intend to rebel against the pékyu?"

Goztan looked at her with pity and contempt. "You are crueler and more harmful than any rebel because you've blinded and deafened the pékyu with your fantasy. But you're nothing but a coward and a worm. I will fight you to my last breath."

"You leave me no choice," said Tanvanaki, weary and pained. "Goztan, you're hereby stripped of all your rank and command. To protect the morale of the warriors from your defeatism, you are to be placed under constant guard until you change your mind."

She turned to Cutanrovo and Noda Mi. "Make it happen."

PAN: THE EIGHTH MONTH OF THE ELEVENTH YEAR OF THE REIGN OF SEASON OF STORMS AND THE REIGN OF AUDACIOUS FREEDOM.

The airship *Grace of Kings* had once been the vessel of choice for Emperor Ragin as he traveled around his realm. It was the ship he had ridden as he departed the Big Island for the last time on that fateful expedition to take back Rui and Dasu from the Lyucu invaders more than a decade ago. It was also the ship that could have carried him to safety as his forces were surrounded by Pékyu Tenryo's army—until he chose to dismount to save the lives of his people.

Sleek, light, and equipped with both kite-sails and feather oars, it was the fastest airship the Imperial engineers had ever designed.

Since then, the airship had been a trophy Tanvanaki displayed from time to time to honor the gods and to rekindle memories of the glory of Lyucu arms. On these occasions, native slaves were brought out to row the airship to take Tanvanaki on a tour of Ukyu-taasa.

Years after its departure from the core islands, *Grace of Kings* was once again winging its way over the turbulent sea between Rui and the Big Island. Only this time, it was on a mission not of conquest, but peace.

The Lyucu warriors onboard whipped the oar slaves mercilessly. The enslaved natives gritted their teeth and didn't cry out. When some finally succumbed to exhaustion and collapsed in their seats, they were tossed into the endless waves below.

Faster! Faster! urged the Lyucu overseers. They were in a race against time. Tanvanaki had dispatched messengers to the Dara armada explaining that she needed time to consider his terms, and Phyro had given her an ultimatum of five days. In the dark of the night, *Grace of Kings* had taken off with a secret delegation headed by Noda Mi, and the ship had made a long detour to the east around the Dara armada before turning for the northern coast of the Big Island.

On the morning of the second day, after half of the galley slaves had died in the mad dash across the ocean, *Grace of Kings* was intercepted by several Imperial airships off the coast of old Rima. The Lyucu ship displayed the white flag of truce and was escorted to Pan.

Upon the eight-foot-tall dais was the lonely figure of Empress Jia sitting in *mipa rari*. The powerful men and women who kept the machinery of the empire running stood in two columns along the sides of the Grand Audience Hall: civil ministers to the east, military officers to the west.

Up front, at the foot of the dais, was the neglected Dandelion Throne, shrouded in its silk veil.

Compared to the days when Emperor Ragin had presided over formal court, the western column was now noticeably shorter and sparser. The ranks of enfeoffed nobles, who had once fought for Emperor Ragin and put him on the Dandelion Throne, had been harshly culled. Years of reduced funding to the military had led to few senior officers being promoted. In the absence of Than Carucono and Puma Yemu, who were away fighting with Emperor Monadétu, the ranking military officer at court was now improbably Prince Gimoto, a proxy for his reclusive father Kado Garu, the titular King of

Dasu. And since even Gimoto was absent today due to an illness—no doubt an excuse contrived by his mother and advisers, who understood better than he that his estimation in the empress's eyes could only be diminished by his voicing of any opinions on matters of state—Princess Aya Mazoti stood at the head of the western column. Though she had been stripped of her command after the debacle that was the aborted peace treaty with the Lyucu, she remained an Imperial princess and had been retained at court as a strategist.

This was undoubtedly the court of Empress Jia, regent and holder of the Seal of Dara.

At the center of the hall knelt Noda Mi, once a Tiro king of Dara and now the voice of the Lyucu. For this occasion, he dressed like an official at the Dandelion Court, save for the vest made of long-haired cattle fur—more decorative than functional—worn outside his silk robe, and the crested mynah skull capping his hair bun—a symbol of his office as the clever-tongued envoy.

"Greetings," began Noda Mi. "My sovereign, Pékyu Vadyu Roatan of Ukyu-taasa, Protector of Dara, bids me to inquire after the health of Her Imperial Majesty, Most August Regent of Dara, Empress Jia."

The more politically astute ministers and generals exchanged meaningful looks. By refusing to address Empress Jia as "*Rénga*," was Noda Mi trying to insult her or merely following formal court protocol?

The empress's face betrayed no reaction. "How is my daughter-in-law? Is she sleeping well these days? I am an herbalist of some skill and can recommend some happy dream recipes for dear Tanva-*tika*."

Though a few of the palace guards tittered at this, most of the ministers and generals managed to suppress their mirth. Phyro's own messengers had brought to court news of the triumph at Crescent Island (as well as the sad news of Than Carucono's passing), and already preparations were underway for Emperor Monadétu's triumphal march through Pan. By completely ignoring Tanvanaki's title and calling her by a diminutive, Empress Jia was toying with this Lyucu lapdog.

Noda refused to acknowledge the insult. "I'm most humbled by

Your Imperial Majesty's solicitousness. My votan sleeps well, knowing that Ukyu-taasa blossoms under Emperor Thaké's gentle rule and the maternal protection of her firm hand."

The ministers and generals glared at Noda Mi, and more than a few wished they could tear the traitor apart with their bare hands.

Zomi, in particular, could no longer hold back. Just remembering the way her mother had died and the stories told by the refugees made her blood boil. She took a step forward, out of the line of ministers on the east. "How dare you lie—"

"Silence," said Jia, without even turning to look at her. Her voice was as cold as the first winds of winter.

Zomi pressed her lips together and stepped back into her place.

Next to her, at the head of the line, Prime Minister Cogo Yelu considered the exchange, his eyebrows furrowed almost imperceptibly. Noda Mi was no great scholar, but he was cunning and devious, and no doubt advised by erudite collaborators back in Unredeemed Dara. Noda's words had to be parsed carefully for hidden meaning, much like those traditional logogram-covered puzzle boxes from Ginpen. Only by pressing the logograms in the correct sequence— usually clued by an obscure poem—would the box open and yield its secrets.

Cogo remembered that Kuni Garu had given his firstborn son a name drawn from Kon Fiji's poem:

> The gentle ruler governs without seeming to govern.
> He honors his subjects as he honors his own mother.

By referring to Timu's "gentle rule" and emphasizing the "maternal," Noda Mi was obviously playing on Jia's concern for her son, Timu.

Still revealing no emotion, Jia spoke to Noda Mi. "I'm sorry to see that you've been away from Dara for so long that you've forgotten the proper use of simple words like 'gentle' and 'protection.' But I am not your language tutor. What is it you want?"

"To negotiate a continuing peace between our two states, Dara and Ukyu-taasa."

Jia chuckled mirthlessly. "To negotiate requires that you have something to offer. My armada has destroyed your defenses. At this moment, liberating Rui and Dasu is as easy for me as plucking a ripe peach dangling before my nose. You have nothing to offer."

"Emperor Monadétu is indeed valiant and cunning," said Noda Mi. At some point during this exchange, he had shifted from *mipa rari* to *géüpa*, as though he were an intimate friend of the empress. "And the pékyu agrees that his armada makes a nice wall sheltering the Great Tent from southerly winds. But to say we have nothing to offer is to gravely misread the strategic situation."

Cogo's eyelids twitched. While Jia had referred to the invasion force as hers, Noda Mi was deliberately emphasizing Phyro's role. Cogo's unease grew.

"A witless cur has no right to speak of strategy," sneered Princess Aya Mazoti. In the aftermath of the humiliation of the botched peace mission in Ginpen, she had become an ardent member of the pro-war party. At court these days, she advocated for Phyro more zealously than just about anyone, as though trying to redeem herself—Zomi was very pleased by this turn of events.

Jia frowned but did not berate her. "Please enlighten us with your strategic vision."

Noda Mi bowed his head. "Permission to approach Your Imperial Majesty."

Surprised murmurs passed through the columns of ministers and generals.

"In open court," said Jia, "there are no secrets. Speak from where you sit or do not speak at all."

Noda Mi looked awkward. "There is much hostility toward me in this hall. Though I am only a messenger, I fear the violence of the mob when I speak a truth that many do not wish to hear."

The murmurs of consternation only grew louder.

After a moment of hesitation, Jia beckoned at Noda Mi. He stood up, approached the base of the dais, and took out a small folded square of silk. Keeping his head bowed, he held the folded fabric above his head with both hands.

Empress Jia shuffled out of her seat to the edge of the dais, plucked the square of silk out of his hands, unfolded it, and began to read.

Noda Mi retreated back to his place in the center of the hall and sat down again in *géüpa*. "There is also a chest containing presents from the pékyu to prove our sincerity. I've left it with the palace guards."

Every breath was held in the Grand Audience Hall as the empress read over Noda's secret message. Whatever was written on that piece of silk wasn't in logograms as the fabric was perfectly flat. Minutes trickled through the water clock as the assembly waited.

At length the empress folded the cloth and put it away in her sleeve. "Idle threats do not a strategy make," she said, her tone as placid as a still pool.

Noda Mi wasn't surprised. He had never thought the threat on the silk cloth would work. His "third path" had only been devised to assuage Tanvanaki's panic and to please Cutanrovo's single-minded devotion to the "Lyucu spirit." He couldn't have survived in Kriphi for so long without being able to come up with tricks that pleased his masters.

Sure, the barbarians were powerful and cruel, but sometimes they weren't cruel enough to come up with the best ideas. Noda Mi had tried his best to devise the most efficient and ingenious design to carry out Cutanrovo's deepest desires. His ostensible plot had won the backing of both the mad hard-liner thane and the pékyu, convinced them enough to allow him to be the ambassador. But no, deep down, he didn't believe such a threat would deter the Empress of Dara.

The trouble with the barbarians, he reflected, *is that they never try to look at the problem from the perspective of their opponent. Why would cold-blooded Jia be moved by the fate of the peasants of Ukyu-taasa? I certainly wouldn't. To her, they must be as insignificant as weeds!*

No, he had always had a *fourth* path in mind.

He and Wira Pin, the *cashima* whose intestines were as knotted as his own and just as full of twisted ideas, had convened in secret on how to persuade the empress. They could see that Jia shared with them the same nature of ambition and desire for *more*. Wira, being far more steeped in the Ano Classics and conversant with logograms than he, had helped him perfect his approach. Almost wistfully, he lamented that the Lyucu were too *stupid* to ever truly appreciate the value he and Wira Pin brought to their cause.

Maybe I will finally have to do something about that.

But first things first. It's time to put my real design into action.

Almost carelessly, he dragged his hands along the floor to describe a circle around himself. In fact, he grew even more insolent as he now looked up to lock eyes with Empress Jia for the first time during this discussion. "The hearts of the people of Ukyu-taasa are united against all external threats."

Emboldened by the fact that Empress Jia hadn't stopped her the last time, Aya Mazoti spoke up. "This 'people of Ukyu-taasa' you speak of consists largely of natives pressed into service to defend a conqueror they despise. In *The Mazoti Way of War*, my mother wrote, 'A volunteer is worth three draftees, and a draftee is worth ten slaves.' How can you possibly imagine that you'll triumph over Emperor Monadétu, who commands an army of volunteers with morale swelling like a tsunami?"

Noda Mi now leaned forward, and quickly swept his hands ahead, once again describing a circle around himself. "It has been a long time since I last saw you, Princess. I was once good friends with your mother, you know? Indeed, I often lament that Gin did not join me and Doru Solofi when she still had the chance. Had she been more clearheaded about her own strategic condition, she might not have suffered—"

"You're not fit to speak the name of my mother!" shouted Aya Mazoti, and she took a few steps toward him, fists balled. Noda Mi was responsible both for her mother's fall from Imperial grace—when he and Doru Solofi had taken shelter with her after their failed rebellion—and also her death at Zathin Gulf, by stabbing her in the back. It was all she could do not to kill the man on the spot.

Like Cogo, Zomi was listening to Noda Mi with growing dread. *What is on that cloth he showed the Empress?* Noda Mi's boast about the defenses of Unredeemed Dara made little military sense, but his sudden appeal to his history with Gin did. Gin was always known to favor Phyro's claim to the throne, and Jia had been convinced that a rebellion from Dara's most powerful warlord was only a matter of time. By referring to Gin, Noda was highlighting the complicated history of mutual suspicion between Jia and

Phyro. Zomi watched the man closely with unblinking eyes. *What exactly is his game?*

Noda Mi showed no fear at Aya's approach. If anything, he seemed satisfied to have provoked her. Once again, he leaned back, dragging his hands along the floor. It appeared to be a nervous tic of some sort. "You speak of morale, but know that the Lyucu will be fighting for their survival with their backs against the sea. They'll fight with more spirit than the Hegemon's berserkers."

Aya took another step forward, raising the ceremonial staff in her hand threateningly. "Your comparison is flawed. You've lost most of your garinafins. No matter how fiercely the Lyucu resist, how can they possibly hope to overcome our dominance in the air?"

Noda Mi stood up and backed away from the princess. He bowed slightly and swept his arms over the circle of land he had been obsessively describing with his dragging fists. "Princess, I invite you to imagine this plot of land as Ukyu-taasa, and to imagine the Lyucu and those loyal to them as ants scurrying across the land. I invite you, as a garinafin rider, to kill all the ants with your mighty staff."

Aya Mazoti looked to the ground, looked back up at him, and flushed with rage and embarrassment.

At court, each minister or military officer carried a ceremonial implement as a symbol of their office. Zomi Kidosu, for example, carried a small silver balance scale for "weighing the fish," the duty of the Farsight Secretary. Cogo Yelu, on the other hand, held a blue jade compass, symbolizing the Prime Minister's responsibility for setting the direction of the Inner Council in policy debates. Military officers generally carried ceremonial weapons made of stiffened paper, coral, or porcelain, depending on rank. As Aya Mazoti had been stripped of all command, she carried a blunt staff constructed from stiffened paper, painted with the stylized winter plum of the House of Mazoti. Such a staff, of course, was not particularly effective against scurrying ants, imaginary or otherwise.

Aya understood that Noda's real point wasn't about the inadequacy of her ceremonial staff, but that air superiority alone was insufficient to secure Rui and Dasu. Noda was suggesting that the Lyucu would fade into the terrain of the islands, and the Dara conquerors would have to be prepared to dig up every tunnel, find each mountain hideout, fight a long and bitter ground war against guerrilla resistance before killing the well-defended queen.

"In a sustained ground fight, Emperor Monadétu will ultimately triumph," said Aya Mazoti. "Once he establishes a beachhead, he will be able to call upon an endless supply of reinforcements to secure his victory."

"Ah, yes," said Noda Mi. "But at what price? You love the wisdom of your mother, so let me quote to you something the Marshal once said to me. 'To kill ten enemy soldiers, we must be prepared to lose at least eight of our own.' A war of attrition will not be any kinder to your side than my side."

"But you'll ultimately lose!" said Aya Mazoti. "Why not skip all the slaughter and surrender so that you can have some hope of our mercy?"

"Mercy is not the Lyucu way," said Noda Mi. "The pékyu has given orders that all the Lyucu, whether pure-blooded, togaten, or loyal native, must resist to the utmost. We will fight you in every valley and on every hill, in every copse and on every pond, in every street and on every roof. We'll die before we'll yield, and so long as we kill enough of you, we'll have no regrets. You ask what we have to negotiate with, and the simple answer is that we possess the eternal, invincible Lyucu spirit."

"A pretty speech," said Empress Jia at last from the dais. "But it would be far more convincing if it came from an actual Lyucu instead of one of their chained dogs. You're about as steadfast as a reed in the wind."

Now it was Noda Mi's turn to blush. "Your Imperial Majesty's wit is as blunt as it is erroneous. Regardless of your assaults on my character, I can assure you that the pékyu's orders will be obeyed to the last syllable. Unless you're willing to watch the sea around Rui and Dasu turn crimson as lava and the fields of Ukyu-taasa salted with the bones of the dead, I suggest that you and I"—once again he locked eyes with the empress—"sit together here"—he pointed to the circle of ground he had been sitting in earlier—"and discuss a peaceful resolution to this unnecessary conflict like civilized human beings." He looked askance at Aya Mazoti, holding her ceremonial staff. "And leave the weapons standing, unused, outside the negotiations."

Throughout, his movements were stiff and formal, and his tone oddly wooden, as though he were a third-rate actor in an unfamiliar role—or, perhaps more likely, terrified at facing the judgment of the people he had betrayed.

Aya Mazoti growled at the hated man, ready to lunge at the turn-coat responsible for her mother's death. But Jia broke in again. "Go back to your place."

Still glaring at the despised Lyucu envoy, Aya backed slowly into her place at the head of the column on the western side of the Grand Audience Hall.

"You've presented your case, Noda Mi," said Empress Jia, sounding distracted. "You may retire so that I and the Lords of Dara may discuss your proposal in detail."

Noda Mi bowed his head. "A quick answer is necessary. Emperor Monadétu is an impatient man and has given us only five days before launching a direct assault on Ukyu-taasa."

Cogo Yelu finally shuffled forward. Years of sedentary living at court had given him a crooked back and a protruding belly, and he no longer looked the part of the expert administrator who had once helped Kuni Garu conquer the world. Yet, his gaze was sharp like an eagle's beneath those bushy, pure white eyebrows, and his voice, though aged, did not tremble.

"Noda, if time is so pressing, why have you not argued your case to the emperor, who is much closer to Kriphi, but decided to cross the sea to come to Pan?"

"Emperor Monadétu may be a skilled field commander," said Noda. "But in a game of *zamaki*, it's always best to keep in mind where the king is."

Empress Jia looked at Cogo, and the corners of her mouth curved up in a bitter smile. "Do you think I like wielding the Grace of Kings, Cogo?"

Instead of responding, Cogo turned slightly, not to face Empress Jia looming high above, but toward the empty veiled throne in front of the dais, and bowed.

The assembled ministers and generals looked at one another. The mood in the Grand Audience Hall crackled with tension like the air before a storm.

Cogo held the bow for a long moment, his hands wrapped around the blue jade compass and extended respectfully before him.

"I promise you, Cogo. Remember the estate you once bought in Rui," said the empress, her tone almost pleading.

Cogo lowered his hands, took a step back into his assigned place at the head of the column of ministers, and stood with his eyes looking straight ahead, his expression unreadable.

Zomi, whose place was next to Cogo's, was puzzled by the enigmatic exchange between the Prime Minister and the empress. *Some kind of understanding seems to have been reached between the two, but what? And why did Cogo choose this moment to highlight the most awkward political fact in all Dara? Empress Jia's unwillingness to hand over the Seal of Dara to the emperor grows daily more untenable, but surely it's a mistake to confirm this tension within the House of Dandelion in front of the Lyucu envoy?*

Unseen by anyone else in the Grand Audience Hall, Lady Soto, ensconced within the small changing room behind the dais, peeked out at the unfolding scene. It was her habit, as Jia's confidante, to secretly attend court this way. There was a time when Jia sought her advice after each session, but these days, she seemed to retreat more and more into herself. Sometimes Soto thought she didn't know her old friend at all anymore.

The empress turned back to Noda Mi almost as an afterthought, waving again to dismiss him.

Noda bowed. "There is just one more thing."

Every pair of eyes focused on the man. *One more thing?*

Slowly, methodically, Noda took out from his voluminous sleeve a small cloth bundle. This he unwrapped to reveal a jade tablet. With both hands, he lifted the cloth, with the jade tablet still at the center, reverently high above his head. Once again, he locked eyes with the empress.

"My dear friend Doru Solofi, once also a Tiro king during the Principate, died at the Battle of Zathin Gulf. I understand that he is buried here in Pan, in the cemetery honoring those who died during the . . . creation of Ukyu-taasa. I'd like a chance to visit his grave to pay my respects, and to leave this tablet carved with his royal name as a token of our friendship. Ah, all power appears mere fleeting vanity in the face of death and defeat."

Empress Jia nodded and waved again impatiently.

Keeping his eyes on the empress, Noda Mi backed away, still lifting the cloth and jade tablet high above his head. When he finally reached the entrance of the Grand Audience Hall, he turned and walked away.

Taking turns, members of the Inner Council examined the square of cloth Noda Mi had handed to Empress Jia.

It was Zomi's turn.

Most of the surface was dominated by a drawing. A cliff loomed over the sea, and from the top of the cliff dangled a large cage. The cage was divided into ten levels, and each level was packed full of people. Small figures in the margin indicated that each level contained one hundred prisoners, for a total of one thousand prisoners in the cage.

She could hear the other ministers of the Inner Council cluster around the chest that Noda Mi had given to the palace guards, containing "presents" from the Lyucu. Already, she had an inkling of what was in the chest.

Above the cliff, the cage was connected, through a block and tackle, to a thick set of cables that ended at a set of harnesses attached to three garinafins. The crudely drawn garinafins strained at the weight and seemed to be walking backward to lower the cage slowly.

"O gods!"

Behind her came cries of horror and revulsion. Retching. Dry heaves.

"Are these ears and noses?"

"Barbarous!"

Resolutely, she forced herself to keep her eyes on the cloth. She would not look at the chest.

The bottom of the cage was packed with stones, and Zomi could

almost hear the despondent cries of the prisoners as they were lowered, inch by inch, toward the cold and merciless embrace of the sea.

Her hands shook as she glanced over the figures at the bottom
of the drawing, a table of calculations. How long it would take to
load the cage with prisoners; how long it would take to drop the
cage from the top of the cliff into the sea; how long it would take for
everyone in the cage to drown; how long it would take to empty the
cage—there was an inset illustration showing the clever mechanism
at the side of the cage that allowed all the corpses to be dumped into
the sea with minimal work; how long it would take to pull the cage
back up to the top of the cliff so the cycle could start again.

*"Can you tell if the ears and noses were cut off from corpses or while the
victims were still alive?"*

"What difference does it make?"

*"If we can determine how the victims died, we may know more about
how seriously to take the threat. . . ."*

The debating voices behind Zomi hushed as the chest was taken
away; the stench of death and decay was replaced by the fragrance
of incense from braziers rushed in by servants; without realizing it,
someone gently took the cloth out of her trembling hands.

The calculations showed how many prisoners could be processed
in an hour, a day, a week. This was an optimized engine of slaughter,
designed to kill as many native captives as possible in the shortest
amount of time.

In her mind she was back on Rui, more than a decade ago.

"Nooooo!" howled Zomi Kidosu. "Mother! Mother! O gods!"

Than Carucono held on to her even tighter.

*The scene before her was incomprehensible. Her mother, burning; her
mother, dying. She had promised to give her mother a better life, and this
was what she had done.*

*Where a hundred people had scrambled and struggled for life a moment
ago, now only a hundred smoldering pyres remained. The charred but still
sizzling bodies maintained the poses of the last moments of their lives: a
mother shielding the body of her child, a husband interposing himself before
his wife, a son and daughter trying to cover the body of their mother—all
three were now fused into one smoldering corpse.*

The Lyucu had perfected their engine of death. Instead of wasting valuable garinafin fire breath, they now relied on inexhaustible water. Instead of a hundred, they could kill a thousand with a single gesture.

She could understand now why Noda Mi had been hesitant about presenting his "gifts" and the drawing in open court. Yes, the assembled ministers and officers would have torn him apart from limb to limb, even though an envoy was supposed to have diplomatic immunity.

An inhuman howl filled the air, a howl of rage, of despair, of utter incomprehension in the face of evil. It wasn't until the pain of tearing at her own throat punctured her awareness that she realized that the howl was coming from herself.

The debate among the Inner Council grew ever more heated, with each side accusing the other of cowardice, rashness, greed, pride, and every other sin known to gods or humankind.

It was clear that Noda Mi's boasting of the prowess of Lyucu warriors was nothing but a smoke screen. The real threat was the ability of the Lyucu to kill as many of the inhabitants of Unredeemed Dara as possible before succumbing.

Should Dara give in and grant peace to the butchers or press on and accept the deaths of hundreds of thousands?

Empress Jia listened to the arguments but said nothing, her face an expressionless mask carved from stone.

Zomi was equally silent. She stared at the evil contraption sketched on Noda Mi's square of silk while the arguments raged on around her, like the incomprehensible murmurs of the gods in her youth.

Finally, Prime Minister Cogo Yelu stepped into the fray. "The welfare of the people of Dara must be our guiding light," he said.

The room quieted, waiting for him to elaborate.

"When Emperor Ragin served as the Duke of Zudi by popular acclamation, he once had to defend the city against the army of the illustrious Tanno Namen of Xana. Namen's practice was to drive civilian refugees before his men as shock troops and living shields. The duke persuaded his friend, Mata Zyndu, to open the gates of the city to let in as many of the refugees as he could, despite the fact that the refugees were not his charge, and the action put the entire city at risk."

The ministers of the Inner Council nodded. The acts of Kuni Garu, as the founder of the Dandelion Dynasty, were constitutive acts, and weighty as precedent.

"When Emperor Ragin first tried to liberate Unredeemed Dara, he achieved great initial success," Cogo continued. "But then he fell into a trap at Naza Pass, and his only route of escape was to board his airship. Pékyu Tenryo drove defenseless peasants to surround the emperor, staked them to the ground, and threatened to burn all of them alive. The emperor stayed to save them, despite the fact that some of the civilians had collaborated with the Lyucu, and despite knowing that his action would make him a hostage, threatening the security of all Dara.

"In both cases, the emperor was guided by compassion. The people of Rui and Dasu are also the people of Dara, even if, as some of you have pointed out, they've collaborated with the Lyucu, some willingly, some not—"

Zomi suddenly spoke up. "Prime Minister, Noda Mi's threat isn't credible."

Everyone turned to her. "Wh-what?" stuttered Cogo.

Zomi pointed to the sketch on the silk cloth. "My job is to weigh the fish. The Lyucu are not engineers, and they have devastated the industrial foundation of Unredeemed Dara. Every piece of intelligence we have points to a consistent pattern in which they have refused to adopt our expertise in construction and engineering, and I do not believe they're capable of building such a machine of death. They are better at tearing down than building up.

"A killing cage like this is a highly challenging piece of machinery. But the drawing here seems to contemplate simply scaling up an ordinary cage, with no structural modifications needed to sustain the weight of the prisoners or to bear up under the stresses of repeated elevations and immersions. I do not believe this represents a real machine at all, but only the imagination of an evil mind with no understanding of what it takes to realize that vision."

Voices cried out in the aftermath of her speech, some in relief, some in disbelief. Zomi seemed to have recovered fully from her earlier loss of control. Facts were the straws she clung to, rebuffing all doubts with explanations of why the killing machine was infeasible.

Jia and Cogo exchanged a long, meaningful look.

Cogo turned to Zomi. "How can you be so certain? Your farseers didn't anticipate that the Lyucu would adopt fire arrows either, to the consternation of the emperor."

"That . . ." Zomi was at a loss for answers. Her knowledge of Unredeemed Dara was necessarily incomplete.

"The Lyucu also adopted novel armor for their garinafins, suggesting that they have in their employ native smiths with skill for invention. How can you be sure that these collaborators haven't overcome the engineering challenges, even if Noda's sketch doesn't show a feasible design?"

Zomi knew that Cogo had a good point. Yet, she persisted stubbornly. "We cannot attribute to the enemy such expertise with no evidence. It's improbable that they—"

"The ingenuity of evil shouldn't be underestimated," said Cogo. "Can you say, with absolute certainty, that they *cannot* construct such a machine? Not just unlikely, but impossible."

"I . . . cannot," conceded Zomi.

"Even if there's only a minuscule chance that the threat is real, we must behave as though it *were* completely real. Besides, even if they have no such evil machine, as the chest of ears and noses shows, the Lyucu have other ways of killing—perhaps less efficient, but workable enough."

Zomi discarded the mask of cold rationality. "But a peace treaty with the Lyucu is the worst decision possible right now! How can you contemplate letting the lives of all the men and women who have died to get us this close to victory go to waste? How can you imagine leaving the enslaved population of Rui and Dasu groaning in their chains? How can you—"

"Zomi, the troops who have sacrificed their lives to get us to this point will not have died in vain. Because of our advantage in arms, we can demand concessions, including better treatment for the enslaved population—"

"That is *not* the right reasoning!" Zomi shouted. "For us to back down because the Lyucu threaten harm to those in their power would encourage them to repeat the tactic again and again. We can't just make enslavement tolerable; we must end it!"

"But the price you speak of . . . Zomi, what of Emperor Ragin's compassion? What of—"

"There are more forms of compassion than the examples you cited. Emperor Ragin broke the peace with the Hegemon in order to end all strife when he had the advantage, instead of inviting another round of slaughter in ten, twenty years. If we're to imitate the emperor, then let's imitate the emperor at Rana Kida, not Naza Pass. We must not think only of those alive today, but also the countless who have yet to cross the Veil of Incarnation. We cannot allow future generations to be born and live in bondage. The interest of the few must yield to the interests of the many, and if we must sacrifice some to secure a lasting peace that is *just*, so be it."

For some time, Cogo simply looked at her, and when he continued, his voice was as anguished as she had ever heard it. "You're talking about the deaths of tens of thousands, perhaps hundreds of thousands. You speak of weighing the fish, but how do you weigh the lives of those who must die for your sense of justice? You speak of the welfare of future generations, but how many of those living now are you willing to kill—"

"We won't be doing the killing! The Lyucu will!"

"How can you evade responsibility by such a legalistic dodge? The chain of causation cannot be severed when the consequences of our decision are so clear and present. The Lyucu *will* carry out their threat if we don't yield. Are you willing to sentence hundreds of daughters to watch in chains as their mothers are burned alive to satisfy the Lyucu's twisted definition of a victory? Are you willing to condemn thousands of fathers to drown while their sons are conscripted to be living shields for the Lyucu? Will the hypothetical happiness of millions unborn always outweigh the deaths and suffering of those already here in the mortal realm?"

Zomi thought back to the moment when she had watched help-lessly as her mother was incinerated by garinafin breath in Naza Pass. What would she not give for Kuni Garu to have yielded a moment sooner, so that her mother could have been spared? Her vision blurred and her voice died in her throat, leaving only an inchoate moan of rage.

Empress Jia looked at the assembled ministers.

"Poti Maji told a story of how once Kon Fiji bought all the fish from a fisherman next to the beach. . . ."

The members of the Inner Council were confused, but they knew that the empress never told a story without a point. They listened.

All the fish in the barrel were still alive. Kon Fiji rolled the barrel back to the edge of the sea, tipped it over, and watched as the fish slithered into the water and swam away.

Onlookers pointed at the old master and laughed at his foolishness.

"Master, you haven't saved them," said Poti Maji. "These are lumber-fin groupers, notorious for being slow and dim-witted. The fisherman will only go out and catch all of them again. Look, he is already preparing his boat and net."

"Then I'll wait here for his return, so that I can buy them from him again," said Kon Fiji.

"But why?" asked Poti Maji.

"Perhaps he will change his mind about making a living by killing. Perhaps some of the lumber-fin groupers will get away. The future is full of possibilities."

Poti Maji shook his head. "Master, even if he decides to leave this trade, someone else will take his place. Even if some of the fish escape, others will be caught."

Kon Fiji smiled and held Poti by the shoulders earnestly. "I know that you're right, but I can't help what I do. It's my nature."

Later, Poti Maji wrote the following in his commentaries on Morality: *"The One True Sage believed that in the heart of every person, from the meanest criminal to the most elevated sage, from the three-day-old babe to the elder on their deathbed, there is a core of compassion and yearning to do good. By following his faith, he accepted the possibility that his actions would sometimes appear foolish or dangerous, but he persisted and never gave up his optimism. By studying Moralism, we aim to change human nature to be closer to the Master's nature."*

Empress Jia finished her story and waited.

"The Lyucu are hated and cruel, but we cannot let hatred be our master," Cogo Yelu said. "If we press ahead with a conquest without regard for the people in their dominion, then all of our hands will be stained with the blood that flows. The Lyucu are taking advantage of us, much the way a rat takes advantage of a man who dares not toss his shoe at the rat lest it strike the delicate vase it shelters behind, yet we have no choice but to acquiesce. To do otherwise would be contrary to our nature.

"In war, we must resist the impulse to become more like our enemies."

A vote was taken, and when Zomi's turn came, she abstained.

The tally was overwhelmingly for peace.

"Thank you, Lords of Dara," said Empress Jia, looking relieved. "Let the Seal of Dara be moved by compassion for the people."

CHAPTER TWENTY-EIGHT

WHAT VALUE DEFEAT?

OFF THE COAST OF RUI, NEAR KRIPHI: THE
EIGHTH MONTH OF THE ELEVENTH YEAR OF THE
REIGN OF SEASON OF STORMS AND THE REIGN OF
AUDACIOUS FREEDOM.

Phyro read over the message from Pan again.

"There must be some mistake," said Puma Yemu. "How could there be a cease-fire?"

"The Lyucu must have sent a delegation to Pan behind my back after they secured the promise of a delay from me."

"But why? We're on the verge of total victory here."

Phyro paced across the quarterdeck of the city-ship. "Bring me my field desk. I'm going to write to Zomi Kidosu for clarification. I must find out what lies the Lyucu have told. It isn't too late to fix the situation."

Just then, an aide-de-camp rushed up and saluted. "*Rénga*, the Imperial envoy has informed all the military monitors of the cease-fire. There is a great deal of confusion among the captains and officers."

Phyro sighed. "Summon the officers and monitors for a meeting. We must stabilize morale."

"What's that?" asked Puma Yemu, pointing at an approaching airship on the horizon to the south.

"Looks like another Imperial messenger airship. Maybe they bring more clarity."

"Somehow I doubt that," said Puma Yemu, shaking his head. The white hair, worn loose, and his snowy beard, made his head resemble a dandelion puff ball in the breeze.

MEANWHILE, IN PAN.

Zomi couldn't concentrate.

While Cogo Yelu was drafting the proclamation from Empress Jia informing the people of a new peace with the Lyucu, Zomi Kidosu had been given the task of preparing a dossier for negotiating the permanent peace treaty. She was extrapolating from the latest farseers' reports on conditions in Unredeemed Dara, which were based on refugee interviews, intelligence gleaned from pirates, Phyro's observations during the Battle of Crescent Island, and educated guesses.

Merely negotiating with the Lyucu already represented total and utter capitulation. She could only imagine how devastated Phyro would be upon hearing this news. All their effort, all the sacrifices made by the volunteer fighters—for this?

But Zomi wasn't only infuriated by her assignment, she was also distracted by her recollection of Empress Jia's behavior during Noda Mi's presentation and the subsequent debate in the Inner Council.

Cogo's arguments had been convincing, but Zomi couldn't escape the feeling that there was some opaque understanding between him and Jia.

What did the empress mean by "wielding" the Grace of Kings? And what was the estate Cogo once bought in Rui?

It doesn't make sense.

She pushed the thoughts from her mind. There was no time for doubt; she had to work on the reports. The cease-fire was a fait accompli. If she wanted the sacrifices of Phyro's soldiers not to have been in vain, she had to make sure they got the best deal possible.

Gori Ruthi and Lady Ragi, due to their experience in dealing with the Lyucu, had been chosen as the chief negotiators with the Lyucu. Jia had authorized the emissaries to offer the Lyucu even more tribute than they had been getting before the war. In exchange, it was hoped that the couple would extract some concessions to benefit the people of Rui and Dasu: the opening of regular passenger and shipping service to allow families separated by the Lyucu occupation to visit each other; permanent embassies; provisions to allow Dara officials to visit the occupied islands to monitor the treatment of natives and the children of Dara-Lyucu unions; cultural and artistic exchanges; perhaps joint exploitation of fishing grounds between the two states.

Bigger concessions, such as freedom for any part of the enslaved population or the cessation of the arbitrary slaughter of natives, weren't even being contemplated. The Lyucu would never agree.

As small as the hoped-for concessions were, Zomi could see their potential. If Tanvanaki agreed to any of them, the farseers would have many more opportunities to extract more accurate intelligence about Unredeemed Dara, a virtual fortress. Zomi imagined a glowing line in the sea around Rui and Dasu, enclosing the islands in an impenetrable circle.

Wait, she told herself. *A circle? Wait.*

The scene of Noda Mi sitting in *géüpa* in the middle of the Grand Audience Hall returned unbidden to her mind. He had sat there, seemingly filled with confidence, but he had betrayed his nervousness by rocking forward and backward, dragging his hands along the ground, tracing out a circle around himself. Maybe it was an unconscious nervous tic.

And then, he had looked up at Empress Jia. They had locked gazes—was Noda Mi concerned about the empress's reaction to the machine of death sketched on his silk cloth? No, the empress had been cool and calm after, seemingly unconcerned.

It doesn't make sense.

Zomi forced her mind to return to the present. She had a job to do; Gori Ruthi and Lady Ragi needed to be well prepared for the negotiations to extract every advantage.

Zomi was hoping to get some military concessions as well, though the possibility seemed to her rather remote: mutual reduction of fleets and armies (though, considering all the Lyucu were warriors, such an agreement would be impossible to enforce), limits on the number of garinafins each side would be allowed to breed, and so on. In exchange, Dara would offer even more economic inducements: shipments of grain, herbs, and manufactured goods beyond the already extensive tribute; maybe the assistance of experts in farming, weaving, irrigation, and such peaceful arts. The hope was that by enticing the Lyucu to profit from such knowledge, perhaps they would grow to be less warlike in time. It was unlikely, but she had to try.

The ivory knife in Zomi's writing hand bit into the wax blocks furiously, racing to keep up with her thoughts. From time to time, she paused to tend to the melting stone over the brazier, wafting the fragrance of top-quality orchid-infused writing wax from Müning, and laid down another column of perfect square blocks on the silk scroll.

As much as she wanted to promote the use of zyndari letters, she had to admit she far preferred to write using logograms. Classical Ano was sonorous, elegant, every phrase patterned to match the shape of thought of generations of sages in dialogue down the millennia. Luan Zyaji had taught her that the logograms were machines for shaping ideas, and she never felt the truth of that statement as much as when she tried to make her thoughts concrete in the form of a well-composed logogram.

At least one of the concessions we must get is the release of scholars who have been imprisoned without any evidence of treason—assuming any remain alive.

Zomi wrote the logogram for "prisoner," which consisted of a stylized figure for "person" in the middle, and a circular wall around it. In formal clerical script, the "person" sublogogram here was usually simplified to a pair of legs striding forward, but Zomi, who learned to write from Luan Zyaji, had always followed the practice of her master: the sublogogram was a full human figure sitting on the floor with feet tucked under, knees pointing outward—a sort of *géüpa*.

She smiled as she remembered Luan Zyaji's explanation for this personal quirk.

"I write it this way to honor an old friend, who has many interesting ideas," Luan Zyaji said. "He thinks it's tiring to always be standing instead of sitting, even in a logogram."

"Maybe your friend is just lazy," said teenaged Zomi Kidosu, brash and confident that she had all the answers.

"You aren't the first to call him lazy," said Luan Zyaji, chuckling. "But it takes more strokes to carve this sitting figure than a pair of striding legs, so laziness doesn't explain it."

"Then why does he write it that way? Just to be different?" Zomi had little patience for the way every great scholar seemed to have his own idiosyncratic version of some logogram—showing off at the expense of students who had to read their books later! Mapidéré's standardization of the Ano logograms was the best thing he ever did, as far as Zomi was concerned.

"No," said Luan Zyaji, his face turning somber. "It's because he used to watch over prisoners during the reign of Mapidéré. He wrote the logogram this way to remind himself that his charges were people who deserved kindness and compassion."

"Oh," said Zomi. "Then . . . I'll write it that way too. Your friend sounds like a good fish."

"He would enjoy hearing that."

She missed her teacher so much—his wisdom, his kindness, his empathy for the universe. She paused as she looked at the logogram and wiped away a tear.

She stopped as a chill flashed down her spine. In her mind, superimposed over the logogram, was the image of Noda Mi sitting on the floor of the Grand Audience Hall in *géüpa*, his hands describing a circular wall around himself.

Empress Jia had dismissed Noda Mi's long speech as a mere smoke screen. The debate among the Inner Council had been focused on his silk cloth.

But what if it was the other way around? What if the silk cloth was the smoke screen and the real message was Noda Mi miming logograms through charades?

This particular way of writing the logogram for "prisoner" had grown more popular in Dara after Emperor Ragin's death because that was the way he wrote it. But there was no reason for Noda Mi, who had spent the last decade in Unredeemed Dara, to write it this way. He must have deliberately done this to send a message specifically aimed at someone in the Grand Audience Hall, someone to whom such a way of writing was particularly meaningful—someone like the wife of the man who once watched over prisoners.

Zomi recalled again how Noda Mi had locked eyes with Empress Jia as he sat before her.

Perhaps her dead teacher's spirit was trying to help her once more.

She got up from the desk, the silk scroll on which she had been writing the report intended for Gori and Ragi forgotten. She needed to talk to someone, and there was only one person in the entire palace she trusted at this moment.

MEANWHILE, OFF THE COAST OF RUI, NEAR KRIPHI.

"*Rénga*," said Puma Yemu, "I, for one, don't believe it. There has been some grievous mistake!"

Phyro stood near the prow of the city-ship, facing his officers and monitors. Gori Ruthi and Lady Ragi, the Imperial envoys, had ordered Phyro to hand over his seal of command.

"The empress has dispatched seven messenger airships to us in quick succession, all demanding the immediate cessation of hostilities and affirming Lady Ragi and her husband's authority," said Ki Aten. "There is no mistake."

"But how can the regent know what is actually happening here?" demanded Puma. "The judgment of the commander on the field is far more relevant than guesses by bureaucrats thousands of miles away in the capital! We need to finish the job lest we betray the sacrifices of our dead comrades."

"What you speak of is treason!" shouted Ki Aten. "The Imperial envoys' orders are clear: We must honor the cease-fire and allow them to begin negotiating for peace."

"It's treason to let Admiral Carucono's death be for nothing! Whoever heard of surrendering when you have your heel on the neck of the enemy? This is snatching defeat from the jaws of victory!"

Phyro stood and looked at each of his officers and monitors in turn. Even though he knew Jia had never favored the invasion, he couldn't imagine why she would try to stop him now, when he was on the verge of liberating Unredeemed Dara. As much as he disliked her, he had always believed that she had the best interests of the people of Dara at heart.

Zomi still hadn't answered him. He had to delay proceedings here, give her a chance.

He held out his hands placatingly to the shouting officers and monitors. "Let me speak to the Imperial envoys in private. Perhaps the empress has plans that aren't apparent from the official orders."

MEANWHILE, IN PAN.

Zomi grabbed a piece of scrap silk and began to drip-form blocks of wax. As she worked through the riddle step by step, she translated Noda Mi's sequence of actions into logograms with the ivory writing knife.

She sat back, the logogram for "prisoner" in the middle of the small table.

Across from her, Lady Soto looked thoughtful.

"Do you think I'm reading too much into it?" asked Zomi with some trepidation.

"I don't know yet," said Soto. "I've been at court longer than you, and every conversation here is an enigma wrapped inside a mystery hidden inside a riddle disguised as talk about the weather. You may be right, or you may be chasing after a phantom."

"I need your help," said Zomi. "I . . . I don't know who else to turn to."

Soto nodded. The court was Jia's court, but Soto was like a second mother to Phyro. Zomi's suspicions could only be voiced to someone she believed would defy the empress for the sake of the emperor.

"So that was the first logogram," said Zomi. After a pause to collect her thoughts, she went on, "The second time Noda looked at Empress Jia, he pointed at her, at himself, and then pointed at the circled piece of ground he had vacated."

Carefully, she carved two sitting figures into a new block of wax.

"This is where I'm stuck. What logogram could Noda Mi have meant? 'Twins'? 'Doubling'? 'Friendship'? But I can't find anything he did that would serve as a motive modifier to narrow the meaning down. And there is no logogram that involves drawing a wall around two persons. Ugh, I feel like such a fool."

Though she was steeped in the Ano Classics, she had come to the logograms late, as a teenager, and had been instructed in an itinerant life around Dara. In many ways, as the empress had pointed out, she remained an outsider to the privileged culture of the literati. She had not grown up surrounded by logogram-infused toys and neither had she attended refined parties at which scholars constructed charades and riddles to entertain one another and to show off their erudition. Despite being one of the most powerful Lords of Dara, at this moment, Zomi felt acutely the shame of her origins as a poor peasant. Class was not something even the best education could erase.

Lady Soto pondered the wax blocks.

"Don't be so hard on yourself," she said gently. "Clever riddles are ultimately just like any other well-crafted machine, and they'll yield before a keen mind driven by persistence. Remember that Noda Mi is not himself a very learned man, so he must have been advised by savvy scholars collaborating with the Lyucu. Thus, the actions they choreographed for him must have been committed to rote memory, and would appear stiff and unnatural. Let's recall in detail what Noda Mi did and said during that sequence."

"Let's see," said Zomi, reassured by Soto's encouragement. She closed her eyes to concentrate on the memory of the scene in the Grand Audience Hall. "Aya was approaching him threateningly, and Noda got up and pointed to the ground he had been sitting on and told the princess to 'imagine this plot of land as Ukyu-taasa.'"

Soto nodded. "So one possibility is that the circled land no longer represented a walled enclosure, but simply 'realm' or 'kingdom.'"

"All right." Zomi poked at a wax block with her writing knife. "As he looked at the empress that second time, Noda invited her to 'sit together' with him in the circle 'and discuss this like civilized human beings.'"

The pair passed the writing knife back and forth, trying out different combinations of semantic roots and motive modifiers. But nothing quite fit.

Soto stretched out her legs in *thakrido* and massaged her calves. "Sorry, I've been sitting for so long that my legs are falling asleep." Then she knelt up and stretched her back. "Age is unforgiving—"

"That's it!" Zomi sat up, her eyes flashing with excitement. "If two diplomats were sitting down to negotiate, they would likely sit in *mipa rari*, which would be the more formal and 'civilized' position."

She quickly carved two kneeling figures facing each other above an "earth" semantic root: the logogram for "contest" or "game."

"Maybe Noda meant to speak of the competition between the Lyucu and Dara?" asked Zomi hopefully.

Soto shook her head. "I feel we're still missing a clue."

Zomi closed her eyes and clenched her fists. *Think! Think!*

"What was it that Noda had said *after* he invited the empress to sit down to negotiate?" asked Soto.

"'And leave the weapons standing, unused, outside the negotiations,'" said Zomi. "Now that you mention it, that sticks out as a very unnatural phrase. Who talks like that?"

Soto took the writing knife from her. "The 'weapon' that Aya was holding wasn't a weapon at all, but a ceremonial staff . . . also known as a banner or standard."

Next to the assembly Zomi had already carved, Soto added a new sublogogram.

"You see this used as a motive modifier in many logograms involving rulership, administration, or the like," mused Soto. "It's a stylized representation of the battle flags that ancient Ano heroes hoisted on their chariots as they rode into battle, rallying their men and calling for the protection of the gods."

The two stared at the new combined logogram at the center of the table and then looked at each other, nodding. This was the right solution. All the pieces were in place.

A motive modifier usually changed the meaning of the base logogram metaphorically. "Competition" modified by "ceremonial standard" therefore meant "winning (or the winner of) the favor of the gods."

Or, as one would say in Classical Ano: *Rénga*.

The honorific used to address the emperor was derived from a classical phrase referring to ancient champions who won athletic competitions honoring the gods of Dara. It was also something that Noda Mi had deliberately refused to say to Empress Jia.

"'Prisoner' and *'Rénga'*—what message was Noda Mi trying to send?" Zomi furrowed her brows. Despite undoing another lock on the puzzle box, they seemed no closer to a complete solution.

"There was still one more time that Noda locked eyes with the empress," Soto reminded her.

This was after the conclusion of the audience, when Noda Mi had been dismissed. He had then lifted the piece of jade wrapped in cloth above his head as he backed away from Jia.

Zomi dripped a new block of wax and sculpted a standing person on the bottom. On top she carved the sublogogram for a piece of woven cloth, and then the logogram for "jade."

"I don't recognize this—" she began hesitantly.

"You forgot that Noda was walking backward the whole time," said Soto. She took the knife and added the motive modifier for "(facing) away."

The audaciousness of Noda Mi's message took their breaths away. They were looking at the logogram for "abdication."

In essence, through a series of charades, Noda had sketched for Jia a vision of the future, that, paraphrased, might go like this:

"Victory by Phyro over the Lyucu will lead to a meteoric rise in the emperor's authority. Imagine him parading through Pan in triumph, at the head of an army absolutely loyal to him. By then, you, Empress Jia, Regent of Dara, will have no choice but to abdicate, and you can look forward to becoming Phyro's prisoner as he exacts revenge for all the years you kept him from the throne that is rightfully his."

Zomi looked at Soto. "Can we be certain that this is right?"

Soto shook her head. "We're piling speculation on guess based on conjecture derived from hunch. Of course we can't be sure. But everything fits, and some of Noda Mi's actions confirm it—"

Zomi nodded. "That bit where he invited the empress to sit inside the 'prison'—"

"Or the way he kept on emphasizing that the victory and the armada belonged to Phyro instead of the empress—"

"Or the way he hinted at the end that the empress was still in charge, but perhaps not for much longer—"

"Or the way Cogo and the empress spoke of who wielded the Grace of Kings—"

"He knew—"

"He knew—"

The two women paused, overwhelmed by the implications. Cogo, by far the most politically cunning member of the court, must have deciphered Noda Mi's true message along with Empress Jia. That would explain the cryptic exchange between the two, after which they seemed to reach some silent understanding.

"What did the empress mean when she spoke of the Prime Minister's estate in Rui?" asked Zomi, her voice barely above a whisper. Reflexively, she looked around to be sure that she and Soto were alone in Soto's tiny bedroom.

"There were rumors, back when Emperor Ragin first ascended the Dandelion Throne, that Cogo Yelu diverted funds from the Imperial Treasury to build himself a luxurious manor on Rui." Soto paused, thinking back to those long-ago events. "I believe he had spread those rumors himself in order to diminish his own stature among the people. He understood that an emperor, even one as trusting as Ragin, would be suspicious of ministers who behaved like perfect Ano sages, since they would steal the people's love away from the occupier of the throne, perhaps in furtherance of their own ambition. By deliberately staining his reputation with a relatively minor act of corruption, he humanized himself in the eyes of Kuni Garu and secured his own political future."

Zomi listened to this account with dismay. Her own patron, Gin Mazoti, never cared to play such political games. She was the unyielding winter plum, and for her directness and overweening pride, she had ultimately been stripped of her fief and imprisoned. Luan Zyaji had warned Zomi of the dangers of court life and the uncertainties of currying favor with suspicious sovereigns, and even after so many years, she found such political maneuvers disgusting.

Yet, the more pressing issue was what the empress meant by invoking that incident. "The Prime Minister used the estate on Rui as a diversion to further his own political goals—" began Zomi hesitantly.

"That might be putting it a bit too strongly," said Soto. "The founding of a new dynasty is a tumultuous time—"

Zomi wasn't listening. "—the goal being to keep himself in power," she concluded. "That's it!"

She thought feverishly back to the scene in the Grand Audience Hall. The Prime Minister had bowed to the empty, veiled throne, as though bidding goodbye to an old loyalty. And after the empress's remark about the estate in Rui, he had then stepped back into his place, and from that moment on, advocated passionately for the empress's preferred view.

"There is a grand conspiracy between the empress and the Prime Minister to keep power away from the rightful occupier of the veiled throne," whispered Zomi. "They will use the lives of the people of Rui and Dasu as a diversion—that's the 'estate'—to serve one overarching political goal: preserving Empress Jia in power."

Soto shook her head. "That's not possible. Jia isn't—"

"But it all fits!" Unable to contain herself, Zomi got up and paced back and forth. "I knew that Noda Mi's killing engine wasn't real, but the Prime Minister and the empress refused to listen—"

"But even if the machine isn't real, the Lyucu can kill many—"

"That's not the point!" Zomi's eyes blazed like stars with the utter conviction of truth. "Don't you see, Lady Soto? For all their talk about mercy and the need to save lives, they're just trying to hold on to their own power, to maintain the status quo!"

"Don't do anything rash!" cried Soto. But Zomi was already gone.

Jia reviewed her calculations again.

It's still not enough! Tiphan Huto needs to work faster!

Based on what Wi and Shido had been able to get out of the despicable, greedy man, the goods she was smuggling into Unredeemed Dara were very much in demand, but the Lyucu simply lacked the funds to buy more than they were already buying. Reducing prices too much would arouse suspicion, so she had no choice but to hope that Gori Ruthi and Lady Ragi could negotiate a treaty that would increase the amount of tribute. The food would be helpful to the starving people of Rui and Dasu, and the gold and silver could be used by the Lyucu to buy more—

"Mistress!"

She looked up. Wi was standing in front of her, her face clouded by worry. Behind her, two Dyran Fins held the bound and gagged figure of Zomi Kidosu.

Her heart skipped a beat. But the surprise didn't show on her face. "What happened?"

"We found her sneaking onto the next Imperial messenger airship, trying to substitute this for your orders to the emperor," said Wi. She handed the empress a folded scroll.

Jia opened it and read over the dense logograms. Then she put the scroll down and looked at Zomi.

"Ungag her."

The empress and the Farsight Secretary stared at each other.

"You're very clever," began Jia. "Perhaps *too* clever. You have a habit of jumping—"

"I *am* a fool!" spat out Zomi. "I'm so naive and blind that I've been deceived by you not once, but twice! I should have known, after what happened to the Marshal, that you crave nothing but power, that you would stop at nothing—"

Jia waved at Shido and Zomi was gagged again.

The empress closed her eyes, trying to think.

This is all the fault of that idiot Noda Mi. Because he is a man moved by nothing but selfishness, he thinks everyone else is exactly like him. Because he is a fool with cunning and no sense, he believes himself the smartest person in the room. His little scheme has been useful to me, but to show off his "cleverness" in open court . . . Ugh!

I should have known that Cogo wouldn't be the only one astute enough to decipher his clumsy riddles. But whereas Cogo has the good sense to understand that sometimes it is necessary to let people think the worst of you in order to do what must be done, Zomi is just like Phyro: Everything is black and white, with no shades of gray.

But how can I blame her? Cogo trusts that I am working toward mutagé; she does not.

To think that I, of all people, have to depend on trust in the end . . . How the gods love to play with us.

"What else does she know?" Jia asked Wi.

Wi shook her head. "We didn't get to interrogate her."

"Do you know about the secret tribute being paid to the Lyucu via Tiphan Huto?"

Zomi's eyes widened at this.

"I guess not," said Jia. *How ironic, since the berries share your name here in Dara.* She turned to Wi again. "Did she share her suspicions with anyone else?"

"She was in conversation with Lady Soto," said Wi.

Jia sighed. That was a problem she would have to solve later. Zomi, as one of the most powerful officials at court, could do incalculable damage with her accusation. Soto, on the other hand, was her friend. She could still be persuaded.

"Bring her to the dungeon, and keep her isolated—use the same cell that once held Gin Mazoti. No one is to see her, not even to bring her food or empty her bucket, except the Dyran Fins. Treat her well but make sure she has no access to any writing implements at all. Tell Cogo that the Farsight Secretary has gone into seclusion for a sudden illness and he is to manage the farseers in her absence."

Zomi stared daggers at her.

"If she tries to contact anyone at all," added Jia, "burn out her tongue and cut off her hands."

Zomi growled in her throat and struggled against her bonds as the Dyran Fins took her away.

MEANWHILE, OFF THE COAST OF RUI, NEAR
KRIPHI.

Phyro left the cabin of the Imperial envoys and looked up at the stars.

He was shaken by the description of the Lyucu killing engine, but a far deeper unease came from his recognition that Goztan had failed.

He had no proof, but he was certain that the box of ears and noses that Noda Mi had brought to Pan were from the families of the native slaves who had immolated themselves at Crescent Island in order to stave off such a fate for their loved ones. The Lyucu were not interested in mercy, not for anyone.

Goztan had given him a rough sketch of politics in Unredeemed Dara, and without admitting it to himself, he had pinned his hopes on the accommodationists winning the internal struggle. But Noda Mi's presentation in Pan showed that was not to be.

Even without the macabre killing engines, he had seen enough at Crescent Island to imagine what a conquest of Lyucu would be like. There would be many more native slaves forced to fight for the Lyucu, and the more of them that died, the more the Lyucu would consider it a victory.

Liberating Unredeemed Dara had seemed so clear a goal at first, but the experience of actually fighting had turned out so different. There was little that was clear, and all was confusion: Noda Mi and Wira Pin, who plotted against their own people and devised cruel methods of torture; the native auxiliaries who killed Than Carucono; the slaves who attacked his own boarding party to defend the Lyucu city-ships, all in the vain hope of pleasing their Lyucu masters so that their families would be spared. . . .

If he were to press ahead with the conquest of Unredeemed Dara, he would have to be prepared to kill many more people of Dara than the Lyucu.

But don't the people have a duty to try to free themselves? he raged inside. *Aren't they complicit in their own enslavement, in the horror that is Unredeemed Dara? How can a few thousand Lyucu control hundreds of thousands, without the conquered people bearing at least some measure of responsibility for their own state?*

He reminded himself that his duty was to the empire, to his army, to people who believed in his vision. Maybe the gods wanted him to ride into Unredeemed Dara on the back of a garinafin and slaughter all who stood in his way. If the people of Rui and Dasu were too cowardly to rise up in arms and save themselves, but would rather serve the conquerors and enslavers, then wasn't it his duty to remove them from the map of Dara as a surgeon hacks off a rotten limb?

How could evil be removed from the world without sacrificing those serving evil, even if unwillingly?

> *Let a man fall with each ten steps you take;*
> *Walk a thousand miles a new path to make.*

He caressed the logograms etched into the blade of Na-aroénna, reading them with his fingers. Once again, he felt the flow of hot lava through his veins. Once again, the world seemed to fade away. He was a colossus like one of the gods who strode through the battle-field in the time of the Diaspora Wars, shaping Dara with his sword much as a scholar carving wax into logograms.

"Freedom isn't free," he said to himself. "The slavish must be consigned to their natures."

He was about to go back to his cabin and summon Puma Yemu to begin plotting the confinement of the Imperial envoys and the military monitors when he heard a sailor singing on the far side of the ship.

> *Is it snow that I see falling in the valley?*
> *Is it rain that flows over the faces of the children?*
> . . .

He stopped. The old Cocru folk song was very familiar to him. His mother, Empress Risana, had once asked Kuni Garu's soldiers to sing it when they had besieged the Hegemon at Rana Kida. It was the song, more than anything else, that had led to the desertion of Mata Zyndu's soldiers and his final fall.

As a child, he had been puzzled by the story.

"*Mama, did you suggest that to Auntie Gin and Da to save the lives of Da's soldiers?*"

"*Only in part, Hudo-tika. I didn't want the Hegemon's soldiers to die either.*"

"*Why? They were fighting for the wrong side! They should have known that Da was unifying Dara so that everyone could live free from wars.*"

"*Maybe they weren't fighting for the best ideals. Yet the Hegemon's soldiers had mothers just like ours. I would want you safe no matter what, and I couldn't bear the thought of those mothers never seeing their sons again."*

"But why do you care about those peasants? They were ignorant and mean—why else would they fight against Da?"

"Oh, that's wrong, my baby. Soldiers always fight out of love: love of life, love of family, love of homeland. Many do end up fighting for the wrong lord or the wrong cause. But your father always said, 'They are not mean in their nature, but made mean by the meanness of their rulers.' Never be so certain that you're right that you can justify the killing of thousands without shivering from doubt."

Phyro imagined the slaves on those city-ships, setting themselves on fire in the hopes that their mothers, fathers, spouses, siblings, children might live a day longer; he imagined the people of Dasu and Rui, trying to endure another day, trying to please their Lyucu masters not out of fear for their own lives, but the lives of those they loved.

He tried to imagine his mother looking at him now, caressing the Doubt-Ender, certain that killing was the answer, certain that slaughter was justified. The lava that had flowed through his veins turned to cold ice. He fell to his knees in shame.

The words of Lady Soto from long ago, like buried seeds, sprouted in his mind.

Killing is a terrible thing, and every time you kill someone, a little bit of yourself dies. In our histories, we call those who kill thousands, hundreds of thousands, even millions, great, but they are often little more than hollow shells, walking corpses into which we project our fantasies of what heroism and nobility look like.

How close he had come to fulfilling that vision! How easy it would have been to give in to that temptation!

He had always thought of his aunt-mother as a coward, an appeaser, a woman who was too scared to confront the Lyucu. But now he saw her in a different light. Had she known, all along, that his dream to liberate Unredeemed Dara would come to naught? Had she always seen that the price for victory would be too great, and that there was nothing to do but to live with evil, to endure an unjust peace?

Under the cold gaze of the stars, Phyro wept the bitter tears of experience, the only value of defeat.

MEANWHILE, IN PAN.

As soon as she found herself atop the Moon-Gazing Tower, Jia knew she was in a nightmare.

It was so difficult these days to stay awake. She kept herself going with various herbal concoctions, and she knew that she was poisoning herself in the process. It couldn't be helped. Sleep, filled with dreams that haunted her, was so much harder to bear.

The rising column of smoke coalesced into the shape of a woman with long sleeves.

Jia faced Risana with dread. The smoke-woman had no eyes, but the stars above seemed like a thousand accusatory eyes, piercing her soul.

Risana approached her and stopped a few steps away. "Sister," she said, "you are troubled."

The voice was unexpectedly kind.

"I've been misunderstood," croaked Jia. It was true, but it was also a dodge.

"So you say," said Risana. "But as you know, I've never been able to read you."

"I accepted peace for the sake of the people of Dara! But I can't let the Lyucu suspect there is a plot. I must let them think that we're afraid, that I'm selfish, that I crave power above all. . . ." Jia's voice trailed off.

"There is a plot, then?"

Jia said nothing. She couldn't count on anyone except herself.

"When you wear a mask for too long," said Risana, "sometimes it's no longer possible to tell where the mask ends and the woman begins."

Jia straightened her spine. The note of pleading left her voice. "So be it."

"Is what Zomi Kidosu suspects true?"

Jia turned away, not deigning to give an answer.

Risana laughed. "You're so paranoid that you can't even be candid in a dream." Then her voice turned gentle again. "But tell me, what was troubling you just now, before you fell asleep?"

Jia relented. "I've sent seven messengers to Phyro, and yet there's been no reply from Gori and Ragi to let me know that Phyro has turned over the seal of command."

"You allowed him to fight this war."

"I never expected him to win! I thought he would suffer a defeat and gain wisdom. But he is too good a field general. Though I starved him of resources, he managed to craft a victory out of thin air—the worst possible outcome for the people of Rui and Dasu."

"Now that he has tasted power, you fear he'll disobey and break the cease-fire you've imposed on him."

"If he does, it will be an irredeemable disaster for all Dara, and I'm afraid we'll lose him forever to the trap of militarism."

Risana waved her insubstantial sleeves mockingly. "If I were still alive, he would listen to me."

Jia shuddered. At length, she said, "Perhaps you're right. But we live with the choices we make."

"Do you really believe that it would be wrong for Phyro to invade Unredeemed Dara?" There was now a cold edge to Risana's voice, as though she were channeling Lady Rapa, the goddess of ice.

Jia turned back to face the faceless apparition of smoke. "With all my heart. I don't know what to do if he refuses my orders. The army is loyal to him, and even with all my attempts to rein him in, he is too like his father."

"If you really want to persuade him, you still have me," said Risana, in that same cold, icy voice.

Jia stared at her. As understanding dawned, her face twisted in horror.

"No," said Jia, backing away. "NO!"

"Teeth on the board," said Risana, pressing forward. "Isn't that what you believe?"

"No, no, no! Please!" Jia was backed up against the edge of the Moon-Gazing Tower. She brought her hands protectively up to her face.

Risana leaned in close and hissed in her face, her breath a blast of darkest winter. "This isn't me. I'm just a part of you. You already know what you must do."

Jia lost her balance and fell—

She gasped as she sat up in her bedroom, drenched in cold sweat. Alone in her room, she wrapped her arms around herself and wept.

～

Soto hurried through the corridors of the Imperial family's private quarters. The ladies-in-waiting and the courtiers bowed as she passed.

Soto's mind was all turmoil. She couldn't find Zomi Kidosu anywhere, and she was afraid that the young hothead had committed some error impossible to fix. She had to go find Jia now.

Whatever Jia's faults were, she was her friend. There was no way that Jia would be plotting with Cogo Yelu to collaborate with the Lyucu just so she could stay in power. Zomi's conspiracy theory was too preposterous to be credited. Every fiber of her being told her it was untrue.

"You promised me," Soto muttered to herself as she followed the winding hallways and through heavy doors. Jia had made her a promise on the day Risana died. She intended to hold Jia to it.

There was a vase in the corner of Jia's bedchamber. Inside the vase were yellow flowers of different varieties: chrysanthemums, dandelions, peonies, sunflowers, eggs-and-noodles. . . .

The petals, made of diaphanous silk, began to spin like tiny windmills, though there was no breeze.

The artificial flowers were connected via silver wires to golden dandelion-shaped medallions embedded in the walls of the long corridor leading to her bedchamber—a common decorative motif throughout the palace. At the center of each of those medallions, however, was a piece of oculium, a little eye. They responded to changes in the lighting in the hallway, and announced passing shadows via the signaling spinners in the vase in her room.

Just because she didn't want Phyro to go to war didn't mean that she didn't appreciate his inventions.

Human guards, however vigilant, could never be as tireless and incorruptible as mechanical ones.

Jia sat up. It was time.

Are you going to finally abandon me, Soto?

Now that the moment had arrived, she felt preternaturally calm. The path she had chosen to walk was a lonely one, and she had always known that none of her mortal loves could survive it. Not her devotion to sensitive, vulnerable Timu; not her care for brave, self-reliant Théra; not her concern for adventurous, idealistic Phyro; and certainly not her affection for Soto, the one and only friend she had left.

She had to find a use for what she couldn't keep. *Had to.*

She remembered once again the terror and isolation she had lived through as a prisoner of the Hegemon. Mata had believed he was reshaping Dara to be better, to cleanse it of the base and low. Who cared if the bones and blood of lesser beings paved his way? War ravaged the land and people died like ants.

Alone, she had saved the orphaned girls who would become the Dyran Fins. Alone, she had managed a household. Alone, she had raised her children.

Until Soto came.

In some ways, she felt closer to her than she ever did to Kuni. Soto was not a lover, but she was the mirror of her soul. Their bond was forged in the most unforgettable, horrific part of her life.

She forced those thoughts away. Risana was right. She already knew what she had to do. The best lies were made from truths.

She had to do terrible things to prevent even more terrible futures. Even if she had to sacrifice her family, friends, those dearest to her heart.

Her heart clenched and she found it hard to breathe.

But she had to. *Had to.* How else could she be sure that Phyro would not seek to emulate the Hegemon, a man who believed that any price was worth paying in order to confront evil? A man who believed in reshaping Dara by the sword, and who deemed all who fell quislings, traitors, cowards, slaves, of lesser natures?

She couldn't trust. She had to *do.* She had to cultivate and encourage his nature, and in that process, save Dara as well as him from himself.

She took a deep breath, and began to speak.

Soto slowed down as she entered the twisting corridor that led to the empress's private suite. Her steps were slow and silent. She knew that Jia had trouble sleeping these days, and she didn't want to disturb her friend if she happened to be napping.

Jia's voice echoed down the corridor.

"Go find Lady Soto and invite her to tea."

There was a pause, and someone seemed to be whispering deferentially before Jia's voice sounded again.

"No. I'll brew the pot myself. Once she is here, guard the door. Do not enter until summoned."

Another pause. More whispers.

"Just one cup. That will be all."

Just one cup.

A silent thunderclap went off in Soto's head. She faltered, having to hold on to the wall for balance. She couldn't hear anything except the rush of blood in her ears.

"Have I finally lost you, Soto? Will you plunge Dara into civil strife?"

"For the sake of the people, I will keep your secret for now. But if you do not give up the reins of power when Phyro is ready, I swear by the Twins that I will proclaim the truth to every corner of Dara."

And here it was, the moment she had never believed would come. Jia, who preferred poison as her way of execution, was inviting her to tea.

Just one cup.

She had to go to Phyro and tell him the truth. She had to get out of here before Jia found her.

Quietly, she snuck away. She didn't stop to return the bows of anyone in the palace, and she didn't care that they looked at her strangely.

For a long time after the flower petals had stopped spinning, Jia sat in her room, staring at the wall as sunlight shifted and shadows chased each other across the floor.

There was no tea set on the table; no pot, nor a single cup.

She was alone in the room.

At length, she roused herself. There was indeed poison to prepare, and horrors only she could unleash. Once the treaty was concluded, the shipments to the pirates would increase. It was time to think about sprinkling the fungal spores she had carefully cultivated . . . perhaps into the next set of crates Wi and Shido would send to Tiphan Huto.

She left her room and strode toward the Imperial Garden, toward her shed. She walked alone, as she always knew she would have to.

LATER, OFF THE COAST OF RUI, NEAR KRIPHI.

Phyro listened quietly as Soto told her story.

For a long time, he didn't respond. He was like a volcano just before eruption, the tension within boiling and building.

"Hudo-*tika*, talk to me," pleaded Soto. She had escaped Pan by bluffing her way onto yet another Imperial messenger airship dispatched to Phyro. The empress's favor for her was well known, and the crew had not dared to question her. Soto had sighed with relief when no guards came from the palace—perhaps Jia had not realized that she had gone and was still searching for her to invite her to tea, thereby burying the secret of Risana's death forever.

Phyro didn't care about the riddles being posed at the Dandelion Court; he didn't care about Cogo Yelu's betrayal; he didn't care about Jia's plot to keep the Seal of Dara for herself.

"She killed my mother?" Phyro asked, pausing between each word. He wanted to be absolutely sure he understood the only thing that mattered.

Soto nodded.

He closed his eyes wearily. So many things that never made sense before were coming into focus now. How else to explain the excessive honors Jia heaped on his mother year after year, while neglecting Fara's mother? How else to explain the constant efforts to deny him power, to prevent him from making any decision that mattered? Jia's conscience was troubled. She was guilty.

The word "aunt-mother" tasted like ashes on his tongue. To think that he had deferred to that unreadable mask of a face for so many years! He was indeed naive, too quick to trust.

She was more poisonous than a viper, more cruel than a wolf, more devious than a spider. She had murdered his mother.

"What are you going to do?" asked Soto.

Phyro didn't know.

He had already decided to abandon the conquest of Unredeemed Dara and hand over the seal of command to Gori Ruthi and Lady Ragi—but he hadn't done so yet. He could still summon Puma Yemu and seize the military monitors; he could announce the sins of Jia to his soldiers; he could march on Pan at the head of his army.

He could rebel against Jia, as she had always feared he would.

"O Mother, my mother," he muttered.

Down that path lay the deaths of hundreds of thousands in civil strife, as brother fought against brother, son against mother. Was he willing to let the flames of war sweep across all the Islands?

He imagined the confusion of his soldiers as they were told that they had turned, overnight, from liberators into rebels.

Jia was not Mapidéré, nor was she the Hegemon. Though she had abandoned the people of Rui and Dasu, she had ushered in a period of unprecedented prosperity in Dara. She was not, to most, an unfit regent and sovereign.

Still, they would follow him, he thought. At least enough would that he would have a viable chance at conquering Dara at the head of an army.

But that would be wrong. They had joined him to fulfill a vision of freedom, to liberate the Islands from the cruel Lyucu. For him to lead them into the horrors of civil war would be a betrayal of that vision, of *mutagé*, of everything his father and mother had believed in.

Risana was born a commoner, and she had always believed it was unjust for the lowborn to die for the ambitions of the great lords. If he were to plunge the Islands into chaos and slaughter to satisfy a private craving for vengeance, he would be no better than Noda Mi.

He was no longer Emperor Monadétu, no longer Prince Phyro, no longer the commander of the army of Dara. Even if he hadn't already decided to abandon the conquest of Rui and Dasu, Soto's revelation changed everything.

Jia had murdered his mother, and it was up to him, as a man, as a son, as Hudo-*tika*, to avenge her. Nothing else mattered. Empire, duty, freedom, *mutagé*—none of these abstractions weighed as much as that one incontrovertible, concrete truth: He loved his mother, and one fought out of love.

"Lady Soto," he said, "I thank you for telling me the truth."

"What are you going to do?" asked Soto again.

"Years ago, my father slew a white serpent, and became the man he was," Phyro said. "I'm going to slay another serpent."

"Are you going to rebel?"

"No," he said. "From this moment on I'm no longer a member of the House of Dandelion, but a fury-driven sword of justice. She may be the most powerful ruler in all the land, but she breathes and bleeds as any mortal."

Jia had killed Risana with her own hands, not with an army; the only honorable response was for him to kill her with his own hands, like the wandering swordsmen of old, righting a personal wrong in person. It was his nature.

"Then I'm coming with you," said Soto. "You'll no longer have your army, but you still need friends."

Phyro summoned Puma Yemu and gave him the seal of command, to be turned over to the Imperial envoys in the morning. Then he handed over Na-aroénna.

"*Rénga!* What is this—"

"I'm leaving. I cannot go back to Pan a prisoner—"

"What!? How can you—"

"Listen to me! There's no time to explain. This sword, a sword to pacify armies, is too heavy and unwieldy for the task I have in mind. Hold on to it for me. When you're back on the Big Island, go find Zen-Kara and give it to her."

"Why?"

A slight hesitation. "If I should succeed, she'll know by this sword that I meant what I said when I made a promise to her. If I should fail, it is something to remember me by."

Puma looked bewildered and crestfallen. "Are you certain you know the right path?"

"I have no doubt."

Accompanied by no one except Mota Kiphi and Lady Soto, Phyro strode across the deck of the city-ship and boarded a tiny messenger airship. The teardrop-shaped vessel soon faded into the predawn darkness.

PART THREE

STONE-TWISTED ROOTS

CHAPTER TWENTY-NINE

THE BONEYARD

THE BONEYARD, UKYU-GONDÉ: THE TWELFTH
MONTH IN THE TENTH YEAR AFTER THE
DEPARTURE OF PRINCESS THÉRA FROM DARA
FOR UKYU-GONDÉ (SEVEN MONTHS AFTER
PÉKYU THÉRA'S ASSAULT ON TATEN AND THE
DESTRUCTION OF THE LYUCU EXPEDITION FLEET).

Before Phyro had launched his failed invasion, before the armies of
Ukyu-taasa and Dara had clashed within the Wall of Storms, before
the Dandelion Court had been shaken to its very foundation for an
old crime, another grand drama was playing out on the other shore
touched by the great belt current . . .

It took Tovo most of the summer and fall to consolidate power in the
chaotic aftermath of the death of Pékyu Cudyu.

The loss of the centralized garinafin army meant that the Lyucu
tribes reverted to their ancient state of war of all against all before
Pékyu Tenryo's unification. Since Cudyu was too young to have designated an official successor, surviving thanes fought over the young
pékyus-taasa like living symbols of the pékyu's office, each harbor-
ing dreams of becoming the next ruler of the scrublands.

All across the scrublands, the long-subjugated Agon tribes, sensing a power vacuum, began to raid some of the lesser Lyucu tribes.
Refugees from the defeated Lyucu tribes streamed to Taten for aid.

This gave Tovo the opportunity he had been craving. Naming
himself Protector of the Lyucu, he rallied the dispirited remnants of

Cudyu's army and the refugees at Taten. Though there was much mutual suspicion among the surviving Lyucu thanes, he persuaded them to put their power struggles on hold until the Agon-Dara alliance under the upstart Pékyu Théra had been defeated and Pékyu-votan Cudyu's death had been avenged.

That meant an assault on the Boneyard, where Théra had established her new rebel base, even if the war had to be fought in the heart of winter, the harshest season in Ukyu-Gondé.

While Tovo had on hand only a small number of garinafins, scouting revealed that the Agon-Dara alliance also had few garinafins of their own. Tovo decided that they couldn't afford to wait. Recapturing the escaped garinafins would take years, and with each passing month, he risked having Théra grow stronger.

The assault on the Boneyard would then have to be conducted mainly from the ground, which didn't frighten Tovo in the least. Even at the height of the Lyucu-Agon wars, when both sides fielded giant armies of hundreds of garinafins in each battle, the ground assault remained an important part of warfare. Garinafins could unleash great destruction on a ground army with no air support, but air superiority alone was insufficient to subjugate a determined enemy.

About two hundred miles to the northeast of Taten lay the Boneyard.

If the terrain of most of the scrublands resembled the rough but flat hide of a garinafin, then the badlands of the Boneyard were the massive battle scars. The torn skin and muscle had healed imperfectly over cauterized blood vessels, leaving the surface full of deep gouges, ridges, bumps, and cords.

Thunderstorms in spring and summer caused flash floods and raging torrents that carved deep gullies and ravines into the landscape, and the constant howling winds deepened and widened these, leaving mesas and buttes towering over the treacherous maze. In winter, water trapped in seams turned into relentless ice, and entire cliff sides and rock spurs fell away like calving icebergs. The patient sculptor that was nature turned the region into an uninhabited metropolis of monumental architecture: mountainous arches as breathtaking as rainbows, precipitous bridges sized for city-ships, buttes and spires whose profiles brought to mind the ancient monsters at the end of the Fifth Age of Mankind, lofty hoodoos that rose like the columns of ruined temples erected by larger-than-life heroes for unimaginable gods.

The latticed landscape, alternating parts exposed to the merciless glare of the sun and parts in permanent, deep shade, created a thousand different miniature climate regions, each no more than a few miles squared. While the parched side of a ravine felt like the middle of the Lurodia Tanta, a few hundred feet away, inside one of the caves, a salty spring bubbled and left crystalline growths on the rocky walls like the ice blossoms of Nalyufin's Pasture.

The drastic microclimate variations also meant that the badlands, as well as the scrublands immediately bordering the region, brimmed with constant, strong, but also unpredictably shifting winds in all seasons. Updrafts, downdrafts, tornadoes, wind shears . . . there was perhaps nowhere else in Ukyu-Gondé where navigation and sustained flight were so difficult for birds as well as garinafins.

Viewed from above, the badlands resembled the skeleton of some gigantic, mythical creature whose desiccated skin was in the last stage of sloughing off. But that was not how the region got its name.

Across the frost-encrusted scrubland, ten thousand Lyucu warriors marched with Tovo.

"Ten dyudyu cupéruna?" he shouted, to keep up their spirits.

"Lyucu kyo." The responses were scattered, lackadaisical.

The warriors, clad in thick furs, marched uneasily, their moods as varied as their mismatched banners and weaponry. This was no longer the professional army of Pékyu Tenryo, buoyed by the vision of conquest, nor was it the disciplined brigade of Pékyu Cudyu, determined to crush all outbreaks of rebellion; rather, Tovo's troops were like a collection of raiding parties temporarily united by a common prey, with each thane barely acknowledging the authority of the "Protector" because they trusted him just a little bit more than they trusted one another.

Tovo knew he must not fail. A victory would cement his stature as the pékyu-maker of the scrublands, but a defeat would plunge the Lyucu into internecine warfare from which they might never recover.

The scouting reports brought him some comfort. Repeated fly-overs of the Boneyard showed that despite the intervening seven months, during which the chaos among the Lyucu should have rekindled the Agon dream of overthrowing their conquerors, Théra's rebels were still outnumbered and outmatched.

The absence of a large rebel garinafin force showed that Théra's claim to be Pékyu of the Agon had by no means been acknowledged by all the scattered Agon chiefs. Still cowed by the memory of Tenryo and Cudyu's harsh reprisals and as suspicious of one another as the Lyucu thanes, most of the Agon chiefs had decided to wait and see how Théra's rebellion would play out before taking a stand. The Boneyard held only a ragtag collection of freed Dara slaves, young Agon fighters with nothing to lose, and their ice tribe allies.

Tovo vowed to add the bones of the rebels to the famed white scree heaped at the bases of many mesas in the Boneyard. He would become a second Tenryo, a unifier and savior of the Lyucu people.

"Ten dyudyu cupéruna?" he shouted again.

On the twentieth day after Tovo set out from Taten, the Lyucu host arrived at the edge of the Boneyard.

A dusting of snow covered the ground like a fresh piece of garinafin skin stretched atop the cactus drums for the storytelling dance. It was the perfect setting for a new voice painting in the re-rememberings of Ukyu-Gondé.

A thick wall of smoke barred their way, rising high into the sky like a curtain. Though wildfires sometimes swept across the scrub-lands in the dry heat of high summer, here and now in deep winter, the smoke was obviously artificial. A long line of heaps of dung and bone had been set alight, generating the thick smog that obscured what lay behind. It was no easy matter to maintain so much smoke in the presence of the constant winds.

The flames were being tended by the rebel army, about a thou-sand strong. Compared to the ten thousand Lyucu warriors under his command, the rebels, some too young, some too old, all poorly equipped, appeared as a bunch of ill-prepared tanto-lyu-naro huddling around campfires, not much of a threat at all.

What are they doing? wondered Tovo. *Are they hoping to create the illusion that they have many more fighters than they actually do?*

"Ten dyudyu cupéruna?" Tovo shouted.

"Lyucu kyo! Lyucu kyo!" The response was powerful, united, full of bloodlust. Warriors pounded their weapons against the ground; the din was deafening, bone-shaking.

Tovo grinned, reassured. Nothing boosted morale like seeing the sorry state of their enemies. The unified war cry should strike fear into the hearts of the rebels, and perhaps they would surrender without even a fight.

Oddly, the rebels didn't show any sign of being intimidated by the sight and sound of the Lyucu host, despite their clear disadvantage in numbers, fighting readiness, and garinafins. They continued to attend to the fires: shoveling fuel, fanning smoke, raking ashes. They acted as if maintaining the smoke was the most important thing in the world and ignored the Lyucu completely.

Gusts of wind blew across the field, stirring up eddies of snow. The smoke wall swirled, churned, thickened.

What lies behind that wall?

Briefly, Tovo wondered if he should have sent up the garinafins earlier so he would now have a better sense of what was going on. But for the last few days, he had deliberately kept the garinafins earthbound and marched them alongside the foot soldiers in order not to give away his position to the rebels.

The Lyucu host, realizing their attempt at demoralizing the rebels had failed, began to murmur in confusion.

Tovo would have liked to have more time to investigate, to probe and test. But he knew that morale was like the tides, rising and ebbing in accordance with forces far more powerful than the will of an individual commander. He had to act *now*.

He gritted his teeth and waved his signaling spear to launch the garinafin force. The best way he knew of confronting the unknown was to hold to the tried and tested. He knew he had air superiority; he would use it.

Instead of piloting one of the garinafins himself, he decided to remain on the ground. The loss of his left arm made him less effective as a pilot. Besides, he had done enough already for the cause of the Lyucu, hadn't he? It was time for others to take risks.

Nonetheless, he ordered that one garinafin be held back.

Just in case.

Thirty garinafins took off from behind the Lyucu lines. These were the entirety of the garinafin force, remnants of the thousand-plus that had once been corralled at Taten. The fearless riders guided their mounts toward the billowing wall of smoke, heedless of any peril. They were the masters of the sky.

Something stirred behind the wall. The smoke thinned, curled, parted.

Five rebel garinafins burst through, heading straight for the Lyucu aerial assault.

The Lyucu stared at this sight in disbelief. They knew that the rebels had few garinafins. But to counter thirty with five . . . that was surely suicide.

The rebel garinafins fought with a ferocity that the Lyucu were unprepared for. Toof piloted Ga-al, the aged garinafin that had once served the Lyucu. Théra's rebels had augmented his claws with sharpened metal sheaths, and the veteran garinafin wielded them like the swords of Cocru dancers, slicing and stabbing like a bestial version of the Hegemon reincarnate. The other rebel garinafins, roused by Ga-al's example, fought just as fiercely.

Yet, five garinafins, no matter how skilled and ferocious, could not overcome thirty. It was a simple matter of mathematics. Claw marks soon scarred the mottled hide of the rebel war beasts, and thick blood oozed from their wounds, precipitating upon the snowy ground far below like crimson rain.

Ga-al gave a long, loud moan, defiant as well as desperate. The bone-chilling cold affected the garinafins even more than humans, making them sluggish and reducing their supply of lift gas.

Apparently deciding that discretion was the better part of valor, Toof guided Ga-al into an abrupt turning dive. Once free of the throng of attacking Lyucu garinafins, Ga-al winged away from the battlefield, heading straight north. The other rebel garinafins, seeing their leader flee, followed.

The Lyucu garinafins, scenting victory, gave chase. Tovo had instructed the riders that it was vital that all remaining rebel garinafins be destroyed as quickly as possible to guarantee victory on the ground.

Besides, the rebel garinafins were flying erratically, a couple favoring one wing. They were injured, scared, on the verge of falling out of the air. It would not take long for the Lyucu garinafin force to dispatch them before returning to support the ground assault.

Soon, all the garinafins had departed from the battlefield, leaving the sky eerily empty.

Once again, the Lyucu host roared and pounded the ground.

Tovo, even in his wildest dreams, couldn't have anticipated such a quick aerial victory. He was almost sorry that the battle was over so soon; how could his courage and strength be properly celebrated in future voice paintings with so little material?

He looked over at the rebels at the base of the wall of smoke, and the wolfish grin on his face faded. As if sensing his mood, the celebratory cheers around him subsided as well.

Instead of clustering together in preparation for a desperate last stand, the rebels were rushing about to douse the fires that they had so carefully tended until now.

Tall, imposing figures gradually materialized behind the dissipating smoke.

Tovo sucked in a deep breath and shivered, not purely from the cold.

Behind the ragtag rebels stood a row of towering skeletons, creatures of nightmare, monsters revived from the legends of the end of the Fifth Age.

There was a gigantic garinafin, easily twenty times the size of a regular garinafin. Seven massive skulls armed with ferocious canines menaced the Lyucu host from the ends of seven columns of vertebrae. The wings, each as large as the entrance flap of the Great Tent, shimmered like the wings of some oversized insect in the bright sun, and through the translucent material one could glimpse the bones, flexing—though the Lyucu would not have made this comparison—like the frame of a silk airship. It squatted on six bony feet, each the size of ten cattle, tipped with craggy stone claws.

There was a monumental eight-legged tusked tiger, whose head was pieced together from hundreds of real tusked tiger skulls, its two tusks as long as the hundred-year-old trees in Kiri Valley. The eight thick legs, shaped like the waterwheels of Dara, were each composed from hundreds of interlocking bones.

There was a gargantuan shark, whose jaws seemed wide enough to swallow hundreds of warriors in one bite. Instead of fins, the shark had dozens of walking appendages shaped like the legs of wolves and tigers. The tail fluke, as large as the wings of garinafins, glinted with a metallic sheen.

Numerous other monstrosities defying description joined their ranks, and all of them had huge sails that undulated gently on their backs, as though city-ships had been transformed and sailed onto land. Rebels clustered around the giant skeletal beasts, holding on to thick cables attached to the bones as though they were restraining the monsters, who, at any moment, might explode into motion.

The creatures were clearly arucuro tocua, but no living bone construction of this scale had ever been seen in the scrublands.

Around Tovo, the Lyucu warriors whispered in terror and awe.

"What manner of sorcery is this?"

"Do the gods favor the Agon and Dara slaves?"

"Is this the end of the Sixth Age?"

Tovo was not a superstitious man. However these bone statues came to be, he was certain they were the work of human hands, not divine in origin. The alternative was simply inconceivable to his stunted imagination.

Yet, could he count on such steadfastness in all his warriors? How were they supposed to fight monsters they had never thought were real?

The rebel warriors let go of the ropes tethering the arucuro tocua beasts. As the wintry wind filled the sails at the top, the giant statues swayed in place, their articulated bones creaking, grinding, groaning, scraping.

The Lyucu raised their weapons uncertainly.

Smoke swirled; the ground quaked; the gods of the scrublands began their dance.

MONTHS EARLIER.

After the death of Takval, Théra spent much of the winter studying the myths of the scrublands and consulting with her advisers: Dara, Agon, as well as the tribes of the ice.

Using Takval's body to assassinate Cudyu had only been the first step in the plan. The demise of Cudyu would plunge the Lyucu into temporary chaos and put a stop to any plans for a reinforcement fleet to Dara.

The second part of the plan involved Thoryo, who would infiltrate the Lyucu and attempt to free as many of the garinafins as possible.

But even if both of those plots worked, the Lyucu would remain masters of the scrublands. It was only a matter of time before a new leader emerged among the Lyucu thanes and rallied Cudyu's army. To truly free the scrublands, it was necessary to deal the Lyucu army a decisive defeat, one that would convince the scattered Agon tribes to rise up en masse.

The third and final part of Théra's plan, also inspired by the visions she had experienced in the moments before taking Takval's spirit portrait, was perhaps the boldest step of all. It involved fusing the native engineering tradition of the scrublands, arucuro tocua, with Dara art and craft. It would embody ancient myths in modern machinery, combine the knowledge of two peoples in a new language of living bones to tell a story that neither could tell on their own.

Çami, the most creative of Théra's Dara engineers, and Gozofin, the most skilled of Théra's Agon arucuro tocua practitioners, were assigned the duty of making Théra's vision come true.

After weeks of debate, they settled on the Boneyard as the site.

The Boneyard was so named because it was a rich source of that most useful construction material on the scrublands: bone.

Eons ago, perhaps during the mythical previous Ages of Mankind, the region had been inhabited by monstrous creatures who no longer walked the earth. Their bones, turned to stone, would sometimes emerge from an eroded cliffside after a spring flood or poke out of a pile of scree after a summer landslide. Shamans of the scrublands had long prized these as signs confirming the truth of the ancient sagas.

The treacherous terrain, full of sheer precipices and steep ravines, also made the region the favorite hunting ground for packs of horrid wolves and ambushes of tusked tigers. By strategically chasing and corralling, predators could stampede entire herds of mouflon or aurochs over a long drop, leaving a meal to be feasted on for days. Sometimes wounded garinafins met their ends here as well, often taking down wolves or tigers with them in their death struggles.

Human hunting bands later on imitated this practice, and it wasn't uncommon to have hundreds or even thousands of game animals fall to their deaths at once.

After the meat and skin were eaten, carried away, or picked clean by scavengers, the bones remained. Year after year, scoured by insects, washed by the rain, bleached by the sun, the white bones piled up in thick layers at the foot of the cliffs. Tribes that needed more bones than their own herds could provide came here to obtain what they needed, much as prospectors and miners in Dara sought glints of gold or rich veins of useful ores.

After the Lyucu came to be the lords of the scrublands, the Boneyard fell into disuse. The Lyucu at Taten had all the bones they needed from tribute, and the scattered Agon tribes were forbidden to come into the heart of the scrublands.

And so, at the end of last winter, unbeknownst to Cudyu, Théra's little band traveled to the Boneyard and established a new secret base. In the aftermath of Cudyu's death, while Tovo busied himself with subduing ambitious Lyucu thanes, the rebels continued to recruit and grow. While the larger Agon tribes hesitated, unwilling to accept the authority of this foreign woman who claimed to be the pékyu, some of the smaller Agon tribes, made more desperate by Lyucu oppression, decided to take a chance and join her.

Théra sent them to raid Lyucu tribes all around Ukyu-Gondé. Since the Agon possessed few garinafins, these strikes had to be extremely limited in their objectives and be concluded quickly so as not to invite a Lyucu reprisal or give away the location of the rebel base. The raiders focused on freeing skilled Dara artisans who had been taken prisoner at Kiri Valley and then enslaved, as well as acquiring as much metal and silk—spoils from Admiral Krita's expedition and Kiri Valley—as possible.

Meanwhile, back at the base, Théra selected Agon warriors and shamans skilled in the art of arucuro tocua and put them under the guidance of Gozofin and Çami.

Adyulek, serving as artistic director, sketched portraits of the ancient monsters at the end of the Fifth Age. Théra made copies of some of the sketches, thinking that Kunilu-*tika* and Jian-*tika* would enjoy them—should she see them again someday.

Gozofin and Çami then translated these images into practical designs that could be realized with bone, sinew, and hide. Where bone offered insufficient strength or flexibility, metal would be added for reinforcement. The two then directed teams of expert arucuro tocua crafters and freed Dara artisans to gather the necessary materials and to begin work on the oversized sculptures.

The project was fraught with difficulty. No arucuro tocua construction of such scale had ever been attempted in living memory, and there were numerous challenges to be overcome, technical as well as cultural. Gozofin and Çami, as practitioners of two very different engineering traditions, had to learn to trust each other. Whereas Çami drew on knowledge gained by centuries of mechanical and civil engineers in Dara, Gozofin called upon generations of experience with bone as a material and inventions unique to arucuro tocua, such as socket joints, wheel-feet, sail-wings, tooth-gears, spine-racks, rib-trains, and so on. They often came at the same problem from two entirely different perspectives, and it took time for them to learn to appreciate each other's expertise.

The abundant piles of bone around the badlands provided the raw material; the strong but shifting winds, more prevalent than elsewhere in Ukyu-Gondé, supplied ample energy. The gods themselves seemed to have picked this place as the roaming grounds for walking fortresses of articulated bone.

After practicing with a variety of scale models and prototypes, Théra's people finally began to construct art that could imitate life.

But a new obstacle arose. Many of the Agon harbored doubt whether it was sacrilege to reconstitute monsters that had been created by the gods to punish humankind for their arrogance. No matter how much Théra assured them of the propriety of their actions, they could not entirely put their faith in a woman who was not by blood an Agon and spoke their language with an accent.

Adyulek then came to Théra's rescue. Again and again, she recounted the last moments of Takval's life, and held up the pékyu-votan's spirit portrait as proof of Théra's favor in the eyes of the gods.

"She fears and trusts our gods," the old shaman said.

"But nothing like this has ever been done!" the warriors fretted.

"When Afir and Kikisavo strode into the wilderness to demand answers from the gods, they also did many things that had never been done," said Adyulek. "Our ancestors didn't know how to herd long-haired cattle or how to ride garinafins, yet here we are."

The shaman who had once thwarted all of Théra's attempts at reform now became her fiercest advocate, and the Agon were convinced. Side by side with their Dara comrades, they threw themselves into the work with gusto.

Leading by her own example, Adyulek even persuaded some of the shamans to share secret arucuro tocua techniques that had been reserved for ritual implements in the mysteries.

"Taboos were established by our ancestor heroes to protect the people and honor the gods," declared Adyulek, "and they may be broken for the same purpose."

As workers swarmed over the massive frames, and living bone beasts based on the most frightening visions of shamans and storytellers gradually took shape under them, Théra was reminded of the busy scene at a Dara airship-yard. Luckily, when occasional Lyucu garinafin patrols flew over the region, it was easy to disguise the constructions-in-progress as piles of bones littering the floors of many valleys in the Boneyard.

Çami was assigned her own dedicated team to craft some of the most intricate and mysterious mechanisms in the bone monsters. When other workers wondered about the purpose of these mechanisms, Adyulek and Gozofin assured them that all would be revealed in time.

THE EDGE OF THE BONEYARD, UKYU-GONDÉ: THE TWELFTH MONTH IN THE TENTH YEAR AFTER THE DEPARTURE OF PRINCESS THÉRA FROM DARA FOR UKYU-GONDÉ.

Filled with wind, the wing-sails swayed from side to side; the reciprocating motion drove giant double-action bellows that pumped compressed air into bone-and-hide chambers throughout the living skeleton; the compressed air, released through valves, provided steady, regulated power, even during lulls in the wind, to drive the rest of the arucuro tocua mechanisms.

Théra's engineers, Dara as well as native, had converted the unpredictable wind into a dependable ally.

The arucuro tocua beasts rumbled and shook, as though awakening from slumber; a noise like the sighing of gods filled the air; bone levers, pistons, hammers, pinions, racks, cams, and gears rattled and pounded and ground against one another.

With earsplitting screeches, the beasts shambled forward, their polygonal wheel-feet deforming, flexing, expanding, contracting, thumping along the hard, frozen earth, throwing up clouds of snow and mud. Rebel warriors retreated behind the beasts, waving their weapons and roaring in chorus, endowing the beasts with even more semblance of life. Accompanied by drumming, their voices gradually coalesced into a hypnotic chant drawing from shamans' visions at storytelling dances, promising the rage of the gods against the arrogant Lyucu, who had defiled the order of the scrublands.

As the mountainous beasts advanced, the Lyucu were by equal measures fascinated and frightened. Could the bone beasts breathe fire? Could they cover hundreds of yards in a single leap? Nobody knew what they were capable of, and that made them even more terrifying.

The Lyucu could see men and women climbing inside, outside, up and down the walking skeletons. They adjusted sails, pumped levers, greased joints, dislodged rocks from stuck gears—participants in an arcane ritual like shamans tending to the voice-painting drums at storytelling dances. The naros and culeks were reminded of fireside stories of the dark magic of Dara, a magic that had created the awe-inducing city-ships and brought the scrublands so much woe before Pékyu Tenryo seized the vessels from Admiral Krita. Could they be witnessing the manifestation of an even more terrifying magic from Dara, a magic fused into the very bones of the scrublands?

Tovo could see that the sight of the gigantic arucuro tocua, giving form to ancient legends, had overwhelmed his warriors. Their will to battle was waning.

But there were other fighters he could call on. Tamping down his own anxiety and incipient terror, he waved his signaling spear, infusing all the determination he could summon, real as well as feigned, into his voice.

"Ready the fire cattle!"

The authoritative voice awakened the discipline instilled into every Lyucu by Tenryo and Cudyu. Even in their stunned state, warriors obeyed without question, doing the bidding of the pékyu's signaling spear. They parted to the right and left, creating a wide, open lane in the center of their formation.

Behind the warriors, at the far end of the open lane, was a herd of eight hundred long-haired bulls. All the bulls had their horns capped by keen stone blades, and attached to their legs were rings of menacing wolf teeth and sharpened bone fragments. The long tails of the bulls were encased in bundles of scrubland moss soaked in grease.

War drums rumbled behind Tovo. As the drumbeats came faster and louder, the spirits of the Lyucu warriors lifted. They began to shout and slam their weapons against one another in time to the beat, trying to drown out the chanting of the rebel fighters. When the drumming seemed to have turned into one long tremulous roar, Tovo threw down his signaling spear, tipped with the fiery tail of a red fox.

The naros behind the herd of cattle touched torches against the bundles of moss tied to the bull tails. Soon, thick, pungent smoke swirled around the herd.

The use of fire cattle had a long history among the people of the scrublands, though it tended to be a tactic of desperation. The long-haired cattle herds were the basis of the wealth of the tribes, the prime bulwark against long winters. To use them as living weapons in this manner, which virtually guaranteed their death and the loss of valuable property, was not a measure to be taken lightly.

But fire cattle formations could be extremely effective. Crazed by pain and heedless of their own safety, fire-driven cattle could mow down entire armies, destroy camps, scatter enemy herds, and even overwhelm and trample garinafins that didn't take off in time.

Tovo's bulls snorted and thundered down the broad open lane, stampeding straight at the rebels.

Inside the cockpit of the Seven-Headed Garinafin, located within the middle skull suspended high above the battlefield, Théra blanched.

Though the cockpit was a cramped space designed for only one pilot, a second figure—Thoryo—was packed inside with Théra. The horrors of witnessing death up close in Taten, caused by her own actions, had drained the young woman of her vitality. Ever since then, Thoryo had refused to be parted from Théra, clinging to her like a child.

The two looked through the eye sockets at the scene outside. Despite the heat from a bull skull packed with burning embers that the women held between them, their teeth chattered, and not just from the frigid air.

The stampeding bulls had divided into separate streams, each rushing toward one of the living bone beasts. Their sharp horn tips glinted in the pale light of the winter sun like raised swords, and the billowing smoke trails were roiling tornadoes that promised death and destruction.

Incoherent noises emerged from Thoryo's throat. Théra held her tighter, but the young woman refused to quiet.

Next to Théra was a bank of levers made from the antlers of garinafins, each dyed a different color. She reached for the one colored red.

And hesitated.

The walking beasts were never meant to survive a direct assault like this. Even joints made of metal would break if the enraged bulls crashed into them, let alone bone. Yet, Théra knew that the Lyucu were still too far away. If she invoked the Divine Voice now, she risked losing everything they'd accomplished so far.

"Shhh . . . it's all right." She caressed Thoryo's back. "Don't look."

"Death . . . ," muttered Thoryo. "I don't want to see any more death!"

Théra felt her heart ache as though pierced by blades. It was impossible not to be affected by Thoryo's distress. Yet, how could she free the scrublands and ensure the survival of those she loved without killing?

How can I know what I'm doing is right?

The gods didn't answer. But the charging bulls were so close now she could see the wisps from their flared nostrils.

Still trying to comfort the weeping Thoryo with one hand, Théra's other hand moved away from the red lever and gripped the black one. She pulled hard.

A set of signaling spears began to wave frantically, both inside and outside the Seven-Headed Garinafin.

Down in the rib cage of the beast, where one would find the heart in a real garinafin, was the seat of the chief animator.

An arucuro tocua beast was the fusion of a vast, articulated bone frame and a human crew that endowed it with intelligence and soul—in principle no different from a soaring silken airship or diving mechanical cruben. In each bone beast, the most important member of the crew was not necessarily the pilot, responsible for directing the walking fortress in broad strokes, but the most senior arucuro tocua crafter, responsible for coordinating the rest of the crew to implement the pilot's instructions. On a Dara airship, the equivalent position was chief engineer, but Théra had settled on the title of "chief animator" to reflect the Agon tradition of articulating inanimate bone into living machines.

As soon as he received Théra's signal, Gozofin, chief animator of the Seven-Headed Garinafin, sprang into action. As he hollered orders, a team of culeks selected for their loud voices repeated them, ensuring that they were disseminated to crews spread across different stations in the vast articulated skeleton. The white steam from their mouths filled the cold interior air, as though the arucuro tocua itself were breathing.

Actuators—culeks responsible for the physical manipulation of the bone mechanisms under the direction of naro crew chiefs—rushed to the gigantic leg cams, which were fashioned from fused bundles of cattle femur and pelvic bones. As Gozofin and his assistants chanted rhythmically to coordinate the separate teams at the six wheel-feet stations, the actuators lowered heavy and strong jammers made from garinafin ribs into the bone-gears. Despite the cold, sweat from exertion beaded every forehead.

Rattling, quaking, the Seven-Headed Garinafin knelt down gracefully on the ground. Around it, the other bone beasts imitated the maneuver.

Théra watched tensely from the cockpit as her order was carried out. In this crouching position, the bone beasts would be more stable with lower centers of gravity, and the folded locomotion appendages served as additional armor to protect the crew inside from a ground assault.

The fire cattle were even closer now, their thunderous hoofbeats reverberating inside the cockpit.

Théra reached out and pulled down the white lever.

More signaling spears came to life inside and outside Théra's flag beast.

In the cavernous belly of the Seven-Headed Garinafin, Çami, the chief musician, shouted, "Storm pipes, sing!"

The center of this immense space inside the bone beast was dominated by a huge sac, roughly the shape of an elongated egg, sewn from the hides of hundreds of long-haired cattle. Located approximately where the stomach of a real garinafin would be, the sac had taken days to be inflated with sail-pumped air. Right now, it billowed in the middle of the bone beast like an airship gasbag, its surface undulating gently from the pressure of the air within.

The long sac rested on top of a cradle constructed from the inverted arches of dozens of whale jawbones. On each side of this bone cradle were long oars connected to the jawbones via a set of ratchet jaw gears and levers.

At Çami's command, teams of Agon culeks began to pump at the bone oars. Inexorably, the jawbones began to contract, pressing against the large sac from both sides. The pressurized air was forced out through a set of massive garinafin bone pipes at the front of the sac, resulting in a sonorous, booming noise. Oversized trumpets, fashioned from curved garinafin and cattle scapulas glued together, then directed the sonic blast out the front of the Seven-Headed Garinafin.

This was one of the mysterious mechanisms that Gozofin and Çami had built into the arucuro tocua fortresses. Essentially a scaled-up version of the traditional storm pipes of the scrublands, the instrument gave the arucuro tocua beasts a voice to match their size.

Çami stepped to the back of the long sac and placed her lips against the flutelike mouthpiece of the pilot pipe and began to play.

Instantly, the sound emerging from the horde pipes at the front changed. As Çami alternately pushed the pilot tube deeper into the sac and pulled it back out, altering the pitch of the note, the horde pipes roared in sync, making a deafening din like the war cries of a hundred garinafins.

Compared to the immensity of the sac and the horde pipes up front, the pilot pipe, as thick as Çami's arm, was comically small, almost insignificant. Yet the genius of the traditional scrublands instrument was such that the horde pipes would chant resonantly with the pilot pipe, albeit at a far louder volume. Çami, though only one woman, was able to sing with a voice powered by all the pressurized air inside a sac that exceeded the lung capacity of a hundred real garinafins.

Around the battlefield, other bone beasts, the Thousand-Faced Tusked Tiger, the Clawed Shark, the Many-Limbed Wolf, the Two-Faced Bull . . . all began to roar.

It was as though a hundred garinafins, a thousand tusked tigers, ten thousand horrid wolves had all joined the Agon and Dara, and the moaning, screeching, howling, trumpeting shook the ground and split the air with thunderous ferocity.

Even some among the Lyucu host, far on the other side of the battlefield, covered their ears. Many stampeding fire bulls, startled by this sudden aural onslaught, veered away from the kneeling bone beasts. The rest slowed and began to slam and bump into one another, driven mad by the searing pain in their tails but also confused and terrified by the wall of noise ahead.

A cold, mirthless grin, however, appeared on Tovo's face.

So far, the bone beasts had not impressed him. They were clumsy and slow; they rattled as though about to fall apart any moment; they roared and howled, but showed no claws or teeth that could do real damage.

It was the habit of Dara barbarians to prize deception and surprise rather than strength, and he sensed, shrewdly, that the giant arucuro tocua creations were far more fragile than suggested by their appearance. Why else would they have gone to their knees at the first sign of trouble? Where were the fire tongues and lightning strikes of the fabled monsters of the Fifth Age, able to deal death to thousands in one blow?

Using loud noises to confuse and divert fire cattle was hardly an unknown tactic on the scrublands. Granted, bone trumpets and hide drums typically were not as loud as these bone beasts, but a counter was easily devised.

"More fire cattle!" he shouted. "Plug up their ears!"

Another eight hundred fire cattle stampeded toward the crouching bone beasts. With their ears sealed with suet and grass, this new wave of frenzied bulls was immune to the blaring noise coming out of the bone beasts. The reinforcements crashed into the remnants of the first wave, and jostling, snorting, lowing, a combined tidal wave of fire cattle charged at the bone beasts.

～

Théra pulled down yet another lever, this one yellow. As the signaling spears waved inside and outside the Seven-Headed Garinafin, the music played by Çami changed: the moaning of a herd of garinafin, mournful, with a hint of desperation in it.

Then, the moaning ceased. Silence descended over the battlefield, save for the pounding of fire-cattle hooves over the frozen ground.

Hundreds of rebel Agon warriors, who had until now remained behind the line of bone behemoths, ran forward. Faces grim, they gathered before the crouching bone beasts. Those in the front-most rank knelt down and propped their clubs and axes against the ground, while those behind them remained standing. With practiced movements, they unfurled large pieces of garinafin skin over themselves, holding the thick hide over their heads like tents.

With their own bodies, they constructed living skirt-dams.

The tidal wave of fire-crazed bulls crashed against them. As bulls slammed into the barriers, the tough garinafin skin held and did not allow the blade-tipped horns and hoof-claws to tear through, but their weight and momentum pressed the warriors back. Some fell under the garinafin hide and were trampled to death. But more warriors ran under the hides to take their places and prop up the tent-shield.

The first bulls leapt onto the inclined surface of the living dams, running up like soldiers trying to scale a city wall.

Tipo Tho, running back and forth across the thick spine of the Seven-Headed Garinafin, directed the defense of the bone beast, now a fortress under siege. The fleet-footed ex-aviator found the experience of riding inside a walking arucuro tocua to be eerily similar to a Dara airship. In both cases, the crew had to navigate the space using skeletal support as catwalks and ladders, fending off threats from outside.

Nméji, she thought to herself, smiling wryly, *I wish you could have seen this day. What would I not give to hear you argue with me once more about the merits of submariners and aviators?*

Her infant son, Crucru, was waiting for her inside one of the caves in the badlands behind them, along with the wounded and aged who could not fight. She had felt her heart bleed when she had bid him goodbye—oh, how much, how much had she wanted to stay, to ensure that the child would not be deprived of both a father and a mother.

Adyulek, the old shaman who had once despised all of Théra's Dara reti-nue, approached her in the cave. "You will see your son again."

Tipo looked up at her, teary-eyed. "Is this what your gods tell you? He's Dara, not Agon. Maybe your gods won't protect him."

Adyulek shook her head. "This is not a revelation from the gods, but a promise from me to you." *Leaning against her staff, she raised one hand to show Tipo a bone dagger and sliced it through the air a few times.* "So long as I breathe, he will breathe. Should we not see another sunrise, you may be certain that I will personally pilot the cloud-garinafin to carry your child to the feast of the gods so you may be reunited."

"But I neither fear nor trust your gods."

"You have the heart of an Agon, whether you acknowledge it or not."

Tipo swallowed the lump in her throat. She had a job to do; she would never allow her son to think her an unbrave woman, especially not at the banquet of the gods.

She waved her signaling spears and shouted commands, adapting airship tactics for the present moment. Dara archers and Agon slingshot scouts peeking out from the rib cage of the bone beast shot at the bulls below, aiming for eyes and noses; culeks scrambling over the massive skeleton poured sacks of grease onto the garinafin-hide dam below; the ice tribespeople guided their dogs to attack out of holes in the wheel-feet, fending off any bulls that got too close.

The oil-slicked surface provided no purchase, and the bulls who had leapt onto the garinafin hide slipped and began to fall back. But more bulls surged behind them, forcing them forward, pushing them up the slick tent sides.

"Second wave, now!" shouted Tipo Tho.

More culeks emerged at the sides of the bone beast and tossed down torches. The oil caught fire, and the barrier tents turned into a sea of flames. Protected by the garinafin hides over their heads, the warriors holding up the dam remained unharmed. This was an old trick of the scrublands, useful for ground troops defending against garinafin assaults.

All around the battlefield, the fire skirts around the bone beasts drove the stampeding bulls back. The fire cattle, panicked and crazed with pain, kicked and bit and gored their bovine comrades with their sharp horns.

Above, in the skull cockpit of the Seven-Headed Garinafin, Thoryo clutched Théra even tighter. The screams and howls of the dying and wounded, both animal and human, assaulted her relentlessly.

Memories of the corpse-strewn sea around *Dissolver of Sorrows* and the fiery ruins of Kiri Valley came to her. *How many more people must die? Is there an end to this interminable slaughter?*

Finally, as fast as the tide had come, the fire-cattle wave receded. Many bulls lay dead, necks skewered with arrows, skulls smashed by dropped stones, bodies trampled by other bulls, bellies gored with entrails strewn across the snowy ground. The stragglers turned and charged back at the Lyucu lines. As they approached, the Lyucu greeted them with axes and spears, felling them before they were close enough to do damage.

Théra pushed up the black lever.

Çami stepped to the pilot pipe and played a new tune. This time, the massive air organ of the Seven-Headed Garinafin let out a booming cry of challenge.

The surviving Agon warriors retreated behind the bone beasts, taking the garinafin hides with them. Gozofin and the other chief animators shouted directions to their crews. Jammers were knocked out from between the gears of the wheel-feet; wing-sails once again filled with the wind.

Swaying, grinding, rattling, the bone beasts climbed to their feet and began, once more, to march toward the Lyucu host.

The cry of the Seven-Headed Garinafin carried far across the scrublands.

Miles away, the pursuing Lyucu riders were frustrated. Somehow the rebel garinafins kept on eluding them. They had dispersed in different directions, forcing the pursuers to divide as well. But each time a hunting party got close enough to a fleeing rebel garinafin to roast it with fire breath, it somehow found a fresh burst of strength and flapped away—even those with apparently injured wings!

Toof guided Ga-al into a long, wide turn. The rebel garinafins had heard the call to return.

Tovo laughed.

The fire-cattle charge had never been meant to bring down the bone beasts. He had merely been probing, assessing the capabilities of these strange engines. The oversized arucuro tocua were revealed to be better at psychological intimidation than winning a battle.

How pathetic!

The noises from the walking skeletons would only frighten dumb animals, not disciplined Lyucu warriors. When they were threatened, they showed no extraordinary magic. The fire cattle had been repelled only with standard scrubland tactics, and at the cost of the lives of many rebels.

The Dara barbarians, true to their nature, always tried to turn every battle into some version of siege warfare. Tovo had already seen this at Nalyufin's Pasture, when Théra and Takval built a fort out of ice and cost him his left arm. Now the Agon, led by that Dara witch, were resorting to the same tricks. Like moving towers, the bone beasts were mobile, raised platforms for slingshots and archers.

But that was easy to counter. His own warriors could raise garinafin tent-shields as well. A rickety bone tower was nothing like an ice fort, and he could already envision his own fighters climbing up the skeletons with ease, dealing death to those cowering within.

There was nowhere for the rebels to escape to on the endless scrublands. They were outnumbered by more than ten to one. They would not survive a determined, general charge from the Lyucu.

The glee of imminent victory surged through him.

Loud trumpeting in the air.

He turned and saw that the rebel garinafins, pursued by his own garinafins, were returning from the north. The rebel fliers, their lift gas drained, could barely stay aloft. Swaying from side to side, they crashed to the earth behind the lumbering bone beasts, as though seeking their protection. They would not lift off again today.

Tovo laughed even harder.

The gods are truly with us!

He waved his signal spears frantically, demanding that the Lyucu garinafin pilots cease pursuit of the useless rebel garinafins. Then he climbed onto the last garinafin. He would lead them into this final assault personally to secure full credit for the victory.

With laboring wings, his mount slowly rose into the air. The other Lyucu pilots pulled their mounts into long, graceful arcs to circle behind him, forming an aerial triangle formation with Tovo at the tip.

Just as he was about to toss out the antler-tipped signaling spear to call for the garinafin force to dive at the towering arucuro tocua, Tovo hesitated.

What if the Dara witch has yet more tricks? What if she has booby-trapped the bone fortresses against me, the same way her death boxes were booby-trapped against Pékyu Cudyu?

He felt shame stir in his heart for this hesitation, so he strove to justify himself. The victory would be aesthetically displeasing to the gods if he deployed so many garinafins against a foe with no air support; if he didn't get the ground troops involved, too many rebels might escape; if he sent in the ground troops along with the garinafins, many of his own foot warriors might be hurt by friendly fire; it was best to keep the garinafins in reserve to hunt down survivors and escapees after a ground assault. . . .

The rationalizations were contradictory and unconvincing, so in the end he accepted the shame as part of the burden of being the supreme leader of the Lyucu. He was too important to the Lyucu cause, too precious to the dream of his people, and too indispensable to the future of the scrublands to risk himself by riding against the rebels as the head of an aerial shock assault corps.

The warrior who laughed last would laugh the loudest. There will be plenty of time for planned heroics—once I can be sure I'll triumph.

Tovo put away the antler-tipped signaling spear and pulled a different spear off his back: one with seven feathers of different colors at the tip.

Gripping the shoulders of his mount with his knees, he heaved the new signaling spear in the direction of the lumbering bone beasts.

The spear traced a long arc through the air before thunking into the ground.

"Charge!"

Like a flood released from a crumbling dam, the Lyucu host on the ground erupted.

This was the day the Agon would be wiped from the scrublands and the Lyucu spirit achieve its ultimate triumph.

Théra looked out through the eye sockets of the skull cockpit.

The ground, as far as the eye could see, was covered by a solid sea of surging Lyucu warriors, weapons raised and garinafin-hide tent-shields at the ready. In the air, the returning Lyucu garinafins dove toward her and the other walking bone beasts, keeping pace with the ground assault.

Closer. Closer. Still closer.

Next to her, Thoryo whimpered.

Still, Théra waited.

Çami's calculations had shown that the power of sound declined with the square of the distance from the source. The closer the Lyucu got to the bone beasts, the better her chances.

She had only one shot.

She pulled down on the white lever painted with red stripes. The Seven-Headed Garinafin slowed down and then stopped. Six of its seven heads—all excepting the skull cockpit—turned in unison away from the enemy, as though desperately seeking an escape route from the Lyucu onslaught. Across the battlefield, the other bone beasts engaged in similar displays of fear.

Agon warriors who had been marching alongside the bone beasts fell back, finally realizing that they could not withstand the Lyucu charge. Like ships stranded on the beach by a receding tide, the abandoned bone beasts looked isolated and vulnerable.

The Lyucu host cheered at these signs of an imminent collapse among the Agon and sped up. They had run out of tricks! The Lyucu could already see themselves scrambling up the bone beasts to drag the rebellion leaders out of their secure perches and throw them to the ground, where their faces would be held against the earth and the backs of their skulls bashed in so that they could die in the most shameful manner possible.

They had almost reached the feet of the bone beasts. The earlier fire-cattle attack had trampled the snow-blanketed earth to slick mud, forcing everyone to slow down. Up close, the arucuro tocua creations resembled just hills of bones, not terrifying engines of war. The Agon riders inside the bone beasts were apparently so frightened that they weren't even launching any weapons at the attackers—perhaps they were clutching at each other and praying to the gods that their lives would be spared by the righteous fury of the Lyucu.

No mercy! No mercy!

The Lyucu thanes leading the charge grinned wolfishly. There would be no mercy on this day, no more than Nalyufin, the hate-hearted, showed mercy to any creature who refused to kneel in submission to winter.

Théra pulled down the red lever.

All the heads of the Seven-Headed Garinafin snapped forward.

The aggressive pose was echoed by the other bone beasts around the field.

In the rib cage of the Seven-Headed Garinafin, some of Gozofin's actuators released the valves that led to auxiliary "lungs"—more skin sacs suspended throughout the interior of the bone beast. As the sails overhead swayed in the wind, their back-and-forth motion had driven pumps that filled the bags. Now that the valves were open, the pressurized air followed the hollow bone tubes into the central air sac, replenishing the powerful singing lung. The lung expanded and strained against the whale-jaw cradle.

Other actuators, under Gozofin's direction, had taken advantage of the time during which the beast's six singing heads were turned away from the enemy to connect the horde pipes at the front of the central lung to pipes leading up each neck. Now that the heads had snapped back to face the enemy, they cranked and rocked and pulled and pushed until the necks lowered the yawning maws near the ground, level with the charging Lyucu.

In the belly of the Seven-Headed Garinafin, Çami worked

quickly. She pushed the pilot pipe all the way into the singing lung and locked it in place. Then she detached the small mouthpiece from the end of the pilot pipe. In its place, she inserted a new, long bone pipe that led farther back, where it ended in a flared trumpet made from the preserved ear of an adult garinafin.

The ear was pressed against the front of a large bone cage, whose occupant was concealed by hide flaps on all sides.

For safety, Çami and all her fellow chief musicians had plugged their ears with deer-antler moss, though they knew such protection would do little good should things go awry.

Çami took a deep breath and gestured for the actuators stationed at the bone oars on each side of the whale-jaw cradle to begin pumping. Bones strained and groaned; the jaws slowly pressed against the sides of the billowing central lung; air under high pressure was forced out the horde pipes; and a low, booming roar emerged from the six singing heads of the bone beast, facing into the tide of charging Lyucu.

The Lyucu didn't slacken their pace. They had already seen how harmless the noise was. They would not be fooled.

Çami pulled aside the hide flap that had concealed the occupant of the cage from the trumpet-ear until now.

The tusked tiger inside had been trapped days ago by skilled Agon hunters and then kept in a semi-comatose state with meat marinated in tolyusa juice. However, starting last night, the tusked tiger had been kept in darkness and deprived of all sustenance, and by now the tiger was hungry, angry, and very awake.

As soon as Çami removed the cage cover, the tusked tiger blinked against the sudden light and tried to free itself. But the bone cage, barely larger than its torso, held it firmly in place. Its limbs were tied with twisted bundles of sinew, and a heavy bone collar, anchored to the bars of the cage, held its head immobile. Moreover, its robust snout was tied with another bundle of sinew, muzzling it completely.

All that the tusked tiger could do was to glare malevolently, its field of vision narrowed to the giant garinafin ear immediately on the other side of the cage. Gradually, the images painted inside the ear penetrated its consciousness: prancing moss-antlered deer, fat aurochs, flocks of juicy mouflon. The smell of fresh blood and meat drifted into its nostrils.

The puny human captors, cowardly out of sight, were taunting it.

Furious, perplexed, mad with hunger, the tiger strained against its bonds. The cage rattled and flexed, but held.

Standing to the side, careful to keep herself out of the tiger's sight, Çami reached in through the bars of the cage and cut the sinew muzzling the tusked snout with a sharp stone knife.

Instantly, the tusked tiger began to roar.

But there was no sound inside the Seven-Headed Garinafin except the creaking of bone oars, the clacking of bone gears, the hissing of pressurized air through bone tubes as the massive central sac was compressed to force air through the horde tubes.

After all, the roar of the tusked tiger was silent, a voice evoking the divine but that could not be heard.

Çami stared at the apparatus in front of her, perhaps her proudest invention since the time she had summoned the whales to protect *Dissolver of Sorrows*, and imagined what was happening inside.

The tusked tiger's silent roar, collected and channeled by the garinafin ear, traveled down the pilot tube deep into the singing lung until it struck a thin membrane at the end. Made from a piece of garinafin gut lining, this film ordinarily served as the reed of the pilot pipe—it was how earlier Çami had produced the music that imitated the roar of real garinafins. Now, however, the membrane behaved more like an eardrum, vibrating in sympathy with the inaudible voice of the tusked tiger.

On the other side of the membrane, a series of thin bones, linked together by traditional arucuro tocua techniques, transferred the vibrations to multiple fine-toothed bone combs, constructed from the spines of the beaked needlefish that lived in Nalyufin's Pasture. Each bone comb was placed at the opening of one of the horde tubes leading to the singing heads of the Seven-Headed Garinafin. A second comb, also made from the spine of the beaked needlefish, was affixed over the tube opening. As the vibrating comb slid over the fixed comb, the gaps between the two sets of teeth changed in sync with the vibrations of the garinafin gut membrane at the end of the pilot tube.

The combs, in effect, served the same function as the reeds of simple wind instruments or the vocal cords of animals. As powerful jets of air sped through the shifting gaps between the teeth of the combs, a thundering voice boomed from the horde tubes.

Since the bone combs vibrated in sympathy with the membrane at the end of the pilot tube, this meant that the music emerging from the horde pipes was a copy of the music played into the pilot pipe. However, since the compressed air being forced past the combs was a hundred—nay, a thousandfold more powerful even than the roar of the tusked tiger, the music blasting from the horde pipes was also a thousandfold more powerful than the voice of the singer chanting into the pilot pipe.

This was the secret of Péa pipes, which Çami had unlocked long ago in Kiri Valley.

"It is similar in principle to the copying machine used by architects at the academies," she had explained the idea to Théra. "There, mechanical linkage amplifies the movements of the tracing brush to the inking brush, resulting in a bigger copy of the traced drawing. Here, mechanical linkage and the additional energy of compressed air amplify the input sound, resulting in a louder copy of the song. The Péa pipes are auditory enlarger-copiers."

Çami seemed to be back at that last Winter Festival in Kiri Valley, when she had watched as the colorful pigment powder atop the voice painting canvas jumped in sympathy to inaudible voices from afar.

And it was Théra who had crystallized the insight that just because they couldn't hear the silent roar of the tusked tiger didn't mean that it wasn't also music, music that followed the same rules as the drumming of the shamans, the cry of the garinafin, or the song played into a pilot tube.

The tusked tiger continued to roar.

The actuators continued to pump at the bone oars.

The whale jaws continued to squeeze, forcing the air from the central lung past the vibrating combs, into the resonant horde tubes.

The silent roar, amplified a thousandfold by the energy of the compressed air in the massive lung of the bone beast, blasted across the scrublands through the yawning maws of the Seven-Headed

Garinafin's singing heads. Snow and smoke swirled, driven by a silent, eerie storm.

It was the Divine Voice, the song of the gods.

As soon as the heads of the bone beasts snapped forward and lowered toward the charging Lyucu host, Tovo kicked the shoulders of his mount hard, directing it to gain altitude.

He tried telling himself that it was proper for the Protector of the Lyucu to survey the grand victory from high above. But in his heart, he knew he was reacting to fear.

Memories of the horrors over the ice at Nalyufin's Pasture rushed back with a vengeance. The stump of his left arm throbbed. He had suffered too much at the hands of the crafty Dara barbarians and their scrubland allies to trust that the unexpected maneuvers of the bone beasts didn't presage some trap.

He chided himself. *Fool! You can't be afraid of mirages. The barbarians are deceivers, devoid of real strength!*

The few surviving rebel garinafins were huddled behind the line of bone beasts, surrounded by the Agon cowering under garinafin-hide tent-shields. His own garinafins, not having received the order to attack, circled the air behind him impatiently, eager to join the fray at a moment's notice. Meanwhile, the crews of the bone fortresses skulked inside their pathetic, flimsy contraptions, doing gods knew what. But he could see nothing emerging from the lowered heads of the bone beasts: no fire, no ice, no lightning storm, not even a wisp of smoke.

It has to be another empty attempt at intimidation.

His troops were about to overwhelm the arucuro tocua like a tsunami slamming into rickety shoreside huts. He was only moments away from ushering in a new world, a world in which the Lyucu would be masters of the scrublands forever.

Reassured, Tovo banished fear from his heart and refilled it with cruel pride. He reared back and laughed, showing his face to the Eye of Cudyufin, inviting the goddess to witness his supreme triumph.

For Lyucu warriors at the front of the charge, the world changed in an instant.

One second, there was the howling of the winter wind, the wet thunking of running feet in crimson mud, the blood-frenzied shouting of comrades, the moans of garinafins far above. . . .

The next, nothing, nothing but peace.

The monstrous bone heads dipped close to the ground before them, swinging from one side to the other. The skeletal jaws were wide open, like bottomless caverns of ice.

All sounds faded away, save a constant, comforting droning that seemed to come from deep within each warrior's heart, not outside. All sensations—cold, exhaustion, the weight of weapons in their numb hands—grew distant, unreal.

Warriors looked at one another, the same eerie smiles on every face. Belatedly, they realized that they had stopped running. The thought caused them no distress. Why had they been running anyway? What was the rush?

A magnificent *presence*, a presence so much greater than each individual Lyucu, loomed over them, pressing down upon them, sinking into their bodies and heads, crushing the air out of their lungs, squeezing the blood out of their hearts. They were connected to one another, to the muddy snow, to the swirling smoke, to the lumbering beasts of bone, to the distant figures inside the beasts, to all Creation.

Was this what it was like to hear the voice of the gods? Was this what it was like to be welcomed into the ranks of great heroes?

They fell to their knees, their hearts and breaths slowing.

The movement of the great walking arucuro tocua slowed down as well, as though time itself was turning to ice. The sky seemed to be filled no longer with clouds, but cloud-garinafins that were descending to take up new passengers. Great pillars of smoke danced and swirled across the winter scrublands, telling an eternal story that had no ending.

The pressure inside their skulls built steadily, as though a great Idea was seeking an outlet. The pressure turned to pain, and the pain sharpened until it became unbearable. The warriors dropped their weapons and pressed their hands against their ears.

It did no good. The Voice could not be kept out, not when it was infused into every bone, coursing through every vein, tingling down every nerve.

How could the voice of the gods be held in mortal minds?

They begged, pleaded, prayed for the singing to stop, to be let go. But their voices were inaudible in the overwhelming silent song of the divine.

They gasped and pounded their chests, trying to take in another breath, trying to restart their stopped hearts. But their struggles were useless against the numinous. The Voice blanketed the battlefield more completely than any snowstorm.

The white forms of the mountainous arucuro tocua gleamed even brighter. Color drained from the world, leaving only the stark, lifeless light of bones and the shadow of everything else. The dance of the formless swirling columns of smoke and snow intensified.

Warriors touched their noses and gazed at the blood on their fingers in wonder; they coughed and spat crimson foam onto the muddy field; they tried to get up and found the act beyond their strength.

Time to embrace the Voice, they thought. Without protest, they fell to the earth. Their eyes looked into the sky, waiting for cloud-garinafins to bear them away.

CHAPTER THIRTY

THE TEMPLE OF STILL AND FLOWING WATERS

DEEP IN THE RING-WOODS OF RIMA: AT THE SAME TIME (THE TWELFTH MONTH OF THE TENTH YEAR OF THE REIGN OF SEASON OF STORMS AND THE REIGN OF AUDACIOUS FREEDOM, ONLY ONE MONTH BEFORE THE EXPIRATION OF THE PEACE TREATY BETWEEN UKYU-TAASA AND DARA).

Once, it was said, much of the Big Island was covered by forests. The natives who had lived here before the coming of the Ano hunted deer and boar, pheasant and *phaméten* (large, flightless birds with splendid, peacock-like tails and powerful legs ending in sharp talons that could kill a wolf in a single kick), aurochs and woolly, dwarf elephants. Over time, as the game grew scarce and the dwarf elephants and *phaméten* faded into legend, they began to burn down patches of wood to create fields for taro and wild rice.

After the arrival of the Ano, the denuding of the Big Island accelerated. Forests turned into rice paddies, sorghum fields, apple orchards, pastures for sheep and cattle. The live oaks and white pines turned into swaying ships, rattling carts, sprawling palaces, and moon-gazing towers. Game migrated deep into the mountains, refugees from a gridded and tamed land.

Except for the Ring-Woods.

Here, the rough terrain and unpredictable weather prevented dense settlement, and warlords and kings, in order to stave off more populous rival states, promoted hunting and raiding as national pursuits. The primeval forest survived, bearing silent witness to a chapter of the Islands' history forgotten in other parts.

As Rima faded from prominence among the Tiro states, it turned inward, gaining in reputation as a land of mystics and hermits. Refugees, much like birds, flocked here to escape the incessant warfare that raged across the Islands. To reach the heart of Rima, one had to pass through successive layers of defenses, all designed to discourage the idly curious and the irresolute.

Visitors were warned to not venture deep within the dark Ring-Woods without local guides. Besides wolves, screeching *phiphi*, swinging pythons, and other perils, the Ring-Woods were populated by fierce woodsmen and hunters who lived in hewn-log huts they built with their own hands and who guarded their independence jealously.

Should anyone make it through the dense Ring-Woods, they would be greeted with the sight of the rolling foothills and rugged ridges that led up to the towering mountain ranges, the cruciform spine of the Big Island. In these verdant hills—tall enough to be deemed mountains elsewhere in Dara—one found misfits and eccentrics, rebels and heretics, misunderstood geniuses who preferred the company of monkeys to men, and fortune's stepchildren who sought nothing except the right to be left alone. Suda Mu, the legendary master chef of the Xana court, set up his kitchen here late in life to delve into culinary magic without having to compromise his art for any patron. Suma Ji, the greatest bladesmith of the Seven States, moved his forge here to be close to abundant high-quality charcoal and away from ambitious though unworthy sword twirlers. Zato Ruthi, the most renowned Moralist scholar of modern times, came here in his youth to live in solitude in a hewn-log hut in search of enlightenment through immersion in the simplicity of nature and the elevated logograms of dead Ano sages. (To be clear, it was said that his mother hired maids to come to his hut to do the laundry and sweep the floor every week, and that his sisters visited him regularly to bring him air-shipped Müning tea and homemade honey cakes—evidently not all the conveniences of modern civilization were corrupting or vulgar, though it would take a mind as great as Zato Ruthi's to sort through which was which.)

Should anyone climb past the foothills, they would find themselves staring up at the pathless peaks of the Shinané Mountains and
Damu Mountains. Here, in hidden valleys and on remote summits,
those who followed faiths and visions unacceptable to established
temples and Tiro kings built mist-shrouded shrines, cloud-hidden
monasteries, cave-walled hermitages.

Like rare orchids found on distant isles, whose outlandish forms
revealed the limitless potential inherent in the basic floral form, the
sects that populated these secret shrines professed beliefs that filled
every niche and nook, thereby hinting at the vast range of conceivable faiths by wandering far from the beaten path.

There were sects who worshipped mountains and streams, believing that each rock and pebble held a spirit; sects who adored Kana
the Unbuilder, preaching that the world would soon end when the
goddess of death unleashed her fury; sects who prayed to Tututika-
in-Frenzy, an aspect of the goddess of beauty that could only be
approached through fasting, alcohol, dream herbs, and sensory
deprivation, and whose rites involved carnal pleasures and exhaust-
ing days-long dances; sects who exalted Fithowéo Patiens, blinding
themselves and flagellating one another to deliver the world from
the evil that lurked in every heart; sects who followed Lutho-of-
Uncountable-Names, dedicating their lives to the enumeration of
every possible combination of Ano logogram components in order
to compile an inventory of all knowledge, encompassing the known
unknowns as well as the unknown unknowns. . . .

Savo trudged through the knee-deep snow.

For more than a year now, he had wandered around Dara. It
had been so long since he had last looked into a mirror or groomed
himself that his beard and hair had merged into one matted and
shaggy mess, full of entangled twigs and grass. Stiffened by frost
from his breath, the beard hung before his neck like a pearl-studded
gorget.

At first, he had no goal in mind except to get as far away as possible from his sister, from Fara, from his teacher and friends in the
Blossom Gang and at the Splendid Urn. Convinced that Zomi would

send the farseers after him, he kept to the wilderness and avoided cities and towns, survival and escape the only thoughts in his mind.

But how could he escape from the demons in his own lungsqueeze and heartbeat? How could he make peace with the warring emotions that threatened to sunder his mind?

As the days grew shorter and colder, he had no choice but to turn to the cities and towns for shelter and sustenance. Begging, taking on odd jobs as a stevedore or farmhand, hiding out in cellars and stables, he managed to stay alive and unnoticed. As Dara celebrated a new year, he felt mired in time, hopelessly entangled in truths that he wished were lies, lies he wished were truths.

The mild spring and hot summer brought some relief. Disguised as a laborer from the countryside in search of work, he visited sites that he had known only through Master Nazu Tei's poetic descriptions: the Hegemon's Shrine, Princess Kikomi's Tomb, the floating spires of Müning, the mist-drenched forums of Boama. As Master Rati Yera's engineering lectures replayed in his mind, he gazed upon the windmills of Cocru in wonder, tracing the path of power from the ethereal spinning silk vanes, through the articulated skeleton of levers and gears, down to the plodding yet relentless millstones. As Arona Taré's lessons on performance and storytelling echoed in his ears, he took in street performances and folk operas, transported by the temporary respite from reality. As Fara's bright smile and dulcet voice haunted his dreams, he looked for traces of her in every dandelion in the fields, every brush painting in the art markets, every sweet or savory or spicy dish in hawker stalls.

But as the peace treaty with the Lyucu was set to expire at the end of the year, the chatter in teahouses turned to talk of war. Crowds gathered in markets to hear veterans tell tales of heroism and sacrifice. Playhouses and indigo houses put on shows commemorating old battles and promised to donate the proceeds to veterans' societies and war orphans. Young scholars spoke of abandoning the writing knife for the honed sword, of leaving the embroidery needle for the airship oar. The very air seemed charged with silkmotic force, crackling with martial spirit.

How could he watch as his father's people went to war with his mother's? How could he wander unconcerned through a world careening toward the horrors of Kigo Yezu, multiplied a thousandfold? How could he bear to see the varicolored beauty of Dara, the kaleidoscopic bouquet whose brightest flower was Fara, fade into the chiaroscuro of blood crimson and bone white, wilt in the logic of war in which to kill or be killed were the only stark choices?

Fara's words in Ginpen came back to him.

Even though they're free to move around Dara, they never feel at home. . . . They try to find shelter at temples and shrines deep in the mountains, where monks and nuns are more compassionate.

Fara was speaking of refugees from Ukyu-taasa, but wasn't he also such a refugee himself? The mountain shrines of Rima were far from every reminder of Fara, from veterans prophesying war, from Pékyu Vadyu's garinafin fires, from the empress's spies and guards.

He fled into the Ring-Woods, into the foothills, into the mountains.

The fall had been relatively easy, with an abundant supply of berries and squirrels fattening for the winter. But as the weather chilled, he had to resort to stealing from woodsman huts and hamlets. His leggings had belonged to a huntswoman, his borrowed deerskin coat was much too short, and his stolen boots did not fit, rubbing his toes bloody and raw.

He shivered. It had been three days since he had last eaten, and he saw no signs of habitation in the snowy country he was hiking through. At this point, he was slogging on more out of instinct than will.

The world is so large, yet where is my place?

He collapsed at the foot of a pine tree, tore away the strips of cloth wrapped around his frostbitten fingers with his teeth, ate a handful of snow to slake the thirst, and chewed on the collar of his deerskin coat to fool his body with the illusion of nourishment. His teeth ached from the tough hide.

Reaching into his coat, he pulled out a small sandalwood letter box carved in the shape of a carp. With numb, disobedient fingers, he finally fumbled it open to reveal a folded piece of silk. He held it up to his nose and inhaled deeply—the fragrance of dandelion, mixed with a hint of beach rose.

He shook the handkerchief free and gazed at the painting. Though working in the style of traditional Dara brush painting, the artist seemed less interested in representation than mood, trading accuracy for fidelity to feeling. A dandelion and a caterpillar grass wound around each other like an intricate bit of Dasu knotwork. The dandelion was lithe, elegant, the flower at the crown in full bloom, as regal as a miniature sun, the brushstrokes at the tips of the petals fading into a translucent, ethereal wash. The *thasé-teki*, on the other hand, done in thick inky dabs from a bristling brush, yielded a form at once clumsy and spirited, brash as well as reserved, with the caterpillar root merging seamlessly into the fungal stalk, giving the impression of a single organism rather than a chimera of two. Long, jagged dandelion leaves, like yearning hands, rested gently against the rough, gangly form of the caterpillar grass, while the pitted stalk tip gazed up into the petaled disc, two mirrored faces seeing while pining to be seen.

Tears welled in his eyes.

In one corner of the handkerchief was a poem. Though his vision was blurred, he could picture every delicate logogram in his mind, as clearly as he remembered every moment in her presence. The calligraphy was in torrent script, a style that eschewed legibility for expressivity. The energetic strokes, combined with a slightly dull blade, had left jagged gashes in the wax, as though the writer's racing heart was almost too wild to be restrained by writing.

> *Liru, Liru, what is love?*
> *I stand at your source;*
> *He stands at your mouth.*
> *Let me take a drink from you*
> *So you can send him a kiss.*

> *Damu, Damu, what is love?*
> *The wild goose, storm-hoarse,*
> *Wings his lone way south.*
> *Take him a message, will you?*
> *Does he fret? Does he me miss?*

The cold had taken the feeling from his fingers, so he held the silk handkerchief close to his face and caressed the wax logograms with the tip of his nose, reading and rereading each. Having been stored next to his breast, the wax was still soft and warm from his body heat. It was as though he were nuzzling again the supple skin of the author, the woman who he yearned for with every heartbeat and breath.

The tears froze on his cheeks. The wax hardened in the snow. He and she were destined to miss each other, like a wild goose winging over a golden carp in the pond below, neither able to live in the realm of the other.

He folded up the handkerchief, placed it back into the letter box, and tucked it into his jacket, right next to his heart. He sat very still, letting snow and twilight descend around him, shrinking into himself.

Time passed.`

An owl hooted somewhere in the woods. Startled, he looked up from his torpor. There was a column of smoke in the distance.

He struggled to get up, but fell back down, his numbed and hunger-weakened legs twitching and unable to support his weight.

Perhaps a hunter stuck away from home by the snow, he thought. *I'll rest a little, gain some strength, and then go beg for some food.*

The snow didn't seem so cold anymore. His arms and legs had stopped shivering. In fact, he could no longer feel his limbs.

Terror set in. If he fell asleep here, he might never get up again. Yet, no matter how much he strained, he couldn't make his body obey. Finally, like a drowning man, he gave in to the warm embrace of the icy snow.

He felt very warm, very comfortable.

Am I dead?

He didn't want to open his eyes. Until he tried, he could still pretend to be alive. If he failed, he would *know*.

But he had to try. Had to face the truth. Gingerly, he willed his eyelids to open, not expecting them to obey.

A demonic face loomed at him out of the darkness: bulging eyes, pupil-less like those of a shark or garinafin; angular ears perched forward like those of a wolf; dagger teeth lining a gaping jaw ready to lock around some unfortunate prey's throat; and a lolling tongue that drooped for a foot out of the mouth.

He screamed and tried to scoot backward, but his back bumped into a wall, leaving him nowhere to go.

Footsteps, flickering lights, cries of consternation.

He was grateful to sink into unconsciousness again.

It was daytime the next time he woke up. An old man in a plain hempen monk's robe sat next to him, spooning something warm and nourishing into his mouth.

He sputtered and coughed. The old man set the bowl down to help him onto his side.

"It's all right," he said. "You're very hungry; let your body adjust."

He coughed even harder, not from the soup, but from disbelief.

The old man was speaking to him in Lyucu.

He realized that he was no longer in the rags that he had worn for months. The old man must have changed him in his sleep and recognized the scars on his back, the scars that marked him as a thane-taasa of the Lyucu.

"At dusk two days ago, I suddenly had the urge to go outside to gather snow for tea. I saw a white hare, its ears twitching like the wings of a dove, hopping outside the temple gates. Since the dove-hare is a holy creature, I followed it, and it led me to you. You were almost frozen dead. Praise be to Rufizo Mender—ah, I suppose in your case it would be Toryoana-Rufizo—that you pulled through."

He had not heard the name of the combined deity since he left Ukyu-taasa. "Who are you?" he asked, his voice trembling with wonder.

"I'm Abbot Shattered Axe, and you're at the Temple of Still and Flowing Waters, where we follow the path of Rufizo Mender." Seeing the confusion on Savo's face, he turned and lifted his robe, revealing the scars on his own back, etched by the shamans with a heated stone when a warrior was deemed worthy.

Dropping his robe and turning back, he added in a voice at once placid and emotional, "I was once called Cu Curoten, Wolf-Thane of the Tribe of Singing Sand. I fled Ukyu-taasa when I became a tanto-lyu-naro."

Though the people of the scrublands worshipped the same gods, both before and after the unification of the tribes under the Lyucu and the Agon, there were as many distinct versions of the sacred deeds of gods and heroes as there were ripples in Aluro's Basin or stars in the sky.

As shamans who followed great leaders like Tenryo Roatan and Nobo Aragoz gained power, their lore also came to be dominant, replacing other versions in the memories of the people. But that didn't mean the old stories faded out completely. Sometimes, the very fact that the pékyu's shamans told you something wasn't true made you want to hear it even more.

One of these stories concerned Toryoana, usually described as "the merciful" or "he of healing hands." In most stories, he took the form of a giant long-haired bull, and like the other gods, he had been born to the All-Father and Every-Mother in the time before time.

But there was another story, much darker and more detailed, about his origins.

After the great heroes Kikisavo and Afir had stolen the secrets of thriving on the scrublands from the gods and returned to the people, Kikisavo roamed throughout the land, meting out justice and recruiting the most worthy warriors to join his band.

One day, while traveling near the World's Edge Mountains, he saw a trapped star. Like other stars, this one had tried to depart the mortal world by climbing into the sky from a tall mountain. However, she had been snared by a jagged bit of crystal at the peak and could not free herself.

Kikisavo rode his garinafin up through the clouds until the air was too thin for the flapping wings; then, he jumped onto the mountain and began to climb. He hung on to dangling vines and defeated howling eagles who slashed at his face with talons made from obsidian. He scrambled up lichen-encrusted cliffs to wrestle bulls with six horns and tusked tigers with nine tails, who growled and snorted in his face. He fought through fog-wraiths and wind-beguilers, defeated light-limbed ice warriors and thunder-voiced fire witches. Finally, he reached the apex of the mountain, where he freed the trapped star with a single punch to the crystalline peak, shattering it into a thousand-thousand pieces.

The freed star shone as brightly as the waters of Aluro's Basin at noon. Grateful for his help, she decided to couple with him and bore him a son. This child Kikisavo named Toryoana, which literally meant "the glowing one."

Because Kikisavo needed to roam the land to teach and protect the people, he took the baby Toryoana and entrusted him to the care of the chief of a tribe living near the foot of the mountain on which Kikisavo had met the star. When the child grew up, he became a great hero.

Toryoana had the strength of a bull, the sharp eyes of an eagle, the sensitive nose of a wolf, and the keen hearing of a tusked tiger. He was the greatest hunter and warrior of the scrublands, and he led his people to victory after victory over neighboring tribes.

But one day, during a battle, his foster-father was grievously wounded, his right arm burned to a charcoal-black stump by garina-fin breath. As the man lay groaning in Toryoana's arms, the young hero challenged death to fight him for his foster-father's life. He called on the aid of his heroic birth father. But death refused to meet his challenge, and Kikisavo didn't answer his call. His foster-father took one last breath and stopped moving.

Toryoana held his foster-father's body and didn't move for seven days and seven nights. Though his eyes were open, he gave no answer as his warriors called to him.

When he finally emerged from that numbed state, he became a different person. During the time he had sat immobile in mourning, he had tried to understand the nature of suffering. Death, sickness, old age, starvation, injury—these were the constants of life in the scrublands, and no one had ever questioned their necessity.

My father is a great hero, yet he cannot bring me comfort, he thought. *My foster-father's lungsong is silenced, and my heart bleeds. I've killed many mothers and fathers in battle, and their children's hearts were as wounded as mine. Though the gods and nature already inflict so much suffering on all, why do we still add to the burden?*

He lay his war club on the ground and broke the bone with a black, heavy stone that had fallen from the sky, a piece of star-matter. He asked his warriors to put down their weapons and never to fight again.

Elders and warriors declared him a madman and drove him away. He wandered the scrublands, homeless, tribeless, as lonely as the morning star.

Wherever he went, he tried to preach his new faith in the necessity of peace.

"What if our enemies come to raid us?" asked the warriors.

"If you lay down your arms and they strike you, only you will suffer," said Toryoana. "But if they strike you and you strike back, there will be twice the suffering."

Most warriors laughed in his face and spat at him; some robbed him of his possessions and beat him. But a few, especially those who had lost loved ones in war, joined him in a roaming band, calling him their guide. Toryoana fell in love with one of the women, a shaman named Diaki and favored by Aluro, the Lady of a Thousand Streams, and together they had three sons.

Because Toryoana forbade his followers from possessing weapons or hunting, his band begged for milk and jerky from camps and passing herders, and sometimes they dug up wild roots and ate the carcasses of animals that had died from natural causes. It was a difficult life, and many of his followers eventually lost faith and left, saying that Toryoana was indeed mad.

One day, Toryoana saw a pack of wolves chasing a ewe and her young lambs over the scrublands. Toryoana ran to stand in the way of the wolves and begged them not to harm the mouflon.

"There is already more than enough suffering in the world," said Toryoana.

"You seek to reduce suffering," said the she-wolf that led the pack. "But you are a hypocrite because you don't hunt for your own food but live off the fruits of killings committed by others. Look at how gaunt we are, how flat our bellies! If we don't feast upon the mouflon, my pack and our pups will go hungry tonight, and some of them may die. By protecting the mouflon, you've doomed me and mine to suffer. Are you really reducing suffering in the world?"

"Then I will feed you," said Toryoana.

He held out his left arm. The wolf bit off the appendage in one bite.

"That is barely enough to sustain me," said the she-wolf. "My pups will still be hungry tonight."

Toryoana held out his right arm. The she-wolf bit it off at the shoulder and tossed it to one of her packmates.

"That's still not enough," said the wolf. "The rest of my pack also need to eat."

Toryoana sat down on the ground and offered the wolves his two legs. The pack rushed up and gnawed at them until even the bones had been crushed and the marrow licked clean.

"They also have pups who must be fed," said the she-wolf. "You are still causing suffering."

Toryoana's wife and children pleaded with the wolves to spare him. Diaki's tears flowed and pooled into a giant lake—and that was the origin of the Sea of Tears.

The ewe bleated and huddled with her lambs.

"Do not grieve, beloved," said Toryoana. "The world is a dark place, but we must strive to make it brighter. I see but one path through the unending waves of suffering, like a cattle trail through the grass sea, and I must follow it to the end. So long as a single star shines, the darkness has not won."

He lay down and invited the wolves to eat the rest of him.

Just then, Cudyufin, always gazing upon the world with her single, unblinking eye, intervened. She filled the wolves' bellies with sunlight and starheat, and the pack, satiated, howled with pleasure and left. The blazing goddess made new legs and arms for Toryoana with shrub branches, and fashioned new hands for him from the segmented roots of the cogon grass. The new limbs had none of the strength of the old, but from then on, whenever Toryoana touched a wound, it stopped bleeding and healed over without scars.

More people came to follow Toryoana.

One day, Toryoana arrived at the shore of Aluro's Basin, where two tribes had gathered to wage war. As garinafins circled overhead and warriors lined up in two opposing formations, Toryoana ran between them, begging them to stop fighting.

"You're a fool, a coward, and a weakling," one of the chiefs said. "You shame the name of Kikisavo."

"You're turning young warriors away from a life of glory and honor, the only path that is worthy of a human being," said the other chief.

"There is more than enough suffering in the world," said Toryoana. "More killing is never the answer to killing."

"It's easy to give up war when you're incapable of fighting," said the first chief, glancing contemptuously at his shriveled shrub-branch arms and legs.

"I was once a skilled killer," said Toryoana, "but that didn't make me great."

"It's easy to seek peace when you're afraid of pain," said the other chief, looking with disdain at his wormlike fingers and palms.

"I once fed myself alive to a pack of wolves," said Toryoana. "The pain was indescribable, but I would do it again without hesitation if it would reduce suffering."

"His people drove my people from our grazing grounds and forced our grandparents to walk into the winter storm," said the first chief, pointing at the second. "How can the spirits of the dead be propitiated without taking away the breath of their enemies?"

"His people raided us when we were asleep and trampled nursing children and toothless elders," said the second chief, pointing at the first. "How can the hate-fire in our chests be quenched without the blood of those responsible?"

"Mercy is the only answer, lest spilled blood be answered with crushed lung," said Toryoana. "Do not continue this, I beg of you."

"It's easy to preach mercy when you aren't tormented by the thirst for vengeance," said the chiefs together. "Anyone can adhere to a false faith while enduring mere agony of the flesh. We'll see how you do when your spirit is tested."

They stopped fighting and ordered Toryoana's followers bound with twisted ropes of sinew. But they left Toryoana unbound and placed a war club, finely crafted from star-snout bear bone and wolf's teeth, at his feet.

They took hold of Toryoana's sons. The boys fought back in terror, scratching the faces of their captors before they were overcome. Warriors from both tribes, their faces streaked with blood, tortured the children in front of their father. They broke the bones of one boy one by one, flayed the skin from another, and roasted the third over an open fire. Even shamans wearing human-skin masks turned their faces away at the horror, wishing they could silence the howls of pain.

The chiefs taunted Toryoana, asking him to pick up the club to fight, to save his children, to make their torturers pay.

But Toryoana lashed his own legs together and cut off the loose ends of the sinew to hold himself in place. "I'm sorry, children," he muttered. "I'm sorry."

As the last of his sons' death screams faded, he broke down and tried to free himself. But his cogon-grass-root fingers, soft and boneless, brushed uselessly against the hard sinew, unable to untangle the knots.

As warriors laid the three mangled corpses before him, Toryoana slumped to the ground. "More killing is never the answer to killing," he whispered.

He beckoned the men and women who had killed his children forward, and they approached wearily, thinking that he was finally ready to pick up the war club to fight. But instead, he ran his hands, the hands that had not been able to save his own children, over the faces of the torturers, over the scratch wounds that were the last marks of his children's final terror-filled moments.

The wounds healed. The warriors shrank back in shame.

Toryoana's voice grew stronger. "To take even the smallest amount of suffering away is to give the world more light."

The enraged chiefs placed a bone dagger at the feet of Toryoana. They took hold of Diaki and began to slice off parts of her body, a finger, a toe, an ear, an eye. As she screamed and shrieked, the chiefs pointed at the bone dagger.

"Pick it up," said one. "Come on, pick it up and free yourself!"

"What good is your faith if you cannot protect your wife and children?" said the other.

Toryoana looked into Diaki's eyes. "I'm sorry, beloved," he croaked. "I'm sorry."

"Vengeance is a demon that will never sleep until it is satisfied," said one chief. "There is no salve for the pain you feel unless you deliver more pain."

"Even a god cannot deny the needs of vengeance, much less a mortal," said the other chief.

Toryoana howled at the sky, at the unfeeling stars, at the inconstant gods, at his own powerless father, the great Kikisavo. His lungs could catch no breath, and his howl was silent.

"If you won't fight, then pick up the dagger and use it to put out your eyes and slice off your ears," demanded the chiefs. "Admit that you are weak. Show us that you are a coward. Prove to us that you submit. And you'll no longer have to witness her suffering."

Toryoana writhed over the ground, but his hands never reached for the bone dagger. He kept his eyes locked on his dying wife and clenched his teeth until they shattered.

Finally, after her screams had faded, Toryoana stopped writhing and slumped to the earth.

"Why didn't you turn your face away?" asked one of the chiefs.

"To blind one's eyes and deafen one's ears against the suffering of the world is also error," said Toryoana. "To avert one's face, to hide behind the excuse of ignorance, is also a sin that increases suffering."

As soon as he said this, Toryoana's heart stopped beating and his lungs stopped pumping. The pain he had experienced was too much for his mortal body, even though he had limbs and hands of bark and grass, not flesh and blood.

It was said that the waters of Aluro's Basin then turned to blood, and the very heavens wept with a raging storm that lasted seven days and seven nights. Only on the eighth morning did the thunder, downpour, and contending gales cease and the lake water clear, and the two chiefs, huddled in terror under a single tent throughout the ordeal, realized that the All-Father and Every-Mother had spared them only in honor of Toryoana's wish to add no more to the suffering of the world.

Members of the two warring tribes were so overcome by Toryoana's courage and dedication to his faith that they stopped fighting and gave him a lavish funeral. They built a grand bier of bone and earth and laid his body atop, surrounded by the most precious treasures of the two tribes. The shamans then danced and called out to the wolves and vultures to begin Toryoana's pédiato savaga.

However, long before his body could be consumed, a star descended to earth and took him into the heavens, where he became Toryoana of Still Hands, the Pacific, the god closest to human suffering.

Savo gazed up at the face of the statue in the shrine's sanctum.

Seated in *géüpa* on the altar, the life-size statue was of a young man, fair-skinned and lanky, with a handsome face that looked back at the viewer with serenity. A pair of curved horns, like the horns of the long-haired cattle, protruded from his temples. Although the sculptor had carved him a muscular body out of ironwood, his green, flowing cape was draped over delicate arms that were disproportionately thin, like the legs of a crane misplaced upon an elephant. The sticklike arms ended in oddly misshapen fingers, as though they were made from half-melted wax—though a closer examination revealed them to be fashioned from young lotus roots.

"You think the statue is too small to be the main idol for a temple, don't you?" asked the abbot.

Startled, Savo smiled awkwardly. Considering that the temple was the home for over two hundred monks and nuns, he had indeed been struck by the rather unimposing appearance of the effigy.

"Rufizo Mender is not a god of power, but of compassion," said the abbot. "A representation of him shouldn't awe or overwhelm. His approachability may be his most important quality."

Savo nodded, knelt down on the cushion before the statue, and offered a silent prayer. Having spent a few days recuperating with the hearty food at the temple, he was feeling much stronger physically, though the frost wounds on his feet and hands would take time to heal.

"Who is Rufizo Mender?" he asked. "I don't think I've ever heard of that particular deity in Dara."

Instead of answering, the abbot posed a question of his own. "It's been a long time since I left Ukyu-taasa. Does the worship of Toryoana-Rufizo persist there?"

The various cults of deities fused from Lyucu and Dara traditions had begun under Pékyu Tenryo, and much of Savo's religious experience in his formative youth had been centered around them. With a somber expression, he answered the abbot, "I cannot tell you how things are in Ukyu-taasa now. However, when I left two years ago, Thane Cutanrovo Aga was advocating against the interpretation of the native god Rufizo as a facet of Merciful Toryoana of Healing Hands. In response, I believe most of the natives returned to worshipping Rufizo in private, while the Lyucu and . . . collaborating natives prayed to the Toryoana of the scrublands they were familiar with."

The abbot nodded, a trace of melancholy in the sag of his spine. "I had heard rumors of such a rejection of fusion. . . . Well, no matter, the gods have always transcended the foolishness of mortals."

Savo knew that the tanto-lyu-naro followed a different aspect of Toryoana than he of Healing Hands. Though he had been circumspect during the past few days, refraining from prying into Abbot Shattered Axe's personal history, he decided that the abbot's reference to life in Ukyu-taasa showed a tacit consent for the subject to be broached.

Just how did a Lyucu tanto-lyu-naro—once a thane, even—come to be the abbot of a Dara temple?

Taking a deep breath to steel his own determination, he asked, "Have you always followed the path of Toryoana Pacific?"

"That depends on what you mean by 'follow,'" said the abbot wryly.

The aspect of Toryoana sanctioned by Pékyu Tenryo and followed by most of the shamans of the scrublands was a deity of bounty and fertility, the male counterpart to Cudyufin. Called Merciful Toryoana of Healing Hands, he was the god of health, virility, and medicines—an obvious favorite of most low-ranking shamans, responsible for administering to the sick and wounded.

According to the most common legends, Toryoana had been born in the time before memories and gained his healing powers when he defeated his enemies and bathed his hands in their blood. The mercy he dispensed was of the battlefield kind: to give a respected enemy a clean death; to enslave the spouses and children of the vanquished rather than killing them; to maim and exile a thane who had offended the chief rather than cutting out her heart.

Toryoana Pacific, on the other hand, felt like an altogether different deity. Over time, the pacifist cult waned and waxed in popularity, though the ranks of believers generally swelled in the aftermath of major wars on the scrublands, when survivors found strength and comfort in a god who understood the unspeakable pain of losing loved ones to cycles of vengeance.

But the war chiefs and senior shamans couldn't abide such developments. A tribe that permitted the cult of Toryoana Pacific to proselytize and grow unimpeded among its elders, thanes, naros-votan, naros, culeks, and children was also a tribe sure to lose its next war. On the scrublands, pacifism was collective suicide.

Therefore, the chiefs and shamans treated the followers of Toryoana Pacific like the victims of a deadly, virulent plague. The tanto-lyu-naro, or "warriors who do not make war," were stripped of their possessions and driven away from their native tribes. The homeless wanderers gathered into roaming bands for protection and lived on charity and begging, preserved from being massacred only by the superstition that it was unlucky to have their honorless ghosts haunting a tribe's hunting grounds.

After the unification of the scattered scrubland tribes under charismatic leaders like Nobo Aragoz and Toluroru Roatan, the tanto-lyu-naro were subjected to even more persecution. Those found possessing Toryoana Pacific talismans or fetishes, such as cogongrass-root dolls or figurines with fused legs, were beaten, marked with scars on their faces, and then exiled, often with their minor children taken away from them. And those proselytizing for the god or advocating pacifism were sometimes executed on the spot as traitors.

Nonetheless, even among the regimented Lyucu tribes under Pékyu Tenryo and his descendants, the cult survived in secret.

To be sure, most people who sympathized with the pacifists or found solace in the cult's ideals didn't go so far as to join the wanderers. Giving up all weaponry and acts of violence meant also giving up hunting and butchering, subsisting only on tubers and roots and wild fruits—a prospect even lowly culeks found revolting. (The Agon rebels at Kiri Valley had resisted a Dara-style diet, dominated by grains and vegetables, in part because they felt the taint of the tanto-lyu-naro in such foods.) Higher-ranking naros with herds of cattle and sheep and slaves captured from war, on the other hand, couldn't be expected to abandon their wealth, security, and status.

Thus, the semi-believers gave food to roaming bands of tanto-lyu-naro and prayed to Toryoana Pacific in private, but continued to participate in hunts and to fight in wars. Cu Curoten and others like him thus became part of Pékyu Tenryo's expedition to Dara despite their spiritual distaste for the pékyu's war.

"I thought I could learn to reconcile my faith with the pékyu-votan's dream of a better future," said the abbot, his gaze distant, "but the reality of what he demanded of us . . .

"I was put in charge of pacifying a village on Rui. After a short battle in which my eldest son lost his life, my band of warriors overcame the native rebels. The villagers who fought were all dead or had dropped their weapons to plead for mercy, while the rest, too terrified to even speak or cry, huddled silently in one clump like sheep in winter. I cradled the body of my son, my heart heavy and my hands slick with his blood.

"Mutely, I watched my warriors approach the surviving villagers to carry out the pékyu-votan's orders. The men under my command raped the native women while the women under my command bashed in the skulls of every child so that the natives would then have to bear and raise our seed. There were no ear-piercing screams, no lung-bursting howls of protest. What I heard was worse: the dull, wet thunking of crushed skulls and the inhuman whimpers from scarred minds that had lost all hope.

"Before we set out on that mission, the pékyu-votan had reminded us of the outrages committed by Admiral Krita in Ukyu, of Luan Zya's perfidy, of the brothers and sisters who had died to gain us a foothold in this new world. Again and again, I repeated the pékyu-votan's words in my head to drown out the horrific noises around me: 'We come to avenge and to free; we must secure an enduring future for Lyucu children.'

"But it was no use. What I wanted most of all was not vengeance, but for my son not to be dead. No one could give me that, not my warriors, not my enemies, not the pékyu-votan, not even the gods.

"I could not block out the reality of my son's cold corpse, nor the crimes we were committing in his name. A voice that I had never heard before, deep and compassionate like the sea, spoke in my head then. 'There is more than enough suffering in the world.'

"I looked down at my child, at my bloody hands, and I couldn't understand how I would ever feel clean again. With these acts, what kind of future were we securing for our children?

"But I was a coward, and I saw no way to escape. I vowed to minimize the suffering I caused directly, and I shattered my bone axe by bashing it repeatedly against an unyielding cliffside. From that point on, I did everything I could to avoid going into battle. Passing up all chances for promotion and enduring the contemptuous glances of my fellow thanes, I begged for assignments like retrieving wounded Lyucu warriors from the battlefield, watching over the aged and the feeble, guarding prisoners far from the front lines.

"But then, Kuni Garu invaded Ukyu-taasa to avenge his people, and the pékyu-votan had to invade the Big Island in turn. I had no choice but to join the invasion fleet. During the Battle of Zathin Gulf, a burning airship collided with my ship, and as I tried to evade death by jumping into the sea, I was struck by a falling spar and lost consciousness.

"When I came to, I found myself alone on a deserted beach in Rima. Not knowing what else to do, I fled on foot inland, avoiding the natives and staying alive with stolen food, until I came to these mountains, desperate with hunger and cold, and saw this temple.

"That voice, that sea-like voice, spoke again. 'There is more than enough suffering in the world.'

"It was a sign, I realized. I crawled to the gate of the temple and knocked, willing to accept whatever fate the inhabitants had in store for me."

A sign, thought Savo. *Master Nazu Tei named me Kinri, which also means "a sign."*

"And they took you in," the young man whispered, "just as you took me in."

Abbot Shattered Axe nodded. "The monks and nuns nursed me back to health, and I learned that this temple is dedicated to Rufizo, the native god of healing and pastures. But their version of the deity is distinct from the patron of Faça. As heretics, they are often persecuted by authorities in Dara."

"Why?" asked Savo.

The abbot sighed. "That is a story both complicated and simple."

It is a truism that no religion or spiritual movement, no matter how concerned with matters beyond the mortal realm, can be wholly free from entanglement with temporal authorities. In the time of the Tiro states, the various kings encouraged the worship of local patron deities as a way to legitimate their own power, while high-ranking priests and monks became members of political courts, currying favor with secular authorities in exchange for grander temples, endowments of land, and privileges for the clergy.

Mapidéré's conquest of the Six States not only decimated the ranks of the old nobility, but also upended the established clerical hierarchies in the conquered territories. Mapidéré declared Kiji, the patron of Xana, as the first deity among former equals. Priests and monks of the other gods who acquiesced in this official position were left in place or promoted, while resisters were punished.

It was natural, in such an environment, for peasant rebels, deposed nobles, and resentful clergy, whose interests were often in conflict, to become allies of convenience. But that didn't mean all religious opposition to Xana rule came out of self-interest.

Since Rufizo was a god of healing, doctrines of his faith drew liberally on medical metaphors. By tradition, low-ranking temple priests and itinerant monastics who served Rufizo also preserved and developed medical knowledge as a part of their religious duties. Unlike more senior priests, whose long involvement in politics made them more akin to cynical bureaucrats than spiritual guides, many of the junior priests and monastics lived in daily contact with starving and afflicted corvée laborers, military widows forced to resort to begging, orphans sold into indentured servitude in indigo and scarlet houses, men who had been maimed and disfigured for petty crimes under Xana's harsh laws, and others who suffered under the new regime. While old Faça's temple leaders quickly made peace with Mapidéré, a group of these junior clergy began to argue that the Xana conquest was a cancer that was destroying the very body of Dara itself as a living being.

Poring through old scrolls in temple libraries, they discovered stories about Rufizo bringing peace to lifelong enemies locked in deadly combat, offering to jump into boiling pots in place of condemned criminals, melting away hatred by self-sacrifice. They found ancient divination records detailing Rufizo counseling Tiro kings and hegemons to retreat from the battlefield, pacifying angry hearts with tears of compassion, persuading tyrants to step down from their despotic perches. They argued that those who followed Rufizo needed not only to heal individuals, but also to mend and restore a broken and sick body politic. Mapidéré had to abdicate in order to remove the source of violence and infection; Xana soldiers had to put down their killing swords and slave-driving whips to give the world a chance to heal. To emphasize this aspect of the god, they gave Rufizo the sobriquet "Mender."

As these voices of protest gained strength, the high priests of Rufizo in Boama grew alarmed. A grand council of senior priests and abbots was held, and after seven days of debate, the doctrine of Rufizo Mender was declared a heresy, and its followers would be expelled and driven from all the temples.

"Did the heretics put up a fight?" asked Savo.

Abbot Shattered Axe shook his head. "They accepted the decision of the council and left quietly, promising to withdraw from Faça altogether."

"So they were afraid," said Savo quietly. The sect of Rufizo Mender sounded to him like cowards.

The abbot shook his head. "No, you misunderstand. The priests who drove the Mendists away weren't merely peeved at having their own authority challenged. They were also concerned about far graver consequences. Given the high esteem in which the people held Rufizo's priests and monks, an anti-Xana movement among the clergy would almost certainly have inflamed peasant rebellions in Faça—despite the avowed pacifism of the Mendists. It was easy, all too easy, for messages of peace to turn into justifications for righteous war. And rebellions—which had no chance of overcoming the might of the Xana Empire in its prime—would have led to brutal reprisals by the emperor and great suffering for the people. The Mendists left so that their faith would not be exploited by armed insurrection, even if many considered such rebellions just.

"To believe in Rufizo Mender was to dedicate oneself to the alleviation of suffering, not to its aggravation, not even in the name of justice."

Savo listened intently. A dim understanding began to take shape in his mind.

"The exiles hiked deep into the Ring-Woods until they arrived here and built the one and only temple dedicated to Rufizo Mender," said the abbot. "In the years that followed, secluded here in obscurity, away from the all-dominating wing-oars of Mapidéré's airships, away from the thundering hooves of the Hegemon, away from the prosperity and intrigues of the Dandelion Court, away from the threat of Lyucu garinafin fire breath, they devoted themselves to saving strangers, to reducing suffering, to healing the world."

"They *chose* not to fight," Savo muttered.

The abbot nodded. "They chose to be *hidden*, but that doesn't mean they chose to *hide*. Have you noticed the carved masks of demons throughout the temple, even in the sleeping quarters?"

Savo recalled the mask hanging at the foot of the bed in the abbot's room that had terrified him in his delirium.

"As my predecessor, Abbot Discarded Butcher Knife, said to me on the night he rescued me, the masks remind the monks that suffering is everywhere, that the world is broken, and that we cannot avert our eyes."

Savo gazed at the statue of the sitting god and shivered, feeling a tingle down his spine like the ones he had experienced as a child watching shamans dancing around the beachside bonfire. He could only imagine how the despondent Cu Curoten must have felt to hear the tenets of his own faith echoed in a foreign land, in the name of another god.

"What good is knowing that the world is in shambles, that it is full of horror?" asked Savo, his heart heavy. He felt it straining against the carp-shaped letter box. "We're powerless before history, before legacies we didn't choose."

Abbot Shattered Axe looked at him, and Savo had the feeling that the abbot *saw* more than he had revealed.

Without directly addressing Savo's query, he went on. "On the evening I was rescued by Abbot Discarded Butcher Knife, I fell to my knees before him and confessed all I had done. Though I was unskilled in the speech of the natives, with the help of drawings I divulged death, rape, slaughter, torture—the horrors I had committed rivaled the sins of those who had killed Toryoana Pacific. I asked to be punished. I asked to be tortured and put to death for the suffering I had caused the people of Dara.

"But the abbot shook his head and put his hands on my shoulders. 'It isn't my place, nor that of any Mendist, to punish you.'

"I lowered my head in shame, thinking I understood. 'Then tell me how to ask your god to punish me.'

"He shook his head again. 'Rufizo Mender has no power to punish.'

"My heart swelled with confusion. 'Without punishment, how can I be forgiven?'

" 'It isn't my place, nor that of any Mendist, to forgive you. Rufizo Mender has no power to forgive. His only commandment is to heal, both yourself and others.'

"Outrage made my breath and voice ragged. 'Then what good is your god? Without being forgiven, how can I heal?'

"He met the anger in my eyes without flinching. 'What is

punishment but another name for vengeance? What is forgiveness but an illusion?'

"I was aghast. His words made no sense.

"Looking into my eyes, his expression neither rebuking nor sparing, he went on. 'Before I became a monk, I was a bandit, as was my father before me. I butchered without remorse; I dealt pain without regret. One day, my band attacked a caravan that seemed to promise much wealth, but the merchants were well-defended with armed guards, and I was cut down and left to die.

" 'When I came to, I found a Mendist monk tending to me. He had been traveling with the caravan, and I had swung my butcher knife, my preferred weapon, into his shoulder, injuring him grievously. But instead of leaving me to the wolves, he had stayed behind to dress my wounds.

" 'Something changed in me in that moment, though I was too ashamed to speak to the monk, who brought me to an inn and cared for me like a brother. When I was fully recovered and we were ready to part ways, I told him that I would abandon my profession and devote the rest of my life to making restitution to the families of my victims.

" ' "If the families of the men you killed wish to strike you and kick you, what will you do?" he asked.

" ' "I will bear my deserved punishment silently," I said. "Even if they wish to avenge their loved ones by killing me."

" ' "And how will you know when you've made enough restitution?" he asked.

" ' "When the families forgive me," I said.

" ' "But how will their forgiveness wipe away the deeds you've done? How will your agony erase the pain you've already caused? Even if you could secure the forgiveness of the survivors, you can never be forgiven by the dead. Even if you could bear a measure of pain equal to all the pain you dealt, you cannot undo the past."

" 'He pointed to the neat pile of chicken bones on the table, the remnants of our last supper together. "We didn't kill that chicken with our own hands, but we benefited from its suffering." He pointed at me. "When you were a baby, you didn't go out to raid or rob, but you grew strong and hardy from the wealth obtained from your father's crimes. Will you seek forgiveness from the chicken? Will you ask to be punished by your father's victims? All of us are entangled in webs of suffering and pain, and there is no power in the universe that can mete out enough punishment or offer sufficient forgiveness to free us."

" 'I stood rooted to the spot like a statue carved from ironwood, my mind swirling with the implications of what he said. The world seemed to me a sea of suffering with no way out. What was the point of knowing that we, all of us, were the beneficiaries of conquests and crimes committed before we were born, in our names, that vengeance only led to more pain, that forgiveness brought no relief?

" 'But then the monk looked at me and shouted, "Drop the butcher knife! Discard self-serving illusions! Heal thyself and the world with thee." ' "

Finally, Abbot Shattered Axe had come to the conclusion of his tale.

The words that the nameless monk had once used to enlighten a bandit, who had then used them to enlighten a Lyucu thane, were now etched into Savo Ryoto's mind.

He wasn't sure, yet, what to do with them.

Gently, the abbot brought Savo back to his room and left him to sleep.

CHAPTER THIRTY-ONE

CLOUD-GARINAFINS

THE BONEYARD, UKYU-GONDÉ: THE TWELFTH
MONTH IN THE TENTH YEAR AFTER THE DEPARTURE
OF PRINCESS THÉRA FROM DARA FOR UKYU-GONDÉ.

Still looking up at the sun from the back of his garinafin, Tovo noticed the sudden hush that had descended over the battlefield below him.

Why have my brave warriors stopped their war cries? Have they already overwhelmed their enemies? Why am I doomed to such short battles, leading to un-danceworthy victories?

Tovo looked down, determined to bask in the moment of his triumph despite his own underwhelming performance, and froze.

Across the battlefield, the Lyucu host had stopped, barely steps away from the bone beasts.

Warriors in the front-most ranks lay curled on the ground, fists clenched at the sides of their heads. Farther back, some staggered around the field, arms waving, seemingly inebriated. Even farther back, naros and culeks alike had dropped their weapons to kneel and pray, as though they had witnessed some miraculous act.

What happened?

He could see no lightning bolts zigzagging across the flat landscape; he could hear no thunderclaps portending dark magic. The battlefield was eerily silent.

Cautiously, he guided his mount lower. He squinted and concentrated. The ground under the Lyucu nearest to the bone beasts was stained with blood, blood that continued to pour from noses and ears. The warriors were dying.

The bone beasts shambled forward, their heads suspended low over the ground, their necks sweeping from side to side, roaring silently at their enemies. Wherever their maws pointed, men and women fell like grass and shrubs scythed down to be feed for the winter.

It was impossible. It was incomprehensible. Yet it was true.

As Tovo glided over the stunned Lyucu army, the formation collapsed. Terrified naros and culeks broke in every direction, their only thought to get away from the cursed breath of the oversized arucuro tocua. Ancient legends spoke of the gods ending the Fifth Age of Mankind with monsters who could wound from afar, kill with a glance, turn people to stone with mere breath.

The legends were true. All true.

Tovo could not accept it. He *would* not accept it. To believe that the gods were on the side of the rebels would negate all his plots, all his maneuvers, his lost arm and toes, his victories and triumphs and dreams. It would make a mockery of the dream of every Lyucu, of the accomplishments of Tenryo and Cudyu.

A story told by Toof and Radia, the traitors who had surrendered to Théra long ago, surfaced in his mind. *Dissolver of Sorrows*, the cunning barbarian princess's flagship, had frightened and distracted the pursuing Lyucu city-ship with kites painted to resemble tusked tigers and an elaborate performance of shadows on a screen.

Tovo's heart lifted. Yes, that must be it. How could the barbarians from Dara possess real magic? This had to be merely another act of deception, another pageant of illusions designed to frighten the gullible.

The other Lyucu garinafin riders, shocked by the chaos on the ground, circled aimlessly over the battlefield, uncertain what to do.

Swooping above them, Tovo dug his heels into his mount's shoulders, spurring it to emit a long, high-pitched screech to get their attention. Wielding his signaling spear like an immense finger, Tovo pointed in turn at the Seven-Headed Garinafin, the Thousand-Faced Tusked Tiger, the Clawed Shark, the Many-Limbed Wolf, the Two-Faced Bull. . . .

"Everything burns!" he shouted. "Ten dyudyu cupéruna?"

The other riders understood. "Lyucu kyo!" they shouted in unison.

The bone beasts were mere symbols: illusory terrors, painted tigers, outsized children's toys. They might paralyze superstitious culeks who had to fight on foot, but they had no effect on disciplined garinafins guided by noble riders. The flying beasts knew nothing of the stories told by shamans, and their pilots were imbued with the invincible Lyucu spirit!

Tovo heaved his signaling spear in a long arc, and the last of the Lyucu garinafins, disregarding the terror-stricken ground troops stampeding from the battlefield, dove toward the arucuro tocua.

Keeping her eyes on the incoming garinafins for as long as possible, Théra pulled down another lever, this one tipped by a turtle shell.

Instantly, garinafin-hide shades descended over the eye sockets of the skull cockpit, sealing Théra and Thoryo within.

Inside every walking beast, teams of actuators rushed to carry out the order to fortify the bone fortresses. They withdrew from the exposed backs and abandoned the power-generating sails and their lookout posts. Scrambling, sliding, tumbling, they congregated inside the belly and strung up sheets of garinafin hide around the central singing lung. Théra had commanded the rebel fighters to retreat to protect the organ responsible for the Divine Voice, like a turtle retracting every limb against a menacing predator.

The attacks began.

Again and again, Lyucu garinafins dove at the artificial beasts, devoid of defenders on spines and wings, lashing them with tongues of fire in an effort to set the bone structures aflame and fry the crews within. The garinafin-hide barriers held, but the exposed wing-sails and wheel-feet blackened, charred, burst into flames.

"We've got to get the fires under control!" cried Gozofin. "If we lose mobility, we're done for!"

From behind the arucuro tocua, rebel culeks and naros emerged from the protection of their garinafin-hide shelters and rushed forward, each carrying a bundle of earth wrapped inside cattle hide. Wielding these awkward tools, they beat at the roaring flames, trying to smother them. Soon, their hair was singed, their eyes blinded by the smoke, their forearms covered in boils and blisters. When their fire-beaters began to burn, some jumped onto the smoking wheel-feet, trying to suppress the raging flames with their own bodies. Agonized screams and the stench of burned flesh permeated the bellies of the walking beasts.

Inside the skull cockpit, Thoryo whimpered.

Théra hugged her, muttering comforting words into the young woman's ear.

"Fear and trust the gods," she said, "but never fear our mortal enemy. We *will* triumph."

"What good is victory?" the young woman asked. It wasn't terror that made her voice tremble, but despair. "So many deaths already, and so many more still to come."

Théra didn't know what to say. At length, she whispered feebly, "The killing will end . . . when the Agon are free."

"Will it?" asked Thoryo, her eyes glazing over. "The ice flowers . . . the sea . . . the endless waves . . . colliding to shatter . . . one after another . . ."

The pékyu fought to stave off panic and helplessness. This was no time to debate philosophy. The garinafin assault was far worse than she had anticipated.

Where is Toof?

She didn't know if Toof's idea would work; she didn't know if he was having trouble carrying out the plan. There were just too many unknowns, too many ways for things to fail.

The inside of the skull cockpit, frigid as a Dara winter cellar just moments earlier, was already uncomfortably warm from the constant fiery blasts against it.

Reluctantly, and then resolutely, Théra let go of Thoryo, leaving the girl to huddle by herself.

"We can't just wait to be rescued," she said to herself. "We've got to try to bring down the garinafins ourselves."

Théra coaxed the nearly catatonic Thoryo into a garinafin-hide cloak that covered her from head to toe. She put on a similar cloak herself, and then crawled over to the protective shades covering the eye sockets. She pressed her ear against them in turn to be sure no garinafin was hovering outside, and then, taking a deep breath to steady herself, she drew the shades.

Instantly, a blast of furnace-like air surged into the cockpit, along with swirling smoke. The ends of her hair began to curl.

Squinting against the eye-watering smoke and heat, she looked out through the eye sockets at the swooping garinafins. Like a scout in the conning tower of the submerged *Dissolver of Sorrows*, she tracked the flight paths of the winged beasts. Gritting her teeth, she reached back into the cockpit and pulled and pushed a set of levers located over a painted image of a spiderweb. . . .

Deep within the belly, Çami continued to guide the silent roar of the tusked tiger; culeks at the bone oars strained to maintain the pressure in the singing lung.

Everyone had the same thought: *Keep on singing!* It was all they could do not to give in to despair.

Gozofin paced around his command station, his hands balled into fists in helpless frustration. There was nothing he could do. With all the lookouts pulled back within the safety of the arucuro tocua fortress, the Seven-Headed Garinafin was blind and deaf at this moment. Théra's plan had included turtling as a temporary answer in the event of a direct garinafin assault, but it was never intended to last this long.

He didn't even know if the pékyu was still alive. The skull cockpit was armored with thick fire shielding, but perhaps Tovo had recognized it as the seat of the leader of the rebellion and decided to concentrate . . .

"We can't wait anymore," said Tipo Tho. "I and the other spotters must go out to direct you."

Exposed to garinafin flame on the Seven-Headed Garinafin's back, the spotters would not survive for long. But what other option did they have? Gozofin nodded reluctantly.

Just as Tipo Tho was about to lead the lookouts back to their posts, a cluster of signaling spears hanging above Gozofin's head began to wave and twirl, thunking into various locations on a large web over his station woven from long strands of sinew. Gozofin looked up and whooped with delight.

"The pékyu is alive!"

Like the other signaling spears, these were controlled by Théra up in the cockpit. However, rather than general directives, their dance in the web conveyed the location, distance, velocity, and angle of approach of attacking garinafins. Inspired by the way spiders sensed their pray by vibrations in the strands of their web, Théra had devised this system for lookouts to signal the arucuro tocua animators.

Gozofin's joy was tempered by the realization that for Théra to be signaling him this way, she must have removed the protective covering in the skull cockpit. Exposed, she wouldn't last long. He had to make the risk she was taking count.

With a hunter's instinct, he kept his eyes on the dancing spears and calculated in his head, imagining the unseen garinafins swooping far above. He shouted directions, which his assistants repeated at the tops of their lungs. Crews of actuators stationed around the vast air sac strained against their bone oars and cranks. . . .

Six long bony necks twisted and turned, lifting their resonant-chambered singing heads toward the sky, aiming the Divine Voice at the diving garinafins.

Despite the swirling smoke that made it hard to breathe, despite the waves of heat that singed her hair, Théra watched the dance of the singing heads, mesmerized.

Only too late did she realize a Lyucu garinafin was diving straight for the cockpit. She scrambled back, shoving the still-whimpering Thoryo to the rear of the cockpit, as far from danger as possible.

She grappled with the signaling levers frantically, trying to sketch the location of this latest threat.

It was too late.

The Lyucu garinafin reared up right before the skull cockpit, a winged demon that filled her field of vision. Time seemed to slow down as gusts from its powerful wings cleared out the smoke inside the cockpit, and its jaws snapped open in preparation to bathe the entire interior of the cavernous skull in a conflagration, immolating the two huddling occupants.

Théra squeezed her eyes shut and wrapped her arms around Thoryo, placing her own body between the oncoming fire and the girl. It wasn't much, but it was all she could do.

"I'm sorry," she whispered into the girl's ear. "I'm so sorry."

The pilot of the garinafin laughed, and shouted into her bone trumpet.

Abruptly, two of the singing heads, one on either side of the hovering garinafin, swung over like the pincers of a crab. The maws of the bone heads snapped open. Silent roars, hundreds of times more powerful than the natural roar of the tusked tiger, slammed into the head of the Lyucu garinafin from both sides.

For a moment, the garinafin hung suspended in midair, its jaw frozen open in a surprised yawn. The Lyucu riders on its back sat stock-still, their faces fixed in rictuses of shock.

Then the garinafin's eyes rolled up inside its eyelids; blood spewed from its nose; the wings collapsed as though the bones had been shattered.

Slowly, and then faster and faster, the massive creature plunged down, dead before it had hit the ground. As the mountain of flesh crashed into the earth at the foot of the Seven-Headed Garinafin, riders tumbled off its back and lay still, as lifeless as the moss-stuffed dolls of scrubland children.

From beneath their garinafin-hide tent-shields, the Agon and Dara rebels let out a thunderous cheer.

Unexpectedly, Tovo found that the loss of the first garinafin calmed him and strengthened his resolve.

Whatever the nature of the invisible breath the Seven-Headed Garinafin had used to bring down the attacking garinafin, it followed rules. And rules could be learned and taken advantage of.

He rallied the remaining garinafin riders and changed tactics. The powerful witchcraft evidently emanated from the jaws of the arucuro tocua, and its effect seemed to diminish with distance. Therefore, he dispatched a few of the garinafins to distract the bone beasts from the front, but he directed them to stay deftly just out of the range of harm. Meanwhile, other garinafins dove close to the ground to circle stealthily behind the bone beasts, where they proceeded to attack the hide-clad backs and tails with their claws. Once the protective covering was wrenched away, the garinafins inundated the interior of the arucuro tocua with fire, frying human crew and bone machinery alike.

Though the rebel crews fought valiantly to save their burning fortresses, they were overcome, one by one. The Many-Limbed Wolf howled defiantly toward the sky as its thick limbs, weakened by the intensifying blaze, buckled and collapsed, leaving a giant bonfire whose smoky tendrils reached high into the sky. The Clawed Shark threshed against the harassing garinafins and broke apart, fragments of bone beams and struts tumbling into a raging inferno in which men and women clung to their posts and did their duty until the very end.

Tovo cackled in delight. For generations to come, shamans would dance the tale of the One-Armed Protector of the Lyucu who extinguished Dara witchcraft. He would be remembered as a greater warrior than even Tenryo and Cudyu.

Inside the skull cockpit, Théra knew that her final gamble had failed.

Three of the singing heads had been incinerated. The Seven-Headed Garinafin was wounded and dying.

No matter how quickly she passed the coordinates of the attacking garinafins down below, no matter how hard Çami and her crew pressed the singing lung, no matter how fast Gozofin and his actuators swung the serpentine necks, the Lyucu garinafins were too fast, too nimble, too numerous.

Still shielding Thoryo with her body, she redoubled her efforts at the levers. Even if defeat was certain, she would not give up.

It was her nature.

"Yee-haw!" Toof shouted into Ga-al's ear. For the tenth time? For the hundredth time? He had lost count. His voice was hoarse.

Ga-al and the last few rebel garinafins stretched out their necks and stared intently into space, sending their silent pleas to the west, to the east, to the south, to the north.

They had started their calls many hours ago, as soon as the Lyucu army had been sighted. They had led the Lyucu garinafins on a fruitless chase, hoping to see the results of their petition. They had continued their inaudible appeal upon return, their lift gas exhausted and their muscles and lungs aching from exertion.

There was no answer.

Before them, towering bone monsters stumbled and fell, unable to withstand the Lyucu garinafin assault. Columns of black smoke, like the tornadoes that plagued the scrublands in winter, surged from the collapsed ruins. Around them, Agon warriors shouted defiantly and waved their weapons, trying to draw the attention of the swooping garinafins in order to save their arucuro-tocua-bound comrades, heedless of their own safety.

Come on! Toof screamed inside. Fervently, he prayed to Péa, the god of garinafins. But what good was prayer from a man who had always preferred the company of garinafins to shamans, found singing to the flying beasts more soothing than dances honoring the gods?

"Yee-haw!" he shouted at Ga-al and the other garinafins again, his voice cracking.

Silently, the garinafins screamed into the smoke-filled, unrelenting sky.

A Lyucu garinafin swooped slowly overhead, surveying this voiceless choir with its cold, pupil-less eyes. The beast and its riders seemed to conclude that this band of mad rebels and frenzied beasts didn't even deserve the courtesy of a strafing. It swerved away, intent on bringing down another walking arucuro tocua.

Toof laughed. He *was* mad. He was mad to have suggested this plan, and Pékyu Théra was mad to have trusted him. How could he think this was ever going to work? The battle was lost.

Vara was dead, Alkir was dead, Radia was dead—everyone he had ever loved had died because of his mad obsession with garinafins, because he thought he understood the beasts better than anyone.

He was neither Lyucu nor Agon; he was a man without a tribe.

Tears of rage and regret spilled from his eyes. Impulsively, he wrapped his arms around Ga-al's neck and began to sing.

> *Tents sprout across the scrublands like mushrooms after rain,*
> *People roam the endless grass like stars through the cloud-sea.*
> *Feel my arms around you, my eyes on you;*
> *Feel my breath against you, my voice through you.*
> *You're never alone when you hear the tribe's lungsong.*

Ga-al and the other garinafins kept on howling inaudibly into the void, even as walking bone towers burned and toppled around them, even as the singing lungs of the arucuro tocua beasts emptied, even as warriors and actuators and singers exhausted their last reservoirs of hope.

It was their nature.

The Seven-Headed Garinafin's remaining singing heads drooped. The long, serpentine necks had become entangled with one another, like the tails of a nest of moonfur rats.

Tovo felt giddy, as though his blood had transmuted into kyoffir. It was time to deal the final blow, to destroy this most redoubtable bone beast, the symbol of hope for the alliance.

He raised the antler-tipped signaling spear, ready to hurl it and end the battle.

The air darkened. Shadows loomed above him, blotting out the sun.

He looked up, and his heart stopped.

Hundreds, no, perhaps more than a thousand garinafins, had congregated from every direction, their wings a dense cloud that turned day into night. For a moment he wondered if the Dara witch did know real magic after all, and had conjured the cloud-garinafins as her allies.

The truth was both far stranger and less so.

The garinafins that had been freed by Thoryo, Toof, and Radia had spread the tale of their rebellion in Taten across Ukyu-Gondé. In the retelling, the tale had mutated, soared, grown from re-remembering into legend. But beneath the flapping wings of exaggeration and elaborate antlers of embellishment, an articulated skeleton of hard truth remained: *It was possible to fight to be free.*

The inaudible call of Ga-al and the others had carried across the flat scrublands and been passed on by those who heard it. The cry that had once rallied the enslaved garinafins of Taten to rise up now demanded aid.

And the call had been heeded. The wild and feral garinafins had come to fight not as enslaved war beasts for an unjust empire, but as free creatures making a stand.

Hot tears spilled from Toof's eyes as he watched their arrival. His faith in the sentience of garinafins had been rewarded; his belief that they would make a choice had been justified.

As columns of smoke over the battlefield swirled in the wing-gusts of the new arrivals, he seemed to see the wispy form of a star-eyed cloud-garinafin, piloted by the insubstantial figure of the woman who had been his dearest companion through the years.

"Thank you, Radia," he muttered, his vision blurred. "Thank you, my friends."

The wild garinafins descended upon the stunned Lyucu garinafins like a pack of wolves upon a few frightened dogs. Tongues of fire filled the sky like lightning bolts; roars and trumpeting sundered the air like thunder. The scrublands had never seen such a large gathering of garinafins united by a single purpose, not under Pékyu Nobo Aragoz of the Agon, not under Pékyu Tenryo Roatan of the Lyucu, not under any god or hero known to the shamans.

The Lyucu fell from the sky, slisli flies swatted down by cattle tails.

Tovo's own mount had lost all will to fight. Its only thought was to escape the carnage. Flapping its torn wings, the terrified garinafin screamed as it lurched out of the sky, skimming close to the ground, tumbling, rolling, threshing. Tovo, too stunned to even realize what was happening, found himself sliding off the saddle, and though he scrambled to hold on, lost his grip.

The last thing he remembered was watching two wild garinafins locking their claws around the neck of his mount. The scene receded, growing smaller in his field of vision. Then his body struck the earth, and everything blacked out.

Thoryo opened her eyes, shuddered as though awakening from a long nightmare, and looked out at the pandemonium.

The remaining arucuro tocua beasts, limping and staggering, had begun to march forward again.

To the west, the remnants of the Lyucu host were retreating as fast as possible toward Taten, while freed garinafins dove at them, roasting small groups of Lyucu warriors as payback for all the torment they had suffered at the hands of their enslavers.

The Agon rebels charged after them, shouting, cheering, celebrating. They had routed the dreaded Lyucu army from the field, and they imagined the devastation they would deliver to Taten and the cries of lamentation that would follow.

Behind the Seven-Headed Garinafin lay a muddy field strewn with bodies: human, cattle, and garinafin. The giant articulated-bone war engines stepped over the dead, crushing their bodies and pressing the bloody smears into the dirty snow and earth. Nothing stood in the way of these creatures powered by wind and gods' breath. They were invincible.

The skull cockpit was filled with smoke. Straining to govern her unsteady limbs, Thoryo climbed out of one of the eye sockets to perch between the towering antlers. Looking upon the slaughter field, she didn't feel the joy of triumph; she felt only weariness and despair.

When will the cycles of killing end? Why must we mortals be compelled to aid the cause of death when death is guaranteed to be the final victor?

She looked behind her, intending to remember the dead before climbing back down into the cockpit to rejoin Théra.

She froze.

Tovo opened his eyes and found himself in a nightmare.

In the distance, skeletal monsters from myth and legend strode across the scrublands. Garinafins fell out of the sky like sere leaves caught in a storm of fire. He was in the middle of a wasteland filled with carcasses and wreckage and charred remains.

Staggering to his feet, he realized that he was the only living being for a thousand paces in every direction. He must have lost consciousness when he fell from the back of his mount, and thinking his unmoving form merely another corpse, the Agon warriors had marched past him without sparing another glance.

The limping hulk of the Seven-Headed Garinafin was not as far away as it had seemed when he had been lying on the ground. Slowly, it labored forward, its burned wheel-feet and torn sail-wings impeding progress. The Agon foot warriors had run far ahead to chase down the routed Lyucu. He was alone behind enemy lines.

Hope flared up in his heart again. The gods had given him a chance for vengeance, to strike a last blow to redeem the dream of the Lyucu.

He ran after the lumbering tail of the straggling bone beast.

The crew of the Seven-Headed Garinafin banged on drums, danced, and chanted, taking turns at the pilot tube of the singing lung. Their victory song, thus amplified, reverberated across the field.

So absorbed were they in celebration that no lookouts were posted, and no one noticed the determined figure clambering up the spine of the bone beast, heading for the skull cockpit.

Thoryo screamed for help, but her voice was drowned out by the clamor of the victory choir. She scrambled to back away, to retreat into the safety of the skull cockpit, but the massive walking bone engine chose that moment to stumble, throwing her off balance.

She tumbled down the long central neck, scrabbling for purchase. Halfway down, she finally halted her fall. Only a few outsized vertebrae now separated her from the intruder.

She felt her limbs turn to ice. The man's gore-drenched visage and the gleeful bloodlust in his eyes made him appear more demon than human. He was a hunter, a predator, the very embodiment of the forces of death.

And he was coming for Théra.

Strength and will fled from Thoryo. She couldn't move, couldn't breathe, couldn't even scream. What could she do in the face of this personification of death? She had never fought. She didn't even carry a knife, as was the custom in both Dara and Ukyu-Gondé. She abhorred the very idea of fighting, of violence.

For an instant, Tovo tensed, thinking that his sneak attack had been discovered. But he relaxed and grinned wolfishly when he realized how weak and small his would-be opponent was. The dark complexion indicated that she was from Dara, and everybody knew that barbarians were helpless in single combat. They had no real strength.

He climbed up to the terrified girl clinging to her bone perch, as still as a corpse. Almost as an afterthought, he casually kicked her out of the way and continued his ascent up the spine.

As she rolled off the neck of the heaving beast, the instinct for survival kicked in, freeing Thoryo from her dazed state. Her fingers gripped onto the protruding knobs of a neck vertebra. Suspended above the dizzying, wobbling ground far below her, she clung to life by the thinnest of threads.

Gratefully, she sucked in lungfuls of air, savoring the sensation of her heart pounding in her chest. The frayed sail-wings swayed powerfully from side to side; the pillar-like wheel-feet deformed and pounded against the ground, ready to grind her into flesh-meal should she fall.

Suspended between life and death, dangling from a simulation of life crafted from the remnants of death, she allowed relief to wash over her, sinking into the pure joy of having *survived*.

How precious was life, how very irreplaceable. She could not conceive of anything more important than to live on. That had always been the spine and thread of her conscious life, the one constant bass note of her lungsong, from the first murky moments in the hold of *Dissolver of Sorrows*, where she had learned what it meant to be alive, to the traumatic day in the garinafin corrals of Taten, where she had witnessed unspeakable horrors unleashed by the best of intentions. She did not want to die; she did not want to kill.

She looked up and saw Tovo continue his climb toward the skull cockpit, his single arm pulling his body up and forward in an uninterrupted, fluid motion, vengeance incarnate.

How easy would it be to do nothing, to survive and to also let him survive.

But then Théra would die.

That frigid beach to the far north returned to her awareness, superimposed over the smoky, shimmering air above the battlefield, still burning with garinafin fire. Flowers of ice tumbled through the haze, achingly beautiful and fragile, ephemeral shards of the eternal Flow spoken of by Ano sages, holding a solidified pattern for the briefest of moments before shattering into oblivion.

"Then how do you know what is right?" asked Thoryo, *tears frozen on her face. "Do you make an appeal to blood? But I am not Dara or Agon, whether by birth or marriage. Do you pray to the gods? But I neither fear nor trust the gods."*

"I can't tell you the answer," said Théra, *"for conscience is the only scale that can tell truth apart from lies, separate gold from dross. But conscience belongs to you and you alone, and can be calibrated by no philosophy or religion, only experience."*

"I don't know what to do," muttered Thoryo. *"I love you, I love Takval, I love the people who have become my tribe, though I know not my origins. But I also know that I will never kill."*

It was killing, more than dying, that she feared. Though she had lived among Dara, Lyucu, Agon, and the tribes of ice, she had also kept herself apart.

She had learned the philosophy of the Ano sages and memorized the storytelling dances of the scrubland shamans; she had tilled the fields next to Théra and flown on the back of a garinafin with Takval; she had succored the wounded and buried the dead; she had emulated flawlessly the accents of tribes at war and tasted cooking fused from divergent traditions. She had lived a life grander than most mortals. Yet, there was one thing she had never done.

Though she came of age among warriors, she had never killed, not since the instant she became aware of death.

Tovo was above the skull cockpit. Carefully, he positioned himself between the antlers, ready to leap down and swing through an eye socket. He pulled out his bone knife and examined it to be sure it was sharp, sharp enough to maim, to kill.

Thoryo pulled herself back onto the neck of the arucuro tocua. She began to climb after Tovo.

A sense of peace descended over her. She wondered if this was what Théra had felt, when she had been under the power of the silent roar of the tusked tiger. She wondered if this was what people meant by the presence of divinity. She wondered if this was what Adyulek felt as she contemplated ancestral spirit paintings, what Tipo Tho and Nméji Gon felt as they listened to stories of ancient heroes, what Théra felt as she tried to plant the memory of the Ano logograms in her children, what Takval felt as he offered his life to Théra so that a dream would not die.

She did not belong to any tribe or people; she was not a link in a chain of generations stretching backward into the mists of time and forward into the unknowable future; she had not the comfort of a greater cause that she believed in.

This was the mortal condition, she realized. She would never know with certainty the right path; she would never experience enough to act with absolute conviction; she would never be able to eliminate all suffering.

All she could do was to act in the here and now, to live and die for love, to fight and battle for friendship, to trust in a conscience that was never perfect but capable of being perfected, to scintillate in the bright light of winter on the frozen beach suspended between the eternal ocean and the inconstant land for the brief instant allotted to us all.

She climbed faster. She had reached the skull. She leapt at the figure of the crouching man, screaming and shouting and making as much noise as she could.

Tovo turned and snarled, plunging his knife into her belly and slicing it across. Steaming entrails spilled from the gash. Thoryo could feel the very essence of life slipping out of her.

Her instinct was to push the organs back in, to flee from this horror, to eke out a few more greedy drops of this fragile beauty called life.

She held her own intestines in her hands. It would be so easy to remain aloof, separate, alone. But that was a state reserved to the gods. To be human meant to be entangled with other humans, equally mortal and equally ignorant, stumbling about in love and hate. So instead, she threw herself forward, entangling Tovo's lone arm with the loops of her intestines.

"I don't hate you," she croaked, bloody foam pooling between her lips. "I will never kill—"

Tovo cursed and tried to kick her away, but Thoryo embraced him, locking her arms and legs around his torso and refusing to let go even as she felt the vitality seep out of her wound with her blood, even as she felt life leaving her lungs with her last breath.

The victory song of the warriors drowned out all noise; blood and gore dripped down the top of the skull cockpit, through the eye sockets, falling onto the startled figure of Théra.

"O gods! O gods!" wailed Théra.

She was drenched in blood, her hands slick with gore. She cradled the cooling body of the dead girl, the girl who had given her life to save her.

Climbing up out of the cockpit, she had run to the crouching figure of Tovo and delivered a kick to the back of his head. The man had crumpled, dropped his knife, and then tumbled off the top of the skull cockpit. Wordlessly, she had watched as his body slammed into the ground. A giant wheel-foot had then rolled over him, pressing him into the earth, hiding his face from the Eye of Cudyufin forever.

It was the final blow of the battle.

Voices of the victorious Agon boomed around her.

> *Ten dyudyu cupéruna?*
> *Agon kyo!*
> *Ten dyudyu cupéruna?*
> *Gondé kyo!*

Sitting atop a monstrous engine of articulated bone that sang with the Divine Voice, Théra wept.

The Lyucu had been scattered to the winds. She had triumphed over them as Mapidéré had once triumphed over the Six States, as Tenryo Roatan had triumphed over all his foes. Overhead, wild garinafins wheeled in the air, screeching with the pleasure of vengeance. She had fulfilled her promise to Takval. But her heart felt like ashes.

They were shouting her name, calling her the greatest pékyu the scrublands had ever known.

She tightened her arms around the dead girl.

"O gods! O gods!"

The work took Théra a full twenty-eight days.

She collected the gash cactus juice herself, though she was not skilled at the task. She cracked a giant turtle shell and polished the central fragment into the shape of a memorial tablet in sandpits filled with progressively finer grains. She rubbed the acid onto the smooth tablet with a sponge and scoured it with rough coral. By the end, her forearms were covered in wounds from the burning acid, her fingers scarred by stinging needles.

She refused to let anyone else help.

Since the stowaway from Dara had never declared herself to fear and trust the gods of the scrublands, Théra had decided to inter Thoryo's body after the manner of Dara. Instead of a tombstone, there would be a shell tablet, etched with logograms recounting who she was: Many-Tongued, World-Traversing, Lamb-Kind, Tiger-Fierce, Garinafin-Wise. . . .

The inscription seemed so inadequate. How could a life be summed up in a few logograms? How could all her laughter, sorrow, doubt, determination be captured in one story?

Yet it was the fate of all mortals to end in dust. Whether it was the pédiato savaga or a mound of earth, every journey concluded in the disintegration of the flesh and the fading of our memories in the minds of those whom we touched.

After burying Thoryo, Théra undertook a journey to the seashore. There, giant turtles were captured and a design etched into their living shells: a blooming lotus floating above a tranquil pond.

Théra stood under the moon and watched as the turtles were released into the sea. Tears spilled from her eyes and added trails to her lined face.

How far will they go? What will they behold?
What distant shores will they touch and visit
Before they sink and sprout and grow and bloom—
To sway over sun-dappled waves anew!

It would be her last message home, to her mother, brothers, sister, Zomi. . . .

She had succeeded. The Lyucu threat was no more.

She would also never see her family and lover again, and her memories of them would fade in time, just as their memories of her would fade or had already faded with the passing years. Life always went on, no matter how close death loomed.

She braced herself and turned resolutely away from the sea, toward the scrublands. She still had much to do.

CHAPTER THIRTY-TWO

HEALING

THE TEMPLE OF STILL AND FLOWING WATERS IN
THE MOUNTAINS OF RIMA: AT THE SAME TIME
(THE TWELFTH MONTH OF THE TENTH YEAR OF
THE REIGN OF SEASON OF STORMS AND THE
REIGN OF AUDACIOUS FREEDOM, ONLY ONE
MONTH BEFORE THE EXPIRATION OF THE PEACE
TREATY BETWEEN UKYU-TAASA AND DARA).

Over the next few days, as Savo continued to recuperate, out of a sense of curiosity as well as boredom, he began to attend the morning and evening lessons given to the novice monastics.

He learned about Rufizo Mender's compassion for all mortals, victims as well as torturers; he learned about the god's empathy with the universe, from every glowing star to each wriggling worm; he learned about the duty all human beings owed to one another to reduce suffering.

The old nun delivering the evening lesson struck a mallet against a bronze bowl filled with water, and the clear ring reverberated around the instructional hall. "The universal sea is vast and boundless," she intoned. "And in that unceasing ebb and flow, we are all votan-ru-taasa and votan-sa-taasa."

The nun's use of the Lyucu phrase wasn't a surprise to Savo. Abbot Shattered Axe had explained why.

Back when the rescued Lyucu refugee was still called Cu Curoten, Abbot Discarded Butcher Knife had invited him to deliver a morning lesson. It was the custom among the Mendists to ask strangers they had taken in to give lessons from time to time, for the followers of Rufizo Mender believed that their god cared little for hierarchies, revealing himself to the faithful and the doubting, the learned and the ignorant alike.

Instead of repeating one of the few stories he had learned about Rufizo Mender, the former Lyucu thane had felt an urge to speak of Toryoana Pacific. He struggled to recount the deeds of this god foreign to Dara and his audience, having to act out some sections when words failed him.

Afterward, the novices thanked him, declaring it one of the most moving lessons they had attended in many months. Cu Curoten broke down in tears.

"We should all drown in the shoreless sea of suffering," said Abbot Discarded Butcher Knife, "but for the barge that is faith—faith that the world can be healed, that we are not trapped by the sins of our fathers or the crimes of our youth. Don't you see, Cu Curoten, that Toryoana Pacific is but another name for Rufizo Mender? Your coming was indeed a sign."

The monks and nuns asked Cu Curoten to join them and become a brother.

"But I have sinned," Cu Curoten cried. "I have killed and maimed and tortured and added greatly to the store of suffering in the world."

"You told me that Toryoana Pacific was once a mighty warrior who took pride in slaughter and bathed himself in blood," said the abbot. "Yet, when he set down the war club and refused to pick it up again, he became a great teacher. I was once a bandit with a stone heart who butchered out of avarice, yet I could drop the knife and find peace in each act of healing.

"When we decide to dedicate our lives to Rufizo Mender, we leave behind our old names and old lives of strife and violence and start anew. Our new names remind us that it isn't what you did in the past that matters, but where you wish to walk in the future."

That was how Cu Curoten became Brother Shattered Axe. And over time, the deeds of Toryoana Pacific were added to the lore of Rufizo Mender, and the words of the new Lyucu brother became part of the liturgy of this Dara sect.

"It is vain to seek vengeance, foolish to pine for punishment," the aged nun continued. "In the name of justice, new injustices are done. Retribution does not restore, and neither does hatred heal. To blame is to be trapped in cycles of recrimination from which there is no escape."

Savo remembered the horrors of Kigo Yezu; he imagined the terrors still to come when Fara's brother invaded Ukyu-taasa; he recalled the stirring speeches of Pékyu Tenryo, vowing conquest and vengeance for the crimes of Admiral Krita; he recollected the bloody campaigns of the Hegemon, driven by a desire to right wrongs.

I myself am the child of a conquest, of a union lacking in consent, he thought in despair. *Even if I have not killed with my own hands, my life is the fruit of violence committed in my name. I can no more undo my existence than I can stop the war between my two peoples.*

The old nun struck her mallet against the bowl again, sending vibrating ripples across the placid surface as the clarion ringing filled the hall.

"Step out of the stream of time; stand apart from the claims of history. Face the horrors squarely, and dedicate yourself to healing and mending."

The Lyucu had invaded Dara and caused unprecedented suffering. Yet, the monks and nuns of this temple had not given up their faith. The statue in the sanctum returned to Savo's inner vision: It combined features of Toryoana Pacific and Rufizo Mender, embraced the faiths of the foreign invader as well as the native victim. A tanto-lyu-naro had become the new abbot upon the passing of the old, and the convocation on that occasion had renamed the shrine Temple of Still and Flowing Waters to commemorate the pool of tears in Ukyu and the waterfall here in Dara that were sacred to the dual aspects of their one god.

As Savo bowed his head, joining others in the instructional hall, he felt his heart grow still and peaceful, resting warmly against the carp-shaped letter box. He had not felt so comforted, so welcomed, in a long time.

We leave behind our old names and old lives of strife and violence and start anew.

A pang of longing and loss pierced him. He had found home, but to enter it, he would have to renounce his old life.

In the morning, Savo found the abbot. In a voice both hopeful and trepidatious, he explained his wish.

Expressing no surprise at all, the abbot took him down the long wooded path leading from the monks' sleeping quarters to the temple's sacred inner halls, the core of the order's spiritual life.

There were three sacred halls in all—Silver Fleece, Ivy Cape, and Snowy Feather—reflecting three different facets of Rufizo Mender's mission.

The Hall of Silver Fleece was an imposing building the size of a giant warehouse such as one might find in the docks of Dimushi, and equally plain in external appearance. But instead of a single open space, the interior was partitioned into multiple floors and rooms of different sizes. As the abbot guided him through the different areas, Savo realized that it was organized like a hospital, with wings and wards and operating theaters. Dozens of robed monks and nuns practiced the healing arts: medicine derived from matter animal, vegetable, and mineral; massages and chiropractics; cupping and stimulation of meridian points; surgery; silkmotic shocks and baths. . . .

"The largest portion of our votan-ru-taasa and votan-sa-taasa, including myself, work in this hall," said the abbot. "Medicine is the traditional province of the followers of Rufizo, and all temples dedicated to the green-eyed god across Dara have hospitals attached to them. However, as the temples have gained in power and prestige under Empress Jia, herself a healer, some of the temple leaders have forgotten their original charge: to care for the stricken without regard to wealth or desert. By word of mouth, patients turned away by the mainline temples come to us as a last resort. We tend to the destitute and the shunned: lepers, criminals, *raye*, fugitives, persecuted refugees, those racked by pain on the shore of the River-on-Which-Nothing-Floats, whose only desire is palliative care before that last ferry ride.

"As well, we share our knowledge freely with all who wish

to learn the healing arts but who lack the wealth or credentials to apprentice with a proper doctor. When they've learned what they want and are ready to go back into the world, we ask only that they promise never to turn their faces away from suffering, to always reserve some of their time for the patients other doctors pretend not to see."

Savo imagined himself as a healer of the body; he didn't feel the call.

"Let us go on," said the abbot.

The Hall of Ivy Cape was much smaller. Constructed of bamboo columns with a thatched roof, it had no walls at all. The empty framework reminded Savo of trellises in a vineyard or the airy fences at a nursery. Here, about twenty monks and nuns tended to herbs and flowers in planters and cultivated the fields and gardens outside the hall. In one corner of the hall, a small group worked on minia-ture landscape models of mountains and valleys, islands and reefs, pouring buckets of water over them and blowing at them with large bellows.

"The votan-ru-taasa and votan-sa-taasa here study the art of heal-ing the land," said the abbot.

"What . . . what does that mean?"

"The pékyu-votan claimed—and Tanvanaki continues to claim—that the natives of Dara enslave and harm the land," said the abbot. "The followers of Rufizo Mender happen to agree with her, in a manner of speaking. Felling forests, plowing up the sod, and plant-ing crops do exhaust and harm the land. By studying the nature of that harm and how to ameliorate it, we treat the Islands of Dara as a living being to be cared for and healed."

Savo felt dizzy. "That must be a monumental task."

"Indeed, and very difficult. Besides the effects of agriculture, the monks and nuns also study the damage done by fishing fleets to the coral reefs and whale pods and the decimation of wildlife from overhunting and land reclamation. The very prosperity of Dara has accelerated these harms, leaving the land and the sea little chance to recover on their own. Much as we inherit the crimes of our ancestors committed against other human beings, the stuff of re-rememberings,

our legacy is also bound up with the suffering to every other creature caused by our fecundity, even unto a blade of grass or dandelion
flower."

Savo flinched at this. But the abbot didn't notice his reaction as
he went on.

"But it isn't only the people of Dara who harm the land. In Ukyu-
taasa, our own people's garinafins and long-haired cattle have
brought their own brand of misery. Refugees from Rui and Dasu tell
me that they're trying to level Mount Kiji in order to create more
pastures by filling in the sea?" The abbot shook his head with horror.
"Such vanity! The wounds dealt to the land will take generations to
heal."

"Have the brothers and sisters here discovered useful techniques
for healing the land?" asked Savo hopefully.

"The Dandelion Court and other temporal authorities have
largely left us alone because we don't interfere in politics," said the
abbot. "When we learn something useful for restoring the vitality
of the land, we cannot petition the court in Pan or the governors
of the various provinces. Instead, we try to convince scholars; the
Cultivationists are particularly receptive to our ideas. So far we've
not had a great deal of success, since it's difficult to convince people
to change habits—just remember how difficult it is to convince
our own people to abandon pasturing for farming! But we'll keep
trying."

Savo imagined himself as a healer of the land; he didn't feel the
call.

"Let us go on," said the abbot.

The Hall of Snowy Feather was the third and smallest of the
sacred halls. The tiny building, constructed from thick blocks of
granite quarried from the mountainside, was warm and cozy inside.
A system of clever light-wells on the roof, lined with diffusion mirrors, filled the space with light. One half of the hall was lined with
tall shelves that reached the ceiling, packed with flat sandalwood
boxes made for the protection of fragile manuscripts, not unlike
Savo's letter box. The other half of the hall was furnished with about
a dozen low, wide desks with tilted tops, at which monks and nuns

sat, concentrating intensely on spread-open scrolls, wielding strange implements and instruments that Savo had never seen.

"What kind of place is this?" asked Savo, amazed.

"Even after years of living in Dara, I'm not as comfortable with matters involving the written word as one born to it," the abbot conceded, hesitating. "I suppose the best way to describe this place is . . . a hospital for books."

Because proficiency in Ano logograms required years of training, literacy was low in Dara and books cost a great deal of time and effort to produce. As a result, most Ano Classics existed only in fragments and competing versions. Books were very precious artifacts, and even the wealthy and erudite owned few.

Most students, in fact, never studied the classics in full. During their school years, they copied the few books owned by their masters and studied this personal collection in detail. As for other books, they had to rely on memorized passages written out by their masters or chance encounters with the collection of another scholar. Errors accumulated with each imperfect reproduction. The very wealthy and privileged might have access to a library maintained at one of the expensive private academies, but most scholars only gained access to a comprehensive collection after attaining the rank of *cashima*, when they were granted the privilege of entering the libraries of the Imperial academies.

Books, never very numerous to begin with, were vulnerable to natural agents of decay: flooding, fire, the teeth of rats, and the intestines of wax-loving bookworms. But they were even more vulnerable to the man-made disasters of war and anarchy.

Emperor Mapidéré, who had ordered old books deemed useless to the new empire burned, was an unprecedented calamity for the world of learning. Though he did command that one copy of each interdicted book be preserved, in practice this was not quite as helpful as it might have seemed at first glance.

Each copy of one of the Ano Classics was unique, containing commentary and annotations from generations of learned scholars in its chain of title and accumulating errors and emendations as it was copied from hand to hand. One fragment of Kon Fiji's *Morality* retrieved from an ancient tomb, for instance, might contain stories about the One True Sage not found in any other copy, while a manuscript of Ra Oji's *To Delectate and to Teach* passed down from the court library of old Métashi might contain epigrams found in no other specimen. Dutifully, Mapidéré's bureaucrats chose one instance of each book, almost at random, as "the copy" to preserve, but that meant other fragments and competing editions of the old classics were doomed to fiery oblivion.

Yet, not all was lost. Mapidéré's soldiers and bureaucrats couldn't get their hands on every book. Book lovers across the Seven States—yes, even in Mapidéré's own Xana—resisted in ways grand and small. Books were handed to trusted servants leaving on long journeys, buried under ancient pagoda trees, covered by ashes in temple incense braziers, disguised as wall tapestries or carpets, sewn into robe liners, smuggled out from under the eyes (and noses) of city garrisons in night soil carts. . . . Men and women who loved learning, officials and clerks who couldn't bear the thought of desecrating the voices of the past, and even illiterate peasants and soldiers who loved the magic of logograms with a tender reverence risked fines, imprisonment, and sometimes even their lives to protect these gossamer records of elevated thought from Mapidéré's censors.

With the ascension of the House of Dandelion, learning and scholarship recovered in Dara like vibrant flowers springing up after a harsh winter. The book rescuers retrieved their prizes, and in time, ancient academies recovered substantial portions of their library collections. But many books that had been hidden never resurfaced—stolen by thieves, destroyed by the elements, or simply forgotten, like caches of nuts buried by squirrels in autumn. As well, many more books disappeared like rare birds hunted to extinction, with all extant copies destroyed by Xana censors or the wars that followed under the Principate. Mapidéré's fiery catastrophe would leave a permanent and indelible scar in the literary heritage of Dara.

The monks and nuns of Rufizo Mender saw it as part of their duty to heal this wound in the world-mind. They journeyed across the Islands for clues and troves of literary refugees, scoured ruins and midden heaps to rescue silk-and-wax fugitives, redeemed scroll-formed hostages at high ransom from pirates and grave robbers.

"By the time these books are recovered, most have been heavily damaged," said the abbot. "Thus, as Abbot Discarded Butcher Knife explained to me, in the Hall of Snowy Feather, we Mendists repair and copy books. Instead of the body or the land, we try to heal the mind."

Savo watched as the monks and nuns reverently and carefully laid out the damaged books on their work surfaces, unfolding the aged scrolls with gloved hands. Aided by bright beams of light channeled down from the ceiling with mirrored tubes and magnifying lenses, the book healers examined the scrolls column by column, logogram by logogram. When a damaged logogram or hole in the substrate was found, they repaired the flaw with wax and knife, with heated probe and iced spatula, with paint and ink and thread and needle, striving to re-create the original scribe's hand and calligraphic style. From time to time, the monks and nuns gathered around the desk of one of their fellowship and conversed in low voices like conferring doctors, musing and debating how to reconstruct a missing logogram or section.

"How do you fill in a lost section?" Savo asked one of the nuns, a young woman in her twenties working on a book of poetry. He pointed at a large blank space on the scroll, where dozens, perhaps even hundreds, of logograms had been destroyed by the ravages of wax-eating mice and worms.

"We try to look through our library to see if we have other editions of the same book or if the missing section had been quoted in other books," said the nun.

"What if you find different editions don't agree on the missing passage?"

One of the last conversations between Master Nazu Tei and himself, concerning apocrypha, surfaced in his mind. His nose twitched and his eyes stung. Was it a sign?

"That happens more often than you think," she said. She put down her tools and looked up at him, her voice kind. "You seem to know much about books."

"I . . . I've picked up a few things here and there."

"I'm working on the poems of Suzaré," the nun said. "Are you familiar with her work?"

"The Amu Imagist?" asked Savo, his heart quickening.

The nun nodded. "Her poems survive only in fragments in other books, and sometimes the quotations don't agree with one another. I've been collating these fragments into a collection, in which I hope to preserve the conflicting versions, note their sources, and include any commentary I find. I may not be able to re-create all her poems, but at least I can gather all the known fragments into one place, and in that way, something of her voice is preserved, even if incomplete and non-authoritative."

"I wish I knew more about her poetry," said Savo. His cheeks felt hot. "A . . . friend once quoted a few lines to me."

"She wrote about love in all its complicated forms: the easy infatuations and difficult devotions; the jealousies, the misunderstandings, and the intrusion of our sublunary, flawed world into the perfect flow of that eternal yearning to merge with another; parting too early and meeting too late; the drive to seek out the mirror of our soul, despite all obstacles erected in our path by gods and mortals."

Savo read over the lines on the nun's desk.

> . . . *white hempen sleeves* . . .
> . . . *aimless willow catkins adrift* . . .

> *Cruel sweet maid,*
> *You've fastened my heart*
> *To the shaft* . . .
> . . . *clop clop* . . . *the racing chariot* . . .
> . . . *tug tug* . . . *your proud eyes* . . .

> . . . *a scattering of dew,*
> *Little blue birds with arrowed beaks,*
> *The green grasshopper: a jade hairpin*
> *Lost in the dune roses clamoring*
> *For your hand* . . .

> *. . . jealous of*
> *Dawn with her coral-hued toes and ruddy ankles*
> *Tiptoeing down the pebble-lined beach . . .*
> *. . . blushing, quick!*
> *. . . your careless breath . . . your salty-plum lips . . .*
> *. . . heart-tickling chin . . . lung-kneading cheeks . . .*
> *. . . lash me again, my huntress . . .*

Savo seemed to hear the fragments being recited in the voice of Fara.

"You're going to miss out on a lot life has to offer if you focus only on wars and politics."

The logograms on the page blurred, and he had to swallow the lump in his throat. He put a hand against his breast, where the gift from Fara nestled against his skin.

Resolutely, he forced his hand away.

More than anything else, he wanted to be Thasé-teki to Dandelion, but that was an impossible dream.

He didn't want to be Savo Ryoto, thane-taasa of the Lyucu, destined to slaughter his father's people to preserve his mother's conquest; he didn't want to be Kinri Rito, brother to Zomi Kidosu, destined to aid his father's people to overthrow and ruin his mother's.

He wanted to be here, *needed* to be away from the world, *needed* to discard the past, to start anew.

"Please." He turned to the abbot. "I hear the call of Rufizo Mender. Let me join you."

CHAPTER THIRTY-THREE

NOT ONE OF US

THE BONEYARD, UKYU-GONDÉ: THE SIXTH MONTH
IN THE ELEVENTH YEAR AFTER THE DEPARTURE OF
PRINCESS THÉRA FROM DARA FOR UKYU-GONDÉ
(SIX MONTHS AFTER THE BATTLE OF THE BONEYARD).

A new year had arrived in the scrublands.

As the defeated Lyucu scattered to every corner of Ukyu-Gondé, news of the fall of the Roatan clan traveled with them. Years of centralization in Taten had deprived most Lyucu tribes of their traditional company of war garinafins, and the demoralized Lyucu were no match for the newly invigorated Agon tribes. The empire that Pékyu Tenryo had built up over decades collapsed in a matter of months.

Meanwhile, from her new Taten in the Boneyard, Théra dispatched messengers to every corner of the land to gather the Agon thanes for a grand council. Pékyu Takval's death should be properly mourned and the triumph over the Lyucu properly celebrated.

Besides passing on the orders of the pékyu, the messengers were also charged with looking for the children of Kiri Valley. Toof had told her that he and Radia had last seen Tanto, Rokiri, and the others near the Sea of Tears, and Théra hoped that the young pékyus-taasa had been taken in by kindhearted Agon herders or perhaps even a wandering band of tanto-lyu-naro.

One cloudless summer night, Théra left her brand-new Great Tent, dismissed her guards, and summoned Ga-al.

She rode until the lights from the tent city were below the horizon before landing. Leaving Ga-al to graze by himself, she sat down on a rock and looked up at the stars.

The flatness of the scrublands made the stars seem both closer and farther away than they had in her childhood in Dara. She immersed herself in that solitude, in conversation with distant, brilliant lights that seemed to pierce her with their merciless gaze.

Gently, she took out a package from inside her vest and laid out the contents on the ground: a few wisps of silk that had once been a mask; a bone dagger that had drunk her husband's blood; a few baked clay Ano logograms. . . .

How much I miss you, Kunilu-tika and Jian-tika! I swear I'll never make you learn any logograms or eat lotus paste if I can have you back. . . .

How much I miss you, Takval . . . your gentle hands on me, your strong arms around me, your warm body next to mine, skin to skin, your steady voice in my ears. . . . I've tried to fulfill your dream, but I don't know if I'm walking the right path. There are so many unknowns. . . .

How much I miss you, Zomi . . . if I can but feel your lips on mine again, your hand holding my hand, staying in bed with you all night but not asleep. . . .

How much I miss you, Father and Mother . . . your counsel, your lessons, your strength and love . . . and what a terrible daughter I am, to not even have anything of yours to remember you by. . . .

How much I miss you, my sister, my brothers. If I haven't miscalculated, the Wall of Storms should have already reopened to show that there will be no Lyucu reinforcements, and preparations for an invasion of Dasu and Rui should be well underway. Will you finally liberate Unredeemed Dara? Will you bring peace to the Islands?

Two shooting stars crossed the sky, like brilliant dyrans passing each other in the deep. An omen.

She strained to make sense of it. Was it a revelation of the future of two peoples, Lyucu and Agon, so closely bound by shared history and yet so far apart, divided by that same re-remembering?

Was it a foretelling of the health of the flocks and herds, the bounty of the hunt?

Was it a concluding statement about the alliance between the Agon and Dara, an affirmation of their victory?

Or was it something far more intimate? Was it a message from Kunilu-*tika* and Jian-*tika*? In which direction did the stars point? Was it a prophecy that she and Zomi would never see each other again, like two parallel celestial trails destined to never meet? Was it a celebration of the love between Takval and herself, as brilliant as the immortal stars? Or was it in fact an eye-catching sign from her parents, reminding her of the family motto: *Do the most interesting thing*? Like a shooting star.

Just because we're apart doesn't mean our love ends.

We're defined by the web woven from all our loves, not one grand romance.

She meditated in the cold light of the stars, her hands caressing the objects laid out on the deerskin on the rock, like a scholar reading ancient logograms, like a shaman deciphering spirit portraits, like a woman trying to assure herself that the past was real in order to step into the future.

As the days passed, none of the search parties returned with the information Théra craved: the whereabouts of her children.

They did, however, bring news of a far less welcome nature. A new kind of wildfire, the fire of vengeance, was burning out of control. Agon victors tossed entire Lyucu tribes, from great-grandmothers nearing ninety to babes nine days old, into water bubbles in the grass seas and forced the captives to swim until they drowned from exhaustion. Defeated thanes and naros-votan had been pierced through the soft flesh under the clavicles and then strung together like grasshoppers, after which they were made to dance for the amusement of the Agon raiders before being roasted alive by garinafin fire. Mass slaughter, castrations, and rapes were ordered in the name of wiping out Lyucu bloodlines.

"The killing will end . . . when the Agon are free."

"Will it?"

Théra was horrified. The Agon had achieved Takval's dream, but like a receding winter wave that promised an even greater crest to come, she could already see a bloodier future being written.

"The ice flowers . . . the sea . . . the endless waves . . . colliding to shatter . . . one after another . . ."

The pékyu's messengers now demanded restraint and mercy from the victors. But her words seemed to have little effect.

As well, many Agon chiefs, after unleashing their fury upon the Lyucu, had begun to turn against one another. In the name of reclaiming the dream of Pékyu Nobo Aragoz, the chiefs jostled for status, grazing rights, captured garinafins, cattle, sheep, and slaves. The disputes often turned violent; raids and counter-raids threatened to escalate into civil war.

The upcoming grand council of mourning and celebration would also have to decide the future of the Agon people.

> *Ten dyudyu cupéruna?*
> *Agon kyo!*
> *Ten dyudyu cupéruna?*
> *Gondé kyo!*

From the rich grasslands near Aluro's Basin, from the oases in the arid expanse of Lurodia Tanta, from the snow-fed streams in the foothills of the World's Edge Mountains, from the harsh salt plains near the Sea of Tears, from the icebound tundra near Nalyufin's Pastures . . . the proud chiefs and haughty war thanes of the Agon people, several hundred strong, gathered in Taten.

They were all curious about this new Pékyu Théra, by marriage a member of the Aragoz clan, though not by birth. She was a foreigner from Dara, and it was said that her witchcraft had been instrumental in the victory over the Lyucu. Though there were many stories of the heroic deeds of her warriors, she herself was not known for prowess in battle.

The moon was almost full.

The silver light spilled across the Boneyard, filling the canyons and gulches like mercury poured into ancient river channels. Piles of bone glowed peacefully in the shadows, an approximation of the stars far above.

The western edge of the badlands was a towering cliff hundreds of feet in height. Above and beyond it lay the endless scrublands, all the way to the sea. Perched on the lip of the cliff was a city of tents, stretching for miles to the north and south. The white structures, differing in size and shape, glinted under the moon like an island of mushrooms in the grass sea. Here and there, giant mounds of bones, remnants of the arucuro tocua creations that had awed the Lyucu host, sat mutely among the tents like the ruins of an ancient civilization or the petrified remains of prehistoric monsters.

Although Théra's rebellion had found refuge in the canyons and caves of the Boneyard, the need for concealment had vanished with their complete victory. Besides, new arrivals didn't like the idea of living in the badlands, where flash floods and mudslides were common in summer. Thus, the field on which the final, bloody battle against the Lyucu had been won, just beyond the edge of the Boneyard, also became the site of the new Taten.

Singing, carousing, laughing, speechmaking filled the air, along with an occasional snort, bleat, or moan from the sleeping flocks and herds. The grand celebratory banquet would take place tomorrow night, and everyone was busy with last-minute preparations.

Beyond the northern border of Taten, separated from the tents by a band of empty space about five hundred paces wide, glowed numerous bonfires, as though the stars had descended to join the revelry. They burned brightly, fed by dry dung and old bone, and fanned by the ever-present winds.

A group of Agon warriors approached the bonfires from the direction of the tents, dragging bone sleds piled high with meat. The woman in the lead stepped cautiously and slowly, clearly unaccustomed to her tall garinafin skull helmet. An old woman kept pace with her, aided by a staff taller than herself.

"Do I have to wear this every moment?" asked Théra, adjusting the clumsy helmet once more to prevent it from falling. "Everyone knows I'm no warrior."

Adyulek sighed. "We've gone through this many times, votan. You can do as you like in front of me and others who know your heart, but for most of the thanes, you're a stranger. You must act like the pékyu for them to treat you as the pékyu; you must look like the pékyu for them to believe you are the pékyu. Until these habits of the mind have grown as natural for them as breathing, you cannot set aside these symbols, uncomfortable as they may be."

"Theater," muttered Théra.

"What?" asked Adyulek, as Théra had spoken just now in the language of Dara.

"Nothing," said Théra, a wry smile turning up the corners of her mouth. "I was just thinking my parents would have liked you."

They arrived at the bonfires.

"Come, share in the feast!" Théra called out. Gaunt figures stood up in the shadows of the fires, their furs tattered. But none approached.

Théra tried again. "The gods demand that we share our good fortune!" Still, the figures in the shadows hesitated.

Théra turned to Adyulek. The old shaman took a deep breath and raised her voice. "Normally, I speak for the Every-Mother, but today I speak for Théra Garu Aragoz, wife of Takval Aragoz, son of Souliyan Aragoz, who serves the Agon as Pékyu. Come and share in the bounty of peace."

At last, the hesitating figures emerged from the shadows and approached. The naros, led by Tipo Tho, who had taken over as Théra's captain of the guards, began to distribute the meat on the sleds to the gathering families.

"It's my accent," said Théra to Adyulek in a low voice. "Even the tribeless find it too jarring and hard to understand."

As part of the celebration, Théra had asked that bands of roaming tanto-lyu-naro also be invited. She hoped that the gesture would find favor in the eyes of the gods, and specifically, Toryoana Pacific. Considering the arduous task of persuasion ahead of her, she could certainly use some divine aid.

"You speak well and clearly," said Adyulek. "But it takes time for those not used to your speech to adjust to the unexpected cadences and bent syllables. I remember straining to parse your words when I first met you, but that passed in time. Besides, there are tribes from all over Gondé gathered here, and as many topolects are spoken as there are stars wheeling above us. Even I have trouble understanding some of the thanes from tribes from corners of the scrublands I'm unfamiliar with. It will be no more difficult for them to accept your speech than to accept one another. It just takes time."

Théra shook her head, her brow furrowed. "Time is what I don't have. The accent of the First Family, of the Aragoz clan, is what they'll be expecting. How can I sway the haughty thanes with a first impression when I cannot speak like Takval? You said yourself that what is needed is a perfect performance."

During the last week, as Théra greeted the visiting Agon chiefs and war thanes, more than a few had had trouble understanding her (and some had openly mocked her). She wondered if there wasn't a measure of pretense in some of these misunderstandings.

"No, not perfection," said Adyulek, "conviction. If you believe you're the one and only pékyu, others will follow your lead."

"If it were only that easy," muttered Théra. "I wish I had Thoryo's gift." Recalling the death of the young woman so adept at languages and accents made her even more morose.

"It's no use to envy others when we each have our gifts," said Adyulek. "You can no more force your voice to be free of the sounds of your native tongue than I can erase the scars of my youth from my flesh. But remember, you came to us as a stranger and dissolved our sorrow. What does it matter if you cannot speak of your own deeds like a child of the scrublands? *You* wear the garinafin skull helmet; *you* hold the garinafin antler signaling spears; *you* are named in Takval's spirit portrait. We who have fought and stood by you will add our voices to yours. *I* was there; *I* witnessed the moment Takval's blood and breath fused with yours."

After her heart had finally calmed, Théra held out her hands to the old shaman. "Thank you."

Then, after a pause, "You speak of adding your voice to mine. Does this mean you—" She didn't finish.

"After you told me of your vision, I prayed to the Every-Mother many times for guidance."

"And she asked you to support me?" Théra's heart felt close to bursting.

Adyulek shook her head. Théra's heart sank.

"She gave no answer at all," said Adyulek. "The path you wish the Agon to walk is new. Like the fog-shrouded beginning of the Sixth Age, the gods do not provide answers when the answers must be found by the people themselves."

Théra waited, cautioning herself against hope.

"I fear and trust the gods, votan, but sometimes that isn't enough," said Adyulek. "I believe your unfamiliar accent will lead the Agon into a new age, in the same way the bold Afir and Kikisavo led the people of the scrublands into a new way of life."

"I . . ." Théra couldn't finish. The pékyu and the shaman embraced. Surely that was how Afir and Kikisavo had embraced before setting forth on their journey to find a path where there had been none.

Théra spent the rest of the night walking among the tanto-lyu-naro, inquiring after their travels. For a long time she did this, taking pleasure in their tales of wonder. Her only disappointment was that no one could recall seeing two children matching her description— she had hoped that the wanderers would have good news.

At last, it was time for Théra to depart. Before retiring for the night, however, she wanted to visit the gravesite of Thoryo in one of the sheltered canyons below the tall cliff.

"I'd like to tell her that her words didn't fall on deaf ears," said Théra.

Adyulek did not join her. She still found the notion of being buried under the earth rather than undergoing pédiato savaga abhorrent.

"Don't exhaust yourself," said Adyulek. "You must get plenty of rest tonight."

Théra nodded. A grand political performance awaited her on the morrow. "Are you going to sleep now?"

"I'll stay a bit longer among the tanto-lyu-naro. They have stories about the gods and heroes of old that I've never heard before, and I never tire of learning new stories about Afir and Kikisavo."

Théra smiled. "I hope to remain as curious as you when I'm your age."

Adyulek smiled back. "It's the only interesting way to live."

Théra offered to leave Tipo Tho and a few naros behind to guard her, but the old shaman declined. Months after their defeat, there was little concern that the remnants of the Lyucu would dare to assault Taten. And no one could conceive of any act of ill will toward an old shaman from the pacifist wanderers.

"Good night, votan."

"Good night, Tongue-of-the-Every-Mother."

Neither noticed the pair of baleful eyes that glared at them from the flickering shadows by a bonfire.

"I was not born of Gondé; I had to become Agon. . . ."

Théra began the banquet by recounting the long re-remembering of their rebellion: how Takval had risked everything to be on the expedition to Dara; how he had faced down the Dandelion Court to demand an alliance cemented with a royal marriage to her; how the couple, aboard *Dissolver of Sorrows*, had led the fleet through the Wall of Storms, escaped the pursuing Lyucu city-ship, and then arrived in Gondé; how they had established a base in Kiri Valley, where the Agon and their Dara allies had built up their strength, until the despicable sneak attack by the Lyucu. . . .

She forced herself to speak slowly, to articulate and project, to shape the words as free from the influences of the tongue of Dara as possible. She did all this deliberately, to give herself and her audience the time they both needed.

Gradually, as she continued her account, the thanes stopped paying attention to her unfamiliar accent; instead, they became immersed in the story. Their hearts sank with the desperate flight of Takval and Théra as garinafins deluged Kiri Valley with flames; their spirits rose as the ice tribes joined them to make a stand by the frozen sea. They laughed with her as she remembered the first time she climbed into the sky as a garinafin pilot; they wept with her as she spoke of the last moments of her husband. They slammed their weapons against the ground to simulate the thudding of arucuro tocua wheel-feet; they howled and ululated to re-create the lung-stopping moment a cloud of feral garinafins materialized to fight for their cause. . . .

For the briefest of moments, Théra considered shrouding the use of Takval's body to assassinate Cudyu and the deployment of arucuro tocua armed with the Divine Voice in mystery and mysticism. Superstition and magic had, after all, been useful tools in the march to power of many kings and pékyus in both Dara and Ukyu-Gondé, and her task in convincing the Agon to follow a new path would be so much easier with blind obedience out of awe and fear at her witchcraft.

But she rejected the thought. She was going to be a pékyu who led by conviction, not a tyrant who imposed her will through deception of both the people and the gods.

So she was frank about her initial skepticism, about the moment she first felt the power of the gods of Gondé descend upon her, about her gradual embrace of the Agon way of life, of the voices of the ancestors of her adopted people. She didn't claim to possess any magic from Dara, but revealed to all that the magnificent and terrifying weapons that had brought down the Lyucu had been built by brave and clever fighters originating from two lands divided by an ocean, animated as much by Dara engineering expertise as by Agon arucuro tocua skill. Yes, the weapons were wondrous, but they were the result of knowledge, not magic.

"Long ago, Afir and Kikisavo set out into the pathless waste in search of knowledge," she said. "And it is knowledge, knowledge of ourselves, of our allies, of our foes, of garinafins, of our land, that led us to victory and freedom. Knowledge still will lead us into the future."

Finally, she was done.

> *Ten dyudyu cupéruna?*
> *Agon kyo!*
> *Ten dyudyu cupéruna?*
> *Gondé kyo!*

Against the swirling smoke and shimmering air, the ecstatic clamor seemed to shake the star-studded firmament itself. Tears spilled from every eye. They were indeed favored by the gods; the Agon spirit had been proven to be invincible. They gazed upon the woman who had led them to this place, who had vanquished the hated Lyucu with guile and strength, with a fervent adoration even more ardent than the central bonfire that illuminated the grand circle of sitting rugs.

Théra, on the other hand, looked about her with some anxiety. Adyulek still hadn't arrived.

But she couldn't wait any longer. As the noise slowly subsided, Théra spoke.

"Votan-ru-taasa, votan-sa-taasa, I ask now that we honor those who gave their lives to overthrow the Lyucu."

She picked up her skull bowl, filled to the brim with fragrant kyoffir, and stood up, her spine whalebone straight to keep the garinafin skull helmet, much too big for her, from tilting over. At Théra's insistence, the banquet so far had been free of kyoffir and tolyusa—rumors were that the new pékyu wanted everyone present to be absolutely sober, for she had an important announcement to make. There were many guesses—a comprehensive plan for how to dispose of the defeated Lyucu, a new scheme of tributes and titles to consolidate her rule, a proposal for the conquest of the ice tribes, a levy of troops to build a new garinafin army—but no one knew for sure.

The chiefs and thanes picked up their bowls and stood up as well. As soon as the pékyu drank, the proper celebrations would begin.

But instead of raising the bowl to her lips, Théra leaned forward and, slowly and carefully, poured out the contents on the ground.

The hundreds of Agon chiefs and thanes gathered around the roaring bonfire looked at one another, astonished and confused.

"Why is she wasting good kyoffir?"

"The gods will be angry!"

"I hear that she doesn't take tolyusa either."

. . .

There were many rumors about the new pékyu, though few of the chiefs and thanes knew her. As much as they were troubled by her strange gesture, they were still too spellbound by her tale and too wary of one another to dare to challenge her.

After a moment of hesitation, a few chiefs followed her lead, pouring their kyoffir also upon the ground. Soon, the others did as well.

Théra let out a held breath. Her gamble had succeeded. Her audience had taken the first and most important step: defying tradition. That it was a tiny step didn't matter. She would enlarge upon the breakthrough.

"But today is about the future," said Théra, shifting into her new theme. "Long were the days and nights when we suffered in darkness and cold, when we had no comfort or hope to offer to our children, when we had to abandon the aged and infirm as we moved camp, because there was not enough food for all."

The assembled Agon leaders nodded, many eyes moistening at the memory of loved ones who never got to see this day of celebration and joy.

"The Lyucu drove us away from the heart of Gondé. They multiplied, grew fat, and enlarged their families and herds by enslaving and starving us. I know many of you look forward to exacting vengeance, to making them suffer as we did."

The chiefs and thanes slammed their weapons against the ground and shouted again.

"Ten dyudyu cupéruna?"

"Agon kyo!"

Théra held out her hands, bidding them to be quiet.

"But the Lyucu also have grandparents who have lost all their teeth and babies who have yet to acquire any," said Théra. "The Lyucu also have parents who wish the best for their children, and children who wish to care for their parents in their old age. They also must eat when hungry; they also must drink when thirsty; they also must find shelter from storms; they also must build fires to keep the frost at bay.

"The Agon and Lyucu are descended from a great pair of heroes and companions, Afir and Kikisavo. Our languages are mutually intelligible, and our customs similar. We worship the same gods and retell the same stories.

"We are also linked by the bonds of blood and ancestry. Do not forget that Lyucu blood flowed through my husband's veins too, for his mother, the wise and compassionate Souliyan, was the child of Nobo Aragoz and an enslaved Lyucu woman. Many of you can recall similar unions in your own lineages, as can many of the Lyucu thanes and warriors. We are all victims; we are all oppressors. These re-rememberings are not marks of shame, but reminders of how we dishonor ourselves when we forget the pain and suffering of our own ancestors in the insistence of *us* and *them*, in the rejection of the truth of our shared experience.

"We must now strive to reclaim and re-remember that most precious bit of knowledge: the knowledge of peace. Agon and Lyucu, we can learn to live together again."

As she spoke, shouts of rage and disbelief erupted from the audience.

"The Lyucu are nothing like us!"

"How can you bring up our blood-taint? Shame! Shame!"

"They deserve everything we've done and will do to them!"

"Where were you when *they* showed *us* no mercy?"

. . .

The shouting gathered strength until the cacophony was like a summer thunderstorm, and Théra's voice drowned in the noise.

But a solemn and booming melody, like the moaning of a hundred garinafins, erupted from beyond the circle around the bonfire. Gozofin, chief animator of the Seven-Headed Garinafin, had erected a set of Péa pipes not far from the assembly. And now Çami Phithadapu was using them to enforce Théra's will. The smaller torches at each of the sitting rugs flickered, threatening to go out, while the central bonfire leapt taller, throwing up sparks to challenge the stars.

The thunderous music quieted the rebellious uproar for the moment, and into that silence, Théra spoke.

"If compassion will not move you, then perhaps fear will.

"Like you, the Lyucu also have hearts that crave vengeance.

"When Pékyu Nobo Aragoz defeated the Lyucu, he didn't foresee the rise of Tenryo Roatan. When Pékyu Tenryo subjugated the Agon, he didn't foresee the rise of Takval Aragoz. Who among you can foresee that there won't be another to rise among the Lyucu in twenty years to avenge the wrongs you insist on committing against their people? Who among you can deny the justice of their claim?"

More cries of outrage.

"That is why we must show no mercy and exterminate the Lyucu once and for all—"

"We must have our vengeance! To renounce it is to be weak—"

"The Agon spirit will not be frightened into submission!"

. . .

Once again, the somber, deafening notes of the Péa pipes muted the raucous crowd. The very ground seemed to shake, the fires swayed and danced unsteadily, and the chiefs and thanes covered their ears against this aural demonstration of Théra's power.

"I know that few of you have fought for me or know me," said Théra, her voice calm but bone-hard. "So let me remind you of what I've done. *I* watched as my dearest companions in Kiri Valley died in an inferno of Lyucu creation. *I* lost my mother-in-law and children in a desperate flight to preserve the hope of Agon revival. *I* marched through the World's Edge Mountains and Nalyufin's Pasture to earn the respect of the gods and our ice tribe allies. *I* held my husband's body as he died while being pursued by the Lyucu across the floes. *I* commingled my blood with Takval's to become the pékyu. *I* planned the assault on Taten to kill Cudyu and free his garinafins. *I* led my warriors to triumph over a Lyucu army ten times the size of my own, summoned the voice of the gods to be embodied in arucuro tocua, earned the aid of a thousand free garinafins, and fulfilled the dream of the Agon people. Do not misjudge *me* as weak."

While some of the Agon thanes and chiefs lowered their heads in shame as they recalled their own cowardice and vacillation when Théra had needed them the most, others looked even more defiant and contemptuous. Since they hadn't been at the Battle of the Boneyard in person, they viewed most of the legends about Théra as self-serving exaggerations. The new pékyu didn't look like a mighty warrior, didn't claim to possess powerful magic, and yet, she was advocating a path of cowardly accommodation toward the Lyucu! That simply couldn't be tolerated.

Fractious voices filled the air, demanding justice, vowing vengeance, insisting on the right to punish. . . .

Théra grabbed one of her signaling spears and thrust the tip into the torch flame next to her sitting rug. The spear's tip had evidently been soaked in oil, since it flared into a bright blaze almost instantly. Théra waved the spear overhead: once, twice, three times.

From the darkness beyond the brightly lit banquet circle, thousands of voices chanted in unison:

> *Ten dyudyu cupéruna?*
> *Théra kyo!*

The chanting came from Théra's warriors—the ice tribespeople, the Agon rebels, and the Dara survivors—the ones who had dared to hope and had come to the Boneyard to fight for her the previous winter.

The gathered thanes and chiefs looked about them with expressions of fear. Finally, they realized who they were dealing with.

Théra sighed inside. She had wanted to persuade the haughty Agon leaders through reason, but Adyulek, Gozofin, Tipo, and Çami had all urged that she plan a demonstration of force.

"I am asking for your cooperation," she said. "But do not mistake my solicitousness for frailty. There has been enough suffering. All acts of vengeance against the Lyucu must cease instantly, and neither will you fight amongst yourselves for selfish advantage. I, with your counsel, will find an equitable way for the children of Afir and Kikisavo to share Ukyu-Gondé. I am your pékyu, and my will is the law."

She hated the idea of enforcing a peace through intimidation and force, but it seemed that the law of the scrublands left her no choice.

Many of the thanes and chiefs looked sullen and resentful, though a few seemed comforted by her words. Théra was glad that, despite Adyulek's absence, she had been able to accomplish her goal at the banquet. At least, the Agon leaders all seemed willing to accept her authority.

All, except one.

"Before we follow the orders of the pékyu, we must first determine who *is* the pékyu."

The voice was cold, calculating, and full of hatred. Just hearing it made the hair on the backs of many of the Agon leaders stand up. As everyone turned to gaze in its direction, an old man stood up from one of the sitting rugs and stepped out of the shadows into the light.

"Volyu," cried Théra, utterly amazed.

After Pékyu Cudyu wiped out the rebel base at Kiri Valley, he returned the Agon informer, Volyu Aragoz, to Sliyusa Ki as an ignominious prisoner in a cage. Cudyu knew that Volyu had betrayed his own nephew not out of any sense of loyalty to the Lyucu, but because he was afraid of losing power as a Lyucu puppet among the Agon should Takval succeed in his rebellion. The Lyucu pékyu wasn't going to make the mistake of trusting such a fool.

After the Lyucu guards left, the council of elders of Sliyusa Ki kept Volyu inside his cage and out of sight as they debated what to do. That a descendent of the great Nobo Aragoz could be so cowardly, so devoid of the Agon spirit was beyond shameful—it also spoke poorly of the judgment of the elders and shamans at Sliyusa Ki that they had trusted and backed the man for so long. Therefore, the council voted to keep Volyu's betrayal of Takval and Théra a secret.

To have Volyu remain the Pé-Afir-tekten was out of the question, but the embers of the Aragoz name still glowed brightly enough that the elders couldn't contemplate executing him. Therefore, the decision was made to denounce Volyu for vague charges of dereliction of duty and to exile him from the settlement with only three days' worth of food and water, leaving his fate up to the gods.

On the seventh day after his exile, as Volyu lay dying in the pathless expanse of Lurodia Tanta, a passing band of tanto-lyu-naro rescued him. The son of Nobo Aragoz, once the self-styled chief of all the Children of Afir, thus became a wanderer for peace.

But the fire of vengeance burned in him brightly, and he was sure the gods would give him another chance.

The thanes on the sitting rugs on either side of Volyu Aragoz stared at the man, stupefied. Each had thought the unremarkable old man part of the retinue of the other. They couldn't imagine how the youngest son of Nobo Aragoz, rumored to have been killed by Cudyu in a fit of rage, had suddenly appeared among them.

Every pair of eyes in the banquet circle was on Volyu.

Slowly, Théra's face reddened. Memories of the horrors at Kiri Valley, which she had struggled to suppress, now resurfaced with fresh pain. More than anything else, she wanted to leap at the craven man and lock her fingers around his neck until he stopped breathing.

But she held herself back. She was calling for mercy in place of vengeance, and she had to live by the rules she was imposing on her people. Besides, to reveal the full extent of Volyu's betrayal would bring shame to the Aragoz name, the very name through which she claimed her own legitimacy as the leader of the Agon.

Sensing her hesitation, Volyu smirked and spoke again.

"I am called Volyu Aragoz, son of Nobo Aragoz, son of Akiga Aragoz, once the Pride of the Scrublands. I serve my people now as the Pé-Afir-tekten, but my rightful place is the Pékyu of the Agon."

Fury and disbelief warred in Théra's heart. Volyu's challenge was so absurd that she could only respond with helpless laughter. It was like watching a slisli fly proclaiming itself the leader of a pack of wolves.

"You *dare* to claim to be the pékyu? After what you did in Kiri Valley—"

"It's a good thing you bring up Kiri Valley," intoned Volyu. "I blame myself every day for not seeing through your plots earlier, Dara witch!"

"What are you—"

"Votan-ru-taasa and votan-sa-taasa, we've been betrayed by this woman—"

"Silence, traitor!" Blood surged into Théra's head with a deafening roar, and the garinafin skull helmet teetered, threatening to topple. She took a deep breath and tried to force her trembling lips and tongue to obey her will. "You—you—li-li-lie—"

But the assembled chiefs and thanes, cowed but a moment earlier, suddenly rose to their feet in support of the challenger.

"Let him speak!"

"We want to know what he knows!"

. . .

Théra looked around at the jeering faces around the banquet

circle and realized that she had no allies present. She had made a deliberate choice not to bring any of her senior thanes or advisers to the banquet except for Adyulek in order to emphasize the legitimacy of her own claim, to show her trust in the gods of Gondé, and to display her confidence in her own authority. But that also meant there was no survivor from Kiri Valley here to back up her accusation against Volyu.

Volyu strode into the center of the banquet circle. Like a shaman at a storytelling dance, he paced and strutted around the bonfire, recounting his own version of the rebellion.

Théra whispered into the ear of a young naro guard near her and sent her away into the darkness. By the time she turned her attention back to the assembly, Volyu was already in the middle of his tirade.

". . . At first, she tried to seduce me, attempting to use her beauty to convince me to disregard the interests of our people and turn the Agon into mere tools of the strangers in Dara. But I, mindful of the teachings of my noble father and fearful of the gods, rebuffed her advances. Only then did she turn her attention back to Takval, an inexperienced young man beguiled by her exotic looks. . . ."

"Mo-more lies! How—how—could—"

Théra swayed unsteadily on her feet as dark blotches swam in her vision. But the assembled thanes and chiefs shouted at her, drowning her out.

"Let Volyu finish!"

"Sit down!"

"Why are you so afraid of having him tell his story?"

Théra quieted, realizing that the initiative had been lost. The more she protested, the more she would seem to have something to hide.

Let the cur lie for now, she said to herself, smiling bitterly. *The truth will be out as soon as Adyulek and the others arrive.*

But a sense of cold unease took root in her heart and grew.

As Volyu continued his story, his voice grew more sonorous and his movements more confident. ". . . Despite my misgivings, I allowed them to leave Sliyusa Ki in the company of some of my best warriors, hoping that with the passage of time Takval would come to his senses and see the evil lurking in his bride's heart. For years I sustained their settlement in Kiri Valley with supplies, braving the arduous journey through pathless Lurodia Tanta. . . ."

Théra had to admire the man for the boldness of his lies as well as their crafted intricacy. Mixing three parts truth with seven parts fiction, he was constructing an alternate reality like an articulated arucuro tocua.

". . . Finally, the chance that I had been waiting for for our people, the opportunity that I had been planning for years, came. Cudyu and his thanes were gathering at Aluro's Basin, and with one fatal strike, the Children of Afir would be free! But when I presented this plan to Takval and *that* Dara woman, do you know what happened, votan-ru-taasa and votan-sa-taasa? She refused! Isn't that true, *Princess* Théra?"

Surprised by the sudden question, Théra blurted out, "Yes, but—"

Volyu raised his voice. "Ah, but do you know why? It was because she wanted us to attack Cudyu at Taten, so that we would destroy the city-ships. Yes, you heard that right, she was planning all along for Agon warriors to bleed and die for Dara. She is a princess of Dara, *not* a sa-taasa."

Théra opened her mouth to answer, but no words came. She had, in fact, rejected Volyu's plan because she wanted a chance to destroy the Lyucu city-ships. The best lies always contained a kernel of truth. As the assembly turned to look at her, guilt and frustration colored her face.

Volyu pointed at her, wielding his finger as though it were a spear. "It's because of you, because of your insistence on not launching an attack until Cudyu had returned to Taten, that our brave warriors had to die at Kiri Valley. *You* are the traitor to the Agon! *You* are not one of us at all!"

Théra recoiled as though each accusing stab from Volyu physically struck her. "It's not . . . not trow—not true!" Her tongue seemed to have a will of its own, and she couldn't make it form the words she needed. "I a-afraid—I mean, I fear the gods—"

Volyu laughed at her mockingly. "Listen to you! You cannot even speak our language properly. How can you hope to speak to the gods? You claim to be Agon? Then let me ask you. While you were at Kiri Valley, did you not try to force our warriors to abandon the freedom of pasturing in order to slavishly dig for food out of mud? Did you not try to persuade our children to disregard the wisdom of our ancestors in order to worship the idols of your word-scars? Did you not attempt to instruct the children of Takval in the language of your homeland, the speech of foreigners?"

With each new accusation, the faces of the assembled thanes and chiefs grew colder.

Under this relentless verbal assault, Théra could do nothing but shake her head in denial. The more angry, wronged, and desperate she felt, the more the language of the scrublands seemed to desert her. The very thing she had been afraid of was happening, and she was powerless to stop it.

"You're trying to turn us away from the voices of our ancestors, the gifts wrested from the gods by Afir and Kikisavo, the practices and customs that have made the Agon great. Your Dara nature will never allow you to understand our love of freedom!"

"No, it's not true. You are twisting—"

"You wish to enslave us the same way Admiral Krita tried to enslave the Lyucu. You wish to corrupt us with the foreign ways of your homeland and make us your thralls. You are *not* Agon, but Dara, and a woman of Dara can *never* change her nature, can never be our pékyu!"

The faces of the Agon thanes and chiefs hardened as they watched the would-be pékyu shrink away from Volyu's thunderous words.

Even more than the import of the words, it was Volyu's voice that moved them. Volyu was speaking the topolect of the Tribe of the Sea of Tears, in the accent of the First Family. The older warriors present could dimly recall hearing Pékyu Nobo Aragoz in their youth, and the great pékyu had sounded just like Volyu. The contrast with Théra's foreign accent and imprecise enunciation couldn't be stronger.

A pang of fierce longing struck Théra as she heard echoes of Takval in his uncle's oration. She forced herself to focus on the present, on the task at hand.

"I *am* Agon! I've risked everything for the people—"

"If you really are Agon," said Volyu, his voice as insinuating as the undulating body of a scrubland snake, "why don't you prove it by drinking kyoffir, as all Agon do?" He strode up to Théra's sitting rug and filled the skull bowl in front of her from a kyoffir pouch.

Théra stared at him with hatred as well as despair. He was taking advantage of her inability to consume kyoffir, but she had no good answer. To refuse the drink was to confirm his accusation; but to accede would be to show weakness. Besides, consuming the kyoffir would likely make her sick before the end of the banquet, further eroding her authority. She decided to resort to the truth.

"It's true that my body cannot tolerate kyoffir," she said, her voice anguished. "But whether I am Agon shouldn't be determined by what I can eat or drink—"

"Listen! Listen, my fellow Children of Afir," cried Volyu triumphantly. "The Dara princess admits it. This is why she pours the precious kyoffir on the ground—it is all part of an act to fool you. Her body rejects the gift of our gods!"

Cries of consternation all around the circle. The idea that a pékyu of the Agon could not—or perhaps, *would not*—drink kyoffir was unbelievable, was sacrilege.

Théra couldn't believe how much the banquet had slipped out of her control. Would all the deeds and sacrifices by her, by Takval, by those who risked everything to follow them, be for nothing? Though she had defeated the Lyucu, could she now lose to this viper-tongued traitor because she spoke with an accent and couldn't drink kyoffir? The very idea was intolerable.

She stood up, heedless of the fact that her sudden motion caused the teetering, ill-fitting garinafin skull helmet to tumble from her head. Volyu, surprised by this sudden show of defiance, stumbled back a step.

"*I* am the designated successor of Takval, my husband," said Théra. In one hand she held a thick bundle of rolled-up garinafin stomach lining, and in the other a bone dagger covered in dried blood. She unfurled the stomach lining, revealing the gray-black surface etched with a single undulating line, like the path of a wanderer across a pathless wasteland. "This was his spirit portrait, in which he named me as the Pékyu of the Agon! This was the dagger that mingled his blood with mine, adopting me into the lineage of Afir!"

The restless throng quieted.

Théra looked around the bonfire, her face gradually settling into a mask of authoritative indifference. But a tumultuous storm raged in her heart, mixing grief with deep disappointment.

All that I've done matters less to them than the stain of blood; all that I've said weighs less than the words of my dead husband. How am I to bring peace to the scrublands? How?

Volyu collected himself and approached her again, a feral glint in his eyes.

"I do not accept these as proof."

Théra stared at him. A cold dread crept up her spine.

"Do you challenge the blood custom of the Agon, the voices of our ancestors?" she demanded.

"The objects you hold are mute, and therefore may be forgeries," said Volyu, speaking slowly and deliberately. The throng, shocked by such an accusation, quieted even more, straining to catch his words. "Pékyu Takval died in suspicious circumstances. Who was there? Who witnessed the moment Takval's blood fused with yours?"

The feeling of dread grew in Théra. Volyu's questions sounded so familiar. . . .

"Adyulek, Tongue-of-the-Every-Mother, was my guide and witness," said Théra. She tried to keep her voice steady, to enunciate and project, but her lips and tongue trembled as though it were deep winter. "She took Takval's spirit portrait; she instructed me in the right words and deeds; she can attest to the truth of my claim."

"Where is she?" asked Volyu. The voice was icy, but his eyes burned with excitement, as though he were a wolf who had finally locked his jaws around the throat of his victim. "Why is she not standing with you at this moment? Why does she not add her voice to yours?"

Where are you, Adyulek? Théra closed her eyes despondently.

"I was there as well," said a new voice. "I witnessed the moment spoken of by the pékyu."

Théra opened her eyes. "Çami!" she cried out in relief.

The Dara scholar had abandoned her post by the Péa pipes. But Théra was too happy to see her to object to this act of disobedience.

"Have you found her?" Théra whispered urgently to Çami.

Çami shook her head slightly, looking grave. "Tipo Tho is leading the search. Apparently she never returned to her tent last night. Her apprentices thought she was out to seek the guidance of the Every-Mother and didn't raise an alarm."

The Agon were whispering among themselves at this new development.

Volyu addressed himself to Çami.

"You?"

"Yes, me," said Çami. "I assisted the Tongue-of-the-Every-Mother at her request. I saw Théra plunge the dagger into Takval's heart and take his last breath into her lungs. She is the Pékyu of the Agon."

Shock and terror flitted across Volyu's face but were soon replaced by renewed confidence. "Tell me, idolator of word-scars from across the ocean, do you fear and trust our gods?"

Çami's spine stiffened. She knew the answer that was expected— even required—of her. But she was dedicated to the ideal of a knowable universe, and like many Dara scholars, she would not yield in the face of a threat. "I do not. All gods are mere super—"

"Do you hear that, votan-ru-taasa and votan-sa-taasa? Princess Théra claims as her witness a fellow foreigner who neither fears nor trusts our gods! Why should we listen to anything this 'witness' says? Indeed, I hope she is lying, for the presence of such an idolator at our most sacred mystery would be desecration! It would be a grave misjudgment by Tongue-of-the-Every-Mother if it were true!"

Théra wanted to scream at the gods with frustration. The extraordinary circumstances under which she had become pékyu were the source of this standoff. Çami, as a nonbeliever, could not authenticate Théra's claims. Thoryo, whose perfect Agon would have gone some way to make up for her own flaws, was dead. The only person who could persuade the doubting Agon thanes and chiefs was the missing Adyulek.

"Open your eyes, Children of Afir! Actions speak louder than words. She asserts that she fought for our freedom, but all along her only concern was the destruction of the city-ships, the obsession of her homeland; she pretends to fear and trust our gods, but she pours sacred kyoffir on the ground; she feigns respect for the voices of our ancestors, but she taught her children to prize barbarian word-scars; she claims devotion to the Agon people, but she cannot speak our language without the taint of her native tongue; she professes love for Takval, but she murdered him and enclosed his body in an unholy box, away from the Eye of Cudyufin. The evidence is clear: This princess of Dara has always been *using* us to secure the safety of *her* people, *not* ours."

Volyu spun around triumphantly, looking into the eyes of every thane and chief. He knew he had them. "Do you know what I think happened in the ice floes of Nalyufin's Pasture? I think my poor, deceived nephew finally saw through her deception and tried to thwart her plots against us. The evil-hearted witch then murdered him, and usurped the title of pékyu!"

"How can you make up such lies!" Çami shouted. "I was there, along with Thoryo."

"Thoryo is already dead. Besides, you are both of Dara, and there-fore her coconspirators. It does not surprise me in the least that a skilled witch like you helped the princess with the forgeries."

Çami refused to take his bait. "Adyulek, Tongue-of-the-Every-Mother, was also there."

"Then let her come and add her voice to yours!"

"You will accept the testimony of Adyulek then?" demanded Çami.

"I will," said Volyu. "Everyone here knows the great shaman's strength and courage. She will speak the truth!"

Théra said nothing. Her mind was all confusion. She tried to pray to the gods of Gondé, but she could not find that feeling of peace, of a grander presence enveloping her in the flow of history, of the dance of gods and heroes across the scrublands. All she felt was a bleak sense of doom.

A keening rose in the darkness beyond the flames of the banquet circle. Everyone turned.

Four young shamans, Adyulek's apprentices, entered the banquet circle bearing a bone-and-skin stretcher. Upon it lay the body of an old woman, her eyes wide open, her face frozen in a rictus of surprise and agony.

Gozofin, walking by the stretcher, fell to one knee. Wailing, he announced to the assembly, "We found Tongue-of-the-Every-Mother on the northern border of Taten. She was killed last night by a blow to the back of her head. Her body was then buried under a layer of sand, and that was why we didn't find her until now."

Théra ran up to the stretcher and fell upon the lifeless corpse, weeping. Adyulek had been the hardest among the Agon for her to win over, but she had also been her fiercest ally. They had traveled together for thousands of miles, survived countless dangers natural and Lyucu, won an inconceivable victory together. For her to die from a sneak attack by a worthless traitor was beyond unjust.

She turned to regard Volyu. There was no surprise or doubt in her gaze. The longer Volyu had gone on, the greater her unease had grown. Now his confidence throughout his performance made perfect sense. He knew Adyulek would never be able to stand with her, to add her voice to hers.

She staggered to her feet and grabbed a signaling spear. She would point it and bring down vengeance against the despicable killer who had been responsible for the deaths of those dear friends and family in Kiri Valley, who had scattered her sons to who knew where, who had murdered in cold blood the wisest—

"Votan-ru-taasa, votan-sa-taasa!" Volyu screamed, his features fixed in an expression of outrage. "So this is why the Dara witch isn't afraid that her lies would be shattered by our beloved Adyulek! She murdered our noblest shaman just as she had murdered my dear, dear, foolish Takval. O gods! O gods!"

"*You* are the killer!" Théra screamed. She pointed her signaling spear at Volyu. "I call upon all Agon to seize this murderous traitor and bring him to justice!"

To her horror, none of the thanes and chiefs around the banquet fire moved to obey. The looks that greeted her were full of contempt, suspicion, even hatred.

"Still lying to the bitter end?" sneered Volyu. "As Afir once said upon uncovering Kikisavo's betrayal: The one who raises a hue and cry is also most likely the thief herself. All true Agon know that to bury a corpse so that the deceased would be kept away from the Eye of Cudyufin, unable to complete pédiato savaga, is a desecration one wouldn't even visit upon one's worst enemies. Only a barbarian from Dara would do such a thing to her victim!"

Théra stared at Volyu. The depth of the man's cunning and carefully woven plot took her breath away. "But *why*?" she asked plaintively.

The shouts of the furious thanes and chiefs demanding for *her* to be seized meant that only Volyu and her own guards could hear her.

"Why are you doing this? Surely you can't really believe that they'll make *you* the pékyu."

Volyu locked gazes with her, the corners of his mouth curving up in a smile.

Théra pressed, making one last effort at persuasion. "You have no warriors of your own, and the best you can hope for is to become the puppet of another ambitious thane, a figurehead. A far worse fate awaits you because the truth of what you did at Kiri Valley won't be hidden forever; the Lyucu will reveal who was the traitor."

Volyu began to laugh, a noise that sounded like the howl of a wolf.

"If you destroy my authority tonight, you'll do more than bring suffering to the surviving Lyucu," pleaded Théra. "You'll be plunging our own people into civil war as they contend for the prize of being the next Pride of the Scrublands. Please, don't do this, uncle."

Volyu stopped laughing. "What do I care if I cannot be the pékyu? What do I care what happens to the rest of the Agon?" he hissed, his voice as quiet as hers. "So long as you lose, I will have had my vengeance."

He dodged out of the way of a furious club swing from Gozofin. "Help me!" he screamed at the top of his lungs. "The murderous foreign witch is trying to silence me for revealing her evil plot against Takval!"

Gozofin ran after Volyu, but Théra cried after him. "Don't! The more we try to harm him, the more we give weight to his lies!" Reluctantly, Gozofin halted.

"His lies have already become the truth," observed Çami, her hands balled at her sides helplessly. "How can these people be so foolish as to believe him? And after all you've done!"

Like a bolt of lightning piercing through the stormy murk, Çami's words lit up the confusion in Théra's heart. The Agon leaders present had all survived the Lyucu conquest while maintaining their hold over their own tribes; they weren't fools. It was likely that only a few were truly outraged by the lies of Volyu. Most knew, in their hearts, that Théra was telling the truth. But they were happy to join the mob, act the fool, and pretend to believe Volyu because it offered a convenient excuse to maintain the status quo.

Without vengeance against the Lyucu, where would they get the slaves and cattle to reward their own followers and consolidate their own rule? Without incessant warfare against an enemy, how could they justify their own decades of cowardice and continuing privilege? Only by getting rid of her before she had established her authority firmly, before she could impose her will on the scattered tribes, could they maximize their own power, bought at the price of present suffering and future bloodshed.

The "Agon spirit" was a cover for their cynical calculus. She could never have persuaded them. She had nothing to offer them but ideals, and ideals rarely benefited those already in power.

Théra's mother, Empress Jia, would have berated her for making this simple political mistake. Human nature was unchanging, whether in Dara or Ukyu-Gondé.

As Théra's heart turned to ashes at this realization, Agon thanes and chiefs rushed forward, swarming around her in a disorderly mob. Behind them, Volyu shrieked and screeched.

"Seize *her*! Don't be afraid! The Dara witch has no powers— she admitted as much when she said that she had no magic, but exploited the knowledge and skill of our own warriors in arucuro tocua. The murderer of Takval and Adyulek must not be the pékyu! The foreign seductress who tries to preach mercy, to turn us away from vengeance and justice, to defy the voices of the ancestors, to sap our Agon spirit *must not be the pékyu*! Agon kyo!"

Volyu's hysterical cries were taken up by the mob, now completely inflamed by a combination of Volyu's lies and their own selfish cravings.

"Agon kyo! Avenge Pékyu Takval!"

"The foreign witch must not be the pékyu!"

"Tear her tongue out! She has tried to deceive us!"

Çami, Gozofin, and Théra's guards, drawn from the rebels who had fought with her against Cudyu and Tovo, formed a barrier around her with their bodies. They would breathe their last before they'd let Théra come to any harm.

Théra was despondent. She could see no way to get the situation under control. Gozofin and Çami had both wanted her to bring more warriors to the banquet, but she had thought such a naked display of her power an ill omen for a celebration intended to bring about peace. Once again, her inclination to mercy, to not shed blood, had placed her friends in danger.

Gods of Gondé, why do you play with us so?

Ear-piercing screeches overhead; the bonfires danced wildly, buffeted by sudden gusts of wind. The mob and Théra's guards halted, looking up in astonishment, their eyes stung by the wildly swirling smoke.

Five garinafins, crewed by Théra's loyal warriors, thumped down inside the banquet circle. Giant dogs, directed by Kitos, revered chief among the ice tribes, leapt off their backs and snarled on the ground, forcing the Agon thanes back. Toof, pilot of Ga-al, directed the old bull garinafin to brandish his long neck menacingly. Behind Toof sat Tipo Tho, her son strapped to her back.

A pang convulsed Théra's heart. At any other time, Tipo would leave Crucru with Adyulek, but now . . .

Toof leaned down and shouted, "Drop your weapons and step back. Now!"

Relief washed through Théra. The situation could still be saved. If only she could restore order and convince the assembled throng to slice through Volyu's lies with reason, until even they could no longer persist in willful blindness—

There was no fear on Volyu's face, only ecstasy. He made himself look as tall as possible and spoke in his booming voice, in the accent of the First Family, in the manner that reminded Théra so much of her Takval.

"Listen to this Lyucu slave's accent! Look at these who would fight for the Dara witch! Lyucu slaves, ice fleas, Dara idolaters, Agon traitors—she calls on them for aid in her shameless usurpation of the title of Pékyu of the Agon! Now we finally know why she tries to peddle us the defeatist ideas of the tanto-lyu-naro: She has sold us out to our enemies. She is not one of us, never one of us—"

Toof moved.

Théra screamed. "No!"

But it was too late. Ga-al leaned down, snapped his jaws, and spewed a glowing lance of fire at Volyu. Instantly Volyu, and those nearest him, turned into burning pillars.

Screams. Curses. Thanes and chiefs scattered, shouting for their own garinafins to be launched.

"Votan, we must go!" shouted Tipo Tho.

Théra allowed herself to be lifted onto Ga-al, her mind blank.

She is not one of us, never one of us.

Wings flapping, necks craning, the garinafins lifted into the air and headed to the east, leaving behind a panicked Taten, leaving behind the ruin of Théra's dreams.

CHAPTER THIRTY-FOUR

THE WRITING ZITHER

She strode wearily through the narrow streets of the ancient Tiro capital, paved with strips of sandalwood laid across a bed of crushed pumice. Though her face was covered in grime and her dress patchy and ragged, none of the other pedestrians in the street dared to treat her as a mere beggar. The way she carried herself, her gaze steady and spine straight, each step light as the breeze and certain as the fall of a meteor, spoke of inner strength, of self-knowledge, of a nobility of character as obvious as a glowing pearl.

And so would-be thieves left her alone, haughty scholars with swords mutely stepped out of her way, and crowds parted as she approached, though their curious gazes followed her long after she was through.

She stopped in front of the Shrine of King Jizu just outside the city walls, built on the site where the ideal king had immolated himself to save his people.

The shrine was in the form of a simple fishing shack, a large bubbling fountain in front, fed by a natural spring. A steady stream of pilgrims stopped to pray to the spirit of the good king, leaving behind tiny clay figurines in the king's likeness. The rim of the fountain was covered by rows of these crude figurines, like an army of miniature Jizus waiting to wade into the eternal sea.

The figurines were supposed to repeat the pleas and prayers of the worshippers, amplifying them in the ears of the gods. Unlike the gold and jade statues of the gods molded by master sculptors in grand temples, these humble charms were kneaded by devout peasants and fisherfolk and sold for a few coppers at temple fairs. Even the lowly and the mean could whisper their hopes and fears to King Jizu, who loved his people and who had once been as poor as they. The king would intercede on their behalf with the distant gods. He, unlike the great Lords of Dara, never closed his ears to the pleas of the common people.

She watched the pilgrims, the clay figurines, the bubbling fountain, hoping for a sign, a direction, a hint of where to go.

He liked history, liked stories of heroes. You're a hero. Do you know where he is?

There was no answer.

Where are you? Where are you?

It had been the same at the Temple of Fithowéo earlier, with the god's colossal statue looming over her, his face barely discernible through the haze of incense. Lord Fithowéo was blind but could see, and she thought that would make him a better guide than most. But the god, like the king, had given her no guidance.

She had never been particularly pious, but she found the silence in the wake of her prayers oppressive, weighty. Lately, all her prayers had seemed to fall on deaf ears. It was as though the gods had retreated from Dara, leaving the people to fend for themselves.

Wearily, she listened, taking in the hubbub of conversation around her.

"Get your knives sharpened! Get your kettles and pans patched! I can do it all!"

"Have your future told! I can decipher your fate from the logograms in your name. . . ."

"Did you hear? The emperor won a great victory near Crescent Island. The Lyucu may surrender in days!"

"So soon? I was hoping the war would drag on for a few years. . . . I just put in three hundred silver on ore and sinew futures—"

"Follow the path of Rufizo! The monks will be at the Eastern Gate to collect donations at noon. Be there early to get the best blessings—"

"I told you to wait, didn't I? You'd better swallow the loss and invest in sorghum futures. I hear they're starving over there in Rui and Dasu. Once the islands are redeemed, I bet the Prime Minister is going to have to buy lots of grain. . . ."

The young woman frowned but didn't berate the speakers. She had been away from home often enough and seen enough of the world to be more accepting of human frailties. There would always be those who profited from death and misery, and the sins of these two were lighter than most. Like her, they could do nothing to change the course of the war; they could only pursue goals they found worthwhile, the same as she.

At least Phyro seems all right, and that is some comfort.

He knows who he is. Do I?

A lone wild goose flew high overhead, winging southwest. A few desultory honks; almost gone before they could be heard.

As though sensing something in the air, she turned in the direction the goose was headed in, and walked away from the shrine.

While war raged in the sea north of the Big Island and the inhabitants of Rui and Dasu were plunged into a new realm of suffering, life in much of the rest of Dara continued as before. Merchants and officials went on hosting lavish banquets at the Splendid Urn; pirate ships, laden with mysterious goods from the Huto clan, braved the dark waves; plays were put on at theaters and indigo houses; storytellers entertained rapt audiences at teahouses; monks and nuns knocked at the doors of the wealthy and asked for donations; scholars expounded upon the wisdom of the Ano sages as well as the mysteries of the universe.

Was it just or unjust, the sign of a golden age or of misrule, that a nation could be so prosperous, so secure, that while some of its sons and daughters died fighting on distant shores, the rest of its citizens could go on to enjoy luxuries, speak of love, compose poetry, scheme and plot for profit, carry on with the grand performance that was civilization?

It was a question that even the Ano sages and the gods could not answer.

∾

THE TEMPLE OF STILL AND FLOWING WATERS IN
THE MOUNTAINS OF RIMA: THE EIGHTH MONTH OF
THE ELEVENTH YEAR OF THE REIGN OF SEASON
OF STORMS AND THE REIGN OF AUDACIOUS
FREEDOM.

An hour before dawn, Brother Thasé-teki got up with the other novices.

There was much to do. The novices had to sweep the yard; dust the shrines, figurines, and prayer instruments; polish the idol of Rufizo Mender; draw water from the well to fill the cisterns; and prepare breakfast for the senior monks and nuns.

Today, Thasé-teki was assigned kitchen duty. Fried "sheep tails" were on the menu. While another novice monk prepared the dipping sauce with herbs cut from the temple's garden and aged fermented bean curd, Thasé-teki, the sleeves of his robe rolled high up on his arms, mixed and kneaded the dough. To feed hundreds of monks and nuns required a lot of dough, and his face and body were soon covered in a thin film of perspiration. The labor felt satisfying, calming.

After the dough was ready, the two young monks rolled it into thick ropes and pulled off chunks that they pressed by hand into flat ovals. They slapped the cakes in bowls of sesame seeds and dried monkeyberry flakes, making sure both sides were evenly coated.

A large pot with bubbling oil stood ready on the stove. They slid the pastries into the oil bath, as carefully as they would release white-bellied fish back into a pond. Soon, golden-brown cakes floated above the oil lazily, fringed with delicate, crispy fins. With a pair of long eating sticks, Thasé-teki and his fellow cook picked out the puffy pastries, now fat and tender like their namesake, and set them out on a rack to dry.

All meals at the temple had to be prepared without ingredients that required slaughter or the spilling of blood. Some of the older monks and nuns even eschewed eggs, fearful that a fertilized egg might slip through. But following the tenets of Rufizo Mender didn't mean that the food had to be bland—in fact, Thasé-teki thought the cooking here at the temple some of the best he had ever tasted.

But it wasn't just the taste of the food that brought him comfort. The work reminded Thasé-teki of the Splendid Urn, and sometimes he hummed the work songs he had learned as a kitchen boy there, wondering how Mati, Lodan, and Grand Mistress Wasu were doing.

And always, he thought of Fara.

Only after breakfast and cleanup did his workday truly begin. He went to the instructional hall first for an hour of prayer and meditation, at which a senior nun recounted Rufizo Mender's deeds and unraveled their spiritual significance.

Some of the stories and mysteries seemed familiar. He recalled similar plots and tropes from another life, when he had been a child in the dark belly of a city-ship, and his culek nurses had told him secret, forbidden tales about Toryoana Pacific to lull him to sleep.

The tales familiar to him had not all come from Abbot Shattered Axe. Thasé-teki didn't find this particularly surprising. After all, he and his mother, mere mortals, had journeyed across the ocean to this new land, so who was to say that the gods had not traversed the same expanse in eons past? The desire for peace was universal, he thought, no rarer among the gods than mortals.

He had finally found a place he could call home, though he no longer went by his old names.

The morning lesson over, he reported to the Hall of Snowy Feather. He sat down before his workstation and let out an excited cry as he examined the ancient manuscript laid out on his desk.

After months of tutelage by the other brothers and sisters of the hall, he had been assigned his own grand task: to heal a volume of Ra Oji's epigrams and acts.

In his old age, Üshin Pidaji, Ra Oji's biographer and student, retired to the mountains of Rima to brew tea from dew, to converse with the monkeys and wolves, and to put together a collection of epigrams and stories about his master that would eventually become the foundation of an entire school of philosophy.

Pidaji's manuscript was composed in an idiosyncratic hand that exhibited his unconventional character: novel logograms devised to express new ideas whose meaning could only be deciphered by context; simple logograms chosen for their phonetic values substituted in place of complex, traditional logograms (in effect, a kind of writing-by-punning); free-flowing verse forms that followed no known antecedents; semantic roots and motive modifiers abstracted into shorthand that could be carved with fewer strokes; an emphasis on adapting the knife stroke to the natural flow of the solidifying wax rather than proper sharp corners and clean edges.

It was as if Üshin Pidaji's thoughts flowed too quickly for the heating brazier and the writing knife, and he needed to write like a passing spring breeze or the flash flood after a summer thunderstorm. The ornate, formal clerical script, prized by Moralists, was no match for his wild, rebellious mind that viewed hierarchy and decorum with contempt, and he had to invent his own "torrent script."

It was sometimes said that in torrent script could be found the roots of the zyndari letters that, in a later age, would be invented to write the vernacular.

After his death, Pidaji's book, copied and memorized by his students, spread around Dara along with the Fluxist school of philosophy. Compared to the other Ano Classics, the preservation of Pidaji's works, written in a script unfamiliar to most scholars, posed an even greater challenge. The fragments of his compositions that survived were shorter, and there were fewer copies.

With a frustrated sigh, Thasé-teki scraped away the remnants of his latest failed effort at imitating the hand of the ancient scribe.

Calligraphy had always been his least favorite subject. It wasn't that he didn't understand the importance of the art; Master Nazu Tei had told him many tales of how writers are judged by their script, in the same way actors are judged by their looks. But more than that, for the truly cultured and erudite, calligraphy was a way to unify form with function, medium with message: a reader knew the spirit of a writer by the proportions of the logograms in a manuscript, the sharpness of the corners, the straightness of the edges, the smoothness of the curves. A messy mind led to a hesitating hand.

But the young Kinri—already, the name felt strange to Brother Thasé-teki, as though a summer grass were recalling its time as a winter worm—could never summon enough patience to reproduce the logogram models carved by his master with exactitude. What was the point of practicing calligraphy so long as his master could decipher what he meant (albeit with some trouble)? He preferred to hear stories of Mata Zyndu's matchless strength and the magnificent cities of the Tiro kings, gleaming with a splendor that he longed for as well as feared, filled with sword dancers, debating poets and philosophers, and windmills that labored like giants with vaned arms.

In contrast, calligraphy was boring, repetitious, rote. To write properly, each logogram had to be carved through an exacting sequence of knife strokes. To shape the logogram for "king," for instance, the scribe was supposed to start with a block of dripped wax and shape it into a cube with five cuts that embodied the Moralist worldview: front, back, left, right, and then top ("first, bow to the sovereign seated before you; second, show reverence to the ancestors standing behind you; third, pay respect to your family, who bring comfort and aid to your sinister hand; fourth, honor your friends, who stand ready to fight on your dexter hand; last, you praise the heavens above so that the gods may bless your righteous deeds"). Next, the scribe was supposed to chisel the side of the block of wax facing the reader into four parallel layers—matching the four stacked realms of fire, water, earth, and air—but leaving the back of the block intact. This should be done with three long swaying horizontal strokes, moving from the bottom of the block to the top. Finally, the scribe would bevel the edges with seven quick strokes, again moving from the bottom to the top, before adding inflection glyphs—though in artistic calligraphy such marks were often omitted.

By following the correct stroke order, it was easier for the scribe to write with beauty and economy, resulting in logograms with classic, standard proportions. For reasons such as aesthetics and history, different schools of calligraphy employed different stroke orders, and there were variations in diverse locales across Dara as well.

Thasé-teki never memorized the stroke orders—though he understood that they followed patterns, the patterns felt to him obscure and confining. His mind was always racing to the next idea, the next piece of the puzzle, and he wrote as though he were hacking and whittling blocks of wood: a chop here, two whacks there, desperate remedial cuts to cover up his mistakes. . . . The resulting logograms looked like bones gnawed over by a hungry dog or shacks erected carelessly by underpaid laborers: uneven columns, slanted roofs, crooked walls, misplaced doors and windows.

"You have good ideas," Master Nazu Tei used to say as she sighed. "But I'm afraid only I can bear to read them."

Thasé-teki had to agree that she was right. When he occasionally tried to read over one of his earlier compositions, even he had trouble recognizing the misshapen logograms and had to puzzle them out like some secret code.

Though he was now working in the Hall of Snowy Feather, his script hadn't improved much. No matter how much he meditated or tried the patience exercises taught by the senior monastics, his clerical script remained barely legible. Instead of the delicate work of mending ancient manuscripts, most of his assignments had been copying already repaired books. But even so, the senior brothers and sisters often had to stay up late to redo the passages he had copied, and Thasé-teki felt terrible about the trouble he caused.

But the abbot didn't give up.

"Sister Covet-No-More tells me that you are as impatient as a colt, always running to the next clump of grass before the one in front of you has been thoroughly grazed," the abbot mused. "That wildness in your nature should be channeled rather than dammed. . . . I understand that Pidaji's torrent script gives many brothers and sisters trouble, but perhaps the unrestrained thought trails of the Fluxist master require an equally restless book doctor."

Thasé-teki assented, though not for the reasons suggested by the abbot. He couldn't care less about Üshin Pidaji, but torrent script was the favorite calligraphic style of Fara, who saw in it a match for the tendency toward the expressive rather than the representational in her own art.

To write like her, he thought, *is a little like being with her.*

The experiment, however, wasn't going so well. Replicating the loose, flowing script of the Fluxist sage (and the young Dara princess) had been just as difficult, if not more so, than writing in the neat clerical script better suited to other Ano classical masters.

Weeks had passed since that first excited cry in the Hall of Snowy Feather. Thasé-teki had devoted all that time to mending a single manuscript retrieved from the grave of a duke of Cocru who had died six centuries earlier. Sometimes it took him all day to re-create a single column of logograms, and still the result felt dead, clumsy, without any of the liveliness of the original scribe.

Having cleaned off the last residue of wax, he set down the knife, leaned back, and took a deep breath. Almost time for lunch.

The kitchen was preparing something he hadn't tasted before, and his mouth watered at the delicious aromas. There was a fruity scent—maybe a rose-pip-and-monkeyberry coulis—as well as something richer—perhaps roasted pine nuts sprinkled with sea salt and Faça lantern peppers stuffed with stone ear mushrooms and cacanut flakes. His stomach growled in anticipation. The summer breeze carried other scents that painted vivid pictures in his mind: flat bread pockets filled with taro paste, lotus roots, and dried berry chunks; lightly toasted seasonal wild vegetables; hearty soup made from eight types of gourds and four herbs. . . .

No matter how much frustration he encountered in his work, the pleasures of good food always cheered him up.

He swallowed and closed his eyes, savoring the names of the dishes: Listen, Ye Faithful, the Master Awaits; the Shepherd's Cornucopia; Wandering in the Divine Garden; Eight Delights and Four Strictures. . . .

The names were allusions to Rufizo Mender's deeds and teachings. At first, he had been confused by them, for they didn't reveal the ingredients or methods of preparation.

In fine cuisine, the key is to invoke all five senses. But the best dishes must draw upon a sixth sense, often described as "mind-pleasure."

How right Fara had been. Now that he understood the stories behind the dishes, just reciting their names was like meditating upon the god's wisdom, a delight that transcended the merely sensual.

He smiled as he recalled scenes from his life at the Splendid

Urn: chopping and bringing in firewood in the morning; running to the market to purchase something Mati needed at the last minute; busing the dishes and even helping out the waitstaff when Lodan needed him; learning to play the zither with Fara; the contest against the Treasure Chest . . .

Wait, he thought. *Wait.*

Images of Rati Yera's machines chopping, dicing, carving, stirring, frying, flipping in the kitchen of the Splendid Urn filled his mind.

One of the recipes had called for cubes of winter melon that would then be marinated in sauce and wrapped in dough for frying. It was important that the winter melon pieces be identical so that they'd be cooked to the same degree. Mati had been worried that the Blossom Gang's mechanical assistants couldn't accomplish the task with sufficient precision.

"Anything you can do, my machines can be taught to do," declared Rati with pride. *"The trick is to decompose your motion into its most basic constituent pieces."*

On the night of the second competition, the winter melon cubes had been perfect, more uniform even than Mati herself could have made them.

Master Nazu Tei had taught him to engineer ideas with Ano logograms; Master Rati Yera had taught him to engineer deeds with mechanical contrivances. Might there be a way to marry the two to reproduce the beauty of Fara's hand?

Thasé-teki's eyes snapped open, the mind-pleasure of lunch forgotten as a torrent of new ideas took its place.

"You've been absent from the Hall of Snowy Feather for the last three weeks," said Abbot Shattered Axe.

The abbot had found the missing novice in the carpenters' workshop. Like any community away from the bustle of large cities, the brothers and sisters of the Temple of Still and Flowing Waters had to craft the necessities of life with their own hands, making well-stocked workshops a requirement.

Scattered around the floor now was evidence of a furious bout of construction: adzes, saws, planes, chisels, nails, hammers, squares, sticks of charcoal, plumb lines, bubble levels, rulers . . . bits of lumber of various sizes and wood shavings. On a workbench in the middle of this mess sat a contraption about the size and shape of a nine-stringed zither. Thasé-teki knelt next to it, filing the rough edges.

"Sorry," he said, a smile of apology on his sweaty face. "Been busy."

Instead of berating the young monk for his dereliction of duty, the abbot nudged aside tools and lumber to clear a space for himself and sat down in *géüpa*. "Tell me."

"Well," began Thasé-teki hesitantly, "I've been having trouble with writing in torrent script. . . ."

Thasé-teki thought of his own mind as a swallow in spring: comfortable with sharp turns and quick dips into the warming water, but incapable of long, sustained flight. He became bored soon from repetitive tasks that required precision and endurance. He far preferred to create the new than to refine the old.

These habits of the mind were at the root of his poor handwriting, but likewise, they provided the solution.

Rati Yera's motion-copying machines had allowed Chef Mati to chop twenty winter melons at once by having the mechanical arms replicate Mati's own expert movements exactly. Her instructible carts had allowed a skeletal staff to run a full dinner service. Could these seemingly unrelated machines come to the aid of Master Yera's disciple? Could he teach a machine to write in beautiful torrent script, and therefore save the world from his own clumsy writing knife?

Though Thasé-teki was no master calligrapher, he had plenty of examples of the best calligraphy at his disposal (including one in the letter box next to his heart). He began by studying these specimens not as artifacts, but as solidified motion.

The process of writing could be analyzed into constituent parts. Each logogram was a compound machine composed from sub-logograms, sub-sub-logograms, and so on until you reached the basic semantic roots, motive modifiers, phonetic adapters, and inflection glyphs. These, in turn, could be broken down into individual knife strokes: the vertical chop, the horizontal slice, two types of diagonal slashes, a twist to hollow out a hole, a turn to sculpt a protrusion, a scrape to smooth a surface, a swipe to bevel an edge, and about a dozen additional flourishes for incising, carving, scoring, slitting, roughening, and so on.

In the same way that each fall of the cleaver brought the cook closer to the finished dish, each knife stroke brought the writer closer to the completed logogram. If he could replicate the individual movements, he would have the raw ingredients for the long sequences needed to build logograms, sentences, paragraphs, books.

He experimented. By consulting the monks and nuns in the Hall of Silver Fleece, he studied the anatomy of the human hand and arm as well as the principles of joints and degrees of motion. These he then reproduced through mechanical linkages, springs, gears, ropes, silk strands, wound-up sinew. Many failed prototypes later, he was in possession of a mechanical hand that could, when the right ropes were pulled and the right levers pushed, replicate the movements of a knife-wielding scribe.

Next came the matter of control. Locking gears and escapements confined the motion of the hand to precisely measured gradations; twisted sinew and compressed springs stored energy for metered release. By coordinating the tensing and relaxing of multiple control lines, his mechanical hand could be made to perform various predetermined gestures: a slow back-and-forth motion to saw a wide horizontal gap in the wax; a powerful, quick downward chop to leave a clean vertical face; a gentle, slow twist to gouge a perfect circular hollow.

The cheremes of this language of motion in hand, Thasé-teki now had to devise a way to transmit the will of the writer-with-no-knife to the hand-with-no-mind.

"You've been trying to replicate a scribe in wood and silk?" the abbot interrupted the novice's excited presentation in disbelief. "But why? You have hands of your own!"

"Because the mechanical hand can write with more beauty than my own," said Thasé-teki, looking at once embarrassed and proud. "Watch. I'll show you."

Moving with suppressed excitement, he placed an empty silk scroll on the tilted platform at one end of the machine, melted and dripped a lump of wax onto it, and swung the writing arm— fashioned out of wooden dowels and bundles of cords in place of muscle—over the wax.

Then, Thasé-teki walked to the other side of the machine and sat down in front of a contraption that resembled a zither—except that instead of the common nine strings, this one had many more. Grinning at the abbot, Thasé-teki began to pluck at the strings.

Gears clacked and meshed, twisted sinew snapped and groaned, silken cords tensed and loosened, and the mechanical arm swung through the air, wielding the knife against the solidified wax.

Much as martial arts masters taught students to combine basic punches and kicks into set forms and poses, calligraphy masters taught students to combine basic knife strokes into compound strokes such as the box form (four vertical chops and a horizontal slice on top), the ladder form (two chops with two, three, or four slices), the cross form (a dexter-to-sinister diagonal slash followed by another, sinister-to-dexter), and so on.

Thasé-teki realized that the compound forms were similar to chords composed of basic notes, and the musical metaphor inspired him to adapt the standard nine-stringed zither for a new use. The strings of the zither, tied to the silken sinews of the mechanical arm, translated the musical notes into the cheremes of the writing hand: while plucking the first string led to a hard chop, fretting the string halfway resulted in a half chop; strumming the eighth string swung the knife to the right, but strumming the ninth string swung the knife to the left; playing a chord on the first, eighth, and ninth strings, with fingers positioned at the correct frets, then resulted in a box-form stroke that carved the nascent wax logogram into a perfect cube.

As the abbot's jaw dropped in amazement, Thasé-teki played on the zither the opening bars of the tune for "The Silk Maker," a popular work song among spinners and weavers.

> Pick the cocoons, soak, boil, stir, reel.
> Spin the wheel, sister, spin that wheel!

Whirring, clacking, groaning, creaking, the knife at the end of the mechanical arm danced through the air, leaving a perfectly formed logogram for "silk" in torrent script on the scroll.

The abbot approached the logogram gingerly. Though Shattered

Axe was no scholar, even he could tell that the curves were smooth and flawless, the edges undulating with grace, and there were none of the chips and notches that even the best scribes sometimes left on a logogram.

"I doubt anyone has ever written torrent script with such perfection, perhaps not even Üshin Pidaji," declared Thasé-teki with pride.

He had deliberately avoided the word "beauty." It was believed that a great calligrapher wielded the knife with their spirit, so that part of their soul was captured in wax. The best calligraphy specimens, therefore, were celebrated as much for their imperfections and seeming "flaws" as for their adherence to standard aesthetic rubrics. The mechanistic logogram produced by the machine was indeed perfect, though that perfection also removed it from the realm of the human.

He placed his hand over his heart, over the letter box.

These mechanical logograms are neat and clean, better than any I can write by hand. But only your writing can be called beautiful.

"Does the music always match what is written?" asked the abbot, after he had recovered somewhat from the shock.

"Sadly, no," said Thasé-teki, shaken from his reverie. "That was just a bit of whimsy for demonstration purposes. The 'music' that would have to be played to write most logograms isn't very musical at all, at least if you follow standard stroke order. But if one adjusts the sequence of strokes and notes, almost all logograms can be rearranged into something pleasing to the ear."

"Pleasing to the ear! But writing is meant to be a silent activity—"

"Writing is so boring that I have to find a way to entertain myself."

(The abbot, not being a native of Dara, did not realize that only someone who had not been immersed in logograms since before reaching the age of reason would treat standard stroke order with so little reverence. It was akin to speaking the syllables of a lexeme out of sequence or spelling a word-square's zyndari letters last-to-first—innovative, original, interesting . . . but not the sort of thing children continued to do after some time under standard schooling. The writing machine, as unique as Thasé-teki, was animated by the spirit of its inventor.)

The abbot shook his head, bemused and amused, but before he could raise another objection, Thasé-teki rushed on.

"This machine not only makes well-formed logograms and entertains the writer, it is also fast!"

Once again, he walked over to the tilted writing platform and swung over a second dangling arm, at the end of which was a cone-shaped receptacle. Carefully, he nudged and adjusted the arm until the tip of the cone hovered just above the silk scroll, a little distance ahead of the writing knife.

Returning to the zither on the other side, he resumed playing.

His hands danced like a pair of swallows in spring, swooping and diving above the vibrating strings. The tune shifted in mood and tempo precipitously, joyous one moment, wistful the next; dark and somber one instant, lively and bright the next.

As he played, the writing platform slid along a rail below it, bumping by exact fractions of an inch. Wax dripped from the cone onto the silk scroll, solidifying into a series of lumps as a gentle breeze wafted through the workshop. The writing knife followed along, spinning, slicing, chopping . . . carving each into a new logogram.

When the writing hand reached the bottom of the scroll, a mechanism ticked inside the machine. Both the writing arm and the wax-dripping arm stopped as rolling axles advanced the scroll one column to the right on the tilted writing surface, while the platform itself clacked back to its initial position, leaving the cone and the knife at the top of the next column.

Lines of well-known Fluxist epigrams, written in the most flawless torrent script, appeared on the scroll:

> Silkworm! Are you such a good model? You labor every second
>   until death, but only another bride will appear in the splen-
>   dor of your shroud.

> A Moralist is someone who can tell you how everyone ought to
>   behave except himself.

> It's easier to ascend Mount Kiji than to know the mind of a
>   king;
> And safer, too.

Thasé-teki lifted his fingers from the zither strings, and the final notes lingered in the air of the workshop. The scroll was filled with neat columns of torrent script—a full day's work even by the most skilled scribe.

"You could have practiced with the knife until you were finally a decent calligrapher, able to carry out your duties," said the abbot, eyeing him thoughtfully. "Surely inventing a new machine required more work? I understand you skipped meals and went to bed long after all the others."

"But this is more . . . ," protested Thasé-teki, ". . . *interesting*."

"Avoiding the work assigned to you is a kind of laziness, don't you think?"

Thasé-teki lowered his head in shame. "I know. But—"

"If only we could all be as lazy as you!" said the abbot. Thasé-teki looked up in surprise, but the abbot was laughing. "Your writing zither isn't useful for repairing old books, but it *is* good for copying them. Now we can make a new book in about one-twentieth the time it would have taken the old way, and perhaps we can make so many copies of every book that we'll never have to worry about the extinction of a book due to war and decay. And these new copies will be more legible and well-made than all their predecessors."

Thasé-teki grinned back. "I was worried that you might find my actions too frivolous—"

"You *were* having fun"—the abbot waved away the novice's objections—"but who says that the task of mending the world must be *un*interesting?"

CHAPTER THIRTY-FIVE

FLIGHT

UKYU-GONDÉ: THE NINTH MONTH IN THE
ELEVENTH YEAR AFTER THE DEPARTURE OF
PRINCESS THÉRA FROM DARA FOR UKYU-GONDÉ.

Summer turned to fall as Théra's party continued its aimless flight across the scrublands.

In the wake of the disastrous banquet at the new Taten, the Agon had splintered into multiple factions vying for dominance. Some of the new self-proclaimed pékyus tried to rally followers with promises of harsh punishment against the Lyucu; others sought to re-create the empire of Nobo Aragoz; still others—with fewer warriors and garinafins at their disposal—promised clemency for the defeated Lyucu if they would fight for new masters. Plots, schemes, alliances, and betrayals spread across Ukyu-Gondé wherever there were herds and tents.

But all the Agon factions were united in their denunciation of Théra, the foreign witch who had tried to corrupt the Agon spirit and who had murdered Takval, her husband, for power and to benefit Dara. The heartless woman had even killed her husband's uncle in order to silence him when he had revealed her evil schemes.

So, wherever Théra's party landed, Agon pursuers soon followed. The capture (and subsequent torture and execution) of Théra—mariticide, usurper, traitor, witch, enemy of the Agon—would add immensely to the legitimacy and prestige of whichever thane or pékyu accomplished such a thing.

Théra's command was always to flee, even when it seemed clear that the five garinafins in her party would more than hold their own against the pursuers. Gozofin and Tipo Tho, seething against Théra's refusal to make a stand and fight, came to see her together.

"These ungrateful traitors have desecrated the Agon spirit," said Gozofin, gritting his teeth. "They must be made to pay!"

"Our forbearance will not kindle in our enemies feelings of shame or mercy," said Tipo Tho. "It will only be perceived as weakness."

"The only thing they respect is strength," said Gozofin. "We cannot flee all the rest of our days. Let's raid a few tribes to show the squabbling thanes that we have teeth and claws, and then perhaps we can negotiate—"

"Better yet, let's plan a surprise attack on one of the pretender pékyus," said Tipo Tho. "Once we have taken their warriors and garinafins, we can build a secure base from which to—"

"You speak of plots for vengeance, of schemes for rebuilding an empire," said Théra. "But I do not wish for vengeance or empire. I wish for the people of the scrublands to live in peace."

"Only the unquestioned master of the scrublands can demand peace," said Gozofin.

"To make peace, you must first make war," said Tipo Tho.

"How many have already died?" demanded Théra. "How many more must die still? The words of my mother-in-law, Souliyan, haunt me.

"'What is justice? My father slaughtered thousands to bring the Lyucu under the shadow of Agon garinafin wings, and Tenryo then slaughtered ten times as many to reverse the situation. My mother was born a Lyucu, but when the Lyucu overran her adopted tribe, they killed her for having borne an Agon child. I have neither the skill nor the interest to restore my father's domain by killing yet ten times more.'"

Gozofin and Tipo both interjected. "But you promised to lead—"
"You vowed to rejuvenate—"

"I promised Takval to free our people; I vowed to Thoryo that the cycles of killing will end; I pledged to Adyulek that I would lead the Agon down a new path. But how can I keep these promises with your advice?

"If we obtain power through killing, then we must be ready to continue killing to hold on to it. My heart is weary. Perhaps the thanes are right: I am not one of them."

"I am a mere soldier," said Tipo Tho, unconvinced. "Moral philosophy and regret are luxuries afforded only to the victor and survivor."

"Luxuries they may be," said Théra, "but that doesn't make them any less true or weighty. My sorrows are too great to be dissolved by claims of expedience."

The only one who didn't try to convince Théra to fight was Çami Phithadapu, the scholar who did not fear or trust the gods.

They were resting under the stars. The days were shorter and the nights colder. They'd have to plan for the winter.

Théra was praying to the gods of the scrublands when Çami sat down before her.

"Do you ever regret what you've done?" Çami asked, drawing up her knees in the manner of the Agon.

Startled, Théra opened her eyes. Since her escape from Taten, the gods had offered no guidance in the form of visions or that sense of the presence of the numinous. But praying made Théra feel better, and so she had continued.

Théra took a moment to compose herself. "How do you mean?"

"Had you not granted mercy to Volyu back in Sliyusa Ki, none of this would have happened."

Théra thought back to that long-ago moment, before the fires that consumed Kiri Valley, before the final fight of Tipo's husband and her own mother-in-law, before her children had been taken away, before the long march through the World's Edge Mountains, before the desperate escape over the ice, before Takval's blood stained her blade, before Thoryo's eyes saw their last sunrise, before Adyulek's lungs drew their last breath, before the sacrifices of so many dear ones had come to naught.

"I cannot deny the justice of your charge," she said, her voice weak. "Volyu lived to betray us, and more than once. My mercy has come at a great price, a price many others have had to pay."

"Your father would have chosen differently," said Çami. "He

could have granted mercy to the Hegemon on the shores of the Liru, but he betrayed him instead. He loved his sworn brother, but he killed him, thereby saving Dara from decades of war."

Though not entirely unanticipated, the blow struck Théra hard. Çami, who always prized truths over sentiments, had plunged the most persuasive of daggers into her heart. So many had already died for her mercy, which was indistinguishable in effect from weakness. By refusing to fight now, was she being weak again? Did she lack the courage to prevent the deaths of the many by killing the few?

"Had I not offered mercy to Volyu, I wouldn't have been who I was, who I am still." It took all her strength to speak. "I am not my father. Volyu is right: I cannot change my nature. I am sorry, but I do not regret."

"You have nothing to be sorry about, *Rénga*." Çami's voice was still unsentimental, but full of heat. "We, all of us, the survivors and the dead, chose to follow you because of your compassionate nature, a grandness of spirit that called forth something equally grand in our own hearts."

Théra broke down in sobs, and Çami embraced her.

"So many dead, O gods, so many—"

"We fool ourselves in thinking that history has a set course, or that the future can be determined like a well-engineered machine," said Çami. "I do not think even the gods, if they exist, can be so arrogant as to proclaim, free of doubt, that Mata Zyndu would have gone on fighting had your father not betrayed him, or that we would have won the war against the Lyucu earlier had you not let Volyu go as you did. A thousand-thousand decisions by a thousand-thousand men and women make up the links of causation, not only yours. I say this not to excuse you or to lighten the load of responsibility on your shoulders, but to affirm that to live a life true to one's nature, and to accept the consequences, seems to me all that can be demanded of us."

Long did they sit under the stars, listening to the howling of the scrubland winds.

"I know there is much doubt among you," said Pékyu Théra.

Around her stood what was left of her band: Kitos, Toof, Gozofin,

Tipo Tho, Çami Phithadapu . . . less than two hundred who still believed in her.

"We have no friends, no allies, no refuge. The Lyucu view me as the cause of their downfall, and the Agon view me as a traitor. All would like to see me and those who follow me dead. I have no plan for a turnabout victory, no secret plot to snatch success from the jaws of defeat.

"If you wish to leave me now, I understand. You may take one of our five garinafins. I thank you for coming so far, and promise you there will be no pursuit."

She waited. And waited. And waited.

"But if you wish to follow me still, then know this: From this moment on we are no longer Dara, Lyucu, Agon, or the ice tribes of the north. We are a new people without a name. I intend to lead you on a new course, a path that leads not to glory or triumph, not to domination or vengeance, not to empire or power. I can offer you only hardship, uncertainty, and the remote hope of living in accordance with your true natures."

For much of the night, the band talked and debated. Where could a new people with no name go in the scrublands, where every knoll, hill, oasis, grassland, river, lake . . . was already contested by multiple claims? Where could they find refuge for the winter and beyond without fear of pursuit? Where could they escape if they were willing to think the previously unthinkable, they who had already broken so many taboos and prohibitions, reanimated monstrous beings from the mists of legend, repurposed sacred arucuro tocua techniques for war, made allies of foes and foes of blood?

In the morning, five garinafins took off and headed for the forbidden grounds of Taten-ryo-alvovo: the City of Ghosts.

CHAPTER THIRTY-SIX

WINTER WORM, SUMMER GRASS

THE TEMPLE OF STILL AND FLOWING WATERS
IN THE MOUNTAINS OF RIMA: THE NINTH
MONTH OF THE ELEVENTH YEAR OF THE REIGN
OF SEASON OF STORMS AND THE REIGN OF
AUDACIOUS FREEDOM.

The Hall of Snowy Feather sounded different.

In the past, one would have heard only the soft scratching of writing knives and the gentle hissing of charcoal braziers heating bowls of wax. But now, into the mix was added the strange music of zither strings, muffled by downy pillows.

Some of the older monks and nuns, proud of their own handwriting, eschewed the use of Thasé-teki's newfangled writing zithers. But other scribes, especially younger ones, favored the perfectly proportioned logograms and fast writing speed made possible by the instruments and quickly adapted to their use. Old, original manuscripts could be left alone to decay in peace, like ancient ruins silently bearing witness to another age, while new manuscripts gathered the fragments and collected the competing versions into a single, comprehensive volume.

Upon becoming a novice and taking up a temple name, every nun or monk took the following vow:

"I leave behind the world of strife and pain so that I can help mend it. Though I do not avert my face from the suffering, I will not add to it."

To heal, a doctor must stand apart from the patient while retaining empathetic attachment. Thus, the Mendists had to be detached from the world while also keeping a finger on its pulse.

The world had grown more strife-ridden. From traders and peddlers who trekked to the temple to sell goods that the brothers and sisters could not produce themselves, they had received news of Emperor Monadétu's failed war against Ukyu-taasa and the subsequent humiliating peace.

Some of the monks and nuns from the Hall of Silver Fleece departed the temple to tend to wounded veterans returning after their defeat. They brought back rumors that the emperor had gone missing after the war, perhaps kidnapped by pirates or turned bandit himself out of dissatisfaction with his regent and aunt-mother. There was no way to confirm the truth of any of these stories.

Abbot Shattered Axe, Brother Thasé-teki, and other monks and nuns who had Lyucu roots sighed with relief at the news that the invasion had not resulted in mass slaughter.

But there was nothing they could do to directly alter the actions of ambitious thanes and elevated lords. They could only pray, meditate, heal each broken limb, mend each torn page, hope for the restoration of a more vigorous, fecund world.

As peddlers and traders departed the temples, they carried new books and medicines produced by the order. The stream of commerce would spread them far and wide across Dara, much like dandelion seeds.

Each scribe concentrated on the manuscript in front of them with the same dedication due a patient from a nurse. The original writing zither was too loud to be used in an open scriptorium, and Thasé-teki had modified the prototype with a muffler so that the writing music was mostly felt and heard only by the writer. Since each monk or nun developed their own unique way of arranging the notes in each logogram, their writing-song was as distinct as their mind.

On the slanted desk next to Thasé-teki sat several unfurled scrolls full of Üshin Pidaji's deeds and sayings, recorded by his students. His task today was to resolve conflicts among competing versions of one of these stories—among the most famous of Fluxist tales—and to record the unified version in a new manuscript, complete with commentaries and interpretation by scholars from later.

THE TALE OF THREE SWORDS

Let a man fall with each ten steps you take;
Walk a thousand miles a new path to make.

The crown prince of Métashi was a martial arts enthusiast and craved skilled sword fighters in his service. Gathering thousands of sword fighters in his castle, he asked them to dance and duel for his entertainment. Dozens were maimed or killed in bouts each day, while he lavished gold and jewels on the victors. The people whispered that the crown prince intended to start a war against the other Tiro states as soon as he ascended to the throne.

Üshin Pidaji went to the crown prince's castle, demanding an audience.

"Why have you come to see me?" asked the prince, taken aback because the itinerant scholar did not bow to him.

"I heard that you like to meet heroes," said Pidaji.

"Are you a good swordsman then?" The prince was skeptical. The man in front of him wasn't very tall and his shoulders weren't very broad. He didn't look like a powerful sword fighter at all.

"A man falls with each ten steps I take, and I've walked a thousand miles without anyone being able to stop me. I haven't bowed to you because my sword is too thirsty for blood—I fear as I bend my waist it will fall out of its sheath and demand a life meal."

Impressed, the prince immediately asked Pidaji to dine with him.

As they feasted on platters of sliced fish and quaffed flagons of rice beer, the prince asked Pidaji to describe his fighting skills in more detail.

"I have three swords," said Pidaji, "the Courage of Brutes, the Ambition of Nobles, and the Grace of Kings."

"Tell me about the Courage of Brutes," said the prince, his eyes wide with excitement.

"This is a sword forged from bronze, shaped by hammer, and sharpened on stone. To wield it, one needs bulging muscles and a lust for blood. You

can use it to lop off an opponent's head and spill his entrails on the ground. Fighting with it makes one no better than a beast baring teeth and brandishing claws. In its wake are dozens of bodies and wasted potential."

The prince's expression turned somber. "Tell me about the Ambition of Nobles."

"This is a sword forged from determination, shaped by cunning, and sharpened on pride. To wield it, one needs the support of able strategists and the humility to listen to them. You can use it to conquer vast territories and humble your rivals. Fighting with it makes you one of the colossi striding across the land in every age. In its wake are widows and orphans, cries of lamentation and cycles of vengeance."

The prince's mien grew even darker. "Tell me . . . tell me about the Grace of Kings."

"This is a sword forged from hope, shaped by experience, and sharpened on wisdom. To wield it, one must have a heart that can empathize with the meanest peasant as well as the proudest prince, to bear compassion for the loyal friend as well as the overweening foe. But one must also climb high enough and walk far enough to see beyond the here and now, to not be blinded by mere sentiment, to not mistake convention for truth. You can use it to defeat your enemies without fighting at all and to realize the golden visions of ancient sages."

The prince's eyes lit up. "Is it a very hard sword to learn to wield?"

"Very. Alone among the world's blades, it has no hilt, no grip, no handle. To grasp it, the wielder will bleed first. To unleash its power, you may be required to harm those you love and to compromise with those you hate; you may be obliged to kneel before the conqueror and to sacrifice the innocent for a greater good. When you hold the Grace of Kings, a man will fall with every step you take; yet you may be compelled to march a thousand miles without stopping to mourn."

The prince shuddered. "Then . . . does fighting with it leave you a name praised and honored down the ages? In its wake are there celebrations, dances, songs and poems, admiring children and devoted elders?"

"No," said Pidaji, shaking his head resolutely.

"No?" The prince was confused.

"No," affirmed Pidaji. "How can you foretell the shadow you'll cast upon the future when the future is a new river carving its own channel even as it flows? While the Grace of Kings will reshape the world, what it leaves in its wake cannot be predicted. If you fight with the Grace of Kings, you may leave behind a golden age that will, in ten generations' time, swell into a tide of sorrow to overwhelm the world, or a wasteland of devastation upon which, ten springs after the winter, a fresh, vibrant garden will sprout. If you wield it, be prepared to be remembered as a tyrant or a sage, a despot or a lawgiver, and perhaps all at once."

"But why is this?"

"Because we are mortal and imperfect. Because no wielder can stand high enough to take in all the suffering of the world or to see far enough ahead to predict the flow of years beyond the horizon. Because doubt is the only constant of our brief sojourn between the Veil of Incarnation and the River-on-Which-Nothing-Floats. To act, even with the best of intentions, may lead to an evil greater than that which was to be prevented. But to hesitate, even with the purest of designs, may lead to a proliferation of horrors worse than at first imagined. What is virtue today may one day be seen as vice; what is right today may one day be seen as wrong. It is folly to judge the rightness of an action solely by its consequences, for consequences beget consequences, and none can see to the end of all time or tally up the accounts of all souls."

"I thought you had come to persuade me that my enthusiasm for martial glory is misplaced, that I should not lean upon the Courage of Brutes or the Ambition of Nobles," said the prince. "But the Grace of Kings doesn't sound much better. I'd rather not wield it at all."

"The Grace of Kings has far more power than any other sword, for both good and ill," said Pidaji. "My master, Ra Oji, used to say that perhaps it would be best if the Grace of Kings could be cast into the ocean and allowed to sink out of sight, never to be recovered by mortal hands at all."

"I'm beginning to think that Ra Oji was right," muttered the prince.

"But we do not live in the world of parables and fables," said Pidaji, his voice firm but kind. "So long as the Courage of Brutes and the Ambition of Nobles exist, the Grace of Kings will always be forged, and it will be wielded by the deserving and the undeserving alike."

"I don't know what to do!" cried the prince plaintively.

"Accept the necessity of doubt," said Pidaji, "but know also that you must end it before it ends you."

He bowed—the sheath at his belt, it turned out, was empty—and departed.

Afterward, the prince dismissed all the swordsmen in his employ and drove them from his castle.

SELECTED COMMENTARIES

SÉTI FAÇA OF MÉTASHI, ROYAL TUTOR:

After ascending to the throne of Métashi, the crown prince in this story, better known to us as King Maso, the "Conscientious," dedicated himself to the study of the art of good governance and became one of the most lauded Tiro kings of all time.

He surrounded himself with Moralist philosophers and listened humbly to their sage advice. He refrained from waging war, preferring to inspire his enemies with the propriety of his actions and to shame them by the reverence he displayed for the moral path. He worked from sunup to sundown to bring to life the golden vision of Kon Fiji, where every man knew his place in the chain of being, and all lived in accordance with the proper rites. Tragically, King Maso worked so hard that he passed away from exhaustion at the young age of forty.

In King Maso's example can be glimpsed the boundless potential of a true Moralist sovereign.

SUYE OF GAN:

Though King Maso died centuries ago, he remains a figure of some controversy.

Some praise him for his lenient treatment of several peasant rebellions during his reign, sparing many lives. Others argue that by negotiating a compromise, he dissipated the reformist sentiment among the nobility and allowed land ownership to grow even more imbalanced, paving the way for a much deadlier rebellion after his death. Some laud him for lowering taxes and encouraging private commerce. Others denounce him for so depleting Métashi's treasury and weakening its army that it was almost conquered and partitioned by neighboring Tiro states less than a decade after his passing.

How should history judge him? One's conclusion changes depending on one's perspective, just as the arguments of the litigators before the magistrate shift based on who pays the bill. And since no one is paying my bill in this case, I will offer no opinion.

But I will, free of charge, offer a few words on the "Three Swords" story itself. Many scholars have argued that this tale of a purported conversation between Üshin Pidaji and King Maso was most likely a forgery produced decades after Üshin and Maso had both died. For evidence, they point to the verse forms used in the tale, the odd Classical Ano grammar (showing Neo-Faça influences), and the anachronistic use of reduced-stroke logograms.

As I am no philologist, I will not opine on the strength of the evidence (except to point out, in passing, that the same sort of evidence can be compiled against the veracity of many stories about Kon Fiji, beloved by teachers across the land, and that the many points of doubt can be just as easily read as the natural consequences of the devolution of a piece of reportage, accumulating mutations down the ages as it is copied from scribe to scribe). I am more interested in what the story means, *even if it's more fiction than history.*

It will not surprise you to learn that the tale's most avid debunkers are Moralists. The point of the story is commonly understood to be mockery of the Moralist commitment to ancient rituals and classical modes of thought. Üshin Pidaji claims that the "Grace of Kings" can be used to "realize the golden visions of ancient sages"—a most succinct summary of Moralist political philosophy—only to deflate it a few lines later by pointing out the unpredictable consequences of even the most idealistic reforms. Moralists throughout the ages have thus tried to counter this piece of Fluxist propaganda by elevating King Maso himself into an ideal Moralist sovereign, emphasizing the positive consequences of his reign and burying the negative, in effect substituting one piece of historical fiction for another.

But I think it's error to view the story as merely a Fluxist parable. While it's true that the story shows a great deal of skepticism toward concentration of political power—I think that is the true tenor of the metaphorical "Grace of Kings"—Üshin Pidaji does not advocate its destruction as a practical solution (consigning the sword to the bottom of the sea, of course, stands in for the Fluxist political goal of governance in accordance with the Flow, that is, that which governs the least, governs the wisest); rather, he claims that the Grace of Kings is unavoidable, and so the best that can be hoped for is for its wielder to embrace doubt before acting, but then to be free of doubt once committed to action.

This is neither Moralist nor Fluxist, but evinces a practical mind resigned to the reality of human nature.

The time of Pidaji and Maso was one of great violence and constant warfare. It's easy to imagine that even the most idealistic philosopher, when faced with the depravities of the human animal, would lose hope and fall back upon the comforts of pragmatism. To my ears, even if the grammar is faulty and the logograms anachronistic, Üshin Pidaji's words glow with the inner light of authenticity.

Litigators are often accused of cynicism toward the truth, and I suppose my lack of interest in whether Üshin Pidaji and King Maso actually had this conversation or not will only prove the charge. But as I have clients waiting for my services, I will indulge my wasteful habit of commenting upon the classics no more today.

LÜGO CRUPO, DISCIPLE OF GI ANJI AND
PRIME MINISTER OF XANA:

Suye of Gan, one of the most renowned paid litigators of his generation, has been roundly mocked by subsequent generations for his defense of the "Tale of Three Swords" as "true-ish" (or, as he put it in his inimitable style: "glow[s] with the inner light of authenticity.").

The general charge levied against Suye is one of narrative fallacy. Suye seemed to suggest that the story was true because it was a "good story," but as his detractors point out: History has no plot, and kings do not follow character arcs.

The critics of Suye are far too harsh, and they have quoted their target out of context—whether out of ignorance or malice I cannot say. I do not read him as claiming that the entirety of the "Tale of Three Swords" is his-torical fact, merely that Üshin Pidaji likely made similar arguments, even if not in those exact words. Suye was pointing out that the doctrines of the various philosophical schools, formalized after centuries of evolution, may in fact be more limited and narrow-minded than the thinking of the original masters who founded the schools. That Üshin Pidaji, perhaps the second most important figure in Fluxism, could have a thought that was not, by later definitions, strictly "Fluxist" must have made many uncomfortable.

(I do note, however, that Üshin Pidaji's pragmatism, which treats the "Grace of Kings" (or concentrated political power) as a necessary concession

to human nature, seems to show the seeds of modern Incentivism. Whether Pidaji may be claimed as a prefiguration or a Proto-Incentivist would be an interesting topic I intend to take up another time.)

In the process of rereading Suye, however, I've been struck with a new insight. What if we took the misquoted Suye at face value? What if we actually treated the "Tale of Three Swords" as real history, not parable?

We do know that the reign of King Maso was marked by restraint and nonaggression—a rarity among his contemporaries! We also know that in his youth, as crown prince, he did seem to be far more militaristic (see, for instance, the Hall of a Thousand Skulls and the Field of Ghost Sword Dancers, both attested locations in his fief-castle when he was crown prince). So let's give in to the desire for a good story and assume, for the moment, that all of it was true: The prince was obsessed with warfare and sword fighting; Üshin Pidaji really did go try to persuade the prince to see the errors of his ways; the itinerant Fluxist actually succeeded. The story was recorded (though very much embellished).

Despite the unpredictable vicissitudes of life, each of us cannot help but construct the random events of our experience into a coherent narrative. The autobiography of individuals, the histories of the great lords, and the myths of nations are but manifestations of the same impulse.

However, that a story is too neat doesn't mean it's also not true.

If there is anything to be learned from this interpretation of the tale, it's the power of this desire for a good story. Kings and dukes may be motivated to do great deeds by the desire to leave behind a memorable narrative about themselves. Üshin Pidaji, perhaps without even understanding what he did, incentivized the future King Maso to peace with the promise of a moving tale to be told about him.

TAN FÉÜJI, DISCIPLE OF GI ANJI AND
PRIME MINISTER OF HAAN:
The more one reads commentaries upon the classics, the more one wishes they could all be expunged.

Every time Thasé-teki plucked the zither strings, his fingers tingled and a trickle of warmth filled his chest. In a world of chaos and uncertainty, to write was a luxury, a refuge as well as an escape.

Calligraphy styles generally fell into broad schools: clerical script, torrent script, seal script, mirror script . . . and so on. Each scribe, however, also put their own unique twist upon the adopted style, which was why no two scribes' writing looked exactly the same, making it possible to identify specific writers even thousands of years later.

Thasé-teki had tuned each writing zither to replicate the hand of the user—albeit a more elegant, clean version. But his own machine was the exception. Rather than his own hand, it imitated the hand of another.

He had reverse engineered the way *she* had wielded the knife to produce each protruding flourish, each hanging lip, each slanted surface, each leaning vertical. Then he had tuned the machine to reconstruct those strokes, so that as he wrote, he could feel that he was seeing *her* hand.

A gentle tap on his shoulder. He looked up. The abbot.

"Brother Thasé-teki, the world has come in search of you."

In the middle of the vast, empty visitors' hall stood a young lady, a yellow shawl around her shoulders, a bit thin for the chill evening. She was facing away from him, shivering despite the heat of the charcoal brazier at her feet. In the rays of the westering sun through the portico, she was poised like a summer dandelion, or perhaps a chrysanthemum blooming defiantly against the first winds of winter.

He took a step forward, his heart beating wildly, a storm raging in his ears.

She turned at the sound of his footfall, and he saw the face he had dreamed about every night: a bit wan, a bit gaunt, signs of miles of hard journey and months of heartache.

"Fara," he croaked, swallowing.

She looked at him, and for a moment she held still. Then she ran into his arms, and he embraced her, but she held back and beat her fists against his chest, tears streaming from her eyes.

He stood, letting her rage and sorrow run its course.

He felt like the happiest man in the world.

∾

She had been wandering around Dara for months, raging against the gods and cursing the world.

She felt utterly alone. Her brother had gone missing after the failed invasion of Unredeemed Dara, and rumors spread among the people that her aunt-mother was a tyrant who was willing to conspire with the Lyucu to secure her own place on the throne. Admiral Than Carucono, who had always loved her like an uncle, had died on the battlefield. Zomi Kidosu, who had cared for her like another sister, had disappeared from public view. Her secret attempts to contact Lady Soto, who had raised her like a second mother, had gone unanswered. And she dared not reach out to Aya Mazoti, her sister-friend, lest she send the farseers after her.

The political storm she had warned Aya of had inundated everyone she cared about and cast her adrift. Away from the stifling intrigue that permeated the palace, she felt even more lost and confused. Why had Empress Jia recalled Phyro's expedition when it was on the verge of victory? Where were her brother and Zomi? What was really going on in Pan? Paranoia made her want to connect everything, but she didn't know how.

While the people of Unredeemed Dara continued to suffer, ships filled with tribute grain and meat sailed for Rui and Dasu, proclaiming Dara's shame. There were whispers of rebellions and revolutions, often involving the name of her brother. Security at city gates increased, and soldiers with unsheathed swords scrutinized the papers of passing caravans and pedestrians. Veterans' societies became centers of anti-regency sentiment, with many veterans voicing disapproval of the humiliating end to the war. In response, government inspectors began to harass these societies, shuttering them for violating various construction codes or minor regulations. For the first time in years, Imperial airships patrolled the sky over Pan, perhaps a reminder that the empress was watching.

But she was powerless to influence politics. She couldn't save the world; she could only devote herself to her own task.

She continued the quest that she had already begun while still in Pan. She visited fishing hamlets in Wolf's Paw and hillside ranches in Faça, seeking news of a young man who traveled alone and liked to gaze at windmills. She trekked to distant shrines in Amu and remote isles off the coast of Cocru, following rumors of a stranger who spoke with the accent of Dasu. She hiked through mountains and waded through streams, strode down broad avenues and meandered up narrow alleys, thinking she was trying to find Savo.

But no, Lady Soto was right. Savo was only an excuse. She was, in fact, looking for herself.

The golden dandelion crest that was everywhere she looked as she grew up; the incessant mutterings of tutors, ladies-in-waiting, and Cousin Gimoto, reminding her how a princess of the House of Dandelion should behave; the very name of Garu and all the intrigue, heroism, betrayal, and sacrifice that it implied . . . everything told her a story of who she ought to be. She had lived under the weight of these expectations for so long that she had not realized how stunted they had made her.

She had sought refuge in plays and songs about love, in the poets' notion of romance. Love, for her, was something that could belong to her and her alone, not to Phyro, not to Théra, not to Lady Soto or Empress Jia, not to the imposing memory of her father, a man she barely knew at all, or to *mutagé* and the welfare of "the people of Dara," ideas that had been drilled into her from birth.

The happiest time of her life, she realized, was the period when she had lived at the Splendid Urn in Ginpen, when she had been *seen*, truly *seen*, by friends she loved and a boy who loved her. Savo had loved her not because of her name, but because of *who she was*.

Someone she hadn't even known.

It was that sense of being seen, of being truly understood, that had kindled her affection for him. It must have been the same with the Hegemon, a man who had been told from birth of the path he must walk. Lady Mira was the first woman to truly see him, and only in her company could he be free of the weight of family and history.

But affection wasn't quite the same as love, not exactly.

Only when she had lost him, when the weight of history had pushed them apart, did she realize the difference. She had come to depend on him for that sense of freedom, of being "Dandelion" instead of Fara Garu, Imperial Princess.

And so she had put away childish things and idle pursuits. As she departed the pomp and intrigue of the court and traveled around Dara, accompanied only by herself, she had to learn to *see* herself, to love herself.

She was not the cleverest student, nor the most skilled artist; she had no ambition to start a revolution or to rule an empire; she had no aptitude for leading an army to victory; she didn't enjoy plots and schemes, nor did she crave to do grand deeds and leave a name that cast a long shadow on history.

But she was confident about which poems were worthy of being memorized, and which weren't; she loved music and painting, and took delight in her own work; she was a loyal friend, sister, child; she was an ordinary person of average talent, and she deserved happiness as much as anyone.

The words of the lady by the shore of Lake Tututika on that day long ago resurfaced in her mind.

"What are the four great pleasures?" asked Fara, instantly curious.

"That would be sitting by a cozy fire in winter while snow falls outside the window; climbing onto a high place after a spring rain to admire a revitalized world; eating crabs with freshly brewed tea next to the fall tides; and dipping your feet into a cool lotus-covered lake in the middle of summer."

"You didn't mention the love of a handsome man!" said Fara. "That's the most important thing."

The lady chuckled. "Each of the pleasures I mentioned is better with a friend. A real friend is a mirror that reflects the truth back to us."

The mysterious lady had been right, but so had Fara. There was nothing ordinary about being ordinary; to love and to be loved: That was the quintessence of the extraordinary.

Only by being apart from her beloved did she finally love herself; only when she had learned to love herself did she truly begin to love.

"I am the Hegemon," she whispered to herself. "And you my Mira."

It was a bold claim, but that didn't mean it wasn't also true.

In a small trading post in the mountains of old Rima, she ran into a caravan of merchants resting their horses. She struck up a conversation with the merchants, and upon discovering her love of poetry, they showed her their latest acquisition, a manuscript they were sure would fetch a good price in Ginpen. It was a collection of Fluxist tales and epigrams, not so rare by itself, but done in so fine and perfect a hand that even calligraphy masters would admire it.

She gazed at the torrent script on the scroll in astonishment. It was . . . her own hand. To be sure, the logograms were too clean and neat, almost eerie in their perfection; indeed, it looked like an idealized version of her own writing, a reflection from a mirror in love with the subject.

In answer to her query, they pointed her to the path leading deeper into the mountains, to the temple that hid itself away from the world.

For days Fara stayed as a guest at the Temple of Still and Flowing Waters. She instructed him in advanced zither techniques, while Savo spoke to her about his new faith, reciting the deeds of Rufizo Mender and Toryoana Pacific.

They avoided discussing the future; the present was enough.

One dusk, after a day of hiking in the mountain to pick monkeyberries, they sat down together in front of the temple. Clouds in the west, wispy, diaphanous, glowed gold and red, like the tail fin of Tututika's *pawi*.

"Look, the goddess of love is waving at us."

"I've always thought her the wisest of the gods, though the youngest."

No one was about, so they shared a long, lingering kiss.

"I like who I am when I'm with you," she said.

"Me too."

They sat and held each other, like a dandelion and a caterpillar grass leaning together, watching as the light of the sun faded second by second. A shadow darkened Savo's face.

Time didn't stop, not even for lovers whose hearts vibrated in sympathy.

"History doesn't end for love," he said, struggling with words that pained his heart. But love had no place for lies. "I am still Lyucu, and our peoples, the people we love, are still at war."

She pulled back. "Do you want me to leave?"

"No!" said Savo. "How can I lose you again when you finally found me? But . . . I've finally found peace. No one here wants to add to the suffering of the world." He swallowed and forced himself to go on. "Would you join me here, forever?"

"You want me to become a nun?"

"No. Not at all!" Savo's head shook like a rattle drum. "That's . . . not what I meant. But maybe we can live away from all the rest of them, to escape the broken world?"

"I can't do that," said Fara gently. "And neither can you. Can you truly bear never to see your mother and sister again? Can you ask me never to see my brother or Aya again? That would be asking us to cast off parts of ourselves. We wouldn't be who we are without them."

"We cannot avert our eyes from the suffering of the world," muttered Savo.

A discreet cough. Abbot Shattered Axe appeared at the temple gate.

Awkwardly, the pair pulled apart. Celibacy was one of the Mendist vows.

"It's all right," said the abbot. "Lovers mending and tending to their bond would surely please Rufizo Mender."

Blushing, Savo and Fara grinned.

"It's time for you to go, Savo," said the abbot, not calling the novice by his temple name.

"No," he pleaded. "Please don't send me away. I'm still Thasé-teki, and there must be a way for us to stay—"

The abbot shook his head. "The winter worm is destined to become the summer grass. You found refuge with Rufizo Mender when you needed it, but your life's path leads elsewhere. You remain attached to the world of pain and strife. Do not force what cannot be."

"But I want to mend the world—"

"There are many ways to mend the world," said the abbot. "You don't have to stand apart from the world to tend to it. Some who follow Rufizo Mender are called to serve in the Three Sacred Halls, but many more must work in the world itself. To tarry at the temple as an excuse to escape from your attachments, your responsibilities, is also to avert your eyes from the suffering of the world."

Savo and Fara looked thoughtful.

"I cannot choose between Dara and Lyucu," said Savo, his voice subdued.

"Then don't choose," said the abbot. "Whenever there seem to be only two impossible choices, you must find a third path."

"That's the most interesting way," said Fara.

And though the last ray of the sun had disappeared, the world seemed to glow with her smile. He knew then that whatever happened next, he would be able to bear it.

"Do you know where you want to go?" she asked.

"Anywhere you wish," he said, "so long as I'm with you."

A SECLUDED SEASIDE VILLA BY LUTHO BEACH: THE NINTH MONTH OF THE ELEVENTH YEAR OF THE REIGN OF SEASON OF STORMS AND THE REIGN OF AUDACIOUS FREEDOM.

It was not surprising at all that they should return to the Splendid Urn, the site of their happiest memories.

But it *was* surprising to be whisked away by Widow Wasu, to be told to be quiet inside the secret smuggling compartment at the bottom of the carriage, to leave the city in the dead of night, only to emerge at dawn inside the walls of a secluded seaside manor.

"No one knows I own this place," said the aged widow. She had made the tiring journey with the young couple. No matter how they pressed her for information, she had refused to tell them what was going on. "Ah, there he is."

Fara and Savo looked at the figure emerging from the house, tall, broad-shouldered, a wide, confident grin lighting up his face.

"Hudo-*tika*!" Fara cried.

PART FOUR

THE FRUITS OF KNOWLEDGE

CHAPTER THIRTY-SEVEN

THIRST

PAN: THE TENTH MONTH OF THE ELEVENTH YEAR
OF THE REIGN OF SEASON OF STORMS AND THE
REIGN OF AUDACIOUS FREEDOM.

"Mistress, it is done."

"You're quite certain?" asked Jia. There was no light in the room except the faint glow of stars.

"We stayed on Mount Rapa for three days after the fire and made sure there were no surviving specimens. The entire field is gone."

"Good. And the processing plant where the goods were roasted before shipment?"

"After an acid bath to scour everything, we sold the equipment to a tea roaster, and the building was then burned to the ground."

"Well done."

"What should be done about Tiphan Huto?"

A pause. "Leave him be."

"But we didn't actually implant any magical mushrooms in him—"

"Oh, I'm sure he was stealing and sampling the goods himself," said Jia. "He'll have his just deserts soon."

Since the empress said nothing more, Wi and Shido bowed and merged into the shadows.

Jia sat, thinking. It was impossible to go to sleep again; she was afraid that Timu would visit her in her dreams. It hadn't happened, not yet.

The new peace has whetted Lyucu appetite for more. . . .

Based on Tiphan Huto's shipping records, I've finally waited long enough. Will it work? Or must Unredeemed Dara continue to groan and suffer?

The field is gone, but there's still the secret in the medicine shed in the Palace Garden. I don't know why I've kept it . . . I'll never use it. I must clean it.

I've done all I can. The rest is up to chance.

No, not quite. There's still the matter of Phyro, foolish, hot-blooded Phyro.

TOAZA: A FEW WEEKS LATER.

Tiphan Huto was thirsty. He had never been so thirsty in his life.

It wasn't a thirst that could be quenched by water, by beer, by sweet monkeyberry juice. His throat burned; his skin was on fire.

Though it was autumn and cool at night, he couldn't bear to wear a strip of clothing. Naked, he lay on the floor of his room, surrounded by blocks of ice that had been purchased at exorbitant prices. Still, he felt like he was going to be consumed by flames from within.

A rumble in his stomach. He turned over and heaved. Nothing came out as he gagged like a fish thrown onto a rocky beach. He had already emptied his stomach hours ago; he hadn't been able to keep anything down for more than a week now.

Doctors had been summoned from as far away as the Big Island. They had tried everything: expensive medicines, silkmotic shocks, ice baths, bloodletting, leeches, dream herbs, exorcisms performed by priestesses from the Temple of Tazu, tubes stuck down his throat to force him to eat and drink and take his medication.

Nothing had worked. By now his family had given up and no longer entered his room, fearful of contagion.

"Ungrateful wretches!" he croaked. "Without me, do you think you'd have all this gold?"

Covered from head to toe in thick canvas and working quickly, servants brought him ice and took away his bedpan.

"You fools! There's nothing to be afraid of!"

But they skittered out of the door, not daring to come anywhere near him.

He knew what was wrong with him, of course.

It was those cursed bandit queens.

Every month, in accordance with their secret pact, they brought him boxes of mysterious goods as well as the medicine to keep the infestation of Blooddrinker mushroom in his body under check. He had faithfully kept up his end of the bargain, passing the goods onto the pirates to be smuggled to Unredeemed Dara for trunks of gold, which he had shared with the bandit queens—he didn't even cheat them . . . except just a little.

Curiosity had gotten the best of him, and so he had opened one of the mysterious chests to see just what was so valuable. It turned out to be red berries and dried leaves of some plant, one with a smoky scent. He couldn't resist sampling some, just a *tiny* amount out of caution.

Oh, how the magical berries had made him fly! There was nothing like it. When he ingested or smoked them, he felt as though he was twenty feet tall, a veritable living Mata Zyndu. He could tear up mountains with his bare hands and negotiate business deals with the gods. He could fly to the moon and dive to the bottom of the ocean. He could ride crubens and roast garinafins for dinner. He was *invincible*.

No wonder the Lyucu were willing to pay so much for the plant. He took a bigger amount.

He sold every box he received from the bandit queens and asked for more. Obligingly, they increased the shipments but told him to be cautious—as though he needed to be told how to conduct business!

The secret trade had made the Huto clan powerful again. He was once more a respected member of the clan, and elders begged him to give his opinions on the renovation of the ancestral hall, the layout of the new mansion, the investment of the clan treasury. . . . *Tiphan Huto has risen again!*

And then, two weeks ago, at the appointed time and place, the bandit queens failed to show up. Not to take their share of the gold, not to deliver him more of the magical berries or leaves, and most important: not to bring him the medicine that would keep the Blooddrinker in check.

That was when he began to feel thirsty.

At first, he experienced the strange sensation of always lacking energy. No matter how much he slept, he didn't feel refreshed. Thinking it a matter of his humors being ill-regulated, he ordered lavish meals filled with exotic ingredients—wild boar testicles, shark gallbladders, jellyfish stingers—intended to give him more strength and vitality. But rather than restoring him to vigor, the meals had sharpened an inchoate craving in him, a thirst for a drink that he couldn't name.

It had to be the Blooddrinker those bandit queens had forced him to ingest. Had to be!

In a panic, he confessed everything to his family, and they had reacted with horror. Though they had praised him like a genius when he brought wealth and status to the Huto name, they now turned on him and declared him a degenerate who was going to bring catastrophe upon the whole clan. Trading with pirates! Had he forgotten that he had come *this* close to being convicted as a traitor?

So they had imprisoned him in his room. Though the elders were willing to pay to bring doctors to tend to him, they refused to go out in search of those bandit queens and beg them for the only medicine that could cure him.

Worst of all, he didn't even have the magical berries to comfort himself. He should have saved some when he had the chance, but he had been greedy for the gold, and why should he bother when the bandit queens were always on schedule and brought him more?

O gods! End this torture!

He could no longer stand it. He was going to die of thirst. He screamed, pounded the ground, slammed his head against the ice, rolled around the room, but there was no relief, none. He could picture how the evil mushroom's mycelia, entangled in his entrails, were sucking the blood from him, draining him bit by bit.

Wait. What is that? Wait!

In his struggles he had managed to dislodge a dresser in the corner of his room, revealing a few dried red berries. They must have rolled there when he had been sampling the goods in secret.

Ah, sweet relief! Even if I were to die now, I would die on clouds!

Oddly, though he couldn't keep anything else ingested in his stomach for more than a quarter of an hour, the berries stayed down. The horrible feverish heat that roasted his body seemed to recede a smidge, and even the ever-present thirst slackened slightly.

He felt his mind clearing. Once again, he was invincible.

The bandit queens had said that there was no way to be free of the mushroom unless his viscera were removed with it.

We'll see about that, won't we? I will be my own doctor!

He began to cackle. Yes, he would save himself and then go seek vengeance against those bandit queens. He would use the gold to hire the best sword fighters and martial artists in all of Dara and hunt down the heartless women. He would torture them and find out where they got their supply of those magical berries so that he could continue his trade.

Tiphan Huto will rise again!

After a rushed and private funeral (supposedly the body didn't even get to lie in the mourning hall for a full week, as was the custom), the clan declared Huto's cause of death to be a mysterious disease.

Years later, long after the Huto clan had faded into obscurity, if one were to ply an old mortician in Toaza with plenty of drink and silver, he might sometimes break the vows of his profession and describe for bar patrons the most terrifying corpse he had ever prepared for burial.

There had been nothing left of Tiphan Huto's throat and neck except a bloody, pulpy mess. If it weren't for his spine, the mortician was sure Tiphan's head would have separated from the rest of his body. He had to wrap layers and layers of silk around the base of the head to secure it to the torso.

"Did a wolf sneak into the Huto manor?" one patron asked in a frightened whisper.

"Was he attacked by a demon?" asked another, gulping rice beer for courage.

"No, no!" the mortician said, looking around at his audience slyly. "You'll never guess."

After another full tankard of rice beer had been set down in front of him, the mortician licked his lips and said, "It was him! He'd done it with his own fingers.

"He had scratched and clawed at his throat until he had torn away most of his neck! I cannot imagine his state of mind. Tazu must have been in his head."

CHAPTER THIRTY-EIGHT

A REBELLION
THAT ISN'T A REBELLION

PAN: THE ELEVENTH MONTH OF THE ELEVENTH
YEAR OF THE REIGN OF SEASON OF STORMS AND
THE REIGN OF AUDACIOUS FREEDOM.

The rain had started at sundown and grown heavier as the evening deepened. By the time bells at the Temple of the Twins tolled the second watch, rain was pouring in sheets, and waterfalls cascaded from every roof in Pan. Everyone, from merchants to ministers, from scholars to scullery maids, was home. Even the night watchmen shirked their patrols; not even gangs of thieves would work in such weather.

But on Pan's city walls, soldiers of the empire maintained their vigilance. The Harmonious City was full of dissonance, and even the lowest foot soldier could sense the tension in the air.

In a watchtower over the Gate of Toyemotika, the westernmost gate of the city, two soldiers huddled next to a stove, fighting off the late autumnal chill by drinking hot tea so thin that it was indistinguishable from water.

"Do you think Prince—er—Emperor Monadétu is still alive?" asked Asulu, a young man of eighteen from Arulugi's countryside.

Égi, a career soldier in his forties from the Tunoa Islands, chuckled at the question. "Of course he's alive."

"How do you know?" asked Asulu eagerly. "Did you hear something from a friend in the navy?" All available warships, excepting those needed to escort the tribute fleet to Rui, had been dispatched to hunt for pirates in the hopes of finding the missing emperor.

"No," said Égi. "But I don't think his disappearance had anything to do with pirates. What? Do you really believe that on the way home from Rui, the emperor decided to take a skiff out to fish away from the fleet and was kidnapped by pirates? Only children and fools would believe that preposterous story."

Asulu's face flushed. "But Prime Minister Cogo Yelu issued a proclamation for all fishing boats on the northern coast of the Big Island and Arulugi to stay home so the navy wouldn't mistake them for pirates. My cousins back home wrote to me to say they are worried. Every day they have to stay away from the sea is a lot of coppers they aren't earning."

"You know how to read and write? Ha! I underestimated you."

"I just know the zyndari letters, good enough to keep in touch with home without having to pay a letter writer. My cousins and I were among the first winter school students when Secretary Kidosu started building them."

Égi retrieved a tiny flask from under his armor and poured the contents into his cup and Asulu's. "Here, you need something stronger for the chill. I'm not saying that the navy isn't out there hustling, but I don't believe they are trying to catch pirates or find the emperor."

Asulu took a sip and grimaced as cheap sorghum liquor, even diluted, burned his throat. "So what are they doing?"

"Do you remember how during the summer, right after the empress recalled the invasion fleet and signed a new peace treaty, there were all sorts of protests against the resumption of tribute shipments to the Lyucu?" asked Égi.

Asulu nodded. "I happened to be on leave in Ginpen when some scholars occupied the city-ships seized from the Lyucu by the emperor and chained themselves to the masts to stage a hunger strike, demanding the empress continue the emperor's unfinished work."

"Ah, yes, those hunger strikers. Didn't Lady Ragi, the empress's emissary, have to drug them to get them to eat in the end? Anyway, another group of scholars raised money and hired a fleet of fishing boats to try to stop the tribute shipments to Rui at sea."

"I heard about that, too," said Asulu. "The scholars' boats got in the way of the tribute fleet and refused to budge, even when the navy escorts fired warning shots with stone-throwers. When marines finally boarded the fishing boats to seize them, several scholars jumped into the sea and drowned to show their resolve. Now those men and women had mettle!"

Égi sipped his tea. "Careful, you sound almost as if you admire those agitators."

Asulu didn't like contradicting a senior soldier, but he felt he had to say something. "I *do* think they were heroes. Usually, I only see bookworms debating nonsense in teahouses or cavorting in pricey indigo houses, their noodle-like arms draped around the girls. But those *toko dawiji* weren't afraid to die, and they tried to stand up for the common people."

Égi snorted. "How were they standing up for the common people? The tribute was going to feed the people of Rui and Dasu so they wouldn't starve to death."

"But the tribute ships were also sending over gold and silk for the Lyucu wolves! The scholars were saying that we should continue the emperor's mission to fight the Lyucu and free our people, not work like dogs to appease them so they could demand more—"

"You really want an all-out war?" asked Égi. "I was just a kid when the Hegemon and Emperor Ragin were fighting to see who would be lord of all Dara, and let me tell you, nothing compares to the suffering back then. The empress was right to put a stop to the emperor's military adventures. Better to be a minnow in peace than a cruben in war."

"But those poor people in Rui and Dasu—"

"I'm not saying they don't matter," said Égi. "But it's their tough luck to be born there instead of here. I'm not ashamed to say that I'm selfish, all right? I want to wake up safe and sound next to my Amo every day until I can't get up anymore, and to see my four girls grow up happy and start their own families."

Asulu didn't agree, but he didn't want to make the older soldier angry. "So what does this have to do with the navy and pirates?"

"Do you know who was leading those troublemaking scholars? It was Réza Müi, a bona fide *firoa*! After she and the other arrested scholars were brought to Pan, she refused to admit fault and apologize. I was surprised that the empress didn't have her executed as a traitor right away but instead just imprisoned her and let her go after a month. Anyway, the empress and the ministers must be concerned about more copycat rebellions—you know how bookworms love dramatic gestures for 'the good of the country' and *mutagé*, and a high-ranking bookworm like a *firoa* is an irresistible symbol to them. That's the real reason why fishing boats have been forbidden from going to sea, and the navy is patrolling to keep the waters clear for the tribute ships."

"So . . . if the emperor wasn't kidnapped by pirates, what do you think happened to him?"

Égi took a peek around the watchtower to be sure they were alone. Nonetheless, he lowered his voice as he continued, a cunning look in his eyes. "You have to use your head! Don't just listen to what the palace says; watch what it *does*. Farseers are swarming all over the veterans' societies; martial law has been imposed in the big cities; security in Pan has never been tighter. Why?"

"I thought we're watching out for Lyucu spies and bandits," said Asulu, looking bewildered. "To . . . protect the empress and the ministers."

"Why would the *Lyucu* want to harm the empress? She's basically their biggest ally and advocate here. And bandits? Why would anyone turn to banditry now when the harvests are good, taxes are light, and there's plenty of money to be made in honest ways? But there is *someone* who, if he were still alive, would be plotting against the empress."

A silkmotic lamp seemed to go on over Asulu's head. "Wait . . . are you saying the empress is trying to defend against . . . against . . . *a rebellion by the emperor*?"

"Shhh," shushed Égi. "Keep your voice down! There's a difference between knowing the truth and speaking it. The emperor has been seething under her iron fist for years. Why are you surprised that he might now be raising an army against her?"

"But to rebel against his aunt-mother!? She raised him after his own mother died—"

"Do you think the Imperial family is anything like our families?"

asked Égi. He spat contemptuously into the fire in the stove. "All that grand princes and Imperial consorts care about is power, and filial feelings are meaningless. Remember what happened to Mapidéré's children after he died? Now *that* was some bloody family drama. In any event, Empress Jia has been holding on to power for so long that it's clear she never intends to give it up to Prince—see, even you and I don't think of him as the real emperor."

"But what is the empress holding on to power *for*? She's not going to live forever."

"I don't pretend to understand the mind of a woman like that. But as best as I can figure, she's still trying to pass the throne to her son, Prince Timu—"

"The puppet emperor over there in Rui?"

"She was always scheming to have the succession go that way, back when Emperor Ragin was alive. And when he passed the throne to Princess Théra—who people say was closer to her father than her mother—I bet you ten silvers that Jia had something to do with how she drowned soon after—"

"Grand Princess Théra was sailing with her Agon husband to get us help from beyond the Wall of Storms—"

"Right, and if you believe that story, you probably also believe that Luan Zyaji once rode a balloon to the moon and brought back the secret of the silkmotic mill. Come on! There never was any Agon prince, no alliance with barbarians from beyond the seas, no crazy plan to sail through the Wall of Storms—what a fairy tale! It was all a sham manufactured by the empress and her cabal after they got rid of Théra, probably because the princess refused to be her mother's willing puppet."

The cascade of revelations was coming so fast that the younger soldier felt dizzy. "Uh . . . if there was no Agon alliance, how did we get the garinafin eggs?"

"Easy! Given how much tribute the empress has paid to the Lyucu, don't you think they'd be happy to give her some garinafin eggs in secret to help her secure her own power?"

"You think our garinafins came from the *Lyucu*? Our sworn enemy?"

"Why does that surprise you? Remember, ravens are as black in Tunoa as they are in Dasu; all grand lords and ladies wanting to hold on to power think alike. We commoners may find it hard to trust the Lyucu because of what they did—are still doing—to our people, but that kind of history wouldn't bother an ambitious person like Empress Jia."

"It's just so twisted and shocking—"

"You and I eat something and poop it straight out the day after. But the intestines of people who crave real power have eighty-one coils so that they can really let the shit ferment into cunning plots. Also, don't forget that Tanvanaki is Jia's daughter-in-law; they probably admire each other. If the Lyucu pékyu thinks giving Jia some garinafins will benefit them both, why should she hesitate?"

"That just doesn't make any sense! Our garinafins fought theirs!"

Égi sighed. "You are so naive. I imagine when Tanvanaki first gifted the garinafins to Empress Jia, it was a secret. But eventually, Phyro discovered the garinafins and took them over, which was how he was able to force the empress to let him go to war. Or maybe Tanvanaki and Jia had some kind of disagreement, and Jia decided to let Phyro go to war to show Tanvanaki that she still had teeth. Anyway, the point is: You can't believe anything the government tells you. There's always some kind of conspiracy behind it, which you can only decipher with experience and close observation."

Asulu took some time to digest all this information. "So . . . if I'm understanding this right: The empress was always bent on having Prince Timu on the Dandelion Throne. That's why she engineered the death of Grand Princess Théra, maintained the peace with the Lyucu, and refused to step aside as regent for the emperor. The peace treaty with the Lyucu is a smoke screen for a secret understanding between the empress and Tanvanaki to help each other stay in power. The garinafins are bargaining chips. And the emperor's failed invasion is really just the manifestation of a family power struggle."

Égi smiled and nodded with approval. "*Now* you're getting it. You gotta think for yourself. I bet you fifty silvers that once he reached the shores of Rui, away from the empress's eyes, the emperor was hoping to turn the army against the empress and march on Pan. But the empress was the more skilled plotter and got the control of the army back from him just in time. That's why he's in hiding now, trying to raise a new army against her."

Asulu felt chills going down his spine at this completely new view of politics. "Then . . . that means the empress didn't end the war out of concern for the people!"

"And the emperor wasn't invading Unredeemed Dara out of concern for the people either," said Égi. "They were—are both just fighting each other for more power."

"Surely it can't be as bad as that!"

"That's politics, kid. You must have heard plenty of teahouse storytellers. Emperor, duke, minister, general—they may talk of *mutagé* and 'the welfare of the people of Dara,' but ultimately, the only thing that matters to them is power."

Asulu pulled his cape tighter around his shoulders. He hated this new view of the world. He wished he had stayed home by his parents' side and never volunteered to join the army after seeing that inspiring play. . . . A new thought popped into his head.

"If you're right, then we're expected to fight against the emperor himself! That would be—"

"Treason?" Égi eyed him and chuckled. "I'm sure you're not the only one bothered by the thought. That's why the empress doesn't openly say that the emperor is rebelling against her. Bandits and Lyucu spies make convenient excuses."

"How can you be so calm about this? If you're right, we're fighting for a usurper! Kon Fiji always said—"

"I don't give a sheep's fart about what Kon Fiji said. The empress is the regent, and as long as she holds the Seal of Dara, I've got no problems with fighting for her against *anyone*."

"But the emperor is the legitimate—"

"I don't care about all that *legitimacy* nonsense," said Égi. He took a moment to calm himself down. "Look, I know you must be confused why I bother to defend the empress when I think she's a heartless, power-hungry schemer."

"I do wonder."

"All the Ano sages that the bookworms quote talk about serving the people of Dara, right? The way I figure it, it doesn't matter who sits on the Dandelion Throne, as long as they don't start wars, keep taxes low, preserve the roads from bandits, and let me and mine work honestly to fill our rice bowls. *That's* serving the people of Dara, and everything else is just noise."

"That's like saying a baby should call anyone who gives it milk 'mother.' Life has to be about more than just having full bellies. Whatever you say, I still believe the emperor was fighting to free the people of Rui and Dasu, and that's a cause worth rallying behind."

Égi sighed and looked at Asulu with pity. "Freeing the people of Rui and Dasu . . . eh, but have you thought through what that would cost?"

"The Lyucu aren't as invincible as some—"

"I'm not talking about the cost of the war itself—the lives lost would be impossible to measure for the families involved. I'm talking about something less lofty, but easier to measure. If somehow the emperor had succeeded and the Lyucu surrendered, do you realize how much it would cost to rebuild those two islands after what the Lyucu have done to them? Just taking care of the refugees from Unredeemed Dara now is bad enough, but multiply that by a hundredfold, a thousandfold! All of Dara would have to ship food, clothing, medicines, construction material . . . it'd be a lot more than the tribute we pay the Lyucu now, and I'll bet you a hundred silvers that taxes would go up through the roof! All of us would have to pay to clean up that mess."

Asulu was stunned. To be sure, he had never thought that far about what would happen after the war. He just felt that saving the people of Rui and Dasu was the right thing to do. Now he was having second thoughts because of Égi's speech, and he felt . . . ashamed.

As though reading his mind, Égi continued. "Trust me. Most people, especially those who own a little property, think like this. Even over the summer, when scholars and veterans seemed to be whipping everyone into a frenzy to support the emperor's invasion, I think most people remained opposed to the war. They just held their tongues because they didn't want to be shamed. But I'm shameless and I'll speak my mind."

Asulu gulped his alcohol-infused tea instead of saying anything.

"You're still young and foolish," said Égi. "When you're older and wiser, you won't be so contemptuous of a peace that you find . . . objectionable."

Asulu took a deep breath and said nothing. An awkward silence hung between them. At length, he tried to change the subject. "You . . . think the empress is a good ruler?"

Égi nodded. "Whatever her faults and schemes, Empress Jia *has* done well for all of us. The cattle herds are fat; the granaries are full; people are having lots of children; the markets are bustling with goods from every corner of Dara; the workshops and mills are booming and offer good wages for workers; the restaurants and indigo houses are full of customers; I can argue with the constables and magistrates and not feel terrified; if someone wrongs me, I can hire a paid litigator to get my due in the courts; the bookworms in the Imperial academies are told to come up with inventions that are useful instead of empty philosophy—and I have to admit, they do; and even I, a lowly soldier, have made enough to hire my girls a tutor to read some Ano Classics—me, who started as a peasant on a rocky isle in Tunoa, where even migrating wild geese wouldn't stop to shit!"

"What good is learning the Ano Classics for a soldier's daughters? I thought you said you didn't give a sheep's fart—"

"*I* may think Kon Fiji farted more than he talked sense, but you have to study him to move up in this world. And my eldest is smart! The Twins be praised, she's even taught me a few logograms—did you see me sign my name in front of the paymaster last week? Her tutor tells me she's got a real gift with book learning. If she keeps up her hard work, I'll pay to send her to an academy and have her take the examinations. Can you imagine? Me, the father of a *toko dawiji*?" Égi's face broke into a wide grin, as though he could already see that glorious future.

"May your daughter be like a golden carp of legend," said Asulu, and raised his teacup in a toast.

"I'll drink to that. But really, ask yourself: Doesn't everyone you know live better now than they did ten years ago?"

"That's true," confessed Asulu. "My parents sold their fishing boat and moved to Müning to open a tea stand. They picked a good spot, and have done well with all the merchants and scholars stopping by on their way to visit Princess Kikomi's Tomb."

"Exactly. So you ought to support the empress too."

"I don't know if I'd give her credit for everything," said Asulu. "She doesn't do much, does she? Seems all I hear is how she enjoys picking handsome young men to fill the Palace Garden—"

"Hey, maybe one day her carriage will pass through the Gate of Toyemotika, and she'll look up, and there you'll be, with your armor and helmet all polished, striking a pose like Fithowéo—"

"Shut up!"

When the two had recovered from their bout of lascivious laughter, Égi went on, "Anyway, Prime Minister Cogo Yelu and Farsight Secretary Zomi Kidosu probably deserve the bulk of the credit, and anyone can see they've straightened out the bureaucracy and got the officials *working* for us instead of *squeezing* us. Still, if anyone wants to start a war against the empress and mess up what we have, I'll fight them, even if they wave the banner of the emperor."

"You may sound all cynical, Égi, but I think you quite admire the empress—"

A loud boom outside the watchtower, not quite like thunder.

"Oh, by the Twins—do you see that?"

The two guards peered out from the watchtower and were astonished to see a firework explosion in the western sky. It was bright, golden, and the streaks persisted despite the rain: a gigantic, blooming dandelion.

A second boom, then a third. The multiple fireworks illuminated hulking shadows over the western horizon in the direction of Lake Tututika—airships? Yes, they had to be airships!

"He's really done it," muttered Asulu. "The emperor is really marching on Pan."

Égi struggled to pull on his helmet. "Don't just stand there! Sound the alarm!"

Soon, bright warning signal fires flared in the watchtowers along the western wall of Pan, and urgent bells reverberated over the city.

CHAPTER THIRTY-NINE

MADNESS

KRIPHI: THE ELEVENTH MONTH OF THE ELEVENTH
YEAR OF THE REIGN OF SEASON OF STORMS AND
THE REIGN OF AUDACIOUS FREEDOM.

Goztan climbed atop the hill and took in the field of rubble and weeds: all that remained of the ancient city of Kriphi.

Here and there, clumps of mushroom tents sprouted from the rubble, though they looked dirty, ill-maintained, leaky. There were no columns of cooking smoke or roaming riders to soften the monotony of the landscape, nor songs from young herders to relieve the oppressive air. The emaciated herds had long since escaped into the foothills to fight over what little vegetation remained near the once-bustling capital of Ukyu-taasa.

All she could hear was a faint chorus of desperate groans and dream-fervent mutterings of yearning, the pleas of hundreds of Lyucu warriors for their thirst to be slaked, for their hunger to be satisfied, for the burning lava coursing through their veins to be cooled by a soothing ambrosia that they no longer had access to.

How did this happen? What went wrong?

A young naro-votan ran up to her and saluted wearily. "Votan, there was another fight in the old market district. By the time we got there, six culeks had been injured. Two of them aren't likely to survive."

Goztan's face twitched. "What happened?"

So many thanes had fallen to tolyusa-madness that Cutanrovo had to turn to disgraced political rivals, even an old foe like herself, to help maintain order.

"One of the culeks saw her companion sneak out of camp, and she suspected he was hoarding tolyusa. She followed him out, and when she saw him duck down behind a broken wall without coming back up, she thought he was consuming the berries in secret. She gathered a few other culeks from the same camp and attacked him."

"But how did the fight become fatal?" asked Goztan. "My orders were to confiscate all weapons from camps where tolyusa use had been heavy."

The naro-votan looked revolted, but he forced himself to go on. "She bit him in the throat, thinking that she could get some of the potency of the tolyusa from his blood—"

Goztan flinched and gestured for him to stop.

It had been only three weeks since Cutanrovo issued the order to forbid the use of tolyusa in Kriphi except by shamans in religious rituals. It was an odd decision, since she had been the one to greatly expand the consumption of the berries at festivals, storytelling dances, and the various rallies she held to "enhance the Lyucu spirit," at which kyoffir and tolyusa flowed as freely as water—at least for those who professed hard-liner beliefs.

At first, the consequences of Cutanrovo's decision were unremarkable. Some warriors became irritable, and incidents of brawling and feuds increased. Thinking it merely a case of spoiled naros fuming over being denied a luxury, the thanes lectured the instigators severely and increased the punishment for those who fought privately and disrupted military discipline.

Among the tribes of the scrublands, it was not unheard of for warriors to occasionally fall prey to a kind of mad craving for kyoffir and tolyusa, but such incidents were rare and generally viewed as a manifestation of weakness. The sufferers were usually ostracized and denied the craved good until they recovered on their own, or, if they were powerful, simply given enough of it to function. Tolyusa-madness had never been a big problem.

No one could have anticipated how those early brawls and arguments would grow into an unprecedented crisis a week later. So many warriors—and even thanes—were now suffering from the worst case of tolyusa-madness in living memory that Kriphi was virtually paralyzed. The afflicted spent most of their time mired in a spiritless torpor, with no appetite or drive, flailing about on the ground and muttering for tolyusa, unable to rouse themselves to do anything useful. But once in a while, as though possessed by some demonic energy, they would lash out violently and need be subdued, before sinking back into that listless languor.

Worst off were the children of the afflicted. Some of them, mere babes, had been born with the madness in them. They now wailed, their fists balled, their faces red with a craving that they neither understood nor could name. The screams and cries nearly drove the nurses mad with their own helplessness.

Only culeks and low-ranking naros who had not been important enough to be granted a regular supply of tolyusa in the first place kept things running.

It was no longer possible to ignore the questions. Cutanrovo finally had to reveal the reasons behind her recent about-face on the use of the sacred berries.

She had been trading with the pirates—Cutanrovo was quick to point out that the pékyu herself had set the precedent—and among the goods she obtained were supplies of wild tolyusa from outside Ukyu-taasa.

Tanvanaki cursed Cutanrovo, and then she cursed herself.

She had never objected to the garinafin-thane's expansion of tolyusa use because the positive effects had been so obvious: at the spirit rallies, the battle dances had been so frenzied and the chanting so thunderous that Tanvanaki felt her warriors loving her more than they loved her father. Considering how many of the projects for making Ukyu-taasa to be more like Ukyu had failed, the spirit rallies were one of the few bright points in her increasingly dreary life. She had even taken tolyusa a few times herself and joined in the celebration, returning to her sleeping mat later with multiple virile thanes in tow, all ready to please her, all in tolyusa-haze. (The sullen Timu not only offered no comfort, but seemed to deliberately provoke her with constant questions about trivial subjects such as whether the cattle-breeding reports were accurate and whether the harvest figures could be trusted. She had banished him from her sleeping mat entirely.)

She should have known! The sparse patches of tolyusa on lava flows on Rui and Dasu—barely enough to maintain the garinafin force and to sustain sacred rituals—could not possibly have supplied enough berries to support Cutanrovo's largesse. She had willfully refused to ask Cutanrovo questions because she had been afraid she wouldn't like the answers, and she didn't want her one pleasure taken away.

"As of two months ago," Cutanrovo added reluctantly, "none of the pirates had any to sell, no matter how much gold I offered."

Tanvanaki shivered. Ever since the revelation that Dara proper had its own secret garinafin force, she had been wondering how Jia and Phyro had been able to breed and maintain the creatures without their own tolyusa—a decade ago, Tanvanaki had destroyed the source patches on Crescent Island after obtaining the berries for Ukyu-taasa. Now that it was confirmed that tolyusa was flourishing in Dara proper and being smuggled into Ukyu-taasa, Tanvanaki was confronted by a new question: Given that Jia and her ministers must have understood the military value of the plant and taken measures to keep it under strict control, how could there be so much "wild tolyusa" for the pirates to gather?

"I've been rationing the store of tolyusa, waiting for the supply to resume," said Cutanrovo, sounding defensive. "However, the success of repelling the Dara-raaki invaders and the increased tribute from our foes seemed to justify more celebrations. I fear and trust the gods, and so I ordered more festivals—"

"Enough excuses!" said Tanvanaki, gritting her teeth. "Divert all the tolyusa we're growing for military use to alleviate this madness. It will pass soon enough, and we can always delay garinafin breeding by another season."

"There is . . . uh . . . another problem."

Right before the pirate fleets stopped bringing more wild tolyusa, a mysterious blight had struck tolyusa patches all around Rui. A white powder, perhaps a kind of fungus, covered the plants like frost. Leaves withered, flowers wilted, berries shriveled, and entire lava-flows' worth of plants had died within days. As of now, there was no living tolyusa anywhere in Rui.

"Why didn't you report this?" demanded Tanvanaki, feeling dizzy. The nightmare scenario that the evil Luan Zya had tried to foist on the Lyucu more than a decade ago returned to the pékyu's memory. Without tolyusa, the Lyucu were utterly doomed.

"I thought we could replenish the stock by scattering some of the wild tolyusa obtained from Dara proper," said Cutanrovo. "But . . . but they turned out to be sterile."

Tanvanaki erupted out of her seat and faltered as she felt the blood rush to her head. "Sterile?"

"The berries would not sprout," Cutanrovo said, her voice sullen. "I . . . I don't know why. Some of the native slaves claimed that the berries had perhaps been roasted ahead of time to remove their vitality, but what do the mud-legged slaves know of our sacred berries?"

Is it the will of the gods to end us? Tanvanaki thought in despair. *Or is it . . . a plot? No, impossible!*

The existential threat to the garinafin force finally forced Tanvanaki to do the previously unthinkable. She turned to her old friend, Goztan Ryoto. The garinafin-thane had been sidelined since the defeat at Crescent Island, but there was no one that Tanvanaki trusted more on matters involving garinafins or tolyusa. Goztan was restored from disgrace—and even Cutanrovo couldn't object.

"There remains another way," offered Goztan, after having been informed of the crisis. "We should still have patches of tolyusa on Dasu—not many, since exposed lava flows are scarce on the island, but at least a few. If they've been preserved from the blight, we can use the harvested berries to help the warriors suffering from tolyusa-madness and replenish our stock."

And so Goztan had been dispatched on her errand. To prevent inadvertently carrying the blight to Dasu, Tanvanaki prohibited all traffic by air, water, or tunnel between the islands. To get to Dasu, Goztan and her crew bathed themselves in scalding water, and then boarded a boat naked. They were met in the middle of the channel by another boat from Dasu, and before stepping across the gang-plank, they bathed themselves once more to be sure that when they stepped onto the new boat, not even a single speck of dust from Rui came with them.

Fortunately, the tolyusa in Dasu *had* escaped the blight. Goztan and her crew returned, laden with all the tolyusa berries they could carry.

But a quick meeting with Cutanrovo led to more bad news. In Goztan's absence, the decline in Kriphi had been precipitous. The Lyucu capital now resembled a camp of invalids more than the heart of Ukyu-taasa. She had seen similar sights at other encampments across Rui on her way back.

Everywhere, thanes and warriors dozed in their tents or in the shade of broken walls, dreaming of tolyusa, the general lethargy punctuated only by bursts of violence. Abruptly, someone would lash out at those around them, demanding that they yield up the precious berries. With bloody eyes and frothing mouths, they fused into paranoia-fueled mobs, attacking the teams of thanes and warriors attempting to maintain order.

"Where is the pékyu?" asked Goztan.

Cutanrovo looked away, saying nothing.

Goztan sighed. She knew that Tanvanaki felt no joy at the triumph over Phyro. It had not been an honest victory obtained by force of arms, but the result of a threat made against the hapless natives that destroyed the last shred of credibility in the notion that the Lyucu were "liberators." Moreover, Tanvanaki and Goztan both suspected that Jia had recalled Phyro because the regent was more afraid of the young emperor than she was afraid of the Lyucu. It was about as shameful a way to "win" as could be imagined.

No wonder Tanvanaki didn't want to face the reality of this never-would-be Taten, to acknowledge how much she had failed to achieve the dream of her father and fallen short of the goals she had set herself.

Ukyu-taasa craved the comforting presence of some sign of authority, and in the gap created by Tanvanaki's refusal to engage, others had stepped in. Cutanrovo, who had staved off the madness herself because she could still access a tiny reserve of ritual-use wild tolyusa in her capacity as chief shaman, had declared the general malaise a punishment imposed by the gods for the decline of the

Lyucu spirit. To propitiate the gods, she ordered more human sacrifices. A thousand native slaves had been slaughtered in an elaborate multiday ritual.

It had not helped. There was no sign that the madness was lifting at all from the panting, groaning, fever-tossed bodies of the afflicted.

The corpses of the sacrificial victims were heaped high at the former site of the palace, a macabre echo of the demolished Mingén Tower. Falcons circled the decomposing bodies, their stench shooting straight into the sky. Clouds of flies buzzed and swarmed.

But the sacrifices did accomplish something: While most able-bodied Lyucu in Kriphi had been summoned to witness and celebrate the slaughters, a fire had broken out in the granaries and icehouses near the floating wharves, where the tribute of grain and meat from Dara proper was stored. Whether it was an act of sabotage or simply the result of a madness-stricken naro knocking over a torch, no one could say. By the time the fire was put out, most of the tribute had been ruined.

Goztan hoped the gods, whichever ones kept watch over this cursed land, were well satisfied.

For now, ad-hoc patrols consisting of low-ranking culeks led by naros and thanes with accommodationist sympathies managed to frighten the slave population into docility. (Since these naros and thanes had been disfavored by Cutanrovo, they had not shared in the generous portions of tolyusa that Cutanrovo had been doling out to her supporters. They were thus mostly free of the madness.) As yet, there had been no organized native uprisings.

But Goztan dared not think of the consequences once the enslaved realized the true precarious state of the ruling race in Ukyu-taasa.

"Start distributing the tolyusa," Goztan ordered her crew. "It's time to clear the madness from their minds and restore the Lyucu to some semblance of a fighting force."

Then she stared at the imposing form of the Great Tent. It had been days since Tanvanaki had emerged from her self-imposed seclusion.

Timu cowered in the corner of the small tent that served as his present sleeping quarters, the imprint of Tanvanaki's hand a pale shadow against his face as he shielded his head with an arm.

Dyana threw herself on her father's body. "Mother! Mother! Please don't hit him. Please! Whatever he did, he's very sorry."

Tanvanaki ignored her daughter. She stood glaring down at the frail, curled-up body of her husband, her hand trembling as she held up a scroll in her left hand. "Cutanrovo found this in the possession of one of your guards as he was trying to steal a fishing skiff near the coast. Is this your hand?"

Slowly, Timu moved his arm away and looked up at his wife. He swallowed. "Yes," he croaked.

Tanvanaki tore the silk scroll in half, balled it up so that the wax logograms crumbled and sloughed off, and threw the mess away. She took two steps forward, lifted a screaming Dyana off the body of Timu, and proceeded to deliver a series of kicks to his ribs and stomach.

"How dare you plot against me!" raged Tanvanaki. "You speak of trying to build a Dara in which the Lyucu have a place, and yet behind my back, you would invite your mother's army to come and slaughter my people!"

Timu grunted and groaned as the kicks landed, but he made no effort at resisting, only shielding his face and head. "I was not plotting against the interests of *our* people. I only wrote to ask for another shipment of food and clothing for Ukyu-taasa—argh!" He screamed as a rib broke.

"Mother! No! Please—" Dyana wrenched free of Tanvanaki's hand and dropped to shield her father again with her body. "You're hurting him!"

"It's code!" shouted Tanvanaki, looming over the curled-up body of Timu. "I know how your devious mind works. Everything is buried under layer after layer of allusions and word games and hidden references; nothing is as it seems. You're trying to tell Jia that we're weak, inviting her to invade!"

"But we *are* weak—"

"Father, stop talking! Stop—"

"Lies, all lies!" Tanvanaki leaned down to scream in Timu's face. "The tribute grain and meat may be gone, but there have been no reports of food shortages at all! We *have* put down roots in Ukyu-taasa.

Once Goztan has secured a domestic supply of tolyusa, we'll be back to full health in no time. How dare you make false claims about our peerless strength, about our indomitable spirit—"

"Vadyu," Timu croaked, his voice unsteady from the pain, "listen to yourself. . . . Have you really *looked* at the world outside the Great Tent? The day of reckoning is coming, whether you like it or not."

Cutanrovo Ago and Goztan Ryoto stood before the pékyu in council. The Great Tent was otherwise deserted.

"You knew?" Tanvanaki roared.

Goztan's clinical summary had felt like a physical blow to Tanvanaki. Cutanrovo, on the other hand, had looked bored as she listened to the report.

Cutanrovo inclined her head defiantly. "I had long heard sporadic reports that the tolyusa we find in the military reserve lava flows lacks the potency of the wild tolyusa obtained from the pirates."

Upon her return, Goztan had immediately distributed the precious Dasu tolyusa to the afflicted. Though at first the berries appeared to revive them, the effect soon wore off. In fact, the berries only seemed to have sharpened their craving, and upon sobering from the haze, they became even more violent than before, lashing out at family and friends with inhuman strength and fury. They had to be restrained.

"Why didn't you do something about these reports?" demanded Tanvanaki.

"I did!" protested Cutanrovo. "I suppressed these reports and disciplined those who dared to speak of the difference between domestic and imported tolyusa."

Tanvanaki stared at her in disbelief. "You *suppressed* the reports and hid them from me? What were you thinking?"

"Votan, consider the matter from a dispassionate perspective," said Cutanrovo. She didn't act as though she had done anything wrong; instead, she began to stride around the Great Tent, waxing eloquent as she gestured animatedly.

"Tolyusa is the heart of Lyucu spirituality. While I believe the fact that wild tolyusa from Dara proper is more potent than the berries found on Rui and Dasu is a sign that the gods favor our settlement in *all* these Islands, not everyone is as stouthearted or clearheaded as me. I realized that rumors that tolyusa from Dara proper was more powerful than the domestic variety would have demoralized our warriors, feeding into a defeatist narrative that perhaps the gods favor the natives and lavish them with gifts."

Cutanrovo took a quick glance at Goztan before continuing. "An adjustment to the facts was necessary to combat a certain biased attitude against our own inevitable dominion over all Dara, especially among thanes and warriors who have been corrupted by native influence. I thought there was no harm in concealing from everyone the source of the potent tolyusa, since we would soon control all Dara."

"'An adjustment to the facts,'" repeated Tanvanaki mockingly. "Oh, Cutanrovo, you are no less cunning with words than the native scholars you so despise."

Before Cutanrovo could respond, Goztan broke in. "I don't think the gods have anything to do with the potency of the tolyusa from Dara proper."

"What do you mean?" asked Tanvanaki.

"Tolyusa, named zomi berry by the natives, was unknown in Dara before the pékyu-votan's expeditions," said Goztan. "Therefore it seems reasonable to suppose that the wild tolyusa in all Dara is derived from stock brought from Ukyu. Given how little time has passed, I don't think it's likely that different strains of the plant could have developed between the islands. After all, even our tolyusa here in Ukyu-taasa was derived from wild stock retrieved from Crescent Island."

Tanvanaki's expression was hard. She already had an inkling of what Goztan was going to say. "Go on."

"The natives are skilled in cultivation," said Goztan, "an art we are ignorant of. Cultivation and breeding can change the nature of plants, as attested by the many varieties of sorghum and rice that the natives grow—each with traits desired by the cultivator amplified. I've compared the little imported tolyusa we have left with the domestic tolyusa from Dasu. I don't believe that the imported tolyusa was wild at all, but *cultivated*, and cultivated specifically for the potency of its delirium."

"That's preposterous!" exclaimed Cutanrovo. "Tolyusa is the very embodiment of our free spirit. How dare you claim that its powers can be tamed and subjected to Dara-raaki manipulation? This is sacrilege! It's defeatist—"

"There is yet more evidence of manipulation," said Goztan calmly. "I've also reconstructed the progress of the tolyusa blight across Rui. The first outbreaks were near the floating wharves of Kriphi, where the tribute ships dock, and then spread from there. I think it's possible that the blight came with the imported tolyusa, and the intent was to make us completely dependent on the manipulated supply, which has now been cut off."

"You sound like a native with all this talk of 'cultivation' and enslaving nature! If you know so much about their ways, you clearly have too much idle time on your hands—"

"One does tend to have more time to look into the truth when one isn't immersed in a tolyusa-induced delirium and killing slaves for sport—"

"More sacrilege! More defeatism—"

"That's enough!" roared Tanvanaki again. Goztan had voiced aloud the greatest fear in her heart, facts that she had been trying to deny.

Have I been played? While I've been fending off Phyro's garinafin riders, was it Jia's apparent submission that I should have been far more on guard against?

"Goztan's suspicion is . . . reasonable," mused Tanvanaki. "You never did ascertain from the pirates that the tolyusa they shipped you was found in the wild, did you? And how do you explain the fact that the berries are sterile without manipulation?"

Cutanrovo seemed stumped, but only briefly. "If, and I emphasize *if*, Thane Goztan's outrageous conspiracy theory is true, then all the more reason for us to conceal the real source of the tolyusa. Can you imagine the average naro or culek knowing that the sacred berries that bring them close to the gods are the product of native *craft*? Such knowledge would further sap the Lyucu spirit and bias our warriors against our own proud traditions, making them think that cultivation and enslaving the land were acceptable or even superior practices—"

"It is reality that has a bias against our traditions, you fool!" The world seemed to reel about her as Tanvanaki felt the blood surge into her head.

A pékyu must be able to tell true stories apart from false ones.

"No!" countered Cutanrovo heatedly. "Appeal to so-called 'reality' is the most seductive call of the accommodationists. But we *make* our reality, not the other way around. If the pékyu-votan had been saddled by this defeatist worship of 'facts,' we would never have defeated Admiral Krita or conquered Ukyu-taasa. The Dara-raaki are superior to us in armament and numbers, yet, he persisted, and that is why we—"

"You will not lecture *me* about my father!" Tanvanaki shouted. "He learned all he could about the natives so that he could defeat them, while you refuse to learn from them even to survive!"

But I'm no better than Cutanrovo. She's blinded by her contempt for the natives, but what excuse do I have? I've allowed Ukyu-taasa to become dependent on our enemies for sustenance, for spiritual nourishment, for self-regard. We crave what they supply.

How can I face my father among the cloud-garinafins?

She took a deep breath to calm herself. This wasn't the time to berate and blame, but to act.

"Your 'adjustment' of facts has come close to dooming us. Fortunately, we still have tolyusa from Dasu to maintain the garinafins. Keep the afflicted under watch so that they don't harm themselves. Give them plenty of water but no berries. Only when the last traces of the manipulated tolyusa have left their body and they've become docile can you start giving them small amounts of the pure variety, if necessary, to revive them. We know how to deal with such madness, even if the scale is unprecedented."

Jia, you may think you have crippled us. But we've put down roots in Dara, and you will not eliminate us like so many weeds from your garden.

"Now that the tribute grain and meat have been ruined, both of you need to work together to implement a rationing scheme to allow us to last through the fall until the next shipment. Our flocks and herds, thin as they are, must carry us through. And the harvest cannot be disrupted. We can weather this storm."

"There's nothing to it," said Cutanrovo. "Votan, don't let the weak-willed deceive you—"

"Keep the natives fed." Tanvanaki gave Cutanrovo a hard glare. "With so many of our warriors laid low by the madness, we cannot afford any uprisings. Do you understand?"

Cutanrovo and Goztan nodded.

CHAPTER FORTY

THE BATTLE OF PAN, PART I

PAN: THE ELEVENTH MONTH OF THE ELEVENTH
YEAR OF THE REIGN OF SEASON OF STORMS AND
THE REIGN OF AUDACIOUS FREEDOM.

Prime Minister Cogo Yelu and Princess Aya Mazoti dashed through the palace, heading straight for the private quarters of the Imperial family. To minimize delay, both held up the symbols of their offices—Cogo's blue jade compass and Aya's ceremonial bamboo sword—so that they could be identified from a distance.

At this late hour, most of the courtiers and ladies-in-waiting were asleep, and the guards on duty retreated out of the way of the running pair without challenge.

Just as the two were about to pass through the gate in the Wall of Tranquility, however, a pair of swords crossed in front of them, missing Cogo Yelu's nose by an inch.

Cogo tried to come to a stop, but Aya crashed into him. The swords followed the Prime Minister's tumbling figure and cut into his robe, drawing blood.

Clumsily, Cogo knelt up. One hand shielding his face against the harsh beams of the silkmotic lamps held by the Dyran Fins, he raised his blue jade compass with the other hand. "There is an urgent matter that needs the empress's attention."

The two women, heedless of the heavy rain, looked at him without expression. "The empress is not to be disturbed."

Ever since Phyro's disappearance, Jia had increased security in the palace and secluded herself. Not only had formal court been suspended, but she no longer even called sessions of the Inner Council. Even the palace guards had been put under the command of the Dyran Fins, and Wi and Shido had altered the protocol to forbid anyone from entering the Imperial quarters at night.

The empress's paranoia had become the subject of much whisper at the court, and fueled the feverish speculation among teahouse storytellers.

Cogo pointed up at the raining sky. "Can't you hear the bells tolling? Pan is being invaded!"

The Dyran Fins looked at each other, and one of the women pointed at Aya. "She's armed."

"This is a bamboo sword!" cried Aya. "Look, it doesn't cut anything!" She held it out so that the women could examine it.

Since the days of Emperor Ragin, court protocol forbade anyone, save the palace guards, to be armed inside the palace—with Gin Mazoti, Aya's mother, being a notable exception. Since Marquess Puma Yemu had been placed under house arrest upon his return to Pan, Aya Mazoti, the most senior military commander who still held the empress's trust, had been put in charge of the city's defenses. Thus, her paper staff had been exchanged for a bamboo sword.

"It doesn't matter," said one of the Dyran Fins. "The empress won't allow anyone except us inside the private quarters at this hour. If you have a message, we'll pass it on."

"We're not *anyone*!" Aya Mazoti said, frustrated. "We're her Prime Minister and the general defending Pan! We have to talk to her, now!"

"Anyone could be an assassin," said the Dyran Fin, unmoved.

Cogo, still trying to brush off the mud from his robe, looked thoughtful. "What about . . . the young men who warm her bed at night?"

"They strip here, and go to her naked," said the Dyran Fin.

"To show that they have no concealed weapons," mused Cogo.

The Dyran Fins nodded.

Aya strove not to stare as the three nude young men scrambled away, escorted by the Dyran Fins.

Her own nakedness was distracting. Like a pair of newborns, she and Cogo had run through the Palace Garden in the pouring rain without a stitch of clothing, surrounded by four Dyran Fins. Water had pooled at her feet, and her hair was plastered against her back. She shivered, not just from the cold, but the sense of humiliation.

There must be a way to make visitors more comfortable if the empress insists on this . . . treatment. Perhaps a set of screens around each person so that only the head is visible, like rabbits peeking out of their holes. . . .

Cogo Yelu had to do most of the talking; she was too embarrassed to speak.

Empress Jia was sitting up in bed. Without her makeup or Imperial regalia, draped in a simple silk gown, her head lowered in thought, she looked frail and vulnerable. For the moment, she was no longer the most powerful person in all of Dara, but an old woman, alone and very mortal.

And then the moment was gone.

Jia looked up, and her steely eyes, the color of aged plum wine, locked onto Aya's. There was no weakness or mercy in that gaze, and Aya shivered again.

"What have you done so far in response?" Jia asked, her voice unperturbed.

Silence.

Cogo turned to look at her. He didn't look any more dignified than she did, but he seemed to be accepting their state with far more grace. He coughed discreetly.

"Oh . . . oh!" Aya didn't know where to put her hands, so she performed a *jiri*, which at least had the benefit of allowing her to avert her eyes from the empress's unrelenting glare. "I've dispatched three Imperial airship squadrons to Lake Tututika."

"Have you?" Jia's voice remained placid. "Don't you think that's a bit excessive?"

Aya's heart sped up. "Marshal Mazoti wrote, 'When stronger in numbers, bring the war to the enemy; when weaker, let the enemy come to—' "

"Don't quote Gin at me," snapped Jia. "I need you to *think*, not fight a war on paper. Did it ever occur to you that these shadow airships so far from the city might be a diversion?"

"Your Imperial Majesty," Cogo broke in, "I think Aya's strategy is sound. Fighting near Pan will lead to panic and far greater destruction to the city, whereas meeting the . . . rebels out there will minimize casualties. A diversion is unlikely since we know that the emperor does not have a large army—"

"Do we?" Jia turned her cold gaze on him. "We now know that Zomi had been conspiring with Phyro for years to push us into a war. You and Gori have taken over the farseers for only a few months. Can you be sure they're telling you the truth?"

"Phyro does not wish to plunge Dara into general civil war—"

"So you're basing everything on the goodwill of my son, a son who is now in open rebellion?"

"He could have mutinied off the coast of Rui and led his army to march on Pan," said Cogo. "But he chose to go into exile alone. Even now, he has not openly rebelled, and most people believe he is simply missing, perhaps a hostage of bandits—"

"I think you overestimate how many people believe that story," said Jia.

"Nonetheless, Phyro has not called on generals loyal to him to rally to his cause. He is angry with you for the peace with the Lyucu, but I don't believe he wishes to destroy the prosperous peace of the House of Dandelion. His aim . . . appears to be only you."

"Only me . . ." Jia's voice trailed off. Then she regarded Cogo coolly. "Since you're such an expert on his thinking, perhaps you've been in closer communication with him than I understood. Do you wish to initiate a coup and bring me, shackled, to see him?"

Cogo knelt down immediately. "Your Imperial Majesty, I've always served the people of Dara. For the emperor to illegitimately seize the Seal of Dara by force from you, Emperor Ragin's appointed regent, would set a terrible precedent. It would encourage endless acts of ambition in the future and sunder Kuni's legacy. I swear by the spirit of my departed old friend that I do not support the emperor's rash actions."

"You still believe peace with the Lyucu was the right decision?"

"With all my heart," said Cogo.

Jia sighed. She turned to Aya. "What about you?"

Aya fell to her knees as well. "My charge is to secure Pan against enemies both foreign and domestic, and I will do so to my last breath."

She had been more shocked than anyone else when she found out that Phyro had disappeared after the failed invasion of Rui and Dasu. Having become a proponent of Phyro's military plans, it was difficult for her to choose between her instinctive desire to obey Jia, the holder of the Seal of Dara for most of her life, and her admiration for the man who had always been like a brother to her.

But so long as Jia was the holder of the Seal of Dara, she was the regent, the one and only rightful ruler. Her own mother had ended up as a traitor for promoting the claim of Phyro to the throne over the claim of Timu, for trying to arrogate to herself an authority that she didn't possess. She would not make that same mistake, even if her heart bled in sympathy with Phyro's rage.

Mother, I won't let the Mazoti name be once more associated with betrayal.

Jia sighed and resumed speaking in measured tones. "You're right that the only head he wants is mine. He doesn't want to start a general civil war and give the Lyucu an opportunity to take advantage of the chaos. He also has a romantic yearning for the kind of direct confrontation that the Hegemon preferred. . . .

"Therefore, he's most likely to wage a quick, concentrated assault on Pan with a small but elite force, with the aim of reaching me in as little time as possible—"

"Which means he will prize speed and aerial access," said Aya. "In other words, airships."

Jia nodded, though it was unclear if she was really convinced.

"Aya has sent an overwhelming force to meet him," continued Cogo. "There is a good chance we'll defeat him quickly and capture him without the loss of many lives. The emperor is rash to resort to violence to seize the throne from you, though it is perhaps to be expected given his warlike nature. I trust that, once he has been seized, in time he will come to understand your wisdom in seeking peace with the Lyucu to save lives."

"Understand my wisdom . . . ," muttered Jia. Then she laughed bitterly.

A Dyran Fin appeared at the door of the bedroom. "Mistress, there's a group of ministers and generals clamoring to see you at the Wall of Tranquility. It might take too long to ask them all to strip—"

"It's all right," said Jia, getting up off her bed. "Dress me. I'll hold court. If my son wants a direct confrontation, then I'll give it to him."

Never before in the records of the court historians had the Grand Audience Hall been filled for formal court at such a late hour.

Well, "formal" was probably not exactly the right word. Silkmotic lamps—a recent addition by Princess Aya to the Grand Audience Hall to reduce the risk of fires from open-flame torches—revealed a less-than-solemn scene. The ministers and generals had gotten dressed in haste, and many were not in proper court regalia, missing a symbol of office here or a piece of ceremonial armor there. A few had even put on their robes inside out.

As Empress Jia sat atop the dais, presiding over the veiled Dandelion Throne and two columns of unkempt civil officials and military officers, farseers and soldiers streamed in to deliver their reports.

"Airships near the coast of Lake Tututika are holding their positions," reported one farseer.

"New airships sighted to the north of Pan at a distance of ten miles," said another farseer.

"More airships?" Aya blurted. "How is that possible?"

The farseer had no answer to that. "Commander Dün of the Fourth Air Squadron requests permission to launch and engage."

"No!" said Aya, the empress's warning blaring in her mind. "We have to maintain an air cover over the capital itself."

"Multiple fireworks sighted to the south of Pan," said a third farseer. "Precise launch point is unknown, but they don't appear to be from any known town or village. Commander Mutu of the Gate of Kana requests permission to send a scouting party of five hundred-chiefs and their units to investigate."

"Permission denied," said Aya, blood draining from her face. "We . . . we don't know if this is a diversion. . . . Signal for the three squadrons heading for Lake Tututika to return immediately!"

"Disturbance at the Gate of Tazu. A large group congregated at the gate, banging on drums and cymbals, playing coconut lutes, and singing lines from *The Women of Zudi*."

"In the middle of this storm?" Aya was incredulous.

The young gate guard delivering the report nodded. "They were also shouting that . . . that . . ." The guard glanced at Empress Jia with frightened eyes.

"They called me a usurper and tyrant and running dog of the Lyucu, and probably worse," said the empress. "It's all right. You're just the messenger."

The young guard swallowed gratefully. "The garrison commander sent a detachment of men down from the tower to arrest the troublemakers, but the soldiers . . . hesitated, and the mob was able to disperse and escape."

"Why did the soldiers *hesitate*?" demanded Aya.

"The group used some trick to fill the air with smoke, and a bright, giant image of Emperor Ragin materialized in the haze. Some of the soldiers knelt down to pray to the emperor, and the rest refused to advance against the mob. The garrison commander is having them whipped."

"Risana would be pleased with her son," said Jia in a faint voice, sounding rather amused. No one else spoke.

"Thick smoke and foul odors from several warehouses in Market Square . . ."

"Reports of ghost sightings of Emperor Ragin and Empress Risana in the auditorium of the Imperial Academy . . ."

"Soldiers at the Gate of Fithowéo have barricaded themselves in the watchtower. They claim that the iron railings are charged with silkmotic force and will bite them. The garrison commander requests engineers. . . ."

"Multiple members of the College of Advocates are kneeling outside the palace, demanding to know the whereabouts of Farsight Secretary Kidosu. . . ."

. . .

"Not a very large army, did you say?" Jia looked at Cogo, a bitter smirk on her face.

Cogo bowed. "The emperor is resourceful."

Aya felt the claws of panic scraping against her throat. The intelligence from the farseers had never indicated that Phyro had the manpower or resources to assault Pan from multiple directions, or that the city was filled with saboteurs. Her defense plan was in shambles.

"It is very clever of him to invoke the name of his father against me," said Jia, almost admiringly. "He's always known how to reach the hearts of soldiers."

Cogo bowed again. "Military monitors at all levels remain loyal. Though many of the younger soldiers are impressed with the emperor's martial prowess, the senior commanders can be trusted. There will be no general mutiny."

"He won't need a general mutiny. It'll be enough for the soldiers to *hesitate* when he shows up."

"*Rénga!*" Aya finally found her voice. "It's inconceivable for the emperor to launch an assault on Pan from every direction. Most of these disturbances *must* be diversions. He's concentrating his real attack in only one direction."

"Maybe," said Jia. "But we can't afford to send airships and soldiers after every phantom threat to be sure. He may indeed have only a tiny corps of die-hard followers, but by inundating us with ghosts, he's neutralized our advantage. We can't tell where his true strength lies."

"Yes, we can," said Aya.

I am the daughter of Luan Zyaji and Gin Mazoti. I will not *be outplayed.*

Cogo and Jia looked at her.

"The emperor was a close student of my mother's tactics," said Aya. "She was skilled in the use of feints and surprises, and she always said one should confuse the enemy by making apparent feints the real strikes, and apparent weaknesses strengths."

"Go on," said Cogo.

"The airships in the west were sighted first, and they remain the farthest away," said Aya, gaining confidence as she ticked through her reasoning. "In fact, lookouts say that they haven't moved at all. It's natural to conclude that they pose the least threat."

"They are undoubtedly mere bait, as I suspected at first," said the empress. "The intent is to draw our air force away from Pan."

"That's exactly what the emperor wants us to think," said Aya. "Because the assault from the west appears most like a feint, it must therefore be the only true attack."

Jia and Cogo looked at each other, hesitating.

"Emperor Ragin always said that once you have worked out all the odds, you still have to toss the dice, to take that leap of faith," declared Aya. "I am certain that the emperor is in the west, and we can end this quickly if we focus our efforts there."

After a perfunctory debate among the other generals, the consensus sided with Aya. (Truth be told, no one was going to gainsay the daughter of the legendary Marshal Mazoti, especially not after she quoted both her mother and Emperor Ragin.)

"Belay the order to recall Admiral Temururi," Aya commanded. "Launch the last two squadrons of airships to the west as well to aid her. Maintain stealth, but make all haste. We'll catch the emperor with a surprise of our own!"

"Make sure Phyro isn't harmed," added the empress.

LATER THE SAME NIGHT, NEAR LAKE TUTUTIKA, WEST OF PAN.

Admiral Temururi, a thirty-year veteran of the air force, had never fought a battle as confusing or with as conflicted a heart.

The incessant rain lashed the hull of her flagship, *Rana Kida*, sounding like the drums of war. She strained to peer through the windshield of the bridge for shadows of enemy airships. Below and behind her, the entirety of Pan's air force followed in a tight cluster.

She had flown only a few miles on this stormy night, but Temururi thought about how far she had journeyed to get to this moment.

The illegitimate daughter of a Gan merchant's son and his chambermaid, she and her mother were kicked into the streets to fend for themselves before she was a week old. "Temururi" was the name of the merchant's biggest competitor, and this bit of symbolic revenge was all the girl's mother could muster.

Mother and daughter drifted through towns in Géjira, scraping by as laundresses, fruit pickers, field laborers, scullery maids, and sometimes beggars. When neither work nor charity could be found, sometimes her mother dug up tough wild roots for the two to chew to keep the pangs of hunger at bay. And the girl would climb trees—terrifying her mother as she swung from branch to branch like a monkey—to find bird eggs as a treat.

The powerful dictated the lives of the poor. She never dreamed the world would be otherwise.

"We're approaching the location the enemy fleet was last sighted," the navigator whispered.

"Full stop," ordered the admiral, keeping her voice low as well. In stealth mode, airships ran silent and dark. No silkmotic lamps or torches were lit; even the use of signaling bells and clappers was forbidden. Orders had to be passed by whispers among the crew. Ship-to-ship communication would have been impossible but for Temururi's innovation: the signaling lines that dangled between the tightly clustered airships, attached to muffled clappers at each end.

"Keep your eyes peeled," Temururi ordered. Then, knowing the question that was silently echoing through the mind of everyone on the bridge, she added, "I don't know either."

How are we supposed to see anything through all this rain?

Nighttime aerial battles were rare in Dara. Airships, their translucent hulls lit up from within, glowed like luminescent jellyfish drifting leisurely through an inky sea lit only by stars, making them easy targets. Thus, airships that had to fight at night operated in stealth mode, much like underwater mechanical crubens. These tended to be small skirmishes involving a single ship on each side. The two combatants, circling each other in darkness, practically blind, instinctual, slow-moving, resembled creatures of the deep far more than inhabitants of the sky.

Large fleets generally avoided maneuvering in stealth due to the risk of collisions and friendly fire. But Princess Aya Mazoti had demanded that a fleet of five squadrons engage the enemy in stealth.

At night.

In the middle of a storm.

It was a ridiculous order. The princess had no understanding of how airships worked, but there had been no chance for Temururi to raise her objections.

"Do you hear that?" whispered the navigator.

"What do you mean?" demanded Temururi.

"It's a buzzing . . . or . . . more like a fluttering."

The bridge staff held their breath and listened. But it was impossible to tell if they were really hearing anything through the thumping of raindrops against the varnished silk hull, or if they were merely imagining things.

"What are we waiting for?" asked the military monitor. "We saw those fireworks but half an hour ago. They must be straight ahead. We should break stealth and flood the area with light!"

"Aren't you even the least bit suspicious that the rebels care so little about stealth that they would launch fireworks *every ten minutes*?" Temururi tried to keep the scorn out of her voice but wasn't having much success. "Do you think maybe, just maybe, they *wanted* us to rush here like moths drawn to a flame?"

"But . . . Princess Aya's orders were—"

"I wish the empress trusted *real*, experienced military commanders," Temururi muttered.

The rest of her bridge staff nodded but said nothing. The empress's suspicion of military commanders was legendary. Puma Yemu, despite all that he had done for the House of Dandelion and the victory at Crescent Island, was currently under house arrest. And he was only the latest example in the long line of generals and enfeoffed nobles who had been stripped of power during the last couple of decades.

But what good would it do to gripe to one another about the obvious? Besides, while the admiral could speak her mind in front of the military monitor, the junior officers didn't want to be reported for treason.

"So what are your intentions?" asked the red-faced military monitor. "You've been dragging your feet the whole way. But whether you respect the princess or not, orders are orders."

"Stop nagging. Let me think."

Temururi closed her eyes and prayed to Lady Kana and Lady Rapa.

To prevent the airships of her fleet from colliding with one another in the dark, Temururi had clustered the vessels tightly so that lookouts on each ship could keep their eyes on the nearest sister ships. The formation also enhanced stealth by reducing the profile of the fleet as a whole. However, airships packed so densely could proceed only slowly, which, as the monitor pointed out, contravened Aya's directive to "make all haste." It didn't matter. Temururi wasn't about to risk the lives of her crew by blind obedience to Aya's nonsensical orders.

The golden fireworks that had guided her here, erupting regularly like dandelions blossoming in the sky, had ceased half an hour ago—probably a casualty of the worsening rainfall. They had been flying by dead reckoning since then.

How are we supposed to see anything through all this rain?

Her eyes snapped open.

The emperor's airships were likely no more than a few hundred feet away. In a blind fight like this, whoever gave up stealth first would be at the mercy of the other.

"First squadron, increase altitude by two hundred feet. Second squadron, decrease altitude by two hundred feet. . . ."

Her plan was to deploy the ships of the fleet at different altitudes and slowly press ahead, much like a trawling net sweeping toward a school of fish. The fireworks had revealed the enemy airships to be few in number. Absent an unforeseen plot, her advantage in numbers ought to be decisive.

She peered into the darkness, her heart racing.

As Mapidéré's conquest and the rebellions in the aftermath of his death turned Dara into a hell on earth, work for the rootless and landless became harder to find. Looting armies and marauding bandits were constant threats, and landlords and tenant farmers alike looked on the vagabond with suspicion. Unwilling to sell themselves to an indigo house, the pair had little choice but to turn to thieving. Temururi was quick of mind and fleet of foot, and many were the times she managed to outrun dogs and angry vendors to bring a steamed bun or a roasted chicken drumstick to her mother, huddling in the ruin of some wrecked temple.

And as the Hegemon filled the land with petty Tiro kings, who warred with one another incessantly and raised taxes month after month, there still seemed no hope for the common people. Temururi couldn't remember a single night as a young girl where she slept untroubled till the morn. She got better at thieving, and now she could scale tall walls and run along steep roofs, diving, climbing, leaping, swinging, rolling, tumbling, until she emerged with gleaming jewels, plucked from well-guarded estates.

"I worry about you," said her mother. "It's too dangerous. Someday you'll be shot by an arrow or cut down by a guard's sword."

"It's no more dangerous than stealing bird eggs," she said. But in her heart she knew that her mother was right. Yet, what could they do? What chance did people like them, as common as weeds, have in a world where the colossi strove for power and glory?

And then came the call from Kuni Garu, King of Dasu, for all men and women of talent to go join him. Dasu was where a woman who grew up in an indigo house could become a marshal, and where a novel and useful idea—like using steam from heated rocks to drive a paddled wheel—could earn the inventor hundreds of gold. Even if these were just exaggerated tales glorifying another petty, ambitious Tiro king, what did they have to lose? Temururi and her mother found passage on a smugglers' boat and made their way to Dasu.

There, her mother became one of the laundresses in Marshal Gin Mazoti's auxiliary corps, and Temururi herself joined the all-women air force. She learned how to live and fight on gigantic machines that were as complex as they were delicate. She had to submit to a military diet (at least it was filling) and exercise constantly to keep her body in fighting shape and make the required weight. She shaved her head to avoid entangling hair in cables and rigging. She learned to pull oars for hours at a time until her back screamed, to patch leaking gasbags in a storm thousands of feet above the roiling sea, to close valves and clamp hoses under fire, to launch battle kites and drop burning oil bombs while surrounded by chaotic shouting and conflicting reports. She learned to read gauges and adjust trim, to repair the lacquered hull and mend the silk rigging, to make the dangerous leap onto a thin mooring mast to anchor the ship and to cut away the ballast cables for an emergency takeoff. She scrambled up poles, swung from girders, raced across precarious catwalks that groaned and clanged as her vessel buckled and twisted in the wind.

She undertook these duties with joy because her acrobatic skills, developed out of the need to survive as a thief, made her a valued member of her crew—her new family. Watch chiefs and executive officers asked her to demonstrate her climbs and flips, and shipmates viewed her with admiration. The captain put her in charge of training and conditioning so the whole crew could move about the ship as nimbly and as quickly as she did.

For the first time in her life, her mastery of body and space was no longer a mark of shame, but a source of pride.

She had found a clan and tribe.

Webs of lightning shattered the dark air as though *Rana Kida* were inside a giant Ogé jar. For seconds, everything was illuminated in stark shades of black and white.

"Multiple unknown vessels in north-north-west!" a lookout whispered urgently.

Temururi had caught sight of the strange ships herself, and the vision had taken her breath away. About five in all, they were impossible creations: sleek, shimmery, each almost ten times the size of *Rana Kida* herself.

But their size wasn't the quality that stunned Temururi—it was the way they moved.

During that brief window of light, Temururi found herself transported to another world. She was no longer in a tempest-tossed airship, but somewhere under the sea.

Gargantuan forms writhed above her, covered in silver scales that shone like mirrors. They could not be machines, but organic embodiments of Lord Tazu's strength and grace. The massive ships—was that even the right word?—seemed to hold no definite shape. Moment to moment, they deformed from bulbous disks into slender spindles and back again, sprouting fins, tails, wings, flukes, before resorbing them. They twisted, arched, ascended, dove, swept through space. For a moment, she believed she was viewing the essence of crubens, freed from the constraints of mortality.

There was no question in her mind that these ships were capable of feats of aerobatics unattainable by her own clumsy airships. These were the supremely confident sovereigns of their domain. To imagine that she could fight them was madness.

Thunder rumbled and crashed through the night, the laughter of gods and demons.

The last time she had felt such awe at flying ships was more than a decade ago.

During Temururi's time in the Dasu air force, she volunteered for the most dangerous jobs and never backed down from a challenge. But she was neither reckless nor ambitious. She protected her crew like her family.

For acts of bravery and dedicated service, she was promoted steadily up the chain of command: squad leader, watch chief, boatswain, executive officer, until she was put in command of her own ship in the last days of the Chrysanthemum-Dandelion War.

On the day she was given her commission, King Kuni presented her with the short bronze ritual sword that all airship captains wore as the symbol of their rank. She had looked into his face—familiar from his speeches but never seen so close—and not known what to say. Then he had smiled and bowed to her.

Shocked, she had dropped into *jiri* clumsily, unused to the formal ceremonial armor that she never wore in air and unsure what to do with her hands.

"Gin tells me that you're a brave and talented commander," King Kuni said. "Risana tells me that you move with more grace on a swaying airship's girders than she does on a dance stage. I'm honored to have you fight on my side."

She mumbled something that she couldn't even understand herself.

"What is the thing you dream of most?" he asked.

She debated what answer he expected from her. That she dreamed of serving him until her dying breath? That she wanted to be an admiral of the fleet, commanding dozens of ships flying the banner of Dasu, a blue-black cruben breaching from a red sea? That she wished one day to be named a duchess or marchioness, with a title as well as a fief to be passed on to her children and grandchildren, ensuring generations of pomp and wealth?

"To not have to fight at all," she blurted. "To see my sisters who serve with me safe and sound, living in comfort as well as obscurity. To watch my children earn an honest living from tilling the soil or crafting Ano logograms with a writing knife, instead of having to aim arrows at another beating heart or to scale walls and climb roofs to steal food to fill hungry bellies."

She didn't think this was the kind of answer the Marshal would have given, or the sort of daydream the king wanted to hear. But she wasn't the Marshal, and she didn't want to tell him something untrue.

"That may be the hardest but also worthiest dream of all," he said.

She was surprised, and for some reason, her eyes stung, though she was in no pain and there was no death to mourn.

"I'm no great warrior nor skilled tactician," he continued. "But before the commissioning ceremony, I read your service record with care. Many were the times you spread the credit for success broadly and shouldered the blame for failure yourself. You've never shied away from a fight, but you've also never sought a brighter war cape for yourself, stained with the blood of those who followed you. You fight not for personal glory, but for love of your comrades. I bow to you now not to flatter your considerable talents, but in recognition of your grandness of spirit. Never forget your dream. It's equally important to know why we fight and why we *don't*."

Before, she had looked on the king from a distance with admiration but little love. He had given her mother, her comrades, and herself ways to make a living, opportunities to prove themselves. But in that moment, as he, one of the grandest lords in all Dara, showed her a respect she did not know she craved, she came to understand that he had given her and others like her far more: a chance to reshape the Islands as members of a new nation, to fight for their own future, to stand up and make the great lords hear their voices instead of merely lying down to be trampled as weeds.

With the Hegemon's death and the peace that followed the founding of the Dandelion Throne, many fighting-men and -women were discharged from service. She and her mother retired to Géjira, the fief of Queen Gin Mazoti. There, they bought a large farm with their pension, and Temururi married a man who took her name and treated her mother as his own. They had children, and she loved that they were surrounded by affection and security as they grew up. She would have been happy to spend the rest of her life in obscurity, for she had seen more than enough slaughter and violence to last her many lifetimes.

But the coming of the Lyucu changed everything again. As the Islands mobilized for war, there was much fresh terror and anxiety. The Marshal, freed from prison but still charged as a traitor— Temururi would always lament that Gin's legacy was marred by her ambition—sent out word that veterans of the Chrysanthemum-Dandelion War were needed to fight against a seemingly invincible foe. She and her husband held many heated debates, but in the end, she decided that she could not leave her children behind. War was for the young and the foolish, for those who had nothing to lose.

Her mother came to her and told her she must go fight.

"What about you? What about Phy? What about Nagi-*tika* and Luna-*tika*?"

"We'll be fine," said her mother. She hadn't heard that steely edge in her mother's voice in years. "Emperor Ragin once bowed to you. Do you remember that?"

She lowered her head in shame. How could she forget? "But we have no lift gas, no way to overcome fire-breathing monsters—"

"The emperor could have saved himself," her mother broke in. "But he stepped off his airship so that he could be one of us. He's now languishing in a Lyucu holding cell while they threaten to undo all that he has wrought. I'm a simple woman, and I don't pretend to know the Moralist virtues. But I do remember the Marshal saying that men and women should be willing to die for great lords who recognize their talent."

It's not about talent, she had whispered silently. *He saw in me something I had only dreamed of. And then he told me never to forget that dream.*

And so she had left her mother, left her children, left her husband to volunteer for the Marshal's hopeless cause.

The sight of the Marshal's new Imperial airships astonished her. Deprived of the lift gas from Mount Kiji, they stayed aloft by the power of a new gas extracted from fermenting manure. They were armed with novel silkmotic weapons, complex, delicate, deadly, like the human heart. They had the capability to transform, interlock, combine into aerial fortresses that would stem the Lyucu tide and preserve the beauty of Dara.

But her awe came from none of these things—her eyes stung at the sight of the aviators who would give the machines life. So many comrades, old and new, had decided to fight not because they thought there was glory to be gained, but because not to fight and make their voices heard was intolerable.

At the Battle of Zathin Gulf, she had commanded the Imperial airship *Vigor of the Twins*. She and her crew had fought valiantly, downing multiple garinafins. In the end, as her ship disintegrated into a flaming wreck around her as a result of Noda Mi's treachery, she had stayed at her post, refusing to abandon ship as she had ordered her crew to do.

The fiery wreckage crashed into a Lyucu city-ship, and miraculously, she survived that encounter and was rescued, though her left arm, mangled and burned, had to be amputated.

She regretted only that she hadn't been able to give more of herself.

"Searchlights!" Temururi shouted. "Battle stations! Brace for evasive maneuvers!"

Now that they were practically on top of the opposing fleet, there was no point in maintaining stealth any longer.

Bawled orders reverberated through speaking tubes as signaling bells and clappers added to the noise. Crews scrambled over girders and catwalks. Silkmotic torches came to life and their brilliance was focused by curved mirrors into sharp beams that probed into the dark storm. Archers crouched next to fortified slits, arrows notched and ready. Crossbow crews paired up at the base of the tillers, poised to crank the winches to draw the mighty strings.

The bright beams sought out and locked onto the shimmering, sinuous forms of the rebel emperor's airships, their alien beauty at home in the raging storm.

Temururi's confused heart grew no clearer.

Jia's regency had embittered many in the armed forces. Pay was stagnant or had been cut, and many seethed at the imposition of the system of civilian military monitors, a plain declaration of Empress Jia's distrust of soldiers. Veterans—at least those who were in the armed forces for more than just coin—had applied for discharge in droves as it seemed clear that no opportunity for fighting the Lyucu would be forthcoming.

Temururi had stayed on out of a sense of duty: She was certain that the Lyucu would attack again, and she could not bear the thought of young soldiers fighting against the wolves from the north without the benefit of veteran knowledge, bought with spilled blood and charred bones. She held fast, training new crews year after year, visiting her children and husband only during leaves and holidays.

When Phyro finally forced Empress Jia to go to war, Temururi's heart had soared. More than a few aviators she had trained volunteered to join him. The young prince was, in so many ways, just like his father. A compassionate, charismatic lord, he had made it his cause to confront the Lyucu and free the people of Unredeemed Dara. Starved of resources and manpower, he had nonetheless cobbled together an invasion force that achieved an impossible victory on the shores of Crescent Island.

Oh, how Temururi had grieved in the aftermath. Not only for all the aviators who would never return; not only for all the patriots whose bodies would never rest under the earth of their ancestral villages. The young emperor's dream, which was also her dream, had been thwarted, inches short of the ultimate goal, not by the enemy, but by the regent empress herself.

"They're n-not attacking," said the military monitor, her voice trembling. "They are just . . . flying."

And how they flew! Temururi was mesmerized as beams from the searchlights struggled to keep the fast-moving enemy airships illuminated. Their scaled hulls seemed to be made of some liquid metal that did not belong to this sublunary world; the ships did not so much fly as *flow*. One moment, the rebel ships were misshapen spheres that loomed over the Imperial fleet like shrunken moons; the next, they transformed into elongated serpents that slithered away from the Imperial fleet like the mounts of legendary immortals. She could not detect any structures that resembled gondolas, arrow slits, or weapons platforms. She saw nothing that looked like oars, sails, paddles, jetting flames or propellant streams. They followed no principle of engineering she understood.

Her first impression had been confirmed. These were otherworldly crubens performing in front of a school of gaping lumber-fin groupers. She was both glad that she got to see such incredible machines and sorrowful that it had to be in such circumstances.

What was she supposed to do?

Despite Empress Jia's persistent mistrust of military officers, Temururi admired her. Jia was a skilled regent who oversaw Dara's recovery from the devastation of the war with the Lyucu. She carried on the legacy of Emperor Ragin with tenacity. Her insistence on peace, though often criticized and ridiculed, was a sentiment Temururi understood—Dara at peace was what allowed her to dream her fondest dream: *to not have to fight at all*.

To look for war was also to look for death and suffering. She scoffed at the Moralists, who protested the empress's reforms that elevated Imperial examinees into positions of power regardless of connections and birth, that transformed the bureaucracy from a collection of petty fiefdoms governed by vague precepts of tradition, privilege, and deference to an elaborate, well-oiled machine that functioned through clear laws and carefully balanced incentives. She cared not for the whispered insinuations concerning her scheming character or her many lovers—the empress had not, as far as she could tell, allowed her private excesses to spill into public misrule. To fight for such a steady hand on the Seal of Dara against all insurrection and rebellion, against all who would plunge the Islands into lawless chaos, was a cause she believed in.

Yet wasn't the emperor's cause also just and admirable? He was Emperor Ragin's favorite son, who had been deprived of his birthright to rule by his aunt-mother. To avenge his father, to defeat the hated Lyucu and free the people of the northern islands from their cruel enslavers, was also to carry on the legacy of the lord she most cherished in all the world. She felt the humiliation and injustice of Empress Jia's appeasement of the Lyucu in her very bones. To fight against the man who wanted to free those suffering in bondage revolted her.

What was the right thing to do? Who was more true to the legacy of Kuni Garu, the emperor who had once bowed to her, urging her to remember *why* she was fighting or not fighting?

"Admiral, what are your orders?" The military monitor broke into her reverie. "The crew is tense and confused. We must do our duty."

Temururi drew a long breath. The nerves of the crew aboard *Rana Kida* were too taut for her to remain in this state of indefinite suspension. With each passing moment, the chances for an unfortunate accident increased, even if so far the emperor's ships were merely flying, not attacking.

She had to commit to a course of action.

"Full stop. Tell the crew to stand down. We'll launch no weapons and initiate no boarding attempts."

"Admiral, I must remind you that our mission is to seek out and engage the rebels, defeating them swiftly," said the military monitor, a note of warning creeping into her tone. "The Throne does not tolerate vacillating loyalties."

"I'm well aware of that," said the admiral. "However, let me remind *you* that our orders also included the admonition not to harm the emperor, who may be deceived by or under the control of rebels."

"But we can't just sit here and do nothing!"

"I didn't say we'll do nothing. We will . . . sing."

"Sing?" The military monitor, as well as the entirety of the bridge staff, stared at her in disbelief.

"We will all sing," said Temururi, her voice resolute.

> *Is it snow that I see falling in the valley?*
> *Is it rain that flows over the faces of the children?*
> *Oh my sorrow, my sorrow is great.*

One by one, the command staff joined in. And as the order was passed via speaking tubes to the rest of the crew and through signaling lights to the rest of the fleet, the singing voices swelled.

The military monitor looked around at her comrades, hesitated, and finally added her voice to theirs.

> *It is not snow that covers the floor of the valley.*
> *It is not rain that washes the faces of the children.*
> *Oh my sorrow, my sorrow is great.*

> *Chrysanthemum petals have filled the floor of the valley.*
> *Tears have soaked the faces of the children.*
> *Oh my sorrow, my sorrow is great.*

> *The warriors, they have died like falling chrysanthemum*
> *   blossoms.*
> *My son, O my son, he is not coming home from battle.*

Everyone in Dara knew that once, sung by the women auxiliaries who accompanied Kuni Garu's army, this old folk song from Cocru had shattered the resolve of Mata Zyndu's army at his last stand on the hill near Rana Kida.

Very few in Dara knew that once, sung by a single sailor on Emperor Monadétu's flagship, this song had reminded Phyro Garu of his mother's wisdom and stayed his hand from launching an invasion that would have led to the deaths of hundreds of thousands in Unredeemed Dara.

The singing voices of the Imperial fleet swelled into a raging torrent that crossed the stormy air to assault the shifting, twisting, shape-shifting rebel airships.

Temururi prayed that the song would once more save lives. The emperor's rebels and the empress's soldiers were brothers and sisters. How could a son take up arms against his aunt-mother, or a regent go to war against the young sovereign she was charged to guide and protect? It was wrong whether viewed through the eyes of Kon Fiji or an illiterate peasant child. It was a deed that would comfort Dara's enemies and dishearten the spirits of departed Emperor Ragin and Marshal Mazoti.

But the rebel ships continued to maneuver through the air as though they weren't crewed by flesh-and-blood daughters and sons of Dara, as though the emperor, unlike the Hegemon, had plugged up with wax the ears of the rebels who followed his cause.

Disappointment. A psychic oppression more aphotic than the starless night. Blood would be spilled uselessly, like the senseless wars among the Tiro kings.

Temururi heard a buzzing . . . no, more like a fluttering.

This must be the noise the navigator heard earlier.

A realization, at once terrifying and hopeful.

"Bow archers, launch a volley at the nearest enemy ship."

Bells and clappers passed her orders to those on the battle decks. Leaning forward tensely, Temururi watched as fiery trails crossed the space between *Rana Kida* and the strange, roiling, shimmering mass off the port bow. She squeezed her fists, uncertain whether she hoped for the arrows to bounce off harmlessly or for the hulls to erupt into flames.

The shooting stars sank into the liquid metal skin and instantly disappeared as though they had never existed.

"Primary crossbow stations, fire!" she barked.

The four crossbow teams near the front of the lower floor of the gondola had already winched the strings as far back as they'd go. Long bolts with thick bamboo shafts and thousand-hammered steel tips were loaded into the flight grooves, and with loud twangs, shot off toward the strange ship.

The bolts were swallowed by the silver skin of the airship without effect. There was no hissing scream from torn gasbags, no blinding flash from a silkmotic-force-triggered firework explosion. The bolts simply disappeared as though they had sunk into water.

The rebel airship continued to deform and soar, oblivious to the stings.

The air on the bridge of *Rana Kida* chilled. Panic began to crawl onto each face. Were the emperor's ships armored by Fithowéo himself, impermeable to mortal weapons?

But the admiral showed no fear. Her expression was enigmatic, suspended halfway between madness and faith.

"Engage all oars," ordered Temururi. "Collision course."

For a moment, the military monitor looked as if she wanted to object, but in the end, she pressed her lips together and nodded. The executive officer shouted into the speaking tubes. The navigator and rowers carried the order out. Slowly, *Rana Kida* began to move, accelerating toward the enemy.

"Brace for impact," yelled the military monitor, and everyone on the bridge grabbed a handhold or dangling harness—except for Temururi, who stood with her legs apart, her one arm casually at her side, her face preternaturally calm.

Rana Kida rammed into the hulking rebel ship, still twisting and turning like a living storm. Like a pond's placid surface yielding before the sharp prow of a racing scull, the shimmering skin parted around the Imperial airship's round bow.

A loud series of cracks resounded throughout *Rana Kida*'s hull, as though the ship was sailing through hailstones, or pearls were being dropped onto a sandalwood tray.

Temururi stared through the windshield. Dozens, hundreds of tiny silvery wings slammed against the glass, blocking out all sight.

Relief. Joy. Understanding.

"That's . . . that's not a ship!" cried the military monitor.

Temururi laughed. Her guess had been right.

Spidery cracks appeared in the windshield. "Duck," shouted Temururi, falling to the floor herself.

The glass shattered, and silvery shadows, each no bigger than a bird, poured in. They fluttered through the bridge like bats through a cave, and the bridge staff scampered out of their way. The military monitor, recovering first, gingerly knelt up and caught one of the "bats." She brought it to Temururi.

It was a tiny machine constructed from bamboo and silk, covered in silver paint and trailing silk ribbons and flexible thin reeds. There was no razor-sharp beak, no acid-spewing spigot, no firework-powder bomb. The mechanical bird was entirely unarmed.

As the bridge officers picked up disabled ornithopters from the floor and admired them, the tiny wings continued to flutter without cease.

"Launch the signal fireworks," Temururi ordered. She held up her arm, both to shield her face from the still-fluttering mechanical birds darting about the bridge as well as to hide her wide grin. "The emperor isn't here."

TIRO COZO: MORE THAN A YEAR EARLIER.

"What good is teaching ornithopters to fly like a flock of birds?" demanded Phyro impatiently.

A cloud of ornithopters swarmed over the courtyard at the center of the workshop complex. The swarm changed its shape as it drifted from one side of the open space to the other and then back again, sometimes resembling a loose, flat disk; sometimes a tight sphere; sometimes a long, sinuous belt. It reminded Phyro of a flock of real starlings at dusk.

"Aren't you even a little bit curious how it's done?" asked Rati, grinning mysteriously. "What if I told you that I did *not* instruct all these ornithopters to fly the same course? In fact, the cork instruction cylinders inside each only try to keep the artificial bird aloft, essentially holding its position."

Phyro relented. "You've aroused my interest. Lecture away."

"I've always been interested in bird flocks and the intelligence they show. How can thousands of individual creatures, amassed so close together, coordinate their flight as though they're a single organism? Can you imagine guiding hundreds of airships clustered as closely as the birds in a flock?"

Phyro grimaced as he tried to imagine the accidents that would no doubt follow if he were to attempt such a thing.

"Yet birds, far less intelligent than airship captains, perform such feats with no trouble."

"So what is their secret?" asked Phyro.

"I don't really know how birds do it, but I suspect they're like soldiers marching in formation. The individual soldier inside a formation doesn't think about the big picture, the path to be taken by the group as a whole; rather, his concerns are limited to keeping pace with the man before him, neither too fast nor too slow, and not bumping into those on his left and right. All that the individual soldier or bird needs to do is to react to its neighbors."

"And that's what you've done here?"

"Pretty much. I equipped the mechanical birds with reed feelers and connected them together with short bits of string. They were then instructed to stay aloft and maintain position. As they bump into and pull against their neighbors, the gyro stabilizers adjust their positions automatically. Yet, though the motion of each mechanical bird is essentially random, the flock as a whole moves as though it has a collective will."

"But what can we do with this?" asked Phyro. "It looks impressive, but the feelers and ribbons reduce the amount of weapons they can carry. A tethered flock like this is not nearly as useful against the Lyucu as ornithopters individually instructed to attack a target. At most it's a curiosity."

Rati shrugged. "Not everything has to be useful, *Rénga*. Sometimes it's enough to build something just because it's fun."

For a long time after, the two gazed up as the flock overhead changed direction and shape, moving about as a single, shimmering, shape-shifting creature in the bright sun.

"Shark!"

"Jellyfish!"

"Elephant!"

"Airship!"

CHAPTER FORTY-ONE

REUNION

The last of the viridian barley had been harvested, threshed, and winnowed. The cereal would be turned into beer as well as flour. The flour, roasted and mixed with a buttery soup made from the milk of the small mouflon flock, would be hearty and filling over the long winter. Added to the ample store of pemmican and game jerky, the settlement on the edge of the Barrows was well prepared for the winter.

Even the garinafins would be well cared for. Viridian barley stalks made good bedding as well as feed. Supplemented with hay harvested from the rich, thick vegetation in the valleys between the mounds, dried berries and fruits, viridian barley grains, and wild tolyusa from the edge of the salt flats, the new winged members of the nameless tribe would winter as well as the humans.

"Sometimes, I still can't believe that I'm not living in a dream," said Théra, wiping her brow as she rested against the bone pestle, almost as tall as she was, which she had been wielding to pound the barley into flour. Around her, everyone—Lyucu, Agon, Dara, ice tribes—was laboring at agricultural chores without complaint.

"I'm so proud of you," she said to her sons, laboring next to her. The pride in her voice was laced with a tinge of sorrow—the failed settlement at Kiri Valley would never be forgotten. "You've achieved what I couldn't't."

Tanto understood the complicated feelings behind her simple declaration. "Parents begin by dreaming their children, Mama," he said, "and in time, children dream their parents."

The attempt at quoting a Dara aphorism was sincere, even if Tanto's limited knowledge of the tongue of Dara led to several errors. These days, he tried to speak the language to his mother as often as possible. Next to him, Rokiri, whose knowledge of Dara was even more inadequate, lifted up one of the charms he wore around his neck in mute support of his brother.

The charm was the logogram for *mutagé*, made from bone fragments cemented together with ochre-gum glue. Both Tanto and Rokiri wore several charms like this one, as did the other children in the settlement. The two pékyus-taasa had begun to make them as a way to comfort themselves when they missed their mother, the same way they wrestled and practiced with small war clubs when they missed Takval. But over time, the game took on its own significance, a craft through which they expressed their fears and hopes. After they had exhausted the logograms they knew, they invented new ones: "heart" plus "hole" to mean *I miss you*; "cruben" enclosed in "wind" and "fire" to mean *garinafin*; four "hair" sublogograms supporting "dog" to mean *horrid wolf*; "bone" stacked on "air" stacked on "mouth" to mean *arucuro tocua*, the living breath animating a creation of bone.

Though constructed using principles derived from Classical Ano, the new bone logograms belonged to a new language, native to the scrublands and consonant with its rhythms. The other children, who learned the art from Tanto and Rokiri, called the bone logograms arucuro sana, or "talking bones."

Théra knelt and wrapped both her sons in a fierce and tearful embrace, heedless of the angled, dangling arucuro sana pressing into her face.

What words could be adequate to describe the reunion of long-parted friends and fate-sundered kin? What poetry could be up to the task of capturing the laughter as Théra embraced her sons, or the tears of Kunilu-*tika* and Jian-*tika* as they kissed their mother and learned of the death of their father? What song could catalog the expressions and sentiments as Sataari mourned Adyulek, Tongue-of-the-Every-Mother, but also grandmother-who-could-never-be-acknowledged? What dance could do justice to the manner in which Gozofin and Nalu clung to each other, refusing to let go? What word-scars could record the incoherent noises that emerged from throats and the tumultuous emotions that drowned hearts as Razutana, Toof, Çami, Tipo, and others gazed upon one another in wonder?

Better to leap ahead in the stream of time, to the aftermath, when passions had subsided and coherence had been restored.

After screams of disbelief and prayers of thanks came feasts and stories.

It took many nights for Théra to recount the deeds of the departed, the sacrifices, the triumphs, the mistakes, the betrayals, the discoveries, and mysteries.

"I knew it!" exclaimed Tanto. "Mama, you brought back the weapons at the end of the Fifth Age. I was looking for them!"

"You are indeed my son," said Théra, smiling and bringing out the sketches of the walking arucuro tocua to show her boy.

It took many days for Sataari and Razutana Pon to familiarize the newcomers with the patterns and routines of the settlement.

After Tanto's exploration into the heart of the Barrows, Razutana had experimented with the recovered seeds and discovered several varieties that were well-suited to cultivation. There was a hard tuber that became palatable only after much pounding and cooking, which Razutana called stone taro. There was a cereal, barley-like, with a blue-green husk, which Razutana named viridian barley. There was a vegetable, its leaves curled tightly like a cocoon dress, holding its freshness indefinitely when buried in frost, which Razutana designated Rapa lettuce. Along with these names derived by analogy with crops from Dara, Sataari gave them Agon names as well, though she wished she had known what Kikisavo and Afir had called them.

The paintings in the tomb had shown Sataari that the legendary heroes of the scrublands had also been farmers, and her prayers to the gods had not yielded a contradictory answer. She supported

Razutana's attempts at enlarging the fields of the settlement, and the children, their prejudices against farming not nearly as deep-seated as their elders', had taken to the agricultural work with curiosity and ease.

"Supplemented by hunting and gathering, the fields have yielded more than enough nourishment for these growing children," Razutana declared with conspicuous satisfaction to the band gathered around the bright fire. "In fact, the harvest this year is so good that even with all of you to feed, we shouldn't have a shortage."

Since their first trip, Sataari and Razutana had entered the Barrows several more times to gather seeds and to study the farming implements of the original inhabitants. With each trip, the taboo around the area had grown weaker for Sataari, and she had also been motivated by an intense curiosity over the lives of the people who had once lived there.

"If Kikisavo and Afir and their people had been farmers, how and why did they become the Agon and the Lyucu of the scrublands?" Sataari asked. She shook her head in frustration. "I've studied the paintings many times, but cannot make sense of them. If only the voices of our ancestors could speak again!"

Setting aside such abstract unsolved mysteries, Théra's band of refugees drifted off to sleep on the warm ground around the fire. Here, in this forbidden land, they were safe from the elements as well as their pursuers. Souliyan's wish had come true. The warring Agon and Lyucu tribes were very far away, their violent obsessions unable to penetrate this bubble of secure tranquility that was in, but not of, the scrublands.

At Théra's insistence, the settlement began to send small bands of warriors to the edges of the vast salt flats. Their mission wasn't to raid, but to collect the small groups of refugees who came to the salt flats to die.

With war raging everywhere among rival Agon thanes and the remnants of the Lyucu empire, those who wished to fight no more sometimes thought it was better to expire in the lifeless wasteland while they still had a choice rather than waiting to be enslaved or murdered. Whether the refugees were Lyucu, Agon, or tanto-lyu-naro, Théra promised them protection and sustenance from the imminent hard winter.

More than a few of Théra's followers objected to this plan. "We are doing just fine by ourselves," said Gozofin. "But our stores are not inexhaustible. Why should we be concerned with the welfare of these people, who are neither kin nor friend, who never fought for you?"

"How can we ever trust them?" demanded Toof. "Once they've had enough to eat, they may decide to betray us to the Lyucu or Agon so that they could be tiger-thanes."

"Or they could grow ambitious and hateful," added Tipo Tho. "They may seek to become the overlord of a farming people, and subjugate us as the Lyucu did in Dara."

"I cannot change my nature," replied Théra, as if that explained everything.

The others sighed but did as she asked.

Slowly, the settlement on the edge of the City of Ghosts swelled.

While Théra insisted that she no longer wished to assert her claim to be the Pékyu of the Agon by force, her followers weren't nearly as ready to give up as she was.

"The Barrows can serve as a base, much like Kiri Valley," said Tipo Tho. "This place can support a large force of like-minded warriors, enough to enforce the pékyu's claim—should she decide to fight again."

"If we're going to take in all these extra people," grumbled Gozofin, "they better be ready to fight for the pékyu."

"If we could prove the validity of Pékyu Takval's final will designating Théra as successor," said Sataari, "her claim would be much strengthened." She contemplated Takval's spirit portrait reverentially. Unfortunately, with Adyulek, the shaman who had taken the portrait, dead, there was no way to authenticate the portrait to the satisfaction of the warring Agon.

The others said nothing. They already knew what Théra would say.

"The breath is gone with the life that made it," said Théra. "What would I not give to hear my beloved's voice again? But he is already among the cloud-garinafins, and we will hear his voice no more."

What would I not give to hear my beloved's voice again?

Théra's wistful declaration reverberated inside Çami's mind, refusing to let go.

Never prone to mysticism, she treated the persistence of the idea not as a sign from the gods, but as a plea from the inchoate parts of her mind. There was a problem that demanded to be solved, a fish that craved to be weighed. When she became obsessed with an interesting problem, her mind would work on it in dream-space even when she wasn't consciously thinking about it.

After more than a decade living among the people of the scrublands, she had come to appreciate the power of the voice in a way she never could have in writing-dominated Dara. A writer wrote for an imaginary audience, divided from them by space and time, reshaping and refining the logograms in solitude. But an orator spoke to a living audience gathered in the same place and moment, her heart beating in sync with theirs, her breath commingling with their anticipation. The speaker was the lead bird in a swooping, soaring, diving flock, the voice the magic that transformed the Many into One.

The living word demanded much of the speaker. She had no choice but to put her whole soul into each breath. To speak was to take on the apathy and inertia of the crowd, to challenge the very silence of the gods and the hush of the universe itself.

It was, in other words, akin to fighting, and thus self-authenticating for a warlike people.

On long, cold nights, Sataari held storytelling dances for the children. The drums, fashioned from what bones were available at the middens, were small and crude. The paint, derived from material at hand, lacked the vibrancy and brightness of a shaman's proper repertoire. But she believed it was important to begin the process of committing the deeds of the new heroes—Souliyan, Nméji, Takval, Adyulek, Radia, Thoryo . . . and so many others—to memory and voice painting. Every legend began with a first dance, no matter how humble or clumsy; every re-remembering built upon the first remembering, no matter how halting or incomplete.

Adults, along with the children, gathered to watch and listen to Sataari's performances.

One night, as the paint on the drums vibrated to the rhythm of Sataari's striking staff, as junior shamans fixed the records of her leaps and turns in glue, Çami watched the scene, transfixed.

The Ano logogram for "writing" was said to have been derived from the patterns left on a pond as a wild goose passed over. One popular kenning for "writing" was "substantial speech."

Sounds are vibrations; patterns across space and time. Is it possible to read a voice the same way one reads writing?

Çami brought her idea to Sataari.

"If Adyulek allowed you to assist with the mystery of taking Pékyu Takval's spirit portrait," said the young shaman, "then the Every-Mother must have approved your involvement. This, then, must also be her will."

Together, they constructed a smaller version of the arucuro tocua machine used for taking spirit portraits. Some concessions had to be made to the lack of good raw materials: instead of the ear of a gari-nafin, they used the preserved ear of a muntjac; instead of garinafin stomach lining, they used mouflon tripe; instead of a bone needle polished from a garinafin wing tip, they used a fish rib. Since they were interested in painting strong, living voices, instead of the faint whispers of a dying warrior, they hoped that the substitutions would be adequate.

As Sataari cranked the smoke-coated tripe-tape, Çami shouted words and phrases into the muntjac ear. Afterward, the two pored over the patterns etched into the deposited smoke, hoping to associate the squiggly patterns with specific words and syllables.

At first, they thought they were making progress, and Çami drew up elaborate charts to record their successes. But Çami knew that in research, there was nothing so dangerous as seeing what one wanted to see. She asked Sataari to take portraits of herself reciting some phrases without telling Çami what she had said, and when

Çami tried to decipher the resulting portraits, she did no better than random guessing.

Reading the patterns on the tape was at best like lipreading, closer to an art than a science. When she already knew what was being shouted into the muntjac ear, she could almost convince herself that she was reading the sounds from their trails. But without that crutch, she was utterly blind.

Staring at the wavy patterns on the tape, she fell asleep. In her dreams, she was back on *Dissolver of Sorrows* at sea, and beneath the waves, the whales sang to her.

To take advantage of the last spell of good weather before winter ensconced itself, the settlement planned another gathering trip. Although there was already plenty of food stored up, Théra wanted as much variety from stone taro and viridian barley as possible to ensure the health of her people. All kinds of mischief resulted when people became dependent on one type of food.

The settlement divided into small bands to concentrate on hunting, fishing, gathering, and the like. Tanto and Sataari took Çami to collect late-season wild berries. Çami was glad for the chance to get away from the unsolvable puzzle of spirit portraits for a bit.

They hiked into the Barrows. The wilderness that had reconquered the human-altered landscape was no longer as mysterious as it had been when the children first arrived. Frequent subsequent explorations had even left some trails.

"Watch your footing," cautioned Sataari as they came upon a treacherous patch of wetland. The mud and grass concealed numerous sinkholes that would have swallowed the unwary traveler. "Step exactly where I step."

Tanto and Çami, walking in a line behind the young shaman, dutifully watched where she set foot and followed.

The hike was pleasant. The monotonous task of placing her feet into the prints left by Sataari and Tanto, over and over, caused Çami's mind to wander. She listened to the chorus of birds, frogs, and insects. One bird's singing was picked up by another, who trilled the same few notes, and then by a third. One frog's croak was answered by a friend or foe, and then a third joined in. Çami wondered what legends were being told and retold if she could decipher their speech.

"Watch out!" Sataari cried. One of the stepping-stones that had proven so reliable in the past had wobbled, and she splashed through the knee-deep mud as she tried to regain her footing.

"Watch out!" Tanto, close behind, had stepped on the same wobbly stone. Even as he splashed through the mud, he managed to insert his feet into the same holes Sataari had made. Arms wheeling, he collided into Sataari, who had finally come to a stop and was struggling to remain upright. The two collapsed into a muddy heap.

Çami, absent-mindedly emulating Tanto's steps, could not avoid the same wobbly stone. "Watch out!" Squishing through the mud, she instinctively plunged her feet into the same line of holes until she fell on top of the other two muck-covered figures.

Sataari lifted her face out of the wet mud and spat a mouthful of slime. A baby frog, glad that it had not been crushed by this sudden calamity, hopped away from her chin and croaked in joy. Other frogs, concealed around the swamp, croaked in response.

"I didn't mean that you needed to copy everything I did," said Sataari, wiping the mud from her face.

Tanto was laughing too hard to get up.

"It's all too easy to follow along blindly, retracing the steps of those who come before us—" Çami stopped.

"What's wrong, Çami?" asked Tanto. "You have to get up before I can get up."

Çami's eyes widened. Wordlessly, she climbed off the other two. And without even attempting to brush off the mud that was all over her, she began to run.

"Hey, come back! That's not the way to the berry patch! Don't you want to . . ."

Çami wasn't listening. She was racing back to the camp, where the arucuro tocua machine that could take living spirit portraits waited.

CHAPTER FORTY-TWO

THE BATTLE OF PAN, PART II

PAN: THE ELEVENTH MONTH OF THE ELEVENTH
YEAR OF THE REIGN OF SEASON OF STORMS AND
THE REIGN OF AUDACIOUS FREEDOM.

"Report from Admiral Temururi," said the messenger. "Attack from the west is a feint!"

The floor of the Grand Audience Hall seemed to buckle under Aya. Only with a great effort did she maintain her footing.

Her gamble had failed. She had tried to follow in the footsteps of her famous mother, but the emperor had outwitted her.

"This isn't entirely unexpected," said Cogo. "How could Phyro have obtained the resources to construct a fleet of airships in secret? If we simply reinforce the gates—"

He couldn't finish because a farseer had dashed in, leaving a trail of wet footprints on the stone floor. Falling to one knee, he shouted, "*Rénga*, urgent report from Tiro Cozo: The garinafins have escaped!"

Even Jia lost her composure at this news. She leaned forward, her face ashen. "What?"

"Earlier this afternoon, there was a surprise assault on the base by bandits. They freed Ofluro and Lady Suca and took off with all the garinafins. Before leaving, they destroyed the messenger airships and pigeons at the base, which is why it has taken this long for the news to reach Pan."

Aya Mazoti collapsed to the ground, so shocked that she couldn't breathe. Jia had placed the garinafin caretakers and trainers at Tiro

Cozo under guard as soon as Phyro disappeared, uncertain of their loyalty. But now, the entirety of the empire's garinafin force was under the emperor's control, and Pan itself was without even a single airship for defense.

Jia glared at Cogo. "Apparently he didn't need to construct an air force of his own. He just had to steal ours."

"*Rénga*, we must immediately recall Admiral Temururi's airships!" Aya finally found her voice again.

Jia laughed bitterly. "Even if there's enough time for that, how do you think they'll fare against garinafins?"

Blood drained from Aya's face. The empress was right. Conventional airships would never be a match for garinafins. That was true more than a decade ago, when Pékyu Tenryo first invaded Dara; it remained true now.

Fear now even crept into Cogo's voice. "I confess that I never believed the emperor would resort to such a drastic, abominable plan. To unleash the fury of the garinafins upon the people of Pan! Even the Lyucu . . ."

Aya shook herself out of her paralysis. She was the daughter of Gin Mazoti and Luan Zyaji. She was in charge of the capital's defenses. She had to *do* something.

"Even I miscalculated," said Jia. "I never could have imagined . . . When you play with fire . . ."

When you play with fire. Aya repeated the empress's words silently. Her eyes roved over the bright silkmotic lamps in sconces all around the Grand Audience Hall. The sconces, designed for torches, were sculpted in the shapes of the gods: Those behind the civil ministers on the eastern wall took the likeness of Lutho, the god of calculation and foresight; those behind the military officers on the western wall took the likeness of Fithowéo, the god of war and intuition. . . .

"*Rénga*," she blurted out. "It's not hopeless yet! Garinafins may be fierce, but they still must *see*!"

She explained her plan.

Jia and Cogo looked at each other. After a moment, the empress nodded.

"Place Pan under martial law." Aya dispatched messengers

confidently. "All fires are to be doused. We'll shroud the city in darkness so that the garinafins won't know where to go."

All they had to do was to survive the night. Aya knew that exhausted garinafins wouldn't stay aloft. Once they were forced to land in the morning, she would equip the airships with silkmotic lances and go after them. As for before then, she had other tricks. . . .

Jia turned to the other ministers and generals. "Go home and seal the gates of your manors. Wait for the chaos to be over. I will go into hiding in the palace as well. May the gods help Dara through this stormy night."

The gates in the city walls were sealed. Even the grates over sewers discharging into the moat were triple-locked. Eyes in watchtowers peered vigilantly into the storm. No one would enter the capital tonight—unless they shattered its defenses.

All over Pan, soldiers raced through the rainy streets, announcing the order from the palace. Lights were extinguished, torches doused, hearths banked. The city soon disappeared in inky darkness.

But in some of the dark, twisty alleys, small groups of men and women dressed all in black snuck along in obscurity, wending their way toward the academic quarter of the city.

Composed of impoverished veterans, thieves, indigo house girls, grave robbers, Adüan gangsters, and other denizens of the shadowy side of life in Dara, they were united by one ideal: belief in Emperor Monadétu, the dashing, rightful heir to the veiled Dandelion Throne.

Phyro had not wanted to turn his quest of vengeance against the woman who had murdered his mother into a civil war that would slaughter the innocent, but he could not refuse the aid of his dear friends—the Blossom Gang, Widow Wasu, and most of all, Zen-Kara—who were as outraged by Jia's duplicity as he was.

The Blossom Gang had recruited for the emperor's vendetta.

The recruits were not Moralist scholars, who could reason that the Grace of Kings was not the same as morals governing individuals. They were not Incentivist officials, who could justify murder in the name of the greater good. They simply knew that a son had a duty to avenge the death of his mother, and that people were bound to stick knives in their own ribs if that would help a friend in need. It was not a sophisticated code of ethics, but as in so many other things, what was sophisticated and complex wasn't necessarily better than the simple and direct.

Earlier, they had slipped through deserted streets and slithered through waterlogged sewers to stir up chaos in all quarters of the city: starting fires, pretending to be ghosts, putting on shows with smoke, mirrors, and gongs.

Now that the city had been plunged into darkness, it was time for the next phase of the plan. Like drops of rain zigzagging across a pane of glass to commingle at the trough at the bottom of the window, they congregated at the deserted plaza before the Examination Hall.

While the best of Dara's scholars gathered here once every five years to fight for a chance to be elevated into the upper echelons of Dara's machinery of government, it was hardly a target of military importance. There were no garrisons of soldiers, no guards keeping watch.

But Mota Kiphi was waiting for them. He waved his arm decisively.

Half of the rebels began to build barricades around the cylindrical hall. Levering up paving stones, breaking down nearby shops and stalls, they constructed defenses on the perimeter, settling in for a long siege.

The rest, led by Mota, crashed through the thick oaken doors of the Examination Hall and climbed up the catwalks along the inner wall. The locked door leading up to the roof hardly slowed them as they rammed through. There, heedless of the relentless rain, they pried up the roofing tiles and assaulted the battens until they had made a gaping hole. The interior of the Examination Hall, now accessible to the sky, was soon drenched by torrents of cascading water.

There was no time to rest. Mota rallied the rebels to disassemble the whale-oil lamps and curved mirrors located around the rim of the ceiling and install them on the central platform from which officials in charge of the examination kept an eye on the examinees. The lamps were filled with barrels of whale oil and lit.

Normally, these bright lamps were used during the three-day examination to illuminate the interior of the hall and to prevent cheating. Now, however, Mota and his rebels had turned the curved mirrors to direct all the light into a single beam that shot upward and out of the hole in the roof, piercing the rainy darkness.

In the middle of the obfuscated metropolis of Pan, a single bright eye had opened, gazing into the abyss.

"There it is!" cried Aya Mazoti, pointing in the direction of the pillar of light that had suddenly materialized.

She was just outside the eastern gate of the palace, next to a giant gimbaled crossbow, like those Gin had wielded to beat back the Lyucu tide a decade earlier. Beside the crossbow lay half a dozen diamond-tipped silkmotic bolts, recovered from the waters of Zathin Gulf and lovingly restored by Imperial artisans to commemorate one of the most important battles of Emperor Ragin's reign.

Similar crossbow stations had been erected on the other sides of the palace as well. Aya Mazoti would use her mother's weapons to defend the city against a new garinafin threat.

But she had also been prepared for another possibility: sabotage.

The strange disturbances around the city earlier in the evening had alerted her to the presence of rebel sympathizers in Pan. If Phyro intended to invade the city by garinafin, then it was almost certain that the saboteurs would act as his guides and spotters, eyes and ears. Her order for all the lights in the city to be extinguished, besides taking away garinafin sight, had also been a trick to force the saboteurs to reveal themselves.

"Go, go, go!" she ordered, waving her arms as she leapt onto her horse. A detachment of palace guards, the most elite soldiers of the empire, followed her. They rode toward the academic quarter of the city, intent on capturing the rebels and leaving Phyro's garinafins blind.

"You can't just seize the Seal of Dara by force, Hudo-*tika*," Aya muttered to herself as she rode through the rain. "It isn't *mutagé*; it isn't *right*."

Soon after the bright beam pierced the rain-drenched sky over Pan, a dark missile rose into the murk from the tallest peak in the mountains east of the city.

The missile had been launched by a Fithowéo's arm. Though modeled on the engines that had first demonstrated their power as Puma Yemu faced off against the Lyucu fleet in the waters south of Rui, this one was far larger and propelled its load a thousand yards up into the air.

Fashioned from a bundle of stout but light bamboo poles, about the size of a ship's mast, the lofted missile reached the apex of its arc and began to fall. Only at that point did the most powerful silkmotic mill ever fashioned by Rati Yera, charged with the power of lightning from the storm earlier that night, whir to life inside. Driven by spinning propeller blades at the tail, the missile jerked forward under its own power, like a colossal dyran coming awake.

Moonless, starless, the sky was as obscure as the deep. The missile swayed left and right, its single, transparent, domed eye peering into the dark. Then, with a rumbling *shudder*, it locked onto the bright pillar of light at the center of Pan, its polestar. The spinning blades *kicked* hard, accelerating the missile until it was faster than any Mingén falcon, any airship, any garinafin. No human being had ever flown with such celerity.

"Are you scared?" shouted Phyro. Secured by tethering belts at his waist and chest, he clung to the side of the missile like a furry baby bear cat hugging a towering bamboo stalk.

Arona Taré was right next to him. Firmly strapped to the missile with thick strips of silk, she resembled a silkworm in the last stages of sealing herself in a cocoon, with only her head peeking out the top.

"Ter-ter-rified!" she managed through chattering teeth. Behind thick glass goggles, her eyes were squeezed tightly shut.

It was cold up here, in the realm of birds and cloud palaces. The unrelenting rain lashed every inch of exposed skin, and each drop stung.

Phyro, drenched hair whipping about his face in the turbulence of the missile's speedy flight, laughed heartily. "Good. This will get the blood flowing before we reach the empress."

The great silkmotic dyran arced through the sky, its sunflower-inspired oculium eye locked unwaveringly on the bright glow at the heart of Pan. Faster and faster the missile flew, its beacon brightening ahead.

Arrows crisscrossed the rainy night.

It was a most eerie fight. To be illuminated was to make oneself a target; to make noise was to abandon the protection of darkness. The defenders crouched behind their provisional ramparts, bearing up against a hailstorm of arrows that gave substance to the falling rain.

There were no lights save the sparks of arrowheads striking iron shields; there were no battle drums to rouse the spirit, only the quiet grunts of exertion and the screams of the dying.

Aya grew impatient. The rebel saboteurs were far more skilled than she had anticipated, and her own soldiers had made little progress at breaching the Examination Hall. The bright beacon glowed tantalizingly above and before her. With every passing minute, the likelihood that Phyro's garinafins would be summoned to the scene increased.

A new idea entered her head. If the rebels were calling the garinafins here, then this was where she would hunt them.

Messengers were dispatched, and in less than a quarter of an hour, one of the giant gimbaled crossbows and a set of silkmotic bolts had been brought from the nearest palace gate to the Examination Hall Plaza.

And just in time, too. From high in the eastern sky came the faint strains of a shrill whistling, like the cry of some animal. It was insistent, minatory, summoning forth every horror-filled dream about fiery breath laying waste to entire city blocks at one blow.

"Incoming!" she shouted. While some of the palace guards continued their assault on the makeshift lighthouse that was the Examination Hall, the rest rushed to wind and load the crossbow, tilting a long bolt into the sky.

The shrill whistling grew louder. The unwavering beam at the top of the cylindrical hall, crosshatched by the rain, finally revealed the source of the otherworldly music: a slender tube with stubby fin-wings that wiggled through the sky as it approached. The tube gleamed the silvery figure of a sprinting fish, and its whirling tail left a long, vapory trail.

This wasn't at all the garinafin assault Aya had imagined; it was, rather, a mindless fantastical simulacrum of a rainbow-tailed dyran.

Phyro wasn't coming to Pan after all, not personally. He was going to deal death to the capital from afar, using weapons meant for the Lyucu.

Rebels and palace guards alike stopped their fighting, stunned by this new development. A moment later, the rebels scurried to take cover under their barricades. Did they know that their lord would discard their lives with so little care?

"Lock on target!" shouted Aya, her heart inflamed by outrage as well as anguish. *Phyro, do you know how disappointed my mother would be by you?* "We will do our duty!"

Her fearless determination staved off panic among the palace guards. Some of the guards interlocked their pavises to form a protective barrier around the rotating crossbow platform. Those on the platform struggled to aim the mammoth silkmotic bolt at this fast-moving, constantly swerving target.

"Hold it," Aya said, forcing her racing heart to steady. "Let it get closer." The dyran, being much more slender than a garinafin, presented a difficult target.

This must be how my mother felt during the Battle of Zathin Gulf, as she ordered her soldiers to hold their fire until they could see their own reflections in the cold, pupil-less eyes of the garinafins.

The dyran swerved and dipped its head, locking its eye onto the beacon atop the Examination Hall. It began to dive, speeding up.

"Hold it . . ."

A scene from long ago, when she had only been a little girl and Fara's playmate in the Palace Garden, surfaced in her memory.

Phyro, tall, broad-shouldered, a severe expression on his face, berated her for playing instead of studying her mother's manual on military strategy.

"Mutagé is everything, Aya. You must live up to the weight of the expectation on your shoulders. Do what is right for Dara."

She shook her head to dispel the past.

Her vision narrowed. Everything in the world disappeared except that gleaming missile plunging toward her through the relentless rain. This was the moment that would mark her place in the history books. This was the moment when the Mazoti name would be cleansed of its taint of treason. Aya Mazoti would live up to Phyro's admonishment—one that he himself had betrayed—prove herself loyal to the Dandelion Throne, even against the very man who had been like a brother to her, who had told her how important it was to be loyal.

"Hold it . . ."

So many books memorized and recited; so many lessons with the sword and bow; so many *cüpa* and *zamaki* sessions in summer heat and winter frost—they all led to this moment. Dara must not be allowed to descend into chaos; the veiled throne could not be claimed by force. She grasped her ceremonial sword tightly and raised it high. There was no doubt in her heart that she was doing the right thing.

The mechanical dyran was so close that she could hear its whirling tail and see the torrents cascading down its reflective surface. It loomed like a bubbling scar, a lightning-seared gash in the flesh of night.

"Fire!" She swung the sword.

The giant silkmotic bolt lurched out of the flight groove, flexing as it sped at the approaching missile. It reminded Aya of a scene from some old shadow puppet play, the kind that she and Fara used to sneak out of the palace to see: misunderstood, moody swordsmen wandering the earth in search of injustice; two skilled opponents dashing at each other, their swords leading the way, until the two sword points collided, and in a shower of sparks, only one would emerge the victor.

Her eyes snapped shut as a blinding flash erased the night, followed a moment later by a deafening explosion.

Arona screamed as the distant explosion seemed to shatter the very substance of the night air that she was plunging through.

Phyro hugged her tightly to his chest. "It's all right. We're safe."

He pulled the cord, and with a loud *thwump*, their precipitous fall slowed.

The pair descended in their harness, gentle as two leaves falling together in autumn, shielded from the rain by the silk balloon overhead that had been dyed black to blend in.

Phyro had delayed deploying the silk balloon as long as possible to get out of the light cone from the beacon at the Examination Hall. The palace was east of the academic quarter, and he had plotted the flight path of the missile to take them directly over the palace.

Zen-Kara's Adüan warriors, skilled at navigating pathless, dense woodlands, had had no need of airships to make their way into Tiro Cozo. They overcame the surprised garrison in short order and freed the prisoners. Though Zen-Kara had not met Ofluro or Lady Suca before, her possession of Na-aroénna convinced them that she was working for the Emperor of Dara. The garinafins were now safely hidden in the Wisoti Mountains, resting after their strenuous escape.

Phyro had no interest in laying waste to Pan or harming its people. That would not be *mutagé*, not be right. He simply needed to convince the cunning but cowardly Jia that he *would*. With her air force lured away, the paranoid empress would scurry into hiding, would plunge the city into darkness, leaving Mota Kiphi the opening to light the beacon and summon his true aerial steed.

Pulling on the strings that tethered their harness to the balloon, Phyro adjusted their glide toward the dark expanse of the palace, illuminated now faintly by the embers of the wreckage of the single-eyed mechanical dyran that had taken them here.

Once, Mata Zyndu had ridden into Zudi on just such a balloon to capture Jia and hold her captive. Now, Phyro was riding into Pan to avenge his mother and to make the duplicitous tyrant who stole the veiled throne pay the ultimate price.

Throughout Pan, residents huddled in their homes, doors and windows barred, their ears against the wall.

Something terrifying was happening in the city. A ghostly army had invaded the capital, and for the first time in decades, war had come to the streets of Pan.

The explosion over in the academic quarter of the city, near the Examination Hall, had drawn the attention of all the patrolling detachments near the palace. Congregating around the Examination Hall, they reinforced Aya Mazoti's palace guards and laid siege to the building.

Though its main purpose had been fulfilled, Mota Kiphi continued to maintain the bright beacon and rallied the rebels to hold the makeshift fortress. Their task now was to draw the attention of Jia's defenders, buying Phyro and Arona time to do their work. As long as the defenders believed that more missiles or garinafins would be summoned by the beacon, they would have to focus their efforts on Mota's diversion.

While her troops continued the assault on the Examination Hall, Aya examined the wreckage of the massive silkmotic dyran.

"We've found no signs that the missile carried any firework powder or armaments," reported one of the farseers, an engineer. "In fact, the explosion was entirely the result of the firework powder carried on the intercepting silkmotic bolt. The emperor's missile was unarmed."

Aya furrowed her brows. Something felt very wrong.

"Keep attacking!" she ordered the soldiers laying siege to the Examination Hall. "Put out that beacon and try to capture as many of the rebels alive as possible. I'm going to see the Prime Minister."

Phyro gazed at the portrait of his mother.

In the red glow from the incense brazier—its faint light could not be seen outside the sanctum, and its warmth was much needed after that frigid flight—the simple, abstract lines that Fara had used to evoke the idea of Risana rather than a strict likeness seemed to flow and spread, dancing through the smoky haze.

He was a little boy again, and his mother, as gentle as her chosen medium of smoke, was smiling at him with love.

Mama, I haven't forgotten you. I finally found out the truth of what that woman *did. Her blood will flow tonight and you'll finally find peace.*

After crash-landing in the deserted Palace Garden, Phyro and Arona had packed up the silk balloon and hid it inside Fara's camera obscura. Then they had made their way here to the Pellucid Cocoon Shrine, the highest point in the whole palace. It was a convenient perch from which to survey the palace, but Phyro had also wanted to get a blessing from the spirit of his departed mother.

The portrait gazed back at Phyro. Risana's expression was serene, impossible to read.

In the semidarkness of the brazier's glow, Phyro and Arona dried each other quickly with the sitting mats on the floor.

"Ready for the next step?" Arona asked.

"Why don't you prepare first?" Phyro said. "I'll go scout a bit."

Arona nodded and began to strip off her wet clothes. Phyro left the sanctum to give her some privacy. He went down a level on the spiraling staircase of the shrine, lifted the gossamer shade over a window, and peered outside.

In the distance, he saw the palace's western wall, dark and deserted. Beyond the wall, he could see the bright beacon of the Examination Hall. He imagined the fierce fighting taking place around the besieged structure. Mota's orders were to hole up inside and defend the beacon as long as possible, to keep up the pretense that more aerial invaders would be coming.

Earlier, when he and Arona had landed, the palace grounds had also been dark and deserted. That was no longer the case.

The order to obscure all Pan in absolute darkness had apparently been revoked, at least within the palace walls. While the ramparts remained shrouded in shadows, columns of soldiers, bright torches held aloft, snaked between the buildings. There seemed no discernible pattern in their movements.

After a moment of reflection, Phyro nodded in admiration. *A good trick.*

Aya was an inexperienced military commander and too book-bound—in fact, his plan had counted on her reacting as she had done so far. But the Imperial princess was not foolish. His ruse wouldn't deceive Aya forever, especially if that old fox Cogo Yelu was advising her.

Phyro was now certain that atop the dark walls, there were many soldiers crouching behind crenellations, bows and crossbows ready. Aya and Cogo must already suspect that the exploded mechanical dyran had not been without passengers, and this was their way to ferret out intruders within the palace. The moving patrols with torches were bait, intended to lure him and his band into making a rash move. Though the patrols moved about seemingly at random, they left gaps in between that were too tempting. As soon as he emerged to take advantage of them, however, thousands of arrows would greet him.

He didn't blame Cogo and Aya for siding with the empress. As far as they were concerned, he was an ambitious prince no longer content with waiting to be declared ready to reign. He was a usurper trying to wreck the carefully regulated machinery of empire.

They didn't know what Jia had done; they didn't know he was here as a son carrying out his unshirkable duty to avenge his mother.

Suddenly, he noticed several columns of torch-lit soldiers converging toward the shrine. Heart pounding, he dropped the shade and crouched lower.

Have we been discovered? How?

Voices came from below. Feminine, resolute, the topolect of Boama.

"Have you found anything?"

"Nothing."

"Not us either."

"Maybe they're wrong."

"Better be careful than sorry."

"Comé, take Teké with you and go to the Second Fin. She needs help at the Examination Hall."

"But who's going to watch the Grand Audience Hall then?"

"Leave that to the palace guards. Not important."

"Raing, let's go to the eastern gate. I don't trust the commander there. He was close to Phyro as a boy."

"Phia, Wi said that we should keep an eye on the Plaza of the Four Seas. Take two detachments but no torches."

. . .

Phyro pondered the situation. Some of the voices sounded hoarse, either from exhaustion or illness. The empress must have been pushing her bodyguards hard. Now, in her paranoia, she was sending the Dyran Fins out to take over defense duties in the palace. This was an unexpected stroke of luck.

He had rejected Mota and Widi's suggestion that he lead a direct assault on the palace, surrounded by a corps of skilled veterans in heavy armor. His argument had been that he wanted to minimize casualties, but in reality, he also thought such a blunt use of force would have marred the purity of his vengeance. Jia had murdered his mother by her own hands; nothing would do unless he killed her with his own. He didn't want an army; it wouldn't feel *right*.

He had convinced them (and himself) that *his* plan minimized the chances of detection as well as loss of lives. But in his heart, he knew that dropping into the palace from afar as a lone assassin (except for Arona, whose help he couldn't do without) appealed to his romantic yearning for a pure moment of confrontation.

He had to be alone. He had to pluck the empress from the middle of her web of deceit and lies with his bare hands. It was the only way for him to fulfill his destiny.

The voices outside the shrine faded.

Cautiously, he lifted the shade and peeked out again.

Columns of soldiers continued to march about the darkened palace, glowworms in a maze of undersea tunnels. Like a spectator next to a giant *zamaki* board, he was watching a skilled player marshaling her pieces, covering every vulnerability, protecting the commander in the castle against an assassin dropped from the sky.

Where was the empress hiding? He concentrated on the glowing columns . . . they seemed to cluster with especial care around the western gate.

That made sense. The western gate of the palace opened onto a military airfield, where a squadron of airships was normally stationed. If Admiral Temururi's airships were on their way back, they could land here and whisk the empress to safety. The empress was likely hiding just inside the gate right now, waiting to be rescued. Even with Arona's help, it was inconceivable for the two of them to fight their way through all those soldiers. Besides, Arona was more of a sword dancer than a sword fighter.

Phyro shook his head in frustration. No. That couldn't be right. Jia would never entrust her life to the military like that. It wasn't in her nature.

He was thinking about this the wrong way. Cogo Yelu was an avid player of *cüpa*, not *zamaki*. The two games differed not only in scale, but also in focus. While *zamaki* was a game of skirmishes in which it was paramount to preserve the strength of one's army, to pay attention to the pieces, *cüpa* was a game about territories, spaces, empires. A skilled *cüpa* player focused not on the stones, but on the empty spaces around the board.

He squinted and tried to take in the movements of the soldiers with a more distant gaze. Instead of watching where they were, he tried to see where they *weren't*.

There! Though the glowing columns seemed to crisscross every inch of the palace grounds, there was a lacuna near the Hall of Ten Thousand Flavors, where palace chefs prepared meals for the Imperial family. The patrols skirted it, perhaps because it was too unimportant a structure for even assassins or rebel emperors to be interested.

There was a story from the early days of the Chrysanthemum-Dandelion War, concerning how the Prime Minister had discovered the talent of Marshal Gin Mazoti by playing a game of *cüpa* with her. Cogo Yelu had presented Gin with an old, famous game in which one side seemed to have all the advantage of position. Instead of fighting to preserve a doomed army, Gin had deliberately killed off a large swath of her own stones in order to clear up the territory for a new contest.

In that empty space lay danger, possibility, temptation, redemption.

"I'm ready, *Rénga*," Arona whispered from the sanctum above. "Your turn."

Phyro smiled to himself and climbed back up.

CHAPTER FORTY-THREE

THE FALL OF UKYU-TAASA

KRIPHI: THE ELEVENTH MONTH OF THE ELEVENTH
YEAR OF THE REIGN OF SEASON OF STORMS AND
THE REIGN OF AUDACIOUS FREEDOM.

There was no light and no breeze in the dank underground cell, the stale air thickened by the odor of excrement and rotting food. To stay out of the slimy mud that was the floor, the captive squatted on a raft woven from bones. Some of the bones were from dead young garinafins that had once been imprisoned here as hostages to ensure the obedience of their parents—the cell's original purpose. Others, more delicate and slender, were from people who had been imprisoned here in the early days of Cutanrovo's campaign of cleansing Ukyu-taasa of native influence, when execution had not yet been automatic.

Sores covered the captive's body. It had been days since he had been given clean water or food. He had tried to stave off hunger and thirst with maggots and worms dug out of the mud, but even these, perhaps sensing the danger of his presence, were now impossible to find.

Even as a lowly member of the labor gangs, he couldn't escape Cutanrovo's notice. Someone had reported him trying to sculpt a logogram out of mud, and so here he was, denied the rays of the Eye of Cudyufin and the comforts of Lord Kiji's breath, forgotten and left to rot.

The darkness didn't hinder the captive's composition. Scooping up handfuls of mud, he formed a row of lumps along a ledge in the rough wall, and shaped them into individual Classical Ano logograms by feel.

Gaunt long-haired cattle wander the rubble;
Next to the wharves, barnacles encrust
The chains of city-ships too decrepit to trust
To brave the waves; fish whisper of trouble.

No one tends to the cooking fire.
Neglected garinafins low with need and hunger.
In abandoned fields choked by weeds, younger
Barbarians seethe and their plots grow dire.

Elaborate grow the sacrificial murders,
While thanes and naros pine
For something stronger than wine,
Dreaming of days when they were simple herders.

The delirium of desiring the despairing
Serves as the temple incense of a half-pacified land.
Reaching for an imaginary berry, a man extends an unsteady
*   hand,*
Haunted by the ghosts of deeds of daring.

A wild-eyed shaman in a skull dress yells
Syllables from ancestral voices prophesying war;
A native girl squats along the muddy shore
Scooping scraps from stubborn shells.

The ancient and inhumane eagle
Sits in her eyrie alone,
Eyeing the growing tower of bone,
Absolutely serene and regal.

A world and an ocean away, beyond the wall-shaped storm,
Whale pods hunt in the lightless deep,
Unconcerned with whether we reap or weep
Or our inconstant form.

He finished the last logogram and caressed the poem with trembling fingers. Though written in Ano logograms, this was a poem that followed no classical form from Dara and could never have been sculpted by any native poet. He longed to know what the scholars on the Big Island would think of it, longed to converse with the poets of Müning and Çaruza as they sipped floral tea together and posed riddles for one another, longed to join in their shared love for an ancient art form remade anew with each generation. . . .

But such an opportunity would never come. His people had crossed the ocean in the hopes of achieving a dream, and somewhere along the way, that dream had changed for him. He had fallen in love with this land, with its people, with its culture and art. In place of conquest he longed to . . . belong.

For that dream he had been imprisoned. And, it seemed now, that dream, along with Pékyu Tenryo's dream of empire, would never come true. His heart throbbed with an ache at once dull and keen.

He didn't know whether his recent neglect was the result of a deliberate decision or an accident. He had, at first, tried to shout and bang on the cell door to get the attention of his jailers. But he lacked the strength now to even crawl up the slimy slope to the door, much less to shout from his parched throat.

For daring to preserve the memories of this land, for wishing to become part of its living heart rather than a mere scar, for wanting to write poems like this, Cutanrovo had declared him a traitor.

And now, a poem was all he would have left.

Running his left hand over the logograms one last time to remember their beauty, Vocu Firna closed his eyes and tried to dream again.

Tanvanaki felt that all she did these days was scream.

The tolyusa-madness had only grown worse during the last few weeks. Rather than gradually sobering out of their haze, the afflicted had grown even more violent. Some tore their throats or slammed into walls, cracking their own skulls; others fought their guards, not yielding until they had been fatally injured. Goztan had no choice but to shackle and bind the rest for their own safety. In that state, they refused to eat or drink, demanding only tolyusa. In the end, to prevent them from wasting away, Goztan had to give them the tolyusa from Dasu, which calmed them enough for them to accept nourishment, but the berries, evoking the far more entrancing effects of the enhanced tolyusa, sharpened desire and plunged them even deeper into the madness.

Even the garinafins were showing signs of thirst for the manipulated tolyusa. Several garinafins, lashing out destructively upon being denied the drug, had to be put down. Others grew more recalcitrant and jittery. It was only a matter of time before the heart of the Lyucu war engine would shut down completely.

As if all that weren't enough, the latest report from Cutanrovo made Tanvanaki's blood boil.

"What do you mean we've run out of food?"

"It's the fault of native officials," Cutanrovo protested. "They've been lying to me about the harvest figures and the state of the herds."

"Don't blame *them*," said Goztan. "They knew what you wanted to hear, so they simply followed your example and adjusted the facts to suit your version of reality. The truth would have gotten them whipped or executed."

"And we lost all the tribute grain . . ." Tanvanaki cursed. "How did it get to this? What about all the land you've reclaimed?"

"The weather has not been cooperative this season," said Cutanrovo, "and land reclaimed from the sea yielded grass that sickened cattle and sheep—"

Goztan interrupted. "Any native farmer could have told you that such salty soil would be useless for either crops or grazing—but since you executed any who dared to speak up—"

"Those who objected were Dara-raaki saboteurs!" declared Cutanrovo. She actually sounded aggrieved. "We've had to slaughter more of the herds than usual to keep the warriors fed, and when that wasn't enough, we tapped into the stored grain usually left to the natives. Only my continuing rallies—though less effective now without the tolyusa—have revived the Lyucu spirit and sustained the warriors despite their substandard diet—"

"What. About. The. Natives?" Tanvanaki broke in. "If our warriors have been eating the last of the villagers' winter store, what are the natives eating?"

"The natives are not our concern," said Cutanrovo, her expression stubborn.

"I've made them your concern. I told you they must be kept fed!"

Reluctantly, Cutanrovo answered. "Naturally they've had to yield to the superior claims of our people. Certain unfortunate events have come to pass due to the natives' lack of faith in the Lyucu spirit—"

Goztan could no longer stand it. "There have been multiple uprisings due to starvation." She glared at Cutanrovo. "Your responses have added fuel to the flames."

Tanvanaki scowled.

"When native villagers complain of starvation, it is almost always due to laziness and lack of imagination rather than real need," said Cutanrovo, once again sounding as though she had been unfairly misunderstood. "The harvest this year was worse than usual because of the sloth of the mud-footed—"

"It's hard to keep the fields tilled when villagers were conscripted to fill the sea with rubble dug from the mountains during the busiest farm season," said Goztan.

Cutanrovo ignored her. "However, mindful of your charge to keep the good-for-nothings alive, I gave the order that any village that genuinely could no longer feed itself could apply for relief from us. Despite the difficult and demanding work of tending to the tolyusa-mad and upholding the Lyucu spirit, I devoted considerable energy to devise creative solutions to keep the swine alive. For instance, natives could volunteer for labor gangs. In exchange for work, they'd be fed."

"Why don't you tell the pékyu what sort of work the labor gangs were doing and what you were feeding them?" prodded Goztan, her face a mask of rage.

Tanvanaki waited.

Cutanrovo shrugged. "I assigned Noda Mi and Wira Pin to set the work gangs to building the cliffside engines—"

"You mean the slaughter cages?" Tanvanaki's eyes widened. "But one of the concessions we agreed to in the treaty was—"

Cutanrovo waved the pékyu's concern away. "Who cares what promises we make to Dara-raaki? The mere mention of these engines forced Jia to sue for peace; they will deter Dara-raaki adventurism in the future. We *must* have them."

Tanvanaki trembled with fury at Cutanrovo's open defiance of not just the treaty, but her own orders. She had promised Goztan that these killing engines would not be built when the garinafin-thane was restored to power.

"Even . . . even if you thought it a good idea to build these machines, you should have done so in secret! Once the natives find out about these machines, they will rebel all at once! How can you keep a secret when you've brought labor gangs from all over Ukyu-taasa to work on—"

"The slaves were told that the cages would be used to catch whales," said Cutanrovo. She snickered. "They are too stupid to understand what they're building anyway. As for food, since I couldn't use beef, mutton, or grain, I turned to the next best thing."

Tanvanaki stared at Cutanrovo's proud smirk, sensing fingers of ice closing around her own heart. "Go on."

"I began with the bodies of sacrificial victims. Even if a bit rotten, after sufficient boiling the flesh could be rendered suitable for consumption, and the smell was easily disguised with pepper and caca-nut. When we ran out of corpses, I instituted a work quota system. Any worker who couldn't meet his quota for the day was executed and used to make that night's dinner—"

As Cutanrovo recited all this in a matter-of-fact tone, Tanvanaki's features twisted with horror. Turning away, she retched violently. When she finally recovered, her face was ashen. "How . . . what . . . why did you think that would be an acceptable solution?"

Cutanrovo looked baffled. "Votan, *you* are the one who insisted that they must be fed! I would have preferred to let the swine starve or fill their bellies with dirt and dung—that isn't too different from how they normally get their food anyway. But since you wanted to be merciful, I decided not to let perfectly good meat go to waste—"

"Even you cannot pretend not to understand the depravity of your act," Goztan interrupted, her voice breaking with fury. "To force enslaved people to build the very machines intended to slaughter them en masse . . . You . . . you are a mon—"

"If it's any comfort to you, we haven't completed any of the engines," said Cutanrovo with a hint of regret. "Noda Mi's drawings turned out to be worthless, or maybe the laborers engaged in sabotage. The first cage fell apart before it could even be finished—"

"How did you get away with feeding the laborers human flesh?" Tanvanaki broke in.

"Oh, that's not hard. You overestimate the sensitivity of slaves' palates—"

Goztan was fed up with her rival's callous tone. "To disguise the source of the meals, Thane Cutanrovo had the overseers grind the corpses until they were unrecognizable. The work gangs did the work and ate the stew, thanking the Lyucu overseers at first, not realizing what they were building or eating. But when one of the cooks grew careless and left a child's hand intact in the stew, the workers realized the truth and rebelled. They captured the guards, who confessed the true purpose of the engines—"

"I had no choice but to order a speedy suppression," said Cutanrovo. "However, since so many of my warriors had been laid low by tolyusa-madness, I had to rely on fighters with accommodationist sympathies. They were not as effective as I had hoped, and Thane Goztan must take responsibility for allowing some of the laborers to escape—"

"Even the sober warriors are weak from the harsh rationing," said Goztan, her voice frosty and brittle. "Besides, how were less than a hundred warriors supposed to hold back a tide of four thousand workers fighting for their lives?"

Despairingly, Tanvanaki looked at Cutanrovo. "I asked you to *stabilize* the situation, but you've accomplished the very opposite. When what you've done spreads among the natives—"

"I am *not* afraid of swine with two legs!" Cutanrovo exclaimed. "Votan, you act as if feeding the natives with their own flesh is beyond the pale, but the pékyu-votan once suggested the very same thing—"

"I told you, never lecture me about my father—"

"*I will never stop reminding you of who you are!* You have grown soft because of your native concubine, but it is my duty to remember the pékyu-votan, to inspire you with his spirit—"

Tanvanaki leapt forward and wrestled the older woman to the ground. Immobilizing Cutanrovo with her own weight, Tanvanaki locked her hands around Cutanrovo's neck. As the garinafin-thane gasped for breath, her fingers prying at the pékyu's viselike grip, Tanvanaki leaned into her face and growled.

"You keep tormenting me with my father's name, but you don't seem to understand the difference between his world and ours. My father taunted the natives with that suggestion of cannibalism when he had thousands of warriors and dozens of garinafins at his side ready to enforce his will, and the natives still believed that obedience would buy them a measure of mercy—even coexistence."

Cutanrovo's eyes bulged, and her jaw slackened, showing her tongue. As the pékyu's choke hold continued, the garinafin-thane's attempts to throw her off weakened.

"How many warriors do we have now who can still fight, free of the tolyusa-haze? How many garinafins have survived that massacre at Crescent Island? You may be deceived by your own fantasy of turning the natives into an army of mindless drudges through a campaign of terror, but even the most docile sheep will bite if you push them hard enough. A general rebellion will finish us, do you understand? *Finish us!*"

Finally, as Cutanrovo's movements slowed, and her limbs fell to the ground, limp, Goztan stepped forward and gently touched Tanvanaki on the shoulder. "Votan, let go. Too many of us have already died."

For a long while, it seemed as if Tanvanaki would ignore Goztan. But abruptly, she let go and stood up. The older woman gasped and coughed as air, long denied, finally returned to her lungs.

"You are the most dangerous kind of fool," said Tanvanaki as she stepped away from Cutanrovo's curled-up form, "the kind that believes her own lies. You *thought* you were doing the best for the Lyucu in Ukyu-taasa, and for that reason alone I am sparing you—"

She stopped as self-loathing overwhelmed her.

Have you really looked at the world outside the Great Tent?

Timu's words felt like a slap to the face. *She* herself was the most dangerous kind of fool; *she* thought she was doing the best for the Lyucu; *she* had believed her own lies. While Cutanrovo made a mess of things, she had been paralyzed by fear and hope, instead of doing the only thing worth doing: confronting reality.

Cutanrovo panted as she lay on the ground, recovering.

Tanvanaki turned to Goztan. "*If* there is a general rebellion, how long can we last?"

"We have nominally less than half of our fighting strength, due to the tolyusa-madness," said Goztan. "But in reality, it's much worse since most of the thanes and naros-votan have been afflicted, and there is much fear among the remaining warriors that the gods are displeased with us."

"And the native garrisons?"

"They are hated as much by the common people as we are, so for now they remain obedient. But once our plans for the slaughter-engines are revealed and a general rebellion is sparked, I suspect many of them will turn to fight for the rebels in order to save their own hides."

"We've got to give the natives hope; defuse the tension some-how," mused Tanvanaki, pacing around. Now that she had finally accepted unbending reality, a new strength seemed to suffuse her limbs. She was still the pékyu; she had to think about what was best for Ukyu-taasa.

Think! What do the natives want?

"Set the slaughter-engines aflame and destroy them in front of as many witnesses as possible. We'll need a good scapegoat. . . . Blame the slaughter-engines and the corpse-meals on Wira Pin and Noda Mi. Flay them alive and parade the skins around the islands to pacify public anger."

Goztan nodded.

"Send Timu to tour around Rui and Dasu to further calm the mood," continued Tanvanaki. "Let the people know that I am sorry to have been deceived by Noda, Wira, and Cutanrovo—"

"Votan! No!" Cutanrovo struggled to sit up. "You cannot show such weakness—"

"Silence!" said Tanvanaki. "The only reason I'm not throwing you into a lightless cell immediately is because too many warriors are stricken with tolyusa-madness, and I need every able-bodied Lyucu—"

Ignoring the pékyu, Cutanrovo glared balefully at Goztan. "It's the false counsel of faint-hearted advisers like you that has led the pékyu astray—"

Tanvanaki strode up and loomed over her. Cutanrovo flinched.

"If you weren't Lyucu, I'd flay *you* and parade *your* skin around Ukyu-taasa. It would honestly do more good," said Tanvanaki calmly. She turned back to Goztan. "Slaughter the remaining cattle and distribute the meat to the native villages. We can only hope this will stave off a rebellion long enough for us to go beg Jia for more aid."

Even Goztan looked surprised. "Beg? But you said that Jia would show no mercy if she knew our true state—"

"No, votan," croaked Cutanrovo, desperation overcoming her fear of Tanvanaki. "You cannot mean beg. You must threaten—"

"I *do* mean beg," said Tanvanaki quietly. She looked from Cutanrovo to Goztan, a bitter smile on her face. "Don't you get it? This was her plan all along. We became addicted to her tribute, and then we became addicted to her tolyusa. She was never afraid of our threats; she just didn't want her people to die needlessly. All she had to do was to cut off the supply of manipulated tolyusa, and she knew Ukyu-taasa would fall apart in a month. We have nothing left to threaten her with—not even the despicable act of killing hostages, not when our warriors waste away in dreams of tolyusa-haze!

"Without launching a single ship or garinafin, she has subdued us. She is a far more skilled warlord than her husband or son."

Tanvanaki gazed into the distance, a look of genuine admiration on her face.

"There is nothing we can do now except . . . beg her to grant us mercy, even if it's against her nature. When all the possibilities have been closed off, the only path left leads through the impossible."

Neither of her thanes, one standing, one lying on the ground, said anything for a long time.

"Who do you want to be the envoy?" asked Goztan.

"The best choice is of course Timu," said Tanvanaki, ". . . assuming I haven't shattered his heart. We should send Vocu Firna with him—he has done the least against the natives and knows the tongue of Dara best of us all."

"Vocu is dead," said Goztan. She glanced at Cutanrovo and choked back the rest of her bitter speech.

"Dead?" After a brief, melancholy pause, Tanvanaki went on. "Then we'll need to spare Noda Mi to go as the emperor's assistant. Timu is too pure; he'll need someone like Noda at court to help him. I'll start drafting the letter to my mother-in-law."

She didn't say it, but both Cutanrovo and Goztan understood that such a letter was likely the first step in the ultimate surrender of the Lyucu in Ukyu-taasa. Cutanrovo's expression was one of utter despair, but for the first time in a long while, there was hope in Goztan's eyes.

Tanvanaki walked away, her shoulders hunched under an enormous, invisible weight.

Cutanrovo paced in her tent like a caged animal.

The pain and humiliation from Tanvanaki's rebuke had faded with another dose of the precious, dwindling supply of omnipotent wild tolyusa—no, she refused to accept Tanvanaki's conclusion that this sign of the blessing of the gods of Ukyu had been part of a Dara-raaki plot. To accept such a theory was to accept that she had been at fault, which was the same as admitting weakness, just as those who had succumbed to tolyusa-madness were confessing their weakness.

She was *not* weak.

Yet . . . she *had* lost. Everything the pékyu-votan and his brave Lyucu warriors had fought for and bled for and died for over the last decade and more: gone. Lost because a weak and young pékyu, beguiled by the corrupt accommodationists, lacked the courage to do what had to be done.

She was certain that if only Tanvanaki could see further, like her father had, she would understand that Cutanrovo was right. So long as the Lyucu spirit remained unbowed, victory was always possible.

The more desperate the situation, the more the Lyucu needed to remain resolute.

That Tanvanaki had been so cowed by Jia that she was ready to surrender was incomprehensible. One had to view the Dara-raaki with utter contempt; so-called reality had to be filtered through faith, through the absolute truth of Lyucu superiority—anything else was a lie.

If Noda Mi were dispatched to Pan with another threat to slaughter the native population of Ukyu-taasa—or even better, the slow and painful torture of Timu, though unfortunately Tanvanaki could never be persuaded to go that far—Cutanrovo was sure another tribute fleet would soon be arriving in Kriphi. In fact, she would have him demand that Jia scour the rest of the islands and bring Ukyu-taasa more of the precious wild tolyusa.

And even if Jia somehow had grown a spine, she believed the Lyucu would survive the winter with no problems: There were plenty of two-legged swine for everyone to feast upon.

As for the specter of a rebellion by the native garrisons and villagers, the risk was obviously exaggerated. The natives were cowardly, craven, divided—how could they possibly be a threat? And even if they tried to fight, a single wolf was as good as a hundred sheep, and the invincible Lyucu would overcome them with barely any loss—so long as the softhearted accommodationists weren't there to sabotage the effort.

She squeezed her fists tightly until the nails dug painfully into her palms. *If only I could make the pékyu see . . . if only I could make her feel . . . if only I could make her believe . . . if only I could force my mind into her body and awaken the blood of the pékyu-votan—*

The string of bones hung over the outer entrance to her tent chimed, announcing the arrival of a visitor. She looked up sharply, eyes red from tolyusa-haze, as the visitor opened the inner flap of the entrance and—

—there was no one standing at the entrance.

Slowly, she lowered her gaze and realized that her visitor was crawling in on hands and knees, his nose against the ground.

Her mouth curved up in a wide grin. It was Noda Mi, Loyal Hound of the Lyucu.

～

"Most August and Merciful and Magnificent and Sagacious Pékyu, a calamity! A disaster! Such terror! Much sadness! There is no time to waste! You must go to Kigo Yezu right away!"

Tanvanaki looked at the prostrate figure of Noda Mi, trying to suppress the blend of disgust and suspicion from her face. After being spared from Wira Pin's bloodcurdling fate, Noda had turned even more groveling and simpering in his manners, his speech a nigh-incomprehensible admixture of pseudo-formal Lyucu high speech and badly translated Dara honorifics. If before he had acted like a dog of the Lyucu, he now most closely resembled a maggot. A caricature of himself.

"How did Cutanrovo get captured? She has always been so careful."

Noda Mi slammed his forehead into the ground before her again and again, heedless of the sharp pebbles poking out of the soil. "Thane Cutanrovo was deceived—beguiled—no, *entrapmentational-ized* by the crafty, despicable, Dara-raaki slaves! Oh, heart bleeds, weeps, erupts with regret and indignation—"

"She ought to know better than anyone how much the natives despise her."

"Every word from the most Transcendent and Pulchritudinous and Awesome and Circumspectful Pékyu Vadyu is like a drop of the purest truth that sates the parched throat of this most loyal subject—"

"Get to the point!" With great effort, Tanvanaki kept herself from kicking him.

"Certainly! Certainly! Thane Cutanrovo went—progressed—no, *bipedal-pre-per-throughambulated* to a gathering at Kigo Yezu to commend slave elders from several nearby villages for voluntarily slaughtering five children as a sacrifice to the gods of Ukyu and to reduce the number of people the local garrison must feed. Since the Dara-raaki slaves were so loyal and close to a garrison, the thane didn't bring a detachment of warriors to guard her; instead, she only brought me in case the slaves needed an interpreter to understand the thane's opulent, coruscating pearls of wisdom.

"However, it all turned out to be a dirty trick. Such despicable! Much surprise! The elders had not slaughtered any children at all, but sculpted simulated corpses out of hunks of beef distributed to them by the local garrison! As the thane offered the elders a sip of kyoffir to reward them for their submission to Lyucu supremacy, a group of rebels emerged—erupted—no, *explode-vomited* from ambush and captured her. I was released to bring you the news—"

"Careless!" seethed Tanvanaki. "So arrogant and careless! And at a time like this!"

Noda Mi prostrated himself even more violently against the ground; his bloody forehead stained the pebbles. "It is all my fault, Most Omnipotent and Omniscient Pékyu, Most Panoramic and Pansophical Protector of Dara . . ."

Almost subconsciously, Tanvanaki shuffled back, unwilling to have this fool stain her feet with his blood.

She tried to sort through her tangled thoughts—it was so hard to think with Noda's constant patter! A nascent rebellion like this was a test. Unless handled properly, it could erupt into a general conflagration that would ruin the fragile peace she had been maintaining.

As much as she hated Cutanrovo, if she allowed these rebels to kill her, long the most powerful thane in all Ukyu-taasa, it might send a signal to the natives that the Lyucu were like an arrow near the end of its flight, and precipitate a general rebellion. But a violent, all-out assault might undo all the goodwill that the public execution of Wira Pin, the distribution of food to the hungry, and Timu's visits had built, and lead to general rebellion as well.

There was no doubt that she had to save Cutanrovo—she was, after all, a Lyucu. Yet she had to walk a delicate balance and keep the natives in just the right amount of suspense. She had to maintain the peace until Timu could go to the Big Island and beg for mercy from Jia and Phyro.

Meanwhile, Noda Mi's tongue never stopped wagging. ". . . Thane Cutanrovo is like the main mast that powers the ship of state of Ukyu-taasa—oh, no, no! Forgive me! The Peerless and Brightest Jewel of Heaven, the Priceless and Firmest Jade of Earth, Sovereign of Sovereigns, Queen of Queens, Mistress of Mistresses, Pékyu Vadyu, is *actually* the main mast. But the thane is a little like a mizzenmast, which is also crucial . . ."

Tanvanaki rubbed her throbbing forehead in frustration. Telling him to stop this nonsense was useless. At most, he would shut up for a few seconds, before beginning the absurd groveling again. As much as she despised him, she also pitied him: He acted like this only because he was a parasite; his very survival depended on pleasing his Lyucu masters. She forced herself to try to be kind to him.

"Noda, I'm perfectly aware of Cutanrovo's importance in the hearts of my people. Perhaps Goztan could rescue her through a surprise assault, with a few naros on a garinafin—"

"Oh, no! Pékyu, that must not be! Thane Goztan is away to bring in a new shipment of tolyusa from Dasu. And these black-hearted rebels are cunning, sly, and crafty! They've posted lookouts in every direction, and at the first sight of an approaching garinafin, they will execute the poor, loyal, magnanimous thane for sure."

Tanvanaki bit her bottom lip. She hated how volatile the situation was, leaving her no good choices.

Noda Mi waited a beat before continuing, a note of hope creeping into his voice. "The rebels *did* say that if you and Emperor Thaké, all by yourselves, would go to Kigo Yezu in person, listen to their complaints, and grant them a full pardon, they would release the thane unharmed. Is it worth a try, votan?"

"Only a child would fall for such a trap," Tanvanaki scoffed. "They clearly intend to capture me and Timu and hold us as hostages."

Noda slammed his forehead against the ground again. "Oh how close I came to falling into their evil schemes a second time! I was preserved from ruin only by the unfathomably keen insight of the Magnificent and Many-Hearted Pékyu. . . ."

Tanvanaki looked away, disgusted. Before falling out of her favor, Noda had been her most ruthless and sly adviser. His recent brush with death had apparently straightened out his intestines and taken away his ability to think.

". . . of course it's a trap. How could I have been so stupid! Stupid! The pékyu should never ever be put into the position of taking any risks. . . ."

Tanvanaki's face flushed. Noda's prattle bothered her more than she cared to admit. Was this really how he and her thanes saw her? A coward who didn't dare to take risks to save her own people, a petty queen no different from the native tyrants the Lyucu so despised?

Whatever Cutanrovo's faults, she was loyal. She was Lyucu; and she had to be saved.

"Maybe Timu and I *should* go meet the rebels," she mused aloud. "Otherwise people would really think that I'm afraid of some peasants."

"Who would dare to think such a thing!" cried Noda Mi. "Who? Show me who! I will bite anyone who dares to doubt—"

"You don't have to spare my feelings," snarled Tanvanaki. "I know there is much confusion among the warriors and anxiety about the future of Ukyu-taasa. Naros and culeks, especially those who love Cutanrovo, whisper that I am no longer the stouthearted fighter that I was, that I've lost the favor of the gods, that I am drained of the Lyucu spirit. Maybe it is time for me to do something to show them that I am still Flash-of-the-Garinafin."

She drew a deep breath, feeling a fresh energy coursing through her veins. She had missed the feeling of fighting with her own hands, of being in charge of her own fate. Let them try to trap her and hold her hostage! She would show them what she was made of.

". . . those mud-legged peasants would be no match for your strength, for your mighty war club! They are so weak that they can hardly stand! They'll tremble before you. . . ."

Tanvanaki gave a wan smile. Was this how it would all end? The Pékyu of Ukyu-taasa brought down by a few emaciated peasants who overwhelmed her by sheer numbers?

Why did she feel no fear, no regret?

She needed to stop thinking like Cutanrovo, treating every move by the natives as some sly scheme to destroy the Lyucu. She needed to exercise a long-dormant capacity: empathy.

Why did the rebels demand to see her *as well as* Timu? It was because they still believed in him as a symbol, still thought of him as their emperor. They were desperate enough to rebel, but they still had hope. They could . . . be trusted.

"It isn't a trap," she declared, her confidence surprising even herself. "The rebels just want to be heard and seen. There will be no more killings, no more massacres."

Noda Mi stared up at her, mouth agape.

She could already picture the scene: She would take Timu and go to the rebels to listen to their complaints without an escort. The rebels, awed that she would actually show up, would fulfill the promise of releasing Cutanrovo.

And then they would rant and accuse and she would listen: perhaps the last time as their pékyu. There was little chance that Timu's trip to the Big Island would secure the Lyucu anything except a most ignominious fate—she wasn't even sure Jia would allow her to live.

But she would look them in the eye and listen to their plaints. She owed them that much.

". . . Such unparalleled courage! Such unprecedented love of her people! Ukyu-taasa is blessed to have such a pékyu! Ten dyudyu cupéruna? Ukyu-taasa kyo! . . ."

She knew that far from freeing the people of Dara, she had brought them endless suffering. Step by step, error after error, she had turned Ukyu-taasa into a hell on earth.

There was too much history between the two peoples, too much bad blood. Lyucu supremacy was the fundamental tenet of the conquest of Ukyu-taasa, and neither Timu nor Goztan had been able to find a way for the two peoples to coexist without it. How could the Lyucu, so few in number, divided from the people of Dara by language and culture, hope to maintain their rule without resorting to the harshest form of enslavement? Once she had agreed to take up her father's dream, there was no other way for it to end except as a nightmare.

". . . I know of no sovereign more merciful and brave in all the annals of Dara! I know of no ruler with a more caring hand! . . ."

She could blame Cutanrovo's inflexible devotion to tradition (or at least an imagined version of it); she could blame the selfish counsel of advisers like Noda Mi and Wira Pin. But in the end, she was the pékyu; she was responsible. In her relentless drive to protect and preserve the Lyucu, she had doomed them, and in that process victimized countless others.

For so long she had been hiding from the truth, terrified that her compassion would be aroused by the fate of the enslaved—a reminder of the Lyucu's own suffering under Pékyu Nobo Aragoz of the Agon and Admiral Krita of Dara. She had isolated herself lest her natural empathy manifest itself as weakness and lead to the destruction of her own people. But the time for hiding was over. She was no longer in search of victory, but a dignified defeat. It was the best that the Lyucu could hope for.

". . . There is no wiser counselor than the emperor . . . no purer soul . . ."

And Timu would be there, by her side, to hold her up and give her strength as the rebels lobbed their accusations against her and heaped her with scorn. She was grateful for that. The bond between them had been strained, but not yet broken—more due to his efforts than hers.

The least she could do was have the courage to face the truth, to stand before the people she had enslaved and harmed, to listen to them and mutely plead for a measure of mercy—a mercy the Lyucu didn't deserve but needed, to let Cutanrovo go, to let her and Timu go, to preserve the peace until the arrival of Jia's judgment.

"Summon the emperor," she said to Noda. "And prepare fast horses."

Cutanrovo sat in the middle of the clearing that was the former site of the village of Kigo Yezu, her feet tied together in front of her, hands bound behind her back to a stake driven into the ground, mouth stuffed with a gag made of hemp rope.

She looked around. The villagers' once-lush fields were choked by bramble and weeds. The dry weather over the summer had left little good grazing, and now, in the cold winds of late autumn, everything was dry, withered, worn. The burnt remains of the villagers' huts peeked out of the rotting leaves like skeletons.

The destruction of this village had marked the beginning of her bid to displace Goztan Ryoto as Tanvanaki's most trusted adviser.

She wasn't sure if Noda Mi had selected this site because of the re-remembering, but the choice did suggest to her good fortune: The scene of her first triumph would serve as the setting for the greatest gamble of her life.

It was so easy to manipulate the natives. They thought themselves clever, but their intelligence was like that of the garinafins: selfish and shortsighted, driven by hunger for security and fear of pain. A simple promise to adopt Noda Mi into her own clan, to marry him to a Lyucu thane and give him a Lyucu name, honors unknown to any slave, had been enough to secure the loyalty of the simpering fool. But how could Noda Mi ever really be Lyucu? He lacked the Lyucu spirit, a supreme pride and courage that nature never saw fit to waste upon the natives.

Never mind that. It would be easy enough to get rid of him after the deed was done.

Thumping hoofbeats carried over the dune. She listened carefully. Though she was dedicated to the ways of the scrublands, after more than a decade in Ukyu-taasa, she was not ignorant of useful animals tamed by the natives. She could discern two horses, one heavily laden, perhaps with more than one rider.

She smiled to herself. Noda Mi's plan was working to perfection. She readied herself for the upcoming performance.

The first rider to emerge atop the dune was Noda Mi. "The pékyu is here! The emperor is here! Do not harm Thane Cutanrovo!" His panicked tone was so convincing that Cutanrovo could even picture tears of anxiety streaming down his face.

Cutanrovo understood the real source of Noda's anxiety. Though Tanvanaki claimed that the man had been spared in order to act as the Lyucu's tongue at the Dandelion Court, Noda had almost immediately realized that his real value to Tanvanaki was as a bargaining chip. He was certain that as soon as the delegation arrived in Pan, he would be bound and presented to Jia as a pledge of Lyucu goodwill. The people of Dara hated a traitor like Noda Mi even more than they hated the Lyucu.

How did Noda Mi put it? Oh, right, "Throw them a bone."

Cutanrovo chuckled inwardly at the image the lapdog Noda had picked to evoke his pitiful fate. No wonder the furless cur was willing to do whatever he could to thwart Tanvanaki's plans.

A second horse appeared at the top of the dune. Tanvanaki, as always, held the reins. Her husband rode behind her, hanging on with all his might.

What a weakling. A sneer flashed across Cutanrovo's face. *But also useful.* As soon as her plot succeeded, she would sail right up to the Big Island with Timu naked and caged like some filthy animal and demand all the meat, grain, feed, and tolyusa she wanted from Jia. And if Jia balked, Cutanrovo would personally bite off Timu's fingers and toes one by one until either the weakling died or his mother complied. Cutanrovo would do what Tanvanaki couldn't.

Two horses stopped next to the clearing, and the riders dismounted.

"Where are the rebels?" demanded Tanvanaki, looking about in confusion.

"They . . . they must be nearby," said Noda Mi.

Cutanrovo struggled against the ropes and made angry noises in her throat.

"We should free Thane Cutanrovo first," said Noda Mi, but he remained where he was, next to the horses.

"Emperor Thaké and I have come alone, as you demanded," Tanvanaki shouted, looking around the deserted clearing.

"Pékyu Vadyu and I have come to listen to your demands," Timu shouted. He held Tanvanaki's hand, a look of contentment on his face. This was what he had always wanted: his beloved Vadyu and himself standing side by side, trying to find a way for the people of Dara and the Lyucu to live together in peace. It had taken a long time for Tanvanaki to find her way back, but she *was* back.

Tanvanaki looked at her husband pityingly. She didn't have the heart to explain to him the real consequences of a Lyucu surrender. *Let him dream on,* she thought. *Let's keep the peace, even if it's just for a little longer.*

Ever alert, she realized that something didn't seem right. There were no footpaths through the bramble-covered fields, no signs of a rebel encampment, no traces of a celebratory banquet that had been held to lure Cutanrovo here.

Tanvanaki's hand tensed around Timu's. Everything screamed *trap* at her. *Where were the rebels she was supposed to meet?*

Cutanrovo moaned through the gag in her mouth. Her body strained against the ropes as though she was in pain. There was a pleading look in her eyes.

"They must have poisoned Thane Cutanrovo," Noda Mi shouted. "Oh, such black-hearted cowards!"

"Let's free her first," said Timu. "Maybe the rebels just stepped away for a bit."

Wordlessly, Tanvanaki let go of Timu's hand and retrieved her war club from the horse.

"What are you doing?" Timu demanded. "You promised that we wouldn't be fighting!"

"You and Noda should get on the horses and go back to the top of the dune," said Tanvanaki.

"I'm not leaving you alone," said Timu. "You can't fight them, Vadyu. They're just peasants who want to see us and tell us their troubles."

Tanvanaki hesitated. Every instinct in her screamed at her to get out, that this was an ambush.

Gurgling noises emerged from Cutanrovo's throat as her eyes rolled up into her skull. Her body arched like a bent bow, straining every muscle.

"We've got to free the thane," said Noda Mi. "She's going to die!"

"Stay near the horses with the emperor," said Tanvanaki, finally making up her mind. "Protect him with your life."

With her war club raised defensively, Tanvanaki approached the bound thane slowly, glancing around as though she expected enemies to leap out of the bramble in the fields at any second. Gingerly, she tested the ground with the tip of her foot before shifting her weight with each step.

Finally, she was standing next to Cutanrovo. Still gripping the war club with her right hand, she looked into the woman's agony-filled eyes. Carefully, she reached out with her left hand to pull the gag out of Cutanrovo's mouth—

Cutanrovo's right leg whipped out—the loops of rope around

her legs had not been knotted—and struck Tanvanaki in her ankles. With a cry of pain and surprise, the pékyu fell prone to the ground.

In a second, Cutanrovo had freed herself—the ropes around her hands had been for show as well—and pulled the stake out of the earth. Before Tanvanaki could recover, Cutanrovo swung one end of the stake, tipped with a stone like a hammer, against Tanvanaki's feet, shattering her ankles. As Tanvanaki screamed, Cutanrovo swung the other end, wrapped in layers of cloth, against the back of the pékyu's head. A few muffled blows later, Tanvanaki lay still on the ground.

Everything had happened so fast that Timu didn't even have the time to react beyond a cry of anguish. Cutanrovo left the prone figure of Tanvanaki and strode up to him, a bit unsteady on her feet after having sat immobile for so long.

"Your writing dagger," she demanded.

As though awakening from a dream, Timu dodged around her and fell on the body of Tanvanaki. "Vadyu-*tika*, Vadyu-*tika*!" He caressed her cheeks, leaning in to feel for her breath.

Cutanrovo walked up and hoisted him up by the back of the collar like a hawk lifting a baby chick. After pulling the small writing knife free from his belt, she tossed him aside.

Tanvanaki groaned and tried to lift her head.

"Stay down," said Cutanrovo, and casually pressed a foot against her back. Tanvanaki moaned, her limbs floundering weakly.

Timu screamed and crawled over, pushing Cutanrovo's foot aside to shield his wife with his body. Finally, he remembered Noda Mi. He shouted at the man, still standing by the horses. "Stop her!"

Noda Mi shook his head and smiled. "*Rénga*, that's the last thing I want to do right now."

Timu looked from Cutanrovo to Noda Mi, and understanding finally dawned. "There never were any rebels."

"It's a coup," declared Cutanrovo. "The pékyu is no longer fit to rule Ukyu-taasa."

"You've lost your mind!" Desperation made Timu's voice crack. "It's the tolyusa, isn't it? You suffer from the sickness too. Listen—"

"I've never been more clear-minded in my life!" roared Cutanrovo.

Once again she picked Timu off Tanvanaki and tossed him aside like a doll. "She's contemplating surrendering to your mother, to the filthy Dara-raaki swine who eat food that is grown from their own excrement! You've corrupted her, made her forget that she's a daughter of Tenryo Roatan, the greatest pékyu who ever lived!"

"You will doom all the Lyucu if you kill her," said Timu. "Ukyu-taasa is hanging by the thinnest of threads. How can you handle an uprising by the peasants when you'll be fighting amongst yourselves? And what will you do when my brother returns with his invading army? With so many warriors laid low by the tolyusa-madness, you can't even carry out the depraved threat of mass slaughter, the only reason my mother recalled Phyro's invasion last time. Tanvanaki and I are our last chance at negotiating tolerable terms for a surren-der, to preserve the lives of the Lyucu. Don't do this!"

"Negotiate?" Cutanrovo laughed. "The Lyucu don't negotiate; we conquer." She knelt down and placed a knee against the small of Tanvanaki's back. Grabbing Tanvanaki's long hair, she pulled her head back, revealing the bare throat. Tanvanaki sputtered, her arms flailing uselessly, too dazed to fight the garinafin-thane off.

"Stop! O gods, stop!" Timu screamed, trying to reach Tanvanaki again. Noda Mi stepped in and restrained the emperor.

"You will never understand us," said Cutanrovo, as though lec-turing a child. "A little tolyusa-thirst is *nothing*. A rebellion by every mud-legged native in Ukyu-taasa is *nothing*. Your brother's invasion, no matter how many witchcraft-infused weapons he brings, is *noth-ing*. The Lyucu spirit, on the other hand, is *everything*."

"You are mad . . . utterly mad—"

"You're right that you're very valuable, my mud-legged emperor. We may not be able to build the slaughter-engines, but we can still strike Jia where it really hurts. Oh, don't worry, I'll keep you alive, but you may not enjoy your existence very much. I'll cut off a piece of you every day and send it to your mother until she sends us all the meat and tolyusa I want."

Timu's struggles against Noda's grip subsided. "Then you don't understand my mother. She was willing to order her own marshal to kill my father at the Battle of Zathin Gulf so that he couldn't be used as a hostage." Despair filled his eyes as he struggled to make Cutanrovo *see*. "Do you really think she'll give up the opportunity she has engineered for the defeat of the Lyucu on account of *me*? Weighed against the welfare of the people of Dara, she won't flinch at letting me go. Teeth on the board. You'll never defeat her with such threats."

"Then we'll die as warriors, as is our nature," declared Cutanrovo, sounding not only proud, but overjoyed. "It's better than begging for mercy from people fit only to be slaves. Wolves must never become dogs."

Timu softened his voice, straining to reach what was left of the rational part of Cutanrovo's feverish mind. "You have no legitimate claim to be the pékyu, and the other thanes will not support you. If you kill her to seize power by force, what's to stop the others from doing the same to you?"

"Why would they think *I* killed her?" asked Cutanrovo in a mocking voice.

Timu looked at her, uncomprehending.

"You really are stupid." Cutanrovo raised her right hand high in the air, and something metallic flashed in the sun.

"Nooo!" Timu screamed.

Cutanrovo leaned down and plunged Timu's small writing knife deep into Tanvanaki's throat. She pulled it back out a second later, and blood gushed from the wound in powerful spurts, instantly drenching Cutanrovo's face and upper body.

As Timu screamed and fought against Noda's iron hold, Tanvanaki gurgled and flopped against the weight of Cutanrovo like a hooked fish. Blood filled her nose and mouth. Cutanrovo methodically plunged the small writing knife into her throat again and again, and the bloody fountain gushed to the rhythm of Tanvanaki's fading heartbeat.

"When the body of the dead pékyu is presented to the other thanes," said Cutanrovo in a detached, methodical voice, "they'll see that the wounds are not from the weapon of a brave Lyucu warrior, but the toy knife of the pékyu's cowardly concubine, who abused the pékyu's trust to commit the most heinous of crimes against his wife and lord."

The convulsions ripping through Tanvanaki's body grew more sporadic and less intense. With a final spasm, the body of Flash-of-the-Garinafin, Pékyu of Ukyu-taasa, Protector of Dara, stilled.

Timu slumped against Noda's hold. "O gods! O gods!"

Slowly, Cutanrovo climbed off Tanvanaki's corpse and tossed the writing knife away. Her face, shoulders, chest, arms, hands were covered in blood.

"And now, it's your turn," said Cutanrovo, a ravenous grin splitting her blood-covered face. "I was going to keep you alive to bargain with your mother. But since you're so sure of your worthlessness, let me send you to join your dear, departed wife. I'll bash in your skull and take it back with me to show that I've avenged the pékyu, and in their gratitude, the thanes will proclaim me her successor. . . ."

Timu howled. The gods were blind and without justice. He turned his face away from that demonic visage to gaze upon the still body of his wife, the mother of his children, the woman he loved and also regretted loving.

". . . I'll become the greatest pékyu of the Lyucu people," said Cutanrovo. She swayed unsteadily on her feet, dizzy from the exertion of killing Tanvanaki. Slowly, she bent down to pick up Tanvanaki's war club. "I'll carry on the true legacy of the pékyu-votan—"

Timu felt Noda's arms, until now locked tightly around his chest, abruptly give way. Unsupported, he began to fall, and as he looked up in confusion, time seemed to slow down.

A blurred shape rushing by him—

Cutanrovo, still bent over, wrapping her fingers around the war club—

The blurred shape stopping next to Cutanrovo and resolving into Noda Mi, unsheathing a sword and lunging forward—

Cutanrovo's head snapping up as she looked, uncomprehending, at Noda Mi's sword sliding into her body—

Timu felt his head strike the hard earth. Time continued to flow at an agonizingly slow pace as his view bounced and shook. He could not make sense of what he was seeing; he couldn't think.

Noda Mi jumping back; the sword's handle snapping off, leaving the blade in Cutanrovo—

Cutanrovo roaring and swinging the war club at the retreating Noda Mi, losing her footing as the club left her hand—

Noda Mi dodging, but not fast enough; the heavy bone head striking him in the shoulder, bringing him to the ground—

Cutanrovo stumbling forward, grunting and gurgling as blood pooled in her lungs, trying to catch Noda—

Noda scrambling and rolling away from her—

Cutanrovo wrapping her hands around the inch of blade not buried in her chest; failing to get any purchase as the sharp edges cut into her fingers, slipping against the blood oozing from the wounds—

Noda getting back to his feet, crouching defensively.

Time snapped back to its normal flow. Timu gasped and filled his lungs with air.

"Why?" he cried plaintively at Noda. "Why didn't you stop her earlier?"

Without waiting for an answer, he crawled to Tanvanaki's body, trying to cradle her head in his lap.

Cutanrovo's mouth opened, and instead of words, blood spurted out. With every ounce of strength left, she clamped her jaw shut and locked her gaze on Noda's face, skewering him with a silent inquiry.

"Wolves must never become dogs," said Noda Mi, panting, answering both of their questions at once.

Cutanrovo straightened her back, the broken sword sticking out of her chest absurdly like a toothpick in a canapé. She tried to laugh, and bloody spittle sprayed from her mouth. She coughed and clawed against her throat, choking. Her knees buckling, she fell to the ground, unable to draw another breath, her legs spasming and kicking uselessly.

Noda Mi picked up the war club that had struck him and gingerly approached the dying thane, intent on finishing her.

Just as he raised the club to bash in Cutanrovo's head, the woman sprang up and slammed into his legs with her whole body, bringing him down. As Noda Mi screamed and squirmed, Cutanrovo held him down and climbed on top. Opening her bloody mouth, she bit him in the face.

Noda howled like a lamb about to be slaughtered and pummeled Cutanrovo's cheeks with his fists. Cutanrovo held on with her teeth and increased the pressure in her jaws. Noda twisted and turned, and finally managed to bring his knees up between the woman and himself. As he heaved her free, he let out another bloodcurdling shriek.

Cutanrovo rolled along the ground and came to a stop next to the stunned Timu. Noda Mi scrambled up into a sitting position, whimpering as he stared at the dead thane in terror. A chunk of flesh had been torn from his face, revealing bone.

For a long time, Timu and Noda simply sat across from each other, the bodies of the two dead Lyucu bleeding and cooling between them.

At length, Noda staggered to his feet, limped over to Cutanrovo, and slammed the war club down on her skull.

Thwack! As blood and brains splattered onto Timu, he flinched and lifted his face from the cold body of his wife to gaze at Noda.

"*Rénga*, it's all right," Noda Mi croaked. His face was covered in blood, some of it coughed up by Cutanrovo as she lay dying on top of him, but most of it from the hole in his cheek. White bone glistened through the crimson gore, and air hissed through the hole with each breath. "You're now safe."

Timu's eyes were devoid of will and comprehension.

Noda sat down with a grunt, ripped off his leggings, and began to wrap the strips around his head to stanch the bleeding. "It's funny how easy these barbarians are to fool, isn't it? All I had to do was to swear a few oaths and kill a few peasants while chanting in their coarse tongue, and they thought I was truly their loyal hound. And promising me a barbarian wife like some prize—the very thought is revolting! Cutanrovo thought she could use me, but only Noda Mi gets to use anyone."

Timu said nothing.

"A couple of barbarian whores thinking they could throw away *my* life . . . ," said Noda, wincing as he tied off the bandage. He spat at Cutanrovo's body. "Fighting Empress Jia when most of the Lyucu are incapacitated in a tolyusa-haze? It would be like striking a rock with an egg. Good thing I never touched the stuff."

"But Tanvanaki wasn't going to fight a senseless war," said Timu, his tone betraying no emotion. "She was going to sue for peace with my mother. She had a chance to preserve the lives of the Lyucu."

"That's all fine and good for the Lyucu," said Noda. "But what about *me*? Those Moralist ministers in Pan—spouting 'loyalty' and 'honor' and *'mutagé'* all day—have probably been dreaming of drinking my blood and eating my flesh ever since my little trick at Zathin Gulf. No, I couldn't let that happen. Better all the Lyucu die. I've got to think of *me*."

"I see," said Timu. The corners of his mouth twitched as he focused on Noda. "What's going to happen next?"

"We're going to hide near the shore for a few days," said Noda. "There will be much confusion after the rest of the thanes discover that the pékyu and Cutanrovo are missing. While they fight over who gets to be in charge, the two of us will find a boat and escape to Dara proper, where we'll be greeted as heroes."

"Heroes?"

Noda Mi laughed. "You must be too shocked to think straight. Because we killed the barbarian chiefs Tanvanaki and Cutanrovo and avenged Emperor Ragin! Can you imagine the celebration in Pan when we show up? You'll instantly have more than enough political capital to challenge your brother for the throne, and your embarrassing marriage to that semiliterate brute will be forgotten, or even better, described as part of a long, secret scheme to behead the Lyucu! There will be plays, operas, statues—"

"Challenge my brother?" Timu seemed to have trouble keeping up.

Noda suppressed his annoyance. It was really no surprise that a naive bookworm like Timu couldn't wrap his head around betrayals and counter-betrayals, and work out the political implications. The more books someone like Timu read, the more foolish they became.

During all the time that Noda Mi had played the role of lapdog to the Lyucu, he had never neglected to cultivate his relationship with emissaries from Empress Jia on the tribute fleets. A cagey hare always made sure to have no less than three exits from its warren, and a clever crimson-tailed woodpecker didn't cling to just one tree. He was certainly smarter than both.

As long as he thought he could still get *more* from serving the Lyucu, he would do whatever was needed to keep them in power. But when the Lyucu tree was rotted through, he was not going to hesitate to give it a final toppling peck if such an act would land him a better perch.

Lady Ragi, Jia's tribute emissary, had repeatedly dropped hints that Noda would be rewarded if he chose the right time to strike a fatal blow against the Lyucu—but Timu didn't know that.

He would have to explain this game of *zamaki* to the confused emperor step by step.

"Yes, I've just given you the key to challenge your brother to the Dandelion Throne! You're very welcome, *Rénga*. Of course, I didn't plan all this just for your benefit. When I present Empress Jia with the heads of Tanvanaki and Cutanrovo, as well as the living, breathing form of her favorite son, she'll have no choice but to treat me as the savior of Dara."

"No choice?"

"Heh! Think! Jia's ultimate goal has always been to put you on the Dandelion Throne; that's why she's been refusing to let Phyro rule all these years. But you've been away from Pan for so long that most of the generals and ministers must prefer Phyro as the heir. She'll have to build you up by emphasizing your heroic efforts to undermine the Lyucu from within, and that requires cultivating *me* to become part of your story and your party. You and I are two crickets tied to the same string. The more power I have, the better I can counterbalance the ministers and generals loyal to your brother."

Noda's voice grew even more excited as he imagined that glorious future. "Your mother will probably make me a duke right away . . . no, a king, just like Gin Mazoti! My deeds will live on in Dara's lore forever in song and story. 'Noda Mi, Cruben of the Dandelion Throne' has a nice ring to it, don't you think?"

"What about Dyu-*tika* and Zaza-*tika*?" muttered Timu, still sounding lost. "They'll ask about their mother—"

"Forget about them," said Noda Mi, growing more impatient. *What is wrong with this idiot?* "Being Lyucu spawn, they'll have no place at the Dandelion Court. You can take as many consorts as you like once you're the real emperor in Pan to produce children for you—I certainly intend to. I'm sure you're looking forward to real girls after years of sleeping with *that*—"

He kicked Tanvanaki's corpse.

This seemed to have finally broken through Timu's near-catatonic state. "Don't you dare speak of my wife or children that way!"

Noda looked at him curiously. "Surely you jest. Are you willing to jeopardize your future for a couple of half-breeds?"

"They are *my* children! And there are tens of thousands of children just like them! What will happen to the people of Ukyu-taasa while you and I run off to the Big Island? Leaderless, the Lyucu will not be able to keep the peace. How many will die in a general rebellion—"

"Who cares? The more people die, the more glorious will appear our victory and your miraculous rescue—"

"How can you speak so casually of death and suffering—"

"The people who are about to die are like weeds. If they are cut down, more will spring up in their place in twenty years."

"They are *people*!" Timu's face was contorted by fury. "They're not weeds, not tokens in some game! They *deserve* better than your cold calculus of personal gain."

When Noda Mi spoke again, his voice was slow and deliberate. "*Rénga*, the world is divided into those who play the game, and those who are merely pieces on the board. I don't expect you to understand, having been born a prince. But I've had to fight and scheme all my life to avoid the fate of becoming a token in someone else's game. Do not speak to me of what is *deserved*.

"Did the people of Dara deserve Mapidéré's tyranny, foisted upon them like a frost-hearted winter? Or did they deserve Pékyu Tenryo's fury, unleashed upon them like a volcanic eruption? The world is a horror-filled sandpit, and each of us must claw and gnaw and stomp on our fellow men to delay the doom that awaits us all at the bottom. The words of the Ano sages and appeals to the gods are equally worthless. There is no higher ideal than this: Anyone who gets in my way is my enemy."

Timu looked away in despair. He could not conceive of a mind that worked like Noda's. A gulf divided them, as wide as the sea between Ukyu-taasa and his homeland.

" 'You must do the right thing,' " he muttered to himself, " 'even if it hurts you.' " The words of Kon Fiji felt to him like a salve, a ray of hope against Noda Mi's lightless vision.

"You do understand that I saved you?" said Noda Mi, a hint of menace creeping into his voice. "I hope obsession with the Ano Classics has not made you blind. That dirty sow who shared your bed never saw you as anything more than a useful *cüpa* stone in her own game.

"Do you not understand how she would have used you as a bargaining chip to secure the best terms for herself and her people? Why, had she not turned on me, I would have advised her to ignore Jia and go to Phyro! After selling your life to your ambitious brother, removing the main rival to his claim to the throne, she could then promise to help him launch a coup against Jia. With Lyucu aid, Phyro would become the emperor in fact as well as in name in no time. . . ."

Timu stopped listening. In his own way, Noda was as dangerous a fool as Cutanrovo. They both thought everyone else's minds worked just like theirs, guided by nothing but the naked craving for *dominance*, for *supremacy*, for *power*. . . .

But maybe he was the bigger fool for daring to think that there was *more* to be desired in the world, for believing in the Ano sages and the judgment of the gods, for taking ideas like "the good," "the right," "*mutagé*" seriously. After all, Noda Mi was now triumphant, while he was powerless to stop him.

And as for what Noda was saying about Tanvanaki—he turned to the dead body cradled in his arms—could he be sure Noda wasn't right? From him to her, there was nothing but an unreasoning, unjustifiable love, no matter how she treated him. But from her to him, the emotions were complicated. There was tenderness, affection, duty, perhaps even love—but he knew, from the very first time she took him, that her first love would always be a dream, the vision of conquest that her father had insisted that she carry on even after his death. She would always do what she thought was best for the Lyucu people, stranded beyond the Wall of Storms, lost among the Islands of Dara. Nothing was going to get in the way of that duty, not herself, not him, not perhaps even their children.

He had tried to convince her that there was another path for the Lyucu beyond conquest and slaughter, but he couldn't be sure, even at the very end, that she believed him. Indeed, how could he blame her? When the world allowed people like Cutanrovo and Noda Mi to triumph, what right did he have to insist on the viability of any other course?

"... Now, are you going to do as I say?" asked Noda Mi. "Or do I have to persuade you through some less pleasant means?"

Timu shivered, not from fear of pain or the late autumn wind, but a weariness that infused his bones.

He was not a man who knew how to fight. Indeed, he had always wanted to emulate the good king, Jizu of Rima, who died to uphold the ideal of the Moralist philosopher-king, burning up as a beacon of hope and compassion in a time of violence and darkness.

But his death would not help the people of Ukyu-taasa now, whether Lyucu or native. Perhaps it was time to look to another figure for emulation: Princess Kikomi, who had concealed her true intentions under a mask of frailty and gotten close to Phin Zyndu, the Hegemon's uncle, to strike a fatal blow to save her people.

"You make a very convincing case," he said, swallowing revulsion and hatred with every syllable. "I . . . am grateful for your help. When I am Emperor of Dara, your services will be amply rewarded."

He imagined himself plunging his writing knife into the pulsing neck artery of a sleeping Noda Mi. Afterward, he would return to Kriphi and let the thanes know the truth of Cutanrovo's and Noda's betrayals. He would then carry on the unfinished task of his wife and secure a future for the Lyucu *alongside* the natives.

"Good," growled Noda Mi. "Glad to see your brain hasn't been entirely rotted by books."

Gently, Timu lifted Tanvanaki's head off his lap and set it on the ground. The gesture pained him more than if he were cutting out his own heart. "We'll come back for this . . . later," he said, trying to make himself sound uncaring.

He picked up his writing knife and wiped off Tanvanaki's blood with a handkerchief. Carefully, he folded the handkerchief and put it, as well as the knife, away. Then he climbed onto the horse that Tanvanaki had ridden here. As he held the reins himself for the first time—Tanvanaki always did so when they rode together—his hands trembled.

He realized that Noda Mi hadn't mounted his horse.

Turning, he caught Noda's eye. The man was standing between the corpses, staring at Timu intently.

Timu was nervous. He couldn't tell what was going on inside that calculating, devious mind. He forced a measure of authority into his voice. "We should leave immediately before they come in search of the missing."

A smirk slowly appeared on Noda Mi's face. "We still have some unfinished business."

"What do you have in mind?" asked Timu, his voice quavering.

Noda Mi knelt down next to Cutanrovo's corpse. He wrapped a piece of cloth around the broken sword and, with a grunt, pulled the blade out of her chest. Tying the cloth to the blade to fashion a make-shift handle, he sheathed the sword. "Can't leave behind too many clues that lead back to us, now, can we?"

Next, he picked up Cutanrovo's stake-club and proceeded to methodically smash it against the woman's body. "Have to make it look like she was in a fight against other Lyucu. Have to leave behind a good story."

"But they'll still suspect us when they find the bodies without finding us," Timu protested.

"That is true," said Noda Mi. He dropped the stake-club and approached Timu. "*Rénga*, your knife, please."

"Why?"

Noda Mi continued to smile, saying nothing.

Timu handed him the knife.

Noda returned to Cutanrovo's corpse and began to hack at the wound in her chest. Soon, the single wound from the sword was gone, replaced by a bloody mess from the dull knife.

Timu's heart sank. Something was very, very wrong about all this. He strove to keep his voice calm. "Stop messing about." He tried to think the way a man like Noda would think. "We . . . could dig out the bodies of a couple of villagers from a mass grave and dress them in our clothes. If we . . . bludgeon the faces until they're unidentifiable, perhaps the thanes will think that you and I also died in a fight between Cutanrovo and Tanvanaki."

Noda Mi laughed heartily. "Ah, so you're capable of scheming and plotting as well! But you should have begun earlier. Much earlier."

Satisfied with his gruesome handiwork, he put the writing knife in his belt. Then he unsheathed his sword, and with another grunt, lopped off Cutanrovo's head. More blood spilled everywhere, and now his legs and feet were as gory as the rest of him.

Timu cried out in alarm. "What are you *doing*?"

"Empress Jia will demand proof that I killed the Lyucu leaders," said Noda Mi. He strode toward the corpse of Tanvanaki, sword lifted high.

The idea that his wife's corpse would be mutilated in this manner was intolerable. Timu screamed again, scrambled off the horse, and fell on top of Tanvanaki.

"Just as I thought," said Noda Mi, sounding amused and satisfied. "You're not with me after all."

Timu turned to face him, no longer bothering to disguise his hatred. "You won't get far with my mother if you don't have me, even if you do bring her Tanvanaki's head."

Noda Mi looked down at him in pity. "That's true. But if I can't have the cooperation of your mind, I'll have to settle for the cooperation of your corpse."

Timu glared at him. "I'm not afraid to die."

"Oh, of course you aren't. Just like Cutanrovo is infused with the Lyucu spirit, you're fortified with the words of the Ano sages," Noda Mi mocked. "I, on the other hand, am a mere man of flesh and blood, so I have to make sure I survive above all. I do need to thank you, however, for reminding me of another way to get what I want."

"What—what are you—"

"Your children! I'll bring your head as well as Tanvanaki's with me. With you dead, those two sniveling Lyucu-spawn will be all that remains of your bloodline. That has to be worth something to Jia and Phyro. One of them will make me a king, even if you won't."

"But then you'll have to go back to—" Timu stopped, finally understanding.

Noda Mi sheathed his sword and took out the writing knife again. Carefully, meticulously, almost as though he was putting on makeup, he cut himself: on the forehead, on his upper arms, on his thighs . . . Blood oozed from the wounds until it was no longer clear whether the blood covering him came from him or his victims.

Timu shivered uncontrollably. He should have known that he was no match for Noda Mi when it came to plots and schemes. Rather than getting a chance to avenge Tanvanaki, all he had accomplished was to put his own children at risk. He was no Jizu; he was no Kikomi; he was nothing but a fool, a failure. He couldn't protect Dara; he couldn't protect Ukyu-taasa; he couldn't protect his family. All he knew were useless words, useless books, useless ideals not worth the price of the wax they were written in.

As Noda Mi approached, Timu closed his eyes in despair.

"There is one more thing you will do for me," said Noda, his voice as cold as the glint from the edge of his sword. "Write a note to the children, so that they'll come with me without resistance. It's the only thing you can do unless you want them to join you soon on the other side of the River-on-Which-Nothing-Floats."

CHAPTER FORTY-FOUR

THE BATTLE OF PAN, PART III

PAN: THE ELEVENTH MONTH OF THE ELEVENTH
YEAR OF THE REIGN OF SEASON OF STORMS AND
THE REIGN OF AUDACIOUS FREEDOM.

Prime Minister Cogo Yelu hurried along the twisting, unlit paths, a single Dyran Fin at his side. It was good that he was so familiar with the layout of the palace; all the silkmotic and whale-oil lamps had been extinguished in order to make life as difficult as possible for intruders.

The heavy doors to the Imperial kitchen swung open on silent hinges. Cogo and the Dyran Fin stepped through and found a vast, long hall, deserted and silent. Even the incessant rain outside was muffled by the thick walls, made of stone to reduce the risk of fire.

A column of soldiers marched past behind them, half the distance of an arrow's flight from the kitchen. The faint glow from their torches spilled inside the open entrance, revealing the hulking shadows of stoves, ovens, frying stations situated along the two long walls, with pots, pans, fire-stokers, bamboo steam cages, skewer racks, and all manners of cooking utensils hanging above them. The long island down the center, where ingredients were washed, peeled, chopped, skinned, deboned, and filleted, loomed like an oncoming ship.

Cogo shut the door behind him and his Dyran Fin guard.

The room erupted. Silkmotic lamps sputtered to life, buzzing and humming, along with whale-oil torches that blazed like miniature suns. Cogo shielded his face with his long sleeves, temporarily blinded.

Dozens of fighters in sleek leggings and woven-silk body-fitting armor dropped from the ceiling and emerged from hidden pits as though materializing out of the air, all of them women. Swords and crossbow bolts pointed at Cogo, their tips glinting coldly.

Wi, her face covered by a black silk cloth so that only her expressionless eyes showed, stepped forward to face the Prime Minister.

"No one is supposed to come here until the rebels have all been caught," she said, her tone tense.

Cogo lowered his sleeves and blinked. He tried to speak, but the mad dash through the rain to reach here had been hard on his aged lungs, and he hacked and coughed instead, bent over, his arms flopping helplessly.

The Dyran Fin who had accompanied the Prime Minister took a step forward to stand next to him. She was dressed the same as the other Dyran Fins in the Imperial kitchen, save that she held no weapon. Most of her face below the eyes was hidden by a black cloth. A soaked headscarf sat low over her forehead and strands of wet hair peeked out, plastered against the little skin left showing. Her eyes shone with an intensity that matched Wi's.

"I've returned from the Second Fin," she said, her voice hoarse. "The Prime Minister must see the empress."

It was hard to tell the Dyran Fins apart when they wore their night fighting clothes, but Wi recognized her as Teké by the distinctive plum-shaped birthmark next to her right eye. Wi's heart clenched in sympathy at Teké's strained voice. Many of the sisters had fallen ill from the intensity of the recent all-night patrols and the cold weather—and the mistress had been too preoccupied to brew them curative brews. But she had no choice but to continue sending them out night after night.

"It's urgent, First Fin. The mistress's safety hangs in the balance."

Like all the Dyran Fins, who had grown up in the care of Empress Jia, a Faça native, Teké spoke in the accent of Boama, distinct from the rest of the palace, who tended to copy the Central Cocru topolect of Emperor Ragin and his old coterie.

Wi considered the request. If the Prime Minister made some argument based on the fate of the empire, she wouldn't have been moved.

But a plea from one of her sisters, absolutely loyal to the empress, was a different matter. This deviation from the agreed-upon plan had to be accommodated.

"Come with me," she said, turning around. Cogo rushed to follow her. Four other Dyran Fins fell in step behind him and Teké, while the rest of the Dyran Fins faded back into their hiding places.

Wi stopped by one of the large stoves in the back of the kitchen. A clumsy old-style stove that required coal, it had clearly not been used in some time. She took a ladle off the wall and struck it against the large semispherical-bottomed pan resting on the stove: two quick bangs, a pause, three quick bangs, a pause, another two quick bangs.

With a deep rumbling, some machinery under the stove was activated and the stove slid out of the way, revealing the entrance to an underground tunnel.

Though Cogo's face remained unperturbed, Wi caught the look of surprise in the old man's eyes and was pleased. "I guess even the Prime Minister doesn't know everything about the palace."

Cogo inclined his head in agreement, betraying no emotion in his expression.

Wi went into the tunnel, followed by Cogo and the five Dyran Fin guards. As soon as the last in the procession had disappeared into the tunnel, the heavy stove slid back into place.

The torches and silkmotic lamps went out, and the Hall of Ten Thousand Flavors once again was plunged into darkness and silence.

The assault on the Examination Hall was not going well.

Shido listened impassively as the commander of the palace guards explained the lack of progress.

Aya Mazoti's directive that as many of the rebels be captured alive as possible was a great hindrance—it was like being told that you had to fight with one hand tied behind your back. To be sure, the rebels seemed to be fighting only halfheartedly as well, turtling behind their barricades until the palace guards got too close, at which point they forced the attackers back with a barrage of arrows, most of which seemed to miss the mark—likely because the rebels were just a ragtag collection of untrained gangsters—

"Sounds to me like your men are simply putting on a show without any urgency," interrupted Shido.

While Wi was protecting the empress in her hideout, Shido had taken on the task of surveilling defenses outside the palace walls. They couldn't trust anyone who wasn't a Dyran Fin to do their job properly.

Shido narrowed her eyes at the commander. "Is it because none of you want to face Phyro, even though he is in open rebellion?"

"Err, tha-that isn't—um—" The commander swallowed and wiped his face. The Dyran Fins were rumored to be quite ruthless. "Lady Shido, you have to un-understand that many of the palace guards have served the Imperial family since the time of Emperor Ragin. I myself watched the emperor grow up as a child. This rebellion . . . is perhaps a misunderstanding—"

"The empress is the regent of Dara, and your one and only legitimate sovereign," said Shido severely. "Have you forgotten your duty?"

In truth, Shido couldn't have cared less about *legitimacy*. Jia was her mistress as well as the closest thing she had to a mother. There was nothing that mattered more than Jia's safety and well-being. Even when Shido and Wi were still girls, they wouldn't have hesitated to defend Jia with their fists and teeth had Kuni expressed any displeasure at Jia's liaison with Otho Krin, the steward. Jia had intimated that Phyro intended to kill her; that meant Phyro had to die.

The mistress, always kindhearted, had said that Phyro was not to be harmed. Yet Shido also knew that there were certain orders that the mistress could never issue, but nonetheless had to be understood by her loyal Dyran Fins.

"I really don't think the rebels are desperadoes," the commander pleaded. "I think they are putting on a show with that beacon and all the shouting and singing. We should talk to them. Maybe persuasion—"

"If you cannot protect the empress, then I'll find someone else who can." Shido whipped out a small metal tablet with a stylized dyran carved into it—the symbol of the empress. "As Princess Aya is consulting with the Prime Minister, I'm personally assuming command of this assault in the name of the empress. If the palace guards cannot fight the rebels wholeheartedly, then summon the city garrison. These rebels *must* fall."

The commander of the palace guards bowed in resignation, more than a bit relieved that he was no longer in charge.

The underground tunnels they passed through were lit by widely spaced, spinning, buzzing silkmotic lamps. This was a part of the palace that no one except the empress and her Dyran Fins knew existed; the laborers who had dug the tunnels were condemned criminals who had been executed as soon as the work was finished.

Finally, they arrived at a small antechamber before heavy oaken doors.

"Strip," ordered Wi.

Cogo looked at her. Though his face remained placid, his posture was one of exhaustion and suppressed fury. After all that he had been through on this tense, confusing night, this final indignity was too much. He was like a volcano that had been pent up for too long, and as his eyes flashed, he was ready to blow.

But Teké stepped forward before he could speak. "Eldest Sister, there is reason to believe that intruders have already breached the palace's defenses. The Prime Minister has absolutely vital information that the empress must know immediately. We don't have time for this."

Wi hesitated. If it were anyone else, she would have stood her ground, but the fact that a fellow sister was vouching for him and that he had already stripped earlier in the empress's bedchamber made her waver.

"Fine," she said, and gestured for the other Dyran Fins to open the heavy doors on the other side of the antechamber. The thick panels creaked open to reveal a narrow, dark tunnel. Warm light spilled from the exit at the other end.

One hand on the handle of her sword, Wi swept her other arm out in an inviting gesture.

Cogo nodded in thanks and proceeded forward. Teké tried to follow, but Wi stopped her. "What are you doing?"

Teké looked at her, puzzled.

"You're wearing armor."

Teké bowed in embarrassment. "Sorry. It's been a long night. I just wanted to make sure the empress is safe."

Wi looked at her kindly. "Soon it will be morning, and all the rebels will be captured. The mistress has planned for every eventuality."

Cogo hurried on through the tunnel, paying no attention to the exchange behind him. Wi followed him with her eyes, tilting her head to listen intently.

The walls of the narrow tunnel were built from powerful lodestone, and no iron weapon could pass through without being pulled to the wall and stuck fast. Even the Dyran Fins couldn't step inside the tunnel with their light armor and slender steel swords.

There was no clang or jangle as Cogo made his way through the tunnel, ending at a curtain of coral beads and pearls. He paused for a moment, gently parted the strands, and stepped through.

Satisfied that the empress's mechanical contrivances had verified her trust, Wi ordered the heavy doors closed.

Beyond the curtain was a large underground room brightly lit with four whale-oil lamps. Other than those concessions to Imperial luxury, the rest of the furnishing was simple and plain: rough hempen sitting mats, a low bamboo-and-wicker table, unvarnished wooden chests, bare stone walls devoid of rich tapestries.

The empress's secret lair reminded Cogo of a middling merchant family's sitting room rather than the heart of the palace. Some kind of hidden ventilation system must be circulating fresh air through the place, for it didn't feel musty or damp at all.

The empress was reclining on a daybed, browsing through a bundle of old letters in a box. She looked up expectantly as Cogo entered.

The Prime Minister glanced behind him to be sure that the heavy doors at the end of the tunnel were shut. He reached up behind his ears and began to pull.

The wrinkled skin over his face crumpled; the aged features

deformed and shifted; the sparse white hair lifted to give way to dark, thick locks.

Cogo Yelu's face peeled off, revealing the determined visage of Phyro, Emperor Monadétu.

Jia sat up in *mipa rari*, her face showing no hint of surprise; she had been waiting for him.

"Your guards will never get in here in time," said Phyro, gazing at her with a look of pure hatred. "So don't even try to summon them."

"I have no intention to," said Jia. "It's time that you and I talked, just the two of us."

Phyro's posture remained tense, but this was clearly not the answer he had expected. Jia looked him up and down.

"Clever," she said at length. "I should have known that Cogo's trick of putting on a show around an empty nest wouldn't fool you. . . . You've put into practice one good scheme after another tonight. Did you come up with all of them by yourself?"

"I have no empire," said Phyro. "But I have loyal friends."

Now that he was finally face-to-face with his mother's murderer, Phyro was filled with gratitude and admiration for his companions: Widow Wasu, who lent him material support at great personal risk, motivated only by an old friendship with his father; Zen-Kara, who refused to retire to Tan Adü but instead led the daring assault on Tiro Cozo to free Ofluro, Lady Suca, and the garinafins; Rati Yera, who devised the swarming ornithopters and built the speedy silkmotic dyran; Widi Tucru, who clouded the sight of the farseers with false and contradictory rumors; Mota Kiphi, who rallied the gangsters and discharged veterans in Pan to sow confusion throughout the city and lit the guiding beacon; and of course Arona Taré, who perfected the disguise that finally persuaded the empress's most trusted guards to lead him right to her.

And he bore no ill will toward Fara and Savo, who refused to condone his act of vengeance, but who would, perhaps, be his most valuable allies in the aftermath of tonight.

"Your father would be proud," said Jia. "He was a lot like you, with a way of drawing people to him and keeping them loyal. He built his empire on bonds of friendship, on links of trust." Her fingers ran lovingly over the old letters in the box. "Did you know that he always took the time to write to me during that period when I was the Hegemon's captive, no matter what else was happening—"

"Stop it," growled Phyro. "Don't you dare bring up my father now to soften my resolve. It is my *mother* that you should be thinking of. I will never understand how my father married a woman like you, with a heart crueler than a scorpion's sting and a mind subtler than a snake's coils."

"Give me some credit," said Jia. "It was that very same mind and heart that kept your siblings safe from the wrath of the Hegemon, that eliminated the danger to the throne posed by ambitious generals and nobles your father elevated but lacked the will to subdue, that kept Dara from tumbling into an obsession with vengeance, devoted to warfare and death—"

"Lies! More lies!" Sparks seemed to shoot from Phyro's eyes. "I will not retread these tired arguments with you. You've always clothed your actions in noble-sounding reasons, but the truth is that you simply wanted power—for yourself, and for Timu. I used to believe that you made your choices based on a vision of what was best for Dara, even if I disagreed with that vision. But Auntie Soto has told me the truth."

"For Timu?" said Jia, softly, a wry and bitter smile convulsing the corners of her mouth. Then, she met Phyro's eyes and raised her voice. "Without Soto's intervention, you would have ridden the garinafins into Rui and Dasu and turned the soil of those islands carmine with the blood of the helpless. No messenger from me could have stopped you—except Soto, with a message to divert you to vengeance."

For the first time, doubt crept into Phyro's heart. "You . . . sent Soto?"

Jia's smile was ghastly. " 'Sent' is perhaps too strong a word. It's in Soto's nature to do what she believed was right; I just took advantage of that nature to accomplish a greater good, as I have of Timu and . . . even you."

The helpless feeling that Jia was still somehow in control was intolerable to Phyro. He roared, careless if he could be heard outside the empress's hidden lair. "For once in your life, tell me what is true! Did you kill my mother?"

"Yes," said Jia.

The very simplicity of the response stunned him. There was no attempt at prevarication, at deflecting blame, at trying to paint a confusing smoke-scape constructed out of layered pretexts wrapped in reasons piled upon justifications.

"Then I'm here to avenge her," said Phyro. From deep in his robe, hidden next to his skin, he pulled out a bone dagger fashioned in the Lyucu manner, warm from the heat of his wrath.

"You have every right."

Again, the simplicity of her response threw him off. There was no plea for more time, for a chance to explain.

Doubt, hateful, unwanted doubt, grew in his mind.

Jia began to fold up the letters, placing them one by one neatly back in the box. "Let me put your father's letters out of the way. You shouldn't spoil them with my blood. Someday, you may want to read them—if you wish to understand how the lives of your father, me, and Risana were bound together in a common vision for Dara—"

"You are *not* fit to speak the name of my mother!" Tears of rage and pain spilled from Phyro's eyes. But he made no move as the empress closed the letter box, got up slowly, and gently set the box down on the small stand at the head of the daybed. "Why did you kill her? She was kind as a rabbit and devoid of ambition, deferring to you in every way. *Why?*"

The box's weight depressed a tiny protuberance atop the stand with the faintest of clicks.

A bell in the ceiling of the antechamber chimed.

The sound was so soft that one could have been forgiven for thinking that the otherworldly tinkle was an illusion, or the result of a passing draft.

Wi and all the other Dyran Fins instantly sprang into motion, stripping off their light armor and unhooking their sword belts.

All, except for Teké, the Dyran Fin who had accompanied Cogo Yelu here. She stood rooted in place, uncertain what to do.

Until now, Phyro's plan had been working to perfection. She had prepared the costume and the disguise based on the emperor's descriptions. She had practiced the accent of Boama and the movements of a Cocru sword dancer until she could walk among the Dyran Fins without arousing suspicion. They had led her and Phyro to the empress's secret refuge.

The plan had then called for her to depart as soon as Phyro entered the empress's lair. She was supposed to go back into the Palace Garden, find a secluded spot, and launch a signal firework to let Mota Kiphi and the others know that the plot had succeeded. Mota and the others would then surrender, their mission to distract the garrison and give the emperor an opening to sneak into the heart of the palace accomplished. She would hide in the Palace Garden until Phyro avenged his mother, secured the throne, and restored order to the chaotic palace and capital.

But she had stayed and waited in the antechamber. Something about that dark tunnel beyond the heavy doors made her uneasy. What if Phyro needed her help? The empress was cunning and resourceful.

It was a risk, she knew. Oh how she wanted to be out there launching the firework that would tell her dear Mota to lay down his arms, to stop risking his life! But it was a risk that Mota would want her to take. One stayed behind to help friends. Wasn't that the right thing to do?

Wi noticed her confusion and was on her in three long, quick strides. Her hand darted out and ripped the veil off to reveal the face of Arona Taré.

"You're not Teké. You're not one of us at all!"

Arona leapt back, picked up one of the swords the bodyguards had discarded, and dashed in front of the heavy doors to the lodestone tunnel, barring the Dyran Fins' way. She danced in front of the doors, spinning her sword into a cold, deadly chrysanthemum.

"*Rénga*, do it now!" she screamed.

"Push!" Égi screamed. "Push!"

True to her word, Shido had summoned the city garrison through the dark, rain-slicked streets of Pan to put down the rebellion.

Urged on by the implacable Dyran Fin captain, the soldiers had hastily assembled a crude arrow-tower out of odd bits of lumber lying about the wrecked shops and stalls surrounding the cylindrical Examination Hall, the rebels' improbable stronghold.

A team of a hundred soldiers chanted, braced their shoulders against the foot of the arrow-tower, and pushed. Slowly, the heavy structure, mounted on rolling logs and reinforced with sandbags, rolled toward the Examination Hall like a moving watchtower. Archers ensconced at the top took advantage of their elevation to shoot at the rebels behind barricades.

"This feels wrong," whispered Asulu. He and Égi had been assigned to the first story of the arrow-tower, where their task was to wield long spears through arrow slits to prevent any rebels from getting too close to the tower and setting it on fire. "We are fighting against our own people, when we should be fighting the Lyucu!"

"Don't let your mind wander," said Égi, posted next to the younger soldier. "We have a job to do, and the sooner we put down this rebellion, the sooner everything returns to normal." He turned to scream at those behind the tower, "Push! You lazy greenhorns. Push!"

Relentlessly, the arrow-tower pressed forward, crashing through the rebel barricades like an icebreaker in the northern ports in winter. The rebels' arrows bounced harmlessly off the fortification, and, as the siege engine advanced, the rebels scattered, retreating back into the Examination Hall itself.

"Onward! Onward!" shouted Shido. "Kill them all!"

Once the arrow-tower connected with the Examination Hall, soldiers would leap through the windows and catch the rebels like trapped rats with nowhere to go.

"I killed your mother to keep power away from you."

Even more than the content of her disclosure, Jia's matter-of-fact tone by turns chilled and boiled Phyro's blood.

The empress went on. "Risana might be devoid of ambition, but as your mother, she would have been a living standard. As long as she lived, those unsatisfied with my decisions at court would have a banner to rally around, and she would have, by choice or not, become a rival center. I had to make you, a mere child at the time, dependent on me entirely. Her death gave me the time to consolidate the machinery of state, to build up enough strength of my own so that I could keep the throne from you as long as it was necessary."

The thumping of Phyro's heart was a raging storm in his ears, and a faint voice seemed to be calling to him from somewhere in the distance, through the bead curtain, through the dark, narrow tunnel, through the thick oaken doors, through the twisting maze of tunnels beyond—was it the spirit of his dead mother, calling for vengeance?

Do it now!

He took a step forward, brandishing his bone dagger.

He stopped.

His mother had always counseled him that anger was dangerous, like the smoke that she manipulated in her art to obscure reality. To avenge her properly, he had to extract from her killer a full and proper confession, to reveal the extent of the dark plot that had cost her life. He had to *understand* and weigh the fish.

"But to what purpose? To pass the throne to Timu or Gimoto?"

Jia shook her head. "Gimoto is nothing more than a distraction, a way to force you to learn and . . . to draw out the poison in the restless hearts of the Lords of Dara through court politics. As for Timu . . . I love my son, but he can never be emperor. The only true heir to your father and Théra is, and has always been, you."

Another shock. The empress's lament seemed genuine, not another wisp of deception. "Then . . . why keep the Seal of Dara from me? What were you waiting for?"

"For you to be ready to wield the Grace of Kings, to understand the need for cruelty in the service of a greater mercy, to accept the world as it is, not as it ought to be. So long as you believe the solution to Dara's problems is war and conquest, so long as you heed the seductive song of militarism in the service of liberating Unredeemed Dara, you must not be emperor. The people of Dara, *all* the people of Dara, deserve better."

Phyro began to laugh, howls of despair. "You think you see everything, yet you cannot see into my heart. I've accepted the need to maintain the peace with Ukyu-taasa, to pay the Lyucu tribute to save lives. Did you know that even before Soto arrived, I had already decided to call off the invasion on my own? And it was at the counsel of the spirit of my departed mother, the woman you murdered."

Through hot tears, Phyro saw a sight he never thought he would witness: doubt and confusion on Jia's face.

Can it be? Jia wondered. Can it be that Phyro is already the good emperor I've been hoping he'll one day become?

He's not so blinded by notions of honor and glory to treat the lives of the people like weeds. He's not so in love with tales of triumph and romance to disregard reality, which requires compromise, submission, and sacrifice.

How long had she been wishing for this day, when she could unburden herself and let go of the crushing weight of responsibility! If Phyro truly understood the horrors of war, the impossibility of achieving victory by mere force of arms, the futility of gaining liberation through certain death, then . . . perhaps she could finally let him know the truth.

She could explain to him the years of plotting to lull the Lyucu into a sense of complacency; she could reveal the secret field of engineered zomi berries in the mountains; she could explain all the manipulations, all the schemes, all the feints and counter-feints.

But was Phyro strong enough for the aftermath? To understand the price of war alone was not enough—he also had to know when it must be paid. In the chaos after the fall of Unredeemed Dara, would he be so consumed by notions of fairness, justice, mercy, honor that he would forget the need to be cruel?

She had to trust him. Could she?

"Hudo-*tika*," she began, her voice quavering, "let me ask you a question."

Mota kept glancing at the sky in the direction of the palace.

He could hear shouted orders and cries of alarm; he could see the unsteady glow of torches carried by invisible columns of soldiers. But he could not see the one sight he craved above all: Arona's firework signaling that she was safe.

The arrow-tower, spitting missiles and bristling with spears, lumbered toward the Examination Hall like some monster from a fairy tale. The rebels shot fire arrows and tossed torches at it, but the wet sandbags absorbed every blow.

"Mota, what are we going to do?"

"How much longer do we have to fight?"

"They killed my sister! Is the emperor going to win?"

Mota looked at the anxious faces around him: discharged veterans, Adüan gangsters, the *raye* . . . men and women who had rallied to the emperor's cause, who had joined him to do the right thing, who had believed that they were meant to create a distraction, not to make a last stand.

"Retreat back into the Examination Hall," he shouted. "We don't know if the emperor has succeeded, so we have to draw their attention for as long as we can!"

Then he ran toward the lumbering monster, heedless of the cries of consternation behind him.

Arrows rained down around him; torches atop the arrow-tower lit everything bright as day. One arrow thunked into his shoulder. He stumbled, pulled it out, tossed it aside, and ran on.

There was still no firework in the direction of the palace. The plan had gone wrong.

Four or five spears poking out of arrow slits challenged him. He brushed them aside as easily as an ox would flick away bothersome flies with its tail. He was at the foot of the tower. Planting his feet in the ground and leaning against the tower, he *pushed* back.

The tower ground to a halt. Mota, alone, withstood the strength of a hundred men.

Soldiers atop the battlement cried out in surprise. Stones rained down around him. Arrows slammed into the ground, inches from his feet.

He looked in the direction of the palace, hoping, praying.

That moment from long ago, in the air above the roiling Zathin Gulf, came back to him.

"Captain, do you think they'll remember us in the future like they remember the Hegemon?"

"*Probably not. Most soldiers who die are quickly forgotten. But we don't fight to leave a name; we fight because it's the right thing to do.*"

An arrow slammed into his back, and the pain was so sharp that his knees buckled. The tower slid forward an inch. He howled like a wolf, and forced the pain from his mind, willing himself to push back even harder.

The tower stopped again. He had to hold on. So long as he pinned the attention of the mighty empire here, Phyro would still have a chance.

But truth be told, he wasn't thinking about the emperor at all. The face that filled his mind belonged to Rona, and he was thinking of the last time he had seen her, a few days earlier.

"*Are you scared?*" *she asked.*

"*I'm never scared,*" *he lied.* "*Are you?*"

"*I am . . . but not for me. I have a feeling that I might not see—I don't want to say it.*"

"*Then don't. One should never speak words of ill fortune before taking to the air.*"

"*I'm not a superstitious aviator like you.*"

He gazed into her eyes and made a decision. "*How about this? I promise you that after this, we'll never fight again. You and I will go buy a taro farm near Ginpen, and we'll go to the city to see new plays every month.*"

Her eyes lit up. "*Really? But what about . . . your mission? Haven't you always wanted to redeem the Marshal's name? Don't you want to be a part of the emperor's rise?*"

"*Dara will be fine once the emperor is in power,*" *he said.* "*There are worthier things for men than dying for great lords who recognize their talent, Rona. I prefer to live with the woman who touches my soul.*"

Another arrow sank into his back. Then another. He could see the blood pooling at his feet, feel himself weaken.

He howled again, gazing into the sky over the palace, willing for her to be safe.

The Dyran Fins closed in on Arona. She glared at them and spun her sword faster.

Any minute now, she knew, Phyro would emerge from the tunnel, triumphant with the news that he had avenged Empress Risana and restored the veiled throne to its rightful owner. As the Dyran Fins cowered before him, she would stand next to him, beaming with pride. Of all his companions on this journey, she was the one who had walked with him nearest the end.

And then, she and Mota would be able to live the life they wanted in a land of peace, with everything the way it should be.

"Back off!" she growled. "Emperor Monadétu has returned!"

All she had to do was to hold them off a little longer.

The outcome was never in doubt.

All Arona's fighting skills were learned on and for the stage, beautiful to look at but of little avail against fighters trained to deliver the killing blow.

With a few deft turns of the sword, Wi disarmed her. Before the tumbling sword had even struck the ground, the other Dyran Fins had thrust their swords into her chest, belly, side, the blades buried deep.

Arona fell, writhed feebly on the ground, and stopped moving.

The Dyran Fins didn't even spare a glance at her lifeless body as they dropped their swords. Clad only in black silk, they opened the heavy doors and crept noiselessly down the lodestone tunnel toward the bead curtain at the other end.

"After the Battle of Crescent Island, you didn't slaughter the Lyucu who surrendered to you. Why?"

This was the last question in the world Phyro expected. "Because . . . because I needed Goztan to act as emissary, to persuade the Lyucu to surrender in the face of overwhelming force."

"Is that it? You kept them alive out of expedience? If you had no more use for them, would you have killed them?"

"No!" Blood rushed into Phyro's face. "Of course not! Goztan had fought me with honor. She and her army surrendered upon losing the duel, with no conditions. To slaughter her and her warriors in such a state would be despicable, revolting beyond the ken of gods and mortals. Dara must not be stained so."

"Even though Goztan could have simply been deceiving you?

Even though she could have plotted to lose the duel in order to preserve her strength to fight you another day?"

Phyro shook his head resolutely. "I fought her hand to hand, wing to wing. That is not in her nature."

Jia sighed. So that was it. Phyro did not understand the nature of the Lyucù. There were enemies to whom mercy couldn't be granted. He was still a child who saw the world in black and white, in honor and betrayal. He couldn't tolerate the reality that all sovereigns, in order to protect their people, must sometimes tear up peace treaties, slaughter prisoners, be cruel. She couldn't trust him to finish the task she had started.

Still, she felt she had to try, one last time.

"Let me explain, Hudo-*tika*—"

"No," shouted Phyro, wiping away his tears. "You've explained enough. No matter how grand the ideals, nothing can justify murder in cold blood. There are some crimes that cannot be forgiven. When I have avenged my mother and propitiated her ghost with your blood, I will be the good emperor that my father and mother always wanted me to be."

He lifted his bone dagger once more.

Or perhaps he understood the need to be firm only too well. She couldn't trust him, and he didn't trust her.

She stared into his eyes, willing him to understand.

You may be the good emperor Kuni and Risana always wanted you to be, but a good emperor isn't enough. Against the Lyucu, at this moment, Dara needs an evil empress more than a good emperor.

"By cutting me down, you will have proven only your skill with the Courage of Brutes," she said, her voice pleading as she shuffled backward. "Yet, you must learn to wield the Grace of Kings. Is it in your nature to understand true *mutagé*?"

She pictured the trap she had prepared for this eventuality—she had thought of everything, after all. The poison at the tips of the bamboo skewers would not be fatal, but they would tranquilize him almost immediately. She needed time, needed time to complete the last piece of her plan before passing him the Seal of Dara.

Behind Phyro, the strands of beads making up the curtain shook ever so slightly.

Phyro wished he could shut his ears against Jia's incoherent babbling.

She appeared to be just an ordinary old woman, spine crooked, skin wrinkled, hands that shook even as she tried to keep them steady. She seemed so helpless; she was his aunt-mother. Was it right to kill her in cold blood?

Yet, what could be more right than to exact vengeance? To right the horrible wrong that had been committed against his beloved mother?

How he wished he was wielding Na-aroénna at this moment, so that he could end all the doubts warring in his heart.

Suddenly, Jia leapt backward, out of his reach. She scrambled into the corner behind the daybed and held up a sitting cushion as though it were a shield.

Behind him, Phyro felt the air stir. He cursed himself. Jia had been playing for time, distracting him as she had alerted her guards.

Without looking back, he lunged, landing right next to the daybed. One more step and he would be able to plunge the dagger into her heart.

But the rug at his feet gave way and crumpled. He tried to leap up, but his toes found no purchase against empty air, and he was falling, falling into a pit.

Wrath filled his heart. Once again he had been outmaneuvered, fooled, trapped. He was still the helpless child, unable to do a thing against the powerful aunt-mother who barred him from his destiny, from being a worthy warrior, a dutiful son, a good emperor.

He felt his feet touch the bottom, where something sharp pierced them. A moment later, hot lances of pain skewered his mind.

The Dyran Fins rushed into the room, heading straight for the pit where Phyro had fallen—

Shadows loomed overhead, above the rim of the pit. Fighting through the pain, Phyro reached into his robe—

"Don't injure him!" He could hear Jia shouting. "He's harmless now—"

Phyro's fingers wrapped around a ceramic pot about the size of a man's head, packed with firework powder and glass shards. In his disguise as Cogo Yelu, it had served as the aging Prime Minister's rotund belly. In the center of the pot was a tiny Ogé jar, storing the silkmotic force in two layers of silver so that it wouldn't trip the lodestone detectors.

Rati Yera had not wanted to make such a thing, but Phyro had insisted.

"You should always plan to live, not to die," said Rati Yera.

"Sometimes prudence is not a virtue," said Phyro. "My father always said that if you are going to gamble, don't hold anything back."

A haze was descending over his mind.

Arona is dead, as likely is Mota. I've failed my companions, dear friends who have given me all, who have seen me as I am, as I wish to be. Men should be willing to die to live up to the stories they wish to be told about them.

Slowly, as though moving through some viscous liquid, he freed his feet from the long, bloody bamboo skewers—

"Mistress!" Wi shouted. "Get down!"

With the last of his strength, he leapt up, holding the pot tight against his beating heart, slamming the triggering mechanism home as he reached the rim of the pit—

The Dyran Fins jumped on the rising emperor—

In the heart of the pot, the Ogé jar broke, and sparks arced through the darkness of the tightly packed firework powder: heat, bright light, expanding gas, a grand explosion that heralded the creation of a new world and the ending of the old.

CHAPTER FORTY-FIVE

TRACE, RETRACE

TATEN-RYO-ALVOVO: THE ELEVENTH MONTH IN
THE ELEVENTH YEAR AFTER THE DEPARTURE OF
PRINCESS THÉRA FROM DARA FOR UKYU-GONDÉ.

Çami invited the leaders of the settlement to a demonstration.

The apparatus, the result of days of debates, prototyping, and experimentation among Çami, Sataari, and Gozofin, was brand new in design but incorporated components from Sataari's ritual arucuro tocua device for taking spirit portraits. The preserved muntjac ear, complete with the eardrum and the osseous linkage, was embedded in a complicated frame of articulated bones, terminating in a slender wing-tip needle.

However, under the needle, instead of a blank roll of garinafin stomach lining as would be found in a spirit-portrait-taker, lay Takval's spirit portrait.

"What is this?" asked Théra, once everyone had settled around the fire.

Çami and Sataari shared a meaningful look. Sataari nodded and began to tap a steady beat on a heartbeat drum, singing quietly to herself. Théra recognized the tune—the same chant that Adyulek had intoned when she took Takval's portrait.

To the beat of Sataari's chant, Çami cranked the bone rollers so that the membranous scroll wound from one axle onto the other.

Çami nudged the sharp needle down to touch the moving tape.

"No—" Théra gasped. The thin, translucent membrane seemed so delicate, and the wing-tip needle so sharp. The idea that this last trace of her husband, this final portrait of his inimitable voice, could be at risk filled her with terror.

"Votan, it's all right," said Gozofin, putting a comforting hand on her elbow. "The portrait will hold. It's strong."

Théra watched the machine with unblinking eyes.

The needle pressed into the layer of hardened glue-ash over the tape, the tip resting inside the serpentine groove down the middle. As the tape wound on, the needle retraced the path sketched by Takval's final words.

Pausing in her chant, Sataari said, "Çami realized that rather than trying to read the portraits of the dead like word-scars, we should be listening to their voices by retracing the steps of their vocal dance. The ear that hears vibrates in sympathy with the throat that sings."

She resumed singing; Çami continued to crank.

The needle inside the groove vibrated; the tremors amplified as they traveled up through the linkage of bones; the garinafin eardrum at the end quaked.

Everyone held their breath.

A faint buzzing emerged from the flared pinna.

"What—" Théra didn't get to finish her question because Çami was waving for her to be quiet. She beckoned the pékyu to come closer.

Taking a deep breath and willing her heart to slow down, Théra leaned in, placing her head inside the inviting cone of the garinafin auricle.

The crackling of the bonfire, the murmuring of the throng, the susurration of the breeze among the grass . . . everything faded away, leaving her alone with the voice inside the garinafin ear.

Her face froze; the crowd leaned forward.

A confident, reassuring voice, a voice she never thought she would hear again, filled the air around her, seemed to speak to her from the middle of her head.

Tears flowed down Théra's face without restraint. "O gods!"

"*. . . son of Souliyan Aragoz, daughter of Nobo Aragoz. I serve the Agon people as pékyu. Hearing the call of the cloud-garinafin, I now voice my spirit to be painted . . .*"

There was no substitute for the self-authenticating voice, for the thinking-breath that filled the listener's head and compelled faith.

"Votan," Gozofin said, "with the aid of the speaking bones, we now possess the proof you need to legitimate your claim. You *will* have the support of all the Agon warriors. Will you go to war?"

"*Rénga*," Tipo Tho said, cradling the sleeping form of toddling Crucru, "I know you do not wish to see death and mayhem, but it is the law of the scrublands that only the victor may dictate to the vanquished. The gods have given us a chance to be victorious. Will you go to war?"

Théra pulled her head out of the giant garinafin ear to meet the expectant gazes of her tribe.

"No," she said resolutely. "There is something else far more important we must accomplish first: Retrace the steps of our people."

CHAPTER FORTY-SIX

GARINAFINS OF DARA

DEEP IN THE WISOTI MOUNTAINS: THE ELEVENTH
MONTH OF THE ELEVENTH YEAR OF THE REIGN
OF SEASON OF STORMS AND THE REIGN OF
AUDACIOUS FREEDOM.

The cold mist thinned with the rising sun, revealing a lone figure standing atop the peak.

She had climbed up here every morning without fail, gazing west until the setting sun forced her to look away. She gazed as though her eyes could speak, could call forth the man she wanted to see by sheer force of will.

Below her, hidden in the dense woods in the lee of the mountain, the garinafins moaned restlessly, their bellies swollen with lift gas. It had been days since they were allowed to fly. Enforced grounding didn't accord with their nature.

"He's not coming."

Zen-Kara whipped around. It was Lady Suca.

"We can't wait here forever," said Lady Suca. "The emperor has failed."

Zen-Kara said nothing. A sudden gust of cold air made her shiver like a lone, sere leaf. So long as she didn't acknowledge it, perhaps it wouldn't be true.

"Phyro is either imprisoned or . . . dead."

Zen-Kara growled at her, balling her hands into fists.

Suca didn't flinch. "Is it his?" She moved her glance to the swell in Zen-Kara's belly.

After a pause, Zen-Kara nodded. The baby had been conceived the last time they were together, on Crescent Island.

"Then you know what you must do," said Suca. "You carry the legitimate heir to the Dandelion Throne."

Tears flowed down Zen-Kara's face, the drops glistening in the wintry sunlight as they traced the lines of her blue tattoos. As Suca wrapped her arms about her, she collapsed into the embrace, weeping openly and inconsolably.

An hour later, the garinafins took off and winged west, toward Pan, the Harmonious City.

PAN: THE ELEVENTH MONTH OF THE ELEVENTH YEAR OF THE REIGN OF SEASON OF STORMS AND THE REIGN OF AUDACIOUS FREEDOM.

The Inner Council met again, as they had done each of the last seven days.

"How is the empress?" asked Doman Gothu, Head of the College of Advocates. "Is she almost ready to resume her duties?"

Gori Ruthi, Acting Farsight Secretary, shook his head. "Her injuries are too extensive. Wi tells me that though she's awake, she must be kept in constant dream-haze to dull the pain. She cannot be bothered with affairs of state."

"Any progress on catching the assassins?"

Gori Ruthi's face flared red momentarily. "Interrogation of the survivors who assaulted the palace continues. They refuse to betray their coconspirators."

"If you would apply some more rigorous techniques of interrogation—"

"It was this very council that abolished the use of torture, with both the emperor and empress assenting," said Gori. "I'm not going to violate the rules just because it's expedient."

"But everyone here knows that the empress's story is prepos—"

"That's enough!"

Silence. The members of the council stared at one another, none willing to voice aloud what was on their minds.

The empress, during brief bouts of lucidity, had been adamant that her injuries were the result of an accident, and that no assassin had succeeded in breaching the palace defenses. Though everyone suspected that Phyro had been behind the nighttime attack, there was no proof.

"What are we going to do?" asked Mi Ropha, the Chief Circuit Intendant. "Outrageous rumors are proliferating, and the people are anxious. Dara cannot be without a sovereign."

With the emperor missing and the empress incapacitated, the Inner Council had kept things running by consensus. But everyone was fearful of a crisis erupting: a Lyucu invasion, a pretender rebellion, a natural disaster.

The council couldn't even agree on a member of the House of Dandelion to assume the duties of regent pro hac vice. Princess Fara had always displayed little interest or skill in politics— besides, no one knew where she had disappeared to. The idea of turning to Prince Gimoto—arrogant, cowardly, ignorant—was a nonstarter.

"It seems to this rather foolish man that there is no need to fret," said Cogo Yelu, Prime Minister.

"What?" blurted Gori Ruthi.

"The empress has always said that the welfare of Dara cannot depend on any one person," said Cogo, his eyes half-closed and his tone slow and even. "She may hold the Seal of Dara, but she has always delegated authority and listened to counsel. When the voices of the council are united and she is in the minority, she has backed down. When she has consented to a decree we proposed, she has submitted to its strictures. It seems to me that she has been preparing us for exactly a day like this, when we must act in place of the sovereign until her return.

"The Imperial bureaucracy is a complicated but well-crafted machine. It embodies the insights of the Ano sages, the wisdom of good counselors, and the spirit of the sovereign. It is capable of responding to the needs of the people. So let us be good engineers and carry out our assigned tasks with its aid."

To some of the assembled ministers, Cogo's declaration seemed to verge on treason. A Dara without a sovereign? A disembodied Throne embedded in a "machine"? Yet, when they pondered the words in light of Empress Jia's actions, they seemed to mirror one another.

Reluctantly, the ministers nodded in assent.

"I wish to bring up a new matter for discussion," said Gori Ruthi. "Farseers embedded among the pirates have brought news of domestic strife among the Lyucu. Details are scant, but—"

A palace guard dashed into the Inner Council Chamber, shouting at the top of his lungs. "Invasion! Garinafin invasion!"

Temple bells clanged. Smoke signals billowed from city watchtowers.

Panicked crowds ran through the streets, seeking shelter in deep cellars, stone-walled warehouses, temples where statues of the gods gazed upon the world with sightless eyes. Pan had once before been burned to the ground by the conquering Hegemon; would it again turn into a sea of flames?

Aya Mazoti, her armor and hair in disarray, struggled to guide her horse through the streaming crowds. With Puma Yemu under house arrest, she remained Pan's senior military commander and had to rally its disorganized defenses.

The city garrison, preoccupied for the last few days with hunting down the remnants of the "pirate raid" in Pan, was wholly unprepared for this aerial assault. But despite the absence of clear orders from above, discipline held. Soldiers pushed heavy platforms mounting gimbaled crossbows into the market squares, temple plazas, wide crossroads; silkmotic bolts were loaded and the strings winched taut; bright bonfires roared to life, and bags of specially formulated herbs and spices were tossed in—these had been devised by the Imperial Academy to generate thick columns of soporific smoke to lure and then incapacitate the garinafins.

Overhead, garinafins circled above different districts of the city.

Veterans of the Battle of Crescent Island, piloted by riders who had shared hardship and glory with Phyro, they had come to enforce the claim of their lord, the one and only true Emperor of Dara.

"Scared?" asked Égi, a smirk on his face.

Asulu nodded, keeping his eyes on the garinafin gliding high above. His breathing was labored, and his limbs ached from the exertion of winding the winch for the silkmotic bolts. "Aren't you?" he retorted.

"Everyone dies sometime," Égi said. "This is what we signed up for."

"Feeling good about dying for the empress?"

Égi laughed and spat. "I don't give my life for the empress. But if I can take one of them down before I die, that's one less garinafin to harm my wife and daughters. A good trade."

Asulu glanced to the side, where teams of soldiers were struggling to ready and raise the unwieldy, mast-like silkmotic lances in case the garinafin dove to strafe them. In the distance, he could see the billowy profiles of Imperial airships, like silkworm cocoons, struggling to gain altitude and assemble outside the city walls.

"So many people are going to die today," muttered Asulu. "What a waste."

"I thought you admired the emperor," said Égi. "You were quite sympathetic to the rebels, if I recall."

Asulu thought back to that night of terror, when he had killed for the first time. The memory made his scalp tingle. "It cannot be right to kill so many people just for the throne. Emperor, empress, you, me—we're all people of Dara. We shouldn't be fighting each other at all."

"I wish the great lords could hear you. I do."

The garinafin turned and dove at their position.

"Fire!" shouted the commander. "Reload and aim!"

Égi and Asulu threw themselves into their task.

With each wingbeat, the garinafin Ginki descended lower.

Zen-Kara looked down at the buildings of the palace, looming ever larger in her field of view: the glazed tiles, the sweeping roofs, the statues of guardian beasts perched at the ridges. She was riding a fiery lance aimed at the very heart of Dara.

Ofluro, the pilot, turned and shouted from the saddle, "We're in position for the strike. What are your orders, Lady Zen-Kara?"

The unfamiliar form of address startled her. *I suppose I am a lady now, consort of the Emperor of Dara.* "I . . . don't know."

Untrained in the art of war, she had been of little use in planning the assault. It was Ofluro and Lady Suca who had devised the plan to have the other garinafins approach Pan singly from different directions so as to confuse the defenders, giving Ginki, the most nimble of the war beasts, a chance to streak straight to the palace.

Ofluro had not wanted to put Zen-Kara at risk at all, but she refused to be left out. Somehow, she felt that she had to be there, had to be the one to avenge Phyro personally.

"You have to decide! If the garrison is given enough time to concentrate their anti-garinafin engines at the palace, we won't—"

A loud *twannng*, like the snap of a giant whip. A shiny missile shot up from a platform parked in the middle of the broad plaza before the palace, heading straight for Ginki.

Ofluro jerked the reins and kicked his heels hard into Ginki's shoulders. The young war mount snapped her wings to lurch to the side, then folded them against her body, dropping like a stone.

The missile flashed through the space where Ginki had been but a fraction of a second earlier.

Zen-Kara felt her organs rise up, threatening to erupt from her throat, as the sky and the earth spun around, switching places rapidly. She was grateful for the harness that strapped her tight against the barrel-rolling beast. The last time she had experienced such a wild ride was also on the back of Ginki, piloted by her beloved.

The garinafin pulled out of her evasive maneuver. Ofluro directed her to circle around, dive, and lash the rotating crossbow platform below with a searing lance of flames. Soldiers on the ground scattered just as the garinafin fire breath struck, incinerating the massive crossbow.

Sky and earth returned to their customary places. The world abided, and even the garinafin she was riding was the same. But

Phyro was gone, a hollowness in her heart that could never be replaced.

A muffled explosion behind them, somewhere in the distance. The silkmotic bolt that had missed them by mere inches had completed its long arc and fell to the ground, setting off its Ogé jar fuse. Zen-Kara hoped that wherever the missile had struck, there were as few victims as possible.

Ofluro directed Ginki into another sweeping, wide turn above the plaza as he looked about alertly. He pointed to the columns of thick, black smoke rapidly progressing through different parts of the city, congregating on the palace.

"They've gotten the crowds out of the streets and are coordinating their defenses. We've lost three garinafins already, Lady Zen-Kara. You have to decide now: Do we attack the palace?"

Zen-Kara gritted her teeth. Below her, the wreck that had been the silkmotic bolt launch platform burned brightly. The flames roared like a hungry monster, spitting forth acrid smoke, testifying to the destructive power of Phyro's garinafin force.

She imagined the palace deluged by a fiery flood. Jia would die, as would many others who had had no part in Phyro's fall.

"How can you be so"—she hesitated, struggling for the right word— *"open?"*

"To confront evil, one must be open to all that is good in the world," he said. *It was a Moralist cliché; yet, she had never heard it spoken with such conviction.*

The desire for vengeance drained out of her.

"Don't attack!" she shouted in Ofluro's ear. "Land in front of the palace. I'll assert the right to parley."

The Plaza of the Four Seas, forbidden to non-pedestrian traffic, was the main stage for those performances in Dara's political theater intended for the common people. It was broad enough to be an airfield, bounded on three sides by wide avenues and abutting the palace on the fourth. Here, Empress Jia (and Emperor Monadétu, when he chose to be present) delivered public prayers on solstices and equinoxes and other calendrical milestones. Here, officials, nobles, and generals gathered in neat formation before proceeding through the gates to attend formal court. Here, tens of thousands gathered on major holidays to see fireworks, admire riddle lanterns, enjoy performances, and catch a glimpse of the Imperial family.

Today, however, the plaza was deserted, save for the smoking ruins of a silkmotic bolt launch platform. The wide avenues around the square were packed with soldiers in armor, manning giant crossbows, silkmotic lances, Fithowéo's arms loaded with firework bombs, and all other manners of anti-garinafin and siege weaponry.

The garinafins landed in the plaza one by one, like a flock of wild geese touching down upon a placid lake along their annual migration route.

A single figure emerged from the gates of the palace and approached the lead garinafin.

"I am Cogo Yelu, Prime Minister of Dara."

Ginki lowered her head gently to the ground, and Zen-Kara stepped off.

"I demand to speak to Emperor Monadétu."

Cogo shook his head. "The Seal of Dara is held by Empress Jia, duly appointed regent of the Dandelion Throne."

"I'm here to remove her, to save Dara!"

"This isn't the way to save anything."

"Will you die to defend a murdering usurper, old man? You know the truth about Jia. The people deserve a good emperor!"

"I stand before you not to defend an individual, but a system," said Cogo. His voice, wheezy but strong, echoed over the flagstones. "The Hegemon and the bickering Tiro kings all thought they were good sovereigns. They believed that slaughtering their opponents was the same as winning an argument, and that a foe defeated was an idea disproved. But experience and the words of the Ano sages teach us that even a just claim is tarnished when it is enforced at the tip of a sword or from the back of a garinafin."

Zen-Kara faltered. Quotations from revered Moralist masters flitted through her mind. "What . . . what has happened to Phyro?"

"I don't know the answer to that," said Cogo, pausing in great anguish. "But what I do know is that Phyro loves the people of Dara, and he would never wish to see Pan engulfed in the flames of civil war. The Lyucu remain in Unredeemed Dara, and their spies are no doubt watching right now. Do you believe Phyro wants to see the enemies of Dara celebrate and hear the laments of those who love this land?"

Zen-Kara closed her eyes. Phyro had insisted on seeking vengeance against Jia as an assassin, aided by a band of his trusted companions, rather than as the Emperor of Dara at the head of an army. He had relied on guile and feints in order to minimize casualties and the possibility of all-out civil war. She could not deny the truth of the old man's words.

"Kuni Garu rebelled against a tyrant and yielded his life to the Lyucu to create tranquility, so that the people of Dara would not be slaughtered—either by foreign invasion or domestic strife," said Cogo Yelu. "He wanted the machinery of state to balance the desires of those who disagree, to resolve their differences peacefully. As his father's heir, Phyro knows that his actions will be constitutive acts for future sovereigns, and weighty as precedent. What example will he set for those who come after him? If Emperor Monadétu seizes power by slaughtering and burning the Harmonious City, then his victory will be a defeat. His name will be cursed down the generations."

Cogo's words struck Zen-Kara hard. She was not born of Dara, but she had come of age in it. The ideals that Cogo cited—legitimacy, the weight of history, the constitutive nature of political acts— perhaps didn't move her as much they would have moved someone steeped in Dara's values from birth, but her heart vibrated in sympathy with their hold on the man she loved, the man who had been torn between his duties as a son bound to avenge his mother and his duties as heir to the Dandelion Throne to maintain and sustain a just engine of power.

She looked at the old man standing in her way, frail and vulnerable, but with no trace of fear on his face; she looked at the soldiers clustered around their war engines beyond the edge of the square, nervous but disciplined; she thought about the thousands upon thousands huddled in the densely packed tenement buildings, winding alleys, and spacious manors beyond—servants, officials, beggars, scholars, children, elders . . . all with their own grand dreams and private anguish.

They were the people of Dara, the people Phyro loved.

A people she also loved.

She sighed. Phyro was the mirror of her soul, and she of his. Love made one do strange, beautiful, terrible things.

She turned and beckoned to Ofluro, her pilot. Gingerly, he unbuckled himself from the saddle, stepped onto Ginki's head, and allowed the garinafin to lower him down. He kept a hand on Ginki's antlers, in case he needed to be re-saddled in a hurry.

"Phyro trained the garinafins to defend Dara, not to enforce his ambition," she whispered to him, looking him in the eye. "Do you know what Phyro would ask of you?"

Ofluro was silent. Then, he heaved a great sigh. "Though I am Lyucu, my heart, like these garinafins, has long accepted a new home. I will obey the Seal of Dara, even if it isn't held by him."

Zen-Kara nodded, and tears of relief and grief ran down her face.

"After the Lyucu are defeated, I'll come to Tan Adü with a treasure fleet of gifts and ask your parents for your hand. Then we'll have all the time in the world to surf and cruise around the Islands on crubens. Will you say yes?"

Yes, she said to that mirage in her mind. *Yes I will yes . . . But you were not fated to be the true Emperor of Dara, and I am not fated to find my home here.*

Politics isn't for me, and it shouldn't be for our child. It's time for me to stop interfering.

She turned back to Cogo. "Grant me safe passage back to my people, and I'll not set foot in Dara again so long as I'm alive. There will be no more blood staining the streets of the Harmonious City today. We surrender."

CHAPTER FORTY-SEVEN

A RIDDLE

KRIPHI: THE ELEVENTH MONTH OF THE ELEVENTH
YEAR OF THE REIGN OF SEASON OF STORMS AND
THE REIGN OF AUDACIOUS FREEDOM.

The thanes had their first intimation that something was wrong when Korva, Tanvanaki's aged mount, began to writhe and moan in the pen as though in pain. Uncertain what was distressing her, several grooms tried to approach, but she hissed at them and drove them away.

Tanvanaki could not be found. Her guards explained that the pékyu had departed that morning with the emperor and Noda Mi, leaving in such a rush that she didn't bother to tell them where she was going.

A decision was made to feed Korva some precious Dasu tolyusa. Perhaps she was ill and needed the comfort of the drug. The red berries seemed to revive the ancient war garinafin. Half an hour after consuming them, she staggered to her feet, unfurled her leathery wings, and took off on her own.

Everyone was shocked. Korva was so old and frail that she hadn't flown in weeks. The only reason she hadn't been sent to the slaughter grounds was because Tanvanaki was sentimental. But the tolyusa seemed to have given her one last burst of strength.

The garinafin ascended above the rubble of Kriphi, circling, gliding, as though searching for her mistress. The grooms could see that she was weakening, her wing strokes more labored with each beat. They tried to coax her down with drumming and trumpets, but the garinafin ignored them.

An hour later, Korva was exhausted, losing altitude with every weak flap of her wings. But instead of coming back to the pen, she turned east and then north, gliding over the sea, as though she wanted to head for the Wall of Storms, as though she thought she would find Tanvanaki beyond.

With a last, defiant trumpeting, Korva folded her wings about her like a shroud and fell from the sky. She plunged into the ocean, throwing up a distant eruption like the spout of a cruben. The waves closed over the spot, and she did not reappear.

It was a most inauspicious sign.

Near evening, Noda Mi, covered in blood and sporting grievous wounds, returned to Kriphi with two horses, three bodies, and a most extraordinary tale, which he duly delivered to the assembled thanes and naros-votan.

The pékyu had summoned him out of the blue that morning with a most unusual request: to accompany her, Thane Cutanrovo, and the emperor on a secret mission, whose purpose Tanvanaki would not reveal. Always eager to serve the pékyu, the Loyal Hound of the Lyucu had not questioned her orders.

The pékyu led the group of four riders to the site of Kigo Yezu, a village that had been razed for an act of rebellion years ago.

As soon as they emerged into the clearing in the middle of the ruined village, a band of natives, accompanied by traitorous Lyucu warriors, ambushed them. Though at first terrified out of his wits, Noda soon calmed down due to the inspiring presence of the pékyu. Fortified by her emanation of the Lyucu spirit, Noda shouted and spurred ahead to protect the pékyu and her consort. But one of the Lyucu warriors launched a missile at Noda Mi with her slingshot, and he tumbled off his horse and lost consciousness.

(As Noda Mi recounted this tale through tears and snot, he pulled off his tunic to show the dark bruise where the bullet had struck him on the shoulder.)

The fall might have saved his life. While the traitors and rebel slaves attacked the rest of the party furiously, they seemed to have paid no more attention to his immobile body. Still, as combatants fought near him, an occasional sword strike or club swing must have landed on him.

(Here, Noda Mi pointed to the various wounds covering his face and body. The ferociousness of the battle could well be imagined from these merely accidental hits.)

By the time he finally awakened, the battle was over. The attackers were nowhere to be seen, but they left behind a field of corpses. The shaken Noda Mi crawled through the carnage, wailing at the blindness and injustice of the gods, and managed to find the bodies of Cutanrovo, Tanvanaki, and Timu. The cursed rebels had cut off the heads of all three—no doubt an act of outrage committed because of the native superstition that a headless ghost could not haunt its murderer.

Upon that discovery, faithful Noda Mi cried as he had never cried before. The most merciful, most beauteous, most wise and redoubtable and formidable and revered sovereign in the history of the universe, Pékyu Vadyu Roatan, Protector of Dara, and the most loyal, most thoughtful, most hardworking and farseeing and omniscient and steadfast counselor in the breadth and height of the world, Thane Cutanrovo Aga, wearer of the lurona ryo lurotan, had perished! Oh, dear dear votan! Oh, curse the gods! Oh, woe is us—

(Here, some of the gathered thanes and naros-votan shook their heads impatiently. They looked with undisguised contempt at Noda, face covered in tears and mucus, fists drumming helplessly against the ground. The pitiful cur really could grate on one's nerves.)

But faithful Noda did not forget his duty! No, he searched the field carefully for clues concerning the identity of the surprise attackers. Finally, from Emperor Thaké's tightly clenched fist, he recovered a single piece of silk covered in bloody zyndari letters. As the emperor was no fighter, Noda surmised that he must have devoted the final moments of his life in the midst of a chaotic battle to compose a letter to his children.

Noda Mi read the letter aloud to the assembly.

I do not know who our enemies are. I only know that they're so numerous and so fierce that we will not leave this encounter alive. Yet, what a loyal man Noda Mi is! With what unparalleled bravery

did he rush ahead to defend his pékyu! But he was cut down in only
one blow. Ah, poor, faithful Noda. Only in a crisis do we see the truth
that lies deep within the human heart, like a beam of moonlight illu-
minating the ghostly flocks drowning in the still water at the bottom
of a well, crying out silently.

Dyu-tika and Zaza-tika, know that I love you more than life
itself, and there is so much that I wish to tell you that I fear I will be
unable to.

So, if you ever read this, remember my final advice to you: A ruler
should guide his people without rebuke, like a faithful shepherd who
has renounced the staff for gentle determination. Carry on the legacy
of your father, and hope will glow in your hands like iced tolyusa.
All the people of Ukyu-taasa are your charge, and remember to do
what is right.

Dyana snatched the cloth out of Noda Mi's hands and read the
letter for herself. Recognizing the bloody handwriting as her father's,
she broke down, wailing inconsolably. The horror of her parents'
final moments was unimaginable.

Meanwhile, Todyu stood stoically by the side of his sister. Though
he had always despised his weak father, he was moved that the man
had enough courage at the end to write a message to him in blood.
He pictured his mother killing as many native slaves and traitors as
there were stars in the sky, and only with treachery had they managed to overcome her at the end.

Noda knelt down behind them and wrapped his arms comfort-
ingly around the two pékyus-taasa.

There was immediately a storm of accusations and counter-
accusations.

"This is clearly a plot by Cutanrovo Aga against the pékyu,"
a thane shouted. She was one of the accommodationists who had
returned to power in the aftermath of the plague of tolyusa-madness.
"We know she's been unsatisfied with the pékyu's leadership, and
she no doubt collaborated with native rebels to plan this ambush
against Tanvanaki. She was likely slain by the pékyu herself."

"What evidence do you have for such a preposterous claim?" demanded a hard-liner. The tolyusa-madness had decimated the hard-liner ranks, but as one of Cutanrovo's most trusted followers, he also had a secret stash of enhanced tolyusa that kept him functioning. "Thane Cutanrovo gave her life to defend the pékyu! In fact, I think it's far more likely that this was a plot by *your* side. Colluding with the natives is exactly your style."

"That the emperor's letter doesn't mention Cutanrovo at all speaks volumes," sneered the accommodationist. "The emperor devoted a whole paragraph to praise Noda's loyalty but made no reference to Cutanrovo at all. Why? Because he suspected Cutanrovo's role in the ambush."

"That is absurd nonsense," replied the hard-liner. "We all know that the weakling Timu bore Thane Cutanrovo little love. The letter also makes no mention of the pékyu. By your logic, should we treat this as proof that the pékyu wrought this fatal attack herself?"

"But you can see that Cutanrovo died from multiple blows from a war club. Other than the pékyu, who is skilled enough to overcome the dreaded garinafin-thane in single combat? Cutanrovo had rebelled!"

"I see plenty of wounds on the thane's body from native weapons as well. If Thane Cutanrovo was colluding with the natives—an accusation that doesn't even deserve a response—why would they attack *her*?"

On and on it went.

Even after a fact-gathering expedition returned from Kigo Yezu, there was no more clarity. The investigators found no bodies of the attackers at the site—Noda Mi swore that there had been many, but perhaps the attackers had returned later to remove the evidence of their treachery. The search party discovered no signs of their escape either, but if experienced Lyucu hunters had been among the despicable rebels, it was possible that they knew how to disguise their trails from pursuit. The ambush was an utter mystery.

Noda Mi smiled secretly. His plan to sow confusion was succeeding perfectly. He was especially proud of making Timu write that message. The sentimental fool had been true to his nature even in his death note: It was replete with unnecessary flowery phrases and cloying platitudes pulled from the Ano Classics, even though he was writing in zyndari letters instead of logograms. Noda had dictated the gist (the only part he really cared about was the paragraph absolving himself of any suspicion), but left the terrified emperor to find his own phrasing—the letter would be more convincing that way.

While the Lyucu lords advanced their rival theories and vied for political advantage, Noda Mi embraced the orphans even tighter.

"As the gods are my witness," he vowed, "you will be safe in my protection as long as I breathe."

THREE NIGHTS LATER.

Cold wind, cloudy sky.

Kriphi, the tent-city, was shrouded in silence and darkness.

Noda Mi decided that tonight was the night.

Most of the hard-liner thanes were away. They had taken garinafins and warriors—those who could still awaken from their tolyusa nightmares, at least—on raids throughout Ukyu-taasa. Bursting into towns and villages like packs of hungry wolves, they broke down doors, upended boxes and baskets, ransacked chests and dressers, cut open mattresses and sitting cushions, all in an effort to discover evidence of the plot against the Lyucu and to wreak vengeance for Tanvanaki and Cutanrovo.

They lined up terrified natives and demanded to know if anyone had participated in the rebellion. When no satisfactory answers were given, they picked victims at random and unleashed their wrath. They piled stones on white-haired elders until they slowly suffocated and bashed babies' skulls in front of their parents; they committed ritualized rapes, castrations, disembowelments, flayings.

Confessions poured out of the remaining natives in torrents, and it seemed to the hard-liner thanes as if all of Rui and Dasu were populated by conspirators and spies. More killings led to more accusations, which resulted in more massacres. Bloodlust was a monster that grew more hungry as it fed.

The accommodationists, on the other hand, were preoccupied

with maintaining order. They went to the native garrisons and plied the commanders with treasure and promises of more power, projecting an air of strength and confidence, knowing that the loyalty of the collaborationist soldiers was the only thing keeping Ukyu-taasa from teetering off the edge.

Noda Mi stole through Kriphi, ignoring the groans and moans emanating from the tents he crept past. Kriphi was barely functioning. Lyucu warriors wasted away in feverish dreams; work camps beyond the border of the tent-city were full of restless native laborers, now with nothing to do; native as well as Lyucu refugees streamed into Kriphi from all over Ukyu-taasa, hoping for order or enhanced tolyusa. Military discipline had long since broken down, and there was no night watch.

He approached the small tent where the pékyus-taasa were sleeping. After casting his glance around to be sure that no one was watching, he lifted the tent flap and ducked in.

"Goztan?" asked Todyu in a sleepy voice. Since he lay close to the opening of the tent, the cold gust that accompanied Noda's entrance woke him right away. As Dyana had been waking up several times every night, screaming from nightmares, Todyu tried to shield his little sister in her uneasy slumber by blocking the draft with his own body.

Goztan, as the sole garinafin-thane left, should have been in charge in the aftermath of Tanvanaki and Cutanrovo's deaths. The fractious hard-liners, however, had refused to submit to her authority, and the garinafin-thane had disappeared from Kriphi. Rumors were that she had brought a band of warriors loyal to her to Kigo Yezu in the hopes of ferreting out the truth behind the attack on the pékyu.

"*Shhh!*" said Noda, placing a finger over Todyu's lips. "It's me. You have to wake up Zaza-*tika*. We need to leave now."

"What? Where are we going?"

"There is a plot against you and your sister," said Noda. "Thane Goztan, your parents' murderer, is thinking of forcing you to give up your claim to be the next pékyu and emperor of Dara; instead, she wants to prop up Zaza-*tika* as a puppet. I have to take both of you away to keep you safe."

Sleep left Todyu's voice as he scrambled up to face Noda. "Goztan murdered my mother?"

"I've only just found out," said Noda impatiently. "There's no time to explain everything. Quick! Get Zaza-*tika* ready."

But Todyu refused to move. "Zaza-*tika* and I are nothing like my cowardly father. If Goztan wants to be the pékyu, let her come and fight me. I won't shame my mother by running away. I will claim my birthright in open combat."

Noda cursed himself for misreading the situation—of course the foolish boy would react to a threat this way. But his scheming mind soon settled on a new solution. "The most important quality in a great pékyu is forbearance. Even the great pékyu-votan, your illustrious grandfather, bided his time when he was among the Agon and struck only when he had the advantage. There's no shame in a . . . strategic retreat from the cowardly Goztan! Once we're safely ensconced elsewhere, we'll return to avenge the pékyu."

Todyu's eyes lit up. "So you're saying this is just like when my grandfather escaped from Nobo Aragoz's clutches on the back of his trusty mount, Kidia?"

"Yes, yes!" said Noda, relieved. "Think of me as your Kidia. Come, ride me!"

Satisfied that his actions would not be shameful in the eyes of his legendary grandfather, Todyu turned to waken Dyana and ordered her to get ready to leave. As the young girl muttered sleepily in protest, he shoved her roughly and berated her, exactly the way he imagined his mother would have berated his father.

When Noda Mi looked away for a moment, Todyu dug out a small leather pouch from underneath his sleeping rug and tucked it securely into the inner pocket of his fur vest. Since Cutanrovo's death, it had been emptying at an alarming pace, and he didn't know how he would ever fill it again.

Finally, the two children were dressed, and Noda Mi led them out of the tent.

Pausing from time to time to hide from the few naros out of their tents, pissing or fighting, the three stole away undetected from the tents clustered near the Great Tent. Once they emerged into the ruins of old Kriphi, they sped up. Though the only source of illumination was starlight, Noda seemed to know exactly where he was going as he took the children on a winding path toward the coast.

"How can you see where you're going?" asked Todyu, struggling to keep up.

"A clever crimson-tailed woodpecker doesn't cling to just one tree," muttered Noda.

The answer seemed a non sequitur to the young pékyu-taasa, but before he could ask for more clarification, Noda Mi shushed him and urged them to run even faster.

During the last three days, Noda Mi had scouted this route to the coast multiple times, preparing for various contingencies. The general scarcity of able-bodied warriors in Kriphi left the region near the harbor unwatched, and the beach was crowded with fishing boats abandoned by coastal villagers who had been drafted into work gangs.

Most of the boats had been staved in to prevent escaping refugees, but Noda Mi had hidden an intact boat among the wrecks. It was perfect for the three of them, and he had filled it with provisions for the journey to the Big Island.

Just before they crossed the ruined old city walls, Noda stopped again to demand that the children remove their jewelry and other personal effects: their baby garinafin bone hairpins, the jade pendant that Dyana wore around her neck on a leather cord, the child-sized war club that Todyu always carried.

Noda dropped these items on the ground next to a well.

"Why are you doing that?" asked Todyu. "I'll need a weapon to fight—"

"I will be your weapon," said Noda placatingly. "I'm your Kidia, remember? We need to leave some signs to confuse Goztan when she looks for you in the morning. Come on, let's go!"

Earlier that day, Noda had dumped the headless bodies of two children who matched the ages of Todyu and Dyana down the well. For good measure, he had also added the headless corpse of a native man who resembled his own build. He smiled as he imagined the confusion that would result once the Lyucu found the bodies; even if the barbarians eventually figured out that the corpses were decoys, he and his hostages would long be out of the range of pursuing garinafins.

The harbor was in sight, and Noda's heart soared.

He wouldn't have to keep up the stream of lies much longer, he decided. Once they were safely at sea, he would reveal to the children that he was taking them as bargaining chips to the grandmother they had never met: Empress Jia. If the children had brains, they should recognize that they had little choice but to go along with his plan and become his playing pieces in this grand game of *zamaki*. But if they protested, he would have to resort to more drastic measures. If necessary, he would toss Todyu overboard and keep Dyana, who seemed, at least until now, to be far more compliant, never questioning his actions.

His sloop was straight ahead, resting peacefully on the beach. The coast was deserted. *The gods are with me!* "Faster!" Noda urged the children. "Get in the boat and I'll push us off."

"I don't understand why we need to be on a boat," Todyu said. Like most Lyucu, he wasn't much of a swimmer. "I thought we were going to get a garinafin, just like my grandfather."

"We're going to join the pirates," said Noda. He knocked away the wedges that had been securing the boat against rolling logs, planted his feet against the rocky ground, and heaved against the hull, grunting. Slowly, the boat slid into the water.

"Pirates?"

"That's right," said Noda, grinning wolfishly. "They'll become the core of your army, votan, as you prepare for your triumphant return to claim what is yours from Goztan."

"It will be as glorious as when my grandfather slaughtered his siblings to become the greatest pékyu of the Lyucu people," declared Todyu, clearly excited by Noda's vision.

"It will be more glorious than you can imagine," said Noda, chuckling. "Now hurry and get in!"

Todyu climbed onto the small sloop and reached out for Dyana. Instead of taking her brother's hand, however, Dyana turned to Noda Mi. "Uncle Noda, did my father cry for very long after my mother died?"

Elated with the success of the escape, Noda answered absent-mindedly. "Of course. He wept like a baby."

Dyana's question brought back for Noda the memory of Timu wailing over the barbarian woman. *How pathetic!* He couldn't help a sneer of contempt.

"And he told you to keep us safe?"

"Yes, yes! Now get on board!"

Dyana nodded, as though a final piece of the puzzle had fallen into place. The moon peeked out from behind the clouds, and the sparkling reflection off the waves threw the hulk of the fishing sloop in sharp relief.

Just as the girl turned and started to climb onto the sloop, she stopped. Her eyes widened as she pointed at a pile of rocks down the beach. "Who's that?"

Noda whipped around in the direction of her gaze. A figure was peeking out from behind the rocks, her ragged clothing suggesting a native.

Noda cursed. A witness was the last thing he needed. "Stay back," he told Dyana, and dashed toward the woman, unsheathing his sword as he ran.

The woman ducked down behind the rocks.

Noda sped up. A half-starved peasant wouldn't be able to get away from him. He leapt atop the rocks, sword held high—

—he froze. Ten Lyucu warriors were waiting for him on the other side, enveloping him in a semicircle.

He spun around. More Lyucu warriors had materialized between him and the boat. He was completely surrounded.

Several Lyucu splashed into the water and climbed onto the sloop, subduing a struggling Todyu. Dyana, however, was not on the boat.

The young girl was walking toward him, holding the hand of the woman striding next to her.

Goztan Ryoto.

"Noda." Her voice seemed more tired than triumphant. "Your endless betrayals are finished."

"She's behind the plot against the pékyu and Thane Cutanrovo!" Noda screamed at the Lyucu surrounding him. "Brave and wise lords, listen to me! Goztan is an ambitious traitor who wants to *be* the pékyu. She's going to secure herself a corrupt life of wallowing in native pleasures by selling out the future of the Lyucu people! I've just discovered her plot and was on my way to find you—"

Goztan sighed. "Bind him," she ordered quietly.

Noda's sword was easily knocked out of his hand. The Lyucu caught him and tied his hands behind his back, forcing him to kneel before Goztan and Dyana.

Noda ceased struggling. He had noted that several of the warriors were loyal to Cutanrovo, including a couple of thanes, and they had moved with reluctance during the fight. *There is still a chance.*

"You are hereby charged with treason against Ukyu-taasa," said Goztan, "and the murders of Pékyu Vadyu and Garinafin-Thane Cutanrovo. How do you plead?"

"What proof do you have?" asked Noda defiantly. "I am Pékyu Vadyu's First Garinafin Groom, Loyal Hound of the Lyucu. I am innocent!"

"How dare you desecrate the memory of my mother by invoking her name?" demanded Dyana, her voice trembling. "My father witnessed your crime and accused you in his dying declaration."

"What are you talking about?" Noda asked. His mind buzzed like a disturbed beehive. *Impossible!*

Not only had he watched Timu closely as he scrawled each letter, he had dictated the content. Noda had forced Timu to write in zyndari letters instead of Ano logograms only in part because the idea of the emperor melting and carving writing wax in the middle of a battle would have strained credulity. He had also been leery of Timu attempting some kind of intrigue with Ano logograms; zyndari letters were a much more transparent script for him to evaluate.

"I have to thank the clever young pékyu-taasa," said Goztan. She took out Timu's bloody cloth and handed it to Dyana.

"Read my father's report for yourself," said Dyana. She strode up to the bound Noda Mi, holding up the letter and pointing at a particular line.

"'A ruler should guide his people without rebuke, like a faithful shepherd who has renounced the staff for gentle determination,'" read Noda Mi. "That's the kind of platitude the emperor was always spouting. How does it implicate me?"

"My father took great pride in his facility with language. He never would have written something so awkward unless he meant to hide a message within."

Noda Mi, devoid of literary taste, simply gawked.

"My father's name means 'Gentle Ruler,' correct?"

"Yes," said Noda. Though he was far from being learned, the allusion to Kon Fiji's poem embedded in Timu's name had been one of the facts that Wira Pin had drilled into his head prior to his mission to negotiate with Jia.

"In the sentence you just read, the word 'gentle' has been severed from 'ruler' and placed at the opposite end of the line, much as you severed my father's head and took it away, depriving him of even peaceful rest in death," said Dyana, tears welling in her eyes.

"Ha ha ha!" Noda Mi's forced laughter convinced no one, not even himself. Nonetheless, he licked his lips and went on. If he sowed enough doubt among the warriors loyal to Cutanrovo, he could still get out of this. "Preposterous! If that kind of childish logic constitutes proof of my betrayal, than no one is safe from doubt. You're a poisonous viper striking at phantoms in your imagination."

Dyana ignored him. "My father was a skilled and erudite writer—" She choked back a sob, but went on determinedly. "He and I often entertained ourselves with logogram riddles. Though he couldn't write in logograms for this letter, he adapted his techniques to the phonetic script, as is sometimes done in logogram riddles for children. The phrase that divides 'gentle' from 'ruler' is 'a faithful shepherd who has renounced the staff.' What is a shepherd without a staff?"

"I have no idea what you're talking about," said Noda, but his face blanched.

"The logogram for 'shepherd' is written like so," said Dyana, kneeling down to sculpt the logogram out of beach mud. "It's formed from three semantic roots: a 'hooked staff' on the right, and 'chaser' plus 'fleece' on the left. If we remove the staff"—she wiped away the right side of the logogram with her hand—"what's left is simply 'fleece chaser,' which happens to be a kenning used in the ancient sagas to describe a sheepdog. And a faithful sheepdog is my father's way of referring to you, Loyal Hound of the Lyucu, as his killer."

Noda's mind reeled. He cursed himself for being careless. Timu had trembled and cried the whole time he wrote his letter, and he had been taken in by the man's act! Never could he have imagined that Timu would bury a logogram riddle in a letter written hastily in zyndari letters. Not having grown up in a scholar's family, he had no idea that such a thing was even possible.

The look of disgust and hatred on the faces of the warriors loyal to Cutanrovo told him that his hesitation had been fatal.

Noda turned to Goztan. "Please, Wise Garinafin-Thane, you must see this is a mistake! The pékyu-taasa is reading too much into the emperor's last words. How could I be his killer when I was knocked unconscious as soon as I entered Kigo Yezu?"

"You just told me that you saw my father weeping for my mother," said Dyana, "and that he told you to keep us safe. Lies piled on lies *will* fall apart. I was testing you."

Noda felt the ground give way under him. Desperately, he slammed his forehead into the ground at the feet of Goztan. Spitting sand from his mouth, he sputtered. "I confess that I had lied out of fear. The truth is that Cutanrovo was plotting against the pékyu and the emperor! I tried to stop her but couldn't. I tried to save the pékyu and the emperor—"

"And why didn't you reveal Cutanrovo's role in this plot until now?" Goztan asked coldly.

"Because . . . because I was terrified"—Noda glanced at the angry faces of the Lyucu warriors all around him—"that those loyal to the evil Cutanrovo would silence me for daring to accuse their leader!" He wriggled on the ground like a worm, struggling to slam his forehead into the sand before Goztan as quickly as possible.

"You're right about Cutanrovo plotting against the pékyu and the emperor," said Goztan. "But you're also part of that plot."

Once again, Dyana held up her father's letter and read from it. "'Only in a crisis do we see the truth that lies deep within the human heart, like a beam of moonlight illuminating the ghostly flocks drowning in the still water at the bottom of a well, crying out silently.' Do you know what my father meant or which poet he was quoting?"

Noda Mi shook his head in confusion.

"It wasn't any of the Ano poets," said Goztan. "This was, in fact, a paraphrase of a line from a poem by Vocu Firna, my dead friend and also a confidant of the emperor. He enjoyed writing poems in Classical Ano, but filled them with images and myths of the Lyucu. Among our people, the moon is known as the mouth of the goddess Nalyufin, the Hate-hearted. Vocu Firna sometimes used the image of a moonlit well filled with death as a synecdoche for Cutanrovo, because Cutanrovo was the Thane of the Flock of Nalyufin. Ironic that the Loyal Hound of the Lyucu would know so little of our traditions."

Noda Mi said nothing. He had never paid much attention to Lyucu myths and legends, and that ignorance had given Timu an opening.

"The emperor placed your name within the same paragraph in which he refers to Cutanrovo," said Goztan, her voice placid but implacable. "This was also the same paragraph in which the emperor described the enemies attacking him and the pékyu. In this way, the emperor revealed that you and Cutanrovo were coconspirators."

"No! No! Please—"

"When Zaza-*tika* came to me with her suspicions," said Goztan, "I believed her but couldn't do much. After all, an accusation framed through riddles could not convince the other thanes. So I had to create the impression that no one was watching you, and then observe what you would do. The pékyu-taasa was very brave to agree to be the lure. Like a wolf pretending to be a loyal hound, it was only a matter of time before you revealed your true nature."

At that moment, several of the Lyucu warriors, who had been searching the sloop, exclaimed in horror and rage. Soon, they returned to the assembly and set down their findings reverently.

Three human heads, preserved with lime, rested in a row on the sand. Tanvanaki and Cutanrovo were grimacing, their eyes locked open as though still raging against their foes. Timu's face, on the other hand, was a mask of tranquility. Dyana wailed and leapt to the heads of her parents, cradling them against her chest.

No one spoke in the face of this gruesome scene. At length, Goztan broke the silence.

"You plotted with Cutanrovo to kill the pékyu, and I suspect you then betrayed your coconspirator in order to secure some personal advantage, as is your wont. I don't fully comprehend your scheme, but it doesn't matter. The fact is that the charges against you have been proven—"

"I can help you!" Noda Mi screamed. "I can help you pacify the natives and become the pékyu! Listen, I have lots and lots of good ideas for how to leverage these two children to force Empress Jia to submit to your terms. With me by your side as counselor, Ukyu-taasa will once again rise to greatness. I swear by all the gods that I will be loyal—"

"Treason is in your nature," said Goztan. Without warning, she swung Gaslira-sata and bashed in the skull of the screaming Noda Mi, silencing him instantly. Blood, bone fragments, and brains splattered over Goztan and the kneeling figure of Dyana, still crying and hugging her dead parents. Neither made a move to wipe the gore away.

At dawn, thanes and warriors, healthy or laid low with tolyusa-madness, gathered on the beach to hear Goztan explain Noda Mi's betrayal at Kigo Yezu.

Messengers were dispatched all over Rui and Dasu to recall the marauding bands of warriors. The severed heads of Cutanrovo, Tanvanaki, and Timu were reunited with their torsos and laid upon driftwood funeral mounds. After the requisite mourning period, the bodies would be given to the wilderness so that the departed could begin their pédiato savaga.

"You're not at peace," said Goztan.

Dyana made a sound that was halfway between a laugh and a sob. "The very idea that the woman who murdered my parents will receive the same honor as them turns my stomach."

"Preserving Thane Cutanrovo's reputation is required—"

"Don't." Dyana took a deep breath. "I am my mother's daughter. I understand."

The night before, after Noda Mi's confession and execution, the Lyucu thanes who were present and loyal to Cutanrovo negotiated a pact with Goztan. The truth of Cutanrovo's attempted coup against Tanvanaki would be suppressed, at least for now, and Goztan promised no further investigations to ferret out other coconspirators; in exchange, the hard-liner thanes would lobby the rest of their faction to support Goztan's claim as the first thane among equals and guardian of the young pékyus-taasa.

The compromise, though imperfect, was the most expedient way to prevent a civil war among the Lyucu in Ukyu-taasa.

"The living need peace more than the dead need justice," muttered Dyana. "But I need time to grieve."

"My heart beats in sync with yours, votan," said Goztan, her voice gentle but firm. "However, grief is a luxury the Pékyu of Ukyu-taasa cannot afford at present."

Dyana looked at her, startled. "The . . . pékyu?"

"Your brother cannot be handed the signaling spear for the people of Ukyu-taasa."

Reluctantly, Dyana nodded. Todyu's mind, already fragile from tolyusa-thirst—unbeknownst even to his own family, he had become addicted to the enhanced tolyusa supplied by Cutanrovo—had collapsed under the weight of the revelations of last night: Cutanrovo, the warrior he worshipped as a paragon of Lyucu virtue, had been plotting against his own mother; Timu, the man whose blood-tie he had always despised, had avenged his wife by writing the truth with his blood; Noda Mi, the one native he trusted, had been trying to use him like a hunting trophy. . . . He had erupted into violence, lashing out at his guards and screaming that he would avenge his dead mother by killing everyone in sight. Goztan had had no choice but to have him bound and gagged.

"We won't survive the winter," said Goztan. "Our granaries and smokehouses are empty, and our warriors and garinafins are sick. Long before starvation, there will be a uprising against our people. The Lyucu in Dara will be no more, and many natives will die as well. You must chart a new course for Ukyu-taasa."

"Is it really up to me?" Dyana cast a glance at the towering woman standing next to her, her eyes lingering on the fearsome war axe in Goztan's hand: Gaslira-sata, the Peace-Bite.

Goztan heard the fear in the girl's voice. She sighed. After all that had happened, she could hardly blame the girl for being suspicious. "You have nothing to fear from me. My ambition lies not in rule. I served your mother, and her father before her. Now I will counsel and serve you."

"Because I am young and easy to manipulate?"

"Not at all." Goztan paused to sort through her tangled thoughts. "You know, I met your mother for the first time when she was about your age. And even then, I saw two qualities in her that told me she would become a worthy pékyu. You share her nature."

"Which two qualities would those be? Let me guess: Her skill as a garinafin rider? Her charisma as a war leader? Unfortunately, I have neither."

"No. First, she could tell true stories apart from false ones. Second, she was empathetic, able to see the world through others' eyes, to feel what they feel."

Dyana laughed mirthlessly. "Yet she couldn't see through Cutanrovo's lies, nor could she feel what my father felt as Ukyu-taasa fell into ruin."

"She failed because she lacked an even more essential quality, a quality that your father possessed in abundance."

Dyana locked eyes with Goztan. "Which is?"

"The courage to live true to one's nature."

Dyana heaved a deep breath and looked away.

Goztan went on. "Your mother lived in the shadow of her father, believing that she had to fulfill his dream of Lyucu supremacy. Fearful that she would appear weak, she hardened her heart against the suffering of the native people and willfully blinded herself to the consequences of her actions."

"I am my mother's daughter."

"And also your father's."

Cactus drums had been erected around the largest funeral mound, the one belonging to Dyana's mother. Shamans danced around her body, singing the deeds of the dead pékyu as they banged on the drums. Because Tanvanaki left no spirit portrait, these voice paintings would be the final summation of her life. The voice of Flash-of-the-Garinafin, now merged with the winds, would be heard no more.

"Where does your ambition lie, if not in rule?" Dyana asked abruptly.

"I wouldn't call it ambition, not exactly."

She thought back to her life in Ukyu, to the days when she had fought first to free her clan from the haughty Agon thanes and then to liberate her tribe from the degradations of Admiral Krita. She remembered that heady moment when Pékyu Tenryo first sketched the dream of a new Lyucu homeland in wealthy, temperate Dara. She summoned the memory of the night she parted from her son, a child she had raised to be as much Lyucu as native, when she had sent him into the world to search for home.

She recalled that night on the deck of Captain Dathama's city-ship, when she had conversed with a stranger from Dara whose stories and domestic hopes seemed so familiar, not at all like those belonging to an implacable enemy.

If we can't go home, we'd like to live together, in peace. Paradise may not exist, but we can try to build it, side by side.

She couldn't be sure she had remembered Oga's words exactly. It had been, after all, such a long time ago. Time had a way of reshaping memories much as the relentless sea reshaped the shore, rubbing smooth what had once grated.

Her hand tightened around the handle of Gaslira-sata, her fingertips caressing the strong ribs that spoke of a dream of unity.

"I wish"—Goztan hesitated, searching for the right words—"for the Lyucu in Dara and the natives to become the people of Ukyu-taasa. Cutanrovo thought that a betrayal of my people, but I think it is the only vision grand enough for the Lyucu spirit."

Dyana nodded. "You speak of a devotion to ever-enlarging circles of empathy, of a yearning for new identities that transcend old enmities. Among my father's people, there's a word for that: *mutagé.*"

"*Mutagé*? Interesting. That's not the way Vocu Firna explained the word to me . . . but I see that it fits."

"My father, like his father before him, was prone to new readings of the classics. . . . How do you know serving me will be the same as serving this vision of the people of Ukyu-taasa?"

"It's in your nature," said Goztan.

Dyana smiled. "No. I think it's in all our natures."

Goztan turned to face Dyana, lifting both arms and crossing them at the wrist. Dyana accepted the salute wordlessly, the way a new pékyu should.

"My father had a suggestion for what to do next," said Dyana.

In response to Goztan's surprised look, the young pékyu took out the bloody letter from Timu and read from it. "'Carry on the legacy of your father, and hope will glow in your hands like iced tolyusa.'"

Goztan shook her head. "I don't understand."

"The native word for tolyusa is 'zomi,' given to the plant by the great scholar Luan Zyaji. The Classical Ano word means 'pearl of fire.' But if the fire were put out by ice, then what is left in our hands is simply a pearl."

Goztan gazed anxiously into the empty cupped palms of the pékyu.

"The name of my uncle, the Emperor of Dara, means 'Pearl in the Palm.' My father always told me that unlike my implacable grandmother, his brother has a deep streak of mercy that can be reached. Appealing to my uncle instead of my grandmother is our best chance of surrendering without losing everything."

Goztan felt relief flooding through her body.

"There will be many voices raised in opposition, both native and Lyucu," said Goztan. "Those who followed Cutanrovo think surrendering to the Dandelion Throne worse than death, and native collaborators who betrayed their own people will hardly want to face the consequences."

"Remedying the errors of one's parents is never easy," said Dyana, a steely edge coming into her young voice. "Are you with me?"

"Always."

"'All the people of Ukyu-taasa are your charge, and remember to do what is right,'" Dyana read from the silk cloth. "And that's no riddle at all."

CHAPTER FORTY-EIGHT

BOOKS

A SECLUDED SEASIDE VILLA BY LUTHO BEACH:
THE TWELFTH MONTH OF THE ELEVENTH YEAR
OF THE REIGN OF SEASON OF STORMS AND THE
REIGN OF AUDACIOUS FREEDOM.

They waited.

Slowly, messengers made their way from the capital to the estate by the black sands of Lutho Beach. Mostly escapees from the massacre at the Examination Hall, they recounted the startling flight of the mechanical dyran through the rainy night, homing in on a bright beacon of hope; the long standoff against the palace guards, when morale among the rebels burned as brightly as the whale-oil lamps behind them; the growing anxiety as the promised firework signaling success never came; the sudden assault by soldiers in a moving arrow-tower; Mota Kiphi's last stand. Confusion, terror, death.

Over the following days and weeks, more news arrived from Widi Tucru's spies in the capital. Soldiers patrolled the streets, stopping pedestrians and carts at random. Farseers, disguised as commoners, listened to conversations in teahouses and markets. The disturbances that had crippled the capital on that rainy night were blamed on bandits and saboteurs. Heralds proclaimed that the wise leadership of the empress had quelled the troublemakers before much damage could be done. Even the missing garinafins had been safely recovered after a bit of a scare.

The palace announced that there would be no formal court for a while; the empress was indisposed.

There was nothing said about the emperor.

Savo came to Fara. "I'm afraid the worst has happened."

Fara nodded, acquiescing in the truth but unwilling to speak it aloud.

Although the couple had been unable to convince Phyro to veer from the path of vengeance, they had persuaded the young emperor to authorize certain contingency plans to be carried out should he never return.

Fara carved Phyro's name in wax over a wooden tablet and built a makeshift shrine in the walled garden, among a patch of withered weeds that should be blooming with dandelions come summer. Kneeling before it, she wept. Lady Soto knelt down beside her and pulled her into a tearful embrace.

Leaving the two to grieve, Savo went to the hutch and attached message-holding bamboo tubes to the cooing inhabitants. He released them one by one, watching as they took off and melded against the oppressive, snow-laden winter clouds.

All over Dara, messenger pigeons landed at the story halls of veterans' mutual benefit societies.

The directions contained in the bamboo tubes were cryptic, but as they were signed by the personal seal of the missing Emperor Monadétu, his followers carried them out faithfully.

Under cover of night, tattooed Adüan gangsters snuck into warehouses at Ginpen's harbor to retrieve unlabeled boxes from obscure corners and loaded them onto ships bound for all quarters of the compass. . . .

From Toaza to Müning, from Boama to Çaruza, stevedores unloaded the boxes and stacked them on carts in caravans bound for cities and towns in the interior. . . .

Discharged veterans, employed in private security and public town watches, received the boxes from caravan drivers and unpacked them in the middle of the night. . . .

Then they turned the contents over to their sons and daughters, many of whom were clerks or household servants for people of power: city magistrates, provincial governors, Imperial ministers, circuit intendants, military monitors, grand scholars, and academy researchers. . . .

And when these Lords of Dara, nexuses in the all-encompassing system, cogs and levers in the even-tempered machine that was the bureaucracy of the empire, came to work in the morning, they found stacks of books on their desks.

MEANWHILE, IN ZUDI.

Naro Hun, Mayor of Zudi and the very model of a good official in Jia's system, stared at the stack of books dominating his otherwise empty desk.

Has a storm struck Pan that even the distant reef shrimp cannot escape?

As the spouse of Mün Çakri, First General of the Infantry and one of Emperor Ragin's earliest and most decorated followers, he could have lived a life of ease and luxury after Mün's death at Naza Pass during the ill-fated counterinvasion of Rui. Instead, Naro had volunteered for Gin Mazoti's army, whose cause had seemed hopeless in the face of the mighty Lyucu invasion fleet. Though he possessed little in the way of strength or skill with arms, he was not an unbrave man.

After the Battle of Zathin Gulf, during which he served in the logistics corps, Prime Minister Cogo Yelu asked him what he wanted to do. Mün Çakri, a marquess, had left Naro a generous benefice, and Naro could have leveraged his connections among Mün's friends at court to become a very wealthy man.

"Give me a real task suited to my abilities, from which I can make an honest salary to take care of myself and Cacaya-*tika*," said Naro. "As for Mün's title and benefice, let them escheat to the Throne."

Cogo looked at Naro, his eyebrows raised.

"My son does not need to be a marquess," said Naro. "The starling at the head of the flock sees the first glint in the falcon's eye; the leaf at the tip of the branch feels the first chill of winter."

Cogo nodded. Empress Jia had long harbored suspicions against

Kuni's generals and nobles. As regent, her campaign against them would only accelerate. It was wise of Naro to sense the developing political currents and fade away before the empress's baleful gaze fell on him and his young son. Cogo had only known Naro as a beautiful man who captured his friend's heart; he had not expected him to possess such good judgment. In Naro, Cogo almost sensed a kindred soul.

The Prime Minister helped Naro draft the petition to the empress to yield up Mün Çakri's hereditary title and to donate the benefice to the Imperial Treasury. Then he made Naro the librarian of Zudi, Naro's hometown. It was supposed to be a sinecure that involved little challenge, but in this, the Prime Minister miscalculated.

Zudi, though a backwater compared to the grand metropolises, held a special status in Dara as Emperor Ragin's hometown. The Inner Council and the Governor of Cocru wanted to ensure that Zudi was managed well—otherwise, the political symbolism would cause great embarrassment to the Imperial family. To that end, the city received all sorts of tax relief, collected generous development and infrastructure aid from the provincial capital of Çaruza as well as Pan, and was often assigned top-ranked *firoa* (or even sometimes *pana méji*) as administrators. Cities of Zudi's size rarely got such talent.

However, to these ambitious and inexperienced men and women, fresh from success in the Imperial examinations or a stint in the College of Advocates, being assigned to sleepy Zudi instead of a more prominent post felt almost like an insult. (The top administrator of the city even had the title of "mayor," a relic of the days of the Tiro states.) Eager to prove themselves (so they could be promoted away) and encouraged by Zudi's full treasury, they tried to show off their cleverness by devising all sorts of newfangled policies for the city. Their bold enthusiasm for change would then infect and incense their subordinates, and lead to waves of reforms and counter-reforms.

For instance, one mayor decided to turn Zudi into a Moralist paradise by implementing universal mandatory education, forcing all children to go to government academies and disregarding the fact that many of the city's poorer inhabitants needed the labor of their children to survive. Angry petitioners soon made their displeasure known to the circuit intendant; the mayor was unceremoniously transferred away.

His successor, a pious *firoa*, decided that the way to appease the poor and return Zudi to greatness was to assess a new property tax on the wealthy, the proceeds of which would be used to renovate all the temples in the city to glorify the gods (and to encourage more charitable acts by the various clergies). To further enhance Zudi's esteem in divine judgment (and her own reputation), she ordered all pubs and indigo houses shuttered for the duration of the renovations. The gentry flooded the College of Advocates with complaints; within the month, the mayor was "promoted" to overseeing the Hegemon's Shrine in remote Tunoa.

Her successor, a Fluxist, then criticized both of her predecessors for excessively intruding into the lives of the people and furloughed the entire city government staff to realize the ideal administrative state envisioned by Üshin Pidaji: the Null State. The subsequent howls of protest from minor clerks and low-level bureaucrats . . . well, your imagination wouldn't need the help of teahouse storyteller to fill in the blanks.

The Fluxist's hostility toward her inherited staff wasn't really unexpected. Each time one of these air-dropped genius mayors launched a campaign of massive reform, they were inevitably met with great resistance from the local bureaucracy, composed of career civil servants with deep roots in the city. In order to push through their agenda, the mayors then had to apply a strategy of divide and conquer, winning the support of some local power brokers by promising to implement their own pet projects. Officials grouped into alliances and factions, backed by powerful patrons at court, and politics in Zudi soon rivaled Pan for its cutthroat intensity.

To be sure, the tension between reform-minded Imperial appointees and status-quo-preserving local career functionaries was a persistent feature in every city in Dara. The beneficial conflict, intuitively grasped by Kuni Garu, was later codified into the system by Empress Jia and the Inner Council. Besides striking a balance between centralization and preserving local character in a federated empire, the push-and-pull between representatives of the capital and local elites had the virtue of reducing corruption, enhancing stability, *and* preventing stagnation. But Zudi's special status and excessive solicitousness by the court pushed the system out of balance, like a body that had turned against itself as a result of too-rich food.

Naro, though not a ranked scholar himself, proved to be both adept at administration and politically astute—the consummate bureaucrat. He was kind to his subordinates and respectful to his superiors, never flaunting his status as the widower of one of Dara's most legendary generals. He bobbed and weaved, dodged and danced, careful to avoid being drawn into the increasingly treacherous political maneuvering among his colleagues. Incredibly, as Zudi was embroiled in alternate sessions of upheaval and paralysis due to bureaucratic infighting, the library system, his charge, remained an island of stability.

Eventually, the stream of petitions from city elders, guild heads, venerable abbots, and hereditary nobles, all complaining about the local government, forced the Inner Council in Pan and the governor of Çaruza to re-evaluate their approach. The best-ranked fresh examinees, their ambition and intellect untempered with experience, were not the best choices as top administrators, not right away, and not for a small but politically treacherous city like Zudi. Far better to find someone with roots in Zudi, preferably with little ambition, to handle this hot taro. It went against the empress's ideal of discouraging entanglements between Imperial appointees and the local gentry, but compromise was the soul of a good bureaucracy, wasn't it?

That was how Naro Hun, librarian, became the multi-term Mayor of Zudi.

The years since then had been good to Naro and Zudi both. Naro's youthful good looks had faded, to be replaced by a steadfastness and maturity that continued to draw admiring glances. Open to advice from his subordinates and the city elders, he administered the city cautiously, resistant to grand, sweeping changes, but open to small, gradual tweaks and compromises. There were public schools, but attendance was not mandatory and poor students' families received a stipend in addition to waived tuition. The temples were well-attended, but so were the pubs and indigo houses. The staff was small, but the salaries were high to prevent the temptation of corruption. Zudi had prospered and grown, and was often mentioned as a model for good governance.

In his long tenure as mayor, Naro had weathered countless political storms. Whether it was the struggle between Zomi Kidosu and Cogo Yelu, the intrigue between Empress Jia and Emperor Monadétu, or the many debates over war or peace with the Lyucu, he had resolutely attempted to stay out of court politics, focusing only on Zudi and its people.

This latest mystery, however, was unlike any challenge in his memory.

First of all, there were as many books on his desk as could be found in one of Zudi's public neighborhood libraries. A collection like this was worth a fortune.

Who put it here and why?

Naro opened a few of the plain wooden cover-boxes. The silk scrolls were filled with neat, dense columns of Ano logograms composed in authoritative clerical script. To his practiced eye, the script posed a second oddity.

As handcrafted artifacts, each book should be unique. Even two copies of the same book produced by the same scribe revealed a thousand differences when examined closely. Collections of books, unless they were all personally written by the owner, tended to show great variety in material, size, cut-and-fold, and above all: the scribe's calligraphy.

But these mysterious books were all written on the same kind of fresh silk, and cut and rolled the exact same way. The logograms inside showed the identical hand: neat, restrained, trustworthy. The faint fragrance of fresh wax and coloring ink suggested that the books were very new, perhaps not more than a couple of months old. All the evidence pointed to these books having been written by the same scribe within that time frame, but that was plainly impossible. A lifetime of tireless toil by one scribe could not have produced such a quantity of books.

How?

Naro's hands settled on one box, different from all the others. Made of sandalwood, the exterior of the container was not plain, but covered in intricate carvings of chrysanthemums. He opened it and gasped: the silk scroll was woven with golden threads, a most rare and luxurious bookmaking medium.

In contrast to the handwriting in the other books, which seemed to emphasize legibility above personality, the Ano logograms on this scroll proclaimed the work of a skilled calligrapher tutored by the masters of old Cocru. Though not formally schooled, Naro had picked up quite a bit of esoteric philological knowledge as a librarian. He recognized some of the logograms on the scroll as variants that had been outlawed by Emperor Mapidéré. The calligraphy also showed a defiant spirit with unbeveled edges and rough-hewn corners, features that only those most confident in their own place in the world would leave in formal writing.

Naro nodded to himself. During his time living in Pan with Mün, he had seen samples of handwriting from many great lords and ladies. The scroll before him was the work of Lady Soto, the empress's confidante.

Finally, his head filled with questions and his heart pounding with trepidation, he began to read.

Like hundreds of others all across Dara.

"Father, why are you doing this?" asked Caya Çakri. The teenaged boy had been dutifully helping Naro pack up the family's personal effects, which filled only two chests. He and Naro were now in the process of pasting paper seals over the cabinets and closets in the mayor's manor—Naro insisted that they take nothing that hadn't been bought with his personal funds, not the formal robes, not the fine tea from Pan, not even a single sheet of paper that was meant for official business.

"Haven't you always told me that we should stay out of court politics, that the duty of those in the lower echelons of the bureaucracy is to carry on serving our neighbors no matter what storms roil Pan, to be content as the reef-dwelling shrimp rather than seeking to attach ourselves to crubens and whales roaming the seas? You were so cautious that you never sought to reclaim my name-father's title for me. What has changed to make you want to risk everything?"

Naro looked at his son affectionately. The boy was hardworking and kindhearted, but he had no aptitude for books or politics. Knowing that there was no future for Cacaya-*tika* as a scholar, Naro had apprenticed him to a butcher, a choice that he thought his dead husband would have approved.

"You're right, my child," said Naro. "Much of the time, it's wiser to stay focused on the soil at our feet than to imagine grand palaces in the sky, to interfere in the affairs of great lords. But the present matter is different from the title that should have been yours: One is about benefit to a family, a single lineage; the other concerns the fate of the whole nation. There is also a duty we all owe to the truth, to justice and the grandness of every human spirit."

"You're speaking of *mutagé*," said Caya.

"Yes, I suppose I am," said Naro, a little surprised at this display of erudition from his son. He pointed to the pile of new books on his desk. "Now that I know the truth, it would be a betrayal of *mutagé* to continue as before, pretending that I don't."

"But to challenge the Throne and the regent . . . ," said Caya, his voice faltering. "How do you know you'll succeed? Maybe the farseers will arrest you for treason! Maybe the end of the regency will bring much more suffering. Hasn't the empress been good for the people?"

Children always grow up faster than parents would like to believe, thought Naro, glad but also a bit sad. "The empress's good deeds cannot erase her crimes. When your name-father charged at the fiery maws of garinafins, he knew that there was no chance he would slay Pékyu Tenryo. He persisted because he believed in the ideal of a better Dara, and it was an ideal worthy of the ultimate sacrifice, enough for him to give up the chance to ever see you again. How can I shrink back from my duty and stain his good name? We do what is right not because we think we'll succeed; we do so regardless of the consequences, good or bad."

"I understand," Caya said. Then, after a pause, he added, "I'm not afraid."

The pair returned to their packing and sealing, working in companionable silence. As they finally departed the mayor's manor with the setting sun, Naro hung the mayor's seal from the lintel above the front gate.

He had resigned as the Mayor of Zudi, and now he would join a revolution.

CHAPTER FORTY-NINE

BOOKMAKING

THE SECLUDED SEASIDE VILLA BY LUTHO BEACH:
THREE MONTHS EARLIER.

The estate, a vacation villa belonging to the Wasu clan, now served as Phyro's refuge when he wasn't traveling across Dara to plot against Jia. It also sheltered Soto, Savo, and Fara.

"Stay as long as you want," said Widow Wasu. "Back in the day, Kuni Garu basically lived on free handouts from my pub. If I could fill the bottomless pit that was his expanding beer gut, I certainly don't mind feeding you and your young man."

"Thank you, Granny," said Fara, blushing.

"What about me?" asked Soto. "I'm a fugitive running from the empress's wrath. It's treason to harbor me."

Widow Wasu waved her off. "As far as I can tell, this is the story: We have a large, wealthy family with several loving children. However, the first wife is trying to keep the family inheritance out of the hands of the son of the second wife, going so far as to murder the second wife. How can it be wrong to help the son and to protect his faithful old governess?"

Soto didn't know whether to laugh or cry. Widow Wasu had reduced the fate of Dara to the plot of a folk opera. At least Widow Wasu's view of the world had an attractive simplicity to it.

"You just stay put and do whatever you want to do. If that Jia gives me any trouble, I've got a good speech prepared on what Kon Fiji said about the proper role of a first wife and aunt-mother!"

Meanwhile, Savo tried to stay out of Phyro's way. Though the young emperor was friendly and open toward his sister's intended, Savo, knowing the role Phyro played in Dara's war against the Lyucu, found it difficult to face the martial emperor with equanimity. He shrank back from Phyro's embrace of violence in the pursuit of justice—first in regard to the Lyucu, and now to avenge his mother—but he was also keenly aware that his own pacifism was a luxury, made possible only because he was living under the peace of Empress Jia and shielded by Widow Wasu's generous heart. How could he, a Lyucu thane-taasa, presume to tell the people of Dara what was justice? Or counsel their emperor to give up vengeance?

Fara, however, tried again and again to dissuade Phyro from his chosen path. "Dara must be healed, not torn asunder."

"I've gone too far down this route to stop," Phyro replied. "I'm glad that Savo, and now you, have found wisdom in the teachings of Rufizo Mender, but in the real world, a blood debt must be repaid with blood. How can I leave my mother's death unanswered?"

No philosophy could overcome the power of a heartfelt truth, and there was a gulf between the siblings that could not be bridged by words.

Phyro departed, but left word that members of the Blossom Gang might stop by from time to time.

Soto spent much of her time at the villa in isolation, setting down in wax what she knew of Jia's secret machinations and misdeeds. Terrified that Jia was going to find her and silence her forever, she wanted to leave behind a manuscript.

Savo and Fara, restless and anxious, came to Soto to talk.

"What Aunt-Mother did was wrong," Fara fretted, wringing her hands. "But she should be punished according to the laws of treason, not die in an act of bloody retribution that will surely plunge Dara into chaos."

"How can you put the empress on trial?" said Soto, shaking her head. "The sovereign is beyond her own laws."

"What if we simply told the truth?" asked Fara. "What if you found a way to reach the Prime Minister and the members of the Inner Council?"

"That wouldn't do much good," said Soto. "Cogo is a good man, but . . . he's a creature of the system, as are all the high-ranking ministers. Even if they believed me, they wouldn't want to jeopardize the stability of Dara. They may even prefer to join Jia in suppressing my voice."

"Then what if we told *everyone* the truth? Phyro forced the empress to go to war with the Lyucu by changing the minds of the people, didn't he? The people can compel the empress to submit."

Soto chuckled at this bit of naïveté. "I once thought as you do. But Jia controls the farseers, the army, the entire bureaucracy of the empire. Her iron grip on power cannot be loosened by a mere story. Rumors concerning her treachery against Rin Coda, Gin Mazoti, and others have circulated for years without threatening her position—because so many have benefited from her rule."

Fara refused to give up. "But those were just rumors with no source. It'll be different when *you* reveal the truth of what she did to Empress Risana. Testimony from you, the Hegemon's aunt and one of my father's most trusted advisers, cannot be dismissed out of hand."

"Maybe," conceded Soto. "But I'm just one woman. How can I speak to everyone in Dara? The moment I reveal myself, the farseers will track me down and silence me. And when I'm gone, my story will become just another sourceless rumor. The voice dies with the speaker."

"That's why you are writing it down," said Fara, understanding dawning. "The logograms carved in your own hand, imbued with your inimitable style and individual personality, authenticate themselves."

Soto gave her a bitter grin of acknowledgment. "Even so, my case would be bolstered if I had documentary proof—Gin's trial transcript, Zomi's retraction, Rin Coda's suicide note, and so on. . . . Well, no point in pining after the impossible. But even if I could summon such corroborating documents, I can only write one book, and one book is easily destroyed. How many minds can a single silk scroll change? Even if it works, it will take a long time, time we may not have."

"I wish I had better ideas," Fara lamented. "But all I know is poetry, painting, music. I really know nothing."

"That is *not* nothing," Soto chided. "Beauty and art can persuade through the heart even when grand speeches from learned philosophers fail to sway the mind."

Fara forced herself to smile, knowing that Soto was trying to cheer her up. But her spirits had sunk lower than ever. Her brother and aunt-mother were set on a collision course that she was certain would end in disaster, but she was helpless to avert it.

Throughout the conversation, Savo sat to the side, listening but saying nothing. He wanted to help Fara mend a broken family and a country about to be torn asunder, but he didn't know how.

Something Soto said stayed with him, however: *But I can only write one book.*

The seaside villa welcomed a new guest: Rati Yera.

After a brief council of war, Phyro had dispatched the Blossom Gang and the rest of his small band of rebels to different parts of Dara to prepare for the assault on Pan. But Rati Yera, upon finding out that Savo and Fara were sheltering with Widow Wasu, wanted to visit her prized students first. The old inventor was, after all, committing treason, and they might never see each other again.

Though two years had passed since they were last together, Rati and Savo soon fell back into their easy rapport. With pride, Savo showed Rati a writing zither he had taken with him from the Temple of Still and Flowing Waters.

"What a marvel!" exclaimed Rati. Although she couldn't read the wax logograms carved by the machine, she admired its whirling gears, swinging cams, bouncing levers, vibrating strings. "Your invention would surely dazzle even Na Moji, were he to return to life."

Savo beamed. There was no one whose praise of his engineering skills he craved more. "If I am able to soar high in the air today, it's only because a great teacher took care to launch me into the wind."

Rati laughed, but the corners of her eyes were moist. "The cerulean dye may come from the indigo plant, but it glows with a hue far brighter than the flower of the original. The luckiest teachers are those who live to witness their students surpass them."

Savo blushed with pleasure. "The writing zither is a good instrument and may do much good, but it isn't quite enough."

"How so?"

And so Savo described Lady Soto's dilemma, the problem that he had been trying to solve for days with little result. Soto wanted to write a book to reveal Empress Jia's manipulations to the world, but a single copy of the book would accomplish little. Plus, she could not corroborate her account with documentary evidence.

"Ah, I could perhaps help you out there," said Rati, smiling.

She revealed that when the Blossom Gang left Last Bite to join Zomi Kidosu, Mota, Arona, and Widi had secreted some of the most important documents related to Gin's trial in Rati's wheeled chair and snuck them out of the archives.

"What?" Savo couldn't believe his ears. Dimly, he seemed to recall that Rati Yera's wheeled chair had indeed seemed extra heavy and clumsy on the day they departed from Last Bite.

Rati chuckled. "We are, after all, a gang of thieves. And though we agreed to work with the emperor and Secretary Kidosu, we didn't forget about Mota's dream of one day proving the Marshal's innocence."

"Lady Soto will be overjoyed," exclaimed Savo. "The documents will strengthen her case and fill in gaps in her own personal knowledge. The gods are truly with us."

"The gods do get a lot of credit," said Rati, a bit miffed.

Savo's brow knitted again. "But even the documents exist in only one copy. . . . We still cannot reach everyone in Dara. I could construct a writing zither to write in Lady Soto's hand and teach her to use it. The writing zither is faster than the carving knife after one becomes proficient with it. But even if I could teach both Fara and Lady Soto to master the instrument, with all three of us working nonstop, we wouldn't be able to make enough copies of the book and the documents to make a difference."

Rati Yera's eyes lit up. Nothing excited her more than an engineering challenge. "During the war with the Lyucu," she mused, not noticing the way Savo's face flinched at this, "I had to figure out a way to instruct thousands of ornithopters all at once. Mechanizing the process of copying a composition in the language of drilled holes around many cork cylinders, though far simpler than replicating a composition in the language of Ano logograms on many scrolls, is fundamentally the same problem. Here, let me sketch for you what I . . ."

As Rati delved into the details of her invention, Savo's initial instinct was to stop her. He didn't want to hear about machinery invented for war and killing, and he didn't want to arouse Phyro's suspicion that he was, despite everything that had happened to him in Dara, spying for the Lyucu. Yet, a quote that Master Nazu Tei had taught him, attributed to Luan Zyaji, came back to him.

"A knife is not malicious merely because it is sharp, and a plot is not evil merely because it is effective. All depends on the wielder."

Why can't inventions birthed in war be copied and wielded to promote peace?

"Unfortunately, my solution isn't directly translatable to your problem," said Rati Yera regretfully. "I needed only a few dozen pseudo-logograms to devise my flight plans—even navigating the freedom of the skies is but a tiny, bounded domain compared to the vastness of all human experience, a borderless province that could only be described via hundreds of thousands of logograms. My cork-cylinder copying machine is too simple."

Savo's fingers idly struck the strings of his writing zither as he pondered Rati Yera's words. *Copy. Copy. Copy.* As the zither's tiny whirling blades carved out the same logogram over and over, the same musical phrase echoed around the room.

"Can't you play something a little more tuneful?" asked Fara, entering the room bearing a tray of snacks and tea. "You play so repetitively that one could have mistaken you for a puppet in Na Moji's mechanical orchestra. I, after all, am your music master. Your playing reflects on me." She laughed at the wounded expression on Savo's face.

"Sorry," said Savo, fumbling to take the tray from her. "I was too absorbed in—"

"Wait!" cried Rati Yera. "Dandelion—er, Princess, Your Highness, what was it you just said?"

"I was just kidding with Savo—"

"No, no, before that. Something about a mechanical orchestra?"

"Oh, it's from an old account back in the time of the Tiro states. Na Moji supposedly constructed a team of wooden puppets for the King of Xana that was capable of playing the *moaphya*. The witness described the mechanical orchestra's playing as skillful, but I imagine the admiration was mostly from the fact that it could be done at all rather than that it was done well."

"Fara told me about that back at the Splendid Urn," added Savo. "It helped me grasp your instructible carts."

"A mechanical orchestra," muttered Rati Yera, holding up a hand to silence the other two as she squeezed her eyes shut in concentration. "Another level of abstraction . . . yes, another way to teach and learn . . ."

At length, Rati's eyes snapped open as she let out a satisfied sigh. "The answer is automata. Or, as Secretary Zomi Kidosu put it, 'to multiply the work of one adept a hundredfold' through the use of machines."

"Automata?" asked Fara, looking lost. "Do you mean . . . like the cooking automata at the Splendid Urn? You want Savo to build an orchestra of mechanical scribes to pluck at writing zithers?"

Rati laughed. "No, not literally a mechanical orchestra, though a scribe using Savo's machine to write also plays music."

Savo gazed at her intently. "Master, I'm afraid that you've flown too high for me to follow."

"I haven't worked out the details, but here's what I'm thinking. In principle . . ."

Rati explained that in her exploration of the art of automata construction, two principles had proven to be helpful in overcoming most obstacles.

The first principle was higher abstraction. The primitive system of individual wheel turns that defined the capability of the instructible carts threatened to overwhelm the pilot until abstracted into a system of compound knots that could be strung together to represent a map. The primitive language of punched holes that specified each minute aspect of the wingbeat of an ornithopter was impossible to use to write a flight plan until it was abstracted into the higher language of pseudo-logograms that represented numbers, directions, and degrees.

The second principle was imbuing machines with wisdom. Whether it was the self-adjusting feedback loop powering the even-tempered archon or the human intelligence encoded in the knot-map and the master cork cylinder, marvelous automata were made possible by reifying wisdom, by reducing experience and practiced routine into precise instructions that could be carried out by a machine, repeatedly and at high speed.

She beckoned at Savo and gesticulated at the writing zither as she elaborated, "If I understand correctly, for the zither-playing scribe, the musical phrase associated with each logogram is just a mnemonic device. But the music can also be interpreted as a series of precise manipulations of the zither strings. The musical *score* then can be used to control the writing knife and the wax depositor just like the language of drilled holes instructs the wings and fins of the ornithopters. Once we have the score, we don't need to play it *as music*; we just need to feed it through the writing engine as quickly as possible."

Savo tried to imagine such a thing: himself translating each logogram into a musical phrase and compiling Lady Soto's manuscript into a score; mechanical fingers hovering over the zither strings and plucking out the music; cords and levers connected to the zither strings moving the writing knife and wax depositor to carve out new sequences of logograms. . . .

Savo began by developing the "score" format. Based on Rati's experience with ornithopters, he settled on using punched holes to encode the machine-instruction language. However, instead of small cork cylinders, he would use spooling silk cloth hardened with varnish as the medium to account for the increased complexity of logograms.

First, he mapped the individual actions of the writing knife and the wax depositor into distinct patterns of holes. Individual logograms would then be composed from these patterns—essentially a "song" for each word. He compiled long tables mapping the most commonly used logograms to tunes. More obscure logograms would be added on an ad-hoc basis.

Next, he tackled the construction of a writing engine that could read the score and produce logograms. Translating the pattern of holes into lever presses, gear turns, rack slides, and arm swings was a relatively easy matter of mechanical engineering, and by using a comblike row of pins that dipped into the holes as the spooling cloth was scrolled underneath, he rigged a simple reader that could drive the writing zither's wax-carving engine in place of the scribe's string-plucking hands. The matter of replicating the details of Soto's hand in each logogram, however, posed a challenge.

Savo was no skilled calligrapher; he had but the roughest understanding of how a scribe's touch translated into specific artistic effects in the final logogram. When he had devised the writing zither for his fellow Mendist monastics at the Temple of Still and Flowing Waters, his task had been simplified by the relative austerity of the standard clerical script and the extremely loose form of torrent script—it was easy to write in neat cuts or wild strokes. His imitation of Fara's hand, on the other hand, had been much less convincing—though passable due to a lover's idealization of the beloved. As Lady Soto's unique hand was an essential part of the text's claim to authenticity, the machine had to get it exactly right.

Fara came to his rescue. A practiced calligrapher and artist, she dissected the strokes of Soto's handwriting with far more insight. With her help, Savo finally succeeded in tuning the writing engine to replicate Soto's hand with nearly perfect fidelity.

"Once we have your book in the form of a scroll of holes instead of wax logograms on cloth, we would be able to make a new copy of your book just by running the spool through the writing engine," explained Savo.

"But how do we translate my book into this scroll of holes?" asked Soto, looking at the clacking writing engine with suspicion and confusion. "And it isn't just my book; we have to make facsimiles of all the other documents as well."

Savo's face fell. The tables for translating individual logograms into patterns of holes were long and unwieldy. Even he, the designer, could not memorize them all. To create the punched-hole scrolls by hand, one logogram at a time, was beyond daunting.

"Could you build a writing zither that punches holes in cloth instead of carving wax?" asked Fara. She was proposing, in essence, that Savo build an encoder.

"But someone would still have to read each book and rewrite it using the zither," said Savo. He did some quick math. "We have to work slowly and be careful about mistakes, since holes are much harder to patch than errant wax carvings. All of us would have to pitch in—"

"I'm too old to learn a whole new system of writing," fretted Soto.

"It's worse than that," said Savo. "Copying books every hour for the next few months, checking and rechecking for errors . . . that would . . . would bore—"

"—why should we learn to write for machines when machines should learn to read like humans?" said Rati at the same time.

The two looked at each other and burst out laughing as they recognized a kindred spirit of productive laziness.

"So what would be the more *interesting* solution?" asked Fara. "How could we get an automaton to turn a manuscript into a pattern of punched holes?"

"We need to teach the machine to read," said Rati.

Soto and Fara looked at her as though the master engineer had lost her mind. Even Savo didn't see how this was possible.

But Rati kept on muttering under her breath, "If only the oculium eye could see more than a single point of light. . . ."

To occupy herself in the isolated seaside manor, Fara had taken up gardening.

While pruning a beach-rose bush, she noticed a hefty bumblebee crawling over a dandelion flower at her feet. The insect was so large that the thin stalk of the flower was unable to support it, swaying back and forth precariously as the bumblebee shifted from one side to the other, scrambling to hold on like a drunken sailor clinging to the mast or a tyrant struggling to remain on her throne.

Fara laughed at the image. She decided she would turn the scene into the pattern for a knitted shawl. The nights were growing chilly, and she wanted something warm to wear and amusing to look at— besides, knitting would keep her mind off her worries about Phyro.

As she worked in the garden with her sketch pad, bleary-eyed Rati and Savo emerged from the house to have their breakfast in the garden—they had been working on the writing engine all night.

Savo took a bowl of hot porridge, flavored with wild vegetables and pickled caterpillars, to Fara.

"What are you working on?" he asked.

She showed him. She had started with a sketch of the oversized bumblebee on the dandelion. Then she had drawn a grid of tiny squares over a thin, translucent sheet of paper and overlaid this atop the sketch so that she could redo the picture as a mosaic of black-and-white squares.

"Why are you doing this?" Savo inquired in puzzlement. "Your original sketch is much prettier."

"Spoken like someone who's never knitted," said Fara. "This is how you make a knitting pattern."

She explained how each square represented a stitch, knit, or purl, and that by working like this, one square at a time, she converted the scene into the language of loops of yarn on the needle.

"That is a fascinating way to see the world," Savo said. He knelt down to examine the grid, admiring the way Fara had translated thicknesses, curves, and shades into patterns of black-and-white squares.

"I suppose all artists strive to come up with new ways of seeing the world," said Fara. "Lady Mira saw the Hegemon as abstract, geometric shapes, and captured the essence of his spirit in the bold strokes of her embroidery. The mathematical painters of the Tiro states discovered the world seen through the pinhole in a camera obscura, and thereby devised methods for creating the illusion of depth on a flat page. Men and women in past generations learned to visualize the world as a grid of colored knots, and that is how we have pretty sweaters, shawls, and the knotwork of old Xana."

Rati, done with her porridge, joined the pair. Intrigued, the two engineers continued to observe as Fara slowly filled in the grid with a piece of charcoal. When she reached the bumblebee's eyes, she hesitated.

"It's funny," said Fara. "I sometimes wonder whether the bumblebee sees the world the way a knitter does. It has such strange eyes—each seems composed from numerous facets."

"I think each facet is actually a smaller eye, if the zoologists at the Imperial Academy are to be believed," said Rati. She vaguely recalled Kisli Péro telling her something about the so-called "compounded eyes" of bees.

Fara nodded. "If so, then perhaps each simple eye only sees the world in its view as a dot of light and color, which then must be added to the dots perceived by all the other eyes to make up a full picture."

"What an interesting observation!" said Rati. "Though it seems more likely to me that each of the little eyes is like the pinhole on—" Abruptly, she ceased talking, and stared at the pattern under Fara's charcoal intently.

"What's wrong?" asked Savo, concerned.

Rati held up a hand, indicating that Savo and Fara should let her think. The expression on her face hovered somewhere between ecstasy and confusion. Then, she began to laugh and whoop joyously.

"Are you . . . all right?" asked Fara. She turned to Savo. "You really shouldn't have kept Master Yera up so late—"

"No, no! I feel fine. Better than fine, splendid!" shouted Rati. "Ah, Princess Fara, we may yet make a fine engineer out of you!"

A large windmill spun in the breeze.

Based on an old Gan design with improvements from Imperial researchers, the vanes automatically turned to face into the wind and spun at a steady pace regardless of the strength of the air currents.

With a flourish, Rati threw a switch at the foot of the windmill. The spinning worm gear swung over to engage a gear train that had been idling, and with a loud thrumming that brought to mind a swarm of bees, a massive silkmotic generator came to life, sending the invisible force down wires in every direction, and the yard, filled to the brim with machines, erupted to life.

At last, Savo and Rati were ready to demonstrate their new invention to Soto and Fara.

On the eastern side of the yard, a long, thin strip of varnished silk began to spool onto a spindle. The neat pattern of holes in the cloth, read by a comb of retractable pins, directed the action of ten separate writing engines that whirled and clacked in parallel, driven by the animating silkmotic force.

A large tank of wax was suspended above and just ahead of the writing knives. Rati drew the observers' attention to the bright curved mirrors placed around the tank that gathered the rays of the sun to melt the wax blocks in the tank.

"This may be the best-tasting dish to ever come out of your sun stove," quipped Fara, "at least as far as mind-pleasure is concerned."

As the tank shuttled back and forth, the melted wax dripped through ten spigots to end up as soft, doughy dollops on ten unwinding silk scrolls. Blocks of ice placed under the scrolls and silkmotic-powered spinning fans at the sides instantly cooled the wax into solid blocks ready to be carved.

"The wax must be cooled quickly because the writing engines are so much faster than human scribes, even scribes playing writing zithers," said Rati.

Ten sets of writing knives, as though wielded by miniature Cocru sword dancers, spun through the air and bit into the rough wax blocks. Carving, slicing, chopping, smoothing, hacking, gouging, drilling, whittling—columns of neat Ano logograms began to take shape, perfect facsimiles of Lady Soto Zyndu's singular hand.

"It is the oddest feeling in the world"—muttered Soto—"to see one's own handwriting appear under the writing knife of a ghost scribe. Look at them go! At this rate, the machine will finish the whole book by noon!"

The others, even Rati Yera, were similarly mesmerized by the hypnotic motion of the writing engines.

"It's like watching ten cooking automata in the kitchen of the Splendid Urn on that night when we had to serve a full house without a staff," whispered Fara.

Savo squeezed her hand.

"I wish Master Nazu Tei could see this," said Savo. "She always wished I would see the value of calligraphy. Well, I think she would have enjoyed teasing me about how this machine writes more beautifully than I."

"I wish Zomi were here," said Fara wistfully. She turned to Savo, her voice growing excited as a new thought struck her. "You could also tune the engine to write in a standard clerical script, devoid of personality, can't you?"

Savo nodded. "But why would you want to do such a thing?"

"If you make hundreds of writing zithers all tuned to the same handwriting and teach all the examinees at the Grand Examination to use it—"

"Oh, you're right. Zomi would very much want to see that," said Lady Soto.

Zomi Kidosu had always been concerned with fairness at the Imperial examinations. Students wealthy enough or lucky enough to study with calligraphy masters naturally had an advantage—including Zomi herself. But with writing zithers tuned to write in the same, standardized hand, scholars would have to distinguish themselves by ideas alone, another step closer to the perfectly fair examination that Zomi yearned for.

"Now that you've seen the writing side," declared a proud Rati Yera, interrupting this side discussion, "you need to pay attention to the *reading* side."

Heaving herself along in her wheeled chair, Rati led the group to the western side of the yard. In contrast to the mechanical frenzy that filled the other half of the yard, here, a single device stood alone at the center.

Soto's manuscript was being slowly scrolled across the slanted surface of a lectern by a pair of rollers. A cube-shaped box hung above the columns of logograms. The box shuttled back and forth on a track, and as each logogram passed under it, it paused for a fraction of a second, dipped down to cover the logogram, and then sprang back up, ready for the next.

"What *is* that thing?" asked Fara. "It looks like a bee pausing to sample every flower."

"That's exactly right!" replied Rati, laughing. "I call it the Bumblebee, named after you, my favorite knitting princess."

"You better explain how this works."

Rati gestured for Savo to flip the switch at the foot of the windmill to disengage the silkmotic generator and temporarily put a halt to all the commotion. Then she took the Bumblebee off its track so that everyone could get a good look.

The Bumblebee was a five-walled box with an open bottom, and each wall was divided into a neat grid of sixty-four cells.

"What's in each cell?" asked Fara.

"An oculium eye," replied Rati, "just like the ones that guided Phyro's mechanical dyrans."

Gently, Rati lifted Soto's manuscript to reveal a glowing crystal sphere embedded into the surface of the lectern. "This is a small silkmotic light that gives off an intense glow, and mirrors are deployed to direct as much of the light upward as possible."

As the Bumblebee dipped down to cover each logogram, the bright light illuminated the logogram from underneath, casting shadows onto the five walls of the Bumblebee.

"Each oculium eye can see only a tiny piece of the picture," explained Soto. "If the wax is very thick between the silkmotic lamp and the eye, then the light reaching the eye will be very faint; but if the wax is very thin, then the light reaching the eye will be very bright. The amount of light that reaches each eye is measured by the strength of the silkmotic current that flows through the wire behind the eye. Though each eye can see only a tiny part of the logogram and report on how bright or dark it is, by combining the reports from all the eyes—"

"You get a full picture of the logogram!" finished Fara, shivering with the joy of understanding. "This is just like how I make a knitting pattern by shading in boxes in the grid—"

"Exactly," said Rati. "I couldn't figure out how to use oculium to *see* until you showed me."

Rati explained how the hundreds of wires connected to the tiny oculium cells were then gathered together in layers so that the silkmotic currents could amplify and reinforce one another, resulting in distinct patterns. Each pattern (or set of patterns, depending on how neat and standardized the scribe's handwriting was) was associated with a distinct logogram, which could then be translated into the corresponding arrangement of holes that Savo had devised to be punched in the cloth scroll.

It had taken many sleepless nights of calibration and tweaking, but finally, everything had come together. A woman who knew no more than a dozen logograms and a refugee from Unredeemed Dara had created a mechanical scribe capable of copying more books in a single day than most human scribes would produce in a lifetime.

"You've taught a machine to read and write," said Fara, finally grasping and awed by the concept.

"Well, technically I call it optical logogram recognition," said Rati, quite pleased. "There's no *understanding* in the machine, but it does encode the wisdom of Savo's tables."

Savo flipped the switch again to activate the machines. The observers watched as the Bumblebee dipped over every logogram, seeing it and reading it with the aid of the hundreds of oculium cells inside the box, translating the recognized logogram into a pattern of holes, which was then punched into the strip of cloth that spooled into the eastern side of the yard, where the comb-reader deciphered it to actuate the ten writing engines to reproduce facsimiles of the manuscript at a speed that no human scribe could ever hope to match.

"I call this the book-mirror," declared Rati. "It is an insubstantial scribe that makes perfect facsimiles."

"A fitting name for a wondrous machine," said Fara. "You and Savo have found a way to visualize the whole through pinpricks of light, dimly glimpsed; orchestrated a scriptorium staffed by silkmotic ghosts; constructed a mechanical wonder that reads and writes. Is there *anything* that cannot be accomplished by the ingenuity of the silkmotic engineer?"

Rati blushed and grinned. The princess had a way with words.

Savo wrapped his arm around Fara and pulled her close. "No mechanical wonder can ever replace the joy of sharing one's breasthoard with the mirror of one's soul," he whispered into her ear.

CHAPTER FIFTY

JUDGMENT

Dispassionately, Jia folded up the last of the scrolls, placed the neat bundle back into the pisciform box (*a clever little dig on behalf of Zomi,* she thought, *if a bit overwrought*), and slid the box into its place in the stacks of boxes. She winced as the movement irritated the bandages, reminders of Phyro's assault.

Throughout the land, protests raged. Veterans and scholars congregated in front of ministries and magistrates' manors, clamoring for Emperor Monadétu to emerge from seclusion to speak to them. They blocked airfields and docks, waving banners listing the empress's sins. In Pan, Réza Müi, always the troublemaker, led a hunger strike of scholars in the Plaza of the Four Seas. In Ginpen, Lolotika, head girl of the Aviary, put on a new play, *The Innocent,* based on the alleged transcripts of the trial of Gin Mazoti.

Petitions from the College of Advocates covered the palace secretaries' desks like a snowstorm, demanding that Empress Jia terminate her regency and give up the Seal of Dara—"Even if the empress is wholly innocent, she should avoid the appearance of tyranny and yield up power, pending a full investigation. . . ."

More than a few magistrates and governors, following the example set by the famous wartime hero Naro Hun, had closed their courts and shuttered their halls to join the protesters, proclaiming that they would no longer follow orders from Pan until Jia answered the accusations concerning Empress Risana and Marshal Gin Mazoti in Soto's book and the secret Imperial archive documents that had been released.

Phyro's corpse lay in the hidden chamber under the Imperial kitchen, preserved by embalming herbs and blocks of ice. It was a secret known only to herself and the Dyran Fins. Publicly, the assault on the palace had been blamed on bandits and saboteurs—even a lie that no one believed could still be convenient. The protesters would never get their wish: The good emperor they pined for was dead.

Some of the more timid officials, terrified of incurring Jia's wrath, had sent her the mysterious boxes of books left at their residences. In the groveling notes accompanying the materials, they took pains to point out that they had not broken the seals on the boxes and there-fore had not read them.

Whatever lies the enemies of the empress try to spread, they assured her, *will fall on deaf ears. Rénga, you're the sovereign of Dara, and your word is law.*

She had prepared a list of the names of these favor-currying offi-cials that she would send to Cogo Yelu when this was over. Termites could not be allowed to nest comfortably in the incorruptible edifice that was the machinery of state of Dara.

O Phyro, Phyro! she lamented. *Why did it have to end this way? You were so clever, so brave, so compassionate—yet you were not wise enough, not ready to wield the Grace of Kings. You didn't give me enough time. I couldn't trust you.*

This new rebellion from beyond the grave—was it really only Soto's idea? Or did you have something to do with it? How could the Dandelion Throne survive such an assault? Peace and prosperity depend on the sov-ereign wearing a mask, require the throne be veiled. To reveal the secret court intrigues and political machinations that maintain the stability of the system is to strike at the very foundation of the state; surely you were wise enough to know this?

It was odd to read about herself in the third person, as though the deeds being described had been done by someone else. The pas-sionate denunciations from Soto; the shame-filled, self-flagellating memoirs of Zomi Kidosu and Rin Coda; the cold fury in the words of Gin Mazoti, palpable even when filtered through the officialese logograms of the trial transcripts—Jia didn't recognize the strange woman they described: power-hungry, deceitful, manipulative, clothing her selfish ambitions for herself and her issue in the guise of benefiting the people of Dara.

Or maybe she did. It was hard to tell where the mask ended and where the face began, after so many years.

She was tired, very tired. Years of playacting had taken a toll, and even young bedmates no longer provided any pleasure. It was hard to persist along this path alone and in secret, to pursue an idea whose full scope she dared not reveal even to her dearest confidante, to treat even those she loved most as stones that could be sacrificed in the grandest game of them all.

Just a little longer.

As if she hadn't already had her hands full, a Lyucu delegation had arrived in Pan, seeking an audience with the Emperor of Dara.

Yes, the delegation was specific on this point. They did not wish to speak to the regent.

She had to be near the end of her balancing act. *Had to.* The destruction of the zomi berry field and the cessation of shipments to Rui and Dasu must finally be bearing fruit. There was no telling what the Lyucu wanted, but she suspected that they had come to beg. Maybe Timu had even—she pushed away the thought. Hoping for something only made it less likely to be true. She could not afford hope; she had to act.

But her carefully constructed plot had fallen apart at the most critical moment. Her succession plan was in shambles. The ship of state had run aground on shoals that she had not seen and a storm was brewing in the streets—it was as if the gods of Dara were toying with her.

She squeezed her fists until her nails had drawn blood against skin.

Then she forced herself to relax. She could not change the past; the only thing she could do was to react, to plan and plot and scheme for the future.

Was there some way to take advantage of this latest crisis, to make it the keystone of her grandest vision, a strategy even longer running than the plot against the Lyucu, a dream that had first germinated in that house outside Çaruza, when she had been a captive of the mercurial Mata Zyndu?

The people have been told that a good king is all they can hope for. But it isn't enough. Even the best king eventually dies.

She drained the teacup and lay down on her daybed. She would just take a little nap. There was still so much to do.

Jia strolled through the Palace Garden.

She couldn't remember where she was supposed to go. That was so unlike her; she always had a destination in mind. Aimlessly, she picked a path and followed it.

Ahead was a circular stone garden filled with rock formations—Consort Fina preferred them to flowers, as they reminded her of the highlands of her native Faça. Jia, on the other hand, felt at home everywhere and nowhere in Dara, the consequence of a lifetime of being uprooted and uprooting.

Beyond the rock formations, she could hear the voices of two boys.

She crept through the stone garden, hid behind the gnarled formation closest to the voices, and listened.

"Hudo-tika, you cannot play all day! When are you going to work on Master Ruthi's essay topic?"

"Who's playing? I'm practicing fighting moves Uncle Théca taught me. I have to spar with Daf later."

Jia smiled to herself. The children were so small, full of potential, their natures not yet fully formed.

It was nice to have a good dream instead of a nightmare. The injuries she had sustained from Phyro's bomb had made sleep even harder to come by. She had taken twice the usual dose of dream herbs to get some rest.

"Sword fighting and archery are not worthy pursuits for a prince of the House of Dandelion! You should be reading books and learning the wisdom of the sages."

"How is reciting Kon Fiji going to help Da defend the empire? Mark my words, big brother, there'll come a day when you'll wish you'd studied how to wield a steel blade better than an ivory writing knife."

"And mark my words, little brother, there'll come a day when you'll

realize that it takes more to be a good Emperor of Dara than merely winning battles!"

"Ha! So you agree I should be the emperor when we grow up? Should we go tell Da?"

"I agreed to nothing of the sort! I was speaking of . . . a hypothetical. Do you even know what the word means?"

"I'll show you a hypo . . . hypostatical! Watch me bring down this obstinate rebel! Hiiiii-ya!"

A swoosh. The soft sighs of leaves and petals falling to the ground.

"Did you see how cleanly I cut down that bush? Not bad, eh?"

"Consort Risana just had that beach rose transplanted from the greenhouse! Oh, you're really going to get it now. Don't you even think about begging me to lie to your mother—"

"It's just a little chop. Ma will never be able to tell—Ah no!"

The sword clanged to the ground. The clattering of wooden soles over the brick path and then the shuffling of feet through grass.

Jia peeked out from behind the rock formation. The boys were crouched around the beheaded beach-rose bush. Gingerly, Timu cupped his hands around something among the weeds.

"Is it okay? I didn't see it!" Phyro was frantic, nearly in tears. "I'm so sorry, little bird."

His older brother was much calmer. "I don't think you struck it. Best as I can tell, you frightened it, and it fell. Maybe a wing is broken."

"What should we do, Toto-tika?"

"Give me your belt," said the older boy. Phyro untied the silk sash from around his waist and handed it to Timu, who wrapped it around the bird's body to secure the wings in place, careful not to make the loops too tight. "I think we should take it to my mother. She's good at healing things."

"Yes, good idea." Phyro nodded vigorously. "Aunt-Mother always knows what to do."

Timu stood up, cupping the injured bird in his palms. "Do you want to carry it?"

"No, you should do it," said Phyro, also getting up. "You have gentler hands. I'm too clumsy."

"You're not clumsy," said Timu. "You're just . . . a bit impulsive." He paused and then hastened to add, "That's not always a bad thing. Kon

Fiji said that a good ruler must act even when there are no good choices. Sometimes, I don't know how to answer a question that has no right answer—Master Ruthi considers it a fault."

"What does Master Ruthi know?" said Phyro, rallying to his brother's defense. "He's just a sore loser. During the war, Auntie Gin beat him like a cat batting away a mouse."

"Hudo-tika, you can't always . . ." Timu shook his head and sighed.

Still out of view, Jia stifled a chuckle—but her face froze as horror struck.

Why am I dreaming of the boys now? Though she missed Toto-tika with every fiber of her being, he had never visited her in her uneasy slumber, the province of the ghosts of her conscience.

The boys began to walk away. Timu was in the lead, cradling the injured bird. Phyro followed close behind, peeking at it anxiously.

"If you become the emperor," Phyro said, "promise me you'll make me your marshal."

"Of course." Timu's voice then took on a hint of heartache. "But that probably won't happen. Father likes you better."

Phyro didn't object. He was old enough to know that what Timu said was true, but not old enough to pretend that he didn't.

"Maybe we can take turns being the emperor."

Timu laughed. "That's . . . not how it works."

"Why not? Let me hold the bird for a while."

"You just said you were too clumsy! Let's not frighten it."

"But taking turns is more fair! Anyway, why can't you, me, Théra, and Fara all take turns being the emperor?"

"Now you're just talking nonsense."

"All right, maybe not Fara, 'cause she's just a baby. When I'm emperor, I'll make you Prime Minister."

"Uh . . . thanks?"

The voices faded.

Behind the rock formation, Jia remained frozen in place, tears streaming down her face.

Timu must be dead, like Phyro.

She should have been expecting it. With the supply of cultivated zomi berry cut off and her plague spores decimating the local variety, Unredeemed Dara must have already fallen into total chaos and civil strife. She had *plotted and schemed to cut down that tree of evil; how could she expect an egg nestled precariously in its branches to survive intact? From the moment she had decided to goad her son into acting in accordance with his nature, this was the only possible result.*

Teeth on the board.

But it didn't make the grief any easier to bear.

How the gods love to play with us! *she raged.* How you love to torment the mortals in our powerlessness!

As though in response to her silent accusations, the ground rumbled and quaked as the rock formations around her enlarged and rose up. Twisting, flexing, unfolding, expanding, the rocks turned into towering, living statues.

The gods of Dara.

Jia spun in place, staring up at the divine figures around her: dark-haired Kana, eyes aglow like fiery volcanic craters; silver-skinned Rapa, hair frosted over with ice; long-speared Fithowéo, his obsidian orbs unblinking; nine-fingered Kiji, a Mingén falcon and a garinafin over his shoulders; ivy-caped Rufizo, his hands outstretched in supplication; chaotic Tazu, grinning like a toothy shark; pulchritudinous Tututika, her blond tresses undulating like the fins of a carp.

Jia trembled. It was said that the gods of Dara only manifested in council to render judgment to a dying sovereign.

"No!" she screamed. "You cannot do this. I'm not finished!"

The gods gazed down at her, their faces flashing through a thousand expressions. They raised their weapons, summoned their pawi, pointed at her, and seemed to converse with one another in mute council, mind to mind, will to will. But they did not speak to her.

"Please!" She fell to her knees. "Please! I know everyone pleads for more time, but I'm so close! The Lyucu are on the verge of collapse. For the sake of the people of Dara, give me a little more time to see it through. I beg you!"

The gods stopped their silent council. As one, the colossal presences turned to look down upon her.

"I know I have sinned," Jia sobbed. "My victims . . . they haunt me in my nightmares, never letting me rest."

Kana's face melted and reshaped itself to resemble that of Rin Coda, as he hung at the end of his rope, unable to close his eyes from shame and self-hatred.

"I betrayed those who trusted me," said Jia, her voice cracking.

Rapa took on the appearance of Otho Krin, gazing at Jia with unrequited longing.

"I exploited love as a blindfold and leash."

Tazu mutated into the form of Tiphan Huto, his throat a bloody pulp from his own hands.

"I bypassed my own laws, killing without mercy."

Fithowéo was next, metamorphosing into Gin Mazoti as she languished in a dank prison cell.

"I was ready to remove all who stood in my path, regardless of their contributions."

Tututika took on the guise of Risana, with her head grotesquely deformed by impact against the ground.

"I harmed those who did nothing against me, so long as they posed a threat to my vision."

Kiji became Phyro, though the face, so lacerated by shrapnel, was nigh unrecognizable.

"I kept the legitimate heir away from the throne, because I couldn't trust that his hand would be as steady as mine."

Finally, Rufizo appeared as gentle Timu, blood seeping from a mouth filled with broken teeth.

"I disregarded the safety of my own flesh and blood, so long as I was serving a higher cause," Jia wailed.

Each self-denunciation struck Jia like a body blow. She swayed unsteadily on her knees, almost falling over.

"But only I can carry this plan to completion. I meant to pass on the Seal of Dara to Phyro when he was ready, but he . . . I have to finish what I started! I must do what is right for Dara, no matter the consequences. The people of Dara must not ever suffer again as they have before, not at the hands of bloody warlords like Mata Zyndu, not at the hands of barbaric invaders like the Lyucu, and especially not at the hands of a 'good emperor' like Phyro, who didn't understand the need to sheathe the sword when one is weak, nor the need to finish an enemy who can never be reconciled with!"

The gods did not respond. They continued to stare at her, the flitting expressions on their faces unreadable.

Gradually, Jia stopped crying. Some invisible source of strength seemed to revive her, the glow of reality. Straightening her spine, she staggered to her feet. She had never found the guidance of the gods helpful as she felt her way through the dark storm that was life.

She looked at the gods, one by one.

"What right do you have to judge me?" she muttered. "When Mata Zyndu decimated the land with wars of vengeance and ambition, did you blunt his sword or soften his cudgel? When families were torn asunder, brother warred against brother, and orphans filled the streets, did you respond to their pleas for succor? When the Lyucu committed systematic rapes, mass massacres, unspeakable tortures, forced servitude, did you step in to stop them? When they snatched babies out of mothers' arms and tossed them down wells, did you avenge the innocent victims? When they enslaved two islands to construct a hell on earth, did you refuse the Lyucu offering of sacrificial victims?

"No, you have no right to judge me. You are immortals, and you're free from suffering and terror. How can you ever understand our agony?

"I wield the Grace of Kings. I will submit to the judgment of history, but not to you."

The gods stopped moving, their faces rigid as though carved from stone.

Jia strode defiantly up to them, her expression as haughty as the one she had worn when she stared down Tanvanaki at the Battle of Zathin Gulf.

She leaned in to examine the feet of the colossi. The stone was full of chips, cracks, stains, the marks of damaged faith, of vanity wrecked.

Jia began to laugh, a sound of despair and triumph in equal measure.

"You are useless idols, figments of my imagination. I do not fear you! Do you hear me? I do not fear you!"

The statues gave no reply as her voice echoed among them.

She lay gasping, her heart fluttering like a wounded bird.

There was no way to go back to sleep, not now, perhaps not ever.

I've crafted a Dara in which power is channeled and constrained, like the spring flood tamed to irrigate the rice paddies, like the silkmotic force of lightning storms guided through silver wires and pooled in Ogé jars.

The circuit intendants watch the officials for abuse of power; the military monitors watch the generals to check ambition; the paid litigators invoke the laws to protect the illiterate against the privileged; the farseers root out saboteurs and corruption; the College of Advocates criticizes and humbles the Inner Council. The institutions interlock and intertwine, weaving into a web in which none may be captured and turned into an instrument of oppression.

Constitutive acts. Weighty precedent.

The people of Dara must not ever suffer again as they have before.

Not at the hands of great lords wielding the Ambition of Nobles, and not at the hands of invaders dedicated to the Courage of Brutes.

But what about a tyrant who threatens the very system of power channeling by standing outside it, who arrogates to herself a deadly force bound only by personal loyalty, who grips the Grace of Kings and will not let go?

What about me?

Empress Jia rarely hosted formal banquets for the Dyran Fins. No. Not just "rarely." None of the women could remember the last time such a thing happened.

The mistress had plucked them from abandonment and destitution and raised them like the daughters of nobles. They loved her the way children loved a mother, subjects loved a benevolent queen, devotees loved a goddess. To be near her was the highest state of existence they could imagine.

And now, in the private quarters of the Imperial family, she was throwing them a lavish banquet with the finest cuisine and the rarest of beverages: bean curd balls marinated in the juices of seven different kinds of wild game; lotus seeds whose bitter cores had been replaced with eight varieties of sweet and savory fillings; soup made from thousand-year-old homunculus mushrooms; mead brewed from the honey of giant, translucent-bellied bees high up in the Wisoti Mountains. . . .

All the Dyran Fins had been summoned: the bodyguards in the palace, the ones dispatched to Mount Rapa to survey the site of the incinerated zomi berry field, spies who kept an eye on Gimoto and the ministers of the Inner Council.

They ate from golden plates and drank from jade cups. They were feted like princesses and grand ministers. Even before the first sip, they were already drunk with happiness and gratitude.

Carrying a jade jug, Empress Jia went around to every seat, filling each cup with rice beer: spicy, osmanthus-fragrant, and so intoxicating.

Her shoulders and chest remained heavily bandaged. A terrible scar marred her visage, a reminder of the horrors that had transpired last month.

With a grimace, the empress sat back down in the hostess seat in *géüpa*, and the other women followed her pose. She clinked her cup with a silver spoon, and spoke.

"I wanted to gather everyone here today to tell you how grateful I am for all you've done. Filial feelings can be stunted in the rocky soil of an Imperial household, and so it is that sons sometimes take up arms against mothers, and parents sometimes must scheme to keep their children's unsteady hands away from the levers of power. Though we're not related by blood, you are, in many ways, dearer to me than my own children."

Tears welled in the eyes of the Dyran Fins. Their beloved mistress was articulating the truth in their own hearts. Jia was dearer to them than their own half-forgotten birth parents.

"My only regret is that I haven't done this sooner. The empty seats rebuke me."

There were four empty seats scattered around the room, at which the food and drink remained untouched. The women who would have sat in them had died in the underground hideout on that fateful night. With their bodies, they had shielded Jia from the desperate, final strike of Phyro, the unfilial son who had tried to assassinate his own aunt-mother in his hunger for power.

"Let's drain our cups and celebrate our most rare bond. I may be the dyran of the seas, but I cannot glide through sea nor air without you."

What we need are systems and rules to channel the flow of power, Jia thought. *Yet, I've had to rely on you, existing outside the systems and rules I've worked so hard to cultivate, to wield power to protect the people of Dara. I had hoped to resolve this contradiction in time, but I'm a mere mortal. I've run out of time.*

The empress raised her cup, and the Dyran Fins lifted their cups with both hands in response. They drank deeply of the strong rice beer. It had been brewed from the crop of a small farm reserved to the Imperial family outside Pan, grown from seeds harvested from the rice paddy that had once been in the Palace Garden, tended by Emperor Ragin himself. This was a beverage that only the Imperial family and its closest confidants got to sample. The high honor being dispensed to the Dyran Fins was obvious and—more than a few had this thought but dared not speak it aloud—deserved.

The women, intoxicated by the mark of favor shown them, didn't notice that Jia's cup had been empty before she raised it to her lips.

They finished the beer.

"And now, I must turn to a new theme," said Jia, her tone somber.

The Dyran Fins set down their cups and leaned forward, hanging on her every word.

"Even the longest banquet must come to an end, and the closest bond may be severed by fate," said Jia, sounding wistful. "None of us can accomplish all that we wish; each success also brings the day of reckoning closer. It's the fate of those who plan for the long now to be misunderstood in the hasty present."

A few of the Dyran Fins frowned, not from the empress's obscure words, but because an odd sensation was developing in their guts, a kind of numbness that radiated outward. Had something at this sumptuous feast disagreed with their bodies? Reluctant to head to the toilet because the empress was still speaking, they kept their faces attentive and held their hands against their bellies.

Alarmed by the empress's plaintive tone, Wi tried to reassure her, always the First Fin. "Mistress, are you worried about the protests in the streets? Don't waste your time on them. They're just confused fools who don't understand your beneficence, and the Prime Minister will surely restore order soon."

"And if he doesn't, we *will*," added Shido, as the Second Fin always did.

"Whatever happens," said Wi, "we'll never acknowledge any master of Dara except you."

"We'll fight against anyone who dares to challenge you," said Shido, "be he emperor, duke, minister, or general! You can trust us."

"I know," said Jia, a bitter smile on her face. And then, lowering her head, she added in a whisper only she could hear, "I'm so sorry."

The mood in the banquet hall grew bleak. None of the Dyran Fins knew why the empress seemed so sad. The numbness in their bellies grew, spreading into chests, arms, thighs, an enervating absence of sensation. There was no pain. It didn't seem right to grow alarmed.

Jia forced herself to raise her head, looking each Dyran Fin in the eye by turn. She projected her voice to every corner of the hall. "I want to tell you something that may not be known even to you: You've devoted your life not just to my protection, but to the service of a dream, to the realization of an ideal for the future that few can understand or appreciate. Everything you've done has been for the welfare of the people of Dara, though they do not know, and perhaps never will know, just how much you've sacrificed for them and the generations to come after. You are the very embodiment of *mutagé*."

The Dyran Fins were confused by the empress's cryptic pronouncement. Was she praising them for their loyalty? But that was only her due.

"Ah!" one of the Dyran Fins cried out, stumbling up from her seat but falling back down. "I . . . I can't move!"

Exclamations of agreement from around the hall.

All the Dyran Fins felt it: The numbness had spread into their faces, fingers, toes. Muscles that had been honed in years of martial training refused to obey their minds. Fingers refused to close around eating sticks; legs declined to uncurl; arms felt like they belonged to another body, or inanimate prosthetics. Even breathing was becoming difficult.

Plates clattered to the floor; cups shattered.

A few women teetered out of their seats, but their legs wobbled like stilts, and after only a few faltering steps, they collapsed to the floor, gasping for breath.

Wi tried to speak, but nothing came out except a faint hiss and gurgles deep in her throat. Foam spilled from her lips. Staring at Jia with eyes full of confusion and horror, she fell over.

"Mistress, please call for the Imperial doctors!" Shido shouted. She had been the last to finish her drink, wanting to savor the treat as long as possible. But she felt it now, the numbness that sapped all strength, devoured all vitality. "Something . . . someone . . . assassins . . ."

Empress Jia looked at her with pity, her face twitching. "I'm sorry, Shido-*tika*. I'm so sorry."

Shido fell. Her limbs no longer followed her will. The numbness spread into her cheeks, lips, eyelids.

She was being enclosed in nothingness. There was no knife-twisting pain in the gut, no fiery trail down the throat, no thousand-needle whip lacerating her nerves—she wasn't sure whether she would have preferred those agonies to this paralysis of feeling, to this severing of the senses.

"This is the best I could do," muttered Jia. Unable to meet Shido's gaze, she looked away.

Shido grunted and strained to draw air; her chest labored against the invisible weight of emptiness. She felt saliva pooling in her own mouth. Panic gave her a last burst of strength, and she flopped onto her side like a caught fish. Spittle dribbled from the corner of her mouth. As she heaved and coughed, her eyes took in the rest of the hall.

Many of the Dyran Fins had stopped moving, including Wi. Froth spilled from their mouths. Their eyes were wide open in their frozen faces, a most eerie and horrific sight. The rest convulsed on the floor, not far behind their sisters.

Finally, she understood.

"But why?" she wheezed, each word depleting her last breath. Her roaming eyes stopped to focus on Jia. "Mistress, why?"

Trembling, Jia rose from her seat and crawled to her. She cradled Shido's head in her lap and wept. "I'm sorry. I must betray those who trust and love me the most. Everything can be sacrificed in the name of the plan, even if it's my life, even if it's your life. . . . Teeth on the board. I'm . . . so sorry."

Shido's consciousness faded.

She was once again that little girl in the house outside Çaruza, where her kind mistress had stanched the flowing blood and was about to set her broken ankle.

"Mistress, why are you crying?"

"Because I know how much it hurts you, Shido-tika."

"But the wound is on my leg, not yours."

"When a child is hurting, the wound in her mother's heart is deeper, even if it is unseen."

"It doesn't hurt anymore, Mistress. It doesn't."

She looked up at the old woman cradling her. She had given Jia everything in her life, and she was never going to question anything Jia asked of her.

"It doesn't hurt, Mistress," she rasped.

The light in her eyes went out; they remained open.

In the still, silent banquet hall, Jia wailed. Long after the glow from the westering sun had faded, alone among a hall of dead daughters, her howls continued.

Thunder, lightning, a winter storm.

The protesters in the streets, lashed by the snow-laden winds, scattered to their homes. They would return and continue on the morrow. The empress had to give them an answer.

- Jia has always been my favorite mortal. She works slowly and stealthily, like a glacier imperceptibly carving a valley. You can't rush if you want to build anything that lasts.

- Rapa, my dearest sister, you overpraise her. The span of a mortal life is but the blink of an eye.

- Nonetheless, she was so subtle that even I missed her plot against the Lyucu . . . and even now, I cannot discern what she's planning. Do any of you know what she'll do next?

- . . .

- I bet Lutho would have seen through her. He was always the best at understanding mortals.

- What about me? I daresay I'm pretty insightful.

- You!? What do you know of the hearts of mortals, especially a dyran among mere fish like Jia? Tazu, your insight is limited to latrine rats like Wira Pin and Noda Mi.

- Risana was the master of smoke and illusions, and I always thought Jia the boring one. But she works with a medium even more powerful and subtle than smoke—Jia is a powercrafter.

- This may be the most admiration for a mortal I've ever heard from you. But Jia's goal has always been to tame power, to sheathe the Grace of Kings, to pacify the chaotic waves with seawalls and sturdy ships. She works against you.

- It doesn't matter. She's a worthy opponent, and isn't it the way of the mortals to admire a foe who elevates the contest to a new level? The curious turtle would have applauded her for deep calculation and careful planning, while I am impressed by her ruthless dedication to her vision—even if I cannot see the shore she's striving toward.

- We're all in the same boat, my brothers and sisters. Let's remain humble and continue to observe, and perhaps we'll learn something from those we were charged to protect.

- You speak as if the mortals are children who have grown up.

- Aren't they?

JUST OFF THE NORTHERN COAST OF THE BIG ISLAND, NEAR GINPEN: THE TWELFTH MONTH OF THE ELEVENTH YEAR OF THE REIGN OF SEASON OF STORMS AND THE REIGN OF AUDACIOUS FREEDOM.

Grace of Kings, escorted by a squadron of suspicious Dara airships, was winging its way toward Ginpen. The white banner of an emissary of peace dangled under it.

"They want us to land in Ginpen first," explained Goztan. "Once we receive permission from the palace, we'll proceed to Pan."

Dyana nodded, unable to take her eyes from the scene stretching out under and before her.

Fishing boats, as numerous as grains of rice, dotted the sea. Weaving between them were cargo ships, bearing goods from all over Dara, converging on the harbor that was ten times the size of the one in Kriphi. Beyond, she could see the battlements of Ginpen's city walls, and past them the gleaming roof tiles and soaring towers of a grand metropolis, where the buildings were as dense as a primeval forest. Still beyond them, she could see gridded fields, fallow for the winter and studded with hay bales, fading into the horizon.

"I never imagined . . ." Dyana swallowed, and then went on, her voice filled with awe. "Dara is so big, and has so many people in it. . . . There must be as many people in Ginpen as in all of Ukyu-taasa."

"Now you know why your grandfather wanted to conquer it," said Goztan. After a pause, she added, "And why your mother feared it."

Dyana took a deep breath. The Lyucu were about to walk an unexplored path in Dara.

CHAPTER FIFTY-ONE

ANCESTRAL VOICES

TATEN-RYO-ALVOVO: THE TWELFTH MONTH IN
THE ELEVENTH YEAR AFTER THE DEPARTURE OF
PRINCESS THÉRA FROM DARA FOR UKYU-GONDÉ.

Théra proposed an expedition to the heart of the City of Ghosts to retrieve what she believed were the spirit portraits and voice paintings of the ancestors of the people of the scrublands.

She spoke hesitantly because she was afraid. She had not, after all, been born on the scrublands; would her new tribe of castaways follow her in breaking a taboo? Or would they see her still as an outsider, *with* them, but not one *of* them? She wished more than ever for the powerful voice of Adyulek.

A younger voice, no less strong, came to her aid.

"To tell a new story of where to go," said Sataari, "we must first understand the story of where we came from. I have been to the heart of the Barrows, and the gods do not disapprove."

Tanto would retrace his steps, but this time, not alone. He rode on the back of a garinafin piloted by his mother, directing her toward the site where he had come so close to death and found new life.

The barrows, draped in snow and frost, swept under the speeding wings like a giant flock of slumbering sheep, bearing mute witness to this unprecedented expedition.

They returned with scrolls of garinafin stomach lining retrieved from the burial chamber inside the Great Barrow, in which the remains of Kikisavo and Afir lay at rest.

Fearful that the ancient spirit portraits would be unable to withstand the pressure of the reading-needle, Çami suggested that a copy be made. After Çami explained her rationale and the proposed process, Sataari assented.

With great reverence and care, and watched over by Sataari, Çami took a wax impression of the etched trail through the smoky varnish, brittle with age, and then pressed the impression into a new scroll of fresh charcoal-dyed tallow.

Çami loaded the new scroll into the bone-talker and gently deposited the needle into the groove. As she began to crank the rollers, Sataari placed her ear against the garinafin ear.

A voice, as raspy as the sands of Lurodia Tanta, as dry as the skeletons in the Boneyard, as faint as the stars in the long twilight in Nalyufin's Pasture, emerged haltingly from the machine.

Everyone held their breath as they watched Sataari's face, her eyes squeezed shut in concentration.

At length, she held up a hand, indicating that Çami should stop. Confusion and fear strained her features.

"I . . . cannot understand the voice."

"Speech changes from generation to generation," said Razutana. "We know this from studying the Classical Ano texts. Though many in Dara believe that the language of the ancient sages was frozen in its perfection, such was not the case. The phonetic components in many logograms, for instance, diverge greatly from the modern standard pronunciations of the logograms, hinting at shifts in pronunciation over time. By comparing rhyme schemes from the sagas of the Diaspora Wars with the writings of Kon Fiji and his students, and then with neoclassical writers like Suzaré and Nakipo, we can reconstruct—to some degree—how Classical Ano evolved over time, such that later generations could scarcely understand the speech of earlier ones. A language is a living being—it might evolve at the rate of the movement of glaciers through a valley or the accumulation of silt in a delta, imperceptible to each generation, but over hundreds of years, the speech of the dead and the living might as well be described as two tongues."

Sataari nodded. The shamans, charged with keeping the old tales alive through memory, were not ignorant of this fact—to learn the oldest tales, the shamans had to learn what amounted to a different language. But even the mind-fossils of the deeds of Kikisavo and Afir had deformed and changed in the passage through the malleable medium of oral tradition; try as she might, she could not make sense of the voice of the speaking bones. Some phrases, here and there, teetered on the verge of recognition, but comprehension eluded her like the reflection of the sun in a rushing stream.

Théra refused to give up, however. "Zomi Kidosu once told me of an experience she had when she was studying with the itinerant Luan Zyaji. They were traveling through Crescent Island, and Luan remarked that the language of the people there, though derived from the vernacular of Amu, retained old pronunciations and vocabulary that had been lost on Arulugi. Could we . . . do something with that knowledge?"

"You're referring to a phenomenon well-known to philologists," said Çami. "I'm no expert, but I understand that when speakers of one language are divided into groups isolated from one another, their speech begins to evolve in different directions. What is retained in one group may be lost in another, and different aspects of the ancestral tongue are fossilized. This is how scholars conjecture that the vernacular topolects of Dara all evolved from a common ancestor, and perhaps ultimately descend from the speech of the Ano."

"The speeches of the Agon and Lyucu across the vast extent of Ukyu-Gondé are also widely divergent, some of the varieties being not mutually intelligible," mused Théra, thinking back to her experience during the time when the scattered Agon tribes had come together briefly after the victory at the Boneyard. "If each topolect preserves some aspect of the original speech, then it follows that the speakers of different topolects would be able to understand different phrases in an ancient spirit portrait. It may be possible, with enough listeners, to piece together the whole."

"That is an experiment we can attempt with ease," said Gozofin. "We have speakers of varieties of Lyucu and Agon from the most far-flung corners of Ukyu-Gondé. Even the ice tribes and the tanto-lyu-naro may have preserved fragments of the ancestral tongue. Thanks to your policy of welcoming refugees from everywhere, this little settlement may have the most varied and diverse collection of tongues ever found gathered in one place on the scrublands."

"You're proposing using many ears across space to reconstruct a compounded ear that can reach across time," said Sataari, her eyes glinting with excitement. "What a breathtaking idea!"

"Sometimes it takes an ear not immersed in the hubbub of the familiar, an ear not born in this land, to hear the call of that which cannot be heard," said Théra.

By twos and threes, speakers of topolects found in every corner of Ukyu-Gondé were brought to the replica spirit portraits. Again and again, the speaking bones whispered into new ears. The listeners strained to capture fragments of sense from the raspy noise and repeated what they heard to Sataari. Razutana, acting as scribe, recorded these fragments so that they could be collated and compared, their patterns discerned and extrapolated, and the whole put together like a puzzle.

"The word-scars are good for something, after all," acknowledged Sataari grudgingly.

Razutana smiled and said nothing.

After days of hard work, Sataari told Théra that she was ready.

On the night of the Winter Festival, as the air was filled with snowflakes that seemed fragments of the brilliant stars, the settlement gathered around the blazing bonfire to celebrate, to honor the gods, and to listen to Sataari tell a story at once new and old.

"I am called Afir, known to my people as the Lightning-Step, the Six-Toed Mouflon. I speak now of the anger of the gods and the dying of the mother-sea. . . ."

A long, long time ago, Ukyu and Gondé was a lush grassland, laced with streams and dotted with lakes. The Sea of Tears was a vast freshwater lake many times its present size, and upon its shores, nomadic tribes settled and built a grand civilization.

The people learned to plant the wild herbs they sometimes gathered for roughage and bred them until the tubers, shriveled and bitter, became sweet and plump. They cultivated fields of heavy-headed cereal that they turned into flour and meal. The lake itself yielded fish and clams, while herds of fat cattle and sheep roamed the grassy shore.

Great pékyus presided over the construction of monumental mounds, from which astronomers studied the movement of the stars and predicted the weather and the harvest. They orchestrated the assembly of giant paintings from hundreds of thousands of individual stones that could only be seen from the sky, offerings of thanks for the bounty of the gods.

The population swelled; the city of earthen mounds expanded like the bellies of pregnant mothers; ingenious arucuro tocua creations proliferated like sprouting mushrooms after a summer thunderstorm or the fantastic visions in tolyusa-induced dreams.

And then, the world began to change. At first slowly, and then very fast.

Year after year, the mother-sea shrank, the receding water leaving behind cracked salt flats. The flowing rivers weakened and dwindled, and fewer fish leapt out of the ripples. There was much less rain, and fires swept through the flat grassland, whipped into a frenzy by the dry winds. The grass sea grew patchy, replaced by expanding islands of hardy scrub.

Crops and herds died from drought and disease, and there was no longer enough food for everyone.

At first, the pékyus believed that the gods were displeased. Gangs of workers labored to construct ever-grander barrows to map the course of the stars and to build more impressive stone-paintings in the salt flats to glorify the deeds of gods and demigods. They dug more irrigation canals, intensified cultivation, devised more clever ways to capture the dwindling bounty of the dying lake.

But none of it worked.

As the population was ravaged by hunger and disease, the pékyus had no answer except to point to the gods. They demanded more sacrifices, bigger barrows, more magnificent stone-paintings.

When they could no longer pay the labor gangs, they resorted to enslavement, enforced by garinafin breath.

Moved by despair and anger, rebellions flared and divisions took root. Blood drenched the fields and fishing weirs lay abandoned. Garinafins burned the temples of the gods, and storage pits were defiled by rotting corpses. The bones of the dead became the raw material for a new kind of macabre arucuro tocua: engines of war and slaughter, new ways of killing.

Two heroes rose from the ashes of the all-consuming chaos: Afir and Kikisavo. Close as tongue and lips, voice and breath, they complemented each other with their strengths and saved one another from their weaknesses. They fought with the vigor of star-snout bears, the fortitude of wild aurochs, the quickness of spiral-horned mouflon, the wile of tusked tigers, and the ferocity of horrid wolves. Working together, they at long last deposed the old pékyu and brought peace back to a much-diminished Barrows.

"We can't go on as we used to," said Kikisavo. "The world is changing, and we must learn a new way to live."

"We can't abandon the ways of our ancestors," said Afir. "Are you so arrogant as to think that we possess more wisdom than they accumulated over a thousand generations?"

"Humans didn't always live by the shore of the mother-sea," replied Kikisavo. "Nothing lasts forever, not even ways of life."

For seven days and seven nights they argued, neither able to convince the other. The rancorous disagreement cleaved the pair, and divided their followers as well.

Kikisavo and his followers left the Barrows. They took nothing with them that reminded them of the old way of life, a way that had brought so much sorrow: no seeds, no arucuro tocua, no shamans who charted the stars and retold stories of the past. They would live by following the instincts of migrating herds of long-haired cattle. The scrublands was terra incognita, a boundless emptiness into which they would howl their brand-new story.

Meanwhile, Afir and her followers stayed behind. They tried to eke out a living among the devastation of the ruins. They dug long canals to bring water across the salt flats to irrigate the bone-studded fields, but even the sea itself had grown salty. They tried to repair and maintain the barrows and stone-paintings, but the increasingly extreme summers and winters, crumbling earth and cracking rock, made a mockery of their efforts. They tried to keep the old ways alive, but death's choke hold grew tighter every year.

Each thought the other had betrayed them. Memory, filtered by resentment, became as bitter as the Sea of Tears.

Years later, as the remnants of Afir's people struggled against the inevitable, they were surprised by a sudden procession that appeared at the entrance to the Barrows. Though the newcomers brought with them a great number of garinafins and cattle, they weren't invaders. At the head of the procession was a bier, upon which lay the body of Kikisavo.

These were the final words of Kikisavo, as repeated to Afir by his followers: "My dearest Afir, my sa-votan, my people have learned to survive in the boundless scrublands by following the whims of the herds, to ruthlessly discard the weak and the infirm, to accumulate nothing that cannot be carried on the backs of our garinafins. It isn't an easy life, and we'll never be as numerous as our ancestors had been in the paradise of the past. But it is a new way of life suited to a changed world. I was right.

"Yet, my heart isn't at rest. I was angry with the gods for abandoning us, but now I crave their presence again. I was enraged by the weight of the outmoded commands of our ancient heroes, but now I miss the comfort of their words of wisdom and tales of courage. Try as I might, I cannot cast off the pull of our collective memory. Mere survival isn't enough. A people cannot be a people if they don't know where they come from, if they can't fear and trust the gods of their parents, if they've been cut off from the stories of their past. I return to you now chastened, for I was also wrong."

Afir wept. She asked that the people, both those who followed her and those who had followed Kikisavo, work together one last time to convert the Great Barrow into a burial mound for her closest companion and greatest rival.

"We are not stones, doomed to stay in the pattern we're placed in. We are not animals devoid of thinking-breath, fated to repeat the mindless patterns of our progenitors. The gods are capricious, but we're adaptable. It is neither right to discard the wisdom of our ancestors like the molted skin of a serpent, nor right to be trapped by it like the shell of a tortoise flipped on its back.

"My ru-taasa, how I wish we had listened better to each other!"

Afir then encouraged her people to leave the Barrows with the followers of Kikisavo, so that they could learn from the Children of Kikisavo how to live on the scrublands. Kikisavo's people, on the other hand, reacquainted themselves with what they had left behind by learning from the Children of Afir.

Ideas that were useful and comforting in that vast emptiness—prayers to the gods, dance-stories of ancient heroes, techniques for fashioning arucuro tocua, edible plants and medicines that could also be found in the wild—were kept; knowledge that wasn't suited to the new way of life—seeds of crops that couldn't tolerate drought, implements for farming, methods of construction suited only to a permanent settlement—was sealed up in the mounds and forgotten, perhaps to be recovered when the land had changed again to make it viable.

Upon her death, Afir chose to return to the Barrows herself and to be buried next to Kikisavo. Her passing would mark the end of the Fifth Age of Mankind.

"What happened next?" asked Tanto and Rokiri, their eyes wide with fascination.

"That's where the story ends," said Sataari. "The speaking bones don't know everything, and already I've filled in too many blanks with mere guesses."

But Razutana, less reverent toward the gods and re-rememberings of the people of the scrublands, wasn't so restrained. Drawing upon what he had learned from the widening and narrowing of tree rings in Kiri Valley, the farming techniques of the proto-Lyucu-Agon, the accumulated layers of silt on the shore of the Sea of Tears, and other similar pages from the book of nature, he freely speculated for the benefit of the pékyus-taasa.

The spirit portraits of Afir and other ancient pékyus conjured up a vision of cataclysmic changes in weather patterns that led to the

drying out of the grasslands and the Sea of Tears, leading to the ultimate collapse of the civilization at the Barrows.

After the inhabitants abandoned the site and adapted to a
nomadic way of life, they spread out far across the scrublands, until
the City of Ghosts was only a forbidden place of semi-coherent legends, which warned the descendants of Afir and Kikisavo never to
adopt the farming life again, never to settle.

The resentment between those who had chosen to leave with
Kikisavo first and those who had chosen to stay with Afir first didn't
fade with time, however, but grew. Each tribe believed itself to be the
true heir of the greatness of the Barrows. Small differences accumulated and festered until they became irreconcilable.

Over the centuries, weather patterns shifted again. Heavy rainfall
returned to parts of the eastern edge of Ukyu-Gondé, and that was
why the valleys in the foothills of the World's Edge Mountains and
the alluvial plains along the eastern shore of the Sea of Tears had
recovered a lush and hospitable climate, complete with ample fresh
water and wetlands.

Though the ancient site of the Barrows was suitable for farming
again, the people of the scrublands didn't return, believing that settlement was itself a taboo act. Though they remembered fragments
of the stories of their ancestors, they had forgotten their true import.

"Is it the nature of our people to either dominate or submit, to be
master or enslaved, with no escape from cycles of retribution and
vengeance?"

By the light of the blazing bonfire, Théra looked each of her loyal
advisers in the eye: Dara, Lyucu, Agon, ice tribe, tanto-lyu-naro. . . .
Behind them, nearly a thousand refugees held their breath, their
hearts beating in sync with hers.

"No! Our ancestors dared to adapt, to change as the land changed
around them. They strode away from a dying city and into the endless storm raging across the scrublands. They dared to forget, to
remember, to leave behind, to hold on—when one way of life was no
longer viable, they carved out a new one.

"Votan-sa-taasa, how can we be any less courageous?"

CHAPTER FIFTY-TWO

A TEMPEST OF GOLD

For the first time in months, Empress Jia announced there would be formal court.

The mood throughout Pan was somber. Airships patrolled the overcast sky, with an occasional circling garinafin to add to the show of force. The protests in the capital had been suppressed, and detachments of the city garrison, accompanied by farseers, stood at every street corner, watching the traffic and subdued pedestrians with suspicious eyes. Even the animals seemed to sense the tension in the air. Dogs did not bark, horses did not neigh, and cats refrained from chasing after the birds that pecked listlessly for crumbs in the streets.

Nonetheless, the people whispered. There was talk of the mysterious books that had been delivered to the officials and generals, accusing Empress Jia of high crimes and dark treason. There was talk that Secretary Zomi Kidosu, long out of the public sight, had been imprisoned arbitrarily, and the College of Advocates was working feverishly to free her. There was talk of secret orders being given by Emperor Monadétu to all the ranked scholars, salaried officials, the fighting-men and -women of Dara's armed forces. There was talk of some political crisis in Unredeemed Dara, with a child pékyu taking the place of Tanvanaki and the captive Prince Timu.

And so, on that bright winter morning, as the chill wind whipped feathery snowflakes through the streets, as golden chrysanthemums from hothouses bloomed defiantly and filled opulent manors with their fragrance, as the people of the Harmonious City huddled in teahouses and markets while gazing surreptitiously in the direction of the walled palace, the Lords of Dara filed into the Grand Audience Hall.

All the governors of the realm, all the enfeoffed nobles (though there were now so few of them), all the generals, ministers, Imperial scholars, and titled lords with the right to appear at court came. This was the most well-attended session of formal court that anyone could remember for years. Something momentous was about to happen, every soul was sure.

The herald chanted his opening lines and the trumpets played their ritual bars. The herald stepped forward and asked if anyone had business to bring to open court.

Despite the blazing bronze braziers scattered about the hall—an innovation from Princess Aya Mazoti to make winter formal court more bearable—the air seemed frozen. No one stepped forward.

Jia studied the assembly, gears and levers in the engine that administered Dara. They had all, she knew, read Lady Soto's book. Would it make a difference?

Phyro's rebellion had failed.

The ship of state had sailed through a great typhoon unscathed; the machine that channeled and regulated Dara's power had held up under an unprecedented load; the system of institutions she had built up to maintain stability had not buckled under pressure.

There would be no bloody coup, no change of power accomplished by civil war. Cogo, and the bureaucracy he represented, had stood up for her against what many might have seen as a superior claim.

She still held the Grace of Kings.

But there was no joy in Jia's heart, only exhaustion. She could no longer tell if she was wielding power, or if Power was wielding her. She was a powercrafter, but power was a dangerous and unstable medium, and no individual will, even one as strong as hers, could withstand its relentless assault forever.

The only thing she wanted was to finish the task she had started, to complete her long and patient plan, to see through the utter destruction of the Lyucu.

"What shall we do, Lords of Dara?" intoned Empress Jia. "Rumor and gossip fill the streets, casting aspersions on my name. The Lyucu have come to bargain, but they do not wish to speak to me. We're beset by domestic turmoil and foreign strife. What is your counsel?"

She waited.

As she looked around the hall, everyone avoided meeting her gaze.

"Will you let me speak to the Lyucu, Lords of Dara?" she said, the pleading tone in her voice unfamiliar even to her own ear.

There was an empty space where Prince Gimoto was supposed to be. She suppressed the urge to smile. Foolish though he was, the young prince seemed to understand that formal court would be a battlefield today, and ever the coward, he had decided to plead an illness.

His absence makes everything so much easier. He would be leading chants of "Rénga! Rénga!" now if he were present.

Jia stopped her roaming gaze on Cogo Yelu. The aged Prime Minister, a veteran of three reigns, the consummate politician and bureaucrat, stood with his hands folded together, hidden in his voluminous sleeves. His face was placid and his eyes half-closed, reminding Jia of a dozing turtle.

She had to force him to act, to play his role.

"Cogo, do you wish to speak?"

She could see his mind warring with itself under that shell of equanimity. Loyalty to the House of Dandelion; concern for domestic tranquility; the instinct to preserve what was working, however imperfect; the yearning for moral clarity.

You always want to avoid conflict, to compromise and preserve the peace. But sometimes harmony isn't what Dara needs. You must choose.

"Cogo, what is your counsel?"

The Prime Minister's sleepy eyes snapped open, meeting Jia's eyes with a cold light. He drew a deep breath and stepped forward.

Turning to the empress, he bowed.

The assembled ministers and generals stared at him, their hearts in their throats. The empress's request was almost absurd in its reasonableness. Who else could speak for Dara except its sovereign?

She had just survived a coup attempt and now controlled the gari-nafins; her power was as overwhelming as the midday sun and her hold on the court as secure as Mount Kiji.

Lady Soto's book . . . what difference could it make?

The Lyucu's demand to bypass the regent to speak to the emperor—wherever he was—had to be rebuffed, hadn't it?

Saying nothing, Cogo straightened back up. Then he turned, shuffled up to the empty Dandelion Throne at the foot of the dais, and knelt before it, his back to the empress.

Jia's face was impassive. "What is the meaning of this, Prime Minister?"

Still silent, Cogo touched his forehead to the ground before the throne.

"There is no one in that veiled throne," intoned Empress Jia. "I am the regent. I hold the Seal of Dara. I speak for the people of Dara."

Cogo knelt up, his back straight as an arrow shaft. Still keeping his back to the empress, he looked around the Grand Audience Hall, gazing at the shocked ministers, generals, governors, nobles in turn.

"Answer me, Prime Minister," said Jia. "Do you still serve me?"

Cogo took off his formal court robe, folded it neatly, and placed it on the floor before him. Then, reverently, he placed the blue jade compass, the ceremonial symbol of his office, upon the folded robe. Now stripped of his courtly finery, clad only in his plain under-tunic, he was just an old man with a head of snowy white hair, like a dandelion puff ball trembling in the wind, an ordinary member of the Hundred Flowers. He bowed again, touching his forehead to the floor in front of the empty, veiled throne.

Jia's heart pounded. Though she had worked with Cogo all these years, she still couldn't see into his heart—that was Risana's gift, not hers. A powerful wave of emotion, compounded of ecstasy and terror, arose from the bottom of her heart like Tazu's whirlpool, threatening to overwhelm her mind.

"This is your last chance, Cogo," Jia said, barely able to keep the tremors out of her voice. "If you continue to resist, I will declare your act one of treason."

"The Dandelion Throne is a kite that rides upon a special wind, the will of the people," proclaimed Cogo Yelu to the assembled lords.

"Aya Mazoti," said Jia, "seize that babbling fool."

Cogo Yelu looked over at the confused Aya, her mouth agape. "The will of the people can lift that kite up to unimagined heights, if the kite follows the rules of balance and just construction. Or it can tear that kite to shreds if it is ill-constructed or rotten from within.

"The people of Dara speak for themselves. I have never served you; I serve the people of Dara."

"Arrest the traitor!" shouted Jia.

The word "traitor" seemed to startle Aya from her stunned state. She took a step forward, raised her ceremonial bamboo sword in one hand, and looked to the palace guards.

"You're not mere actors with assigned roles," shouted Cogo Yelu. Though he was looking at Aya, he seemed to be speaking to everyone in the Grand Audience Hall. "Strip off your costumes, drop your props, forget your memorized lines. We cannot be forced to attend a sovereign who claims power through slaughter, nor can we continue to serve a despot who has lost the trust of the people."

Aya hesitated. Like everyone else, she had also read Lady Soto's book and the documents that revealed the truth of what had happened to her mother. Gin Mazoti was not a traitor, and she hated the scheming Jia with all her heart. Yet, Jia was the legitimate regent, appointed by Emperor Ragin before his death. If she were to defy her, she *really* would be committing treason. Her bamboo sword wavered in the air, and she struggled to swallow the lump in her throat. Her voice, like a rusty sword, refused to emerge from her throat.

"Aya, do not force me to summon the Dyran Fins," said Jia. "I expect you to do your duty."

Aya tried to imagine what her parents would do, but she could recall no applicable strategy from Gin's book or guidance from stories of Luan Zyaji. She was alone, a frightened child, a girl who was trying to do the right thing but didn't know how.

Cogo continued, his voice growing louder. "Under all the trappings of power and performance, there is an inviolate voice that belongs to each of you, the same as any mean peasant or lofty scholar, any wealthy merchant or indigo house servant, any beggar or Lord of Dara. It is our voices, combined in chorus, that make up the will of the people of Dara. You must do what is right."

Then he pointed at the stylized golden dandelion atop the throne, and at the many smaller versions of the insignia embedded in the walls and pillars of the Grand Audience Hall like so many eyes compounded into one gaze looking down upon Dara, and began to sing:

> *Cold winds rise in Pan's streets, wide and austere:*
> *A tempest of gold, an aureal tide.*
> *Our humble fragrance dares to climb the sky.*
> *Bright yellow armor surrounds every eye.*
> *With gentle hearts, ten thousand voices sing*
> *To secure the grace of kings, to hail spring.*
> *A noble assembly, loyal and true.*
> *Who would fear winter when wearing this hue?*

Gori Ruthi, Acting Farsight Secretary, was the first to break from the long ranks of civil and military officials and kneel down next to Cogo, taking up his song.

Jia looked at him in wonder. Gori had always been so loyal to her, not questioning any of her moves—even when she had ordered him to negotiate a humiliating cease-fire with the Lyucu.

Puma Yemu, who had been released from house arrest in order to attend formal court—though he had been told to remain silent on pain of death—was the next. The aged warrior sang heartily at the top of his lungs, and met Jia's gaze defiantly.

Jia struggled to keep her composure. Of course Puma would rebel—she always knew he would. Better to have him rebel at the right time for the right reasons.

Next to join them were the ministers of the Inner Council, and then the governors of Cocru and Haan, two of the most important provinces. A dam seemed to break as the rebellion reached a critical mass, and ministers, governors, generals, nobles rushed in a flood to Cogo's side. They stripped off their formal robes and placed the neatly folded bundles before the empty, veiled throne, carefully placing their ceremonial implements on top. They knelt around the throne, circling it.

"Seize them! Seize them!" shouted Jia. A part of her mind, cool and dispassionate, seemed to be watching her own performance from somewhere high above, admiring her own hysterical screams. How long had she been waiting for this moment? Perhaps the day she pushed Risana off the top of the Moon-Gazing Tower, or even before?

The machinery of power must be able to watch its engineer. The body politic must be healthy enough to purge poison from within. No one can claim to be free from the safeguards and constraints I designed to rein in power, not even me.

That cold, calculating part of her mind noted the few officials who remained standing awkwardly in their assigned places, trembling likes leaves in winter. She would remember their names, cowards who didn't understand that a system had to be more worthy of respect than the person at the top, had to transcend notions of personal loyalty.

"Palace guards," Jia cried, her voice quaking—though it was impossible to tell whether it was from excitement or fear, "arrest all these traitors before you commit an error from which there is no recovery."

The bamboo sword in Aya's hand stopped wavering.

"Palace guards," shouted the woman who had trained all her life to live with, and live up to, her name, "form a line around the Lords of Dara! No harm will come to them from the Dyran Fins or anyone else."

(Later, Puma Yemu would tell everyone how much the Imperial princess, in that moment, resembled her mother, the peerless Gin Mazoti.)

The palace guards looked at one another. After only a moment of hesitation, they rushed forward. The kneeling ministers closed their eyes, preparing to be yanked away violently.

But the soldiers formed a wall of shining armor around the kneeling officials. They unsheathed their swords and crouched determinedly, ready to meet the legendary onslaught of the Dyran Fins. "We serve the people of Dara," they shouted, staring at the empress.

Seconds passed. The terrifying Dyran Fins did not materialize. Jia stood up.

Everyone tensed, waiting for the Regent of Dara to unleash her fury—the empress always had a backup plan, didn't she?

Jia descended the dais and approached the wall of palace guards. When they refused to budge, she simply looked at two of the soldiers imperiously. Though she was so much shorter and old and frail, they were intimidated by her implacable air and stepped aside.

She approached the kneeling Cogo Yelu, reverently placed the Seal of Dara on the ground next to him, and whispered into his ear, "Thank you, old friend."

No plan is perfect, and I won't be able to see the ultimate end to the Lyucu threat. But my system has survived the greatest of threats: me.

I am so tired.

She looked up toward the ceiling, at the painted scenes of the gods.

"I am not afraid of you," she muttered.

They watched, disbelieving, as the empress walked away.

She paused at the entrance to the long hallway leading to the private quarters of the palace.

"Phyro is dead. You can find his embalmed body under the Imperial kitchen." There was infinite exhaustion and grief in her voice.

Gasps, cries, curses—a truth, even if universally suspected, was nonetheless shocking when confessed.

She went on, and as her footsteps retreated down the hallway, they could hear her howling, a noise halfway between laughter and sobbing.

"Secure the private quarters of the palace," a relieved Aya ordered the palace guards. "Arrest anyone who resists. The Dyran Fins are skilled fighters—bring crossbows!"

The guards departed. The Grand Audience Hall, after the tumult of a moment ago, seemed eerily quiet.

"What . . . shall we do with the Seal of Dara?" Puma Yemu broke the silence, looking lost. The regency was over, but the veiled throne remained empty.

"We must send messengers to Prince Gimoto at once," declared Gori Ruthi. "Emperor Monadétu left no heirs, and Prince Timu is still imprisoned in Unredeemed Dara. The only branch of the House of Dandelion that remains—"

"No!" Cogo Yelu's voice was firm. "Prince Gimoto will not be needed."

"But the empress has always asked Prince Gimoto to come to court. . . ." Gori Ruthi's voice trailed off. As much as he believed in the importance of the traditional rules of succession, he found it hard to advocate for Gimoto with any measure of conviction. Besides, after what had just occurred, Jia's endorsement had no persuasive power.

"We already have a proper heir."

The assembled Lords of Dara stared at the Prime Minister in confusion.

"We'll free Secretary Zomi Kidosu first, so that we can have the benefit of her wise counsel." Cogo Yelu's voice had returned to its habitual serenity. "As she will confirm and attest: The precedent has been set by Emperor Ragin, and it is weighty."

Understanding unknitted the brows of the puzzled Lords of Dara, one by one. Emperor Ragin had designated Grand Princess Théra as his successor, and Théra didn't just have brothers.

"I'll send all the farseers to look for Princess Fara immediately," Gori Ruthi said. Then, he added under his breath, "The Lyucu delegation will just have to wait a little longer."

The cheer that filled the Grand Audience Hall was subdued, tentative, anxious. Dara was in treacherous waters, and a heavy fog had just descended.

CHAPTER FIFTY-THREE

PERSUASION

Lady Soto took Zomi to the Hall of Cultivated Minds, which also served as the mourning hall.

There, they found Fara alone.

The walls and floor had been covered in white silk, and in the middle of the hall was an elevated platform upon which rested the embalmed body of Emperor Monadétu. Since Na-aroénna, the sword that he had wielded during his military campaigns, couldn't be found, a paper-craft replica lay next to him.

Stretched out on the other side of the sword was a young man's silk robe, embroidered with images of breaching crubens. Since Timu's body had undergone pédiato savaga in Rui, there was no choice but to substitute a robe he had worn as a prince in Dara in place of the corpse.

Around the pair of emperors were planters of golden chrysanthemums and dandelions taken from the hothouses in the Palace Garden.

Fara, dressed all in white, knelt before the bier. Incense from braziers shrouded her body in a haze.

Zomi paused at the entrance and put her hand against the lacquered doorframe, grateful for the support. Physically, she still hadn't fully recuperated from the imprisonment in the dungeon. Mentally, she suspected that the process of recovery would take even longer. She still couldn't sort out her complicated feelings about Jia, didn't fully understand the empress's layers of schemes and plots. Jia had been her mentor as well as adversary; her sentiments toward the empress were both filial and resentful. She resolved to go to Cogo later to voice her unease and to see if she could help him unravel the mysteries.

But that had to wait. Fara came first.

Zomi felt something rough in the otherwise smooth, mirrorlike surface of the doorframe. She lifted her fingers and looked closer.

Carved into the wooden frame was the drawing of a young woman, clearly done with a writing knife wielded by a childish hand. Under the drawing was an inscription in neat zyndari letters in word-squares, slanted at an audacious angle, like windblown rice seedlings in a paddy: *Kikomi was wronged.*

Zomi looked at it, stunned. The face of Théra resurfaced in her mind, passionately explaining to her how the Amu princess had been misunderstood.

"This was where Master Zato Ruthi instructed the Imperial children," said Lady Soto in a soft voice. "Fara wanted a place with . . . happier memories for her brothers' souls."

Zomi nodded. The weight of history was heavy upon the Imperial family, a family doomed to be perpetually misunderstood.

She took a few steps into the hall, realized that Lady Soto wasn't following, and looked back questioningly at her.

"There's no need to gang up on her," whispered Soto. "Besides, there's someone else I need to see." She bowed in *jiri* and walked away.

Zomi turned back. The princess, still kneeling in silence, made no sign of having heard her entering. Quietly, Zomi approached the bier and knelt down next to Fara. She lit some incense sticks and offered a prayer to the dead emperors.

Then she turned to Fara.

"I've been waiting for you," Jia said. Sitting at the low table, she was gazing outside the window, her back to the door of the bedchamber.

Soto glanced down at her cloth shoes. They had made no sound against the stone floor. The guards posted at the far end of the twisting hallway that led to this chamber had also made no sound as she showed them the authorizing tablet from Cogo Yelu.

Abandoning the attempt at stealth, she strode quickly into the room, her sleeves swishing and her feet scraping against the polished wooden floor.

Jia didn't turn around.

Soto's eyes were drawn to a vase in the corner. Inside the vase were yellow flowers of different varieties: chrysanthemum, dandelion, peonies, sunflowers, eggs-and-noodles. . . . Jia had always enjoyed intricate flower arrangements, but these were no ordinary flowers: The petals were slowly spinning.

Rati Yera, who had examined Jia's suite for hidden tunnels and secret chambers, had been right: Jia had installed a system of oculium eyes to warn her of intruders by watching for passing shadows in the hall. The master engineer had been full of admiration at the arrangement. Even the inventor of a new kind of machine could not anticipate its every possible application.

"Are machines the only things you trust, Jia?" Soto asked.

"Don't," croaked the young princess, her voice hoarse. "I know why you're here. The answer is no."

"I know that," said Zomi evenly. "I come not to persuade, but to mourn with you."

"Thank you," said Fara, after a moment. "They haven't even been buried, and everyone at court seems determined to forget about them and move on."

Zomi waited a beat. The princess was kneeling on the side of the bier closest to Phyro's corpse.

"You were close," she offered tentatively.

A faint smile appeared on Fara's tearstained face. "When I was little, Timu and Théra were both too busy with their own schemes and projects to play much with me. Hudo-*tika* was the only one who would listen when I wanted an audience for my make-believe stories. One time, I wanted to make a book with my stories in it—when I barely knew how to write my own name in logograms. Hudo-*tika* told me that I could write my book in pictures and stole some makeup from Aunt Risana for me to use as paint. He said I was a good artist."

With a pang, Zomi realized that she had never really appreciated the strength of the bond between the two siblings. Among the Imperial children, Phyro was closest to Fara in age. After Timu and Théra had both departed the Big Island more than a decade ago, Phyro was the only sibling who remained as Fara came of age. "What kind of stories did you tell?"

"Oh, mostly fairy tales featuring wise dyrans, a vast and stormy ocean, big bad sharks, and impetuous princesses who wanted to escape from the palace and visit faraway lands. Sometimes he would do the voices of the characters with me."

"Was he a good actor?"

"No, he was terrible. He always wanted to be the wise dyran, even though I told him wise dyrans were women."

Zomi chuckled. "He did like to fight with your sister over who got to play the better parts. Do you remember that time—oh, I think you were four then—during a Palace Examination, when some scholars put on a show with monsters like cruben-wolves, falcon-carps . . ."

And in this vein the two shared memories of Phyro Garu, from his days as a mischievous schoolboy, worshipful of his older sister and always competing with his older brother, to his boastful and boisterous time as a young prince, dreaming of the romance of honor and martial glory, then to his turbulent reign as emperor only in name, seething under the thumb of his aunt-mother's regency, followed by his transformation into a brilliant general, stunning the Lyucu with guile as well as strength, until, finally, his bold rebellion against Jia, falling short of achieving his goal literally by one step.

Fara's grief was so intense and overwhelming that Zomi despaired of her mission. Yet, she had to go on.

"He was the emperor Dara deserved but didn't get," Zomi said. The incense sticks in the brazier had almost burned down to ashes, and so she renewed them with a fresh bundle.

"No," said Fara, after a pause. "He would not have been a good emperor."

Zomi looked over at her. *Perhaps there is hope after all.*

"Phyro always wanted to live up to an ideal," said Fara. "He yearned to be like the Hegemon in honor, implacable in the pursuit of vengeance; to be like Marshal Mazoti in martial prowess, leaving no foe undefeated as he strode across the Islands; to be like Father in grandness of spirit, earning the loyalty of the most talented women and men of the realm. But he never could accept that his heroes were figures from stories, and a real person of flesh and blood could never live up to the glorified portraits painted by poets."

"You don't think it's a good thing to strive to be better than we are?"

Fara shook her head. "You misunderstand me. My interest is in art, and it's the nature of narrative artifice that even those striving to tell the truth must flatten reality to a sketch, to reduce the heft of logograms to mere zyndari letters. The Hegemon's honor was inseparable from his cruelty; Auntie Gin's martial prowess was the twin of her overweening pride; my father's pragmatism cannot be celebrated without recognizing that it led him to betrayal, first of his sworn brother, the Hegemon, and then of the many generals who laid the foundation for his throne. My brother yearned for the light in those portraits but refused to acknowledge the darkness."

"He demanded as much from himself as he did from his followers," said Zomi.

Fara shook her head again, frustrated. "His failing wasn't hypocrisy, but a reluctance . . . to accept imperfections, shades of gray, human frailty. The world for him was black and white, like one of my knitting patterns. He loved ardently and hated passionately, with nothing in between."

"Some might say that is exactly how an Emperor of Dara should be," said Zomi. "How can you trust a sovereign who only ever shows the people a mask?"

"These are qualities one seeks in a good brother, filial son, loyal friend, faithful lover, and charismatic warlord. But are they what the people need in a just sovereign?

"If someone didn't take up arms for their freedom, Phyro considered them a willing slave and traitor. If someone didn't devote themself wholeheartedly to his cause, Phyro dismissed them as worthless.

"He was once willing to let nine out of ten die in Rui and Dasu, so long as he liberated the conquered islands. He was once willing to grant mercy to all the Lyucu, so long as they surrendered to him with honor. He risked everything, including his life and the stability of Dara, so long as he could avenge Empress Risana with his own hands."

"But he was also able to grow and change," said Zomi. "I understand from Puma Yemu that he gave up the invasion of Unredeemed Dara at the last possible moment on his own, out of concern for the people who would have been harmed, before Lady Soto had arrived with the truth behind Empress Risana's death. I do not think I could have re-sheathed the sword of righteous rage, had I been in his place. Was that not wisdom?"

Fara broke down in deep, heaving sobs. "That is the grandest tragedy of all. He could have been, would have been, should have been— but he wasn't. We'll never know how his nature could have grown, how he would have nurtured his wisdom. Though I love my brother dearly . . . I'm glad that he was never trusted with the Seal of Dara during his lifetime. My heart breaks because in the end, he could not live the life he wanted and deserved to live, but was reduced to a caricature of vengeance and all-consuming hate.

"He lived up to the story he wanted others to tell about him, instead of a story that was true to his soul."

We have all underestimated you, thought Zomi in wonder, *even me.*

"Machines are predictable," said Jia, "far more so than the human heart."

Soto turned from the vase of spinning silk flowers to look at the erstwhile regent of Dara.

"This was how you sensed I was coming to see you, hoping to catch you unawares, on the day I escaped from the palace."

Jia gestured for her to sit at the table.

Her back was straight as a pillar in the Grand Audience Hall, her white hair pulled into a perfect bun, not a strand out of place, her expression regal, calm, in control. She didn't seem like a prisoner at all; she still looked like the Empress of Dara.

Soto settled into the seat opposite from Jia and looked around. The room had been stripped of long sashes, writing knives, sharp hairpins—any implement that might be used to commit suicide. But Lady Ragi, who had volunteered to care for the prisoner, had striven to make Jia's cell homelike within the constraints. The sitting cushions were thin but comfortable; the absence of a charcoal brazier was barely felt, as the walls were heated with stoves on the other side; in the corner was a small shrine with a tablet engraved with Timu's name. The winter sun cast a pale glow over Jia's wrinkled face, reminding Soto of statues portraying Lady Rapa in her crone aspect.

On the table sat a pot of tea and two bamboo cups. Soto shuddered involuntarily. If Jia really intended to kill herself, no one could stop her.

She was still alive. There was still hope.

"You put on a performance for me on that day. You *wanted* me to think you were going to poison me. You manipulated me into running to Phyro to reveal the truth about Risana to him. Why?"

Jia poured tea into the cups and drank from hers. "Why linger on the past? What's done is done. Phyro is dead."

"Because intentions and motivations matter! Officials are vying with one another to denounce you, calling for your blood to pay for regicide. Teahouse storytellers call you a treasonous usurper, a selfish tyrant blinded by ambition. Why won't you defend yourself?"

"Defend myself?" Jia repeated, her tone placid. "How? Perhaps they're right."

"I don't believe you killed Phyro! Though you claim to put more trust in machines than people, your schemes have always centered on the frailties of the human heart.

"Ever since I found out you were using me, I've been consumed with the compulsion to untangle your plots. I think . . . despite the web of deception you've spun, you remain a worthy empress of Dara, motivated by concern for the people—especially the powerless and the base.

"On that day, you must have been worried that Phyro would overcome your elaborate apparatus of military monitors with charismatic appeals to the common soldiers' love of country and desire for vengeance. If Phyro, his confidence newly boosted by the victory at Crescent Island, had been determined to march on Rui and Dasu, hundreds of thousands—collaborators, prisoners, the enslaved, peasants, fisherfolk—would have died in the Lyucu's mad plan to kill the civilians of Unredeemed Dara rather than surrender. Goading me into revealing to Phyro the truth of how his mother had died was the only way you could be sure to turn his impulsive heart away from conquest, redirecting his rage at *you*.

"And knowing that you intended for him to rebel to save the people, you must have tried everything to trap him, to capture him, to incapacitate him—but not to kill!"

"A good story," said Jia, blowing gently at her cup of tea. "But it is just that, a story."

"Then tell me your story. Tell me the truth!"

"The truth?" Jia seemed puzzled by the word. "What is the truth? Why does it matter?"

"Phyro's dream of redeeming Unredeemed Dara may yet come to pass," said Zomi. "The Lyucu have come to plea for peace."

"What changed?"

"Years of misrule have taken their toll. The people of Rui and Dasu cannot survive the winter without a massive injection of aid."

"I didn't think the Lyucu cared about that."

"The hard-liners wouldn't have," said Zomi. "But Tanvanaki's passing has resulted in a new leadership that may be more compassionate. As well, the Lyucu are beset by a plague that has killed some of their warriors and crippled many more."

"An illness?"

"Not quite. It is more like a poison—but they're unwilling to go into details. They blame it on the empress. That is why they demand to see Phyro. They believe that your brother, a man of honor, would be merciful to a foe sincerely offering submission and give them the antidote."

"They think Aunt-Mother, sitting here in Pan, poisoned them from across the sea?" Fara shook her head in disbelief. "An absurd

conspiracy theory. As for their faith in the mercy of my brother . . .
I do believe they've judged his character correctly. But that is all
beside the point. Phyro is dead, and we have no miraculous antidote
for whatever is ailing them."

"Whether their belief in an antidote is reasonable, the prospect
for reunification and the surrender of the Lyucu cannot be ignored.
Since the throne remains empty, the Inner Council has appointed
Gori Ruthi as chief negotiator. Through preliminary conversations,
he has confirmed that even the wildest rumors of hard-liner policies in conquered Dara fell short of reality. Starvation, enslavement,
massacre, systematic rape and castration, destruction of culture and
erasure of history—the Lyucu intended to eradicate the people of
Dara and replace them with their own seed."

Fara shuddered with revulsion. "The evil . . . How can we heal
from this? . . . What are we—what is the Inner Council going to do?"

"Opinions are divided. Some, with Incentivist leanings, advocate lying to the Lyucu about an antidote, accepting their surrender,
and then slaughtering them to avenge their victims. Others, citing
Moralist axioms, argue that we should tell them the truth and see if
we can nonetheless work out a new peace treaty. Still others, more
Patternist in their thinking, want to investigate this poison—though
the Lyucu are reluctant to discuss specifics—and see if we can work
out a cure. Yet others suggest that we drag out the negotiations to
gain maximum advantage. There are as many opinions as there are
voices, a cacophony with no emerging consensus."

"There is no hand holding the Seal of Dara . . . ," muttered Fara.
"There is no plank to dampen the agitated waves in the bucket. . . ."

"What is your counsel, Ada-*tika*?" asked Zomi. She called the
princess by her nursing name, as though they were simply two
friends discussing an abstraction, not the fate of millions.

"My counsel? I have none."

"I don't believe that. You are not someone who would avert her
face from evil, nor someone who would shirk a burden that is hers
by law and custom."

Fara's face flushed with heat. "Law and custom? I never wanted
this! I am not Timu, steeped in the wisdom of the Ano sages. I am

not Théra, endowed with the rare courage to leave everyone and everything she loved to undertake a journey into the unknown. I am not Phyro, blessed with charisma and martial talent to dream of redeeming the Islands by his own strength. I am not Aunt-Mother, so skilled with schemes and plots that even her enemies would tremble at her name. I have no ambition for power, no craving for glory, no desire to ever sit upon the Dandelion Throne and determine the fate of the people. I have nothing in my heart but doubt!"

"Then I've not misjudged you," said Zomi.

Fara glared at Zomi. Slowly, understanding softened her features. "Ah, a test."

"You speak of submitting to the judgment of history," said Soto. "What good is history without the truth?"

A bitter smile on Jia's face. Instead of answering, she asked a question of her own. "Do you remember the years that we spent together as captives of the Hegemon?"

Soto nodded. That was when her friendship with Jia had first taken root, and when she had first decided to throw her lot in with the House of Dandelion.

"How much I hated him then! But had Mata died immediately after the sacking of Pan, history would have remembered him fondly as a great war hero, not the tyrant who presided over the decade of chaos and unceasing war that was the Principate. Had Huno Krima and Zopa Shigin died in the early days of their uprising, they would have been recalled as champions of the people against cruel Mapidéré, not pusillanimous gangsters who pretended to be kings. Had Gin Mazoti died in her prison cell, before her victory over Zathin Gulf, would so many now care about redeeming her name? Had Kuni been shot down in his airship when he abandoned me and the children at Zudi, would so many Moralists now cite him as an exemplar of the ideal sovereign? The nature of these men and women did not change, but history's judgment of them was accidental, contingent, divorced from the truth."

"Only a long journey can reveal the true strength of a horse," Soto insisted. "Only when we are given all the facts can we make a sound judgment. My book brought you down, but it isn't the whole story. Give it to me, and trust in the judgment of the people."

"There are no whole stories, only fragments that suit the purpose of the moment," said Jia. She shook her head. "I grow weary of tests and judgments. I know what I've done; I know why and how. That's enough. I care not to justify my actions to any god or man."

"Yes, a test," said Zomi. "But not only for you."

For the first time, Fara's eyes betrayed surprise.

"You spoke of evil. For more than a decade, we've been faced with an evil that shook the very foundational faiths of our people. To appease the Lyucu and preserve the peace meant sacrificing the people of Unredeemed Dara; to confront them meant plunging all of Dara into war and heading down the path to militarism. The gods didn't answer our prayers, and the wisdom of the Ano sages offered cold comfort. Empress Jia chose one path, and Phyro another. No choice was good."

"Neither harbored any doubt as to the righteousness of their choice," said Fara. "That is what a sovereign must do: to commit to a course of action alone and end all doubts."

Zomi shook her head. "No one wields the Seal of Dara alone, not even Empress Jia. I and the other ministers of the Inner Council are the sovereign's compounded eyes, aggregated ears, thousand-handed arms, hundred-fragmented mind—but in the end, the sovereign can only guide, not compel; persuade, not coerce.

"It is precisely because your heart is filled with doubt that I believe you'll be the pilot to sight the shore through the storm, the scout to discover the path through the murky maze."

"I don't understand what you're saying," Fara said, shaking her head. "It sounds . . . mad!"

"We're at a crossroads, Fara," said Zomi. "The Lyucu are on the verge of surrender, but we are paralyzed with indecision."

"Isn't the redemption of Rui and Dasu what we've been waiting for all these years?"

"But on what terms? The Lyucu demand an antidote to the poison before they'll permit shipments of aid. Do we devote our resources to saving torturers, enslavers, killers? Or do we refuse and watch as Unredeemed Dara starves?"

"Don't ask me. I'm not—I can't—"

"The surrender of the Lyucu is but the first question of many to come. What shall we do with the liberated islands? Those freed from enslavement will demand retribution. How will we channel their righteous rage? Some of the Lyucu were responsible for the torture and slaughter of tens of thousands; others tried to save who they could. Some of the Lyucu have formed families with the islanders, and even if some of these families began in rape and murder, the children, with their mixed blood, have a birthright claim to these shores.

"What of the collaborators? Some of them, like Noda Mi, tried to accrue wealth and power upon the bones of their fellow island-ers, but others genuinely believed that collaboration was the only way to save lives. How will we tell them apart and all the shades in between?

"Should we promise the surrendered Lyucu blanket amnesty, thereby leaving the ghosts of the dead in unpropitiated fury and the spirits of the living in unslaked thirst for vengeance? Or should we punish them all and bathe Rui and Dasu in Lyucu blood? What—"

"I don't know! I don't know! Stop asking me!" cried Fara.

"This is a test not for you, but for all Dara!" Zomi was relentless. "What kind of people will we be? How will we be judged by his-tory?"

Fara shook her head, overwhelmed.

"No one knows the answers to these questions," said Zomi. "The past is no guide to the future, and the court is in discord. Every par-tial voice is certain that it alone speaks the truth; every simple eye is certain that it alone sees reality. But in terra incognita, what use are maps drawn from familiar shores?

"Emperor Ragin and Empress Jia have left us a sturdy ship, a system that can weather the storm. But no system, no matter how perfectly designed, can sustain itself for long without the animat-ing spirit of a constitutive story that feels true. The most important choices in life are not made by logic, by the tallying of pros and cons, by measuring and weighing, by naming and mapping, but by yielding to the eternal yearnings of the heart and renewing the foundational myth of our mortal condition—this is as true of individuals as of peoples.

"What Dara needs now is not the Doubt-Ender, but the emptiness of doubtful potential. When the bitter core of the lotus seed has been removed, it is ready for all the flavors of the world. When the old words in *Gitré Üthu* have been washed away by the sea, new stories may be written upon the blank pages. When the heart has been cleansed by doubt, every hope becomes a possibility.

"Doubt gives rise to humility, and humility leads to empathy. It is empathy, more than anything else at this moment, that we need in the hand that wields the Seal of Dara. It is the plank that calms the agitated water in the bucket, the salve that comes after iron and blood, the spring dandelion that blooms after the ice of winter.

"To be born to the House of Dandelion may be a curse rather than a blessing. Your brothers gave their lives for this land, and your sister is lost beyond the Wall of Storms. You are the rightful heir to the throne.

"But we cannot force you to take up this burden. You must do so willingly."

Fara kept her eyes on the bier. If she refused, the Inner Council would have to turn to Gimoto, the side branch of the House of Dandelion. The very idea of that arrogant fool on the throne filled her with horror.

She never thought this day would come. No one had ever cultivated her for a life of politics, to rule and decide from the throne. She wanted a life of art, stories, laughter, love.

She thought of her time at the Splendid Urn. How free she had been then! She was not a princess of Dara, not a daughter of Kuni Garu. She was simply Dandelion, unofficial member of the Blossom Gang, favored by Granny Wasu, cherished by Mati and Lodan, adored by "Thasé-teki," an ordinary young woman having fun in a grand metropolis, living a life filled with all the flavors and mind-pleasures undreamed of in the palace.

How she loved them! Loved them then, loved them still. The

love, born of experience, was an ache, a longing, a craving that made the world more vivid, beautiful, *real*.

The voice of Phyro echoed in her mind. *"You can't force anyone to live a story that doesn't feel true to them."*

But what story feels true to me?

She thought of her beloved Savo, who had stayed behind at the seaside villa of the Wasu clan, waiting for her to return.

"We're not characters in epic romances. You love your brothers, your sister, your aunt-mother, your parents. I love my mother, my sister, my playmates from childhood, the naros who taught me how to wrestle and ride. Yet your brother and my sister wish to drive my mother's people, who are also my people, into the sea, and take pleasure in their cries of lamentation.

"We are embedded in strands of love and hatred, a web that glows in the sunlight of history, bedecked in pearls of blood and fragments of bone. How can we truly see each other the way we deserve to be seen without acknowledging the truth?"

The Blossom Gang was no more. Arona, the sister she never had, who taught her how to inhabit each disguise as though she were embracing a new life, was dead. Mota, the silent, strong friend in whose singular presence she felt as safe as though she were surrounded by all the palace guards, was dead. Phyro, her stubborn, brave, silly brother, who would tease her but also back her up against anyone, against the world, was dead.

They died believing that they were fighting for more of that love that she could never get enough of, the love that enlarged the soul, the love that made the world *real*.

The people of Dara was no longer an abstraction to her, and *mutagé* no longer an indefinite word.

She was a daughter of the House of Dandelion. She could not avert her face from the horrors of the world.

What Dara needs now is not the Doubt-Ender, but the emptiness of doubtful potential. When the heart has been cleansed by doubt, every hope becomes a possibility.

I want to tell a story that the people don't expect, a story of empathy that encompasses the world.

She nodded, almost imperceptibly, and did not hear as Zomi

backed away on her knees and bowed down, touching her forehead to the ground, saying, *"Rénga."*

Soto pleaded, threatened, shouted, reasoned. She pointed at the tablet with Timu's name; she invoked the memory of Kuni Garu. She spoke until the tea was gone, until her throat had grown parched and her voice hoarse.

But Jia's will was iron. She would not defend herself, reveal her plots, explain herself, justify her accounts.

"You were the one who persuaded me to go into politics, do you remember?" Jia said. "In this art, the highest accomplishment is silence. Let future generations tell what stories they like about me; it's my gift to them."

"Your mind has always been too subtle for me," said Soto, a hint of bitterness in her voice. "Yet I believe you were trying to do the right thing for Dara. I never lost my trust in you."

"Ah, but you did," said Jia, a smile on her face, "as I always knew you would. I counted on it."

There was no answer to that.

"Come, old friend, let us speak of more pleasant things."

And so the teapot was refilled, and Jia and Soto reminisced about their time in the house just outside Çaruza, where Toto-*tika* and Rata-*tika* had been born, where Otho Krin had pined after his mistress, where Wi and Shido had found a refuge, where the two of them had carved out a pool of tranquility in the midst of devastation and war.

CHAPTER FIFTY-FOUR

TRUTH

PAN: THE FIRST MONTH OF THE TWELFTH YEAR OF
THE REIGN OF SEASON OF STORMS.

In the extreme northwestern corner of Pan was the Sunspot District, the quarter of the city farthest from the palace and also least developed. When Kuni Garu rebuilt Pan from the ruins left by the Hegemon's fires, Cogo Yelu had designated the area to be reserved for farmland and woodland so that it could function as a strategic reserve within Pan's walls in case the capital was subjected to a long siege.

There were no bustling markets here, no prominent restaurants or indigo houses, no temples dedicated to the gods filled with incense smoke and chanting monks, no sprawling manors of nobles or officials. The city garrison left the farms fallow and maintained the woods as wilderness, occasionally using them to conduct war games. Children came here in spring and summer to fly kites or play soldiers and rebels, while groups of elderly citizens gathered in mornings and evenings to admire the wild birds that made their home here.

There was, however, a single large, walled compound in the middle of the Sunspot District. Its ramparted walls were patrolled day and night, and the land around it had been cleared of covering vegetation for hundreds of paces. A single road led to it from the populous center of the city, guarded by multiple checkpoints. This high-security miniature city-within-a-city was where the Dandelion Court housed certain kinds of important visitors to the capital— high-ranking enfeoffed nobles with their own armies, chiefs and ambassadors from Tan Adü, prominent leaders of pirate fleets or rebellions who had surrendered in exchange for amnesty and titles, and envoys from Lyucu-occupied Rui and Dasu.

In Emperor Ragin's time, such guests would have been housed in quarters right outside the palace walls, but Empress Jia had constructed the new walled compound at the beginning of the regency, arguing that separation of such visitors from the heart of the city enhanced the dignity of the Throne and improved security. From confidence verging on arrogance to caution shading into paranoia, the shift in location, as much as anything else, neatly marked the difference in ruling style and substance between Kuni and his first wife.

The only visitors living in the walled compound at this moment were members of the Lyucu delegation. Although weeks had passed since the Lyucu's arrival and Dara had welcomed a new year, there was no answer from the Dandelion Throne concerning their demand for an audience with Emperor Monadétu. Gori Ruthi, assigned to liaise with the Lyucu, fended off their increasingly impatient queries with perfunctory excuses. Though Gori Ruthi insisted that the Lyucu were not prisoners, he gently rebuffed all their requests to be allowed to tour Pan proper, instead offering to bring the Lyucu whatever they needed.

Pékyu Dyana and Goztan Ryoto knew they were being kept in the dark about something—perhaps a fierce political contest of wills between Empress Jia and Emperor Monadétu. But despite their growing anxiety about the imminent collapse of Ukyu-taasa, they had no choice but to wait until summoned, fretting like crabs skittering about a pot getting hotter by the minute.

Sounds of shattering porcelain, cries of surprise, the noise of furniture being smashed . . .

Dyana strode down the long hallway toward Todyu's bedroom, the source of the ruckus.

. . . rushing steps, angry shouts, a full-throated roar of rage from a boy . . .
Dyana began to run.

At first, Todyu's condition had improved. In response to Dyana's pleas, Gori Ruthi and Lady Ragi summoned the best physicians of Pan to cure Todyu of his tolyusa-thirst. The learned doctors, unfamiliar with the source of the dependence, tried everything that was effective or said to be effective against forms of addiction: expensive decoctions of rare herbs; secret recipes passed down through generations; specially treated varieties of tobacco, dream herbs, silkmotic shocks. . . .

. . . scuffles, sounds of struggle, cries of pain . . .

Some combination of these treatments had seemed to work. Todyu seemed to emerge from the alternating bouts of languid slumber and mindless fury and recover his wits. Dyana's heart soared. There was hope for the thirst-stricken Lyucu!

But as soon as Todyu had eaten, recouped some of his strength, and figured out where he was, he began to denounce Dyana.

"You are a traitor! You are a Dara-raaki! Mother will bash in your skull when you see her. You'll never ride the cloud-garinafin!"

He attacked the doctors, scratching, kicking, punching, screaming that he would never touch the medicine of the mud-legs. There had been no choice but to subdue him by force, bind him, and continue his treatment by pushing a tube through his nose and down his throat.

But the treatments had not worked. The earlier amelioration in his symptoms had been temporary, and the tolyusa-thirst had returned with a vengeance. The periods of oblivion had grown longer, and the episodes of wakeful rage had grown more violent.

. . . another heart-wrenching howl: "Traitors! Traitors. Dyana, I will kill you. . . ."

There seemed to be a knife twisting in Dyana's heart; she couldn't breathe; her vision grew blurry; she faltered.

A powerful pair of arms wrapped around her, stopping her in her tracks. It was Goztan.

"Don't, votan," the thane said. "You can't do anything."

She kept her arms locked around the girl even as she struggled, punching and kicking, wailing helplessly for a brother who she had always known and no longer knew.

At length, her struggles slackened, and then stopped.

Goztan let go.

"Summon Gori Ruthi," said the young pékyu, her voice icy. "We've waited for my uncle long enough. Let's see if my grandmother has a heart of stone or flesh."

~

The pale light of the heatless wintry sun suffused the window, frosted over so that nothing could be glimpsed through it. Against this milky screen, two seated silhouettes could be discerned: one with her back straight as a pine, unyielding; the other leaning forward, supplicant.

"Gori and I have both seen the boy," Lady Ragi pleaded. "It's not a Lyucu trick or plot. He stands on the shore of the River-on-Which-Nothing-Floats. Will you not even see him, *Rénga*?"

"Don't call me that," said Jia in a whisper. "Never let them hear you call me that."

Ragi went on as though she hadn't heard. "He *is* Prince Timu's child, your flesh and blood. He looks the spitting image of Toto-*tika* at that age. I remember when—"

Jia flinched for the briefest of moments, but she instantly brought herself under control. "What good will seeing him do? I know nothing of what ails the child. The Lyucu suffer a plague from the gods; no mortal hands can stop that."

Ragi hesitated.

Jia could see that the young woman she had raised like a daughter was struggling with an emotion she had never associated with Jia: doubt.

A wisp of joy seeped into Jia's heart, like a trickle of spring water dripping into a desiccated root. *I was right to send her away when I did, and also right to spare her from the fate of the Dyran Fins. She is free of me.*

She can and should doubt me, but she, like the Lyucu, will never have confirmation that I was responsible for the tolyusa-thirst.

Ragi made as if to speak again, but Jia held up a hand.

"I'm tired," she said, and that wasn't a lie. "I wish to be alone."

Lady Ragi bowed deeply. Then she was gone.

Jia waited until the silk flowers had stopped spinning, indicating that the long, winding corridor leading to her bedchamber was empty. Only then did she allow her face to crumple and her posture to slacken, aging ten years in an instant.

Silently, she faced the tablet in the corner with Timu's name. She squeezed her eyes shut, but thick, hot tears spilled from beneath the lids, refusing to be held back.

*We're moved irrationally by the sight of individual anguish, our com-
passion aroused by empathy. Even Laughing Skeleton's twisted face haunts
my dreams.*

*But what of the suffering of thousands, of millions? What of the elders
whose skulls were bashed in by the Lyucu, of parents forced to eat the flesh of
their children, of wives compelled to castrate their husbands? The nameless
and faceless souls find no rest under the earth, their deaths unavenged.*

*I must avert my face from my grandchild so as not to be corrupted by
the weakness of blood-bond, so as not to betray the memories of all the other
victims.*

It was an extraordinarily cold and dark night. Unexpected heavy
snow obscured the stars and the moon. Wells and cisterns were sealed
by solid ice. The guards who were supposed to patrol the ramparts
of the walled compound huddled in the watchtowers, trying to keep
warm with cheap sorghum liquor that burned the throat. . . .

It was an extraordinarily busy night. Preparations for Princess
Fara's ascension to the throne occupied everyone in the capital, and
the streets were filled with caravans heavy with goods and workers
braving the snow to put the finishing touches on celebratory banquets, performances, fireworks displays, processions. . . .

It was an extraordinarily tiring night. After another day of tense
negotiations with Gori Ruthi and fretting over the declining condition of her brother, Dyana fell asleep as soon as her head touched the
pillow. Goztan and the other thanes went to sleep as well, and even
the naros keeping watch over the bound figure of Todyu dozed off. . . .

It was difficult to know whether the confluence of events was a
matter of divine intervention, mere coincidence, or the ineluctable
playing out of the nature of the universe.

What was certain was that by the time the fire in the guest compound had been discovered, it was beyond control.

Coughing, crying, struggling, the startled-awake young pékyu
was carried out of the smoke-filled corridors until she shivered in
the desolate yard, watching helplessly as the buildings were consumed by tongues of roaring fire leaping toward a sky full of swirling snow, like a horde of warring garinafins.

"Dyu-*tika*! Dyu-*tika*!"

Goztan restrained her as she fought to dive back into the conflagration. Todyu must have managed to free himself and started a fire.

The frozen wells yielded no water. Messengers dispatched to summon the city's fire brigades were blocked by the traffic. By the time carts laden with water drawn from the city's central cisterns, kept free of ice with constant-burning stoves, arrived at the scene, there was nothing left to save.

"She did this," Dyana muttered, voice barely audible, eyes burning with hate. "She did all this."

"I wasn't expecting to see you," said Jia. The sun had barely risen, and the bedchamber was suffused in a dreamy, golden light. "Isn't today Fara's coronation?"

"Empress Shizona insisted on a quick and simple ceremony." Cogo Yelu slipped into the seat opposite from hers. He was dressed not in formal courtly regalia but a plain robe that made him look like a teacher at one of the private academies.

"She should know better," said Jia. "The pomp and circumstance aren't for the benefit of the sovereign, but the people. She cannot inspire the necessary awe—never mind; it's no longer my place to speak of such things. Shouldn't you be at the post-coronation celebrations?"

"The empress has canceled all the celebrations. Even as she's still mourning her brothers, new grief has stricken like last night's fresh snow. Todyu, Timu's son, has died from tolyusa-thirst."

Jia stiffened. After a few moments, she gave up the struggle and slumped.

"Pékyu Dyana, your granddaughter, has forced her way into the palace at the head of the Lyucu delegation, carrying the corpse of her brother."

A flash of anger on Jia's face. "Are the palace guards so useless?"

"Empress Shizona ordered that they not be harmed. Dyana is demanding that you produce the antidote for tolyusa-thirst."

Jia sighed. *Fara has always been soft. But it doesn't matter. I am not soft. I made sure it wouldn't matter who sat on the Veiled Throne.*

"The Lyucu can persist in their delusion that a divine punishment has a mortal origin," she said. "But I no longer wield the Seal of Dara. Why do you speak to me of matters of state?"

Cogo tilted his head, as though mulling over his words. "True. This isn't the Inner Council Chamber. I've come to visit an old friend." He settled into informal *géüpa*, as though they were back in Zudi, before he became the Prime Minister and she the empress, a lifetime ago.

There he goes again, never saying what he truly means.

"A last visit before I'm either executed or exiled to Tan Adü?" Jia asked. A newfound strength seemed to fill her, and she straightened her back, kneeling up into formal *mipa rari*. A serene smile appeared on her face. She was going into battle, perhaps one last time.

Cogo looked at her. In contrast to him, the empress was dressed in bright, courtly finery, though with her posture and air, it resembled more a defiant suit of armor. But she was aware that her steady, cold facade was belied by the objects that surrounded her on the floor: a bundle of old letters, the logograms half-melted, as though they had been subjected to heat, with dark, crooked zyndari letters filling the blank spaces; two baby blankets—one red and one green, with thick, colorful embroidered letters spelling out "Toto-*tika*" and "Rata-*tika*"; a toy wooden sword that had often been seen in the hands of a toddling Phyro; a small scroll with childish drawings done in vivid colors taken from makeup: lip rouge, brow ink, cheek blush. . . .

"The list of charges against you is long," said Cogo Yelu. "Abuse of power as regent, betrayal of the nobles and generals of Emperor Ragin, appeasement of the Lyucu, usurpation of the Dandelion Throne, slaughter of the Dyran Fins when they refused to sustain your misrule, and heaviest of all, treasonous murder of Consort Risana and regicide against Emperor Monadétu."

"I'm well aware of the charges against me," said Jia. After a pause, she added, "They're all true."

"You won't tell your side of the story at trial?"

"My side of the story?" Jia smiled coolly. "History has little regard for those who make excuses for themselves. Let the storytellers in teahouses speak of me as a tyrant, a selfish woman drunk with power who tried to steal the Seal of Dara from her children."

Cogo looked thoughtful. "Selfish? I was also once accused of selfishness because I sought to build myself a large manor with money from the Imperial Treasury. We all wear masks."

Jia's heart pounded. Cogo was referring to that incident from long ago, when he had deliberately sullied his own name so as to allay Kuni's suspicions that he harbored grander ambitions.

Why is he bringing that up? Does he really know?

"Sometimes there is nothing beneath the mask," she said. Silently, she berated herself for the quaver in her voice. *Why do I still yearn for understanding when misunderstanding is my goal?*

"On the night I took the Seal of Dara away from you, I had a dream," said Cogo. "The gods of Dara appeared to me, towering figures of stone, but more lifelike than any statue carved by mortal hand, and insisted that I pursue the truth."

Jia kept her face placid despite the thunderous roar of blood rushing through her ears. "You've always been free and easy in your interpretation of oracles. Dreams of the gods are figments of idle fancy, not substantive enough to be weighed."

"Perhaps. But can a message seemingly from the gods really be disregarded so lightly? You insist that the gods have lain our enemies low with this tolyusa-thirst and delivered us a most improbable victory. You also proclaim, like the Hegemon did, that you were not removed from power because you miscalculated, but because the gods were against you. Vanquishing the Lyucu without us having to dispatch a single ship *and* removing Your Imperial Majesty from power without a tide of blood . . . each by itself would be wondrous; together, they feel miraculous."

"I can't say I'm the most pious person in the world," said Jia. "But I think it's best not to look too closely into miracles lest we find ourselves undeserving."

To disguise her agitation, she tried to brew tea. But as she placed the pot over the brazier, her hands shook so much that water spilled into the glowing charcoal, hissing and filling the room with steam and fragrant smoke, softening the harsh glow of the winter sun and bringing to mind the smoke-fog of Empress Risana, a medium that could as easily lead to truth as fantasy.

"The ways of the gods are mysterious," she said, swallowing to moisten her parched throat.

"The ways of the mortals, however, follow discernible patterns," said Cogo, his tone as serene as the surface of Lake Tututika on a breezeless summer day. "After waking from my dream, I decided to probe deeper into this 'miracle.' I found much that is surprising, enough to make me doubt the prosecution's case against you."

Cogo, don't do this. Don't.

"Are you offering to be my paid litigator?" asked Jia, quirking an eyebrow mockingly. "I have no desire to drag out the inevitable. My scheming days are over."

"I don't have much skill when it comes to farseeing or plotting, my old friend," said Cogo, bowing his head slightly. "Of Kuni's old retinue, I'm without a doubt the least impressive. I lack Gin's knack for reading a battlefield like a *cüpa* board and inspiring an army with her dauntless courage. I want Luan's capacity for devising ingenious strategies and inventing marvelous machines. But I *am* endowed with a mulish capacity for doing plodding work: reading ledgers from start to finish, double-checking shipping records, trawling a sea of the quotidian for a few elusive clues, reconstructing a story coded in numbers instead of being told in words. Experience as a stodgy bureaucrat has its advantages."

Jia sighed. Her hand steadied as if she had, by an act of sheer will, calmed the storm raging in her heart. "And what fantastical story have you divined from the oracular bones of these mute records?"

Cogo persevered in his methodical, emotionless tone. "I think it best to lay out the facts, to pile up the fish on the scale. There must be a solid foundation for the fanciful castle I'm about to conjure in thin air."

Carefully, Jia measured powdered tea into two cups and gestured for him to continue.

"I began at the end, when you whispered a word of thanks to me as you gave up the Seal of Dara."

Jia's heart clenched. She regretted that impulsive act in the Grand Audience Hall, like adding feet to a drawing of a snake. But it was too late. "I was grateful to you for not ordering the palace guards to kill me on the spot."

Cogo shook his head. "We've known each other too long for such crude lies, Jia."

Jia accepted the rebuke silently.

"What were you thanking me for? The question refused to go away. The bloodless coup was not what it seemed. I summoned the coroners who examined the bodies of the Dyran Fins—"

"There's no mystery there," said Jia. "I poisoned them. I brought these girls up to fight for me, against anyone who would do me harm. But they abandoned me at the moment I needed them the most, refused to cut you and the other rebelling ministers down when I ordered them to. The price for that unforgivable act of betrayal is death."

Cogo waited until Jia was finished with her outburst. "The coroners agreed that the Dyran Fins were poisoned, but they also told me that based on the stiffness of the bodies, the women had died long before the start of formal court, perhaps a day or two earlier. By the time you claimed to summon them, they had long crossed the River-on-Which-Nothing-Floats."

Jia said nothing.

"The Dyran Fins were utterly devoted to you," continued Cogo. "They would have done anything for you, including removing my foolish head if you had demanded it. Indeed, even if you had ordered them to cease all resistance, they would have fought against us to the last woman standing, believing that you were under coercion. I don't believe they were capable of betraying you at all."

Jia stared into the teacups.

"Rather, it seems that someone had anticipated the rebellion of the ministers and killed the Dyran Fins ahead of time, to make sure that our coup would succeed with minimal resistance and loss of lives."

"You wrong them," declared Jia, a hard edge in her voice. "They were good girls, and they deserve to be remembered as heroes of the revolution—" She stopped, but it was too late.

Cogo nodded. "In your own fashion, you are as devoted to them as they are to you. They had to die, but you wanted them to be remembered as heroic figures who stood up against tyranny, not pawns who had to be sacrificed for a secret plot, not as traitors to the Dandelion Throne. You wanted tablets with their names in the Hall of Mutagé so that even though they have no children, they'll receive offerings every year at the Grave-Mending Festival."

The water was boiling. Jia tried to pick up the ladle to fill the teacups, but her fingers seemed stiff, clumsy, disobedient. She could not wrap them around the handle. She gave up.

"Why would I kill the only people who could keep me in power?" she asked.

"That is only a mystery if staying in power were your goal," said Cogo.

Steam obscured Jia's face from Cogo's gaze. Nonetheless, he went on.

"The deaths of the Dyran Fins also silenced them forever. They weren't subject to the control of any general or minister. They came and went as they pleased, obeying only you. So what secret did they take with them to their graves? Naturally, I started by examining the sections of the palace accessible only to them and to you, especially the medicine shed in the Palace Garden, where you practice herbalism."

"It's a hobby . . . ," murmured Jia.

"Several drawers in the shed were left slightly ajar, and there was some residue at the bottom of one of the cauldrons. When I consulted the College of Imperial Physicians, they informed me that the ingredients from those drawers matched the recipe for the poison that took the lives of the Dyran Fins, and remnants of the very same decoction were left in the cauldron."

"I already confessed that I poisoned them," said Jia.

She seemed calmer. Picking up the bamboo ladle, she scooped just enough water from the boiling pot to fill the two teacups.

Cogo shook his head. "The floor of the medicine shed was spotless; the ladder for accessing the high shelves was secure in its bracket; the kneeling stool was pushed under the workbench; notebooks were stacked neatly on the desk, the edges perfectly aligned, everything at right angles; stalks of dried herbs in the drawers lay in parallel bundles, as neat as combed hair; even the pestles resting in the mortars all pointed in the same direction, like the shadows of sundials at the same hour."

Jia felt like a cornered rabbit. She was running out of room to deflect, evade, dodge. "My teachers always stressed the importance of leaving a clean work area. A neat workbench led to a neat mind."

But Cogo was relentless. "How could someone so obsessed with a clean work area leave those drawers open or that cauldron unwashed?"

"A moment of carelessness."

"You are never careless, Jia. When a letter consists of a few logograms on a scroll much too large for them, the blank space must contain the real message. When an herbalist shed is perfectly clean except for a few stray items, they must be intended to mislead. The absence of clues in the rest of the shed is the real clue."

Jia closed her eyes.

I was too clever, or not clever enough. But it's too late to remedy now.

"Whatever you were truly working on in that shed, you had to rely on the Dyran Fins to get it out of the palace," Cogo said, his tone unperturbed as though he were describing another refinement to the bureaucracy. "The Dyran Fins, of course, did not report their movements to the palace guards. However, the Imperial kitchen does maintain meticulous records."

Jia looked at him, confused.

"Wi and Shido grew up as orphans, and they never lost their habits of economy and deep respect for the effort it took to keep bellies full. When they ordered from the Imperial kitchen, they never asked for more meals than there were Dyran Fins in the palace on that day. By combing through these requisition orders, it was easy to derive the number of Dyran Fins in the palace on any day, and the dates when groups of them were sent away on missions."

Jia chuckled helplessly. *Who would have thought to check the kitchen records? . . . Kuni was right to value Cogo so.*

"Once I had that, I issued writs to shops around Pan and obtained their sales ledgers. By matching the sizes and durations of expeditions to purchases of equipment and supplies on relevant dates, it was possible to draw educated guesses as to their destinations. For example, furs and crampons would be needed if they were going to scale a snowy peak like Mount Rapa—and the guesses could be confirmed by asking inhabitants at the foot of the mountain if they recalled strangers matching the descriptions of the Dyran Fins on those days. A trip to Wolf's Paw, on the other hand, would require the hiring of a ship. . . ."

Jia sipped at her tea as Cogo continued his recitation of facts. He made it sound easy, but she could imagine how much effort it had taken to trawl through a sea of useless information for a few glimmers of the dyran's tail. Only a master at wielding the bureaucracy, at crafting a singular sight out of thousands of pairs of disparate eyes, could rise to the task.

". . . It would not surprise you, I suspect, to know that Tiphan Huto kept detailed records of his transactions with the pirates—the Huto clan was only too glad to offer them up when they realized they could be charged as accomplices. Though Tiphan kept the ledgers in code, speaking of 'red rice' and 'gold rice,' it was easy to crack the code once we had interrogated his middlemen, the pirate fleet leaders, many of whom had decided to surrender now that the Lyucu smuggling business was gone and the seas were being patrolled more effectively. . . ."

So many clues that she could not erase, or else the erasure itself became a clue. No matter how much she wanted to control everything, the unexpected always happened: Phyro's appeal to the people, Zomi's recognition of hidden talent outside the Imperial examinations, Cogo's relentless desire to discover the truth. . . . The gods must have been working against her.

". . . A survey conducted by garinafin and airship flyovers finally yielded a charred field near the top of Mount Rapa," said Cogo. "I went there to examine the remains, which proved intriguing. For instance, I discovered some wreckage that might have been giant parasols, the sort used by plum flower merchants to simulate winter sunlight in summer. As another example, Imperial botanists combed through the ashes taken from the burned field and identified a new variety—no, a cultivar—of zomi berries that showed the hand of an expert breeder—"

"That's enough," Jia broke in. "Prime Minister, you sound like one of those teahouse storytellers who think every little innocuous detail is evidence of some grand conspiracy. You've piled speculation upon conjecture upon guesswork upon hunch, all tied together with wild leaps of fancy. You have no proof."

"The trouble with conspiracy theories," said Cogo, locking eyes with Jia, "is that sometimes they are true."

"This audience is over," said Jia. For a moment, she sounded again like the Empress of Dara. "You should leave."

"I still haven't told you my story, the story that I read in the blank spaces."

"I'm tired of stories," said Jia. "Leave!"

I cannot bear this. I cannot bear it.

"Some stories require a special teller, but this one requires a special audience. I've never demanded anything from you, old friend. I ask you to listen to my story now. Will you grant me this one request?"

Jia stared at him for a long time. And then, as her shoulders sagged and her body slumped in defeat, she nodded.

Cogo sipped from his cup. Keeping his eyes on the empress, he began to speak.

The gods endow each of us with different gifts, and it is the lot of mortals to make the most of them. We describe these gifts as our nature.

There was once a woman named Jia Matiza, who was born in Faça, fell in love in Cocru, and came into her own as the borders between the old Tiro states dissolved. Her gift was in cultivation. But she was not one who knelt over the soil, eyes locked on the square around her feet. She needed to soar high, higher than any kite, any Mingén falcon, any airship, so that she could contemplate and tend to the whole, grand garden that is Dara.

During the chaotic years of the rebellion against the Xana Empire and the Chrysanthemum-Dandelion War, her mind was indelibly scarred by the slaughter and suffering, much of it due to the Ambition of Nobles and the Courage of Brutes. Therefore, when she became empress after the founding of the empire, she strove to prune Dara into a land of peace, to clip away those men and women who would use violence to achieve their selfish ends.

"*The Hundred Flowers deserve better than that,*" she said to herself. It was her duty to make the dream come true.

But then an unexpected fleet came from beyond the Wall of Storms, unleashing an invasion force that gave no quarter and followed no rules of war. And so, unexpectedly, she had to unsheathe the Grace of Kings and resort to the blood and iron she had forsworn, lest the garden be consumed by the Lyucu's insatiable greed and boundless cruelty.

Like many others, she endured pain and loss. Her husband died in the war, as did her most valiant war duke. Her son became a captive, and her daughter departed Dara to pursue a most remote chance at striking the enemy in their homeland. She put her own life and the lives of her family on the line, seeing it as her duty.

In the end, a fragile stalemate was achieved, with the Islands partitioned in halves. One half was the dominion of the invaders, who desired nothing less than the annihilation of the native population. To achieve this goal, they would blink at no act of cruelty, shudder at no policy of atrocity.

Jia, on the other hand, found herself in charge of the charred remains of the other half, teetering on the precipice of collapse from insecurity. Voices cried out for war, for vengeance, for salvation of the people being butchered across the sea. How could their just demands be denied? But Jia also knew that fighting the Lyucu meant certain death for the captive population. Total war had a logic of its own, and a people consumed by war became more like their enemies. That way lay the madness of militarism, the desolation of deaths by the millions, and finally, the terror of tyranny justified by the thirst for conquest.

How could she redeem Unredeemed Dara without leaving behind a field of bones? How could she triumph over the Lyucu without dyeing the sea with blood? How could she cultivate a harvest of just victory without sterilizing the seeds of compassion, without salting the soil of hope, without incinerating the frail sprouts of new dreams of a better Dara? How could she triumph over an enemy that threatened the very annihilation of the people of Dara without corrupting and destroying Dara's soul in the process?

She had to devise a plan that would be as subtle as the movement of Lady Rapa's glaciers, as merciless as the will of the Hegemon, and as difficult to detect as the sting of Lady Mira's dagger, the Cruben's Thorn. It was her duty.

She cleaved herself in twain. One half would become the fabled Patternist patron who boosted innovation and invention, the ideal Moralist sovereign who reified virtues through rituals, the sage Fluxist guide who ruled the best by intervening the least, and above all, the master Incentivist lawmaker who reformed codes and systems to encourage healthy growth and to suppress cancerous corruption.

The other half, however, would work in darkness, plotting and scheming, conspiring and misdirecting, deceiving and deflecting, committing acts that the Moralists would denounce as heinous, playing a long game whose true objective was obscured from friend and foe alike.

She turned, as always, to the art of cultivation.

She removed Empress Risana so that the young emperor would not challenge her power as regent. She sued for peace with the invaders, abasing herself to plant in their minds the seeds of arrogance: a belief that she was selfish, craven, a coward; an opinion that the people of Dara were weak, soft, terrified of war. In time, these would grow into unshaken articles of faith, unquestioned dogma, convictions for the foundation of Ukyu-taasa.

While free Dara grew stronger year after year under the peace of the regency, in the conquered lands, the invaders grew indolent and indulged in misrule. Jia reacted by sending the invaders ever larger shipments of tribute and by spreading rumors of reinforcements from beyond the Wall of Storms. The shipments and rumors served as fertilizer and water for the worst tendencies of the Lyucu. They became addicted to the fruits of Dara's apparent submission, which disguised their own weakness.

Appetite, when indulged excessively, mutated into addiction, a disease that would lead to self-deception, self-destruction, self-defeat. It would be Jia's greatest ally.

The Lyucu traditionally enjoyed the hallucinogenic effects of tolyusa, which we call zomi berries. A skilled herbalist, Jia knew how to concentrate the nature inherent in the seeds into ever more potent cultivars. The Dyran Fins smuggled these into Unredeemed Dara with the help of pirates and unscrupulous merchants who would betray Dara for profit, not realizing they were stones in the empress's grand game of cüpa.

Just as the invaders had come to rely on shipments of tribute to feed their bodies, they also came to rely on shipments of enhanced zomi berries to sustain their spirit, sinking ever deeper into a dream in which they were indomitable, the favored children of the gods.

She had to keep the plot to herself. Tanvanaki was no fool, and there were many traitors in Dara willing to sell her what she craved: information, know-how, even kidnapped engineers to be enslaved. But there was an even more important reason for the secrecy: Her plan required actions that the people would not contemplate taking, costs that the people were not ready to bear.

To perfect the addictive strain of zomi berries, she had to experiment upon live prisoners. To guarantee that she could personally see her plan through, she had to keep power away from the legitimate heir to the throne. To accelerate the fall of the Lyucu, she needed to nudge her son, the captive puppet emperor who had a pacifying effect on the natives, to overreach in his zeal for Moralist ideals—even if that meant risking his life without his understanding or consent.

Most horrifying of all, to deliver the greater portion of mercy, she had to prevent the Lyucu from grafting themselves onto the rootstock of Dara, forestall them from budding onto the bough of the people of the Islands, block them from building an efficient machinery of state that would permanently enslave native invention, knowledge, and skill in the service of Lyucu supremacy in Ukyu-taasa. That meant she had to undermine the accommodationists and prop up the hard-liners, leave the captive population of the conquered islands in unspeakable suffering.

She saw it as her duty. Teeth on the board.

And when Emperor Monadétu defied her and launched an expedition to liberate the conquered islands, she had to force his army to retreat and abandon all the fruits of their sacrifice so that a greater sacrifice could be averted. It led to the death of the emperor, though she did not wish for it and would have done anything to avoid that outcome, if only she could have trusted anyone other than herself.

She violated every precept of Moralism, every rubric of ethics. If the truth of her actions were revealed, she was certain she would be stopped by her own ministers and generals, especially by Phyro, the child who saw the Grace of Kings as a romance, not a terrible blade with no hilt that harmed the wielder as much as the foe.

To prevent anyone from suspecting her true intentions, she distracted observers by sullying her own name. She pretended to be a usurper, dispensing favors upon a prince whom she had no intention of promoting over the true heir; she surrounded herself with beautiful young men, letting others conclude that she indulged her appetites without care; she repressed the generals and mistreated discharged veterans, adding to the impression that she aimed only to appease the Lyucu.

It would take time for the Lyucu to become fully addicted, not just to the enhanced zomi berries, but also to their own self-deception. But when the fruit of her scheme had finally ripened, the empress would pluck it without mercy. Like all great poisoners, she practiced her art with precision and discretion. The tolyusa was a drug available only to the Lyucu and high-ranking collaborators, sparing the civilians. And the poisonous effects required two components: consumption of the enhanced tolyusa, followed by its withdrawal.

But the empress was not satisfied. Because she peered so far beyond the horizon, she saw the danger of her own actions.

Her dream had always been to create a Dara in which it didn't matter who was the sovereign. A good king always died; only a good system could secure the happiness of the people beyond one mortal span. But her plan required her to carry out hidden designs beyond the reach of the law, to maintain a secret military force not subject to civilian oversight, to hold on to power without the constraints of legitimacy, consensus, the institutions that channeled power.

To defeat the Lyucu while keeping Dara free from the tyranny of militarism, she had turned into a tyrant. To save the people while preventing Dara from being corrupted by total war, she had corrupted herself. The paradox had to be resolved.

The actions of those who found an empire are constitutive acts for subsequent generations, and weighty as precedent. She could not let her own example become a guide for future tyrants, for a would-be Hegemon, Gin, Phyro, or even—especially—another Jia.

So she embarked upon a second, parallel plan: cultivating, pruning, shaping, training the living machinery of the state. Gathering able advisers and pitting them against one another in teams of rivals, she implemented the Incentivist insight that people were motivated by desire for gain and aversion to loss without disregarding the Moralist hope that individuals could be inspired to strive for ideals grander than their immediate needs. Stepping back and giving up power as the bureaucracy grew and refined itself, she fulfilled the Patternist belief that out of many disparate components, each *molded for a different purpose, a grand, coherent machine could be assembled to carry out a single goal, thereby also enacting the Fluxist archetype that harmonious Flow emerged from random chaos.*

While she veiled away the Dandelion Throne to separate it from its rightful heir, she also placed the fingers of the many upon the handle of the Grace of Kings. The people have always had the right to rise up in violent rebellion against a tyrant, but she wanted there to be another way, a way for the garden to thwart the straying gardener without the death of millions. She plotted for her own downfall by planting the seeds of an institutional rebellion, a systematic coup, a bloodless, loyal act of treason.

The moment arrived. The field on Mount Rapa was burned to the ground; Tiphan Huto tore out his own throat; the Lyucu were plunged into tolyusa-thirst, and practically overnight, an invincible empire built upon cruelty and the worship of death crumbled.

And almost simultaneously, the seed that Jia had planted, Lady Soto's conscience, had sprouted and bloomed. Soto proclaimed the truth—or at least the part of the truth Jia wanted to be known—of the empress's betrayals and murders to the world.

Jia had succeeded, but she was also exhausted. The weight of years of plotting against an implacable foe strained her heart; the guilt of cruel acts against innocent victims stained her conscience. She was glad that the self-regulating, self-correcting machinery of state that she had worked so hard to build was finally strong enough to constrain the power of the sovereign, ready to challenge herself.

Like a silkworm spinning out the last loop of thread to seal herself into the cocoon that would be her shroud in the boiling vat, she killed off her most faithful defenders, the women she loved as her own daughters, and unleashed a revolution with herself as its target. She wanted to take the secret of her long plots to the grave. She would become the last, lone sacrifice necessary to initiate a new reign, a reign in which the empire no longer relied on a wise ruler, but could be wise in itself.

A well-crafted plan is indistinguishable from a miracle, especially if the plotter can be as cruel to herself as she is to her enemies.

Cogo stopped.

Jia's face was streaked with tears.

She had been understood; she had been seen. Though she had tried to encase her heart in ice, to submit to misunderstanding, the craving to have one's heart vibrate in sympathy with that of a kindred soul never died.

"You spin a wondrous tale," she said, wiping her face clean and putting up a last, desperate fight. "But it is only a tale."

"I cannot claim full credit as the author," said Cogo. "Zomi shared my suspicions, and we pooled our evidence and poked holes in each other's conclusions until we were satisfied that the fish had been properly weighed. True tales are always the most wondrous."

"Extraordinary claims require ironclad proof," Jia protested, her voice barely a croak.

Cogo's eyes were full of compassion. Her face provided all the proof he needed.

"You were the playwright and lead actress in that last performance in the Grand Audience Hall," Cogo said. "It was the culmination of a lifetime of deception engaged in to benefit the people of Dara, to reify *mutagé*. It was a grand work worthy of an Empress of Dara." Cogo knelt up in *mipa rari*, straightening his back with difficulty. The weight of age, of the vicissitudes of history, was unforgiving.

His voice took on a severe tone. "But it was also, in the end, a staged performance. The bloodless revolution is a lie."

"*Every* act from the sovereign and the Lords of Dara is a performance," said Jia. "That is the nature of politics. But even staged acts, when validated by the belief of the audience, reify into records of history and become patterns to constrain and guide future behavior. These constitutive acts are not 'lies,' but the very foundation of a better life for the people of Dara."

"I've already tendered my resignation as Prime Minister," said Cogo Yelu.

"Why?" Jia demanded, absolutely shocked.

"Because I knew that your case against Gin was fabricated but backed you anyway; because I suspected that you had murdered Risana but did not act on my suspicion; because I turned a blind eye to your schemes, until Phyro died. I was your accomplice, even if I didn't know."

"Phyro killed himself!" Jia's hands balled into fists. "I wanted to stop him; I tried. He was too strong-willed, too black-and-white, too—" She stopped. It was long past the time for explanations. "I deceived you precisely because I hoped—"

"I understand," said Cogo. "I know that you wanted to keep me and the other members of the Inner Council from the price of such a victory over the Lyucu: the murders, betrayals, the suffering of the people under Lyucu misrule while you cultivated the hard-liners. You wanted to pay for all of it yourself, playing the role of the villain and hoping to insulate the rest of us from responsibility. But we were all complicit. None of us was clean."

"O Cogo, Cogo! You once understood the value of performances and roles and necessary deceptions. What has happened to you?"

"I've grown old and less cynical," said Cogo. "A more just future cannot be built upon a foundation of lies."

"You want the truth?" Jia's voice cracked, and she stood up, a trembling finger pointed at Cogo. "How do you think my granddaughter and her thanes will react when they receive confirmation that their suspicions were true, that I poisoned their bodies to sap them of the will and ability to fight? How do you think the people of Unredeemed Dara will react when they discover that I was in part responsible for their suffering by encouraging the excesses of the Lyucu? The atrocities committed by the Lyucu hard-liners exceeded even my dark imagination— O gods! O gods . . . How do you think the common people will react when they hear that Soto's accusations against me only scratched the surface, that I committed far more heinous crimes in their name?"

Compulsively, she rubbed her hands to rid them of the invisible stain.

"You did what you did to avert a worse fate for millions," said Cogo. "Your actions cannot be judged by a court of law, only by the hearts of the people and the long shadow of experience. You've always said that you submit to the judgment of history; history begins in the present."

"You have too much trust in the common people," said Jia. "The truth will make them lose faith in the Dandelion Throne, in the Inner Council. They are shortsighted, selfish, governed by their hot passions—"

"And you trust them too little," said Cogo. "You want to con-struct a system of interlocking institutions that will serve the people of Dara long beyond your lifetime, but a system is nothing unless it is *reconstituted*, act after act, generation after generation, by a free people who choose what they do based on full knowledge of the facts. You think you see far, but no individual, no matter how wise, can see as far as the compounded eyes of their children and their children; you have no power to foretell the future. The people of Dara must be allowed to see for themselves and chart their own course, to tell their own story."

All right, she thought. *I've done all I could; at least I kept the most important secret.*

"Let the people have their truth," she said, with infinite weari-ness, "for all the good it will do them." Though she was no longer the Empress of Dara, she couldn't help asking one more question of policy: "What about the Lyucu? What has Fara decided to do with them?"

"Ah," said Cogo, "there is one more thing. Empress Shizona is negotiating the terms of the Lyucu surrender directly with Pékyu Dyana. The Lyucu have one demand before they'll discuss anything else: the cure for tolyusa-thirst."

"They have no right to ask for any terms at all!" Blood rushed into Jia's face. "Besides, they cannot have any more of the enhanced zomi berries. I made sure they were eradicated."

Cogo shook his head. "They're asking for a cure, not more poison."

"There is no cure."

Cogo looked at her in the eye, saying everything and nothing.

Impossible, Jia screamed silently in her head. *Not even the Dyran Fins knew. How could he know?*

"The tolyusa-thirst plagues the worst of the worst," she said. "The hard-liner thanes, the high-ranking collaborators, those who believed in the annihilation of our people. Let them die."

"The tolyusa-thirst also struck thanes who obeyed Cutanrovo Aga out of convenience rather than zeal, collaborators who tried to curry favor with the Lyucu to save the people, and those like Todyu, your grandson, too young to understand what they did."

"Excuses," said Jia, her voice cold. "What of their victims? Why aren't you pleading for them? Why aren't you speaking for justice?"

"The surrendered Lyucu will also be the people of Dara," said Cogo. "A cure is an act of good faith, and weighty as precedent."

"Fool! The Lyucu can never become the people of Dara!" This was exactly what she had feared Phyro would do. "I beg of you, do not undo all that I've done. The Lyucu cannot be reasoned with, accommodated. If you allow them and their descendants to live among us as equals, then you're choosing generations of hatred, the endless poison of the desire for vengeance, the undying dream of the revival of Lyucu domination. Only their utter and complete submission, only by driving them into the sea—"

"You speak like Cutanrovo, like Tenryo," said Cogo.

Jia felt as though she had been slapped in the face. Her mouth moved, but no words emerged.

"How can we dismiss an entire people in one judgment?" said Cogo. "Dara has produced individuals like Gin and Luan, Timu and Théra, heroes who left their teeth on the board, heedless of sacrifices for the people. Dara has also produced individuals like Wira Pin and Noda Mi, butchers and cowards who lived on the blood of their victims. That same variety is true among the Lyucu. For every cruel Cutanrovo Aga, there is an Ofluro, who trained the garinafins to defend the Dandelion Throne; for every merciless Tenryo, there is a Vocu Firna, who gave his life to save a few native scholars.

"Fara has chosen mercy over justice. It is the will of Empress Shizona and her new Inner Council that you yield up the cure for the tolyusa-thirst. She wishes that her nephew, Todyu, will be the last to die of the sickness instead of one of the first."

Jia closed her eyes. In her mind she pictured the thirst-ravaged body of Todyu. Because she had never seen her grandson, she naturally substituted the face of his father as a boy. The son of her son, flesh of her flesh, lay dead by her own hand, and she had refused to even see him once before he passed beyond the River-on-Which-Nothing-Floats.

Her face crumpled. No matter how much she tried to close herself to human feelings, she was only mortal.

"I had to climb high enough until I could see the whole picture, to enlarge my heart to contain the fates of millions, to harden my soul for the unforgiving edged grip of the Grace of Kings," she said, as tears spilled from her eyes. "But as I climbed, I also watched myself changing from a dandelion into a towering pine, a shrimp into a cruben, a sparrow into a Mingén falcon. I could no longer discern the lives of individuals, Dara or Lyucu. They became entries in tax ledgers, figures in assessments of relative military strength, anonymous stones on a *cüpa* board whose fate depended on which side they were on, black or white. O Timu, my son, I've failed you. My son!"

Cogo sat with her in empathetic silence. Tears flowed from his eyes as well.

At length, as her sobs subsided, he spoke again. "With only an herb as your weapon, you've achieved a victory over the Lyucu that will rank with the greatest campaigns by Gin Mazoti; with only experience as your guide, you've constructed a self-instructing, self-reflecting, self-correcting engine of state for collective decision-making that is the equal of any invention by Luan Zyaji. In a world of terrible choices, you chose a path that minimized suffering. You preserved the soul of Dara against the horrors of total war."

"I cannot sleep, old friend." Jia shrank into herself, inconsolable. "I cannot close my eyes without seeing the faces of all those I harmed."

"I know, old friend," said Cogo. "You and I are both old and our consciences stained. It's time for us to step aside for a new generation.

"It's the lot of mortal beings to see but a short way into the future, no matter how much we strive, and it is both a curse and a manifestation of grace that children must make their own path, independent of their forbearers.

"Those who plant saplings will not live to enjoy the shade of the full-grown tree; those who build the city-ship will not get to steer it into the unknown storm. I'm asking you to let go of the Grace of Kings, and trust that the Wisdom of the People will be wielded well by the people you saw as your duty to defend. The living machine of the state is endowed with its own intelligence, its own foresight.

"Free yourself from the arrogance that you can see the end of history, design a perfect system, plot for the best ending. Embrace the humility of doubt. You're one pair of hands among multitudes, one pair of eyes among myriads. You're no longer the empress, but one of the people of Dara. Only then can the revolution you desire truly succeed. Only then can you, by your own act, reify *mutagé*."

He, like the rest of the room, had become blurred in Jia's eyes, but she made no effort to wipe away her tears.

A long line of figures, larger than life, seemed to parade before her. She was about to shout defiantly at them again, but then she realized that they were not the gods of Dara at all.

Friends, foes, lovers who had passed beyond the River-on-Which-Nothing-Floats: Kuni and Risana, Otho Krin, Gin Mazoti, Timu and Phyro, Wi and Shido, Laughing Skeleton, Nazu Tei, Todyu, Tiphan Huto. . . .

She couldn't tell if their expressions were of forgiveness or hatred, compassion or enmity. No matter how much she strained, their faces refused to resolve into clarity. They simply beckoned at her, asking her to see herself as flawed, merely mortal, but one of the people of Dara.

One by one, the figures faded into a tapestry of the Islands of Dara, a teeming mass of humanity, a grand, living machine that no longer needed her hand, and perhaps had never needed her hand.

"Just one more question," she said. "How did you know that I would have a cure?"

"You're an herbalist, Jia, a healer. It is in your nature never to design a poison without an antidote."

The gods endow each of us with different gifts, and it is the lot of mortals to make the most of them.

She nodded and composed herself. "Let the empress know that I'm at her service. I submit to the judgment of the present."

CHAPTER FIFTY-FIVE

SURRENDER

By tradition, the first decree from a new sovereign should announce a reign name, one that would be auspicious and set the tone of the administration. But Empress Shizona declined to do so. Instead, her first official act was the production of a book.

A nameless mysterious young engineer trusted by the empress, and his teacher, Master Rati Yera, supervised the construction of multiple book-mirrors. The machines, connected to the silkmotic mills of the Imperial Academy, ran day and night. Thousands of copies of the new book were produced and distributed by airship to every corner of the Islands.

The book, simply titled *Confessions*, was divided into two parts. The first part was carved by Jia Matiza, detailing her decade-long plot to bypass the legitimate institutions and laws of the Imperial bureaucracy to carry out a secret war against the Lyucu. The second part was dictated by Goztan Ryoto and translated into Classical Ano, laying out the sequence of bloody policies carried out against the native population by the rulers of Ukyu-taasa.

In the grand avenues of Pan, drivers of hired carriages argued with their passengers; in the suspended teahouses of Müning, patrons debated heatedly over snacks and floral infusions; in the wide expanse of Temple Square in Ginpen, orators stood on makeshift cargo-box platforms to deliver passionate speeches, both pro and con; even in the bustling markets of pragmatic Toaza, shoppers and vendors couldn't help but mix in a few observations about politics as they haggled over the price of the daily catch. . . .

Everyone seemed to have an opinion on Jia Matiza, once the Regent of Dara, and the peace with the Lyucu.

While Pékyu Dyana and Empress Shizona were locked in heated negotiations concerning the final terms of the Lyucu surrender, as a preliminary step, a temporary armistice was reached to bring aid to the long-suffering inhabitants of Rui and Dasu. Dara's Imperial army would assume control of Ukyu-taasa, but with a guarantee that the Lyucu would be unharmed until a permanent treaty had been ratified.

The shipments of food and medical supplies reached the two islands just in time. As teams of doctors and soldiers fanned across the islands, they found the survivors of this last merciless winter, both Lyucu and native, both oppressor and enslaved, to be as emaciated as skeletons. There were more than a few reports of cannibalism.

Many of the natives were severely injured. Years of hard labor, torture, and random acts of cruelty from Lyucu overseers had taken their toll. Thousands upon thousands had been blinded, maimed, castrated. . . . The doctors could tend to these victims, but mere medicine was helpless against the invisible wounds in their psyches.

Herbalists trained by Jia administered a special brew to the Lyucu and high-ranking native collaborators in the throes of tolyusa-madness. It was a complicated concoction whose main ingredient turned out to be a specific variety of fungal spores, the white powder that had decimated the Lyucu's own fields of tolyusa.

"Surprising that a poison should grow so close to its antidote," said Cogo in admiration.

"Pairings of opposites embody one of the fundamental principles of herbalism," said Jia. She was reminded of a similar lecture she had given once to Kuni in their youth. "The deadly seven-step snake of Faça nests in shady coves where the crying boy mushroom, which secretes an antivenom, likes to grow. The fiery salamander weed, a good, hot spice for cold winter nights, grows better next to the snowdrop, known for its power to relieve fevers. Creation seems to favor making friends of those destined to be enemies."

The concoction brought immediate relief and sobriety to the tolyusa-plagued, but they would have to deal with a lifetime of chronic sequelae and aftereffects. As well, they would have to strive for the rest of their lives not to fall back into tolyusa-thirst—even the unenhanced variety would be dangerous to them. They would, in effect, be forever cut off from an aspect of traditional Lyucu spiritual practice.

The garinafins suffered from withdrawal of the enhanced tolyusa in their own fashion, and curing them presented unique challenges. Fortunately, the Lyucu garinafin riders and grooms, relieved from tolyusa-madness, could help calm the massive beasts as herbalists poured cauldrons of antidote down their maws.

The rescue workers also came across unexpected good fortune. An old man, who had once been a servant of Thane Vocu Firna, led them to the site of the ruins of his former master's manor in Kriphi. Following his directions, the workers dug deep under the latrine pit until they found a collection of sealed chests. Inside, they found ritual vessels, manuscript scrolls, veneration figurines, knotwork tapestries, ceremonial weapons—all taken from the royal collection of old Xana and the Temple of Péa-Kiji. After the devastation wreaked by Cutanrovo's purification packs, these artifacts were practically the only surviving physical evidence of Rui and Dasu's long history, the only remnants of the islands' literary and cultural heritage, of their soul. After the discovery of decoy treasures of lesser cultural worth that had led to his downfall, Vocu Firna, even under torture and threat of death, had not revealed the existence of this deeper, more precious trove. The rescue workers and the gathered natives fell to their knees, weeping from sorrow as well as joy.

The erasure of a people's history was the most important step in the destruction of that people; the salvaging and restoration of that history was the first step in the long road to recovery.

Meanwhile, the freed natives, after briefly celebrating their liberation, were shocked to see that the hated Lyucu suffered no punishment after turning in their weapons. Doctors from the core islands tended to the surrendered Lyucu as well as native villagers, and the food was being distributed to all equally. In fact, the Lyucu were sequestered from the natives and protected by the soldiers. When questioned, the aid team commanders explained that the Throne had ordered that the Lyucu be given comfort and aid, as well as full protection against native reprisals.

Men and women fell to their knees, wailing for the dead and the disappeared. They couldn't understand why they had been abandoned by the Dandelion Throne for so long, and now that they had finally been freed, why the Throne refused to allow them vengeance.

Officials among the aid workers tried to explain to the stunned villagers the grander meaning of the policies of Empress Jia and Empress Shizona, first relinquishing them to the predation of the Lyucu and then keeping them from tearing the Lyucu apart. That these policies had minimized and would minimize suffering and death was intellectually understandable to them, but it provided no comfort.

Some scholars accompanying the aid teams decided to interview and record the stories of the survivors. These narratives, the first draft of history, began to spread around the core islands, revealing the full extent of the horrors committed against the people of Unredeemed Dara during the occupation.

Angry crowds filled the streets of every metropolis and town across Dara: veterans' societies, craft guilds, workers' leagues, ranked scholars, merchants, stevedores, waitresses, musicians from the indigo houses. . . .

They demanded that their voices be heard.

Some demanded that Jia be executed in the most gruesome way possible; others pressed for Jia to be freed immediately and declared a national hero. Rival protests clashed in the streets and the army sometimes had to be called in to restore order.

Some wrote screeds urging the Imperial army to slaughter every surrendered Lyucu and collaborator, cleansing Lyucu influence from the freed lands once and for all; others insisted that the ideals of Moralism be upheld, and that leniency be the overarching guideline in structuring the peace to come.

Petitions from the College of Advocates piled up thickly on the desk of Empress Shizona, forming a miniature model of the Islands.

Only days after the effigy of Timu and the corpse of Phyro had been buried in the Imperial cemetery near Pan, the Hall of Cultivated Minds was once again covered in white.

The charred remains of a young boy lay on the bier. At Dyana's insistence, the body had been prepared in the Lyucu style, wrapped in the skin of a yearling calf so that only the head was exposed to the gaze of Cudyufin, with a replica of his favorite weapon, a child-sized war club fashioned from a piece of garinafin antler, next to him.

Fara and Dyana knelt together next to the bier. Fara lit a bundle of incense sticks and offered her prayers; Dyana reached out with shaking fingers to paint the burnt face of her brother's corpse with earthen pigments. Each moved awkwardly, aware of the other but unwilling to acknowledge her.

The negotiations were not going well, and even at this private moment, when the two were supposed to be members of a family, not opposing leaders of nations, the tension was palpable.

"You won't reconsider?" asked Fara.

Dyana shook her head resolutely.

The final moments of her brother's life were seared into her mind's eye.

"A Lyucu warrior never surrenders!" Todyu shouted. He was standing on the roof of the guest compound. Thick smoke and flaming cinders swirled around him, mixed with wind-whipped snowflakes.

Dara officials and soldiers scrambled on the ground below, helpless. Multiple attempts had been made to save the boy, with ladders extended to the roof or carts filled with hay below. But Todyu had hacked at the ladders with his war club and burning pieces of wood, forcing the would-be rescuers to retreat. An airship circled overhead, draping a long rope ladder, but Todyu had run to the part of the roof where the fire was most intense, as though the flames offered protection, not death.

"Dyu-tika!" Dyana screamed. "Don't do this!"

"Traitor!" he shouted at Dyana, spitting in her direction, his eyes filled

with hatred. "Coward! My only regret is that you escaped the fire. Mother should have drowned you when you were born."

The words lacerated her heart. Her brother, the one person in the world who shared her memories and should be closest to, saw her as not even human.

A second airship approached through the night, moving slowly. Its gondola was filled with ice water taken from Pan's central cisterns. The airship aimed directly for the boy on the roof, ready to drench him and the burning canopy, now on the verge of collapse.

"I am Todyu Roatan," Todyu screamed through the thickening smoke, his voice hoarse and wild, "son of Vadyu Roatan, daughter of Tenryo Roatan, Pékyu of Ukyu-taasa. I will not bring shame to my ancestors. I will purify my tainted blood with fire. I die a Lyucu, not a Dara-raaki."

He dove into the sea of flames and disappeared.

"My brother must be given the Lyucu rites," said Dyana, choking back a sob. "His body should be left in an open field in the wilderness, to be reclaimed by tooth and nail, beak and claw. Pédiato savaga is the only way for his spirit to find peace."

"Would you consider a compromise?" asked Fara. "He is, after all, as much a child of Dara as of Ukyu. Suppose the body is placed in an open field within a fenced enclosure and covered by netting for three days, before—"

"No!" said Dyana. She paused to bring her voice back under control. "Todyu cannot be buried within the Imperial tombs. He hates everything . . . Dara; I cannot betray him after his death." Tears spilled from her eyes as her shoulders heaved with a new wave of grief.

Fara sighed. Dyana was a most difficult negotiating partner. Intense, serious, a masklike face concealing all emotions, she fought hard over every concession, every article, every logogram, determined to wring out every possible advantage for the Lyucu. The girl, despite her affinity for and knowledge of Dara culture—no doubt the result of Timu's tutelage—sometimes acted as though she had no connection to her father's people at all.

The empress sometimes forgot that Dyana was a child, her niece. She resisted the impulse to wrap her arms around the crying girl.

A yawning gulf of diverging interests and experiences divided them, and it couldn't be bridged so simply.

Tentatively, she tried again. "A burial would do much to bring a measure of reconciliation between the Lyucu and the natives. Funereal rites mean more to the living than the dead. To inter Todyu as a part of the Imperial family will have great symbolic meaning for both the Lyucu and the people of Dara—"

"He is not a *symbol*," Dyana spat between gritted teeth. Todyu's face, contorted with hatred and despair, persisted in her vision. As much as she believed that surrendering was the only option left for the Lyucu, she couldn't dispel her brother's accusation. *Traitor! Coward!* Guilt burned in her throat like bile. "He is my brother, and he is not a part of *your* family."

Fara stiffened. "Take care with your words."

She took deep breaths to calm herself. She must try to reason with the young pékyu. "The negotiations have dragged on for too long, and you must see that public sentiment is turning against both of us. The court is under enormous pressure from the people to take a vengeful stance against the Lyucu. Meanwhile, in Dasu and Rui, sur-viving hard-liners are fanning the flames of Lyucu supremacy again, now that the immediate plague of tolyusa-thirst is under control.

"Just earlier today, protesters in Ginpen almost blocked an aid fleet from departing, demanding that we cease curing the Lyucu. And I've just received word that a group of Lyucu thanes in Dasu killed their guards and escaped into the jungle, calling for a general uprising—"

"Can you blame them?" Dyana gazed at her aunt defiantly. "Jia perverted the sacred tolyusa into an instrument for the destruction of the Lyucu people. Do you have any idea of how many Lyucu have died in the most shameful way possible, not on a field of battle, but from fighting each other in the madness of tolyusa-thirst?" Looking away, her eyes fell on the burnt face of Todyu. She shuddered, and focused her baleful gaze on Fara once more. "Do you have any idea of the pain we endured, watching proud warriors reduced to the walking dead, pining and groaning for another dose of the poisoned berries? Do you—"

"Enough!" Fara said. "I *do* blame them." Her voice was sharp and searing.

The empress strained to keep her body from trembling. She had been solicitous of Dyana, but the young pékyu playing the victim had pushed her patience to the breaking point.

Again and again, Fara reminded herself that the child had grown up surrounded by Lyucu hard-liners who fed her a steady diet of a twisted view of history and reality. Even if she had been aware of Lyucu atrocities against the natives, the events were distant, abstract. But the tolyusa-thirst had struck those closest and dearest to her: her mother's loyal thanes, respected shamans, her own brother. What horrors she must have experienced as Ukyu-taasa crumbled around her. It was natural for her to overcompensate for the fact that she was only half-Lyucu by wholly taking up their cause. How else could she, a mere girl, secure the support of her mother's thanes as she negotiated for her people's future?

And . . . Fara couldn't help but see traces of Timu in Dyana's self-righteousness, in her stubborn defense of the Lyucu. Dyana was indeed her brother's daughter, and it was heartbreaking to see her fall into the same trap as Timu.

But appeasement was getting her nowhere. She needed to try a new approach.

"And I blame *you*," Fara added, her voice now cold as ice.

A disbelieving Dyana opened and closed her mouth several times. Finally, she squeaked out, "What?"

"I blame you for behaving like a foolish child blinded by grief, instead of a leader of a people and a princess of Dara."

"I am *not* a princess of—"

"Yes, you are! Being born to both the lineage of Tenryo Roatan and the House of Dandelion may feel to you like a curse—believe me, I know—but that is what the gods have decreed for you. With that comes responsibilities, duties, the weight of history. You and your brother are both symbols, and you must choose whether to use that symbolism for good or ill."

"Fine! I choose to reject you, same as my brother—"

"Then you've chosen the Courage of Brutes," said Fara. "And

you've doomed the rest of the Lyucu. If the armistice is broken, then the only thing that awaits all of them is death."

"You are as bad as that witch Jia!" screamed Dyana. "You are evil!"

Fara slapped Dyana hard across the face, and the crisp sound reverberated in the mourning hall. After a moment of stunned silence, Dyana leapt at the Empress of Dara like a wounded animal, growling, biting, scratching. She switched to speaking in Lyucu entirely, showering her aunt with the worst curses she knew.

Palace guards at the entrance of the mourning hall rushed in, but Fara shouted for them to stand down. It took some time before she subdued her niece, pinning the girl's hands behind her and holding down her kicking legs by kneeling on them with one of her own.

Fara breathed heavily. Her white dress had been torn, and her hair was a mess.

The girl stared at Fara contemptuously, and then spat at her.

Fara did not bother wiping the spittle away. "You speak of the suffering of the Lyucu thanes from tolyusa-thirst. But you've said not one word about the mountains of corpses near Kriphi, victims of starvation, overwork, and outright massacre. What about the cries of despairing parents diving into the sea to drown themselves when they found that they had been fed the flesh of their children? What about the terrified sobs of children forced to dig graves for their grandparents before they were buried alive in those same mass graves? Have you forgotten the rapes, tortures, maimings, and killings authorized by Cutanrovo, your mother, and grandfather?"

The fierce hatred that had lit Dyana's eyes faded, replaced by a growing despair. "Not so many would have starved if you had kept on sending food instead of poison. *I* blame Jia—"

"Don't you dare," hissed Fara. "Don't you *dare*. You're a very clever girl, Dyana, but take care that you don't deploy your intellect to evade responsibility, to draw false moral equivalences, to seek the refuge of dishonest relativism. To cling to the lies of a narrative of Lyucu victimhood is an act of contemptible cowardice beneath you!

"Empress Jia cultivated the worst tendencies already present among your mother's thanes and warriors to accelerate the fall of a corrupt empire, and she exacerbated the suffering of the people in Unredeemed Dara in order to prevent the deaths of millions in a general, all-out war. But Cutanrovo's aim was enslavement, subjugation, the extermination of the people of Dara. She wanted to cleanse the land of all traces of the people who were already living there. If you pretend not to understand the difference between them, then you are an utter disgrace to your people, and especially to your father."

Tension suddenly drained out of Dyana's limbs as she ceased struggling and began to cry. Fara let her go, and the young girl collapsed to the floor in a heap.

A moment later, Fara pulled her into a fierce hug.

"My father," Dyana sobbed. "O my poor father. He thought there would be another way."

"Your father was gentle in nature, and he tried to reason his way to the impossible. He sought to make the lives of the enslaved people of conquered Dara more bearable through more abject submission. But had the accommodationist faction gained the upper hand, do you really believe the natives in Unredeemed Dara would have been free? Lyucu supremacy was the foundation of Ukyu-taasa, and a gentler, kinder enslavement would still have been enslavement."

Dyana wanted to argue, but she couldn't. In her heart, she knew that Fara was right.

"Timu couldn't accept that evil cannot be appeased away. By the time he realized the role he had played in aiding and abetting evil, it was too late."

"My mother was a good person," sobbed Dyana. "She had to preserve the conquest of my grandfather, to bring about a better life for her people."

"The greatest evil is often committed in the pursuit of the good," said Fara.

"Would you say that about . . . my grandmother then?"

Fara hesitated. "I don't know if I can judge her. It's common to see powerful lords sacrifice the lives of the common people to benefit their loved ones, but Empress Jia sacrificed everyone she was close to—including herself—to benefit the lives of the common people. In her single-minded pursuit of the goal of freeing the people of

Unredeemed Dara and building a lasting empire of peace, she committed terrible acts."

"I can't forgive her."

"To understand is not the same as to forgive," said Fara. "I understand why Pékyu Tenryo and Tanvanaki did what they did, but that doesn't mean I forgive them either. Your grandfather and mother dreamed of a better life for the people of the scrublands, but they tried to achieve it by killing and enslaving others, and that cannot be countenanced. However, you can still realize their dream through another path."

Dyana broke from her aunt's embrace and sat up, looking confused. The two had, perhaps unwittingly, fallen into the poses of negotiating partners again.

"The Lyucu must become part of the people of Dara," said Fara. This was the heart of the impasse in the negotiations. Dyana and her thanes, fearful of the loss of Lyucu identity, insisted on some measure of autonomy—preferably a separate territory—for the surrendered Lyucu, but the idea of a state within a state was a nonstarter for the Inner Council.

"If the Lyucu transformed into part of the people of Dara, then the Lyucu would be no more," said Dyana.

"Listen to me," said Fara. "The ways of the scrublands cannot be the ways of the Islands. You've seen yourself the consequences of trying to impose on this land a way of life unsuited to the conditions: the destruction of farms for open range, the loss of soil and vegetation under trampling herds, the ruination and starvation. Ukyutaasa is an impossibility."

"You want the Lyucu to live like the natives," said Dyana. "But that cannot be. Our culture, our nature—"

"There is no such thing as unchanging nature," said Fara. "How can the Lyucu become part of the people of Dara if they insist on standing apart? If you seek a better life for them in the generations to come, if you don't wish for cycles of vengeance and reprisal to echo down the ages, if you want to stop violence being committed in the name of purity of blood and immaculacy of tongues, then the Lyucu must change."

"You are demanding my mother's people to submit, to no longer be Lyucu," muttered Dyana.

"No," said Fara. "I'm asking the Lyucu to have the courage to become *more* Lyucu."

Dyana looked at her, uncomprehending.

"I know you are haunted by your brother's dying words, accusing you of treason," said Fara. "But when he started the fire that night, he wasn't just trying to kill himself, but to murder all of you. He would rather slaughter all those he claimed to love than to see them begin a new life in Dara. He would rather doom all Ukyu-taasa than to give its inhabitants hope. *That* is the true betrayal of the Lyucu people."

Dyana flinched. Fara had spoken aloud the doubt in her heart, a doubt that she had not dared to confront.

"How can such a cult of death be the Lyucu spirit, point the way to the future?" asked Fara. "The people of the scrublands are survivors. I know the tales of Afir and Kikisavo, who would not yield even to the gods in their quest to learn a new way of life. Pékyu Tenryo once led the Lyucu to rebel against the Agon against all odds, transforming the scattered tribes into one united, unstoppable force. Tanvanaki learned to speak our language, to worship our gods, to take off on the back of a garinafin launched from the swaying decks of a city-ship. My intended learned to become an engineer as skilled as any to be found in all the Islands. The Lyucu have never been afraid of change, of hope, of new dance-stories."

Dyana's heart thumped. There was truth in her aunt's speech— Goztan had said the same thing using different words. "But the demands of honor . . . the wishes of my grandfather . . ."

"Honor, pride, the commands of our ancestors—these are not unalterable laws of nature we must submit to. History is like the string of a kite: It tethers us to the ground, but it is also what allows us to fly. Will you try to lead your mother's people to soar to happiness? Or will you commit them to an irreversible plunge into oblivion?"

"How . . . how can you be so certain that your vision is right?"

"I can't be certain," said Fara. "Many in Dara advocate a hard line toward the Lyucu, to do unto them as they did us. They say that the Lyucu can never become part of the people of Dara. Can I foretell the future and say they're wrong? No, I cannot. But I am not my aunt-mother; we cannot become the monster we strove so hard to defeat, even if I cannot see the farther shore."

"So you are also . . . full of doubt."

Fara nodded. "Where doubt ends, evil begins."

Dyana pondered. To give up on a separate enclave for the Lyucu . . . to abandon the dream of even a tiny version of Ukyu-taasa where the people of the scrublands could live apart, pure . . . Was that something her mother would have contemplated? Was that something her grandfather would have tolerated? What was the right thing to do?

"I must . . . speak to my thanes," said Dyana. "But meanwhile, I'll send Thane Goztan to pacify the rebelling Lyucu in Dasu."

Fara nodded, and the two continued tending the corpse of Todyu.

The tension in the air seemed to have dissipated just a bit, like the air after a thunderstorm.

A new day. The formal negotiations resumed.

"Let's begin with Todyu's burial," began Fara.

Dyana shook her head.

Fara's heart fell.

"He has made his choice," said Dyana, "and we cannot unmake it for him, to lie through his bones. But while the dead have run out of choices, the living must still go on."

Hope flared in Fara's heart again.

"I don't deny the importance of symbolism," said Dyana. "I will become a Princess of Dara, if you wish to grant me that title. I am a daughter of the House of Dandelion, a child of these Islands. My father's dream matters as much as my mother's."

"I'll draft the proclamation right away—"

"There is one condition," said Dyana. "I'll also retain the title of Pékyu of Ukyu-taasa."

"What?" asked a confounded Fara. "There is no more—"

"The fear among the Lyucu is that they'll be scattered to the ends of Dara in small pockets where they'll be at the mercy of the natives, that their children will forget the existence of their ancestral land, their language and customs, their gods and traditions. They fear to be erased."

Dyana waited. Complete integration of the Lyucu was indeed the favored proposal among the Inner Council.

"So let Ukyu-taasa remain a separate province, with me as the pékyu. I won't have an army, but otherwise give me the powers of one of your governors. Let me attempt to accomplish what my father could not. Let me find a way to encourage the Lyucu to live next to the people of Dara as neighbors, but remain their own people, connected to their own community."

Even before Dyana was finished, Fara was shaking her head. "They must become part of the people of Dara. For them to remain separate is to invite conflict, hatred, mutual suspicion, certain ruin down the years. One nation cannot belong to two peoples."

"How can you be so certain? Are you one of the gods, able to see down the years, decades, centuries? How can you have no doubt?"

Fara was at a loss for words.

"You can no more force a people to call themselves by the name of their enemies at point of sword than you can force my brother to call himself a child of the House of Dandelion," said Dyana. "But the heart is a living thing that grows and learns, and with time, the unimaginable becomes real. The mightiest thunderstorm will not leave a single mark in the stone floor of the courtyard of this palace, yet the Islands are full of valleys carved by the flow of trickling springs over eons.

"My father told me that there was a time when merchants from Wolf's Paw would refuse to trade with merchants from Xana, a time when the inhabitants of Haan would be outraged to be thought of as belonging to the same nation as those from Cocru. Who knows if the descendants of the people now living in Dasu and Rui, whether of native descent or Lyucu blood, will not all one day proclaim themselves the people of Dara by carving logograms from wax as well as etching figures in turtle shells?

"If you have faith in the way of life of a free Dara, then do not force the Lyucu to become Dara, but let them choose."

Fara closed her eyes. Dyana's dream was lovely.

"How can you think you'll achieve the dream that failed both of your parents?"

"I am tethered by their history, but I am not bound by their path. I was born to this land, but the blood of two peoples flows in my veins. I am a child of Ukyu-taasa in Dara, the first generation free to choose. I am not afraid of an empathy that encompasses two worlds."

"The path you've chosen is full of obstacles and traps, terror and dread, perhaps even blood and iron. Are you certain?"

"No, I am . . . full of doubt. But it is the more interesting path."

Fara smiled. She stood up, regal and erect, the bright red Imperial dress cascading around her like a shimmering fall of fire in which golden crubens and dyrans swam and danced, striving to rise up to meet the uncertain future.

"It's time," said Empress Shizona.

Dyana stood before this most august sovereign of the reunified Islands of Dara, raising both arms to cross them at the wrist, saluting in the Lyucu manner. Then she fell to one knee, placing both hands atop the other knee. She gazed up at the empress, and for the first time, she saw the resemblance between her aunt and her father, and her heart broke again.

My heart accepts.

Shifting into full *mipa rari*, Dyana bowed down in *jiri*, hands crossed in front of her chest, eyes lowered. The movements were awkward. She had practiced the gesture with Timu as a little girl, but this was the first time she had ever had to perform it.

"*Rénga,*" she whispered, "I, Dyana Roatan, daughter of Vadyu Roatan, daughter of Tenryo Roatan, serving the Lyucu as Pékyu of Ukyu-taasa, surrender."

Empress Shizona placed a hand on Dyana's head, and the girl felt the warmth of her palm, steady and steadfast, the hand of a helmswoman who had glimpsed a way out of the raging storm.

"Rise, Dyana Roatan Garu," intoned Empress Shizona. "Henceforth you shall be known as Princess Dyana, newest flower of the House of Dandelion—"

A shiver went through her body. Dyana took a deep breath and held still.

Leaving her hand over the young woman's head, Empress Shizona went on, "And also as the daughter of Timu and Vadyu, descendant of Kuni Garu and Tenryo Roatan, serving her people as the Pékyu-Governor of the Province of Ukyu-taasa.

"Your people shall be my people, my home your home.

"Welcome home, Zaza-*tika*."

Before the Seal of Dara could be applied to the scroll, the terms of the surrender negotiated by Empress Shizona and Pékyu Dyana had to be debated in formal court. The debates lasted three days.

Ministers, generals, nobles, governors, the Lords of Dara in full assembly, listened to testimony. Victims from Dasu and Rui were brought in by airship to describe their suffering under Lyucu occupation; farseers returning from investigative trips gave their frank assessments of the physical conditions in Ukyu-taasa and relations between the natives and Lyucu tribes; military officers reported on nascent rebellions and Lyucu hard-liner remnants who had turned to piracy and banditry; surrendered Lyucu thanes on the mend testified to the horrors of tolyusa-thirst; and many, many scholars, philosophers, officials, and orators presented plans to address various aspects of the crisis.

After many heated exchanges in open court and whispered discussions in backrooms, the broad outlines of the plan were adopted, but with numerous refinements.

The Province of Ukyu-taasa, consisting of Rui and Dasu, would be subdivided into multiple counties, each to be administered by a magistrate appointed by Pékyu Dyana with the Inner Council's consent. Each county would also be garrisoned by a detachment of the Imperial army to keep order and peace, with the commanding officers and military monitors reporting directly to Pan. Weapons of every kind, whether metal blades or bone clubs, would be forbidden to the civilian population in Ukyu-taasa.

The surrendered Lyucu tribes would be given land of their own around both islands, mostly taken from villages that had been depopulated by the Lyucu massacres. The settlements would be large enough to maintain a sense of community, but not so large as to create a sense of self-sufficiency. Most of the counties would be majority native, but some, concentrated around Kriphi—which would be rebuilt with funds from the Imperial Treasury—would be majority Lyucu. But there would be no exclusively Lyucu counties; most Lyucu villages would be sited near native villages.

The proposal to give the land of the dead victims to the surrendered Lyucu was extremely controversial, and the veterans' societies as well as a majority of the College of Advocates argued strenuously against it. They contended that the move amounted to yet another act of violence against the memory of the victims.

The empress pointed out that the Lyucu and their descendants had to be settled somewhere, and this solution disturbed the existing population distribution in the islands the least. But the objectors refused to yield. A few advocates vowed to call upon the people of Dara to protest in the streets again if the empress did not withdraw her proposal.

In the end, Zomi Kidosu, who had lost both of her parents to the Lyucu, proved the decisive voice. She volunteered not to seek title to the land in Dasu that had belonged to her parents, instead dedicating it to the resettling of a Lyucu family. "This isn't an act of forgiveness, for it is neither my place nor desire to give absolution for the horrors committed by the Lyucu. But the dead do not need land; the living do. Let those who will now live on the land I was born to refill it with hope and love."

The proposal passed, with the additional requirement that the resettled Lyucu must repair the desecrated ancestral graves in the depopulated villages and tend to the graves of their victims, especially when the lineages had been entirely cut off.

Fara came to see Zomi in private to thank her for her support.

"Perfect timing," said Zomi. "I was about to come see you to tender my resignation as Farsight Secretary."

Fara looked in shock at the scroll she had been handed. "I thought you had agreed to help me. With Uncle Cogo also resigning, I need you more than ever!"

"Gori Ruthi has done great work as Acting Farsight Secretary;

indeed, he's far more suited to be chief spy than I ever was. Cogo and I both are too much associated with Empress Jia. A new reign needs new voices; you need ministers who are dedicated to your vision, actors associated with the future rather than the past."

Fara knew that Zomi was right, but she couldn't help looking betrayed.

Zomi chuckled. "Like my teacher, Luan Zyaji, I was never suited for dancing in the crosscurrents of power. I've given half my life to the Dandelion Court; I'd like to spend the rest of it for myself."

"I thought you wanted to reform the Imperial examinations—"

Zomi held up a hand. "Let me show you something."

She left for her bedroom and returned carrying a chest—the kind scholars used to store their libraries when on the move. She held it reverently, as though it held treasures of inestimable value.

She opened it and took out the objects one by one: a thick codex with stained and warped pages, a jar of pickled caterpillars, pots of candied lotus seeds, a few turtle shells etched with strange patterns.

"Your sister doesn't write much, both because it's hard to pass a message through the Wall of Storms and because the most important message of all—that she succeeded in her mission to stop Lyucu reinforcements—is best conveyed by the very absence of anything coming through. However, she did write me a few times over the years." Zomi pointed at the shells.

Fara examined the patterns etched on them: a three-legged *kunikin*, a blooming lotus over a tranquil pond.

"I don't understand."

"Ignorant of the progress of the war against the Lyucu, she couldn't write explicitly lest the letters be intercepted. So she wrote in code, in a language that only I would understand."

She went on to explain the role the *kunikin*-engraved shells had played in Jia's deception of Tanvanaki. The *kunikin*, a reminder of where Zomi and Théra spent their first night together, was a private message of love, but the Lyucu had read it literally upside-down and saw in it a promise of more garinafins from the homeland.

". . . And then this last letter, an etching of the blooming lotus, arrived just a few days ago."

Fara caressed the shells that spoke mutely, imagining the life of her big sister, a legend in her own right.

"Théra has put down roots in Ukyu-Gondé. She is the lotus seed that has carved out a new life on distant shores."

Fara looked for signs of sadness in the older woman, for hints of regret. She found none.

"She's telling me to live this mortal span to the fullest," said Zomi. Her eyes moistened but she was smiling. "'A withered branch still remembers the caress of the wind; the salty main still recounts the dance of departed fins.' We're dyrans streaking past each other in the vast deep, but our shared lightning flash will illuminate the darkness ahead until we are embraced by the eternal storm."

Fara was struck by the depth of love in her voice. Carefully, she set the shells down. "What . . . will you do?"

"Luan Zyaji was an exceptional teacher, but he took few students. I will not have children, but I'd like to spread his wisdom and my insights to many more. When the peace with the Lyucu is concluded, I'd like to spend some time with Savo—I don't know my brother well, and he's the only family I have left now.

"Then I'll travel back to Dasu with the remains of my parents so that they can find peace under the earth of their ancestral village. There, I hope to start an academy where all may attend for free."

"I suspect you'll have eager parents wearing grooves into your threshold," said Fara, laughing. "To study under a former head administrator of the Imperial examinations is every scholar's dream."

Zomi shook her head. "There are plenty of places focused on the examinations. I don't intend to teach the Ano Classics at all. I would like to focus on subjects that are more *interesting*. Empress Jia defeated the Lyucu with an herb, and Emperor Monadétu drew on the help of companions who disdained the system. There should be ways for men and women of talent to find happiness and success in Dara beyond one path, even if that path was laid down by the One True Sage."

"You don't believe the Imperial examinations can be reformed to be perfect?"

Zomi looked thoughtful. "Could the Imperial examinations ever have elevated Rati Yera and her companions? Could constructed models ever capture every facet of the irreducible irregularity of reality? Could any scheme of artful testing ever replace the nature of suffering and the qualia of experience?

"No matter how much we reform them to be more equitable, more fair, more relevant, the examinations will always have to serve the system. But a system of bureaucracy, the fruit of mortal design like any other machine, can never be perfect. Over time, it is compelled to grow more elaborate, more intricate, more layered, its organs and authority expanded and its institutions and ideals ossified. Even as it constrains the power of would-be despots through interlocking levers, it also insulates those in power from the consequences of their decisions, makes them unaccountable. An individual may leave their teeth on the board; a bureaucracy, never.

"A totalizing system turns always into tyranny, and there must be room for the absence of system, the province of freedom. There should always be flowers blooming outside the walls of a garden, for to cultivate away all wilderness is also to harvest death. Ra Oji was right: *Gotha co malo co pirupha, luphy-ga ça düsén co crucogéü ki othu ro üa rén né, dotrodo racrulu micru ga théthutefinélo.* 'The cored lotus seed should be most prized, for in that emptiness lies infinite potential.'"

Fara pondered, and then smiled. "You are a better farseer than you admit."

Zomi smiled back, and the two sat and discussed her plans long into the night.

The ratification debates continued in formal court.

Under the resettlement plan, the Lyucu tribes could choose to use their allotted land as they saw fit. If they wished to continue the herding of long-haired cattle, that was within their right. But as the amount of land attached to each village was not large enough to provide for the grazing of massive herds, the Lyucu would have to negotiate with their neighbors for grazing rights, trade for additional food, or take up farming themselves.

"Many Lyucu fear that they cannot remain Lyucu if they must farm," fretted Princess Dyana to the empress in private.

"Many natives fear that Dara cannot remain Dara if the children of invaders are granted the same rights as natives," replied Fara. "Some fears must be confronted, rather than appeased. Herding simply cannot provide as much food as farming, and the Lyucu cannot depend on handouts. We all must change."

"Then there must be support for the Lyucu to adopt farming," said Dyana. "They'll need seeds, tools, experienced farmers to provide instruction, and Cultivationist experts to help with the recovery of natural tolyusa."

"As governor and pékyu, these will be matters within your province," said Fara. "But do not single out the Lyucu for special treatment. Such aid would be necessary for all the citizens of Ukyu-taasa, including those whose farms were expropriated by the Lyucu."

Dyana nodded. "Speaking of power . . . will I be allowed to promote the Lyucu into positions of power?"

"Of course," said the empress, a little taken aback by the question. "Lyucu magistrates and officials would be not only allowed, but perhaps even necessary. You'll need them to maintain not just the appearance of fairness, but also the substance. A fair Ukyu-taasa, welcoming to all, cannot be exclusively administered by only one people."

Dyana breathed a sigh of relief. Her thanes were afraid that Pan would impose various limits on the surrendered Lyucu, similar to the abolished ancient restrictions on the *raye*, war captives and their descendants.

"But any Lyucu officials must be held to the same standards as the rest of Dara," added Fara. "Special favors and relaxed standards would only promote a sense of separateness, destroying the very foundation of the peace."

"That means they must pass the Imperial examinations to become *toko dawiji*," mused Dyana, "or even *cashima*, for the senior posts."

"That is right."

"They will have to learn the language of Dara, and to become proficient in the patterns of thinking encoded in the Ano Classics. Some Lyucu parents will never permit their children to go to school to study the logograms."

"That is also their right," said Fara. "But the Ano Classics and officialdom will not be the only means to success." She thought of Zomi Kidosu's plans. "Dara is changing, and all talented individuals will have a path toward elevation."

"Many Lyucu will see this as an attempt to pressure them to become more like the natives."

Finally, the meaning behind the pékyu's line of questions became clear. The empress answered carefully. "Different parts of Dara are different, and it was Emperor Ragin who set the precedent of tolerating local variation. To this day, many in Cocru continue to prize writing in the old logograms that Mapidéré abolished, and the cult of the Hegemon in Tunoa flourishes without interference.

"Our policy in Ukyu-taasa will not be a mirror image of the Lyucu's. There will be no laws against the Lyucu language or religious practices; there will be no legal distinction between subjects of native or Lyucu ancestry; terms like 'togaten' or '*Anojiti*' will receive no official recognition.

"But there must be one standard across the Islands to bind its various peoples, and if the Lyucu see advantage in entering government service, they will learn the Ano Classics and other new forms of knowledge."

"Well said, *Rénga*." Dyana bowed. "Then you'll no doubt be glad to consent to my request for tax relief and Imperial assistance for building schools all across Ukyu-taasa."

Fara stared at the grinning face of her niece. "We . . . can certainly discuss that." She had been tricked, she realized. Princess Dyana was a fast learner in the ways of bureaucratic maneuvering for the advantage of the people of Ukyu-taasa.

Never had she been so happy to discuss taxes.

"But I warn you," she said, "as governor, you'll be subject to the same oversight by the circuit intendants as any other official. No special favors."

The most difficult proposal of all was held back until the third day.

Other than the execution of about a dozen of the most senior hardliner thanes and leading collaborators for the atrocities committed in

Ukyu-taasa, everyone else involved in the Lyucu invasion of Dara would receive a full and unconditional pardon.

There would be no trial of Lyucu warriors for the murder and enslavement of the population of Rui and Dasu, no trial of the native collaborators who saved their own hides by working with the invaders, no trial of Jia Matiza, who killed many and engineered the downfall of Tanvanaki's regime.

"What about reparations?"

"What about vengeance?"

"What about justice?"

Empress Shizona spoke through the beaded veil of her crown.

"You've heard the testimony from Ukyu-taasa, Lords of Dara. Can you find any Lyucu in Dara, even children as young as six, who didn't participate in one of Cutanrovo's killing gangs? Can you find any native who survived without having had to inform, desecrate, sell out, or otherwise aid and comfort the invaders? Yet, many collaborators and Lyucu accommodationists also strove to save lives, even as they carried out the policy of Lyucu supremacy. How do you weigh merits against sins? Shall we sentence them all to death?

"Many families in Ukyu-taasa are the result of rape or forced concubinage. Indeed, the Imperial family is one of them. But children have been born from such unions. The families of the abducted claim the right of vengeance, but many of those taken as well as their children now plead for mercy for their Lyucu captors. Each family is a capsule of the oppression and resistance, the crimes and acts of salvation, the horrific contradictions of Ukyu-taasa. What do you think is the Moralist path through such thickets?

"And we here in the core islands cannot claim full innocence. The merchants who grew wealthy, the scholars who succeeded at the examinations, the indigo house partners who rose to prominence, the farmers and tradespeople who enjoyed the fruits of peace—even if we hadn't personally traded with the Lyucu through pirates, all of us benefited from the peace bought at the price of the suffering of the people of Ukyu-taasa. My brother, who never forgot the shackles binding Rui and Dasu, was the exception rather than the rule. How many of us can claim to have rallied behind him, yielding up blood and treasure for freedom? Our omissions, no less than our acts, condemn us.

"How do you achieve justice, Lords of Dara, for all the victims, without drowning the sea in blood and choking the land with bones?"

The walls of the Grand Audience Hall reverberated with her voice, but was otherwise silent.

"Show trials cannot bring justice when so many have died and so much has been lost," the empress went on. "The Hegemon sought vengeance for the death of Cocru soldiers by murdering Xana prisoners at sea, and that only brought more death and cycles of violence. Noda Mi and Doru Solofi sought to rebel against Emperor Ragin by exploiting grievances felt by those who had once fought for the Hegemon, and the result was more injustice. More blood is not the answer to a gaping wound. We cannot be trapped by history."

Puma Yemu stepped out. "The victims must not be forgotten."

"No, absolutely not," said Fara, her voice cracking. "To forgo the pursuit of justice isn't to resign ourselves to blithe oblivion and shouldn't be taken as a gesture of absolution. The Imperial Treasury will allocate funds dedicated to the goal of remembering.

"The testimony of the victims and perpetrators of the horrors in Ukyu-taasa will be transcribed, and book-mirrored copies of these records will be distributed to every corner of the Islands and made accessible to the public to ensure that these horrors are never forgotten.

"Legal formalisms for apportioning blame and justification are inadequate in the face of extraordinary horror, where suffering exceeds mortal comprehension. But that doesn't mean we abdicate the duty for moral judgment. Let the debates of the legacy of Tenryo and Tanvanaki, of Empress Jia and Emperor Monadétu, continue down the annals of history.

"May the gods watch over Dara, and may our descendants judge us with care and compassion."

No one was happy with this non-resolution clouded in doubt, but they accepted its necessity.

Fara stared at the young woman standing before her, her heart tied in knots. In some ways, this was the hardest task yet in her young reign. It was never easy to punish a friend, much less a friend who had grown up with her like a sister.

As difficult as it had been to convince the Dandelion Court to accept the terms of the surrender, not all the Lyucu were content with what Pékyu Dyana had wrought either.

Uprisings erupted. Some were hard-liner loyalists seeking to resurrect Cutanrovo Aga's fantasy; others were inspired by rumors of the death of Pékyu-taasa Todyu—to them, death was better than life.

Aya Mazoti and Goztan Ryoto had been dispatched to quell them. The military monitors' report of Princess Aya's performance was scathing. She had been hesitant, vacillating, reluctant to engage with the rebels. Had Goztan not decisively assumed command, many more lives, both Lyucu and native, could have been lost.

"I am relieving you of your command," the empress said. "You are also hereby stripped of all military rank and fined three years' benefice." The worst was yet to come. "The Inner Council has determined that you should be expelled from the College of Strategists so that you'll never be given a military command again."

Aya's shoulders slumped.

Fara's heart convulsed. Aya, the daughter of the great Gin Mazoti, had been groomed from childhood for a life of martial glory. That path was now forever closed to her. What was she going to do?

To Fara's amazement, when Aya looked up, the empress saw in the eyes of the princess only gratitude, not resentment or despair.

"Thank you, Ada-*tika*," whispered Aya. "You don't know how long I've been hoping for a day like this."

"What?"

"All my life, I've lived in my mother's shadow. Zomi and Phyro expected me to become another marshal, and because I couldn't bear to disappoint them, I made myself think it was what I wanted, too. But the first time I was sent out to a real battle, I realized what a mistake it was. I hate military strategy; I hate riding and shooting; I hate killing."

Fara nodded. *You can't force anyone to live a story that doesn't feel true to them.*

"What will you do, sister?"

"I don't know," said Aya, looking lost, but not distraught. "But my mother's name has finally been cleared. I feel I can say goodbye to her."

Fara approached and hugged her, and the two sat together for a long time, talking of inconsequential things.

The final sealing of the treaty of surrender and reunification was to take place on the day of Empress Shizona's wedding. The empress was going to take as her consort the son of the most important thane among the surrendered Lyucu.

Teahouse storytellers and ranked scholars nodded thoughtfully and pronounced themselves satisfied with the new empress's strategic acumen. A political marriage was clearly helpful at such a tumultuous time to reassure the jittery Lyucu tribes. It was rumored that the consort-designate was a young man favorably inclined toward Dara culture, perhaps even an adherent of the Mendist faith. That reassured the skeptics in the streets.

No one asked whether the empress loved the consort-designate; how was that relevant in a marriage intended as political theater? Besides, the empress would surely take other consorts and lovers as she pleased in the future, as soon as the situation in Ukyu-taasa stabilized. That was the way of the great lords.

The young man in question had in mind something he wanted to do, and he went to speak to his mother to get her blessing.

Goztan told him of the latest round of horrors in Ukyu-taasa: of naros-votan who refused the antidote for tolyusa-madness and killed the messengers; of thanes who killed their children before committing suicide; of rebels who leapt into the sea and drowned rather than surrender to a future they saw as dishonorable.

The young man listened mutely to the account of pain and suffering, not averting the eyes of his imagination. This was the real world, not the world of myths in which a god could redeem the whole world by his own suffering.

She also told him of signs of hope: of itinerant Mendist monks who healed all they met, regardless of the tongue they spoke; of naros and culeks who, though weaponless, tried to defend native villagers from rebel raids; of native villagers who sheltered Lyucu orphans and hid them from roaming vigilante gangs.

The young man listened mutely to the account of small steps and tender beginnings, not averting the eyes of his imagination. This was also the real world, in which we should all drown in the shoreless sea of suffering but for the barge that was faith—faith that the world could be healed.

For her part in quelling the rebels, the Inner Council had awarded Goztan the rank of Third General of the Cavalry. She would be in charge of the squadron of garinafins seized from the surrendered Lyucu, an extraordinary vote of confidence.

"General Gozotan Rito." He switched to Dara, and used the form of the name adapted to the habits of the tongue. "Goztan Ryoto" was too hard for the people of Dara to say, and there was no Lyucu word quite matching "general." "It has a nice ring to it."

She replied likewise in the tongue of Dara. "It is something to get used to. Thank you for picking out the logograms for my name."

He took a deep breath and fell to one knee, placing both hands atop the other knee. The formality felt necessary, comforting.

He told her what he was planning.

"I will never forget who I am," he added.

Then he said it again, this time in Lyucu, as if affirming it in one tongue was not enough.

She looked at her son in wonder. What he was asking could be seen as a betrayal, a rejection of her. Perhaps this outcome had been inevitable the moment she had sent him into exile from Ukyu-taasa on that dark night, or even earlier, when she had begged a Dara scholar to teach him the ways of this new land.

She thought back to that sleepless night long ago, when she herself had a different name, and when she had swapped stories with a peasant named Oga Kidosu on the deck of a city-ship, when they had come so close to understanding each other and remained so far apart.

She thought about what it meant to be called "Obedience" versus "Gozotan Rito"; to war against Admiral Krita versus to surrender to Phyro Garu; to have one's name taken from them versus to take up a foreign name willingly; to be coerced to become someone else versus to learn to change for a better future; to hold on to things out of fear versus to enlarge the self to new experiences out of hope. Some things could look so similar superficially, but be so different in nature.

"I know," she said. "And you have my blessing."

She repeated it again, this time in Dara.

"You are certain?"

"I am. An Imperial Consort is also a symbol, and weighty as precedent."

Fara held his hand, moved beyond words. Her intended had decided to formally adopt the Dara name "Kinri Rito" before marrying her. Like Dyana being given the title of Imperial Princess, Kinri's gesture would do much to reassure everyone of the sincerity of the Lyucu desire to become part of the people of Dara.

Names didn't matter, but they also mattered a great deal.

"My teacher, Master Nazu Tei, gave me that name, 'a sign.' I never realized, until now, that it is the act of naming, not the name itself, that is the sign."

Though he assured her that he had come to the decision willingly, she couldn't quite dispel a twinge of guilt.

"I know this wasn't the path you envisioned for us—"

He held up a finger against her lips. "I haven't forgotten what you taught me about poetry; I understand your Imperial name."

The Classical Ano logogram in Fara's new name was usually translated as "observant." But for those familiar with the history of old Xana, the local topolect reading for the logogram, "shizona," was an onomatopoeia for the sound made by the rustling knot-bells worn by dancers at the court in Kriphi.

> Words lie, but not the music of your limbs
> Sweeping over me, moonlit ocean waves.

Centuries ago, the Imagist poet Suzaré had composed those lines about her lover, Lady Jito of White Sleeves. One could readily imagine the gentle susurration of the knot-bells as the legendary beauty twirled, glided, and leapt across the flagstones of the Grand Audience Hall, enchanting the king, the ministers, the generals, and the admiring poet alike.

Fara had continued the musical theme of her family in choosing an Imperial name, but it was coded to allude to the moment when she and Kinri had fallen in love. The dream of a life free from obligations, duties, politics, and the weight of history and re-remembering was not dead, only put on hold.

"Whatever names we are known to others by, I will always be your Thasé-teki and you my Dandelion. You're the mirror of my soul, my wakeful weakness."

She pulled his face down and locked their lips in a long, fierce kiss.

PAN: THE THIRD MONTH OF THE TWELFTH YEAR OF THE REIGN OF SEASON OF STORMS AND THE REIGN OF AUDACIOUS FREEDOM.

For the first time since her wedding, Empress Shizona came to see Jia Matiza. Kinri was occupied with seeing to Zomi's departure, and Fara suspected that he wasn't eager to meet this particular in-law.

With the help of Lady Ragi, Jia was packing for her departure as well. She had few possessions, and one trunk was more than sufficient. Dressed in a plain hempen robe and wooden walking shoes, the former empress looked like any other aged herbalist from fog-shrouded Faça. Having been stripped of all titles of nobility and rank, she was now simply referred to in the official court histories as "Jia Matiza, first wife of Emperor Ragin, a commoner."

"*Rénga*," said Jia, bowing in *jiri*.

"Aunt-Mother," said Fara, bowing back. "I wanted to see if you had everything you needed."

After her pardon, Fara had offered Jia the choice to stay in the palace the rest of her life in seclusion. The former empress was such a controversial figure that it was hard to imagine her emerging from these walls. But Jia had petitioned Fara to be allowed to travel to Ukyu-taasa, where she thought she could conduct research on the sequelae of tolyusa-madness and the various chronic conditions suffered by victims of Lyucu torture and hard labor, and devise cures. She also volunteered to help with the effort to bring back the unenhanced varieties of tolyusa that had been devastated by her engineered blight.

The people of Dasu and Rui need healers.

The empress had consented. But Fara also noticed that Jia refused to call the new province by its formal name, Ukyu-taasa. Jia accepted the empress's policy toward the Lyucu, but that didn't mean she agreed.

"The Imperial Academy has been most helpful," said Jia. "Ragi and I have all the equipment and herbs we need. I expect we'll be ready to leave for Ginpen this afternoon."

Fara nodded. She had a thousand things she wanted to say to Jia, and yet, none seemed adequate. Her aunt-mother was going to live among the very people whose lives she had done the most to harm. Was it an act of courage? Of contrition? Of defiance? Of seeking absolution? She suspected that even Jia didn't know. The heart was complicated.

"I suspect we'll never see each other again," said Jia. "But there are a few words that I wish to be relieved of, lest they stick in my throat like fish bones. May I be frank?"

Fara nodded.

"What you've done will cause endless strife and suffering down the ages," said Jia. "To leave in our midst a population full of contempt for our traditions, to allow those responsible for massacres to pass on their language and desire for supremacy generation after generation, to give them the room to assert their own identity and to hold themselves apart—you have buried the seeds for a future rebellion, a disaster that will lead to the deaths of thousands.

"If that were all, it would be bad enough. But you've done worse and more. You've chosen to commemorate the victims of Lyucu misrule rather than allow the atrocities to be forgotten, thus ensuring that the wound of history will remain ever-open and suppurating.

There is nothing more powerful than constant reminders of the past to push the descendants of victims to demand justice and descendants of the perpetrators to feel themselves victims. You've set Dara up for unending cycles of mutual hatred and vengeance.

"Kuni Garu knew that some enemies cannot be lived with; he had to pursue the Hegemon to the bitter end. Your act of mercy today may in decades to come be seen as an act of cruelty, a gesture worthy of that Moralist fool who tried to show compassion to the wolves, Zato Ruthi."

Fara's face turned stony. Jia had spoken aloud her deepest fears.

She was plagued by doubt that she had been too soft, too accommodating, that she lacked the edge of cruelty necessary for a good sovereign, that empathy was not, in fact, enough.

Terror flooded her heart. The lives of the countless future victims of her weakness, of her compassion, formed a bloody sea, a sepulchral storm. She felt like a woman on the verge of drowning, a kite about to be ripped apart.

The voices of Phyro and Kinri spoke in the maelstrom of her mind.

The world may not be fair, but we must strive to make it so.

The world is a dark place, but we must strive to make it brighter.

Like Lord Lutho's helpful turtles, they kept her afloat; like twisted silken strands, they tethered her to the ground.

"You speak of possibilities, of tendencies, of potentialities, not certainties. You cannot see the future. You can be wrong." As she spoke, her faltering voice grew stronger. "You were so fearful of the threat of militarism that you did everything you could to weaken the army, to keep Phyro from fighting.

"Yet, he convinced the people of Dara to back his war, despite your interference. And when the fatal moment came, when the lives of millions hung in the balance, he stayed his hand on his own, without your manipulation.

"Do you also know that because he defeated the Lyucu with honor, he is viewed with great admiration among them? It was out of that sense of trust he had earned that the Lyucu, after the fall of Ukyu-taasa, believed they could come to Pan to seek peace rather than to struggle on, saving hundreds of thousands from senseless deaths.

"You never foresaw what kind of man Phyro would become. You never foresaw that even in death, Phyro would do his part to defend and preserve the lives of the people of Dara.

"You cannot read that which has yet to be written."

Jia stood still, looking impassive. Was she surprised? Or had everything, even Phyro's aborted invasion and the effect it had on the Lyucu, been part of her plans?

At length, Jia said, "Neither can you."

"No, I cannot see the future," Fara shot back. "I cannot be sure that my decisions will be judged by history to be right.

"But to deem only that which guarantees survival to be virtuous is to think like Cutanrovo; to believe that only that which leads to victory and conquest is of value is to follow the faith of Tenryo.

"Compassion and empathy are not safe and easy paths, and they require the striving of all the people of Dara, Lyucu and native alike, for generations. But such is the lot of mortals. Even the wisest, most far-seeing leader cannot hope to determine the fate of their descendants.

"Step aside, Aunt-Mother. I will resolve the crisis facing Dara my way, not yours."

For a long, tense moment, Jia remained still.

" 'It is both a curse and a manifestation of grace,' " she muttered to herself, her eyes unfocused, looking into the distance.

Gradually, her face relaxed. She bowed deeply to the empress.

"You sound just like your sister."

After a pause, she added, "I once thought it best for Dara to be a land in which it didn't matter who was the sovereign, but I'm glad it is your hand that holds the Seal of Dara."

Fara breathed hard. Had that been a test? Had she passed? She wondered if she would ever understand Jia, the most subtle and fearsome leader of Dara.

A faint peal of thunder overhead, as though the gods wanted to break the tension.

It was time to get on with the business she had come for.

"I wanted . . . to offer you a ride to Ukyu-taasa."

She turned and summoned the future pékyu-governor through the door.

"Grandmother," said Princess Dyana.

A variety of emotions flickered across Jia's face. "You look just like my Toto-*tika*."

"My father spoke often of you," said Dyana. "He always regretted not being able to carry out the proper duties of a son."

Jia forced back the tears. "What is your name?"

"Dyana."

"A Lyucu name," muttered Jia.

"Yes," said the princess, "for I am a child of the Lyucu as well. But my father also gave me a nursing name: Zaza-*tika*."

As in Mati*za*.

"Sit by me, Zaza-*tika*. I . . . am glad to know you."

Unobtrusively, Fara retreated from the room. A winter's worth of ice could not melt in a single spring day, and neither could a wound lasting half a lifetime heal in a single meeting. But it was a start.

I think I've just found the name for my reign.

CHAPTER FIFTY-SIX

SPEAKING BONES

UKYU-GONDÉ: THE THIRD MONTH IN THE TWELFTH
YEAR AFTER THE DEPARTURE OF PRINCESS THÉRA
FROM DARA FOR UKYU-GONDÉ.

Spring.

Life returned to the scrublands, as did wars. The remnants of the Lyucu and the scattered Agon tribes fought and clashed, killed and died.

The chiefs and thanes fought for the memories and dreams of dead pékyus, for grievances lost in the mists of mythological dance-stories, for titles and honor and treasured artifacts of long-vanished fleets. They fought, in other words, for grand, epic stories.

But the naros and culeks, unmoved by such high ideals, fought for a much simpler story that was no less compelling. The scrubland was a harsh and unforgiving place; there were always too many people for too little food. Those who won had garinafins, cattle, sheep, pemmican, fire-dung; the victors didn't have to push their grandparents into the eternal storm; the conquerors didn't have to leave their babies behind as they chased the green grass sea.

It had always been this way, and so it had to be a true story, didn't it?

Rumor sped across the scrublands on the wings of garinafins and by the mouths of the wandering tanto-lyu-naro. Something was happening in Taten-ryo-alvovo, the City of Ghosts, the land of forbidden mounds on the shore of the salt flats.

As the spring winds blew across the salt flats, stirring up columns of white smoke, hulking beasts of pure white bone emerged from the haze.

Comparable in size to adult garinafins, the walking arucuro tocua were cobbled together from the bones of aurochs, mouflon, and dead warriors. In form they brought to mind not so much the warlike monsters that had ended the Fifth Age, but fantastic beings of grace, lightness, playfulness: ethereal whales with wing-fins, wobbly muntjacs with stilt-like legs, turtles with wise-seeming heads looking in six directions . . . and many beasts that had no earthly analogs at all.

In place of hearts, the beasts had in their empty rib cages massive, dangling charms. Fashioned from articulated bones that rattled and clacked with each step, the charms were enlarged versions of the talking bones invented by Théra's sons: "fire" plus "movement" to mean *dance-story*; "mouth" over "air" over "mouth" again to mean *re-remembering*; "lifted empty hand" enclosing "heart" to mean *hope*.

Propelled by the strong wind that undulated the membranous sails over their backs, the arucuro tocua beasts, devoid of pilots, strode resolutely out of the salt flats and spread in every direction. Every few hundred steps, when the bone gears inside had revolved a preset number of rotations, the beasts stopped, and began to sing.

The singing mechanism had been adapted from the Divine Voice, the aural weapon that had once devastated the Lyucu host. Inside each beast, as a garinafin wing-tip needle ran through the groove in the unwinding scroll, the tiny, trembling voice that emerged was transmitted to the sympathetic vibrating membranes of a set of mammoth storm pipes. Powerful cords of twisted sinew then squeezed the sail-pumped air sac, driving the compressed air through the garinafin bone pipes, vibrating the vocal cords, until the beast amplified the voice a thousandfold, and a thunderous spirit portrait boomed across the land.

The scrolls animating the bone beasts had been prepared by Çami and Sataari.

By having a spirit-portrait player sing into the ear of a spirit-portrait taker, they made many copies from one original by tracing and retracing. The copies weren't perfect—fidelity was degraded, extraneous noises introduced, the *now* indistinctly layered onto the *already*, becoming a whole *always*. Such was the nature of all stories passed from lips to ear, whether the organs were of flesh or bone. But the truth in the voices, through the hisses and skips and distortions, remained intact.

The score consisted of multiple voices, spliced and wound together, a chorus of the re-rememberings of the Lyucu and the Agon, of ancestral voices and present thinking-breath: ancient heroes of the Fifth Age, Afir, Takval, Théra, refugees in the City of Ghosts. . . .

The voices spoke of the past, of the beauty that had once been and the beauty that was still within reach. They spoke of the glory that had once illuminated the city of mounds on the shore of a Sea of Tears teeming with life, of fields of viridian barley and patches of marrow tubers. They spoke of the drying of the rivers, the shrinking of the lake, the coming of starvation and strife, the fall of a way of life.

They spoke of the ascension of Théra, and the love that allowed Takval to give her his last breath. The body was gone, but the breath lived on.

Adapt, adapt, sang the voices. *Discard old enmities. The way forward is not to be afraid of change. We have always changed; we always will, to be who we are. The best way to honor our nature is to re-remember the future.*

Come to the Barrows. Gather on the revitalized shore of the Sea of Tears. The scars of drought have healed; the water of life has refilled. Here you'll learn a new way of life, which was once the way also of Afir and Kikisavo. Here you'll join a new people, a people who cultivate hope from long fallow fields, who conjure living breath from silent bones, who have turned the City of Ghosts into the Gathering of Life. For us to triumph doesn't mean they have *to lose.*

As the singing bone beasts wandered the scrublands, passing herders, Lyucu, Agon, and tanto-lyu-naro, stopped to listen. Long-haired cattle lowed; garinafins moaned; dogs yelped. The hearts of the people were moved, enticed by the spirit portrait of the soul of a people.

The warring chiefs and thanes, alarmed by the singing beasts, ordered their warriors to attack with fury. But the feral garinafins that had been released by Théra came to their rescue. Survivors of the feral garinafin assaults affirmed that the singing arucuro tocua were protected by the gods. Legends grew; myths multiplied.

In time, some of the beasts would become tangled in the grass sea and collapse; others would be destroyed by storm and rain; still others would fall prey to fire-cattle stampedes or garinafin breath, commanded by the ambition of thanes and the pride of chiefs.

But once the story of the Gathering of Life had been told, it couldn't be untold. Tyrants could burn books and bury scholars, slaughter story-dancers and mutilate spirit portraits. But a lung-song passed from mouth to ear, from heart to mind, could never be silenced.

CHAPTER FIFTY-SEVEN

THE REIGN OF ENDURING SPRING

The wine-dark sea was dotted with ships.

Once, the waves this far north of the Big Island had been the favored hunting ground of pirates. But city-ship battle groups now patrolled the shipping lanes, their complements of garinafin riders ready to take off at a moment's notice to enforce the freedom of the seas. The merest glimpse of General Gozotan Rito's standard—a stylized depiction of Gaslira-sata, the Peace-Bite—was enough to make every remaining pirate captain flee beyond the horizon.

Four years ago, in the immediate aftermath of the Lyucu surrender, most of the ships heading to Ukyu-taasa had ridden low in the water and returned empty. Supplies and workers had to be brought to the devastated islands of Rui and Dasu: rice, sorghum, jars of pickled vegetables to feed the hungry; bolts of cloth and stacks of blankets to clothe the cold; seeds and implements for the empty fields; tools and construction material for the rebuilding of Kriphi—and many, many skilled artisans and workers needed to put everything to use. The Imperial Treasury's program for the reconstruction of Ukyu-taasa had been like a rich banquet at which everyone wanted a seat, and merchants of every description competed for a lucrative government contract.

Nowadays, the shipping was more balanced. While silk, lacquerware, metal tools, bamboo furniture, porcelain, and other goods from all over Dara continued to flow to Ukyu-taasa, plenty of goods were flowing the other way as well. Free-range long-haired cattle beef, for instance, had become a delicacy prized by many in Dara after Lady Gina Cophy, Ginpen's leading food critic, published a loving essay praising the Splendid Urn's "Lyucu Brisket," consisting of long-haired cattle beef grilled on a sun stove (or, as Lady Cophy put it, "Under the sizzling gaze of the Eye of Cudyufin"), flavored with "authentic Dasu spices" that made the eye as well as the mouth water. For an extra thrill, she suggested that the tongue-scorching grilled meat be complemented with an order of creamy, frozen Lady Rapa's Feast.

(The cynical claimed that Cophy had been so over-the-top in her praise only because she was trying to curry favor with the Throne. Empress Shizona and Consort Kinri had paid a special visit to Ginpen shortly after their wedding and stopped at the Splendid Urn for a meal. The food—by all accounts just simple home cooking—had so impressed the empress that she had presented Lodan Tho and Mati Phy, the Splendid Urn's manager and head chef, with a logogram sign in her own calligraphy: "First in Dara." The empress had also given Widow Wasu, the restaurant's owner, the title of Lady of the First Rank by Writ on account of "extraordinary achievements in hospitality." No one could figure out just what the widow had done to deserve such an unprecedented honor, and most rumors that attempted to explain—the widow had presented the empress with a thousand-year-old homunculus mushroom of immortality; the widow was actually the empress's long-lost grandmother; the empress and her consort had once worked for the widow as a waitress and a busboy—were too ludicrous to be credited.)

In any event, the chef responsible for the dish, once a culek relegated to the drudgery of mess duty for Lyucu garinafin riders, suddenly found himself the most desired guest of Dara noble households. Every master chef in Dara seemed to be rushing to explore the craze for hybrid Lyucu-Dara cuisine.

(To be sure, not all Lyucu cuisine was proving to be popular with the rest of Dara—"sheep sponge," for instance, remained revolting to most whether served hot or cold, and there were even movements by some public health officials to ban the dish entirely.)

Likewise, the long cattle hair, when spun into yarn, was soft and warm, and possessed a unique shimmer that proved very much in demand by the fashionable. It helped that researchers based at the new Imperial laboratory in Daye had developed a mix of hardy native grasses suited for sustainable ranching of long-haired cattle. Shippers were bringing live cattle as well as meat and wool to every port, and fortunes were minted in Ukyu-taasa as Lyucu herders and native traders worked together to buy up more land for grazing.

Even kyoffir had become big business. Though the beverage was traditionally incompatible with the constitution of most natives of Dara, Jia Matiza had devised an herbal supplement that, if ingested shortly before consuming kyoffir, allowed them to enjoy the intoxicating drink without suffering any of the ill effects. Craft breweries, both Lyucu and native, had sprung up all over Dara like bamboo shoots after a spring storm, and ranked scholars vied with one another to come up with fanciful names for different types of kyoffir to increase the mind-pleasure of connoisseurs. It was considered the mark of high fashion and good breeding to hold kyoffir-tasting parties.

Above the surface ships darted speedy airships, transporting perishable goods and passengers who couldn't bear the long sea journey. Some of the airships still relied on manure gas, but others had been upgraded with the pure lift gas from Lake Dako. While many commercial air carriers still relied on rowers with bulging muscles straining against massive feathered oars to get their passengers to Ukyu-taasa as quickly as possible, a few particularly bold carriers— the adjective applied both to their adventurous engineering and the exorbitant prices they charged—had outfitted their airships with silkmotic mills and spinning dyran fins so that their vessels rumbled and dashed across the skies, leaving other airship captains in their tail turbulence looking on in envy.

One of these speedy airships was *Soaring Kunikin*, owned and operated by the Wasu clan.

~

Far in the stern of the gondola, away from the hubbub of the observation lounge at the bow, a mother and her son sat quietly at a table in the cafeteria, two cups of tea and a small dish of candied lotus seeds between them.

"Have a lotus seed," urged the mother. "They're really good. You haven't eaten since we got aboard. Are you not feeling well?"

Dutifully, the boy, about seven years of age, picked up a sweet treat and ate it. But he seemed not to taste it at all; his brows remained knitted in a deep frown incongruous with his years.

"Well," he said, at length. His voice was so faint and raspy that one could have mistaken it for a throat-clearing croak.

The mother caressed his forehead affectionately, smoothing a stray lock of hair into place. She was used to his laconic nature. It was, after all, the reason they had been on the Big Island for the past year.

"Pain," the boy croaked again, pointing at his stomach.

"What happened?" The mother got up and knelt down next to her son, anxiously rubbing his stomach. "Was it the mock duck we had at the monks' canteen? How long have you been in pain?"

The boy shook his head. He pointed at the front of the gondola, then wrapped his arms around himself, rocking forward and back.

The mother understood. "You are afraid of seeing *them* again because we're going home."

The boy nodded.

He had been born in a fishing village in Dasu, near the end of the terrors in Ukyu-taasa. He learned to talk early, and was a great pleasure in the lives of his parents. When he was three, his village was visited by a group of rampaging Lyucu culeks in search of sport. His father hid the toddler in a wicker fish basket and told him to be quiet, no matter what. His father had then been castrated and disemboweled, and his mother raped, and he saw everything from his hiding place. From that day on, he never uttered another word.

After the liberation of Ukyu-taasa, his mother had begged the healers from the core islands for a cure for his muteness.

"The injury is in the mind, not the tongue," a Mendist nun told her.

"My art is not enough. But if you can go to the Temple of Still and Flowing Waters, the brothers and sisters there may be able to help."

She had scrimped and saved, begging for coppers from the reconstruction workers sent from the core islands to rebuild Ukyu-taasa. Finally, she had enough to take her son on a journey to the Big Island to visit the temple of legend.

The nuns and monks tried everything they could think of to heal the boy. They gave him solitude and silence; they bathed him in warm spring water; they massaged him with silkmotic wands; they immersed him in the company of children his age at play; they chanted the stories of Rufizo Mender and Toryoana Pacific; they played the *moaphya* and held his small hands against the vibrating bronze slabs. Above all, they tried to make him feel secure, safe, free from the terrors that clouded his mind and sealed his throat.

She had needed the respite too, to heal herself.

After a year of work, the boy was able to speak a single word at a time. The abbot, with defeat and compassion in his voice, explained to the mother that they did not think they could make any more progress.

The abbot wondered if the pair would prefer to stay in a big city on the Big Island, where there were many more opportunities.

"No," the mother said. "We want to go home."

So the abbot had bought them tickets on *Soaring Kunikin*, which was supposed to have the smoothest ride and the best accommodations.

"Them," the boy said, and wrapped his arms around himself even tighter.

The mother's heart broke. His terror was manifesting as a physical ache. She didn't have to imagine the effort it took for him to speak past the horror, the pain that would not let go. She felt it, too.

"They can't hurt you again, baby," she said, hugging her son tightly. "They are no longer allowed to do what they did."

The words of comfort felt hollow, ineffective. She couldn't even bring herself to say the word "Lyucu." Besides, how could she promise that they would never hurt her and her son again? As far as she knew, the culeks who had slaughtered the village remained alive and well. Empress Shizona had granted them all an unconditional pardon, and Princess Dyana, daughter of Tanvanaki the Butcher, was the Pékyu-Governor of Ukyu-taasa.

"Why?" the boy said.

She didn't know what he meant. *Why had the Lyucu done what they did? Why had the people who killed his father and raped his mother not been punished? Why was the world the way it was?*

But the answer to all the questions was the same. "I don't know, baby. I don't know."

The great lords strutted and posed on their stage, claimed to speak for those whose voices were too faint. They went to war or made peace, asserted the right of vengeance or granted pardons. They thought they did what was right. But who gave them that *right to decide*?

Was she right to bring him back to Dasu, to the place where he had witnessed those horrors?

"They wanted to destroy me and your father," she said, whispering into his ear in a fierce plea. "They wanted to erase us. The Hundred Flowers like us don't have much, but no one can erase us from the earth."

"Home," the boy said.

"Yes, home!" she said. She pressed her face against his, and their tears mingled. "The monks told me that the former Prime Minister has set up a benefit fund for survivors of the terrors, and once we claim our portion, it will be enough to buy a new fishing boat, one of those with a silkmotic winch. I will teach you to fish, the way my mother taught me. We will make a living, a good living. Your father will smile even on the other shore of the River-on-Which-Nothing-Floats."

"Love," the boy said. He unwrapped his arms from around himself and put them around his mother's neck.

It would take time, perhaps a lifetime, for the child to recover his voice fully. But they would never give up, and he had already made so much progress.

With a tearstained face, she began to sing him an old children's song.

When Dara falls, the people hope.
When Dara rises, the people hope.
When Dara is strong, the people hope.
When Dara is weak, the people hope.
We survive, the Hundred Flowers.
We survive.

In the observation lounge at the front of the gondola, a group of passengers admired the view out of the wide, floor-to-ceiling windows. Wisps of clouds passed by from time to time. Far below, the endless sea was like a wrinkled piece of blue water silk.

"What line of trade are you in, sir and ma'am?" asked a burly man dressed in the homemade clothes and white leggings of a laborer—rather surprising that he had chosen to travel by this expensive means. An honor tablet prominently tucked into his belt revealed him to be a discharged veteran of the Imperial army. The name "Égi" could be seen on the protruding part of the tablet.

Égi was talking to an old woman sitting in a wheeled chair and a middle-aged man behind her, his hair in the double-scroll of a *toko dawiji* and his flowing, well-cut robe incongruously covered by patches in every color, shape, and material.

"I work with machines," said Rati Yera.

"I guess you could say the same about me," said Widi Tucru. "We just work with different sorts of machines."

The two shared a meaningful smile. After a period of mourning for Arona and Mota, the two surviving members of the Blossom Gang decided to carry on the group's legacy. Empress Shizona wanted to give both important posts in the Imperial bureaucracy, but they declined.

"Some flowers do best outside the garden," said Widi.

"We prefer to be friends of Dandelion, not servants of Shizona," said Rati.

"Then it shall be," said the empress. *"We'll always be the extended Blossom Gang."*

The three then stayed up all night, discussing Fara's vision for Dara and Ukyu-taasa. Rati and Widi would help her as they had helped Phyro, using their talents to bring about change. They would take no salary, accept no official title, carry out no Imperial decree. They would travel and work incognito, taking no advantage of their connection with the Dandelion Throne.

They even paid for their own passage on *Soaring Kunikin*—though the Wasus did give them a friends-of-the-clan discount.

"Oh, engineers! That is a good trade to be in," said a woman who wore the triple scroll-bun of a *cashima*. "I have a friend who works at the Imperial laboratory in Ginpen, and she tells me workshops are always begging her to quit government service and join them because they can't find enough skilled engineers. She tells me she likes her work too much to quit, though she'd make much more in a private workshop. You've heard of Kisli Péro, right? She was once my friend's colleague at the laboratory before she quit to become chief designer at Princess Home Furnishings. I heard that she now makes more money than the Prime Minister, just for designing self-heating bathtubs!"

"Don't buy anything from Princess Home Furnishings," interjected Égi. "They're fancy and luxurious, but overpriced and not very practical. Who needs a fan powered by the silkmotic force? Don't people have hands?" He shook his head, clearly contemptuous of anyone who'd waste their money on such gadgets.

The *cashima*, apparently a fan of Princess Home Furnishings, looked annoyed. "*I* think their designs are very thoughtful, functional, *and* nice to look at. For example, they wrap the switches for their silkmotic lamps in glowworm silk so that you don't have to fumble for them in the dark. Imperial Princess Aya has attracted a lot of talented people to work for her. You may have to pay a *little* more for their goods—"

Égi was having none of it. "Pshaw! If you ask me, people buy from them only because of that 'Princess' mark—oh, and because her biggest investor, Cogo Yelu, that sly old fox, had the princess hire Lolotika to be their spokesperson and use their furnishings as props in shows at the Aviary. It's all just marketing to separate fools from their hard-earned silver."

The *cashima*, unwilling to engage further, turned back to Rati and Widi. "Are you going to Ukyu-taasa to build silkmotic mills? I've heard that Pékyu Dyana has a tax credit for them."

"Hmm . . . not exactly," said Rati. To deflect the focus away from herself and Widi, she asked of Égi and the *cashima*, "What about the two of you?"

"I was the deputy treasurer of Toaza"—the *cashima* smiled as the others exclaimed in admiration—"but I've resigned. I'm now headed to Dasu to open a school."

"Really?" Widi looked very interested. "Forgive me for prying— but I would have thought someone with your scholastic credentials would prefer to remain in Imperial service."

"I got tired of climbing the bureaucratic ranks," said the *cashima* with a laugh. "My love is poetry and philosophy, and I have little patience for the minutiae of accounting and the intrigues of office politics. The students in Ukyu-taasa are hungry for knowledge, and they say the Lyucu thanes treat learned teachers with great respect. The salary promised me by the wolf-thane who invited me to tutor his children is many times what I'd get in my old job, and I'd have plenty of time to work on my poems."

"That's why I'm heading off to Dasu, too," said Égi.

"To write poems?" asked Widi, unable to keep the skepticism out of his voice as he glanced over the man's plain clothes and scroll-bun-less hair.

"No, no!" Égi laughed so hard that his eyes turned into crescent moons. "I barely know how to read. My eldest daughter is the real scholar in the family. I meant that I'm going to Dasu to make a fortune!"

Rati's glance fell on the man's honor tablet. "You served in the armed forces? Thank you for your service."

Égi nodded. "Just doing my duty, ma'am. I was a member of the capital garrison."

Widi's face darkened. If the man had served in the capital garrison, then he had likely fought against Phyro's followers during the surprise attack on Pan and possibly played a role in Arona's and Mota's deaths.

Rati put a hand on Widi's arm. When he looked at her, she gave him the slightest of head shakes.

Let it go. That's not what Mota and Arona would have wanted.

Widi sighed. Even after the circumstances surrounding Phyro's death had been made public, it was no clearer who was right or wrong. Everyone had . . . done their duty.

"What trade will you be pursuing in Dasu?" Rati asked Égi, to keep the silence from growing awkward.

"That . . . well, I have some ideas, but nothing fixed in stone. Like I said, I'm from Pan and I've served in the army all my life. When Empress Shizona and the Inner Council announced last year that the army didn't need to be so big anymore now that we're no longer at war and offered to pay some of us old-timers to retire early, I took the deal. My wife and I talked over what we wanted to do. I suggested we settle in Ukyu-taasa since neither of us has aged parents tying us to Pan, and Pékyu Dyana is offering a stipend for people from the core islands to move there."

Rati nodded thoughtfully. Fara didn't share Jia's contempt for the military, and motivated in part by the memory of Phyro, she had been extra solicitous of the welfare of active-duty soldiers and discharged veterans.

I may be moved by the path of Rufizo Mender and Toryoana Pacific, she had told Rati in private, *but I'm no Zato Ruthi. The Courage of Brutes and the Ambition of Nobles remain at large, and the people will need a sword as well as a shield.*

"I suspect there's more to your decision than just a small stipend from the pékyu," said the *cashima*, grinning. "You said your daughter is a scholar? Those who take the Imperial examinations in Ukyu-taasa are given extra points."

"Heh, you know how parents are, always wanting their children to be the golden carp that leap over Rufizo Falls." Égi chuckled, scratching his head. "Since I never saw any action against the Lyucu, my children can't benefit from the empress's new policy giving preferences to decorated veterans of the Lyucu wars and their descendants. That makes the geographical preferences from moving to Ukyu-taasa even more attractive. . . . But, it's not *just* about the extra points. I want my daughter to get the best education possible. Former Farsight Secretary Zomi Kidosu has an academy in Dasu—"

The *cashima* shook her head. "Secretary Kidosu is most learned, but I'm afraid that I cannot condone her teaching methods. She doesn't make her students memorize the Ano Classics, and she encourages them to write in the vernacular and even in Lyucu in zyndari letters—how are they supposed to master their logograms with their attention so divided? . . ."

Rati thought the *cashima*'s objection too shortsighted. It was true that Empress Shizona had put Réza Müi in charge of the committee to reform the next session of the Imperial examinations, and she was well known as a proponent of using only Classical Ano at the examinations to ensure standardization and a level playing field for scholars of diverse backgrounds. But Réza had also always shown a radical streak in her, and now with Empress Shizona pushing forward all sorts of reforms, who knew what Réza was going to do?

The *cashima* went on. ". . . I've even heard that she takes them on random balloon trips to places like Crescent Island and Écofi, filling their heads with useless knowledge about animals and plants. No, no, the One True Sage remains the only suitable subject for a scholar of ambition. If you really want your daughter to do well in the examinations, I can recommend some of my friends' academies."

"Much obliged," said Égi, clearly not very impressed by the offer. "As I was saying, once we get to Dasu, I intend to make a fortune. Everyone knows there is a lot of empty land in Ukyu-taasa, uh . . ." He stopped, realizing that he had unwittingly broached a sensitive topic.

Everyone fell silent. The deserted land plots in Dasu and Rui, as well as Dyana's interest in filling them with more people, were the legacy of the mass graves that dotted the landscape of Ukyu-taasa. They were as much scars in the terrain as in the psyche of the people.

Égi shook off the awkwardness and pressed on. "I'll use the stipend and my savings to buy a big tract. I figured I could set up a long-haired cattle ranch. That's a big business now and likely to grow bigger."

"That's not an easy business to get into," said Widi, his tone stiff and a bit cold. "The long-haired cattle are very different from the cattle in Faça, and you'll need someone who knows what they're doing to help you."

"I know it," said Égi. "Ideally, I'd like to partner with a Lyucu naro-votan. I'll put up the money, and they'll put in the skills. I hear that the Lyucu like to work with veterans because they think we're more honest and trustworthy than the average civilian, on account of their experience with Emperor Monadétu. Once I get the ranch set up, though, I've got other business ideas I want to explore."

"Such as?" asked Widi.

"You know how Lyucu thanes like to collect antiques and calligraphy scrolls to be more cultured? Well, when I was in Pan, I noticed that the lords and ladies like to wear acid-etched bones and shells to be more cosmopolitan. I bet I can figure out a way to sell Lyucu handicraft in the core islands for their weight in gold. I've also seen these very intricate toys that the Lyucu make for their children out of articulated pieces of bone. . . . Anyway, can't let all my secrets out. I've been learning Lyucu in preparation for all these schemes, though it's hard to learn without a partner."

"I'll practice with you," said the *cashima*.

"You're learning Lyucu too?" Though Égi hadn't exactly clicked with the *cashima* so far, this offer piqued his interest. "But I thought you were just going to teach the kids the Ano Classics?"

"How can I explain the full intricacy of the Ano Classics without some knowledge of the native tongue of my students?" said the *cashima*. "I've also found that trying to translate the Ano Classics into Lyucu gives one new insights. Besides, I'm interested in collecting more Lyucu folklore and myth. The mythology collection published by Empress Shizona and Consort Kinri is very popular."

"My daughter read some of those stories to me!"

"Oh, which story is your favorite?"

"I'd have to say Merciful Toryoana of Healing Hands. . . ."

Rati smiled to herself. Though she was still not very proficient with logograms, she was proud of the book-mirror, the joint invention of her and her student Kinri. The book-mirrors had flooded the market with cheap, high-quality books. Any scholar now could own a complete set of Ra Oji's epigrams and Kon Fiji's treatises without paying much more than half a year's rent. It was a luxury generations in the past could only dream of.

"You never explained what sort of machines you two work with," said the *cashima*, looking at Widi and Rati.

Fara had told Widi that Princess Dyana was plagued by a thorny problem in Ukyu-taasa: Land ownership in the two islands was a tangled mess. After the tumultuous changes wrought by the Lyucu conquest and the mass resettlement plans post-liberation, almost every plot of land, empty or occupied, was subject to overlapping and conflicting claims by displaced original inhabitants, resettled Lyucu and natives, distant heirs of the massacred, collaborators, squatters, speculators, and even the government itself. No matter how thorough the bureaucrats' investigations or how impartial the magistrates' adjudications, justice that satisfied everyone was impossible. There would be years of legal wrangling, and in such fights, those with interests more aligned with the state's desire for stability usually won.

There were also other problems beyond the horizon. To secure a lasting peace, the empress had pardoned all the Lyucu, leaving many thanes and naros-votan, as well as their native collaborators, in positions of wealth and power. For the foreseeable future, it was unlikely that claims for reparations by the victims and survivors would receive much attention from either the Throne or the pékyu-governor. But that legacy of pain and suffering would last for generations; the demands for justice could not be silenced forever.

Widi was going to Ukyu-taasa to train paid litigators, especially those willing to take up the cases of the destitute, the powerless, the unheard. Stability was important, even more so in the aftermath of the horrors that the people of Ukyu-taasa had gone through. Without it, nothing else, no reforms, no improvements, no *progress*, could be advanced at all. Yet stability couldn't be its own end. It needed the dynamism of purposeful agitation to seek a new equilibrium. Sometimes the best way to endow the organs of collective decision-making with more intelligence was to stir up trouble, to destabilize, to give those without weapons or voices a way to fight.

But Widi didn't want to openly discuss his thoughts for tinkering with the machinery of government from the outside; he looked to Rati for help.

"Well, I've been working on making the lives of farmers easier,"

Rati said, falling into a lecture. She always did have a professorial side. "As you know, a lot of the land in Dasu and Rui was ruined by erosion and overgrazing, and to make the land productive again requires building retaining walls, irrigation, regrading, fertilizing, seeding . . . a lot of labor. And there aren't enough people in Ukyu-taasa to do the work. So I've been thinking of building machines that could be taught to do some of this work—"

"You know how to work with instructible machines?" asked the *cashima*, eyes wide. Instructible machinery was the most advanced form of engineering, and Imperial Consort Kinri Rito had been put in charge of advancing the art. Not just anyone got to work with such engines. "You must be famous!"

"Err . . ." Rati realized that she had said too much. "I . . . I'm really just a beginner. Oh, look down there! Is that one of those new ships driven by steam? How wondrous! I was fortunate enough to learn a bit about their engineering principles. . . ."

While spinning dyran fins drove *Soaring Kunikin* northward toward a land of not only anguished memories and traumatized bodies, but also of long-flowing hope and infinite potentials, the audience listened, rapt, to Rati sketching for them visions of fantastical machines and clever inventions, as magical as anything in the tales of wandering bards.

PART FIVE
FALLING
LEAVES

CHAPTER FIFTY-EIGHT

THE GATHERING OF LIFE

TATEN-RYO-RUNA ("GATHERING OF LIFE,"
ONCE KNOWN AS TATEN-RYO-ALVOVO, CITY OF
GHOSTS): MANY, MANY WINTERS LATER.

Garinafin riders wearing skull helmets stained the hue of viridian barley arrived in every corner of Ukyu-Gondé.

Each messenger brought a tightly wound scroll of garinafin stomach lining. The scroll was inserted into the arucuro tocua chanter and pulled across to the empty axle. The shaman gently brought the wing-tip needle down so that it just touched the groove etched into the smoky surface. Then, as the shaman kept time with heartbeat and lungbreath, they began to crank the chanter.

The voice of Pékyu Rokiri, aged but strong, commanding but tinged with sorrow, emerged from the chanter's polished trumpet, a blooming bone-flower.

Pékyu-votan Théra Garu Aragoz, the Breath of the Scrublands, Interpreter of the Dead, Re-Rememberer of the Future, was gravely ill.

They came.

They came from the north, where hunters pursued toddling auks across ice floes and warriors proved their mettle by facing off against star-snout bears. Southbound dogsleds sped over Nalyufin's Pasture, laden with fermented ice-shark flesh, marinated star-snout bear liver, auk eggs with double yolks . . . the best and most potent medicines of the people of the ice tribes.

They came from the long western shore, where fisherfolk speared silver gulpers from coracles and coastal villages hauled icebergs from the sea with towering arucuro tocua cranes every spring to irrigate their viridian barley fields and marrow tuber patches. Eastbound cattle teams brought dried seaweed cakes, etched turtle shells, arucuro sana made from bone as well as corals and pearls . . . the best and most pious offerings to the gods.

They came from the east, where Lyucu and Agon settlements dotted the misty valleys in the foothills of the World's Edge Mountains. There, tribes that had decided to take up farming cultivated a mixture of crops that had been domesticated in the time of Afir and Kikisavo as well as new seeds from Dara. The settlements sent westbound delegations laden with sweet tubers, barley-sorghum bread, varieties of tolyusa bred to bring about dreams dedicated to particular gods . . . the best and most precious fruits of the reinvigorated land.

They came from the south, where the oases in Lurodia Tanta were no longer the province of exiled, defeated tribes, but communities of pioneers who had decided to explore a new way of life suited to the desert. They farmed drought-resistant varieties of dates and sorghum, and tended to gash cactus fields. The brave went on long journeys to the south by garinafin in search of new oases. Slowly but steadily, the descendants of Afir and Kikisavo had begun to explore lands unknown to their ancestors. Now, to the north, garinafins carried sun-bleached skulls of animals unknown in the scrublands, cactus spices, sky iron chunks . . . the best and most prized discoveries of a new frontier.

They also came from all over the scrublands, where Lyucu and Agon tribes continued to live in the ancient ways, herding and migrating, advancing and retreating with the seasonal tides of the grass sea. Sometimes, the tribes raided one another, especially when times were lean—but far more often they traded with those who had settled down to farm. A pastoral family might one day decide to join one of the settlements, and a farming family might one day decide to uproot themselves and follow the herds again. Ukyu-Gondé was big enough to support a multitude of ways of life, each adapted to its locale. Even without the stained bounties of conquest, babies didn't have to be left behind because the grass sea retreated too fast one summer, nor grandparents be asked to walk into the eternal storm in a particularly harsh winter. To the Barrows, the pastoral tribes sent skins of kyoffir, polished bones suited for arucuro tocua, pure white fat cattle, sheep with horns rolled in perfect triple-spiral knobs . . . the best and most proper gifts of the scrublands.

Even the wandering tanto-lyu-naro came, bearing no gifts save dance-stories and songs of gods and heroes.

Though Pékyu Rokiri exacted no tribute, demanded no allegiance, led no conquests, the people came to Taten-ryo-runa, the Gathering of Life, where they deposited their presents in heaps as grand as the monumental constructions at the end of the Fifth Age.

Here, fresh water again flowed through the ancient irrigation channels, centuries-fallow fields and orchards again were tilled and tended, and tunnels and caves in long-abandoned barrows were once again filled with song and laughter. Gigantic arucuro tocua structures bowed and straightened, swiveled and dipped, maintaining the old barrows and constructing new ones. At night, shamans congregated on platforms atop the mounds to gaze at the stars and to record their positions in voice paintings.

Here, re-rememberers debated and teased out the meanings of old stories and chanted new ones. Scrolls of garinafin stomach lining were cut apart and pieced back together into a living transcript of the arguments, the elaborations, the compromises. On the Winter Festival and other sacred occasions, the scrolls would be played for days so that everyone would remember that the past, present, and future form not one long monologue of ambition and power, but a living debate of many voices, of cacophonous thinking-breath, to be carried on across the generations.

The epic of Afir and Kikisavo was not over. So long as there were human beings, there would be struggles against the gods and pacts with nature. The Lyucu-Agon would change and resist change, as stubborn as their own hearts and as adaptable as their children.

The people of the scrublands gathered at Taten-ryo-runa prayed for the health of Pékyu-votan Théra, the woman who had united the tribes of the scrublands not into one empire, but one story.

Théra, lying on her side, could hear the prayers of her people in the distance.

It was late autumn; scapula-tree leaves fell from branches framed in the opening of the tent. They made a thick carpet on the ground: vermillion, crimson, ruby, bright red. The fallen leaves would rot into the earth, and then they'd nourish the roots of the trees so that next spring, the new buds would be even greener.

Rokiri, along with the pékyus-taasa, his own children and the children of his brother, were out there thanking the delegates. She would like to join them, but her body, after decades of gradual decline, no longer obeyed her will.

Her glance fell to the pile of bones and clay blocks in the corner of the tent. Her great-grandchildren sometimes played with them. Théra loved to see the youngsters experimenting with arucuro sana as well as the old Ano logogram blocks. They would never know these clay blocks the way she did: poetry tied to the nostalgia of childhood, repositories of the wisdom of a whole people, machines for engineering a whole way of thinking. To them, the clay blocks were no more than curious artifacts, half-understood traces of an exotic and foreign land.

It's all right, she thought. *Such is the fate of all mortals: The life of the parent, no matter how glorious and vivid in their prime, is destined to fade, to fall, to disappear into the soil of memory of the child.*

I should try to record some stories of Dara for them.

She'd have to do it in the language of the scrublands, the only language the children knew, and with which she was now more comfortable than with Dara. It would be difficult; there were still so many things where the perfect word only existed in Dara: the way a student bowed to a teacher, the way a daughter looked up to her father, the stance of a general as she was about to unleash hell. She would have to use awkward paraphrases, inadequate translations, shades of color achingly off from the vivid hues of her memories from that other land.

Even if the children don't care about them now, they might like to have the stories someday, to re-remember the war between the House of Chrysanthemum and the House of Dandelion, to learn about wily Kuni Garu and indomitable Mata Zyndu, to know something about the courage of Gin Mazoti, the steadfastness of Cogo Yelu, the brilliance of Luan Zyaji, the silly escapades of their great-grandmother as a little girl, her schemes and adventures with Timu, Phyro, and Fara. . . .

Sataari—no, she's gone; I'm thinking of her and Razutana's daughter, Leksa. Leksa is going to come soon to take my spirit portrait. Her heart convulsed as she thought of the web of names and loves and regrets and hopes that made up her life. *It has been a good one.*

One name in particular surfaced in her mind like a breaching cruben, a soaring dyran, a diving garinafin; a name that still brought as much longing and soul-ache as that of her cloud-garinafin-riding husband. One was her breath, the other her heartbeat.

She focused her eyes on the bare branches in the opening of the tent, all their leaves gone.

A withered branch still remembers the caress of the wind; the salty main still recounts the dance of departed fins.

Her vision blurred, and the murmured prayers of the people grew until they sounded like the howling of the wind across the emptiness of Ukyu-Gondé, a vast land covered by a vaster sky.

The spiraling, falling leaves turned into storms careening across a grander-than-life stage, dancing-telling stories of gods and heroes.

The air was heavy like water; lightning bolts crisscrossed the heavens; she was adrift in a sea of the numinous.

She allowed her mind to open, to receive, to fall into the fear and trust of the gods.

No, I don't know if the peace will last beyond my death. I don't know if another Tenryo Roatan will emerge in the future, reviving the cult for conquest and death. A people bound by a story of change is both stronger and weaker than an empire held together with blood and bone.

I can only hope, and let the people choose to wander where they will.

I've given all my life to this land, to my people. I have one last request. Please.

Please.

A falling leaf yearns to return to the root.

The storms danced and swerved, gathered and parted. Thunder boomed across the earth-stage, majestic, exalted, magnanimous.

Thank you, she thought.

She sat up, a new vigor infusing her aged limbs.

CHAPTER FIFTY-NINE

HOMELAND

DARA: TWO YEARS LATER.

A falcon stepped off from its eyrie on the new stone tower in the heart of the reconstructed palace of Kriphi.

This tower, housing artifacts and books taken from the famed Vocu Firna Collection, was not a part of the administrative functions of the palace, but a museum open to the public. Alongside the precious physical record of the long history of old Xana, the museum also archived and displayed voice paintings, weapons, and ritual arucuro tocua donated by the Lyucu of the Conquest Generation, as well as shackles, homemade memorial tablets, and knotwork diaries donated by their victims. The full story of Ukyu-taasa would take generations to tell and to make sense of; this was only the beginning.

Every effort had been made by the rebuilders to make this new tower as grand and impressive as the old. Not that it mattered to the falcon—this was the only tower it had ever known.

An adventurous sort, the falcon closed its wings and dropped like a stone, only snapping them open as it neared the ground, lifting off at the last possible second. The falcon was headed for the wetlands outside the city, where juicy loaches and fat bream teemed.

The falcon didn't know that those wetlands yielded such good hunting because they formed a wild preserve sacred to Péa-Kiji, closed off to human development. It was also the site where Garinafin-Duchess Gozotan Rito had undergone pédiato savaga many years ago, riding on a cloud-garinafin into the world beyond the River-on-Which-Nothing-Floats.

The turbulence from the falcon's remiges loosened a clump of dandelion seeds at the foot of the tower, scattering them into the air like a floral snowstorm.

One of the seeds, its tiny fuzzy parachute caught by a breeze, rose high into the air.

Gently, the seed drifted over the market squares: hawkers offering kyoffir tea and tolyusa smoking herbs, skewers of roasted long-haired cattle beef flavored with Dasu spices, silk from Toaza; tea from Müning; antiques from Ginpen; acid-etched turtle shells from Daye. . . .

The Hall of Calculation and Contemplation was where clerks and deputies and undersecretaries researched policy proposals and drafted recommendations for the pékyu-governor, a sort of provincial answer to the Imperial College of Advocates in Pan.

Halting music drifted out of the window of a third-floor office, grew discordant, and then stopped. A young official took her hands off the strings of her silkmotic writing zither and rubbed her tired eyes.

At twenty-five, Tenra Aga was a rising star in the government of Ukyu-taasa. Over a blue water-silk robe, she wore a light fur vest to fend off the morning chill. Her hair was put up in the triple-scroll bun of a *cashima*, held in place with a garinafin-tooth hairpin. She looked out the window, her unfocused gaze taking in the dance of swooping birds, twirling catkins, floating dandelion seeds.

There was no formal court today because the pékyu-governor had gone to the Big Island for a special occasion. But the work of the provincial bureaucracy never stopped.

In fact, Tenra Aga was glad that the pékyu-governor was away. It meant she had more time to finish her difficult task: analyzing two vexing policy proposals. Her sterling academic pedigree—she had studied under Master Péi Thu, one of the most famous graduates from the legendary Academy of Daye founded by Zomi Kidosu—offered little help through the tangled thicket.

The first had to do with a long-standing tax break colloquially known as "the harmony subsidy." Enacted years ago by Grand

Princess Dyana, Ukyu-taasa's first pékyu-governor, the provision reduced the taxes of any household that had at least three Lyucu neighbors as well as three native neighbors. The intent had been to encourage the integration of the population of Ukyu-taasa by discouraging the formation of large mono-ethnic enclaves.

But decades later, with the intermarriage rate ever rising, the policy had become a source of tension. Neighboring households would often coordinate their answers on the annual census to get the tax break. A household with only one Lyucu grandparent might claim to be Lyucu, while a household with three Lyucu grandparents might claim to be native. Families fell into acrimony as members argued over which classification made "more sense." Attempts by the government to impose some order on this chaos and to prevent tax dodging had resulted in voluminous regulation but little harmony.

The gaze of the state has a special power, thought Tenra Aga. *Whatever it looks upon tends to freeze in stone.* The Province of Ukyu-taasa had been founded upon the principle that terms like "togaten" and "*Anojiti*" would have no official recognition, but the very process of pushing against discrimination tended also to perpetuate it. The sorting and classifying of people, even if once motivated by benign reasons, was no longer consonant with the feelings of the people. It ought to be abolished like the extra points that had once been added to the scores of those taking the Imperial examinations from Ukyu-taasa.

But could she foresee all the consequences of eliminating the harmony subsidy? Relations between households claiming Lyucu identity and those claiming native identity were amicable in Kriphi and Daye, but did she really know what things were like in rural villages? Might the yearning to be part of an imagined community of myth and blood triumph over the reality of a shared experience? Would those mono-ethnic enclaves of constructed "purity," so feared by Empress Shizona and Grand Princess Dyana, emerge in the aftermath?

The second proposal was no less complicated. It had to do with a series of portraits of the life and deeds of Pékyu Tenryo and

Tanvanaki produced decades ago in the immediate aftermath of the surrender. The oversized portraits, some of them voice paintings of dance-stories by shamans, some of them traditional brush paintings done by hired artists in the Dara manner, some of them ancestor poles carved from whalebone as well as jade, had been enshrined in the great tents of the first Lyucu villages. To those of the Conquest Generation, the portraits were community symbols, commemorating heroes of the Lyucu people and strong leaders who had struggled valiantly to ensure Lyucu survival in a hostile land. Grand Princess Dyana had tolerated these portraits with little comment—after all, they preserved the memory of her grandfather and mother. In fact, when survivors of Lyucu misrule had tried to deface these portraits, troops had been dispatched to protect them, thereby giving the portraits a quasi-official status.

With the passing of the Conquest Generation, the significance of the portraits shifted. Book-mirrored records of the atrocities committed by the Lyucu under Tenryo and Tanvanaki were available for all to read, and descendants of the perpetrators and victims began to see the portraits as relics of a bygone age, monuments to a repudiated past. The meaning of the portraits grew more sinister still when several riots and rebellions, led by disaffected thanes hoping to revive a "pure Lyucu" Ukyu-taasa, used the portraits as their rallying standard. The "Thanes of Pékyu Todyu" rebels had been quickly suppressed, but the portraits remained the focus of contentious debate.

The policy memo before Tenra Aga, drafted by about a dozen young staff of the Hall of Calculation and Contemplation, proposed the removal and destruction of the portraits. "The Ano sages and the wise tales of Kikisavo alike teach that propriety cannot be judged as the consequences of a fortunate fall. They who brought so much suffering to our people must not be remembered as heroes, even if they were our ancestors." They had signed their names in the Lyucu manner, showing lineages going all the way back to the Conquest Generation.

A counter-memo, drafted by elders in several of the villages with these portraits, argued for their preservation as historical artifacts and apolitical emblems of Lyucu heritage.

Tenra Aga pondered the implications. Given her name, she could hardly be neutral on this matter. All her life, she had lived in the shadow cast by her notorious ancestor, and more than once, she had thought of adopting a Dara family name, freeing herself from the legacy of the hated architect of Ukyu-taasa's darkest years. But in the end, she had decided to keep her name, embracing the dictum attributed to Grand Princess Dyana: *We cannot hope to free ourselves from re-remembering through oblivion. The past is never past; it is the tether that anchors the present and gives us strength to soar into the future.*

Destroying the portraits would surely inflame passions and open old wounds, but keeping them around was hardly better. Arguably, the problem had been seeded back when Grand Princess Dyana appeased Lyucu sentiment of the Conquest Generation by allowing them to be enshrined in Lyucu villages. But the princess had ruled during a different time, with different fears and hopes, threats and promises; was it Tenra's place to condemn her constitutive acts? Doubt, the mother of humility, counseled compassion for the past as well as the future.

And the public, enshrined portraits were but the tip of an iceberg of other controversies: What of the small, private portraits of old Lyucu leaders (including even of Cutanrovo Aga) that some wore as talismans of good luck? What of the growing clamor by descendants of victims for reparations by descendants of native collaborators and Lyucu thanes, many of whom had become prosperous in Ukyu-taasa in part because they continued to occupy positions of power after the surrender? Would the destruction of the public portraits lead to even more rancor and strife?

A bold thought came into her mind. Was it right, even, to continue to have a pékyu-governor of Ukyu-taasa, one of the last hereditary titles of nobility endowed with substantial political power? The system ensured that Ukyu-taasa would always be governed by a descendant of Tenryo Roatan, setting the province apart from all others. This compromise had been necessary to stabilize the nervous surrendered Lyucu, or so it was believed, but those inside an outdated system were also the least likely to see its flaws. Perhaps the time had come to treat Ukyu-taasa no different from any of the other provinces.

The Lyucu spirit is mutagé. Such had been her faith. But how was she to reify that ideal?

Could a full reckoning with the legacy of the atrocities of the conquest and enslavement be delayed forever? Was a full reckoning even possible?

Master Zomi Kidosu was right: History was the hardest subject of all to weigh.

Despair threatened to overwhelm her. She forced herself to pull back, to cling to hope by focusing on the here and now.

A northerly breeze picked up, sweeping the air clear of catkins and dandelion fuzz. A last, lonely dandelion seed drifted across her field of vision, leaving the window empty, like the fresh scroll on the desk in front of her. *Every generation must compose its own destiny. There is no shirking of this duty. Teeth on the board.*

She sighed and then placed her fingers resolutely back on the humming strings of the writing zither. The musical strains, hesitant at first, grew more confident and euphonious as the writer fell into her impassioned logogram-song.

The seed continued south over the island of Rui.

The seed drifted over sorghum fields and rice paddies. Some were terraced along mountainsides, so steep and narrow that they seemed carved by the hands of gods, rather than mortal-kin. Human figures could be seen tending to the crops, tiny ants crawling around a tiered cake. Surely there were too few of them to care for the vast tracts?

The answer could be found in the teams of oxen marching steadily across the fields, boustrophedon. Constructed from wood and iron, they were powered by rumbling heat engines in their bellies. Gears clanged and rasped; pistons pumped and rattled; steam puffed out of their nostrils. The oxen, refined descendants of long-ago proto- types made by the great Rati Yeraji, could be instructed to plow, dig, irrigate, harvest. . . . With the aid of a team of mechanical oxen, a single family could now do the work that used to take fifty.

The seed drifted over broad swaths of land filled with lush but fibrous grasses and bushes, a unique blend of flora specifically cul- tivated for the guts of the herds of long-haired cattle and flocks of knob-horned sheep. Ranch hands on horseback kept watch, most wearing skull helmets to keep the sun out of their faces.

These days, much vaster herds could be found on Écofi, where adventurous herders migrated with thousands of cattle across the vegetal sea, guarding their animals on the backs of garinafins or elephants. But it was said that the best beef and mutton could only be found in Ukyu-taasa, where the ways of the scrublands had found a new life.

The seed drifted over a valley in the foothills of Mount Kiji. This valley, far from the main path winding up the mountain to the Temple of Péa-Kiji, didn't see many pilgrims passing through. But occasionally, Mendist pilgrims devoted to the art of healing did take an extra half day to stop by. They weren't here for a shrine dedicated to a forest spirit or lake deity, but for a tomb located at the very end of the valley.

The tomb was simple, almost crude: a mound of earth reinforced with a circle of stones at the base. The tombstone, only waist-high, held a few sparse lines of logograms:

JIA MATIZA GARU, HERBALIST.

BELOVED WIFE OF KUNI, CHERISHED MOTHER OF TIMU

AND THÉRA, AUNT-MOTHER OF PHYRO, HONORED AUNT-

MOTHER OF FARA, GRANDMOTHER OF TODYU, REVERED

GRANDMOTHER OF DYANA, ESTEEMED TEACHER OF RAGI,

WI, SHIDO, ZOMI, AND OTHERS, DEAR FRIEND OF SOTO.

ONE OF THE PEOPLE OF DARA.

LOVE MAKES US DO TERRIBLE THINGS.

There was no string of elaborate, extravagant, tongue-twisting posthumous titles; no imposing mausoleum filled with carvings of protective spirits and demons; no forest of stone tablets commemorating all her victories in ornate calligraphy. It didn't resemble the tomb of a sovereign at all.

It was Jia's own wish not to be interred in the Imperial cemetery—some thought she was too guilt-ridden to be buried next to Emperor Ragin and Empress Risana. The epitaph, on the other hand, had been composed by Zomi Kidosu—in the end, the one-time Farsight Secretary thought it most appropriate to define Jia not by the controversies that would long outlive her, but by the web of her mortal loves.

In truth, Jia Matiza's reputation had undergone something of a rehabilitation in recent years, especially after the publication of Lady Ragi's biography of the erstwhile regent: *The Silkworm*. Ragi, who accompanied Jia in her work and travels after the Bloodless Revolution, devoted many chapters to Jia's so-called "third act": the research that led to the kyoffir-neutralizing supplement; the refinement of prosthetic limbs for the maimed; the treatment of tolyusathirst sequelae; the recipes for supplementing the nutritional needs of children whose development had been stunted as a result of Lyucu-made famines; the dream-herbs to relieve the survivors of the occupation from unending nightmares; the close bond she built with her granddaughter, Grand Princess Dyana; and finally, the years as a Mendist nun at the end of her life, during which she composed a book of meditations on the tales of Toryoana Pacific, *Amends*.

Though many continued to blame Jia, at least in part, for the suffering of the people of Ukyu-taasa during the Lyucu occupation, and soldiers and veterans held her in disdain for her anti-militarism as well as her treatment of Gin Mazoti and Phyro Garu, the view that Jia was a decent, even heroic, sovereign was ascendant among historians as well as teahouse storytellers.

But it was still much too early to know the judgment of history.

The dandelion seed flitted away from the tomb and glided over a village nearby.

Young children sat in neat rows inside a schoolhouse, and, following the lead of a master, chanted in unison in Classical Ano,

> *A world and an ocean away, beyond the wall-shaped storm,*
> *Whale pods hunt in the lightless deep,*
> *Unconcerned with whether we reap or weep*
> *Or our inconstant form.*

At home, some of them spoke in the Dara vernacular (mostly the local topolect, but a few in topolects from the core islands), some in Lyucu, and still others in a mixture of both. They were one people, all brother-and-sister, votan-sa-taasa. No one knew what the future held, but for now, at least, their voices were in harmony.

As though satisfied, the floating dandelion seed spun up to catch a stronger breeze, and swayed its way toward the other end of Dara: Tan Adü.

Canoes bobbed in the waves. Their rowers were at rest, panting from the exertion of blowing into the whalebone trumpet. Zen-Kara, her hair so white that it resembled the snowy peak of Mount Rapa, sat at the head of the largest canoe, frowning in puzzlement.

An unprecedented number of crubens had been sighted near Tan Adü recently, heading north. Concerned that there was an impending catastrophe, Zen-Kara had demanded to be taken out to the open sea over the vociferous objections of her son, Chief Ra-Garu, so that she could talk to the crubens.

The breaching crubens had not sung any of the songs of danger known to the Adüans, and neither had they seemed distressed. To Zen-Kara's anxious queries, they had responded with mirth. Free and easy in their movements, spouting in delight, they had reminded Zen-Kara of nothing so much as the crowd lining up outside a theater in Ginpen in anticipation of some wondrous new show in her youth.

What are the crubens heading north to see?

The unexpected reminiscence of her youth, triggered by the sight of the crubens, unsettled her. It had been a long time since she had last left Tan Adü or thought of the dreamlike wanderings of her youth.

In the intervening years, she had devoted herself first to the creation of a logographic-phonetic script for Adüan, and then to the composition of a narrative poem recounting the foundational mythologies of the Adüans in that script, the first and most important step in the transformation of Adüan into a grapholect, a language grounded in and strengthened by writing. She had slowed down and then halted the sending of Adüan children to the Big Island for study, believing that they first needed a secure foundation in who they were.

But she hadn't told the entirety of the story of her people. How could she? There was another chapter, a chapter whose full meaning she could barely glimpse through the mists of time. Her people had gained much and lost much, as had she herself, in commerce with Dara. They were of the Islands but also outside of them. Was it time to reengage?

A flicker in the corner of her eye. She looked up. A dandelion seed hovered above her, a tuft of fuzz limned in gold by the sun. Beauty, courage, grand-spiritedness.

Phyro.

"Head back," she ordered the rowers, her voice cracking with age and emotion.

She would retrieve Na-aroénna. She would find Ra-Garu. She would tell him the story of his origin, of the man and the people who had given him half of his being, and let him decide what to do with that knowledge.

She had no idea what would happen next, and she felt utterly free.

The dandelion seed drifted north.

It passed over the Tunoa Islands. There, it took a wide arc to sweep over Zyndu Castle, the Hegemon's Mausoleum. This was a place for worship and veneration of the martial spirit, and favored by enlisted soldiers, sailors, and aviators. They came to offer incense and prayer, to listen to stories of the deeds of the Hegemon told by veterans, and to buy the gilded chrysanthemum charms that would offer protection in battle.

To the side of the main memorial tower was a smaller shrine, in which visitors could view the portraits embroidered by Mata Zyndu's consort, Lady Mira, and read the biography written by his aunt, Lady Soto, titled *By the Time I Bloom*. These offered different views of the Hegemon than the narrative in the main memorial tower, and they moved some visitors, infuriated others, and left still more unsettled. It was hard to say which depiction of the man was closest to the truth.

On and on, the seed rode the wind, gliding over the narrow Tunoa Channel, reaching the Big Island.

Outside Çaruza, the seed lingered in the air above a towering pagoda tree standing alone in the middle of a rectangular plot of rubble. Sweet strings of white flowers dangled from the branches, the low-slung boughs so thick that they could easily have supported the weight of a squad of soldiers, let alone the five or six girls scampering over them now. Their clothes were simple but well-made and clean, marking them clearly as the daughters of well-to-do farmers in the area.

"Have you tried these? They're so sweet!"

"—pfffft, *yuck*—"

"I told you *not* to pick the greenish strands—"

"—don't eat all the good ones! We're supposed to make soup for Mother—"

"Hey, look at this!"

One of the girls hopped down from the tree branch, squatting down at an angular stone half-hidden in the grass. "There are drawings here."

The other girls clambered down from the tree and gathered around her. The rubble-filled plot had once been a modest-sized manor. Abandoned and unmaintained, the house had collapsed and then rotted away, leaving behind only bits of stone foundation and ceramic tiles. The broken stone the girl was pointing at had once been the top of one corner of the foundation. It was covered in childish drawings, evidently done with makeup powder dipped in sap.

The girls, curious, pulled away the tall weeds around the stone, revealing more of the foundation and more drawings.

"Look at that! Two daughters and their mother."

"I don't think she's their mother. See how she's got a halo around her head? I think she's supposed to be a goddess."

"A goddess! Which one? Lady Kana or Lady Rapa?"

"I don't know. . . . Neither . . . See how she's got red hair?"

"Maybe she's not supposed to be a goddess. Just a grand lady."

They chattered like a flock of magpies, trying to make sense of the pictures. Judging by the gradually maturing style, the drawings had been done over a significant period of time. They showed various scenes involving the two girls—sisters, the gang decided—and the grand lady: the sisters sewing while the lady was telling them a story; the three of them cooking together; the sisters climbing over a pagoda tree laden with strings of flowers while the lady watched. . . .

It was a diary, the girls realized. Each sketch was an entry. Below each drawing was a rectangular area filled with dense columns of tiny pictures—the painter had evidently not known how to write, either in stylized flat logograms or zyndari letters, and the simplified pictograms formed a private code, a script for those who already knew the story.

"What's that oval thing with a flap? A purse?"

"I think it's supposed to be a duck. You know, roasted, with the neck bent over?"

"What about that one? A cloud? With drops of rain?"

"No! Ah . . . ahahaha! I think that's a mouth drooling!"

Squeals and giggles of delight. The girls were getting into this game.

"Help me with this! Look at these circles—coins?"

"Nah. Obviously they're grapes."

"Oh . . . wait, what do you mean, 'obviously'?"

"Haven't you noticed? The diary painter was obsessed with food."

"You're right! I guess they must have been hungry a lot. . . ."

The girls themselves had never known hunger, and starvation was but an abstract word taught by their schoolmaster, a monster of indefinite form. But they were faithful attendees at the monthly shadow puppet show at the local veterans' society. The show last month had included a song describing the horrors of the Principate, when the Hegemon had stridden across Dara, lopping off a hundred heads with each stroke, and people had starved to death by the thousands. The way the puppet players turned the flat puppets slowly perpendicular to the screen to show them growing thinner and thinner, until they faded into nothing, had made a huge impression on the girls.

"The sisters are making soup for the grand lady!"

"Hey, look at that bubble coming out of the lady's mouth. I think that's supposed to be her talking."

"What's she saying?"

"Smiling face—upside-down pointy hills—drooling mouth."

"Uh . . . thanks for that *insightful* reading. Do you have an actual interpretation?"

"Well, we saw smiling face means 'happy, good,' right?"

"And those aren't pointy hills—that's supposed to be a crown."

"Oh! Drooling mouth means 'hungry.'"

"Or 'I want more.'"

"Or 'Not enough.'"

"That's it! 'A good king isn't enough.'"

The girls fell silent, awed by the somber message.

"Do you think they lived during the time of the Hegemon?"

"Maybe . . . or at least another time when people were hungry a lot."

"That grand lady kept them fed."

The thought of two little girls from long ago being hungry felt intolerable. The girls climbed up the pagoda tree and stripped it of virtually all flowers. The sweet blossoms were then piled up in front of the broken stone foundation, a fragrant mountain of delicious treats.

A passing breeze, carrying faint voices from the direction of the village.

"Pépé-*tika*! Where are you?"

"Zya-*tika*! Time for dinner!"

"Your brother's going to finish all the pork buns if you don't get back now!"

The girls looked at the pile of flowers. They wouldn't be bringing any home, but that seemed all right.

"I guess I should head back, too."

"See you tomorrow!"

By ones and twos, they ran toward the swirling columns of cooking smoke, toward warm light and unconditional love, toward home.

"A good king isn't enough. . . . A good king isn't enough. . . ."

The dandelion seed nodded and dipped in the air, and then sped away on the breeze.

The seed skimmed over Dimushi, the Capital of Magic.

The Gilded Cage, the Islands' largest theater, with a seating capacity of fifty thousand, was packed. Snow-haired Lolotika was the star tonight, kicking off her fifteenth tour of Dara—following the same route that had once been traveled by Emperor Mapidéré. A decade had passed since her last tour, a revival of *The Women of Zudi*.

Lolo had promised her fans, new and old, a never-before-seen performance.

The curved-mirror spotlights went out one by one, like dying stars; the silkmotic lamps overhead hissed out, like the veiling of the moon. Total darkness filled the Gilded Cage. Every breath was suspended, every pair of eyes focused on the invisible stage.

Something seemed to take shape in the murk. The audience rubbed its eyes.

Phosphorescent phantoms, green and blue and indigo, wriggled in the gloom like fantastic creatures of the deep, or perhaps the first gods of the Lyucu. Even knowing that Lolotika was likely using costumes made of glowworm silk didn't detract from the stage magic.

The sound of pumping, panting, deep breathing, at first faint, then louder and louder until the whole theater reverberated in sympathy, the contraction and expansion of some universal lung. Unwittingly, the audience found itself breathing in sync with this thumping metronome.

A fiery streak, red-orange-yellow-white, lanced through the darkness, a shooting star arcing across the empyrean. The audience gasped, seeming to feel the heat of that celestial fire even from their seats high up the theater walls.

The streak held, thickened, solidified into a curling, flaming tongue. The brightening glow pushed back the gloom to reveal an old woman as the wielder of the burning whip: Lolotika, nimble, lithe, triumphant, a smile that rivaled the sun itself. And, giving the audience barely enough time to cheer, Lolotika sprang into the air, twirling to the rhythm of the thunderous pumping of the mechanical lung.

The sinuous fire tongue, some twenty or thirty yards in length, became an extension of her as she leapt and spun and soared and dipped. Sometimes it coiled around her like Empress Risana's famed long sleeves; sometimes it shot straight out from her like the spear of Lord Fithowéo; sometimes it roared and snapped, a garinafin's breath; sometimes it dipped and delicately nipped, a chef's miniature fire-thrower in the preparation of Lady Kana's Feast.

Lolotika's movements felt impossible. How could she leap up

and stay suspended in air, a faint starry glow around her feet? How could she bend and snap the fire tongue like a wandering hero's sword? Sparks scattered and twirled, fireflies swarming around a dark forest. The fire tongue forked and forked again, lightning bolts flickering in stormy clouds. The audience sat, mesmerized, as a most unlikely couple, the dancer and her flame, lived out one grand romance on the stage.

The mechanical thumping stopped; the fire tongue hissed out; Lolotika stood still in the middle of the unlit stage, a goddess in the darkness before dawn, the Chaos before Creation.

Brilliant silkmotic lamps snapped on. The audience gasped again. The stage was dominated by a gigantic block of ice, full of holes, bevels, tunnels, channels, grooves, cuts—this was the structure upon which Lolotika had been dancing, climbing, sliding, skating. . . . During the dance, she had been wielding the fire tongue like a writing knife, and the ice was her wax.

Lolo bowed, basking in the deafening tide of applause.

Colorful spotlights roamed around the stage, illuminating the edifice of ice from every angle, revealing fluid logograms that shifted and transformed like living beings: Pain, Love, Home, Redemption, Pleasure, Heartache, Fulfillment, Pride, *Mutagé*. . . .

The seed glided over Pan, the Capital of the Empire.

The city itself teemed with humming silkmotic carriages and rushing pedestrians. Performers put on shows in temple and market squares, vying for the attention of the capital's jaded audience. Ranked scholars in teahouses debated rarefied philosophy in top-floor suites, while downstairs, among the noisy open tables, ambitious youth who had decided to seek success outside the Imperial examinations showed off their new inventions to suspicious investors.

Outside the city walls, the Imperial procession was being readied at the airfield. *Grace of Kings*, the emperor's new ship, bobbed gently at the central mooring mast, a cruben at rest. It had ten times the volume of its predecessor and was powered by nine sets of spinning silkmotic dyran fins. Around it, smaller airships were tethered to other masts, a pod of whales eager to plunge into the aerial sea.

Hundreds of crew dangled from cables and crawled over catwalks, busy with last-minute prelaunch routines.

At the edge of the field, the Lords of Dara milled about, waiting for their turn to board. Governors and nobles had been summoned from all around Dara, and ministers and generals had been exempted from their official duties for the day. The excitement was palpable.

The crowd rustled like the tentacles of a sea anemone: silkmotic wires from Ginpen had confirmed the news.

They are here.

The seed glided over grain-heavy fields and rice-fragrant paddies, fish-laden lakes and lotus-filled ponds. It glided over kite-driven carriages and self-driving cargo caravans. It glided over work-shops filled with instructible looms and teams of automata. It glided over libraries filled with books and publishing houses filled with book-mirrors. It glided over humming power plants, where fleets of windmills generated the silkmotic force needed to power modernity. It glided over lone Mendist monks and nuns walking steadily along winding country roads, intent on the unending task of healing the world.

The seed arrived at Ginpen, the Capital of the Mind, where scholarship and research were no longer confined to the Imperial laboratories and academies, but also found in the bustling factories churning out novel silkmotic home furnishings; the private mind-tanks disseminating big ideas through their own book-mirrors; the innovation theaters where inventors presented their impractical prototypes to panels of investors, with the public cheering on their favorites as though at some boxing match. "Ogé Jar" had become a nickname for this city, where sparks proliferated not just between wires, but also between the abundance of brilliant minds.

A city-ship battle group was sailing out of Ginpen's harbor.

The city-ship had begun its life, nearly a century ago, as *Xana Exalted*, a ship built to look for immortals; it had passed through the Wall of Storms, reached Ukyu-Gondé on the great belt current, and returned to Dara as *Ukyu kyu*, a ship of conquest; now, rechristened *Gin Mazoti*, it was tasked with the defense of the Islands.

In the city-ship's long life, its planks and sidings and masts and spars had rotted and been replaced countless times. It was doubtful any timber from the time of Mapidéré remained—a living embodiment of the old philosophical debate over whether it was in fact proper to call the ship the same ship.

Would Mapidéré think this Dara the same empire as the one he had created? Would Kuni? Would Jia?

A city-ship battle group was a most puissant display of military force. Mechanical crubens, now freed from reliance on underwater volcanoes by silkmotic reservoirs, stealthily patrolled far ahead of the fleet. Airships and lookouts in high-altitude kites made sure that the command staff on *Gin Mazoti* was aware of every vessel, shoal, whale, or even school of fish for miles and miles around. Warships with short-range Fithowéo's arms and long-range guided silkmotic dyrans protected the city-ship, ensuring the safety of the launch platform for the battle group's main weaponry, the fire-breathing garina-fins and their phyroites—skilled riders who crewed the living war engines.

The battle group was headed north. Where was it going? What had aroused its interest?

The seed, after the briefest of hesitations, rushed ahead of the fleet.

Such a task would surely have been impossible for an ordinary dandelion seed, but you didn't think this one was ordinary, did you?

The seed soared over roiling waves. Ahead could be glimpsed the impossible magnificence that was the Wall of Storms: a living wall of wind and water reaching from the sea to the heavens.

But the waters below the drifting seed weren't being churned by a rogue storm.

Hundreds of crubens had gathered here, breaching, spouting, circling, eager, expectant, nervous. In their midst, thousands of dyrans cavorted and skimmed over the sea, their long, graceful, rainbow-hued tail fins crisscrossing like trails of fate.

The audience had been assembled. Where was the show? The sea beyond the crubens was calm and flat, almost like a mirror.

The seed dipped and bobbed, waiting.

The sea erupted.

Dissolver of Sorrows gently undulated with the waves, like an iceberg at rest. Sunlight glinted from its salt-bleached surface in dewdrop shimmer.

Assembled from hundreds of thousands of pieces of bone, shell, horn, antler . . . the skeleton ship was the greatest feat of arucuro tocua in anyone's re-remembering. It was sleek, supple, simply splendid.

Decades of advancement in arucuro tocua construction, inspired by Dara engineering, were on display. The articulated triple-keel, assembled from chains of garinafin vertebrae, allowed the ship to flex and bend with the waves, resulting in a smooth ride even in choppy, rough seas. Sleek sharkskin and stretched garinafin leather formed a watertight hull that parted the water with little resistance. Besides battened sails inspired by Dara examples to catch the wind, *Dissolver of Sorrows* also featured "water wings," bone-framed fins whose up-and-down flapping motion, imparted by passing waves, could be translated via bone gears and levers into forward propulsive force.

Besides cargo holds and sleeping quarters, the interior of the skeleton ship also featured a large, empty rib cage occupied only by air sacs—the ship's lungs. The compressed air in these sacs powered the Divine Voice with which the crew could speak to cetaceans, and, crucially, also gave *Dissolver of Sorrows* the capacity to dive under the sea when necessary—such as when escaping from a typhoon or swimming under the Wall of Storms.

Théra stood on the bridge, greedily gulping down lungfuls of the salt-scented air.

"Granny, are you all right?" The speaker was her granddaughter, Pékyu-taasa Lurofir.

"I am," Théra said, her voice hoarse. How could she explain the emotions buffeting her heart now? She had last breathed this air when she had been younger than Lulu-*tika*.

The Wall of Storms was behind her, streaked through with lightning and rumbling faintly with thunder.

"Look!" Lurofir pointed.

Ahead, hundreds of crubens, the scaled whales unknown in Ukyu-Gondé, were putting on a show: rainbow-sheened bodies, each as massive as *Dissolver of Sorrows*, leapt to and fro above the waves, always heading south, as nimble as a school of dyrans.

"I think they want us to follow them," said Crucru, the captain. He turned to Théra. "Pékyu-votan, your orders?"

Théra nodded. "Follow them south."

Crucru turned to issue orders to the crew. The corners of Théra's mouth curled up as she looked at the dependable captain, recalling how Crucru's parents, Nméji and Tipo, used to bicker over the relative merits and deficiencies of submariners and aviators. Crucru, who flew on the back of a garinafin and dove beneath the Wall of Storms, was both.

Then, somberly, Théra whispered, "You're home."

She wasn't talking to herself, but to the bones in one of the cargo holds. Though many from her original expedition had decided to put down roots in Ukyu-Gondé: Razutana Pon, Nméji Gon, Tipo Tho . . . there were also those who had never trusted and feared the gods of Ukyu and Gondé: Admiral Mitu Roso, Çami Phithadapu, Thoryo. . . .

A falling leaf yearns to return to the root; rest is found under the soil of home. It didn't feel right to leave the bones of these sojourners of Dara in a foreign land. And so, while *Dissolver of Sorrows* was under construction, Théra had also sent people to scour the scrublands for Dara graves and remains: the cemetery in Kiri Valley, the plot near the Boneyard, the scattered resting places for those who had been enslaved by Pékyu Tenryo and Pékyu Cudyu. . . .

Besides the bones, *Dissolver of Sorrows* also brought back the spirit portraits, the frozen voices, of many of the old crew. These recordings, re-remembering a grand life in a grander land, would make a most wondrous gift to their loved ones and descendants, occupying a permanent place of honor beside the incense-shrouded memorial tablets.

Hugolu pha gira ki. She had fulfilled her promise to Mitu Roso. She had brought them home, so that they could step across the River-on-Which-Nothing-Floats.

Unnoticed, one set of bones in the cargo hold had quietly vanished.

∾

The dandelion seed circled in the air, almost insolently. Abruptly, it stopped, and vibrated in place, thrumming with excitement.

- *Do my eyes deceive me? Are there truly immortals beyond the Wall of Storms? Is it really you, my brother, Lutho?*

The very air seemed to coalesce with substance and weight. A vague outline of a sea turtle.

- . . .

- *Oho! You have no idea how long I've been waiting for this! There's a betting pool, you know? I'm the only one who never doubted you'd return. . . . Well, there's also Rufizo, but he thinks the best of everything, and that makes it no fun at all.*

- . . .

- *Have you lost the power of speech? Am I going to be the sole god of wisdom? Will all the scholars now have to worship me? How will—*

- *Tazu, stop your prattling for just a second. Please.*

- *I've never known you to back down from an argument.*

- *It's not that . . . You . . . have to give me time and space to recover my wits. . . . After all, I've just gone through a whole cycle of life and death, of being mortal.*

- *Was being a mortal everything you thought it would be?*

- *Yes! Yes . . . and no. When I was a mortal, I remembered nothing of my life as a god. But now that I'm back, that mortal span looms in the mind as an eternity. It will be a while before I can tell you how I feel. All I can do for now is to tell you the story of what I went through, a tale of epic grace and sublime love—*

- *Save the poetry for the banquet. We also have stories to tell you of what happened here while you were gone, and I'm willing to bet ours will have more sex and betrayal, the spices that give the most mind-pleasure.*

- *To be an observer of the mortals is nothing like to be one. . . . There's no substitute for experience. . . . Never mind, I mean this in the best way, my brother. You really haven't changed at all.*

- *What are you talking about? The mortals have given us all makeovers— you should see Rufizo, ahaha, you may not even recognize him now, with those hands made of floppy roots.*

- *The mortals have much to teach us.*

- *Doubtful. Let's just say that I'm glad that they haven't imposed their cursed bureaucracy on us yet. Come, Tututika and Rufizo have laid out quite a spread in the Damu Mountains. Little sister sent me to fetch you, and admonished us to not be late.*

- *Oh? Our little sister is now in charge?*

- *Eh, I humor her since she claims it's the age of love and healing.* . . . *Don't worry, if you're bored, I have some schemes brewing for having fun with the mortals, and you can plot against me—*

- *I'm quite certain the days of my plotting with or against mortals are over. Like children who have grown up, they need us less than we think.*

- *Surely the mortals need drama as much as we do—it keeps life interesting. Come on, brother, it's no fun plotting alone.*

- *If I didn't know better, I'd say you missed me. I certainly have missed you.*

- *Ugh. Please don't let this be the new normal.* . . .

Dissolver of Sorrows pulled up to the black sands of Lutho Beach.

Behind, anchored off the coast, was *Gin Mazoti*, whose garinafins and phyroites circled the air, an aerial honor guard. The city-ship battle group had not been launched in anticipation of a threat at all.

A year earlier, hundreds of turtles had found their way through the Wall of Storms, a simple message etched in their shells:

Coming home.

The Lords of Dara, dressed in their finest courtly regalia, were arrayed in dense ranks on the black sands. Bronze *moaphya* rang majestically, accompanied by long toots from the Péa pipes.

Théra, helped by Lurofir, climbed down from the skeleton ship.

She took a first, tentative step, faltered, and almost fell. The strength that had reinvigorated her limbs for the last two years seemed to have drained out of her in an instant. She was walking again on the land of her birth, breathing the air of her childhood. Her heart beat so fast that she feared her rib cage would crack.

Her eyes roamed around in wonder, her failing eyesight veiling everything in a luminous haze: the billowing, mountainous form of *Grace of Kings* like a beached whale in the distance; garinafins dressed in golden armor swooping overhead, the skull helmet of each pilot emblazoned with a stylized dandelion; batteries of fifty-yard-long spears pointing at the sky, either celebratory fireworks or some kind of unknown weapon. . . .

Everything was familiar and yet alien.

A young man emerged from the center of the assembly of the Lords of Dara and approached her. He wore a crown with dangling strands of coral and pearl beads that obscured his face.

Théra's breath quickened.

The young man stopped before her, lifted off his veiled crown, and, holding it before him reverently, bowed to her.

"*Rénga.*"

Shocked, Théra had to take a few moments to compose herself before realization sank in. When she had departed, all those years ago, she had not formally abdicated. Now that she had returned to these shores, she was once again the legitimate sovereign, Empress of Dara.

She accepted the crown but didn't put it on.

"What . . ." She had not spoken the language of her youth for so long that her voice sounded strange to her own ears. She strained to recapture the old rhythms, the unfamiliar-familiar syllables, the half-forgotten words. "What is your name, child?"

"Coto-*tika*, Great-Grandaunt," the young man said, grinning as he looked up. After a pause, his tone turned formal. "I am called Danhu, son of Çafidi, daughter of Dyana, daughter of Timu. I served the people of Dara as Emperor Darokin in your absence."

Théra peered closely at the young man's face. She could see hints of her siblings, traces of her parents, but infused with the natural vigor of the young and hopeful. In Danhu's accent she could hear the shy laughter of Timu, the confident whoop of Phyro, the mischievous giggle of Fara, the delighted guffaw of Kuni, the calculated chuckle of Jia, as well as a joyous strength that was wholly new.

The temptation of power stirred in her for the briefest of moments before dissipating. She wielded power once, but Power would never wield her.

"Lower your head, Coto-*tika*," she whispered. The young man was too tall.

Danhu bowed. With trembling hands, Théra placed the crown back on her great-grandnephew's head, making a few adjustments so that it sat snug and proper. Then, ignoring the protests of her aged limbs, she bowed deeply in *jiri*. *"Rénga."*

Emperor Darokin straightened, his face once again obscured by the dangling beaded veil. Théra noticed that tiny skulls of birds and voles hung from a few of the strands of coral and pearl.

Standing erect and regal, the emperor intoned, "Welcome home, Théra, Grand Princess of Dara."

The formalities over, Théra felt even more tired. Her mind was a confusion of emotions; she had wanted to come home, but the home she knew was no more.

She didn't notice that the emperor had stepped back to make room for a silkmotic wheeled chair that had hummed its way onto the black sand in front of her.

"I brought these for you," said a voice, trembling, hoarse, but oh so familiar. An outstretched hand held a plate of lotus seeds.

Théra's eyes focused on the face of the occupant of the wheeled chair. The skin was lined, the hair sparse and silver, but the smile was exactly how she remembered it.

"Zomi!" She fell to her knees and embraced her wakeful weakness, the mirror of her soul.

While the music swelled and fireworks were launched, while kyoffir and plum wine flowed freely, while eating sticks clacked and knives scraped, while sheep sponge was served alongside compote of wild monkeyberries and ice melon, Pékyu-taasa Lurofir and Emperor Darokin began the first tentative steps toward drafting a new chapter in the joint history of the people of the Islands of Dara and the people of Ukyu-Gondé, one to be woven from the commerce of arucuro tocua skeleton ships and silkmotic-powered mechanical crubens, with the exchange of goods and ideas, the sharing of recordings and scripts, the movement of peoples and tongues.

Offshore, crubens breached and spouted in starlight, a most auspicious sign.

Two figures, one walking and the other seated in a wheeled chair, moved away from the commotion, finding a quiet corner of the beach under the stars.

They recounted to each other the stories of their time apart—though only the barest of outlines, and there would be many nights ahead to fill in the blanks. They made plans to visit the graves of Kuni and Jia, Timu and Phyro, Luan and Gin, Aki and Oga. They made plans to stay with Fara and her family at the remote mountain estate of her dear friend Mozo Mu, Dara's legendary recluse chef.

"Fara abdicated in favor of Dyana as soon as she felt things were stable enough," said Zomi, feeding Théra another lotus seed. The bitter green core had been replaced with sweet fillings of aged honey, marinated monkeyberries, candied ginger. "She and Kinri then took their kids to travel the Islands in disguise, refusing all invitations to visit the court—that's also why she didn't come with me this time, saying that she only wants to see her sister, not perform in political theater."

Théra laughed. "Fara never did like politics. Her time as empress must have been hard for her."

"She was good at it, though. Though her reign was too brief, the precedents she left were weighty in the constitution of Dara."

"I can't imagine she stayed idle after her abdication," said Théra. "She was always restless, romantic to the core."

She fed Zomi a lotus seed, this one with a filling of salted plum. Zomi smiled at her. The very air seemed to vibrate in sympathy with their joy.

"You know her well," said Zomi. "There are theories that Fara was the anonymous author behind a most popular book of love poetry as well as the unnamed playwright for *The Chrysanthemum and the Dandelion*, the Aviary's longest-running show. I asked, but she would never admit these accomplishments."

"I'm just glad she lived, and still lives, the life she wanted," said Théra, a hint of wistfulness in her voice. "We'll have to make her cook us a sumptuous meal to make up for not coming to greet me."

Impulsively, Zomi grabbed Théra's hand. "Sometimes I wonder if we should have done as she had done."

Théra heard the unspoken lament for the life together that could have been.

She loved the life she had lived, as Zomi did hers. But it was the lot of mortals to live with regret, to never be free from doubt.

"We've enlarged our souls with many loves and devoted ourselves to many duties, instead of consuming ourselves in one grand romance. We have more lines on our faces than there are breaths left in our lungs." Théra placed a hand on Zomi's face, her fingers gently caressing the wrinkled, beautiful skin, now stained with tears. "Though we stand within sight of the River-on-Which-Nothing-Floats, we would not exchange our places with the immortal gods."

They kissed, embraced, and held on tightly, abandoning themselves to an empathy with the eternal tides.

GLOSSARY

ANOJITI: a neologism formed from Classical Ano roots to describe the people of Dara, created in response to the Lyucu invasion.

CASHIMA: a scholar who has passed the second level of the Imperial examinations. The Classical Ano word means "practitioner." A *cashima* is allowed to wear his or her hair in a triple scroll-bun and carry a sword. *Cashima* can also serve as clerks for magistrates and mayors.

CRUBEN: a scaled whale with a single horn protruding from its head; symbol of Imperial power.

CÜPA: a game played with black and white stones on a grid.

DYRAN: a flying fish, symbol of femininity and sign of good fortune. It is covered by rainbow-colored scales and has a sharp beak.

FIROA: a *cashima* who places within the top one hundred in the Grand Examination is given this rank. The Classical Ano word means "a (good) match." Based on their talents, the *firoa* are either given positions in Imperial administration, assigned to work for various enfeoffed nobles, or promoted to engage in further study or research with the Imperial Academy.

GÉÜPA: an informal sitting position where the legs are crossed and folded under the body, with each foot tucked under the opposite thigh.

JIRI: a woman's bow where the hands are crossed in front of the chest in a gesture of respect.

KUNIKIN: a large, three-legged drinking vessel.

MINGÉN FALCON: a species of extraordinarily large falcon native to the island of Rui.

MIPA RARI: a formal kneeling position where the back is kept straight and weight is evenly distributed between the knees and toes.

MOAPHYA: an ancient Àno instrument of the "metal" class, consisting of rectangular bronze slabs of various thicknesses suspended from a frame and struck with a mallet to produce different pitches.

MUTAGÉ: variously translated as "faith-mercy" or "loyalty-benefaction," one of the most important virtues to the ancient Ano. It refers to a dedication to the welfare of the people as a whole, one that transcends self-interest or concern for family and clan.

OGÉ: drops of sweat. The Ogé Islands were supposedly formed from drops of sweat from the god Rufizo.

PANA MÉJI: a scholar who has done especially well in the Grand Examination and is given the chance to participate in the Palace Examination, where the emperor himself assesses the qualities of the candidates and assigns them a rank. The Classical Ano phrase means "on the list."

PAWI: animal aspects of the gods of Dara.

RAYE: descendants of prisoners of war, the lowest social caste in the days of the Tiro states.

RÉNGA: honorific used to address the emperor.

THAKRIDO: an extremely informal sitting position where one's legs are stretched out in front; used only with intimates or social inferiors.

THASÉ-TEKI: literally "winter worm, summer grass," a hybrid organism consisting of a fungus and a particular species of underground caterpillar that the fungus infects. The mycelia slowly spread throughout the body of the caterpillar, eventually killing it to sprout aboveground in a grass-like stroma. Called "caterpillar grass" in the vernacular, it has many uses in herbal medicine.

-TIKA: suffix expressing endearment toward younger family members.

TOKO DAWIJI: a scholar who has passed the first level of the Imperial examinations. The Classical Ano phrase means "the elevated." A *toko dawiji* is allowed to wear his or her hair in a double scroll-bun.

TUNOA: grapes.

ZAMAKI: a game of war between opposing armies composed of tokens representing pieces such as the king, consort, ship, advisor, assassin, horse, kite, and so on.

LYUCU/AGON

ARUCURO SANA: literally "talking bones"; logograms constructed from animal parts using principles derived from arucuro tocua as well as Classical Ano.

ARUCURO TOCUA: literally "living bones"; articulated creations made from bones, sinew, horn, antler, and other animal parts.

GARINAFIN: the flying, fire-breathing beast that is the core of Lyucu culture. Its body is about the size of three elephants, with a long tail, two clawed feet, a pair of great, leathery wings, and a slender, snakelike neck topped with a deerlike, antlered head.

KYOFFIR: an alcoholic drink made from fermented garinafin milk.

PÉDIATO SAVAGA: literally "stomach journey," the scrublands funeral practice of leaving a body exposed to the elements and scavenging animals.

PÉKYU: title given to the leader of the Lyucu or Agon.

PÉKYU-TAASA: title given to the children of pékyus; sometimes translated into Dara as "prince" or "princess."

TANTO-LYU-NARO: tribeless wanderers of Ukyu-Gondé who do not follow the ways of either the Lyucu or the Agon and who renounce all warmaking. Literally "warriors who do not make war."

TOGATEN: literally "runt"; a slur used against those of mixed Lyucu and native Dara ancestry.

TOLYUSA: a plant with hallucinogenic properties; the berries are essential for the garinafins to breed successfully.

VOTAN-RU-TAASA: "older-and-younger"; brothers.

VOTAN-SA-TAASA: "older-and-younger"; sisters (or siblings).

LIST OF SELECTED
ARTIFACTS AND MOUNTS

CRUBEN'S THORN: a dagger made from a cruben's tooth and therefore undetectable to lodestone detectors, a favorite weapon of assassins. A rebel from Gan first attempted to kill King Réon of Xana with it. It was later wielded by Princess Kikomi against Phin Zyndu, and finally by Consort Mira on herself.

NA-AROÉNNA, THE DOUBT-ENDER: an extraordinarily heavy sword constructed by the master bladesmith Suma Ji for Dazu Zyndu, Marshal of Cocru. With a heart of bronze and a coat of thousand-hammered steel, it was quenched in the blood of a wolf. Later, it became the weapon, successively, of Mata Zyndu, Gin Mazoti, and Phyro Garu.

GOREMAW: an ironwood cudgel made more fearsome with rings of teeth embedded in the strike-head. Wielded by Mata Zyndu, it was the companion to Na-aroénna.

RÉFIROA: Mata Zyndu's war steed, the "Well-Matched."

GITRÉ ÜTHU: the Classical Ano title means "Know Thyself." Legend has it that Luan Zyaji received it as a gift from the gods. The book supposedly showed divine revelations, but only of what the user already knew. Luan carried it with him beyond the Wall of Storms, and later gave it to his disciple, Zomi Kidosu.

BITER: a toothed war club given to Dafiro Miro by Huluwen of Tan Adü.

SIMPLICITY: once the sword of Mocri Zati, champion of Gan. When Mata Zyndu defeated him, the sword was gifted to Ratho Miro, the Hegemon's personal guard.

LANGIABOTO: a war axe fashioned from garinafin rib and talon, it had been in the hands of the Aragoz clan, the ruling family of the Agon, for generations. The name means "self-reliance" in the language of the scrublands. Later, it was seized by Tenryo Roatan and became the symbol of Lyucu domination.

GASLIRA-SATA, THE PEACE-BITE: Goztan Ryoto's war axe, made from a tusked tiger's fang and four baby garinafin ribs bound together with horrid wolf sinew.

NOTES

The Veiled Throne and *Speaking Bones* were conceived of as one continuous narrative, and should be read as such.

A few notes specific to this book:

Fara's poem for Kinri is in part reworked from the Song Dynasty poem 《卜算子•我住長江頭》by 李之儀.

Ro Taça of Rima's poem about the lute player is in part reworked from the Tang Dynasty poem 《琵琶行》by 白居易.

The song from the mother who survives the Lyucu occupation of Dasu is in part reworked from the Yuan Dynasty poem 《山坡羊•潼關懷古》by 張養浩.

Fithowéo's arm, the stone-throwing machine deployed by Phyro during the Battle of Crescent Island, is essentially a counterweight trebuchet based on a modification of the design of traction trebuchets used in ancient China, as early as the fourth century before the common era. Traction trebuchets were described in Mohist texts, but probably had been invented earlier.

The Péa pipes (and the various arucuro tocua devices derived from them, such as the Divine Voice) are inspired by the Auxetophone, a pneumatic amplifier invented by Horace Short and Sir Charles A. Parsons. The device for taking spirit portraits is inspired by the phonautograph invented by Édouard-Léon Scott de Martinville. Alexander Graham Bell created a version of the phonautograph using a cadaver ear.

I'm deeply grateful to the following individuals for their help in the production of this book: Joe Monti (editor extraordinaire); Russell Galen (bestest of agents); Danny Baror and Heather Baror-Shapiro (foreign rights); Angela Cheng Caplan (media rights); John Vairo and Lisa Litwack (art direction); Tony Mauro (cover); Robert Lazzaretti (map); Valerie Shea and Alexandre Su (copyediting); Lauren Truskowski and

Kayleigh Webb (publicity); Madison Penico (manuscript assistance); Caroline Pallotta, Kaitlyn Snowden, Kathryn Kenney-Peterson, Alexis Alemao (managing editorial and production).

I also wish to thank the many people who helped me during the drafting of this book, whether by reading drafts, giving me ideas, providing research assistance, or keeping up my spirits: Anatoly Belilovsky, Dario Ciriello, Elodie Coello, Elías Combarro, Kate Elliott, Nathan Faries, Barbara Hendrick, Crystal Huff, Emily Jin, Allison King, Leticia Lara, Anaea Lay, Felicia Low-Jimenez, John P. Murphy, Erica Naone, Tochi Onyebuchi, Emma Osborne, Bridget Pupillo, Achala Upendran, Alex Shvartsman, Carmen Yiling Yan, Christie Yant, Florina Yezril, Caroline Yoachim, Hannah Zhao.

Above all, I couldn't have done this without my family. Lisa, Esther, Miranda, I love you.

Finally, thank you, readers, for coming on this journey with me. I've long held the belief that fiction is a co-creation between the author and the reader. While the author sets the scene and describes the action, introduces the characters and sets forth their lines, it's the reader whose imagination brings it all to life. Just as the author must put something of themselves into the world to build it, the reader must also take a leap of trust to devote their attention wholly to the fantasy world, to live a life separate from reality.

Dara began as a joint creation of my wife, Lisa, and myself. We wanted to make a world together that honored the wuxia fantasies that played such an important role in our childhoods. Later, I expanded Dara and told the story of the Dandelion Dynasty in it. The saga was conceived of more than a decade ago, and the very last scene of the series was actually the first scene that took shape in my head. It's a great privilege for a creator to find a world so absorbing as to spend such a big portion of a lifetime laboring in it; but without you, the story of Dara would remain nothing but printed words on a page, as inert as blocks of congealed wax carved by a clumsy hand.

May you find a place in this fantasy world to live out an interesting life, a life with an empathy that encompasses the world and at the end of which you leave your teeth on the board, content that you served *mutagé*.

Ukyu & Gondé

Lower Peninsula

Luan Zya's
Landing Site ⚓

Péa's Sea

Admiral Krita's
Landing Site ⚓

Taten
(Pékyu Tenryo Roatan)

GONDÉ

Tenryo & Diaman
⚔

Lurodia Tanta
(The Endless Desert)   🌴 Sliyusa Ki

Blood River

*Sea
of
Tears*

Ghost River

Wing
(Agon)   Foot
(Lyucu)

Kiri Valley   Tail
(Lyucu)

Antler
(Agon)